I0760802

THE ARTIFEX AND THE MUSE

BOOKS BY AUDREY AUDEN

The Voice in All

The Path of Mysteries

The Many Worlds

Realms Unreel

The Artifex and the Muse

For author news and release updates, please visit
audreyauden.com

THE ARTIFEX AND THE MUSE

AUDREY AUDEN

LOVE THAT BOOK
An imprint of Love That Labs
Independent Publisher Since 2022
Bethlehem, New Hampshire

THE ARTIFEX AND THE MUSE
Version 1.1.6

Cover design by Audrey Auden in collaboration with DALL·E

Published by Love That Book, an imprint of Love That Labs LLC

ebook ISBN: 978-1-937262-40-2
paperback ISBN: 978-1-937262-41-9
hardcover ISBN: 978-1-937262-42-6

Discover story soundtracks, book club guides, and audiobooks
for *The Artifex and the Muse* at
audreyauden.com

For Eden Hill Farm

CONTENTS

There is a land of the living and a land of the dead and the bridge is love, the only survival, the only meaning.

— Abbess Madre María del Pilar, *Bridge of San Luis Rey* (1927) by Thornton Wilder

THE ARTIFEX AND THE MUSE
PART ONE

THE VOICE IN ALL

It's queer how out of touch with truth women are. They live in a world of their own, and there has never been anything like it, and never can be. It is too beautiful altogether, and if they were to set it up it would go to pieces before the first sunset. Some confounded fact we men have been living contentedly with ever since the day of creation would start up and knock the whole thing over.

— Charlie Marlow, *Heart of Darkness* (1899) by Joseph Conrad

Is life so dear, or peace so sweet, as to be purchased at the price of chains and slavery? Forbid it, Almighty God! I know not what course others may take; but as for me, give me liberty or give me death!

— Patrick Henry, rally speech to the Second Convention of the American Revolution (1775)

AVA

I CROUCH MOTIONLESS beside my mother at the edge of the cedar forest. We peer out at the high stone wall of the temple city through a screen of ferns. Our mud-smeared faces and dust-covered hoods should be enough to conceal us from the watchful eyes of the gatekeeper atop the wall. But my mother said there could be other Mohirai watching from anywhere, so we've had to keep still and silent all through this long hot afternoon. I'm desperate to move my legs. Thank the spirits that sunset's approaching, and with it the protective cover of darkness.

My mother's fingers sign, *Ava, look.*

I follow her gaze, searching for whatever she's spotted.

Ahead of us, the relative safety of the forest gives way to an exposed meadow that slopes a long way down toward the sea. About a dozen girls and boys around my age swim near the small crescent beach beside the city docks.

Above the beach looms the great wall enclosing the temple city. The wall stretches from the shore to the forest edge, and the bronze-clad gate at its center stands closed.

Ah, there it is: a flash of movement atop the wall, backlit by the sinking sun. I squint against the glare. A lone Mohira passes behind the narrow gap of a crenellation. The gatekeeper is on the move.

I tap my mother's rough, sun-reddened hand, which looks massive beside my own small brown one. She watches my fingers as I sign, *Is this the expected time?*

She glances at the sun's position and signs, *Yes. Perfect silence now.*

The city gate swings slowly inward. Three Mohirai step out onto the rutted dirt road, dressed in identical dark cloaks over sky-blue robes. They follow the road a short distance across the meadow before turning onto a narrower footpath that climbs uphill toward the forest.

Despite the hoods obscuring their faces, I think that's the High Priestess Serapen walking in front, flanked by the other two women. I've never seen anyone else with this gliding gait and peculiar way of clasping her hands as she walks, like she can't swing her arms.

I glance at my mother. Her square, muscular jaw twitches. She signs, *That's Serapen and two of her healer initiates. Three more healers remain inside the wall.*

I repeat the message back to confirm I understand, then sign, *I await your command.*

My mother signals for me to continue waiting.

Serapen and her healers enter the woods about a hundred paces west of our lookout spot. The forest now hides them from us as well as it hides us from them, so we've lost one of our advantages. It's a calculated risk. The only way we could be absolutely sure Serapen is out of the city is to see her leave, and the safest place for us to watch the gate is here at the forest edge.

My mother closes her eyes and draws back her hood just enough to expose her ears. She listens, and I know she hears the three women's footsteps passing somewhere through the woods behind us. When she inhales silently, I know she detects their scent in the air. Those Mohirai could hear us, too, if we made the slightest sound in the underbrush. They could even smell us, if we hadn't thoroughly masked our scent with soil and forest debris.

I wish I could perceive everything like my mother and the Mohirai, whose senses are enhanced by the arts of pharmaka. Unfortunately, with my unaided perception, I hear nothing but sea breeze in the canopy and smell nothing but sweet bracken ferns, spicy cedar needles, and the occasional pungent whiff of low tide.

Despite all my mother has taught me about the risks that accompany the use of pharmaka, I can't help but envy her powers of perception, her size, and her strength. Her body has so many advantages over mine because of pharmaka. At least once per moon, I plead with her to teach me the basics of these arts, enough at least that I might protect myself if I ever have the misfortune to encounter a Mohira without my mother beside me.

But no argument I've tried on this subject has ever moved her. She always says, *Abstinence from pharmaka gives you an essential advantage over all the Mohirai: freedom from the Voice in all.* I don't understand how this is an advantage, though. I've heard the Voice a few times, and to me it seems like nothing more than a disembodied whisper in my mind, insubstantial as a daydream. The Voice can't possibly be as dangerous as facing an initiate Mohira on my own.

The forest shadows lengthen as I wait for my mother's signal. I distract myself from my restless impulse to move by watching the girls and boys playing together in the waves. As sunset approaches, they swim ashore, dispersing in little groups of two and three and four, disappearing into the orchards and gardens outside the wall. One boy lingers behind on the beach, watching the fiery glow of sky and sea as the sun dips toward the horizon.

Inside the temple city, the bells for the evening silence toll, a sweet chord of three notes repeated three times. My gaze drifts toward the magnificent bronze dome of the Children's Temple at the city center, one of the few buildings visible over the wall. The sound of the bells and sight of the dome recall memories of a more innocent time, when this temple city was the only home I knew and I looked forward to nothing more than becoming an initiate Mohira myself.

The girls who had scattered across the grounds gather promptly at the sound of the bells. They converge on the meadow outside the temple city. The bronze gate opens to admit them. As the girls pass through the gate in a silent line, I wonder whether my two former trio sisters are among them. Neither would remember me now, I suppose. The Mohirai probably took those memories from them after my mother escaped the sisterhood with me.

The gate swings shut, cutting off my view of the girls, so I turn to watching the boys instead. They're reappearing slowly from the orchards and the gardens, making their way in little groups toward the rambling stone house of boys on the far side of the meadow, outside the city wall. I glance toward the beach and see the lone boy still standing there, watching the last of the sunset.

My mother opens her eyes, and my attention snaps back to her. She looks at me and signs, *It's time. Serapen is past hearing. Be careful.*

Unable to suppress the excitement I always feel at the start of a job, I grin at my mother and sign, *Next stop, freedom!*

Her thin lips press into a stern line, and her ice blue eyes bore into mine. *Don't get cocky*, she signs.

We've done this job so many times before that I'm inclined to wave away her warning. There's nothing much different about this time, except that it's the last time. But my mother's grim expression is sobering, so I sign, *I'll be careful.*

DOM

I SIT AT THE BEACH on the last day of summer, distracting myself from thoughts of tomorrow with a final sketch before I lose the light.

Today was hot—too hot for clothes—and this little crescent of sand between the rocky tide pools and the docks is the best place to swim within an easy walk of the city gate. About a dozen of the sixteenth summer girls and boys splash and dunk each other, their naked bodies rising and falling together in the gentle swells. Shouts of laughter merge with the shrill cries of the gulls fishing for their evening meal and the throaty barks of the seals lazing on the rocks.

I glance from the scene before me to the scrap of oak plank I balance on my knees as a makeshift drawing board. In my left hand, I grip a tiny nub of charcoal pencil I found in the meadow after one of the younger girls tossed it aside during her drawing instruction. I smooth my free hand over the wrinkled surface of my parchment, a sour-smelling cheese wrapper I salvaged during kitchen chores a few days ago. Sometimes I wonder what it might be like to draw on new parchment like the girls do, but this piece actually isn't too bad. With my bold charcoal lines now covering its surface from edge to edge, I hardly notice the grease marks.

As I focus on the sea, my shoddy materials fade from my awareness. The steady inhale and exhale of the waves leads my hand in a gentle rhythm, stroke after charcoal stroke over parchment.

I love the sea in any of her moods, from the rage of a winter storm to the calm of a windless summer day, from cheerful mornings to melancholy sunsets. I can almost always lose myself and any troubled thoughts in her presence. Now I study how she transforms at the edge where day approaches night, wave approaches shore, boy approaches calling.

My hand jerks to a stop. I've managed to evade most thoughts of my calling for the past moon, but it's impossible now that tomorrow's the day.

I try to resume sketching, but I've slipped out of the flow. My hand feels stuck. Resigned, I set down my drawing board on the sand beside me.

I study the faces of the boys out there enjoying the waves on our last day together. Not one of them seems to share my dread of tomorrow. If anything, the approach of our Calling Day has stirred them into a frenzy. Each boy knows today is his last opportunity to seize the easy pleasure of our lives here among the Mohirai. The sailors who deliver supplies to the temple city often visit the house of boys, and they make no secret of the rougher conditions in the villages where we'll spend the rest of our lives among the men.

Two of my friends, Balashi and Hanu, break away from the rest of the swimmers and ride a wave back to the beach. Hanu picks up a towel from the sand, shakes it clean, and dries herself. Balashi bounds after her like an energetic puppy but doesn't bother with a towel. He shakes his wet hair, spraying her with seawater. She swats his arm lightly, and he inclines his head in apology. She gestures for him to follow her. They turn in my direction.

Hanu spots me and waves. "Dom!" she calls. "I was wondering where you'd gone." She walks up the beach toward me, Balashi close at her side. Hastily, I pull my tunic from the pile of discarded clothes beside me and drape it over my drawing board, concealing my sketch from view.

She stops before me, a naked silhouette against the sunset. Her eyes rest a moment on my hand, which hovers nervously at the edge of my tunic. I know she knows what I'm hiding, but she won't force me to show the sketch to her, not in front of Balashi. Instead, she wraps her towel around her waist and sits beside me, stretching her long legs out in the sand and leaning back on her hands. The coppery light glistens on the warm brown skin of her smooth shoulders, generous breasts, and gently rounded belly.

Balashi, entirely naked, flops down on my other side and slings his damp arm around me companionably. Despite his fair complexion, he's managed to retain the faintest bronzing after a long afternoon in the sun. His handsome face and indomitable confidence make him a favorite among the girls. They've kept him busy today, but it's clear from the way he eyes Hanu that he's hungry for more.

"What are you thinking, spending today alone, brother?" says Balashi, shaking me by the shoulders as if to wake me from sleep.

"Do you want to come with us?" says Hanu, looking at my unclothed body with frank interest. Balashi's expression clouds at her invitation, but the decision is hers, not his.

"I'm all right," I say. "You two should go ahead."

Balashi shoots me a grateful look, then offers some brotherly advice. "Better make a proposition before the bell rings and the girls are all locked up inside the city again."

"Go," I insist, waving him off.

He shakes his head in bewilderment. "I'll never understand you, Dom."

"Some find as much pleasure in the mind as the body, Bala," says Hanu.

"Easy for you to say." Balashi laughs and claps me on the shoulder. "We men have to get what pleasure we can while we still can."

"You boys, you mean," Hanu says mildly. "Well, come and get it then."

Hanu stands, and her towel slips off. She wraps it back around her hips, taking her time. Concealment only adds to the attraction of her figure, and I can see that she knows it. She catches my gaze, making clear that her offer still stands. I lower my eyes, grateful she's not being as aggressive as some of the other girls have been toward me over the last few days.

I enjoy Hanu's company most of the time. But lately, with her growing excitement at the approach of Calling Day, I've found it impossible to forget the chasm between us. It's not that she flaunts her advantage, not exactly. The Mohirai teach the girls from an early age to be kind to boys and men. And most of them are. At least, most of them try. And Hanu is better than most.

But even Hanu takes for granted things that are forever out of my reach. Her unconsciousness of this is sometimes unbearable. I would give anything for just the basic instruction every girl receives from the Mohirai. Reading and writing, historia and poetika, tekhnologia and pharmaka—all of these and so much more will remain among the mysteries for me. And the sixteenth summer girls haven't even started their novice training in the higher mysteries, which will be followed by centuries of deepening practice through their service to the Voice as initiate Mohirai. So of course Hanu is excited about her path ahead, especially now, on the eve of our Calling Day. But her excitement amplifies my dread.

Hanu pulls Balashi up by the hand and leads him along the beach toward the orchard path. Their laughter drifts back to me as I remain sitting, watching the crimson and gold melting into the west and the deep purple rising in the east.

A little while later, Hanu returns to the beach alone. She searches for the clothes she left on the sand earlier this afternoon and dresses herself. She comes to sit beside me again and looks out at the waves.

I can't help myself from asking. It's always more interesting to hear this story from a girl's perspective, especially Hanu's. I say, "How was he today?"

Hanu chooses her words carefully, savoring each. "Like a summer sunshower. Lovely, invigorating, over almost before he's begun."

I chuckle. Hanu tips her head to the side and looks at me, the corner of her mouth curving in a hint of a smile. She rests her warm hand on my bare thigh and says, "You're another thing entirely, Dom."

I study Hanu's familiar face, committing her to memory—her thoughtful brow, her kind eyes, her sensuous mouth. I may never see her again after tomorrow, but there's still enough time to learn what words she might choose for me today. Clearly she's willing. But I'm not in the mood.

When I make no move toward her, she lifts her hand from my leg and taps the tunic concealing my drawing board. "May I see?" she says.

She waits, curious but not insistent. It's demoralizing to show my work to a girl who's had so much instruction in the arts. But perhaps Hanu will teach me something useful, even though strictly speaking the girls aren't supposed to share instruction with boys. I pull back the tunic and hand her the sketch. She examines it for a long time. When she looks up at me, her brow is furrowed and her eyes are troubled.

"What's wrong?" I say.

She's probably thinking this is an utterly useless way for a boy to spend his time. But what she says is, "I wonder why the Voice has given you such gifts. You would have been better off as a girl."

I try to laugh, but it sounds hollow. I say, "Wouldn't we all have been?"

"Not all of you, I think," she says. She gestures toward the boys coming ashore with other girls. They split off in twos and threes and fours to seek their pleasure, making their way toward the forest, or the orchards, or the gardens. "None of them have the inclination toward the arts and mysteries. They'll live out their days as happily in the villages as they've grown up here in the house of boys. The Voice will give them all the sense of purpose they need, and pharmaka will give them all the courage they need to make the journey into Death."

My heart sinks at her words. It's not that I'm afraid of Death. I've known since I was a small boy that Death is where all uninitiated creatures go after we've served our purpose to the Voice. And I've seen firsthand that the lives of the creatures we care for are pleasant. Of course I've also seen the awful flash of knowing in the eyes of the countless sheep and rabbits I've slaughtered, in that brief moment before the fall of my knife. But their deaths are as painless as it's possible for us to make them, and their fear is over in an instant. The Mohirai handle boys and men with even greater care than we give our animals, so I can't really fear Death.

It's the prospect of what happens before Death—or, rather, what won't happen—that saddens me. It's the sense of loss, knowing all I might have done as a Mohira. The life of an initiate continues for as long as the Voice requires the initiate's service—centuries, even millennia. Spirits, what a life that would be! But training in the arts and mysteries is wasted on lives as short as men's, and the Voice requires a different service from us. We must pay with our hands, our sweat, and our lives the debt incurred by men who came long before us, the men who brought about the destruction.

Seeing my expression, Hanu takes my hand, her long brown fingers soft and smooth against my work-hardened palm. "Don't be troubled, brother. The Mohirai teach that all find purpose in their callings, men as well as women. The Voice works through you with purpose, as it does through us all, whatever our paths."

Hanu's words reawaken the one bit of genuine excitement I feel as I face tomorrow. Calling Day is the one day in my life when I'll hear the Voice in all for myself, like the Mohirai do. The Mohirai teach that hearing the Voice brings the clarity, contentedness, and courage each man needs to walk his path. I take comfort in this teaching as Hanu and I watch the last of the sunset together.

Inside the temple city, the bells for the evening silence toll, a sweet chord of three notes repeated three times, summoning the girls to return to their dormitory. Hanu stands, pulls me up by the hand, and kisses me lightly on the cheek. "Good night, Dom. Safe passage on your journey tomorrow. I'll miss you."

THE LAST JOB

I REMAIN AT THE BEACH, and Hanu departs. I watch her walk back up to the meadow, where she rejoins the other girls returning from their dalliances here and there about the grounds. Their chattering ceases as they enter the temple city, passing through a gate that will remain locked to me forever.

I look down at my sketch one last time before crumpling it into a ball and burying it in the sand. There's no point keeping it, since I can't take anything with me to the ceremony tomorrow. I pick up my tunic, breeches, belt, and shoes and dress myself, preparing to return to the house of boys.

A creak, splash, and thump catches my attention, and I look toward the docks. A small fishing boat slows to a stop alongside the outermost mooring slip. A tall, slim man hops out of the boat with a line and ties it loosely around a cleat on the dock while a burly man onboard lowers the foresail. It's late for a boat to arrive. Perhaps they've had some mishap out at sea.

"Good evening, brothers," I call as I walk toward them. "Do you need help? I can take a message to Hedi Mohira at the house of boys if you need assistance."

The slim man and the burly man both look toward the boat's stern, where I notice a third man with a thick, dark beard seated at the tiller. All three men wear caps low over their foreheads, so I can't make out any of their faces in the fading light. The bearded man murmurs something to the burly man, who calls back to me in a lilting accent I don't recognize, "Tanks kindly, lil' brother. We'll just sleep de night and be on our way. No need to trouble a priestess."

"I'm sure it's no trouble," I say. "Hedi loves to welcome any man who returns to the house for a visit. Wouldn't you rather come up for a meal and a proper bed?"

The burly man says, "We make an early start. And we heard de bell ring already. Should'na you be abed, yourself?"

His question puzzles me. He can't possibly think I'm as young as that. There's no curfew for boys my age. Perhaps the rules have changed since this man grew up here. Although, in my experience, the Mohirai don't tend to change their rules about much, especially not Hedi Mohira, who has run the house of boys for centuries.

I shrug off my confusion and say, "I'm just heading back to the house now. Are you sure you don't need anything?"

"Not a ting," he says.

"Well … Good night, then."

"G'night."

I walk back to the house of boys from the docks. The first evening stars appear as I cross the meadow. I follow the worn footpath along the split-rail fence of the paddocks, continuing past the stone animal enclosures. The path passes through rows of trellises and terraces and raised garden beds luxuriant with summer growth, soon to be harvested. I have a thousand memories of hauling and sweating, weeding and pruning, milking and shearing in every corner of these grounds outside the city.

Ahead of me stands the house of boys. The house backs into the steep hillside just below the edge of the cedar forest, and its wide arching windows and front door face a magnificent view of the sea. The dormitory windows on the upper two floors are dark. The younger boys on those floors are already in bed, sleeping the pharmaka-deepened sleep of the newly unbound. But golden light flickers from many windows on the lower two floors, where the older boys, our unbindings years behind us, are mostly still awake.

Three lit candles stand on the windowsill of the ground floor bedroom I share with my trio brothers, Balashi and Kuri. Our window's open, and as I pass by on my way to the front door, I hear Balashi speaking in an animated undertone punctuated by Kuri's occasional deep chuckle. This is our last night together as a trio after eight years in the house of boys. I'm sure we'll be up talking half the night, between speculating about what calling each of us will receive from the Voice tomorrow and hearing Balashi rehash his exploits from today.

I don't particularly relish the thought of discussing either right now. If I can delay my return to our room just a bit longer, maybe Balashi will be nearing the end of a tale I've heard a hundred times before with minor variations.

I waver at the front steps of the house. A breeze stirs, and I inhale the sweet and spicy scent of the cedar forest, redolent of childhood memories. An overwhelming desire strikes me to visit my special place in the woods one last time before tomorrow. So I turn away from the front door and walk around to the back of the house, up the steep hillside, into the ferns that grow at the edge of the forest.

A faint animal track through the ferns leads me to the ancient cedar at the forest edge west of the house. It's not obvious from here, but this cedar's massive trunk is hollow. I've always found it strange that, despite so many clear memories of playing around this tree, I don't remember how I discovered that it's hollow. The opening in the trunk is completely hidden by the underbrush. But when I was small, I used to climb up through the heart of this cedar and step out through the top of the hole onto a high branch. The view of the sea is amazing up there, and you can even see a bit over the city wall.

I'm far too big to climb up through the trunk any more, but I still enjoy sitting here when I want to be alone. I pull myself up onto a low, broad branch and lean against the trunk, breathing in the scent of its bark and needles, listening to the familiar nighttime sounds of the forest insects and the more distant sound of waves rolling ashore.

These sounds have lulled me to sleep for as long as I can remember, and this perch is surprisingly comfortable. I've almost nodded off before I realize with a start that I should return to the house. The Calling Day ceremony starts before dawn, and I don't want to fall asleep in the woods and miss Hedi's wake-up call. I hop down from the branch.

I've taken only one step when I hear something unfamiliar amidst the usual nighttime sounds. I pause to listen. There it is again: shallow, panting breaths. Another lover's tryst, most likely. Perhaps some pair failed to hear the bell or lingered behind on purpose. Either way, I have no interest in disturbing them, so I resume my walk back to the house.

There's an abrupt crunch and snap of branches. I turn slowly toward the sound, reconsidering what I heard. Perhaps it's an animal moving through the underbrush. I listen more closely. There's a soft rustle, a light thud, a hissing intake of breath, and a whimper. I feel a protective instinct, like I do whenever a lamb or kid goes missing from the herd. Maybe one of the younger boys wandered off into the woods.

"Hello?" I call out to the shadows.

△▽△

I'll be careful, I sign to my mother.

Still crouching, I creep back into the forest. My mother remains in our lookout spot in the ferns, so she can create a distraction for me if she detects Serapen or the other healers returning to the city earlier than expected.

Once I'm deep enough in the woods that I can't be seen by any Mohira who might look this way from the wall, I stand. I unlace and roll up my dirt-encrusted cloak and stuff it into the bottom of the small leather pack I'm carrying. The linen shirt and riding breeches I'm wearing don't provide any camouflage, but they're less likely than my cloak to catch branches if I need to hide up in the trees.

Barefoot, I follow a faint deer track upslope through the underbrush until it joins a wider footpath. It's just past sunset, but the dense canopy in this part of the forest blocks almost all of the twilight. Fortunately, my feet know each twist and turn of this path, and I find the darkness relaxing. Darkness is a thief's best friend.

I know I'm approaching my destination when cedar gives way to beech. Beech leaves rustle in their branches at a lower pitch than cedar needles and feel softer underfoot. The path disappears into a patch of young beeches, and I push my way through the pliable saplings, feeling my way forward in the darkness until my fingertips brush the cool face of a high boulder. I slide my hands in both directions along the boulder until I find the cave opening.

I kneel before a loose pile of leaves beside the cave entrance and uncover the two bundles I buried here in daylight. The first bundle contains my worn leather riding boots, and I stuff them into my pack for later.

The second bundle contains my disguise. I unroll this bundle on the ground, stand up, and strip off my shirt, belt, and riding breeches. I take the little waterskin from the bundle and pour out just enough to wash the mud off my hands and face. To the Mohirai, dirtiness would be a conspicuous sign of something amiss. I gulp down the rest of the water. It's been a hot day, even in the shade of the woods, although the night air is cooling fast.

I change quickly into the undyed cream-colored wool tunic, roughspun breeches, and cloth shoes that all the girls and boys wear. I rake my fingers through the dark tangle of my unbound curls, plaiting my hair in a single long braid like the girls inside the temple city often wear. A braid can be quickly stuffed inside my tunic to keep it out of the way, or to make me look like a boy from a distance. If all goes well, the disguise won't matter because I won't be seen at all, but looking like just another girl or boy could be decent camouflage in a pinch.

I re-buckle my belt around my waist to keep my tools handy, stuff my riding clothes and the empty waterskin into my pack, sling the pack over both shoulders, and spread the leaf pile around to erase the signs of my presence here. I double-check my mental inventory of what's in my pack and what's in my belt. I think that's everything. Taking one last breath of the sweet forest air, I enter the cave.

I keep my hand above my head to avoid hitting the low cave ceiling, feeling my way forward with my feet as best I can despite the cloth shoes muffling the sensation in my toes. Although it was quite dark outside already, about ten paces inside the cave I enter total darkness. I close my eyes, since I know from experience they're good for nothing beyond this point but catching cobwebs, dust, and—if I'm unlucky—panicking bats. I keep walking forward until the soft soil beneath my shoes gives way to a rough-hewn but level stone floor.

I've reached the start of a long tunnel bored through the hillside. I sweep both hands around me in the pitch darkness, tracing the rounded shape of the tunnel from its high point above my head to the walls beside me. There's about half an arm's length of clearance around me on all sides. Most Mohirai would struggle to move through such a small space; that's why I always do this part of the job.

The cool stone beneath my fingertips is my only guide through the darkness as I walk the steep downward slope in this first section of the tunnel. My hand slides over hundreds of ancient chisel marks with each step. The slope flattens out after a few dozen paces, and then I run. I prefer to move fast through these tunnels. It helps me shake off the feeling that I'm walking into a trap.

The echoes of my running footsteps change as I approach the intersection, and I slow to a walk. My fingertips slide off the wall, grasping nothing but air. If I tripped or turned or became disoriented here at the five-way intersection, I would be in real trouble. I only know where two of these tunnels lead. I rein in the unhelpful thought and walk steadily forward, keeping my hand outstretched. I seem to float through a void without an anchor, with only my heartbeat and my breath for company in what's otherwise complete silence and utter darkness. In ten heartbeats, the fingers of my right hand catch the chiseled stone wall on the other side of the intersection. I allow myself a tiny sigh of relief. The storerooms aren't much farther now.

I walk the rest of the way with my left hand out ahead of me, until my palm lands on a rough wooden door. I grin. Almost halfway done, and I'm making great time.

I fish out a leather drawstring bag that I keep in a buckled pouch on my belt. Carefully, muffling any sound of jingling, I pull out two bronze rings. Each holds a collection of long iron pins. By touch, I locate the pins I need, then kneel before the door. Another ten heartbeats is all I need to pick this lock. The tunnel door swings open, and I step into an unlit storeroom.

I make my way across the dark room by memory. I reach its front door without crashing into anything, and I press my ear to the doorframe. Hearing nothing, I lift the latch and push gently. To my relief, the olive oil I rubbed into the hinges last time pays off now as the door swings silently open. I step out into the dim, flickering light of the corridor and shut the door behind me, double-checking that it remains unlocked for my return.

I glance left and right, double-checking my mental map of my exits while I'm free from distraction. Three locked doors stand to the left of my exit door, and beyond them the wider central corridor that connects a warren of storerooms beneath the Children's Temple. Five locked doors stand to my right, and beyond them a dead end. I face eight locked doors on the opposite wall.

Satisfied that I'm properly oriented, I hurry to the fourth door from the left on the opposite wall. Picks in hand, I kneel before the lock and set to work. I've never entered this particular storeroom before, but the lock sounds about the same as all the others, and my mother has described what the room looked like the last time she went inside seven years ago. The Mohirai tend to make changes on a timescale of centuries, so I'm hoping to find everything within basically unchanged.

Padding footsteps echo softly to my left, coming from somewhere in the central corridor. *Three more healers remain inside the wall*, I remember, and my mouth goes dry. Perhaps my mother misjudged, and the pharmaka preparations for tomorrow's Calling Day ceremony aren't complete after all. Maybe one of the healers forgot some ingredient and she's coming back here now. I close my eyes, forcing back the distracting thoughts, blocking out all sensation other than the sound of my picks inside this lock. Almost there.

Snick. My door unlocks just as the padding footsteps stop. A door in the main corridor creaks open. Relief washes away some of my nerves. That must be some Mohira visiting a food storeroom. I'm safe here, at least for now. I risk lingering in the corridor a moment longer to light a candle stub from my pack at the nearest oil lamp. Then I slip into the storeroom and lock the door behind me.

I'm exultant, having reached my destination without a hitch and gained the advantage of light, which should speed things up considerably.

The urgent need to sneeze nearly blows out my advantage. I clap my free hand over my nose and mouth, squeezing hard. Tears stream from my watering eyes, blurring my vision. My mother warned me about the smell, but the powerful melange of aromas emanating from the pharmaka ingredients in this room is more pungent than I'd expected. I switch to breathing through my mouth like a swimmer, which seems appropriate because my head is starting to swim. I need to move fast. Even the raw ingredients of pharmaka can have powerful effects on the uninitiated, like me.

I hold up my candle to examine the room. Four large barrels stand in the four corners of the room. Wooden shelves mounted on iron brackets line the stone walls from floor to ceiling. Large clay jars fill the shelves. Each bears a wax label neatly lettered in cuneiform with a description of the jar's contents. My mother explained the organization system: jars grouped chronologically by moon of harvest, then by moon phase. I skim the labels shelf by shelf. Ah, here they are: ingredients harvested near the first full moon after the summer solstice.

I can't suppress an indignant grumble when I spot the jar I need—dried amanitai—on a top shelf. Of course my mother wouldn't have anticipated this problem. That shelf would be well within her reach, within reach for almost anyone but me. Children raised by the Mohirai grow up eating a rich diet laced with many forms of pharmaka, which generally produces tall bodies, long arms, long legs. Not for the first time, I curse my mother's adamant stance on raising me without pharmaka.

I scan the room for possible solutions. The shelves appear solidly built, and they're already carrying considerable weight. It's possible I could step up onto a lower shelf to reach the top one. But I imagine the difficulty of hopping down with such a large jar and the risk of upsetting a whole shelf full of jars. I'm an excellent climber, but the risk seems too great. There must be a better option.

I could try to use a jar from a lower shelf as a step stool. I'm not confident one of these jars could bear my entire weight, though. If there were a plank, perhaps I could safely spread my weight across several jars and use that as a step, but I don't see anything like a plank.

There's that large barrel in the corner beside the shelf, though. I approach and examine it, wondering whether the barrel might be safe to stand on. I slip my fingers into the grooves carved into the barrel's circular top and discover to my delight that the top lifts off. I'm now holding the bit of plank I need for my step stool.

I glance inside the open barrel. It's about half full of what appears to be pure water. Seems odd to store water all the way down here in the storerooms. Healers usually require fresh spring water to prepare pharmaka. I risk a tentative sniff over the barrel. I still think it's water, but I really can't be sure with all the other bizarre smells confusing my nose.

I shake my head to clear it. All this pharmaka in the air must be getting to me. Of course it doesn't matter what's in this barrel; I need to focus on getting the amanitai and getting out of here.

I quickly construct a makeshift tripod stool from three jars and the barrel top. I step up, pull down the jar I need, set it carefully on the floor, and pry off the wax-sealed lid. The mushroom powder inside appears just as my mother described: rust in color, almost as fine as dust.

The jar's nearly full—over a bushel of powder, easily twice what we've agreed to pay the free men in exchange for our westward passage. Usually, I take only what we need, to minimize the risk of the Mohirai noticing what we've taken. But we're never coming back here again, so it seems foolish to leave behind something that could be so useful for bribes. I rummage through my pack and withdraw an empty linen-lined leather sack. I slip the sack over the mouth of the jar and upend the jar's entire contents into it.

A little cloud of mushroom dust rises as I set the empty jar back down. Holding my breath to avoid inhaling any of the airborne amanitai, I knot the sack closed and shove it into my pack. The overfilled sack is a little too big to fit entirely inside my pack, unfortunately. I hadn't accounted for the extra volume. Maybe I should empty some of the amanitai back into the jar so I'll be more streamlined for the run back out through the tunnels.

Unfortunately, I've run out of time for that. I hear footsteps again: two sets. My stomach churns, but I keep calm. It could be more visitors to the food storerooms.

But no, I realize with dismay—these footsteps are too loud to be in the adjacent corridor. They're coming this way, along with the voices of two women chatting.

The first woman says, "Do you need anything while I'm in here, sister?"

The second says, "A handful of withania root should do it."

I curse inwardly. I recognize this ingredient name, because I just saw it on a shelf in this room.

"More withania?" Something jingles like a hundred keys on a ring. The jingling pauses, and the first woman calls out, like she's now separated from her companion. "Did something go wrong with the preparation of the unbinding pharmaka?"

The second woman calls back, "No, but Serapen told me before she left for the clearing that we need more doses."

The jingling stops. The first woman says, "Spirits, it would have been nice for the Voice to tell her that a bit earlier, wouldn't it? We'll be up all night making a second batch."

"Ah, well," says the second. "The Voice works in mysterious ways."

A chuckle, then the first says, "Did she say why? Is it possible there'll be a novice Artifex called tomorrow?"

"She didn't say, though I can't think of another reason."

The first woman says, "Can you imagine a boy in the house of novices?"

Laughter from both of them, then the second woman says, "Hard to say whether that's good fortune or bad for the boy, but the girls will enjoy it, I'm sure. I certainly would have."

The first woman says, "I can't even remember when the last one was called. What do you think? Over a century? Maybe two?"

To my relief, the women seem to be in no hurry to conclude their chat about the novice Artifex, whatever that means. I have a moment to consider my options. I still have the advantage of surprise. If I burst out of this room, I can escape through the door I left unlocked across the hall. There's little chance these women can catch me in the corridor, and I can move much faster than they can through the tunnels. Even though my pack is now a bit unwieldy, the amanitai powder is light and won't slow me down much.

Unfortunately, I'll be seen if I step out into the corridor. Once I'm seen, the Mohirai will send out an alarm. With an alarm out, my mother and I can still escape through the woods, but that's not where we need to go this time. We need to get to the docks, where the boat is waiting to carry us far from here. Getting to the docks was going to be tricky enough without an alarm, but with an alarm out it will be nearly impossible. Even if we did get to the docks, there's almost no possibility our boat would wait for us after an alarm. No sailor would be foolish enough to cross the Mohirai openly by helping runaways.

And once that boat leaves, it won't be easy to find another. It took my mother years of careful preparation to arrange this departure for us. It could take years to arrange it all a second time.

Think, Ava, think.

If only there were somewhere to hide in here, I could stay put, let this Mohira gather what she needs, then slip out after she's gone. No one would be the wiser until someone notices all the amanitai is missing. By then, my mother and I will be safely out at sea. I like this plan far better than the first. The only problem is that there's nothing in here large enough to conceal a whole person.

Except … there is a perfect hiding place for someone as small as I am. I spring into action, swift and silent as I return the storeroom to the condition I found it. It's no good hiding if it's obvious I was here.

The keys jingle outside the door again. There's a scrape of metal on metal as a key enters the lock. My stomach drops. I still need to get into my hiding place, but she'll be in here in three heartbeats. She's going to catch me. I get ready to run for it.

There's a faint crunching sound in the lock. Relief washes over me. She tried the wrong key. The jingling resumes.

Her mistake gives me just enough extra time. I lick my fingers and put out my candle, plunging the room into darkness. Stepping toward the opened barrel in the corner, I grasp the lip of the opening with both hands, swing my legs over the edge, and lower myself carefully inside. I gasp involuntarily at the shock of icy water rising up my legs. I bite my lip hard—too hard—to silence myself. I taste blood.

I lean over to pick up my pack and the barrel lid from the floor. Holding my pack tight over my head with one arm and balancing the barrel lid above me with my other hand, I sink quickly until I'm sitting on the bottom of the barrel. The bone-chilling water rises to my neck as I pin my knees to my chest. I try and fail several times to close the barrel lid above my pack. It would be easy if I could just let the pack get wet, but I'm pretty sure a bag of wet amanitai will be worthless to us. At last I manage to close the lid by dropping my head so far forward that my bleeding lip is submerged in the water.

The storeroom door creaks open.

THE VOICE IN ALL

Hiding inside the barrel, with frigid water rising all the way up over my mouth, I breathe as silently as possible through my nose, trying not to blow bubbles. I listen as the Mohira steps into the storeroom and bustles about for what seems to be an impossibly long time, opening and closing at least half a dozen jars as she mutters to herself.

I'm losing sensation in the arm holding the pack above my head at this awkward angle, so I make a minuscule adjustment. To my horror, something powdery spills from the top of my pack into the water. The overfilled bag of amanitai has come untied. How could I have forgotten to double-check that knot?

A scent like dark forest soil floats toward me across the surface of the water. I press my lips tightly shut, but not before a taste of something bitter, sweet, and musky slips over my tongue. The cut on my lip where I bit myself tingles strangely.

I stew in amanitai for I don't know how long, until at last the Mohira departs. The door closes and locks. Footsteps retreat down the corridor. I'm relieved that my plan worked, but I'm worried because I don't know how much of the amanitai I've spilled into the water.

I climb out of the barrel in the pitch dark, dripping everywhere, but there's no help for that or for the amanitai I'm leaving behind in the barrel. My soaked clothes cling to me, and I wedge my tongue between my teeth to stop them from chattering with cold. I feel my way across the room toward the door. Fortunately, this lock only prevents someone from coming in, so I don't have to pick the lock to get out while I'm shivering.

I open the creaky door and step into the corridor. There's no point trying to re-lock the door with my picks. The wet mess I'm leaving behind is an unmistakable sign I was here.

By the light of the oil lamps, I quickly check the contents of my pack. My riding boots at the bottom are wet. But to my relief, the leather sack containing the amanitai remains dry. About a third of the amanitai spilled into the water while I was in the barrel, though. I suppose it's good that I took so much extra, after all. What remains is still more than we need. I retie the top of the sack quickly, triple-checking my knot this time.

I cross the hall, take my exit, and hurry across the unlit storeroom. Chilly air pours over me as I open the back door into the tunnel. Despite my soaked clothes and shivering, my skin tingles with a strange warmth. Probably just nerves. Quickly, I step into the tunnel and pull the door closed behind me.

The rough tunnel wall slides faster and faster beneath my fingertips as I race ahead. Unfortunately, I can't outrun the inner voice, which sounds like my mother, chastising me for my mistake. It's not my narrow escape that bothers me —that Mohira's unexpected appearance in my storeroom was no fault of mine.

But the failed knot and lost amanitai were entirely my fault. It's been years since I've made a mistake like that on a job.

I cross the intersection, running at full speed all the way until I reach the last little rise in the tunnel. A smudge of dark grey appears in the void ahead of me: the cave opening. I've made it.

I pause just inside the opening. The forest outside sounds unusually loud for this time of night, full of animal calls and hums and chirps, some of which I recognize, but many of which I've never heard before. The unfamiliar noises make me uneasy, but there are definitely no human sounds, so I step outside cautiously. I'm surprised by how bright it seems beneath the canopy. It's almost as if dawn's approaching.

My breath comes in short, panting gasps, and I sway on my feet, lightheaded. Sprinting such a short distance shouldn't have winded me like this. Instinctively, I drop to a crouch, pressing my hands to the ground to steady myself. My wet palms tingle where they touch the soil.

As I struggle to catch my breath, an icy understanding washes over me. That taste in the barrel—maybe I swallowed some of the amanitai that spilled into the water. Or that smell—maybe I breathed in too much of that pungent aroma floating around the storeroom.

Stay calm, Ava. Whatever it was, I couldn't have swallowed or breathed in very much of it. I was in the storeroom longer than planned, but not that long. At least, I don't think it was that long. I'm struggling with my sense of how much time has passed. The forest does seem oddly bright for this time of night. How long have I been crouching here?

Confusing impressions swirl through my head. The trees seem to grow taller. Or am I shrinking? Wait, are my arms growing longer? I hold up my hands—dirty again—and stare at them, momentarily awed by the sight of these familiar, wonderful, strange instruments. I wiggle my fingers. They're so far away. All of my body feels far away. I touch my face tentatively to make sure it's still there, and cool mud smears my cheeks.

Focus, Ava. I need to keep moving. I need to find my mother before this gets any worse. She'll know what to do.

The strange distortions of my sight and hearing do nothing to help my rapidly worsening balance. I remove my soaked cloth shoes. Feeling the forest floor under my bare feet again anchors me somewhat better to my surroundings. I know I should bury the shoes, but I'm not sure whether I'll be able to stand up again if I lean over, so I simply throw them as far away from the path as I can.

I walk, much more slowly and carefully than before, back the way I came. If I just keep going downslope, I'll reach the lookout spot. I narrow my focus to the step ahead. But step by step, I'm slowing down. Slower and slower. I try to remember where I'm going and why I'm going and how I'm supposed to get there.

At last I stop, rooted to the path. My throat goes dry. I tremble. A tingling warmth rises up through my feet. My awareness sinks down into the ground, spreading slowly out toward the trees. A profound calm settles over me, and though a small voice inside of me cries out, it's swallowed up by stillness. I've lost myself. All I can do now is listen.

So I listen.

I listen.

I listen.

And I hear the Voice in all. The Voice speaks inside of me, but also in the rustle of leaves and needles above me, in the touch of the strange breeze stirring around me, in the wink of stars peeking down at me through the canopy. The Voice conveys pure meaning, speaking the language within language.

We are the bridge joining light to darkness. We are the wheel turning season to season. We are the threads binding realm to realm.

No, no, no. I slam my hands over my ears. But the Voice in all can't be shut out. It is inexorable.

We are creator, preserver, destroyer of worlds.

"No!" I cry, trying to drown out the Voice with my own voice. "No, no, no." I somehow tear one foot from the ground and take a step, then another, then another.

Together you shall seek us, find us, know us.

Together you shall amplify us.

"Mama!" I call. I know I'm far from the lookout spot, but maybe she can hear me. Maybe she'll come to me.

Together you shall weave us through the many worlds.

The dark forest around me disappears in a flash of blinding light.

I stand before a smooth wall of reflective glass. The glass wall rises straight up from the hard, flat surface beneath my feet. I recognize myself in the reflection, although I look so strange, wearing clothes I've never seen before, the upper half of my face and my eyes entirely covered by a shiny mask. The glass wall rises all the way up into the clear blue sky, like a bridge to the sun.

It's the glass tower. I've seen this tower before, but only in dreams—never before in such vivid detail.

I rise up slowly through the air like I'm floating to the surface through deep water. I rise faster and faster, until I'm not just floating but flying. I look down and see my strange shoes, striped in brightest blue, white, and green. Between my feet, I see the tops of many glass towers rising from the heart of a beautiful unwalled city. The city sprawls over many hills, bounded only by a vast ocean to the west and a sparkling bay to the east. It's larger than any city I've ever seen in all my years of roaming with my mother through Dulai.

My awareness flows through every part of the city, inside and outside its buildings, above and below broad avenues, over bridges, across the bay, up into the hills beyond. Everywhere, I see strange creatures speeding through the streets. No, they're carts, or some kind of machines, rolling on shiny wheels, though there are no horses or oxen pulling them.

And the people—so many people! I never knew there could be so many people, and here they are all gathered in one place. So many colors and styles of clothes and hair. So many eyes concealed, like mine, behind shiny masks. Even the Mohirai from the most distant temple cities don't look so strange.

But the strangest thing of all is seeing men and women and children of many ages together in one city. I see from the way they speak to each other and look at each other and touch each other that these people belong to each other. I recognize what I'm seeing from what my mother has taught me. These people are bound in kinship, a bond forbidden since the time of destruction, forbidden by the Mohirai, forbidden—I thought—by the Voice in all.

I'm stunned by what the Voice has shown me. The vision fades. The Voice says, *Together you shall answer our call.*

When the Voice departs from me, I find myself lying face down in the dirt, tangled in the underbrush. I open my eyes, and the dark forest spins in my peripheral vision, nauseating me. It feels like I've broken half my ribs, and there's a stabbing sensation below my heart. I whimper involuntarily at the pain in my chest, then bite my lip to silence myself, then wince when my teeth dig deeper into the cut already there. I taste mud and blood.

I need to calm down. Anyone could hear me crashing about the woods and moaning like this. I raise my head a little to scan my surroundings. To my relief, I see the footpath not far behind me. I'll retrace my tracks from there. Maybe I haven't wandered too far from the lookout spot.

I push myself up. Even this tiny exertion makes me start panting again, and the panting rapidly worsens the pain in my chest. I take a tentative step forward, but a root catches my foot, and my balance deserts me. I fall hard onto my knees and try to suppress a cry at the agonizing pain that shoots out from my heart.

"Hello?" calls a voice.

I freeze. It's not the Voice in all, and it's not my mother.

△▽△

"Hello?" I call out a second time, peering into the forest shadows, searching for the source of that last whimper.

Silence. If it is a lost boy, he should answer my call. But he might be hesitant to show himself, since it's past the younger boys' curfew. A scolding from Hedi can be intimidating, even to me.

"It's all right, little brother," I say, speaking loud enough that he can hear I'm not Hedi or one of the other Mohirai. "You can come out."

No answer.

"It's all right," I say again, in the voice I use to soothe skittish horses. "I'm coming to get you. We can go back to the house together. I'll tell Hedi I kept you out late for chores."

The forest ahead is quite dark, but I should be able to find him. The sound wasn't far away. I walk forward, listening carefully. The rapid shallow breathing resumes, closer than before. I sense eyes on me but can't see anyone.

The breathing stops again, but it was coming from the dense patch of leafy underbrush directly ahead of me. I extend my hand, saying, "It's all right. Don't be afraid."

The leaves burst into motion as a shape springs away from me. It's a small figure, clad in the undyed wool tunic all of the children wear. So it is one of the younger boys from the house, though I have no idea why he'd run from me. I call out, "Wait!"

The boy doesn't stop, so I jog after him. He's unsteady on his feet, and he doesn't get far before he trips and falls flat on his belly. He gasps in pain.

I hurry toward the fallen boy and put my hand on his shoulder. He flinches. His tunic is sopping wet and ice cold to my touch, and there's a strange smell about him that reminds me of mixed wine, although I don't smell alcohol.

I piece together what might have happened. Hedi keeps the storerooms in the house kitchen locked, but even with the ever-watchful eyes of the house Mohirai, certain bottles have a tendency to go missing. This boy will probably have an awful headache tomorrow, but he'll have learned his lesson. Meddling with pharmaka never ends well.

"Are you hurt, little brother?" I ask. Again there's no answer. With both hands, I turn him gently onto his side to take a look at him.

A curtain of dark curls obscures his face. His lips, rather full and feminine for a boy, are smeared with blood. He pants rapidly through his mouth. A long, wet braid matted with cedar needles and twigs lies across his chest. That's when I realize he's not a little boy. She's a little girl. I brush her hair back from her eyes. Actually, maybe she's not so little. It's hard for me to tell her age. She's no taller than a twelfth summer girl, but her face is closer to a woman's.

"Stay … away … from …" She speaks in gasps. Her face contorts in a grimace, and she shivers so hard her teeth chatter. She's soaked head to toe and clearly in pain, although her only obvious injury is her bleeding lip. As I lean over her, that pharmaka smell gets stronger, but I can't identify exactly what kind of pharmaka it is. The scent is woodsy, maybe floral, but with a musky undertone that's almost animal. I wonder what she's gotten into. Nothing good, from the look of her.

Maybe I should leave her here and come back with help. But she seems very disoriented. She might try to run off again and hurt herself even worse before I can return. I could easily carry her back to the house of boys, though. Hedi Mohira will know what to do.

"Easy there, little sister," I say. "I'm taking you to a healer."

She moans softly, "No … don't … I …"

I slip my arm under her shoulders and raise her to a sitting position. She resists, wincing with every movement, so I try to be gentle. I scoop my other arm under her knees and stand up. She's even lighter than I expected. She's cold against my chest, and her wet clothes soak into mine. The pharmaka scent intensifies, filling my lungs.

Her shaking right hand reaches for her belt. I look down to see what she's doing, and her hand flashes swiftly toward my neck.

The edge of a blade digs into my throat. Every muscle in my body tenses at once. She continues to shiver in my arms, her face so close to mine that I taste her breath on my lips. With a strange sense of detachment, I notice there's no scent of pharmaka on her breath, only a sweetness like spring water. I wonder where that strange smell is coming from, then.

"I don't want … to hurt you …" She's still gasping, but her words come more easily than before. The cold point of her knife quivers on my skin as her hand trembles, tracing a wandering line toward the pulsing artery just below my jaw. "Let me go."

Her eyes and tone are fierce, despite her apparent weakness. My mouth is dry, and I try to swallow, but it's difficult with the knife's pressure against the sinews of my neck. My entire awareness seems to shrink down to the edge of her blade.

"All right," I say, trying to stay calm, hoping this will calm her, too. "All right. I'm putting you down."

She doesn't lower her blade as I lower her feet carefully to the ground. She tries but fails to keep her balance, then pitches toward me, her raised knife hand swinging erratically. I catch her without thinking, and for a moment we're locked in a dangerous embrace, the length of her body pressed against me, her clothes soaking even more into mine, her blade pressed to my throat. Her heart races against my chest, or perhaps that's my heart racing against hers.

I'm afraid to hold on to her because she might try to kill me, but I'm afraid to let her go because with another stumble like that she might still kill me accidentally. I compromise and step back from her, holding her by the shoulders at arm's length. Her knife is still extended toward me, but at least my neck is beyond slashing distance of her hand.

"Careful," I say, as much to myself as to her, as I realize with shock what a near miss I've had. I might not be afraid of Death, but I have no desire to go there yet.

She stares at me, her eyes flickering over my face. She leans back slightly, losing her balance again. I tighten my grip on her shoulders so she won't fall. She glances down at my hands and back up at me. The fierce look fades from her eyes.

"Let me go," she says softly, wincing as she speaks, like her chest hurts her. Maybe she's broken a rib.

"How about this," I propose, doing my best to sound completely non-threatening. "You sheath your knife, then I'll let you go."

"No," she counters, her voice growing stronger. "You let me go. Then I'll go."

I doubt this will work. She's clearly in no condition to go anywhere. But I'm not in the best position to negotiate, because she still holds the knife.

"Fine," I concede. "I'm letting go."

I slowly let go of her shoulders. She slowly lowers her knife. Shivers wrack her small frame again, and the knife falls from her hand, plunging into the soil beside her bare foot. We both look down at it for a heartbeat, then grab for it.

She drops to a crouch, moving with incredible speed considering her unsteadiness a moment ago. Her right hand closes tight around the handle. I grab her wrist, squeezing hard until she winces and releases her grip on the knife. She tries to grab for it again with her left hand, but I see this coming and catch that wrist too.

"Let me go," she growls. But my negotiating position is rather improved, so I don't let go this time. Instead, I haul her by the wrists away from the knife and push her down onto her back. I've never handled anyone, boy or girl, so roughly before. My stomach turns at the sickening thud of her body against the ground. She's simultaneously furious and gasping in pain, thrashing and kicking and even trying to bite me until I splay her arms out beside her so my arms are clear of her teeth. She's stronger than she looks, but not nearly as strong as I am, and she's wearing herself out without managing to inflict much damage on me. I climb on top of her, straddling her thrashing legs.

"Stop," I say firmly. "Calm down."

"You're hurting me," she gasps through clenched teeth. I loosen my crushing hold on her wrists and take some of my weight off her. But when her knees take aim at my groin, I reverse course quickly and pin her legs even tighter between mine.

We're both panting shallowly now, and that pharmaka scent seems to be coming from everywhere at once. Whether it's residual shock from my near miss with the blade or something else, I'm not quite sure, but my vision swims. A sea breeze sweeps through the trees, chilling the wet front of my tunic, and I shiver.

I focus on the girl beneath me, trying to ignore the forest around us, which is slowly spinning. She stops shivering, even though she's more soaked than I am. For the first time, I get a clear look at her face. She glares up at me, her dark eyes fiery, fearless, and calculating. Her cheeks are dirty, and she bares her teeth at me, her bleeding lips quivering with fury. Her expression would be terrifying if she weren't so clearly in pain.

Despite the blood and mud obscuring her face, she looks familiar. Of course I should know her, since I know every girl in the temple city. My mind skims over the names and faces of them all, from the youngest girls in their eighth summer to the girls my age in their sixteenth. But she is none of them. There's a fog in my mind as I try to remember her.

"Who are you?" I ask at last, mystified.

Her expression softens. The look she gives me is resigned, almost pitying, as she says, "Have they taken that from you, too, Dom?"

The question disorients me, but the sound of her voice saying my name cuts through the fog. I struggle harder to remember. A tingling sensation spreads through my palms where they dig in to her bare wrists. She turns her head from side to side, looking at my hands pressing hers into the dirt.

"What are you doing?" she says.

Fragments of memory gather before me. A little girl with a scarlet ribbon at the end of her long dark braid, smiling down at me from a high cedar branch, her bare toes tracing circles in the air. Climbing up through the hollow trunk, learning from her the handholds and footholds on the way to the top. Her animated hands gesticulating in storytelling. Her fingers laced through mine, pulling me along a forest path, pointing the way toward some special place she wants to show me. Her spicy sweet scent of cedar, ferns, and sea salt. Her voice in my ear, whispering secrets, giggling, saying my name.

I stare down at her, stunned. It can't be. "Ava?"

She looks surprised.

"But …" Confused, I shake my head. This turns out to be a bad move, because it worsens the spinning at the edge of my vision. "Where have you been?"

She hesitates, then says slowly, "I've been with my mother."

"Your what?" I say. Whatever is affecting my vision must be affecting my hearing, too.

"Never mind. Get off me."

Her imitation of the trained voice of a priestess is near perfect, and I almost comply without thinking. Boys learn to obey the Mohirai from an early age, and my deeply ingrained habit of obedience extends even to the uninitiated girls much of the time.

But the skin at my throat prickles in warning. It's been years since I last saw Ava. I have no idea what's happened to her or what she might do to me. Even though we were friends when we were little—at least, that's the memory inexplicably trickling back to me—I'd be mad to trust her now.

"Are you going to kill me?" I ask. The question sounds foolish even to me, but I want to hear her answer before I decide what to do next.

She glances over at the knife, then back up at me. "Not tonight," she says.

Not exactly reassuring, and I'm not going to take her word for it. But it also feels ridiculous sitting here on top of her while she's not fighting back.

"All right," I say. "I'll get off, but hold still or we're going to end up right back here."

I reposition her wrists and pin them over her head with one hand. I retrieve her knife with my free hand and slip it into my belt. I pat down the front and sides of her tunic and examine each pouch on her belt. She doesn't appear to have any other weapons. Except for her hands, her feet, her knees, her teeth … Well, at least she doesn't appear to have any other blades.

Keeping a hold on the knife handle with my left hand, I carefully climb off her. My peripheral vision is still spinning, and my balance is unsteady, so I remain in a crouch, one hand pressed to the ground. She sits up and massages her wrists.

"Sorry about that," I say, gesturing to her wrists. I didn't mean to hurt her, but she didn't leave me many options.

"I'm fine," she says, to herself more than to me, tugging down her wet sleeves over what will likely be some ugly bruises. She looks at me warily and says, "But what was that?"

"What was what?" I say.

She reaches for my right hand and taps my palm with her forefinger. "That tingling. Did you do that?"

I'm surprised she felt that too. "I don't know," I say. I'm confused by everything that just happened. "I was trying to remember your name, and then my hands felt … strange … and I remembered …" I trail off as more bits and pieces of memory float through my mind in a jumble.

She looks like she's about to ask another question, but she shakes her head quickly and says, "I have to go."

This cuts through my confusion, and I refocus on her. "Ava, you can't. You're—I don't know what exactly. But you're barely able to stand. You're hurt. You need a healer."

"I'm fine," she says again. She climbs to her feet, much steadier now than she was a few moments ago. She searches the nearby underbrush and picks up a leather pack she must have dropped when she fell. She inspects its contents carefully and slings it over her shoulder, preparing to leave.

"Wait!" I can't believe this. She can't leave. I have so many questions. I rise from crouching to standing too fast. The ground seems to lurch to the left, and I stagger to the right. Ava's eyes widen as she watches me struggle to keep my balance.

"Are you all right?" she asks, putting her hand on my chest to steady me, her voice sounding farther away than it should. She looks from me to the footpath behind her and back to me. With a wordless sound of frustration, she grabs my hand. "Come on. I'll take you back to your house first. Listen to me, Dom. Tell Hedi you were exposed to amanitai. Do you hear me? Amanitai."

She looks at me, waiting for me to respond. I'm vaguely aware I should answer, but it's hard to remember what she just said. She pulls me in the direction of the forest edge. I wish she'd slow down. How can she walk so easily now while I'm barely able to stand? And why is she in such a hurry? If she'd just wait a moment, maybe my head would stop spinning.

But she hauls me forward. I follow only a few paces before I sway. In a blur of motion, she darts back to my side, wedges her shoulder under my arm, and wraps her arm around my waist. She tries to hold me up, but she's much smaller than I am. As my legs give way, my weight overwhelms her. We both fall hard to our knees.

I'm vaguely aware of her colorful cursing as I stare up through the little gaps in the canopy that reveal the stars winking down at us. My mind wanders. It's getting late. What a strange way to spend the last night before my Calling Day. It's nice to see Ava, again, though. I've been missing her, even though I didn't remember she existed until just now. Where did she say she was all these years? I try to remember, but it slips away like water through my fingers.

THE DOUBLE BIND

Damn the Voice, curse the sisters, and spirits blast it all. This job has gone badly sideways.

Dom's a dead weight around my shoulders, and when he stumbles, he pulls both of us down hard. I swear under my breath continuously as I heave up with all my remaining strength. The powerful arms and long legs he used to wrestle me to the ground are somehow useless now. I'm not nearly strong enough to lift him, and there's no way I can drag him all the way through the underbrush back to the edge of the forest so he can be found by the Mohirai.

But I can't leave him here. Even though it's been years since I last saw him, as soon as I recognized Dom all I could think of was that sweet little boy trailing me around the grounds for the year I lived here in the temple city, before my mother took me on the run. Somehow I've exposed him to this pharmaka, and it looks like he's starting to go through the same sequence of side effects I was having earlier. He's apparently not feeling the stabs in his chest yet, but I can't bear the thought of him lost and alone in the woods, writhing in pain on the ground like I was before he found me.

Dom's head tips back, and I worry he's lost consciousness. But his eyes are open as he says in a wandering, delighted voice, "Look at the stars. Do you hear them? Don't they sound beautiful?"

I remember the strange things the Voice said to me when I first emerged from the cave, and how I seemed to see in vivid detail the city of glass towers where I often find myself in dreams. Somehow even in that dreamlike state I managed to wander far past the lookout spot where I'm supposed to be meeting my mother. So even if Dom is having some similarly weird experience, maybe he can walk while it's happening, too.

I ease his heavy arm off my shoulders and stand to face him. To my relief, he stays upright, though he's still on his knees. I take one of his hands. His rough, strong palm feels nothing like the soft child's hand I remember holding when we were small. I set my other hand on his cheek and steer his gaze back down from the patch of starry sky he's staring at. He refocuses on me, his expression peaceful and open, more like the boy I remember now that we're not grappling with a knife between us. His deep-set eyes sparkle in the shadows, framed by level brows and long lashes. He's changed a lot, but I recognized him by these eyes, which look out at the world with such intensity—far more curious and perceptive than other boys' eyes, even now, veiled in a haze of pharmaka.

"Come with me," I say firmly, doing my best to imitate the priestess voice my mother uses when she needs me to obey without asking questions. It must be a poor imitation, though, because Dom immediately starts asking questions in that same wandering voice.

"Where are we going?" he says.

"I'm taking you back to the house of boys, to Hedi, so you can get help," I say, pulling on his hand. To my enormous relief, he stands. We haven't made it three paces, though, when he stops.

"But … where are you going?" he says.

This is too complicated to explain to him, especially in his confused state, and anyway of course I can't tell him where I'm going. So all I say is, "I'm going away from here."

I pull on his hand, but now he won't budge. A deep crease forms between his eyebrows as he searches my face. His voice is clearer, more insistent, his words coming faster as he asks,"Why don't you stay here? Tomorrow is our Calling Day, remember? You've always wanted to be a Mohira."

I was surprised that Dom had remembered even my name, but it seems he's remembered far more. This was all we used to talk about, in long afternoons playing together in the forest. I dreamed of being a Mohira, skilled in the arts, initiated into the mysteries so frustratingly locked away from children. He dreamed of being a Mohira, too, at first, until the reality of every boy's fate became impossible for either of us to ignore, even in play.

I don't understand how he could be remembering any of this, though. My mother told me that unbound memories can't be recovered. And Dom's memory of me was definitely removed by unbinding pharmaka. He didn't recognize me, not at first.

Of course we've both changed a lot in the last seven years, but his lack of recognition was deeper than that. He had that foggy look and those flickering eye movements of someone trying to recall an unbound memory. I'd anticipated that look. When troubling things happen, especially when they happen to children, the Mohirai often use unbinding pharmaka to smooth away the difficult memories. My disappearance would certainly have been troubling to some of the other children, especially to Dom, who was my closest friend while I lived here.

I'll have to discuss this with my mother when this wretched job concludes. Maybe this means I could someday recover my memories of her, from the years before my unbinding. But this is irrelevant right now. We'll have moons of leisure time to talk this all over once I leave Dom somewhere safe and she and I are on the boat.

"Where are you going on a boat?" Dom asks, tilting his head, his eyes widening, his fingers tightening around mine.

Did I just say that aloud? I shouldn't have told him that. I must still be in a haze of pharmaka myself.

Dom watches me with intense interest, awaiting my answer, and there's that tingling again where my hand touches his. My thoughts rush on, strangely difficult to stop.

The boat will take us to the land on the far side of the ocean, far beyond the reach of the Mohirai and the control of the Voice in all. It's a circuitous route, and we'll sail for many moons.

My mother has described the journey to me many times over the last seven years. She knows more about the route than the destination, though. In the absence of better information, I've constructed my own picture of what lies beyond the ocean from bits and pieces of my mother's teachings and my own imagination. I know it's little more than a dream, but the city of glass towers is what I always see when I imagine the place where she's promised we'll be safe, where we can be a family, where people live in freedom from the Voice and the Mohirai who enforce its will. The breathtaking vision of the city that I saw shortly after hearing the Voice flashes in my mind again. For a fleeting instant, I'm flying over the towers.

"Beautiful," Dom says, staring at me in wonder.

I stare back at him in disbelief. He's certainly not talking about me. Somehow, I know he's talking about the city of glass towers. With a sinking feeling, I look down at my tingling fingers entwined in his, my wet sleeve dripping water into our palms. Oh, spirits. This is not good.

I drop Dom's hand and step away from him. I hurriedly strip off my wet wool tunic and breeches, running my hands over my naked body. Everywhere I touch is covered in a slightly gritty, sticky residue of amanitai. I hadn't felt how much of it was on my skin, with my clothes so wet. I have no water to rinse with, so I tear handfuls of leaves from the underbrush and try to scrub off the mushroom dust. It doesn't work; I'm only moving the sticky grit around.

Dom's gaze travels up and down the length of me while I do this. Nakedness is utterly routine among the Mohirai, but he is a teenage boy, after all.

I'm thankful for the little breeze stirring through the trees that slowly dries my skin, though it makes me shiver again, which stirs the ache in my chest again, which makes everything harder again. I clench my teeth and work through the discomfort. To my relief, as my skin dries, brushing my hands over myself causes some of the amanitai powder to crumble away. I clean off as much as I can, until I'm too cold to bear it any longer. I kneel before my pack, my hands shaking badly as I rummage for my riding clothes. I change into them quickly. Dry clothes are a major improvement, but every part of my skin still feels gritty. I'll need to wash myself as soon as my mother and I are on the boat.

"Come on," I say to Dom. "Arms up."

"Why?" he asks. He looks at me with the same wondering expression he had while staring up at the stars. The pharmaka must be hitting him pretty hard now.

"I think there's pharmaka absorbing through our skin," I say slowly and clearly, uncertain whether he's already too far gone to understand me. "You need to take off these wet clothes."

Dom doesn't resist as I pull his tunic off over his head. Bare-chested, he looks as strong as an ox. The Mohirai have clearly prepared him well for the life of manual labor that lies ahead of him. I run my hand over his ribs where the tunic had absorbed the most water. My palm tingles where it touches him, but I don't feel any mushroom residue on his skin apart from what's rubbing off onto him from me.

Dom leans down and whispers, "Ava—"

Just as my mother's voice booms right behind me, "Ava!"

△▽△

Ava's face was a blur while I was having the strange sensation of overhearing her thoughts, but my vision sharpens when she strips off all her clothes.

I've studied a lot of girls' figures as I've taught myself to draw. Most of the sixteenth summer girls are long-limbed, curvaceous, beautiful in a decidedly feminine way. Ava's body is different. She's lean, muscular, small-breasted, narrow-hipped. Every line of her is diminutive and delicate. Her fascinating beauty is more feral than feminine, and it's amplified in motion. She's graceful like the Mohiran dancers, and she moves with precision and speed like a hunting falcon, especially now that she's so focused on whatever she's doing with all these leaves, which is a complete mystery to me.

It's a shame she clothes herself so quickly, but she re-captures my attention when she says, "Come on. Arms up."

I have no objection to her undressing me, but still I ask, "Why?"

"I think there's pharmaka absorbing through our skin," she says, tracing the damp imprints she left on my tunic during our scuffle. "You need to take off these wet clothes."

Before I can sort through the implications of either statement, her hands are at my waist. In a rush of panic, I grab for the knife at my belt and raise it high over my head, out of her reach. But she doesn't even seem to notice the knife. She's too intent on unbuckling my belt and pulling off my mud-smeared tunic. Keeping a firm grip on the knife, I lean forward and let the tunic slide over my head.

She tosses my tunic aside and runs her hand over my chest. Her palm is slightly gritty, which isn't surprising after all our grappling in the dirt. That tingling sensation follows the movement of her hand over my bare skin.

Over her shoulder, something looms in the shadows. Startled, I tighten my grip on the knife.

"Ava—" I whisper in warning.

A massive cloaked woman steps toward us, her eyes locked on the knife raised high in my hand. Her deep voice calls out in warning, "Ava!"

Ava relaxes visibly and turns toward the woman. "Spirits, I'm glad you found me."

The woman rushes forward and stands between me and Ava. "Drop your weapon," she says to me.

My hand drops immediately to my side, and I let go of the knife. I would have complied even if the woman hadn't used the priestess tone of command, because her face is so terrifying, with her teeth bared and her wide eyes staring down at me. She's at least half a head taller than I am, square-jawed, shoulders broad as a man's. Wisps of the fair hair framing her face seem to glow in the dark, along with the streaks of unusually pale skin visible beneath the mud on her cheeks. Physically, she appears in every way to be Ava's complete opposite, apart from the mud and the ferocity.

Ava seems confused by the woman's command until she looks back and sees the knife I've dropped on the ground beside me. Her eyes widen, and she grabs the woman's arm. I notice for the first time that the woman is gripping something beneath the folds of her cloak. "No!" Ava exclaims. "Mama, wait. It's not what it looks like. Please listen. I—"

The woman seems unmoved by Ava's protests, but she also seems satisfied that I present no further threat now that I've dropped the knife. She lets go of whatever she's gripping under her cloak and raises her hand to interrupt Ava. In a low, urgent voice, she says, "Later, Ava. You've been gone far longer than we planned. We can still make it, but we must go now."

"But I—" Ava begins, then starts shivering so hard she can't say another word. A moment later, I'm shivering, too.

I would normally defer to a girl to speak first, but Ava seems unable to proceed, and given the circumstances I suppose it's all right to interrupt her. I don't recognize this woman, and I've never heard of a sister named Mama before, so I decide to use the respectful form of address for a priestess of unknown rank.

"Mama Mohira," I say. This must be the wrong form of address, because Mama and Ava both give me a strange look, but I push on given the urgency of the situation. I don't understand who this sister is or why she needs to take Ava anywhere in such a hurry, but I'm sure she'll help us once we explain. "Ava needs a healer. We both do. We've had some accident with pharmaka."

Mama looks from me to Ava, then takes Ava's shivering shoulders in her hands and says, "Tell me what happened. Quickly."

"I had to … hide in a barrel of … water while I was in the storerooms." Ava's words are halting, and she winces with each breath. "I had … the amanitai … I still have it … but some … spilled into the water … I think I … swallowed some … but mostly … it stuck on … my skin … I was … confused … in the forest … trying to get … back to you … Dom … found me … and now it's … happening … to him too."

Mama looks up at me, at my shaking bare chest and arms. She jerks back her hands from Ava's shoulders and brushes her palms thoroughly on the outside of her cloak.

"Think, Ava," says Mama, her voice hard. "How much amanitai fell into the water?"

"Maybe … maybe a … third of a bushel?" says Ava. Mama curses under her breath, and Ava hurries to say, "But there's … plenty left … for the boat … I made sure."

"Were you barefoot?" says Mama.

"What?" Ava looks as perplexed by this question as I am.

"While you were walking through the woods. Were you barefoot?"

"Yes … Yes … Of course."

"You said you were confused. While you were confused, did you hear the Voice?"

Ava stares up at Mama, her expression fearful.

"Focus, Ava!"

"Yes," Ava gasps quickly.

Mama takes half a step back from Ava. Her broad shoulders slump as she says quietly, "There won't be a boat. Not for you. Not tonight."

"But you said … there's still time … if we hurry," says Ava, argumentative despite her shivering. "Can't you … give me … counter pharmaka … Once we're … on the boat?"

Mama shakes her head and says, "You've had an overdose of amanitai, Ava. It's the main ingredient in the binding pharmaka. There's only one thing to counterbalance it: unbinding pharmaka."

Finally I'm hearing something that makes a little bit of sense. I know the unbinding pharmaka, of course. The younger girls and boys drink unbinding pharmaka every night for the first few years after they arrive here. The Mohirai say it gives sweet dreams from the Voice, though in my experience it mostly gives very deep sleep, and you tend to remember no dreams at all when you wake up afterwards.

I've never heard of binding pharmaka before, though.

"But …" Ava winces, as her pain appears to worsen. "Maybe … I could … take just a … little bit of … unbinding pharmaka … Just enough to … stop this … this pain … this dizziness."

Mama says, "Even if I had unbinding pharmaka to give you, the amount you'd need is too much for someone so young. You need initiate training, and centuries of memories, to be able to tolerate high doses of unbinding pharmaka."

"Then … what will … we do?"

Seeing the contortions of pain on Ava's face, I feel an echoing pain in my own chest, under my heart, needling at first, then a stab. I suck in a breath through clenched teeth. Ava hears me and looks at me in concern, and my pain grows worse, and then her pain seems to grow worse, and then both of us are hunched over, clutching ourselves.

Mama looks from one of us to the other, then curses again.

"Go to him," says Mama, in a tone of disgust, gesturing toward me while keeping well back from Ava. "Take his hand."

"But why?" says Ava.

"Now, Ava."

Mama's tone of command is so harsh I cringe. Ava stumbles toward me and grabs my hand. I heave a sigh of relief at her touch. My pain gradually eases, and Ava's seems to as well. Cautiously, we both straighten up.

"What is happening?" Ava says to Mama, gripping my hand tightly.

Mama shakes her head, massaging her mud-streaked forehead with a broad hand, studying Ava like she's trying to identify a strange mushroom. She says, "In small doses, binding pharmaka amplifies the connection between two awarenesses. The longer the contact and the larger the dose, the stronger the connection. Too much connection with another awareness can cause great pain, even deadly pain, for one untrained in the arts."

"But—" Ava drops my hand quickly. She winces, and pain prickles in my chest. To my relief, she takes my hand again before it worsens. "But then shouldn't I be trying to get *away* from Dom, to stop the pain?"

Mama's pale eyes flick briefly my way. Frowning, she says, "An awareness like his shouldn't be enough to cause pain." I have no idea whether this is an insult, though her tone is certainly dismissive.

"But he's the only person I've touched since I left the storeroom," says Ava.

"He's the only human you've touched," says a voice, but it's not Mama's.

△▽△

"He's the only human you've touched." The clear, resonant voice of the High Priestess Serapen flows out of the forest behind me. I clench Dom's left hand in my right as my mind reels. How on Dulai could she have managed to get this close without my mother hearing her? She continues, "But he's not the only awareness you've touched."

My mother inhales sharply, and I can see she's realized something, but I don't know what it is, and she makes no sign to me. Slowly I turn around, searching for Serapen. I see nothing but trees. Damn, I wish I had my blade right now.

"Muse Serapen," Dom calls loudly, sounding relieved and taking a step in the direction of Serapen's voice, pulling me after him. "Please, we need your help."

I yank Dom backwards and curse his foolishness. He looks at me like I've kicked him. I suppose I've already kicked him several times, but seeing his expression, I feel a twinge of contrition for my harsh language. It's not his fault he doesn't know who Serapen really is, or that we need to get away from her, and it's too late to explain now.

The tall, slim figure of Serapen glides out of the darkness a few paces ahead of us, hands clasped before her heart in that peculiar rigid posture. She walks unhurriedly and silently toward me and Dom. The rustling of the forest seems to fade, until the only thing I hear is my own racing heartbeat.

Serapen stops halfway between us and my mother. She pushes back her hood, and tendrils of long snow-white hair spill out around her shoulders. Her dark complexion and the forest shadows make it difficult to see much of her face except for her gleaming eyes, twin pools that reflect every color of the nighttime woods from black and violet to deepest blue. There's something unsettling in the contrast between the fluid movement of Serapen's body and the birdlike flight of her gaze, which flicks precisely from place to place, transitions nearly imperceptible.

Serapen's strange eyes lock on my mother, and there's a crack in the underbrush as my mother steps back. I glance at her, and the tumultuous display of emotions on her usually stoic face confuses me. Is that fear? Grief? Rage?

"Lilith," says Serapen, drawing out my mother's name so it lingers in the stillness. "For seven years I have wondered what work the Voice was doing through you."

"Damn the Voice," my mother says. "The free people serve no Voice."

Calmly, Serapen says, "None of us walk free of the Voice, Lilith, though some choose not to listen."

Two hooded women appear in the shadows behind Serapen, flanking her. I glance sidelong at my mother, expecting her signal. Her eyes never stray from Serapen's, but behind her back, one of her hands signs to me, over and over, *Throw me your pack. Throw me your pack.*

My pack is still looped over my shoulders by both straps. I'll have to let go of Dom's hand to get it off and throw it to her. There's no way to do it without drawing attention. I wonder why she wants it right now. She must want me to be carrying as little weight as possible for whatever comes next. The contrast between her strength and my weakness has never seemed as stark, or as consequential, as it is right now.

"You fools who blindly worship the Voice are doomed to fail, Serapen," my mother says. "There is no purpose to a human life without freedom."

"You speak out of great ignorance, Lilith. What freedom exists may be found only in the Voice."

I mentally rehearse each movement I need to make. We may have only one chance to get it right. I'll drop Dom's hand, shrug the straps off my shoulders, swing the pack toward her. My mother will have to sign to me whatever I'm supposed to do next, but based on what I see, I'm guessing the plan is to run for it. Maybe she's going to make a distraction of some kind. I have no idea how far I can run away from Dom before the pain takes me down, but there's no way to find out except to try. I'll have to go as far as I can on my own, but my mother is strong enough to carry me on her back once I fall.

"Your world is destined for destruction," says my mother, keeping Serapen's eyes on her to buy me time. "You will see."

Serapen makes a long, low, wordless sound, something between a hum and a sigh. She says, "Indeed. I have been called to witness much. So I have. So I shall."

I spring into action, pulling away from Dom, slipping off the pack, tossing it to my mother. It flies in a perfect arc, and she catches it easily by one strap. In an instant, the pack is secure on her back, and she's flying toward the forest edge at full speed on her long, strong legs. She's made no sign to me, though, and I'm so surprised by this that I freeze uncertainly, a moment too long, before I spring after her. Each step brings pain, pain, more pain. I clutch my side.

Behind me, Serapen says calmly but firmly, "Stop her, Dom."

I don't make it ten strides before Dom catches me. I kick and scream and curse at him, but he wraps me in his long arms, pinning my hands to my sides, lifting me right off my feet. I can't get a hold on anything, so I kick his shins as hard as I can with my bare heels. He grunts in pain, but he keeps his hold on me. Each time I land a kick on him, I feel an echoing pain on my own shins. It's awful.

"Mama! Mama! Mama!" I shout.

The forest swallows up my voice. My mother does not return.

RESISTANCE IS FUTILE

Wrestling Ava to the ground wasn't easy the first time, and she seems to have recovered more of her strength since then. It takes me plus the two healers to hold her down this time. I pin her hands above her head, and a healer holds down each of her legs. My shins ache in a dozen places where Ava kicked me as I hauled her back here. She more than returned the damage I did to her wrists in our first scuffle. She shouts so loud that I imagine she'll wake everyone in the house of boys, and maybe the girls inside the wall, too.

"Mama! Mama! Mama!"

The woman who ran off—who Ava seems to think is named Mama but Serapen seems to think is named Lilith—is clearly not returning, and Serapen hasn't commanded anyone to follow her. I don't understand who that woman is or why Ava is so distraught, but she's clearly furious at me more than anyone else, because she alternates shouts of Mama with cursing my name.

When Ava stops shouting to catch her breath, I say hurriedly, "Muse Serapen, there's something wrong, something happened to Ava in a storeroom—"

The High Priestess makes a small gesture with her hand to stop me. She says, "I know, little brother. I heard what Ava said."

"Oh ..." I say. I don't understand how Serapen heard, but I press on. "Can you help her?"

Ava resumes shouting. Serapen looks like she's in pain, though she's probably just reacting to Ava, who's gradually growing hoarse but is still excruciatingly loud.

Serapen kneels beside me. She uses two long brown forefingers to probe the exposed undersides of Ava's wrists under my hands, pressing there for a few heartbeats. I've seen Hedi do this before. There's a nerve somewhere in the wrist that the healers manipulate to calm children. Ava stops shouting to look at Serapen's hands, then thrashes with redoubled energy. I guess whatever Serapen is trying to do doesn't work on Ava.

Serapen's hand moves to Ava's forehead. She closes her eyes, pressing her palm against Ava's furrowed brow as she intones, "Listen. Listen. Listen."

Ava moans quietly. "No, no, no. I want my mother. I want my mother."

Serapen opens her eyes again. Her voice is soft as she says, "I know, child. I miss her, too. But she's gone."

Ava stops moaning. Her dark eyes search Serapen's. She says, "Please, Serapen. Please let me go to her. We'll never trouble you again. We'll never return here. Why would you hold me here?"

Serapen sighs. "I am but a servant, Ava. Only the Voice can hold you here."

Ava resumes struggling. Serapen stands and makes a resigned gesture to me and the two healers as she says, "Let her go."

The healers comply immediately, but I look up at the High Priestess uncertainly. I keep my voice deferential but still dare to question her command. "Are you sure, Muse Serapen?"

Serapen nods and extends her hand to me. I look down at Ava, who glares up at me with such fury I flinch. I hope Serapen doesn't change her mind, because I really don't want to catch Ava again. My shins are throbbing.

Cautiously, I release Ava and step back from her. Serapen's fingers close around my wrist. Ava springs to her feet and runs after Mama. This time, to my enormous relief, I feel no pain in my chest as Ava departs. Even the pain in my shins subsides. That tingling resumes on my wrist under Serapen's hand, though.

We listen to the swift rustle of Ava's passage through the underbrush. The sound fades, restoring peace to the forest. I'm relieved, as though I've woken from a nightmare to find myself safe in my bed.

I glance up at Serapen. She listens for something, eyes closed. When she opens her eyes again, she says to me and the other two healers, "Come."

Keeping a gentle hold on my hand, Serapen leads, and the healers and I follow her through the trees. We walk a short distance in the direction Ava ran, until we reach the ferns at the forest edge. Ahead of us, in the meadow, Ava lies curled on her side. She holds her knees to her chest, gasping for breath.

Without further instruction from Serapen, the two healers kneel beside Ava. One draws out a little flask from within her cloak and lowers it to Ava's mouth. Ava presses her lips tight together, refusing to drink it, so the healer lets it drip onto her muddy forehead, hands, and feet instead. The second healer uses a blue cloth to massage the liquid into Ava's skin.

Ava's clenched hands slowly relax, and her labored breathing eases. She stares up at the night sky, limp and unresisting. Moonlight glistens on the tears sliding silently down her cheeks. Seeing her pain subsiding gives me some relief, but I feel yet another kind of pain at the sight of her grief.

"What's happened to her, Muse Serapen?" I ask, looking up at the High Priestess.

Serapen gazes at Ava and says, "She is on a more difficult path than most."

That doesn't sound good. I look back at Ava. "But … why?"

"Hmm." This soft sound of the ineffable resonates somewhere between Serapen's throat and her heart. "Why. That is a very great mystery indeed. A question worthy of the initiate's path."

I lower my head, suddenly aware of my impertinence in questioning the High Priestess. The initiate path is not for boys, so this mystery will remain a mystery to me.

Serapen turns to me, and her voice is kind as she says, "Do not be downcast, little brother. All will be well in its proper time. You will see."

I see myself reflected in Serapen's strange eyes. For a brief moment, I have the sensation—at once exhilarating and frightening—that I'm looking down at the world from a very great height, through her.

She lets go of my hand, and the strange sensation fades. I blink, disoriented and uncertain whether Serapen has dismissed me. Over Serapen's shoulder, I see two windows remain lit on the ground floor of the house of boys: my bedroom and Hedi's. I'm exhausted, and the thought of my soft bed calls to me. Even the prospect of listening to Balashi and Kuri's inane conversation is appealing, after so much shouting and struggling. I could also use a hot bath.

The sea breeze blows over my bare skin. I forgot to grab my tunic before Serapen led us out of the woods. I shiver, then wince at the prickle of pain that returns to my chest now that Serapen has let go of my hand. I roll my shoulders forward slightly to ease the pain. It's uncomfortable, but not yet as sharp as before.

"Should I return to my room, Muse Serapen?" I ask.

"I think not," says Serapen, her observant gaze flicking from my chest to my eyes. "It will be some time before the binding is eased enough between you and Ava to separate you. I cannot keep you with me tonight, and you cannot go inside the city with her. So she must go with you."

I frown. "With me where?"

"Back to your house," says Serapen, as if this is obvious.

"But won't Hedi—"

"Don't worry. I've already sent word to Hedi."

I don't know how the High Priestess could have sent word already, but I nod.

"Stay with Ava," Serapen continues, speaking slowly and clearly to me, waiting for my acknowledgment after each instruction. "Take her to your house when she's recovered enough strength to walk. Attend Hedi's instructions, and make sure Ava does, too. Try to get some sleep."

I nod again, though that last instruction worries me. My mind races ahead. I ask, "What will we do tomorrow, for Calling Day?"

Serapen looks at Ava, limp on the grass between the healers, and says, "Tomorrow will be a long day for you both, I imagine."

"And after that? Will she be all right?"

Serapen turns to me with a softer expression than before. I hesitate to meet her strange gaze again, but when I do I see only the somewhat tired and quite ordinary brown eyes of a woman looking back at me with compassion. She says, "It will take some time to counterbalance the more extreme effects of the dose she's had. A moon at least to get through the worst, I expect. But it will take years of training for her to learn to manage the residual effects. Perhaps centuries. The good news for you is that, since you cannot bind to the Voice in the same way a woman can, you only need to manage the effects of the binding with Ava. Not a small task, either, but you're a strong boy. You'll manage. And you'll both be more comfortable if you stay together for now. Do you understand?"

I don't understand at all. I have so many more questions.

But Serapen raises her hand over me in the sign of blessing and says, "Safe passage tomorrow, little brother. Good night." She departs with the other two healers, slips into the forest, and leaves me in the meadow.

Reluctantly, I approach Ava once more.

△▽△

She left me. My mother left me. Why did she leave me?

I stare up at the stars in shock as the healers' hands move over me. I can't move my arms or legs to struggle—everything hurts too much—but I won't let them pour their damned pharmaka down my throat as long as I can keep my mouth closed.

But a part of me knows my resistance is futile. Serapen made her point. That final sprint took every last bit of energy I possessed, and the pain that followed was unendurable. As I emerged from the forest, I glimpsed my mother briefly in the moonlight, the shadow of her cloak flying far ahead of me across the meadow. She never slowed, never even looked back, before she disappeared. I think I lost consciousness for a moment, because the next thing I knew I was curled up in the grass shivering, in so much pain I couldn't open my eyes.

The pain eases a little, and I'm vaguely aware of Serapen's voice. The healers rise and go to her. Dom has been standing with Serapen, and now he approaches me. Serapen and her healers slip away into the woods.

Dom sits in the grass at my side. The healers left my hands folded over my heart, and he tentatively takes one of them in his own. He winces at the sight of my wrist, runs his thumb lightly over the place where I'm starting to feel the throbbing bruises he left there. He looks ashamed. Good. I hope his shins are throbbing, too. I hope he feels a knife digging under his ribs just like I do.

But as he sits there, my hand in his, the hunched tension of his bare shoulders eases. The throbbing in my wrists eases. The pain near my heart eases most of all, which is a huge relief. But something else starts seething in its place.

"Ava—" Dom's eyes meet mine, and I see his concern for me in that innocent, open expression. That's what pushes me over the edge. I feel a surge of fury at him: this hand, that voice, those eyes, every part of him a trap. I was supposed to be flying across the sea by now, and instead I'm caught in a snare.

"Go away," I say. I would pull back my hand if I could, but I'm utterly spent.

He sighs. "I can't. Serapen says—"

"Don't," I say. "I don't want to hear what Serapen says. If you won't go away, then be quiet."

There's enough venom in my voice to put down a horse. Dom cautiously releases my hand. He stays quiet, but he doesn't leave. I try to hold my face expressionless as the pain starts up again in my chest. It's not as bad as it was before—whatever the healers did helped a little—but it grows steadily worse and worse, breath by breath. His back and shoulders tighten again, and his jaw clenches, and I know it's hurting him too. I refuse to ask him to take my hand again, but I'm relieved when at last he does.

"I'm sorry, Ava," he says. "I was only trying to help. I don't understand what's happening."

That strange tingling resumes between our palms, and I feel the unfamiliar sensation of ... is that humility? I'm not sure I've ever felt that before. But this feeling combined with his words unlock other feelings and thoughts I've been evading. None of this is his fault, not really. I've trapped him as much as the Voice has trapped me. I'm the one who exposed him to pharmaka. I'm the one who screwed up the job.

He looks at me curiously and asks, "What does that mean? The job?"

My mind is clearer now than it was in the forest when this happened before. I'm sure this time that I didn't say anything aloud about the job. The pain in my chest has subsided enough that I can push myself halfway up to sitting. I try to ignore the fact that Dom helps me up the rest of the way. I study his face, my curiosity momentarily stronger than all my other uncomfortable feelings. "I didn't say anything about the job," I say. "How do you know about that?"

He runs his free hand over his face and rubs his eyes before he meets my gaze. He looks almost as exhausted as I feel when he says, "I just … hear you. Somehow. I guess it's the binding pharmaka, isn't it?"

I guess he's right. Spirits, I wish my mother had taught me more. If I had known, if I'd understood what could happen, maybe I would have done things differently back in the storeroom. None of this needed to happen. Why didn't she tell me what could happen? Why did she leave me here? Anguish at the memory of her running away rips through me, followed by confusion, followed by anger.

Dom winces, stopping my spiraling emotions in their tracks.

"You're not only hearing me," I say, my understanding growing. I remember the jarring sensation of kicking him in the shins and hurting myself. A dozen places on my own shins are still aching. "You're feeling what I'm feeling, too, aren't you?"

Dom nods. "You're … mostly angry. At that woman."

"At my mother," I say slowly.

"What does that mean?" he asks. "Your mother?"

The question is so ridiculous, but it cuts straight to the heart of the matter. I feel sorry for him, but also sorry for myself. Maybe it would have been better for me if I'd never known the answer to this question, either.

The thought of my mother's betrayal brings on a feeling of crushing weariness. I sigh and say, "I'll tell you, Dom, if you really want to know. But not tonight. It's too much. I think … I really just need to sleep right now."

"All right," says Dom, looking relieved.

We glance down awkwardly at our joined hands, as the particulars of this come into focus. Should I—should we?—sleep in the woods?

Dom, overhearing my thoughts again, shakes his head. With confidence that sounds forced, he says, "No. Hedi will sort us out. Come on, little sister." He offers his arm and helps me to my feet. We walk slowly together toward the house of boys, his arm around my shoulders, mine around his waist.

"You can't call me that, you know," I say, after we've figured out a way to manage his long stride beside my short one.

"Call you what?" he says.

"Little sister," I say. "We're the same age. I'm even a little older than you are. I was already here the day you came out of the woods with Serapen."

He inclines his head, a perfect imitation of deferring to a Mohira. Perfect, except for the mischief in his eyes as he looks pointedly down at me. Something about that look makes me laugh.

△▽△

When Ava laughs, so many memories light up inside my mind that for a moment I'm stunned.

Her laughter fades. "What's wrong?" she says.

I open my mouth to answer but find no words. Ava reaches for my cheek and tilts my face down toward her, studying me with concern. Soft moonlight illuminates her features, and her dark eyes reflect the stars. I remember so many times I've looked into these eyes and held this hand. But most of all I remember that laugh. Even after she stops laughing, sparkling echoes of the familiar sound seem to drift out from the woods, where we spent so many long afternoons playing together as children.

My gaze turns toward the old cedar, a looming silhouette against the starry sky. I blink, and the shadows of night seem to dissolve into daylight as a memory returns to me.

I'm eight summers again, and I'm sitting beside Ava on the high branch of the old cedar. Ava looks out to sea, but my eyes keep returning to the high stone wall enclosing the temple city. I say, "What's it like, inside the wall?"

Ava turns to me with a delighted expression, eager to share a secret. "Come on!" she says. "I'll show you."

She stands, gripping the branch beneath us with her bare toes as she returns to the opening at the top of the cedar's hollow trunk. She climbs down through the tree, and I shimmy after her. We emerge from the shrubs at the base of the cedar.

I follow Ava along an animal track that leads deeper into the forest. We stop at a sandy hollow beside a clear stream. I've never been here before, but clearly Ava has. Her small footprints cover the sand.

She walks up to an oak snag beside the stream. Its ravaged trunk is full of holes bored by woodpeckers and other creatures. Ava pulls out treasure after treasure from these holes: smooth river stones, acorns and pinecones, curling strips of bright white birch bark. She arranges her collection in little piles before her, then points out the place where I should stand in the middle of the sand.

I watch closely as Ava places river stones in a curve around my feet.

"Imagine this is the wall," she says.

I recognize the shape immediately. For the first time, with Ava's help, I stand inside the wall.

A golden chip of bark shed by a nearby yellow birch catches my eye, reminding me of the bronze gate in the wall. I pick it up and poke it into the sand so it stands upright where Ava left a gap between two stones. The shape and color of the chip are just right. Ava laughs and says, "Yes, exactly! There's the gate."

Now that I understand the game, I gather new bits and pieces for Ava's collection: iridescent shells dropped here and there by seagulls, bright flowers blooming in patches of sunlight, elegant fronds of ferns, glossy bird feathers, anything I think she might find beautiful. Ava so enthusiastically admires everything I find that my chest swells a little.

She narrates as she places the pieces one by one into their places. "The biggest building behind the wall is the Musaion," she says, arranging a large circle of pinecones some distance behind the wall.

"That's the one with the big dome?" I say.

"That's right," she says. "The sisters give our instruction in reading, writing, historia, and poetika in the library halls of the Musaion."

She carefully arranges curls of birch bark in a ring around the pinecone Musaion as she says, "And these are the workshops where we practice the arts of tekhnologia." She taps one of the birch bark workshops and says, in an aggrieved tone, "Here's where I was the last few days—the house of weavers. The sisters wouldn't let any of us outside the wall to play until we'd spun all the wool from the spring shearing. Spirits, I hate spinning."

I'd love to learn to spin, but I don't tell that to Ava. She always looks sad when I talk about the things I'm not allowed to do.

Ava considers our collection and selects one of the big fern fronds I gathered for her. She breaks it apart into littler fronds and pokes the pieces into the sand, forming two neat lines of green running east to west inside the wall of the miniature temple city. "These are the kitchen gardens where we learn the arts of pharmaka," she says, running her fingertip along the top of one ferny line. "They're so beautiful, Dom! Walled gardens, and open orchard terraces, and glass houses like enormous jewels. When it's cold and grey outside, the glass houses stay warm and green inside, and they always smell like summer."

I struggle to imagine entire houses made of glass. Perhaps they look like enormous bottles of pharmaka.

I point to the second ferny line and say, "Are these gardens, too?"

Ava says, "Yes, but the girls never work in those. Those gardens are for pharmaka ingredients that only the initiates are allowed to tend."

Ava lays a grid of pebbles on the east side of the city. She says, "The girls' dormitory is a big stone house through the gate here. Here's where I sleep." She taps a spot near one corner.

From our collection, I select a tawny kuku feather to represent Ava. I poke it into the sand beside her fingertip, so it stands at attention before her. She smiles down at the feather, pleased. My chest swells a little more, until a critical expression flickers over Ava's features.

"But there should be two more, for Hanu and Eumelia," she says, pronouncing Eumelia's name with mild distaste.

This seems easy enough to fix. I examine our collection and select two flowers: one pink for rosy-cheeked, sharp-tongued Eumelia; one violet for solemn, soothing Hanu. I set these beside Ava's feather. Ava claps her hands in approval, then says gleefully, "My turn!"

She steps over the wall and lays a foundation for the house of boys. She searches through our collection and selects two new objects.

First she places a plain dark pebble inside the house of boys. "For Kuri," she says with a giggle, "because he's about as clever as a rock."

She could be right. Kuri never says much, though, so it's hard for me to know for sure.

Next, she places a delicate, perfectly spiraling snail shell beside the pebble. "For Balashi," she says with a more thoughtful expression, "because he's very beautiful."

She's certainly right this time, but I'm deflated, hearing her speak of Balashi this way.

Ava pores over the rest of our treasures, searching intently. I await her judgment on me. At last, her eye falls on an acorn riddled with holes and etchings—the signs of beetles' work. This ruined acorn looks like nothing special compared to the flawless shell she chose for Balashi. But Ava beams at me and holds the acorn up between us, turning it slowly in her fingers.

When the angle is just right, I see what Ava sees: two dark eyes staring out from a round brown acorn shell face, beneath a thick mop of acorn cap hair. She places the acorn between the pebble and the shell. "And that's for you," she says, "because I see you. Always looking."

Ava glances at me with a teasing smile and catches me at it again. I quickly drop my gaze to my lap, trying to hide the hot embarrassment rising in my cheeks. Maybe I do look at her too much. But how can I stop? Does she want me to stop?

"Dom." She says my name playfully. When I don't look up, she takes my hand. Reluctantly, I meet her eyes again. She says, "I like the way you look. It makes me want to show you everything."

My embarrassment ebbs. Our peace is restored.

I say, "Are we friends, then?"

She laughs, and I smile. "Best friends," she says.

△▽△

"What's wrong?" I say again, examining Dom's eyes closely. He's looking at me with a dazed expression, and I brace myself for another unpleasant round of pharmaka side effects.

He opens his mouth, closes it, swallows. At last he says, "I just … I remember your laugh."

I relax. Maybe that is some sort of pharmaka side effect, but at least he's coherent this time. I wrap my arm back around his waist, he wraps his arm around my shoulders, and we keep walking. Wistfully, I say, "What does it feel like, remembering something you've lost?"

"It's a relief," he says. "I'm grateful to have it back."

His gratitude is as sweet as it is heartbreaking. What the Mohirai have done to him—to all of us—should make his blood boil. But I bite back my impulse to shout in frustration at the night sky. I'm too spent for another fight tonight.

We don't say anything else as we make our way up the rest of the path to the front door of the house of boys. There's a light moving behind a ground floor window, and the heavy arched door swings open as we reach the front steps.

I remember Hedi Mohira, the stout, red-cheeked sister who must have raised tens of thousands of boys in this house over the centuries since the time of destruction. I often saw Hedi bustling about around the house when I'd come here to play with Dom. I remember her in the blue healer's dress with the sleeves rolled up above her muscular forearms, herding boys all about her, often with the aid of the long wooden clapper she used to ring the meal bell.

Now she stands before us holding a large candle, wearing a white sleeping tunic and loose leggings under her unbelted sky-blue healer's robe, her frizzy curls peeking out under a white sleeping kerchief. She blinks at me in astonishment, but I can see she recognizes me. The Mohirai who raise children remember us all.

"Ava," she says, shaking her head, softly clucking her tongue. Her expression is hard and wary. "Spirits, I could hardly believe Serapen, but here you are. Really, you should be taken back into the city. But all the temple healers are so busy with preparations for tomorrow. I ..."

She raises her candle to look at us more closely, and she sees the state I'm in, the state both of us are in. Her expression softens when she looks at Dom. I understand—that face of his would melt a heart of stone.

Whatever Hedi's feelings may be toward me, seeing that we're in trouble elicits the no-nonsense manner I remember, the pragmatism of an initiate healer. She says, "I suppose there's a first time for everything. Come along."

△▽△

By the light of the oil lamps in the entrance hall, Hedi inventories our injuries. We're both muddy and bruised. I'm half-clothed and have a few scratches on my neck from Ava's knife. The cut on Ava's lip has reopened and is bleeding, and her wrists are covered in bruises from me, but the worst of the damage seems to be to her bare feet, which are filthy, covered in scratches, and leave crimson smudges on the grey stone floor wherever she walks. Hedi wakes another of the house sisters for assistance, then leads us to the bathing rooms.

Bathing proves more complicated than the healers anticipate. At first they try to help us bathe in separate tubs, but we both shiver and wince after only a short time apart. Ava and I are starting to understand our predicament better, though, so we quickly sort out that we have to take the bathing in turns. I sit wrapped in a blanket beside Ava's tub, holding her hand when she needs it. It takes two full tubs of hot water to rinse all the sticky residue from Ava's skin, with both healers using long-handled scrub brushes to keep the amanitai off themselves.

Then I have my turn. Ava sits beside my tub holding my hand as Hedi scrubs me down. I have no idea how we're going to keep this up tomorrow, but I'm too delirious to think much further ahead than a bed right now. Hedi puts us in winter sleeping tunics of fleecy wool after watching all our shivering, although I feel warm again after the hot bath. She keeps us in the bathing room to attend to our cuts and bruises with healing pharmaka. My injuries are superficial, but Ava's feet require some time to bandage properly.

Hedi leads us down the corridor toward one of the spare bedrooms where visitors usually stay. She drags the two single beds together and lights two candles for us. From the washbasin stand in the corner of the room, she retrieves two small wooden cups. These she sets on the bedside table.

Withdrawing a silver flask from her robe, Hedi pours a small measure of golden liquid into each wooden cup. I know this routine well; I drank a cup of unbinding pharmaka like this every night at bedtime for my first three years in the house of boys.

Hedi taps the bedside table beside the cups, then looks from Ava to me. "Listen, little sister, little brother," she says. "Any other night, seeing the shape you two are in, I'd say you should drink the full dose and sleep through the whole day tomorrow. But given the circumstances, I suggest you avoid it unless absolutely necessary for the pain. If you must, take the smallest dose you can. Otherwise, you'll be asleep on your feet through the ceremony. Do you understand?"

"I have listened and I have heard, sister," I say automatically. But Ava only stares at Hedi, making no sign of acknowledgment. I wonder whether she's forgotten the correct response.

To Ava, Hedi says, "Listen, little sister. I know you haven't received the proper instruction for Calling Day. But the most important thing to remember is to keep the silence until the High Priestess calls you, and to follow her instructions carefully. You and Dom will walk behind all the others at the end of the lines so you can stay together. You'll see the ceremony repeated several times before you're called forward, so listen carefully and I'm sure you'll learn the correct responses. They're all very short."

Hedi gestures to a shelf holding two folded piles of glossy white clothes, then points to two dark cloaks hanging from pegs by the door. She says, "You'll wear these for the ceremony."

"I can't," says Ava, her voice quavering. "I can't be called." Her expression as she looks at Hedi reminds me of a cornered animal.

Hedi's demeanor toward Ava softens, seeing her fear. She pats Ava's cheek and says, "Don't be afraid, child. The Voice has returned you to us now so you may be called with your sisters and brothers at the proper time. Resisting the Voice will do you as much good as resisting the approach of spring. There's no escaping it, whatever that foolish woman may have told you. All will be well. You will see."

That's more comfort than I've ever seen Hedi offer to anyone, even to the youngest boys. Briskly, Hedi concludes, "The ceremony starts at dawn, despite the night you've had. There's no delaying the equinox. Try to get some sleep."

Ava's hand clenches in mine. Anger seems to pour into me. In the same way snippets of her thoughts flashed in my mind before, her emotion rushes to my head, hot and tumultuous and overwhelming. I'm afraid she's regained enough energy to start another scene with Hedi, so I say quickly, "Thank you, Hedi Mohira. We'll try to sleep. Good night."

Hedi withdraws and closes the door. I turn to Ava and say, "Please, Ava. Please don't fight this. It's a long ceremony tomorrow, and I can't make it through without you. I need you there."

"You don't have any idea what's going to happen after you're called, do you?" she says.

Ava's tone with me is as harsh as Mama's was with her. But it's the note of derision in her voice, not her anger, that sparks my own anger. My voice is louder than I mean it to be when I say, "Just because you're a girl doesn't mean you know everything, Ava. Tomorrow is the one and only time I will ever hear the Voice for myself. You don't know what it will say. I don't know what it will say. No one can know until it happens. But …" I falter, not recognizing this cutting tone in my own voice and alarmed by what I see boiling behind Ava's eyes as she hears it. I've never spoken to a girl this way, or to anyone else for that matter. My anger cools a little, but what follows close behind it is a sickening mix of fear, frustration, and longing that's been accumulating in me for years. I manage to lower my voice somewhat as I finish my thought and say, "It's the closest I'll ever get to knowing what it might have been like to be a Mohira. You can't take this from me."

The small point of Ava's chin rises as she tries to glare down at me, though she has no choice but to look up at me from her little height. Her nostrils flare. She bites back something she's about to say, drops my hand, and turns from me. She blows out one of the candles, climbs into one of the beds, and buries herself in the blankets.

Now that she's let go of my hand, I can't tell what she's thinking or feeling any more. It's a relief to be alone with my own thoughts, which are far less tempestuous than hers. I want to go down the hall to my own bed, listen to Kuri's familiar snore and Balashi's steady deep breathing, and forget this day ever happened. Maybe I could manage it, despite the pain.

But Serapen specifically told me to stay with Ava. As kind as Serapen has always seemed to me, I don't want to find out what she's like when she's disobeyed. And as frustrating as Ava is, I really don't want to cause her any more pain, after all I've seen her go through tonight.

I sigh, climb into the other bed, and blow out my candle. Ava and I lie side by side, not touching, as the pain builds up inside us. I can't bring myself to reach out to her to make it stop, because I dread that burning anger of hers coursing through me again. Sleeping this way is going to be impossible. I close my eyes, trying to relax as the pain grows steadily worse.

But this time, to my surprise, she's the one who ends it. She turns over and reaches tentatively toward me under the blankets. Her fingertips slide down my sleeve until she finds my hand. Her fingers lace through mine, and she squeezes her palm to my palm. The pain trickles out slowly between us.

She whispers something, in a voice so small I can't hear it. I turn my face toward her and whisper back, more sharply than I mean to, "What?"

"I'm sorry," she says a little louder, quite slowly, like she's never said these words before. "You're right. I don't know what will happen. All I know is what I've been taught by my mother, and ..." Her eyes shine with tears, but she blinks them back and simply says again, "I don't know."

I'm stunned by her apology. I don't think a girl has ever apologized to me for anything. My irritation toward her fades. I still feel upset, but most of what I'm upset about has nothing to do with her, really. Ava's anger just unlocked my own.

"All right," I say at last.

The pain ebbs until it's almost gone. She curls up into a ball facing me, her head deep in her pillow. She's asleep almost instantly, and her fingers twitch against my palm. Despite her thick woolen sleeping tunic, Ava's hand feels cold in mine, and occasionally she shivers.

In sleep, the tension around Ava's eyes and lips disappears. I study her face in the moonlight for a while, waiting for my exhaustion to turn into sleep. She looks much younger now than she did before. Long-forgotten childhood memories of Ava drift through my mind, out of sequence and out of context. My eyelids grow heavy, but each time I'm about to drift off I'm reawakened by Ava's shivering or a glimpse of her dreams. Her dreams frequently include jolting flashes of Mama's stern face and ice blue eyes, which sets my heart pounding. I consider taking a sip of the unbinding pharmaka Hedi left for us to help me sleep, but I don't want to wake up Ava by letting go of her hand. Everything is so much more peaceful while she's sleeping. So I watch her sleep, hoping this will help me fall asleep.

Ava's hand grows colder and colder, until at last I pull her toward me, wrapping our two blankets around us, hoping this will stop her shivering. She relaxes against my chest, and for the first time since I picked her up in the woods, her skin feels warm to my touch.

It's nearing sunrise when my exhaustion finally overcomes all the other strangeness, and I slip straight into dreams. But whether they're Ava's dreams or mine, I cannot tell.

THE MORNING AFTER

I STARTLE AWAKE at the sound of footsteps approaching. Heavy arms wrap around me. A warm chest rises and falls against my back. Soft breath courses down my neck.

Overwhelmed by the sense that I'm caught in a trap, I spring away, heart racing. I fall out of a strange bed, tangled in blankets, onto a hard stone floor. My knees and hands and entire body throb, and I moan softly in pain. Where am I?

Dom sits up in the bed, the window silhouetting his mussed halo of curls. Even in the dim pre-dawn light I can see the dark circles under his eyes. He looks down at me with the same expression of concern I remember from last night. It all comes back to me at once. I moan softly again, this time in defeat.

The soft footsteps that woke me stop outside the door. Three loud knocks, and the door swings inward. Hedi stands at the threshold wearing a dark ceremonial cloak over her blue robe. Her deep voice resonates in the room as she says, "Awake, awake, awake. The day of your calling has arrived."

Dom jumps out of bed like it's a reflex, which I suppose it might be, considering all the pharmaka the sisters use to train these boys to the routines of their life. Hedi looks sharply at me sitting on the floor. Wordlessly, she gestures for me to stand up and hurry.

Hedi withdraws, and Dom stumbles groggily toward me. He looks even more exhausted than he did last night, and I feel sorry for him. I open my mouth to speak, but he shakes his head quickly and raises a finger to his lips, reminding me of the ceremonial silence. I wince a little at the prickling pain returning to my chest, and he sees the wince and takes my hands until the pain subsides. Then he pulls me up to stand.

I know this is real, but it feels like a bad dream. My mother spent the last seven years trying to prevent this from ever happening to me. She taught me that Calling Day is the beginning of a woman's unending service to the Voice. It's the end of freedom, the end of choice. It's worse for men in most ways, of course. They have no choice about their calling either, and they have to live almost entirely without the arts and mysteries. Dom should fear this day even more than I do. At least a woman has a life full of comfort and learning, even if she has no control over her path. But both paths are paths of servitude. This is not what I wanted for myself, and not what my mother wanted for me.

But my mother isn't here. She left me. With the clarity of a partial night's sleep, I'm starting to think it makes sense—in a cold, calculating way—that my mother chose to keep her freedom. She's taught me to think that way, too. She must have known from her priestess training what I learned by brute force when I attempted to run after her last night. I couldn't have endured the pain of separation from Dom for long, even if she'd carried me all the way to the boat and we'd managed to sail away.

The boat, my mother, the entire life I thought I was beginning yesterday—all of them are gone. My mother understood, as I'm beginning to understand, that there's no way out for me, at least not until I find out how to counter this overdose of amanitai. My mother couldn't help me, and spirits know what Serapen would have done to my mother had she stayed with me. Whatever it is must be pretty bad for my fearless mother to have looked as frightened as she did. Although ... she never actually told me what would happen if Serapen caught her. My mother only told me what would happen if Serapen caught me. Which is what's happening now.

I try to let go of thoughts of my mother. I need to figure out what I'm going to do about what's happening to me now. I take a breath, centering myself in the present. I'll have to get through this like I'd get through anything else, like it's just another job. Of course I don't have a plan yet, but at least I can consider my options.

I look up at Dom, who's still holding my hands. All my options at this point include him. He can't go anywhere without me, and I can't go anywhere without him. The only thing that feels entirely under my control right now is how much pain he experiences and how much pain I experience. I try not to think about the fact that this works both ways, so he has as much control as I do.

Yesterday, I was willing to cause Dom—and myself—any amount of pain in my attempt to follow my mother. But I failed, and we've both paid a heavy price for it. I'm weakened from my ordeal last night, and although Dom is clearly far stronger than I am, he's in much worse shape than he was when he found me. I need to figure out a smarter way to manage the pain for both of us. Any escape will be easier with both of us at full strength.

But Dom made it clear last night that escape is the last thing on his mind. He wants to go to his Calling Day ceremony. He's foolish to want it, perhaps. But how can I blame him? He's been raised to know nothing else, just as I would have been if I'd stayed here. I suppose I could try to stop him, but if he truly wants to be called, he'll find a way. The autumn equinox is considered the most auspicious day to hear the Voice, but the Mohirai could help Dom hear the Voice on another day. I can't think of anything I gain from ruining today's ceremony for him, and I don't want to drive a wedge between us now when I know I'm going to need Dom's help later.

I don't know what I'll do at the ceremony myself, though. Maybe Dom can receive his calling and I can pitch a fit to avoid receiving mine. I'm not sure. I'll have to improvise once we get there.

My hands tingle, and Dom speaks to me, though his lips don't move. *Ava?* His voice sounds tentative, searching, somewhere in my mind. It's an odd sensation, hearing him while the room remains silent. This must be how I sounded to him yesterday.

I don't know exactly how to answer, so I simply think, *I hear you.*

Dom looks relieved. I glimpse a flash of his memory, of Hedi giving him and his trio brothers instructions for today. Dom thinks, *We need to wear the ceremonial clothes with hoods up. Hair stays unbound—no braids or ties of any kind. There's a long walk at the start of the ceremony, and we can't wear shoes. We can't eat until the evening meal, but we can drink water if we need it. And ...*

His voice seems to fade away in my mind, so I adjust my hold on his hands and think, *We can drink water. And ... what?*

Apprehensively, he thinks, *Well ... There's more pharmaka in this ceremony.*

I sigh. Of course there is. I think, *Spirits, I'm not sure I can handle any more pharmaka.*

Dom's worried expression is enough to tell me he's not sure he can either. Hedi's soft footsteps move on to an adjacent corridor, and he thinks, *She's waking the rest of the sixteenth summers. We'll have to leave soon. Do you mind if I ...* He gestures at the door to the privy closet.

I wave my hand for him to go. After everything that's happened already, and whatever is bound to happen next, there's no point in being shy.

△▽△

Step by step, Ava and I figure out how to make ready for the day ahead. Taking turns at the wash basin, her hand on my back, then mine on hers, to give each other two free hands. Stepping back to give each other privacy, stepping forward quickly to touch the other's hand before the pain becomes too bad.

Undressing and dressing is the most intricate of these dances. Ava dresses first, and in such close proximity, I can't help watching her. I place my hand on her waist as she pulls her fleecy wool sleeping tunic up over her head. The brightening twilight reveals the warm hazelnut tone of her skin as she slips into the white ceremonial silks embroidered with golden threads. I touch the soft skin above her collarbone as she wraps herself in the white robe. The long black curls loose around her shoulders tickle the back of my hand. All these clothes are far too big on her, though I imagine they're the smallest Hedi could find on short notice. Each movement of Ava's hands and feet seems to linger in the air as excess fabric floats behind her, golden threads gleaming at her wrists and ankles.

Ava's hand moves lightly from my shoulder to my back to my neck as I change into new leggings, new tunic, new robe. The silk against my skin feels cold, almost liquid, until it warms up. I've never worn anything this fine, so smooth and weightless, and I don't expect I ever will again. Usually only the initiate Mohirai wear dyed clothes and delicate fabrics. It's been eight years of undyed wool and leather for me as a boy, and most of the men I've seen wear much the same.

Ava and I argue briefly in the silence when she glances toward her leather belt on the bedside table. She refused to be parted from it last night when Hedi took our other muddy clothes away. I see her visualizing possible ways to hide it under her robe. She reaches for it, but I touch her wrist and think, *We're not allowed to take anything with us to the ceremony apart from the clothes we've been given.*

She thinks, *It's the only thing I have left.* Her emotions, which have been fairly calm until now, grow agitated.

Please, Ava, I think. *I'm sure the Mohirai will give us everything we need after the ceremony.*

She bites her lower lip, wincing when her teeth dig into the deep cut already there. She takes a last look at her belt, looks up at me, and sighs in resignation.

Thank you, I think, relieved she's not putting up a fight this morning.

The footsteps of the sixteenth summer boys shuffle down the adjacent corridor toward the front door. I hurry to put on the cloak of undyed black wool, but I can't figure out the intricate laces, which are different from the children's cloaks. Ava takes over, somehow knowing how these work. Her fingers fly over my heart, tying the little series of knots on my cloak before she laces her own. The footsteps are gone by the time she's done. We're running behind.

I look at Ava and gesture toward the door. She nods and takes my hand. Her lips tremble. Even if I couldn't feel that she's frightened, I would have known it from the look in her eyes as they meet mine.

I squeeze her hand and think, *It'll be fine. You'll be fine. We'll be fine.* Although I have no idea whether this is true. Her lips curve into a wry smirk. Oh spirits, she overheard me thinking that. This isn't going to be easy.

Nope, she agrees.

I try to stop thinking, and we step out the door.

Dawn brightens behind us as Ava and I hurry hand in hand down the path through the gardens, catching up to the cloaked and hooded line of boys following Hedi. My bare feet sting, but I realize quickly that it's not my pain. I glance down at Ava's bandaged feet, just visible beneath the hem of her white robe, and I feel the rough gravel of the path digging into all her cuts and bruises. I wonder how she'll manage the long walk ahead.

Don't worry about me, she thinks. *Compared to all that pain yesterday, this is nothing.*

No one is supposed to look back once the ceremonial walk begins, but Kuri and Balashi decide it's worth risking the wrath of Hedi. As soon as we approach the end of the line, their heads swing back toward us.

Under their hoods, Balashi and Kuri's eyes widen at the sight of Ava holding my hand. Kuri looks confused. Balashi looks impressed. Their faces hold an expression somewhere between, *Who is that?* and *How did you get away with that?* But neither dares to speak, and eventually they have to face forward again so they don't trip over themselves.

They haven't changed much, Ava thinks. I feel her amusement like a warm ripple through my chest, and I have to suppress a laugh.

I realize as we step out onto the meadow that, in our rush to catch up to the others, Ava and I forgot to raise our hoods. I quickly pull the fleece-lined hood up over my head. Ava sees me and raises hers as well.

The hood envelops me in an aroma of pharmaka so intense that for a moment I'm light-headed.

Spirits, here we go, Ava thinks.

It'll be fine. You'll be fine. We'll be fine, I think again, but now it's more for my benefit than hers.

She squeezes my hand and thinks, *Whatever happens, it can't be worse than yesterday.*

I hope she's right.

NOT TOO LATE

HAND IN HAND, DOM AND I FOLLOW the line of cloaked boys walking across the meadow toward the temple city gate. Dawn light gleams on the great bronze dome that peeks over the top of the city wall. I remember standing under that dome many times, looking up at the beautiful ceiling mosaics. The vaulted space beneath the dome connects many different halls of the Children's Temple Musaion, including the library halls. Those endless shelves of parchment scrolls and clay tablets were my favorite place to roam on days the girls weren't allowed outside the city. I remember that when we were little, Dom used to ask me so many questions about the Musaion, and about everything else behind the wall. I spent a lot of time describing the temple city to him as we played together in the woods. I wonder whether he remembers any of that.

More bits and pieces started coming back to me last night, Dom thinks, startling me. He's so quiet when he's listening that I almost forget he's there. But when I focus, I can feel him: a little stillness amidst the churn of my own thoughts.

Across the meadow, the city gate opens inward. Serapen glides out, leading a silent line of eight cloaked girls toward us. The line of boys converges with the line of girls at a footpath that turns upslope into the woods. I scan the shadows beneath the girls' dark hoods, wondering whether I might see either of my old trio sisters. I can't pick out Hanu, but I think I see Eumelia's round, freckled cheeks and smirking half-smile beneath one of the hoods. She and I used to quarrel endlessly, and I feel a flicker of annoyance at the memory, even though I haven't seen her in seven years.

Hedi and Serapen lead the boys' line and the girls' line onto the footpath toward the forest, so we're walking in parallel lines. I realize only as I take my place at the end of the line beside Dom that I complete the trio of trios. Nine girls to match the nine boys.

When we reach the forest edge, Serapen turns to face us. Hedi turns away and walks alone back toward the house of boys. I'm startled by an impulse to cry as I watch Hedi depart. But it's not my impulse—it's Dom's. I catch glimpses of his memories: Hedi introducing him to Kuri and Balashi on his first day here, Hedi leading the blessing in the meal hall, Hedi tending to scraped knees, Hedi kissing his forehead before bedtime. He's realizing he may never see her again.

I feel a pang of sympathy for him, followed by a rush of memories of my mother that rekindle my grief and anger from yesterday. Dom's hand tenses around mine, and I try to calm myself so he won't need to share these painful feelings again. Inadvertently, I take a deep breath of the potent pharmaka in my hood. Dom's memories and mine drift away from me, blurring with distance. His hand relaxes. Although I worry about what this pharmaka might be doing to me, its calming, numbing effect does make me feel better in this moment.

Sorry about Hedi, I think, through the slight fuzziness in my mind. *It's hard to lose someone like her.*

Hedi wasn't warm toward me, probably because she cares about Dom and doesn't like seeing him tangled up in this situation with me. But despite that, she was efficient, pragmatic, even kind. I understand why Dom would miss her, how he could love her, especially since he doesn't know what she's done to him.

I even notice some similarities between Hedi and my mother. I love my mother not because she's ever been particularly warm toward me, but because I admire her knowledge, strength, and self-reliance. I've wanted to be like her since the day she led me out of the Children's Temple and explained what had happened to me. She taught me everything I need to be self-reliant like her, and to trust myself over anyone else. All that will be useful now that she's gone, since all I have left is myself.

And me, thinks Dom.

Spirits, it's so weird having him overhearing all this. It's hard to tell when he's listening and when he's not.

Sorry, he thinks. *Do you want me to let go of your hand?*

Even the thought of the stabbing pain returning makes me feel tired. *No,* I think. *You feel even more exhausted than I do. Let's not make it worse.*

Thanks, he thinks. His gratitude soaks into me like warm sunlight, so disproportionately strong in response to my very small kindness that I'm ashamed of everything I put him through yesterday.

Let's also try not to think about yesterday, Dom thinks.

Good point. No need to re-live any of that right now. Better focus on what's ahead.

The eighteen of us stand facing Serapen. The first light of dawn peeks beneath Serapen's hood, revealing the sharp lines of her jaw beneath the shadows of her hood. In a ringing voice that fills the meadow, she says, "The sun rises on the day of your calling. Listen well, for I tell you a mystery.

"There is a Voice that speaks within all. Within each stone, within each tree, within each breath of the wind. The Voice speaks clearest in stillness. Give yourself to stillness, and listen for the Voice that calls within you."

Serapen turns and walks into the cedar forest. We follow her, walking in silence along a wide footpath through the trees. I know this forest well, having found food and shelter and safe passage beneath its canopy in every season over many years of travel. But I've never seen the forest look as beautiful as it does this morning.

The sun rises, transforming the dark violets and blues of morning twilight into the bright greens and blues of full morning. As we walk deeper into the woods, my toes sink into soft beds of star moss. I look down at the velvety mosses, tenacious lichens, and mysterious fungi springing up around my bare feet. I'm a giant passing over this tiny world, even as I'm the tiniest field mouse scampering beneath towering trees.

I breathe in the resinous sweetness of the cedars. For a moment, I forget to step forward. I stare up at their ancient forms in simple awe. Each one of their vast trunks holds a shape unique from all the rest. This one twists like the muscled torso of a farmer straining against a plow. That one bends like a Mohira over her lyre. Their branches spread overhead in a dance with the dazzling sun, weaving a canopy so dense that only a rare sunbeam penetrates to the forest floor. Drifting shafts of light illuminate tiny motes of dust and winged insects spiraling overhead. The late summer birds call out to one another from perches all around us, gossiping about what we're doing here, occasionally revealing themselves with a flutter of wings or a darting flight from one treetop to the next.

Every familiar tree, herb, mushroom, insect, and bird call seems so mesmerizing to me this morning that I wonder whether the pharmaka in my hood is affecting my senses. I certainly felt some strange distortions in my vision and hearing last night. I glance at Dom, wondering whether this is happening to him, too. He gazes upward with that look of intense focus, the look he turned up at the stars last night, the look I caught him giving me as we were getting dressed this morning. That look is now focused on the canopy. Is this how Dom sees the forest? Does he see like this all the time?

Dom glances back at me.

Don't you? he wonders.

No, I think, astonished. *Not even close.*

Serapen turns off the wider footpath onto a narrower trail. The girls' line and the boys' line press closer together, our long cloaks brushing against each other and catching sometimes on the tips of the branches on either side of the path.

The trees grow ever larger, older, grander. I step carefully over the gnarled roots that surface more frequently through the soft soil here. Herbs reach out with tender green fingers into the opening of the trail, tickling my bare feet and ankles.

Bright sunlight streams through the thinning trees ahead, and we follow Serapen into a grassy clearing. At the center of the clearing lies a large spring, its surface reflecting the blue sky. On a flat rock beside the pool stand a large silver chalice and a tall silver ewer, gleaming in the sunlight.

Serapen turns to face us and pushes back her hood. Her eyes reflect the blue and green of the clearing. In the morning sun, her long snow-white hair shines brighter even than the chalice behind her. She unlaces her dark cloak and lets it fall around her bare feet, revealing her dazzling white robes, her ornate sleeves and collar worked in golden thread. Looking at her is like staring at the sun.

Serapen says, "Keep your silence until the Voice calls for you. Remember your instructions as you approach. Do not look down into the waters as you step into the sacred pool. It is dangerous to look upon the waters unprepared. Look only to me, listen only to me, as I receive the Voice's words for you."

Serapen approaches the pool. We stand waiting. She lifts the silver ewer from the flat rock and bends to dip it into the pool. The glassy surface of the water, now disturbed, shimmers in the sunlight. I struggle with an impulse to look down at the surface, but I remember Serapen's warning and keep my eyes locked on her.

Serapen pours a stream of clear water from the ewer into the chalice. From within the folds of her white robe, she withdraws a small cloth pouch and empties it into the chalice. She lifts the chalice in both hands, swirls it slowly, drinks deep, and lifts it up toward the sun.

She carries the chalice back toward us. She nods, and all the girls and boys around me push back their hoods, so I follow their lead.

Serapen walks along the line of boys, holding the chalice to each boy's lips in turn. Each boy drinks until she withdraws the silver cup. My apprehension of whatever is in that cup builds. I'm afraid of what might happen to Dom, and to me, if we drink. What if we get sick? I saw that happen many times during ceremonies in my year at the Children's Temple. Would we both feel each other's sickness? What if we start seeing things or hearing things or become confused? Will we both feel that way? Will we amplify those feelings between us? My stomach churns.

Calm down, Dom thinks. *Serapen's the most experienced healer in all of Dulai. She wouldn't give us anything that would hurt us.*

Poor Dom. He still doesn't know the first thing about Serapen.

What do you mean? he thinks. *What do you know about Serapen?*

I know that she takes away memories and people and choices that should belong to us. My mother showed me how the men in the villages live, how the initiates in the temple live, how the priestesses called to bear children live. I've heard what some of the men say in secret about the injustice of the sisters, about all that was stolen from them when the Mohirai took control of Dulai after the time of destruction.

The withered faces and voices of the old men I've seen die, the sounds of women in childbirth, the look in the eyes of the mothers and children as they are unbound—all flash before my eyes, the things my mother showed me so I could understand what she'd learned through centuries serving the Voice as an initiate priestess.

I feel Dom's confusion as he glimpses my memories without context or explanation. But I also feel his desire to understand.

I'm sorry, Dom, I think, growing frantic. *There's not nearly enough time to explain it all at once. But …* Serapen is approaching Dom fast, working her way down the line of boys with the chalice in her hands. A desperate plan forms in my mind, spilling out from me to him.

No, Ava, he thinks. *Don't. Don't run now. Please.*

Do you really want to spend your entire life as a slave to the Voice? I think.

I don't know what that means, he thinks.

A slave … I try to remember the words my mother often used. *A slave is someone whose body and mind and life belong to someone else. A slave is someone who must obey commands. A slave is someone who makes no choices of their own.*

But everyone has to obey the Voice, even the Mohirai, he thinks.

No, I think. *That's just what the priestesses want you to believe.*

Dom's jaw clenches, and I feel his resistance to this thought rising between us like the wall around the temple. Serapen reaches Kuri, two boys ahead of Dom. Kuri drinks from the chalice. We're almost out of time. I pour every last drop of my conviction into my next thought, willing Dom to believe me.

Please listen to me, Dom. It's not too late. We can escape from here, if we run together. I know these woods like the back of my hand. But I can't go without you. You saw what happened to me last night.

Dom turns to me, and despite the tired circles under his eyes, his acorn brown complexion looks rosy, glowing with the effects of whatever pharmaka we're breathing in from these hoods. His eyes are bright but unfocused. He looks at me with that awed expression again. I wonder whether he's heard me, or whether the pharmaka has him in its grip, making him compliant, unresisting, unthinking.

Inside my head, I scream in frustration. Dom overhears me and winces. His eyes refocus as he searches my face.

You're wrong, Ava, he thinks. *The Mohirai would never do anything to hurt us. The Mohirai don't lie. I don't understand what you saw, but you must be mistaken.*

The lamb. The fool. The damned fool lamb. The vitriol surges inside me until Dom drops my hand like I've burned him. Serapen stands before him, and he looks up at her.

The pain in my chest prickles as the High Priestess raises the chalice to his lips.

ANSWERING THE CALL

AVA'S WORDS ECHO in my mind even after I drop her hand: *Do you really want to spend your entire life as a slave to the Voice?*

Each thought that spills from Ava into me feels like another push toward some dangerous precipice. And I don't want to follow her there. She thinks she's telling me the truth, but somehow I know she's wrong. I've received nothing but kindness from the sisters my entire life. As much as I've wished for another fate than my own, I trust the Mohirai. I believe the Voice has a plan for me just like it does for every other creature in its care. I want to give myself over to the Voice. I want to know my purpose.

And I definitely don't want to run away with Ava. Most of what I've experienced with her since yesterday has been pain, pain, and more pain. The life of an uninitiated man may not be the richest or fullest life, but it can't be nearly as painful as a single day bound to Ava this way.

Ahead of me in line, Balashi finishes drinking from the chalice, and Serapen moves on from him to me. Even though I've let go of Ava's hand, somehow I still feel her agitation. I try to shut out my thoughts of her, which is easier when I look up into Serapen's eyes. The High Priestess raises the silver chalice before me. I look down into a swirling brew of dark blood red.

I breathe in a faint bitterness, but when the cool liquid meets my lips, the taste is mostly sweet. I swallow and swallow until Serapen pulls away the cup. A buzzing sensation spreads over my tongue, down my throat, into my belly.

Serapen turns from me and walks back to the front of the line of girls. She passes her hand once more over the chalice and raises it to the first girl's lips.

The needling pain has been rebuilding in my chest since I let go of Ava, but now she tentatively takes my hand again. My pain eases at her touch.

I'm sorry, Ava, I think, *but this is what I want. You can't take this from me.* A feeling like grey fog sweeps through me, and I recognize Ava's grief. But this time, her grief is for me, not for her mother.

I never wanted to take anything from you, she thinks.

I look down at her, and she looks up at me. The morning light reveals flecks of yellow, amber, and green in her dark brown eyes, which gleam with unshed tears.

She thinks, *I wanted to share everything with you. Don't you remember?*

I search Ava's face, trying to remember. In her eyes, I see my reflection—impossibly young—as a memory returns to me.

Ava and I are small children again, and I smile shyly at her as we sit side by side in the high branch of the old cedar on a warm, clear afternoon. Ava smiles back at me, then looks out toward the sea. She tips her head to the side and says, "I wonder if we can see all the way to the ocean from here."

"What's the ocean?" I say.

Ava gasps with delight at having a new secret to share with me. She sweeps her hand across the watery horizon to the south and says, "The sisters say the ocean is an even greater sea beyond the sea. And," she looks at me for emphasis as she shares the best part, "beyond the ocean, they say there are whole other worlds beyond Dulai!"

Awed, I say, "What's in the other worlds?"

Ava frowns and says, "I don't know. The sisters won't tell me. But," her voice rises with new conviction, "I'll be a Mohira one day. And when I find out—" she leans toward me, dropping her voice to a conspiratorial whisper, "I'll let you know."

The whisper fades back into my memory as Ava thinks, *Please, Dom. Come with me. Where I'm going, you won't need to serve the Voice. I'll hide nothing from you. We'll share everything as equals. I promise.*

I struggle to hold my focus on Ava's words. *I'll hide nothing … We'll share everything … I promise.* I want to ask what she means. But the pharmaka is hitting me hard. It's difficult to think of anything except how beautiful this clearing is, how this is the only place in the world I want to be.

Ava's hand relaxes in mine. Distantly, I wonder whether she's experiencing some effect of the pharmaka through me, even though she's taken none of it herself.

Serapen reaches the end of the line of girls and looks down at Ava. A profound stillness falls over the clearing. Even the dust motes swirling in the sunlight seem to cease their motion. The High Priestess raises the chalice to Ava's lips. I hold absolutely still, listening intently to Ava's thoughts, expecting an explosion of some sort from her. What will she do? Throw the chalice back at Serapen? Break away from me again to run?

Ava's awareness coils like a snake preparing to strike. My whole body tenses in anticipation of whatever is coming. But I hear nothing in her mind but a rippling reflection of my own memory, the sound of her child's voice overflowing with confidence: *I'll be a Mohira one day.*

I can't believe my eyes when Ava accepts the raised chalice in Serapen's hands without a single protest. And yet there she stands: swallowing, swallowing, swallowing. I feel her tasting the bittersweetness of the dark brew, the tension melting from her awareness.

At last Serapen lowers the chalice from Ava's lips.

What am I doing? Ava thinks.

Serapen returns to the pool, pours out the last of the pharmaka onto the soil, and returns the chalice to its place beside the ewer on the flat rock. She turns to face us and closes her eyes.

"Listen," she says.

"Listen," she says again.

"Listen," she says a third time.

We listen. A breeze stirs in the clearing. A prickle runs down my neck.

Serapen steps into the pool, wading in until she stands submerged to the waist. She turns back toward us and calls Ubar, the first boy in the line ahead of me.

Ubar unlaces his cloak, and the dark folds drop around his ankles. He makes his way toward the High Priestess. His gaze doesn't stray to the forbidden surface of the pool as he steps in and takes her outstretched hands. His white silk robe rises around him, floating on the surface like a lotus blossom.

Serapen looks down at him. "Listen, Ubar, for the Voice that calls to you," she intones. "Listen."

"I listen," he replies in a low, soft voice.

Holding hands, they close their eyes and wait. The breeze stirs. Serapen says, "Listen, Ubar, for you are called as farmer. Will you answer the call?"

"Yes," he says, in a voice more confident than before. "I will answer."

They open their eyes. Serapen smiles at Ubar, embraces him lightly, and kisses his cheek. He allows her to lower him gently into the water, so he floats face up toward the sky. He closes his eyes and mouth tightly just before Serapen presses him briefly down beneath the surface.

He re-emerges with a gasp, wet hair hanging over his eyes. Serapen helps him find his footing and leads him by the hand out of the pool. His soaked ceremonial garments gleam in the sunlight.

I'm startled when a man steps out from behind a large tree at the edge of the wood behind the pool. He calls in a deep voice, "Welcome, Ubar, to the order of farmers."

Ubar turns toward the man, who holds out a new cloak dyed a rich chestnut brown. The man wraps the dry cloak around the wet boy and leads him off into the woods.

And then Ubar is gone.

Serapen calls the next boy, and the next, and the five that follow. One by one, they're called to join the farmers and fishermen, hunters and gatherers, masons and smiths. Kuri disappears under a dark green gatherer's cloak. My last sight of Balashi is of his handsome face disappearing beneath an inky black smith's cloak with silver threads.

My head swirls. My heart races. At last, I'm going to hear my calling. As if from a great distance, Serapen calls, "Dom."

I let go of Ava's hand. My fingers fumble on the cloak laces Ava tied for me this morning. Vaguely, I wonder when the prickling pain will return to my chest, but all I feel is the tingle of pharmaka in my belly, radiating out along my arms, steadying my hands. The heavy cloak falls from my shoulders.

I step out into the bright sunlight of the clearing, walking forward until my bare feet reach the rocky edge of the pool. When I step in, the water closes cool around my toes, and Serapen's fingers close warm around my hands.

The water ripples at the bottom edge of my vision, enticing, but Serapen's words of warning were very clear. I hold my gaze steadily on hers, never looking down into the pool.

Serapen looks back at me through eyes that reflect all colors of the rainbow. I feel so connected to this woman, and through her to the stones beneath our feet, to the water rising up around my body, to the trees holding up the sky above us.

"Listen, Dom, for the Voice that calls to you," she says, in a voice that holds more richness, more certainty, more promise than any single voice can hold.

The breeze encircles us. Nothing moves, and yet I lose all sense of my body's orientation above the ground, of the ground's orientation beneath my feet. I find myself standing alone in the wood. Even Serapen is gone. Panic flares in me for a moment, but her unseen hands grasp mine tight.

She says, "Listen."

The reply rises within me. "I listen."

I don't know how long I stand in this place where the wind blows between layers of the unseen.

The Voice calls up from the depths of the pool, from the height of the sky, from the tips of every branch, but I can't make out the words.

I strain to listen. The sun and moon and stars swirl in the bowl of sky, dissolving time and space. Their passage fills me with wonder. I know for the first time that the Voice calls not only within this world, but within all the worlds.

The sky's swirling stops. I gaze up at an infinite darkness pierced by innumerable stars, and I listen.

I listen.

I listen.

And then I hear.

You have asked it. We may give it. But there is a price. Do you accept it?

As the Voice says this, I feel Ava's hand in mine. She's with me here, and at the same time she's elsewhere. I'm not sure whether I've asked for Ava or Ava is the price of what I've asked. In this moment there are no such distinctions. All I comprehend is that the choice—to have all I've asked—lies before me.

So I choose. I think, *Yes. Yes. Yes, I do accept the price.*

The Voice says, *Listen, Dom, for you are called as Artifex. Will you answer our call?*

Artifex. I've never heard this word before. But it resonates within me, and I've never been more certain than I am when I say, "Yes. I will answer."

The stars wink out above me. I look no longer into the infinite darkness, but into the twin reflecting pools of Serapen's eyes. She doesn't smile at me like she smiled at the other boys. Instead, she looks at me with knowing. Her face draws near to mine, and she kisses my cheek.

"May you find peace on your long journey, Dom Artifex," she whispers in my ear.

She holds me gently in her arms and lowers me into the pool. I see the blue sky above for just a moment before I close my eyes and sink beneath the surface.

When I step out of the spring, no man steps out of the forest to claim me. Confusion clouds the certainty I felt just a moment ago when I heard the Voice. Serapen takes me by the hand and leads me back to the place I was standing before, beside Ava. Serapen picks up the dark cloak from the place I left it. I had expected it to be replaced with one of some other color, after seeing what happened to all the boys before me. But Serapen simply wraps this cloak back around my damp shoulders, re-tying the laces with practiced fingers.

I reach for Ava's hand, and her cold fingers grip mine.

△▽△

Dom stands beside me, dripping beneath his cloak, his warm hand wrapped around mine. I overhear him thinking, *Why am I still here? What's an Artifex?*

I have no idea what's going on, but I remember overhearing the word Artifex. This is what the two healers in the storerooms were discussing last night while I searched for a hiding place. What does it mean? Why hasn't Dom been sent off with the other men?

It's hard for me to focus on these questions, though. I'm still reeling from the fact that I drank Serapen's pharmaka. All I could think about as the awful chalice rose to my lips was how desperately I want to be a Mohira, even though I know that's not what I want. I haven't wanted that for seven years. I want to get out of here. But somehow Serapen's gaze pinned me in place as easily as Dom's strong arms did yesterday.

I also can't make sense of what happened when Dom walked away from me into the pool. Why was there no pain in my chest? Has Serapen given us some kind of antidote to the binding pharmaka? Could it be safe for me to run away now?

There are so many unknowns, so many risks, and the buzz of pharmaka seems to be slowing down my thoughts, making reasoning difficult. Still, as I've watched all the other boys follow different men off into the woods, a plan had been forming in my mind. It seemed so simple, really. I'd follow Dom, go to whatever village he was destined to labor in for the rest of his life, and work out my next steps far from Serapen's watchful eyes. It didn't seem likely that Serapen would try to stop me—I'd be senseless with pain if Dom left without me, anyway.

But now Dom's here, and he doesn't seem to be going anywhere. So I'm stuck here, too. Spirits blast it all, what game is the Voice playing with me now?

Calm down, Dom thinks. *It's wonderful. You'll see. You'll see.*

His conviction floods through me, and I feel my resistance disappearing like the tide pools beneath the waves.

Narua is the first of the girls called to join the Mohirai. She's followed by her trio sisters Bel and Tashlu. Kor, Piroza, and Kishar follow in their turn. Hanu is called. Eumelia is called. Mohira after Mohira after Mohira.

And then Serapen calls, "Ava."

I try to resist one last time. But Serapen's eyes watch me steadily across the clearing, and I find my fingers trembling as they untie the laces at my throat. My dark cloak falls around my bandaged feet. I walk unsteadily toward the pool, step into the water, and look up into the uncanny eyes of the High Priestess.

"Listen, Ava, for the Voice that calls to you," she says.

The reply rises unbidden to my lips. "I listen."

The strange breeze that accompanies all of the callings stirs again around me. But here in the sunny clearing I don't hear the Voice, even though I heard it easily last night in the woods. There is no call for me, at least none that I can hear.

The long silence stretches. I feel a tentative sense of relief. Perhaps the Voice doesn't want me. Perhaps the Voice is going to let me go. Perhaps I don't have to be a Mohira after all. Serapen says she's a servant of the Voice, so if the Voice doesn't want me, who is Serapen to force me to do anything?

I'm about to laugh in triumph, to pull away from the High Priestess, to step back out of the pool with my freedom, when a cloud passes briefly over the sun. The sun re-emerges, momentarily dazzling me, and its light flashes bright on the surface of the pool, drawing my eye irresistibly downward. I gaze into the reflection.

I find myself in a bed in a room I've never seen before, looking out a window toward a sparkling bay. Beyond the bay, across a bridge, behind a pinkish haze, rises the city of glass towers.

A man sits in a chair at my bedside. Though he's changed from the boy I know, I would recognize the concerned expression in those deep-set eyes anywhere. The worried crease between his eyebrows is chiseled deep. The look he gives me breaks my heart.

I look more closely at the face of this Dom, who is at once familiar and unfamiliar. Yes, they're the same eyes in some ways, but they're shadowed by … is it grief? Is it anger? Is it hunger? It's a feeling far too complicated for me to identify. Instinctively, I want to reach out and touch him, so I can feel what he's feeling and understand it. But somehow I know this Dom before me is far, far away—in every way that far can be measured.

I open my mouth to speak to him, but the room vanishes, and I'm trapped in Serapen's long, sinewy arms. She whispers in my ear, "Don't look, Ava. It's too much, too soon."

I look across the clearing at Dom, who gazes at me with an open, hopeful expression. I struggle a bit in Serapen's grasp, unsure what's happening.

In a louder voice, Serapen says, "Listen, Ava, for you are called as Mohira. Will you answer the call?"

I stare up at her in shock. I didn't hear the Voice say that. She must be lying. But the response again rises unbidden to my lips, "Yes. I will answer."

Before I can even close my eyes, Serapen presses me down beneath the surface of the pool. For a heart-stopping moment, I'm sinking an unfathomable depth, water piling over me, pulling me under.

The strange sensation vanishes, and I gasp for breath as Serapen helps me back onto my feet. I sway dizzily, leaning on the High Priestess as she leads me out of the pool, across the clearing, back to Dom's side. The girls' eyes follow me as I pass, though none of them dares turn her head.

At the end of the line, Dom smiles at me. My heart aches as I look into the eyes of this eager, hopeful boy while the gaze of that intense, grim man I saw in the pool lingers in my mind. What's happening? What have I done?

△▽△

Ava and Serapen stand in the pool across the clearing from me. Just like all the other girls before her, Ava says, "I listen."

The silence stretches so long after Ava speaks that I grow uneasy. Serapen takes Ava into her arms and whispers into her ear. Nothing like this happened to the other girls.

But then Serapen says the words, "Listen, Ava, for you are called as Mohira. Will you answer the call?"

And Ava says, "Yes. I will answer."

I can't see Ava's face, but I imagine that if she heard the Voice like I did, she must feel elated. I'm happy for her and eager to have her by my side again so I can find out what the Voice sounded like to her.

As I watch Serapen lower Ava into the water, I'm jolted by the bizarre impression that Ava has slipped like a stone through Serapen's hands into the depths of the pool. This must be some trick of the light or of the pharmaka, though, because as soon as I blink, I see Ava on her feet again, soaked and leaning on Serapen's arm. She looks pale and stricken, and my residual awe at having heard the Voice gives way to worry.

Serapen takes Ava's hand. The pair step out of the water and return across the clearing to where I stand with the rest of the girls. Serapen's white hair flows over the shoulders of her long robes, white and gold threads reflecting the sunlight. Ava's wet clothes cling to her like moonlight, her long dark hair trailing gleaming droplets like falling stars behind her.

Ava returns to her place beside me. Serapen draws Ava's dry cloak up over her small shoulders, tucking the warm folds around her shivering body. I take Ava's hand, and I overhear her thinking, *What is happening? What have I done?*

Serapen returns to the center of the clearing, the sun directly above her at its zenith on the autumn equinox. She faces us and says, "Today you have listened, and you have heard the words of the Voice in all. Remember this day. Remember the Voice. Remember the Voice speaks loudest in the stillness.

"I wish you every blessing on your journey. Be patient with yourselves. Be helpful to one another. Be open to the mysteries you will encounter.

"The Voice has called you all to paths rich in mystery. Not every step will be clear. You will find yourself lost at times. Remember to listen, when you are lost, for the Voice is in all.

"But for now, your path is wide and clear. Today, your training begins. Today, you depart for Velkanos."

THE CARAVAN

SERAPEN LEADS ME AND THE NINE GIRLS out from the clearing by the same narrow trail that led us in. Ava's hand remains ice cold in mine despite the dry heat of midday. I wonder whether it would be all right for me to give my cloak to her now that the ceremony is over.

Overhearing my thought, Ava thinks, *You don't have to take care of me.*

I'm just trying to help, I think.

No one can help me now, she thinks.

A numb sensation spreads from her to me, so different from the afterglow of excitement I feel. I wonder, *Didn't you hear it? The Voice?*

Not today, she thinks. *But I saw something.*

An image forms in her mind. It's a bedroom, though the furnishings are unlike any I've ever seen. A man sits beside the bed, and through the window I recognize the city of glass towers I saw in Ava's thoughts last night.

Where is that? I wonder.

No idea, she thinks, *but I think that's you, sitting beside me.*

I take a closer look at the man in her memory. I don't recognize him, and he looks far too old to be me. But I suppose she could be right. I've only glimpsed my own face occasionally in a watery reflection, and never from this perspective.

What do you think it means? I wonder.

No idea, she thinks again.

She and I walk in silence. Well, everyone has been walking in silence, but Ava and I also manage to silence our thoughts for a while, too.

I look sidelong at her, walking unhooded beside me, her wet hair dripping down the back of her cloak. I hazard another thought. *Thank you.*

For what? she thinks, meeting my eyes.

For staying here with me, I think. *For letting me hear the Voice.*

Ava's curiosity feels like tentative fingers in my mind. *How was it for you?* she thinks.

I remember what I saw, standing alone in the woods beneath the vast night sky, hearing the stars speak. The Voice's words return to me. *You have asked it. We may give it. But there is a price. Do you accept it?* And my answer returns. *Yes. Yes. Yes, I do accept the price.*

Ava frowns, puzzled. *What do you think it means?*

No idea, I think.

I don't like it, she thinks.

What's an Artifex? I wonder.

No idea, she thinks.

We reach an intersection between the footpath and a wider dirt road with deep cartwheel ruts. Twelve horses munch the grass beside the road, while two Mohirai I've never seen before stand by chatting. A few of the horses and both

Mohirai turn curious eyes toward us as we approach.

Serapen embraces her sister priestesses in greeting, then turns to introduce us to them.

"Today the Voice has called nine new sisters to the house of novices," says Serapen, gesturing to each girl in turn. She names Narua, Bel, and Tashlu; Kor, Piroza, and Kishar; Hanu and Eumelia. The two Mohirai greet each girl with friendly nods. Serapen concludes with Ava. Several girls ahead of us in line glance back at the sound of her name, but no one dares to fully turn around.

Next, Serapen introduces the two Mohirai from Velkanos.

First is Thalia, Muse of the house of poetika. She wears a robe of summer green. Her sash, richly embroidered with gleaming copper threads, coils artfully around her figure, displaying her ample bosom to advantage. Her laughing eyes twinkle brighter still when she catches me looking. She tosses her long auburn braid behind her shoulder, her painted rosy lips curving into a smile that reveals perfect rows of bright white teeth.

Second is Arkhi, Muse of the house of tekhnologia. I've never seen a complexion like hers: the color of the night sky between the stars, deepest blue-black. She wears a robe of inky black, and around her shoulders hangs a fine black stole with a delicate pattern worked in silver threads. She doesn't smile like Thalia, but her expression is kinder.

Arkhi raises her hand toward us in greeting, revealing a pale palm painted in swirling patterns of dark blue dye that spread all the way out to her fingertips. Her eyes fall on me. "And who is this?" she asks Serapen.

Serapen settles a hand lightly on my shoulder and says, "The Voice has called a novice Artifex to the path of mysteries today. This is Dom."

My heart rises to my throat at Serapen's words. I must have misunderstood. Did she say that I've been called to the path of mysteries?

That's what she said, Ava thinks.

But … how is that possible? I wonder.

Arkhi and Thalia examine me with interest. The girls seem to take this as permission at last to turn around and satisfy their own curiosity. I squirm under their collective gaze. I've known these girls for as long as I can remember, but in this moment they remind me of nothing so much as a pride of hunting lionesses —beautiful but terrifying.

△▽△

Thalia observes the group of girls staring at Dom like they've never seen a boy before. "What a stir we'll cause in the house of novices," she says slyly, winking at Dom. A hot wave of his embarrassment floods through me as Thalia's tinkling laugh fills the air. I want to smack the smile off her painted mouth, but I don't quite dare to strike a Muse. Not yet, anyway.

These girls are another matter, though. "Leave him alone," I say, glaring at each of them in turn. "Can't you see you're bothering him?"

Kor returns my glare with a distant, disinterested nod. Her younger trio sisters Piroza and Kishar look at me and, to my immense irritation, burst out laughing. Narua ignores me completely and takes her time studying Dom. Her younger trio sisters Bel and Tashlu avoid my eyes, sneaking glances at Dom when they think I'm not looking. Hanu searches my face for a long time with a confused, foggy expression. I wonder whether she'll remember me like Dom did last night, but she doesn't seem to. None of these girls seem to recognize me. That's a relief. Hopefully we can all remain strangers and avoid difficult questions.

Hanu's gaze travels down to my hand gripping Dom's. She and Dom look at each other, and an image flashes in my mind of Hanu's gorgeous naked figure lying on the beach at sunset. I'm confused for a moment before I realize what's happening. I stifle a giggle when Dom realizes, too. He looks away from Hanu quickly, and I feel his desperation to distract himself before he accidentally shares any more intimate memories of Hanu.

In a tone of perfect kindness, Hanu says to me, "Never fear. Dom will come to no harm at our hands, little sister."

"Don't call me that," I say sharply.

My rudeness startles her, but Hanu recovers quickly, inclines her head peaceably, and says, "Of course. My mistake. Sister."

Watching this exchange with undisguised delight, Thalia says, "Truly there is no joy greater than sisterhood." Each syllable shimmers with her amusement.

My anger fades into embarrassment. I realize I've made a spectacle of myself in front of all the other girls and the Mohirai, and I hate Thalia for enjoying it.

I open my mouth to return some choice words of my own to the Muse of poetika, but before I say anything, Arkhi cuts in, saying, "Peace, Thalia." All eyes turn to the Muse of tekhnologia, who speaks with a quiet composure that commands attention. "We have a moon of riding ahead, long enough already without your teasing."

Thalia tips her head in deference to Arkhi, though her eyes still sparkle with mirth. I step back beside Dom, feeling foolish for standing up to defend him against what I realize now are just a bunch of silly girls. Though I'm wary of all Mohirai, Arkhi's deft handling of Thalia earns her my respect. Arkhi appears to be the complete opposite of Thalia, who has about as much substance as a butterfly.

Arkhi continues, "None of you have ridden before, I assume?"

The girls and Dom all shake their heads. Determined to avoid any more unnecessary attention, I suppress a sigh of resignation and say nothing. I guess Arkhi's right—this is going to be a painfully long journey. I've been riding since my ninth summer, but for some reason girls and boys at the Children's Temple aren't allowed to ride.

Arkhi introduces each of the horses by name and demonstrates the proper way to approach them, how to mount the saddle, how to use the reins. She's very thorough in her instruction and answers questions patiently. It's all quite tedious, except for the feeling of Dom's excited anticipation spilling into me through our joined hands. I smile to myself. Riding is one of my great pleasures. Perhaps it will be one of his, as well.

As Arkhi's lesson wears on, I study the horses. Three of them appear to belong to the Mohirai, judging by the saddle blankets that match the patterns of the Muses' sashes and stoles. Serapen's horse is the speckled grey mare called Amisos. Arkhi's is the pure black mare Khaos. Thalia's is the white mare Rurata. So I probably won't be riding any of those. I eye one of the smaller horses, a spirited-looking palomino called Nisaba. She and I would be pretty well matched. I wonder whether I'll be allowed to choose my horse.

A few of the other girls look as eager to ride as Dom, but most seem apprehensive. The girls' nervous energy around these obviously gentle creatures is ridiculous, but I suppose none of them have handled horses before. Dom should know his way around a horse, though, since the boys keep the stables outside the Children's Temple.

"Looks like you forgot a horse," says a bored voice behind me. "Or does Dom have to walk all the way to Velkanos?"

I look back over my shoulder. For the first time since early this morning, I see Eumelia. Where has she been standing all this time? Her hood is pushed back, so I can see her face clearly now. Her round freckled cheeks have slimmed down since we were little, but she still has that mocking half-smile and pert nose I remember taking more than one swing at. She's quicker than she looks, though; I never landed a punch. In our eighth summer, I was the only girl smaller than she was, and she loved finding ways to demonstrate her incremental superiority over me at every opportunity. I'm glad she can't remember me.

I feel Dom's disappointment at the realization that Eumelia must be right, that he's not going to ride. I'm about to feel sorry for him. But then I have a sinking realization: I can't ride without Dom. Maybe we're both going to have to walk for the next moon.

Arkhi looks at me like she's read my thoughts. Spirits, can she read my thoughts? I hope not. I don't think I can bear having yet another person in my mind, and having a Mohira in my mind would make planning an escape impossible.

In a calming voice, Arkhi says to me and Dom, "Nothing has been forgotten, though we do have an unusual situation to manage with you two." Despite my distrust of the Mohirai, I can't help appreciating how Arkhi addresses Dom, without overlooking him or dismissing him like sisters often do while talking around brothers. She continues, "So you'll be riding together on Eridu for this journey."

Arkhi gestures toward a tall chestnut gelding, the largest of the horses by far, who stands behind her mare Khaos. Eridu has a star on his forehead, four white socks, and a calm intelligence in his big brown eyes. He's a larger horse than I would have chosen for myself, but I've ridden horses his size without difficulty. I'd be quite happy with Eridu on my own, but the prospect of riding him with Dom is not appealing, especially not for such a long journey. Dom doesn't even know how to ride.

Sorry, he thinks. I curse inwardly. Yet again, I've forgotten he's listening. His humility is so complete and sincere that I'm appalled by his servility, but not nearly as appalled as I am at myself. I'm as bad as any Mohira, ignoring and forgetting him when it's convenient for me.

It's all right, Dom, I think. *We'll … figure it out, I guess.*

Maybe it'll be fun? he thinks. *You can just hold on to my back.* He looks from Eridu to me, and I glimpse that teasing expression I remember from last night.

Vastly preferring his teasing to his humility, I smile and think, *Not a chance. I'm holding the reins.*

He inclines his head deferentially. I roll my eyes and think, *You don't have to treat me like them. I'm not a Mohira.*

Not yet, he thinks.

Not ever, I think.

Arkhi matches each of the remaining girls with a horse. I'm impressed by the speed with which she pairs the more skittish girls with the steadiest mounts, accounts for size variations between the girls and the horses, and redistributes the saddlebag weight more evenly once she's completed the pairings. She's clearly done this many times before. I agree with all her pairings, except that she gives Eumelia the spirited palomino I wanted.

Some of the girls pet their mounts, tentatively getting to know them. Others flinch every time a hoof stamps or a tail swishes or an ear flicks. None of these novices look like they're going to be great riders any time soon, but hopefully the horses and the Mohirai know what they're doing.

In a voice that carries surprisingly well considering her lightweight laughter, Thalia calls out, "Your riding clothes and boots are here, novices." She demonstrates where to look on her own horse's saddlebags. "Go ahead and change out of your wet things. Then, onward to the Mountain of Muses!"

△▽△

Changing into riding clothes requires me and Ava to repeat our undressing routine from this morning in front of all the other girls. Despite the unwanted audience—or perhaps because of it—we're more efficient the second time. Most of the girls shoot only occasional curious glances our way, but Hanu and Eumelia stare at us openly. Eumelia studies Ava with intense interest. Hanu's gaze drifts often to my hands on Ava's body.

I swallow, trying to keep my focus on Ava so I won't think of Hanu again.

Ava glances at me. Embarrassed heat rises to my ears as I realize she's overheard this. I lower my gaze to my feet and try to clear my mind completely. Ava taps my hand. Reluctantly, I look at her again. She thinks, *Don't be embarrassed. I wish I could give you more privacy, but I really don't mind if you think of Hanu. She's always been the best of these girls, anyway.*

Ava's sincerity helps me relax, but her own irritation grows as Eumelia's eyes linger on her. At last she wheels around, still half-dressed, and snaps, "What?"

Hanu immediately looks away from us both. But Eumelia doesn't flinch, back down, or even acknowledge Ava's tone. She continues studying Ava's face as she says, "Where did you come from? And what on Dulai are you doing to Dom?"

Before Ava can answer, Serapen steps up behind us and says calmly, "The Voice has returned Ava to us after a long time away. She and Dom had an accident with binding pharmaka last night. It will take some time for them both to recover, and until then they need to remain close to each other. But all will be well again in time."

From Eumelia's expression, it's clear that this answer only multiplies her questions. But Serapen's tone of finality invites no further questions.

△▽△

Arkhi, Thalia, and Serapen untie the lines of horses so each novice has plenty of space to mount for the first time. The Mohirai walk among the girls giving pointers and adjusting saddle straps.

Dom and I stand at Eridu's side. After considering our unique situation, Arkhi adjusts the stirrups to Dom's height, but I've insisted on keeping the reins. I've lost control over pretty much everything else in my life since yesterday, so I'm not giving this up without a fight. There's also no way I'm looking at Dom's back for this entire journey. Fortunately, neither Dom nor Arkhi pushes back on this.

Do you need help getting up? Dom wonders, looking from me to the high saddle. In answer, I drop his hand, grab the saddle pommel, and swing myself up easily. I pat Eridu's glossy chestnut shoulder and take the reins, then move as far forward as I can in the saddle to make room for Dom.

Dom mounts with surprising grace for someone who hasn't ridden before. He and I adjust our bodies against each other in the saddle while Arkhi makes a second check of the stirrup length for Dom. Eridu's saddle accommodates two, but it's close quarters. Dom's warm chest against my back reminds me of waking up in his arms this morning. The feeling of entrapment and the memory of my clumsy tumble out of bed follow close behind. Hopefully I can avoid any more falls like that while we're riding together.

Even pressed this close to Dom, the pain in my chest returns because we've lost skin contact. I gather the reins in my right hand and set my left hand on Dom's knee where he can reach it. His palm presses the back of my hand.

How do you want me to hold you while we're riding? he wonders.

Let me think … The last time I shared a saddle, I was a small girl holding on to my mother's back, but I remember the basic mechanics of how it felt to ride that way. I imagine how Dom's body and mine will collide as Eridu walks, trots, canters, and gallops. I imagine the difficulties he'll have without the reins, and the difficulties I'll have without the stirrups. I consider the added complication of maintaining skin contact throughout the ride. I visualize what I think might minimize our saddle soreness tomorrow, sharing the idea with Dom.

I untuck the front of my shirt, and he slips his right arm inside and across my waist, his right hand resting over my left hip. I noticed while we were grappling with my knife last night that Dom's left-handed, and I think he'll want that hand free. He pulls me gently back into him with his forearm, anchoring me to the saddle. He rests his left hand on my thigh, so he can reach forward for the saddle pommel if he needs it.

How does that feel? I think.

Against my ribs, the pulse in his wrist speeds up. He remembers the way my body looked to him this morning as we dressed. He jerks his hand quickly out from under my shirt, but not before I feel another wave of his embarrassment.

"Sorry," he says quietly.

I dig one of my elbows playfully into his ribs and say, so only he can hear, "Relax. It's just another body. But if you have to think about one, better stick with Hanu's. She's more fun to look at, anyway."

Dom doesn't answer, and I glance up at him. He meets my eyes briefly with an expression I can't quite decipher. I wonder why he feels so embarrassed. Seeing my body from his perspective is a little strange, but it's nothing I haven't seen before, and it's certainly not embarrassing to me.

Dom keeps his hands to himself long enough that the prickling pain resumes in my chest. I want to give him as much privacy as I can, because I know it's tiring to have someone else always observing what you're thinking. But eventually my shoulders twitch involuntarily in pain. As soon as Dom feels that, he wraps his arm around me again. My hip tingles under his palm.

Thanks, I think, as the pain eases. *It's not quite as bad as yesterday, but it still hurts.*

I know, he thinks. *Sorry I made it worse.*

Stop saying sorry, I think. *None of this is your fault, remember?*

Fortunately, there's not much time to dwell on these pointless apologies. Arkhi mounts Khaos, glances back at us, and says, "That looks like it should work. Ready to go?"

Are you? I think to Dom.

His eagerness to ride floods through me in answer, and I can't suppress a smile as I call out to Arkhi, "Ready!" I won't deny myself—or Dom—the pleasure of a ride after the wretchedness of the last day. I'll just have to keep my eyes open as I start working out my next plan.

SHELTER FROM THE STORM

Arkhi leads the caravan north on the cart path. Ava and I follow behind her on Eridu, and the rest of our company spreads out in a long line behind us. I'm unfamiliar with the motion of a horse beneath me, so at first I sway in the saddle, pulling Ava off her balance. She patiently shows me how to make small adjustments in my posture to complement Eridu's movement. This helps a lot, and the ride becomes more comfortable for both of us. Her body fits against mine perfectly in the saddle, though I try to avoid thinking about her body. Fortunately, I can see everything easily over Ava's shoulder, so there's plenty for me to look at to keep my mind off of her.

The girls behind us call out to each other occasionally, but most of us ride in silence after the long, tiring day.

Ava's awareness feels lighter and happier as she rides. When the cart path widens, she thinks, *Want to try something fun?*

Curious, I think, *Maybe? Yes?*

Without waiting for me to change my mind, she tugs Eridu's reins, and he steps out of the plodding line of the caravan.

Hold on tight, she thinks, leaning forward and tapping her heels against Eridu's sides.

Eridu springs forward. Instinctively, I grab for the saddle pommel in front of Ava with my left hand and hold her tight in my right arm so she and Eridu don't both fly away from me.

The combination of Ava's breathless laughter and the delight spilling from her into me is intoxicating. Eridu's gallop transforms the forest around the path into a blurred tunnel that shimmers with every shade of summer green. I've never moved so fast before.

Arkhi calls out behind us, almost too faint to hear. Ava urges Eridu onward, but he slows to a trot, then to a walk. Ignoring Ava's indignant tugs on his reins, Eridu turns and walks slowly back toward the caravan.

Although she's a little disappointed by the abrupt conclusion of our ride, Ava mostly radiates exhilaration. "Thanks," she says to Eridu, scratching between his shoulders. "I needed that." She twists slightly against my tight grip on her waist and reaches up to touch my cheek, laughing as she says, "And you need a shave."

I realize only now that the rough stubble on my chin has been digging into her neck since Eridu started galloping. "Sorry," I say quickly, before remembering she hates apologies. I loosen my hold on her and make space between us. "I'll ask one of the Mohirai for a blade when we make camp."

She glances up over her shoulder at me, a mischievous look in her eyes, and says, "Or I could lend you mine."

"What?" I say, astonished. "Where did you get another blade?"

"Never lost the first one," she says.

I try to remember what happened to her knife after I dropped it in the woods last night. I can't imagine how she's kept it with her all this time without me noticing. "You're full of surprises," I say.

She shrugs. "Isn't everyone?"

Eridu comes to a stop when we near Arkhi at the front of the caravan. Some of the girls riding behind the Muse watch us with interest, probably wondering whether we'll be reprimanded, but Arkhi only adjusts the silver-threaded stole around her shoulders and makes a clicking noise with her tongue. All along the caravan, horses' ears flick forward at the sound. Eridu turns and falls into step alongside Arkhi's horse Khaos.

"You've trained them well," Ava says to Arkhi, clearly impressed. But there's a bite in her tone as she adds, "Is that to keep us from running away?"

Arkhi says impassively, "It's to keep the caravan together. There's a vast wilderness between here and the temple lands of Velkanos, far too vast for novices untrained in the arts of navigation to travel alone. But you're welcome to ride Eridu as you please, as long as you don't lose sight of the caravan or wear him out. Remember he needs to carry you both for an entire moon, not just today."

Ava inclines her head slightly in a gesture of obedience, chastened by the reminder of Eridu's welfare. She guides Eridu back in line behind Arkhi, and we ride on for a while in silence.

A landscape of rolling grassy hills dotted with trees opens before us as the narrow cart path emerges from the dense cedar forest and joins a wider road. The road is intermittently paved, so the steady thud of hooves on dirt alternates with the ringing clop of hooves on stone. There are few other sounds besides our horses and the occasional call of a kuku bird. The rainclouds Arkhi predicted earlier gather on the southern horizon, and now even I can feel the approaching storm in the air. Arkhi leads the caravan a short distance east before she calls us to a halt at a small clearing beside the road.

We all dismount, and Arkhi gives instructions to each novice to help make camp. Kor, Piroza, Kishar, Tashlu, and Eumelia unload the horses under Arkhi's supervision, settling them for the night under the shelter of some trees on a grassy stream bank. Narua, Bel, and Hanu gather wood to build a fire and help Serapen prepare the evening meal. Ava and I are useless for many tasks in our present condition, but we can carry gear while walking hand in hand, so we attend Thalia as she lays out the camp. The wind picks up as the rain approaches, so she chooses a spot on the leeward side of a stand of trees, and we help her stake out four canvas tents.

The rapidly darkening sky looks ominous, but Arkhi says we have enough time to eat outside before the rain begins. So the nine girls and I sit in a circle around the fire. Most of the girls chat in little groups. Ava and I sit apart from the others in a comfortable silence. Her hand rests lightly on mine. She watches Serapen with close attention as the High Priestess draws ingredients out of a leather satchel and carefully pours and mixes them into whatever she's brewing over the fire.

I'm not as hungry as I'd expect after the daylong fast, but I'm completely exhausted now that it's been almost two days since I've had any real sleep.

Ava overhears me and thinks, *You do look exhausted. Do you want us to just go to bed? I'm not really hungry.*

Serapen looks over at us and says, "The evening meal will help restore you, and afterwards I'll give you instruction to help you ease your binding. Just stay put a bit longer, all right?"

"All right," Ava says cautiously, thinking, *Do you think she can hear us?*

Not sure, I think. *I don't notice anyone else in my head besides you, though.*

I don't like it, she thinks.

I glance at her, amused.

What? she thinks.

There's a lot you don't like, Ava.

She gives me a playful shove, and I laugh.

Hanu and Eumelia have been speaking with Thalia on the far side of the fire from us. They stand up and cross over to our side.

Ugh, Ava thinks, looking at Eumelia. *Not again.*

Hanu sits facing me, her back to the fire. I try to focus on Eumelia, who takes a seat facing Ava, just out of her arm's reach.

"What do you want?" Ava says to them, not quite civil, but not as rudely as before, either.

Hanu glances at me, then looks at Ava and says, "Thalia says the tents usually hold three. And the other trios want to stay together. So that leaves us four to share the last tent."

"Should be fine," Eumelia says to Ava with a shrug. "You take up hardly any space at all."

Ava manages to hold her tongue, but I feel her distaste for smirking Eumelia like a knot in my throat.

Take it easy, I think. *None of us will get any sleep in that little tent if we're fighting.*

"But also, you would complete our trio," Hanu adds gently, seeing Ava scowling at Eumelia. "Will you be part of ours, Ava? We've always been missing our third sister."

Not always, Ava thinks.

In the awkward silence that follows, Hanu looks hopefully from Ava to me and back again. I hope Ava says something soon, because I'm struggling to fend off more thoughts of Hanu. She's leaning a bit forward toward Ava, awaiting an answer. Hanu's riding shirt, slightly damp with sweat, is translucent over her breasts now that she's backlit by the fire.

Are you going to say something? I think.

Ava glances at me, then at Hanu. Her scowl fades. Her lips twitch in a mischievous smile. I would be apprehensive if I weren't so exhausted.

All right. Fine. Maybe it'll be fun, she thinks, tossing my earlier words back at me.

"Sounds good," Ava says, with an indifferent shrug that's almost a perfect imitation of Eumelia's. Hanu beams at Ava, then at me. Eumelia continues to watch Ava through slightly narrowed eyes. I'm relieved when Serapen announces to the group that food is ready. Hopefully this will give all the girls something else to focus on for a little while. And maybe Hanu will turn around to face the fire so I can safely look up again.

Serapen ladles out a fragrant stew. Bowls pass hand to hand around the circle. The three Mohirai stand around the fire and turn their palms up toward the darkening sky. We all join them in speaking the familiar words of the meal blessing.

We give our thanks for gifts of sun
Of water, soil, and seed
For gifts of many seasons
Gathered here to meet our need
To build our strength so that our hands
May in their time return
The gifts received from mother land
Improved with gifts our own

The ritual is comforting, even spoken in this unfamiliar setting beneath the open sky. When I say the words, I'm transported to my old table in the meal hall packed with boys, where I recited this blessing a thousand times before.

Do you miss them? Ava thinks, pressing my hand in sympathy.

I think, *Everything today happened so fast. I haven't had time to think about them until now. But I'll miss them, in some ways, yes. Things are ...* I feel Hanu's eyes on me, Ava's hand touching mine, Eumelia's quirking half-smile that Ava keeps avoiding. I keep my eyes on Ava's hand as I think, *Things are simpler when it's just boys.*

Ava's amusement at my predicament with Hanu drowns out most of her other emotions at the moment, but she's trying to be encouraging when she thinks, *Still, you always wanted to be a Mohira, right? Seems like the Voice gave you exactly what you wanted. Or as close as you could get as a boy, anyway.*

It's the first time I've thought of it that way, that the Voice gave me what I wanted. I've always thought of the Voice as something wise and powerful but completely indifferent to what I want. Ava's words make me realize I should be feeling deeply grateful. And I do feel grateful, in a way. But I also feel regret, which confuses me. Maybe that's Ava's regret I'm feeling, though.

What about you? I think. *This was what you wanted once, wasn't it?*

Ava sighs. *It doesn't matter,* she thinks. *This is what I have to work with now.*

But what did you really want? I think.

An image of the sea flashes before me. A deep blue vastness beneath a brighter blue bowl of sky. A green headland rising in the west. Wind through my hair. Freedom.

I'm sorry, I think. *I wish you could have that.*

Don't apologize, she thinks, bumping my shoulder with hers. *I'm happy for you, anyway. From the looks of it, you're going to be much better off as an Artifex than you would have been in the men's villages. Although ...* she glances at Hanu, and at some of the other girls looking at me. *I still think you should have made a run for it with me. These girls look like they're going to eat you alive.*

She and I both laugh at this, and we catch some puzzled glances from the others.

My stomach growls, reminding me of the untouched bowl of stew I'm holding in one hand. Ava and I decide through a quick exchange of ideas that the best way to manage eating at the same time is by making use of our feet. We each pull off a boot, and Ava rests her bare foot alongside mine.

"You're so weird," Eumelia says, more bewildered than malicious, as she watches Ava's toes wiggling absent-mindedly beside mine in the grass.

Ava ignores her, and the four of us eat in silence for a while. Ava hardly touches her food, but the rest of us dig in with good appetites.

"I always wondered why we were missing a girl in our trio," Eumelia says thoughtfully, her eyes still fixed on Ava. "What did Serapen mean, when she said you were lost? Where were you?"

△▽△

"What did Serapen mean, when she said you were lost? Where were you?" says Eumelia.

She, Dom, and Hanu all look at me. Spirits, the last thing I need right now are shrewd questions from Eumelia drawing more attention to me. The less anyone knows about where I've been and where I'm going, the better.

I struggle to think of an answer that would put an end to further questions. Fortunately, I don't have to say anything, because the High Priestess stands up from where she's been sitting with the other Muses and approaches us.

"Have you had enough to eat?" she asks me and Dom. We both nod. I'm grateful for the well-timed interruption, even coming from Serapen, whom I'd otherwise be trying to avoid. There's a hint of concern in Serapen's expression as she looks at my nearly untouched bowl beside Dom's empty one, but she makes no comment about it. Instead, she gestures for us to follow her and says, "Very well. Come walk with me."

We quickly pull on our boots and hand our bowls to the girls helping Thalia and Arkhi wash up after the meal. The first few raindrops fall as we follow Serapen across the clearing, toward the grassy stream bank where the horses are sheltered beneath the trees.

I've been expecting something like this to happen. Now that Dom has to stay with the girls, and I have to stay with Dom, I figure the Mohirai have to silence me in some way. Serapen can't possibly want the other novices to find out what happened to me or learn what I know about the Mohirai. So what does she plan to do with me? Negotiate for my silence? Manipulate me with one of her arts?

Dispose of me somewhere in the wilderness?

I've allowed the pleasure of riding this afternoon to keep my mind off these darker thoughts, mostly for Dom's sake. I'm worried about the trouble I've already caused him, and how much worse it could get the longer we're together and the more he learns of my plan. He seems determined to stay among the Mohirai, so the sooner I can escape from here, and from him, the better everything will be for both of us.

But where would you go? Dom wonders, looking at me with that worried expression again.

It's good I have no escape plan right now, since Dom seems able to overhear so much of what I'm thinking. But this overhearing is going to be a real problem.

Serapen leads us to a large beech tree by the stream and turns to face me. From inside her robes, she withdraws a silver flask. The surface of the flask reflects her sky-blue sleeves with their delicate embroidery of golden threads.

Holding out the flask to me, she says, "I suppose you know what this is."

Warily, I say, "Unbinding pharmaka."

She nods and says, "Keep this with you at all times. If you experience acute pain from your binding, you can take the unbinding pharmaka to weaken the bond, which should reduce the pain."

I know very little about the arts of pharmaka, but most of what my mother taught me is about the effects of unbinding pharmaka. I would have been willing to take unbinding pharmaka from my mother's hand, but not from a priestess, and definitely not from the High Priestess Serapen, whom my mother fears more than any other Mohira. I say, "I don't want it."

Patient but unyielding, Serapen says, "It's wise to be cautious. The use of unbinding pharmaka comes at a cost to memory, and it is challenging even for a skilled initiate to control what memory is lost. These arts require time to master, but the only way to attain the skill is through practice."

"I'm not going to take it," I say. "I want to remember."

Serapen says, "You do not need to fear the arts of pharmaka, little sister. Pharmaka is a gift to us all from the Voice. Accept the gift. No child under my care will be left helpless, as you were in the forest last night."

I detect reproach in these words, but the reproach doesn't seem directed at me. It occurs to me suddenly that Serapen must be speaking of my mother, and of what my mother has taught me—or not taught me—about pharmaka. Why did my mother leave me so helpless? I chew my lip, worrying this is a trick of some kind. Perhaps Serapen's trying to confuse my thoughts. Still, I can't see the harm in accepting the flask as long as I don't drink from it, and I can see Serapen won't take no for an answer. So I take the flask, securing it to my belt with a leather strap.

Serapen continues, "Your amanitai overdose is unlike any case I've seen before, Ava. There's always an experimental component to pharmaka, but usually experimentation is done by an experienced initiate with small incremental changes in dose. Your overdose was extreme, and you had no prior tolerance to moderate the effect. Even among my most experienced healer initiates, no one has ever taken such a large dose all at once.

"The overdose alone would have made the healing work significant, but it's complicated by the fact that you formed not just one bond, but two."

"Two?" I say. I've been so focused on managing my bond with Dom that the thought of a second bond is truly awful. How on Dulai could I have formed a second bond? As soon as I wonder this, a memory from last night resurfaces. Apprehensively, I say, "I told my mother that Dom was the only person I'd touched, after my accident. But then you said …" I struggle to remember exactly what Serapen said, given all the confusion that followed.

"He's the only human you touched," says Serapen. "But he's not the only awareness you touched."

I frown. "I don't understand."

Serapen says, "Surely Lilith taught you where the Voice in all dwells."

"Well … It's in everything, isn't it?" I say.

"It is," says Serapen. "But in some places the Voice's awareness is much stronger. It's more concentrated in rich soils, like a forest floor. That's why forests are sacred to the Mohirai. Even without binding pharmaka, walking barefoot through a forest creates a weak connection with the Voice. But walking barefoot through a forest under the influence of binding pharmaka, as you did last night, would create a connection far stronger."

So this is why my mother asked if I was walking barefoot. Why didn't she warn me this could happen?

Serapen continues, "Connecting awareness with binding pharmaka safely takes years of training, even with low doses of binding pharmaka, even for initiates of the mysteries. Too much connection creates overwhelming sensation. Imagine the pain if you tried to swallow the ocean all at once. In a way, that's what happens when an unprepared human awareness connects too fast with a non-human awareness like the Voice in all."

The warmth drains out of my face and hands as I remember the excruciating pain I felt when I tried to run after my mother for the last time. I don't think I could have endured it a moment longer than I did. Shutting my eyes, I struggle to suppress the memory so I can think clearly again.

Dom squeezes my cold fingers in his warm hand as he thinks, *You're all right. It's over now.*

Is it? I wonder. I'm afraid to ask my next question, but I summon my courage. This may be the only question that really matters. I take a deep breath and look up at Serapen. "Are you saying I'm bound to the Voice in all?"

My heart pounds louder and louder as I wait for Serapen's answer. I sway dizzily on my feet. Dom wraps his arm around my shoulder to steady me, and Serapen reaches out and grips my wrist. Briefly, I feel her awareness probing mine —light, swift, and precise as a hummingbird—but she withdraws her hand even before I react. I look at her suspiciously, wondering what she did to me with that healer's touch. Despite my worry, I'm relieved when my dizziness passes.

"All are bound to the Voice, little sister," Serapen says. "But you …" Her gaze drifts upward as she searches for words. I notice her long fingers moving absent-mindedly through the air between us, like she's untangling invisible threads. "The depth of connection you formed with the Voice should have been fatal. In truth, I don't understand how you survived. But perhaps it has something to do with your double binding."

I have no idea what to make of this. I say, "If one bond should be fatal, wouldn't two be worse?" Can anything be worse than fatal?

Thoughtfully, Serapen says, "Two are more complex to manage than one, certainly. But complexity creates possibility. Every bond presents unique possibilities, for good and ill, and one might offer counterpoint to another.

"For example, humans are far more similar to each other in their awareness, and far less complex than the Voice in all. A human mind has fewer sensory perceptions, less attention, less memory to manage.

"So your binding to Dom, even though it formed without preparation, is far less painful than your binding to the Voice in all. Dom's awareness is concentrated in a single human body with only sixteen summers of memory, not spread out over a vast area of ancient perceptive awareness like a forest, certainly not as vast as the entire perceptive awareness of the Voice that dwells in all. And Dom cannot hear the Voice as you can, so it cannot overwhelm him the same way it overwhelmed you. For you, Dom's awareness might therefore be like … the calm at the eye of a storm. As long as you're within the eye, you're safe from the storm."

"Muse Serapen," says Dom. He's been listening so quietly that I'd almost forgotten he was here, even while his arm is wrapped around me, supporting me. I'm not sure whether he has an uncanny ability to fade into the background or I have a deplorable tendency to forget him.

"Yes, Dom?" says Serapen.

He says, "The Mohirai teach that men can't hear the Voice in all, apart from our Calling Day. And you said it again now, that I can't hear the Voice like Ava does. Why not?"

It's a good question. There are few advantages to being a boy, but I suppose this might be one. If I'd been a boy, maybe I couldn't have formed an accidental bond with the Voice in the woods last night. If I'd been a boy, maybe I would have succeeded in my escape.

Serapen says, again in the tone of instruction, "Listen, novice Artifex. You, and all the men of Dulai, pay the debt of the men who came before you. Ever since the time of destruction, men have been cut off from direct experience of the Voice. The Artifexi alone among men may live and work among the Mohirai, but even an Artifex may experience the Voice only through his Muse.

"You will learn more of this mystery in the proper time, from the Muses as well as from your brothers among the Artifexi."

This answer only multiplies my questions, but I suppose I should let Dom ask these questions. They do pertain to him more than me. So I'm surprised when he asks nothing else, reciting only the ritual response to instruction. "I have listened, and I have heard, sister."

I'm disappointed by Serapen's answer, and even more disappointed by Dom's failure to question. How typical for a Mohira, to cloak something so important in mystery. And how typical for a boy, to accept what is given and ask for no more. Ah, well. I suppose that's none of my concern. Dom can muddle through the mysteries however he likes, but I want answers.

To Serapen, I say, "So … If Dom is like the eye of the storm, and the Voice is the storm, what can I do to get out of the storm?"

"I'm not sure," says Serapen. "There's little we can do to escape a storm around us, other than take shelter. But I think the work ahead of you might be the inverse of most novices' work. The usual goal of novice training is to ensure the connection to the Voice deepens slowly and steadily over time without becoming overwhelming. Usually it is only when the mind and body have been suitably prepared by pharmaka that a novice seeks deeper connection to the Voice through initiation.

"But the Voice has set you on a different path. You have begun your novice training with a connection that's far too deep. Dangerously so. Your work will be to change this connection into one you can manage safely on your own.

"The other Muses and I will do our best to instruct you in this work. But even we will not always know how to help you. Only you will be able to judge when you've found the right balance for yourself between connection to and freedom from the Voice in all."

Everything about Serapen's voice and presence conveys knowledge so deep that my instinct is to trust her. Yet I can't trust her words. She speaks of connection and freedom as if they complement each other and can coexist peacefully. But my mother taught me that connection to the Voice is the trap that holds an initiate back from true freedom, that the Voice's will eventually subsumes the initiate's own. Once that happens, there is no way for an initiate to judge for herself the path she should take. She can only follow the Voice's call.

My mother also warned me about the subtle ways the Mohirai maintain the Voice's control over initiates. I've stumbled upon the least subtle way by overdosing on binding pharmaka. But the Mohirai practice many arts drawn from their mysteries, and they have many tricks up their richly embroidered sleeves. Maybe Serapen's apparent trustworthiness is one of these tricks. Maybe trusting her will ensure my own enslavement to the Voice.

But, as impossible as I find it to trust the High Priestess, I know I need her help. I have to ease this painful bond with the Voice. I can't remain tied up with Dom forever. Cautiously, I say, "What exactly is this work?"

The rain falls a little faster, but the old beech above us offers adequate cover, so we remain dry. Serapen sits at the base of the tree, in a crook formed between its gnarled roots. She gestures for us to sit like her. Dom and I find similar spots at the base of the tree and sit, then peer around the trunk to watch Serapen. She pulls off her riding boots and tucks her legs beneath her. The tops of her bare feet and her ankles press into the soft, dark soil. She presses her back against the trunk and extends her hands, palms up, on either side of her, inviting me and Dom to join her. He and I pull off our boots again, lean back against the trunk, and take her hands. Serapen's fingers are strong, warm, and dry like Dom's, but much softer and smoother than his, like fine oiled leather. We form a ring around the tree, facing outward.

"Listen, novice Mohira," Serapen says to me, raising her voice over the patter of the rain. She speaks in the tone of instruction, though from her it sounds far gentler than it ever did from my mother. "Close your eyes, if you like. The work of unbinding is not so different from the work of binding. Both are works of transformation. One is the complement of the other. Unbinding inverts binding. Binding inverts unbinding. In either case, whether you work to bind with or unbind from another awareness, you must first focus on the connection you wish to change. In your case, the connection you need to change is between your awareness and the awareness of the Voice in all.

"When we speak of awareness, it is helpful to imagine it as a whole with many parts, like a year has many moons, or a lyre has many strings. But most often, the Mohirai speak of awareness like a soil with many layers.

"Each layer of an awareness creates the possibility for some aspect of experience. The more layers an awareness possesses, the richer those experiences may be, just like the richest soils may support the most life.

"We give names to the more familiar layers of our human awareness. There are passive layers of bodily sensation and emotional reaction, like sight and hearing, touch and scent, fear and desire, anger and joy. There's the sense of self—those many inner voices speaking words we think are our thoughts, telling us stories we believe are our identities. There's imagination—that most active part of awareness, always generating ideas, meaning, and purpose with the help of the other layers. And there are some layers that remain cloaked in mystery, like intuition and the sense of knowing.

"Every creature possesses some layers of awareness, though not all creatures share all the same layers. The Voice in all differs from other creatures because its awareness includes all layers—many beyond our human ability to experience.

"Each layer of an awareness has the potential to connect with a layer of another's awareness. Awareness in fact hungers to connect in this way, so it may receive more, give more, experience more.

"Awareness grows in power through expanding connection. But in that power lies the danger. It is easy for us to damage another awareness, and for another awareness to damage our own, especially when that awareness is deeply connected to ours through binding pharmaka. Binding pharmaka strips us of the protection that comes from separation and unawareness. Without separation, one awareness may flood into another in unexpected ways.

"You have experienced a bit of the consequence of this, Ava. You experience pain because your awareness is unprepared to receive the awareness of the Voice. But pain is not the only possible consequence of a poorly formed connection between two awarenesses. Without the protection of separation, it becomes easier to manipulate another awareness, or to be manipulated. It becomes easier to force an idea or a desire upon another awareness, or to have one forced upon our own.

"It is possible to injure and even to destroy layers of awareness through such ill use. Just as rich soil may turn to desert, or an eye might be blinded, or skin might be burned away."

I cringe at these vivid images. The High Priestess continues, "We sit now in a place where the Voice's awareness is more concentrated than most, at a living intersection between water, soil, air, and sun. The Voice's awareness travels beneath us, above us, and all around us. Your pharmaka-amplified connection to the Voice would be too strong for you to endure here alone, Ava. You would be aware of everything connected to this tree across all of Dulai, and you would have none of the protection from that awareness that comes from initiate training. You would experience pain from all this unfamiliar sensation, and that pain would quickly become deadly, for an unprepared mind cannot hold so much awareness.

"Here and now, however, you have shelter from your awareness of the Voice. All initiate Mohirai learn to bond lightly to a new awareness on contact, and we learn to manage connection to the Voice without allowing it to overwhelm us. So while you hold my hand, my awareness offers yours shelter, as would the awareness of any other initiate Mohira. Dom's awareness offers shelter to yours as well, while his awareness resides in you and yours resides in him.

"Your work of unbinding will require you to find places like this one, where you can practice the art of connection to the Voice with enough shelter to protect yourself from ill effects. Most of the work is simply observation, allowing yourself to encounter the awareness of the Voice. The best way to encounter another awareness is without resistance and without using force, letting each layer of your awareness find balance with its counterpart within the other awareness. You will know when you have found balance—it will feel like pain easing, like awareness expanding.

"Finding the balance takes practice and self-discipline, like any art. You may find that some layers of awareness reach balance with another's easily. But sometimes you will struggle, and many times in the beginning you will fail. When the struggle seems too great, or when you find you're no longer making progress, that is when the unbinding pharmaka is useful. You can use the pharmaka to weaken your bond to another awareness while you're in contact, and this will reduce the intensity of painful connection, like wrapping yourself in a cloak to protect yourself from the elements.

"But you should not rely on unbinding pharmaka alone to protect you in this practice. Memory should never be given up lightly, and the amount of unbinding pharmaka you would need to counterbalance your overdose all at once would have catastrophic effects on your memory, since you are so young and have so few memories. The Voice has given you a gift in Dom. Let him help you in your practice. In time, you should be able to manage your connection with the Voice without great loss of memory."

I consider Serapen's instruction carefully, comparing it to what my mother said in the woods. If I had any hope before that this unbinding work could be done without Dom, that I might be able to take care of this predicament on my own, it's now gone. Whether or not I trust Serapen, her guidance and my mother's seem to agree on this point: I can't risk using unbinding pharmaka alone to counteract my overdose. I'll need Dom's help if I want to remember who I am when this is all over.

I say, "If I do need to take the unbinding pharmaka, will it weaken my connection with Dom as well as my connection with the Voice?"

The gentle rain transitions into a downpour, and a translucent grey curtain falls over our view of the camp. All the other girls and Mohirai withdraw to their tents. The beech boughs above still manage to keep us dry, though.

Over the rushing sound of the rain, Serapen says, "The unbinding pharmaka will work most strongly on the connection with which you have the most physical contact. If you take unbinding pharmaka while you're in a place like this, with a high concentration of the Voice's awareness, the bond with the Voice should weaken more than if you were to take it in a desert, for example. However, since Dom's awareness is so concentrated in his body, you may also affect your bond with Dom, especially if you need his contact soon after you've taken the unbinding pharmaka. This is why it's important to do the work in small steps. You must keep your connection with Dom strong enough to offer shelter as you work to balance your bond with the Voice, to minimize the need for unbinding pharmaka."

I say, "And then, when this work is done, will I be like I was before? Able to walk on my own, free of this pain?"

The High Priestess takes so long to answer that I grow alarmed. At last she says, "There is no returning to the condition you were before, Ava. A thing once known can never be fully unknown. An awareness once experienced can never be entirely forgotten. But the bonds between awarenesses can be strengthened and weakened, relative to one another, once they are connected. The art lies in balancing the strength of your bond and your freedom from the bond."

Serapen stops and looks at me expectantly, and I realize she's waiting for the proper response to her words of instruction, which means this is all that I'm to learn tonight. This would all be fascinating, if it weren't so hopelessly complicated. Dispirited, I say, "I have listened, and I have heard, sister."

"Good," says Serapen. "Then it is time to act."

"I'm still not sure I know what to do, though," I say.

She says, "Sometimes the only way to know is to do."

Well, at this point doing seems preferable to knowing. My mind can't possibly hold much more than the knowledge Serapen's already poured into me. So, tentatively, I let go of Serapen's hand. I hold on to Dom's hand a moment longer, anticipating the unwelcome return of the pain, but then I let him go too. I lean back against the trunk of the tree and close my eyes.

I'm aware of nothing at first but the sound of the rain in the leaves above me.

Next I feel the tingling where my ankles press into the soil, the same feeling that comes when Dom and I share thoughts in a particularly vivid way. My insides clench as I remember how this feeling came over me for the first time last night when I touched the forest floor outside the cave, just before I heard the Voice in all. Fortunately, the memory prepares me somewhat better this time for the disorienting sensation of my awareness slipping away from me and sinking down into the ground. I have an impulse to panic, but Serapen's words return to me. *Observe ... without resistance ... without force.*

So I try to relax, despite my disorientation. My body drifts away from me, and I let it drift. Freed from my body, my awareness spreads outward through the ground. I feel my awareness drawn into the tree. I stretch deep down along old roots through the soil, toward rock. I rise up along strong branches through the air, toward the sun. My young leaves tremble in the wind. My tender rootlets soak in the rain.

The Voice, when it returns this time, is louder than before. The weight of it slams into me from all directions. The pain comes on fast, much faster than before, so fast I only fleetingly perceive it as pain before I'm lost inside of it. A tiny voice inside me screams as I shrink to a grain of sand, a point of nothingness, swallowed up in an infinite vastness. There is no I. There is only ...

We are the bridge joining light to darkness. We are the wheel turning season to season. We are the threads binding realm to realm. We are—

The Voice fades. There's a hand. My hand, pulled out of nothingness by another's hand. Dom's hand. The rest of myself returns in pieces, slowly reassembling. I am an I again.

Are you all right? Dom thinks.

Am I? I wonder, dazed.

Serapen takes my other hand and says, "Breathe, Ava. Breathe." I gulp air, and each breath seems to draw blades deeper into my back. My pulse is erratic. Dom's and Serapen's hands on my skin feel so hot they might burn me, but it must just be my fingers that are so cold. I lean weakly back against the trunk of the tree and look up into its branches. For a strange moment, I think, *up into my branches*. The wind stirs the leaves, and I'm nauseated by their motion.

Serapen and Dom wait silently at my side as I attempt to recover my composure. The rain pours down harder, at last breaking through the protective cover of the beech boughs. Warm raindrops patter on my upturned face, sliding down my cheeks.

Eventually my breathing steadies. The stabbing pain ebbs. My pulse returns to something like normal. Serapen squeezes my hand and says, "It will get easier with practice, little sister. Head back to the tents, when you're ready. Try to get some sleep tonight. You both look like you need it."

Serapen stands, pulls her dark hood low over her forehead, and runs through the rain back toward the camp.

I remain sitting, uncertain whether I'm strong enough to stand yet. Dom reaches toward me and lifts up my hood to cover my head from the rain. I hadn't noticed how much water was running down my neck until he makes it stop.

"Thanks," I whisper.

Dom studies me with worried eyes. He says, "Do you want me to carry you back?"

I say, "Do I look that bad?"

"You look … not good."

"Still better than you, though," I say, forcing a weak smile.

He chuckles. "Can I give you a hand up at least?"

I nod. Dom pulls me up. I stand without too much difficulty, but when I try to step forward, my legs move like a newborn colt's, as though I've never walked before. I wobble, grip Dom's hand hard, and throw out my free hand to catch myself against the beech trunk. I grit my teeth and breathe sharply through my nose, trying to focus. I feel almost as weak as I did last night when I collapsed in the meadow, and my sense of helplessness infuriates me. Propped up here between Dom and the tree, I hunger for their strength.

Both my palms tingle, and warmth floods through me. To my surprise, I feel steadier on my feet. Tentatively, I withdraw my palm from the tree and look up at Dom.

"Did you feel that?" I ask.

"I felt your hand get warmer," he says. "Is that what you mean?"

I nod and say, "Do you feel all right?"

"Me? Same as before, I guess. Just tired."

Whatever happened, it's a relief, and the exhilaration of my renewed strength rushes straight to my head. I look out at the curtain of heavy rain separating us from camp.

"Shall we run for it?" I say.

"Maybe we should take it slow," he says, his brow furrowing.

I disagree. I pull him after me into the downpour.

THE TROUBLE WITH TRIOS

Hand in hand, Ava and I run back toward camp. Her bright laughter as the rain pours over us reminds me of galloping with her on Eridu this afternoon. Hearing her, I can't help myself from laughing too.

But despite her apparent recovery from whatever just happened to her, I haven't recovered from my alarm. When Serapen and I let go of her hands beneath the beech tree, Ava had closed her eyes and briefly relaxed. I watched her, waiting for the prickling pain to return in my chest like it usually does when we're separated, but at first I felt nothing amiss, so I thought Ava must be fine. Then all at once she'd gone so pale. I'd felt a crushing sensation, an unbearable pressure all around me, so I'd grabbed her hand. Her fingers were ice cold, and although her body sat beside me, I could tell some part of her was gone. For a terrifying moment, I thought she might not return. Even after her eyes opened again, she looked translucent, as if some part of her had dissolved into the air.

It's like none of that ever happened, though, as we burst through the door flap into the fourth tent, breathless and soaked.

"Ugh!" Eumelia shrieks as a light spray of rainwater from my riding cloak splashes her in the face. Hanu catches a bit of it as well, but she only laughs in surprise.

"Sorry, sorry," I say to Eumelia, wiping water out of my eyes. Eumelia grumbles but accepts my apology.

Ava attempts to use the hem of her damp riding shirt to dry her drenched hair. I shift my hand to her bare hip to free up both her hands. Hanu's eyes follow my every move.

Eumelia asks, "Where did you two go with Serapen?"

I wait for Ava to speak, but she seems preoccupied, so I say, "Over to the stream."

Dom, Ava thinks. *Let me handle this. We need to be careful about what we say to them. I don't want anyone else tangled up in this, all right?*

Sorry, I think automatically.

You don't need to be sorry, she thinks. *I'm the one who got you into this mess.*

Eumelia raises an eyebrow, then says, "What did she want to talk to you about?"

Ava's thoughts churn with possible answers to this question, evaluating the risks and advantages of each possibility so fast I can't keep up. I wait. At last she says, "She's teaching me and Dom how to ease the binding between us."

"Oh, I'm glad there's something she can do to help you," says Hanu. "Did she say how long it will take?"

How long do you think Hanu can tolerate? Ava thinks. A hint of a smile plays at the corner of her mouth as she glances at me.

Please stop, I think.

"She didn't say," says Ava. "I don't think she really knows. I hope it won't take too long."

Hanu nods sympathetically and says, "It must be difficult for you both to manage."

"It is," says Ava. "I wish I could trade places with you." Her tone is all innocence, but her mischief feels like a squirrel on the loose inside me.

Hanu says, "Tell me if there's anything I can do to help. Really. If you need extra hands, or anything like that."

Ava surveys the tent. Hanu and Eumelia have already laid out their bedrolls on one side, leaving the other side open for me and Ava. All I want right now is to spread out my bedroll at the far edge of the tent and collapse into it.

But Ava says, "You know, there is one thing that would be helpful."

I see what Ava's thinking before she says it. I grip her hand. *Please don't,* I think urgently. *Please, Ava.*

Oh come on, she thinks. *I'm doing you a favor.*

Ignoring my silent protests, Ava says, "One of the side effects of the binding pharmaka is that I get cold very easily, and Dom does too. Could we sleep between you and Eumelia for warmth?"

"Of course!" says Hanu. She looks at Eumelia. "Is that all right with you, Mel?"

Eumelia shrugs. "Fine with me as long as you sleep on Dom's side. No offense, Dom, but you smell like boy sweat. That's more Hanu's taste than mine."

Ava and Hanu laugh. I want to say that I'll be fine sleeping on the outside edge of the tent, that actually I'd prefer it. But there is some merit to the idea that we two should sleep in the middle for warmth, at least until we've both recovered more of our strength. And Ava knows, because she can hear what I'm thinking, that I don't want to hurt Hanu's feelings by saying I don't want her next to me. I'm irritated that Ava's put me in the middle of this situation, but her amusement pours into me, drowning out my annoyance.

You're terrible, I think.

You're welcome, Ava thinks.

Hanu folds up her bedroll and moves to the other edge of the tent beside me.

Ava and I help each other get ready for bed. In these tight quarters, with Ava and Hanu undressing on either side of me, there's not much that's safe to look at. I keep my eyes on Eumelia's side of the tent. There's no risk of any uncomfortably intimate memories popping up involving her. Eumelia and I have always been friendly enough, but nothing more than that.

Eumelia's face is less mocking, less guarded, and more thoughtful when she thinks no one is watching. Her gaze follows my hands on Ava's back with undisguised enjoyment as Ava pulls a dry sleeping tunic over her head. Eumelia catches me looking at her, and I'm so surprised that I don't think to look away. Eumelia winks at me. I suppress a laugh.

Ava glances up at me and thinks, *What?*

I do my best not to think about Eumelia's expression. *Just appreciating how clever you are*, I think. Ava narrows her eyes suspiciously, but I manage to keep a straight face.

Ava and I spread out our bedrolls, and Hanu lends a hand when we need help. The rain and wind pick up outside the tent. Darkness falls. There's nothing left to do for the night but try to sleep as best we can. So the four of us crawl under our blankets.

Ava curls into a ball, pulls her blanket up over her nose, and reaches for my hand. The damp chill from the rain creeps inside the tent, emanating up from the ground through my thin bedroll. The warmth drains slowly from Ava's fingers, and eventually she's shivering even harder than she was last night.

I'm delirious with exhaustion, but I feel her growing discomfort like it's my own. I overhear Ava's thoughts as she chastises herself for weakness and tries to fall asleep despite the cold.

Come here, I think. *I'll warm you up.*

I'll be fine, she thinks. *I'll ask Thalia for an extra blanket tomorrow.*

Come on. I reach for her sleepily. *I can't sleep if you can't. You'll be doing me a favor.*

Her gratitude overcomes her resistance. She lets me draw her against me, her back to my front. She grows warm again and relaxes. I fall almost instantly into a deep and dreamless sleep.

△▽△

Before sunrise, I wake to the familiar sound of the first morning birds outside the tent. I recognize the weight of Dom's arms around me and the steady cadence of his breathing against my back. Yesterday returns to me through all the scents still clinging to him: pharmaka, sweat and leather, grass and campfire. His hand rests on the bare skin of my hip. Being held this way still feels like a trap, but this morning I have no impulse to spring away from him. For a moment I simply enjoy his warmth and the feeling of a good night's sleep. I guess even a trap can become comfortable, once it's familiar.

But I can't let myself get comfortable. I can't let myself forget that Dom, innocent though he may be, is just another tool the Mohirai can use to hold me here against my will. When I asked him to come with me yesterday, to run from the Voice's calling, I was driven by an impulse to save him as much as to save myself. How foolish I was. Of course he trusts the Mohirai more than he trusts me. Of course he wants to stay here; he knows nothing but what they've taught him. I need to focus on saving myself, before the Mohirai have me lulled into complacency the way they've lulled him and all the rest of these girls.

I open my eyes to find Eumelia watching me, her nose a handspan from mine. I'm so surprised that for a moment I simply stare back at her. I never before noticed the ring of blue encircling her hazel irises, or how pretty her mouth is when she's not smirking at me.

Her expression has changed dramatically since yesterday. Yesterday, Eumelia and Hanu both studied me with the same foggy look Dom gave me the first time he saw me in the woods. Neither of my former trio sisters could remember me. But the fog is gone from Eumelia's eyes this morning.

The soft, smooth hand on my hip slides away, and I realize that what I thought was Dom's hand is actually hers. She finds my hand beneath my blanket, and my fingers tingle against her palm.

I remember, she thinks. A memory of my younger face flashes before me. Eumelia's memory.

My eyes widen. *How do you remember?* I think.

I don't know, she thinks, shaking her head slightly against her pillow. *I was dreaming that I was flying over a beautiful city made of glass. When I woke up, I could still see it so clearly in my mind. Then I realized I was touching you, and I pulled back my hand, and the city disappeared. Then I touched you again, and I saw the city again. So I knew that image was coming somehow from you.*

And now when I look at you, I remember all sorts of things. I've seen you before. We know each other, don't we?

It hadn't occurred to me earlier that anyone who touches me, not just Dom, might experience some effect of the binding pharmaka. Serapen didn't warn me about this. Perhaps she didn't know; she did say she's never seen an overdose like mine before. In my head, I curse extravagantly.

Eumelia's lips twitch into her usual smirk as she overhears me, and something about that familiar expression erases the years that have separated us. A memory returns to me.

I'm eight summers old, standing with Dom in a crowd of children outside the sheep paddocks. Eumelia's exasperated voice calls out from behind me, "Ava! Where were you? Why are you never where you're supposed to be?"

I look back over my shoulder at Eumelia, irritated by everything about her, from her plump freckled cheeks to the infuriating way she always talks to me, like I'm hers to command. Eumelia and Hanu stand waiting for me as the crowd of children disperses around us. I gesture sharply for Eumelia to wait, then turn back to Dom and say gently, "I have to go."

Dom looks crestfallen, and I feel guilty for leaving him. It's his first day here, and I can see he's nervous to be left alone among all these unfamiliar boys. I remember my first day, coming out of the woods with Serapen, so I know how confused he must be feeling. But he's not allowed into the temple city with me, so there's not much I can do. He has to go with the other boys back to their house outside the wall.

"Don't worry," I say, doing my best to sound cheerful. "The sisters will let us back out after we finish preserving the temple garden harvest. Should only take a quarter moon or so. I'll look for you at the old cedar when we're done, all right?"

"Ava, come on!" Eumelia marches toward me. She looks at Dom shrewdly and says, "Don't let her get you into trouble. She has a lot of funny ideas in her head."

My hands clench as I resist the urge to push Eumelia to the ground. Why can't she ever just leave me alone? I say, "You couldn't fit an idea in your head if you tried, Eumelia."

Eumelia rolls her eyes at me and says to Dom, "You'll see."

Dom looks uneasily from Eumelia to me. Hanu approaches, stepping between me and Eumelia, joining hands with us. She's much taller than both of us, with large, watchful eyes in her dark, solemn face.

"Come on," Hanu says in a soothing, grown-up voice. "You'll both feel better once you've eaten."

I refuse to look at Eumelia as Hanu draws us back toward the city gate. I cast one last look over my shoulder at Dom, who stands alone beside the paddock, looking completely forlorn as he watches us go.

The memory fades, and I'm back in the tent, lying nose to nose beside Eumelia. *Ugh,* she thinks. *You're such a sucker for that sad puppy face of his.*

I blink, horrified to realize Eumelia's just witnessed that entire memory. I try to pull back my hand from her, but she tightens her grip around my wrist, inadvertently digging into the bruises Dom left there yesterday. I wince, and she loosens her grip slightly but doesn't let me go.

Wait, she thinks. *I want to know what really happened to you.*

It's difficult to stop my thoughts from spilling into her while she's holding on to me. I consider wrenching my arm away, but she's always been stronger than me, and I don't want to cause a scene that wakes up Hanu or requires the intervention of the Mohirai. The last thing I need right now is more hands touching me, more awarenesses tangled up in mine.

Let me go, Eumelia, I think. *Whatever's happening to me with the binding pharmaka is dangerous, and Serapen doesn't really know how to fix it. I don't want to hurt you, all right?* More importantly, I don't want to be worrying about yet another person overhearing my thoughts while I need to be planning my escape.

Eumelia studies my face. *You're not going to hurt me,* she thinks. Her confidence is as infuriating as it is misguided, considering all the ways I managed to hurt Dom yesterday. I briefly consider slipping out of Dom's arms just to give her a taste of the awful pain, to prove I can hurt her. That seems unnecessarily cruel, though. There must be a better way.

I consider the memory of Dom's sad puppy face, which, however pathetic it may seem, is pretty effective at arousing sympathy. Maybe a little bit of his submissiveness would do the trick. Eumelia always seemed to enjoy being superior to me when we were little, after all. *Please let me go,* I think, summoning up the closest thing I can find to humility and hoping it feels authentic. *Please, Eumelia.*

You can tell me, she thinks insistently. *We're trio sisters, Ava. You can trust me.*

I stifle a derisive laugh. How could I trust Eumelia? For the brief time we lived together, she was nothing but a constant source of torment. Just looking at her fills me with irritating memories. She's the most unlikable person I've ever known.

Eumelia's lips tremble slightly. Oh, blast, she overheard that. *Sorry, Eumelia,* I think. *You're just … Well …*

Listen, Eumelia thinks, setting her lips in a firm line. *I can't change what I did when we were little. Maybe I was irritating. Maybe I was unlikable. Maybe I still am. But I promise you can trust me. Just give me a chance.*

I chew the inside of my lip, considering. *You want me to trust you?* I think.

She nods.

I think, *Then don't tell anyone about what happens when you touch me, all right? Not Hanu. Not the Mohirai. Not the other girls. I don't need anyone else in my head right now. Dom's too much as it is.*

All right, thinks Eumelia, *I promise. I won't tell anyone else. So tell me what happened.*

Prove you can keep a promise first, I think. *And let me go when I ask you to let me go.*

To my relief, Eumelia finally lets go of my wrist. But just as she withdraws her hand, a series of confusing sensations swirl through my awareness. The curves and colors of my face, lips, and body. The smoothness of her skin against mine and mine against hers. Arousal stirring deep inside of me—or is it inside of her? Understanding dawns on me, followed by awkwardness. Heat rushes to my cheeks. I curse inwardly.

My agitation seems to disturb Dom's sleep, and his waking sensations unfold clearly in my awareness. First he's so cozy that he doesn't want to open his eyes. Then his arms tighten slightly around me, and he's glad I'm still here and still warm. Then his pulse speeds up when he realizes the reason he's so cozy is that Hanu is draped around him, still asleep. He recognizes the feeling of her long legs tucked behind his, her full breasts pressed against his back, her forehead touching his shoulder, her hand resting on his thigh. Then he's alarmed because he realizes I'm awake and overhearing all this.

Good morning, I think, amused enough by Dom's predicament to momentarily forget my own. Eumelia's expression softens, and I realize with dismay that I'm smiling at her as I'm thinking of Dom. She's smiling at me because she thinks my smile is meant for her. And she's happy because this is how she wants me to smile at her. I curse inwardly again.

Now it's Dom's turn to be amused. *Good morning,* he thinks. *Turns out two can play at this game, eh?*

I roll over to face him so I don't accidentally send Eumelia any more mixed messages. Dom only half-opens one eye at me, but it's enough for me to see his teasing expression. I can't begrudge him his amusement. I was the one who thought playing games with our sleeping arrangements would be harmless fun, after all. This was a more serious mistake than I could have imagined. I need to get out of here before this gets any more complicated.

Dom's drowsy expression sharpens into wakefulness, overhearing me. *You can't get out of here without me,* he thinks. *You need to tell me what you're planning to do.*

Spirits, he's almost as irritating as Eumelia. I flop onto my back and stare at the canvas roof so I don't have to see Dom's concerned eyes or Eumelia's eager smile while I try to think.

My abrupt movement wakes Hanu. Through Dom, I feel the warmth of her body stretching alongside his, the gentle touch of her fingers on his side, the light kiss she presses to the back of his neck. All of these sensations seem familiar to him; I guess they've woken up together like this before. Her sleepy hand trails up Dom's thigh, and his concern for me disappears into a panicked surge of arousal.

He sits up, letting me go and extricating himself from Hanu's arms.

"Sorry," he says hoarsely. "I'll be right back."

Dom rushes out of the tent wearing nothing but his sleeping tunic. I sit up, my chest prickling in pain as soon as the tent flap falls closed behind him. Hanu yawns softly and sits up. "What's wrong?" she asks, looking from me to Eumelia.

Eumelia's expression is a perfect imitation of complete mystification.

All of this might have seemed funny to me yesterday, but now all I can see is how reckless I've been, tangling myself even deeper in this web of complications. I hastily pull on my boots, wincing alternately at the stabbing pain in my chest and the stinging pain in my bandaged feet. Eumelia watches me, and when our eyes meet I can see what she's thinking, almost as if she's still touching me. *Your secret is safe with me. I promise.*

I don't like the idea of anyone being the keeper of my secrets, especially not her, but there's no help for it now. I knot my boot laces, hop to my feet, and head out after Dom.

GOOD INTENTIONS

AVA CALLS OUT from behind me, "Dom! Wait! Please, wait!"

I'm already halfway across the clearing, heading toward the stream. A few of the grazing horses look up at my approach, and Eridu whinnies a friendly greeting.

I walk faster. As the distance grows between me and Ava, the ache in my chest returns, although I notice my pain doesn't escalate as fast today as it did yesterday. It occurs to me for the first time that I shouldn't think of this pain as mine. It's Ava's. She feels this pain because she's able to have a connection to the Voice. I feel the pain indirectly through her, and the idea that my feelings are only an echo of hers bothers me.

Knowing these are her feelings does nothing to lessen their intensity for me, though. I wince as the pain sharpens, and I know this means her pain is growing worse too. But I can't go back to her yet. I don't want an audience while I sort through my confusion.

Yesterday, when Ava pleaded with me to run away with her, she thought, *I'll hide nothing from you. We'll share everything as equals. I promise.*

Yesterday, I wanted so deeply to hear the Voice that I couldn't imagine doing anything that might interfere with my calling, especially not running away. But when I woke with Ava in my arms this morning, her words were the first thing I remembered. *We'll share everything as equals.* Those words give shape to a desire I've felt for a long time but never really understood until now. I want to know what it feels like to be treated by Ava as an equal.

But how can I trust her words? It's clear from all I've overheard her thinking that she's hiding plenty from me. She has yet to explain where she's been for the last seven years or what happened to her. She does exactly what she pleases with no regard for how it affects me. She seems to forget I'm here one moment, then toys with me for her own amusement the next. I don't know what it's like to be treated as an equal by a girl, but I can't imagine it's like this. With other girls, at least I know where I stand, what to expect, how to behave. With Ava, I'm completely confused.

It's not only confusion I feel, though. I also feel regret, wondering whether I made the wrong choice. What might have happened, if I had agreed to run with her? Maybe the reason Ava doesn't see me as an equal is because I didn't have the courage to go with her. Maybe if I'd agreed to go, she'd treat me differently. Maybe I deserve to be treated this way.

"Dom," Ava says breathlessly, catching up to me as I stop beside the stream.

I sit on the grassy bank. "You didn't need to come out here," I say, not looking at her. "I would have come back before the pain got too bad for you."

"That's not why I came," she says. She sits beside me, but she doesn't take my hand, even though I can feel her pain worsening. "I came to apologize. I'm really sorry, Dom. You asked me to leave things alone with you and Hanu, and I ignored you. I shouldn't have done that. I wish I hadn't. I honestly thought it was just a bit of fun, and that you'd like having her close to you after having to spend so much time with me. But I see now that …" She trails off.

I look at her straight in the eye as I say, "What? What do you see now?"

She shrinks back a bit but holds my gaze. In a small voice, she says, "What's between you and Hanu is private. And I forced you into a situation where I'd see things you didn't want me to see. I wouldn't want you to do that to me, but I did it to you. I'm really sorry. I won't do it again."

Her eyes as she looks at me are wide with contrition. She tries not to look away, but her eyes close briefly in a wince as a searing stab of pain pierces both of us.

"All right," I say, relenting. I take her hand, and when her skin touches mine, her awareness floods into me. I feel her relief as the pain subsides, but mostly she feels guilty about all the pain she keeps causing me, uncertainty about why she decided to play games with me and Hanu in the first place, and anxiety about something that happened between her and Eumelia this morning. Ava's thoughts are as confused as mine, and this, even more than her apology, somehow makes me feel better.

You know, I think, *you've misunderstood, about me and Hanu.*

What do you mean? she thinks.

I hesitate, then think, *You thought I'd rather have Hanu close by, after spending so much time with you. But I …* Ava watches me, waiting for me to finish my thought. Embarrassed heat rises to my ears as I think, *I like being with you. I don't feel like I need to hide anything from you about Hanu. But I thought those sorts of memories might bother you.*

I feel Ava's genuine surprise as she wonders, *Why would that bother me?* Then her eyes widen as she thinks, *Oh …*

She slips her hand out of mine, so we're both alone with our thoughts when she says, "I like being with you too, Dom. But this is so difficult already, hearing each other's thoughts and seeing each other's memories. I think anything more would be unbearable."

My throat tightens. I run my hands over my face and rub my eyes, trying to decide what to say. Thoughts are so much easier to convey when I'm touching her than when I try to find words to speak aloud. The words I settle on are entirely inadequate to express what I mean when I say, "I know. You're right."

She says, in a hopeful tone, "I think once I've practiced more of what Serapen showed me last night, this will get easier."

I look down at my bare toes in the grass, trying and failing to match her tone as I say, "Yeah. I hope so."

Ava shifts uncomfortably beside me, clasping and unclasping her hands in her lap as the pain rebuilds. At last, she says, "May I touch you?"

I hold out my hand uneasily, wondering which of my emotions might spill into her next. She takes my hand and thinks, *I just don't want to hurt you, Dom.*

I can feel that she means it, but I'm beginning to realize that no matter what she does, it's going to hurt me.

△▽△

My heart sinks as Dom thinks, *No matter what she does, it's going to hurt me.* I worry he's right. The sooner he's cut loose from me, the better for him. Unfortunately, my silly prank and its aftermath have used up what little free time we might have had this morning to practice what Serapen taught me. Now the Mohirai are stirring back at the camp, rousing the girls from their tents, instructing us to make ready to leave.

A number of girls, Hanu among them, hurry toward the stream where Dom and I sit. They strip off their clothes and wash away yesterday's dirt and dust as best they can, chatting amiably with one another. Hanu glances occasionally at me and Dom, but we both avoid her gaze.

I long to bathe, and I can feel that Dom does too. But I'm uncomfortable at the thought of joining Hanu and the other girls now that I understand Dom's feelings about her and me a bit better.

Please can we think about something else right now, he thinks, keeping his eyes fixed on his toes.

Right, I think. *Quick—give me something else to think about.*

How about Eumelia? he thinks.

I laugh, then he laughs, and that makes everything easier.

"Come on," I say, hauling Dom up by the hand. I lead him to a spot a little farther downstream from the other girls, behind a screen of trees, so he doesn't have to look at any of them while he's also in contact with me.

"Is this all right?" I ask.

He nods. "Thanks."

I'm self-conscious undressing in front of him now, even though I've done it several times already without a second thought. But I can't do much to minimize the awkwardness of this apart from turning a bit away from him and averting my eyes. Once we've shed our sleeping tunics and I've gingerly removed my boots and bandages, I take his hand and lead him into the water. I rest a hand on his shoulder as Dom scrubs his hair and body with sand and lets the current rinse him clean. He does the same for me as I wash up and make a quick check of all my little injuries. The cuts on my feet are healing cleanly, thanks to the salves Hedi used, though it'll probably take half a moon before it's entirely comfortable to walk barefoot again. My lower lip is swollen under the scab where I bit myself, but that will heal even faster than my feet. Delicately, I wash my arms, examining the purplish shadows around my wrists and the darker purple spots where Dom's fingertips dug in hardest. They're going to take a while to fade, but they don't hurt much today.

I feel Dom's shame as he sees me looking at my bruises. I look up over my shoulder at him. "Don't feel bad," I say. "You didn't mean to hurt me."

"I still did, though," he says.

I run my fingertips lightly along his shins, which look far worse than my wrists. "I actually did mean to hurt you when I did this," I say, wincing as the ache of the tender marks on his legs echoes in my own shins. "Sorry."

"We need to be more careful with each other," he says.

I nod. "I'll try to do better. I promise."

"Me too," he says.

We hurry to follow the other girls back to camp, change into our riding clothes, and help Thalia break down and pack up the tents. Arkhi and Serapen set out a cold meal. My stomach felt strange all day yesterday after drinking the Calling Day pharmaka, but I'm ravenous this morning.

After we say the meal blessing, I sit in the grass with Dom. I tuck my bare foot under his bare ankle and start to eat. He chuckles, watching me.

What? I think, chewing an enormous mouthful of delicious dark bread spread with soft goat cheese. It's pretty useful to converse this way right now, since I don't have to pause eating for talking.

That bread tastes as good to you as harvest cakes do to me, Dom thinks. *It's like you've been fasting for half a moon.*

I shrug and think, *It's been a while since I've had bread. Or cheese.* My mind flicks back over the few small foraged meals I ate with my mother in the forest on our last few days on the road to the Children's Temple. I'm used to going days at a time without eating much.

Really? Dom thinks, and his amusement fades.

I roll my eyes at him and think, *Don't feel sorry for me. I've always had enough to eat. Maybe not as much as you have, but I don't need much. And there's always something to eat in the forest, if you know where to look.*

Dom looks up, and through his eyes I see Arkhi approaching behind me and glimpse a bit of his perspective. In her inky black silks, she weaves through the bright morning light like a ribbon of midnight.

Like a ribbon of midnight? I think, delighted by Dom's impression of Arkhi. I glance over my shoulder at her, and I hardly even notice her clothes. What I do notice is how she's looking at me, with that uncomfortably perceptive expression. I turn back to Dom and smile. *Everything is more beautiful through your eyes, Dom,* I think. He shrugs, looking a bit embarrassed, but I can feel he's pleased.

"Good morning," says Arkhi, taking a seat across from the two of us on the grass. "Did you manage to sleep, all four of you in that little tent?"

"We did," I say.

No thanks to you, Dom thinks. I can't suppress a giggle, which turns into a choke as I inhale a bit of the bread I'm chewing. Dom thumps me on the back.

Arkhi waits until I've recovered, then says, "The two of you are sharing thoughts quite frequently."

Dom and I glance at each other. I wonder how Arkhi knows this. She hasn't really asked a question, but she seems to be waiting for an answer. I can't think of anything I'll gain by lying to her about this, so I say cautiously, "Yes. I guess we are."

"Listen, novices," says Arkhi. She speaks in the tone of instruction, but in her voice it's more inviting than it ever sounds from my mother, or from Serapen—like we're friends, not just her wayward little sister and little brother. "I know it may seem easier to share thoughts directly with each other. And sometimes sharing this way will be unavoidable, especially while you both must remain in such close contact.

"But every shared perception, emotion, and thought strengthens your bond, just like using the binding pharmaka itself. Strengthening the bond between you two may not seem dangerous, compared to the far greater danger posed by Ava's bond with the Voice. But a binding between two human awarenesses should not be taken lightly. Awareness is unruly by nature, and most novices find it challenging enough to manage their own awareness without the added trouble of another's. This is why initiate Mohirai approach binding with great caution and allow the bond to form slowly over time. You and Dom have already formed a far deeper bond than any initiate would create by choice, and the more you use the bond between you, the stronger it will become."

I don't like the sound of this at all. My chest prickles painfully, and I realize I've unconsciously withdrawn my bare foot from Dom while Arkhi's been speaking.

Arkhi must see my apprehension, because she continues in a slightly more encouraging tone. "Even the most unruly awareness can be shaped by the arts of mindfulness—especially the art of intention. Intention will serve you well in the house of novices, but it will make the journey ahead more comfortable for you both, too. You'll receive deeper training in this art from the Muses at Velkanos, but there's no need to wait. To begin building an intention, simply choose an intention, focus on it, and remember it.

"I'd suggest you choose an intention to use your bond with each other in a disciplined way. As you focus on that intention, you might practice distilling your thoughts into speech rather than allowing unfiltered thoughts to spill into each other. Or you might choose carefully which experiences you allow yourself to have, knowing both of you must share them. Or you might try to anticipate which of your actions could create which sensations for the other."

I can't help remembering what happened in the tent this morning, and I feel guilty about it all over again. "I didn't mean to hurt Dom, by sharing thoughts this way," I say.

"The absence of good intention can be as dangerous as the presence of bad intention," says Arkhi. She says this kindly, but her expression is deadly serious. "You can still hurt each other, even if neither of you intended to."

I glance down at my bruised wrists and nod slowly. "All right," I say. "I'll be more careful."

"We both will," says Dom.

Arkhi nods and rises from her seat beside us. She calls out to the rest of the group, "Grab your saddlebags, novices. It's time we're on our way."

△▽△

Only after Arkhi's warning do I realize how much of Ava's awareness I'm perceiving, and how much of mine I'm sharing with her. I have no idea how to stop sharing while we're still touching each other. I try to clear my mind entirely of thoughts, but this only seems to make thoughts spill out faster.

Ava, overhearing all this, says wryly, "I'd never shared a thought with anyone two days ago, and now it feels like a hard thing to give up. Speaking is so much harder, isn't it?"

I chuckle ruefully and say, "I was thinking exactly the same thing."

But, even as I say these words, I realize that Arkhi's suggestion—*practice distilling your thoughts into speech*—works. The search for words, and speaking them aloud, temporarily stops the flood of shared thoughts between us.

Ava and I hurry to finish eating, then stand and brush crumbs off ourselves. Following Arkhi's instruction, we head toward the pile of packed camp gear to pick up our saddlebags.

Ahead of us, Kor grabs her saddlebag and turns in the direction of the horses. She pauses mid-turn, a puzzled expression on her face. Following her gaze, I look back to see a tawny female kuku bird pecking at the breadcrumbs Ava and I left behind in the grass. The dark bars across the kuku's chest tell me it's her first autumn.

Kor lowers her saddlebag and walks slowly toward the bird, kneeling in the grass a few paces away. Girl and bird study each other for a moment. In a sweeter voice than she ever uses with humans, Kor says, "Hello, little sister. What are you doing here so late in the season? Have you lost your way?" She extends her open hand toward the kuku, offering her a few dried bits of fruit from our morning meal. The bird hops toward Kor and eats out of her palm. When all the fruit is gone, Kor points toward the south and whispers to the kuku, like she's sharing a secret, "The sea's that way. Off you go." The kuku takes wing, flying off into the clear blue sky.

Ava watches this exchange with wide eyes. Muffling a giggle, she whispers to me, "Getting stranger by the year, isn't she?"

Kor does have an odd way about her, but there's a gentleness to her that I like. I see no need to make a joke at her expense, so I say nothing and pick up my saddlebag. I reach for Ava's bag automatically, from long habit of carrying things for sisters, but she stops me and picks it up herself. "I've put you through enough already without making you my packhorse, too," she says.

Hand in hand, we walk toward the horses. Eumelia and Hanu fall into step on either side of us carrying their saddlebags.

Eumelia says to Ava, "I saw you teaching Dom how to handle himself in the saddle yesterday. He was riding beautifully by the end. Would you teach me how to do that?"

"And me, please!" says Hanu. "You and the Mohirai seem to be the only ones walking normally this morning. My whole body aches from riding."

Ava's happy to share something she loves with an eager audience. She says,

"I'll show you some things that can help with the saddle soreness once we're out on the road."

Eumelia and Hanu thank her and say they'll rejoin us once the caravan is underway. They hurry off toward their horses.

"Oh," says Ava, looking at me with dismay. "I've done it again."

"Done what?" I say, as she and I quickly part ways to buckle our saddlebags on opposite sides of Eridu.

"I didn't ask what you wanted," says Ava, taking my hand again once her bag is secure. "Is it all right with you if Hanu rides near us? I can make some excuse if you'd rather she doesn't."

I'm so rarely asked what I want that Ava's question takes me by surprise. She waits a long time for me to speak, and her touch conveys her worry that she's hurt me again, right after she promised to do better. I wonder whether this is what it might be like to be treated by Ava as an equal.

At last, I say, "I want you to teach them what you taught me. You're a good teacher."

Ava smiles. "All right. Thanks."

"And—" The next words slip out before I have a chance to consider all they might entail. "I want the four of us to be friends."

An image of Eumelia's most irritating smirk flashes in Ava's mind. Ava sighs dramatically, then says, "Well. I'll try my best."

"Thanks," I say. It would be nice if she'd try to be friendlier to everyone else, too, but I decide not to push my luck. Peace in our tent would be a good start.

She squeezes my hand and says, "Ready to go, then?"

I nod. She mounts Eridu. I give her a moment to settle herself up there while I treat Eridu with some apples I pocketed from the morning meal.

"No fair!" says Ava. "He's going to like you better."

"He already likes me better," I say, swinging myself up into the saddle. She laughs, and the sound makes me smile.

I settle myself in the saddle and start to wrap my arm around Ava's waist. But the memory of what happened when I did this yesterday stops my hand at the hem of her shirt. My self-conscious hesitation stretches into an uncomfortably long pause.

At last Ava says, "It's all right, little brother. You can come out." I hardly recognize her voice as she speaks in this steady, soothing way. Then it hits me that she's mimicking my voice. These are the words I called out to her in the forest the other night. It's a pretty good impression, and I chuckle. She takes my hand and slides it under her shirt, settling my palm lightly at her hip. Her skin feels cool under my hand. Not as cold as she was last night, but not as warm as she should be, either.

"Do you want your cloak?" I say.

"I'm fine, Dom. Don't worry about me." She taps Eridu lightly with her heels, and we follow Arkhi back onto the road.

△▽△

Dom and I haven't been on the road long before Eumelia calls my name. I turn to see her trotting toward us on Nisaba, followed by Hanu on an elegant silver mare called Baba. I wince at the sight of the two girls bouncing along in their saddles, their bodies jarred by every movement of their horses. It's obvious why they're so sore after yesterday's ride.

"What, you don't think I'm as graceful as the Muses?" says Eumelia, seeing my expression. Her mocking half-smile is clearly meant only for herself now, and we share a laugh.

I call out to Arkhi at the head of the caravan, "Is it all right if we ride behind so I can give Eumelia and Hanu some pointers?"

Arkhi raises a hand in assent and says, "Just stay in sight of the caravan."

I pull Eridu out of the line, and Eumelia and Hanu follow me. We stand at the roadside and wait for the rest of the caravan to pass.

Using the open space on the wide road, I give the girls a lesson I received from my mother long ago. I show them four paces on Eridu, passing back and forth before them at a walk, trot, canter, and gallop. It's a bit complicated with Dom behind me in the saddle, but I manage to demonstrate certain postures and leg grips that can jostle a rider at each pace. Then I show them how I can move more smoothly with Eridu, sitting deep in the saddle, opening up my legs and hips. I ask first Eumelia and then Hanu to ride back and forth at a walk and trot, calling out suggestions. The caravan seems unlikely to move much faster than a trot for a while, so I figure the other paces can wait.

Ahead of us, the caravan begins to disappear around a bend in the road. I'm about to tell the girls we need to catch up when Eridu, Nisaba, and Baba all trot ahead without our direction.

"How is Arkhi doing this?" I mutter to myself. The Muse must have summoned the horses to keep us close, but I didn't see or hear her do anything.

Nisaba trots so close beside me that Eumelia overhears. "Don't you know?" she says, looking at me with genuine surprise. "Why were you using binding pharmaka, if you don't know what it's used for?"

I want to protest that I wasn't using binding pharmaka—at least, I hadn't meant to—but that would only raise more questions about what I was doing, so I remain silent.

Hanu, riding on my other side, says kindly, "How could you know, without a Mohira to teach you?"

For once, Hanu's words annoy me even more than Eumelia's, because they remind me that my mother could in fact have taught me, but instead chose not to. I ask Eumelia, "Do you mean Arkhi is controlling the horses with binding pharmaka?"

"The Mohirai would say communicating, not controlling," says Eumelia. "But yes, essentially. The main use of binding pharmaka is communication at a distance. After the destruction, with so few people spread out across such a large region, communicating with binding pharmaka was much more practical than sending messengers.

"The Mohirai use bonds to communicate directly with each other, but they also use them with animals, to send deliveries between temple cities without using riders. Once I even saw Muse Serapen send a dove out from the aviary to forage for her."

I'm fascinated by this. I also wonder why my mother never told me that the Mohirai could communicate with animals. "But how does it work?" I ask Eumelia. "Does Arkhi have a bond with all the horses in the caravan?"

Eumelia shrugs and says, "I'm not sure how it works, exactly. The Mohirai don't teach any advanced pharmaka until we start novice training. But I have a general idea from watching the sisters in the Children's Temple. You've seen Arkhi's stole, haven't you?" I nod, remembering the long silver-threaded black stole the Muse wears over her robes. Eumelia says, "Some of the higher arts involve weaving with pharmaka. I've seen sisters use ribbons, robes, stoles—all sorts of things, really—to communicate with each other. I'd guess some threads in Arkhi's stole let her communicate with the horses the same way. See this?" Eumelia pats her saddle blanket.

For the first time, I notice the subtle gleam of silver threads in all three of our dark wool saddle blankets, much like the silver threads in Arkhi's stole. Then, with a jolt, I recall the golden threads worked into the white ceremonial silks all the novices wore to the Calling Day ceremony, and the ornate golden embroidery of Serapen's robes. During the ceremony, I'd been conscious of the effects of the pharmaka I inhaled from my hood, but I'd assumed that pharmaka had been smeared or soaked into the hood. I hadn't considered that pharmaka might be woven into the fabric itself.

I look down at the riding shirt I'm wearing, which Thalia gave me yesterday. I think of the coppery threads of the long sash she winds so artfully around her green robes, and I search my sleeves and hems for any gleam of copper, silver, or gold. I see nothing but undyed linen, without ornament or embroidery of any kind. I examine the legs of my riding breeches and the tops of my leather riding boots. Are any of these things what they seem?

My mind races through all my memories since my overdose. I consider Arkhi's uncanny perceptiveness, my suspicion that Serapen was somehow reading my thoughts, my unaccountable decision to drink from the chalice at the Calling Day ceremony. Struggling to keep the alarm out of my voice, I say, "Do the Mohirai use binding pharmaka to control us, too, then?"

With ambivalence I find both shocking and impressive, Eumelia shrugs and says, "I doubt the Mohirai would use binding pharmaka on novices. Only initiates are supposed to use it, because of the tricky side effects. You've already broken that rule, of course. But you're not the first." Eumelia flashes a cheeky smile at Hanu. Hanu looks back at her coolly. Puzzled, I look from one girl to the other.

"That mouth of yours is going to get you in trouble one day, Mel," Hanu says with dignity. She urges Baba ahead with a light flick of the reins, leaving the three of us behind.

Eumelia groans. "Oh, come on, Hanu!" she calls. "You can't have thought that was a secret!"

What do you think that's about? I wonder. Dom shifts uneasily behind me, and I sense more of his embarrassment. Must be something else to do with him and Hanu. Well, let him keep his secrets. I have no desire to revisit the awkwardness from this morning. I have far more pressing concerns.

Hanu's parting words chasten Eumelia somewhat, and her mocking expression fades. She changes the subject. "Thanks for the lesson," she says to me.

It's hard for me to focus on Eumelia as my mind churns with all these new questions about pharmaka. But I did tell Dom I'd try to be friendly, and it's a little easier to be kind to Eumelia after Hanu's put her in her place. "Glad it helped," I say. "You and Nisaba ride well together."

Eumelia brightens at my compliment. She leans forward and pats Nisaba's shoulder, saying, "Well, that's more to her credit than mine. Nisaba's splendid. She looks like she'd be fast, too, doesn't she?"

Eumelia's landed on one of the few subjects I find irresistible. For a moment, I forget my other concerns, looking longingly at Nisaba, imagining how well she and I would ride together, if I weren't stuck with Dom and Eridu. "She sure looks fast," I say.

"Want to find out?" Eumelia says, giving me a sly smile. "I seem to remember you love racing."

Dom's hand tingles at my waist, and I feel his surprise as he thinks, *Eumelia remembers you, too? When did that happen?*

I didn't have a chance to tell you, I think, showing him my memory of what happened between me and Eumelia this morning. *It's my fault. I'll stay at the edge of the tent from now on so there's no more accidental touching.*

Dom's amusement is palpable. *You think that was accidental?*

I ignore him, lower my voice, and say to Eumelia, "You can't tell anyone you remember things like that. It's a secret. You promised."

Eumelia's smile widens. She guides Nisaba so close to Eridu that her knee almost touches mine. I look at her warily. So swiftly that I don't have time to pull away, she reaches out, taps the back of my hand lightly with her fingertips, and thinks, *All right. I don't remember all those times I beat you.*

A jumble of memories, mine and hers, flashes before me. Foot races across the meadow. Swim races at the docks. Climbing races in the woods. Races up the stairs of the city alleyways, through the kitchen gardens and temple orchards, even in the library of the Musaion. In most memories, I'm half a stride or half an arm's length behind Eumelia.

I'm stunned that so much can be shared through such a brief touch. Thoughts and emotions seem to flow between me and Eumelia even more easily than they do between me and Dom. The strangest part of re-experiencing these memories through Eumelia's perspective is that, while they look nearly identical to mine, they feel entirely different. I understand for the first time that I love racing because moving at speed feels like freedom. Winning isn't the point, for me. But Eumelia craves the feeling of triumph as much as I crave freedom. Winning is the entire object for her. There's something intriguing about this difference between us. Something that could be useful.

I study Eumelia with new interest. Slowly, I say, "I'd love to race, but the roads through these hills are too winding for an inexperienced rider. And there's Dom to consider. We're not evenly matched with two riders on Eridu and one on Nisaba."

Eumelia dismisses these concerns with a wave. "Arkhi told me we'll be on open plains for days, until we cross over the Purattu. And Serapen told me you should be able to go brief stretches without Dom soon, if you practice what she showed you properly. So practice! Whenever you're ready, I'll be waiting."

Eumelia winks at me and rides off after Hanu. I stare after her, stunned by the idea Eumelia just planted in my mind. A smile spreads slowly over my face. Of course. The Purattu.

Overhearing me, Dom says, "What's the Purattu?"

"Oh …" I think fast. Talk, Ava. Talking makes the sharing stop. "The Purattu. It's a river. It's the outer boundary of the Velkanos temple lands." I try to think of other innocuous facts about the Purattu, but fortunately Dom has more questions.

"Have you been to Velkanos before?" he says with interest.

Not in the way that Dom's thinking, but that's a bit too complicated to explain right now. I say simply, "No. I've crossed the river before, though."

"Is the river far from here?" he says.

"Maybe half a moon's journey," I say, more to myself than to Dom. Half a moon. Will that be enough time?

CHILDREN OF THE VOICE

Dom and I ride at the end of the caravan. Dom has endless questions about the places I've traveled in Dulai, and I'm grateful for all his questions now, since the longer we keep talking, the longer I can keep my thoughts of escape planning to myself.

So I chatter on to Dom, hoping he doesn't notice my divided attention as I study the road ahead, looking for landmarks to help me estimate more precisely how far we are from the Purattu river crossing. I've tramped through quite a lot of Dulai, and I've had a general idea of our location since Arkhi called us to make camp yesterday afternoon. The lightly forested hills we're approaching are distinctive, so now I know exactly where I am.

There, on the north side of the road, is the hilltop grove of oaks where my mother and I made our last camp together three days ago. It was warm and cloudless that night, so we hadn't raised our tent, and we'd had a good view of the surrounding terrain. I remember lying awake past midnight, looking up at the stars through the branches of those oaks, wondering what it was going to feel like to sleep on a boat among the free men.

We hadn't built a fire at that camp because my mother said we might be spotted by Mohirai on the road. Her concern had seemed strange to me at the time, because we'd so rarely encountered anyone on the roads, in all our years of travel. But she must have known the route of the three Mohirai I'm following now. She would have been familiar with the usual comings and goings of the sisters around the time of the autumn equinox. She likely made this very journey herself, centuries ago, after her own Calling Day ceremony. It's possible she too led a caravan of novices like this one back to Velkanos when she was a priestess, perhaps many times. Perhaps that's how she came to know the roads of Dulai so well. I never thought to ask her. Maybe, if I manage to pull this off, I'll have another chance to ask.

My eyes linger on the hilltop grove as I remember many routes I've taken with my mother that passed by this place. I think I may have estimated right the first time: at the pace our caravan is moving, it should be about half a moon's ride from here to the Purattu ferry crossing that the Mohirai use on the route to Velkanos. My mother and I always steered clear of that ferry crossing—my mother said the ferryman Urshanabi couldn't be trusted—but there's a men's village upriver from Urshanabi's crossing, at the edge of a wide ford. My mother and I crossed the river there several times. I remember a boatwright in that village, with fair hair and pale eyes like my mother's. He accepted a bribe from her about a year ago to pass a message to a sailor headed downriver. My mother never allowed me to speak to the men who were involved in arranging our westward passage, and she usually prevented me from even seeing them, but I still managed to glimpse a few of their faces. If I could find that boatwright, or any of the other men who helped my mother, maybe they would help me like they'd helped her. Maybe they could send a message to my mother. Maybe I could tell her I'm working to counter the effects of the amanitai. Maybe once this work is done, I can return to her, if I can only find out where she's gone.

"Ava," says Dom. I straighten up in alarm. I realize I fell silent some time ago, and my mind has been wandering. I'm not sure how much of this he's overheard.

"A lot of it," he says. "It's hard to block it out. But I don't understand much. Would you just explain it to me? I won't tell anyone else. I promise."

After Arkhi's warning, I'm worried about how much of each other's thoughts we're overhearing, and how much worse our binding is becoming. My thoughts seem to be private only when we're talking or separated. It's going to be impossible to talk indefinitely for the entire journey to the Purattu. And so far I can only endure separation from Dom for very brief stretches of time. Under the circumstances, it's inevitable that I'm going to let something slip. Eventually, whether I like it or not, Dom's going to know something I'll need him to keep secret.

But can I trust Dom? As a boy, he has the most to lose by staying among the Mohirai, and therefore he seems to be my most likely ally as I plan my escape. He's instinctively obedient to the Mohirai, which presents difficulties for me, but it's obvious that he cares about me, too. More than that, he's genuinely curious about what I know. Perhaps, even though he refused to run with me on Calling Day, he might still be persuaded to help me get away on my own.

My stomach twists indecisively. I wish I could trust him, but all my instincts tell me it's foolish. This entire situation is impossible. I yearn for the days when escaping a job gone sideways was as simple as disappearing into Dulai's endless trackless wilderness. Unconsciously, I rein Eridu to a stop, overcome by the desire to dismount and run back toward the woods from which we've come.

"Please don't," says Dom. "You know you can't go without me."

I sigh. He's right. I'm being ridiculous. And if I had even a shred of hope remaining that I might escape here, it's stripped away when Eridu resumes trotting ahead after the caravan without my direction. Arkhi must have summoned Eridu again through this damned saddle blanket. He's as much a part of my trap as Dom, it seems.

"I never meant to trap you," says Dom. "I want to help you, Ava. But how can I help if you keep me in the dark?"

I'm struck by the familiarity of Dom's frustration as it spills into me. It's the same frustration I always felt when my mother withheld something in an effort to protect me. But despite all my mother's efforts, here I am, trapped in a situation that could have been avoided entirely if she'd just been more open with me about what the amanitai could do. As much as I want to protect Dom from the consequences of what I must do, keeping him in the dark is no guarantee he'll be protected from anything.

So I decide I'm going to trust him. What other option do I have? I glance ahead to confirm we're still out of earshot of the others. I say, "All right. I'll explain."

How did my mother explain this all to me for the first time? I think back to that day she found me alone in the woods outside the temple city, at the start of my ninth summer. I remember that she started with what was possible for a child to understand. Dom's a lot older than I was that day, but he can't really know much more than I did then.

So I guess I'd better start with the basics. "Do you know where children come from, Dom?"

△▽△

Ava glances over her shoulder at me. The emotion that spills from her into me is a peculiar mix of apprehension, amusement, and pity. She says, "Do you know where children come from, Dom?"

Feeling foolish, I say, "I've only ever seen children come out of the woods with Serapen."

"You must have seen hundreds of lambs and kids and calves born, though," she says.

"Sure," I say. "I've had to help plenty of their births along."

"Did you ever think we too must have been born, like every other animal?" she says.

I consider this. There are many similarities between us and our animals. They have most of the same basic needs we have—water, food, shelter, companionship. We separate them by male and female for their separate purposes—meat or milk, work or breeding. It's not so different from how the Mohirai separate boys from girls and how our paths diverge.

And like all boys, I've managed the breeding of animals. The way animals conceive and bear young is no mystery to me. However, even if there are some similarities between the sexual appetites of humans and animals, sex seems to serve a different purpose for us than it does for them. Animals rut by instinct, and the act seems to serve no purpose other than breeding for them. But the Mohirai treat sex like music, painting, or pharmaka—an art to be practiced and perfected, one of many ways to experience the mystery in all. No girl or Mohira has ever given birth after sex, to my knowledge. So the purpose of sex for humans, if I had to guess, seems to be pleasure, not breeding.

At last I say, "I guess, if I ever thought about where we came from, I assumed it's another mystery the Mohirai keep. You know how few of the mysteries are explained to children, especially to boys. But I never heard anyone say we're born like the animals are. I've never seen a child born. And I don't remember being born myself."

"It's true, though," says Ava. "All of us were born. I've seen children born."

"You have?" I say, fascinated. "Where?"

"In the villages," she says.

"What? Among the men?" I say.

She laughs and shakes her head, "No, not in the men's villages. There are other villages, outside a few of the larger temple cities, where Mohirai give birth to children."

"I never heard of those villages. Are they another one of the mysteries?"

"I don't think the existence of the villages is a mystery, not exactly," she says. "But very few of the Mohirai are ever called by the Voice to bear a child. How the Voice calls for a child is among the mysteries kept by the initiates, according to my mother."

There's that word again. "Your mother," I say. "Will you tell me what that means? I've only ever heard of mother land, like we say at the meal blessing."

"Mother," Ava says the word softly. "It's an old word. Maybe the oldest word. But the Mohirai don't use the word mother any longer in the old way. The Mohirai changed the meaning of kinship words—mother, sister, brother—after the time of destruction.

"But before the destruction, a mother meant any creature who gives birth and raises young. So my mother is the one who gave birth to me. Your mother is the one who gave birth to you."

"My mother." I say the phrase slowly. The possessive word sounds strange in this context. How can a mother belong to me, when I've never even known such a person existed? "But I don't remember having a mother."

"You're not supposed to remember her," says Ava. "That's why all the young children receive unbinding pharmaka. The Mohirai use it to weaken the connection between mothers and children, so our memories of them and their memories of us are lost."

We ride in silence for a long time as I consider this, searching my memory for some sign of this supposed mother of mine. My mind roams through eight years in the house of boys. Hundreds of identical repetitions of wake-up calls, meal blessings, chores, and bedtime pharmaka blur together across the seasons. The faces of Balashi, Kuri, Hanu, Eumelia, and all my other brothers and sisters grow younger and younger the further back I go, while the faces of the Mohirai remain always the same.

Somewhere in the early days of my time at the house of boys, I reach a place in my memory that seems cloaked in fog and shadows. Vague forms hover just at the edge of my perception here, and whenever I reach out for one of these memories, it retreats from me, always just beyond my grasp. Focusing on this unsettling fog requires enormous effort, and it's a relief to give up trying to remember.

I say, "But why do the Mohirai do this, unbinding children and mothers?"

Ava doesn't answer me as quickly this time as before. I recognize the feeling spilling from her into me. It's grief—silent tears in the moonlight as she realizes her mother has left her. But now her grief is for me, feeling the loss of my mother on my behalf. I wonder whether I should be feeling this for myself. But I can't grieve the loss of something I can't remember. She squeezes my hand and says, "Did any of the Mohirai ever say to you, when you were sad, something like this? Peace, child …"

I repeat the familiar words of soothing, "Peace, child. The Voice loves you. You belong to the Voice."

Ava nods and says, "The Mohirai teach that all children born since the time of destruction belong to the Voice in all. They teach that our purpose is to serve the Voice. The Mohirai unbind children from mothers to ensure that the strongest bond we'll ever know is the bond with the Voice that's formed on Calling Day."

I don't understand Ava's anger as she says this. Tentatively, I say, "But isn't it better for all of us to have a strong bond with the Voice? Doesn't that make it easier to answer our calling and perform our service to the Voice?"

Ava says, "It's only better if you believe what the sisters teach: that we belong to the Voice. But that's not what my mother taught me. My mother says we belong to ourselves. We can choose how to live our lives. We don't have to serve the Voice in all."

Of all the strange things Ava's told me, this is the strangest by far. The Mohirai say that the purpose of my life is to serve the Voice in all, and they've never given me reason to doubt their trustworthiness or truthfulness. Ava contradicts the sisters' fundamental teaching with deep conviction, but what she's saying doesn't make sense to me. I say, "If your mother is right, then why are you here?"

"What do you mean?" she says.

"Well, Serapen said the Voice is the only thing that keeps you here. If it's true that you don't have to serve the Voice, why can't you leave?"

MUTUAL FEELINGS

"If it's true that you don't have to serve the Voice, why can't you leave?"

Until Dom asked this question, I thought I was persuading him to help me. I'd hoped that once he knew what I knew, he'd believe what I believe: the Voice must be avoided and the Mohirai can't be trusted. Now I realize I've persuaded him of nothing. Instead, he's turned my own conviction into doubt.

Why can't I leave? The most obvious answer may be the right answer, and I'm afraid of this answer. But my mother always says that understanding comes from facing reality without fear. Reluctantly, I let myself consider that maybe my freedom from the Voice ended with my overdose. Maybe this unwanted bond is irreversible. Maybe I've lost, the Voice has won, and all that's left to me now is the life my mother tried so hard to save me from.

Dom's arm tightens around my waist, and I realize I'm swaying in the saddle, shivering. He takes Eridu's reins from my shaking hands and pulls us to a stop. "What's wrong, Ava?"

I grip the saddle pommel to steady myself. "I don't want to talk about this any more right now," I say, pushing away the hopelessness that's closing in on me from all directions. "Can we just ride?"

Dom keeps the reins and nudges Eridu onward. After a while, he says, "I think I understand a little of what you're feeling. I was feeling the same way, just before I found you."

My curiosity dispels some of my gloom. For the first time, I wonder what happened to Dom that led him to be in the woods the night he found me.

Dom says, "For almost as long as I can remember, I thought I'd spend my life far from the arts and mysteries. I didn't want that life, but I knew I had to go where the Voice called me." As he remembers how this felt, I feel it too: dread, uncertainty, powerlessness.

I say, "But if you felt like that, why didn't you come with me when I asked you to run on Calling Day?"

"The whole idea seemed like madness," he says. "It still does. Even if we weren't bound together this way, how far could we possibly get on our own, without supplies, without horses, without any help from the Mohirai?"

"I would have figured it out," I say. "I've done harder things than that before."

"Have you?" he says. "Well, I haven't. And I wasn't going to risk my one shot at hearing the Voice."

I overhear a bit of his next thought and say, "You think it was the right decision, not to come with me."

"Not exactly," he says. "It's more that I'm glad I heard the Voice. I've never been more certain about anything than I was in the moment I answered my call."

"And I'm happy for you," I say. "But you don't even know what it means, to be an Artifex. How do you know that's what you want?"

Dom shrugs. "I don't know whether it's what I want. Like you said, I have no idea what it means to be an Artifex, apart from the little bit Serapen told me. But … I don't know if this makes sense, but have you ever wondered whether wanting something is useful? I spent so much time wanting to be a Mohira because I thought that was the only way I'd ever be allowed to learn the mysteries. Now it seems like all that wanting—and all the unhappiness I felt because I wanted something impossible—was such a waste. None of it changed what's happened to me, and what's happened is actually better than I'd expected.

"I might have been happier all this time if I hadn't been so focused on what I thought I wanted. Maybe it's better to accept things as they are and trust in the Voice, like the Mohirai teach. Maybe it's better not to worry so much about what I want."

I shake my head in disbelief, disagreeing with so many aspects of what Dom's said that I don't know where to begin.

Dom chuckles and says, "So you think I'd be better off worrying about it?"

"You know I don't think worrying is useful," I say. "For that matter, I wish you'd stop worrying so much about me. But wanting is useful. If you don't want anything, how can you ever know what you need to do next? Until this accident with the amanitai, I knew what to do because I knew what I wanted. I wanted to escape from the Voice and the Mohirai. I wanted to get on that boat."

"But your wanting to get on the boat didn't matter in the end," he says. "You've ended up in exactly the same place you would have been if you'd never heard of that boat."

"That's not true," I say, growing heated. "I'm not in exactly the same place as the rest of you. This—" I sweep my hand in a gesture that encompasses me and him, the caravan, this entire situation. "This isn't permanent. Eventually, I'll find my way out of this. And when I do, it will be because I wanted to find a way out."

He says, "You think that wanting to find a way out will be enough?"

I say, "I didn't mean that wanting is enough. But it's a start. I'll need your help, too."

"Only mine?" he says.

Clearly Dom is trying to get me to see something, but I'm not sure what it is. I consider the vague outline of the plan I'd been contemplating earlier: making my way to the nearest coastal village, negotiating a deal with the boatwright, sending a message to my mother through the sailors on the delivery routes. "Well, no," I say. "I'll need a lot of people's help."

"And you think all of those people will help you, if it's not something the Voice wants, too?" he says.

"What are you trying to say, Dom?" I can't keep the frustration out of my voice. "That I should accept there's nothing I can do about any of this? That I'm helpless?"

"No, no, that's not it at all," he says. "Sorry, it's so much harder when we're trying to talk this way. What I mean is—" His palm tingles against my waist as he thinks, *The Mohirai teach that the Voice works toward its own purposes, in its own time. If the Mohirai are right, shouldn't you try to understand what the Voice wants? Maybe you can work with the Voice, rather than fight against it.*

My fear of the Voice runs so deep that I've never really tried to understand what it might want, beyond its desire to control me. Imagining the Voice as an ally rather than an opponent is an intriguing change in perspective, opening up many possibilities. I'm surprised by Dom's insight.

"Why are you surprised?" he says, in a tone that would sound joking if I couldn't also feel the bitterness behind his words. "You think because I'm a boy, I can't have ideas of my own?"

Gently, I say, "Of course I don't think that, Dom." I know Arkhi warned us against sharing thoughts and feelings, because we could hurt each other. But something has already hurt Dom, and I want to understand what it is. I close my eyes to focus, searching for the source of Dom's bitterness. He lets me find it, and the feeling flows into me: his frustration with being always underestimated, always assumed to be less capable, always treated as less worthy of respect.

I know this feeling. For both of us, the frustration is rooted in the constraints of our bodies—mine so small, his so male. Neither of us fits into our world the way we wish we did.

I wish there was something I could do to change these constraints, for Dom and for myself. But I can't change his physical form any more than I can change my own. I think, *It always seemed wrong to me how the Mohirai treat the boys so differently from the girls. I never really understood why it was wrong, though, until you and I were connected this way. What we have in common is so much more than what separates us.*

Something about my thought sends Dom's own thoughts reeling. I don't understand why until I overhear, *I'll hide nothing from you. We'll share everything as equals. I promise.* I recognize these words as my own. But hearing them from his perspective, feeling his reaction to them, I realize they mean so much more to him than I could have imagined. Despite all Dom's said about how pointless it may be to want anything, I feel how desperately he wants the inclusion every girl can take for granted.

Did you really mean it? he wonders, *Would you have treated me as your equal, if I had gone with you?*

Dom's desire for me to say yes is almost strong enough to pull the words out of me before I'm ready to answer. I resist, alarmed by the sensation of his awareness trying to control mine. For the first time I understand the danger Serapen described, how the bond between us could be used to manipulate each other. Fortunately, this time, what Dom wants to be true is the same as what's actually true.

I did mean it, I think. *And I still want to share everything as equals, even if you don't want to come with me.*

Dom's awareness usually feels much calmer than mine, but my words stir a whirlwind of conflicting desires in him. He wants to trust the Mohirai, and he wants to trust me. He wants to follow his calling, and he wants to follow me. I'm momentarily drawn toward this fascinating tumult in his mind, until I realize I'm losing the ability to differentiate his thoughts from my own. It's an unsettling sensation, far too much like the loss of my self-awareness that happens when I hear the Voice.

I panic at the thought that I've accidentally erased some critical boundary between myself and Dom. Frantically, I try to remember what Arkhi said to us this morning, when she warned us of the risk of sharing thoughts. *Choose an intention, focus on it, and remember it.* I grasp for something that seems like a good intention: for Dom to decide for himself what he wants, whom to trust, whom to follow. I focus my entire awareness on this intention as best I can.

Though my focus wanders again and again, I pull it back to this intention, and the intensity of Dom's thoughts slowly recedes from me. I become more aware of the steady clop of Eridu's hooves, the distant sound of girls' voices from the caravan ahead, the rush of wind through the grassy hills. Gradually, I relax. I can't quite block out my awareness of Dom's agitation, since he's still holding on to me, but the boundary between our innermost thoughts seems to have solidified once more.

I'm still struggling with my unruly focus when Dom says, "I believe you. And I'll help you leave, when you're ready to go. But not as a brother obeying a sister's command, or as a man serving a Mohira. Just as a friend helping a friend."

I hadn't considered that he might want to help me purely for friendship's sake. Over the last seven years, I've learned to see everyone else as either an opponent or an ally. To secure an ally usually requires shared interests, persuasion, sometimes bribery. I've been so focused on turning Dom from an opponent into an ally that I'd failed to see he might be something else entirely.

"So we can be friends again?" I say, surprised by how much I want this. It's been so long since I last had a friend.

"I don't think we ever stopped being friends," says Dom. "It's more like our friendship was lost, and now we've found it again."

Dom speaks with the same unguarded sweetness as the little boy who sat beside me in the forest seven summers ago, playing with river stones. I'm startled by my fierce protectiveness of his innocent openness, because I fear that somehow it must lead to that grim-faced Dom I glimpsed on Calling Day, a man so changed from the boy I know. As much as I want Dom's friendship, I worry that my friendship will do nothing but harm him.

Overhearing my thought, Dom says, in a bright, animated voice utterly unlike his own, "I'm fine, Ava. Don't worry about me."

I look over my shoulder at him and shoot him a mock glare. "Is that supposed to be me?" I say.

He grins. I elbow him in the ribs. "Ow!" he exclaims. "I thought we agreed to be careful with each other."

"I thought you wanted me to treat you like any other girl," I say.

"Is this how you treat other girls?" he says.

"I'm not this gentle with other girls," I say, and he laughs.

△▽△

Ava and I settle into a routine over the next several days on the road. Our mornings begin well before dawn. Ava always wakes first. She tries to keep perfectly still beside me, to let me sleep as long as possible. But as soon as she's awake, her mind begins to race. She's always eager to start the new day, hoping for some breakthrough in her work to ease the binding between us. Her anticipation spills into me, making it impossible for either of us to fall back asleep, so we make our way together out of the tent, as quietly as we can.

Each morning, we see Serapen somewhere at the edge of camp in the predawn twilight. She's nearly invisible in her dark cloak, seated cross-legged on the ground, facing east. Sometimes she raises a hand to us in greeting, but she always remains silent, listening as the early birds herald the sun. I have no idea when, or whether, the High Priestess sleeps.

Each morning, Ava finds a new spot to practice her unbinding. There we sit until sunrise. I stay close beside her, so she can reach my hand if she needs me, and I can reach hers if I need to intervene. The work consumes all of Ava's focus, so we speak very little until she's done. At the end of these morning sessions, when Ava takes my hand, I often notice residual effects of her time alone with the Voice. I feel traces of unfamiliar sensations, overhear peculiar thoughts, and glimpse strange images. Sometimes I ask her what these things mean, but she seems as mystified by them as I am.

After each session, as the sun rises, we return to camp, make ready for the day's travel, and resume the long eastward march.

Each evening, we raise the tents and eat the evening meal. The other novices and the Mohirai often relax around the fire if the weather is clear, but Ava always wants to resume practicing, no matter how tiring the day's journey has been or how bad the weather might be. Our evening sessions are longer, continuing long past sunset, until she's completely spent.

Although the work is exhausting, Ava's progress is rapid. Each day, she's able to sit apart from me for longer before the pain becomes too much to bear. Sometimes we practice walking along the road, back and forth, without holding hands. Each time, we walk farther before Ava's breathing turns into painful gasps.

Almost every day, she tells me how much better and stronger she feels, her eyes bright with hope, even though the rest of her looks pale and weakened. Often, after particularly difficult sessions, I notice that strange translucency about her that I noticed our first night on the road, like some part of her has dissolved into the air. And every night, she needs more and more time to warm up in my arms before she falls asleep. I worry that she's pushing herself too hard, but every time I suggest we take a break this evening, or end a session sooner, she pleads with me to continue. "You said you'd help me, Dom. Please, do this for me." I find it impossible to refuse.

Between these morning and evening sessions, we ride. We use all sorts of tricks to pass the time and practice shielding our thoughts from one another. We join in enthusiastically, if not particularly tunefully, with the rest of the girls whenever Thalia proposes a caravan song. We listen to Narua recite epic poems in a rhythmic voice that carries over the hoofbeats of the caravan—poems that hold Ava's attention long after I've gotten lost in all the unfamiliar names and places. On flat stretches of road, we race ahead on Eridu, often chased by Eumelia on Nisaba, until Arkhi recalls us.

Despite our best efforts, though, it's impossible to maintain perfect mental discipline all the time, and these games and distractions have their limits. At times, I catch glimpses of unguarded thoughts in Ava's mind that show me she's still keeping secrets from me, even though I've promised I won't tell anyone about her escape plan. I wish she would trust me. Things would be easier between us that way. But I know trust is built over time, and it can be destroyed in an instant. Ava's trust has been destroyed so many times in so many ways that I can't blame her for distrusting me.

Increasingly, as the journey wears on, Ava slips into long silences. When she does, it's hard for me to stop myself from following her wandering thoughts and daydreams. Her mind fascinates me. It's so entirely different from my own.

What I notice most about Ava's awareness is how she questions the meaning of everything. When a Mohira says something mysterious, or we pass a ruin at the roadside, or Eumelia and Hanu exchange a look, Ava's mind generates a hundred penetrating questions before I realize there's a question worth asking. She can be deeply perceptive when she focuses her attention.

And yet Ava often fails to see what's directly in front of us. To me, each landscape we pass appears entirely solid and real, full of color and texture and movement. But through Ava's eyes, this solid reality seems to melt away into abstractions. What surrounds Ava is a bright foreground of the possibilities she finds most interesting, against a blurry background of uncertainties, complexities, and interconnections still to be untangled.

Where I see picturesque roads winding through forested hills, Ava notes specific patches of woods thick with beechnuts and blackberries, worth remembering for a return journey if she manages to escape before the winter snows. Where I see washouts that mar the level symmetry of the ancient paving stones over which we ride, Ava focuses on the dried-up streambeds that lead to a river that leads to a village where she once raided the food storerooms. Where I see the interplay of light and shadow on a rocky scree, Ava marks the cave openings where she could take shelter from rain, wind, and cold. Ava sees the world as a collection of opportunities to be seized and risks to be avoided.

I understand now why Ava was so frustrated with me when I suggested that perhaps it's better to simply accept things as they are. She spends so much time imagining how things could be and what she needs to do to make those things happen. She's always planning ahead.

But Ava's thoughts aren't all as practical as planning her escape. When she daydreams, she always seems to return to the place I glimpsed the night I found her in the woods: that beautiful, improbable, monumental city of glass towers.

Unlike the world around us, which often fades into abstractions in her mind, this city seems entirely solid and real to her. It's so real to her that if I don't resist, I'm drawn in after her.

There's a beauty to this strange other world in her mind—an order and a scale and an energy quite unlike the woods and fields and shorelines where I've spent my life. I marvel at the tall buildings, at the crush of people and their strange machines, at the many languages and peculiar sounds and smells of this place. When we fly over the city from a great height or pass through the streets at speed, there's a grandeur to it unlike anything else I've ever experienced.

But when Ava moves through the city of glass towers more slowly, my impressions are more complicated. I feel the complete absence of wilderness and wild creatures, which makes this place feel untethered from the land beneath it. I see human filth that turns my stomach. I'm horrified by the sight of all the sick and infirm tucked in doorways and alleys, untended and unnoticed. I'm puzzled by the people drifting past one another in the streets like they don't see each other. And everywhere, eyes are covered in strange masks, locked on glowing tablets, turned inward. The people in this world are blind to their surroundings in the same way that Ava often seems blind to hers. As I look into all these unseeing eyes, I can't help feeling sorry for them.

And yet, despite all the flaws of this world, I envy the men living here. Everywhere I see them doing forbidden things: wearing bright colors, reading books, playing instruments, caring for children, commanding women. Some of them clearly hold as much power as initiate Mohirai, perhaps even more.

Ava's daydreams inspire my own, and I often find myself unconsciously modifying what I've seen in her mind, preserving what's beautiful about the city, removing what seems broken, adding what seems missing. I can lose myself in reimagining like I lose myself in sketching. When I listen, the city of glass towers calls to me, revealing its proper form and scale. Streets grow wider and greener, people and machines move more slowly, masks disappear from eyes.

I'm not sure how long I've been wandering through these imagined streets one morning when Ava murmurs, "Beautiful."

"Hmm?" I blink, and my daydream fades away. I'm surprised to see the sun's almost directly overhead. The caravan stands stopped at a crossroads, and the girls ahead are dismounting. Somehow half the day has slipped by in what felt like an instant.

"The way you imagine the city," says Ava. "It looks so beautiful."

"You could see that?" I ask. I'm pleased by Ava's praise, but self-conscious at the realization she's been observing me at work this whole time.

"Sorry for peeking. You just seemed so focused—I didn't want to interrupt. But Arkhi says we need to water the horses quickly now, before the windstorm."

"Windstorm?" I say.

Ava laughs. "Spirits, you really drifted off, didn't you? Arkhi said there's a windstorm coming. We need to make camp and take shelter before it hits."

I dismount, and Ava hops off after me. She doesn't take my hand, so I know she wants to practice separation while we're out of the saddle. I follow as she leads Eridu toward the small pool by the crossroads where the other girls are gathering. The horses crowd along the cracked mud banks in the shade of a few scraggly trees, drinking deep from water that looks decidedly unappealing to me. Whorls of sand skitter around our boots and between the horses' hooves, following the breeze.

"Where are we?" I say. Ahead, a dusty plain stretches as far as I can see—golden sand and clumps of tenacious silver-grey scrub beneath a cloudless blue sky. The sight of this barren landscape devoid of trees unsettles me. The familiar ache of separation from Ava rebuilds in my chest, adding to my uneasiness.

"The Subartu Desert," says Ava, wiping the dust from her face with her shirtsleeve. "Not my favorite place."

"You've been here before?" I say, wondering why anyone would come here by choice.

Ava nods, squinting against a gust of gritty wind. "It's not an easy crossing," she says. "But we should be on the other side of it in a few days, if this windstorm isn't too bad."

A few days? I don't like the sound of that. I shade my eyes and look toward the eastern horizon. So much of my energy has been consumed in helping Ava practice unbinding that the days have started to run together. I've lost my sense of where we are on the route. But I vaguely recall Arkhi's description of the desert, and of the Purattu river that runs down its middle. Arkhi said the Purattu marks the boundary of the temple lands of Velkanos, though the temple city itself is another half moon's journey eastward from the river crossing.

No amount of Arkhi's description of the desert could have prepared me for the actual sight of it, though. I'm alarmed to see nothing green east of here beyond the few blades of grass growing in the shade around this murky pool. "What will we do for water until we reach the Purattu?" I ask, struggling to suppress my growing anxiety.

△▽△

I'm squinting at the eastern horizon, looking for signs of Arkhi's predicted windstorm, when Dom says, "What will we do for water until we reach the Purattu?"

My stomach twists strangely. It's not the prickling or stabbing chest pain that's become so familiar since my amanitai overdose. There is a little bit of that pain, too, but it's so familiar now that I hardly notice it. No, the feeling I'm noticing is anxious apprehension of the road ahead, a sense of foreboding.

Usually I trust intuitive feelings like this one. Intuition has saved me from many mishaps. But I've crossed this part of the Subartu Desert a few times with my mother. The road isn't difficult, and although some of the watering holes will be dry at this time of year, there should still be plenty between here and the Purattu. It's really only the wind we need to worry about. Even on a relatively easy crossing, the wind is a formidable opponent, and a major windstorm can be dangerous without shelter. However, if there's one thing I've learned to trust on this journey, it's the remarkable accuracy of Arkhi's predictions. If she says we'll be able to weather this particular windstorm at camp, I'm not going to worry about it. I have plenty to worry about already.

I turn back toward Dom, who looks out at the desert with a troubled expression. Ah. This is not some anxious intuition of mine. This is his anxiety I'm feeling, even though we're not touching.

I'd wondered whether this might happen. It's been clear to me almost from the start that the bond between me and Dom works at a distance. How else could he feel my pain when we're not touching? But until recently, the severity of my pain while we're separated has been so intense that it drowns out my awareness of anything but the pain itself. After nearly half a moon of practice, though, I'm growing more adept at managing the pain that comes when I hear the Voice. Perhaps as that pain lessens, it creates more space in my awareness for what Dom's feeling.

Until this moment, I'd allowed myself to hope that as my awareness of the Voice became less painful, my awareness of Dom would lessen, too. But that was wishful thinking. Arkhi's warning at the start of the journey was pretty clear. *You and Dom have already formed a far deeper bond than any initiate would create by choice, and the more you use the bond between you, the stronger it will become.*

Of course the only alternative to using the bond with Dom is to use the unbinding pharmaka from Serapen, and that's not much of an alternative. What's the point of freeing myself from the Voice with unbinding pharmaka if it makes me forget who I am and where I need to go?

My amplified sense of Dom's anxiety, although unwanted, is definitely better than memory loss or mind-obliterating pain from the Voice. This is a feeling I can handle without any special arts.

I take Dom's hands in mine and say, "Don't worry. There's water in the desert, if you know where to look, and the Mohirai know where to find it. You're safe with them."

Dom and I smile at each other, and gratitude floods through me, unusually strong because it's a mutual feeling. Dom's grateful for my words of comfort, and I'm grateful for the chance to return a small bit of the comfort he's given me on every step of this journey. I wish there was more I could give him before I have to go.

Dom's smile fades. I bite my lip when I realize I let my guard down long enough for him to overhear that.

Dom's grip on my hand tightens. "You're planning to go soon, then?" he asks quietly.

Of course it's no secret between us that I'm leaving. Every day is full of my preparations for departure, most of which I can't hide from Dom. Still, I've avoided sharing specifics about my plan, and Dom hasn't pressed me for details, which I appreciate. I do trust Dom, and it means a lot that he's offered to help me, but there are already so many unknowns in my plan without the added risk that

Dom might—wittingly or unwittingly—give away my plan to the Mohirai.

I can't see any point in denying what he already knows, though. So I say, "Yes."

Dom's head and shoulders drop together, a resigned posture that reminds me of his obedient deference to the Mohirai. Some essential part of him withdraws behind that lowered gaze. I hate to see him looking like this, especially knowing I'm the cause. Am I just as bad as any other Mohira, using Dom while it's convenient for me, casting him off when he's served his purpose, making him feel invisible? My guilt at this thought is unbearable.

"Listen," I say, and his eyes meet mine again. I reach up and smooth away the worried crease between his brows with my thumb. "My offer from Calling Day still stands. If you want to come, just tell me. I'll take you with me. I promise."

I'd hoped this reminder would make Dom feel … I'm not sure what, exactly. Better, somehow. Less like I'm abandoning him. But instead, he's unhappier. "What's wrong?" I ask, dismayed that I've done the opposite of what I'd intended.

He studies my face. "Do you want me to come with you?" he says.

"I want you to decide for yourself what you want, Dom," I say. "I can't decide for you."

He continues to struggle with something, until finally he says, "Would you feel like I'd trapped you again, if I came with you?"

I chuckle, hearing in this question how well Dom knows me. I say, "Maybe I would sometimes. Spirits, especially when you're looking at me with those awful worried eyes! But if you really wanted to come with me, I'd never leave you behind."

His expression brightens. At last, it seems I've managed to say the right thing. I don't want to give away too much, but I also want to make sure I've been clear, so I add, "You need to decide soon, though, Dom. Can you do that?"

"How soon?" he asks.

My gaze drifts eastward as I say, "The sooner, the better."

△▽△

I've grown accustomed to exhausting days and rough nights over the first part of our journey. There's been the ongoing struggle to manage Ava's pain, cold, and weakness; her grueling practice sessions with the Voice morning and evening; the effort required to minimize shared thoughts while riding; the strange glimpses of each other's dreams that disturb our sleep. But the cumulative exhaustion of all that is nothing compared to the delirium brought on by our caravan's grinding march across the windswept Subartu Desert.

I might have expected a flat, straight road to make for easy riding after so many days on steep, winding, crumbling roads through the hills. Unfortunately, though the windstorm Arkhi predicted passes quickly over us the night we camp at the edge of the desert, there's no reprieve on the vast plain from the ceaseless shifting winds.

At the start of the desert crossing, Arkhi shows us how to tie cloths over our noses and mouths, how to wrap scarves around our heads and shoulders to protect our skin from the scouring wind. She gives us devices to protect our eyes, which she calls eye glasses. I examine the glasses Arkhi hands me with confusion, but Ava seems to know already how they work, and she shows me how to position the glass discs over my eyes and secure the leather straps behind my head. It takes me half a day to grow accustomed to looking at the world through this strange green darkness, and I never grow entirely accustomed to the bizarre appearance of Ava or the other girls when they're wearing these glasses. Still, wearing the glasses is much better than squinting through dust clouds as we travel through the dazzling expanse of sun-bleached desert.

Despite these protections, the wind drives dust, grit, and sand into the eyes, mouths, and noses of every horse and rider, until at last even relentlessly high-spirited Thalia is subdued. The desert works its way into every crevice of our clothing, saddlebags, and bedrolls. It's impossible to wash anything, even when we do encounter the little watering holes Ava promised we'd find, because the windblown sand immediately adheres to any clean surface. We resign ourselves to a weary cycle of chafing riding, gritty eating, and itchy sleeping. To my relief, Ava reluctantly decides we should stop our morning and evening practice sessions, at least until the wind subsides.

The discomfort wears us down, making it harder for me and Ava to shield each other from sharing sensations, which amplifies the discomfort for us both. After the first half day of riding in these miserable conditions, I propose riding in front on Eridu. Ava's too small to shield me from the wind, but I could shield her from it if she'd let me, and then at least one of us would be a bit more comfortable. She humbly agrees to ride behind me, and this turns out to be an even greater improvement than either of us expects, because Ava quickly discovers that by focusing on her own comparative sense of well-being, she can share it with me, too. She also discovers a new use for her vivid daydreams: sharing them distracts both of us from our present circumstances.

So I'm riding in front on the early afternoon of our third day crossing the desert. I've been hunched into a headwind for some time, and I lift my head for a moment to roll my shoulders and stretch my aching neck. Ahead, I notice something new on the horizon for the first time in days. I push the tinted glasses back on my forehead and squint through the dust. I'm not imagining it—there's a dark green line in the distance.

Ava? I think. At Ava's insistence, I've given up speaking while riding. Shouting over the wind is difficult, and my throat is raw and sore from breathing in so much dust. *Is that a forest?* She can't easily see around me, so I share what I'm seeing with her. My skin tingles where her hand rests on my hip.

She straightens up. "That's the west bank of the Purattu!" she exclaims, squeezing me around the middle with such excitement that I start to laugh, which immediately turns into dusty coughing.

THE GREAT PURATTU

As soon as Dom shows me his first glimpse of the Purattu, all I want is to gallop the rest of the way to the river's edge. But that would be cruel to both Dom and Eridu, who've borne the brunt of the terrible wind for almost three days. So I wait as patiently as I can, and the caravan plods on at a pace that's even more excruciating now that relief's in sight.

What's the river like? Dom wonders, offering a distraction for me as much as for himself.

My face is completely covered by my headscarf, my cheek nestled in the space between Dom's shoulder blades, so I don't bother trying to answer him aloud. Instead, I remember the last time I crossed the Purattu with my mother. What stands out in my memory most clearly is how I pretended to clumsily spill an entire waterskin down the back of the helpful man who thought he was transporting a Mohira and a novice across the ford on his skiff. How my mother pretended to chastise me as she helped him dry the water off with a bright blue cloth. How the expression in his eyes grew distant as my mother slowly erased his memory of us and of our crossing with a series of subtle touches. But I suppose none of that answers Dom's question about what the river is like.

I close my eyes and try to focus on what Dom might have noticed, had he been with me that day. He observes so much form and movement, color and texture, sound and scent when he looks at the world. So I think of the long shoreline hugged by cool, shady groves of rustling willows. The scents of fresh water and river weeds. The sparkling blue current carving smooth hollows in steep stone cliffs and curving languidly around sandy grey beaches. The luff of a patched canvas sail above me, and the dip and splash of oars beside me. The indignant calls of *krek krek krek* from an enormous floating flock of ducks, their comical faces striped amber and emerald. My sudden exhilaration as the entire flock takes flight around me, a whirlwind of wings ascending into the blue sky. Even now, this memory makes me smile.

Dom wants to linger in that moment, so I do, and he steps inside it with me. The harsh desert wind recedes from our awareness. We sit together instead at the bow of the little skiff, and I grin up at the birds, pleased that I've remembered something that pleases him. I glance at him, and my pulse quickens at the expression in his eyes, which I've seen once before, but not on this boyish face. My memory falters, and the whirlwind of wings slips away.

Unsettled, I think, *Sorry. I … I guess I'm so tired that it's hard to hold the memory steady. You'll love it, though. The river's magnificent.*

It's late afternoon by the time the caravan reaches the outermost stands of oak and pistachio that line the river. The choking clouds of dust subside as the road descends toward the water's edge. Dom and I push back our hoods, remove our filthy headscarves, and let our glasses hang loose around our necks. By the time the road reaches its end at the river's edge, all that remains of the wearying wind is a gentle breeze off the sparkling water.

"We'll make camp downriver, not much farther," Arkhi calls back to me and Dom. I pass the message down the line behind us. Arkhi turns south onto a narrow, well-worn trail that weaves through the enormous willows along the water's edge.

When Eridu unexpectedly prances forward, cutting ahead of Arkhi, I grip Dom tight around the waist to catch my balance. "Where are you going?" I say.

"It's not me!" he says, bewildered.

I cast a suspicious look at Arkhi as we pass her. She chuckles and says, "It's not me, either. But don't worry, Eridu's not going far." She nudges Khaos to a trot and follows close at our heels.

I peer around Dom's shoulder to see where Eridu's taking us. We emerge from the willows onto a wide stretch of lush grass that edges a sandy beach. The beach is enclosed on three sides by short, tawny cliffs. Atop the cliffs stands a small stone house with whitewashed walls, a blue door, and two little windows that look out across the river. A staircase carved into the cliffside descends from the house to the beach.

A sandbar divides the broad, clear shallows near the beach from the darker blue current beyond, and a long wooden dock spans the distance from the beach to the deep water. A boat with a high, curving bow and a low, flat stern is secured to the dock by two heavy ropes.

On the raised platform at the bow of the boat, a man sits on a little stool. He mends a section of canvas sail that flaps around him in the breeze. The man looks up at our approach, and a broad smile spreads across his deeply lined face.

"Urshanabi!" Arkhi calls, waving excitedly at the ferryman.

Eridu prances up to the dock and whinnies at Urshanabi, who promptly rolls up the sail he was mending and jumps over the side of the boat onto the dock. He offers Eridu a small apple from his pocket and presses his forehead to the white star on Eridu's. "Hello, old friend," he says. He turns with open arms toward Arkhi, who has already dismounted and rushes up to embrace him. "How goes the journey, Ark?" he says.

It's hard for me to reconcile the harmless-looking little man before me with the mental picture I had of the ferryman my mother said must not be trusted. I study Urshanabi as he and Arkhi exchange their news—his of the river, hers of the road. He's at least a head shorter than Arkhi, perfectly bald, barechested, and barefoot. His trimmed white beard forms a bright contrast to his brown skin, which gleams like a polished acorn shell in the sun. A dark tattoo of some intricate pattern, like tree roots, winds around the left side of his sinewy torso. He wears loose, knee-length, bright white breeches secured at the waist by a worn leather belt.

Dom and I dismount and stand behind Arkhi on the dock. Urshanabi turns toward us, and I expect Arkhi to introduce us now, but instead she looks from us to Urshanabi with an inscrutable smile. "Hmmmm," he says, tapping the side of his nose with one long finger, the wrinkles around his eyes deepening as he examines us. "My, my, my, how the time slips by, swift as the river herself. How are you, Dom? And you, Ava?"

Arkhi and Urshanabi smile at each other as if they've shared a joke. Dom and I glance at each other, confused. I'm too perturbed by all the questions this greeting raises to figure out how to respond. Has Arkhi told him our names somehow that we couldn't hear? Has this man met us before, but we can't remember him? Who is this man, exactly?

"Sorry … how do you know our names?" asks Dom, his voice still raspy with dust.

Urshanabi smiles, revealing gleaming white teeth. He settles one hand on Dom's shoulder and the other on mine, drawing our three heads together as if to share a secret. His oiled skin gives off a spicy scent of pharmaka, and his voice is merry as he says, "Every child of the new generation is a gift that I remember well."

"But we don't remember you," I say warily.

Urshanabi's expression turns more thoughtful as he looks at me. He nods as he says, "Yes, yes, yes. It's a gift sometimes to forget, as well. But I trust you'll remember me from now on."

He claps our shoulders companionably and turns to welcome Thalia and Serapen, who approach the dock with more of the novices. By way of explanation, Arkhi says to Dom, "Urshanabi's been a ferryman on the Purattu since the time of kings. Every child takes his ferry on the westward route to the Children's Temple, and he takes great pride in his long memory."

Urshanabi repeats his trick several times, surprising one girl after another by knowing her name. I wonder how many times Urshanabi has done this before. Spirits, it would be countless times if he's really been ferryman since the time of kings. That would make him as old as Serapen. I've never heard of a man living for so many centuries.

After a while, Arkhi raises her voice over the noise of all the greetings and says, "I'm sorry to cut this short, but we should make camp before the rain so everyone will have time to prepare for the feast."

This is the first I'm hearing of a feast. Clearly it's intended as a pleasant surprise, and the news elicits a delighted response from the other girls. It's not such a pleasant surprise for me, but I try not to let it show. There's no such thing as a job without complications, and I imagine this will be the first of many. I'll have to make it work.

"Quite right, quite right, quite right," says Urshanabi. "All is ready on my end, but of course you must refresh yourselves after the desert crossing. I look forward to the pleasure of your company tonight."

Thalia clasps Urshanabi's hand and says, "Our revels make this journey worth the trouble, dear brother."

"You are the essential ingredient, sweet Muse," Urshanabi says, inclining his head.

"Careful, brother," Arkhi says dryly. "Flattery will get you everywhere with her."

For the first time in several days, Thalia's bright laugh rings out. She drops a kiss on Urshanabi's shiny bald head and says with a wink, "Until tonight."

Arkhi calls us to follow her to the campsite. I take Eridu by the lead and Dom by the hand, and we walk with the rest of the girls from the dock toward a row of shallow alcoves worn into the base of the cliffs. The alcoves look like they should offer good shelter from the predicted rain. Arkhi points out where we should unload the gear and where each trio should set up their tent.

"What was Arkhi saying before?" Dom asks as we unload Eridu. "Urshanabi's been ferryman since the time of what?"

"The time of kings," I say. I remember first learning about the ages of Dulai from the Mohirai in the Children's Temple, and my mother continued instructing me in historia after she took me away from the sisters. Of course Dom wouldn't have learned any of this, since historia is kept among the mysteries for boys. I thought it was kept as a mystery from men, too. But based on what the Mohirai have said so far about the Artifexi, and especially now that Arkhi has mentioned the time of kings to Dom, I suppose he'll be permitted to learn some of the mysteries that are withheld from other men.

"What does kings mean?" Dom asks as he unbuckles our saddlebags.

"The kings," I say, removing Eridu's bridle, "were men who ruled all the lands and peoples of Dulai, before the destruction."

"Men ruled?" Dom says, looking astonished. "The way the Mohirai do?"

"Well," I say uncertainly, "my mother always says the Voice rules Dulai, so maybe the kings were more like the Voice in all. In any case, whatever the kings commanded, the people had to do. So the people were slaves of the kings back then the way people are slaves of the Voice now."

Dom says, "Have people always been slaves, then?"

"Most people, I guess," I say with a shrug, "except for the ones who manage to escape."

Dom unsaddles Eridu, and we carry our tack and saddlebags into one of the alcoves. All our practice of walking apart for short distances makes this easier; we've been able to work independently for longer stretches every day. It's still nerve-wracking to lose sight of each other, though, because we sometimes need to reach each other quickly if pain comes on unexpectedly.

I'm still not feeling any significant pain in my chest, though, so we take advantage of having four free hands. We grab two currycombs and give Eridu a thorough rub down, his first in three days. Clouds of dust come out of his coat, tail, and mane, and by the end he looks like a new horse. He nuzzles our shoulders gratefully before we turn him loose on the grassy bank beside the willows with the rest of the horses.

With Eridu settled, we set to work raising our tent. Hanu and Eumelia rejoin us and help finish the job.

"Anyone else ready for a bath?" I say. I don't think I can wait a moment longer to strip every scrap of this itchy, sandy clothing off my body.

Hanu makes a sound somewhere between a sigh and a moan of pleasure. "Yes, please, yes. I haven't seen my skin in three days."

The four of us make our way eagerly to the sandbar. We peel off our boots and socks, glasses and headscarves, riding clothes and underclothes, leaving them in little heaps at the river's edge. As I stand looking out across the water with my bare toes in the wet sand, I feel a bit like my old self. It's almost possible to forget what's happened, to forget my tether to Dom, to forget where I'm headed and what I'm leaving behind. Embracing this rare sensation of freedom, I close my eyes, dive into the dark blue current, and let myself sink into the cool depths.

For the first time in a long time, I seem to be completely alone with my thoughts. It's so pleasant here beneath the surface. I linger, spreading my arms as the current picks me up, like I'm flying underwater. How far would the river carry me, if I let it?

I've grown used to all the strange ways the Voice can find me, so I'm not surprised to hear it now within the liquid rush and chortle of the great river, saying, *Together you shall seek us, find us, know us.*

My awareness flows out of me, racing ahead through the current at an impossible speed.

Together you shall amplify us.

The shape of the river draped over the landscape feels as familiar as the shape of my own body, which drifts somewhere far behind me. I yearn to join the sea.

Together you shall weave us through the many worlds.

I spill out into the oceans, spreading out in all directions.

The familiar needling ache in my heart returns, tugging me back toward my body. I ignore it, even as the sensation grows more insistent, because I'm searching for the city of glass towers. I can sense it there, so close now that I—

A rush of Dom's anxiety pulls me back into my body with force.

Ava? he calls from somewhere deep inside me. *Where are you?*

My heart pounds frantically against my ribs, and I realize I need to breathe. I kick back up to the surface and fill my lungs. Despite the pain in my chest, I'm exhilarated. My entire body tingles with my residual awareness of the river, that tantalizing taste of the sea, that glorious expanse of the oceans. I'm certain that the Voice would have shown me where the city of glass towers lies, if only Dom hadn't called me back. I cast a last longing look downstream.

I turn around to see Dom, Hanu, and Eumelia standing in waist-deep water off the sandbar, scanning the river some distance upstream from me. Dom looks frantic, and Hanu rests a comforting hand on his arm. Eumelia spots me, points, and says something to the others. I wave and call loudly, "Over here!" Hanu smiles and waves back. Dom's posture relaxes a little, but even from this distance it's clear that he's upset.

I swim back toward them, and Dom swims out toward me. We meet halfway. I dig my toes into the sandy river bottom to stop myself from drifting in the current, reaching for Dom's outstretched hand. He pulls me back toward shallower water, until we reach a depth where we can both stand, but where we're still out of earshot of the others.

Though I wish Dom hadn't interrupted me, I'm eager to tell him what I saw, because we've spent so much time daydreaming about the city of glass towers together on the road. But, as we usually do after longer separations like this, we have to wait to speak until the pain in my chest subsides, until I've caught my breath, until my pulse returns to its normal rhythm. As we wait, I'm surprised by my acute awareness of Dom's naked body so close to mine in the water. Usually he's the one who has thoughts like this unbidden. After so many days of near-constant contact with him, I'd expect to be blind to his body by now. He'll probably tease me about this later.

I push the pesky thought away and say, "I saw …" My eyes meet Dom's, and the words die on my lips. The exhilaration of my close encounter with the city's possible location fades. I've been so caught up in my own excitement that only now do I see how truly frightened he is.

Dom says, in a voice barely audible over the river, "I thought you'd gone."

His hands shake, and the sensations he's been holding back now flood into me: icy fear, wrenching loss. It's not my brief plunge into the river that's upset him. It's the anticipation of my departure.

"Not yet," I say softly. And I wait, listening, hoping he'll tell me what I've been waiting to hear from him for days. He must know that this is the moment to speak, if he's ever going to speak. But he doesn't speak.

I sigh. On Calling Day, I didn't know how to persuade Dom to come with me. I could definitely persuade him now, though. I've spent enough time in his mind to know where he's susceptible to pressure. There are many ways to use the bond between us, and I'm pretty sure I could force him to come with me. Of course I would never do that. That would make me no better than the Mohirai. No, I can't decide for him how he'll live his life. If he wants to be free, he has to want it for himself.

I have to let him choose, and it seems he's made his choice.

URSHANABI'S FEAST

Ava and I swim back toward the sandbar, where the rest of our party has gathered at the water's edge. Novices and Mohirai in various states of undress come and go, washing sand from clothes and hair and skin, discussing the prospect of Urshanabi's feast with great anticipation. Kor sits alone at the edge of the camp near the horses, looking up into the branches of the great willows lining the riverbank, apparently enthralled by the sight of some bird. Ava joins in occasionally with the girls chattering about the feast, smiling and nodding as if nothing has happened, while I remain silent, still shaken by her sudden disappearance into the river.

I've been consumed by exhaustion for the last three days, and maybe I've used that as an excuse to put off thinking about the choice Ava set before me at the start of the desert crossing. Being on the road has changed my sense of time, and maybe I let myself pretend the journey would go on forever, so I'd never have to make a choice at all.

I consider the choice now, but I still don't know what I want. Well, I do know what I want, but what I want is impossible. I want to stay here among the Mohirai, answer my calling from the Voice, learn what it is to be an Artifex. And I want to follow Ava. For all her faults, she makes me think and feel and experience so much more than anyone else I've ever met. She exhilarates me.

Which of these things would I choose to live without? It's an impossible choice, and I'm running out of time to decide.

Eumelia sits in neck-deep water, eyes half-closed with pleasure. Hanu stands behind her, gently massaging some fragrant, foamy concoction into Eumelia's scalp. Eumelia lets Hanu lower her head into the water to rinse her hair clean.

"What's that?" says Ava, as a ribbon of suds drifts by us. "It smells so good."

"Thalia gave us some of her bathing pharmaka," says Hanu. She gestures toward the buxom Muse, who lounges naked in the shallows with Bel and Tashlu. The two girls watch me with admiring eyes, giggling with each other, trailing ribbons of white bubbles and shimmering oil into the river. I lower my naked body a little deeper into the water. Hanu continues, "She wants everyone to look pretty tonight. And Arkhi said this is our last chance for a decent bath until we reach Velkanos, so we might as well make the most of it."

Hanu lifts Eumelia back out of the water, then smiles at Ava and says, "Want me to do yours next?" Eumelia and I exchange a sidelong look over Ava's head, probably both thinking how much touching that would entail. Clearly Ava's thinking the same, because she thanks Hanu but says she'll wash her own hair. Hanu tosses a little bottle toward her, and Ava and I each take a dollop of Thalia's bathing pharmaka and set to work cleaning. It's strange to cover myself in a scent I associate so strongly with the Mohirai, but it's much better than the pungent smell of sweat and horse that's permeated every pore of my skin and scrap of clothing after so many days on the road.

By the time we've scrubbed every last bit of the desert off ourselves and our bodies are smooth with scented oil, Arkhi's promised rainclouds are closing in on us from the southwest. Ava and I pick up our riding clothes from the sandbar and walk a little way downstream from the bathers.

Hanu and Eumelia join us, and the four of us kneel at the river's edge, scrubbing soap into our filthy clothes. Crusts of dirt dissolve into grey plumes and flow away, but no amount of washing will entirely remove the dun color of the desert from these clothes.

"If I never see another grain of sand it will be too soon," Eumelia says irritably, wringing out her riding shirt and rising to her feet. "If anyone needed convincing that the Voice's plan for men is just, that blasted desert should do it."

"Mel!" Hanu says sharply. "That's an unkind thing to say."

Before I've fully registered what Eumelia said, a hot wave of anger rushes to my head, followed by a prickle of pain in my chest. Alarmed, I look over to see Ava glowering at Eumelia. In a harshly mocking imitation of Eumelia's voice, Ava says, "If anyone needed convincing that you deserve to be breeding stock, that enlightened view should do it."

Hanu looks shocked. Eumelia's expression wavers between amusement and contrition. "Come on," Ava says, picking up the dripping pile of her clothes and holding her hand out for mine. Hastily, I gather my things and take her hand. The prickling pain in my chest subsides, but Ava's anger still burns.

"Ava!" Eumelia calls, hurrying after us. "I'm sorry, I shouldn't have said that. Dom, I wasn't talking about you." She tries to catch Ava's arm to stop her, and Ava repeatedly shakes her off. "Ava, please, I—"

Ava lets go of my hand and wheels around toward Eumelia so suddenly that Eumelia's chin slams into Ava's face, cutting off her next words. I wince, feeling a sharp echo of the painful collision. Ava and I both touch the same tender spot below our right eye, while Eumelia rubs her jaw.

Ava glares at Eumelia and squares her shoulders. Eumelia raises both of her hands in a placating gesture and takes a step back. Hanu catches up to us and looks from Ava to Eumelia in dismay. I settle my hand on Ava's shoulder, prepared to hold her back if she gives in to her almost overwhelming desire to slam her clenched fist into Eumelia's nose.

Don't do this because of me, I think.

It's not just because of you! Ava thinks, seething. *She shouldn't have said that. She shouldn't even think that. It's not right.*

"Spirits, I hate you," Ava says to Eumelia, in a low, dangerous voice. "I've always hated you."

Don't say that. You don't mean that, I think.

You think I don't?

"Ava—" Eumelia begins again.

"Shut up!" Ava exclaims. "Can't you ever just shut your damn—"

"Ava," Hanu interrupts, slipping between Ava and Eumelia. She joins hands with the two other girls and says gently to Ava, "Mel didn't really mean that. She speaks without thinking sometimes, but …" Hanu trails off, lips parted, eyes widening in startled recognition as she looks at Ava.

My fingers tingle against Ava's shoulder. For a disorienting moment, I feel Ava's fingers tingling against Hanu's palm, and Hanu's fingers tingling against Eumelia's. I'm not sure where my body ends and Ava's body begins, or where Ava's body ends and the other girls' begin.

Spirits, what is this? Ava thinks, pulling her hand quickly out of Hanu's grasp and stepping away from me. The disorienting sensation subsides.

"Everything all right there?" Serapen's voice appears out of nowhere. Dazed, I turn to see the High Priestess emerging from a little copse of oaks carrying an armful of gathered firewood, heading back toward the tents.

Ava, Hanu, Eumelia, and I stand silent as Serapen's perceptive eyes sweep over the four of us. Hanu stares at Ava in surprise. Eumelia's jaw twitches, but for once she holds her tongue. I glance uncertainly at Ava. Ava says tightly, "Just a misunderstanding. Everything's fine now."

Serapen's eyes linger on Ava. She nods, then says, "Better get dressed, then. Thalia wants to see everyone in ceremonial silks tonight." With that, Serapen continues on her way.

△▽△

My cheek throbs painfully where Eumelia ran into me, and my mind churns with the knowledge that Hanu's remembered me. I'm relieved that Serapen departs without asking me any more questions. I'm not sure what I might have said, or whether I could have lied to the High Priestess if I'd wanted to.

As much as I want Eumelia to regret her thoughtless comment about the justice of men's subjugation by the Voice, I have no desire to tattle on her to Serapen. But another part of me wishes I'd told Serapen more; maybe she could explain what just happened when Hanu joined hands with me and Eumelia.

At first it had felt similar to what happens right before I hear the Voice in all. When I practice using my connection to the Voice, my awareness usually slips out of my body into some part of the landscape. When Hanu took my hand, I'd lost the sense of my body's boundaries, as the edges of me somehow expanded into her, Dom, and Eumelia. But when I'm connected to the Voice, this sensation of losing my body is usually followed soon afterwards by pain. Although that pain is unpleasant, and sometimes frightening, it also helps me keep track of my body, so I can return to myself. The boundary between myself and the landscape can blur and even briefly disappear when I let my awareness expand, but pain is always there to help re-establish the boundaries.

When Hanu took my hand, it wasn't painful. It was unexpectedly pleasant. But without the pain to remind me where my edges should be, I'm not sure they've all returned to their original places. Even now, after taking a step back from Hanu, Dom, and Eumelia, my awareness of them seems amplified. The three of them look more solid, more detailed, more intensely alive than they were just a moment ago. I can't tell if something about them changed, or something changed about how I see them.

Hanu's surprised recognition turns into effusive delight. "Ava! Spirits, Ava," she says. She wraps me in her warm, soft, sweetly-scented arms and kisses me on both cheeks.

Hanu was always my favorite among the girls. Even though she's treated me as kindly on this journey as she ever did when we were little, I've missed our old familiarity. Dom's constant presence at my side and his feelings about her have led me to avoid her for his sake, even though I greatly enjoy her company.

So it feels good to be remembered by her now. I hug her back for a moment. That odd blurring feeling returns, as I lose the sense of where I end and where she begins. Dom's reaction to seeing Hanu's naked body pressed against mine further complicates this embrace, so I extricate myself from Hanu before it gets worse for him.

"But why didn't you tell us who you were?" says Hanu. "Mel, Ava's our—" Hanu turns to Eumelia to explain who I am. She sees the knowing look on Eumelia's face, and on Dom's. "Wait. You knew?" Hanu touches her forehead as understanding dawns. "Both of you knew?" She looks at the three of us with a slightly hurt expression. "But why didn't any of you tell me?"

"I asked them not to," I say. "It wasn't because I wanted to exclude you, Hanu. It's because the binding pharmaka makes every connection with someone else so much harder to manage. I didn't want any more trouble."

Hanu appears more puzzled than upset by this. She gives me a sympathetic smile and says, "Well, whatever the Voice's plan is in all this, I'm just glad it's brought us back together again. We can be a proper trio now, like we were always meant to be." She presses my arm happily. My skin tingles beneath her fingertips, and Hanu's smile fades. With a sinking feeling, I realize she, like Eumelia, perceives my thoughts with even greater ease than Dom when she's touching me. Quickly, I drop a veil over my thoughts and pull away. But Hanu's already glimpsed the essential thing.

"You don't want to stay with us," she says sadly, letting me go. Briefly, I worry that Hanu might have seen some part of my plan. But I've been very careful to suppress those thoughts because of Dom, and she says nothing more, so I think my secret's safe.

Hanu, Dom, and Eumelia look at me with variations of the same expression. They want me to stay, each for different reasons. I look away, feeling guilty. But why should I feel guilty? I never promised any of them I'd stay. They were fine before I got here, and they'll be fine after I'm gone.

Spirits blast it all. This would have been so much easier if none of them had ever remembered me.

As we stand in awkward silence, the first of Arkhi's predicted rainclouds passes over us, and a shower of raindrops dissolves the desert heat. I shiver miserably as cold rainwater trickles down my naked back.

"Come on," says Dom, touching my arm to lend me some of his warmth.

"Let's get ready for the feast."

The four of us run back toward the cliffs, into the stone alcove where we raised our tent. Sheltered from the rain, we hang our wet riding clothes out to dry, then head into the tent, where we rummage through saddlebags for our ceremonial clothes. Somehow, the white silks and thick woolen cloaks from our Calling Day have remained almost entirely free of dust in the bottom of our saddlebags. It feels unbelievably luxurious to pull dry clean clothes over smooth clean skin. I don't think I've been this clean since Hedi put us to bed that night in the house of boys.

Unfortunately, even after I'm dressed, I'm still freezing, and there's a throbbing ache all through the right side of my face where Eumelia collided with me. I tug the heavy folds of my wool cloak around my shivering shoulders and press my icy hand over the tender part of my face. I know Dom will give me his warm hand as soon as he works out how to tie those complicated laces on his ceremonial cloak, so I try to wait patiently. I wish I didn't have to rely on him so much for body heat.

"May I?" says Hanu, extending her hand toward me.

"May you … what?" I say, still apprehensive of her touch after my accidental sharing earlier.

"May I help you feel better?" she says.

"What do you mean?" I say.

With a wry smile, Hanu says, "Oh, you don't have to keep the mystery from me, Ava. Like Mel not-so-subtly implied …" She shoots a mildly exasperated look at Eumelia, who smirks back at her. "I've had my share of binding pharmaka. I know the basics."

I'm curious what Hanu may know about binding pharmaka that Dom and I haven't figured out already. "How can you make me feel better?" I say, holding out one hand toward Hanu. "Would you teach me how it works?"

"Of course," she says eagerly. She kneels in front of me and takes my cold fingers between both of her warm hands. Slowly, she slides one of her hands up along my forearm. I tense again, expecting that disorienting sensation of losing the edges of my body. She says, "Try to relax, Ava. I want to give you a gift. But it's much easier for me to give if you want to receive it."

It sounds like it should be easy. I'm so cold, and I would much rather be warm. My cheekbone throbs where Eumelia ran into me, and I wish it would stop. The difficulty is that I'd much rather take care of myself than accept help from Hanu. I don't want to need her for something. I don't want to owe her anything.

Hanu lightly massages my hand, my wrist, my forearm. Warmth travels from her practiced fingers up my arm a short distance before retreating back into her hand.

"Hmm," Hanu says, tilting her head to the side and studying me as her fingers continue their work. *May I show you something that might help?* she thinks.

I nod, curious. Hanu takes my awareness in hers as gently as she holds my hand in hers, and I follow its pull. Again the edges of my body blur, then disappear. It's much less alarming now than when she intervened between me and Eumelia. This time, I'm prepared for the change, and it's much calmer somehow, when it's just me and Hanu, not four awarenesses joined unexpectedly together all at once.

Hanu's awareness feels very different from my own, and from Dom's. I explore her perspective with interest. She's exquisitely sensitive to her own body, and to mine. She relates to everyone around her with such sympathy because she's fascinated by what others feel, by all the varied causes and effects of sensation. She loves to feel good and for others to feel good. She's an artist of pleasure.

She lets me see how witnessing my suffering causes her pain. The pain she feels isn't as acute or as deadly as the pain I often feel, but it's still a kind of pain. All this time, when I've been suffering, it's not just Dom who's shared my suffering. Hanu has shared it too, though she's never complained about it.

I had no idea I had this effect on her, that I could have been hurting her with my own attempts to be stoic. The realization makes me feel awful, but it also makes the solution obvious. If I can make her feel better by accepting her help, then of course I want to. By accepting Hanu's help, I'm giving her a kind of gift as well.

As soon as I think this, my arm, my shoulders, and my back all relax. I luxuriate in the delicious warmth that suffuses my core and spreads all the way out to my toes. Once my entire body feels warm, Hanu's soft fingers move to my cheek, and the ache there melts away under her palm. Clean and warm and miraculously free of discomfort, I feel completely renewed.

How did you learn to do this? I think.

Hanu lets me in on her secret, showing me all the experimentation she's done with small doses of binding pharmaka spirited away from the personal stores of Mohirai in the Children's Temple. I see Dom has been the subject of a few of these experiments, along with many other girls and boys.

I envy her experience with binding pharmaka, which has been far more pleasurable and far less complicated than my own. The memory of the awful pain I experienced that first night after my overdose returns to me unbidden. I hasten to suppress it, as I've learned to suppress so many other thoughts, but some part of my memory still spills into her. Hanu's eyes glisten with tears as she looks at me.

I had no idea binding pharmaka could feel like that, she thinks. *I wish that hadn't happened to you.*

Her deep sympathy makes it easier to let the memory pass. I focus instead on what she's given me: this radiant warmth, this sense of well-being, and this new perspective on pain and pleasure.

There you go, Hanu thinks, pressing a kiss to my cheek. She gives my fingers a parting squeeze and lets go of my hand, looking pleased with herself.

"Thanks," I say, rubbing my two warm hands together, then touching my cheek tentatively. I can tell there will be a bruise, but the angry throbbing is gone for now. I reach for Hanu and hug her tight, for once not caring what effect this might have on Dom. "I feel so much better," I say.

"I'm glad," says Hanu, holding me until I let go.

Once we part, I again have the unsettling suspicion that the edges of my body haven't returned to their original places. I feel more anchored to my own body than I did before, and also much more aware of Hanu, of Dom, and even of Eumelia. Seeing the world through Hanu's eyes seems to have rubbed off on me.

△▽△

Hanu and Ava kneel facing each other on the far side of the tent. Hanu's hands move up Ava's arm as she demonstrates some method of sharing body heat through the binding pharmaka. I can't help wondering whether Ava and I have learned through painful trial and error what Hanu might have been able to easily teach us our first day on the road, if only Ava hadn't been so obsessed with secrecy and I hadn't been so conflicted by my feelings about Hanu.

For the first time in a very long time, I manage to look at Hanu without a single sexual thought crossing my mind. It doesn't hurt that Hanu's now fully clothed, but what helps more than anything else is my new understanding of what I'm actually feeling when I see Hanu.

A few days ago, when Eumelia teased Hanu about her illicit use of binding pharmaka, I realized for the first time why sex with Hanu was so different from my experiences with other girls. I wish Hanu had asked me before using binding pharmaka with me. I suppose it's not surprising she didn't—the Mohirai routinely use pharmaka on all of us without our knowledge, after all—but Hanu could have saved me a lot of confusion and embarrassment if she'd told me.

Even before I knew the cause, though, I certainly noticed the effect of having used binding pharmaka with Hanu. My awareness of her body, and her awareness of mine, have been amplified since the first time we had sex. When Hanu's nearby, I can feel what she's feeling, and since she's so aware of her own body, I'm aware of it by extension. This was useful and pleasurable when I wanted to be intimate with Hanu. This is complicated while sharing a constant close connection with Ava's mind, no matter how understanding Ava might be about it.

But knowing my feelings about Hanu are amplified by binding pharmaka has made it easier for me to manage. All the techniques Ava and I practice to discipline our thoughts for each other work equally well on my thoughts about Hanu.

And for all the complications Hanu's presence has caused me on the road, I've started to appreciate how much I unwittingly learned from her that's been useful with Ava. The reason I intuited how to share thoughts with Ava using binding pharmaka was because I'd experienced a similar sort of communication with Hanu before. I think this may also be why I've been able to lend Ava strength, and warmth, and other kinds of help, when she's needed it. It's not so different from how Hanu shared sensations with me while we were intimate.

Hanu finishes her work with Ava, and the change in Ava astonishes me. Her skin looks rosy and warm. The tight lines of discomfort around her lips and eyes are gone. She moves a bit more slowly and fluidly than she usually does, like every muscle in her body has relaxed. When she turns her gaze on me, her eyes linger longer. Her normally piercing expression softens into something more receptive, a look I'm more used to seeing on Hanu's face. I swallow, wondering what lies behind that look, wondering whether—

Thalia pops her head in through our tent flap, her eyes and lips freshly painted, her musical voice full of cheer. "Come along, novices," she says. "Arkhi says this is about to turn into a proper deluge. Hoods up!"

The four of us pull up our hoods and follow Thalia out of the tent, joining the other girls and Mohirai walking up the beach. Although I haven't felt any echoes of Ava's pain in my chest for a while, out of habit I offer my hand to her as we walk. She laces her fingers through mine, and I feel not only the pleasant warmth of her skin but a new kind of warmth in her awareness. She looks up at me from under her hood and says, "I wish I'd told Hanu sooner. She knows a lot of useful things."

"Like what?" I say, a bit apprehensive of what Ava might have seen in Hanu's mind.

Ava smiles and says, "Well, at first, it seemed like most of what Hanu knows is how to have really good sex. And I'm sure that's useful. Looks fun, anyway."

"It is!" Hanu calls over her shoulder.

Ava laughs, then lowers her voice so that only I can hear her. She says, "But what's even more useful is what Hanu knows about communicating using every part of the body. She's so … sensitive. To everything. To everyone."

We reach the base of the stone stairs carved into the cliffs and start to climb. Ava says, "She knows how to listen with the body, to figure out what's causing pain and how to make it stop, even how to turn it into pleasure. I can't help thinking that's what I need to learn how to do. There's so much pain to manage from the Voice. Maybe I can use what Hanu showed me to figure out what's causing the pain. Maybe I could make it stop for good. Or maybe it doesn't have to feel like pain at all, and I could change it into something else."

Ava stops speaking, but her thoughts race on, her face glowing with the excitement of a promising new insight, a possible solution to her problem. I should be happy for her. I am happy for her. And yet the faster Ava gets better, the sooner she'll be gone.

I keep these thoughts to myself, though, and say only, "I hope so."

We reach the top of the stairs and hurry through the rain along a pebbly garden path toward Urshanabi's little white house. The house must have a sweeping view on a clear day, but right now it's closed in on all sides by grey curtains of rain. We pause at the bottom of the steps that lead to the blue front door. Thalia knocks.

The door swings inward, and Urshanabi stands at the threshold in a clean white robe, backlit by the cheerful golden glow of candles and firelight. He beckons us in with a bright smile, saying, "Welcome, welcome, welcome."

I'm not convinced our entire party will fit inside such a small house until Ava and I squeeze inside and Urshanabi closes the door behind us.

We stand elbow to elbow in a warm and cramped single room with a cleanswept stone floor. Urshanabi shepherds us into the bench seats arranged around the long wooden table that occupies most of the room.

I examine the inside of Urshanabi's house with interest. A short wooden ladder on one wall leads up to a narrow sleeping loft with a small mattress. Clearly the ferryman lives here alone. I've lived in shared quarters with other boys for as long as I can remember, until this journey began, so I struggle to imagine what it's like to live alone in a place like this, so far from other people. But the ferryman seems to have a great deal to occupy himself. Shelves line his walls from floor to ceiling, crammed with boxes, jars, parchment scrolls, and a large collection of musical instruments. I wonder where a man could have learned to play musical instruments.

After so long eating out of doors, it feels like a luxury to sit at a table again, even one as crowded as this. Sitting around a table with women adds a degree of novelty, too. The Mohirai who ran the house of boys always dined at their own table in the meal hall, so I only ever ate with the other boys. Now, I sit between Ava and Thalia on a bench. Their warm, sweet-scented bodies press against me on both sides, and I'm quite comfortable indeed.

In the time it took us to make camp, bathe, and dress, Urshanabi has laid out an impressive feast for fourteen. I can't imagine how he did this all on his own. He must have been preparing for our arrival for days.

Urshanabi serves his exquisite food on a humble assortment of plates and bowls. We dine on tender lamb and savory rice, soft breads and ewe's cheese, roasted vegetables and stewed fruits, delicious sweets of creamy almond paste and fresh green pistachios dripping with honey.

Wine flows from a seemingly inexhaustible supply, as Urshanabi retrieves bottle after bottle from the pantry beneath his sleeping loft. The ferryman pours out each new bottle into a large painted mixing vessel at the center of the table, and Serapen stirs in crumbly pharmaka from a leather pouch she carries in her robes. Thalia wields the ladle throughout the meal, ensuring no goblet goes empty.

The mixed wine goes down easily, and the room gradually turns into a noisy, cozy blur for me. I'm not entirely sure how much I've had to drink when I notice Ava hasn't touched her goblet. This must be why her awareness has retained its sharp edge. I realize too late that by partaking in the wine I may force Ava to share the experience, whether she wants to or not.

"Would you rather I abstain?" I ask her.

She dismisses the question with a wave and a relaxed smile. "Enjoy," she says. "It's been a long journey, and we'll be here two nights, anyway. But do me a favor and drink some of this, too. I'd rather not share your headache tomorrow." She pours me a cup of clear water from a pitcher and sets it beside my wine goblet.

The party grows steadily more voluble and boisterous, and Urshanabi prompts each of the novices in turn to tell him stories of what we've seen and done on the road so far.

The eloquence of the other girls impresses me, especially given the strong effect the wine's having on me. But they've all been accustomed since childhood to hearing and reciting poetry, and feasting with Mohirai, so they use language with far greater skill than I do, even as they grow intoxicated.

Piroza describes the unique character of each forest she particularly admired along the way. Bel recalls the dramatic views afforded by some of the winding hill roads we traveled. Narua recounts her favorite origin myths of the mountains we've seen. Eumelia offers a spirited accounting of various mishaps she observed amongst the group, walking a fine line between provoking and entertaining the party. I listen with absorption, laughing at funny anecdotes, murmuring appreciatively along with the others when a girl offers a particularly evocative description of a scene on the road. Otherwise, I remain silent, and so does Ava, though she watches and listens to everything with close attention.

Are you all right? I think at one point, glancing at Ava. I haven't overheard a single thought or felt a single reaction from her in quite some time.

Fine, she thinks, giving me a small smile. Does she look a little sad? I'm tempted to ask what she's been thinking about, or even to peek into her thoughts. But after all the work we've done to make it possible for each other to have any privacy, that seems inappropriate. If she doesn't want to share, I'm not going to force her.

Plates are almost empty and bellies are almost full when there's a lull in the conversation. Urshanabi turns to me and says amiably, "What about you, Dom? How have you found the journey?"

Nothing I say could compare to the cleverness of what the other girls have said already, so I say simply, "I'm grateful to be traveling in the company of such wise and skilled Mohirai. And I'm looking forward to learning more of my calling once we reach Velkanos."

Urshanabi nods slowly and says, "What have you been told of your calling, little brother?"

Thalia falls silent on my left side, and Ava perks up with interest on my right. Across the table, Arkhi and Serapen exchange an unreadable glance.

"Muse Serapen told me I'll learn more of my calling from the Artifexi in the proper time," I say slowly, trying not to slur my words. "But she did say I've been called to the path of mysteries."

"A rare calling indeed, for a man," says Urshanabi, taking another sip of wine.

Seeing his knowing expression, it occurs to me to ask, "Are you an Artifex, brother?"

He shakes his head and says, "I was an old man long before the first Artifex was called. And yet perhaps I may still presume to welcome you as a brother on the path of mysteries. For I too have known communion with the Voice in all."

The rest of the girls fall silent as Urshanabi speaks. Rain patters gently on the roof, and a log crackles in the fireplace.

I say, "So there are other men called to the mysteries, besides the Artifexi?"

Urshanabi leans back in his seat at the end of the long table and says, "None born in this new age. But long ago, before the destruction, the path of mysteries could be walked by all seekers, even men. The arts were widely known and practiced, even outside temple walls.

"There was a priesthood of men, in those days. And I was an initiate of that ancient brotherhood, trained in their mysteries."

I study him with interest. I've never heard of a priesthood before. "Are you a priest, then?" I ask.

"I was, but no longer," says Urshanabi. "I had the great sorrow of witnessing the end of my order. The corruption of my brotherhood eventually ran so deep that I could no longer walk the path I loved, knowing what damage my brothers were doing to mother land and her people."

"So … what are you now?" I ask.

Urshanabi considers this question for a long time before he says, "When I abandoned my vows, I became nothing. Worse than nothing, for all men held me in contempt.

"So I sought refuge in the wilderness outside the great temple city of Velkanos. In the age before the destruction, the sisters of the unnamed priestesshood would still tolerate a hermit in their temple lands, provided he did no mischief. And one day Mohira, the last High Priestess of the age of kings, gave me this post. She said the Voice grants purpose to all, and she revealed the Voice's purpose for me. So here I remain, a humble ferryman, alive by the mercy of the sisters and the grace of the Voice in all."

"You must have seen a lot, in all that time," says Ava, her eyes locked on Urshanabi. She speaks in a tone that cuts through the air like a blade.

"Indeed. Far more than I ever imagined might be seen in a single lifetime," he says.

"Do you miss it?" says Ava. "The rule of men? The age of kings?"

Urshanabi's gaze grows distant, as if he looks across an inconceivably vast landscape. He says, "I've never known such peace or beauty in the land as I've seen in this new age."

Ava's eyes flick to each of the three Mohirai in turn, then back to Urshanabi. She thinks, *It all worked out quite well for him, at least.*

What do you mean? I think, my wine-dulled mind struggling to keep up with hers.

Ava's eyes meet mine. She thinks, *Why would the Mohirai let this man live so long? Did he sell out his brothers before the destruction began? Did he help the Mohirai come to power?*

Arkhi says calmly, "The Voice speaks wisdom as clearly through you as through any Mohira, Urshanabi."

The ferryman's eyes shine as he looks at Arkhi and says, "That is a great kindness, sister."

How very interesting, thinks Ava.

△▽△

I hold my tongue, deciding not to risk asking the ferryman any more probing questions, as much as I'd like to. Dom and the Mohirai watch me with uncomfortably close attention, but I need to fade into the background. Fortunately, Urshanabi chooses this moment to clap three times and rise from his seat at the end of the table. He reaches for a gleaming lyre that hangs from a high hook on the wall behind him.

"It seems you all have satisfied your need for food and drink," says Urshanabi. "So may I ask you to honor us with a song, fair Muse?" He extends the instrument with both hands toward Thalia.

Thalia rises eagerly from her seat beside Dom and accepts the instrument and its small bone plectrum. Urshanabi pulls out a low carved stool for her, and Thalia settles herself there, swinging her long auburn braid behind her shoulder and cradling the turtleshell crescent of the lyre in her lap. She takes the plectrum in the fingers of her right hand and strums it across the seven strings, humming quietly to herself.

It's been many years since I was in close proximity to such a fine musical instrument. Life on the road with my mother left no room for the Mohiran arts of revelry. I know the sound of the lyre well enough, though. I even remember what it's like to hold the instrument, because I received instruction in music like all the other girls during my first year in the Children's Temple.

I remember just enough to fully appreciate that the sound of eighth summer girls plucking at strings and singing has about as much in common with Thalia's music as the rough huts of the village workmen have in common with the temples of the Mohirai.

Thalia's voice, sweet and smooth with wine, fills the room, weaving through the haunting chords she plays. My perception of the Muse of poetika as frivolous, ridiculous, even useless, changes dramatically as I witness her art for the first time. I melt a bit into the bench as I listen.

She sings a mournful ballad of a humble priestess named Shubur, a tale I've never heard before. Shubur's great joy is listening to the Voice in all, until one day the Voice is stolen from Dulai through the trickery of a powerful priestess named Kigal. Shubur sets out on a journey to recover the Voice, which leads her to cross the great ocean that rings the world. At last Shubur discovers that Kigal has taken the Voice into the land of Death and hidden it there. So Shubur makes the journey into Death, and after many strange adventures, she returns the Voice to the people of Dulai.

I'm captivated by the lyrical descriptions of the people and places Shubur encounters on her journey. Occasionally, I recognize the names of old city ruins my mother and I used as landmarks to navigate the wildernesses of Dulai. I wonder whether this could be a true story.

No one else appears to be as gripped by the tale as I am, though this is certainly no fault of Thalia's. Her performance is beyond compare. But the eyelids of the other girls around the table grow heavier and heavier as the song goes on and they succumb to bellies full of rich food and mixed wine.

Even Dom, who drank less than anyone but me, eventually nods off. His head comes to rest on my shoulder. The last three days have been exhausting, so I let him sleep. I rest my cheek against his mop of curls, which are warm and soft and smell sweetly of bathing pharmaka. I observe his sleeping awareness pulled along in the slipstream of the Muse's song.

Dom's dreaming mind reimagines Shubur's journey into Death and back again, casting the people and places we've seen along our own journey into new roles in Thalia's tale. Even in dreams, Dom constructs worlds of breathtaking beauty. I'll be glad to have this memory of him.

A change in tempo and melody signals that the end of the song approaches. Those who nodded off begin to stir. Dom's languid sensations slowly reorder themselves into wakefulness, until he remembers where he is. His eyelashes tickle my neck as he opens his eyes, and his nose grazes my earlobe as he lifts his head from my shoulder.

"Sorry," he whispers. His voice is husky from sleep and the dusty air of the past three days.

"Don't be," I say, smiling at him. I prop my chin up on one hand and rest my other hand on his, listening to the final verses of Thalia's song. Her beautiful voice lingers, then fades into silence. I realize only now that the rain has stopped.

"Thank you, sister," Urshanabi murmurs. "You've given me a gift that will live long in my memory."

Thalia's eyes sparkle at the ferryman as she says, "And the night is still young." She reaches for her goblet and raises it first to Urshanabi, then to the other Mohirai, and last to us novices. She takes a drink, then says, "It seems the Voice has granted us a reprieve from the rain. Shall we honor it with a dance?"

I look around the room, doubting anyone has energy left for dancing. I'm surprised—even a bit envious—to discover that the other girls have emerged from their dozing with renewed energy. Thalia's proposal is accepted with great excitement. I wonder what exactly Serapen mixed into the wine.

It's not too late to find out, Dom thinks, gesturing toward my full goblet.

But I have other plans. As Thalia said, the night is still young.

THE DOUBLE CROSSING

All the other novices and Dom rise with Thalia and spill out of the house in a laughing, singing, somewhat clumsy tangle. They're followed by Urshanabi, Arkhi, and Serapen, who carry a few instruments selected from the ferryman's collection, as well as several more bottles of wine. I hang back for a moment, making a quick survey of the abandoned table. It's a mess of nearly empty plates and goblets, except for mine. I glance at the door to make sure I'm alone, then grab two hunks of ewe's cheese and what remains of the delicious flat breads. These I wrap in a spare linen cloth I tucked inside my clothes while I was dressing.

I slip the packet of food inside my robe and turn toward the door just as Dom reappears at the threshold, his cheeks rosy, his gaze a little unfocused.

"Ah, there you are," he says happily. "Come on!"

I accept his offered hand and close the door behind us. We step out into the cool night air and walk down the garden path, which squishes slightly beneath our bare feet. The rain has washed the desert air clean, and I breathe in the damp, sweet scent of soil with gratitude after so many days of choking dust. I catch a glimpse of Dom's softly blurred perspective as he takes in the river view from atop the cliffs. The rainclouds recede eastward as the waning crescent moon rises into a glittering vault of stars.

Our noisy companions make their way to the stone stairs and descend to the beach. I hang back near the cliffs' edge, looking down at the shimmering river, marking the position of each member of our party. Half of them construct a bonfire on the sand while the other half debate who'd better play and who'd better dance. The plaintive notes of an aulos drift up to us, followed by the beat of a drum and the strum of two kitharas. The drum settles into a dancing beat. As the first flames of the bonfire catch, the dancers join hands in a ring. Dom watches with interest.

With a burst of inspiration, I say, "Do you want to join them?" This would certainly make things easier for me.

"Boys aren't allowed, remember?" Dom says ruefully.

Dom hasn't thoroughly considered all the implications of what's changed for him since he was called as Artifex. I'd guess many of the rules from the house of boys no longer apply to him. And even if the ridiculous rules haven't changed, I'd be inclined to break them. Unfortunately, that's not really Dom's style.

Fortunately, it doesn't seem like any rule-breaking will be required this time. "Look," I say, pointing down at the swirling shadows. "Urshanabi's dancing."

Surprised, Dom looks down to see the ferryman among the dancers, arm in arm with Thalia, crossing hands with Arkhi, spinning around Serapen, weaving his way through the other girls. I'm sure Dom's never seen a man dancing before. For that matter, neither have I. But seeing Urshanabi's skill as a dancer only proves to me how silly all these rules of the Mohirai are. What possible reason could there be to exclude men from these arts? Clearly they're as capable as women.

Dom's eagerness to dance feels similar to his eagerness to ride on the first day of our journey.

"Come on," I say, pulling him by the hand. "It's fun. I'll show you." This will be a good way to say goodbye. At least for me.

The sounds of the revelry grow louder as we descend the stone stairs to the beach. The warm swirl of movement and laughter around the bonfire pulls us in, and we're absorbed quickly into the ring. It's been years since I last danced, but dancing comes to me as naturally as breathing, and the steps seem as familiar as they were when I first learned them in the halls of the Children's Temple. Dom struggles, but he covers for his inexperience with a good sense of rhythm, a lanky grace, and a quickness to laugh at himself and learn from his mistakes. His delight spills into me when our hands touch, and I can't help laughing with him. I feel the effects of the wine in him as he spins and his vision spins and the rest of the party spins around him. I wonder whether he'll remember any of this tomorrow.

When the lead kithara cues the next dance, I seize the moment. I improvise a quick series of steps to swap my position with Hanu in the ring, so she and Dom stand hand in hand. The next dance is long and intricate, requiring close attention even for an experienced dancer. Dom will probably have to look at his feet the entire time.

I step out of the ring for a moment and pretend to rest at the edge of the bonfire's glow as I survey the group. Everyone's accounted for—eight novices, three Mohirai, Urshanabi, and Dom—all of them thoroughly intoxicated. My eyes linger on Dom. He looks at Hanu, who leans in and says something that makes him smile. He answers, and she laughs. They look happy together. Beautiful, really. I realize for the first time how ridiculous it was for me to think he might want to come with me. He must feel like the luckiest boy in Dulai, heading to Velkanos in the company of all these beautiful women for a life in service to the Voice. It's certainly far better than any life he'd ever dreamed was possible. It's not the life I want, but it's the life he wants. It's the life he's always wanted.

So I'm happy for him, though I know I'll miss him. Silently, I wish him well, then slip into the shadows.

△▽△

Hanu's eyes gleam in the firelight as she looks at me. She leans toward my ear and says, "You and Ava dance well together."

I smile and say, "As long as I stand still and she does all the dancing."

Hanu laughs and says, "That's not true. You have a good sense of the music."

I incline my head toward Hanu, then look around the ring for Ava. I've been waiting for a break in the music to pull her aside and talk to her. That moment in the river has been replaying in the back of my mind all through the feast. I'm not sure if it's my memory of that moment, or the wine, or something else, but everything seems clear to me now. I've finally made my decision. I know what it would feel like to be left behind by Ava, because that's what I felt when she disappeared into the river. I never want to feel that again. I don't know what life as an Artifex might be like, so I can't know whether I'd want that life. But I have an idea of what life with Ava might be like, and I want to see more of that life. I want to hold on to our friendship. I want to experience everything she's going to experience on the journey to freedom. And I want to listen to her laugh on the way there.

I search the shadows at the edge of the bonfire, looking for her. My stomach twists when I can't find her. Then I relax. There she is, resting in the sand a few paces behind me, just catching her breath. That's probably a good idea; my own head is spinning from all the wine. I should go talk to her now.

I'm turning to step out of the ring when the music transitions, and Hanu takes my hand. She says, "Would you like me to teach you this one? It's a little bit complicated, but I can show you a simpler version."

"Oh—" I glance back at Ava, but the dancers are moving around us now, and I've lost sight of her. "All right. This is the last dance for me, though."

△▽△

I hurry back to the tent and quickly strip off the bright white ceremonial clothes I'm wearing. I've been wary of the golden threads in these clothes ever since Eumelia explained how the Mohirai control the horses. It's a shame I have to leave such fine fabric behind, since it would be such a useful barter item, but I can't risk the Mohirai using these threads to track me down.

I change into my damp riding clothes and wrap my dark wool cloak tight around me to ward off the night's chill. Thankfully, my spare pair of wool socks are warm and dry on my feet. The desert air should suck the moisture out of everything else by sunrise.

In daylight over the last few days, whenever I could find a moment alone, I carefully examined every scrap of my riding clothes and gear, tearing little holes into cloth and leather seams, checking everywhere for gleaming threads. I found no sign of anything suspicious; as far as I can tell, everything I'm about to take with me is free of pharmaka.

Except for one thing. I double-check my leather belt before I leave the tent, ensuring that my flask of unbinding pharmaka is securely fastened. I hope I won't have to use it, but this pharmaka is the only thing standing between me and catastrophe, if I've overestimated my ability to manage the Voice without Dom.

I cut off the thought of Dom with self-discipline I've perfected only in the past few days, pulling back the part of my awareness that reaches for his. The biggest risk of this whole job is that I'll alert him to my departure inadvertently by letting him into my thoughts, and that he'll let something slip to the Mohirai with his reaction. I know eventually he'll notice I'm gone, but if everything goes according to plan it'll be too late by then for the Mohirai to track me down using

Dom's connection to me.

I stuff my bedroll, my waterskin, my glasses, and the little wrapped bundle of food into my saddlebag; sling the bag over my shoulder; and slip out of the tent. I walk through the shadows beneath the cliffs, toward the alcove where we stored the horse tack. Nisaba's bridle and saddle are right where Eumelia left them, and I pick them up, leaving behind the mare's silver-threaded saddle blanket. Eumelia will have to ride with Dom the rest of the way to Velkanos, I guess. Or maybe Hanu will volunteer to take my place.

I carry the saddle and bridle toward the grassy part of the riverbank near the willows, where the horses are resting. Most of the mares lie sleeping in the grass, but Eridu stands watch over them, as he sometimes does. He looks particularly alert tonight and nickers softly at me as I approach. I offer him the little apple I pocketed at dinner. He nuzzles my shoulder insistently, suspecting I have more, but I need to keep the rest of my food for myself, so I give him only a parting kiss on the nose.

I move on toward Nisaba, who lies on the grass. In a friendly undertone, I say her name, and she raises her head to look at me. She flicks her ears a bit peevishly but nonetheless obeys my gesture to stand. As quickly as I can, I saddle and bridle the little mare, then buckle on my saddlebag. I do my best to guess the right stirrup length for myself, then mount her.

As much as I take pride in my ability to ride any horse, it's clear that I should have been riding Nisaba all along. Eridu's wonderful, but Nisaba's the perfect size for me. Sitting properly in a saddle with full control of my reins and stirrups is a welcome change. Nisaba and I will make excellent time together.

I give Nisaba a gentle nudge to trot on toward the willows, but she sidesteps, catching me off balance. Surprised, I grip the saddle pommel to steady myself.

"Wh—What are you doing?" an indignant voice slurs from the nearby shadows.

Eumelia takes a few unsteady steps away from Nisaba, into the moonlight. Spirits blast it all. How did she manage to sneak up on me like this? She stares at me in confusion as I try to think of anything to say that might salvage the situation. But all I manage to do is repeat her question. "What are *you* doing?" I say.

Eumelia's wine-hazed expression sharpens. Her eyes travel from my riding clothes to my packed saddlebag. Cautiously, she says, "I came to apologize for what I said earlier."

I curse myself. Why couldn't I have just let that go? "It's fine," I say. "Really. It's fine."

Eumelia raises an eyebrow. "What are you doing with my horse?"

"She's not your horse," I say, annoyed.

"Well, what are you doing with Nisaba, then?" she says, her voice growing louder and clearer. If I don't shut her up fast, someone might hear her. Eumelia steps forward and reaches for Nisaba's bridle, but I pull Nisaba back a few steps.

"Stay away," I say, trying to make my voice as commanding as possible while still speaking in an undertone. "I don't want you to get hurt."

Eumelia rolls her eyes and steps directly in front of Nisaba. "What, are you going to run me over?"

I glare down at her.

"Oh, spirits," says Eumelia, with an elaborate sigh. "You can't be serious, Ava. Now? You're going to try to leave *now?* In the middle of the night? In the middle of the desert? With no supplies? I thought you were smarter than that."

I open my mouth for an angry retort, then snap it shut again. This is wasting precious time. Think, Ava, think.

I wish I could make Eumelia forget this ever happened, the way my mother used to do when we encountered inconvenient people on our journeys. I'm sure I have more than enough unbinding pharmaka here in my flask to wipe this moment from Eumelia's memory, but I could just as easily do some major damage to her, and to myself, for that matter. I have no experience using unbinding pharmaka because my mother never trained me with it.

What I do have, though, is plenty of experience with binding pharmaka.

My awareness of Eumelia stirs like a limb waking from sleep. I remember the two times we shared thoughts before. As I focus on those memories, it's almost like I can step inside her, surveying the possibilities of this other mind. My connection with Eumelia isn't nearly as strong as my connection with Dom, or even my connection with Hanu, whom I've always liked better than Eumelia, but it's still there. I know this girl. I know what she wants.

So now I use it to my advantage.

"You know what?" I say. "You're right." I hop off Nisaba and face Eumelia.

She looks confused. "What?"

"You're right," I say again, taking a step forward. "It's crazy for me to try to escape here, now, like this. But … what do you think I should do?"

I reach for a memory I saw in Hanu's mind this afternoon. A practiced look. I fix that look on Eumelia.

Eumelia moistens her lips with her tongue. Her voice is a slightly higher pitch than usual when she says, "I think you shouldn't try to escape."

"No?" I say, taking another step forward. "Why not?"

Eumelia swallows. I keep channeling Hanu. Slowly, I reach up and touch Eumelia's cheek, trace the line from her earlobe, along her jaw, down her neck. I let her feel what I feel: the smooth warmth of her skin, her pulse speeding up beneath my fingertips, the elegant lines of her collarbone. I let her see that I see her beauty. It's easy. I simply look at her the way Dom looks at everything.

Slowly, I take my hand away. Eumelia's desire for me sparks across the tiny space between us. Perfect. I tip my head to the side and smile at her, the way she wants me to smile at her, a smile that's just for her. I wait. Your move, Eumelia.

Tentatively, with a look in her eyes that's almost frightened, she touches my face with both hands. Her eyelashes flutter in a wince as her fingertips trace the bruise she left on my cheekbone. Her thumb runs lightly along the edge of my lower lip. I tilt my chin up ever so slightly toward her.

She kisses me, gently at first. Her lips are so soft, and she tastes like wine and honeyed pistachios. Her hands slide down my back as she pulls me toward her, lifting me to my toes as she presses the length of my body against hers. I let her kiss me for a moment, waiting to feel in Eumelia that feeling Hanu arouses with such expertise.

There it is. Eumelia's losing control.

I return her kiss. Softly at first, then hungrily. I slide one hand into the front of her robe, running my fingers lightly over her breast. Her nipple hardens as she inhales sharply. I run my left hand over her shoulder and down her back, feeling the soft curves of her waist and hip as I untie her sash with my right hand. I draw her robe down her shoulders and let it fall at her ankles, so she stands before me in only her translucent silk tunic and leggings, trembling.

I press my advantage and swiftly unlace the ties at the back of her neck. I gather folds of silk around her waist and lift her tunic off over her head. I let myself feel through her the sensation of the smooth fabric sliding up her back, the touch of the cool night air on her very warm skin. I don't take my eyes off her, focusing on the task at hand, blocking out every other thought but her. I can't let her see anything but what I want her to see.

I take her by the hand and pull her down beside me in the damp grass at the edge of the willow grove. I push her onto her back, and she doesn't resist. I straddle her hips, stroking her body, feeling her reaction through my hands and within my awareness. She closes her eyes. I pin her hands to the ground above her head, lacing my fingers through hers, palm to palm.

This is going to be the hard part. I know it's possible, because Dom and I have shared some pretty vivid dreams and memories, but I'm not sure whether it will work so easily with Eumelia, or how long I can keep it up before she realizes what's happening. But I have to try. Better this than threatening her with my knife or trying to knock her out. She's always been stronger and faster than I am, so I might not succeed that way. I know this will be safer for both of us, but I hesitate nonetheless. Forcing myself into Eumelia's awareness doesn't seem right.

But I don't have to force anything. Eumelia wants me. Badly.

So I imagine the rest and it pours into her: everything I know Eumelia wants from me, everything I know she wants to give to me, elevated by everything Hanu showed me. I grip Eumelia's hands tightly as I let my mind play out the scene. My palms tingle against hers, and I pull Eumelia into my imagination, sharing each sensation, drawing from a well of experience that's entirely Hanu's. And, spirits, does Hanu have some potent memories. So the sex is good. Perhaps amazing. I don't have anything else to compare it to. But I can tell from the way Eumelia's reacting that she's deep in it.

Quickly, keeping one hand pressed to Eumelia's for skin contact, I use my free hand and my teeth to rip four long strips of silk from Eumelia's discarded tunic. In my imagination, I turn Eumelia over, while in reality I also turn her over, face down in the grass. She moans in pleasure as I tie her hands, and then her feet, and finally gag her. Gently, I pull her up to her knees and bind her hands tightly to her feet behind her.

I'm flushed from the effort of holding this vivid encounter with Eumelia in my mind while tying her up. Even though I know I've imagined almost all of it, I'm breathing as hard by the end as if it really happened.

Eumelia realizes too late how I've tricked her. I touch her cheek and whisper, "I'm sorry." She screams, but I've done a good job with the gag. The sound that escapes her will be impossible for anyone to hear from the bonfire, especially over the music. I'll be long gone before anyone finds her. Eumelia thinks desperately, *Ava, wait, you—*I pull back my hand, cutting her off. I have to get out of here before anything else happens.

Quickly, I hop back on Nisaba and ride away, trying to ignore Eumelia's muffled screams. The sound of her fades quickly enough, but my amplified awareness of her persists for quite a while, until at last I manage to suppress my thoughts of her.

My heart lifts as I think, for the first time in half a moon, that I'm heading in the right direction: toward freedom.

△▽△

When the dance concludes, I let go of Hanu's hand and step out of the ring. I make my way to the place Ava was resting a moment ago, but she's not here.

I'm about to turn back to ask Arkhi whether she's seen Ava when I recognize the small footprints in the sand. The rain has smoothed the beach into an easily readable canvas, revealing that Ava headed back to our tent. Good. We can talk there in private.

I follow her footprints up to the tent and raise the flap. It's dark inside, but it's clear she isn't here. When my eyes adjust, I see what else isn't here: her saddlebag and her boots. My stomach drops.

Ava? I think, reaching out for her. *Where are you?*

She doesn't answer, and I can tell she's shutting me out. I repeat some of the colorful curses I've learned from her as I half-stagger, half-run through the darkness toward the horses. My head spins with wine and anxiety, and it's hard to keep my balance.

The dark shapes of the horses stir on the grassy bank, clearly agitated. A strange sound comes from beneath the shadows of the willows, like a bizarre combination of a kuku bird calling and a dog panting. Has one of the horses fallen ill? I've never heard a horse make a sound like that. Maybe I'm hearing things.

I search the shadows for the source of the sound, and there I discover Eumelia kneeling on the ground, half naked, hands and feet bound behind her, gagged. Eumelia must be even more drunk than I am for Ava to have overpowered her this way.

I crouch behind Eumelia, wishing I had a knife. It takes me some time to loosen the tight knot at the back of her neck. Eumelia coughs when the gag and a crumpled ball of silk finally fall out of her mouth. Her words follow in a rush.

"She took Nisaba on the trail back to the road."

My hands scramble in the darkness around the intricate knot Ava tied at Eumelia's wrists. Where did she learn to tie knots like this? I can't find where it begins or ends.

"Leave me!" says Eumelia. "I can shout for the others. You have to stop Ava! You can still catch her, but you have to go now!"

"But—" I say, my wine-muddled brain struggling to keep up.

"Go!" Eumelia cuts me off with a frustrated shout, chucking her bare shoulder into mine to get me going. "There's no time!"

"All right, all right," I say, jumping to my feet.

I turn toward Eridu, who's unsaddled and unbridled and looking at me with a puzzled expression. I've never ridden bareback before, but I suppose there's a first time for everything.

I grip Eridu's mane as gently as I can and clamber onto his back, then nudge him to a trot toward the trail through the willows. Eumelia's shouts fill the air behind me, and the music at the bonfire stops. I'm relieved she's been heard. It feels awful to leave her behind tied up like that.

It's dark in the willows, but Eridu seems to have a good sense of the trail. I push him to go as fast as I dare given my compromised balance and all the twists and turns and low-hanging branches along the way. Riding bareback is very different from riding in the saddle with Ava, and I use everything she taught me to avoid falling off Eridu as we move faster. There's no way I can ride very far like this. If I don't catch Ava before she reaches the open desert road, I'll lose her.

But to my relief, I hear Nisaba's hoofbeats up ahead. I shout, "Ava! Wait! Please, wait!"

△▽△

Dom's voice is so faint that I'm sure I've imagined it. My elation at having pulled off my escape must be going to my head, making me hear things. I thought I just heard a pair of kuku birds calling, too, which makes no sense at this time of night or this time of year.

But then I hear his voice again, a little louder. Maybe he's reaching out to me using our connection, despite all my efforts to shield my thoughts. I redouble my effort to shut out his awareness until I'm farther along the road.

"Ava! Wait! Please, wait!" he calls, so close behind me there's no way to mistake what I'm hearing. His voice stirs a dull ache in my heart, somewhere between pain and pleasure, quite different from the sharp pain that comes from hearing the Voice in all.

I pull Nisaba to a stop and look back at Dom, ghostly white in his ceremonial robe as he rides toward me through the shifting shadows of the willows. I wonder how in the world he managed to catch up with me. Only when Eridu draws closer do I see he's riding bareback and barefoot. He obviously left in even greater haste than I did. "What are you doing?" I say.

"I want to come with you," he says breathlessly. He looks pale and almost sick with worry, although that might also be motion sickness from the wine.

"You couldn't have told me that a little sooner?" I say. I'm surprised by how glad I am to see him, but I can't suppress the note of irritation. My mind races to rework my plan to include a half-drunk, bootless, saddle-less Dom and the likelihood that the Mohirai will soon be after us, if they aren't already. And, spirits, he's still wearing those blasted ceremonial silks. We'll need to ditch those as soon as possible. He might as well have run after me stark naked.

"I'm sor—" he starts to apologize, then amends it quickly to say instead, "I only just decided. But I do want to come with you. Please, Ava, will you take me with you?"

Even as I fret over my spoiled plan, Dom's words unlock a door inside me that I hadn't fully realized was there. As it swings open, I smile at him. "I promised I would," I say.

For once, the anxious worry in Dom's eyes disappears, and his expression transforms to pure happiness. He says, "I wish—"

Several things conspire to prevent me from hearing Dom's wish. A kuku bird calls directly above us. There's a sharp rustle in the leaves of the willow behind Dom. Nisaba whinnies shrilly and lurches beneath me. Eridu rears and kicks. I cry out in alarm as Dom flies off Eridu's back and through a heavy curtain of low-hanging willow branches. His body thuds to the ground somewhere unseen beneath the tree.

"Dom?" I call, hardly recognizing my own voice in this high pitch of terror. He doesn't answer, and Eridu—the traitor—turns and canters back to camp. I try to calm Nisaba so I can dismount, but she's moving beneath me as erratically as if she's stepped into a hornet's nest. I jump clear of her, landing in a crouch on the trail, then dash toward the tree where Dom fell. Nisaba's hoofbeats follow Eridu's.

I shove my way into the bower of hanging branches that ring the enormous willow trunk. Urshanabi's entire house could fit twice over in the open space beneath these branches. I peer around in the darkness, hesitant to move in case I step on or trip over Dom, who must be injured or unconscious. But I don't see him anywhere, even though the white silk he's wearing practically glows in the dark.

"Dom?" I call again, and when he still doesn't answer, I instinctively reach out for him through our bond. To my enormous relief, his awareness floods into mine, and my frantic questions start flying. *Where are you? Are you hurt? Can you hear me? What—*

In my mind, his voice rings out so loud and commanding that—for the first time—he drowns me out entirely. *GET OUT OF HERE!!!*

There's a muffled grunt, then a snap of twigs. Confused, I wheel around toward the sound and see a thrashing white blur on the ground less than ten paces ahead, moving away from me. Is that Dom? Is he … being dragged?

A dark figure emerges at the edge of my peripheral vision, moving with a rapid but irregular gait toward me through the branches. I spring back, but a strong hand clamps down hard above my right elbow. All my instincts kick in at once, and I lunge straight toward the person who's grabbed me.

I drive my knee with all my strength into what I discover is a man's groin. He cries out in pain and drops to the ground as I dodge away from the second figure lunging at me. A hand grabs the edge of my cloak, momentarily snaring me. I yank at my collar with both hands until the laces rip open, freeing me from the cloak. I burst out through the curtain of willow branches and hit the trail at a run.

I have no idea where I'm going. Back to camp? Into the river? Out to the road? Spirits, I can't just leave Dom! I have to get help. Back to the camp, then. Fortunately, that's the direction I'm already going.

Light footsteps pursue me. Just one set, I think, but my heart pounds so loud in my ears I'm not sure. I look back over my shoulder and catch a glimpse of a tall, slim man rapidly closing the distance between us. When I face forward again, it's too late for me to swerve to avoid the massive hooded man who seems to have materialized out of nowhere into the center of the trail. His fist swings out from beneath his cloak and lands hard in my gut, knocking the wind out of me. Dazzling pain radiates from my core along every nerve of my body, and stars explode behind my eyes. I crumple to the ground at the feet of my assailant, unable to breathe.

My pursuer slows to a stop close behind me. I struggle to push myself up to my knees, but my assailant presses his heavy boot into my back and pushes me down onto my belly. I wriggle helplessly beneath his crushing weight on my spine, my cheek grinding into the damp sand, my mouth filling with grit as I try desperately to inhale. I gasp as the first tiny gulp of air returns to my lungs, and as soon as I'm able to take a single full breath I try to scream. All I manage to get out is a wounded yelp before my assailant pins his knee into my back, grips a fistful of my hair, pulls back my head, and closes a callused hand over my mouth. There's a peculiar scent on his fingers, something sharp and astringent. I can't scream. I can barely breathe. But I can still think, so I try to focus. Think, Ava, think.

A single desperate idea presents itself, and I seize it. My lips tingle against my assailant's rough palm as I imagine my tiny body overpowering this enormous man, throwing him off my back. It's so improbable, even to me, that I struggle to make the image vivid enough to feel real. His hand jerks back like I've burned him. I take another breath to scream, but his hand returns swiftly to my mouth, this time wrapped in a thick woolen rag drenched in whatever it was I smelled before on his fingers. I briefly try biting his hand through the rag, but all I manage to do is taste bitterness.

"Well, it's a feisty one, innit?" says my assailant, as if this is all very amusing. He adjusts his grip on my hair, wrenching my neck and sending a spasm of pain down my spine. I stop struggling and focus on taking minuscule breaths through my partially-covered nostrils. I'm going to black out if I don't get more air. A troubling darkness swirls around the edges of my vision.

"Spirits, I tought de boy would be de trouble," says my pursuer, panting as he catches his breath.

"Never underestimate the little ones," says a third man, who speaks in a deep, resonant voice that's a bit hoarse, as if he's in pain. There's a strange creaking sound, and then he adds, "Take it easy on her neck there, would you?"

My assailant loosens his grip on my hair, and my forehead touches the cool sand. I focus on inhaling and exhaling through the soaked cloth. The scent in my nostrils is so overpowering I want to gag. My limbs grow weak. Rough hands hoist my limp body off the ground. The swirling void around the edge of my vision consumes what's left of the moonlight, and everything goes black.

UP THE RIVER

I CLAW MY WAY OUT of the awful nightmare, back toward my waking reality. As the heavy fog of sleep slowly dissipates from my mind, I'm relieved to find myself cozily buried in my blanket, safe inside our tent, my arms wrapped around Dom's waist, my cheek nestled against his bare back. Drowsily, I hug Dom to reassure myself that everything's all right.

But when I try to let him go, I realize everything's not all right.

I can't let go of Dom because my wrists are tied in front of him. There's some kind of bag over my head, so I can't see where we are, but we're definitely not on our bedrolls in the tent. We're covered in a damp blanket, lying on a hard wooden floor that rocks and creaks. Wind rushes over us, carrying the moist green scents of the river.

Are you awake? Dom thinks.

I hope I'm not. This has to be a dream. Or another nightmare.

Unfortunately not, Dom thinks.

I open my mouth to speak but find my lips, tongue, and throat too painfully dry to make a sound.

Better stay quiet, Dom thinks quickly. *Are you hurt?*

I take a quick inventory of myself. I'm desperately thirsty. My head aches. I can't see anything through this bag, but just enough dim light penetrates the cloth to make me think that the frightening swirl of darkness in my vision has cleared. My left arm is numb where Dom's weight presses it into the floor. My stomach aches with every breath, and I remember with a wince the awful gut punch, although nothing feels like it's broken or seriously damaged inside of me. The skin around my wrists stings, chafing under the tight bindings that hold my arms around Dom.

Apart from that, everything's great. *I'm all right*, I think.

The muscles of Dom's back relax a little under my cheek. *Thank the spirits,* he thinks. *I didn't know what they did to you.*

They … I think, remembering the shadowy figures under the tree, the slim man who ran after me, the massive cloaked man who took me down. *How many of them?*

I didn't see anything before they covered my head, Dom thinks. *But there were definitely two who tied me up under the tree, and one who ran after you. They've all been pretty quiet, except for the man in charge. He's sitting right behind you.*

That sends a shiver down my spine. I notice for the first time the sound of breathing behind me, occasionally audible over the wind. And that might be the toe of his boot poking the back of my shoulder through the blanket, although it feels oddly hard and cold to be a boot.

Where are we? I think.

On a boat, Dom thinks.

Ah. The strange sounds and sensations resolve into a mental picture. A riverboat. We're lying on the deck of a riverboat. I don't hear any oars dipping in the water, though. We must be sailing. Trying not to move, I look upward through the pinprick gaps in the weave of the bag and see a bright smudge that must be the crescent moon overhead. It's near midnight, then. I haven't been unconscious for very long.

Are you hurt? I think, remembering in a horrible rush of emotion how I'd thought Dom might have been knocked out, or worse, when he fell off Eridu.

I'm fine, he thinks. *I wasn't hurt when I fell, but as soon as I hit the ground, they were on top of me, and they gagged me. I'm sorry I didn't warn you fast enough.*

I'm appalled that he's apologizing for this. I think, *If it hadn't been for me, you wouldn't have been there. None of this would have happened.*

I'm not so sure about that, Dom thinks. Before I can ask what he means, he wonders, *What did they do to you?*

I glimpse in his mind every awful thing Dom imagined they might have done. Fortunately, what actually happened to me wasn't nearly that bad. I show Dom what I remember.

He used pharmaka to knock you out? Dom thinks, surprised.

I guess so, I think.

But where would a man get pharmaka? Dom wonders.

Now that's a very good question.

△▽△

I'm relieved that Ava's awake again. Ever since they tied us up together, I've been focusing on keeping her breathing regular and keeping her body temperature up. Her mind was blank and dreamless while she was unconscious, and I'd worried they'd hit her on the head and seriously injured her. I'd worried a lot of other things as well.

But now her mind races with questions, so she seems to be returning to normal, if anything about this situation can be considered normal.

Where would men get pharmaka? Ava thinks, running with my question. *And who would have taught them how to use it? And why? It doesn't make any sense. The Mohirai would never teach pharmaka to men.*

You know what else doesn't make sense, I think. *Why did they tie us together like this? That was one of the only things I heard them talk about. The man in charge was very specific that you needed to be tied up to me, and that you needed skin contact with me.*

Ava thinks, *How could they know about the binding between us?* She flicks through possibilities in her mind, dismissing each so quickly I can't keep up. At last, she gives up and refocuses on a more urgent insight. She thinks, *Well, if they think we can't be separated, let them keep thinking that. We can use it to our advantage.*

You think being tied up like this is an advantage? I think, skeptical.

She thinks, *Well, as long as we can't see anything, I'd rather know where you are. And it seems better to stick together until we figure out what's going on.*

I think, *Do you want to keep pretending you're unconscious, too?*

No, she thinks. *I'm going to try to get them talking. Or at least get them to give us some water. I still have grit in my mouth from when the big one squashed me into the ground.* Inadvertently, she shares the feeling of her painfully dry tongue running over the sand in her teeth.

All right, I think, swallowing to clear the strange sensation out of my mouth. *I'll follow your lead.*

△▽△

I twist my head against Dom's back and say, as loudly as I can manage through my parched throat, "Please, I need water."

"She's awake," the man in charge says from right behind me. "And she's thirsty. Pick them up." I recognize the deep voice of the man who told my assailant to take it easy on my neck. I wonder who he is. He sounds close enough that I could reach out and touch him if my hands weren't tied. Maybe that's why my hands are tied.

Two sets of footsteps walk across the deck toward us. They pull the blanket off us but leave the bags over our heads as they hoist us to our feet.

The man in charge steps up behind me, so close that the warmth of his body radiates through the back of my thin riding shirt. He smells like the sea. I consider the advantages versus the risks of ramming my head into his nose while I'm tied to Dom. Before I've made a decision, the man leans down toward my ear. His thick beard brushes the exposed skin of my neck as he says softly, "Don't try anything, child. I'll knock you out again if I need to."

I shudder involuntarily, remembering the suffocating hand over my mouth and the swirling darkness that sucked me under. *I wonder how much more of that pharmaka he has,* I think.

Let's assume plenty, Dom thinks.

"Who are you?" I say over my shoulder, in the general direction of the man in charge.

"A free man," he says.

I frown inside my bag, taken aback. Could he really be one of the free people? My mother and I have been trying to reach them for years. But the free men live across the sea. Why would this free man be here, now, in the heart of Mohiran land? And why would he take us captive?

"What do you want?" I say cautiously.

"A better world," he says.

Someone unties my wrists and pulls me backward, and Dom slips out of my arms. I wasn't exactly comfortable being tied together, but I'm frightened to be separated like this. I grit my teeth to stop myself from crying out for him. I don't want these men to think I'm weaker than they already must think I am.

Bony fingers grip my elbows, holding my arms tight behind me. These hands must belong to the slim man who chased after me. Across the distance between us, I sense a muscular grip wrenching Dom's arms painfully backward. Perhaps that's the big man who punched me.

More of Dom's sensations spill into me as his discomfort grows. He shivers as the damp, chilly night wind off the river courses over his bare skin. I realize with a rush of anger that Dom's been stripped completely naked. I guess these men knew about the pharmaka in those ceremonial clothes, too, although I have no idea how they could know such things. I can't bear that this is happening to Dom, and that it's happening because of me.

"Please," I say. "Please give Dom his clothes back. He's freezing."

No one answers. Our captors reposition me and Dom back to back, interlacing our wrists and binding them tight behind us. They lower us to a sitting position on the deck. Dom's shivers move like tremors through me. I try to share some of my warmth with him, but soon I'm shivering too. I guess I don't have as much warmth to spare as Dom usually does. To my relief, someone at last takes pity on us and wraps the damp blanket back around our shoulders, blocking some of the wind.

A peculiar sound—a combination of creaking, thumping, and footsteps—approaches me, while a normal set of footsteps approaches Dom. I sense bodies standing around us. Someone leans down over me, and again I smell the saltwater scent of the man in charge.

What's happening? Dom thinks nervously.

I let Dom feel what's happening to me so he can't imagine the worst, and he does the same for me. Gloved fingers brush my neck as someone unties the bag covering my head and pulls it partway up. Rough calluses graze Dom's chin as his bag's rolled up to his nose. I look down and glimpse one leather-clad knee kneeling in front of me on the heavily varnished, pitted wooden deck of the boat, alongside an object I don't recognize that gleams in the moonlight. The bag stays low over my eyes, so I can't see more.

Something slips under the bottom edge of my bag, and I flinch away from the sudden pressure at my lips, until I recognize it as a leather waterskin. I grab it eagerly with my teeth and suck in a huge mouthful of cool liquid. Behind me, Dom does the same. I'm just about to swallow when I catch a whiff of flowery sweetness. Dom recognizes the scent the same instant I do.

Don't! he thinks.

Spit it out! I think.

We splutter and cough, and we must have sprayed the unbinding pharmaka everywhere because I hear wordless sounds of disgust all around us. The bag falls back down over Dom's lips, and Dom gnaws on the fabric, trying to wipe the taste out of his mouth. I spit over and over, until saliva runs down my chin, dripping onto my shirt.

"Stop," a fourth voice says wearily. "Let me do it."

I'm so shocked that for a moment I forget how to breathe.

Spirits, Ava, Dom thinks, his heart racing. *Is that* … ?

"Mama?" I say.

△▽△

"Mama?" says Ava. "How—How are you here? Who are these men? Why—"

The man in charge interjects in a low, warning tone. "Keep her quiet, Lilith, or we'll have to gag her. There could be other scouts on the river."

"Listen, Ava," Lilith says quietly, approaching us from the side. Ava falls utterly still behind me, and I feel her listening, waiting, hanging on her mother's every word. "You've done well. I'd feared the worst when I saw you last. But you've made astonishing progress. I saw you walking today and riding tonight almost as freely as if your accident never happened. That will make everything much easier for the boy."

Ava's back trembles against mine. "I don't understand," she says nervously.

Lilith says, "I'm sure you understand why I left the way I did. There was no way to take you with me the night of your overdose, and anything I told you could have been extracted from you by the Mohirai.

"When I met our boat that night, we changed course to sail east, so we could intercept you. Our scouts have been monitoring your caravan, so we knew when you'd be at the ferry crossing. We're heading upriver to rejoin our horses now, and we should make it back to the coast of the Middle Sea in less than two days."

Ava's voice quavers as she says, "Why are we tied up like this, Mama?"

Lilith says, "We weren't expecting you to leave the camp tonight on your own. I hadn't even considered that might be possible so soon after your overdose. We'd planned to take you from the camp tonight while everyone was sleeping. As it was, you took us by surprise. The whole job came off more roughly than planned. The men had to subdue you quickly so we could leave before the Mohirai came looking for you. The Mohirai must not learn the identities of the free people living among their slaves. And since the boy can see what you see, we need to keep both your heads covered until you're unbound."

Cold understanding washes over me. In my panic, I interrupt Lilith and Ava without thinking. "You don't need to unbind us," I say in a rush. "I want to come with Ava. That's why I was following her."

"It's true," says Ava. "Dom wants to be one of the free people, Mama."

"No," says Lilith. "He wants to be with you, Ava. He's powerless to resist you. Even a skilled Mohira would have difficulty resisting a bond as strong as the one between you."

"Why does that matter?" says Ava. "We're managing the bond fine on our own now. Just leave us as we are."

Lilith sighs. She says, "Ava. I've taught you that the Mohirai have many subtle ways to control the children raised among them. To undo the work they've done to this boy would be dangerous to his mind, and still he would never be trusted among free men. He can't come with us."

Ava's silent for a long time. I overhear her working through every scenario that might possibly lead us out of this situation together. One by one, possibilities dwindle, dwindle, vanish, until only one remains. She squares her shoulders against my back and says in a hard voice, "If he can't come, I don't want to come, either. So let us go. Leave me behind."

"You know far too much to be left among the Mohirai, Ava," says Lilith. "Why do you think we've made such an effort to recover you?"

A tempest brews inside of Ava. She says, "How can you do this to him, and to me? All my life, you've taught me that unbinding is the greatest crime of the Mohirai." Her voice rises, until a warning growl from the man in charge hushes her again. She concludes in a furious hiss, "If it's wrong for them to steal memories from children, why is it all right for you to steal memories from us?"

"Unbinding memories isn't right or wrong, Ava," says Lilith. "What's right or wrong is the reason for which it is done. The Mohirai unbind memories to preserve the Voice's power over the people. We unbind to free the people from the Voice."

With contempt, Ava says, "How does tying us up free the people? And what good is your freedom, if you get it by taking ours away?"

"Peace, Ava," says Lilith. "Your resistance will only make the work more difficult for the boy. It's far easier to unbind the willing."

"I'm not willing!" Ava hollers at the top of her voice. "He's not willing! You can't do this!"

"Ava—"

"Enough!" says the man in charge. "It must be done before we reach the ford. Hold them down."

"Stay back," Lilith says in the tone of command. "Forced unbindings can be catastrophic. She's of no use to anyone if she loses her mind."

"She has more than one use to me," says the man in charge.

"She's no use to you without me," says Lilith. "Don't be a fool."

"Say that again," the man in charge says dangerously.

As the argument between Lilith and the man in charge escalates, Ava thinks, *We have to get out of here, Dom.*

But how? I wonder.

We'll have to swim, she thinks.

What? I struggle to even imagine it, bound and blinded as we are. *We'll drown.*

We can't stay here, she thinks. *I don't understand what's happening, but I don't want to stick around and find out. We're both strong swimmers. We'll manage.*

I swallow. *All right,* I think. *What do we do?*

Ava's idea materializes in my mind, as clear as sight. Standing together, rushing away from the sound of Lilith and the man in charge, letting ourselves fall over the side of the boat. It's so vivid I can almost believe we've succeeded already. My confidence grows. Or perhaps that's Ava injecting some of her confidence into me.

Are you ready? Ava thinks.

Ready, I think.

△▽△

With one swift upward thrust, Dom and I drive our feet against the deck, pushing our backs together until we're standing. We've spent a lot of time maneuvering around each other's bodies over the past half moon, but this movement is still challenging, especially with our height mismatch. Despite Dom's effort to slouch, my arms are jerked backward and upward at a painful angle by our bound wrists. The damp blanket falls off us as we scuttle blindly together toward the port side of the boat.

Surprised shouts from my mother and the free men follow our sudden movement. Dom's foot tangles in a line coiled on the deck. My knee rams into some hard protrusion. His bare hip smacks into the port side railing. We're moving too fast to feel the pain of either collision yet.

"Grab them!" the man in charge shouts breathlessly.

Dom and I leap together over the rail and tumble overboard. I think we've made it, until a hand clamps hard around my ankle, trapping me upside down. My submerged head drags alongside the hull of the boat, sending stinging water rushing up my nose and down my throat. A stab of wrenching pain in Dom's shoulder echoes in my own as he's dragged through the water by our bound wrists. The bag over Dom's head, which someone left untied, slips away in the current. He kicks and struggles to lift his head above water. For a moment, I glimpse the clear night sky through his eyes before the dark current swallows him again. I can't see anything myself or get my head above water at all, so I focus on holding my breath as I drive the heel of my free foot toward the fingers clamped around my ankle.

But another hand catches my free foot just before I land a blow. Then another grabs at my knee. Eight hands in all take hold of me and Dom, and no amount of our thrashing can free us from their grasp. They haul us out of the river like a monstrous, unruly fish and drop us unceremoniously inside the boat. The side of my head and the length of Dom's naked body slam hard against the wooden deck. I cough up water while Dom shivers behind me.

It was worth a shot, Dom thinks.

Oh Dom, I think miserably, *I'm so sorry.*

Don't apologize, he thinks. *This isn't your fault.*

Isn't it? I think.

The strange thumping gait approaches my head, and I sense the man in charge looming over me. There's a creak as he crouches by my head, and through the wet bag now plastered over my face I catch a whiff of that astringent smell again. A soaked rag reeking of pharmaka settles loosely over my nose and mouth. I thrash my head from side to side, trying to throw it off, but the man in charge presses his hand firmly against my face to keep it there. I force myself again to stop breathing. My heart pounds and my lungs ache for air. Why is my mother letting this happen? How can we get out of here? Think, Ava, think.

It's difficult to focus while I feel what Dom's feeling and see what he's seeing.

The burly man grapples with Dom's thrashing legs, his meaty palms and forearms wrapping tight around Dom's wet, slippery knees. In the moonlight, I can just make out the man's distinctive crooked nose and a quarter moon's growth of dark stubble on his square jaw. The rough, bony fingers of the slim man clamp down painfully hard around Dom's nose, forcing him to open his mouth to breathe. I glimpse the high forehead and thinning close-cropped hair of the slim man, his brow furrowed in concentration. My mother's broad-shouldered frame looms over Dom as she wedges the waterskin between his teeth, squeezing unbinding pharmaka into his mouth, her broad hand pressing back his forehead to force him to swallow. Dom chokes, coughing and spitting the liquid everywhere.

My eyes widen inside my bag as I realize what Dom's seeing and feeling: all those bare fingers, palms, and forearms pressed against his naked skin.

Let me in! I think to Dom, as I realize what I must do to protect him.

Dom doesn't resist me as I send my awareness flooding through him. The edges between us vanish as all the walls we've carefully constructed to protect ourselves from each other come crumbling down.

△▽△

Our awareness explodes outward, binding to each awareness in our path, consuming all. We're a girl and a boy, a slim man and a burly man, a powerful woman and a man in charge, joined together on a river through a desert surrounded by seas edging oceans of a single world among the many worlds.

Together you shall seek us, find us, know us, says the Voice that calls within all worlds. *Together you shall amplify us. Together you shall weave us through the many worlds.*

We glimpse a far horizon, far in every way that far can be understood. For an instant, all is known.

And then the Voice departs.

Our awareness collapses back toward us, retreating like the ebb tide of the greatest ocean, exposing what lies beneath, setting our plan in motion. A burly man and a slim man and a man in charge, their minds confused, move as one toward a powerful woman. They seize her by the arms and rush together toward the starboard side. All four tumble headlong into the great Purattu. What remains is a girl and a boy on the deck of a boat that floats on a river flowing endlessly toward the sea.

△▽△

"Spirits, Ava," Dom gasps. "What was that?"

"I—" I don't know what I just did to drive my mother and the free men away from us. Even if I did know, there are no words to explain what I saw while I was doing it. All I know is the relief of success. Dom's memories are safe. My memories are safe. We are safe.

I shake my head to toss the pungent, pharmaka-soaked rag off my face.

Through the wet bag still covering my head, I gulp deep breaths of fresh air, waiting for my pulse to slow.

My heart flutters strangely, and my face feels numb. I can't feel my arms or my legs. Something's wrong. Something's seriously wrong.

"Get my knife, Dom," I say weakly, sharing a flash of an image with him. "It's in ..."

Awareness lets go of my body, withdrawing into the incomprehensible vastness where it dwells. Darkness swirls around me and swallows me whole.

△▽△

I have no idea how Ava's managed to conceal her knife from me since the night I found her in the woods. But as soon as she shares her mental image of it, I notice the slight ridge pressed against my knuckles. Ava's removed her knife's handle and embedded the blade in the thick leather at the back of her belt, hiding it in plain sight. Clever.

The image vanishes into blackness as Ava loses consciousness.

Stay with me, Ava, I think. There's no response. My heart pounds in my ears. I say aloud, louder and louder, "Stay with me, Ava. Stay with me."

I try to ignore the fact that she's unresponsive to my thoughts and my voice, focusing all my remaining energy on working the blade free from her belt. It's not easy with both hands tied behind my back and my wet fingers numb with cold, but bit by bit the blade comes loose from the leather. At last it falls into my palm. The boat lines that bind our wrists are tough, but Ava keeps a sharp blade. Eventually, I slice through our bindings.

As soon as our hands are free, I turn to her. She lies curled on her side, her arms limp behind her, her head covered in a wet bag. Carefully, I untie the bag and slide it off Ava's head. Her eyes are closed. Even in the moonlight, I can tell that she's the wrong color. There's a bluish tint to her lips, her eyelids, her cheeks.

I press my hand to her heart, closing my eyes as I focus my entire awareness on her, searching for any sign of breathing, any sign of a heartbeat. There's nothing here but silence and stillness. I touch trembling fingers to her cheek, to her lips, to her neck. She's ice cold. Warmth, movement, awareness—everything that was Ava has escaped this fragile shell.

I don't recognize the voice that cries out as I draw her into my arms. My tears fall hot and fast onto her pale cheeks.

Ava, please, I think, as my breathing turns to choking sobs. *You promised you would take me with you.*

But there's no answer.

THERE AND BACK AGAIN

I CALL OUT FOR AVA until all that remains inside me is emptiness. The wind dies down, and with no one at the tiller, the boat rotates slowly in the current, the sail luffing uselessly. I don't know how long I kneel on the deck rocking Ava's body in my arms.

A hard thump against the hull startles me, throwing me off balance. Dropping one hand to the deck to steady myself, I look up.

I must be dreaming. I blink several times, but the vision persists. Across a narrow channel of calm water, beyond a strip of sandy beach, rise the low river cliffs. Atop the cliffs stands a little house, silhouetted against the dark blue pre-dawn sky, golden light flickering behind the two little windows that keep watch over the river. It's Urshanabi's house.

I cry out, but the sound is nothing but a hoarse whisper. I swallow and try again. "Help!" I call. "Please, someone, help!"

From somewhere on the beach, Eumelia shouts, "Dom! It's Dom!"

Many voices call from many places, and three figures hurry down the beach toward me, while others scatter in different directions. Running footsteps pound the planks of the dock, and in the moonlight I make out the dark cloaked figure of the High Priestess Serapen approaching, flanked by Eumelia and Hanu in their white robes.

When Hanu sees Ava's body in my arms, she stops short, clapping both hands over her mouth. But Eumelia jumps straight into the boat beside me and throws a coil of line from the deck onto the dock. Hanu looks down at the line, dazed. Eumelia says sharply, "Hanu! Wake up, sister." Hanu nods quickly and sets to work securing the boat to the dock.

Eumelia looks down at Ava's motionless form. Her eyes gleam with tears, but her mouth sets in a determined line. "Come on," she says bracingly to me. "We're not letting her get away with this."

Carefully, Eumelia and I transfer Ava out of the boat and into the waiting arms of Hanu and Serapen. They lay Ava down on the dock, and Serapen kneels at her side. She touches Ava's forehead and cheeks, smells her mouth, presses points along her neck, wrists, and ankles. She turns to me with a grim expression and says, "Can you carry her, Dom?" I nod, and she says, "Come with me. Hurry."

I lift Ava in my arms and follow Serapen along the dock, back onto the beach. Eumelia and Hanu follow close behind me. Serapen wades into the shallows of the river and gestures for me to follow her.

In waist-deep water, Serapen turns to me and shows me where to hold Ava, supporting her neck and her lower back so she floats face up between us. She unbuckles the silver flask from Ava's belt. I'd completely forgotten the flask until this moment.

"Think carefully, Dom," says Serapen. "Think back to the last moment you remember before you were taken."

I don't have time to wonder how Serapen knows anything about how we were taken. My mind scrambles backward through my memory, from here to the boat, from the boat to Lilith and the free men, from Lilith and the free men to the dark willow grove.

"Do you remember?" says Serapen.

"Yes," I say. "Yes, I remember."

"Hold that memory," she says. "Let go of everything that happened next."

I have no idea what she means, but I do my best to obey. Serapen uncaps the flask. I close my eyes and focus on the last moment I remember before we were taken.

Ava sits tall in her saddle atop Nisaba, smiling at me in the moonlight, framed by the shifting shadows of the willows. I've told her I want to come with her, and she's agreed to take me. Whatever happens next, we'll be together. This is what I truly want. This is what I've always wanted. There's only one thing I'd change. As I hold the memory clear in my mind, I give myself time enough to tell her, "I wish I'd told you sooner."

In the cool waters of the Purattu, my hand tingles against the back of Ava's neck. I open my eyes and see Serapen holding Ava's head above the surface, trickling unbinding pharmaka through Ava's parted lips, drop by drop. I wait for what seems like an eternity, clinging to hope. But nothing happens.

My thoughts spiral. This is madness. Ava's heart and breath stopped long ago. She's cold as ice. She's gone. She's dead. The word snuffs out whatever hope remains in me, plunging me into darkness. My hands grow cold, and my mind plays tricks on me, as Ava's skin seems to grow warmer against my palms.

I blink. Is it a trick? No … there's definitely some change. It's almost imperceptible at first, but the color slowly warms in Ava's cheeks and lips. My arms tremble, and Serapen says, "Breathe, Dom. Breathe." I take a shuddery breath, trying to steady myself.

"Good," says Serapen. She closes the flask and slips it back into Ava's belt. She grasps my shaking hands firmly beneath the water's surface, so we cradle Ava between us. "The body is ready to receive her," she says. "But the choice is yours, novice Artifex."

It takes a moment for the High Priestess' words to penetrate the numb fog that's only slowly clearing from my mind. I look at her uncertainly. She looks at me expectantly.

"What choice?" I say.

"The choice to call her back," she says.

"Back … from where?" I say.

"From where her mind goes when it wanders," she says.

I look down at Ava, who now appears to be merely sleeping, floating peacefully in the slow current of the river. Where does her mind go when it wanders?

As soon as I wonder, I know. Of course I know. Ava's mind always wanders to the city of glass towers.

Hope rekindled rises in me along with the image of that beautiful city. I've followed Ava there so many times before. If that's where she's gone, maybe she can follow me back from there.

Worry follows close behind my hope. I wonder what Ava would choose, if the choice were hers, but I can't bear to consider this too closely. I know what I would choose. And Serapen says the choice is mine.

"Tell me how," I say.

"Listen, novice Artifex," says the High Priestess.

I close my eyes, and the reply rises within me. "I listen."

Once again I find myself standing alone in the place where the wind blows between layers of the unseen. I gaze up at an infinite darkness pierced by innumerable stars, and I listen.

I listen.

I listen.

And once again I hear.

You have asked it. We may give it. But there is a price. Do you accept it?

I feel the pull of Ava's awareness across an inconceivable distance. My longing for her drowns out all other thought. And once again I make my choice. *Yes. Yes. Yes, I do accept the price.*

△▽△

"OMG, Dom!" I say. I push the immerger glasses back on my forehead and rub my eyes. My vision refocuses on my present reality, and I look across the living room toward the kitchen.

Dom stands at the island prepping dinner as he listens to music. It's been a hot day—too hot for clothes—and there's a light sheen of sweat on his chest. He glances up from the mixing bowl where he's massaging kale with both hands. He speaks in a tone of command to the soundbar on the wall, and the volume drops. He says, "Sorry, love, music was too loud. What did you say?"

"I said: O. M. G. This scene on the Euphrates, where I died the first time. It's some of the best immersion work I've ever experienced."

"You're there already?" he says. He steps to the sink to rinse the green off his hands, dries them on a dish towel, and comes to join me in the living room.

"I cheated a little," I say. "I skimmed some of the older memories at two-x. But, anyway, this scene. The sensory resolution is incredible. Did you augment with other sensory libraries, or did it really happen like this?"

I grab Dom's immerger glasses off the coffee table and toss them to him so he can join me in his memory. He catches them in one hand but doesn't put them on. Instead, he snags my glasses off my head with his free hand.

"Hey!" I protest, reaching up for my most precious peripheral as Dom lifts it out of my reach. He gives me a look that says, *That's enough for today, little girl.* I roll my eyes and say, "Oh, fine."

Dom sets our immerger glasses back onto the coffee table and slides into his place beside me on the sofa. He wraps his long arm around me, and I tuck my feet beside me on the cushions, curling up in the familiar space at his side. Even in this late summer heat wave, I enjoy the radiant warmth of his bare skin against mine.

Dom traces slow circles on my shoulder with his fingertip. Few have earned more accolades for immersive design than I have, and yet no digital signal I've ever crafted comes close to conveying the connection that radiates from a single one of Dom's fingertips on my skin.

He says, "It really did happen like that."

I slip my arms around his waist and hug him tight. "I'm sorry I put you through all that," I say. "And through all this."

"Don't apologize," he says, nuzzling his cheek against the top of my head. "I'd do it all over again."

I prop my chin on his chest and look up at him, considering this. He drops a kiss on the tip of my nose. I see myself reflected in those deep-set, watchful eyes. "Would you really?" I say.

The look he gives me sends a shiver of pleasure down my spine. *As long as you'll have me,* he thinks.

Oh, I'll have you, old man, I think, hopping up from the sofa. He laughs as I pull him to his feet and lead him into our bedroom.

Outside our window, the sun sinks behind the San Francisco skyline across the bay, casting rosy light into the bedroom. I turn to Dom expectantly. He takes my right hand in both of his and tugs each one of my fingertips. My silver-threaded immerger glove slides slowly off, and he sets it down on the bedside table. With equal care, he undresses my left hand, setting the second glove atop the first. Now there's nothing left between us.

I take his hands in mine and study them for a moment, savoring the tingling anticipation that flows between our palms. His hands seem to have little in common with mine in this life. His are strong, perceptive, peaceful. Mine are swift, expressive, restless. And yet within these outer forms—his so constant, mine ever changing—we feel so much the same. I raise his hands to my lips, kissing his knuckles one by one, turning them over to kiss his palms.

When I release his hands, he lays me down on our bed. His fingers and mouth move over me, gentle at first, with growing fervor as I respond. We give and receive in turns. I've spent enough time in Dom's mind in my brief life to rediscover what he likes, and I use the element of surprise to good effect, but he maintains an insurmountable advantage of experience. I gasp with the pleasure of every point of contact between us as his sensations multiply mine and mine multiply his. My pulse races, triggering the all-too-familiar needling pain around my heart.

I try to suppress the gasp of pain that follows, but Dom misses nothing. He pauses. *Are you all right?* he thinks.

Yes, I think, refusing to let the pain steal this moment, when we have so little time remaining.

Dom's hand lingers protectively over my heart. *Do you want to keep going?* he thinks.

Yes, I think urgently, moving his hand from my heart to my breast, willing him to forget my pain, kissing him deeply. *Do you?*

Oh yes, he thinks.

He lifts me up astride his hips, arranging me around him in the precise and practiced way he does everything. His right hand anchors my lower back while his left roams further afield. I see myself through his eyes, fully present here with him in this moment, radiant with my desire for him and his for me. *Spirits, you're beautiful,* he thinks, looking at me as only he can look at me.

The hunger I feel in him amplifies the hunger in me. *I want you,* I think. *I want you.*

Now? he thinks.

"Now, yes, now," I say.

I grip his hands in mine, palm to palm, fingers entwined. My awareness slips into his, and his into mine. I'm within him, around him, beneath him. He's within me, around me, beneath me. Edges blur and disappear as we're swept into motion together, until we're only one, riding the long crest of a wave together until we crash ashore.

We're gone a while. After we've returned, I smile down at him, smooth back the curls from his forehead, and drop a kiss between his brows. He draws me down beside him. I stretch luxuriously from my toes to my fingertips and drape myself over his warm body, completely spent.

"And how was it for you?" he says.

"I think you know," I say.

"Tell me anyway," he says.

No words of mine will do him justice, so I steal the words I need. In a language that died millennia ago, I say, "Our revels make this journey worth the trouble, dear brother."

He smiles. In his mother tongue, he says, "You are the essential ingredient, sweet Muse."

"Not a Muse," I say.

"Still friends, though?" he says.

I laugh. "Best friends," I say.

We lie in a tangle of bedsheets, bodies entwined. I nestle at Dom's side, my cheek on his chest, my hand on his belly. His breath deepens and slows as he sinks into sleep. The last of the sunlight fades outside the window. As the darkness gathers cozily around us, I let my relaxed awareness melt into his, and I glimpse his dream.

He stands alone on a rocky promontory surrounded by a deep blue sea. A ladder of scarlet rope hangs before him, close enough to touch. The ladder stretches endlessly upward into a cloudless blue sky. He faces the dilemma of the ladder with a mixture of awe and wariness. Should he stay on the ground or start the climb?

It's strangely soothing to watch this dream, which I've seen so many times before. I linger unseen behind him on the promontory as he reaches for the ladder. My eyes begin to close as I drift into sleep.

A shadow in the bedroom corner moves, startling me back to full alertness. I sit up, staring wide-eyed into the darkness. There's nothing there, but the rush of adrenaline sets my heart pounding, and the wearisome pain in my chest flares, sharper now than before.

I exhale slowly to calm myself, massaging my eyes. Dom's right. I need to cut down on my immerger time. Those glasses must be messing with my vision.

△▽△

I've been standing in a dark corner of the bedroom for some time when the naked woman in the bed sits up and looks straight at me. Until this moment, she seemed to be a complete stranger, but there's something familiar about her pained expression. I stare back at her in surprise. "Can you see me?" I say.

She doesn't answer. Instead, she sighs, rubs her eyes, and settles back down beside her companion.

I wonder what I should do. Before the man fell asleep, I heard them exchange a few words I understood, which gave me hope that I might be able to communicate with them. But I've been completely unable to catch their attention. They haven't reacted in any way to my speaking, shouting, or waving at them. All I've been able to do is follow them from room to room, listening as they speak their strangely unmusical language to each other, studying the strangely shiny clothes and devices they pass between them, marveling at all the strange lights and furnishings and materials in their house. Their lovemaking is the only thing that seems entirely natural about them.

The soft sound of the woman's breathing deepens and slows. I approach the bedside, looking down at the sleeping couple, the woman wrapped in the man's embrace. In the stillness of the room, I feel the familiar pull of Ava's awareness, the pull that somehow forms a bridge between this world and the world where I stand with Ava's body in the Purattu. Ava's here, somewhere. All I need to do is lead her back across this bridge, back to the place where she belongs.

I reach out to touch the woman's cheek, and I'm overjoyed by the sensation of Ava's awareness swirling into mine.

Hello, old friend, she thinks.

I sense a change between us without knowing its cause, so confusion dims my joy.

I thought I'd lost you, I think.

It's not too late to let me go, she thinks. *We can both be free of this forever.*

Her longing for this freedom terrifies me. *I don't want to be free*, I think. *I want to be with you.*

How long? she thinks.

Always, I think, pouring my certainty into her, pulling her awareness into mine, holding her with me through our bond. She doesn't resist, but though I feel her pleasure in returning to me, I also glimpse unfathomable depths of sorrow as she lets go of her companion.

The man's eyes snap open, startling me. His arms tighten protectively around the woman. For an instant, I'm certain he sees me, but his eyes slide over me as he looks toward the woman. His face contorts in an expression of pain so intense I feel it within myself. He sits up, cradling the woman against his chest, burying his face in her hair. "No, no, no," he moans, rocking her slowly in his arms. "My love, my love."

I try not to hear my voice inside the man's as he calls out for what I've stolen from him. I slip out the way I came.

△▽△

It's almost midday when I wake to the sound of Hanu and Eumelia's hushed voices outside the tent. Dom stirs behind me, but he's so exhausted that he doesn't resurface from sleep.

"Should we wake them?" whispers Hanu.

"Let's just leave these here," Eumelia whispers back.

There's a rustle at the tent flap, followed by soft footsteps departing through sand.

Carefully, I turn over in Dom's arms to face him, trying not to wake him. My aching body protests each movement. When I regained consciousness last night —floating in the river in Dom's arms, the sweet taste of unbinding pharmaka on my tongue—it was immediately obvious that something had gone horribly wrong with my escape plan, but I still don't know what happened. All these new cuts and bruises on my body and Dom's face suggest it's quite a story, but the last thing I remember for myself was my joy at seeing Dom in the willow grove.

Out of habit, I want to blame the Mohirai for the memories I've lost, though I suspect I have only myself to blame this time. I should be grateful I lost only half a night. I should be grateful Dom was there. I have so many questions that only he can answer, and he promised to explain everything this morning.

As I wait for Dom to wake, I study his sleeping form the way he often studies me: with full attention, without turning away. I'm not sure whether the change is in him or in me, but the longer I look, the more I see in him. Somehow he is at once the child who played beside me in the cedar forest by the sea, the boy who set out with me on the road to Velkanos, the man who waits for me somewhere far from here. Somehow I've known them all, and I know them all, and I will know them all again. And somehow they've all known me and know me and will know me. Despite my uncertainty about what lies ahead, I find comfort in these thoughts. To know and be known by someone else is perhaps the only comfort in this world of unknowable things.

The tenderness I felt for Dom when he found me in the willows returns in a rush. *I want to come with you,* he'd said. Whatever else may have happened last night, I'm glad I heard him say that. I want him with me, too.

"That's a relief," says Dom.

Spirits. How much of that did he overhear?

He opens his eyes and looks at me with a hint of a teasing smile. "All of it," he says.

With mock indignation, I say, "We need a rule about eavesdropping."

He says, "First we need a rule about thinking so loud while other people are trying to sleep."

I chuckle. "Fine," I say, extricating myself from his drowsy embrace. "Go back to sleep. I'll take my noisy mind outside."

I sit by the tent flap, sorting through the folded stack of clean, dry, mended riding clothes Hanu and Eumelia left for us. A pang of guilt accompanies the thought that Eumelia might have washed and mended my clothes after what I did to her. I separate my clothes from Dom's and set his down beside him, then push open the tent flap to go outside and dress myself.

The blankets rustle as Dom sits up behind me. "Please stay," he says. "I need to show you what happened last night."

There's a strained note in his voice. I look back at him, and my curiosity turns to apprehension when I see his grim expression. I let the tent flap fall closed and sit at the foot of Dom's bedroll, facing him. He extends his hand toward me, and I take it hesitantly.

His palm tingles against my fingers, and a tempest of Dom's fear, grief, and guilt sweeps through me. My heart aches in sympathy. It seems cruel for me to ask him to revisit whatever memories caused such pain. I remember Urshanabi saying, *It's a gift sometimes to forget.* Maybe the ferryman's right. Maybe Serapen did me a kindness by freeing me from these memories.

I reach out and smooth away the deep furrow between Dom's brows with my thumb. His emotions aren't the only thing hurting him. Despite all the healing pharmaka Serapen gave us last night, his body aches as much as my own. The scrapes and bruises on the side of his face sting where my fingertips brush his skin. I'm about to withdraw my hand, concerned that I'm making the pain worse, but Dom reaches up and keeps my fingers pressed to his cheek. I remember what Hanu taught me, and I focus on Dom's sensations, doing my best to draw out the pain from his bruises, to draw out the pain of his emotions, to let my own sense of well-being pour into him. He closes his eyes, and the clenched muscles of his jaw relax against my palm. I say softly, "We don't have to do this now. I can wait."

"I can't," he says.

He draws me back down beside him on the blankets. We lie facing each other, his left hand covering my right. I close my eyes as his mind returns to the willow grove, the last moment we both remember. His memory picks up where mine leaves off. I see myself on Nisaba and hear Dom's voice saying, "I wish—" The world tilts as Eridu rears, and Dom falls into the shadows beneath the willows. With a mixture of horror and fascination, I witness the dark figures converge in Dom's peripheral vision before he's bound, gagged, blindfolded, and stripped. His impressions unfold rapidly, compressing into the space of heartbeats what took place over half the night, expanding to fill the gaps in my own memory.

When it's over, I open my eyes. Dom watches me, and I feel his awareness in mine, listening silently as I sort through all my conflicting emotions. I'm elated again by Dom's unexpected decision to come with me. I'm profoundly disturbed by all the questions raised by my mother's words and actions on the boat with the free men. I'm mystified by whatever I did to free us from our captors, and by whatever Dom did to revive me afterwards.

Most of all I'm stunned by the change in Dom. I've spent enough time in his mind over the last half moon that I thought I knew his nature: trusting and deferential, hopeful and sweet. But the wrenching anguish Dom felt as he held my lifeless body in his arms has changed him. He's glimpsed a darkness that once seen can never be entirely unseen.

He's quiet for a long time before he says, "Last night, when I knew you were …" I realize he can't bring himself to say I was dead. I understand; it's too confusing. If I was dead before, what does that make me now?

He can't find words, but he doesn't have to. As he remembers, I feel it all: wave after crushing wave of anger and despair. I reach for him, cradling his head against my heart. His arms wrap tight around me. He says, "I'm sorry."

I say, "Why?"

He says, "I couldn't let you go, but I know how much it hurts you to stay."

I close my eyes, stroking his hair, drawing his awareness gently into mine to calm him. I have no idea yet what to think about the last memory he showed me, of the woman and the man he left behind in that other world.

At last I say, "Don't be sorry. I never meant to leave you like that. We're going to find our way out of here together. I promise."

We lie in stillness for a long time. Beneath the soft sounds of our breathing, I hear the Voice. Usually its awareness pulls mine so hard that I lose my sense of self, but with Dom in my arms, I find to my surprise that I remain anchored in my own body. I listen, and Dom listens through me as the Voice says,

We are the bridge joining light to darkness.
We are the wheel turning season to season.
We are the threads binding realm to realm.
We are creator, preserver, destroyer of worlds.

Together you shall seek us, find us, know us.
Together you shall amplify us.
Together you shall weave us through the many worlds.
Together you shall answer our call.

The words repeat endlessly, until at last Dom says, "What do you think it means?"

It's impossible for me to answer Dom without remembering all my mother's warnings. She taught me that the Voice wants to control all, that it enslaves its servants by making them powerless to resist its commands. But how can I trust anything my mother taught me, after what she tried to do to us last night?

I remember Dom's words at the start of our journey. *The Mohirai teach that the Voice works toward its own purposes, in its own time. If the Mohirai are right, shouldn't you try to understand what the Voice wants? Maybe you can work with the Voice, rather than fight against it.* Could Dom be right? Maybe I should try listening to him more.

But there's an awful lot Dom still doesn't know. Maybe the best I can do for now is listen and draw my own conclusions.

So I listen. And as I listen to the Voice for myself, I hear not only its command but its promise. The Voice promises knowledge—and not only knowledge, but companionship on the path to knowledge. For the Voice commands us to answer its call *together*.

Perhaps I'm a fool to trust the Voice's promises or obey its commands. But it seems to me that the Voice has already fulfilled one of its promises. The Voice led me to Dom and Dom to me, so we can answer its call together.

I'm grateful for this gift of companionship, and in my gratitude I find myself truly open to the Voice's call for the first time. I'm not sure whether it's me or the Voice speaking through me when I answer Dom's question.

I say, "The Voice wants to be heard in every world."

Dom considers this uncertainly. He says, "But what does it want from us?"

I'm not quite certain, but I hazard a guess. "Maybe it wants us to find those other worlds," I say, unable to suppress the excitement I always feel at the start of a new job.

Dom gives me a knowing look. "Or maybe that's what *you* want," he says.

I laugh. "So what if it is?" I say. "Two things can be true."

"Fair enough," he says. "But maybe sometimes you could try wanting something a little easier."

I consider him for a long moment. I think, *There is one thing I want that might be a little easier.*

I look at him. He looks at me.

Interesting, he thinks. *Very interesting.*

I decide to lead, knowing he'll follow. *May I touch you?* I think.

He can't help laughing, and neither can I. He thinks, *I thought you'd never ask.*

Tentatively, I reach for Dom's hands. The emotion that flows between us in this moment is warm and bright as sunlight. It's the first time I've let myself share this kind of love with anyone, and it's exhilarating. Each sense awakens fully, amplified by the potent mix of pharmaka and desire.

Dom's fingertips trace the lines of my brow, my cheek, my neck. I close my eyes, feeling what he feels as he memorizes me by touch. He takes gentle hold of my hips and draws me closer. I wind my arms around his neck and draw him closer.

As we kiss, my awareness slips inside of his, and his inside of mine. We glimpse what lies ahead, but it's enough for now to savor this moment, finding the perfect fit between us for the first time, losing our selves together.

THE ARTIFEX AND THE MUSE
PART TWO

THE PATH OF MYSTERIES

Ay, me! For aught that I could ever read,
Could ever hear by tale or history,
The course of true love never did run smooth.

— Lysander, *A Midsummer Night's Dream* (1595)
by William Shakespeare

THE FIRST BRIDGE

As Dom and I kiss for the first time, my desire drowns out my better judgment. The opportunity to have him is too tempting, here in the privacy of our tent, nestled in our cozy bedrolls. The High Priestess Serapen excused us from camp chores this morning to give our injuries time to heal. My trio sisters think we're still asleep, recovering our strength. No one should disturb us until well past midday.

Considering the spectacular failure of our escape attempt last night, perhaps Dom and I should spend this rare time alone plotting our next move more carefully. But after all we've suffered since our journey began, haven't we earned this one moment of pleasure together?

Dom's awareness enters mine through the inner door unlocked by pharmaka, flooding me with his arousal, which amplifies my own. In a single smooth motion, he rolls me onto my back, pressing me into the ground with his weight. I suppress the reflexive impulse to defend myself. The last time Dom pinned me down like this, we were wrestling for control of my knife in the midst of my overdose. I exhale slowly. Relax, Ava. That's all in the past. This is now.

Golden sunlight streams through the canvas tent walls, gleaming on Dom's mussed halo of curls, his long eyelashes, his smooth brown skin. He smiles down at me. Tentatively, I slide my hands around his broad shoulders. After sharing a tent, a saddle, and my mind with this boy for the past half moon, everything about him should be entirely familiar to me. Yet something's different.

Were you always this beautiful? I think, studying his deep-set eyes, tracing the shape of his full lips with my fingertips. His ears redden. His expression turns bashful. I stifle a giggle. Yes, I suppose he was always this beautiful. I hadn't let myself see it until now. I weave my fingers through the curls at the nape of his neck and draw him back down into our kiss, breathing in the layers of his scent: leather and woodsmoke, apples and grass, the incongruously refined note of Muse Thalia's perfumed bathing pharmaka.

I usually avoid manipulating Dom through our bond, but I decide to encourage him a little, lending him my confidence, which restores his own. He slips one warm hand under my tunic, tracing his fingertips along the contours of my hip, my waist, my breast. Did he always touch me with this intoxicating mix of eagerness and gentleness? Spirits, I want him.

It's impossible to decide whether kissing or undressing is more urgent. We compromise by doing both at once, sitting up to wriggle free of unnecessary garments. Tunics, leggings, and underclothes join the tangle of wool blankets at our feet.

The only downside to our nakedness is that it reveals the extent of the damage we took last night. The scrapes and cuts on Dom's cheek and shoulder look painful to me, but he's hardly aware of his own injuries because he can't look away from the livid bruises covering my belly, arms, and legs.

They're all superficial wounds, I think, tipping his chin up so his eyes meet mine. *We'll heal. Don't worry.*

Carefully, Dom embraces me. I fit myself into his lap, wrapping my legs around him, resting my cheek against his unharmed shoulder. Neither of us can see the other's injuries now, which helps us both relax.

I close my eyes, feeling the rhythm of his heartbeat against mine. He unties the leather band at the end of my braid and runs his fingers through my unbound hair as he trails kisses down my neck. I knead the muscles of his thighs with long slow strokes of my palms. The pulse of anticipation that runs through him echoes through me. My mind drifts pleasantly.

Do you want to keep going? he thinks.

△▽△

At last. As Ava and I kiss for the first time, the struggle to restrain my feelings for her is over.

Every moment since our accident with binding pharmaka has been full of Ava—her clever thoughts and quick temper swirling through my mind, her animated voice and bright laughter surrounding me, her body pushing and pulling and pressing into mine. For the past half moon, though, she's tried to keep me at arm's length, despite the near-constant physical contact she needs from me to manage the pain caused by her overdose of binding pharmaka.

Thoughts pass so easily between our minds through our bond that it's impossible for me to keep secrets from Ava. She knew almost as soon as I knew that what I want from her is more than friendship. Until this morning, though, she seemed to want nothing more than friendship from me. I understood her reasons, of course; our three-way entanglement with the Voice in all is difficult enough to manage without the added complication of greater intimacy between the two of us.

Out of respect for Ava's wishes, I've tried to suppress my unanswered feelings for her. But now, as I feel the first stirrings of her desire for me, my own desire rises readily in answer.

I can't abandon all restraint, though; I'm too acutely aware of Ava's injuries. Carefully, I reposition her under me, sensitive to the raw scrapes on her wrists and ankles. She flinches briefly as I roll her onto her back, but she doesn't resist me. Tentatively, I slide my hand under her tunic. As I trace the taut curves of her body, my fingers graze the fist-sized bruise blooming over her navel.

Ava can't remember the three free men who did this to her last night, or what happened to her during our struggle to defend ourselves from them. The High Priestess Serapen had to unbind Ava's memory of all that so she could revive her. But I briefly glimpsed two of the men's faces in the moonlight: the burly man with the crooked nose and the slim man with the high brow. My jaw clenches in fury at the thought of them. With effort, I push them from my mind, focusing on Ava's face instead, calming myself with the knowledge that she's safe here now with me.

I wouldn't usually try to influence Ava using pharmaka, but I can't stop myself from sharing my calm with her through our bond. She exhales slowly, studying me with an expression I haven't seen before. *Were you always this beautiful?* she thinks.

Self-consciousness disorients me. Is she teasing me? Oh, spirits, have I misunderstood what she wants? Her eyes sparkle with amusement. I freeze, mortified.

But she draws me down to kiss her again, driving away my doubt with her hunger. I relax, savoring sensations I've only imagined until now: the sweetness of her tongue between my lips, the softness of her breasts under my hands, the invitation of her thighs around my waist.

Ava pulls my tunic off over my head. I slide her leggings down her hips. We've had to help each other undress many times since our journey began, but never with permission to look and touch this way. So we look and we touch, shedding layers until there's nothing left between us. The pleasure of my anticipation is marred only by the dark bruises on her skin.

They're all superficial wounds, she thinks, catching my eye. *We'll heal. Don't worry.*

So I try not to worry. Carefully, I draw her into my lap. She twines her arms and legs around me, pulling me closer. I kiss her forehead, her cheek, her earlobe, breathing in the salt and cedar scent of her as I work my way down her neck. It takes all my self-control to go slowly as she kneads my thighs, awakening my senses, encouraging my urgency. Ava's tolerance for pain is far greater than mine, but as hungry as she is for me, I don't want to hurt her in my eagerness. *Do you want to keep going?* I think.

She trembles. I pull back a little so I can see her face. "Ava?" I say. "What's wrong?"

Her eyelids flutter. Her lips turn blue. She slumps in my arms. Her skin turns cold against mine.

No, no, no, not again.

△▽△

Dom thinks, *Do you want to keep going?*

His words echo in my mind, thrumming hidden strands of my awareness. A pull in my heart tugs me inward from my edges. For a moment I try to resist the pull, but it's inexorable as the tide. I'm vanishing. Or is it the tent around me that's vanishing? Or the entire world beneath me that's vanishing?

What remains after everything else has vanished is a formless nothingness, outside of time, beyond all trouble, devoid of questions or answers. But at the center of this restful nothingness lies an irresistible energy: a distant light growing steadily closer.

From the light, the Voice in all calls endlessly.

We are the bridge joining light to darkness.

We are the wheel turning season to season.
We are the threads binding realm to realm.
We are creator, preserver, destroyer of worlds.

Together you shall seek us, find us, know us.
Together you shall amplify us.
Together you shall weave us through the many worlds.
Together you shall answer our call.

The light summons me, surrounds me, swallows me.

I am elsewhere. And, at first, I'm too immersed in the delicious sensation of warmth, contentedness, and coziness to bother wondering where elsewhere might be.

Since my overdose with binding pharmaka, I've learned to expect any call from the Voice to end in terrible pain, weakness, and cold. But this time feels different. Has the Voice sent me a pleasant dream for a change? I rest a moment with my eyes closed, wanting nothing more than to linger here, without doing, without thinking, without knowing.

But when strong hands slide over my bare backside, my eyes open wide in alarm. I'm momentarily distracted from the pair of presumptuous hands by what I see—or, rather, by what I can't see. What is this place? It looks like some kind of room, but I can't bring the walls into focus. I blink several times, trying to clear my vision. Despite the bright daylight streaming through the large windows on one wall, everything is so blurry.

I look down and see Dom lying naked beneath me on an enormous bed with pale blue sheets. We're wrapped around each other in an embrace far more intimate than the one I left behind in the tent. Our first kiss must be long past us, given my present position astride him.

I open my mouth to ask Dom what's happened, but as my blurry vision draws him into slightly better focus, I forget my question entirely. I squint down at him in confusion. Although many things about him are familiar, this man looks far older than the Dom I know. The planes of his face are sharper, the muscles of his neck and shoulders hardened by physical labor. He gazes up at me with an expression that makes him look somehow ancient. Innumerable impressions of him flash through my mind; they would feel like memories, except all of them are new to me. I'm overwhelmed by the depth of my feelings for this other-Dom, who is at once familiar and unfamiliar.

I study his face, touching his brow, his cheek, his lips. Playfully, other-Dom catches the tip of my finger between his teeth. I can't help smiling at his mischievous expression, but my smile fades when I notice my hands for the first time. They're strangely pale, delicate hands, with polished fingernails painted in intricate patterns of green and blue.

Spirits! I think. *Whose body is this?*

Other-Dom's brow furrows slightly as he studies my face. He lets my fingertip slip from his teeth. Cautiously, he says, "Ava?"

An apprehensive prickle runs down my spine. "Who else would I be?" I say.

This should be a rhetorical question, but other-Dom's expression suggests a more complicated answer. I hold my unfamiliar hands up before me, studying my palms. This can't be right. These hands are far too soft and weak to be my own. These hands have clearly never climbed a tree, wielded a knife, or held the reins. The warmth drains out of my body. My pulse races. My appallingly weak little hands tremble.

"You're all right. Calm down. Breathe," says other-Dom, using the same tone that my Dom uses to soothe horses. He gently slides my naked body off of his and sits up facing me. Before I've even realized I'm shivering, he pulls a blanket up from the foot of the bed and wraps it around me like a cloak. He rubs my icy fingers between his warm palms in a motion so practiced he must have done it a thousand times before. "Where were you, before you were here?" he says.

"I was ..." My words trail off as a swirling fog envelops my mind. Familiar memories of Dom emerge briefly through the fog, only to be replaced with unfamiliar memories of this other-Dom and this other-self in this other-place. Disoriented, I look up to meet the steady, patient gaze of the man sitting across from me. Is he my Dom, or other-Dom? Or is other-Dom my Dom? Uncertainly, I say, "I was ... with you. We were ... in a tent. On the banks of the Purattu river." But, no, that can't be right. I wasn't with this other-Dom. He wasn't with me in the tent on the riverbank, was he?

Was he?

Other-Dom's expression turns inward, as if he's calculating something. "How old are you?" he says.

Answering this requires another difficult search through the fog in my mind. Why is it so hard for me to remember things right now? I almost say sixteen summers before remembering that the autumn equinox passed on Calling Day. "Seventeen summers," I say.

Other-Dom winces, clearly unsettled by my answer. He climbs quickly out of the big bed. As he turns away from me, I catch a glimpse of his back. Tattooed across the weather-beaten skin of his shoulders is a pair of outstretched wings. These marks should prove this man can't be my Dom. And yet, when he turns to face me, the sight of his naked body floods my mind again with thoughts so vivid they're indistinguishable from my own memories: those broad hands caressing my waist, that massive chest beneath mine, those tender lips grazing my neck. Heat rises to my cheeks. I bite my lip and avert my eyes.

Focus, Ava. Focus. Despite the uncanny similarities between him and my Dom, this man is a stranger. These impressions flooding my mind can't be my memories of him. I shouldn't feel any attachment to him. I shouldn't trust him. Whatever is happening to me right now must be some new trick of the Voice. I need to keep up my guard, control these wild feelings, and focus on the problem at hand. How can I find my way back to the safety of my own body, in my own tent, with my own Dom?

I open my mouth to form a question, but when other-Dom's dark eyes meet mine, I can't recall what I meant to say. I remember him, somehow, as though I've known him forever. I feel a depth of love for him that I've never experienced before. I trust him more than anyone else I've ever met.

He waits for me to speak until at last I shake my head, at a loss for words. Kindly, he says, "Is this your first time traveling between branches?"

Curiosity restores my voice at last. "Branches?" I say. "I don't know what you mean. Where am I? What is going on?"

Other-Dom glances at a white circular object hanging above an open door that connects this room to a room beyond. It's too far away for me to see the object clearly, but the blurry symbols around its circumference and long black stroke across its center remind me of a sundial. He says, "I don't know whether there's enough time for me to explain. You usually can't stay here long, when you're this inexperienced with branch travel."

Perplexed, I say, "You make it sound like I come here a lot."

"You do," he says.

"No, I've never been here before," I say. Although as soon as I say it, I'm not so sure. Didn't I see a room like this, and some other-Dom like him, in my vision on Calling Day?

Other-Dom says, "Even if this is your first visit to our branch, I doubt it will be your last. Emmie and I have recorded hundreds of other-Avas' visits here."

What on Dulai is he talking about? I'd better start with the basics. "Who's Emmie?" I say.

Other-Dom runs his fingers through his hair, as though he's struggling to find the right words. "I guess I should … introduce you," he says. He reaches over to the bedside table, picks up a delicate object made of glass and bright blue enamel, and hands it to me.

I hold up the unfamiliar object, wondering what I'm supposed to do with it. Seeing my confusion, other-Dom takes it back from me, unfolds it, and extends it to me once more. Ah. These must be eye glasses, a bit like the ones Muse Arkhi gave us to protect our eyes from the sandstorms as our caravan crossed the Subartu Desert. I wonder what protection these glasses are supposed to offer; they look far too delicate to shield my eyes from a sandstorm. I slip the blue frames over my ears and nose, blinking in surprise as the bedroom around me snaps into sharp focus.

"Better?" says other-Dom.

"Much better," I say. With the help of the glasses, I see other-Dom more clearly. Fine wrinkles form at the corners of his eyes when he smiles at me. The faint pattern of worry lines that often form on my own Dom's forehead are etched deep into this other-Dom's brow. A few silver threads gleam amidst the darker strands of his close-cropped curls. I try to keep my gaze from wandering beyond his face, but I can't help noticing that, despite these signs of age, the rest of his body radiates vigorous health.

Other-Dom leans over me, snapping me out of my reverie. He wraps his long arms around me, lifting me from the bed like I'm a child. "What are you doing?" I say indignantly. "I can get up on my own." I push against him, but I'm not nearly strong enough to escape his grip.

He looks down at me with a resigned expression. "Go ahead," he says, carefully setting me back down on the bed. He withdraws his hands but remains within arm's reach, watching me.

I toss away the warm blanket bundled around my shoulders, swing my legs over the edge of the mattress, and stand. My heart pounds erratically. I sway unsteadily for a moment before I sink back down onto the bed, gasping for breath.

Stricken, I look up at other-Dom. He looks down at me patiently. "You need my help," he says, as though that's not obvious. He offers me his hand again. I accept it begrudgingly. His palms tingle against my skin as he pours his strength into me through our bond. My heartbeat steadies. My breathing slows. I've resigned myself to relying on my own Dom for strength like this since my overdose, but that doesn't make it any easier for me to accept help from other-Dom. I have no desire to be in debt to a stranger, but I don't see any other choice.

Slowly, I stand. This time, I'm able to keep my balance. Other-Dom leads me across a thick, soft rug of cream-colored wool toward the full-length mirror leaning against one wall of the bedroom. Gesturing toward the glass, he says, "Ava, meet Emmie Bridges."

I gaze at the unfamiliar face and unclothed body in the mirror. Before my overdose with binding pharmaka, I might have been alarmed to see a stranger where my own reflection should be. This isn't even close to the strangest thing I've experienced in the last half moon, though, so I manage to remain calm as I study the woman looking back at me. Her expression—my expression?—is penetrating. Her bright blue glasses accentuate her most striking feature: vivid green eyes, the color of sunlight through spring leaves.

"Emmie Bridges," I say, trying to imitate the accent other-Dom used when saying her name. I wonder whether Bridges is a title, like Mohira or Artifex. Tentatively, I touch the cool surface of the mirror so Emmie and I stand palm to palm, examining each other.

The unpredictable way the Mohirai age makes it more difficult to guess a woman's age than a man's. Other-Dom looks like a man of about forty summers. Emmie looks younger than him, but older than me. Is she twenty summers? Thirty? Hard to say.

A streak of cobalt blue dyed into her dark chin-length hair frames Emmie's face, which is more heart-shaped and less angular than my own. She's a little taller than I am, though still petite compared to other-Dom; her head barely reaches his shoulder. The shadows around her eyes and beneath her cheekbones give the impression that she's lost an unhealthy amount of weight. Access to food has been unpredictable for most of my childhood, so I've always been lean, but Emmie's figure is approaching gaunt. I run my hands—her hands?—down her sides, feeling her ribs and hipbones uncomfortably close to the surface, touching her sharp elbows and knobby wrists. The frailty of her naked body makes me uneasy.

The longer I look at Emmie's face, the harder it is for me to remember my own. I search her wide green eyes in the mirror. Is she inside this body somewhere, waiting for me to leave? Has my awareness pushed hers elsewhere? Or are we simply different parts of a single awareness?

This last question disorients me. Is that my thought or hers?

Emmie? I think. *Are you here?*

I wait, listening closely, but I hear only my own thoughts in my mind. I break eye contact with Emmie's reflection and look at other-Dom. "Does she know I'm here?" I say.

"I don't know," he says. "Sometimes you two are aware of each other, and she remembers you clearly. Sometimes she remembers only fragments. Sometimes she seems to be entirely absent while you're here, and she remembers nothing afterwards. Memory is … unpredictable for her."

"What happened to her?" I say. "She looks sick. Her body feels sick."

Other-Dom nods. "Binding pharmaka overdose," he says.

"How?" I say, dismayed. The circumstances of my own overdose were so improbable. How could anyone else have been as absurdly unlucky as I was?

"It's a long story," he says with a sigh. "It was an accident, years ago. At first, small amounts of unbinding pharmaka helped Emmie manage the worst of the pain from her overdose. But using unbinding pharmaka comes at a cost to memory. Her memory loss has been worsening steadily. It's becoming harder for her to find her way back, when her mind wanders. She still has good days, but …" The muscles around his eyes tighten, as if he's in pain. "There haven't been a lot of good days lately."

I frown at the mirror. Emmie is the only other person I've ever heard of who's experienced an overdose like mine. Is this frail woman in the reflection a glimpse of my own future?

The only thing that stops my mind from spiraling into darker questions is the grief in other-Dom's voice. I'm surprised to find that my desire to comfort him is stronger than my fear for myself. "I'm sorry," I say, squeezing his hand. "I wish there was something I could do to help."

"You are helping," he says, running his thumb gently over my knuckles. "I think Emmie would have given up on our great work long ago without your visits. Every time you return, you build a new bridge between our branch and yours."

Puzzled, I say, "What are these branches you keep talking about?"

Other-Dom meets my gaze in the mirror. "I'm afraid that would take ages to answer and lifetimes to truly understand," he says. "Branches are among the greater mysteries. But what's important about branches is that each one gives us some opportunity to answer our callings from the Voice and deepen our understanding of its purpose. Bridges between branches allow us to combine the knowledge earned on one branch with the knowledge earned on many others. Our great work is to preserve the knowledge of many branches so that someday our knowledge will lead us to freedom from this." The sweeping gesture of his hand encompasses the two of us, the place where we stand, and whatever lies outside this room.

Not all of his words make sense to me, but other-Dom says *freedom* with a conviction that stirs my deepest longing. I grew up believing my mother's dream that she and I would someday live in freedom from the Voice in all and the Mohirai who enforce its will. Unfortunately, my faith in my mother has caused me enough trouble over the last half moon to make me skeptical of anyone chasing dreams of freedom.

Cautiously, I say, "What's this great work you're doing here, exactly?"

Other-Dom glances at the sundial-like circle over the door again. "Maybe there's enough time to explain a little more, at least," he says. "Come on."

He pulls a pair of black bundles out of the chest of drawers beside the mirror and hands one bundle to me. It must be some sort of clothing, though I've never seen fabric like this: finer than silk and stretchy as spiderwebs. I have no idea how to put on these garments, but other-Dom gives me a hand. Once I'm dressed in what I suppose might pass for a shirt, leggings, and slippers, I still feel naked. It's as if I've simply traded one skin for another.

I glance at myself—Emmie's self?—in the mirror. From neck to ankle and shoulder to wrist, I appear to have been dipped in ink. I'd look almost like a shadow, except I'm studded here and there with tiny jewels of green and blue connected by gleaming silver threads. Other-Dom helps me slip the matching stretchy black gloves over my hands, so only my face remains visible, hovering over the dark abstraction of my body.

"Is this really what people wear here?" I say, turning to other-Dom. He's dressed himself in a set of skin-tight black clothes, gloves, and slippers nearly identical to mine.

"Not all the time," he says, sliding black-framed glasses over his eyes. "But these clothes help us immerse ourselves in the alternet." He pronounces *alternet* in the same strange flat accent he used to say Emmie's name.

"What's the alternet?" I say, wiggling my fingers tentatively inside the gloves. A warm tingling sensation runs from my fingertips up to my neck. I can't tell whether the warmth comes from my own skin or from the fabric hugging my body.

"The alternet is easier to experience than to describe," he says, gesturing for me to follow him.

He leads me out of the bedroom and down a bright hallway. Through my slippers, the smooth grey floor radiates heat into the soles of my feet.

We emerge from the hallway into a large sunlit room of honey-colored wood and crystal-clear glass. One wall of the room is made entirely of windows that stretch from the floor to the high ceiling. A half-circle of deep couches and cozy chairs faces the windows.

Outside the windows stand four magnificent trees, unlike any trees I've seen before. Their massive trunks, clad in deeply grooved reddish bark, soar arrow-straight toward the sun. Beyond these trees, the land drops away, as though this room is perched at the edge of a cliff.

I gaze through the trees at an expansive view that stretches to the western horizon. Far below us spreads a flatland, embroidered with roads and encrusted with buildings. To the west, across a wind-ruffled bay spanned by bridges, rises the distinctive profile of the city of glass towers.

My lips part in wonder. I've seen that city so many times in dreams. Now there it stands, solid and real as any place I've ever seen in Dulai. The city must be less than a quarter day's ride from here.

"That's San Francisco," says other-Dom, gesturing toward the city skyline.

"San Francisco," I murmur, amazed to know the city's name at last.

Other-Dom leads me across the sunlit room into an unlit hallway. He says something in a language I don't understand, but before I can ask what he means, a light brightens directly overhead. Startled, I look up to see a glowing white disc in the ceiling.

"What kind of lamp is that?" I say.

"There's no word for that in our language," says other-Dom. "Here on Earth, in the English tongue, that's called a lightbulb. Or a light-emitting diode, if you want to be specific."

I repeat the strange words slowly: *Earth, English, lightbulb, diode*. Other-Dom nods, looking mildly amused.

I follow him down the hallway and descend a flight of stairs. At the bottom of the stairs stands a closed black door.

Other-Dom presses his palm to a shiny black panel beside the door. The panel glows at his touch, displaying symbols in white and green. He taps a pattern onto its surface. An unseen bell chimes, and the door retracts into the wall like a turtle into its shell. He steps through the doorway.

I hesitate outside the threshold, uncertain how the door opened and whether it might snap shut again.

"Don't worry," he says, beckoning me inside. "The door won't close on you."

Cautiously, I step through. The door closes smoothly behind me.

Other-Dom and I stand inside a small windowless room. Every surface is a uniform grey, featureless except for a seam that outlines the door through which we entered. A gentle grey glow like twilight emanates from every surface. The floor appears to be smooth and level, but it's yielding and springy beneath my feet, like I'm standing on the taut muscle of an enormous animal.

I crouch down to examine the unusual floor. On closer inspection, the smooth surface reveals itself to be covered in tiny, tightly-packed wrinkles, like the surface of a brain.

"What's this?" I say, pressing the floor with my gloved hand. My palm sinks about a knuckle's depth into the springy wrinkled surface before I hit a harder layer underneath. This layer pushes back against my hand, vibrating faintly, as if protesting my intrusion. I withdraw my hand. The floor smooths away my handprint, like a wave erasing a footprint from beach sand.

Other-Dom gestures around the room, indicating the floor, walls, and ceiling. "This is a spliner," he says. "The space can become almost anything imaginable. The spliner and these immerger clothes we're wearing help us access experiences in the alternet. It's a bit like sharing thoughts or memories with binding pharmaka, but using arts of tekhnologia instead."

"Wouldn't all this be simpler to do using binding pharmaka?" I say. This room and these clothes add a lot of complexity to something my own Dom and I usually accomplish simply by touching each other and sharing thoughts through our bond.

"It would be simpler in some ways," he says. "But Emmie's mind has sustained a lot of damage from the use of so much binding and unbinding pharmaka. Tekhnologia isn't as elegant as binding pharmaka for sharing thoughts, but its effects on the mind are less invasive and more easily reversed."

I nod, beginning to understand. I've had enough firsthand experience of pharmaka's side effects to appreciate how tekhnologia might be a better alternative.

He continues, "While I'm sharing experiences with you in the alternet, our bodies will stay here. But it will look and feel like we're somewhere else. You may be disoriented at first." He speaks slowly, deliberately, waiting for my acknowledgement. I'm surprised to hear a man using the tone of instruction, which I've only ever heard the priestesses use.

His tone prompts me to respond using Mohiran temple formalities I haven't spoken since childhood. "I have listened, and I have heard, brother," I say. It feels strange to address other-Dom this way, like he's my elder and teacher, since I'm slightly the elder and usually the teacher with my Dom. But somehow, in this place, our roles are reversed.

Other-Dom extends his hand to me. "Let's begin, then," he says, with natural authority, like a priestess wielding the tone of command. The younger Dom I know always speaks with complete deference to women. Hearing the same voice transformed by confidence astonishes me. I'm surprised to discover I like the sound of a man in charge, at least when it's a man I trust. I take his hand.

He speaks several more words I don't recognize, which I suppose must belong to the English tongue. The grey twilight of the spliner dims gradually until we're swallowed by pure darkness.

All right? he thinks, squeezing my hand.

Don't worry about me, I think. *Darkness is a thief's best friend.* The complete darkness amplifies my pharmaka-enhanced awareness of other-Dom's sensations, so I feel the amused smile that spreads across his face in response.

He speaks again. Pure white light swirls into the darkness around us. Our bodies are nowhere to be seen, but the warm pressure of other-Dom's gloved hand clasped around mine remains.

He speaks a third time. Mixed in with the unknown English words are a few words I recognize: *Ava, Dom, Dulai.*

The bright light dissolves like a midday fog, and a new landscape materializes around us. I find myself standing barefoot in dusty soil, surrounded by a rustling grove of fruit trees. Late afternoon sunlight warms my skin, though there's a touch of autumn chill in the breeze. The delicate perfume of fresh water hangs in the air. An unseen kuku bird calls from somewhere nearby. At the center of the grove, beside a clear spring, grows a pomegranate tree, its gnarled branches heavy with ripe red fruit.

I step toward the tree. Silk slides across my shoulders as I move. I look down and discover I'm wearing bright saffron robes. An intricately embroidered scarlet mantle rests on my shoulders.

"Why am I dressed like a Mohira?" I say, glancing back at other-Dom. He's wearing rough workmen's clothing: a dusty tunic, heavy leather toolbelt, sturdy work boots. His short-cropped silver-streaked hair has been replaced by a wild tangle of dark curls that nearly touch his shoulders. The deep lines are all but erased from his brow, the sharp edges and dark hollows of his features softened by youth. He appears closer to twenty summers than forty.

"I made that avatar you're wearing to show what you looked like the last day I saw you, on my branch," he says, nodding toward me. "You were a Mohira then. I'm guessing this is close to what you look like at seventeen summers, on your own branch."

I look down at my fingers, which I've been sliding absent-mindedly along the textured hem of my scarlet mantle. I'm relieved to see not Emmie's soft fingers but my own: brown, lean, and strong. I hold up my hands before my eyes, then pull back the hem of my robe to examine my feet.

I wiggle my toes, laughing at them in delight. "You made this … avatar?" I say, pronouncing the unfamiliar word slowly.

"I did," says other-Dom. "What do you think?"

I run my fingers appraisingly through the long curls of my unbound hair, stretch my arms and legs, and take a slow turn where I stand. Apart from the unfamiliar priestess robes, everything else about this body seems to be in order, down to details I never would have bothered to recall. The constellation of freckles that run down the inside of my left forearm. The hard calluses across my palms. The white scar on the top of my right foot from a climbing accident my eighth summer. I look at other-Dom. "It's wonderful," I say. "Very realistic. Is this the great work you were talking about? Making these avatars, these landscapes?"

"Not exactly," says other-Dom. He beckons me with a gesture. I follow at his side along a narrow footpath through the grove. After only a few steps, a sharp pain flares in my chest. I wince and slow down to catch my breath.

Noticing my discomfort, other-Dom pauses on the footpath and takes my hand. His fingers tug at my wrist. I'm confused by what he's doing until I recognize the sensation: he's peeling off my left glove. I can't see the glove here in the alternet, but I can still feel the stretchy fabric sliding off my skin. He presses his bare palm to mine, lending me more of his strength through our bond.

Other-Dom and I wait together until the pain in my chest—Emmie's chest?—fades. We resume walking along the dirt path until we reach a lookout point atop a rocky outcropping. Here we stop. He takes a seat on the stone ledge, dangling his legs over the edge. I suspect that the sheer drop below his feet can't be real, but even so I'm careful not to stumble as I take a seat beside him. I rest my bare hand on the warm rock alongside other-Dom's hand, maintaining skin contact to keep Emmie's pain at bay.

I look at other-Dom expectantly. He appears lost in thought. At last I nudge him and say, "The work. You said you would explain the great work that you're doing here. So explain."

Other-Dom blinks, returning from wherever his mind has wandered. Slowly, he says, "Before her accident, Emmie was … what we might call in our tongue an artist of tekhnologia. She was a creator of alternet domains.

"After her accident, she became obsessed with preserving memories using the alternet. I think the work made the loss of her own memories easier for her to endure, in the beginning. But the scope of the work has changed as the damage to her own memory has worsened. Lately, she cares less about preserving her own memories and more about finding the patterns in common between memories."

Other-Dom and I look out together at the expansive view before us. A footpath winds down from our lookout spot to a small cluster of stone dwellings gathered at the base of this hill. A tidy patchwork of orchards and fields spreads out beyond these dwellings for a short distance before giving way to the open grassland of a vast plain.

Though the humble farming village below us is unfamiliar to me, I recognize the mountains surrounding us from my years roaming the wilderness with my mother. The profile of the Urashtu Range dominates the western horizon. In the middle distance, rising alone from the grassy plain, is Velkanos, the Mountain of Muses. The temple city just visible on the mountain's lower slopes is the final destination of the Mohiran caravan I've been unsuccessfully trying to escape for the past half moon. The snow-capped summit of Velkanos winks at me in the bright sunlight. I lower my eyes, suppressing a shiver at the memory of the dark tunnels hidden within that mountain.

My gaze settles on the smaller sights within arm's reach. These things near at hand are just as beautiful as the impressive vista beyond, in their way: the tufts of waving grasses growing in the cracks of the rock outcropping, the ants investigating a bird-pecked apple on the ground, the tracks of a lynx that passed this way, headed toward the spring at the center of the grove. I trace a line in the thin layer of sandy soil beside me. The gritty texture, the dusty sweet smell of the sunbaked ground, the soft scrape of my fingernail against the tawny pink bedrock, it all seems so real. I've shared thoughts and memories with my Dom before—intentionally and unintentionally—using binding pharmaka, but most of what we've shared between us has been smaller in scale than this place. I can't imagine what sort of effort must be required to make something so large and detailed.

"So … is this place from one of Emmie's memories?" I say, indicating our surroundings.

"No," he says. "This is a place from my memory, a place Emmie asked me to show her once."

"Why are you showing it to me?" I say, studying his expression closely.

He settles his warm hand over mine. I feel his desire to share something with me through our bond, but for some reason he resists. All he says is, "You made me a promise here, once."

"I'm sorry," I say, shaking my head. "I don't remember."

He gives me a small, sad smile before his gaze returns to the distant mountains. "I think you will, when the time is right," he says. "If I've learned anything, following you life after life, it's that you keep your promises."

Spirits, talking with him is almost as frustrating as talking with Serapen. The more he tries to explain, the less I understand. I focus on the words that seem most significant. "What do you mean, life after life?" I say. "What are you and Emmie—" A piercing pain in my chest cuts off my question. My heart flutters against my ribcage like a panicking bird, making me light-headed. I curl forward, hunching my shoulders, struggling to breathe.

My glasses slip off my nose, falling into my lap. The expansive alternet vista before me vanishes. I'm seated no longer on a rock ledge in the sunshine, but on a little grey step extruded from the previously level floor of the spliner, surrounded by the strange dull twilight emanating from the walls. My blurry peripheral vision spins slowly, dissolving the edges of the room. With every beat of my heart, the pain intensifies, expanding from within my chest until I can no longer tell where it is or where I am. Is this pain rooted in Emmie's ailing body, here on Earth? Or is this my own body's pain, somewhere back on Dulai?

Other-Dom sets aside his glasses and kneels before me. He rubs my hands slowly between his, a patient but weary expression in his eyes. His touch eases the pain in Emmie's chest slightly, but my sensation of spinning and dissolving continues to worsen. "You're all right," he says quietly. "You're returning to your own branch now. Calm down. Breathe."

"Wait," I say through gritted teeth, fighting to hold on to this moment, this place, this body. There's so much more I need to ask him, so much more I need to understand. "I don't want to leave yet. I want to stay here with you."

"I wish you could," he says. "But the art of traveling between branches takes training and practice to control, lifetimes to master."

I squeeze my eyes shut, fighting through my pain, focused on the one question that I realize now is of utmost importance. Through gasping breaths, I say, "Where— Where can I learn this art?"

"The Voice speaks through many teachers," says other-Dom. "Listen, and you will learn."

The kiss he presses to my forehead is the last thing I feel before all sensation vanishes.

I don't know how long I drift through that in-between place of darkness and stillness before I open my eyes with a start. The spliner is gone, and other-Dom is gone, though the sensation of his kiss lingers on my brow. I'm lying naked on my back in the tent, everything in sharp focus, including Dom—my Dom, this time —who looks down at me with a terrified expression on his face.

"Ava? Ava? Can you hear me?" he says, gripping my hand.

It's disconcerting to see Dom's youthful face while the memory of other-Dom's older face lingers in my mind. "D—Did you see th—that?" I say. Only when I hear my teeth chattering do I realize I'm freezing cold.

Dom pulls up the blanket from the foot of his bedroll and wraps it around us. "See what?" he says, pulling me into his arms, sharing his body heat with me.

This, I think, pressing my palm to his chest, letting the memory of what I just saw unreel between us.

Dom's eyes widen.

"Was that your memory?" I say, grasping for some explanation. Earlier this morning, Dom shared with me his memory of our disastrous encounter with my mother and the free men last night. There was a strange part of his memory that included a visit to a room very much like the one where I just saw other-Dom.

Dom shakes his head doubtfully. "I did see that bedroom," he says. "That man. That woman—the one he called Emmie. But everything that happened between them was different. I don't think what you saw is my memory."

I cover my eyes with my hand, wishing I could shut out all the confusing feelings about other-Dom this encounter stirred in me. Another memory of that bedroom flashes through my mind unbidden: the vision from my Calling Day of that other-Dom, sitting by that same bedside, looking at me with an expression of wrenching despair. The words Serapen spoke as she held me in the pool on Calling Day echo in my mind. *Don't look, Ava. It's too much, too soon.*

Icy dread spreads through me. My shivering worsens. I plant both hands on Dom's chest and push him away, even though I still crave his warmth. Through our bond, I feel his hurt and confusion as I distance myself from him. I'm not sure whether I'm trying to protect myself from him or protect him from me.

I sit up and hug my knees to my chest. "I don't think I can do this," I say. "Not yet. It's …" Damn this fickle body. Curse these eerie visions. Blast the—

"Shhh," says Dom, hushing my furious inner monologue. He sits up beside me, though he keeps a little space between us this time. "Look at me, Ava." Reluctantly, I look at him. "All I want is to be with you," he says. "In whatever way feels right. We don't have to do anything you don't want to do."

Oh, but I do want to. Or I did, anyway. It's just impossible while I'm wracked with shivering, drained of energy, so terribly weak. I feel Dom's desire for me fading into a desire to comfort me, but even his sweetness can't overcome my bitterness.

I try to forget my body's thwarted hunger for Dom, focusing instead on the tenderness for him that's taken root in me over the past half moon. I recognize the similarity of this feeling to the one that briefly overwhelmed me in the bedroom with other-Dom. Words can't convey its entirety, but a great deal more than words can pass between us through our bond. I wish I could have given Dom more, but at least I can still give him this.

I take his hand. "I love you," I say. *You know I love you, don't you?* I think.

Dom leans toward me and presses a kiss to my forehead, exactly where other-Dom just kissed me. *I know*, he thinks. "I love you, too," he says.

And I know he does. But the certainty of our love can't drive away my fear of where this love might lead us.

THE PATH OF MYSTERIES

"I LOVE YOU, TOO," I say, wishing Ava would let me take her into my arms again, wishing I could hold her restless mind here with me, wishing that what she just saw was nothing more than her imagination. Unfortunately, I can't cling to foolish wishes like these after what I did last night to bring her back to me.

You have asked it. We may give it. But there is a price. Do you accept it? The Voice's words to me last night, the words I heard first on our Calling Day, echo in my mind. Compelled by my own wish, but without knowing the price, I'd answered. *Yes. Yes. Yes, I do accept the price.* I don't understand what's happening to Ava, but my heart is heavy with the growing certainty that my choice has consequences not only for myself, but for her.

Ava's breathing turns into labored gasps. A cold sweat gleams on her forehead. Quickly, I kneel before her, gripping her wrists. I've helped Ava through many spells like this over the last half moon, and I've developed some skill at lending her my strength until her own returns. I focus all my attention on pouring my energy into her, but she worsens rapidly. Nothing I do seems to help. Her awareness inside of mine—usually so sharp, swift, and bright—now blurs, slows, and fades. Her eyelids flutter. She curls up in pain, dropping her forehead to her knees, swaying where she sits.

Alarmed, I say, "Ava?" She doesn't answer. Louder, I say, "Ava? Ava!"

She makes a wordless, groggy sound. "Mmmmm?"

"I'm taking you to Serapen," I say, hastily gathering up our clothes from the floor of the tent. I pull on my tunic and riding breeches before I attempt to dress Ava. This proves challenging; she's very disoriented.

"No … No …" she mutters, struggling weakly with me as I pull her tunic over her head and tug her hands through the sleeves. "I want … to stay here … with you."

I'm somewhat heartened by her familiar obstinance, until her head lolls to the side. "Mmmmm," she moans. "Why is this happening again?"

My stomach twists guiltily in answer, but I can't indulge my guilt right now. I can't let her lose consciousness again. I can't lose her again. I need to focus on getting her help.

I loop her arm around my shoulders and lift her up with me as I stand. Gripping her tight around the waist, I steer her out through the tent flap. My bare toes sink into the cool sand of the natural alcove beneath the river cliffs where we pitched the tent yesterday afternoon. Although it's a sunny day, there's a stiff breeze off the river. Ava's shivering worsens as the wind sweeps over her bare legs. Maybe I should have tried to dress her more warmly, but taking her to Serapen seems more urgent.

Although I'm bearing most of her weight, Ava makes it only a few steps before she stumbles. "Wait," she says, her voice tight with pain. "Please. Stop." She covers her eyes with her free hand, blocking out the bright daylight beyond the alcove. I've seen her in pretty much every extremity of exhaustion imaginable over the last half moon. I know how far she can push herself. But after what happened last night, I also know how pushing leads to breaking, so I stop.

"Let me carry you," I say. "Please, Ava."

"Not while I can still stand," she says. She takes a shuddery breath and attempts to push on, but her legs wobble under her.

I steady her again. "Can't you just let me—" I break off, seeing the blazing look she turns on me.

"Let you what?" she says, a note of warning in her voice. "Do everything for me?"

Patiently, I say, "You know that's not what I was going to say."

She inhales and exhales slowly. I'm not trying to eavesdrop, but I can't help overhearing as she thinks to herself, *Stop trying to pick a fight with him, Ava. All he's trying to do is help. All he ever tries to do is help. Though if he weren't so damned helpful, maybe none of this would have happened in the first pl—*

My guilt flares up again, interrupting Ava's inner monologue. She looks up at me, her eyes wide with contrition. "I didn't mean that, Dom," she says quietly.

"Thoughts don't lie," I say.

She shakes her head. "No, but still, this isn't your fault. If you hadn't tried to help me, I'd be dead."

Dead. Ava says it so glibly, but I haven't been able to say it yet. It's too confusing. If she was dead before, what does that make her now?

Overhearing my thought, Ava says, "I'm alive because of you, Dom. And I'm grateful. Truly. But you can't spend the rest of your life looking after me. I can take care of myself."

These last words are so ridiculous they would be comical if the reality weren't so depressing. Ava can't take a single step without my help right now. Still, I refrain from contradicting her.

We take a few breaths, trying to calm ourselves despite our innermost thoughts colliding in agitating ways. I focus on pouring more of my strength into Ava. She accepts my help as humbly as she can. We stand together, waiting for her to recover her balance. At last, she looks up at me with a strained smile. "Shall we try again?" she says.

We move forward, step by careful step through the sand until we emerge from the cool shade of the cliffs onto the sunny beach. Ava soaks in the warmth as I scan the riverfront for the High Priestess Serapen.

In a nearby cliff alcove, one trio of tired-looking novices—Narua, Bel, and Tashlu—works alongside Muse Thalia and Urshanabi. The other novices in our caravan weren't given the luxury of lounging through the morning like we did, even though they too lost a night's sleep on our account. Under Thalia's direction, the three girls unload provisions from a pair of wooden crates, portion them into smaller sacks, and load them into saddlebags.

Seeing me, Thalia inclines her head, a subdued greeting for the normally vivacious Muse of poetika. Perhaps the near loss of two novices has had a sobering effect on her. Or perhaps she's not yet recovered from the excess of wine she consumed last night. Urshanabi looks our way with solemn eyes; no trace remains of the merriment with which the wizened ferryman danced around the bonfire. The three girls don't even look up.

I lead us onward, continuing the search for Serapen. Ava leans against me; I keep a firm hold on her in case she stumbles again. Out on the sand, another trio of novices—Kor, Piroza, and Kishar—cleans and repairs horse tack. Alongside them, black-robed Muse Arkhi employs one of her arts of tekhnologia, attending to Nisaba's hooves with a set of sharp metal tools. The little mare must have injured her foot when the free men attacked us in the willow grove last night. Arkhi raises one dark hand to me in greeting as we walk by. The mesmerizing blue swirls on her pale palm flash briefly in the sunlight. The three girls working with her glance our way, but no one speaks to us.

I can't blame any of the girls for their unfriendliness toward me and Ava. Our escape attempt ruined what should have been a festive night for everyone, a chance to recuperate at the halfway point of our long journey to Velkanos.

We walk on until at last I spot the tall, angular figure of Serapen. The High Priestess stands just off the sandbar, knee-deep in the river, wearing nothing but her underclothes, reeling in a fishing net hand over hand. Beside her stand Ava's trio sisters—dark, statuesque Hanu and petite, freckle-cheeked Eumelia.

"Muse Serapen," I call.

Serapen, Hanu, and Eumelia look back at me. Serapen says something to the two girls as she coils her net neatly in her hands. A silvery trout caught in the bottom of her net thrashes as it emerges from the river. My stomach growls at the sight; I haven't eaten anything since I ran after Ava last night.

Hanu and Eumelia watch Ava from across the water—Hanu's expression full of concern, Eumelia's expression full of something I can't interpret. The two girls exchange a brief look before returning to their fishing. Eumelia casts her weighted fishing net far out into the current. Hanu's net doesn't sail quite as high or as far as Eumelia's, but it's still a serviceable cast.

Serapen wades from the sandbar back to the beach, untangles the fish from her dripping net, and drops it with a splash into a large wooden barrel full of water. She rinses her hands in the river and picks up her sky blue healer's robe from the sand, wrapping it around herself and tying it closed with a colorful embroidered sash.

Dressed once more in her High Priestess garments, Serapen makes her way across the beach. She stops before us, enveloping us in the inexplicable stillness that often accompanies her. In the midday sun, her snow-white hair glows like an aura around her dark face, emphasizing the sharp edges of her features. Her clear brown eyes lock onto mine. The rushing sound of the river seems to fade. My breathing and heartbeat grow louder.

"Muse Serapen," I say. "We need your help. Something happened in the tent."

I've been so anxious to help Ava that this is the first time I've stopped to consider what exactly I'll have to tell the High Priestess we were doing in the tent. *Don't worry,* thinks Ava, squeezing my hand. *I'll tell her I was taking advantage of you.*

I shoot Ava an exasperated look, but her teasing reassures me. Although her cheeks are still pale, her lips a worrisome shade of blue, she must be feeling a little better. Surely Serapen can fix whatever's wrong; she revived Ava from a far worse condition last night.

Serapen studies Ava's face. "A great deal has happened indeed," says the High Priestess, extending one hand toward Ava. "Come. Walk with me."

Ava reaches out to take Serapen's hand, but she sways on her feet as she tries to support her own weight again. *Take it slow,* I think, steadying her. *Your balance is terrible right now.*

Hadn't noticed, Ava thinks dryly.

Serapen glances down at Ava's hand gripping mine. Quietly, she says, "Let him go, Ava."

The High Priestess wields the voice of command so deftly that Ava obeys before a single defiant thought can cross her mind. As soon as Ava drops my hand, her entire demeanor changes. Color floods back into her face, turning her lips and cheeks a rosy brown. She sighs in relief, like a heavy weight just rolled off her shoulders.

I feel the change in me, too. Over the last half moon, I've grown used to Ava's thoughts swirling in my mind like an endless murmuration of starlings, even when we're not touching. But now there's only silence and stillness in the place her awareness once was.

Ava? I think, *Can you hear me?*

Ava doesn't answer.

To Ava, Serapen says, "Better?"

"Much better," says Ava, looking at Serapen in amazement.

"Good," says Serapen. "Follow me."

The High Priestess draws us alongside her, leading us toward the dock at a brisk pace. To my relief, Ava keeps up without stumbling. Whatever happened to Ava in the tent, the ill effects seem to have been easily cured by Serapen's healer arts.

Ava? I think again. *What happened?*

Ava must be blocking my awareness from hers like she did last night when she ran away from camp. I'm hurt that she's cut me off again so suddenly, but maybe she's uncomfortable sharing thoughts with me while we're in the presence of the perceptive High Priestess. I know how much Ava distrusts Serapen.

As we approach the dock, Serapen says, "To understand what happened this morning, we must begin with what happened last night."

My relief at Ava's quick recovery gives way to my dread of revisiting what the free men did to us last night. Memories flash through my mind unbidden. Ava's shout of alarm as Eridu rears, tossing me from the saddle. Rough hands binding, gagging, and blindfolding me. My frantic unanswered thoughts as Ava lies unconscious behind me, her arms tied around my waist. The threatening undertone of the man in charge as he murmurs into Ava's ear. The terror of being dragged underwater against the hull of the boat. The painful crash of my body and the awful crack of Ava's head against the deck when the men tossed us back into the boat. The explosion in my mind as Ava somehow used the binding pharmaka to drive our captors away from me and overboard. Ava's limp body in my arms after she collapsed from her effort to save me.

At this last memory, my field of vision shrinks to a pinpoint. My face grows numb. My palms turn clammy. I fight the urge to vomit. Serapen stops, drops Ava's hand, and grips my wrist firmly, probing some point deep between my muscle and bone with her long fingers. My nausea passes; my vision clears.

I glance over at Ava, who watches me with concern. She reaches out toward me, then hesitates, balls her fist, and lets it fall back to her side. Her unexpected withdrawal makes my heart ache. I remember her arms around me in the tent earlier this morning, comforting me after I shared my memory of our captivity, cradling my head against her breast, stroking my hair. I long for that touch again. I wish I could simply hold her and forget everything except that she's here, safe, alive.

Serapen squeezes my shoulder. Her voice is full of compassion as she says, "Such memories are a heavy burden, little brother. But you need not carry them alone. Come, I will show you."

Ava and I follow Serapen out onto the dock, toward the small sailboat moored beside Urshanabi's ferry. Serapen steps into the boat and gestures for us to join her. I'd rather not set foot in that boat ever again, but Ava blithely hops aboard, so I force myself to follow.

Signs of last night's ordeal are strewn everywhere: an open wooden trunk lying on its side beside the tiller, haphazard tangles of lines, fresh scratches all over the thick varnish of the deck. A second wave of nausea hits me when I see the crumpled woolen rag, empty bag, and damp blanket piled against the port side of the boat. I shove down memories of the pungent scent of pharmaka stinging my nostrils, the rough lines cutting into my wrists, the cold wind whipping my bare skin.

Serapen surveys the mess on the deck. While the High Priestess' back is turned, Ava crouches over the ropes our captors used to bind us together. She touches the frayed ends where I sawed through the rope fibers with her blade, which lies beside her bare foot, its sharp edge gleaming in the sunlight. Just before Serapen turns back to face us, Ava straightens up and takes a small step to the side, her toes sweeping briefly over the blade. I open my mouth to call out a warning to Ava, thinking she's about to cut herself, but her eyes flash at me. I swallow my words. When Ava steps back, the blade has vanished.

Serapen looks at me and says, "Tell us what happened here, Dom."

Icy sweat prickles on my forehead. I stifle an urge to run back down the dock or jump into the river. Anything seems better than revisiting this memory. In a desperate burst of inspiration, I hold out my hand to the High Priestess. Serapen told us the initiate Mohirai are skilled in the use of binding pharmaka. Perhaps I can share the memories with her through touch so I can avoid talking about them. "I could show you like I showed Ava," I say. "Then you'll know everything I know."

Serapen shakes her head. "Listen, novice Artifex. Sharing memories through binding pharmaka is an art best left to experienced initiates. Sharing dark memories like these, so full of fear and confusion, is especially dangerous when the memories are fresh.

"We who walk the path of mysteries are often called by the Voice to witness the passage of centuries, sometimes even millennia. Over so much time, the weight of memory can grow heavy indeed. Dark memories are heaviest of all. But there is an art to living with memory, and the art begins with the practice of words.

"Over time, our words transform our memories into meaning. We decide, with the words we choose, what meaning our memories will hold for us. Meaning endures far longer than memory, so it is with our words that we decide how heavily or lightly to carry our memories. When chosen poorly, our words can amplify the harm of dark memories. When chosen well, our words can transform even the darkest memories into meaning that strengthens us."

The High Priestess speaks in the same patient tone of instruction I've heard all my life from other sisters. But the instruction of my boyhood never went much further than preparing my hands and body for the straightforward work of caring for myself and my brothers, for our mother land and her creatures. The instruction Serapen offers now reveals an entirely new kind of work, for which my mind feels unprepared.

Serapen looks at me expectantly. Automatically, I give the proper response. "I have listened, and I have heard, sister."

"Good," says Serapen. "Then it is time to act."

I wait, expecting more instruction. Serapen says nothing; I guess this is all I'm to receive for now.

I glance at Ava. She avoids my gaze. Why won't she look at me? Her mind is so much quicker than mine; she could probably explain to me what I should do. I remember sitting with Ava beneath the beech tree at the start of this journey, listening to other words of instruction from Serapen. Ava hadn't known what to do with that instruction at first, either, but Serapen had said, *Sometimes the only way to know is to do.*

So I do the only thing that comes to mind.

Slowly, pacing from the stern to the bow, I reconstruct what happened here last night, fitting each object on the deck into my memory as best I can. As Serapen and Ava listen, I recount how Ava and I lay bound together in the stern until Ava regained consciousness. How the free men moved us to the middle of the deck when Ava asked them for water to drink. How they almost tricked us into drinking unbinding pharmaka instead, and the struggle that ensued. The moment we realized Ava's mother Lilith was on the boat, unseen by us because our heads were covered. The words of Lilith and the man in charge as they argued, and the argument's escalation. Our failed attempt to jump overboard before the men dragged us back into the boat. The inexplicable way Ava used my body and the binding pharmaka to drive Lilith and the three free men away from us at last. How I freed us from our bonds with Ava's blade.

I stop speaking just before I reach the part where I realized Ava was dead. To my relief, the High Priestess doesn't press me to revisit the sickening panic of that moment. Instead, she nods and says, "I have listened, and I have heard, little brother."

Though her eyes remain averted, Ava's expression shows that she's heard me, too. I still wish she would look at me, but simply knowing I've been heard lifts the weight off my chest. The sick feeling in my gut subsides. These are still dark memories, but they're less frightening now that I've talked through them in daylight, with Serapen and Ava listening.

△▽△

After Dom recounts his memory of last night, Serapen walks the length of the deck, examining each object he pointed out to us. She crouches beside one of the scratches in the deck varnish and traces it with her long forefinger. Looking up at Dom, she says, "Do you have any idea what did this?"

Dom studies the mark. "I don't know," he says, shaking his head. "My eyes were covered most of the time we were on the boat. Maybe it happened when Ava drove Lilith and the free men overboard?"

I crouch beside Serapen, examining the scratch like it's an animal track. I consider the memory Dom shared with me earlier this morning, comparing it to the story he shared again just now. It's confusing from his perspective—sounds and sensations and emotions swirling through darkness. I wish I could remember how it was from my own perspective. Dom tried to share the memory with me this morning, in all its awful detail, but I can't help thinking I'd have noticed things he would have missed. Unfortunately, all my own memories of this part of the night are gone. I suppose it's a small price to pay for my life, but it's still frustrating to have this blank spot in my mind.

I'm at a loss to explain the scratch, but, as I survey the deck around it, one thing at least seems clear. "Whatever made this mark, it didn't happen just once," I say. "See?" I point out the trails of similar nicks and scratches criss-crossing the deck.

Serapen follows the trail of marks along the deck, leaning down to examine them in a few places. She looks around the boat, rubbing her sharp chin, her gaze turned inward. If she understands these marks, she gives no sign of it. Instead, she walks to the stern, where a wooden trunk lies open on its side. The trunk looks empty, but she reaches inside, feels around, and pulls something out by a leather strap.

"My pack!" I exclaim. The unexpected sight of something so familiar delights me, after all the strange things that have happened to me over the last half moon.

My pack, like my blade, has seen me through many jobs and journeys over many years. I wonder whether my boots are still in there. Stepping eagerly toward Serapen, I say, "May I have it back?"

Serapen holds up a hand to stop me, saying, "You carried the amanitai you stole in this, didn't you?" There's no reproach in her voice, but a hot flush rises to my cheeks when Dom glances at me in surprise. Reluctantly, I nod. I haven't yet explained to Dom how I obtained the amanitai that caused my overdose. I refuse to feel ashamed of my thievery, but it's still humiliating to be addressed by the High Priestess like a foolish child. Serapen says, "Let me check it first, then. The last thing you need right now is another dose of binding pharmaka."

I can't disagree with that, so I hang back, watching as Serapen carefully empties the remnants of my old life onto the deck.

My filthy riding cloak tumbles out, followed by my beloved, battered, well-oiled riding boots. There's no sign of the bag of amanitai I stuffed in there the night of my overdose, though.

Serapen runs her hand along the inside of my empty pack several times, rubs her fingertips together, and sniffs her palm. "How much amanitai was in this pack when you gave it to Lilith?" she says.

"About half a bushel," I say. Serapen's eyes pin me in place a moment longer than is comfortable. I know what she's doing—this is one of the arts the priestesses use to reveal deception. My mother turned a look like this on me more than once, and I quickly learned there's no point lying under such a gaze. Fortunately, I'm not lying. I wonder why Serapen thinks I would lie about this.

Eventually, Serapen's piercing gaze releases me. The long fingers of her right hand trace a line of embroidery on the sash knotted at her waist. "Half a bushel," she repeats thoughtfully. I wonder whether she's talking to someone through that sash. After what Eumelia told me about woven pharmaka, I regard all clothing of the Mohirai with suspicion.

Serapen tosses the empty pack to me and gestures to the little pile of my belongings. "These are safe to handle. You may have them back if you wish."

Eagerly, I scoop up my cloak and boots and stuff them into my pack. I slip the straps over my shoulders and stand. Out of habit, I take a step closer to Dom. Too close, I realize too late. The warmth of his arm alongside mine stirs intimate thoughts I'd much rather avoid right now. I edge away from him, wishing I could distance myself from all the feelings swirling through me. The harder I try to avoid thoughts of those hands, those eyes, those lips, the more memories flash through my mind. I can't tell whether these are my memories of Dom, Emmie's memories of other-Dom, or some confusing blend of both.

Serapen watches me for a long time, giving me the uncomfortable impression that she sees straight into me. At last she says, "Shall we discuss what happened this morning, then?"

Avoiding Dom's gaze, I look at the High Priestess and say, "We were—" Serapen's snowy eyebrows rise almost imperceptibly. Is that the faintest hint of amusement on her face? I press on, refusing to be embarrassed by something so banal, even if I would rather have kept it private. "We were kissing," I say.

Perhaps unconsciously, my hand drifts toward Dom. Dom's awareness is generally calmer than mine, but his thoughts have been uncharacteristically silent since Serapen told me to let go of his hand back on the beach. When my fingers brush his, his mind opens to me again. He's remembering that moment between us in the tent, just like I am.

I slip into the memory with him. It begins bright, sweet, and full of promise. But then my face grows cold. That strange inward pull tugs at my heart again. I jerk my hand away from Dom in alarm, swaying slightly before I regain my balance. Dazed, I continue, "Then I felt some change in me. Everything disappeared, and I was … somewhere else."

If Serapen was amused before, there's no sign of it now. "Go on," she says.

I clasp my hands tightly before me to stop them from bumping into Dom's again. "I was in a bedroom," I say, trying to focus on the details that might matter to the High Priestess. "The same room I saw in the pool on Calling Day, with you. I was with Dom. But he was … another Dom, older, like the man I saw on Calling Day.

"This other-Dom asked me where I had been before I was with him. He asked how old I was. He said I'd visited him before, though I don't remember that. And then he showed me my reflection in a mirror.

"I seemed to be inside the body of another woman, somehow. Other-Dom called her Emmie Bridges. He said Emmie had an overdose of binding pharmaka, like me, many years ago, and that she's been losing her memories because she's been taking unbinding pharmaka to manage the pain. He said Emmie is using an art of tekhnologia called the alternet, to help with her memory loss.

"He kept talking about branches and bridges—something about how branches help us answer our callings from the Voice, and how I had created a bridge to his branch. But before he could explain much, everything disappeared again. I was back in the tent. And when I looked at Dom—" I'm appalled by the warm tears that slip down my cheeks. I brush them away and say, "Seeing him after seeing that other-Dom … I felt like a part of me had been ripped out. It was so painful I could barely breathe."

Serapen steps toward me and touches my cheek, tilting my face up toward the sunlight. She examines my eyes closely as she says, "How do you feel now?"

I chew my lower lip, considering. "Better," I say. "At least, not as bad as I felt in the tent."

Serapen gestures toward Dom. She says, "And what happens now, when you look at Dom?"

Dom looks at me hopefully. I look down at my toes. Quietly, I say, "I'd rather not look at him."

"Why is that?" says Serapen.

I let out a long sigh. Slowly, I say, "When I see him … it's like I see through him to that other-Dom, in that other place. It's confusing. It hurts. It makes me feel like I'm going to disappear again."

Serapen says, "Did Dom tell you how he revived you last night?"

Curiously, I glance back up at Serapen. "He showed me that memory," I say. "But I don't understand it."

Serapen nods slowly. "Good," she says.

"Good?" I say derisively. "How is that good?"

Dom stiffens, probably shocked to hear me speak in this tone to the High Priestess. But if Serapen's offended, she doesn't show it. Her expression remains serene as she says, "It is good that you know where you stand, as you begin your novice training. Of course you understand almost nothing. You have journeyed a mere seventeen summers on this branch. What small understanding we may acquire on the path of mysteries is the work of ages."

Serapen's superior tone makes me seethe. Words I've heard countless times from my mother tumble from my mouth before I can stop them. "Damn your mysteries," I say. "They're nothing but cages you've built to keep us enslaved in your cursed new age."

Dom winces. Serapen says calmly, "What cages exist in this world are not the work of my hands, child."

I open my mouth to escalate further when, to my surprise, Dom interjects. He almost never interrupts when women are speaking, so he must be seriously uncomfortable about where this conversation is headed. Hastily, he says, "Please, Muse Serapen, isn't there anything that could help Ava stop seeing these things?"

Serapen's eyes flick briefly to Dom before she says to me, "Do you wish to stop seeing these things, little sister?"

I'm surprised—even begrudgingly grateful—to have the choice presented to me. Serapen could easily change what I see, regardless of what I might wish. A sip of unbinding pharmaka from the silver flask tucked into her robe and a few gestures of her healer hands would probably be enough to erase all of these troubling thoughts from my mind, leaving me oblivious to what I saw in the tent.

In some ways, I do wish I were free of the wrenching sense of loss I feel when I think about other-Dom. But other-Dom is somehow connected to the city of glass towers, a place that, even in dreams, feels more like home to me than anywhere in Dulai. I yearn to see that place again. Thoughts of other-Dom also stir intense new feelings of a love deeper than any I'd known was possible, feelings at least as deep as those I feel for my own Dom. Am I willing to risk forgetting all that?

"No," I say firmly. Surely I'm strong enough to manage these thoughts—or visions, or dreams, or whatever they are—just as I've learned to manage the pain the Voice causes me.

Serapen inclines her head and says, "Very well. You are of age to take responsibility for your own memory."

I frown. "Memory," I say. "What does any of this have to do with my memory?"

Thoughtfully, Serapen says, "Memory is perhaps an insufficient word for what we witness as we walk the path of mysteries. But ultimately, all that we perceive resides within the unified awareness of the Voice in all. Our limited awareness, when joined to the greater awareness of the Voice, has the potential to traverse its memory just like we recall our own individual memories. This is one of our greater mysteries.

"Navigating memories through the unified awareness of the Voice is an art that requires ages to master. Even the most highly trained initiates practice this art with caution, for our simple human awarenesses fall captive to memory quite easily."

The idea that a mere memory could hold me captive irritates me almost as much as this talk of mysteries. These blasted mysteries of the Mohirai multiply everywhere I turn, trap within trap within trap. Struggling to keep the frustration out of my voice, I say, "I want to keep my memories. I just don't want my memories to hurt so much."

"A worthy goal," says Serapen. "Attainable, in time. I can offer you instruction in this, if you wish."

Her words spark my hope. Trying my best to sound as humble as Dom, I recite the response I learned as a small girl in the Children's Temple. "I would hear your instruction, Muse Serapen."

The High Priestess says, "Listen well, then, little sister. The path of mysteries is a path of endless branches, each branch a life unique from every other. The branch of one life may be long or short, but in the end all lives are finite. When one life's service to the Voice concludes, the branch of that life is complete and grows no further.

"But awareness is not constrained to these single lives within these single branches. The unified awareness of the Voice in all flows through the entire path of mysteries, all at once. And though a human awareness may concentrate on a single branch of a single life for a limited time, no awareness ever attends a single branch with perfect focus or forever. Awareness has a curious nature, and in its curiosity it wanders between branches.

"When your particular awareness departed your body this morning, Ava, it wandered to another branch, leaving this branch behind."

This must have been what other-Dom meant, when he spoke of traveling between branches. I say, "These branches—these other lives—you speak of them as though they're real."

Serapen says, "Each branch is as real as any other."

"Is what I saw on that other branch a memory of another life I've lived, then?" I say.

"Not quite," says Serapen, "You—at least, what you think of as you—live and have lived and will live only this one life. But the awareness that dwells in you lives and has lived and will live endless lives. And your awareness of the Voice in all, amplified as it is by binding pharmaka, makes it easier to travel among the innumerable branches the Voice attends.

"But your awareness is also bound tightly to Dom's by the same binding pharmaka. Even when your awareness departs your body, your bond with him remains intact. You two form a kind of bridge between you. This is why Dom could follow your awareness to another branch last night, after you died here, and why he could lead your awareness back to this branch.

"Crossing from branch to branch is among the higher arts you will learn on the path to initiation. But as with all the arts, there can be side effects. Your memory of what you saw on that other branch is one such side effect. When an awareness travels between branches, it may access memories from both branches. It can become difficult to distinguish which memories belong to which branch."

I consider this. "It's like the bond between me and Dom," I say. "Thoughts and emotions spill between us, when we're not careful. Sometimes it's hard to tell which thoughts and feelings are mine, and which are his."

"A fair analogy," says Serapen. "And just as the bond between you and Dom grows stronger every time you use it, the bridge between two branches grows stronger the more awareness traverses it, making it more likely that awareness will cross that way again.

"But memory spilling between branches is not the only side effect you're experiencing from your crossing. The weakness you're feeling is a side effect, too. The body requires a great deal of focused awareness to remain healthy on the branch where it resides. When awareness crosses suddenly to another branch, or stretches across multiple bodies on multiple branches, the neglected body weakens quickly.

"It is possible to strengthen the awareness so it can safely attend more than one body at once, and to strengthen the body so it can endure the departure of the awareness, but these arts require practice. For an awareness and a body unprepared, such a crossing can be fatal, as was the case for you last night, when your awareness departed your body and entered the bodies of Lilith and the men who were holding you captive."

It's been difficult enough managing the complex entanglement of my awareness with the Voice and Dom since my overdose. The last thing I need is this new complication. "How can I control this traveling across all these branches and bridges and bodies?" I say, unable to keep the desperation out of my voice.

Is it the angle of the sunlight catching Serapen's eyes that changes their reflection this way? When she looks at me, I see nothing but my own reflection. Serapen doesn't answer my question, but instead asks me another. "What have you learned thus far about the nature of awareness, little sister?"

Even though I can't sense Dom's awareness inside my own right now, his presence beside me reminds me of all we've shared through our bond, and how we've struggled to manage that sharing over the last half moon. "Awareness is difficult to control," I say. "My awareness, especially. Arkhi told us awareness is unruly by nature."

"Muse Arkhi is right," says Serapen. "And perhaps she also taught you some of the ways we manage unruly awareness?"

"She said awareness can be shaped by practicing the arts of mindfulness. By building intention," I say. Along with Serapen's instruction at the start of the journey, Arkhi's words were instrumental in my ill-fated attempt to sneak out of the camp without Dom noticing.

Serapen nods. "Building intention is a powerful art," she says. "What intention do you suppose might stop your awareness from wandering between branches?"

I think about this for a long time, uncomfortably aware of Dom's gaze, which I've been avoiding. At last, I let myself look up at him. In this moment, to my relief, his face recalls only simple memories from this life on this branch: the warmth of his hands on my skin, the weight of his arms around me, the sound of his voice saying, *I love you, too.* I search his eyes, as though I might find the answer to Serapen's question there. A worried furrow forms between his level brows, like he carries a heavy weight between them. The intensity of his expression makes my heart ache, because I know what he wants, but I don't know whether it's something I can give him.

"An intention to stay," I say softly, more to Dom than to Serapen. My words linger in the strange stillness that emanates from the High Priestess.

"The Voice has given you a great gift of perception, little sister," says Serapen. "I hope you will put it to good use." She raises her hand over me and Dom in the sign of blessing and climbs out of the boat, onto the dock.

"Wait!" I call after her, frustrated. "Isn't there anything else you can tell me? I still don't understand how to stop myself from crossing over the bridge to that other branch."

The High Priestess turns back and considers me. "The Voice speaks through many teachers, little sister. If you do not find what you need in my words, try listening elsewhere."

She heads back to the beach, leaving me utterly mystified.

GONE FISHING

SERAPEN DEPARTS, TAKING THE STILLNESS with her. Ava and I remain alone together in the boat. When the High Priestess is a few paces away, the merry chortle of the river rushes back into my ears, and Ava's anger rips through me. I press my palm to my forehead, wincing at Ava's vitriolic inner monologue. These outbursts are my least favorite part of sharing thoughts with her.

*Damn that blasted witch and her—*Ava blinks, seeing my expression. Her furious cursing stops abruptly. I wonder what a witch is; Ava knows so many strange curse words.

"You can hear me again?" she says.

I nod. "I thought you were shutting me out," I say.

"It wasn't me," says Ava. "More of Serapen's tricks, I guess."

Her disdainful tone surprises me, considering how much Serapen just helped us both. "You mean her healer arts?" I say.

Ava rolls her eyes. "Arts. Tricks. In any case, I wasn't shutting you out. I couldn't hear you, either. Serapen must have been doing it," she says.

"Whatever she did helped," I say, taking Ava's hand. "You're standing on your own again. You're able to look at me again."

Her expression softens. For a moment, she lets me in. Briefly, the day seems a little brighter, the air a little warmer, the colors a little richer. Then her expression clouds. She withdraws her hand.

"Please don't," she says quietly. "I need some space, Dom. I need to think. Alone."

She must realize she can't be left alone after what she did last night. The Mohirai won't let her out of their sight. I won't, either, for that matter.

She sighs, overhearing. "Fine," she says. "Don't let me out of your sight, then. But you can leave my thoughts alone, at least, can't you?"

Gently, I say, "Why do you need to think about it alone? It helped me to talk about what happened last night. Couldn't we just talk about this, too?"

"What else is there to say?" she says irritably. "I showed you everything I saw on that other branch already. It doesn't have the same effect on you as it does on me."

"Isn't that the same for both of us?" I say. "I shared the memory of what happened to us last night, but it doesn't bother you."

"It does bother me," says Ava. "But it doesn't bother me as much as it bothers you, because I know it could have been worse."

My throat tightens. My voice drops almost to a whisper. "You died, Ava. How much worse could it have been?"

"I could have stayed dead," she says. "Maybe I should have."

"What do you mean?" I say, stung by her tone.

She looks away. "Forget it," she says. She tightens the shoulder straps of her battered leather pack with a practiced tug. "I just need some time alone, all right?"

She climbs out of the boat. My heart aches as she walks away.

△▽△

Without looking back at Dom, I walk down the long dock toward the beach. I wish I could take back my words that hurt him, but all I can do now is stop myself from saying anything else I'll regret.

Despite my effort to shut Dom's thoughts out of my head, I can't avoid feeling what he's feeling now that Serapen's no longer shielding us from each other. As he watches me depart, leaving him alone in the boat, his awful memories of what happened there last night flood through him again. I suppress the urge to turn back and invite him to follow me, because I can't bear to look at him. Thoughts of Dom lead too easily to thoughts of other-Dom, and thoughts of other-Dom stir the unsettling feeling that I might disappear again. I need to escape all these problematic thoughts and memories as fast as possible to avoid slipping onto another branch.

I step off the dock and onto the beach. Hanu and Eumelia climb out of the nearby river shallows carrying their fishing nets. Eumelia untangles three fish from her net and drops them into the barrel on the shore. Hanu adds another large fish of her own. I'm sure neither of them wants to talk to me, so I hurry past them, heading back toward our tent, craving solitude.

But Hanu calls, "How are you feeling, Ava?"

Completely raw is how I feel, and Hanu's friendly voice pours over me like a healing balm. I look back at her.

Standing beside Hanu, Eumelia studies me with shrewd hazel eyes. Smirking, she says, "Feeling like giving us a hand, I hope. Or are you still enjoying your special treatment?"

"Mel!" says Hanu. "Could you try being nice just for once?"

Eumelia doesn't take her eyes off me as she says, "You can take it, can't you, Ava?"

I set my trembling lips in a hard line, infuriated by the sting of tears in my eyes. I refuse to cry in front of Eumelia. Without a word, I drop my backpack beside the barrel of fish, seize the net Serapen left behind, and brush past Eumelia. Determined to show I need no special treatment, I splash through the river shallows toward the sandbar.

Behind me, in an exasperated undertone, Hanu says to Eumelia, "Serapen said she needs to rest."

Eumelia doesn't reply. I hear her splashing after me into the water.

I climb up onto the sandbar and untangle my net. My mother taught me how to fish with a net like this, and thoughts of her swirl like oil and water in my mind —my happier childhood memories of her refusing to cohere with Dom's dark memory of what she tried to do to us last night. One image stands out among the rest: my mother's massive figure looming over Dom last night, her ice blue eyes glittering in the moonlight, her unyielding hands forcing the mouthpiece of the waterskin between his lips, preparing to squeeze unbinding pharmaka down his throat. I quiver with anger at my mother, tense as a bowstring.

Usually my cast is perfect, spreading the net weights spiraling out over the water before they plunge beneath the surface, like an eagle scoops up fish with its talons. But my first cast is a disaster—weights tangling midair so the net drops in a useless clump into the river. I grit my teeth in annoyance, reel the net back in, and set to work untangling it again. I need to calm down and focus. Nothing ruins fishing like impatience.

Eumelia climbs up onto the sandbar beside me. Without a word, she casts her net with a practiced flick of her wrist. Her net sails through the air in a perfect arc before sinking into the depths.

I whistle in admiration. Whatever my feelings may be toward Eumelia, I can't help but admire such skill. "Beautiful," I say.

Eumelia's eyes stay fixed on the water, but her hard expression softens. The two of us work in silence, casting and reeling, casting and reeling. I recover my technique after a few more casts, and soon our nets are flying and falling in a steady rhythm together. There's something calming, even mesmerizing, about the sight.

With Eumelia standing so close to me, it's impossible to avoid thinking about what I did to her last night. A part of me wishes that memory had been wiped away by the unbinding pharmaka like my memory of what happened afterwards. But cowardice—especially my own cowardice—disgusts me. I'll have to face Eumelia at some point, and putting it off won't make it any easier.

So I pluck up my courage and say, "I'm sorry about what happened last night."

Eumelia looks at me. Neutrally, she says, "Which part?"

She seems to be seriously asking, so I seriously consider my answer. The memory returns: the taste of wine on her lips, the soft curves of her body under my hands, the energy of her awareness in mine. When I took advantage of her drunken desire for me, all I was thinking about was how I could get past her without injuring her. What we did—and what we imagined we did—wasn't part of my escape plan. But I got something I wanted out of it, and I know Eumelia did too.

So what am I sorry about? Maybe the unwanted complication her presence creates for me. I never expected to see Eumelia again after I fled. But now, with the possibility of escape gone, she'll be a near-constant presence for my foreseeable future. What happened between us will have ripple effects.

Eumelia watches me, waiting for my answer. Telling her I'm sorry for the unwanted complication her presence creates for me doesn't seem like the right move. So I start with something a bit simpler that's also true. "I'm sorry I tricked you," I say.

She studies my face, deciding whether I'm serious. At last she says, "Me too. I'd have preferred the real thing."

I laugh in surprise. Eumelia looks back at the river, but not before I see her expression. She likes making me laugh. This realization saddens me, and my sadness confuses me.

Eumelia's tone is distant as she says, "But that's not what you should be sorry for, Ava."

"No?" I say. "What should I be sorry for?"

With a depth of sincerity I've never heard from her before, Eumelia says, "You should be sorry for dying in Dom's arms, you heartless fool. I hope you never have to see the look I saw on his face last night." She touches my arm, and my skin tingles under her palm as she shows me what she saw: Dom in the moonlight, kneeling on the deck of the riverboat, my dead body in his arms, hollow devastation in his eyes. Eumelia withdraws her hand quickly, but her memory lingers in my mind as she holds my gaze.

With equal sincerity, I say, "I'm sorry for that, too." What I don't say is that I've already seen that look on Dom's face. Just not in this life, not on this branch.

△▽△

Ava walks away from me, leaving me in the boat as she heads down the dock toward the beach. She looks even smaller than usual, with her head bowed and her pack straps gripped tight in both hands, as if that pack is all that's holding her together. The last thing I overhear before she shuts me out again is that she's sorry she gave voice to her troubled thoughts: *I could have stayed dead. Maybe I should have.*

If she'd stayed with me just a moment longer, I would have told her she shouldn't feel sorry for speaking honestly. Anything either of us feels sincerely will find its way across our connection eventually, one way or another. Though her words worry me, and they hurt a little, the greater hurt comes from her leaving so abruptly. But she wants space, and that's the only thing she wants that I can give her right now, so I'll do my best to leave her alone until her pain flares up and forces us back together again.

I climb out of the boat and sit at the end of the dock, dangling my bare feet in the river current. Turning my gaze away from Ava is easy enough, but that's not really what she wants. She's asked for true privacy: separation between our thoughts and emotions. We've both struggled over the last half moon to develop the mental discipline required to give each other privacy despite our connection. Ava's skill in this art is greater than mine. She's learned how to build walls and lock doors in her mind to shield certain thoughts from me until she's ready to share them.

I turn my attention outward, immersing myself in my surroundings, trying to clear my head. I gaze across the sparkling water to the eastern shore of the Purattu. During our last few evening meals around the campfire, the Mohirai described what lies ahead on the road to Velkanos. After a few days' ride, the Subartu Desert will give way to the rolling hill country that rises into the rugged Urashtu Range. In another half moon, spirits willing, our caravan will cross the

Urashtu Pass and descend from the mountains to the open plain where Velkanos, the Mountain of Muses, stands alone.

I'd given up hope of seeing the temple city of Velkanos when I chose to abandon the Mohirai last night. As I followed Ava into the willow grove, I'd known how much I was leaving behind: the privileges granted only to initiates of the mysteries; the comforts of living within temple city walls; the training in the arts that I'd longed for, but never dared hope I might receive, as a boy. The renewed prospect of seeing the temple city of Velkanos reawakens all the hopes that flared within me when I first understood I'd been called to the path of mysteries. Ava's words on our Calling Day return to me. *Seems like the Voice gave you exactly what you wanted.*

Perhaps Ava was right. It seems the Voice has given me everything I ever wanted—not only a calling to the path of mysteries, but the chance to remain with Ava. At the same time, the Voice seems to have denied Ava what she wants: freedom to go her own way. *She is on a more difficult path than most*, Serapen told me the night of Ava's overdose. The surge of pity I feel for Ava surprises me. For as long as I can remember, I've envied women, whom the Voice grants long life and the privilege of practicing the arts and learning the mysteries withheld from men.

Withheld from *most* men, I correct myself. I'm not yet accustomed to thinking of myself as different from other men, as an Artifex. I still have no idea why I've been called to live among the Mohirai, when so many other men must toil far from the path of mysteries, paying the debt of the men who brought about the destruction. I'm grateful, but my gratitude is tinged with guilt, because all of my good fortune seems to have come at Ava's expense. She agreed to come with me to our Calling Day ceremony so I could receive my calling, giving me what I wanted. But while she was there with me, she was called to join the Mohirai, a calling she's been trying to escape since childhood. Now, despite her desperate longing for freedom, she's stuck with her unwanted calling and stuck with me—trapped, she often thinks, though I never meant to trap her.

Sooner than I'd expected, light footsteps approach from behind me. My heart lifts. I turn, expecting to see Ava.

Instead, I see Hanu. She stops, seeing my disappointment. In a small voice, she says, "Sorry. It's just me. Do you mind if I join you?"

I consider her warily. Only in the past few days have I learned how to manage my feelings toward Hanu while Ava and I are sharing thoughts. With Ava's awareness temporarily withdrawn from mine, maybe I could let my guard down a little. It would be a relief to talk to Hanu the way we used to, before Ava's unexpected re-appearance in our lives. I'm not sure whether I'll ever be able to trust Hanu the way I used to, though, after learning how she gave me binding pharmaka without my permission.

To be fair, the initiate Mohirai frequently give us pharmaka without our knowledge, and Ava used a catastrophic amount of binding pharmaka with me by accident. But what Hanu did feels different—a violation of our friendship and my trust. Even though her experiments with me were done with the intention of giving pleasure, the effects are enduring. My mind now has an embarrassing tendency to retrieve extremely vivid memories of her at inopportune moments. Still, Hanu's otherwise been a good friend to me since we were children. Maybe I should make an effort to be friendly again.

I decide to give it a try. "Done fishing already?" I say.

Hanu shakes her head. "I thought I'd try fishing off the dock and leave Ava and Mel to the nets. Those two need to talk."

Despite my resolve to give Ava her space, I can't stop myself from glancing briefly over at the sandbar, a short distance upriver. Ava and Eumelia stand side by side, casting and reeling their nets, deep in conversation. "What do they need to talk about?" I say, surprised by a pang of jealousy.

Hanu raises an eyebrow at me. Her silence is a clear reminder that trio sisters keep each other's secrets, just as trio brothers do.

"Sorry," I say with a sigh. "I just wish she would talk to me, that's all." Now that I think of it, though, of course there's unsettled business between Ava and Eumelia. However Ava managed to overpower Eumelia and tie her up last night before she fled the camp, it must have been quite a fight. Ava may be small, but she's fierce.

Hanu takes a seat beside me, dangling her long, shapely legs over the edge of the dock, stirring the water with her toes. She reaches into the pocket of her tunic and extracts two weighted fishing lines with shiny metal lures. She hands one to me. We tie the lines to the dock pilings on either side of us, tossing the lures far out into the current. The lines slowly straighten.

Hanu touches the line on her side, lightly monitoring the tension. "Give her time, Dom," she says. "Ava's been through a lot."

I turn my attention again to the vast landscape beyond the river, trying to lose my self-pity and my frustration with Ava somewhere out there. But it's more difficult now, with Hanu's words forcing my focus back on Ava.

"You've been through a lot, too, though," says Hanu, pressing my hand lightly. "How are you feeling?"

My hand tingles faintly under hers as she uses the pharmaka-enhanced bond between us. It's not a seductive touch, as it might once have been, but it stirs another kind of desire in me. Sensing what I need, Hanu wraps her arms around me in a comforting hug, resting her cheek lightly on my shoulder. The sweet perfume of Thalia's bathing pharmaka clings to Hanu's long, glossy hair, smelling just like Ava's hair did as I held her in my arms this morning. For a moment, I pretend this is Ava's hair and Ava's embrace. Hanu lets me pretend just long enough to make me feel a little better before she releases me.

"Everything feels impossibly complicated," I say. I'm not sure whether I'm talking about me, or Ava, or that other-Dom, or Emmie Bridges, or the free men, or Lilith, or Eumelia, or Hanu. Maybe I'm talking about all of us.

Hanu listens. Into the friendly silence she opens between us, I find myself pouring out more.

"I feel guilty," I say. "All I wanted was to be with Ava, but everything I do seems to hurt her somehow. Whether I stay with her or let her go, whether she looks at me or doesn't look at me, whether she's touching me or refusing to touch me. She always seems to be suffering somehow because of me. And I feel it, too, like it's my own suffering."

Hanu watches me, her eyes wide in sympathy. "Would you like me to help?" she says.

I frown. How could Hanu possibly help? Her presence makes every situation more awkward for me and Ava.

Hanu's lower lip quivers almost imperceptibly. With a fresh stab of guilt, I realize Hanu overheard my thought. I take her hand and say, "I wish you could help. I just can't see how another person tangled up in all this could help anything."

"You sound like Ava," says Hanu. Although her expression is slightly hurt, I can tell from her tone that she's already forgiven me.

"Well, I have been spending a lot of time in her mind," I say, with a half-hearted chuckle.

Hanu says, "Maybe you two should try spending a little less time in your minds."

"Believe me, we've tried," I say. My thoughts return unbidden to what happened in the tent this morning. For a moment, I'm there again: Ava's body twined around mine, the taste of her lips, the tingling anticipation of having her entirely. Hanu studies me with interest, and I recognize the sensation of her gentle curiosity receiving this memory, which I had no intention of sharing. I jerk back my hand, severing the connection.

Hanu tilts her head to one side, giving me an appraising look. "Is it really so difficult?" she says, in a tone halfway between sympathy and teasing.

Some river spirit spares me from answering her. Both fishing lines pull taut at the same instant. Hanu and I turn our attention to reeling in the catch.

△▽△

As I stand beside Eumelia, casting and reeling, casting and reeling, I can't help watching Dom and Hanu at the end of the dock. When I fled camp last night, I thought I was at peace with the idea of the two of them back together again after my departure. I'm surprised by the prickle of possessiveness I feel when Hanu touches Dom's hand and briefly embraces him. I have an impulse to listen in on his conversation with her using our bond, but I'd be furious with him if he did this to me. With effort, I force myself to look away from them, focusing my attention on the river.

Eumelia glances at me with that knowing smirk of hers. She says, "You don't need to worry about Hanu."

"What do you mean?" I say.

She nods toward Dom and Hanu, never pausing her steady cadence of casting and reeling, casting and reeling. She says, "Hanu knows how you feel about Dom. She would never come between you. Unless you wanted her to."

"Why would I want her to do that?" I say.

Eumelia shrugs and says, "You tell me. Why did you push Dom into her arms last night?"

I'm surprised Eumelia noticed this; she was so drunk at the time. I'm even more surprised I feel the need to explain myself to her. But Eumelia is perhaps the only person I can talk to about Dom and Hanu in confidence. Despite her irritating tendency to deliver her unsolicited judgments on everything, Eumelia's also proved capable of keeping secrets far more sensitive than this one. So I share with her something I'd have trouble sharing with Dom. "I knew Hanu would take care of him, after I was gone," I say.

Eumelia looks mildly surprised. "You're not as heartless as I gave you credit for," she says.

I laugh, uncertain whether I've impressed or disappointed her. "Why did you think I did it?" I say.

Eumelia shrugs. "I thought you'd finally gotten tired of him. That's why I followed you when you left the bonfire."

Ah. Another piece of last night's puzzle slides into place. I'd underestimated Eumelia's interest in me, and she nearly foiled my escape plan as a result. She'd underestimated me, too, though; I'd slipped through her fingers. In retrospect, perhaps I would have been better off failing to escape Eumelia; that would have averted my more spectacular subsequent failure. Dom would have been spared the memory of my death. I would have been spared the knowledge that my mother betrayed me. But it's impossible for me to imagine a world in which I never even tried to escape.

I watch Dom and Hanu chatting at the end of the dock, remembering them laughing together in the ring of dancers around the bonfire last night. Dom had looked so effortlessly happy with her. With me, his happiness is always marred by worry and pain that should never have been his to bear. I'm not sure whether I'm talking to myself or to Eumelia when I say, "Everything would have been so much simpler for us both if he'd just wanted Hanu."

Eumelia's smirk fades into thoughtfulness. She looks at Dom and Hanu, then across the water to the eastern shore. She says, "I don't think any of us can choose what we want. We can only choose whether to go after what we want."

For a moment, I glimpse the wise woman Eumelia will become someday. The impression passes quickly, though, as she looks at me with an expression that has annoyed me since we were little girls. Eumelia knows what she wants, and she's determined to get it.

I sigh and look away from her. We're not so different, she and I. We both know what we want. She wants me; I want my freedom. But as far as I can see, neither of us stands a chance of getting what we want.

The Mohirai always say the Voice works through all of us with purpose. If this is part of its plan, the Voice's purpose seems as cruel as my mother always warned me. What purpose could be served by all these desires at cross-purposes

—mine and Dom's and Eumelia's and Hanu's—and all the suffering they cause us?

After our next casts, my net and Eumelia's come up full. We haul in our catch and wade back to shore.

MESSAGE SENT

For the rest of the afternoon, I give Ava the space she's asked for. We cross paths occasionally on the beach as we deliver our catches to the increasingly crowded barrel of fish. In my chest, the dull ache of separation progresses steadily from twinging to throbbing to stabbing. I don't know how long Ava wants me to leave her alone. I'm desperately hoping it's not much longer.

Hanu keeps me company after we deliver the last of our catch to the barrel, but she becomes increasingly agitated as the worsening pain in my chest echoes in hers through our light bond. She insists on trying to ease the pain, so I let her. She makes a determined effort, working her hands down my arms, across my chest, between my shoulder blades. Unfortunately, whatever causes this pain for Ava, and by extension for me, proves beyond Hanu's novice skill to fix. Touching me only makes the pain worse for Hanu.

After a failed third attempt, Hanu lets go of my arm, wincing as she rubs the sympathetic sore spot at the center of her chest. "I'm so sorry," she says, disheartened. "I don't know how the two of you can bear it."

Hanu hasn't experienced anything close to the worst of it, but I just nod wearily.

Behind me, Ava says, "Thanks for trying to help him, Hanu."

I turn to see Ava and Eumelia approaching the barrel of fish, their nets wriggling and dripping. Hanu goes to help Eumelia untangle the fish from her net. For the first time since we parted at the docks, Ava meets my gaze. I hold back my thoughts from hers, waiting for her to make the first move, determined to show her that I can give her as much space as she needs for as long as she needs it.

At last, a little sheepishly, she says, "Want to give me a hand?"

I step forward eagerly, extending my hand. Ava's fingers close around mine. We stand for a moment in silence, letting the pain drain out of us. I can't stop myself from thinking, *I missed you.*

I was right here the whole time, she thinks.

You know what I mean, I think.

She sighs. *I know,* she thinks. *I missed you too.*

We lift Ava's net between us and set to work untangling five trout and dropping them into the barrel.

Watching us, Hanu relaxes visibly. She says, "Could you please not leave him so long again, Ava? That was awful."

"Better gird your tender heart, Hanu," calls a teasing, sing-song voice. "All who walk the path of mysteries must learn to endure long separation."

It's Thalia, approaching from the cliffs, carrying a large bundle of waxed canvas under one arm and three stacked wooden buckets in one hand. Even though I've witnessed the uncanny, pharmaka-enhanced perception of the

Mohirai many times, I'm still surprised that Thalia could overhear Hanu from so far away. Thalia pauses at the barrel of fish and looks inside. "Ah, the Voice is generous!" she says. "You'll need to make quick work of it, though, novices. All of this must be cleaned and set to brine before sundown. Serapen calls for a council tonight."

"A council about what?" says Ava.

There's a sharp edge to Thalia's tinkling laugh. She says, "What do you think, little sister? About you."

Ava's distaste for Thalia rises sourly in my throat, and her questions churn like storm clouds through my mind. Hanu and Eumelia exchange a look. Before any of the girls can ask another question, though, Thalia raises her pretty pink hand and says, in the priestess tone of command, "There will be time enough for talk tonight. The High Priestess has bid us all hurry while daylight remains."

"We have listened and we have heard, sister," I say in prompt unison with Hanu and Eumelia. Ava remains silent. The discourtesy doesn't go unnoticed. Thalia narrows her eyes at Ava but says nothing more to her.

Thalia sets down the buckets and the bundle of waxed canvas on the packed sand near the river's edge. She unrolls the canvas, revealing four filleting knives, four metal scrapers, three bucket lids, and a few cloth bags of brining pharmaka tucked inside. "I'll leave you to it, then," she says.

Thalia heads back toward the cliffs, and the four of us set to work cleaning the catch.

Hanu is too sensitive to strike a killing blow, even to a fish, so Ava, Eumelia, and I divide the butchering between the three of us and leave Hanu the work of brining the sectioned fillets with the salty, fragrant pharmaka rub.

A job I would have expected to consume the rest of the afternoon takes half that time, thanks to Ava. She wields a filleting knife like it's part of her own hand, reducing a live fish to perfect sections with a few easy flicks of her wrist. Eumelia and I watch her closely, and our technique improves by imitating hers, but Ava's still twice as fast as the two of us put together.

It's been years since I last felt squeamish about butchering animals, but as we near the end of the work, something about the neat piles of shiny offal and bluish fish heads accumulating in the center of the canvas brings on a flood of disturbing memories. Ava's blade against my neck in the cedar forest the night of her overdose. Ava's lifeless body curled on the boat deck last night. Ava's lips turning blue in the tent this morning. My stomach churns, and my hands tremble so hard I have to set down the fish I'm cleaning. I clear my throat, trying to push past the nausea.

"Are you all right?" says Ava, looking at me with concern. Hanu and Eumelia glance up from their work, too. The three girls watch me intently.

I wipe the clammy sweat off my face with the back of my clean forearm, trying not to drip fish guts onto myself. I know Serapen said memories like these are better to put into words, but I can't bring myself to talk about this in front of Hanu and Eumelia. "I'm fine," I say, a little too loudly. "Your skill with a blade is just a little terrifying."

Ava chuckles. My stomach settles. I pick up my fish and finish cleaning and sectioning it, then set it beside Hanu, who rubs a palmful of pharmaka into the fillets and tosses them into the nearly full bucket before her. I hurry away from the messy canvas to scrub my hands with river sand and water. Mercifully, the girls leave me alone to clear my head, dividing the remaining work between them until I return to help with the cleanup.

We secure wooden lids on the two full buckets of brining fillets and one full bucket of fish heads, protecting our haul from the motley assortment of birds who have been monitoring our work with keen interest. Hanu and I carry the pile of fish offal between us on the waxed canvas, wade into the river, and toss the scraps into the current. We rinse and re-fold the canvas between us. Eumelia and Ava kneel at the water's edge upstream, cleaning the knives and scrapers.

Thanks to Ava, the chore is done with some daylight left, so the four of us indulge in a brief rest. The girls strip and go for a swim off the sandbar. I'm not quite ready to dive back into the river after being dragged upside down against the hull of a boat last night. Instead, I sit at the water's edge watching the swimmers. To distract myself from the memory of my near-drowning, I sketch the three girls in the hard-packed sand before me with a bit of broken mussel shell.

I'm so absorbed in my sketch that I jump in surprise when Ava says behind me, "It's beautifully done."

I turn and look up at her. She's backlit by the sun, her long curls dripping on the shoulders of her tunic. Hanu and Eumelia follow close behind her. As the girls admire themselves in the sandy scene at my feet, I'm torn between self-consciousness and pride.

Ava has just knelt beside me for a closer look when Hanu cries out in dismay. "Oh! Ava, look—your pack!"

Ava turns around quickly, following Hanu's gaze, then springs to her feet. She runs down the beach, waving her arms and shouting, "Off! Off! Get out of here!" I jump up and run after Ava to see what's happened.

A tawny female kuku bird who's been poking around the perimeter of our work area all afternoon has lingered behind. The rest of the scavengers flew off after the fish scraps Hanu and I sent floating downriver, but this particular bird evidently decided to investigate Ava's pack instead. The pack lies open on its side, its contents pulled out onto the sand. The kuku perches atop one of Ava's old riding boots, pecking relentlessly at the leather, untroubled by Ava's indignant shouts and waving arms. Ava lunges to grab the boot out from under the kuku, clearly expecting—as am I—that this will send the bird flying off. But instead, the kuku launches herself at Ava.

Ava redirects herself mid-lunge with the agility of a cat, diving toward the ground and rolling away. The bird misses Ava's neck by a hair's breadth and splashes down in the sand, sending up a puff of dust two paces ahead of me. Ava bounces to her feet and rounds on the bird. The kuku stares up at me and Ava, her beady eyes flicking nervously back and forth between us, calculating the likelihood we'll pounce on her. We stare down at her, calculating the likelihood that she'll go straight for our eyes with that sharp little beak of hers. None of us appears to like our odds. All three of us hesitate to make the next move.

A faint whizzing sound slices through the air between us. The kuku's feathers ruffle defensively before she stumbles beak-first into the sand. She's still breathing, but otherwise she lies motionless. Ava and I look at the bird, then at each other.

What was that? we think, stepping forward to inspect the fallen creature.

Up the beach, near the fire ring, there's a shout, but I can't make out the words. I turn to see the inky black figure of Muse Arkhi running toward us. A small, flat object flaps loose around her neck, hanging by a leather cord. Kor runs after Arkhi awkwardly, hindered by a basket she's carrying.

Ava lets out a low whistle and crouches beside the bird. "Spirits, what a shot!" she murmurs. I'm perplexed. Does she mean that Arkhi shot the bird? How? The Muse has no slingshot, no bow, no arrows.

"Stay back!" Arkhi's shouts resolve into words as she nears us. "Don't touch that bird!"

Ava and I both step back quickly. Seeing that we've heard her, Arkhi slows and continues toward us at a somewhat more dignified pace until she reaches the fallen kuku. She kneels beside the bird. Kor catches up a moment later and joins Arkhi, setting down her basket between them.

"What's the matter?" says Ava, cautiously stepping up behind Arkhi and Kor. I join Ava and look down over Arkhi's shoulders at the motionless kuku. Arkhi reaches toward the kuku, and now I see the gleaming needle with a feathery blue fringe sticking out of the bird's neck. Arkhi plucks the needle out and tucks it inside the flat object that was flapping around her neck as she ran. It's a little wooden case of some sort, no larger than her palm. She wears it like a necklace under her robes.

Arkhi says to Kor, "Well, what do you think now?"

In the vague, wandering voice she uses whenever she's not talking to animals, Kor says, "Mmm … Yes, it's definitely her. I recognize this cross-hatching on her chest. See?" She points toward the right side of the bird's breast. I squint. Perhaps there is some subtle variation in the regular pattern of chestnut bars over the cream-colored chest feathers, but I couldn't differentiate this kuku from any other of the hundreds I've seen in my life. They're as common as squirrels. How did Kor notice such a small detail?

Arkhi looks up at me and Ava. The Muse says, "Kor believes this bird has been following the caravan since the first morning we broke camp."

I remember Kor feeding a kuku at camp that first day on the road. Ava made a joke of it, after overhearing the odd conversation between Kor and the bird.

"Is that … bad?" says Ava. She sounds as confused as I am.

Arkhi considers. "I'm not certain," she says. "It's unusual to see a kuku this far north and this far inland at this time of year. And it's strange behavior, for her to follow our caravan, especially across a desert." Arkhi withdraws a blue cloth from inside her black robes. She drops the cloth over the bird, scoops the creature up carefully in two hands, and deposits her into Kor's basket, closing it securely with a latched cover. "We'll ask Serapen what she thinks, when she returns."

"Serapen left?" I say, scanning the beach. The High Priestess is nowhere to be seen, and her grey mare Amisos is missing from among the horses grazing on the grassy stretch of riverbank beside the willows. Only now, knowing she's gone, do I realize how much safer I was feeling all day, simply assuming Serapen was nearby.

Feeling my anxiety, Ava squeezes my hand. *I'm sure Serapen didn't leave the camp unprotected,* she thinks.

"Don't worry," says Arkhi. "Serapen hasn't gone far. She's only summoning guards for the caravan."

"Has she gone to Upper Ford?" says Ava, perking up with interest.

What's Upper Ford? I think.

A men's village, a bit north of here, Ava thinks. *There's another river crossing there. I think that's where my mother was trying to take us last night on the boat.*

"There are no sisters at Upper Ford right now," says Arkhi. "And until we identify the men who took you captive, we can't trust any of our brothers there as guards."

Ava frowns and says, "But where else would Serapen find guards?"

Arkhi has no time to answer before the outburst of frightened whinnies at the edge of the willow grove. Everyone looks toward the horses.

△▽△

I clutch Dom's hand tightly in mine as I scan the willows behind the agitated horses. His pulse races with fear as he imagines my mother and a horde of free men bursting through the swaying curtains of branches. I don't see anything yet, but instinctively I slip my free hand into my tunic pocket, where I stashed the blade I recovered on the boat this afternoon. The blade has been without its handle since Calling Day, when I broke it off for easier concealment in my belt. I run my thumb along the sharp edge, considering how difficult it would be to wield the naked metal in a fight without cutting myself. I eye the long filleting knives Eumelia set to dry several paces away, wondering whether I have time to grab a pair of them for me and another for Dom before the unknown danger's upon us.

Dom steps in front of me protectively, obscuring my view. I bite back a curse of irritation with him, grip his arm, and step back out from behind him.

Can you see anything? I think, my eyes searching the willows behind the horses.

Nothing, thinks Dom. His arm is tense under my hand, and I feel the restraint he exerts to stop himself from stepping forward to shield me again.

When Serapen emerges from the willow grove astride Amisos, Dom and I share a sigh of relief. I expect the horses to calm down, too, but their shrieks escalate. Only when Serapen's hand moves over her embroidered sash do the horses quiet down, though they continue to stamp and snort anxiously. I have no idea what's bothering them until I notice the movement in the underbrush a few paces behind Amisos: a roiling mass of fur and eyes. The hairs on the back of my neck prickle in alarm.

Serapen dismounts and pats Amisos' flank, sending her off to join the other horses. Alone, the High Priestess faces the willows and lowers herself smoothly to a crouch. She drops her gaze, pressing one palm to the sand, extending her other hand toward the trees.

My eyes widen. The chattering voices up at the camp fall silent as two enormous wolves step out of the willows and walk slowly toward Serapen. They hold their heads high, their great pointed ears facing forward, their postures alert and curious. They're magnificent, with their long legs and snouts, their sharp ears and teeth, their elegant camouflage of grey and brown and black. As they approach Serapen, the golden light of late afternoon catches in their yellow eyes, which sweep over Serapen and take in the rest of us humans scattered around the beach. Behind the pair, at the edge of the willow grove, I see the crouching forms of three lanky juveniles and four little pups hanging back in the underbrush. The younger wolves' eyes follow every move of the older pair; these two must be the luna female and her alpha male.

The mated pair circle Serapen, sniffing her robes and hair. Fascinated, I watch them lick Serapen's outstretched arm, her exposed cheek and neck. The High Priestess moves her hand slowly between them, touching their muzzles lightly with her fingers, keeping her head at their level, eyes lowered. This sniffing and licking and touching goes on for some time, until at last the luna and the alpha seem satisfied. Their alert postures relax, and the younger wolves burst out onto the beach as if at some signal.

Serapen stands slowly, the long fingers of her right hand on her sash. The pack of wolves surrounds and follows her as she walks them toward the camp. Even from here, I see the whites of the horses' rolling eyes as they snort and stamp their disapproval of this whole affair.

As she draws closer to us, Serapen makes a few gestures over her sash, and the juveniles and pups split off and head up the beach toward the fire ring. All the novices working there have long since stopped what they're doing, and they watch in uneasy silence as the seven younger wolves approach them. At some word from Thalia, the novices resume working, keeping a wary eye on the large juvenile wolves, who settle down by the fire with alert expressions while the pups frolic and wrestle harmlessly around them.

The mated pair lingers behind with Serapen, the rangy alpha walking on her right side, the graceful luna on her left.

As Serapen approaches us, the pair trots ahead, straight toward me and Dom. Hanu whimpers, and Eumelia hushes her. Nervously, Dom and I draw close together. But when the two wolves reach us, they only sniff around our legs for a moment. When Serapen stops before us, the wolves return to her and sit down on either side of her. The High Priestess regards me and Dom for a moment with a calm, observant expression in her clear brown eyes. The luna and the alpha look up at us too, and it's unnerving to see that same calm, observant expression in their big yellow eyes.

Gesturing to the wolves, Serapen says to Arkhi, "These were all I could find nearby. How did you fare, sister?"

Arkhi's hand strokes the silver threads of her black stole, and she gestures toward the top of the river cliffs. A pair of falcons takes flight from a little hollow worn into the stone there. The falcons circle once overhead before returning to their perch. Serapen nods and says, "That should do. The visibility will be good across the last stretch of desert, until we reach the Urashtu Range."

"There's something else, Serapen," says Arkhi, nodding toward Kor. "Tell her, little sister."

Kor steps forward, carrying the basket that holds the fallen kuku. Kor says, "This kuku has been following us since the first night we made camp, Muse Serapen. She was hanging around the fish cleaning this afternoon, then started acting strangely. Muse Arkhi took her down with a dart."

"Ah," says Serapen. "Well spotted, Kor. Let me see her."

Kor delivers the basket into Serapen's hands. Serapen kneels on the sand, opens the basket, and lifts the blue cloth covering the kuku. The bird huddles quivering in a corner of the basket, staring up at all of us in fear. Serapen reaches into her robes, and when she withdraws her hand she's pinching a bit of off-white powder in her fingers. She sprinkles this over the kuku, and a moment later, the bird's eyes close. Serapen carefully examines the limp body of the kuku in the basket. She grasps the bird's clawed feet between her fingers and closes her eyes.

"Yes," Serapen murmurs a moment later. "This creature's awareness has been touched by binding pharmaka. I perceive traces of Lilith in her mind." Serapen cocks her head to one side, as if she's struggling to hear something. "And ... someone else, perhaps?"

Serapen opens her eyes and looks at me. I blink, confused. Serapen says, "Did you touch this bird, Ava?"

I've learned enough about the dangers of touch over the last half moon to know the importance of being absolutely sure. I replay the memory carefully. "She flew straight at me," I say. "I dodged away from her. She passed by close enough that I felt the air moving off her feathers. But, no, she didn't touch me."

"Are you sure?" says Serapen.

"As sure as I can be," I say, though I can't resist adding, "but memory can be imperfect."

If Serapen notices my jab, she makes no sign of it. "Yes," she says slowly. "Memory can be imperfect. Well, we must keep a better guard from now on. And we must take care of this bird."

"Take care of her how?" I say.

Serapen withdraws a silver flask from inside the blue folds of her outer robe. She picks up the blue cloth that had been covering the kuku, and she trickles a bit of golden liquid from the flask into it. I recognize the flowery sweet scent of unbinding pharmaka as it soaks into the fabric. "This bird has been scouting for

Lilith," says Serapen. "Since she approached you, she was likely sent to give you a message, or to take one from you."

"But I didn't receive a message, or try to send one," I say, uncertain whether Serapen's accusing me of something.

Serapen makes no response, wrapping her right hand in the damp cloth and reaching toward the unconscious bird.

"Wait," I say, hating the plaintive sound of my voice. I touch Serapen's shoulder, stopping her hand. The High Priestess looks up at me calmly. "Why would my mother try to send me a message now? I told her to leave me here. I told her I wouldn't go with her. I … well, you know what I did to send her away."

Serapen studies me. "Do you truly believe Lilith would abandon you so easily?" she says.

With angry sincerity, I say, "She did it before."

Serapen surprises me with a look of great tenderness. "Oh, child," she says, shaking her head.

I harden myself against an unexpected upwelling of emotion, struggling to keep my voice steady as I say, "My mother would never come back for me after what happened between us last night." I'm not sure whether I believe this, or whether I want this to be true.

"And yet the fact remains that she sent this bird after you," says Serapen.

"Well … even if my mother did send her, what do you have to do to the bird?" I say.

Serapen and Arkhi exchange a look. Patiently, Serapen says, "We cannot allow the bird to continue spying on us. Her memories must be unbound."

"And she has no choice in the matter?" I say, trying and failing to match Serapen's calm, firm tone. Even to my own ears, my voice sounds more like a petulant child's than a grown woman's.

"Our human schemes mean nothing to this creature, Ava," says Serapen. "She will be better off free of us. I will send her on her way, back to the south, where she belongs. What I will take is harmless to her."

"How can you be so sure?" I say. "Maybe the bird wants those memories. Maybe the bird will need those memories."

Serapen reaches out and touches my hand gently. I flinch, but I discover I don't want to pull away from the soothing sensation she pours into me. *I'm sure*, thinks Serapen. *Unbinding is a gift from the Voice, little sister. You will come to know it, too, when you are ready.*

I don't know why I'm sobbing.

Serapen sets the pharmaka-soaked cloth beside the unconscious kuku in the basket and stands before me. "Hush, hush, child," she whispers, embracing me gently in her sinewy arms, enclosing me in the sky blue folds of her healer's robe, redolent of spice and herbs and pharmaka. My breath comes in ragged gasps. Salty tears stream down my cheeks. Serapen tilts my face up to look at her, pressing her thumb to my forehead. A sensation of calm washes over me.

I sniff, catch my breath, and furiously wipe my eyes. Everyone is staring at me, and the heat of shame rises to my cheeks. I stumble back from Serapen, bumping into Dom. The graceful luna wolf cocks her head at me, trying to understand what's wrong with this little human. I wish I knew.

Dom wraps his arm around me, steadying me as I watch Serapen return to her work with the kuku.

It's not so bad, says Dom. *I saw Serapen do this to you, the night of your overdose. You looked peaceful afterwards.*

It's not right, I think, staring down at the bird, feeling dazed. *What right does she have to take anyone else's memories from them?*

Dom's reply has no words, only intention. He wants to comfort me as Serapen did, and what he lacks in skill he makes up for in earnestness. Despite myself, I feel a little better by the time the kuku blinks up at Serapen, coos loudly, and takes flight. The kuku heads directly south, downriver, back to wherever she belongs. I wish it were that easy for me to escape this mess.

△▽△

Ava hangs back on the beach while Serapen and the others rejoin the rest of the caravan up at the fire ring. The wolves, much like me, seem unwilling to let Ava move more than a few paces away from them. Ava speaks to the luna and alpha wolves in a friendly undertone, occasionally stroking their thick fur as they brush by her legs. She clearly finds them more fascinating than frightening, but they make me nervous, especially without Serapen nearby. I've buried more than a few carcasses of livestock attacked by wolves. I hope that whatever Serapen's done to these wolves makes them see us as pack rather than prey.

I push down my worry about the wolves for a moment to focus on Ava. She's mostly recovered her composure after her distraught weeping, though she looks pale and withdrawn. I'm surprised that little kuku bird was able to reduce her to tears, when nothing that happened last night could shake her. "Are you all right?" I say.

"I don't know what I am," she grumbles, her voice still congested from crying. "Just a fool, I guess. I don't know why watching Serapen use unbinding pharmaka bothers me so much more than it bothers anyone else."

"We're all used to seeing sisters use pharmaka like that," I say. "It's hard to be afraid of something so familiar."

Ava shakes her head. "My mother taught me this was all wrong. And now … I just don't know. I feel like I don't know anything any more."

"You still know more than I do," I say.

"Ugh," Ava groans, swinging her pack over her shoulders. "That's not saying much."

I risk giving her a good-natured shove in the arm. To my relief, she's strong enough to keep her balance now. She laughs, which makes me laugh.

"Can we go back to the others now?" I say. "I'd rather not be alone after dark with our new friends here. They look hungry."

Ava laughs again. In a bright, friendly voice, she says to the wolves, "You're not going to eat me, are you? Are you? No, I don't think so." She kneels before them like Serapen did, letting them sniff her arms and hands, giggling as they lick her cheeks and ears.

Though Ava still avoids looking directly at me, she reaches up and grips my hand, pulling insistently until I kneel beside her. Reluctantly, I let the huge wolves snuffle around my face and neck, cringing when the luna wolf licks my cheek and flinching when her mate breathes warm, musky wolf-breath down my neck. Ava seems entirely at ease, but I can't help questioning the wisdom of letting the wolves acquire a taste for our skin. Ava's amusement ripples through me as she thinks, *Don't worry. I won't let them hurt you.*

Exasperated, I think, *I can't tell if you're teasing me or you actually think you could fight off a pair of wolves.*

Why can't I do both? she thinks.

It's a relief to feel a bit of her old spirit resurfacing, but I don't like where this conversation is heading. "Come on," I say, hauling her up by the hand, "Let's get your things and go back to the others."

We gather the items the kuku pulled out of Ava's pack and scattered across the beach. I pick up Ava's old riding cloak and attempt to shake the river sand out of it. It's so encrusted with dried mud from prior adventures that I'm not able to make much of an improvement. Ava collects her riding boots and stands examining a line of scratches the kuku pecked into the leather of her right boot.

"How bad is the damage?" I say.

She spits into her palm and rubs the saliva into the leather. "Definitely left a mark," she says ruefully.

"One of the sisters in Velkanos can probably repair it," I say.

Ava squints, frowning at the marks on her boot. In a strange, slow way, she thinks, *Return … to …*

"Ava?" I say. "What is it?"

She blinks and looks up at me as if I've interrupted a daydream. "Hmm? Oh. Oh, yes. I'm sure it can be repaired," she says.

I hand Ava her pack, and she stuffs her old boots and cloak into it. We return to the others. The wolves follow close at our heels.

A COMPLICATED GIRL

Dom and I rejoin the Mohirai and the other novices working around the fire ring. This evening, a low cooking fire burns where the massive bonfire blazed last night. As the sun sinks behind the cliffs and the moon brightens in the sky across the river, Thalia directs the preparation of the evening meal, calling out orders to each of the novices. A vat of fish head stew, thick with vegetables from Urshanabi's garden, bubbles over the fire. The smoking tent that Kor's trio assembled earlier now stands over the oak coals. Hanu, Eumelia, Dom, and I spread the brined trout fillets evenly across the rack of cedar planks inside the smoking tent.

As we work, I try to keep my mind from fixating on the boot stuffed into the bottom of my pack. At first I thought I was imagining things, but I'm almost positive those scratches in the leather were letters. Dom didn't notice anything unusual, but that's not surprising since boys aren't taught to read.

Unfortunately, whatever message my mother was sending me must have been cut off when I grabbed my boot from the kuku. Beyond the first few letters—*return to*—I couldn't make out anything else. I'll have to find some time alone with Dom to show him the marks. I don't want anyone else to see whatever message my mother was trying to send me.

Once the fragrant stew is ready, Arkhi ladles it out. Full bowls pass from hand to hand. We set down a portion of the trout on a spare cedar plank for the wolves. The three Mohirai rise and stand around the fire, palms turned up to the darkening sky. They lead us in the meal blessing.

We give our thanks for gifts of sun
Of water, soil, and seed
For gifts of many seasons
Gathered here to meet our need
To build our strength so that our hands
May in their time return
The gifts received from mother land
Improved with gifts our own

After so many days of practicing separation from Dom to prepare for my escape, I could sit apart from him for the duration of the meal without much discomfort, but he and I wordlessly agree we're too drained to bother. The long day of working in the sun was tiring all on its own, but the strange ordeal of my departure for another branch is what's truly exhausted us both. Though I continue to avoid looking at Dom as much as possible, I rest my bare foot alongside his in the sand, letting his touch keep the wearisome pain at bay.

Dom and I eat in ravenous silence as the sun sets. Grey coils of fragrant smoke rise up through the tent of fish into the violet sky. Crickets chorus in the grass along the riverbank.

The wolves make quick work of their meal. The four full-bellied pups collapse into a sleepy, contented pile near the fire, their furry ears and toes twitching as they slip into dreams. The alpha and the luna lead the three juveniles away from the fire. They set up a patrol of the camp perimeter, loping silently on their long legs between the river cliffs and the willow grove, back and forth along the water's edge. The horses stir anxiously every time they scent one of the wolves, but Serapen's somehow managed to stop their terrified whinnying.

As the twilight deepens, the patrolling wolves become nearly invisible, except for an occasional startling flash of reflective yellow eyes peering at me through the darkness. Though I'm sure Serapen has as much control over the wolves as she has over the rest of us, every rustle in the shadows still sends a prickle down my spine. Dom seems even jumpier than I am, though I'm not sure whether it's the thought of wolves or free men pouncing that sets him more on edge.

The spicy, savory stew and Urshanabi's hearty flat bread slowly soothe our nerves. A goblet of last night's mixed wine wouldn't hurt, either, but revelry is clearly the last thing on the minds of the three Mohirai, who huddle together with Urshanabi on the other side of the fire ring, murmuring to each other, their expressions solemn. The other girls around us chat in low voices, occasionally glancing my way with curious looks.

Dom and I have just finished eating when Serapen stands. The soft conversations around the campfire fall silent as we all turn our attention to the High Priestess. She takes a step closer to the fire. The coals cast a warm glow over her dark features and snow-white hair.

In her right hand, the High Priestess holds a cedar staff that's even taller than she is. I've never seen a staff like this before. It resembles a shepherd's staff, but it's far more beautifully wrought. Intricate carvings of vines and flowers twine up the shaft, interspersed with stylized forms of snakes and birds. Where a shepherd's crook would be, this staff is topped instead by a roughly spherical natural burl, large as a sweet melon, partly hollow, polished so the swirling wood grain gleams in the firelight.

Serapen waves her staff low over the rippling heat of the coals. A coil of pure white smoke spirals upward from a small crack in the burled top of the staff, emanating a pungent herbal scent. I try to breathe as little and as slowly as possible. After what I saw Serapen do to the kuku this afternoon, my aversion to pharmaka is even stronger than usual.

Serapen looks at me from across the fire, drawing all eyes to me. My heart pounds in my ears. Unconsciously, I reach for Dom's hand. He squeezes my fingers. *You're all right,* he thinks.

Am I? I think.

"Listen well, novices," says Serapen. "Last night, our sister Ava fled our company. She acted out of a mistaken belief taught to her by a woman Ava calls mother."

I narrow my eyes suspiciously, unsettled by the way Serapen said *a woman Ava calls mother*. The other novices around the campfire exchange puzzled glances. They're probably just confused by the word *mother,* though. I explained that word to Dom recently, but it would be unknown to the rest of the novices. The Mohirai keep mothers among the mysteries for the children they raise.

Serapen continues, "This woman, Lilith, walked the path of mysteries among the Mohirai for many centuries. Lilith is lost at present, wandering far from her initiate vows. But any sister may find herself lost on the path at times, and none of us may judge the path of another. In every path, the sum of all."

In every path, the sum of all. My mother despises this ancient saying. When I was a small girl who knew nothing but the instruction of the sisters in the Children's Temple, I thought these words meant that the Voice teaches all of us the same lessons in our lives, even if our callings are very different. But my mother taught me that the Mohirai have twisted the meaning of this saying to justify their subjugation of men and their rule over all the people of Dulai.

Serapen's eyes fix on me. She says, "Lilith no doubt told you that she abandoned her vows to our sisterhood. But I suspect she never told you why. Initiate Mohirai are bound and sworn to speak the truth. Though initiates may keep mysteries from those unprepared to receive them, we may not lead others into error knowingly. By abandoning her vows, Lilith freed herself from such constraints, so she could deceive you."

I frown, weighing Serapen's words against my mother's teaching. My mother taught me that the Mohirai use the mysteries to hide whatever they wish to keep secret, because initiate Mohirai can't deceive one another outright. The Mohiran arts for detecting deception make lying impractical for priestesses. I witnessed my mother deceive many other people—Mohirai as well as men—during our years in the wilderness. But I never considered that she might have broken her priestess vows specifically so that she could deceive me. My mind reels. Could Serapen be telling the truth? Is it even possible for Serapen to lie?

As if overhearing my thought, Serapen says, "I call my initiate sisters here as witnesses." She gestures to Arkhi and Thalia, who gaze at me solemnly. "So you may know that all I say is true."

Serapen's eyes gleam in the firelight as she looks at me. The heady fragrance of the white smoke drifting up from her staff grows steadily stronger. Serapen takes a deep, slow breath of the smoke. Unconsciously imitating Serapen, Dom and the other novices inhale, exhale, and relax. Tense, I scarcely breathe.

Serapen's tone is gentle as she says to me, "Listen, Ava. The last time I saw your mother was seventeen springs ago. She labored long to bring you into this world, as she was called to do by the Voice. She delivered you into my hands. This was the last service the Voice required of her. I did everything within my power to save your mother. But she died the day you were born."

I stare up at Serapen. Softly, I say, "My mother died?"

Serapen nods. Her eyes gleam with tears. The words of the High Priestess seem to come from a great distance as she says in a slow, patient voice, "Yes, Ava.

Your mother died. Her name was Maya. Maya was very dear to me, and to all who knew her. She was dearest of all to Lilith. So it was Lilith who stepped forward to care for you in Maya's stead, in the years before your unbinding. But Lilith is not your mother, not in the way she led you to believe. Maya was your mother."

In the long silence that follows Serapen's words, I hear nothing but a faint, high-pitched ringing in my ears and feel nothing but a growing numbness in my heart. How many times did Lilith tell me the story of my birth, of the lengths to which Serapen had gone to erase my childhood memories of her, of the great wrong the Mohirai commit each time they destroy the natural bond between a mother and her child? She made sure that I saw with my own eyes how the healers unbind children and what happens to their mothers in the years that follow. She had railed against the injustice of the Voice's command to erase kinship ties. She had promised me a future in which we would live together as a family in the land of freedom on the far side of the great ocean, beyond the control of the Mohirai. Why would she teach me all of this, if she has no true kinship tie to me? And if she lied to me about such an important thing, how can I trust anything else she taught me?

The Muses, the other novices, and even Dom seem to recede from me like a tide going out, leaving me alone on a distant shore. Is this how the little kuku in the basket felt as the High Priestess reached down to wipe away her memories?

"But why would my mo—" I trip awkwardly over the word *mother* and have to start over. "Why would Lilith lie to me?"

Serapen shakes her head. "I do not know why Lilith deceived you, or why she allied herself with the men who took you captive last night. All I know with certainty is that Maya bore you in service to the Voice. Maya placed you in the care of our sisterhood with her blessing, intending you to take your place among us. It is your birthright as a child of the Voice to live among your sisters, Ava. Lilith had no right to rob you of your sisterhood, or to rob us of you."

A tremor somewhere deep inside of me breaks through the numbness. Through our connection, I feel Dom's impulse to hug me.

Serapen says, "I am sorry you have learned your mother's name this way, Ava. Most sisters learn their mothers' names only after initiation, when the Voice's purpose is more deeply understood, and our hearts are prepared for such knowledge. But in this, as in so many things, the Voice seems to have called you to a more difficult path."

Unsteadily, I stand, desperate to escape from all the eyes staring at me around the campfire. Dom scrambles to his feet to follow me. To my relief, Serapen stops him, saying, "Let her go, little brother."

I stumble through the shadows toward our tent beneath the cliffs. Futile questions swirl through my mind like the last of the autumn leaves. Could everything I believed in be a lie, then? Even the possibility of freedom from the Voice in all?

Lilith spent years teaching me the importance of questioning everything.

Why didn't I question her more deeply? Perhaps I can forgive my childhood ignorance; I had only nine summers when Lilith first approached me in the woods, capturing my imagination with tales of a new world across the sea. But I'm no longer a child. How did Lilith manage to fool me so completely?

Or did I fool myself, deluded by dreams of freedom that could never become my reality?

△▽△

Serapen keeps the rest of us back at the campfire for a little while after Ava departs, addressing many questions raised by the other girls on the subject of mothers. From all the discussion, I gather that the girls received far more instruction on the subject of human breeding in the Children's Temple than I did in the house of boys. Yet even the girls hadn't known until tonight that initiate Mohirai learn their mothers' names.

I wonder whether I'll learn my own mother's name someday, too, or whether that's a mystery kept from boys. I don't find the right moment to ask, though. I'm still uncomfortable speaking in large gatherings of women, and there are too many girls talking for me to get in a word, anyway. Eumelia's questions in particular are inexhaustible. The High Priestess hasn't answered even half of the girls' questions before she bids us return to our tents, promising that there will be ample time to discuss this more in the days to come, after a good night's sleep.

Hanu, Eumelia, and I return to our tent. We find Ava sitting at the foot of her bedroll near the open tent flap. She doesn't look up as we approach. Hanu, Eumelia, and I exchange uneasy looks, uncertain how or when to speak to her. I'm wary of disturbing Ava further after such a trying day; Hanu and Eumelia seem to share my concern. The three of us file past Ava and prepare for bed in awkward silence.

I can't stop myself from stealing glances at Ava. She combs out her long black curls with her fingers, braiding her hair loosely over her shoulder, as is her habit before sleep. She hugs her knees to her chest, sitting perfectly still for a moment. Her sorrow wells up in me just before her shoulders begin to shake with silent sobs.

Hanu looks at me with gleaming eyes. Even Eumelia, who normally hardens herself against displays of uncomfortable emotion, sighs in sympathy. The familiar pain of separation from Ava prickles in my chest. I reach toward her shoulder to relieve it.

"Don't," says Ava, without turning around. My hand stops mid-air.

"Please, Ava," I say, cautiously moving to sit beside her, but keeping a little space between us.

She shakes her head. In an exhausted voice, she says, "It's too hard to hold back memories of that other-Dom when you touch me. I have to focus, if I'm going to stay here. You want me to stay, don't you?"

Hanu and Eumelia look from Ava to me in confusion. There's a lot to catch them up on since last night, but now isn't the time to attempt an explanation.

Frustrated, I rake my fingers through my hair. "Of course I want you to stay," I say to Ava. "But you can't sleep this way. Neither can I. What are we going to do?" The Voice has placed us in another impossible situation. How can I be both cause and cure for Ava's pain?

Ava buries her face in her knees. "I don't know," she mumbles miserably.

After a long silence, Hanu says softly, "Would you like me to help?" Her voice is sweet as honey, just as it was when she said these words to me on the dock earlier today.

I'm about to tell Hanu again that there's really nothing she can do when Ava raises her head and looks over her shoulder at Hanu. It's hard to see Ava's expression in the darkness, but I feel her desperate hope that Hanu's touch might relieve her pain now that mine cannot.

Hanu gently nudges my arm, prompting me to make way for her. Reluctantly, I make a Hanu-sized space between me and Ava. Hanu slips into the opening and wraps one arm gently around Ava. I can still feel the sharp pain in Ava's chest that comes whenever she's struggling with her amplified awareness of the Voice. Hanu's touch doesn't relieve this particular pain, but her presence does ease Ava's raw grief about Lilith.

I watch the two of them, trying to suppress my jealousy and appreciate whatever comfort Hanu can offer Ava, however small. Then, to my surprise, Hanu wraps her other arm around my waist. Her fingers slip under my tunic, tingling against my bare skin. She draws me gently into the connection she's sharing with Ava.

The bond between the three of us feels different from the bond between either two of us alone—a more balanced blend of Ava's energy, my calm, and Hanu's sensitivity. I wonder whether it's Hanu's influence that causes my body's edges to blur into the other two girls. I feel at once the softness of Hanu's arm around my waist, the taut muscle of my back under Hanu's arm, the cool pressure of Ava's tearstained cheek against Hanu's; the smooth warmth of Hanu's cheek against Ava's. It's disorienting, but not unpleasant. Hanu kisses Ava's cheek, then my cheek. Through Hanu's lips, I taste the salt of Ava's tears and feel my own rough stubble. I rub the prickly sensation off my mouth with the back of my hand. The acute pain in Ava's chest, the echoing pain in my chest, and the sympathetic pain in Hanu's chest gradually ease.

Savoring the relief from pain, Ava and I relax gratefully against Hanu.

Behind us, Eumelia says, "Well, don't worry about me. I'll just be sleeping all alone here in my corner."

Ava's shoulders shake again, but this time it's her silent mirth that ripples from her through Hanu to me. Encouraged by this welcome change in the mood, and energized by the absence of pain, I take inspiration from the wolf pups and float an idea to Ava and Hanu through our connection.

They're both game. The three of us turn around.

Eumelia's startled cry is cut off as first Ava, then Hanu, then I pounce on her, flattening her onto her bedroll. Ava's infectious giggle bursts out from somewhere near the bottom of the pile, setting the rest of us laughing.

There's a jostling of arms and legs and knees and elbows. Eumelia says indignantly to no one in particular, "You are actually crushing me, you know." I sense Eumelia's awareness through Hanu, though, and I can tell she's enjoying having Ava's body pressed against hers. So I keep the girls trapped under me a little longer. Only when the giggles subside do I let the pile disperse.

In the darkness, we wordlessly rearrange the bedrolls. Hanu lies between me and Ava. Ava lies between Hanu and Eumelia. I'd have preferred to keep my place at Ava's side, but anywhere inside this tent is better than most places I've slept in my life.

The four of us lie awake in the darkness, Ava wrapped in Hanu's arms, my hand resting on Hanu's waist, Eumelia's fingers laced through Ava's. The first time the four of us were joined by the binding pharmaka, it was unintentional, when Hanu and I tried to intervene in an altercation between Ava and Eumelia yesterday. That contact was brief, explosive, and confusing. Ava ended it quickly by withdrawing from the three of us. But now Ava remains with us, too exhausted to do anything but simply accept the comfort we're trying to give her.

Hanu, Ava, and I have enough experience with binding pharmaka to be accustomed to sharing thoughts through touch. We've had time to practice the restraint that makes this sharing less jarring. Hanu and I intuit what Ava needs. *We're here for you,* we think. *You'll be all right. We love you.* Eumelia tries to join us. Unfortunately, she has far less experience than we do with binding pharmaka. Her thoughts tumble through our joined awarenesses like a curious kitten: amusing to watch, until her sharp claws inadvertently catch on something sensitive.

Why did Serapen wait so long to tell you about Lilith? thinks Eumelia. *She could have saved you and Dom a lot of trouble if she'd just told you all of that as soon as Lilith left you behind at the Children's Temple on Calling Day.*

Eumelia's thought agitates Ava, stirring her distrust of Serapen, her confusion about Lilith's deception, and her raw anguish over her abandonment. I feel the tears welling up in Ava's eyes.

Hanu attempts to soothe Ava, thinking, *I'm sure Serapen had a perfectly good reason for keeping that a mystery. You should ask her.*

Ava's bitterness floods through all of us. She thinks, *Ask. Don't ask. It doesn't matter. You can't trust any of them. All these women ever do is manipulate what you see, what you think, what you feel.*

Just like you, thinks Eumelia, her wry observation spilling into the shared connection before Hanu or I can do anything to stop her.

Ava's anger at Eumelia flares briefly before fading into sadness. Silent tears roll down her cheeks.

Horrified, Eumelia thinks, *Oh, spirits, Ava. I'm sorry. I don't know why I thought that. I didn't mean it. I'm really sor—*

Ava pulls her hand away abruptly from Eumelia and rolls over to face Hanu, cutting off Eumelia's awareness from the rest of us.

"Ava?" Eumelia whispers.

Ava buries her face in Hanu's shoulder. Hanu sighs, kisses Ava's forehead, and slowly strokes her hair. Gradually, Ava's tears and ragged breathing subside.

I look over at Eumelia on the far side of the tent, her face just visible in the soft moonlight glowing through the canvas walls. She's turned onto her side and watches the three of us in our little sleeping pile. Her gaze lingers on Ava curled up in Hanu's arms. When Eumelia's eyes meet mine, I don't need binding pharmaka to understand her expression. Whatever our differences, Eumelia and I have one important thing in common. We've both fallen in love with a complicated girl.

INTERSECTIONS

I LIE ON MY BEDROLL nestled in Hanu's soothing embrace. Dom and Hanu's desire to comfort me flows through our shared connection like warm bathwater. My grief over Lilith and my irritation with Eumelia slowly dissolve, leaving behind nothing but exhaustion. I relax. I'm almost asleep when there's a pull somewhere deep inside me. Where have I felt that before?

Oh, spirits. No, no, no. I fight whatever it is that's pulling me away from my branch, but it's futile. I descend into darkness faster than falling through a trapdoor.

Falling turns into floating. It's impossible to tell how long I float in this place of darkness and nothingness before light appears ahead. The light pulls me onward, until I re-emerge elsewhere. Below me lies a familiar city, surrounded on three sides by the ocean. Cool wind rushes over my skin like a river current. I relax. Maybe this is just a dream. For as long as I can remember, my dreams have been full of scenes like this one: me soaring like a bird over the city of glass towers.

Elated by the sensation of flight, I swoop down toward the city. Directly ahead of me, amidst the cluster of majestic towers at the center of the city, the tapered pinnacle of one tower stands above the rest: a symmetrical, rounded pillar of gleaming glass framed by the clear blue summer sky.

I'm sailing over this high tower when the faint shout of a woman's voice drifts up to me. With the rushing wind in my ears, it's impossible to make out her words. I pause, hovering, and look down at the rooftop below me. A woman stands alone on the rooftop, waving both arms energetically up at me. "Ava! Ava!" she calls.

Who is this woman? How does she know my name? I descend toward her in slow spirals. At first it seems that I'm flying toward her, but my stomach tightens as I realize I'm unable to reverse course. Is she pulling me down to her against my will?

My bare feet touch down lightly on the pale paving stones an arm's length away from the woman. We stand facing each other. I examine her unusual clothing: an emerald green shirt with a circular white insignia, a single black glove on her right hand with silver threads that run over the back of her fingers, tight black trousers, white shoes striped with blue and green. She wears blue eyeglasses with lenses so dark I can't imagine how she sees through them. But when she taps the side of her glasses with her gloved hand, the lenses suddenly clear, revealing her vivid green eyes. Only then do I recognize Emmie Bridges.

I'm astonished by the transformation in Emmie. No wonder I didn't recognize her at first. She bears little resemblance to the woman I saw in the mirror this morning. Her gaunt angles and frail posture are gone. Her cheeks are rosy and rounded, her vivid green eyes sparkling. She bounces on the balls of her feet, evidently unable to contain her excitement at my arrival.

At last! Emmie thinks, grinning.

Despite my instinctive wariness, Emmie's delight is infectious. I can't help smiling cautiously back at her. *How are we sharing thoughts?* I think.

We share a lot more than that, she thinks wryly. *I can't tell you how good it is to finally meet you.*

But we already met, I think. Or did we? It would be impossible for the Emmie I saw this morning to have recovered so much vitality in such a short time. It makes no sense. But then again, I suppose it doesn't have to make sense. This is just a dream, isn't it?

A dream? she thinks. *Maybe you're dreaming. But I live on this branch, so it's not a dream to me.*

My skin prickles in alarm. If this isn't a dream, I'm in trouble. *I shouldn't be here,* I think urgently, to myself as much as to Emmie. *My body is too weak to be traveling between branches like this. I need to go back to my branch.* But how can I get back? I haven't had any new training in branch travel since my accidental bridge crossing this morning. Can I fly back the way I came? I shift my weight uncertainly from foot to foot, wondering whether I might take flight again that way. Unfortunately, the effortless ability to fly that I possessed just moments ago seems to have abandoned me. I'm anchored to the ground as firmly as any wingless creature. Anxiously, I scan the rooftop for some other exit.

Don't be afraid, thinks Emmie. Her calm flows into me, much like it does when Dom touches me. *Where were you, before you were here?*

Other-Dom asked me the same question the last time I crossed a bridge. Why does this matter? *I was falling asleep in a tent, on the banks of the Purattu river,* I think.

That's good, she thinks. *So you're asleep?*

I thought I was, I say. *I suppose I still am, if I'm here.*

That's good, she thinks. *Dom told me that sleeping is the safest way to travel between branches. The body lets go of the awareness more easily in sleep, and it's usually less of a shock when awareness returns on waking. But ...* Emmie's expression turns puzzled. *How old are you?*

Seventeen summers, I think.

Haven't you learned this already, then, in your novice training in Velkanos? she thinks.

No. I'm not in Velkanos yet, I think. *I'd rather not go there at all, but it doesn't seem like I have a choice at the moment.*

Emmie thinks, *You must be with Serapen, though. Isn't she training you?*

Serapen is no help, I think irritably. *All she told me is that each life is a kind of branch in the path of mysteries, and that a single awareness flows through all the branches. What on Dulai is that supposed to mean?*

Emmie tilts her head thoughtfully. *A single awareness flows through all the branches ...* Her gaze drifts away from me. She flicks the silver-threaded fingertips of her gloved right hand in the air and says something aloud that I don't understand. I remember other-Dom's hands moving like this while we were in the alternet together. Emmie's gaze refocuses on me. *But why don't you want to go to Velkanos?* she says. *Dom told me that you've wanted to be a Mohira since you were a little girl.*

Emmie must have learned this from other-Dom; surely my Dom couldn't have told her. Her knowledge of my childhood wishes is unsettling. My usual instinct is to hide my thoughts and desires from strangers, unless there's a good reason to share them, but it's difficult to hide my thoughts from someone who is already inside my head—especially someone who seems so sincerely interested in me. *I did want to be a Mohira, a long time ago,* I think. *Now … I don't know. All I know is that I need to get out of here fast. Do you know how I can get back to my branch?*

Emmie frowns. *Travel between branches is difficult to control without the training the Mohirai provide,* she thinks. *I've been trying to travel from my branch for a long time, but I haven't managed to do it yet. It only just occurred to me to try calling you to me, instead. I can't believe it worked! But now that you're here, maybe we can help each other. I need information from your branch, and you might be able to use what Dom and I are working on here to help you return to your branch.*

Other-Dom also mentioned some work he and Emmie were doing together, when I visited his branch this morning. Hadn't he called it *our great work*? I was pulled away from him too fast to find out what he meant. But if Emmie thinks this work can help me travel back to my own branch, I want to learn everything about it. *What is it you're working on, exactly?* I think.

It's … As Emmie searches for words, images flash through my mind: glowing spheres and ghostly branches writhing and morphing like some strange plant growing into its final form. The images pass so quickly that I can't make any sense of them. *Well, it's complicated,* she thinks. *But it's a kind of map, a way to see how different branches connect to each other.*

A map? I think, hope flaring in my chest. *Could you show it to me?*

△▽△

Hanu and I lie in silence beside one another, sending comforting feelings toward Ava through our shared bond. As Ava relaxes, Hanu and I relax. What a relief. Maybe we're going to get some rest after this exhausting day, after all.

We watch Ava's awareness slip into dreams. Soon, she's flying high over the city of glass towers. Her dream exerts a strong pull on both of us through the binding pharmaka, amplifying my drowsiness and Hanu's. After spending so much time in Ava's waking and sleeping mind since her overdose, I've grown used to the sight of the city of glass towers. The sprawling unwalled city surrounded on three sides by ocean is new to Hanu, however.

Is that a real place? Hanu thinks sleepily.

I don't know, I think, my eyelids growing heavy. When Ava looked at the city —San Francisco, I remember other-Dom called it—through Emmie's eyes this morning, it certainly seemed real to her. But what is real, really?

There's a long moment of peaceful stillness in the tent. I've just about drifted off to sleep when a rustle on the far side of the tent pulls me back toward wakefulness. My groggy mind conjures alarming thoughts of wolves and Lilith and free men. Heart pounding, I lift my head from my pillow, looking over Hanu's shoulder toward the sound.

It's Eumelia. She's propped up on one elbow, shaking Ava's shoulder gently. "Ava?" she whispers.

"Leave her alone, Eumelia," I whisper, annoyed by the disturbance. "She needs sleep, can't you—"

Eumelia cuts me off. "Ava?" she says, more loudly this time, shaking Ava's shoulder harder. "Are you all right?"

Her tone of alarm wakes me up faster than a bucket of cold water. Hanu's eyes flutter open. I reach over Hanu for Ava's hand. Her fingers are freezing. "Eumelia!" I cry. "Go get—"

But Eumelia is already halfway out of the tent, running toward the Muses' tent, calling for Serapen.

I kneel at Ava's side, gripping her hand in mine. Hanu sits up beside me and rests one warm hand on my forearm and the other on Ava's shoulder. Her soothing energy is all that's stopping my mind from spiraling into the dark memory of Ava's death last night.

"She'll be all right, Dom," says Hanu. "Muse Serapen will help."

Eumelia returns a moment later with Serapen, Arkhi, and Thalia. Serapen sends Hanu and Eumelia outside the tent to wait with the other Muses, but she lets me stay inside with Ava.

Serapen kneels beside Ava across from me and sets a candle down near the head of the bedroll. Despite the warm candlelight, Ava's complexion appears sickly grey. I can just make out the faint rise and fall of her chest as she breathes. Serapen unlaces the collar of Ava's sleeping tunic and presses her hands to the bare skin over Ava's heart.

Outside the tent, Eumelia paces back and forth, wringing her hands, refusing Hanu's attempts to console her.

After a long silence, I can't stop myself from asking in a hushed tone, "Is she going to die again, Muse Serapen?"

Without lifting her gaze from Ava's face, Serapen says calmly, "All must make the journey through Death, when our service to the Voice is complete. Only the time is uncertain. But you need not fear for Ava's life just yet. She is weak, but traveling between branches while sleeping is far less dangerous for the mind and body than traveling while awake."

Less dangerous? I grip Ava's hand tighter, my heart aching with fear. I can't bear the thought of her in danger after everything that happened to her last night. "There must be something we can do," I say. "Can't we call her back like we did before?"

Serapen's eyes reflect the candlelight when she meets my gaze. In the tone of instruction, she says, "The choice is yours, novice Artifex. You may choose to recall Ava again using your shared bond. But consider carefully. Though we may lend our hands to one another in aid, each of us must walk our own path through the mysteries in the end."

Serapen's warning forces me to stop and think. I remember the Voice's words to me on my Calling Day. *You have asked it. We may give it. But there is a price. Do you accept it?* When I accepted my calling, I had no idea what the price might be to have what I desired, or who might be required to pay that price. Over the half moon since then, I've seen again and again how Ava has paid for my desires. My desire to help Ava the night of her overdose bound her to me against her will. My desire to hear my calling prevented her escape from the Mohirai on our Calling Day. My desire to follow her out of the camp last night led her to give her life to protect me from Lilith and the free men. I want nothing more than to call her back to me now, but what might she pay for my wish this time?

Serapen watches me expectantly. At last, I say, "Let's wait. Maybe she'll find a way back on her own."

Serapen nods. "A difficult choice, but a wise one. We will wait."

△▽△

Emmie leads me to a doorway that stands near the center of the glass tower's rooftop. She pauses before the white double doors, pulls a white card from the back pocket of her trousers, and presses the card against a shiny panel mounted beside the doorframe. That card must be some kind of key, because a metal lock unlatches with a prompt *snick*.

Emmie pulls open the doors and heads inside the tower. I follow her for a few steps. Then I pause. The long, windowless hallway ahead of us is unnaturally silent. I'm unsettled by the strange flat light that emanates from the panels in the ceiling. Without the sun overhead, I'm disoriented. My pulse quickens. My eagerness to see what lies inside one of these glass towers fades into apprehension. The doors swing smoothly shut behind me, and the faint *snick* of the latch re-catching makes me jump. I look back. Are we locked in here?

Don't worry, Emmie thinks. *We don't need a key to get out, just to get in. See?* She demonstrates, returning to the door, twisting the handle, and pushing it open again.

I look at the blue sky outside and take a deep breath to slow my heartbeat. Stay calm, Ava. Focus on the job. *Where is the map?* I think.

It's in the alternet, she thinks. *I'll need a spliner to show it to you. There's one in the office a few floors down. That's where I'm taking you. Will you come with me?*

I have no idea what an office is, but a few floors down sounds manageable. I nod.

Emmie walks down the hallway. Out of long habit, I note identifying features of each door we pass along the way. I've had to escape unfamiliar storerooms and Mohiran temples in a hurry so many times before that I always make sure to know my exits.

Emmie turns right at a four-way intersection with another hallway and pushes open the first door on the left. This door leads into a windowless stairwell. I follow her down three flights of stairs. She pauses before the door at the landing. The door is painted emerald green and bears the same white insignia as Emmie's shirt: the stylized silhouette of a leafless tree and its roots, enclosed in a circle. Emmie opens the door with another tap of her key card.

We step into a sun-drenched hallway that's far more cheerful than the windowless one upstairs. Muffled sounds of footsteps and voices carry along the pale beech floorboards. The glass wall to our left looks out over a dramatic view of the glittering bay east of the city. The familiar profile of the hills across the water reorients me. I'm struck by the thought that, as I stood with other-Dom on the far side of the bay this morning, I looked west toward this very tower. I scan the eastern hills, wondering where Emmie's cliffside house might be.

Emmie points. *A little to the left, north of the bridge ... Yes, there,* she thinks. *Those are the Oakland hills.*

We continue down the corridor. The pale blue inside wall on our right is punctuated at regular intervals by glass windows that look into small rooms. Some rooms are empty, but in others I glimpse groups of men and women gathered around tables or standing before white walls covered in colorful handwriting.

Emmie stops at a shiny black door near the end of the hall. She pulls the key card from her back pocket again and reaches toward the panel beside the door. Before she opens it, three men round the corner of the hallway ahead, walking our way.

The first man is older than the other two and wears a rumpled, colorful shirt that bulges over his large belly. The second man is tall and slouching, with a sharp gaze made sharper still by his small, close-set eyeglasses. Both men carry cups of some steaming, deliciously fragrant brew. These two men listen intently to the third, a young man who can't be much older than I am.

The young man wears what I now recognize as immerger clothes: skin-tight black fabric gleaming with silver threads. He speaks in a clear, animated voice. I don't understand what he's saying, but it sounds like the English tongue other-Dom sometimes used. The young man's gloved fingertips light up occasionally with specks of red and green light as he punctuates his speech with precise gestures. When he sees Emmie, he breaks off what he's saying and greets her in a respectful tone. Emmie replies briefly. Though I don't understand her words, the deferential expressions of all three men are easy enough to read. Emmie must be some sort of high-ranking priestess here.

However, none of the men acknowledge my presence as they continue on their way; they behave as though I don't exist. That would never happen in Dulai. Men in Dulai are all trained from an early age to acknowledge, respect, and obey women. Even a novice Mohira like me would rank higher than any of these men. I suppose the rules governing Emmie's branch are different from my own.

Emmie chuckles. *Yes, Earth is a little different from Dulai, in that way,* she thinks. *But that's not why they ignored you. They just can't see you.*

Emmie taps her key card against the panel beside the door, which retracts into the wall. The large, empty, windowless space ahead of us looks like the spliner other-Dom showed me the last time I visited Earth, though this spliner is larger—easily ten times wider and longer, with a ceiling perhaps three times higher. We step inside onto the springy grey floor, and the door slides silently shut behind us.

Where's the map? I think, looking around the empty spliner, eager to see it transform into whatever Emmie is about to show me.

Emmie glances at me with an amused smile. *You're as impatient as I am,* she thinks. *Calm down. We're getting there.* She digs a silver-threaded black glove—the twin of the one she's wearing on her right hand—and pulls it onto her left hand. She touches the side of her eyeglasses, sliding her forefinger along the frame until the clear lenses darken.

Waving one hand, Emmie says something in English. The glowing grey walls dim, and a faint sphere of light gathers between us, as though we stand in a dark cave sharing a single candle. *Let me see ...* she thinks. *So you said you're coming from a tent on the Purattu ... Seventeen summers ...*

Emmie flicks her fingers through the air, and the empty sphere of light between us fills with a perfect landscape in miniature, more realistic than the most detailed painting I've ever seen in a Mohiran temple. Before I have a chance to examine it fully, Emmie sweeps this sphere to one side and conjures another, then another, then another, until we're encircled by gently glowing spheres of little landscapes that float around our heads like so many bubbles. *Do any of these look like the place where you were?* she thinks.

I turn slowly in place, carefully examining the landscape within each sphere. A few of them appear to be ferry crossings on the Purattu river, which I recognize from my travels with Lilith, but I don't see anything close to where we made camp. *No,* I think. *I'm near Urshanabi's ferry crossing, under the river cliffs.*

Oh, thinks Emmie. *I think Dom's recorded a few memories from there before. Hang on.* Her hands move in a rapid series of precise gestures. The circle of spheres around us vanishes, and another set appears. This time, each sphere shows a location near Urshanabi's ferry crossing: the garden outside his little stone house; the carved stone staircase that descends from his house at the top of the river cliffs down to the little strip of beach; the dock where his ferry is tied up, bobbing in the river current. *Are any of these closer?* she thinks.

I point at the little landscape showing the stairs carved into the river cliffs. *My tent is near there,* I think.

Emmie gestures toward that sphere, and the other spheres fade away. She plucks the chosen sphere from the air with one gloved hand, presses it between both her hands, and pulls her hands apart. She now holds twin spheres, each containing an identical miniature landscape of the cliffs near Urshanabi's house. I blink in surprise at this trick. Before I have a chance to ask what she's done, Emmie tosses away one of the spheres, which vanishes into thin air. She raises the remaining sphere before her. The sphere expands rapidly, swallowing first Emmie and then me as the miniature landscape grows into a full-sized landscape that fills the entire spliner around us. The grey spliner walls fade and then vanish. We appear to be standing at the bottom of the stone staircase that connects Urshanabi's house atop the river cliffs to the beach down on the riverbank. The view is as realistic as that of the hilltop grove other-Dom showed me in the alternet this morning.

I scan the base of the cliffs until I spot the little alcove where Dom, Hanu, Eumelia, and I pitched our tent yesterday. Some of the trees and shrubs growing here are different from the vegetation I remember, but the sandy path through the underbrush that connects the cliffs to the beach is the same. I follow the path toward the cliffs, Emmie close behind me. We stop in the empty patch of sand where my tent should be.

Here? thinks Emmie.

Yes, I was in a tent right here, I think, pointing.

Something like this? she thinks. She gestures in the air, and a canvas tent materializes in the alcove right in front of us. It's almost identical to the tent I've been sleeping in for the last half moon, though it's a lot cleaner.

Yes, but the tent opening should face that way, I think, gesturing.

Emmie raises and rotates her hands. The tent rises up and rotates slowly, like river flotsam bobbing in the current. She looks at me for confirmation. *Yes, like that,* I think. She lowers her hands, and the tent comes to rest in the sand.

We continue reconstructing my memory of the tent in this way for a while, Emmie asking me questions about what's inside and around the tent, what time of night it is, who's in the tent with me. With each of my answers, Emmie refines the scene around us, filling the tent with four bedrolls, transforming day to night, placing avatars of Dom, Hanu, and Eumelia in their places. She recreates the sights and sounds and sensations from my memory until at last there's nothing else I can add to make the scene more accurate.

That should be close enough, thinks Emmie, examining her work with a satisfied expression. *Go ahead and lie down there, however you were while you were falling asleep.*

Obediently, I step inside the tent and lie down on my bedroll between the avatars of Hanu and Eumelia, which both lie with their eyes closed, breathing softly. I nestle closer to Hanu, draping her soft arms around me. Were it not for Emmie standing just outside the tent flap, gesturing rapidly with both hands, I could almost believe I'm back on my own bedroll again. Emmie glances at me and thinks, *Hold still there for just a little longer … Almost done.* She makes a precise cutting motion with her right hand, and the scene around me freezes in place. *All right, you can come back out,* she thinks. *Let's find this place on the map.*

I climb to my feet and step over the sleeping figures of Hanu, Dom, and Eumelia, rejoining Emmie outside the tent. She mutters under her breath in English and makes a gathering gesture with both hands. The landscape around us melts away from its edges. The starry night sky beyond the eastern horizon disappears first, followed by the far shore of the river, followed by the sandy beach. At last, only the sphere of landscape surrounding the tent remains. When Emmie raises her hands, the sphere containing the tent shrinks until it's no larger than her head. The sphere rises up between us, glowing faintly, the only light in the endless darkness that now surrounds us.

Emmie speaks, and a bright white beam of light bursts up from the darkness between our feet and connects to the floating sphere. The light fills the sphere, then splits into three branches that spread outward from the sphere on separate courses. When the branches are about as long as my arm, they split at the tips, forming nine new branches. One of these branches grows toward me, and I step aside to make way for it. The branch splits again, and another new branch reaches toward me. Anxiously, I sidestep again. Emmie thinks, *Oh, don't bother. There's no way to avoid them, but they'll pass right through you. See?* She remains standing where she is, and one of the branches grows straight through her shoulder before it splits again, leaving her evidently unharmed.

It's a good thing I don't need to avoid them, because the branching speeds up as the branches grow and split, grow and split, rapidly filling the entire spliner. Emmie and I remain standing near the trunk of this strange tree, watching until the tips of the branches disappear into the endless darkness where the walls used to be. When I make the mistake of glancing down, I experience a moment of vertigo. I seem to be floating above a fathomless darkness criss-crossed at intervals by more white branches that reach into the depths below me. Hastily, I look up at Emmie, trying to forget the dizzying drop below us.

What is this? I think.

This is the map, Emmie thinks.

Lilith taught me to read many kinds of maps during our years roaming Dulai together, but every map I've ever seen represents a landscape on a flat surface, with rivers and roads and mountains and cities marked by symbols. *I don't know how to use a map like this,* I think.

This isn't a map of a normal landscape, she thinks. *This is a map to help navigate through memories. Many, many memories.*

But I don't need to find my way through memories, I think. *I need to find my way back to my branch.*

Your memories and your branch are so closely entwined that you can't have one without the other, thinks Emmie. *If you can locate a memory, you can usually locate the branch it belongs to.*

How? I think.

Emmie thinks, *There are as many ways to navigate through memories as there are reasons to revisit them. I'll show you how I use the map myself. Maybe that will help you find your own way.*

Emmie raises her hand, and the strange white tree vanishes. Before us, where the sphere containing my tent floated just moments ago, a new sphere appears that contains a very different scene. Emmie gestures toward the sphere, and it expands around us until we find ourselves standing inside a harshly-lit, windowless room filled with the sound of beeping. A high, narrow bed on small wheels stands in the center of the room, its occupant partially obscured from view by curtains that hang from the ceiling. A woman in sky blue clothes walks briskly past us toward the curtains and draws them aside. Emmie gestures for me to follow her, and the two of us follow the woman toward the bedside.

A young-looking Emmie, about my age, lies in the bed, tucked under a thin sheet. She wears a too-large shirt with a pale pink and white pattern. Her green eyes look enormous in her face, which is even paler than her shirt. A number of tubes hang from her arm, attached by small bandages. The woman in blue says a few words to this other-Emmie and repositions one of the beeping machines standing nearby. Other-Emmie grimaces and nods. The woman murmurs a few sympathetic words as she sets three small vials on the bedside table. The woman leans down and sticks a needle into other-Emmie's arm. Dark red blood flows from the needle into a narrow, clear tube that the woman uses to fill each of the little vials. When she's done, the woman bandages the pinprick wound on other-Emmie's arm and departs.

For a little while, other-Emmie lies quietly on the bed with her eyes closed. When a spasm overtakes her body, she cries out with a sound that sends chills down my spine. She clutches her chest, her face contorted with pain. I wince sharply; the sound stirs the memory of the heart-stopping pain I experienced the night of my overdose.

I glance at the Emmie standing beside me. She looks down at this acutely suffering memory of herself with an untroubled expression, as serene as Serapen. I wonder why the sight affects me so much more than it seems to affect her. She waves her hands, and the scene before us shrinks back into a little sphere floating in the dark space between us. She thinks, *In the first few days after my binding pharmaka overdose, the pain was unbearable. It was so bad sometimes that I wished for death. My healers—we call them doctors on my branch—had nothing that could help me.*

Don't the Mohirai have unbinding pharmaka, on your branch? I think.

Emmie shakes her head. *There are no Mohirai on Earth, as far as I've been able to determine. The ingredients of binding and unbinding pharmaka do exist on my branch, but the methods for preparing these pharmaka are closely guarded secrets of a powerful brotherhood called the Stewards.*

The thought of a world without the Mohirai would once have appealed to me, but a powerful brotherhood of Stewards who control the use of pharmaka doesn't sound any better than a powerful priestesshood that does the same thing. *Who are the Stewards?* I think.

Emmie thinks, *On your branch, the Stewards don't exist. At least, they don't exist yet. But their predecessors do. You may have heard of them. Dom—my Dom, the one on my branch, I mean—told me that on his branch of Dulai, a long, long time ago, there was a rebellion against the Mohirai by a group that called themselves free men.*

Yes, I've met a few of the free men, I think. Dom's violent memory of our treatment at their hands flashes through my mind and spills into Emmie.

I'm sorry that happened to you, she thinks. *I wasn't sure how the free men on your branch compare to the Stewards here on mine. Looks like their methods haven't changed much.*

Emmie waves her hand and taps her fingertips in the air. A beam of light shoots up from the floor of the spliner again, connecting to the sphere containing Emmie's memory of the stark little room. Another tree grows in the place where the last ghostly tree stood a few moments ago. When the branches have filled the spliner from wall to wall, Emmie gestures with her hands to enlarge, reposition, and rotate the tree around us, working her way downward along the trunk into one of the branches below our feet. She stops at an intersection of branches connected to another glowing sphere. When Emmie gestures toward this sphere, it expands toward us, enveloping us in near-darkness.

We seem to be standing inside some sort of cave. A few paces ahead, a small point of bright light flares from the raised hand of a tall man with a thick mane of white-blonde hair wearing beautifully tailored clothing. He shouts, rushes forward, seizes a small figure out of the darkness, and grapples with it.

Emmie and I walk toward the man. There's a choking sound, followed by the strangled shout of a woman. As we draw near, I see that the man's long arm is wrapped in a tight hold around the neck of another young Emmie. This other-Emmie, only a little larger than I am, is powerless against such a large man. In his free hand, the man holds a small silver object, about the size and shape of a writing stylus. He presses the sharp tip of this silver stylus against the exposed skin of her neck. She struggles to drag the man forward, pointing desperately toward something in the darkness ahead of her. I follow the line of her arm and see the ghostly form of a leafless tree, white as bone, that stands before a circular pool of water. That tree, with its rippling reflection in the pool, reminds me of the branching white insignia on Emmie's shirt.

The tall man hauls other-Emmie away from the tree, lifting her clear off her feet. She kicks uselessly in the air, gasping as the man's arm around her neck tightens. She reaches her arms backward over her head, both hands scrabbling across the man's scalp until at last she seizes two fistfuls of his hair. She yanks forward hard. The man roars in pain and drops her to the ground, but she doesn't release her hold on his hair. Instead, she readjusts her grip and drags him headfirst toward the dark pool at the base of the leafless white tree. The man shouts something in a tone of warning, flailing his long arms awkwardly toward her as he tries to free himself. The tip of the silver stylus in his hand strikes other-Emmie in the center of her chest. It's difficult for me to see what happens next, because other-Emmie and the man suddenly drop out of view with a loud splash, and the pinpoint of light from the man's hand is swallowed by darkness.

Emmie waves her hand. Her memory of the dark cave shrinks back down into a sphere anchored at an intersection of branches in the ghostly white tree that fills the endless darkness of the spliner. She thinks, *I shouldn't have survived my overdose that day. But the Stewards were willing to make a deal with me, for a price. They provided the unbinding pharmaka I needed to survive. Unfortunately, without the arts of the Mohirai, the damage to my memory caused by using unbinding pharmaka was almost as bad as the pain caused by the binding pharmaka.*

I used as little of the unbinding pharmaka as I possibly could, but each time I freed myself from a little pain, I lost more of my memory. It was awful. The memories of my family, of my life with Dom, of all my friends, of all the things I'd done in my life ... everything I thought of as myself was disappearing.

I stopped using unbinding pharmaka entirely for a while. I thought it would be better to live with the pain than lose myself. But the pain was relentless, whittling away my resolve, day after day. I felt trapped inside a shrinking cage.

I struggled this way for years. In the beginning, I was certain there must be some other cure for the pain, or some way to repair my damaged memory. But everything I tried failed. In the end, I could see only two choices: hold on to my old memories until the pain killed me, or let go of my memories and start over, free of my pain.

Emmie pauses. For a moment, her mind feels entirely clear of thought. I've been listening to her account of the aftermath of her overdose with such rapt attention that I've almost forgotten she's supposed to be explaining how this map works. My questions have turned instead to how Emmie faced the very choice that may lie ahead of me. The prospect of losing my own memories fills me with dread, but the pain caused by my bond with the Voice is unbearable. *How did you choose?* I think.

Emmie sighs. *No matter how strong you are, there's a limit to how much pain the body can endure,* she thinks. *In the end, I realized that if I wanted to live, I had to free myself from pain, even if it meant losing all my memories.*

So I decided to use the time I had left as best I could. Ever since I was a child, I've been a designer of alternet experiences. After my overdose, I turned those skills to a new purpose: re-creating my memories in the alternet for later use. I knew that my memories wouldn't disappear all at once, and I was able to preserve the most important memories that remained to me using the same technologies I'd used to create so many other experiences in the alternet. I took some comfort in the idea that I could return to these memories in the alternet in the future, even though I wouldn't be able to find them in my own mind any longer.

Emmie flicks her hand, and we flit from one white branch to another as lightly as birds, hopping into one memory sphere after another in rapid succession. The settings are varied, and the other-Emmies in each scene are different ages, but the people around her are usually the same. A girl with fair hair and Emmie's laugh. A woman with Emmie's heart-shaped face and a careworn expression. A man who beams with pride every time he looks at Emmie. An energetic, wiry man with an intricate branching tattoo on his arm. A grey-haired older man with a dignified air. A white-haired older woman with Emmie's vivid green eyes. And other-Dom. So many memories of Emmie and other-Dom, laughing with each other, smiling at each other, walking hand in hand, curled up together in cozy spaces in their house in the Oakland hills.

Emmie thinks, *I threw myself into the work of preserving what was left of my memories. I focused on the good memories, the important memories, the beautiful memories. My family, my friends, and Dom all helped me—not only with the work of preserving my own memories, but by adding their memories to mine wherever they could fill in what I'd already lost.*

The scene before us shifts to a little room like the ones I saw in the hallway outside the spliner. In this memory, other-Emmie stands at the head of a table, where a group of young men and women sit looking up at her. In the far corner of the room stands other-Dom. Though this other-Emmie looks exhausted and pale, she speaks to the group in animated tones, hands flying to punctuate her thoughts. When the group around the table turns to discuss something together, other-Emmie leans back, averting her face as a faint grimace of pain flickers over her features. Across the room, other-Dom notices and catches other-Emmie's eye, some question in his expression. Other-Emmie gives an almost indiscernible shake of her head, reaches for a cup at the table, and takes a long sip. Her face relaxes. I look down into the cup. It's half full of a golden liquid I know well: unbinding pharmaka.

The scene fades. Emmie and I stand in the grey twilight of the empty spliner. She thinks, *When the pain was too much for me to handle, I took unbinding pharmaka, accepting that whatever I'd lose, I'd lose. Somehow, learning to accept the loss made everything easier. The pain faded, bit by bit, along with my memories. In the end, I lost even my sadness about what I'd lost, because I couldn't remember what I'd lost.*

Emmie seems entirely untroubled, but her story fills me with dread. Desperate thoughts race through my mind. Surely this won't be my fate. Surely there's some other option Emmie failed to see.

Emmie studies me. *Perhaps there is another way, for you,* she thinks. *After all, the Mohirai on your branch know far more about pharmaka than the Stewards know on mine. From what Dom tells me, the pharmaka on your branch seems more powerful than the technology—the tekhnologia, I guess you'd say—on my branch. Still, Earth's technology isn't entirely worthless. After all, I'm standing here telling you all this, aren't I?*

My racing thoughts pause. I hadn't considered this. If Emmie lost all of her memories by using unbinding pharmaka, how could she know about any of these things that happened in her past?

Now you're asking the right question, she thinks. *It's the same question I asked myself as I was losing my memory. How would I be able to live in the future without any memories of my past?*

At first, I didn't have any idea how it would work. I was too focused on preserving old memories before I lost them. But as time went on, I began to struggle with losing new memories too. New memories disappeared from my mind almost as quickly as they formed. I realized that preserving new memories was at least as important as preserving old memories—maybe even more important for daily life.

This started a new phase in the work: recording new experiences as they occur.

Recording and storing new experiences turns out to be fairly straightforward. There have been technologies on my branch for recording all sorts of experiences for a pretty long time. All I needed to do was refine those technologies to make the recording process easier. I added a few touches of my own, too, to make the recordings more immersive, to capture more of the sensory and emotional elements of someone's experience.

Once I had the recording process worked out, I couldn't help thinking that there must be some way to use all these preserved memories—my old ones and my new ones—to bridge the gaps in my own memory. This turned out to be a much harder problem than simply recording and storing the memories, though. No one had ever used the alternet in quite this way before. The human mind is organized for efficient retrieval of relevant memories at the moment they're needed, but the alternet wasn't designed to work like that. The biggest difficulty came down to speed. Selecting the relevant part of a memory from a vast collection of memories is slow, if you have to search through every single memory stored in the alternet. To use alternet memories in my daily life I had to find what I needed fast enough that I wasn't being constantly interrupted or confused by gaps in my memory.

And that's when I made a key discovery. Despite all the damage to my memory, I'm still able to recognize and recall recurring patterns. Unique memories that occurred only once in my life are usually impossible for me to recall. But recurring patterns trigger some other kind of memory, some deeper form of memory that the unbinding pharmaka doesn't erase. As I spent more time studying these patterns, I realized that the recurring patterns in my life were usually the most important things to remember. If I could just recognize the patterns, I could usually find the memories I needed on the fly.

So I started mapping these recurring patterns. I call them intersections, because they're places where multiple memories overlap in some way—like the routine of finding my way home, or the way my mother tells the same story every year on my birthday, or the way Dom says he loves me before we go to sleep. These intersections form a kind of map connecting all of the memories of my life. It's possible for me to navigate quickly from the important part of one memory into the important parts of other memories through the intersections. Whenever I'm lost in some blank spot in my own memory, I search through the largest intersections in my alternet memories that contain patterns similar to what's happening in my present. Most of the time, I can find the memory I need pretty quickly, and I'm able to act almost as though the memory had been there in my mind all along.

Using technology in place of my natural memory doesn't always work perfectly, though. Even with all the optimizations I've made, it's slower than using my own memory once was. And sometimes an intersection leads me to an unexpected memory. I'll find myself recalling memories from a different time or place than I might have done from my natural memory. That can lead to some confusing situations.

But overall, I've been managing surprisingly well these days. Using alternet memories even has some advantages over natural memory. For one thing, it's possible for me to recall far more, and in far greater detail, than I ever could before my overdose. Natural memory changes and fades over time, but memories preserved in the alternet never fade. There's essentially no limit to how much memory the alternet can hold, or how detailed the memories can be.

Navigating the memories of my own life using these patterns has been useful, but I've found that this technology is even more useful when the memories of many people are connected through a single map. Mapping the intersections through the memories of many people reveals some of the most important patterns of all. The memories from a single life contain only a few patterns, but the collective memory contains the patterns that connect all lives.

Emmie's words trigger some pattern recognition of my own. *Serapen told me about a universal awareness that flows through the branches of the path of mysteries,* I think. *She said that bridges can form between branches, where awareness passes between them. Do these intersections you're talking about work the same way?*

Emmie grins. *You're a few steps ahead of me now. Yes, I think navigating through memories using the alternet has something in common with how the Mohirai use pharmaka to navigate between branches. When I'm searching through alternet memories, if I start at an intersection between my present moment and my other memories, I'm usually able to find my way quickly to any other memories I need. So maybe if you start at an intersection between this moment and your last memory on your branch, you can find a bridge back to your branch.*

But every time I've crossed a bridge between branches, it's been entirely by accident, I think. *And even if I could figure out how to cross a bridge on purpose, I don't know where to start looking for an intersection with my branch.*

Emmie waves her hand, and the sphere containing my memory of the moonlit tent reappears, hovering between us. A beam of white light shoots up from the floor, illuminates my memory, and splits apart, expanding until the spliner is filled again with a translucent white tree, its many branches studded with other glowing memory spheres. An inkling of what Emmie is suggesting forms in my mind. I reach out toward my memory at the heart of the ghostly tree. Could it really be this simple to find my way back to Dulai?

The memory I'm reaching for expands around my hand. I'm eager to return there, but something makes me hesitate. I pull my hand back uncertainly, looking up at all the other spheres embedded in the branches over my head. *What are those memories up there? In the branches growing out of this memory?* I think, pointing.

Those branches lead to memories that might follow this one, she thinks.

Astonished, I think, *Do you mean this map shows the future?*

No, thinks Emmie. *This map only shows how your memory may intersect other memories. But because this is the first memory from your branch that I've recorded, there's a vast amount of your memory that's unknown to the map. Wherever there's something unknown, the map makes guesses to fill in the gaps. The map makes guesses about the past and the future in the same way, using its access to all the other memories stored in the alternet. Those branches below your feet contain guesses about what memories might have preceded this memory. The branches above you lead to guesses of the possible futures that could follow your memory.*

Eagerly, I think, *Can you show those to me? Maybe there's a future where I'm free of this pain, and free of the Mohirai. Maybe I could just go straight to that future from here.*

You could look into that future, she thinks. *But that won't make it your reality. The only way to find out what your own future holds is to live your own life. Your future depends on many things that are still unknown, including the choices you'll make.*

But how do I know what choices to make, to reach the future I want? I think.

Sometimes the only way to know is to do, she thinks.

Until this moment, Emmie's youthful energy has made me feel like I'm in the presence of another novice. Her knowing expression now reveals an age and experience beyond my own. *You sound like Serapen,* I think, annoyed.

Emmie chuckles softly. *I've never met Serapen,* she thinks. *But Dom says that to me all the time.*

This doesn't sound like something my Dom would say; Emmie must be talking about other-Dom again. The thought of other-Dom, and of those last few moments in his arms, stirs a powerful longing in my heart for my own Dom. I miss him. The memory of him tugs some part deep inside of me; I can almost feel the pressure of his warm hand around mine. Instinctively, I push my hand back into the sphere of memory hovering directly before me. As the scene of the moonlit tent expands around me, my vision slowly spins. Emmie, the spliner, and the translucent branches around me dissolve into darkness.

Looks like you found your bridge, thinks Emmie.

Thank you for helping me, I think.

But Emmie is already gone.

△▽△

Waiting for Ava to return is perhaps the hardest decision I've ever made. Time slows to a crawl as I watch over her unconscious form. I'm aware of little other than her slow, shallow breathing and the faint flutter of her heartbeat under my fingertips. Each time Serapen repositions her hands on Ava's body, I scrutinize her every motion and expression, searching for any sign that something's gone wrong.

I don't know how long I've been sitting at Ava's side when she takes a gasping breath, as though she's just emerged from deep water. Her eyes open wide and meet mine. "There you are," she whispers, squeezing my hand weakly.

I press her cold fingers to my cheek. "I thought I'd lost you again," I say.

She gives me an exhausted smile. *You can't get rid of me that easily,* she thinks.

Eumelia bursts through the tent flap, followed close behind by Hanu. Serapen makes way for the two girls at Ava's side.

"Spirits, Ava!" says Eumelia, seizing Ava's free hand. "Why do you always have to make everything so terrifying?"

Ava rolls her eyes. "Why do you always have to ask such annoying questions?" she says.

Hanu strokes Ava's pale cheek. Her touch seems to relax the tension and restore the color in Ava's face. "How are you feeling?" says Hanu.

"Like I could use a good night's sleep," says Ava.

"Sadly, sleep must wait for another night," says Serapen, peering out the tent flap toward the Purattu. I follow her gaze. Across the river, the horizon is rosy with the dawn. "The days are growing short, and winter waits for no one. We must press on."

Eumelia groans. Hanu sighs. I stroke Ava's hand. Ava looks at me and thinks, *I'm sorry this keeps happening. I'm trying to figure out how to make it stop. I just … I don't even know where to start.*

None of this is your fault, I think. *Don't worry. We'll figure it out. Together.*

BEYOND THE RIVER

As the sun rises, I do my best to work alongside Dom and the rest of the novices to break camp and prepare for the river crossing. My fumbling fingers, dragging feet, and distracted thoughts slow me down considerably. I can't decide what's weighing on me most: my confusion over Serapen's revelation about Lilith at the campfire last night, the weakness of my body after all this travel between branches, or my fear that I'll accidentally slip over another bridge at any moment. Whatever the cause, I'm infuriatingly clumsy. Dom steadies me when I stumble, corrects knots I've mis-tied, and sends calming thoughts my way when I'm reduced to cursing my own ineptitude.

After we've disassembled the tents and refilled our waterskins for the ride ahead, we saddle the horses. Urshanabi ferried the wolves across the Purattu shortly after sunrise so they wouldn't be underfoot while we pack, but the memory of the wolves, or perhaps the apprehension of seeing them again, agitates Eridu. He tosses his big head and stamps his hooves restlessly as we adjust his saddle straps and secure our saddlebags to him. Seeing the fearful look in Eridu's normally calm brown eyes, I feel a pang of sympathy for him. This sweet gelding has at least as much cause to rebel against the Mohirai as I do. Unfortunately, he has about as much power to resist them as I do, too.

In a soothing murmur supplemented by apple bribes, Dom steadies Eridu, handling him as adeptly as he's been handling me all morning. Watching him irritates me. I was grateful to Dom and Hanu last night for comforting me, but I can't help wondering whether their kindness is just conditioning me to submit, without protest, to Serapen and the other Mohirai.

I ruminate in silence as the rest of the novices chatter around me. Most of them had an uninterrupted night's sleep after the campfire council and are oblivious to the disturbance in my tent last night. Their collective mood is much improved as a result. Still, I preferred their coldness yesterday morning to the compassion they show me today. It's humiliating to be an object of their pity, after I've spent so much of my life disdaining their ignorance. Dom, Hanu, and Eumelia treat me with friendliness, but even they exchange glances over my head when they think I'm not looking. They're hesitant to disturb my equilibrium, probably thinking—with good reason—that I might dissolve into tears or depart for another branch at any moment.

I can't let them be right. I grit my teeth against another wave of sorrow, refusing to cry again. I ward off thoughts of other-Dom and Emmie and Earth, refusing to allow my mind to wander away again. I'm stronger than this. I have to be stronger than this. A reputation for weakness is the last thing I need as I start this new life among the novices. I'll be spending—spirits, how long?—practically an eternity with them, if the Voice has its way with me.

Once Eridu is packed, I help Eumelia re-adjust Nisaba's stirrups, which I'd shortened for myself when I stole the little mare from camp. Giving a final tug to the stirrups, I glance up at her and say, "How's that?"

"Good, thanks," she says, with a tentative smile. I force a tight smile but turn away quickly, avoiding her eyes. Eumelia's been on her best behavior with me all morning after my ridiculous tears last night. I'm grateful that she's refrained from making any snide remarks about my failed escape attempt, but her kindness is just another reminder of how weak she thinks I am.

I return to Eridu, make one last check of the saddlebag buckles, grab the saddle pommel, and swing myself up to mount him. To my dismay, my grip fails. I slip down Eridu's side and fall backwards into the sand. Several of the girls and all three Mohirai turn around to look at me.

Dom hurries around Eridu and kneels beside me. "Are you all right?" he says.

I push myself up to sit, cursing my clumsiness. Countless times since the start of this journey, I've mounted effortlessly. What's wrong with me? I look down at my hands, and I can't help thinking of Emmie's soft little hands. I clench my fists, pushing back the memory of her frail, naked body in the mirror. That isn't me. That can't be me. I need to be strong. Stronger than strong.

I look up at Dom, who looks back at me with those beautiful, loving, concerned eyes of his. A memory of other-Dom's eyes rushes into my mind. There's an ominous blurring and spinning at the edges of my vision.

"Damn it all," I mutter, squeezing my eyes shut, locking every door inside of myself, refusing to let myself slip across another bridge right now. I take deep breaths, focusing on the gritty sand against my palms, listening to the other girls' puzzled murmurs, feeling the river breeze on my cheeks, desperately clinging to this moment, as unpleasant as it is, because I'm afraid that if I don't, I'll disappear from this branch entirely.

"Give her space, Dom," says Serapen.

With my eyes closed, I sense rather than see the High Priestess standing over me. Dom steps back. Serapen kneels in his place. The complex herbal aroma of her healer robes envelops me.

"Why does this keep happening?" I say, my voice quavering pathetically in a prelude to a sob.

Serapen presses her forefinger between my brows. The spinning sensation slowly subsides. Cautiously, I open my eyes. Serapen looks back at me calmly. She says, "Your body and mind have been through an ordeal, Ava. Healing, like the Voice in all, works in its own time. You must be patient."

She grips my hands and helps me to my feet. Her skin tingles against mine, and through our connection, Serapen pours into me a strength like mountain cedars and a calm steadier than bedrock. I briefly glimpse a memory in her mind: a dense grove of gnarled trees shading a deep pool. I wonder where that is. It reminds me of the hilltop grove where I stood with other-Dom in the alternet, but the grove in Serapen's memory is far more lush and shady, the trees far more ancient, the pool larger. Her memory possesses the same quality of profound stillness that often emanates from the High Priestess herself. The image of the ancient grove vanishes from my mind when Serapen lets me go and gestures for me to mount Eridu.

As a precaution, I use a stirrup to climb into the saddle. I haven't had to mount this way since I was a little girl. My grip is weaker than it should be, and I'm winded by the small exertion, but at least I manage to mount on my own this time. Serapen looks up at me, nods, and returns to her own packing.

Dom gives me a moment to settle myself, then swings up behind me with enviable ease. "Is that supposed to impress me?" I say.

Dom assesses my mood before risking a rejoinder. "Bel and Tashlu look impressed," he says.

I glance at the two girls watching us from atop their horses. They look away as soon as I meet their gaze. "All you'd have to do to impress those two is bat your pretty eyelashes," I say, untucking the front of my riding shirt for him so we can maintain skin contact on the ride.

"Are you saying I'm pretty?" he says, slipping his hand under the hem of my shirt.

"Are you fishing for compliments?" I say, grasping for anything to keep the banter going, anything to distract me from his warm hand sliding under my shirt, across my belly, toward my hip. After Hanu's mediation between us last night, Dom and I have avoided touching and looking at each other, so I've mostly been able to keep problematic thoughts of him and other-Dom out of my mind. But now his entire body is molded around mine, his breath tickling my ear when he speaks. It's impossible to avoid thoughts of me and Dom in our tent, followed close behind by thoughts of Emmie and other-Dom in their bedroom. I bite my lip, focusing on my intention to stay. Stay, Ava. Stay.

"You know what helps?" Dom says softly, overhearing all this.

"What?" I say, my voice strained.

Look, he thinks.

My skin tingles where Dom's hand rests on my hip. He shows me through his eyes what he sees ahead. A clear blue sky. The sparkling Purattu. The open road beyond. Eumelia approaching us on Nisaba, Hanu behind her on Baba. It's a beautiful day for a ride. Could be a good day for a race, too. There are endless things to look at, to think about, to talk about. We could lose ourselves in any of them, at least for a little while. We just have to shift our perspective a little.

"Now I'm actually impressed," I say, only half teasing. "What kind of boy can clear his mind of sex that easily?"

"Even the most unruly awareness can be shaped by the arts of mindfulness," he says, quoting Muse Arkhi.

"Spirits," I groan. "You're turning into one of them."

Dom chuckles. "No," he says. "That's your job."

My mood darkens as the truth of his words sinks in. As much as I've been avoiding thoughts of Dom and other-Dom, I've also been avoiding thoughts of the ultimate consequence of my failure to escape from the Mohirai last night. The road to Velkanos leads to the house of novices. The house of novices leads to initiation among the Mohirai. My mother—Lilith, I correct myself firmly—Lilith told me it's within the house of novices that the Mohirai complete the work they begin in the Children's Temple to subjugate each girl's mind to the will of the Voice. Was Lilith telling me the truth, or was that a lie, too?

I don't know what to believe. I don't know whom to trust. Since my overdose, everything I thought I knew and everything I thought I could rely on has been called into question or ripped away from me.

So who am I now? What am I supposed to do?

△▽△

Our caravan is too large to make a single river crossing on Urshanabi's ferry, so Serapen splits us into three groups. Thalia makes the first crossing with Narua's trio; Arkhi makes the second crossing with Kor's.

Ava and I are in the last group, along with Serapen, Eumelia, Hanu, and our four horses. I'm grateful Serapen stayed behind with us. I still can't shake the memory of the free men jumping out at us from the shadows of the willows, and Serapen's presence calms my nerves. Still, as our group dwindles, I feel increasingly exposed, uncomfortably aware of how easily we could become trapped between the wall of cliffs behind us and the river before us, should anything else unexpected emerge suddenly from the dense willow grove.

My worry eases when Urshanabi returns to us for the third and final crossing. He hails me as he approaches the dock. I leave Eridu with Ava and hurry out to help the ferryman. He tosses the mooring lines my way, poling the boat to a stop in the shallows. Serapen leads the line of girls and horses onto the low rear deck of the ferry using the ramp Urshanabi lowers to the dock. I follow Urshanabi's instructions to cast off the lines, hop aboard, and pull in the ramp after us.

Urshanabi climbs up onto his platform behind the high curved bow of the ferry. He partially unfurls the little foresail and moves the long starboard oar in its oarlock, poling the boat out of the slow-moving shallows until we reach the deeper current. The wind catches the little sail, pulling us across the water with surprising speed. The ferryman navigates the current with deft combinations of paddling the oar and trimming the sail.

Standing alone on the port side of the boat, Ava leans out over the rail, gazing across the water toward the far shore. I'm tempted to join her, but she's been so uneasy around me all morning that I don't want to disturb her. Instead, I stay with Hanu and Eumelia on the starboard side, vicariously enjoying Ava's sensation of flying across the river. I'm glad she's found some diversion from her gloom, however brief it may be.

When the boat is on a steady course, Urshanabi invites each of the girls in turn to join him on his little platform and try her hand at sailing. With Urshanabi's assistance, Hanu and Eumelia both manage to maneuver the ferry in roughly the right direction with minimal mishaps. When Ava steps up, she handles the boat with skill that reveals prior experience. This seems to surprise the ferryman, but after everything I've seen her do over the last half moon, I could believe Ava's had experience doing just about anything.

By the time Urshanabi invites me to join him up on his platform, we've already reached the shallows on the far side of the river. All that's left for me to do is pole our way to the dock on the eastern shore. I wish I'd had a chance to try sailing, too, but I'm so used to the girls going first that it's only a passing disappointment.

The ferry pulls in to the dock. Eumelia tosses the mooring lines to Muse Arkhi, who secures the boat. I wait up on the platform with Urshanabi while Serapen and the girls disembark with the horses. I'm about to follow them when Urshanabi touches my arm and says, "I have something for you, little brother."

Urshanabi unlatches a little wooden compartment bolted to the deck beneath his seat. He withdraws a leather-bound book and places it in my hands. It's not very thick, but it's almost as wide across as my forearm, larger than the books I often saw the Mohirai and girls at the Children's Temple reading. The leather cover is worked with an intricate swirling pattern that reminds me of Arkhi's painted palms.

"Thank you, brother," I say, running my fingertips over the fine leatherwork. "It's beautiful. But I don't know how to read."

"No, of course not," Urshanabi says kindly. "The Muses will help you with that in the proper time, now that you've been called to the path of mysteries. But this is not a book for reading. Open it."

I open the book and find it's empty: nothing but page after page of smooth, unmarked parchment. Delighted, I say, "It's a sketchbook!"

Urshanabi smiles. "I saw your work in the sand yesterday and thought you would put this sketchbook to better use than I ever could," he says. "Muse Noa gave it to me from her own supplies long ago, after I admired her work. She told me even an old man might improve his skills of observation, with practice. Despite my best intentions, though, this sketchbook has been sitting on a shelf collecting dust these past few centuries. I think it's time to pass on the Muse's gift to more worthy hands."

"I've never had new parchment before," I say, sliding my hand tenderly over a blank page, imagining all I could capture here, with the right tools. I'll need to borrow a stub of pencil from one of the Muses, or perhaps whittle some charcoal piece from the campfire tonight.

As if he's overheard my thought, Urshanabi reaches into his pocket and produces one more thing. It's a leather pouch made to wear on a tool belt, with neat leather slots holding a dozen new charcoal pencils, each sharpened to a perfect point. He holds the case of pencils out to me. I grin up at him, speechless for a long moment before I remember to say, "Thank you, brother!"

Urshanabi laughs merrily. His sparkling black eyes all but disappear under a pile of wrinkles. "May you always take such joy in simple pleasures, little brother," he says. He sets the pencils in my hand. I slip them into my pocket and tuck the sketchbook under my arm. The ferryman kisses me on both cheeks and raises his hand over me in the sign of blessing I've only ever seen the priestesses use. "Safe passage on your journey, Dom Artifex."

"Farewell, Urshanabi," I say. "I hope I'll see you again before too long."

"Voice willing," says Urshanabi.

I climb down off the platform and disembark across the ramp. Arkhi stands waiting for me on the dock, holding the mooring lines. "Ah," she says with a little smile, seeing the sketchbook under my arm. "Urshanabi has a talent for gifts. Always seems to know just what's needed." She coils the lines neatly and tosses them into the stern of the ferry, then raises her hand to Urshanabi. "Farewell, brother," she says. "Until our paths meet again."

"Safe journey, Ark," says Urshanabi. "I'll keep an eye on the river and send word if there are any signs of free men."

Urshanabi poles his ferry away from the dock. Arkhi and I rejoin the caravan on the riverbank. The rest of the novices are already mounted and ready to depart. I make my way over to Hanu, Eumelia, and Ava.

"What's that?" says Eumelia, gesturing to the sketchbook in my hand.

I hold up the sketchbook for the three girls to inspect, flipping through the empty pages for them. Ava and Hanu admire it, but Eumelia is unimpressed. "Looks almost as old as Urshanabi," she says, pointing out a few mottled pages. "I'm sure we can find you some finer parchment than this in Velkanos, Dom."

Ava and Hanu round on Eumelia to defend the humble merits of my gift, though there's no need. Not even Eumelia can dampen my enthusiasm for my precious new possession, which I tuck safely inside my saddlebag for later.

△▽△

East of the Purattu, the air is windless and clear, with very little of the dust that plagued us on the first half of the desert crossing. I find myself appreciating in retrospect the one advantage the awful wind had over all this fine weather: the relentless physical discomfort it caused left little room for distracting thoughts of Dom's body pressed against mine. Now, by contrast, I constantly have to suppress intimate memories of Dom, because these lead to even more intimate memories of other-Dom, and those memories of other-Dom lead to memories of Emmie. I can't risk my mind wandering across another bridge today. I'm too exhausted already.

Dom understands my dilemma and is as anxious as I am to prevent me from disappearing to another branch. So we work together to steer our conversation from one neutral topic to the next, anchoring our attention in the present moment and focusing on outward things, like spotting our new caravan escorts. We haven't seen any of the wolves since Urshanabi ferried them across the Purattu earlier this morning, but their tracks are occasionally visible in the sand alongside the road. I've spent a fair amount of time hunting, so I'm skilled at picking out signs of the wolf pack amidst the other animal tracks and random markings in the sand. Dom's interested in tracking, so I spend most of the morning teaching him how to read the signs.

Instructing Dom in tracking while riding is challenging, but his eyes are almost as sharp as mine, and he learns quickly, for a boy. Soon, we've pieced together a general idea of what the wolves are doing. Generally, they run ahead of us, following the road east toward the Urashtu Pass. Occasionally, they split apart for side excursions to the north and south before rejoining the caravan. When the pack splits, one group follows the alpha male, and the other follows the luna female. I wonder whether they're moving this way of their own accord, or because of some manipulation by Serapen.

It's easier to track the pair of falcons. At regular intervals, they appear soaring across the clear blue sky. They usually approach the caravan from opposite directions and circle directly above Arkhi and Serapen before parting ways again, to the north and south, or to the east and west. Serapen and Arkhi consult one another occasionally after these visits by the falcons, but their expressions reveal nothing.

Are the falcons or the wolves communicating anything of interest to the Muses? I'd like to know whether there's any sign of Lilith following the caravan, but for Dom's sake I refrain from asking. He's been on edge since yesterday, and I keep glimpsing uneasy thoughts of Lilith and the free men in his mind. I don't think he's ready to face the thought of new dangers.

In some ways, it makes little difference whether the falcons or wolves have spotted Lilith. Lilith taught me the arts of concealment herself, so I know many ways she could evade detection, even in exposed country like this. If Lilith still intends to capture me and Dom, I have to remain on high alert. She could be anywhere. Just two days ago, the thought that she knows where I am and is coming for me would have been comforting; I had been eager to return to her then. Now, the thought of her tracking the caravan makes me uneasy. I don't want to go with her, and I can't bear the thought of further harm coming to Dom at her hands.

"You don't need to protect me from her," says Dom.

I shake my head, exasperated with myself for letting my thoughts wander. "You're eavesdropping again," I say, trying to sidestep unwanted conversation about Lilith.

Dom won't let me off that easily. "Listen," he says. "I don't need protection from Lilith or the free men. I've been thinking about it all morning. As far as I can tell, they weren't trying to hurt me. They could easily have done much worse to me if they'd wanted to. They were just trying to unbind me so they could take you with them. You're the one who needs protection."

"I can take care of myself," I say automatically.

Any girl would laugh, hearing me say this after everything that's happened to me over the last half moon. But Dom, as always, is gentle to a fault. "I didn't say you can't," he says. "All I meant was that you shouldn't worry about protecting me. I can take care of myself, too. But just because we can take care of ourselves doesn't mean we should refuse any help. If you think the Mohirai know something that might be helpful to us, let's ask them. Serapen said on our Calling Day that we're supposed to help each other. We're in this together, remember?"

We. Us. Together. In Dom's words, I hear the echo of the Voice in all: *Together you shall answer our call. We* and *us* and *together* still feel unnatural to me. But if Dom really wants to be in this together with me—and after everything he's done, I can hardly doubt it—then who am I to shelter him from all that entails? He has as much right to make his own decisions as I have. "Fine," I say briskly, nudging Eridu with my heels. "Let's go ask, then."

Serapen and Arkhi ride side by side at the front of the caravan. We trot up the line toward them. The Muses pause their conversation when we fall into step beside them.

"Have your scouts spotted anything?" I say.

Arkhi looks to Serapen, deferring the question to her. Serapen says, "Before we departed the camp, the wolves caught the scents of two men who walked along the riverbank near our camp the night you were taken captive. The wolves tracked them some distance north toward Upper Ford before losing the scent."

I nod, recalling the memory Dom shared with me. "The man in charge on the boat said they needed to unbind me and Dom before they reached the ford," I say. "Lilith said there were horses waiting somewhere upriver to carry us back to the Middle Sea coast. Maybe after Lilith and the three men fell out of the boat, they returned to Upper Ford to reach their horses."

"That is possible," says Serapen. "But the two men's tracks disappear before they reach Upper Ford. I suppose it is possible they met a boat somewhere between the ferry crossing and the ford, but the falcons spotted no sign of such a boat, upriver or downriver."

I wonder briefly what happened to the third man, but I see no reason to concern myself with him, or with any of the men, really. Though Dom is haunted by the memory of the men who ambushed us in the willow grove, I know there's nothing to fear from men while we're traveling in the company of initiate priestesses. Any initiate could disable an uninitiated man—even the strongest man—with a single word, if she chose. No, it's not the free men I'm worried about. "Was there any sign of Lilith?" I say.

Serapen fixes her gaze on the eastern horizon. "None that we have detected," she says. "Of course Lilith could be following us and concealing herself from our scouts. We aren't difficult to track, and she's known our destination and how fast the caravan would travel from the moment we set out from the Children's Temple. But there are other possibilities, as well. It is possible she never emerged from the river at all."

"You think she could have drowned?" I say, incredulous. Lilith is a tremendously strong swimmer. I can't imagine the river being enough to overwhelm her, especially not at this time of year, with the water running so low.

"I doubt that under normal circumstances she would have drowned," says Serapen. "But last night was hardly a normal circumstance, Ava. You used the binding pharmaka to overpower her completely."

Clearly Serapen grasps some implication of this that I'm missing. "Why would that matter?" I say.

"Recall my instruction," says Serapen. As if at her command—perhaps in fact because of her command—I remember her words on the first rainy evening at the start of the journey, as we sat together beneath the beech tree. *It is possible to injure and even to destroy layers of awareness through such ill use. Just as rich soil may turn to desert, or an eye might be blinded, or skin might be burned away.* "Forcing your awareness upon another presents great risks."

I'm stunned by the possibility that I could have seriously injured Lilith, that Serapen thinks Lilith might even be dead. The idea that I could kill Lilith seems as improbable as the idea that I could destroy a mountain.

"I didn't try to hurt her," I say. I'm surprised to realize this is true, despite my simmering anger at her. "I just didn't want her to hurt Dom."

I'm acutely aware of Arkhi's gaze on me as I say this. She too warned me about the risks of using the connection created by binding pharmaka. *The absence of good intention can be as dangerous as the presence of bad intention. You can still hurt each other, even if neither of you intended to.*

Dom says, "But didn't Lilith send that kuku bird to camp yesterday? How could she have sent the bird if she'd drowned?"

I look to Serapen, hoping she'll say that of course this means Lilith can't be dead. My hope confuses me. As much as I worry that Lilith could be following us, I'm eager for reassurance that she could be following us.

"A good question, Dom," says Serapen. "If we knew that Lilith sent the bird after she fell into the river, we might assume she survived her encounter with Ava. But it's also possible Lilith sent that bird on its mission before the events on the boat."

Frustrated by these alternate explanations for the same facts, and by the emotional turbulence created in me by each possibility, I say, "So really we know nothing."

Serapen exchanges a look with Arkhi, who says, "We know *almost* nothing. And yet we do know that three men and Lilith were on a boat with you two the night before last. We know two men walked north a short distance along the riverbank that same night. We know one kuku bird that Lilith handled at some point was at camp yesterday afternoon. And we will continue to observe, so we will know more in due time."

I like Arkhi too much to reply impertinently, but I can't stop myself from thinking, *Knowing almost nothing is the same as knowing nothing at all.*

"Wise words, sister," says Serapen.

I'm not sure whether she's talking to me or Arkhi.

MESSAGE RECEIVED

I SPEND THE REST of the long day's ride overhearing Ava's endless ruminations. She tries to keep her thoughts to herself, but whenever her self-discipline slips, her questions spiral through my mind. *Why did Lilith pretend to be my mother? Why did she let the free men hurt us? What was she arguing about with the man in charge?* I have no answers to any of these questions, so they take their place among the countless other mysteries of my life. By the time Arkhi calls the caravan to a stop, I'm ready to set aside thoughts of Lilith, at least for the evening, if not forever.

Arkhi settles the horses around a nearby watering hole with the help of Kor, Piroza, and Kishar. Thalia raises the tents with Narua, Bel, and Tashlu in the lee of a low rock shelf. Serapen calls Hanu, Eumelia, and Ava to help her prepare the evening meal.

Cooking is the only camp chore I'm never asked to do. I assume this is an extension of the rule that boys aren't permitted to learn pharmaka, although I'm also learning day by day that certain rules from the house of boys no longer apply to me as a novice Artifex.

Serapen directs Hanu's trio to lay out the waxed canvas beside the fire ring, creating a clean surface to prepare the meal. She directs me to haul water from the watering hole by the horses. I help the High Priestess pour several buckets full of the scummy liquid through a fine-woven cloth into the big stew pot and several smaller pots to boil.

Neither of the other Muses call me to attend them, so after Serapen dismisses me I find myself at my leisure with two fingers of good daylight left. I know exactly how I want to use it.

I retrieve my sketchbook and charcoal pencils from my saddlebag and take a seat beside the scraggly pile of gathered desert brush that will serve as our firewood tonight. From here, I can feed the fire for the girls who are cooking and manage the light for my drawing as darkness falls.

I open the sketchbook reverently. Although drawing wasn't forbidden to us in the house of boys, I've never drawn on new parchment before. Eagerly, I set to work, disappearing into the scene around me as I capture it on the page.

Narua, Bel, and Tashlu play a rowdy game of knucklebones with Muse Arkhi on a cleanswept patch of stone beside the campfire. Kishar argues with Eumelia over who must scrub out the charred crust inside a cooking pot that escaped the notice of whoever was responsible for cleanup last night. Eumelia insists Kishar must do it, while Kishar maintains no one must do it because the pot has been like that for a quarter moon, and round and round they go until Hanu steps in and scrubs out the offending vessel herself, to the other girls' chagrin. Kor lies on her back with her feet near the fire and her hands tucked under her head, watching the sunset. Piroza harmonizes with the wandering tune Thalia hums, improvising solo during the occasional stretches when the Muse of poetika pauses to puff her little clay pipe.

While Hanu and Eumelia chop root vegetables, Ava works beside Serapen with the herbs and spices. Ava watches with fascination as Serapen's long fingers dance across the line of little clay jars, glass bottles, and leather pouches arrayed before her on the canvas. Serapen carefully opens and closes, measures and stirs, explaining each step to Ava as she goes.

"Does this look right, sister?" says Ava, holding up a heavy stone mortar for Serapen's inspection.

Serapen takes a pinch of powder from the mortar and rolls it between her fingertips appraisingly. Ava imitates her. In the voice of instruction, Serapen says, "It's easiest to tell by touch whether you have produced a powder of the right fineness. This feels too gritty." Ava examines the powder on her fingertips, then sets the mortar back down and continues grinding its contents with the pestle until Serapen gestures for her to stop. The High Priestess takes a second pinch in her fingers, as does Ava. "Ah, yes," says Serapen. "Do you feel that slipperiness?" Ava nods. "That's what's needed. Now, to determine the correct amount to use, you must also judge the potency. For that, scent is the surest way." Serapen spoons a bit of the ground pharmaka from the mortar onto a shallow iron pan resting in the glowing coals of the fire. She stirs the dry powder over the iron with a wooden spoon, lifts the pan from the coals, and wafts the vapor off the toasting pharmaka toward her nose. She holds the pan out to Ava so she can do the same.

Ava inhales tentatively. Her eyes widen. "Oh, it smells delicious!" she says. The aroma drifts my way: a subtle sweetness like wild carrot, blooming into oak resin, clinging like cumin. Ava leans over the surface of the pan to take a deeper breath. Her expression turns dreamy.

Serapen smiles at Ava and sets the pan down on a flat stone in the fire ring. "That's probably enough for now, unless you'd like to go straight to sleep," she says. "This cooking pharmaka has many ingredients in common with unbinding pharmaka, and it shares some of its effects—relaxing the body, easing the mind's hold on troubled thoughts."

Ava stiffens. The brief flicker of warmth between priestess and novice is blown out. Serapen must sense Ava's distrust like I do, for her tone turns conciliatory. "I said only that it has ingredients in common, Ava. Your memory will come to no harm from this cooking pharmaka." Nonetheless, Ava remains silent for the rest of the meal preparation, continuing to watch Serapen closely, but with suspicion.

As the last of the sunlight fades into twilight, I emerge from the minutiae of my sketch and see it for the first time as a whole. I've captured nine novices and a trio of Muses around a glowing camp hearth, creating warmth, sustenance, and merriment together amidst the vast wilderness.

It's a satisfying image, and yet there's something missing. I wonder whether the observer should be in scene, or remain unseen. What is the proper place for the observer? Perhaps, if I had received instruction in these arts like the girls, I would know.

A sinuous coil of fragrant smoke tumbles over my shoulder and onto the page. I look up to find Thalia standing over me, puffing her pipe as she studies my sketch by the firelight. While absorbed in my work, I'd lost nearly all awareness of myself, but in the presence of critical eyes my self-consciousness flares. I'm sure every mistake I've made is obvious to a Muse, and Thalia's attitude toward me is usually teasing. I dread what she might say about my work in front of all the other girls.

But when she speaks, it's with a warmth more like her singing voice than her teasing voice. "You have a gift, Artifex," she says. "I see why the Voice has called you so."

Whatever she's smoking seems to have softened Thalia's edge, so I venture to ask, "Does the Voice call the Artifexi to draw?"

Thalia exhales another coil of smoke toward the rising moon. She says, "Many of the Artifexi do practice the visual arts, as the need arises. But the arts employed by an Artifex depend on his Muse. An Artifex serves the Voice through his service to his Muse."

This reminds me of Serapen's words, when I asked her why men can't hear the Voice in all like the Mohirai do. *An Artifex may experience the Voice only through his Muse.* "Will a Muse call me to attend her in Velkanos, then?" I say.

Thalia chuckles softly. She leans toward me, lowering her voice as she says, "No doubt many shall call on you. And no doubt you'll have your work cut out for you, choosing from among them. Should you find yourself in need of instruction in these matters, you may always come to me. You can be sure of my discretion."

The scent of Thalia's perfume mingled with her pipe smoke makes me lightheaded. I swallow uneasily. I've spent enough time among girls to recognize the Muse's tone of seduction, though she uses it more subtly than any girl I've encountered. The thought of being seduced by Thalia—and the thought of Ava's reaction—alarms me.

Something of my discomfort must spill into Ava, because she glances up at me. *What's wrong?* she thinks.

"Let him be, sister," says Arkhi. Ava and I both look over to see Arkhi watching me and Thalia from across the campfire. Thalia smiles innocently at Arkhi and leans back into the shadows.

The scent of Thalia dissipates. My head clears. I glance from Thalia to Arkhi. Arkhi seems a safer source of information than Thalia, so to her I say, "Does that mean I have to choose which Muse I'll serve?"

"Not right away," says Arkhi. "There's a great deal you must learn from the Mohirai, and from your brothers among the Artifexi, before you will be ready to choose. But in time, yes. You will choose which Muse best merits your service.

"This choice is the sacred responsibility of the Artifexi. In choosing his Muse, an Artifex chooses which Muse's great work will be accomplished in Dulai. We live in a world of precious few hands, so the work to which we dedicate those hands must be chosen wisely."

Arkhi's words stir my anxiety. Until my Calling Day, I had no meaningful choices in my life; I simply did what I was told to do by the Mohirai. Since my Calling Day, I've been overwhelmed by choices. I'm only beginning to understand how unprepared I was—how unprepared I still am—to make any of these choices. So many choices are entangled with unknowable mysteries and unforeseen consequences. Every choice I make is further complicated by Ava, since everything I do touches her, and everything she does touches me.

"Why would the Voice give me such an important choice?" I say. "Surely the Muses would choose better than I could. I have no great wisdom."

Thalia laughs, coughs, then laughs again. She says, "You're wiser than I was at seventeen summers, to say so."

In a more serious tone, Arkhi says to me, "I too have wondered why the Voice gave the Artifexi this responsibility. For centuries after the destruction, Serapen herself selected every great work to which we dedicated our hands."

Cheerfully, Thalia says, "Well, I find it refreshing. Centuries of service would grow dull indeed if our work never changed at all. And perhaps the Voice found something in Tio that was wanting in Serapen."

"Who's Tio?" I say.

In a chiding tone, Arkhi says to Thalia, "Really, sister, you should address him properly before the novices as Apatio Artifex. He's first of the Artifexi, after all, not just our little brother."

Thalia raises her hands in playful deference. "Forgive me, sister. But surely a man who prefers the rough quarters and rougher company of Lemnos to the comforts of Velkanos cares little for such formalities."

"That's unkind to the men of Lemnos," says Arkhi. "And hardly fair to Tio. You know how difficult it is for him to make the journey to Velkanos now."

Thalia laughs. "Come, sister. If any man can find a way to overcome difficulty, it's Tio."

I'm fascinated by this talk of Tio and the allusion to other Artifexi. I've been told almost nothing about the Artifexi, and I have so many questions. "How was it that the Artifexi came to be?" I say. "Until I heard the Voice's call myself, I thought only women were called to the path of mysteries, as Mohirai."

Serapen glances at Thalia and Arkhi from her place beside the fire, where she sits stirring the simmering pot of stew with a long wooden spoon. Thalia and Arkhi fall silent, inclining their heads deferentially to her. Unhurriedly, Serapen tastes the stew, sprinkles something from a little jar into the pot, and covers it.

Serapen reaches for her staff, which she's kept within arm's reach all day. Gripping the staff in her right hand, the High Priestess stands, wordlessly drawing all eyes up to her. The other novices fall silent.

"You ask a good question, little brother," says Serapen. "And tonight is a good night for answers, now that you have seen the Subartu Desert for yourself."

The High Priestess' tone tells me we're in for a tale. The other novices settle themselves into more comfortable postures around the fire. Hanu gestures for me to join her, Eumelia, and Ava on their side of the fire. I take a seat beside Hanu, and Ava remains seated between Hanu and Eumelia. Hanu joins hands with me and Ava, gently easing the ache of separation that's been gradually building up in our chests since we dismounted and made camp.

Serapen dips the large spherical burl atop her staff into the glowing coals. Wisps of blue smoke drift out through many fine cracks in the wooden burl. A scent—more savory than the one I remember from the camp council last night—fills my nostrils. Serapen's voice fills my ears. "To understand this new age, you must understand a great deal of historia, of the wheel of time that's ever turning. Listen well, novices, for I tell you a mystery: all that lies behind lies also ahead.

"You heard brother Urshanabi speak two nights ago of the age of kings, an age to which he and I both bore witness. There was, as Urshanabi told you, an ancient priesthood of men in those days, men called to the path of mysteries. These priests were beloved brothers to the sisters of the unnamed priestesshood that preceded the Mohirai."

As Serapen speaks, the fragrant blue smoke from her staff sinks to the ground and gathers in a ring around the fire, like a strange fog. Wisps within the ring coalesce into improbable shapes. I frown. Are my eyes playing tricks on me in the darkness? I peek out through Hanu's and Ava's eyes using our shared connection; they seem to be seeing the same strange shapes that I'm seeing. All the other girls stare at the smoke, too, transfixed.

Serapen says, "For many ages, these brothers were equal to their sisters in learning and wisdom. But by the time of my own childhood, the priests had forgotten the ways of wisdom, preferring instead the ways of learning. Learning without wisdom leads often to foolishness, and so it did in the age of kings, as foolish men of great learning probed the mysteries to extract new arts."

Serapen's words weave mesmerizing images from the writhing coils of smoke. I watch with fascination as the smoke solidifies and takes on new colors, forming a scene that grows ever more vivid, transporting us far from this place and time.

A great walled city filled with imposing towers of stone emerges from the smoke. The city streets throng with men, women, and children. Apart from the city of glass towers I've glimpsed in Ava's mind, I've never seen so many people. At the heart of the city stands a magnificent temple crowned with a golden dome. Within the temple, men in elaborate dress stride through grand halls and whisper behind closed doors. I'm fascinated by the colorful finery and commanding bearing of these men, who are so unlike all the men I've known in Dulai.

Serapen continues, "The ambitious leaders of men in those days, who styled themselves kings and chiefs, saw how the arts and mysteries of the learned priests could be manipulated for their own ends. So they enticed the priests with riches and influence, in exchange for the priests' service. Ambitious schemes like these entangled many men."

The smoke closes in around the whispering men, and when it parts again it reveals a new scene: the landscape outside the city walls. Vast expanses of dark tilled soil and fields of waving wheat edged by long straight lines of dug canals stretch to the horizon. I've never seen such enormous areas of land under cultivation.

"And though it did not happen all at once," says Serapen, "the priesthood in time forgot the responsibility that comes with practicing the arts and keeping the mysteries. The priests grew deaf to the Voice in all. They heard instead only the voices of kings and chiefs. With the help of the priests, the unchecked greed of kings and chiefs devastated the land, to the peril of all."

Serapen's strange smoke rolls over the endless tilled fields like storm clouds. When the clouds part, a vast green valley between two great rivers unfurls before us. We look down at this land between the rivers from a great height, flying like a falcon over dark green forests, lush grasslands, and roaming herds.

Far below us, a dark incision, straight as an arrow, appears in the grassland, slicing outward from the river's edge. At first, the wound seems insignificant in a landscape that seems infinite. But the wound explodes outward from the winding river, slicing at regular intervals and sharp angles across the rolling grassland. Rectangular patches of exposed soil bleed out from the wound, consuming the grassland piece by piece. When the grassland is all but gone, the wound spreads outward, climbing into the hills, devouring forested slopes, until all the marbled greens of wilderness are reduced to a single raw shade of reddish brown.

Serapen says, "The people saw how the priests had helped their kings abuse the land, and how the people suffered together in consequence. So the esteem and trust the priesthood had earned through millennia of service to the Voice eroded in a mere handful of generations."

The smoke-tinged image of the once-green river valley pales as the ravaged soil dries, erodes, and blows away in the wind. With a start, I recognize the desert wasteland left behind. It's the Subartu Desert through which we've been traveling these past many days, divided by the great Purattu river whose waters we fished yesterday. I remember what Eumelia said that so provoked Ava the day we reached the Purattu. *If anyone needed convincing that the Voice's plan for men is just, that blasted desert should do it.*

Serapen says, "The Voice in all governs Dulai, as it governs all things, by maintaining the natural order, the balance between what is given and what is received. In the age of kings, mother Dulai gave many gifts to our kind and received much abuse from us in return.

"So the Voice withdrew one of the great gifts of mother Dulai from our kind: the gift of fertility. Without the ability to bring new children into the world, the foolishness of our kind would find its natural end, restoring the natural order. No creature who abuses its mother and destroys its own home can survive long.

"Now, the Voice knows nothing and cares nothing for human concerns like punishment or wickedness. Nonetheless, the people saw their childlessness as punishment for the wickedness of kings and priests. So they abandoned the temple cities of the priests and the capital cities of the kings, hoping to escape what they believed was the Voice's punishment. And yet, slowly, death by death, the people's numbers dwindled. Ancient ways of life unraveled. Villages fell silent.

The destruction of our kind that followed our destruction of the land respected no borders and recognized no kings.

"At first, the kings tried to preserve their power. They tried to prevent the people from fleeing their cities, first by persuasion, then by force, and in the end by pleading. They tried everything the priests suggested to bring back children to the land. But in the end their efforts failed, for the priests could no longer hear the Voice in all, no longer receive its insight, no longer perceive the natural order. And no king could maintain control over a people so overcome by despair.

"However," says Serapen, "the sisters of the unnamed priestesshood had all this time disdained the power of kings. They remained faithful in their service to the Voice, so they continued to receive its insight. The people recognized the wisdom of the sisters, trusting their priestesses even as they learned to despise their priests and kings.

"So when the last generation of children came of age, they gathered around the temple cities of the priestesses, seeking insight from the Voice. They looked to the priestesses for hope that somehow our kind might survive the destruction.

"At that time, the last High Priestess of the unnamed priestesshood lay dying. Her name was Mohira. And though Mohira was weak, she listened to the despairing voices of the people outside the temple walls, and she took pity on them. As her final act of service to the people, Mohira placed her staff into the hand of her successor, instructing her to listen to the Voice on behalf of the last generation."

Serapen stands silent before the fire for a long time before she says, "So I did. I listened to the Voice, and when I listened, I heard it call the last generation to make the great sacrifice that would end the time of destruction."

The figure of a young woman coalesces in the blue smoke: tall, dark, reed-thin, with long black hair and Serapen's clear brown eyes. She walks barefoot across a cleared hilltop, following a deep-worn path that weaves through a forest of sawn-off stumps. Her hands are mangled by some deformity, clutched stiffly before her heart. She kneels on the cracked soil at the edge of a muddy pool in the center of a ring of massive stumps. She looks down at her reflection. Her tears ripple the cloudy brown surface of the water.

Serapen says, "The Voice revealed to me that the foolish greed of our kind, the greed that led us to ravage mother Dulai, is a greed born of fear. Our kind is fearful by nature—fearful of want, fearful of Death, fearful most of all of what we perceive as other. We are not unique in this. Fear serves a purpose for all creatures living in a world of predators.

"But unlike other fearful creatures, humans have received two special gifts from the Voice in all: the ability to acquire knowledge of the arts, and the ability to acquire knowledge of the mysteries. The arts give us the power to manifest our thoughts in the world. The mysteries give us the wisdom to exercise that power with restraint. When used in balance, these gifts can produce great good. When the balance is lost, especially when we place the arts in service to our fears, the harm can be catastrophic.

"The Voice revealed to me that human fear takes root most deeply in our kinship ties. We fear more deeply for those we love than we do even for ourselves. In our fear for those we love, all else is turned to other. In fear, we take what we should give, we harm what we should heal, we see in parts what is in truth a whole. It is this fear that obscures the truth. All are kin. All are one. We live and die together.

"The Voice revealed to me that the old ways of human life must be sacrificed if we wished to see children return to the land. To end the destruction, we must learn to see the oneness in all, giving up kinship ties and families, mothers and fathers."

Ava taught me the meaning of the word *mother* at the start of our journey together, but I've never heard the word *father* before. I suppose it must mean the same thing as mate, as we say with breeding animals, like the wolves.

Serapen says, "For those of us who grew up in the last generation, changing such a fundamental aspect of human life seemed impossible. But after all the losses we had suffered, many of us were willing to sacrifice even our kinship ties for the hope of life's renewal.

"There were many attempts and many failures before we learned how to make the sacrifice the Voice required. We found unbinding pharmaka to be the gentlest way. Dissolving the memory of kinship ties allowed each person to live free of the past in the new age. After unbinding, we remain only sisters and brothers in shared service to the Voice. And the Voice rewarded us for our sacrifice. Many of my generation received the gift of long life, long enough to see the wounds of the destruction begin to heal, long enough to hear children's voices return to the villages."

From somewhere within Serapen's blue smoke, I hear laughing, whispering, shouting. I recognize a few voices among the many: Hanu's gentle murmur, Eumelia's imperative shout, Ava's bright laughter, a cry of victory from my trio brother Balashi, a low chuckle from my trio brother Kuri, some soft muttering of my own.

Serapen says, "All you children of this new age are rare gifts. Ever since the destruction, the Voice alone decides when to call for a child, to replenish or increase our numbers. And the Voice alone decides who among you will receive the privilege of practicing the arts and walking the path of mysteries.

"The Voice works toward its own purposes, in its own time. For centuries, it pleased the Voice to call only sisters to the path of mysteries, and to grant no brother the honors once accorded to kings, priests, and fathers. In this way, we sisters inherited the responsibilities of leadership that men neglected, the privilege of knowledge that men squandered, and the power to rule that men abused."

The haze of blue smoke around the campfire dissolves. I see all the girls and women around me clearly again. Hanu sits with her eyes half-closed. Ava watches Serapen with intense concentration. Eumelia leans back on her elbows, gazing at Ava. Kor looks up at the stars. Her trio sisters Piroza and Kishar refrain from whispering with each other for a change. Serious Narua sits a little apart from her lighthearted trio sisters Bel and Tashlu, who lean against each other sleepily. At the edge of the shadows, Muse Arkhi sits motionless, nearly invisible in her inky black robes, except for the gleaming whites of her eyes. Nearer the warmth of the fire, Muse Thalia in her bright green and yellow robes puffs her pipe, listening with an expression that suggests she's heard this tale a thousand times.

Serapen looks at me and says, "The Voice has called me to witness much in its service. I am one of the few remaining on Dulai who remember the last age. I saw firsthand the damage wrought by foolish men with unchecked power. But I have also known a father's love, a priest's wisdom, a king's charisma. I have grieved the loss of brothers on the path of mysteries. I feel their absence even now.

"So it was an unhoped-for joy to me when the Voice called Apatio as the first of the Artifexi, beginning a new brotherhood for our new age, after so many centuries in which no man was called to the mysteries. The calling of Artifex remains exceedingly rare, even now. But your calling, Dom, is a sign to me that the Voice may someday open the path of mysteries again to all sisters and brothers. The presence of the Artifexi among the Mohirai is to me a sign of healing underway and a promise of healing still to come.

"Healing mother Dulai from the destruction wrought by our kind is the work of ages. But in time, through our service to the Voice, all things are possible. Mother Dulai still grants us many gifts, whatever our callings may be, as each of us works to repay our great debt to her. This is why we say—" Serapen turns the palm of her free hand up toward the sky and speaks the familiar words of the meal blessing.

We give our thanks for gifts of sun
Of water, soil, and seed
For gifts of many seasons
Gathered here to meet our need
To build our strength so that our hands
May in their time return
The gifts received from mother land
Improved with gifts our own

In the silence that follows the blessing, Serapen sweeps an expectant gaze around the circle of novices looking up at her. As one, we say, "We have listened, and we have heard, sister."

"Good," says Serapen. She kneels beside the fire again, sets her staff down beside her, and lifts the lid off the cooking pot. She wafts a bit of the aroma toward her nostrils, inhales, and says, "Yes, very good. And now it is time to eat."

Thalia and Arkhi are passing bowls of stew around the ring when Kor scrambles back from the campfire, pointing directly over my head as she gasps, "Oh! Oh! Look out!"

There's an outburst of startled cries from the girls all around me. I look up to see a flock of winged shadows swooping down toward us. There's no time to run. My instinct to protect Ava takes over without conscious thought. Hanu lets out a startled cry as I hurtle over her toward Ava. I pull Ava under me with one arm, grip my sketchbook in my other hand, and use it to shield both our heads as best I can from the airborne attack. Ava shouts, "Arkhi! Your darts!"

There's a thud directly over my head as something hits my sketchbook at speed. A stunned bird tumbles to the ground beside us. I feel several more thuds, followed by a violent scratching and pecking on the leather cover of my sketchbook, alarmingly close to my exposed fingers.

"Hold still!" Arkhi calls out in the tone of command. Ava and I freeze, huddled together under my sketchbook. The Muse smoothly withdraws the little wooden case from her robes and raises it to her lips. There's a rapid succession of five whizzing sounds, followed by four more soft thuds of feathered bodies hitting the ground.

Cautiously, I lower my sketchbook. Ava and I stare down at the ground. Five hooded crows, with their distinctive black heads and grey breasts, lie in an irregular circle around our feet. Firelight glimmers on the five blue-tufted needles protruding from their limp bodies. I shiver. Ava looks up at me with a stunned expression. We're both thinking the same thing.

Lilith's alive.

△▽△

"But what message would Lilith be sending by attacking you with crows?" Eumelia whispers to me. "Every messenger bird I ever saw in the Children's Temple carried its message on a ribbon or a scrap of parchment."

Inside our tent, I lie on my bedroll facing Eumelia. Hanu's finally drifted off to sleep behind me, her arm draped over my waist.

"I don't know," I whisper back. I wish Eumelia would hurry up and fall asleep. I need privacy with Dom; I've decided to tell him about the message the kuku bird scratched into my boot so we can see what marks those crows might have left on his sketchbook. Fortunately, in all the confusion after the crows attacked, no one was paying any attention to Dom's sketchbook.

Through Hanu, I sense Dom still awake, listening to me and Eumelia. He's never able to sleep while my mind is racing this way. It's long past time for all of us to sleep, but the incident with the crows took a while to resolve. By the time the Mohirai finished examining and unbinding all five of the birds, and Serapen summoned the wolves to patrol closer to the camp, and Arkhi resettled the terrorized horses farther off from the wolves, and we'd all eaten our cold stew, it was close to midnight.

"It really doesn't mean anything to you?" Eumelia whispers. "Like the fact that there were five birds, or … I don't know … Maybe it's some signal only you would understand? Or some secret you had between you?"

"All of her secrets were secrets she kept from me," I hiss, my irritation with

Eumelia momentarily replaced by a flare of anger at Lilith. Why does Eumelia always have to ask so many questions?

She's just like you, Dom thinks, amused.

Eumelia presses my hand. "Sorry," she whispers. "We don't need to talk about this any more. Good night." She rolls onto her other side and drifts off to sleep. Dom and I remain awake, even more acutely aware of each other now that the other two girls are sleeping.

Are you all right? he thinks.

Spirits, I should be asking you that, I think. *I didn't even ask—did the crows hurt you?* The idea that Lilith could still manage to hurt Dom, even now, infuriates me.

I'm fine, he thinks. *The sketchbook took most of the damage. Maybe the crows just didn't like my drawing.*

I suppress a giggle. I sense Dom smiling. My anger at Lilith ebbs, replaced by an upwelling of tenderness for him. Carefully, I turn around in Hanu's arms, looking over her shoulder at Dom. By the faint moonlight, I can just make out the curve of his cheek and the glimmer of his dark eyes locked on mine.

Memories of all the times I've lain in Dom's arms flood through me. My pulse speeds up. I close my eyes tight to ward off the longing for his touch, for his warmth, for his voice in my ear. I've let my guard down at the wrong time in the worst place. The last thing I need right now is to disturb what little remains of the night by slipping away to another branch.

Hanu moves in her sleep, drawing me a little closer to her. Even in sleep, her presence somehow creates a buffer of safety between me and Dom, allowing my feelings to play out without sending me off to another branch. Slowly, I relax again and open my eyes. Dom is still watching me. I risk sharing another thought. *I need to tell you something.*

Dom's curiosity perks up. *What?* he thinks.

I show him my memory of what I saw on my boot after the kuku attacked it.

His eyes widen. *What does that mean?* he thinks. *Return to? Return to what?*

I'm not sure, I think. *I must have interrupted the kuku when I grabbed my boot. Maybe more of the message came through on your sketchbook this time. Did you look at it after the crows attacked us?*

Yes, thinks Dom. He shares what he saw by the light of the campfire. He can't read, so he didn't recognize the letters, but as I peer into his memory, I can make out the words scratched roughly into the leather cover of his sketchbook: *Return to me and all will be forgiven.*

I'm not exactly sure what message I'd hoped Lilith might send. An explanation, at least. An apology, perhaps. How dare she try to command me to return to her after she's betrayed me? I curse Lilith so furiously in my mind that Dom winces. Hanu stirs fretfully in her sleep. I force myself to calm down.

Dom and I lie in silence for a long time before he thinks, *I'm sorry, Ava.*

About what? I think. *You didn't do anything wrong.*

I'm sorry Lilith lied to you, he thinks. *I'm sorry that she hurt you.*

Damn her, I think. *I never should have trusted her. I never should have dragged you into any of this.*

Dom thinks, *You did the best you could with what you knew. You protected me from her. If it weren't for you, she would have taken all my memories of you.*

Lilith's message unleashed my anger, but Dom's kindness unleashes the grief I've struggled to suppress since Lilith abandoned me the night of my overdose. My grief seems as bottomless as it is pointless. I'm a fool to grieve for her, especially now, after everything I've learned about her. Why should I grieve for someone who lied to me, who used me?

Dom is usually skilled at soothing me, but my inner tempest overwhelms his calm. My tumultuous emotions and endless thoughts of Lilith stir his own awful memories of her and the free men. He and I spiral together into dark thoughts. Sleep eludes us. My guilt for robbing Dom of another night's rest only adds to my own grief and anger. He and I toss and turn, trying not to wake Hanu and Eumelia. When we've finally given up all hope of sleep, we lie on either side of Hanu silently debating what to do about Lilith's message. In the end, I persuade Dom that we should keep it a secret between us. As much as I distrust Lilith, I trust the Mohirai even less.

THE FINAL ASCENT

At first light, Dom and I slip out of the tent to ready ourselves for the day's ride. The restless night full of dark thoughts weighs heavily on me, leaving me even more exhausted than yesterday. How I'll manage another half moon's journey in this state, I have no idea.

On our way to the horses, we walk past the three Muses seated together beside the embers of the campfire, deep in discussion. Serapen nods to us before continuing the conversation in an undertone with Arkhi and Thalia. The three of them kept watch together all night after the crows attacked, but they appear entirely unaffected by the lack of sleep. Lilith once explained to me that sleep is more a luxury than a necessity for initiate priestesses. Not for the first time, I long for the advantages the Mohirai acquire through their use of initiate pharmaka.

Dom reaches out and touches my hand as I trudge after him toward Eridu. A current of his strength runs through me, warm and bracing. *How do you have any energy to spare right now?* I think.

He gives no answer, merely squeezing my hand before proceeding to saddle Eridu. I try to help him at first, and he lets me, but eventually I realize the most useful thing I can do is conserve my strength so he doesn't need to keep lending me more of his. Resigned, I sit down and watch Dom at work, envying the ease with which he moves and hauls and lifts. I never thought I would envy a boy, but even a boy's life seems appealing in comparison to mine. I used to be so quick on my feet and nimble with my hands. Will I ever be strong and healthy that way again?

After the rest of the novices emerge from their tents, the Mohirai call us to gather around the fire ring, where they relate the outcome of their little council. Like me and Dom, they've concluded from the crows' attack that Lilith is alive and following us. Rather than spending any more effort trying to spot her, however, they've decided to focus the attention of our animal guards on protecting me and Dom from further encounters with Lilith or her messengers for the remainder of the journey to Velkanos.

The Muses' plan for our protection sounds reasonable to me at first, until I see what this new protection entails. After we break camp, poor Eridu and the rest of the horses must endure the constant anxiety caused by the proximity of the wolf pack. Serapen uses her control over the wolves to maintain a small distance between them and the caravan, but the horses can still see our wolf escort flanking them throughout the day, and not even the High Priestess can entirely erase the horses' fear around their natural predators.

Meanwhile, the falcons circle endlessly over the caravan to ward off potential attack by messengers from the skies. The falcons are easy to track from a distance, which makes me uneasy. I try to reassure myself with the thought that our visibility can't make much difference. Clearly Lilith hasn't had any difficulty tracking us so far, with or without falcons marking our position.

Thalia assumes the lead position in the caravan, which had been Arkhi's place until now. Serapen places me and Dom at the center of the caravan, with Arkhi riding alongside us. Having Arkhi and her blowdarts nearby is reassuring, though I take greater comfort knowing my blade is tucked inside my waistband, with a new leather handle I've fashioned from strips cut off my old pack. I wish I could fashion a sheath from the rest of my pack leather, but I need privacy for such covert crafts. I don't want the Mohirai to know about my blade.

Serapen follows at the rear of the caravan, the better to keep an eye on all of us, I suppose. Today she rides with her long staff in her hand. That staff looks like an unwieldy weapon, so I assume Serapen can do more with it than simply produce tricky smoke around the campfire.

Perhaps the animal guards and Serapen's presence are sufficient to deter Lilith. Perhaps Lilith's simply biding her time. In any case, our desert crossing proceeds without further incident. Four days after Urshanabi ferried us across the Purattu, we approach the hill country that separates the Subartu Desert from the peaks of the Urashtu Range. The wide, dusty road across the desert narrows and begins a winding ascent.

Days pass. The road climbs endlessly upward. I grow increasingly anxious for the journey to conclude. At these higher elevations, even the midday temperatures are cool, and the nighttime temperatures drop precipitously. When Dom shares his warmth with me by direct skin contact, I have a brief reprieve from the cold, but my mind veers toward thoughts of other-Dom. The dilemma is maddening. To be comfortable in my body, I have to risk my mind wandering off to another branch. To keep my mind safely here, I have to push my body to the point of exhaustion.

But I stifle my complaints about the cold and the distance and the difficulty of the journey. Complaining is pointless, and I don't want to make myself any more pathetic to the rest of the caravan than I already am. Every day, the basic tasks of life on the road become more of a struggle for me to complete on my own. Reluctantly, I learn to ask for more help from Dom and my trio sisters and the other novices. For years, I've been entirely at home in the wilderness, living on my own with far fewer comforts than I've had on this caravan. Now I wonder whether I'll ever be able to live like that again: sleeping under the stars, riding fast and free under the sun.

The journey drags on. I grow so weak that no amount of bundling up or sitting by the fire can drive the chill from my bones. Serapen watches me like a hawk, day in and day out. Her attention would once have bothered me, but I have no energy left to conceal anything from her. Nothing of my predicament seems to escape her notice. She starts to prepare special warming pharmaka for me and Dom to drink at every meal. She probably slips extra pharmaka into my food as well, but I'm too tired to protest or resist.

The cold intensifies day by day, so Serapen directs the alpha and luna wolves into our tent at night to keep me warm. Dom, Hanu, and Eumelia find the wolves' presence in our tent unsettling, but I find their company calming. Dom and my trio sisters often inadvertently add a measure of agitation to my mind when they touch me and thoughts slip through our connection. By contrast, the minds of the wolves are quiet and clear, untroubled by anything but the present moment. Unfortunately, even with the wolves' warm, furry bodies pressed against me, I still shiver my way through many long nights in the mountains.

As we near the end of the long road to Velkanos, I'm too worn out to feel apprehensive of my impending life trapped within temple city walls. Perhaps Lilith was right, and the Mohirai have manipulated me through this journey, wearing down my resistance to prepare me for a life of submission to the Voice's will. Or perhaps everything Lilith taught me was a lie, and I'll discover there's nothing to fear in Velkanos. Whatever the case, I face the journey's end with resignation. The only real desire I have left is for warmth and sleep—endless sleep.

△▽△

Though she puts on a brave face, Ava can't hide her accelerating deterioration from me. I can't hide my worry from her, either, though my concern for her health only increases Ava's frustration with herself. She hates any reminder of how weak she's become.

My only diversion from watching Ava's decline day after day is watching the dramatic landscape that unfolds with each bend in the road. Our route to the Urashtu Pass hugs the bank of a clear, rushing river. As we follow the river toward its source in the heart of the mountains, autumn races by at triple speed. Days pass, and color descends from the remote peaks down to us in the valleys, transforming the dark green groves of oak and beech around us to every shade of sunlight yellow. As we climb, the bright leaves fall, paving the road ahead in gold, a parting gift of warm color from the growing season to remember through the stark whites and long nights of winter ahead.

At the start of the frigid final ascent to the Urashtu Pass, the river narrows and disappears at times into the secret ravines and hidden crevasses of the mountains. We're hemmed in on both sides by steep slopes of weathered limestone. What was a road becomes a path, and what was a path disappears entirely at times into crumbling bare rock. The Mohirai lead us in slow single file along narrow rough-hewn stairs and chiseled ledges. I avoid looking down the dizzying drops beside us on the more treacherous portions, gripping Ava tight around the waist and reminding myself over and over of Eridu's sure-footedness. Ava can't resist looking down. The sight of the stairs sparks endless questions in her mind, which makes me wonder, too. Who carved these stairs and smoothed these ledges? How many feet and hooves have passed this way before us? What would drive anyone up into these mountains, with their harsh winters, so far from the gentle seasons of the Middle Sea?

THE CAVE OF DREAMS

We're cresting the Urashtu Pass one full moon after our Calling Day when Arkhi raises her hand and calls out, "This will be our last stop before Velkanos."

There's a relieved murmur from the other girls in the caravan at this welcome news, but I wish for Ava's sake that we could push on through the Urashtu Pass and camp at a lower, warmer elevation. I suppose we have to stop while enough light remains to make camp. The days have grown noticeably shorter in the moon since we left the Children's Temple. We lose daylight even faster here in the mountains, where the steep slopes shroud the valleys in early darkness.

I survey the spot Arkhi's chosen for us to camp. It doesn't look promising to me, but after all the Muse's sound counsel over the course of this journey, I trust her judgment. There are a few level patches of ground on either side of the narrow path here, although they're barely large enough to accommodate the tents and the horses. There's no water that I can see, apart from what we might melt from the icicles encrusting the rocky slopes around us, and that assumes we can gather enough of the scraggly mountain brush to make a fire. I see nothing for the horses to eat apart from a few handfuls of withered mountain grasses here and there, sprouting from cracks in the bare rock.

Any one of these things—perhaps even all of them together—might be tolerable for one night, if this spot weren't so exposed to the wind. At this elevation, the wind blows steadily from the west behind us, whistling through the rocks above as it courses endlessly through the Urashtu Pass. As soon as the sun sets, the temperature will plunge, and the wind will make it impossible to keep warm in the tents, even with the added body heat of the luna and alpha wolves. Despite the extra food and pharmaka Serapen's been feeding us both, Ava's been drawing so much body heat from me during our daytime rides that for the last few nights I've had trouble keeping myself warm, which was never a problem before.

I dismount, and Ava accepts my help dismounting without protest. I lift her carefully down from the saddle, briefly bearing her entire weight in my arms. If she was small at the start of the journey, she's now frighteningly insubstantial. As I lower her to the ground, I can't help noticing how the only softness she once had about her features has disappeared entirely. Shadowed hollows emphasize her temples, her cheekbones, her collarbones. Her dark eyes look enormous in her thin face. Her lips are severely chapped from her nervous habit of chewing them. Her skin, which was rosy brown this time last moon, has a sickly violet cast today as sunset approaches. As difficult as Ava finds it to look at me while she tries to avoid thoughts of other-Dom, it's even more difficult for me to look at her while she's in this wretched condition.

Her eyes briefly meet mine. She draws her hood tighter around her face to hide her gauntness. She's overheard my thoughts on her appearance already, but I make an effort to suppress any further thoughts. I fish out the thick wool blanket from her saddlebag and wrap the extra layer tightly around her to compensate for the loss of skin contact with me. She starts shivering almost immediately, but this is the best I can do for her until I've helped the others make camp.

I turn to Eridu to unsaddle him, but before I've loosened a single buckle, Arkhi gestures for me and the other girls to stop. She calls over the sound of the whistling wind, "We won't unpack out here. Follow me. If you lose sight of me in the passageway, follow your horses. They know the way."

Despite our exhaustion, Ava and I exchange an intrigued glance at this unexpected instruction. I take Eridu's bridle in my left hand and Ava's icy fingers in my right. We hurry to join the end of the line following Arkhi.

The Muse leads the caravan toward a tall boulder that stands embedded in a slope of loose limestone scree that's tumbled down the sheer rock face of the mountain above. Arkhi leads her mare Khaos by the bridle toward the right side of this boulder. To my surprise, the pair disappears into the mountain. Thalia follows with Rurata. Narua's trio and their horses disappear after Arkhi the same way, followed by Kor's trio and their horses. Only as Ava and I draw near do I understand that what I'm seeing is a trick of perspective. What appears from a distance to be a solid boulder actually has an enormous crack on one side, creating a triangular passageway into the mountain.

"Thank the spirits," Ava sighs, realizing at the same moment I do that we're going to have some protection from the wind tonight.

I'm not quite as thankful as Ava, though. Uneasily, I watch Hanu, Eumelia, and their horses vanish into the pitch darkness of the passage into the mountain. I'm not usually afraid of the dark, but this underground darkness is a different thing entirely from a moonless night.

Ava looks up at me. Despite her exhaustion, she gives me a small, encouraging smile. "You know what helps me when it's really dark?" she says.

"What?" I say.

"Closing my eyes," she says.

"That doesn't make any sense," I say.

She chuckles. "Trust me."

And I do. So I close my eyes.

She squeezes my hand. "All right," she says. "Follow me."

Ava steps forward through the opening. I take a cautious step after her. Eridu takes a more confident step after me. My palm tingles against Ava's as I cross the threshold. Through our connection, I feel Ava trailing the fingers of her free hand lightly along the stone walls on either side of us, then over her head, mapping out the space by touch and by sound. Ava's right. With my eyes closed, my other senses—and Ava's—cast their own kind of light into the darkness.

Ava's fingers detect a gentle curve in the wall ahead. Our steps turn slowly to the right, then to the left. We snake through the tunnel toward the heart of the mountain. The tunnel walls close in around us on all sides—so close that Eridu lowers his head and bumps his big nose against my shoulder, so close that the saddle and stirrups scrape against the stone walls on both sides of him at once. But Eridu just manages to fit through, and finally we emerge into a space that feels much larger and much warmer than the tunnel.

There's a loud crack of metal on stone. I open my eyes just as a torch flares in Arkhi's hand, a few paces ahead of us. The friendly glow illuminates a large cave with a low ceiling. Arkhi touches her lit torch to an unlit torch Thalia holds out to her. When the brightness doubles, I see most of the space around us.

The cave is larger across than the meal hall was in the house of boys, where we often sat over a hundred boys together at long tables. Our entire caravan could fit inside this cave five times over with room to spare. I scan all the faces in the torchlight to reassure myself that no one disappeared on the way in. Narua, Bel, and Tashlu stand with their horses near Arkhi. Kor, Piroza, and Kishar with their horses stand by Thalia. Hanu and Eumelia make room for me and Ava as we enter the cave. I look back to see Serapen ducking her head to pass through the opening behind us, followed by her mare Amisos. The wolves snuffle and pant somewhere in the tunnel behind her. We're all accounted for, except for the falcons, but I suppose they can find their own shelter somewhere in the rocky slopes outside.

The High Priestess picks up an unlit torch from a large supply piled inside the cave entrance, beside a massive stack of split firewood. The trees are so sparse near the Urashtu Pass that this all must have been carried up by packhorses from the forests at the lower elevations. The mere sight of so much firewood, and the knowledge that we won't have to spend the last of the daylight gathering it outside in the cold, has a warming effect on me. Here in the cave, the air is already significantly warmer than it was outside in the wind, and the air grows steadily warmer with all the humans and horses shuffling around. Ava's hand relaxes in mine. I'm relieved to feel her own warmth in her fingers for the first time in several days.

The unexpected prospect of easy warmth seems luxurious all on its own, until Eridu pulls hard on his bridle to show me another of the cave's amenities. Ava and I follow as Eridu leads us to water. By the flickering torchlight, I see the glimmer of snowmelt trickling down one wall of the cave, pooling generously at our feet before continuing on its long journey back to the sea. Eridu and several of the mares drink deep from the pool after their thirsty climb.

The night I was dreading looks more promising, as this cave provides for our most pressing needs. I send up silent words of gratitude to the spirits. Maybe Ava and I will manage to get some sleep tonight after all.

△▽△

When the horses are watered and our hands and faces have thawed, Arkhi says, "We'll unload here. Leave everything packed except for your bedrolls and the cooking gear. We'll share a special meal tonight to mark the end of your journey from the Children's Temple and the start of your initiate training."

Dom and I exchange a resigned look. This probably means another pharmaka ceremony of some kind awaits us, when all we want to do is curl up and go to sleep.

We follow Arkhi's instructions to settle the horses on the dry side of the cave. Here we discover another luxury: bales of fresh hay for the horses' feed and bedding. I wonder how many travelers must come through the Urashtu Pass to justify the Mohirai keeping this place so well supplied. This in turn makes me wonder why Lilith never had us stop here when we came through the Urashtu Pass ourselves on several occasions. And this makes me think of something I've been too exhausted to worry about for days.

I leave Dom to finish unsaddling Eridu and make my way through the other girls unpacking, toward Serapen. The High Priestess stands alone near the opening where we entered this cave. In the dark tunnel behind her, close to the ground, nine pairs of yellow eyes reflect the flickering torchlight back at me. Serapen must have commanded the pack of wolves to settle down here, just out of sight of the horses. The wolves might deter an attack by the free men, but Serapen must know they wouldn't stop Lilith if she were determined to get inside.

"Lilith will know we've stopped here," I say to Serapen in a low voice. The High Priestess nods in agreement, which does nothing to calm my nerves. "Are we safe from her in here?"

Serapen says, "Lilith will not enter this cave."

"Why? Because she's afraid of you?" I say.

"Because she fears the Voice in all," says Serapen. "Just as she taught you to do."

I don't know why Lilith's fear of the Voice would make her afraid of this cave. I've spent plenty of time with Lilith in caves. I say, "Even if that's true, she could wait for us outside. She could ambush us when we leave. And ..." I hate to say it aloud, even though it's completely obvious to everyone in the caravan. "I'm not strong enough to defend myself or Dom from her like I did before."

Serapen levels her calm gaze at me, and for the first time I notice the signs of exhaustion in her eyes. Maybe it's foolish of me to bother her with these worries. She must know as well as I do the risks of stopping here while Lilith is following us. Why else would she have been on constant watch for the last half moon? I can't remember a single time the High Priestess has slept since we crossed the Purattu, come to think of it. Yet somehow she still manages to sound patient as she says, "I have put in place every protection I can for you and Dom. Share the meal with your sisters. Let go of your troubled thoughts for tonight."

I bow my head. I wish I trusted Serapen as simply and completely as Dom and the other novices do. But even though I don't trust her, I'm too weak to do much else but obey her, so I rejoin the others.

△▽△

I finish unloading Eridu as I wait for Ava. I'm not trying to eavesdrop on her conversation with Serapen, but it's obvious from Ava's worried expression that she's talking about Lilith again. Is there nowhere that Ava will feel safe from her?

How far must we travel to escape the shadow of that woman?

After we've settled the horses in their cozy new quarters, Arkhi and Thalia make their way to the innermost wall of the cave. Their torchlight reveals the opening of another tunnel, wider and lower than the last one. Arkhi enters this second tunnel, vanishing into the darkness after only a few steps.

Thalia, standing at the tunnel opening with her torch raised high, calls out to us, "Pick up a new torch from the pile there and follow Arkhi through."

The girls and I shoulder our bedrolls and head toward Thalia, who lights each of our torches from her own. Narua's trio, Kor's trio, Hanu, and Eumelia walk on into the darkness of the second tunnel.

Ava and I follow at the end of the line and pick up two torches from the neat pile beside the tunnel opening. Thalia lights Ava's torch, and Ava steps past her, pausing in the tunnel to wait for me.

As Thalia lights my torch, she glances over her shoulder with a half smile and says to Ava, "Afraid he'll lose his way?"

"Only if he follows you in," says Ava.

The Muse's tinkling laughter echoes along the cave walls. Thalia winks at me and says, "She lives again!"

Ava rolls her eyes and holds out her hand to me. I edge past Thalia and take Ava's hand.

We walk side by side through most of the second tunnel. I hold my torch ahead of us, illuminating the low ceiling so we can avoid hitting our heads. Ava holds her torch near the uneven floor so we can avoid tripping. The tunnel itself appears entirely natural, without any signs of chisel marks, although the soft limestone is scratched in places with symbols that must have been carved by human hands.

We emerge from the tunnel into a second cave, smaller than the outer cave where we left the horses. The other girls meander through the space, torches aloft, gazing upward. Ava and I look up too, and Ava gasps softly.

The flickering torchlight reveals a gently domed ceiling. Unlike the outer cave, whose walls and ceiling were the same pale limestone as the mountain slopes outside, the ceiling of this inner cave is blackened with soot. The entire ceiling is covered with images scratched through the sooty layer into the lighter stone surface beneath.

Some of the images are easy to decipher, though they're little more than stick figures. Riders on horseback aim hunting bows at antlered creatures that might be deer. Large groups of human figures perform some kind of ceremony around a bonfire. Warriors wield spears in chaotic scenes of violence. In a few places, the images are abstract shapes that remind me of the painted blue swirls on Arkhi's palms and the delicate pattern decorating the leather cover of my sketchbook before Lilith's crows ravaged it.

"Come along," Arkhi calls out to us. We gather around her near the center of the cave, where a narrow shaft of daylight shines down through an irregular hole in the ceiling. The shaft of light illuminates a smooth hollow on the stone floor that's covered with a thin layer of ashes. A gentle updraft rises through a crack that runs down the center of the hollow, but thankfully the air from below is much warmer than the icy wind we left outside. "We'll build our cooking fire here and tend it until daybreak," says Arkhi. "None of you will sleep cold tonight."

Following Arkhi's instructions, we place our bedrolls in a ring around the hollow. Thalia enters the cave carrying two large buckets of water, followed by Serapen carrying the cooking gear. The three Muses set to work building the fire and preparing a meal for us, directed by Serapen. None of the novices receive any work assignments tonight, so we extinguish our torches in a pile of ashes near the cave entrance and sit on our bedrolls by the fire, warming our hands and feet, sipping the hot pharmaka Serapen passes around to us in little wooden cups.

Delicious warmth spreads from my belly to my fingers and toes. I watch Ava, who sits quietly on her bedroll between Hanu and Eumelia, close to the fire. She still looks exhausted, but there's an encouraging hint of color returning to her cheeks.

Thalia passes full bowls of stew around the circle. Although the meal appears to be nothing more than the same smoked trout, root vegetables, and herbs we've been eating every evening since we crossed the Purattu, Serapen must have added something extra from her supplies tonight. The stew has never smelled this delicious. It requires more self-control than usual for me to wait for the meal blessing.

But it seems we must wait a little bit longer before we start eating. The High Priestess rises and says, "Listen, novices. We sleep tonight in the Cave of Dreams, a place rich in historia, a place held sacred through many ages.

"Long before the founding of our order, and long before even the founding of the unnamed priestesshood from which many of our great teachings come, the ancestors of the Urashtu people lived in these mountains. Among those people were the first to hear the Voice in all.

"Mountains have long been sacred to those who seek the Voice, for in the hearts of mountains it is easier to find the stillness in which the Voice speaks clearly. In this very cave, seekers have received many great teachings from the Voice: gifts of knowledge that revealed many mysteries and inspired many arts that have been passed down through many generations.

"Within our own order, we bring our novices here to help you remember one important teaching. Whatever mysteries may lie ahead on your path, whatever arts you may practice, whatever understanding you may attain, all human insight in the end derives from a common source: the Voice in all. Though we may build grand temples and accomplish great works, the Voice is not contained in any work of human hands. The Voice came long before us, and the Voice will remain long after we depart these lives.

"We visit this place to remind ourselves that, although we may forget to listen, although we may struggle to hear, though our great temples may fall, though arts may be lost and mysteries forgotten, still the Voice dwells in all, ready to renew its teachings to anyone who chooses to listen.

"Tonight we partake in the pharmaka of dreams, which the Voice gave as a gift to all seekers, long ago. Tonight you will sleep in a place full of memories, where many dreamers before you have awoken with new insight from the Voice. Remember your dreams, as best you can, so you may carry their insight with you to your new lives in the house of novices."

We listen to all this in silence, breathing in the fragrant steam from our bowls. Serapen turns her palms up toward the cave ceiling. Together, we recite the familiar words of the meal blessing together. Our voices echo in the cave so that we seem to be joined by many other voices saying,

We give our thanks for gifts of sun
Of water, soil, and seed
For gifts of many seasons
Gathered here to meet our need
To build our strength so that our hands
May in their time return
The gifts received from mother land
Improved with gifts our own

Serapen lifts her bowl, holding it out toward us, and we all raise our bowls to her. We eat and drink. Arkhi keeps the fire burning high and bright, driving out the memory of cold.

Ava relaxes in the warmth, which helps me relax. The voices of the women and girls around me blend together, joined by the echo voices of the cave. I don't remember lying down, but at some point a familiar face leans over me, smiles down at me, kisses my cheek, and tucks the edges of my blanket around me. My languid awareness wonders who she is. Ava? Hanu? Serapen? Or is she that lost woman, the one whose face slipped into shadows long ago, before my memory begins? I drift off to sleep still wondering.

When I open my eyes again, I'm standing high up on a rocky promontory, entirely alone. I'm surrounded by water on all sides, enclosed by the bright blue bowl of sky above and the dark blue bowl of sea below.

The endless blue fills me with an agony of loneliness deeper than the sea and higher than the sky. I cry out in despair, but there's no possibility of answer. There's nothing in all directions but a perfect circle of unbroken horizon.

I look down into the deep water. In my loneliness, I consider seeking comfort in its embrace. But it's a long way down.

There's a flapping sound high above me. I look up. A flash of scarlet, like the wings of a bright red bird, swoops toward me. I cover my head with my hands, closing my eyes, thinking I'm about to be attacked from the sky.

But there's only a soft *thump* on the ground as something falls at my feet. I open my eyes cautiously.

Suspended in the air before me, just touching the ground, hangs a great rope ladder woven from fine scarlet thread. The rope ladder gleams brighter than blood against the blue sky.

Tentatively, I reach out for the nearest rung of the ladder. It's silky smooth under my fingers. I grip and pull the rung. It's strong, definitely able to bear my weight. I notice a throbbing sensation in my palm, which at first I think is my own heartbeat. But as I examine the scarlet rope in my hand more closely, I realize the ladder itself is pulsing.

I look up the length of the ladder. It stretches so high into the sky that it vanishes into a fine line, like a single scarlet thread cast down for me from the sky's zenith.

I long to see what lies beyond that sky. I long to escape this lonely rock.

So I climb. I climb. I climb.

△▽△

My eyelids are so heavy that I can't hold them open. Yet every time I'm about to drift off to sleep, some tiny sound—a sharp intake of breath from one of the girls sleeping near me, a crackle of a log settling in the fire, the whistle of wind at the top of the hole in the ceiling through which the campfire smoke rises—jolts me awake, and all my worries about Lilith flood through me again.

At last, frustrated, I extract myself from Hanu's arms and sit up. Before me, the three Mohirai sit close to the fire on their bedrolls: Thalia smoking her pipe, Serapen sipping her tea, Arkhi tending the fire. The three of them look at me.

In a low voice, Serapen says, "Sleep, little sister. No harm will come to you here. We three will keep watch together through the night."

But I'm wide awake now, so I scoot to the end of my bedroll, closer to the fire, wrapping my blanket around my shoulders. Even though it's warm in the cave, and even warmer this close to the fire, I feel like I'll never have enough warmth again after all these long cold days on the road. I look at the circle of other novices around the fire, sound asleep. "They fell asleep so fast," I say. "What did you put into the food?"

"The pharmaka of dreams," says Serapen, "just as I told you."

"Then why can't I fall asleep?" I say.

Serapen takes another sip of her tea. "The arts of pharmaka are imprecise," she says. "The receiver matters as much as the giver."

"So it's my fault that it doesn't work with me like it does with the other novices?" I say.

Serapen smiles. "There is no fault in you or in the pharmaka, little sister. No two people experience any pharmaka in exactly the same way. But it is true that you affect the way the pharmaka behaves. Emotions interact powerfully with many forms of pharmaka. Fear can amplify the effects of some pharmaka and suppress the effects of others. That is why we withhold many kinds of pharmaka from novices. Preparation of the self is as important as preparation of the pharmaka ingredients, to achieve the most beneficial effects from both."

I study the face of the High Priestess by the firelight. She gazes back at me. It's surreal to sit companionably by the fire with her after spending my childhood running away from her. Her instruction on the subject of pharmaka intrigues me, after so many years listening to Lilith's dire warnings against its use. Lilith refused to teach me any of the arts of pharmaka, requiring me to abstain entirely. My catastrophic overdose of amanitai was due largely to my ignorance of its use. Perhaps if Serapen had been my teacher, instead of Lilith, all of my suffering—and Dom's—over the last moon could have been avoided.

I'm not sure whether Serapen is responding to my thought, or merely continuing her own, when she says, "Yet even the most experienced healer initiate will have unpredictable results with pharmaka, on occasion."

"You mean even you don't know what the pharmaka might do?" I say.

"The effects of pharmaka become more predictable across a large number of people over a long period of time," she says. "But even a skilled healer with the best of intentions cannot control the outcome for every person every time." Her expression turns distant. I remember the gleam of tears in her eyes that night at the campfire when she said, *I did everything within my power to save your mother.*

Some of the riskiest jobs I ever completed with Lilith required me to attend priestesses in childbirth, to help Lilith administer counter-pharmaka covertly to their newborns, for some purpose unknown to me. I've seen three children born, and their three mothers survived, but I've also seen the gruesome injuries childbirth can cause. I felt helpless, witnessing the pain required to bring new life into the world. I can easily imagine how a birth could go horribly wrong. To witness a mother's death after such an ordeal must be terrible indeed. I'm surprised to find myself sympathizing with the High Priestess. Despite her mastery of the healing arts, even she can't control everything.

"How can you know you're using pharmaka the right way, if anything might happen?" I say.

"Sometimes the only way to know is to do," she says.

Serapen told me this at the start of the journey, too, when she gave me my first instruction in managing my connection with the Voice in all. That rainy evening, as we sat together under the beech tree, I acted on her instruction with little hesitation, despite not knowing what might happen. Could I do that again now, after seeing firsthand how much harm I've caused when I've acted without knowledge? "But doing anything without understanding the consequences is so dangerous," I say.

Serapen's eyes reflect the dancing flames of the campfire. "No action produces only harm or only good, when its effects are known in full. But we rarely see in full. We must be prepared to witness the harm that comes from our actions, even as we hope to witness the good. This is one of the many reasons we say *in every path, the sum of all.* The actions of each life on each branch hang in a balance with the actions of every life on every branch. That is the natural order."

"How can you know that for sure?" I say. "Even if you live a thousand thousand years and see every consequence of your actions over all that time, anything might happen after your life is over. The effect of your life could be more harm than good, in the end, and you'd never know it."

Serapen says, "And yet even a life judged harmful in one age might drive change in the next to counterbalance that harm. Who knows what causes greater harm or greater good—a so-called good life, or a so-called harmful one?"

Serapen's words confuse me. I'm more accustomed to Lilith's instruction, which tended toward certainties: right and wrong, good and bad, justice and injustice. I say, "If you're right, I don't understand how anyone is supposed to decide what to do about anything."

She smiles at me and says, "How do you decide?"

I puzzle over this for a while before I say slowly, "I do what seems best to me at the time I have to decide, I guess."

Serapen nods. "And so do I."

"But how do you know whether you're doing the right thing?" I say.

"I don't," she says. "I have yet to discover whether there is such a thing as right. All I have witnessed on my path is the inevitability of the natural order of things."

I sigh. "The more you explain, the less I understand."

Thalia chuckles, exhales a ring of smoke, and says, "You set great store by understanding, little sister. But there are many other ways of knowing."

I'm honing a sharp retort about Thalia's unique deficiencies of understanding when Arkhi says peaceably, "Indeed, there are many ways to know. Each way has its merits and its limits. Some walk the path by instinct. Some by faith. Some by reason. Some walk in joy, others in fear. But walk we must, each in our own way."

Something about Arkhi's low, gentle voice settles over me like a heavy blanket. I don't remember lying back down on my bedroll and nestling into Hanu's arms, but I'm vaguely aware that I'm finally drifting into sleep. The last thing I see before my eyes close is the campfire smoke spiraling slowly up through the hole in the ceiling. My awareness of my body slips away. With a strange sense of detachment, I feel myself rising up with the smoke.

As I rise, leaving the cave somewhere down below me, an awareness of someone else coalesces inside of me. *Ava,* thinks the vaguely familiar someone. *Are you awake, Ava?*

I'm not sure, I think. Am I crossing over to another branch again? If I am, it feels different somehow this time than before.

Listen to me, Ava, someone thinks.

Could this be the Voice, speaking to me in dreams? Serapen has said many times that the Voice speaks to us in stillness. *I'm listening*, I think.

Someone thinks, *Return to me, and all will be forgiven.*

With a shock of recognition, I think, *Lilith?*

We don't have much time, thinks Lilith. *I've come to show you the way out of the cave. All you need to do is follow my messenger.*

Alarmed, I try to open my eyes and call out for help. But I've lost the sensation of my body and have no control over my voice. All I feel is my awareness being pulled up through the hole in the mountain like a fish hauled up by a net. *What's happening?* I think. *Leave me alone!*

Calm yourself, child, thinks Lilith. *Listen to me.*

Anger flares within me, burning bright. *Why should I listen to you?* I think. *I don't know you.*

Lilith's awareness presses into mine, inexorable as the tide coming in. *The Mohirai have confused your thoughts,* she thinks. *You know me, Ava. I'm your—*

No! I push back against Lilith with such force that I manage to surprise both her and myself. For an instant, our positions are reversed. I'm aware of myself inside of her, looking out through her eyes, my vision sharper than it's ever been before. Is this what it's like to possess the pharmaka-enhanced senses of an initiate priestess? I can see for an incredible distance.

I'm spiraling down—or perhaps Lilith's spiraling down?—over a mountain range from a great height. The first light of sunrise spills over the broad plain east of the mountain range. A single mountain rises from the plain: Velkanos.

Ah. Though I have no idea how Lilith could be up so high, I now know where she is: directly above the Urashtu Pass. She sweeps low over one peak, and I glimpse a faint coil of smoke rising from a hole in the side of the mountain. As she passes over the hole, I spy my little body curled up with Hanu beside the fire, where the three Mohirai sit watching over me and the other novices.

Thalia passes her pipe to Arkhi, and her musical voice drifts up through the hole. With impossibly acute hearing, I catch Thalia saying, "You have a way with words, when you choose to, sister. Were you ever tempted to join the house of poetika?"

Arkhi takes a long draw from the pipe and passes it to Serapen. After blowing a slow coil of smoke upward, Arkhi says, "Who would keep the lamps lit and the baths hot in the house of poetika, if none remained to tend the house of tekhnologia?"

"Now that is why you could never be a poet," says Thalia. "A mind full of such practical concerns has no place in my house."

The three Muses laugh. I want to shout down to them in warning, but I have no control over whatever body I've just entered. All I can do is watch in horror as Lilith pulls in her wings—her wings?—to begin a swift, silent dive toward the hole in the side of the mountain.

Oh, spirits. Where is the Voice in all when I need it? I wish someone—anyone—would speak something in the stillness right about now.

Serapen looks up just as Lilith approaches the hole. Her eyes widen. "Arkhi!" she exclaims. "Call the falcons!"

△▽△

My endless climb up the scarlet ladder into the blue sky ends when Serapen cries out, "Arkhi! Call the falcons!"

I wake from my dream with a start and sit straight up on my bedroll. Somewhere high above, outside the cave, I hear the faint screeching calls of the falcons. My first thought is of Ava. I look over and see her lying peacefully in Hanu's arms, sound asleep, wrapped in her blanket.

Hanu stirs. “What’s the matter?” she says groggily, squinting up at me.

I look toward the Muses seated around the fire. Serapen reaches for her cedar staff. Arkhi fumbles with the case of blowdarts under her robes. Thalia stares upward with a dazed expression. I follow her gaze, looking up through the hole in the ceiling.

My mind, still half asleep, struggles to make sense of what I’m seeing. The patch of brightening blue sky at the top of the opening silhouettes the shape of a large bird that’s diving straight toward us, its descent so silent it’s surreal. As its wings spread wide open inside the cave, I recognize the round face and yellow eyes of a great grey owl. The owl swoops toward the campfire.

No, not toward the campfire, I realize with alarm. Toward Ava.

“Ouch!” Hanu cries out as I throw myself across her and Ava, covering both girls as best I can. Ava remains fast asleep beneath me, blissfully unconscious.

Enormous wings beat the air above me just before the owl’s sharp talons touch down on my shoulders, piercing my skin. There’s a ripping sound followed by a slicing sensation across my upper back. A heartbeat later, the stinging pain hits me. I press my forehead to the cold stone floor of the cave to protect my face, anticipating the stab of a beak that must be coming next. Hanu covers her eyes, apparently anticipating the same.

“Hold still!” Arkhi shouts.

I freeze. A blowdart whizzes past my ear. The owl loses its footing and tumbles off my back.

“Spirits, what is this?” Eumelia cries out. Cautiously, I raise my head and see the unconscious owl lying in Eumelia’s lap.

△▽△

I wake with a start, disoriented by an onslaught of sounds, sensations, and smells. There’s Dom’s chest pressed over my face, his familiar scent incredibly strong as my nose is squashed against his shoulder. There’s Hanu’s arms squeezing me so tight around the middle that I can barely breathe. There’s Eumelia’s indignant voice, saying, “Spirits, what is this?” Something warm and wet drips from Dom’s neck onto my forehead. There’s a stinging pain across my back, though I have no idea what caused it.

I manage to open one eye and look in Eumelia’s direction. There’s a big feathery heap of a bird lying in her lap. The sight of the bird recalls the last part of some strange dream I was having, though the details are fading fast. I remember plunging through that hole in the ceiling over us, and something about wings. My wings?

I wriggle weakly against Dom and Hanu to get them off of me. The three of us clumsily disentangle ourselves from each other and our blankets and sit up.

Dom stares apprehensively up at the hole in the ceiling. I’m starting to piece things together. That unconscious bird in Eumelia’s lap looks like an owl. Did Lilith send that owl with another message? That must be why Dom’s watching the hole. Where one owl came in, many more could follow. And if any more creatures with beaks and talons are about to fly in, I don't want to be sitting here.

"Come on," I say, reaching for Dom and Hanu's hands. "Let's get away from —" As my fingers close around Dom's, the stinging pain in my back surges back into my awareness. I realize with surprise that the pain is coming from him, for a change. My alarm at the thought of Lilith and her birds vanishes, replaced by concern for him. The dim light coming through the hole in the ceiling reveals a dark, wet spot gleaming on the collar of Dom's sleeping tunic and a smear of blood on his neck. I scramble to my feet, walking quickly around Dom as my gaze follows the crimson trail of stains across his tunic. "Oh, spirits." I gasp at the sight of the torn, bloody mess of fabric on his back.

Hanu looks from my face to Dom's, quickly assessing what's happened. "You're hurt," she says, reaching out to touch Dom's cheek. His entire body relaxes at her touch.

"I'll be fine," he says, taking Hanu's hand and pulling her up to stand. "Let's get away from this hole."

The other girls, awakened by the commotion, look up at the three of us in confusion, then groggily follow our lead. Serapen hurries toward Eumelia, who dumps the owl unceremoniously into the open arms of the High Priestess before joining the rest of the novices around the edge of the cave.

There's a collective gasp when two more birds swoop in through the ceiling. Fortunately, it's only the falcons, who land near Arkhi's feet.

"And where were you?" Eumelia says irritably. The falcons cock their heads at her and blink impassively. She shakes her head at them and says, "Useless."

To which the falcons reply with an indignant wail.

△▽△

Kneeling behind me by the campfire, Arkhi tends to the cuts on my back with boiled water, healing pharmaka, and bandages prepared by Serapen. Hanu sits at my side, resting her hand on my arm, sending waves of soothing through me whenever I wince. Ava sits across the campfire from the three of us, looking pale and gaunt but better rested than she has in a while. She steals glances at me when she thinks I'm not looking. Through our bond, I feel her concern for my injury, but she continues to avoid my gaze and touch, determined to keep her awareness rooted on this branch.

On the far side of the cave, Serapen examines and unbinds the unconscious owl. With the danger of further bird attacks apparently passed, most of the girls ignore the owl and ready themselves to depart.

Except for Ava. She doesn't protest the owl's unbinding like she did with the kuku, but she watches the High Priestess with a tense expression. Her anxious thoughts are so loud in my mind that I can't help overhearing. *Serapen said Lilith wouldn't enter this cave, but she was wrong,* she thinks. *How will I find anywhere that's safe from Lilith, if even the High Priestess can't keep her away?*

I catch Ava's eye across the campfire. Reluctantly, she holds my gaze as I think, in an attempt to calm her, *But Lilith didn't enter the cave, did she? The owl did.*

She frowns, her brows knitting together uncertainly, as she thinks, *Lilith was inside the owl.*

Puzzled, I think, *What do you mean, inside the owl?*

Ava shakes her head and looks away. *I don't know,* she thinks. *Maybe it was just a dream.*

Arkhi applies the last of the bandages to my back. "We'll have the healers take another look at you once we reach Velkanos, but those should hold for at least another day's ride," she says. "How does it feel?"

I move my shoulders slowly. The healing pharmaka has eased the sharp sting of the deep cuts into a dull ache, nowhere near the intensity of pain I routinely endure on Ava's account. "Better," I say. "I'll be all right for the ride. Thank you, Muse Arkhi."

Arkhi pats my knee and heads off to join the other Muses breaking camp. Carefully, I pull on my riding shirt—which is far from clean, but at least unbloodied—and turn to pack up my bedroll and Ava's. Hanu and Eumelia dress themselves before helping Ava, as they've been doing for the last several days. Eumelia provides a steadying arm to lean on as Ava pulls on her riding clothes. Hanu gently combs out Ava's thick curls and plaits them for the ride ahead. Ava accepts their help as graciously as she can manage, though it's still obvious how much she hates it.

Eumelia wraps Ava's heavy riding cloak around her shoulders. As she laces up Ava's collar, she says, "Do you think Lilith is ever going to quit with those birds?"

Ava shrugs, clearly not wanting to discuss Lilith or the owl with Eumelia. Instead, she kneels beside the campfire and picks up one of the bowls of bread and cheese warming near the coals for our morning meal. She holds the bowl out to each of us in turn, a small act of service that she can still manage on her own. We each accept some food and sit with her to eat. After an awkward silence, Hanu changes the subject. "Did any of you have dreams last night?" she says.

"Hmm ..." Eumelia considers, struggling to chew and swallow a piece of the very dry bread from the last of our provisions. "Oh! It just came back to me," she says. "I dreamed it was shearing season. The three of us were spinning together, like we used to when we were little, remember? But no matter how much yarn we spun, the fleeces kept piling higher and higher around us."

Ava wrinkles her nose in distaste. "So you had a nightmare," she says.

Eumelia laughs. "Well, I guess it's not as fun as flying over your city of glass towers. Is that what you dreamed?"

"Not last night," says Ava, glancing briefly at Serapen. Eumelia opens her mouth, clearly meaning to ask more, but Ava cuts her off by turning to me and saying, "What about you, Dom?"

My dream was driven clear from my mind when Serapen's shout of alarm woke me, but as I glance up through the hole in the cave ceiling, the sight of the bright blue sky above recalls a fragment of it. "I dreamed of a ladder," I say. "A ladder of scarlet rope hanging out of the sky. I was climbing it."

With a playful smile, Hanu says, "How was the view?"

"I don't think I stopped to look," I say. "Did you dream anything?"

Hanu sighs and says, "I dreamed of a hot bath and a soft bed."

Overhearing us from across the cave, Thalia laughs and says, "The Voice granted at least one of you the gift of foresight, then."

After all of us have eaten, we return to the outer cave to saddle the horses. Ava approaches Serapen to ask again about Lilith, and Serapen quietly reassures Ava that the wolves and falcons have detected no sign of Lilith outside the cave. Still, Ava and I hang back at the end of the line with Eridu, allowing the rest of the caravan to exit first.

It's cool, clear, and bright outside this morning, with very little wind through the Urashtu Pass. I help Ava mount Eridu before climbing up carefully behind her, trying to minimize stretching the skin on my back. Arkhi stands protectively near us on Khaos. The wolf pack closes in tight around Eridu, who snorts indignantly but remains peaceable. I settle my hand on Ava's hip to share my warmth with her. The small effort of walking out of the cave this morning has drained her already. She leans back wearily against me, her head resting lightly against my shoulder.

Before she mounts Amisos, Serapen releases the disoriented owl into the clear blue sky. The owl circles overhead a few times before setting off on a westward course. We all stare after the bird in silence until Thalia calls out, in a tone of high spirits, "Onward, then! To the Mountain of Muses!" She tosses her long auburn braid over her shoulder and nudges Rurata to a walk, leading the caravan eastward.

THE END OF THE ROAD

We begin our descent from the Urashtu Pass. For the first time since we crossed the Purattu River, I allow myself to hope that Ava and I are beyond the reach of Lilith and the free men. Ava's very weak, but surely she'll recover her strength once we're safely inside the temple city walls, resting in the care of Mohiran healers. She can make it through one more day, can't she?

Stop worrying about me, Dom, thinks Ava. *I'll be fine.*

"How much farther is it to Velkanos?" I say to Arkhi.

Arkhi glances at Ava and meets my gaze with a sympathetic expression. Examining the sky ahead, she says, "We should reach the city gates well before sundown."

We ride. The sun rises, and the air warms as we descend from the Urashtu Pass. The vertiginous ledges and crumbling staircases we climbed on the western side of the pass give way to easier paths and eventually transition to a well-maintained road. We make good time. Soon, the rest of the caravan is as high-spirited as Thalia, chattering in anticipation of seeing Velkanos.

Around midday, Ava spots the mountain. "Look," she says softly to me. She points with one thin hand toward a gap in the foothills ahead.

Seeing my expression of delighted relief, Arkhi smiles at the two of us and says, "What say you, Artifex? Does the Mountain of Muses please you?"

"It's magnificent," I say, gazing at the mountain in awe, momentarily forgetting even my concern for Ava.

I glimpsed Velkanos briefly, at a distance, in Ava's memory of that hilltop grove in the alternet, but seeing it with my own eyes is a new experience entirely. The Mountain of Muses stands alone on a vast plain, separated from the neighboring Urashtu Range in a way that accentuates its height and amplifies the dramatic white of its snow-covered peak. Nowhere on the journey have I seen another mountain with such beautiful symmetry, so near a perfect triangle. I'm struck by the impulse to grab my sketchbook, but since that's impossible right now, I study the view intently, committing the image to my own memory as best I can.

It's mid-afternoon when we emerge from the foothills onto the road that crosses the plain. From here, we have an unobstructed view of the entire mountain. The temple city of Velkanos climbs the mountain's southwest slope in level tiers. Sunlight glitters on the dark blue roof tiles of the tall buildings of pale tawny stone that crowd each tier of the city.

The Mohirai told us Velkanos is the largest of the temple cities. Even from this distance, I appreciate its scale. Yet the mountain looming over the city forces me to see how small the greatest work of human hands truly is.

On the lowermost slopes of Velkanos, crop terraces hug the city's outer wall. I recognize the colors and textures of many staple crops we tended outside the

Children's Temple: barley and wheat, lentils and flax. At the center of the high wall stands the bronze-clad city gate, glinting in the late afternoon sun.

"Almost there," I say, hoping to rouse Ava's spirits.

"Almost there," she murmurs faintly.

△▽△

This isn't the first time I've laid eyes on Velkanos. Though we never approached on the open road in daylight like this, Lilith and I visited this temple city more than once by a more covert route.

However, it is the first time I've seen Velkanos through Dom's eyes. His perspective makes everything more beautiful. Beneath the clear blue autumn sky, the mountain's towering snow-capped peak and the city's elegant tiers of stone are magnificent to behold. Still, it's difficult for me to be as enthralled as Dom by the sight—not only because of my weariness, but because I know what this beauty costs. I've seen the underside of Velkanos.

You've been to Velkanos before? thinks Dom. *You didn't tell me that.* Perhaps he shares thoughts rather than speaking because Arkhi's riding so near us. Or perhaps he senses what an effort it's become for me to speak.

I've had a lot on my mind, I think.

I hadn't noticed, he thinks. I smile despite myself. *So* … he thinks. *What do you mean, you've seen the underside of—*

Dom's question is cut short by an eruption of barking, which sends my heart racing. The wolf pack, which has been flanking Eridu silently all day, veers away from us, led by the alpha male. The disturbance in our riding formation shatters the fragile peace that Serapen's been keeping between the horses and the wolves. The orderly line of horses at the back of the caravan breaks apart. Alarmed mares sidestep and rear away from the wolves. Eridu remains calmer than the mares, but he's not pleased. Fortunately, all of the other girls have become capable riders over the last moon and manage to keep their saddles. Dom looks back, searching for whatever the wolves have gone after. I gather the reins in one hand and grip the saddle pommel tightly with the other, keeping my eyes forward. It requires nearly all my strength to keep my balance without Dom holding me steady.

Through Dom's eyes, I see three riders on horseback pursuing us at a full gallop from the foothills, led by a rider on a black horse. Dom's mind churns with panic at the sight of them, but my mind focuses sharply as instinct takes over. Careful to preserve my precarious balance, I reach for the blade tucked into the waistband of my breeches. Unfortunately, I can already tell I'll be useless in a fight; I have barely enough strength to keep a hold on my knife.

We're so close to the temple city that we might be able to reach the gate before our pursuers if we urge all the horses in the caravan to a gallop. I'm not confident I have enough strength to hold on to Eridu at a gallop, though, even with Dom holding me in the saddle. I glance at Arkhi, hoping she has her blowdarts ready to defend us, because I'm not liking our odds of escape.

But Arkhi makes no move to grab her blowdarts from inside her robes, and she doesn't urge Khaos on to gallop. Instead, she shades her eyes with her hand, peering back at the approaching riders. She strokes a line of silver threads on the black stole she wears around her neck. "Thalia, wait," she says. Arkhi must be speaking using binding pharmaka, since Thalia rides far ahead, out of earshot even for a Mohira.

Arkhi reins Khaos to a stop and turns around. Puzzled, I rein Eridu to a stop and turn him around, too. Serapen works her way forward from the end of the line, helping the other girls soothe the disturbed horses, herding us all back together. Thalia turns around from the front of the line and rides back to join the other two Mohirai. The three priestesses stand mounted side by side in the center of the road, forming a line between us and the approaching riders.

The three riders close the distance quickly now that the caravan's halted. As they draw near, I make out three men riding three stallions: one black with a white star, one pure white, one bay roan. They fan out and come to a stop, standing side by side, facing the Mohirai.

I study each man apprehensively, looking for either of the two free men I briefly glimpsed in Dom's memory of the night we were held captive. One of our captors was a thin man with a high brow, another a burly man with a crooked nose. None of the men before us bears the least resemblance to those two free men, but Dom never saw the face of the third free man, so I should remain on my guard. Unfortunately, my alarm over the past few moments has consumed the last of my energy. With a shaking hand, I lower my knife and tuck it into the waistband of my riding breeches before I slump back against Dom.

The man in the center riding the black stallion glances my way. He has a weathered face and a watchful expression. His cheeks are dark with several days' growth of stubble, and there's a sprinkle of silver in his short-cropped black hair. In striking contrast to his dark olive complexion, he has bright blue eyes. Lilith is one of the few people I've ever seen with blue eyes. The man wears a black hooded cloak edged in scarlet, which he tosses back over his shoulder to raise his hand in silent greeting to the Mohirai. Most men his age that I've seen in the villages have bodies hardened by lives of physical labor, but even compared to them this man's arms, shoulders, and hands are particularly massive. Yet as the wind blows back his cloak, revealing his leather riding breeches and boots, I notice his legs are as slender as a boy's. I study his face more closely, wondering what sort of work the Voice has called this man to do that creates such asymmetry in his body. The tension around his mouth and eyes suggests that he's suppressing a grimace. Despite my wariness of this stranger, I feel a twinge of empathy for him, recognizing the look of someone else in pain. Perhaps he's endured as wearying a journey here as I have.

To the left of the man on the black stallion stands the man riding the white stallion. He dismounts smoothly. His white cloak, beautifully embroidered with an intricate, colorful design, flutters behind him. He's well-built from head to toe and radiates the good humor of an enormous puppy as he bounds toward the Mohirai. The Mohirai dismount, and before any of them say a word the man grins and sweeps Thalia into a hug, lifting her off her feet and spinning her around before setting her back down. "Sweet Thalia," he says, pressing a long kiss to her lips. "How do you manage to look so lovely after a moon in the wilderness?"

Thalia looks pleased, but she says with a dignified air, "I'll have none of your cheek, Kabir. Give me a night back in my quarters, and you'll find me fully restored to my former glory."

"Let me know if you require any assistance," he says with a roguish smile, trailing his hand along the yellow sash knotted at Thalia's waist.

"You're truly incorrigible, little brother," says Arkhi, shaking her head at Kabir.

"Ah, wise Arkhi," says Kabir, turning to her with a mischievous expression. "Surely eyes as discerning as yours can't be entirely blind to my charms."

"Surely after all these centuries you've noticed your charms are wasted on me," she says.

Kabir laughs, presses a friendly kiss to both of Arkhi's cheeks, and bows his head deferentially to her. Last, he greets Serapen, addressing the High Priestess more respectfully but with no less warmth than the other two Muses. "Greetings, sister. I've missed you."

Serapen steps forward and kisses Kabir lightly on the cheek, smiling affectionately as she says, "As I have missed you, little brother. Welcome home."

Kabir surveys all of us standing silent behind the Mohirai and raises a hand in greeting. "Welcome to Velkanos, little sisters!" he calls out merrily. "I look forward to making your acquaintances."

"Remember yourself around the novices, Kabir," Serapen says in a tone of mild warning. "You're an elder brother now, not a boy of twenty summers."

"You wound me, sister," says Kabir, pressing his hand over his heart. "I assure you all your novices are perfectly safe with me. Though I can't vouch for Tio's young man," he adds slyly, gesturing over his shoulder.

I take a closer look at the last of the three men, the one riding the bay roan. He's hardly more than a boy, really. He's conspicuously handsome, though his expression is withdrawn. He looks from the Mohirai toward the rest of us in the caravan. His eyes widen when he sees Dom.

At the same instant, Dom and Hanu call out together in delight, "Balashi!"

Ah, I recognize Balashi now. He's one of Dom's trio brothers. I knew him when we were small children, before Lilith took me from the Children's Temple. I saw Balashi briefly on our Calling Day before a man led him away to join the order of smiths. I hadn't recognized him wrapped in his dusty black and silver cloak, with his fair skin so tanned. I wonder what he's doing here. Shouldn't he be in one of the men's villages by now, attending some smith?

Dom and Hanu both dismount and rush toward Balashi. Balashi glances at the silent man on the black horse. Only after the man nods does Balashi dismount to greet Dom and Hanu. The three of them embrace in the middle of the road.

"Bala!" says Hanu, kissing him on both cheeks. "What a wonderful surprise."

"Spirits, it's good to see you, brother," says Dom, hugging Balashi tight.

"It's good to see you too," says Balashi, looking from Hanu to Dom. "But I didn't expect to see you here, Dom."

"Ah-ha!" cries Kabir. "So this is Dom?" Kabir steps forward and extends his hand to Dom. The two of them clasp wrists, as brothers do in greeting. "Welcome, novice Artifex. I speak for myself and Tio," Kabir gestures to the silent man on the black horse, "when I say we are thankful to the Voice for calling you to our brotherhood."

Balashi stares at Dom. In a stunned voice, he says, "You were called to join the Artifexi?"

Dismay clouds Dom's delight. Through our connection, I sense fragments of understanding assembling in Dom's mind. My heart goes out to him, because I'm a few steps ahead of him. I've heard nothing more than Dom has about the Artifexi, but it's enough for me to know that Dom's been called to the path of mysteries, while Balashi has not. This difference may not mean much today, but I've seen the men's villages. I know the fate that awaits those men: the journey into Death, unaided by the arts of the Mohirai. Balashi's entire life will pass by in what will be, for an initiate of the mysteries, nothing but a passing season. The difference between Dom's calling and Balashi's will open a chasm between them that neither can bridge. Dom looks back at me with a stricken expression.

Sadly, I think, *You wanted to know about the dark underside of the temple city? You're looking at it.*

△▽△

Balashi and I have been trio brothers for eight years, sharing every aspect of our lives in the house of boys. He looks at me now like I'm a stranger. He says, "You were called to join the Artifexi?"

Ava grasps Balashi's plight more quickly than I do. As her understanding washes over me through our connection, Balashi's entire life—past and future—seems to flash before my eyes. I remember how Hanu described Balashi on our last day together in the Children's Temple. *Like a summer sunshower. Lovely, invigorating, over almost before he's begun.*

At a loss for words, I glance back at Ava, as if she might have the words to answer Balashi. She sits atop Eridu, slumping in the saddle, her expression sorrowful. She meets my gaze and thinks, *You wanted to know about the dark underside of the temple city? You're looking at it.*

With a creeping sense of guilt, I face Balashi again. "Yes," I say. "I was called as an Artifex."

I've been so preoccupied with everything that's happened to me since Calling Day that I haven't thought much about what was happening to Balashi and our trio brother Kuri and all of my other friends from the house of boys. I suppose, if I'd thought about them at all, I'd have assumed they were settled by now in various men's villages throughout Dulai, beginning new lives in the rough quarters and rough company to which Thalia alluded at the campfire a few nights ago. I wonder what Balashi's doing here, in the company of these two Artifexi. I'm too self-conscious to question him right now, though. I feel Ava's gaze—and everyone else's—on me and Balashi.

Tio Artifex raises his hand, drawing all eyes to him as easily as if he's struck a bell. I wonder why he hasn't said anything in greeting. The contrast between his perfect silence and his commanding presence unsettles me. He looks at me with a penetrating but unreadable expression—neither friendly nor unfriendly, neither kind nor unkind. Meeting his gaze gives me an uncanny sensation, similar to what I've felt sometimes when looking into Serapen's eyes. It's like he sees inside of me. But unlike Serapen's eyes, which often seem to mirror her surroundings, Tio's deep blue eyes seem to absorb everything, including me.

Tio beckons me silently with one hand. I swallow, hesitating. Kabir claps me on the shoulder and says in a jovial tone, "Go on, little brother. The old man won't bite." In an undertone, he adds helpfully, "Nor will he bark. His vow of silence won't end until the equinox."

Tentatively, I approach Tio, offering his black stallion one of Eridu's last apple treats. As my eyes trail up Tio's leg, I notice his boot wedged into his stirrup at what looks like a terribly uncomfortable angle. There's something malformed about his leg, I realize, though his black cloak obscures enough of his breeches that it's hard for me to tell exactly what's wrong. I remember Arkhi saying it's difficult for Tio to travel. I wonder if that has something to do with his leg.

Tio lowers his enormous hand to me. My hand looks about as small and delicate compared to Tio's as Ava's hands look compared to mine. I clasp wrists with him in greeting. The exhaustion in his eyes and the hard set of his mouth are similar to the expression Ava's been wearing this past half moon. His palm radiates a heat that seems almost feverish.

My instinctive concern for his well-being momentarily overrides my uncertainty about how to address an Artifex observing a ritual silence. "Are you all right, brother?" I murmur.

Tio regards me for a long moment before he nods. He lets go of my wrist and raises his hand over me in the sign of blessing, like Urshanabi did when he bid me farewell. He gestures for me to return to the caravan. I back away from him, relieved to withdraw from his gaze.

Arkhi and Thalia approach Tio after me. Each of them grasps his hand and offers warm words of greeting. He nods down at them, somehow managing to look courteous despite remaining mounted and silent.

Serapen takes Tio's hand last, kisses it, and says, "Welcome home, Tio. I am glad you received my message. I had not dared to hope you might make the journey this year."

Serapen keeps her hold on Tio's hand, then extends her other hand to Kabir, who takes it. She wears a bright smile unlike any I've seen before on the face of the High Priestess. For a moment, I glimpse the carefree girl she must have been, long ago. She says, looking from one man to the other, "I cannot tell you what joy it gives me to have you among us after these long years apart. For centuries after the destruction, I feared brothers would never again walk the path with sisters. To have even one of you within the walls is a rare pleasure, but to return through the temple city gates with a full trio of Artifexi is a blessing indeed. The Voice is generous."

Arkhi says, in a respectful but firm tone to Serapen, "And there will be ample time to expand our joy when we are all well inside the gates. The bell for the evening silence will be fast upon us, sister."

Thalia, following Arkhi's cue, calls out cheerfully to the entire party, "What say you, sisters and brothers? Is it time to bid farewell to this long road?" The girls in the caravan, perhaps impatient with the delay caused by all these greetings, raise their voices in hearty assent.

Serapen glances at the sun sinking beneath the peaks of the Urashtu Range in a fiery show of sunset. "You are quite right, sisters," she says, her girlish smile fading into the composed serenity of the High Priestess. She lets go of Tio and Kabir's hands. "The time has come."

△▽△

I'm seated alone atop Eridu, watching Serapen over Dom's shoulder, when the High Priestess says, "The time has come."

The time has come. The words echo strangely. Am I hearing through Dom's ears and my own at the same time?

Darkness closes in around the edges of my vision. I sway in the saddle.

Blast it all. This can't be happening now. Not after I've worked so hard to stay here on this branch.

But I'm too weak to resist the pull of whatever has called me away this time. My awareness departs my body faster than before, sliding quickly through that in-between place of darkness and nothingness. The light at the center of the darkness surrounds and swallows me, delivering me this time to a familiar setting: the hilltop grove other-Dom showed me while we were in the alternet.

I stand at the edge of the deep, clear spring that bubbles up through pale rock at the center of the grove. Looking down at my reflection, I see myself in robes of brilliant saffron and scarlet. My face is familiar, but the eyes looking up at me are older—far older—than my own. Behind me stands a huge pomegranate tree, gnarled branches heavy with ripe red fruit, green leaves touched with autumn gold.

I look up from the water's surface and see Dom—or is that other-Dom?—standing before me. He wears a rough workman's tunic covered in dust, like he did the last time I saw him in the alternet.

But this time, I'm holding out one half of a split pomegranate toward him. The pomegranate's ruby seeds glisten in the warm light of sunset. Crimson juice drips down my wrist onto the dusty stone beneath my bare feet. I hold the other half of the pomegranate close to my heart. I speak, and the words come through me like I'm reciting from deep memory. "I see the way on from here, Dom. The river passes through Death. Come with me. I will show you." My voice holds an intensity of longing, of pleading, of desperation that I've never heard before. What on Dulai am I talking about?

The ground rumbles beneath us. Other-Dom looks at me with a terrified expression. "What was that?" he says.

I glance at the sun as it dips beneath the western peaks. "The time has come," I say. "We must hurry."

I let the pomegranate fall to the ground, scattering its ruby seeds across the dusty soil. Taking other-Dom's hand, I step into the clear pool before us. I'm overwhelmed by the certainty that this is what I'm supposed to do, that this is where he and I are supposed to go together. And yet I have no idea where I'm leading him. The water rises around my bare toes, my ankles, my knees. My saffron robes and scarlet mantle spread out across the water. Step by step, I sink into the stillness beneath the surface.

The sinking sensation reminds me of falling.

Falling.

Falling?

Somewhere—though whether it's behind me, or inside me, or somewhere far away from me, I can't tell—Hanu cries out in alarm. I remember myself with a start.

Oh, spirits. I need to get back to my own body on my own branch with my own Dom. Fast.

△▽△

"The time has come," says the High Priestess. Her words echo strangely in my ears.

Hanu's cry pierces the stillness. I turn toward her just in time to see Ava swaying in Eridu's saddle. Eumelia almost falls off Nisaba in her attempt to grab Ava.

"No!" I shout, running toward Ava as fast as I can.

But neither Eumelia nor I can catch her in time. Ava tumbles headfirst from high atop Eridu onto the ancient paving stones of the road to Velkanos.

"No, no, no, Ava," I cry, crashing down on my hands and knees beside her motionless form.

Ava lies curled on her side, eyes closed, her body covered by her dark riding cloak. There's a deep gash between her brows where her head hit the paving stones. Blood rolls down her cheeks like tears. But the wound is small. Surely she'll be all right.

"Ava?" I say. I grip her limp left hand, which peeks out beneath the hem of her cloak. Her fingers are wet and slippery. Confused, I draw back my hand. It's smeared with blood.

I throw back Ava's cloak. My stomach lurches. There's so much blood—soaking through her tunic, oozing along cracks in the paving stones at an alarming rate, gathering into little crimson pools. I'm momentarily stunned. I can't comprehend where so much blood could have come from, until I see the protrusion near the waistband of Ava's riding breeches: the neatly-wrapped leather handle of her blade, buried deep in her upper thigh. The memory of the kuku felled by Arkhi's dart returns to me unbidden. Dizziness almost overwhelms me. I ball my fists and press them into the ground to steady myself.

The long shadow of the High Priestess falls over me. She settles her hand on my shoulder. Her voice sounds muffled through the high-pitched ringing in my ears. I can't understand what she's saying.

With fumbling fingers, I clutch Serapen's hand and pull her down beside me. "Please—Please—Help her!" I say.

Serapen kneels. Carefully cradling Ava's neck, she turns her onto her back. Her hands move gently but swiftly over Ava's body, assessing her neck before moving to the wound on her leg. Serapen presses both hands around the knife. The flow of blood slows, though the crimson pools on the paving stones continue to grow.

Serapen regards Ava's face with a sorrowful expression. She says, "Her awareness has flown this body again." Looking up at me, she says, "But she may return, if you wish it. The choice is yours, novice Artifex."

The choice is yours. The first time Serapen said these words to me, we were holding Ava's dead body between us in the current of the Purattu. I chose to recall Ava that night, and the High Priestess revived her. The second time Serapen said these words to me, we were watching over Ava's sleeping body together in the tent. I waited for Ava, and she found her way back on her own. Both times, Ava returned to me.

But what am I supposed to do this time? I stare down at the broken body lying before me. The first time I called Ava's awareness back from another branch, I didn't know the cost. I can no longer claim ignorance. I know what I want, and I know I can have it, but I don't know what it might cost Ava. I've seen how every time she travels between branches, she returns weaker, more faded, less able to resist the next time she's pulled across a bridge. Despite Ava's promise to stay with me, and despite all I've done to share my strength with her, she's losing her battle to remain on our branch.

I grip Ava's hand. Her skin grows cold between my palms as the chilling river of the evening breeze sweeps over the open plain. In my mind, there's perfect silence and stillness in the place Ava's awareness should be. But everywhere else in my mind is in turmoil. My grief is greater now than it was the night I first lost her on the Purattu. My desire to have her back battles my desire to give her what she wants. What she wants—what she's always wanted—is to be free.

It's clear to me now that, for Ava, the trap is this life, this body, this suffering. I'm the only thing that can keep her here. But I don't know whether I'm strong enough to let her go.

THREE PROMISES

I SHOULD PROBABLY BE BOTHERED by the gash on my forehead, the blade buried in my leg, and my blood spilling out on the road. I can't feel my body any more, though, which leaves me oddly unconcerned about the mess I've made. Staying in the saddle after Dom dismounted was a terrible idea. Failing to craft a sheath for my knife was a big mistake, too; I should have stowed that blade in my boot. My exhaustion was seriously clouding my judgment.

With the weight of my exhausted body suddenly gone, however, my mind is clearer than it's been for at least a moon. I'd almost forgotten what it's like to be free of constant physical pain. It's invigorating. I'm buoyant. I feel like I could do just about anything right now. For a moment, I'm so elated that I expand, reaching out in all directions, sensing new and greater connections to be formed between my awareness and everything else surrounding me.

Is this, at last, my chance to escape from the Mohirai, from Lilith, from my broken body? Is this my chance to find another branch where I can live in freedom?

Perhaps. But, unfortunately, I still have no idea how to travel to another branch intentionally. Could I find my own way, without initiate training, now that I don't have a body holding me back? Maybe. But, even excluding my fatal plunge from Eridu a moment ago, I've had enough accidents over the last moon to make me wary of meddling with mysteries I don't understand. Once, I might have assumed that dying puts an end to the possibility of further mishaps. Now, I'm not so sure.

It's not only fear of mishaps that stops me from setting off in search of another branch, though. It's my awareness of Dom, who kneels beside my lifeless body on the road. Even though I can't feel that body any more, I can still feel Dom's awareness in mine. He's in a state of agonizing grief. I love him too much to leave him behind in the midst of such suffering.

So instead of setting off into the unknown, I let myself sink back into Dom's awareness, slipping into him like a hand into a glove. I look out of his eyes, listen with his ears, feel through his skin. Firmly anchored inside the familiar sensations of his body, my awareness of what's going on around him sharpens.

Eumelia paces frantically behind Dom and Serapen, pleading with them to call me back. I've never seen her so distraught. I wish she'd get a grip on herself; she's making an already awful situation for Dom even worse.

Hanu stands between Nisaba and Baba, clutching their bridles tight in both hands. She watches Dom and Eumelia with an expression eloquent of grief, but she projects calm, sensitive as always to what everyone else needs in this moment. Though Dom and Eumelia are oblivious to Hanu, I sense her steadying influence on them both, for which I'm grateful.

Serapen leans over my body, working with intense concentration as my blood soaks into her blue healer's robe. She's impressively imperturbable. What horrors must she have witnessed to handle a situation like this with such composure?

I wonder whether this is what it was like the last time I died. I don't remember any of it, apart from what Dom showed me. His memory of that death was so intensely emotional that it's hard to compare to what I'm seeing now. Unlike him, I observe the scene before me with detachment, though I am genuinely sorry for putting everyone else through this—not just once, but twice.

What are they going to do this time? Last time I died, Dom somehow managed to recall my awareness to my body, and Serapen somehow managed to revive me with her healer arts. I suppose they might be able to do that again, though my body looks in far worse shape than before.

Dom clings to my limp hand. I listen to his thoughts as his desperate desire to recall my awareness to my body grapples with his knowledge of all the negative consequences reviving me will surely have for both of us.

Do I want him to call my awareness back to that body? I've seen how all my suffering has affected Dom over the last moon, from my overdose to my first death, from the difficult second half of the journey to this second death at the end of the road. There's no reason to expect my life to become easier if I'm revived a second time. My body was in bad shape even before I hit my head and fell on my knife. Recovering from all my injuries won't be easy, and even if I do manage to recover, I'll still be stuck with the long-term consequences of my overdose and this impossible entanglement between myself, the Voice, and Dom. I remember what other-Dom said about Emmie. *She still has good days, but there haven't been a lot of those lately.* I'm too pragmatic to hope that my prospects are much better than hers. It would probably be better for me and for Dom if we just ended my doomed struggle now.

But I remember the promise I made to Dom after I died last time. I think, *We're going to find our way out of here together. I promise.*

My thought cuts through the tumult of Dom's mind. Calm settles over him as soon as he's aware of my presence. His reaction gives me new insight. Although the sight of my lifeless body disturbs him, the source of his deeper distress was his belief that my death would separate my awareness from his. He hasn't realized yet what I'm beginning to understand, after all my accidental coming and going between bodies and branches. Awareness only ebbs and flows, forms and transforms; it never disappears entirely.

Ava? he thinks. *Is that really you?*

I think so, I think.

I'm not just … imagining you? he thinks.

How would you even know the difference? I think.

That stymies both of us, until Dom thinks, *Tell me something only you would know.*

My thoughts have been so open to Dom over the last moon that it takes me a moment to think of something I haven't shared with him already. But the sound of Eumelia's pleading voice as she paces back and forth behind Dom recalls the memory of what happened between me and her the night I fled the camp. This is not what I would have chosen to share, but my old techniques for separating my thoughts and feelings from Dom's don't seem to work very well, now that we're both sharing his body. My memory floods through him before I can figure out a way to stop it.

Dom looks down at my body, dazed by the memory of my encounter with Eumelia. *Spirits,* he thinks.

Is he surprised? Impressed? Jealous?

He rubs his forehead, inadvertently smearing my blood onto his brow. *Mostly surprised, I guess?* he thinks. *Maybe a little impressed. I didn't know you could make someone believe something's happening that's not really happening.*

I think, *If you believe something's happening, it's basically the same as if it's really happening.*

This makes me wonder whether it might have been better for Dom to believe my awareness had disappeared when my body died the first time. He would have grieved for me, I'm sure, but he's had so much trouble on my account already. Would it have been kinder for me to depart then, to have set him free before our entanglement grew even deeper?

That kind of freedom means nothing to me, thinks Dom. *Please don't leave me, Ava.*

Through Dom's eyes, I look down the road toward the gates of Velkanos. He's so close to finishing this journey. For as long as I've known him, ever since he was a little boy, Dom has dreamed of seeing what lies inside temple walls. If I leave him, he could pass through the gates of the temple city entirely unencumbered by my problematic perspectives and impossible dreams. I don't want to be what stands between him and his own dreams, which may be entirely attainable for him now as an Artifex.

Stubbornly, Dom thinks, *I made my choice already. I want to be with you, Ava. In whatever way feels right.*

Dom said this to me before, that morning we were alone together in our tent. I was too distracted at the time by my own frustrated desire for him to appreciate the depth of his sincerity. It's easier to feel Dom's sincerity now, from my new perspective inside of him.

Do you really mean that? I think, an idea slowly coalescing. *In whatever way feels right?*

Without hesitation, he thinks, *Of course.*

Even like this? I think, tentatively showing Dom what's just occurred to me: a new arrangement that might be so much better for both of us. Or, if not better, at least not any worse. I hope.

Dom's brow furrows as he considers a compromise neither of us would have imagined was possible until now.

Well … he thinks, uncertain, but open to the possibility. *I'm willing to try, if you're sure that's what you want.*

Yes, I say, relieved. *Yes. Thank you. Yes.*

"Dom," Serapen says quietly, her hands still pressed to the bleeding wound on my thigh. "Tell me what is happening."

Dom looks up at Serapen. Behind her, Arkhi, Thalia, Eumelia, and Hanu are all staring at him. The sudden change in his demeanor has clearly been noticed by everyone.

"Um," he says, his mind racing. *What should I say?* he thinks.

Dom finds it so difficult to keep secrets that I'm pretty sure keeping something this enormous a secret for long would be impossible. I think, *You'd better just tell them.*

He's relieved. Openness comes far more naturally to Dom than to me. Still, it's not entirely clear how to explain what's happened. Slowly, searching for words as he goes, Dom says, "Ava … she's not going back to that body. But she hasn't gone away, either. She's … here." He touches first his heart, then his temple. "I can still hear her, like I did before, through our bond."

There's a long silence. Serapen gazes steadily at Dom. Arkhi and Thalia exchange surprised looks. Eumelia leans weakly against Hanu. Both girls' grief-stricken expressions waver between confusion and hope. Other voices murmur from the caravan around us.

"You are certain you do not wish to call her back to her body?" says Serapen.

Dom nods. "I'm certain. Ava's made her decision."

Serapen looks deep into his eyes, but she's addressing me when she says, "Very well, little sister. You have chosen a more difficult path than most, but that is not for me to judge."

Serapen leans back on her heels, removing her hands from my body. The pool of my blood on the road has stopped spreading at last, though I don't suppose that matters now. The High Priestess raises her blood-stained hand in the sign of blessing over my body before she stands, gesturing for Thalia and Arkhi to join her a short distance away from the rest of the caravan. The three Muses discuss together for a few moments.

When Serapen returns, she announces to the assembled company, "Our sister Ava has chosen to depart her body, but she remains with Dom in spirit. Ava's new form will require some changes in the house of novices. We will send word to the Muses in Velkanos explaining what has happened, so preparations can be made."

"But what will happen to her body?" says Eumelia.

Serapen pauses, exchanging a look with the other Muses. I'm not sure what the Mohirai might have in mind, but I don't want to leave the fate of my body in the hands of anyone whose motives and arts are unknown to me. Overhearing my wish, Dom steps forward. He speaks to Serapen in a low voice, and she agrees to do what I've asked.

The sunset is fading when Dom lifts my body off the ground. In passing, I think that if it weren't for me, the caravan would have made it to the city gates just when Arkhi predicted. My talent for spoiling plans has outlived me.

Dom carries my body off the road. I look down at my old form through his eyes: so small, so broken, a little bird at the end of her journey. I think, *I really did try to make things work with that body, but I don't think I could have held on much longer.*

He thinks, *I would have carried you all the way to the gates, if you'd let me.* But there's no accusation in his thought, only sadness.

Dom steps out into the waist-high wild grasses of the open plain and walks a short distance from the road. He lays my body down in the rippling field of green and gold, wipes the blood off my face as best he can, and lies down at my side, holding what was once my hand. Alone together in the sea of grass, we watch the last of the sunset turn to twilight.

There's some discussion among the Mohirai and the Artifexi back up on the road that's not quite audible from here. I'm curious what they're talking about, but Dom seems indifferent to them. Perhaps he's in a state of shock. I focus on keeping his spirits up as best I can.

Eventually, a small group breaks off from the rest of the caravan and approaches, rustling through the tall grasses toward Dom. He sits up. Arkhi, Hanu, and Eumelia walk toward us carrying a few of the saddlebags, flanked by the wolf pack. Behind them, Kabir and Balashi walk alongside Tio, who leans on them both as he makes his way forward with a severe limp.

The rest of the caravan rides on toward Velkanos.

△▽△

Hanu, Eumelia, and Kabir set to work raising two tents near where I'm sitting with Ava's body. Following Arkhi's direction, Balashi gathers stones to form a small fire ring and builds up a cooking fire. Seated on the ground with his bad leg stretched before him, Tio watches the proceedings in silence.

Arkhi prepares a simple meal. Everyone other than Tio says the blessing. We eat the meal in silence. I feed the wolves their portion. After they've eaten, the luna and her alpha curl up on either side of Ava's body, as they've done inside our tent for the last several days. The younger wolves in the pack settle down nearby, camouflaged in the tall grass with their grey and brown fur.

Night falls. Kabir retires to one tent with Balashi; Hanu and Eumelia retire to the other. Arkhi, Tio, and the wolves remain outside with me by the campfire, keeping watch over Ava's body.

The silver sickle of the waxing crescent moon rises—the same moon that shone down on us the night Ava and I crossed paths in the cedar forest outside the Children's Temple. I remember our encounter with sadness, wondering whether I could have done anything different that night to avert this outcome.

I've been thinking about that a lot, too, thinks Ava. *Maybe somewhere, on some branch, things go differently for us.*

Despite my experience traveling from this branch to recall Ava's awareness from other-Dom's branch, and despite witnessing Ava's own unintentional travel between branches, I hadn't considered until now how many other branches there could be. *You think there could be some branch where things turn out all right for us?* I think.

Maybe, she thinks.

The mere possibility awakens my regret. I revisit my part in all that's happened to Ava since her overdose. I think, *If I'd just come with you on Calling Day when you asked me to, none of this would have happened.*

She thinks, *It might not have happened exactly this way. But think what else would probably have happened, if you'd run away with me that day. Lilith would probably have found us eventually, using the same scouts she used to follow us on this branch. She would probably have tried to unbind us, and I probably wouldn't have been able to stop her. The only reason I was able to stop her on this branch was because Serapen taught me how to manage my binding with the Voice, and you helped me practice using our bond on the road, and Hanu and Eumelia showed me how many other ways the bond can be used.*

Ava's words make me realize that the web of consequences from even a single action is unimaginably complex. She continues, *I can't stop thinking about all the things I could have done differently, too. Maybe on some branch, I double-checked the blasted knot on that bag of amanitai and never overdosed at all. If I hadn't overdosed, you and I would never have seen each other in the woods that night.*

Is that what you wish had happened? I think.

If you'd asked me that half a moon ago, I probably would have said yes, she thinks. *If I'd never overdosed, maybe I'd be on the other side of the sea by now, free of this bond with the Voice, free of this bond with you, living the life I've been dreaming about since I was a little girl. And maybe Lilith and I would be happy there.*

But knowing what I know now, I'd never choose a life with someone who'd lie to me like Lilith did. And I'd never choose a life without you, Dom, now that I know what it's like to have our friendship.

The sincerity of her last thought warms me from the inside. *So … you're glad it happened this way?* I think.

Well, she thinks, *maybe I'd have changed a few things, if I could. There are some things you can only do with two bodies, you know?*

Her amusement ripples through me, making me laugh. Arkhi and Tio look at me curiously from across the campfire, but they don't say anything.

You're going to make them think I've gone mad, I think.

Maybe you have, she thinks. I stifle another laugh.

I lean back in the grass, gazing up at the glittering vault of stars, my boots near the warm stones of the fire ring. Despite the strangeness of Ava's newly disembodied state, sitting by the campfire sharing thoughts with her feels comforting and familiar.

The magnificent sight of the vast night sky wheeling overhead sinks deep into us. In the shared stillness of our minds, the Voice in all speaks.

We are the bridge joining light to darkness.
We are the wheel turning season to season.
We are the threads binding realm to realm.

We are creator, preserver, destroyer of worlds.

Together you shall seek us, find us, know us.
Together you shall amplify us.
Together you shall weave us through the many worlds.
Together you shall answer our call.

We listen to the Voice for some time together, like we did in our tent the morning after Ava died the first time. I remember Ava speculating then about what these words might mean, and what she hoped they might mean. As we gaze up at the stars, I think, *Do you still want to find those other worlds?*

The question stirs Ava's deepest desire, yet she hesitates to answer. She thinks, *Do you?*

If Ava and I had never crossed paths, maybe I never would have imagined the possibility of other worlds and other branches. Even now, a part of me wishes I could be content with this branch, in this world. Everything would be so much simpler.

But Ava's conviction that there must be something better than this world has taken root in me along with her awareness. Do I want to see what other possibilities exist on the path of mysteries? Do I want a chance to fix the mistakes I made on this branch? Do I want to find a world where Ava and I can both be free?

Yes, I think, *I do.*

Her delight swells in my chest. *I'm glad,* she thinks. *But* ... Her delight fades into sheepishness.

But what? I think.

Well, she thinks, *I don't know where to begin. I don't know what I'm doing.*

I chuckle. *It's been obvious from the moment I found you in the cedar forest that you don't know what you're doing,* I think.

Irritably, she thinks, *Why do you want to come with me, if I don't know what I'm doing?*

Sometimes the only way to know is to do, I think.

She's quiet for a long time before she thinks, *I love you, Dom.*

I smile. *I love you, too,* I think.

△▽△

It's almost midnight when Arkhi rises and rebuilds the fire with a few bundles of brush wood. In a low voice, she asks Tio whether he needs help to stand and retire to his tent. Tio has been so perfectly still and silent that I'd almost forgotten he was there. Tio declines Arkhi's offer with a small shake of his head and remains seated, his eyes reflecting the flames of the campfire.

Arkhi heads toward the tent where Hanu and Eumelia withdrew at sunset and whispers through the tent flap. Eumelia and Hanu emerge promptly. I suppose neither of them were sleeping, either.

The two girls sit beside Dom. Eumelia's eyes are swollen from crying. When she sees my body, she resumes weeping. Dom lets go of my cold hand and wraps his arm around Eumelia's shoulders, soothing her as best he can.

"I still don't understand," Eumelia says, her tears soaking into Dom's tunic. "Why wouldn't you just call her back?"

Hanu, sitting on Eumelia's other side, winds her arm around Eumelia's waist and kisses her cheek. "You must have seen how hard it was for her, Mel," she says gently. "You can't have wanted her to keep suffering like that."

Eumelia sniffs and says, "It's not fair. Now Dom has her all to himself."

Despite Dom's sympathy for Eumelia, her jealousy stings him. I'm annoyed with her; I wish she could see how cruel she's being.

As I think this, I feel a familiar tingling sensation where Eumelia's forehead touches Dom's neck. Until this moment, I've been so focused on remaining with Dom that I hadn't considered entering anyone else's body. I hadn't even considered whether it's possible for me to enter anyone else's body. But as Dom, Eumelia, and Hanu sit comforting each other, I sense each of their awarenesses joined to the others', and mine joined to theirs.

I realize I want to speak to my trio sisters, and reaching out for them comes almost as naturally as reaching out for Dom.

△▽△

The last time I was in Eumelia's mind was a very different time. Every sensitive, eager, hopeful part of Eumelia's awareness that I used to seduce her is devastated now. My annoyance with her fades as I experience firsthand her grief for me.

It's all right, sister, I think, channeling Dom and Hanu to pour every soothing sensation into Eumelia's mind that I possibly can. *You're all right. I'm all right.*

Startled, Eumelia wipes her eyes rapidly. She doesn't want to cry in front of me, I realize.

Ava? she thinks. *Is that really you?*

I think so, I think.

Irritably, Eumelia thinks, *Why are you never where you're supposed to be?*

The same reason you always know exactly the wrong thing to say, I think.

She flinches. Dom loosens his arm around her shoulder, looking at her to see what's the matter. I realize he's not overhearing the thoughts Eumelia and I are exchanging in her head. She and I can exchange our thoughts in private, just as Dom and I do.

My cutting tone has reminded Eumelia of our quarrel on the riverbank, half a moon ago. I overhear myself in her memory, shouting angrily at her. She looks at my body in the grass, her eyes lingering on my face. Sorrowfully, she thinks, *Did you mean what you said that day? That you've always hated me?*

If I could sigh, I'd sigh. Instead, I think, *Maybe you're not the only one who always knows the wrong thing to say. We're sisters, Eumelia, and I ...* I've never admitted this to myself before, so it's difficult to let myself admit it to her. *I love you, all right?*

My words make Eumelia feel a little better, but not much. *Why can't you ever show it to me like you do to Dom?* she says.

She's pushing for more than I can give her. *You bring out a different side of me than he does,* I think. *You sharpen me. Dom softens me.*

Eumelia glances at Dom. Exasperated, she thinks, *You're such a sucker for that sad puppy face of his.*

He needs me in a different way than you do, I think. *He's not strong the way you are.*

The sincerity of my compliment mollifies her somewhat, but she's still unsatisfied. She thinks, *You should have stayed here with him, then. You should have stayed with us.*

I tried, I think. *You saw how hard I tried. I'm still trying.*

She lowers her head wearily, rubbing her puffy eyelids with her palms. *Yes,* she thinks. *I see it. But won't everything be harder now, without your body?*

At first I'm not sure why I'd share with Eumelia the reason I negotiated this new arrangement with Dom. Some part of me wants to distract her from her grief, I suppose. But another part of me trusts her judgment. So I show her how I'm thinking my freedom from my old body will come in handy, how it could help me and Dom find our way to another branch where we can both be free of the complications caused by my overdose on this branch.

That's a terrible idea, she thinks flatly.

I'm not sure whether this is her honest opinion or simple jealousy. Indignant, she straightens up.

Maybe I am a little jealous, thinks Eumelia. *But Dom's my friend, too, Ava. I care about both of you.*

We could really use your help figuring out how to travel between branches, then, I think. *You'll have access to the Mohirai once you pass through the city gates. You'll be receiving instruction in the mysteries. And you're the cleverest of the four of us, Eumelia.*

Clever enough to see it's a terrible idea, she thinks, seeing through my flattery.

Trying a different tack, I think, *Serapen said the initiates learn how to travel between branches. Why shouldn't Dom and I learn to do it ourselves, in time?*

Eumelia's frustration is palpable as she thinks, *Haven't you noticed that every time you depart for another branch, something bad happens to you? You could make everything even worse for yourself, and for Dom.*

You're right, I think. *But that's not what I'm trying to do. All I want is to keep my promise to him. I promised we'd find a way out of here together. Will you help us? For Dom's sake, if not for mine?*

She glances at Dom again. She sighs as she thinks, *Spirits, even I'm a sucker for that sad puppy face of his.*

Thanks, Eumelia, I think. I would hug her if I could. Something of that sensation must wash over her, because she smiles a little despite herself.

Eumelia thinks, *If it works, you don't have to thank me. But if it doesn't …* She shakes her head. *I hope you know what you're doing, Ava.*

△▽△

Before I return to Dom, I decide to speak to Hanu. I want to thank her—not just for all the comfort she's providing to Dom and Eumelia in their grief, but for all the help she's given me for the past half moon. If it weren't for her, I might have died even sooner.

Hanu recognizes my awareness as soon as I slip into her from Eumelia.

I'm glad you decided to stay, Ava. But ... Hanu hesitates before she thinks, *Why not just go? Isn't that what you've wanted all along?*

I promised Dom I wouldn't leave him behind, I think. *I promised him we'd find a way out of here together.*

Tentatively, she thinks, *Maybe he could be happy here, if you let him go.*

I tried to let him go, I think, surprised by my own defensiveness. *But he wants to come with me.*

She shakes her head, looking at Dom. With sincere pity, she thinks, *Poor boy.*

We look at Dom for a moment through Hanu's eyes. I feel what Hanu feels for him. She's loved Dom for a long time, just as she's loved Eumelia and me and many others. Her love is expansive without being possessive. She sees how much suffering Dom has experienced because of me, and though she doesn't blame me for it, she wishes she could ease that suffering for him.

It's because Hanu loves Dom this way that I'm emboldened to think, *I might need to ask you for a favor.*

As much as Eumelia hopes I know what I'm doing, I know I have no idea what I'm doing. There's a good chance that it will be impossible for me and Dom to find our way to another branch together. If we fail, I want to make sure there's a backup plan this time, for Dom's sake. I show Hanu what I'm thinking might need to happen, if it turns out that it's impossible for me and Dom to find our way to another branch together. There's no need for both of us to keep suffering, if we fail.

Hanu's eyes fill with tears as my backup plan unfurls in her mind. *Oh, Ava,* she thinks. *I don't think I could do that.*

Please, Hanu, I think. *You're the only one with the heart to do it.*

Listen, she thinks. *When Dom and I were younger and I gave him binding pharmaka, I thought of nothing but the pleasure I could give him. I never considered how he might see it as a betrayal of trust. If I could do it over, I would have asked his permission. Dom trusts you so much. Be careful with his trust.*

I would never do anything to violate his trust, I think. *The only reason I'm asking you this is to spare him pointless pain.*

Hanu bows her head. She understands me. I knew she would.

All right, she says. *If it comes to that, I'll do it.*

△▽△

Eumelia, Hanu, and I watch the crescent moon sink toward the western horizon.

Ava's awareness flows between the three of us. As the darkest part of the night approaches, Hanu and Eumelia can't stay awake any longer. They wake Kabir to join me at my watch before retiring to their tent.

Kabir rebuilds the fire and takes a seat next to Tio across from me. Gesturing toward Ava's body, he says, "There's still some time before sunrise. Tio and I can stay with her if you'd like to rest, little brother."

I know I should be tired, but Ava's awareness in mine makes me feel impossibly alert. And some part of me worries that if I fall asleep, I'll wake to find Ava's awareness truly gone.

Don't worry, thinks Ava. *I'll stay with you. You should sleep.*

Not yet, I think, looking at Ava's lifeless body. Maybe it's not only my fear of her awareness departing that keeps me awake. Maybe it's the knowledge that, after sunrise, I'll never see her again in the form I first knew her.

"I'm all right, brother," I say to Kabir. "If you'd like to go back to your tent, I won't mind."

Kabir chuckles. In a playful tone, he says, "Will you dismiss me so soon, when I've come all this way to be your teacher?"

Every word of instruction I've received in my life so far has come from a Mohira. If I had to imagine a man as a teacher, I'd probably have imagined a man more like Tio—solemn, commanding, intense—not a man as boisterous and mischievous as Kabir seemed to be while greeting the Mohirai on the road.

"You're supposed to be my teacher?" I say.

In the warm glow of the firelight, Kabir's eyes sparkle with amusement. He glances briefly at Tio, who wears a rare smile as he watches me. I wonder whether my skepticism is written clear across my face.

Probably, thinks Ava, to my chagrin. *You're pretty easy to read.*

"Of course I welcome your instruction, brother," I say hastily. "I was only confused because no one has explained how I'll be trained as an Artifex."

Kabir says, "When it comes to initiate training, the Mohirai and the Artifexi have learned over the centuries that it's best to shape the instruction to the novice. Each new Artifex possesses different gifts from those who came before him and is called by the Voice at a different moment in our historia for a unique purpose. The training of an Artifex must be tailored accordingly.

"That is why I've come—to guide the course of your training, just as my elder brother Tio did for me when I was a novice." Kabir's expression turns serious, which makes him look much older. "I shall endeavor to pass on the gifts of wise counsel I received from him, along with some of the things I've learned myself since initiation."

I wonder what a man has to say about all these mysteries of the Mohirai, thinks Ava.

"Will we be staying together in Velkanos, then?" I say.

"For this winter, yes," says Kabir. "But in the spring, I must return to my work in Phasis, on the Dark Sea coast."

Ava's curiosity ripples through me. I'm not entirely sure whether I'm expressing my own interest or hers when I say, "I would love to see the Dark Sea."

"I'm glad to hear it," he says. "I hope you'll join me and my craftsmen for summers in Phasis as part of your novice training. Phasis is a fine place indeed to serve my Muse. There is no gentler climate to pass the years, which is a blessing since my great work goes slowly with so few hands in service."

"Muse Arkhi said something about these great works done by the Artifexi in service of the Muses," I say. "Which Muse do you serve?"

"Has she never mentioned me?" says Kabir, chuckling. "How humbling. I serve the lovely Muse Thalia."

My surprise is probably written clear across my face again. When Kabir and Thalia greeted each other on the road earlier, they behaved together much like girls and boys at the Children's Temple—friendly, playful, without the deferential respect children pay to the Mohirai. I'm not sure what I expected the relationship might be between an Artifex and his Muse, but it certainly wasn't that.

I'm about to ask Kabir another question when I hear the distant sound of hoofbeats on stone.

"Here they come," says Kabir, looking to the northeast. The dark triangular silhouette of Velkanos is just visible where the sky is brightening from starry black to deep blue. Kabir rises and goes to Balashi's tent, speaking some instruction to him in a low voice. Balashi emerges from his tent carrying a small leather satchel.

"Good morning, brother," I say.

Balashi inclines his head to me in acknowledgment but doesn't make eye contact, instead heading directly to Tio's side. I wonder whether he's still upset from the news of my calling. I'll have to find some way to talk with him in private later; I hope I can make peace between us somehow.

Trying not to stare openly, I watch Balashi and Kabir help Tio remove his riding breeches. I can't suppress a wince at my first glimpse of what's been hidden beneath Tio's clothes. His shrunken right leg is covered in a ropy mass of raised, shiny scars. The scars begin just above his right hip, pour down over his right buttock, wrap around the front and back of his thigh, cross over the front of his knee, and course down to his mid-calf. The pearly white scar tissue is shot through with livid streaks of crimson and violet, a shocking contrast to the smooth olive skin of his left leg.

Whatever caused this terrible injury spared his right foot, but a great deal of muscle is missing from his right leg. What little remains is withered. His left leg is largely intact, though he's lost the smallest toe of his left foot, and the two toes beside it are fused together by scars. No wonder he has such difficulty walking.

Balashi upends the leather satchel he's carrying, and a collection of small salve jars tumbles out onto the grass. Balashi opens the jars, and he and Kabir proceed to rub many layers of salve into Tio's scars with familiar efficiency. Tio's jaw tightens as the other men handle his leg, but he doesn't break his silence. When they've finished, Kabir and Balashi lift Tio to his feet, help him pull on his riding breeches, and walk slowly with him toward the road, keeping pace with

Tio's halting steps.

I remain behind with Ava's body, which lies before me, eyes closed. In the darkness of the night, I could almost pretend she was asleep. The brightening dawn light makes it impossible even to pretend. She is unmistakably, incontrovertibly, irretrievably dead.

My body is dead, but I'm not, Ava thinks. *I'm more than just a body.*

I rub my forehead. This is all so confusing. *You're sure this is what you want?* I think.

I'm sure, she thinks.

Hanu, Eumelia, and Arkhi emerge from their tent. Arkhi looks at me and says gently, "Shall we begin?"

I take one last look at Ava's face before I stand, leaving Arkhi, the girls, and the wolf pack behind with her body. I head toward the road, following Tio, Kabir, and Balashi.

The sound of hoofbeats grows louder as the riders from the temple city come into sight. Thalia rides her white mare at the front of the line. She's followed by Narua's trio, Kor's trio, Baba, Nisaba, Eridu, and Kabir's riderless white stallion. At the end of the line of horses, Serapen drives an oxcart. She calls out to Kabir, Balashi, and me to unload a few barrels and satchels from the oxcart and carry them back to Arkhi, who thanks us and sends us away again. Arkhi, Hanu, and Eumelia remain behind to wash Ava's body and bind it in bands of clean linen.

The other novices and I unload firewood from the back of the oxcart. Under Thalia's direction, we build a pyre of oak logs at the side of the road. When Arkhi calls out to us, Kabir and I return to her. We lift Ava's cloth-bound figure between us, carry it to the pyre, and lay it carefully across the logs.

Weary after the sleepless night and the exertion of building the pyre, I stumble back a few paces. Hanu and Eumelia step up on either side of me, wrapping their arms around my waist to steady me. Eumelia sobs. Hanu rests her cheek against my shoulder. I'm dazed by the thought of what's about to happen.

One full moon after our Calling Day, as the sun rises, Serapen lights Ava's pyre. The dry wood catches fire quickly. We step back as the heat intensifies. Flames rise up from the center of the pyre with a crackling roar, surrounding Ava's cloth-wrapped body.

I can't watch any more. My gaze follows the coils of smoke rising into the clear blue morning sky. My vision swims with tears. For a moment, I'm disoriented by the impression that I'm staring up the scarlet ladder I saw in the Cave of Dreams.

Serapen speaks, quiet but clear. "The Voice speaks to us through many teachers. Loss is a powerful teacher. Loss teaches us that we are all passing seasons in each other's lives. Loss is part of the natural order.

"It is natural to grieve the loss of a sister. Be kind to yourself, and be kind to one another, in times of grief. Remember that grief, too, is a passing season.

"Listen well, now, for I tell you a mystery. No one who walks the path beside us is ever truly lost. Our sister Ava walked among us for a time, and she remains with us, transformed. We are all transformed by the journey, in the end."

And we reply in unison. "We have listened, and we have heard, sister."

When the last of the smoke disappears, the morning breeze ripples through the tall grasses, dispersing Ava's ashes across the plain.

Thank you, thinks Ava.

I follow the other novices back to the road, where we mount our horses in silence. Arkhi resumes her place at the head of the caravan and leads us on toward the gates of the temple city. Hanu and Eumelia ride beside me as our long journey to Velkanos comes at last to an end.

THE OUTER CITY

THE CARAVAN PAUSES outside the tall bronze-clad cedar doors of the temple city gate. A grim, grey-haired Mohira appears at the top of the wall and raises her hand in silent greeting to Arkhi, who rides at the front of the caravan. A moment later, the gate swings slowly inward. I've been half in a daze since watching Ava's body transform into smoke, but the sight of the gate opening wakes up something inside of me.

You're staring like you've never seen a city gate before, thinks Ava.

I can't help smiling at her familiar tone of teasing. *I've never seen a city gate open for me,* I think. How many times did I watch Hanu, Eumelia, and Ava disappear through the gates of the Children's Temple city, leaving me outside the wall with the other boys?

I hope it lives up to your expectations, thinks Ava. Her thought conveys a deep ambivalence toward the temple city, even though she's happy for me. I'm finally about to experience something every girl takes for granted: permission to enter a place where the arts and mysteries are taught openly.

Arkhi leads the caravan through the gate. We ride up a broad avenue of shallow stairs that climbs the lower slope of Velkanos. Wide, level cobblestone streets intersect the staircase at regular intervals, connecting each tier of the city to this main thoroughfare. Each intersection with the staircase forms a circular plaza, at the center of which stands a sculpted stone fountain spilling water into a steaming pool.

A faintly sulfurous scent emanates from each pool, and each fountain sculpture repeats a theme, incorporating four carved figures with distinct faces and dress who pour streams of clear water into their pool.

As we ride past each landing in the central staircase, I peer down the cross streets on either side, expecting to see the Mohirai who live here. Elegant buildings of tawny stone with arching doorways, large windows, and blue tile roofs line the streets. Cleanswept sidewalks and narrow alleyways create paths between the buildings. Yet every street, sidewalk, alley, and window is empty. There's not a single person in sight. The only sounds as we ride are the cheerful gurgle of the fountains, the clatter of our caravan's hoofbeats on stone, and a rhythmic creaking sound I don't recognize.

Even empty—perhaps because it's empty—the city feels enormous. *Could Velkanos be a hundred times larger than the Children's Temple city?* I think, marveling at its scale.

At least, thinks Ava. *Can you imagine how many hands were needed to build a place like this? And how many people must have lived here, before the destruction?*

Ahead, a second tall bronze gate in a second stone wall interrupts the central staircase. Just before we reach the second gate, Arkhi turns left at the ninth intersection, leading us west on one of the level cobblestone streets. This ninth street is less crowded with buildings than the streets below it. Little paddocks of grazing sheep and goats, fenced patches of meadow grasses, and compact orchards with fruit trees and vines fill the open spaces between buildings. Arkhi leads us toward a large four-story stone building with a commanding view, distinguished from its neighbors by a magnificent columned portico.

As we approach this building, I recognize the signs of a stable. Under the sheltering roof of the portico hangs all manner of horse tack, including saddles of unfamiliar design. The wide, arching double doors at the ground level stand open, admitting light and air into the rows of horse stalls inside. I've never seen horses sheltered in a structure so grand—grander even than the house of boys where I grew up. I wonder what this building was used for before it was a stable.

Above the portico of the stables rise three more floors with tall arching windows screened by cream-colored fabric. An unattended farrier workbench stands in the empty sunlit street before the portico with a bit of horseshoe repair in progress. The scents of horses, oiled leather, and hay spill into the street, reminding me of many happy days I've spent tending horses outside the Children's Temple.

A woman with a gap-toothed smile, a long pitchfork, and a dirty leather smock emerges through the double doors. She props her pitchfork against the wall and opens her arms wide. "Ark!" she calls. "Welcome home, dear sister."

Arkhi hops off Khaos and embraces the stablekeeper. "Thank you, Hippolyta," she says. "It's good to be safe within the walls again. This was a more trying journey than most."

Hippolyta's smile fades. "My thoughts have been with you this past half moon," she says. "We've kept watch over the passes since we received Serapen's message that Lilith was tracking you. I was grieved to learn what happened to Ava, and so close to the journey's end."

"The Voice works in mysterious ways," says Arkhi.

Thalia and the other novices toward the front of the line dismount and lead their horses into the stable. Arkhi beckons me to join her and Hippolyta. I dismount and lead Eridu toward them. Hippolyta drops an enthusiastic kiss on Eridu's nose. He nuzzles her chest so hard he nearly knocks her over. She digs out a handful of carrot bits from her pocket for him. "You old scoundrel," she says affectionately, as Eridu munches carrots from her palm. "You act like they've been starving you, but you're as sleek as you were when you left me."

Hippolyta wipes her hand on her dirty smock and extends it to me, gripping my wrist in the friendly way that brothers do. "Welcome," she says. "You must be Dom."

She puts me so at ease that I say jokingly, "What gave me away?" before remembering that I'm addressing a Mohira. I hope I haven't offended her.

"Ah, another cheeky one," says Hippolyta. She claps me on the shoulder with her free hand. "Just as well. It's been awfully dull in the Outer City since Kabir left."

She keeps a hold on my wrist and searches my eyes as she adds, "And welcome, Ava. I wish we'd met in the flesh, but I'm glad you've decided to remain among us, just the same."

I'm not sure whose surprise is greater—mine or Ava's—at being addressed this way. Should I answer Hippolyta on Ava's behalf? Ava and I debate the right response between ourselves. Ava thinks, *Do you mind if I try to answer her?*

I'm not sure how she could answer Hippolyta, but, curiously, I think, *Go ahead.*

A strange sensation comes over me, and I find myself moving without conscious thought. It takes me a moment to realize that this is Ava, moving through me. Ava releases my grip on Hippolyta's wrist and lifts my chin so I look at Hippolyta directly in the eye, as women do.

"Thank you, sister," Ava says through me. I'm usually careful to speak softly and deferentially before Mohirai, so I'm surprised by the sound of Ava's bold tone in my own voice, and by the feeling of holding eye contact so long. I don't think I ever noticed how tall I am until this moment, when Ava stands me up straight. Hippolyta inclines her head in welcome. When Ava releases her hold on me, I feel a bit of residual exhilaration from the confidence Ava injects into even this simple interaction.

Is that what it's always like, when women meet? I think.

Like what? thinks Ava.

Like … I don't know. Like you can take up as much space as you want to, I think.

Ava's amusement ripples through me. *You can take up as much space as you want to, too, Dom,* she thinks.

I don't know how to do that, I think. *I don't even know how you made me do that.*

Ava considers. *I let go of your deference,* she thinks. *It wasn't too hard.*

Hanu and Eumelia dismount Baba and Nisaba behind me. Hippolyta gestures to our horses and says, "Let's get these three tucked in, shall we?" She leads us into the stable and shows us three open stalls. We unload and unsaddle the horses, who set to work eagerly on mangers full of fresh hay and deep stone troughs of water. I spend a little extra time brushing Eridu down. He clearly has everything he needs here, but I'm sad to part ways with him.

When the Mohirai call the novices to return outside, I feed Eridu the last of the dried apples from my pockets and pat his withers in farewell. I sling my saddlebag and Ava's over my shoulders and follow the rest of the girls out to the street, where Arkhi, Thalia, and Serapen stand waiting.

Serapen gathers us before her with a gesture. "Though we have reached the end of our journey together to Velkanos, the path of mysteries continues ever onward," says the High Priestess. "I wish you every blessing on your journey. Be patient with yourselves. Be helpful to one another. Be open to the mysteries you will encounter.

"Not every step on the path will be clear. You will find yourself lost at times. Remember to listen, when you are lost, for the Voice is in all." Her words transport me back to my Calling Day, when Serapen spoke the same words to me and the other girls and boys before we followed her into the woods. She concludes, "I leave you now in the capable hands of your Muses, for I must return to my own halls in the Over City. Farewell."

The High Priestess raises her hand over us in the sign of blessing before she turns and walks alone down the street, back toward the central staircase.

Thalia steps forward and says, "Novice Mohirai, follow me. I'll take you up to the Over City and settle you in your quarters in the house of novices."

What about us? thinks Ava.

Seeing the looks Hanu, Eumelia, and I exchange, Arkhi says to us, "Don't worry. The four of you will still see plenty of each other. Dom will join you for meals and the call to attendance in the house of novices after second bell tomorrow. But the Artifexi are quartered here in the Outer City with the initiates of the house of tekhnologia."

The Mohirai have treated me almost the same as all the other novices on the journey to Velkanos, but being separated from Hanu and Eumelia now reminds me that, just as my calling as Artifex separates me from Balashi, the girls' callings as Mohirai separate me from them. I hug Hanu and Eumelia tightly in farewell, uncertain how things between us are about to change.

"Don't let Ava get you into trouble," says Eumelia, squeezing my hand in parting. "She'll put a lot of funny ideas in your head."

My hand tingles against Eumelia's, and Ava departs from me briefly. Eumelia smirks to herself. Ava's awareness returns to me with a flood of her irritation.

What did you say to her? I think.

I said you don't need her help to make up your own mind about my ideas, she thinks.

What did she say? I think.

Annoyed, she thinks, *She said it's hard to make up your own mind when you're sharing it with someone else.*

Eumelia makes a good point, but I do my best to suppress that thought from Ava. Ava overhears me anyway. Hastily, I think, *You're probably both right*. This does little to mollify her.

Eumelia and Hanu depart with the other novices, leaving me behind with Kabir, Hippolyta, and Arkhi.

Kabir looks from Arkhi to Hippolyta as though they're keeping a delicious secret from him. "Well? Where are we to be quartered?" he says.

Hippolyta flashes Kabir her gap-toothed smile. "The sisters have decided all three of the Artifexi are to be quartered with me this winter," she says.

Kabir rubs his hands together with a mischievous grin. "It'll be like old times again," he says.

"Spirits preserve us," Arkhi says dryly.

Hippolyta says, "Since you all missed the welcome feast for the other novices last night, I thought we might have our own little welcome feast in my quarters to make up for it. I imagine after keeping watch for Ava last night, a quick meal and a bed might be more appealing to Dom than making the acquaintance of hundreds of eager future Muses in the house of novices this evening."

My alarm at this prospect must show on my face. Kabir bursts out laughing. "Would you risk the wrath of Thalia?" he says to Hippolyta. "If I know her, she's been waiting for that scene since the moment she learned a new Artifex was called."

"Would you throw your novice to the wolves unprepared?" says Hippolyta, with a note of scolding. "Perhaps Dom would have been better off attending Tio, after all. Spirits know he could use the extra hands."

Chastened, Kabir says, "Of course I'll do all in my power to prepare Dom to select his Muse, just as Tio prepared me."

We follow Hippolyta to the east side of the stable. She opens a door into a small entryway. To our left, a short hallway leads to a closed door. To our right, a stone staircase leads to the second floor. Hippolyta pauses at the foot of the stairs and says to Kabir, "Could you see if Tio needs help coming upstairs? I offered to serve the meal down in his quarters, but you can imagine how he reacted to that."

Kabir nods and says, "Come with me, Dom. I'm sure Balashi will be glad to share the load after half a moon's attendance on the old man."

Hippolyta and Arkhi head up the stairs. I follow Kabir down the hall. He knocks on the door, which Balashi promptly opens.

"Hello, little brother," Kabir says in a friendly tone. "We've come to collect Tio."

Balashi nods and makes way for us. We step into the small, sparsely furnished room. A low table with a single chair stands before the unlit fireplace. I detect a hint of that sulfurous smell I noticed as we rode by the fountains. The air in here feels quite warm compared to the chilly air outside, even though there's no fire in the hearth. A soft rushing sound like wind emanates from the stone wall beside me. Curiously, I touch the wall. Heat radiates from the stone into my hand.

Why is it hot? I think, surprised.

Lilith told me something about this, Ava thinks. *The original city builders piped the waters of four mountain springs through the entire city. The hot waters flow through the walls and floors of the buildings during the cold months. The cool waters flow through in the hot months. The Mohirai call it the gift of Velkanos.*

Apart from its unusual source of heat, there's nothing else of obvious interest in this room. A small window facing east admits some light and air from an outside alleyway, but even with the oil lamps lit, it's rather dark. A few faded tapestries cover the three windowless stone walls. A thick braided rug lies on the stone floor before the hearth. Small baskets of fresh apples, apricots, and plums grace the low table. Despite these efforts to lend cheer to the little room, it has a gloomy feeling.

Kabir looks around this front room with a look of mild displeasure, then walks toward the open doorway at the back. Two narrow beds are visible in the dimly-lit room beyond. Kabir knocks on the doorframe and says, "Tio?"

There's a creaking, rolling sound before Tio appears in the doorway. He's seated in a narrow leather chair with two large wheels on either side and one small wheel in front. I've never seen a machine like this, but as Tio rolls himself toward Kabir by pushing the large wheels with both his hands, its purpose is obvious.

How clever, I think.

Ava's fascination with Tio's chair spills into me. She studies every detail of the chair's materials and construction, as if it's an animal she's never seen before. I find I'm unable to stop staring at the chair until Tio looks up expectantly at Kabir, interrupting Ava's close inspection.

Kabir says, "Hippolyta invited us to dine. Would you like to go up?"

Tio inclines his head in assent. Kabir says to Balashi, "I'll help him with the stairs. Can you and Dom carry his wheelchair between you?"

"Yes, brother," says Balashi, ducking his head obediently.

Kabir and Balashi step aside as Tio rolls swiftly out from the bedroom into the front room. I scramble backward just in time to avoid Tio's wheelchair running over my toes. Tio stops halfway out the door to the hall and reaches out for a pair of smooth wooden handles bolted to the inside of the doorframe. He hauls himself up easily from his wheelchair, standing on his left foot. With a stiff but efficient push from his right leg, he shoves the wheelchair away from him so it rolls backwards into the room.

On his own, Tio takes a few limping steps down the hall and stops at the foot of the stairs. Kabir joins him there, looping his left arm around Tio's waist while Tio wraps his right arm around Kabir's shoulders. The two men begin to climb the stairs on three good legs and one stiff leg.

I watch the two men ascend, unsure why I can't take my eyes off them, until I realize Ava's taken hold of me again. I'm no longer in control of my body. *Ava?* I think. *Could you let me go?*

Oh! Sorry, she thinks, releasing me promptly. *I just thought …* She trails off uncertainly.

Thought what? I think.

I'm not sure, she thinks. *There's something strange going on here, don't you think?*

I look at Balashi, as if he might tell us the answer. He avoids my gaze again. I notice for the first time how changed he is since I saw him on our Calling Day. The change in his appearance is superficial—his face thinner, his fair skin tanned and weather-beaten from the road. But the change in his demeanor is dramatic. There's no sign of the winning confidence that used to emanate from him.

Tentatively, I say, "Balashi? Is something wrong, brother?"

My question hangs in the silence between us. Briefly, he looks my way, and I glimpse an expression I've never seen before in Balashi's eyes: resentment.

Balashi turns away abruptly, grips the back of Tio's wheelchair, and pushes it out the door and down the hallway. "Come on, Dom," he says. "Tio doesn't like to be kept waiting."

I hurry after him, readjusting the straps on the pair of saddlebags I'm carrying, which are starting to press uncomfortably into the bandages on my back. At the bottom of the stairs, Balashi waits for me to catch up, though he continues to avoid my gaze as we lift Tio's wheelchair between us. The chair's not very heavy, but it's awkward to navigate the narrow stairs carrying it between us, especially without speaking to each other. We both manage to scrape our elbows and knuckles on the stone walls as we carry the wheelchair up to the second floor.

Kabir stands with Tio in the upstairs hallway waiting for us. Wordlessly, Balashi and I set the wheelchair down before them. Kabir helps Tio settle back into the chair. Tio rolls forward and knocks on the door at the end of the hall.

Hippolyta opens the door. "Welcome, brothers!" she says warmly, stepping aside to let Tio roll pass and waving the rest of us in after him.

Hippolyta's quarters are far more spacious than Tio's rooms downstairs. Arching windows fill the front room with southern light. A thick woven rug in swirling shades of green and blue covers the wide oak floorboards. Dozens of in-progress leatherworking projects fill the shelves that line the walls from floor to ceiling, and the pungent scent of leather rosin fills the air. A beautiful saddle, nearly finished, hangs from a hook beside the fireplace. I recognize the pattern worked into the saddle skirt; it's nearly identical to the one tooled into the leather cover of the sketchbook Urshanabi gave me. The open door on the far side of the room leads to a bedroom with faded wall tapestries depicting scenes of women on horseback.

A large table with five seats and six place settings stands in the center of the room. Hippolyta invites us to sit. Tio rolls to the place setting at the end of the table that's missing a chair. Kabir sits at Tio's left hand, and Balashi sits at Tio's right. Arkhi sits on the far side of the table from Tio. Hippolyta takes the open seat by Kabir, so I slip into the last seat beside Balashi.

Hippolyta and Arkhi uncover the three silver tureens resting on the table. I recognize one of Balashi's favorite meals: stuffed grape leaves, spiced roasted eggplant, and lamb meatballs. I haven't felt hungry since Ava died, but my appetite returns to me in a rush at the sight of all this delicious food. I glance at Balashi, expecting to see the expression of delight with which he always greeted this meal when Hedi served it to us in the house of boys. Balashi's face shows no reaction.

Hippolyta portions out the meal and pours tea into our wooden cups. Arkhi leads us in the meal blessing. Tio bows his head but remains silent.

We eat and drink the first few bites in silence. The familiar flavors of the meal are comforting after the long journey. If Balashi's expression weren't so gloomy, I could almost pretend I'm back in the house of boys, sitting with him at our old table in the meal hall after a long day of chores.

Hippolyta refills Kabir's empty cup of tea and says in a friendly tone, "I was surprised to hear that you and Tio arrived together. Lemnos is so far to the west, and Phasis so far to the north. How did your paths happen to cross on the way here?"

Kabir lifts his cup, sips, and says, "Entirely by accident. I wasn't in Phasis when I received Serapen's message that the Voice had called a new Artifex. I was on the Middle Sea coast, overseeing the preparation of a shipment of marble heading from Kebny to Phasis. I left immediately for Velkanos so I could take the route through the Urashtu Pass before the winter snows. I stopped at Upper Ford to refresh my supplies for the second half of the journey, and that's where I met Tio."

As Kabir says this, Tio withdraws a silver flask from within his robes and takes a sip.

Why isn't he drinking the tea? thinks Ava.

I was just lifting my own cup. Ava's thought stops my hand midair. *Do you think it's safe?* I think.

Probably as safe as anything else the Mohirai give you to drink, thinks Ava.

Uneasily, I set my cup down.

Kabir continues, "Tio arrived at Upper Ford in the company of a supply caravan. He was planning to continue on with the next caravan heading to Velkanos. But that caravan takes a much longer and slower lowland route. I proposed we travel together instead through the Urashtu Pass, to shorten his journey. Tio wouldn't ride with me alone—it's much easier for him to mount a horse with two attendants—so I asked the brothers at Upper Ford whether they could spare a hand. They volunteered Balashi, since he'd just arrived there from the Children's Temple and had not yet begun his smith training."

Balashi's jaw tightens.

Hippolyta smiles kindly at Balashi, then says to Tio, "I imagine it's difficult, spending the winter away from your own attendants in Lemnos. I hope we'll be able to make you comfortable here."

Tio inclines his head politely.

Kabir clears his throat and says, "Since you mention it, Pol, I wanted to speak to you about Tio's quarters downstairs. That's hardly more than a cellar. Surely in this vast city of empty rooms there are a hundred places more fitting for the first of the Artifexi to be quartered."

"Of course there are," says Hippolyta. "The Muses had proposed quartering you, Tio, and Balashi with the initiates of the house of tekhnologia, near Arkhi's quarters. But Tio preferred to stay here."

Kabir says to Tio, "Come now, brother. I know you prefer to reside on the ground floor while your injury heals, but there must be far more pleasant options in the great halls. Those dark little rooms downstairs will be downright depressing as winter sets in."

Tio dismisses Kabir's words with a wave and takes another sip from his silver flask.

In a conciliatory tone, Arkhi says, "Humble as those rooms may be, I'm sure Tio appreciates their advantages more than most. We've always quartered the novice Artifexi here with Hippolyta because the stables are central to the workshops, the Over City gate, and the Outer City gate."

Tio nods at Arkhi. Kabir eyes Tio with mock suspicion and says, "Or perhaps the old man's aware that Hippolyta has the most easily accessible wine storeroom in the entire temple city."

Hippolyta smiles. "No longer, I'm afraid," she says. "Your novice years in my house taught me to keep that door locked."

Kabir winks at me and says in an audible whisper, "Yet I'll wager she keeps the key in the same place she's kept it for the past four centuries."

Arkhi and Hippolyta laugh. I chuckle politely. Balashi and Tio remain silent. Kabir sighs, gesturing to the two of them, and says, "I'm afraid my wit has grown tiresome to my travel companions."

"Your travel companions have my deepest sympathy," says Arkhi. "And I suppose all of us could use some rest after our long journeys." She glances at Hippolyta.

"Of course," says Hippolyta, rising from her chair. "Thank you for the reminder, sister. Kabir and I would gab until solstice if someone didn't keep us on task. Come, little brother," Hippolyta says to me. "You sit there so peaceably that I'd almost forgotten the trial you've been through. I'll take you up to your quarters."

Balashi glances at me as I rise from the table. I've known him long enough to recognize that look. He doesn't want me to leave. Troubled, I think, *Should I say something to him?*

Not here, thinks Ava. *There's something strange going on. Let's try to talk with him alone.*

Reluctantly, I bid farewell to Arkhi and the men, then follow Hippolyta out of the room.

Hippolyta leads me up two more flights of stairs to the top floor. We step through the open door at the end of the hallway into a room that appears almost identical in size, layout, and furnishings to Hippolyta's front room, though there are no tapestries on the walls and the shelves are nearly empty. I set my saddlebag and Ava's down on the floor inside the front door.

Hippolyta walks around the room, pointing things out to me. She says, "You probably won't need any extra heat until winter sets in, but I carried up some firewood for you. You can refresh it from the storeroom downstairs." She taps three piles of folded clothes on the shelf over the fireplace. "Here are your work clothes, ceremonial garments, and spare linens." Gesturing to the row of pegs beside the hall door, she continues, "Winter cloak, riding cloak, satchel. And there are your winter boots and temple shoes. The sisters in the house of novices will tell you which days you'll be working indoors or outdoors. You'll probably want to carry the cloth shoes with you for days indoors. There are many places in the temple where you must go barefoot, and the shoes are easier to slip on and off than the boots."

A fine leather tool belt hangs from one of the pegs. Hippolyta takes it down and holds it out to me with a smile. "And here is my gift for the new Artifex. Just finished it this morning. Will you try it on so I can see how it fits?"

Despite my simmering worry about Balashi, I can't help admiring Hippolyta's craft. "It's beautiful," I say. Of all the belongings I had to leave behind in the house of boys on Calling Day, the only thing I'd been truly sad to part with was the old toolbelt I used to wear for my chores around the grounds. The belt Hippolyta gives me now is much finer and larger. The band is deeply etched with swirling patterns and shines with a coat of fresh oil. There's an impressive array of loops and pouches with different closures, buttons, and buckles. The leather pouch of drawing pencils that Urshanabi gave me will fit here perfectly.

I wrap the toolbelt around my waist and figure out the buckle, which is a new design to me. There's some extra length in the band, and Hippolyta shows me how to knot it so it lies flat and won't be in my way. "Plenty of room to grow into it," she says, examining the fit. "From the look of you, you'll need it."

"Thank you, sister," I say.

"Of course, little brother," she says, flashing me her gap-toothed grin. "We can't have an Artifex running about Velkanos without his tools, can we?"

She leads me across the front room into the adjoining smaller room. "Here's your bedroom," she says. There's a narrow bed on one wall covered in a blue wool blanket, identical to the one that covered my bed in the house of boys. A washbasin, a mirror, and a covered privy bucket are lined up on the wall opposite the bed. A locked wooden chest stands at the foot of the bed. To my surprise, the key rests on the lid of the chest, entirely out in the open. Back in the house of boys, locks and keys were the exclusive domain of the Mohirai. I've never had a key to anything.

You don't need keys if you know how to pick locks, thinks Ava.

A linen curtain hangs across the far side of the bedroom. Hippolyta pulls back the curtain, revealing a deep stone bathtub with four bronze faucets.

"The gift of Velkanos," she says, gesturing to the faucets. "There's one tap for each of the four sacred springs. Two hot. Two cold." She demonstrates how to turn the water on and off by the handles and shows me the cork drain stopper hanging from a hook on the wall. When the hot taps are open, a pungent whiff of the steaming water hits me. I cough. Hippolyta laughs and says, "The scent does take some getting used to. The cold waters are sweeter, if you can bear the chill."

She shuts off the taps and stands up. "I suggest you rest as much as you can tonight," she says. "Tomorrow, you'll hear the first bell before dawn. That's when the novice Mohirai wake for morning ceremonies. You'll attend Kabir until the second bell. At second bell, go up to the second gate. Did you see that gate on your way here?" I nod. Hippolyta continues, "The Over City gatekeeper tomorrow will be Py. She can point you to the house of novices. You'll take your meals there with the other novices, and sister Zia will give you your work assignment after you've eaten.

"At the end of the day, when the fifth bell rings for the evening silence, you must return here to the Outer City. Do you understand?"

All the details are blurring together in my sleep-starved mind, but Ava thinks, *Got it. Wake up at first bell and attend Kabir. Go to the second gate at second bell. Return here at fifth bell.* So I simply nod.

Hippolyta continues, "Kabir's quarters are just below yours, and mine are below his. If you need anything at all, even a bit of company, feel free to knock on my door at any time. With so much coming and going in the stables this time of year, I'm up at all hours. You need never trouble yourself about waking me."

I nod and say, "I have listened, and I have heard, sister."

Hippolyta smiles wryly and says, "I'll have to enjoy these fine Children's Temple manners of yours while I still can. Kabir will have you cured of them in no time." She sweeps her gaze around the room one last time. "I think that's everything you'll need for now. Welcome home, little brother." She gives my shoulder a friendly squeeze before she departs through the hall door.

I pace slowly through my new quarters, taking a second look at everything Hippolyta showed me. These rooms are so much grander than the one I shared with my trio brothers in the house of boys. The magnificence of the city, the unexpected luxury of my quarters, and the beauty of Hippolyta's gift would all fill me with a sense of good fortune, were I not so distracted by thoughts of Balashi. I wonder how I can catch him alone, while he's attending Tio.

Somewhere down on the street outside my south-facing windows, a door creaks open and shuts. Hippolyta's friendly voice drifts up through the windows. "Can I lend you a hand?" she says.

"Better leave it to the three of us," says Kabir. "We perfected our mounting technique on the road together."

I step toward the nearest window. A multi-layered wool screen fits snugly inside the window frame to block the chill. It takes me a moment to work out how to unlatch it. The screen swings inward on quiet hinges. I open it a handspan. A gust of cold air spills into the warm room. I peer down through the narrow gap at the street below.

Hippolyta watches as Kabir and Balashi help Tio mount his horse, while Arkhi holds the bridle of Tio's saddled black stallion. Tio rises from his wheelchair, and Kabir and Balashi help him lift his left foot into a stirrup and push him up from the ground. Tio struggles to swing his stiff right leg over the saddle, but he manages to land astride the horse. He manipulates his right knee with both hands to wedge his boot into the other stirrup. Despite his awkward mounting technique, he sits as naturally in the saddle as any Mohira.

Kabir and Balashi disappear into the stables.

"Will you need your wheelchair in the workshop?" says Hippolyta, looking up at Tio.

Tio shakes his head. Arkhi says, "Tio made several versions of his wheelchair after his accident. I've distributed them through the main workshops in the Outer City. We've also kept his handholds in the workshops, so he should be able to get around pretty well on his own."

Kabir and Balashi re-emerge from the stables riding the white stallion and the bay roan.

Kabir says, "Balashi and I will see the old man to his workshop, and then I'll attend my Muse in the Over City."

"Better hurry if you're going to see Thalia today," says Hippolyta. "The evening silence will be fast upon you."

"No need to remind me, Pol," Kabir says with a laugh. "Serapen put the fear of the spirits in me the last time I dallied past fifth bell. I don't think I've ever fully recovered."

Tio nudges his horse to a trot. Kabir and Balashi follow him eastward toward the central stairs. Arkhi and Hippolyta watch them depart.

When the riders are out of earshot, Hippolyta says, "Balashi knows he's to be unbound, doesn't he?"

"I suppose the brothers at Upper Ford explained it to him when they volunteered him," says Arkhi.

"I'll ask Serapen to give me something for his anxiety," says Hippolyta. "I can't bear to watch him suffer needlessly all winter."

"That's a kind thought, sister," says Arkhi. "You've always had a gentle hand with little brothers."

"Should Dom be told?" says Hippolyta. "Balashi's his trio brother, isn't he?"

"He will be told," says Arkhi. "Leave that to Kabir, though. Dom had quite a shock yesterday. After all that's happened to him and Ava, he might find the prospect of Balashi's unbinding distressing."

"It's one thing to unbind children," says Hippolyta. "The Voice requires it. But a young man, so soon after his calling … It must be a terrible thing for him, to know how much of his youth will be lost to unbinding. Wouldn't it have been better to place Dom in attendance on Tio? A novice Artifex may pass in and out of the temple city without unbinding."

Arkhi says, "Kabir has waited patiently for centuries for his own novice. If Dom were to attend Tio now, how long might Kabir have to wait for another novice Artifex to be called? Tio would not hear of it."

Hippolyta shakes her head. "The Voice works in mysterious ways," she says. There's a long pause. In a more bracing tone, she says, "Care for another drink before you depart? Something stronger than tea, perhaps?"

"Another time," says Arkhi. "After the journey I've had, I long for the gift of Velkanos."

Hippolyta hugs Arkhi and says, "You've more than earned it, sister. Farewell."

Arkhi heads westward down the street on foot. Hippolyta disappears inside the stable.

I back away from the open window with a heavy heart. The accumulated exhaustion of the entire journey settles over me. I trudge into the bedroom and lie down on the bed, staring up at the rafters.

I'm sorry, Dom, thinks Ava. *I know how you feel.*

I don't understand, I think. *Why do the Mohirai need to unbind Balashi?*

Sadly, Ava thinks, *The Mohirai only permit those called to the mysteries to know what lies within temple city walls. If Balashi won't remember Velkanos, it's the same to them as if he was never here at all.*

When I thought Lilith was about to forcibly unbind my memories of Ava, I was terrified. How much worse must it be for Balashi, knowing everything that's happening to him will disappear from his mind as if it had never been? For the first time, I understand the sorrow Ava felt as she looked down at the little kuku bird. Why did it take me so long to understand how wrong it is to manipulate memories? I'm such a fool for trusting the Mohirai.

You believed what the Mohirai wanted you to believe, the same way I believed what Lilith wanted me to believe, thinks Ava. *If you're a fool, I'm the greater fool. The Mohirai hid things from you, but Lilith lied to me outright, and I believed her.*

Ava's words make me angry in a way I've never felt angry before. Angry for myself. Angry for Ava. Angry for Balashi. Angry for all the children who have been manipulated by the Mohirai. My anger sparks a desire in me for which I have no name.

Rebellion, thinks Ava.

△▽△

I'm no stranger to anger, but Dom's anger is an unfamiliar and thrilling sensation for me. I'm surprised—even impressed—by the desire that Balashi's predicament stokes in him. I recognize Dom's desire, because I've seen it in the eyes and heard it in the voices of many men Lilith spoke to during our years roaming Dulai. *Rebellion.*

Rebellion? thinks Dom, intrigued. *I've never heard that word before.*

You'd never hear it among the Mohirai, I think. *Rebellion means opposing the established order to change it.*

Opposing the Mohirai, you mean? he thinks.

Yes, I think.

Dom considers this. He thinks, *So rebellion is like … disobedience?*

I suppose this is the closest word Dom would know. Until he and I crossed paths, he spent his entire life trusting the teachings of the Mohirai. He'd obeyed without questioning. The closest he's come to willfully disobeying the Mohirai, as far as I know, was when he abandoned the caravan to follow me. But even then, I doubt disobedience was on his mind. He just wanted to be with me. How can I explain the difference between the small acts of disobedience that might earn children a reprimand and the greater rebellion to which an anger like Dom's might lead?

Rebellion and disobedience are similar, I think. *But all that's needed for disobedience is a single person who disobeys. A rebellion is a lot of people who disobey together for the same purpose.*

Is that what you and Lilith were doing together? thinks Dom. *Were you part of a rebellion?*

Spirits, there's still so much I haven't shared with Dom. At the start of our journey, I did everything I could to avoid thinking about what Lilith and I were doing before my overdose, to minimize the risk that Dom could share any of that information with the Mohirai. Now that I'm sharing Dom's body, it's almost impossible to hide these thoughts.

Stop hiding, then! Dom thinks. *We're in this together, remember?*

All right, all right, I think. *Yes, we were part of a rebellion. Lilith and the free men have been working together to overthrow the Mohirai. They want to build a new society of free people, where women and men can be equal and no one is bound to serve the Voice in all.*

So, the night I found you in the woods, you were doing something for the rebellion? thinks Dom.

Stealing amanitai, I think.

What does the rebellion need amanitai for? he thinks.

I don't know, I think. *I didn't even know what amanitai was for, when I stole it. But I guess they must need to make binding pharmaka for some reason.*

Dom considers all this for a while. He thinks, *But if you and Lilith were part of the rebellion, why did the free men treat you so badly the night they took us captive?*

I've thought about these questions endlessly for the last half moon. I still don't have any good answers. *Maybe Lilith had some plan she never told me about,* I think. *Or maybe everything she told me was a lie. I don't know.*

Dom's calm flows through me, stopping my thoughts from spiraling. *Don't worry,* he thinks. *We'll figure it out. Together. But not right now.* He rubs his face with his hands. *I'm so exhausted I can barely see straight. Is it possible to be too tired to sleep? That's how I feel.*

It's probably my fault, I think. *You never could sleep while I was awake. But I don't know if it's possible for me to sleep any more.*

Dom closes his eyes wearily. *Maybe you could just pretend?* he thinks. *You seemed to do a pretty good job of that with Eumelia.*

The memory of what I did to Eumelia unreels between us. If I could wince, I'd wince. *I wish you wouldn't bring that up,* I think.

Sorry, thinks Dom. *You did see all my memories with Hanu, though.*

I did. More than once. Even so, Dom's memories of Hanu are innocent compared to mine with Eumelia. He never manipulated Hanu with binding pharmaka. I manipulated Eumelia for my own ends—just like the Mohirai and Tio are using Balashi for their own ends. Just like Lilith used me for her own ends. What I did to Eumelia fills me with guilt.

I don't want to deceive you like I deceived Eumelia, I think.

Is it deception if I know we're pretending? he thinks.

Dom's question gives me pause. Against my better judgment, I find his curiosity arousing my own. An idea coalesces between us. I'm not sure whether it's his idea or mine. Maybe such distinctions are impossible between us now. Cautiously, I think, *Do you mean hypothetically, or do you really want to try that?*

We have to figure out how to sleep again at some point, he thinks. *Initiates don't need much rest, but I can't stay awake forever.*

I know he's right, because I can feel him entering a state of delirium. *Won't it be strange for you, though?* I think.

Stranger than having you share my body? he thinks.

Could be, I think.

Dom pushes himself up from the bed and sits on the edge of the mattress. *Come on,* he thinks, unlacing his riding boots. *After everything we've been through, I'm sure we can manage. Maybe it'll be fun.*

He's thinking of the fun we had our first day on the road: learning to ride Eridu together. But my mind turns instead to our ill-fated attempt at lovemaking in our tent half a moon ago.

Dom's pulse speeds up as that memory plays out between us. He exhales slowly. *Relax,* he thinks, to me as much as to himself. He sets his boots down beside the bed and peels off his socks. *We don't need to do anything like that right now. We just need to help each other pretend we're sleeping.*

I look around the room through Dom's eyes as he unlaces his riding cloak. I try to think of something that will help us both relax, that will make me less nervous about manipulating Dom this way. Our gaze settles on the bath.

Would that work? I think.

Worth a shot, thinks Dom, folding his cloak neatly and setting it onto the wooden trunk at the foot of the bed. *Just don't let me drown, all right?*

That's not helping me relax, I think sharply.

Dom chuckles. *Just teasing,* he thinks. *I trust you.*

He waits. I summon all my focus.

All right, I think. *Are you ready?*

△▽△

I'm sitting on the edge of the bed when Ava thinks, *Are you ready?*

Ready, I think. Like I did earlier, when she asked to speak to Hippolyta, I hand over control of my body to Ava. Carefully, she stands. She wiggles my toes and fingers, then takes a few slow steps, testing my balance. I didn't realize it was possible to tread so lightly until I feel how Ava walks. She crosses the bedroom toward the bath, opens three of the four bronze faucets, and stoppers the tub.

Isn't that a little too hot? I think, as she mixes the water pooling in the bottom of the deep stone tub with my hand.

I like it hot, she thinks.

I don't want to boil these cuts on my back, though, I think.

Oh, spirits, I almost forgot, she thinks. She opens the fourth tap of cooler water and tests the temperature again with my hand. *How's that?*

That'll do, I think.

She stands and walks over to the little mirror mounted above the washbasin. I've seen myself occasionally through Ava's eyes over our last moon together on the road, but it's been a long time since I've looked at my own reflection. Shadows ring my eyes. My riding shirt is dark with the accumulated dust, sweat, and dirt of the last half moon. Those brown stains on my sleeves must be Ava's blood. The only thing on me that looks halfway clean is the edge of the bandage peeking up above my collar.

I didn't need a mirror to tell me I need a bath, I think wryly.

That's not what I wanted to show you, she thinks.

Ava returns control of my body to me. I lean toward the mirror, studying myself more closely, wondering what she wants me to see. My brow furrows in concentration. In my worried reflection, I recognize my resemblance to the man Ava thinks of as other-Dom. I wonder whether he's the man I'll be someday, or just a man on another branch who has nothing to do with me.

I rub my eyes wearily. When I look into the mirror again, the bloodstains on my tunic are gone. In fact, it looks like I'm wearing brand new clothes. Startled, I think, *Wait, have you already … ?*

Yes, she thinks. *Do you want to keep going?*

I was confident that I could handle Ava's manipulation of my perception, but it's more disturbing than I'd expected. I thought I'd feel something to warn me when the manipulation began, but it was seamless. Cautiously, I think, *Yes, but … slowly?*

Behind me, Ava says softly, "Slowly, then."

She sounds so real, but the memory of her body disappearing into smoke and ashes this morning fills my mind, confusing me with the impossibility of her physical presence. I squeeze my eyes shut. A tear slips down my cheek. "Wait," I say, my heart pounding in my throat. "Maybe you're right. Maybe this isn't a good idea."

"I'll stop whenever you tell me to stop," she says.

She waits. I say nothing. I feel her hand on my sleeve, impossibly real, solid, warm. It's unbearable to think that she's not really there.

"Maybe it's better just to look," she says. "Your memory is fighting my imagination."

I hesitate. I'm not sure whether I'm afraid to see her, or afraid that when I open my eyes, she'll be gone.

"Come on," she says gently. "You said you trust me. Trust me."

Slowly, I open my eyes. In the mirror, Ava peeks out from behind my shoulder. She waves her fingers playfully at me. I stare at her, transfixed.

She takes my hand and turns me around to face her. I gaze down at her in wonder. Slowly, I touch her face, tracing the line across her eyebrow, down her cheek, along her chin. Her skin is warm and soft, her cheeks rosy and rounded with health. Her expression is completely unburdened by pain, as if even the memory of pain is gone. "I never saw you like this before," I say.

Ava glances at herself in the mirror. "I was never this clean," she says with a shrug.

I laugh. She reaches up and unties the laces at my collar. "How about that bath?" she says.

I look over at the tub, which is about two thirds full. "Is that a real bath, or part of the dream?" I say.

She narrows her eyes in mock annoyance. "Do you want me to help you sleep, or do you want me to explain how I'm doing this?" she says.

I hold up my hands in surrender.

"No more questions, then," she says. She gestures for me to undress. I pull off my tunic, breeches, and underclothes. Ava's clothes simply dissolve in the air.

"That doesn't seem fair," I say, trying to keep my eyes fixed on her face.

"My imagination, my rules," she says.

Carefully, she helps me unwind the bandages Arkhi secured to my back yesterday morning. In the mirror, I catch a glimpse of the long red slashes Lilith's owl clawed across my shoulder blades. I've seen Mohiran pharmaka at work many times, but I'm still impressed by how fast those cuts are healing. I wonder whether they'll leave a scar.

Ava draws me by the hand toward the bath and turns off the four taps. I step over the lip of the tub and lower myself slowly. The water is still quite hot, and the stone basin of the tub radiates a heat of its own, just like the stone walls of the room. The water stings my back at first, but the pain subsides gradually. Ava steps into the far side of the tub and sits facing me.

I try to relax, but my awareness of Ava's naked body so close to mine makes it difficult. "Do you feel the water too?" I say, trying to distract myself with something innocuous before remembering I'm not supposed to ask her any more questions.

She touches the surface of the water with her fingertips, then flicks a few droplets my way. "I feel what you're feeling," she says. She submerges herself briefly in the bath and re-emerges, hair dripping, water streaming off her bare shoulders. Her fingers close around my ankles underwater. She draws my feet into her lap. My skin feels slippery under her hands in the alkaline water. I swallow, wondering whether she feels what I'm feeling now.

A mischievous smile tugs at the corner of her mouth. She circles my heels with her thumbs and flicks her fingernails lightly up my soles before she goes on the move. Her strong hands slide up my calves, over my thighs, up my sides. My pulse speeds up as her face draws near to mine. Tiny beads of water sparkle on the tips of her eyelashes.

She presses a soft kiss to my lips, to my cheek, to my earlobe. "Relax," she whispers.

She settles herself in my lap, nestling her back against my chest. I rest my cheek on the top of her head, breathing in the scent of her hair mixed with the steaming bathwater. She laces her fingers through mine and wraps my arms around her.

Her body relaxes against mine, as if she's fallen asleep. I stop wondering how she's doing this, simply grateful for the familiar sensation of her touch. I'm lulled to sleep by the soft sounds of two breathing as one, of water lapping stone, of wind coursing through the empty streets of Velkanos.

THE GIFT OF VELKANOS

DOM RECLINES IN THE BATH with his eyes closed. He feels my body wrapped in his arms, and he longs to forget that my presence is nothing more than our imaginations at work. His longing is more intense than Eumelia's desire was the night I seduced her, so his perception is even easier to manipulate than hers was then. I only need to make a few suggestions; Dom's imagination fills in the rest.

So I imagine the pressure of my back nestled against his chest in the slippery alkaline water, the scent of my hair, the sound of my breathing rising and falling with his. I'm tempted to imagine far more, but after all the pain and exhaustion of our last moon on the road together, I know Dom needs comfort and sleep more than seduction.

The tether between Dom's awareness and his body loosens. At last, he falls asleep. Carefully, I stop imagining sensations one by one until all that remain are the real sensations of Dom's body alone in the bathtub: the warm water caressing his skin, the pungent mineral scent hanging in the steamy air, the soft rise and fall of his breathing, the whistle of wind in the roof tiles, the low rush and chortle of water through the stone walls. I observe him closely, refraining from further manipulation. He remains sleeping. Spirits, that's a relief. For once, I've managed to use our connection for something good.

I consider moving Dom back into his bed so he won't wake up later in a cold bath. But he seems safe enough here for now, and I'm enjoying the bath vicariously. Hot baths were a rare luxury in the years I roamed the wilderness. Even so, this isn't the first time I've bathed in the waters of Velkanos. Years ago, Lilith and I performed a job in the Over City storehouses. We escaped with our loot through the Under City, the vast cave system beneath Velkanos that's connected by a network of carved tunnels. The Under City is full of natural springs that bubble up into the cave pools and flow out through the underground river hidden beneath the arid plain surrounding Velkanos.

I remember bathing with Lilith in one of those hot pools in the Under City after we'd completed our job in the Over City. She told me then about the age before the destruction, when people used to throng to Velkanos from all over Dulai to soak in these springs and drink these waters. The people of that age believed the gift of Velkanos could cure any illness. When I asked Lilith whether there's healing pharmaka in the mountain waters, she told me that healing came not from the waters themselves, but from the beliefs people carried with them on their journeys to Velkanos.

This memory—Lilith's low voice echoing along dark cave walls as we floated hand in hand in the underground pool—unleashes my grief all over again. I know I'm a fool to grieve for her. But however she may have deceived me, Lilith also showed me many wonderful things I never would have seen without her. With her, I dared to hope for freedom. Hope itself is a kind of freedom, I realize now. I miss that freedom. I miss the person I used to be, back when I believed everything Lilith had taught me.

Dom stirs uneasily in his sleep as my memories of Lilith flood through his mind. I'd better stop this nostalgic reverie before my thoughts of her create nightmares for him. I refocus my attention on Dom. Because his eyes are closed, the entire world around us shrinks to nothing but this bath, this warmth, the delicious health radiating from the body he's sharing with me. I've lost so much over the past moon, but I've gained a kind of peace I never knew before, with my awareness tucked safely inside of Dom. The bath water gently rises and falls around his shoulders as his breathing slows and deepens.

The tranquility of deep sleep fills Dom's mind, driving out the sensations of his body and the room around him, leaving my awareness drifting through darkness. Without the need for sleep myself, my mind fidgets with endless questions. What can I think about while Dom's sleeping that won't risk waking him up? Would Dom mind if I used his body while he's sleeping? Will he remember anything I do while he's sleeping?

When I decided to remain with Dom after my death, I was so eager to be free of my own body's pain that I hadn't considered how it would feel to be trapped inside of his sleeping body, night after night. I wish I'd had time to think this through more carefully. But I suppose there'll be plenty of time to think about it later, with countless long nights like this ahead of me. Maybe it's all right for me to put off any more thinking for now and simply relax here in the bath. Maybe Dom will even start dreaming soon and provide me with some diversion.

I'm not sure how much time has passed when a hand takes gentle hold of Dom's ankle underwater, pulling my awareness back into his body. This must be the start of a dream. Perhaps Dom's about to revisit the very scene I just created to help him fall asleep. How intriguing. Where might his dreaming mind lead us?

The dream-hand begins to massage Dom's left foot. Ah, that's a promising start. Each stroke of the strong, probing fingers opens pathways of sensation that travel up Dom's leg, into his spine, flowing through his torso, spreading out to his fingertips. It feels good, but there's something disconcerting about the sensation, too. It's as if Dom's body has slipped a few inches deeper into the water, or as if the bathtub has changed shape. Hoping not to wake him, I open Dom's eyes a crack to make sure everything is all right with his sleeping body.

Oh, spirits. It's happened again. This isn't Dom's dream. These aren't even Dom's eyes that I've opened. I'm elsewhere, in a different body, lying in a different bath.

Across from me, other-Dom reclines in a bright white tub, submerged to the shoulders in steaming bathwater. He holds my left leg in his lap as he massages my foot. Apprehensively, I raise my right leg just above the waterline, inadvertently sliding my toes up his impressively chiseled chest. Through slightly blurred vision, I recognize the pattern of green and blue painted onto the polished toenails of a small, soft, decidedly feminine foot.

My toes—or Emmie's toes, I suppose—tingle against other-Dom's skin.

Through the binding pharmaka, I glimpse in other-Dom's mind where this bath was heading before I showed up. I briefly consider letting his intimate encounter with Emmie proceed as he's anticipating; I do have an entire night to kill, after all. But now that I have a better idea of what's going on, it doesn't seem right to intrude unannounced. Regretfully, I say, "Sorry to interrupt."

Other-Dom doesn't look startled. His fingers don't even pause their work on my foot. Just like Emmie asked me last time, he says, "Where were you, before you were here?"

It's difficult to concentrate while he's massaging me like this, but I can't bring myself to pull my foot away. His touch feels so good. Struggling a bit more than usual to put words together, I say, "I was with my Dom in Velkanos."

Other-Dom nods as if this is a perfectly normal conversation. Again like last time, he says, "How old are you?"

"I'm … not really sure how to answer that any more," I say. "Yesterday, I was seventeen summers."

"What happened yesterday?" he says.

"I died," I say.

Other-Dom's brow furrows. His fingers pause their work on the sole of my foot. "Didn't your Dom and Serapen revive you?" he says.

"They did once before," I say. "About half a moon ago, when I died on the Purattu. But yesterday I accidentally crossed a bridge to some new branch while I was in the saddle. I fell, hit my head on the road, and stabbed myself with my knife. I think my knife finished me off, but I was in rough shape even before that. Dom and Serapen were there after I fell, but I told Dom I didn't want to go back to my body—it was so badly injured. I asked to stay with him in his body instead. He agreed. So I was with him in his body right before I came here."

Other-Dom lets out a low whistle. He says, "Well, that's a new one. I thought I'd witnessed every possible form of death after following you for so many lives."

"What do you mean?" I say. "You said something like that—about how you've followed me, life after life—the last time I saw you."

"Do you know the name of the branch we were on, when I said that?" he says.

"The name of the branch?" I say. "I don't know what you mean. But you were showing me one of your memories in the alternet. A hilltop grove with a pomegranate tree, somewhere near Velkanos. Don't you remember? It was only half a moon ago."

He shakes his head. "Half a moon ago for you and half a moon ago for me aren't the same thing," he says. "Did we talk about branch travel at all, the last time you saw me?"

"I returned to my own branch before you could explain much about it," I say. "Why?"

Other-Dom says, "You might expect that if you travel to my branch, then return to your branch for half a moon, then travel back to my branch, the same half moon has also passed here. But you may have actually returned to a time before your last visit, or to a much later time. You might even have traveled to an entirely different branch that at first looks the same as one you visited before. It can be difficult to know exactly where you are until you've spent some time on a branch, since many branches are quite similar."

"I don't understand," I say.

Other-Dom glances up at the white tiled wall across from the bath. The wall is too far away for me to see clearly with Emmie's blurry vision, but I can make out another one of those sundial-like circles hanging above the open door, like the one I saw in the bedroom the last time I was with other-Dom. He shakes his head. "There's probably not enough time to explain," he says. "When you're this young, before you've had any initiate training, your body usually recalls your awareness to your branch in just a few minutes."

"What's a minute?" I say, imitating the accent he uses to say this unknown word.

"Oh. A minute. That's … about sixty heartbeats," he says.

Damn. That really isn't much time; I've been here at least five minutes already. My mind races through all the questions I have, considering which I should ask first. Then something occurs to me. I say, "Serapen told me that when an awareness crosses over to another branch, the body it departs from grows weaker. Traveling between branches can even be fatal—it was for me, twice. But my body is dead, and Dom's awareness is in his body back on my branch. Maybe now that my own body doesn't need my awareness back on my branch, I can stay here a while longer?"

Other-Dom drums his fingers on his lips. "I'm not sure," he says. "I've never received a visit from you while you're dead. But you could be right. Maybe you'll be able to stay longer this time, without a body that needs attention back on your branch."

"Could you at least try to help me understand what's happening to me, then?" I say. "I don't know why I keep traveling between branches. I don't have any control over it. You and Emmie seem to know so much more than I do about how this all works."

"I wish we knew more," says other-Dom. "But I'll try to explain what we do know, at least. It'll be easier to show than tell. Come on."

Other-Dom lets go of my foot, steps out of the bath, and dries himself with a blue towel. For the second time, I glimpse the tattooed pair of outstretched wings that spread across his shoulder blades. I rub my blurry eyes and take a closer look. Am I imagining things, or does that tattoo look awfully similar to the marks clawed into my own Dom's back by the owl?

I shake my head to clear it of the strange impression, overcome by the all-too-familiar exhaustion of Emmie's body. I know better than to try to climb out of a slippery tub on my own this time, so I wait until other-Dom leans over and helps me out. It's irritating to be handled like a helpless infant, but it's pointless to resist him with Emmie's body this weak, so I go along obediently. I have no idea how much time I'll have on this branch before I slip back to my own, so I'm not going to waste any precious time being stubborn.

Other-Dom helps me dry off and leads me into the bedroom. We quickly dress in the same black immerger clothes and glasses we wore the last time I was here. Even the small effort of getting dressed leaves me short of breath. He takes my hand, sending a current of strength through me. We walk out of the bedroom, across the big room with the splendid view of San Francisco, into the hallway, down the stairs to the black door that leads to the spliner. He taps a pattern onto the side panel that opens the door.

I follow him into the spliner. He says something in English. The dim grey light fades into darkness. He speaks again, and bright white light fills the space around us. He speaks a third time, calling out some English words along with *Ava*, *Dom*, and *Dulai*. A now-familiar setting materializes around us.

I stand beside the clear spring beneath the pomegranate tree in the hilltop grove, dressed in priestess robes of saffron and scarlet. Other-Dom stands beside me in the avatar of his younger self, wearing dusty workman's clothes.

"Is this the place you saw before?" he says.

"Yes," I say. "You took me here the first time I met you on this branch. And yesterday, right before I died, I returned here again."

Other-Dom waves his hand. The hilltop landscape around us shrinks down into a little sphere that hovers over his open palm, leaving us surrounded by the blank grey spliner walls. He studies the sphere as he says, "It's hard to predict when your awareness might travel between branches, especially without initiate training. But perhaps it's not surprising that your awareness returned here. This memory is at the center of so many intersections in our lives. Did Emmie tell you about intersections?"

I say, "She told me that intersections are recurring patterns in memories. She showed me how she uses intersections between memories stored in the alternet—like a map to help her navigate from one memory to another—now that she's lost so many of her natural memories. She said intersections in memory are like the bridges my awareness crosses when I travel between branches. When Emmie recorded my last memory from my own branch and showed it to me in the alternet, I was able to cross the bridge back to my branch."

Other-Dom's expression brightens. He turns away from the hovering sphere, grips my shoulders, and searches my eyes. "You were able to travel back to your branch using an intersection in the alternet?"

Confused by his excitement, I say, "I'm not sure. Maybe? Is that surprising?"

He laughs. The joyful expression smooths away years from his face. "Emmie's obsessed with the idea that intersections are the key to controlling travel between branches. But even though she's gotten better and better at using intersections to manage her own memory loss, she's never been able to help you return to your own branch intentionally using the alternet." His tone turns sheepish. "I thought it was impossible, without the arts of the Mohirai. I even tried to persuade Emmie to give up the work, for a while. I thought she was exhausting herself with futile work."

"So you've never actually seen it work?" I say.

Other-Dom shakes his head. "Emmie has plenty of theories, but she's never been able to intentionally travel between branches herself," he says. "How did you manage to do it?"

I'm taken aback. I'd hoped that other-Dom could explain what's going on to me. Now it seems I know even more than he does. I think back to my visit with Emmie in the glass tower. "She started by taking me to a spliner, much larger than this one," I say. "In the biggest glass tower in San Francisco."

Other-Dom nods. "That was probably in the Eden offices," he says, gesturing with his hand. A sphere materializes in front of me containing a miniature version of the glass tower. "Were you somewhere in this building?"

"Yes," I say. "Once we were in the spliner, she asked me a lot of questions about where I had been before I came to her branch. She waved her hands around a lot, like you've been doing. It looked like she was … sort of building my memory in front of me, using pieces of other memories that she said belonged to you."

Other-Dom nods and says, "She was recording your memory, using other related memories to fill in the details." He waves his hands again. Many more spheres pop up around us, each containing some miniature scene. "Was she working with pieces that looked like these?"

"Yes," I say. "After she did that—recorded my memory—she put the memory inside a little sphere like one of those. And then she made a sort of tree grow out through the memory."

"Mapping your memory's intersections with other memories," says other-Dom, making a sweeping motion with his hands. All the spheres floating around us disappear except for his memory of the hilltop grove. A beam of white light shoots up from the floor, illuminating the memory before splitting apart into branches that grow to fill the space around us.

"Yes, like that," I say. "And then …"

After a long pause, other-Dom prompts me eagerly. "And then?"

"I'm not sure," I say. "I looked at my memory, and at some of the branches that grew out from it. Emmie told me those branches led to memories that could happen in the future. Then she said something about you that made me think about Dom—my Dom, I mean. And then I was back on my branch."

Other-Dom waves his hands in a summoning gesture. All at once, hundreds of faintly glowing memory spheres appear, swirling through the air around us like a flock of colorful birds. A beam of white light bursts from the floor and illuminates a sphere hovering directly before him. The memory appears to be our present moment in miniature: me in Emmie's body standing beside other-Dom in the spliner, surrounded by a glowing cloud of memories. The beam of light splits as it passes through the sphere that holds our present moment, branching and splitting and connecting to the other memories surrounding us, until the entire room is filled with translucent white branches studded with spheres of memory.

Other-Dom selects a branch that leads from our present moment at the center of the spliner to some memory floating a few paces away. He walks along the branch, studying various points where it splits, tapping his fingers in the air as he murmurs to himself.

"What are you doing?" I say, following close behind him.

"Trying to understand the effect of what *you* are doing," he says. "Because you've just planted an idea in my head. You've told me that somewhere, on some branch, Emmie helped you use an intersection to travel between branches. You've made me believe that something I thought was impossible is possible."

"So?" I say.

He looks at me. "Consider this. Every action you take on your own branch plays a role in determining your future. Your actions change your set of possible futures. The same is true when you act on my branch: anything you influence here changes the set of possible futures for this branch. Every time you travel to another branch, you make some futures on that branch more likely, and others less likely."

"Is that … good?" I say.

Other-Dom runs his fingers through his close-cropped curls. "Is it good that your awareness shapes the future of every branch you visit? I'm not sure. It changes what may lie ahead for me on my branch. That certainly makes you powerful."

I give a half-hearted laugh. "Powerful?" I say. "I wish I were powerful. I've spent the last moon almost entirely helpless. When I travel to other branches, there's always something wrong with the body I'm in, or I'm trapped in some situation I don't understand. Even now, I don't know how I came here or when I'll leave here or what I should do while I'm here."

Other-Dom squeezes my hand. "Sometimes the only way to know is to do," he says.

I roll my eyes. "Everyone keeps telling me that. But … what am I supposed to do?"

"You tell me," he says. "What are you here to do?"

"I don't know," I say, frustrated. "I didn't come here on purpose."

"Didn't you?" he says. He looks at me expectantly. I look back at him blankly. He says, "Don't you remember the Voice's words to you?"

How could I forget? Any time I stop long enough to listen, I hear the Voice calling in the stillness, its words always the same. Impatiently, I recite the words again for other-Dom.

We are the bridge joining light to darkness.
We are the wheel turning season to season.
We are the threads binding realm to realm.
We are creator, preserver, destroyer of worlds.

Together you shall seek us, find us, know us.
Together you shall amplify us.

Together you shall weave us through the many worlds.
Together you shall answer our call.

Other-Dom nods and says, "As far as Emmie and I have been able to determine, every Ava who has visited our branch has accepted that same calling from the Voice and is trying her best to answer it. Your calling seems to be the one thing you all have in common."

It's strange to contemplate the existence of all these other-Avas that other-Dom has met, but the idea that there are others, each on her own journey, trying to make sense of our perplexing calling, is comforting. It makes me feel less alone, knowing they're all out there, somewhere. "But what is the Voice calling us all to do?" I say.

"Exactly what it says, I imagine," he says. "Seek it. Find it. Know it. Amplify it. Together."

I grumble in frustration at this answer that answers nothing.

Other-Dom looks at me with a hint of mischief. "Perhaps a different perspective would help?" he says. He waves his hand, and the sphere containing his memory of the hilltop grove expands around us again. We stand once more at the edge of the rocky promontory, looking out across the plain toward Velkanos. Before I have a chance to ask what he's doing, other-Dom leans forward and jumps off the ledge. I cry out in alarm. But rather than plunging down to the deadly-looking rocks far below, other-Dom drops a mere handspan and lands on his feet, hovering in what appears to be thin air. He turns around to face me.

My heart pounds in my throat, but I manage to say coolly, "Is that supposed to impress me?"

"Worth a try," he says.

"You'll have to try harder than that," I say.

"Challenge accepted," he says with a laugh. He extends his hand toward me, waiting for me—or perhaps daring me—to join him.

I hesitate at the edge of the rock ledge before I take his hand. Keeping my eyes fixed on his, I step out toward him. To my relief, what looks like a sheer drop feels perfectly solid underfoot. We walk onward, hand in hand, spiraling slowly skyward through the air like we're climbing an invisible mountain.

The landscape below us drops away with surprising speed. After we've taken only a few steps, birds are flying beneath our feet. A few steps later, we're rising through a swirling foam of clouds. The Urashtu range far below us appears to be no more than ripples in a landscape of green and gold. We climb higher, and the land reveals itself to be an enormous peninsula edged by a bright blue coastline and darker blue inland seas. Higher still, the blue sky fades and darkens. The flat horizon bends and bends until its curve becomes a circle. When we stop walking, we look down at a world revealed to be a perfect sphere of marbled blue and green floating in a dark sea of glittering stars.

"This is how I remember Dulai," says other-Dom, indicating the world below us.

"It's …" Beautiful doesn't begin to describe it. Magnificent is too small. There aren't any words for this in our tongue, and the word I choose is entirely inadequate. "Awesome," I say.

"Yes," he says. He raises his hand, and Dulai rises over us like a magnificent blue-green moon. He beckons, and Dulai glides toward us, shrinking as it approaches to the size of a pomegranate, landing in his outstretched palm. Other-Dom turns to me and places the whole world in my hand.

The gently glowing globe is cool against my palm, smooth as glass, heavy as stone. I turn it slowly in my fingers, examining the interlocking pieces of land and sea that form this spherical puzzle. I recognize the tiny outline of the peninsula I've roamed for the last eight years with Lilith. The lands I've seen with my own eyes are such a small piece of the whole world, and amidst this sea of stars the whole world is little more than a speck of dust.

With my fingertip, I trace a line across the globe, westward from Velkanos, over the Urashtu Range, through the Middle Sea, across the great ocean, following the route I once believed would lead me and Lilith to the land of freedom. My fingertip lingers over the coastline of an unknown continent. "Lilith told me there were lands beyond the great ocean," I say thoughtfully. "I guess she was telling the truth about that, at least."

"Who's Lilith?" says other-Dom.

I look at him in surprise. "She's my—" I stop. "It's a long story," I say.

He nods slowly. "Well, there's plenty of space for your story in the alternet. Let's make a place for it."

He reaches out and takes the globe from my hand. He squeezes it between his palms, using the same motion I saw Emmie use on my last visit with her. When he separates his hands, he's holding twin globes, each a perfect copy of the other. He hands one globe to me and keeps the other. "We'll need something to call your branch to get started," he says. "Would you like to give it a name?"

"Isn't it … Dulai?" I say, looking down at the new world in my hand.

"In a way, yes," he says. "But we need a unique name for your own branch, to distinguish it from my branch and all the other branches recorded in the alternet. I call my branch The Underground River." His globe glows brighter when he speaks its name, then dims.

"Why do you call it that?" I say.

"That's where Ava—my Ava—died, on my branch," he says. "In the underground river."

I grimace. "Sounds awful," I say.

Other-Dom's expression contains so many layers. Sorrow, nostalgia, and regret barely scratch the surface. There's a hint of joy, though, too. He says, "It was awful, for a while. But it worked out all right in the end."

I consider the little globe in my hand, thinking of my own branch. "Well, if this one's mine, I guess I'll call it The End of the Road."

"The End of the Road," he repeats. He says something in English that I don't understand. The globe in my hand pulses, glows brighter, then dims.

"All right," he says. He tosses away The Underground River, which vanishes before it hits the floor. He gestures for me to return The End of the Road to him. I toss it his way. He catches it mid-air in his free hand, then lets it go. Rather than falling, it hovers before him at eye level. His fingertips dance before him like he's playing an unseen instrument. He talks to himself in English for a while before he says, in our own tongue, "You said you've died twice on your branch? Half a moon ago and yesterday?"

"Yes," I say.

"Were you at Urshanabi's ferry crossing the first time?" he says.

"A little upriver from there, I think," I say. "But Serapen unbound my memory of that night, so I'm not entirely sure."

He nods, tapping the air and muttering something in English. A new sphere containing a bend in the Purattu river appears, floating about an arm's length away from my little globe of Dulai. He says, "And the second time, yesterday, that was at the end of the road to Velkanos?"

"That's right," I say.

He waves his hand, and an image materializes before me, like a translucent sheet of parchment. After a moment, I understand what I'm seeing. It's a map of the road from the Urashtu Pass to Velkanos, as a bird might see it flying overhead. Other-Dom gestures toward the image. "Can you show me where you were when you died the second time?" he says.

I study the curves in the road. Other-Dom enlarges the image a few times with deft gestures until I find the place where the caravan stopped to greet Tio, Kabir, and Balashi. I tap the image, and a glowing red marker appears beneath my fingertip. Other-Dom mutters something in English, and the flat image vanishes. Another floating sphere appears alongside the globe of Dulai, this one showing the end of the road to Velkanos.

Other-Dom says, "And the last time you traveled between branches, you said Emmie helped you record another memory from your own branch? Could you describe what you placed in that memory?"

I describe the memory of myself in the tent with Hanu, Dom, and Eumelia. After a few moments, other-Dom shows me a memory sphere containing what appears to be the memory Emmie and I recorded together. "That looks like it," I say.

Other-Dom places this memory alongside the other two floating near The End of the Road. He says, "And you said the last place you remember being before you were here was Dom's quarters above the stables?" He asks me a few more questions about what Dom and I were doing in the room. I answer, watching other-Dom's hands closely as he rapidly re-creates the scene in another memory sphere. I don't need to supply very much information; other-Dom seems to have most of the details about the room already recorded elsewhere.

At last, other-Dom makes a sweeping motion with his hands and says something in a conclusive tone. The four new memory spheres and the globe of Dulai collapse on top of each other and vanish like a bubble bursting. He turns to me and says, "Good. We have a basic record of your branch now, with four important memories that can distinguish it from most other branches. Whenever you return here, if you need to explain to me or Emmie where you're coming from, you can just say you're from The End of the Road. If you run into an other-Dom who doesn't remember this conversation, try telling him the name of your branch."

Perplexed, I say, "But if I travel to a branch where there's an other-Dom who doesn't remember this conversation, doesn't that mean the record doesn't exist on his branch?"

"That depends on where you return," says other-Dom. "The record we've just made of your branch is stored using a quantum computer. Any record stored this way will be accessible on any other branch you visit where this quantum computer also exists."

"You've lost me again," I say. "What's a quantum computer?"

"A quantum computer ..." Other-Dom rakes his fingers through his hair, searching for words in the same way my Dom often does. He says, "It's an art of tekhnologia on this branch, a kind of machine. In some ways, it's like a library, or like a human mind—you can store information in it and retrieve it later. But the way this quantum computer stores and retrieves information is special. In a library, you can only access information in the books that were stored in that particular library. In your own mind, you can—usually—only access memories created in your own life on your branch. But with a quantum computer, you can access information stored by anyone who uses the computer on any branch, not just your own branch. The information stored in this quantum computer exists in every branch where the computer exists. And, unlike a library or a human mind, the amount of memories that can be stored in this quantum computer is essentially limitless."

Before my overdose, the idea that anything could hold limitless memories would have made no sense to me. Now, the idea of a quantum computer that holds limitless memories reminds me of the most dangerous aspect of my connection with the Voice in all. My occasional glimpses into the Voice's vast awareness have been excruciatingly painful, because the Voice's awareness contains so much more than what my mind can hold. I wonder whether this tekhnologia is equally dangerous.

"So ..." I try to assemble the pieces I've been gathering through all my travel back and forth between Dulai and Earth. "This quantum computer holds all the memories you and Emmie have stored in the alternet, and it maps intersections between memories. Does that mean it's sort of like the awareness of the Voice in all, that connects every branch of the path of mysteries?"

"The principles underlying this quantum computer are more than simply *like* the Voice in all," says other-Dom. He raises his hands and speaks two phrases in English, which I now recognize as The Underground River and The End of the Road. The two worlds re-appear before us, floating about an arm's length apart. A beam of light appears, bridging the two worlds as they begin to circle each other like two dancers in a ring. "Whether we explore the mysteries through the tekhnologia of Earth or the pharmaka of Dulai, the truth underlying all branches is the same."

"What truth?" I say, transfixed by the sight of the dancing spheres before me.

Other-Dom gazes at the twin worlds with me. Out of habit, before I consciously realize what I'm doing, I take his hand. He squeezes my fingers gently and says, "All are one. In every path, the sum of all."

My annoyance breaks the hypnotic spell of the spinning worlds. "That's just more Mohiran nonsense," I say. "I thought you were trying to make things clearer."

"I'm trying to give you a different perspective," he says. "Only you can make sense of what you see."

I roll my eyes. He's no help at all. I stare at our two versions of Dulai, trying to understand what the Voice has called me here to do. So many ideas rise and fall in my mind, but none of them make any sense to me. It's so frustrating.

I wish my Dom were here right now instead of other-Dom. My Dom is usually able to help me see things from a different perspective, too, but he's so much less mysterious than this other-Dom. Dom's words resurface in my memory now, along with a sense of his comforting calm. *Don't worry. We'll figure it out. Together.*

Wait. Is that my memory? Cautiously, I think, *Dom?*

"Ava?" says other-Dom.

"Not *you*," I say, annoyed. "I meant—" I glance up at other-Dom, and the words die on my lips. The avatar he's wearing has changed. Where the long-haired other-Dom in dusty work clothes had stood just a moment ago now stands a younger Dom I know well, naked except for the sheen of bathwater on his skin.

My Dom gazes up at the ghostly white branches filling the spliner around us. "Where are we?" he says, gripping my hand tighter. He looks at me, and his confused expression grows even more perplexed. "Why are you wearing priestess robes?"

Understanding dawns on me. Slowly, I say, "Where were you, before you were here?"

"I was in the bath," he says. "With you. Well, sort of with you. In Velkanos. Ava, what is going on? Is this a dream?"

I swear under my breath. If Dom is here, and I'm here, then who is with Dom's body back in Dulai? I should never have left him in that bath. How long does it take someone to drown? "Listen," I say urgently. "This isn't a dream. I think I've pulled you into another branch accidentally. You shouldn't be here. We need to get you back to your body, fast. Remember what happened the last time I crossed over a bridge?"

Dom's eyes widen. "How do we get back?" he says.

Spirits, I hope I was paying close enough attention to everything Emmie and other-Dom were doing to navigate through all these memories in the alternet. In uncertain English, I call out, "The End of the Road." To my relief, one of the identical globes circling before us glows brighter at the sound of its name. I tap the globe that represents my branch, and the four memories Emmie and other-Dom recorded for me pop out around it, slowly orbiting the globe. Carefully imitating the hand gestures I've seen Emmie and other-Dom use several times, I expand the memory of taking a bath with Dom in his quarters.

Dom and I now stand inside his room again. I pull him toward the bathtub and instruct him to climb in. He does so, then watches me shed my priestess garments and climb into the tub across from him. We stare at each other across the steaming water. "Now what?" he says, giving voice to my own panicking inner monologue.

Now what? How did I do this before? Last time I was on this branch and looking back at a memory of my own branch, the simple thought of Dom had pulled me back to where he was. But now Dom's awareness is here with me on the wrong side of the bridge. How can we find our way back to our branch if neither one of our awarenesses is there?

A strange expression flickers across Dom's face, like something is tickling his nose.

"What's wrong?" I say, reaching for his hand.

Dom opens his mouth, but no words come out. Instead, he makes an awful gasping sound. My heart races. Is he drowning, back on our branch? As I watch, his face morphs smoothly from the youthful face of the Dom I know to the chiseled older face of other-Dom.

Other-Dom looks at me with a surprised expression. "Ava? What—"

There's a hard tug at my core. I lose the rest of other-Dom's words as the scene around me fades to black.

△▽△

The sensation of water filling my nostrils jolts me awake. Heart pounding, I scramble to lift my head above water, banging both elbows and the back of my head painfully against the hard stone wall of the bathtub. I cough up a mouthful of water and gulp air. Only when my pulse and breathing slow do I realize I'm shivering.

It's dark outside my bedroom window. I must have been lying here in the bath for quite a while, because the water's now cold. I'm disoriented, but I'm sure that whatever happened while I was asleep wasn't just a dream. I was with Ava on that Earth branch for a moment, before I returned here to Dulai.

Ava? I wait for her to answer, trying to suppress the panic that rises in my chest as I wait for her response. She'll come back. She promised she'll come back. I just need to be patient. I count heartbeats. One … Two … Three …

Dom! I heave a sigh of relief as Ava's awareness swirls back into mine. *Spirits, you're freezing,* she thinks.

Maybe next time, we should avoid sleeping in the bath, I think. *Or anywhere else that could kill me, for that matter.*

Good idea, she thinks grimly. *Let's get out of here.*

I grip the lip of the tub with my pruned fingers and haul myself out of the water, surprised by the effort this requires. I stand unsteadily, dripping in the tub as I catch my breath. My vision spins slowly at the edges; my mind feels foggy. *I see why you've been trying so hard to avoid crossing branches,* I think, pressing my hand to my forehead.

It's exhausting, isn't it? she thinks. *I'm sorry I pulled you across the bridge so suddenly. I didn't realize I could do that.*

We both need to be more careful, I think. I step out of the tub and pick my way across the dark bedroom toward the door that leads to the front room of my quarters. Soft moonlight glows through the street-facing windows of the front room. I find a towel in the stack of folded linens on the shelf, dry off, and dress myself in clean clothes. I head toward the line of pegs by the hall entry door and find the winter cloak Hippolyta left for me. I wrap the fleece-lined cloak tight around my shoulders and pace back and forth on the rug in an attempt to drive the chill from my bones. The tidy tower of unlit tinder and kindling in the hearth looks inviting, but I don't see any way to start a fire.

There was an oil lamp out in the hall, thinks Ava.

Thanks, I think. I open the hall door and retrieve the oil lamp that hangs from an iron hook in the stone wall. I kneel by the fireplace with the lamp and use a bit of tinder to transfer the flame from the lamp to the hearth. The kindling catches quickly, and I feed the fire until a log catches. I lean back on my elbows with my bare feet to the hearth. Dry warmth spills over me. At last, I stop shivering.

That's better, thinks Ava.

I gaze into the fire. *What just happened?* I think. Ava's memory flashes through my mind, as she asks herself this same question. We pore over the memory together, comparing her latest visit with other-Dom to her earlier visit with Emmie.

I wish I could figure out why I keep crossing over to that branch so I could make it stop, thinks Ava, frustrated.

Could Emmie be right? I think. *Maybe these bridges you're crossing over have something in common with the memory intersections she's mapping in the alternet. Maybe there's some recurring pattern between her branch and ours.*

Maybe, thinks Ava. *Every time I've crossed to another branch, there has been something similar between the moment I left my branch and the moment I arrived at the new branch. This time it was the bath. Before I fell off Eridu, it was the words Serapen said. The time I met Emmie, it was my dream of the city of glass towers. Before that …* Ava's memory of our failed lovemaking, and the rather more successful encounter between Emmie and other-Dom, continues where her thought leaves off. *But I have no way to recognize that there's some recurring pattern between my branch and Emmie's branch until after I cross over the bridge, so that's not much help.*

You have some control over when you return, though, I think. *That time you were with Emmie in the spliner, you were able to return to our branch when you *thought of me.*

I wish it were that simple, Ava thinks. *But when I thought of you this time, it didn't lead me back to our branch. It pulled you into Emmie's branch instead. If you hadn't managed to find your way back in time ...*

Ava hesitates to finish the thought, so I do it for her. *Yes, it could have been bad, if I hadn't found a way back.* I'm not sure whether it's my lingering chill from the bath or my memory of choking on the water that sends a shiver down my spine. *But when my body started to slip underwater, I think that pulled my awareness back here. My body needed me. And then when I thought of you, that seemed to pull you back to me, too.*

Ava thinks, *I wonder whether that means we could—*

A soft knock at the door startles us. A voice whispers, "Dom? Are you awake?"

The spinning sensation in my head has subsided enough for me to stand, so I walk to the door and open it. Balashi stands before me on the dark landing, reeking of mixed wine. We look at each other awkwardly for a moment before he raises his arm to show me the open bottle in his hand. "I could use some company," he says. His voice, dulled by sadness, is a faded echo of the cheerful voice I remember from our boyhood.

"Come in, brother," I say, making way for him.

Balashi shuffles past me. I close the door behind him. He stands before the fireplace and looks around the cozy room. "You've come a long way from the house of boys," he says.

"We both have," I say.

The firelight flashes in Balashi's eyes. "We?" he says, his voice rising slightly. "There's no *we* any more, Dom. Just *you* and *me*."

His bitterness cuts me to the core. I say, "I overheard what will happen, because of your attendance on Tio. It's a terrible thing, to have so much memory unbound."

Balashi scoffs under his breath. "Terrible, yes. It's funny how many terrible things the Mohirai require of men, isn't it?" He takes a long swig from the bottle and holds it out to me.

I'm not sure how to answer him, so I simply take the bottle. "Where did you get this?" I say, sniffing it tentatively.

"Tio left a few bottles out in our quarters before he left for his workshop," he says.

"Won't he be upset with you for taking it?" I say.

Balashi's handsome features harden. He says, "Does it matter, if I won't remember it?"

"Be careful, brother," I say gently, returning the bottle to him. "Meddling with pharmaka never ends well. You could make yourself sick."

He takes another long swig from the bottle. "Even if I do, I won't remember it in the end," he says with a dark laugh.

When we were boys, I often admired Balashi's confidence and charm. This new recklessness is troubling. Perhaps it makes sense, though. How would I feel, in his position? Knowing that everything I'm experiencing will be forgotten probably would make it hard to care much about anything.

Ava thinks, *Will you let me talk to him?*

That might be weird for him, I think. *He probably doesn't remember you from our Children's Temple days. The Mohirai probably unbound the memory of you from him, just like they did from me, Hanu, and Eumelia.*

Do you mind if we just let him think I'm you, then? she thinks.

I can't see what difference it makes, I think. *Go ahead.*

Eagerly, Ava takes over my voice. "How did you end up in Tio's service?" she says through me. "He must have had other attendants with him, if he traveled all the way from Lemnos to the men's village at Upper Ford."

Balashi takes another long drink from the bottle. It's half empty now; he's going to have an awful headache tomorrow. He says, "The smith who claimed me on our Calling Day traveled with me from the Children's Temple to the men's village at Upper Ford. I was supposed to begin my novice training there with him. I hadn't been in the village for even a day when he told me the plan for my training had changed. He sent me to attend Tio Artifex instead. Tio had just arrived in the village, on his way to Velkanos.

"At first, I thought attending an Artifex was an honor—far better than learning from a mere smith. I only realized my foolishness when one of the younger men explained to me that my memories of my time with Tio would have to be unbound after I'd seen the inside of Velkanos. I didn't want to go with Tio after that. I asked whether there was anyone else who could attend him. But who would volunteer to give up his memory, if he had any other choice?"

Ava listens intently, weighing each of Balashi's words, but I can't tell what she hopes to learn from him. She says, "What's it like, attending Tio?"

Balashi shrugs. "It's mostly a lot of lifting and carrying. He needs help getting on and off his horse, or into and out of rooms. He needs help tending to his injured leg with pharmaka. Apart from that, he mostly ignores me. I'm probably about as important to him as a piece of furniture. Kabir's kind enough, but neither of the Artifexi give me much notice. And why should they? Anything anyone tells me, any training I might receive, any attention at all is wasted on me until after my unbinding."

It's clear to me from Balashi's demoralized expression that he'd rather change the subject, but Ava keeps probing. "What are you going to do?" she says.

Balashi sighs. "I've been commanded to serve Tio until he's done with me. What else can I do but obey?"

A series of Ava's memories flashes through my mind: the faces of men in various villages, speaking in low tones to Lilith. I examine these memories with greater interest now than before.

Nervously, Ava thinks, *Stop, Dom. You can't tell Balashi about the rebellion.*

Why not? I think.

All you'll do is give him false hope, she thinks. *Even if the free men could help*

Balashi, there's no way Balashi could escape Velkanos on his own. Not with Mohirai everywhere.

But you've been here before, haven't you? I think, remembering snippets of Ava's thoughts that I've overheard. *You must know some way out.*

There's no way Balashi could get out that way on his own, she thinks.

Who says he has to escape on his own? I think. *Couldn't we all go together?*

Apprehensively, she thinks, *If you get caught trying to leave, what will the Mohirai do with you? You could lose your chance to be an Artifex. They might even unbind you. What will happen to our bond, if you can't remember me?*

That does give me pause. If forced to choose between Ava and Balashi, I know I'd choose Ava. *But I can't just do nothing, if there's some way I could help Balashi,* I think.

Ava thinks, *I know how much you want to help, but the Mohirai are more powerful than you know. They have more ways to control you and Balashi than you can possibly imagine. All you'll do by trying to help Balashi is hurt him.*

Grim understanding sinks into me. *Like I hurt you,* I think. Even though Ava avoided drawing the connection outright, I can see it. I'm trying to do for Balashi the same thing I tried to do for her, the night I found her in the woods.

You never meant to hurt me, she thinks. *But it's impossible to know how you might harm him, if you try to help.*

It pains me deeply to be so useless. "I'm sorry," I say to Balashi. "I wish I could help."

Balashi looks back at me with a glazed expression. Perhaps the mixed wine is starting to take effect. I wonder what sort of pharmaka is in that bottle. He says, "There is one thing you could do for me."

"Anything, brother," I say.

"Remember me," he says. "You'll remember all this, after my unbinding. Even after my journey into Death. Somehow, I think it would all be easier, knowing that you'll remember what happened to me."

A lump rises in my throat. "I'll remember," I say, my voice husky. "I promise."

Balashi clasps my wrist gratefully. We lie back on the rug, side by side. Our conversation turns to well-worn stories from our boyhood. We laugh together as we revisit familiar places and faces in our shared memories. Eventually, Balashi drifts into a drunken sleep. I cover him in a blanket and lie awake, hands folded behind my head, my feet to the fire, listening to the familiar sound of his breathing.

The darkness outside the windows brightens into predawn twilight. Just before sunrise, the first bell tolls, ringing through the stone streets of Velkanos. The sound stirs a thousand memories of first bell in the house of boys, and I rise promptly. When Balashi doesn't wake, I shake his shoulder until he mumbles in protest, "Too early, Dom."

"It's not too early," I say. "First bell just rang. Where are you supposed to go this morning?"

His eyes snap open. He curses under his breath and rises unsteadily to his feet, pressing his hand to his forehead with a grimace. "I'm supposed to deliver Tio's healing pharmaka to him in his workshop. I'd better go."

Balashi departs groggily. I wash up quickly and head downstairs to Kabir's quarters. When I knock on his door, Kabir answers.

"Good morning, little brother!" he booms, waving me in and gesturing for me to take a seat in his front room. "Did you sleep well?"

Could have been better, thinks Ava.

"Well enough," I say, settling into an upholstered armchair by the unlit hearth.

Kabir takes the chair across from me. He says, "I heard Balashi go up the stairs rather late last night. How was your reunion with your trio brother?"

I hesitate. Every answer that comes to my mind is laced with sorrow for Balashi and anger toward the Mohirai. Until I met Ava, I'd rarely needed to conceal my thoughts from anyone, but I'm going to need to learn this skill fast, because I fear the consequences of speaking openly with Kabir. *What should I say?* I think.

As little as possible, thinks Ava. *Your face says too much already. Better to ask questions than give answers.*

Kabir gives me a knowing look. "It's a hard thing, to receive a calling so different from your boyhood brothers. I had trio brothers once, too, you know."

"What happened to them?" I say.

"What happens to us all, sooner or later," he says. "They made their journeys into Death centuries ago."

Is it the contrast between Kabir's soothing tone and the bitterness in Balashi's voice last night that reawakens my rebellious thoughts from yesterday? Perhaps. Or perhaps it's Ava's own rebelliousness coursing through me. "Are we supposed to abandon our brothers like they're nothing, then?" I say. "Why should we receive so much, while they receive so little?"

I can't tell who is most surprised by my outburst: myself, Ava, or Kabir. Heat rises to my cheeks. A part of me is proud that I've raised my voice in support of Balashi, but another part regrets making such a terrible impression on my new teacher.

Who cares if you make a bad impression if you're right? thinks Ava.

"You'd do well to listen more carefully, little brother," says Kabir. "I said nothing about abandoning our brothers. Indeed, it's the responsibility of the Artifexi to ensure that the path of mysteries reopens to brothers in the future, after we've paid the debt of the men who brought about the destruction. It's true that a calling to the path of mysteries comes with a great many advantages that our brothers will not enjoy in their lives. But these advantages come at a cost. The path of an Artifex will require far more from you than most men's callings. You will come to know the weight of memory and the pain of loss in a way your trio brothers need never know."

"Pardon me, brother," I say, lowering my head deferentially. "I spoke hastily. I will listen more carefully."

Kabir waves his hand and says, "There's no need to address me like a priestess or ask for my pardon, Dom. Deference is useful for the uninitiated, but such formalities serve no purpose between Artifexi. My time as your teacher is only a passing season between us, and we will be equals in our brotherhood for many ages. Indeed, you will learn that in the end all are equal in their service to the Voice. In every path, the sum of all."

"That is a mystery to me, brother," I say.

Kabir smiles. "Time reveals many mysteries," he says. "But we will leave that particular mystery for another day. You have a more pressing matter this morning. What have you been told about your duties in the house of novices?"

"Nothing but what Hippolyta said outside the stables yesterday," I say. "That I'm to meet many Muses in the house of novices."

Kabir chuckles. "*Future* Muses, I believe are the words she used. It's an important distinction. None of the novice Mohirai are Muses. Most of the initiate Mohirai aren't Muses, either, for that matter."

"What's the difference between a Mohira and a Muse?" I say.

"The Artifex makes the difference," he says. "When you place yourself in service to a Mohira, she becomes a Muse. You will amplify the arts she practices through the work of your hands. Many great works have been accomplished in Dulai by the Artifexi in service to our Muses."

"Muse Arkhi told me something of this, on the road to Velkanos," I say. "But I don't understand how I'm supposed to choose a Mohira to become my Muse."

"That is why I've come to prepare you," says Kabir. "The decision should not be made lightly. The service of an Artifex gives great power to his Muse, and the bond between you will endure until the Muse's great work is complete. Depending on the work, you may be called to serve her for years. Even centuries."

Centuries? thinks Ava. *What work could possibly require centuries?*

It's equally difficult for me to imagine a work of centuries, but I have more immediate concerns. "How soon do I need to make this choice?" I say.

"You must wait until your initiation to choose your Muse," he says. "The Voice grants the gift of insight to initiates, which should help you make your selection with confidence. Your teachers in the house of novices will decide together when you are suitably prepared for initiation into the higher mysteries. For most novices, the call to initiation comes by the twenty-seventh summer." My relief must be evident, because Kabir adds, "Ten years may seem an eternity, from where you stand. But time is fleeting. Use it well. The choices you make shape the future of our world and all that live within it."

Kabir's words settle on me like a great weight. Not long ago, I would have considered such responsibility a great honor; I never would have dared to hope for initiation into the higher mysteries. Now, a single moon after my calling to the path of mysteries, I'm filled with doubt. How can I serve the Mohirai, knowing all they do to manipulate the people of Dulai?

You don't have any other choice but to serve them for now, thinks Ava. *Better just keep your eyes open and your mouth shut. We'll find a way out of this. Together, remember?*

Together, I think.

Kabir leans forward and presses my knee. "I see you are a serious young man, Dom. And, indeed, there is a serious task before you. But there's no need to carry it all so heavily just yet. The years that follow initiation can be long and lonely. You'd do well to fill your time in the house of novices with as much joy—and as many beautiful women—as you can manage," he says with a wink.

I can't bring myself to match Kabir's playful tone, so I incline my head respectfully. "I have listened and I have heard, brother."

The second bell tolls. "The Muses call," says Kabir, rising from his seat. "Come, I'll take you to the house of novices."

THE HOUSE OF NOVICES

Kabir and I exit the stables and make the short walk east to the central stairs of the temple city. Every window, doorway, and alley we pass along the way is empty. The street is silent except for the sound of our footsteps on the cobblestones, an occasional bird call from the gardens, and that peculiar creaking somewhere in the distance.

"What's that sound?" I say.

"The water wheels of the Outer City," says Kabir, stepping out onto the circular plaza where the street to the stables intersects the broad central stairs. He points south, toward one of the blue tiled roofs in the line of stone buildings on the street below us. There's a great wooden paddle wheel mounted to the side of that building. The wheel gleams wet in the morning sun as it turns, paddles dripping as they slowly rise and fall. Similar wheels are scattered throughout the Outer City streets below us.

"What do the water wheels do?" I say.

"Oh, all kinds of things," he says, turning north to cross the plaza. We pass by the splashing fountain at the center of the plaza, with its four figures pouring streams of water into the clear pool at their feet. Sulfurous steam rises off the surface of the water. Kabir says, "Originally, Muse Noa built the water wheels to drive the carts through the Under City without oxen, which made it much easier to carry materials from outside the city walls up to the workshops in the Outer City. But the initiates of the house of tekhnologia are always finding new uses for the water wheels. Now they power tools in the workshops, grind grain in the kitchens, even drive bellows in the forges."

Kabir stops before the second gate, at the center of the high stone wall that encloses the Over City. The wall is formidable—taller than the one surrounding the Outer City and topped by crenellations—and its gate is astonishingly beautiful. The two closed doors contain four inset panels of intricate relief metalwork painted in bright colors. The top panel of the left door depicts a tiny red-cloaked figure walking through an expansive forested valley blanketed in what appears to be deep winter snow. The top panel of the right door shows a bent figure in the foreground sowing seed at the base of a steep mountain while another smaller figure in the background drives an ox and cart toward the upper slope. The bottom panel of the right door shows three shrouded figures holding hands in a ring, surrounded by a dense tangle of plants and fungi rendered in striking detail.

My gaze lingers on the fourth panel at the bottom of the left door. It's more abstract and harder to decipher than the others. Four stylized trees stand in a line, their dark leafless branches silhouetted against a bright background, which at first appears to be a sunset sky painted in liquid swirls of orange, gold, and crimson, fading to smoky grey at the edges. I take a step closer to the door, examining the detail on this fourth panel until I realize with a start that this is no sunset. The swirls of color are tongues of flame—a great fire surrounding the trees. Worked into the relief texture of the trees' trunks are four vaguely human faces, eyes closed and mouths open in silent screams. I step back quickly from the unsettling image.

"Are you all right, Dom?" says Kabir. "You look pale."

"What do these pictures mean?" I say.

He glances at the panels. "Ah," he says. "You'll see many doors like these dividing the Outer City from the Over City. Each set of doors represents part of the temple city historia. Muse Clio and other initiates of the house of historia can tell you a great deal more about the gates, if you have an interest in such things."

Kabir steps up to the side of the gate and pulls a delicate chain that passes through a gap in the stone wall. A high-pitched bell rings somewhere on the other side of the wall. Kabir waits a moment, then steps back and calls up toward the top of the wall, "Py? Are you there?"

After a long pause, a young woman wearing a broad-brimmed hat and a dark green robe appears at the top of the wall. She waves at us and calls down, "Sorry! Stepped away to feed the dogs. I'll be right down."

A moment later, there's a faint jingle behind the gate. One of the massive doors swings slowly inward. Py steps out through the gap with a large keyring in her hand, followed by three large, fluffy white dogs. They look more like small bears than the lean wolves I've been traveling with for the past half moon. Kabir drops to his knees to greet the dogs, who smother him with licks and nuzzles before turning to me and sniffing my hands and legs with interest. At a command from Py, the three dogs settle at her feet.

"It's been too long, Kabir," says Py, embracing him affectionately. She turns to me with a smile. "Welcome, sister Ava. And welcome, Dom. I must say, little brother, you've been the talk of Velkanos since we received word of your calling. You're the most exciting thing to happen here in a century at least."

"Impossible!" says Kabir. "I was here less than five summers ago for the harvest festival."

Py chuckles. "You've had your time to play the temple darling, Kabir," she says. "The Voice calls you now to serve as elder Artifex. Will you answer?"

Kabir presses his hand to his heart. "Have I ever done anything but render perfect service to the Voice?" he says. His tone is serious, but his eyes flash with mischief.

"Mmm," says Py, pursing her lips. She looks at me and says, "Let's hope Kabir sets as good an example for you as Tio set for him." She makes a hand signal at the dogs, who rise as one and slip back in through the gate. "Come in, then," she says, gesturing to us. "The bell for the morning meal will ring any moment now."

We follow Py through the gate, which opens onto another circular plaza like the one outside the gate, although the four figures standing in this plaza's fountain have their own unique postures and faces. At the far side of the plaza, the central staircase continues its climb through the Over City toward the steeper upper slopes of Velkanos. Intersecting the plaza, running east to west, is a level cobblestone street lined with elegant stone buildings similar to the ones in the Outer City.

The low, sweet note of a bell fills the plaza. The sound is nearly identical to the one that summoned me to meals every day for the last eight years. I turn toward the sound, half expecting to see the stout figure of Hedi Mohira, keeper of the house of boys, ringing the meal bell with her long wooden clapper. Instead, a short distance down the street, a slim woman wearing a sky blue robe and a stole of many colors stands in a high, arching doorway pulling a chain that rings the bell above the door.

A moment later, the doors of several nearby buildings open. Dozens of priestesses wearing robes of many colors—some in familiar shades of sky blue, spring green, and inky black, others in less familiar shades of scarlet, saffron, and purple—spill out onto the street and converge on the arching doorway. They exchange friendly greetings with the slim woman ringing the bell as they pass through the door.

Kabir waits until the last of the priestesses disappear inside the building before he leads me across the plaza. The woman below the bell stands waiting for us.

"Sister Zia," Kabir calls out as we approach. "I come bearing gifts."

"Welcome home, Kabir," says Zia, beaming. "Welcome, sister Ava. And, oh, sweet Dom, how you've grown! What a pleasure it is to see you again. Welcome to the house of novices."

Zia's voice is so warm and her face is so kind that I find myself smiling back at her automatically, though I'm confused by her words. I'm almost certain I've never seen this Mohira before. I scan my memories of all my years at the house of boys. Was she perhaps one of the priestesses who visited the Children's Temple from time to time? She wears a healer's robe, and there were often visiting healers there when I was a boy.

It's possible, thinks Ava. *But it's also possible she attended your birth, or knew you in the villages where the younger children are raised before their unbindings.*

Ava's thought carries with it her usual anger toward the Mohirai, which stirs my own new distrust of them. My jaw tightens, though I manage to say, "Thank you, sister."

Zia gestures for me to follow her through the door. I'm almost across the threshold when I realize that Kabir has remained behind on the street. I turn back to face him, my pulse speeding up at the thought of facing all the women inside the house of novices alone.

Not entirely alone, Ava thinks indignantly.

You know what I mean, I think.

"Don't look so forlorn, Dom," says Kabir. He settles a hand on my shoulder and looks directly into my eyes. "I know it's a difficult thing at first, but you will find your place among the Mohirai in time. The Voice has called you as Artifex for a reason. Trust yourself. Or, if not yourself, then trust the Voice inside of you."

“Where will you go?” I say.

“I have work that requires my attention in the Outer City workshops. But come to my quarters again tomorrow morning, and we’ll continue our conversation. I’ll want to hear all about your first day in the house of novices.”

We clasp wrists. Kabir departs. Zia gestures for me to follow her, and I enter the house of novices.

The entryway is astonishing in its grandeur. A circular domed ceiling soars high above me, inlaid with an elaborate mosaic of tiny tiles in deep blue, purple, charcoal, and pure black. Small holes scattered across the dome admit pinpoints of daylight from outside, creating a marvelous illusion of the night sky overhead, with many summer constellations I recognize. Large spheres of colored glass hover over me like a gathering of many moons, suspended from the ceiling by delicate silver chains.

Three hallways split off from the entryway, and Zia leads me down the hall directly ahead, pointing out the various corridors that branch off the hall as we pass by them. Each corridor is marked by a distinctive wall hanging or floor mosaic, most containing some writing, though I can’t read any of it. Zia says, “That one goes to the novice sleeping quarters, and the one beside it leads to the bathing rooms. Here’s the way to the stairs down to the Under City tunnels. You shouldn’t go in there without a guide until you’re more familiar with the tunnels —they’re useful in bad weather, but most of the novices prefer to use the streets above until they know their way around. Even I get turned around down there from time to time. Now, over there …”

My head swims as Zia continues her tour, pointing out various storerooms, a laundry room, doors to the street outside, doors I may enter, doors I must not enter without a Mohira.

There’s no way I’ll remember all this, I think.

Don’t worry, thinks Ava. *I know my way around pretty well. I can also read the signs for you.*

The hallway leads us to a sunlit inner courtyard full of greenery. A white stone fountain stands at its center, with four faces arranged at the top of a round column. Water pours through the pursed lips of the stone faces into a large circular pool. Waist-high stone garden beds form a kind of maze through the courtyard, each bed overflowing with herbs, vegetables, and flowers that grow only in the warm months of spring and summer. I run my hand over a bed full of sweet basil, leaning down to inhale the scent.

“This is one of our kitchen gardens,” says Zia. “There are many others, indoors as well as outside along the crop terraces. You’re welcome to enter the kitchen gardens at any time, but you must be accompanied by an initiate to enter any of the walled gardens in the Over City where the ingredients of the pharmaka are tended. You must be careful not to—”

I try to pay attention to all Zia’s instructions, but I’m momentarily distracted when I glance up. I’d expected to see the open sky above this sunlit courtyard, but the sunlight filters through a watery translucence held up by an open latticework, almost like an enormous spider's web.

"What's that?" I say, inadvertently interrupting Zia.

"Ah, the glass roof," she says. "The glass lets in the sunlight and holds in its warmth, so we can garden all through the winter. Glassworking is one of the arts practiced by initiates of the house of tekhnologia. You can talk to Muse Noa if you're interested in glasswork."

Zia ushers me across the courtyard, toward another arching doorway with two wide doors that stand open. The sound of many women speaking at once spills out through the doors into the courtyard. My stomach churns anxiously as we approach.

I follow Zia through the doors into a great meal hall. Long tables set with empty plates, bowls, and cups fill the room from end to end. Novices in undyed cloth occupy the benches at most of the long tables. One table at the far end of the meal hall seems reserved for the initiates in their many-colored robes, who sit in high-backed chairs. The heavy wooden benches scrape along the stone floor as novices take their seats.

The girls in the Children's Temple were only ever allowed outside the walls in small groups with a Mohira in attendance, so I've never seen so many women gathered all in one place. I might have hoped that traveling in the company of twelve women over the past moon would have prepared me for this moment, but the sight of all these women is still very intimidating. My anxiety intensifies as the novices at the nearest table catch sight of me. A murmur spreads through the room, and faces turn my way one by one until all eyes in the meal hall are upon me. The room falls silent apart from whispers. My heart pounds in my ears. I ball my trembling hands into fists, which only makes them shake harder.

You don't need to be afraid of them, Ava thinks.

Easy for you to say, I think.

Zia settles her hand on my shoulder. "Good morning, sisters," she calls out in a clear voice.

"Good morning, sister Zia," many voices reply in a practiced sing-song that fills the hall.

"Today we welcome our newest novice, Dom Artifex."

"Welcome, brother," many voices reply, before the whispering resumes.

"Yes, welcome, Dom," a familiar, musical voice says behind me. I turn to see Muse Thalia, who has just stepped into the meal hall in the company of two other Mohirai wearing bright initiate robes. The other two priestesses pass by me, but Thalia pauses at my side. In an undertone she says, "I hope you'll remember my offer. Should you require any instruction as you find your way in the house of novices, my door is always open to you. I live in the house of poetika adjoining the house of novices. You can be sure of my discretion."

I swallow nervously. Thalia gives me a wink and continues on her way.

Well, maybe you do need to be afraid of some of them, thinks Ava.

One of the novices in the sea of women before me waves from a nearby table. I've never been so glad to see Eumelia, who sits beside Hanu at a table filled with the other six girls from our caravan. Eumelia gestures for me to join them, and Zia nods at me to go ahead. Eumelia and Hanu make space on their bench. I slip into the seat beside Eumelia, grateful to be shielded somewhat from the eyes of all these strangers, surrounded by familiar faces once more.

"Please join me in the words of gratitude for the meal set before us," Zia continues. Around the room, novices join hands around their tables. All together, we say the meal blessing.

We give our thanks for gifts of sun
Of water, soil, and seed
For gifts of many seasons
Gathered here to meet our need
To build our strength so that our hands
May in their time return
The gifts received from mother land
Improved with gifts our own

There's a brief moment of silence before a chatter of voices fills the air. Despite the alarming number of women here, there's something comfortingly familiar about the sounds, aromas, and rituals of the meal hall. When a Mohira in blue robes deposits a large copper tureen at the center of our table, I recognize the very same porridge that Hedi usually served the boys at the morning meal. Kor stands up near the center of our table to fill everyone's wooden bowls with porridge, and the nine of us dig in with good appetites.

I've managed to swallow no more than three bites of food before someone taps my shoulder. I turn around. A pair of Mohirai in initiate robes look down at me with eager expressions. A line of other initiate priestesses gathers behind them.

"Welcome, Dom," says the first Mohira, a woman with a dark complexion and striking dress. Long black lashes and golden painted lines accentuate her large, almond-shaped eyes. A small ruby ringed by five golden petals glitters between her arching brows. Her robes of crimson silk are draped in a bewildering complexity of folds that float around her petite figure. She wears a great deal of golden jewelry: a fine ring in one nostril, rings and studs in her ears, bangles around her wrists and ankles. Only the delicate fingers of her folded brown hands are unadorned. "I'm Aisa, initiate of the house of weavers. I look forward to presenting my gift to you at the harvest festival, young Artifex." The bangles on her wrists tinkle as she takes my hand and presses it to her lips. My pulse speeds up a bit.

I have difficulty tearing my eyes off of Aisa, but courtesy requires it when the second Mohira steps forward. She wears plain blue robes and a kindly expression. "I'm Irini," she says, pressing her two plump hands around mine. "I look forward to making your acquaintance when you attend us in the house of healers, little brother."

There's no time to respond to Aisa or Irini before the next Mohira presents herself, and the next, and the next. There's also no hope of remembering the names of all these new priestesses, or of finishing my meal, because as soon as the first wave of initiates subsides, the older novices arrive to introduce themselves. I recognize the faces of a few of them—girls I'd seen occasionally outside the walls of the Children's Temple when I was a boy—but most of them are strangers to me.

The contrast between these women's keen interest in me and my experience in the house of boys couldn't be greater. No girl at the Children's Temple besides Ava ever showed the least interest in me, much less introduced herself. And besides Hedi, the Mohirai at the Children's Temple rarely paid any attention to boys. Most of the priestesses probably didn't even know our names.

Ava's irritation mounts as woman after woman steps up to my side, often touching my arm or hand or cheek in passing as they greet me. *What a bunch of ninnies,* she thinks. I suppress an impulse to roll my eyes, although I'm pretty sure that's Ava's impulse, not my own. When the next eager novice steps up, Ava's words slip out of my mouth before I can stop them. In a voice dripping with disdain, I say, "What's the matter with you? Never seen a man before?"

Ava! I think, horrified.

Sorry, she thinks. *I couldn't help it.*

The novice's expression turns angry, and she departs in a hurry. Embarrassed, I call after her, "Please, I didn't mean to—" But she's out of earshot before I can finish. Eumelia bursts out laughing. Overwhelmed by the need to explain myself, I turn to Eumelia and say, "That wasn't me! It was—"

"Oh, there's no mistaking Ava's voice," says Eumelia, still laughing. "Didn't I tell you she'd get you into trouble?"

"Shut up, Eumelia," Ava says through me.

I clap my hand over my mouth to stop Ava from saying more. I'm about to apologize to Eumelia, but she says, "Take a look around, Ava. There's no way you can keep Dom all to yourself here. Even if he weren't an Artifex, and even if he weren't so good-looking, no man could avoid attention in a house full of women who are about to be locked up in the city all winter."

I blush. Hanu leans over and says gently, "Eumelia's not trying to embarrass you, Dom. She just doesn't think before she speaks."

Eumelia opens her mouth to protest, closes it, then says, "You know, she's right."

The three of us laugh. Hanu's smile is warm and inviting as she meets my eyes. It's a look I saw many times as I held her in my arms back in our days in the Children's Temple. A series of intimate memories of her flashes through my mind, and my cheeks grow warm again. *Please don't say anything,* I think, briefly covering my eyes with my hand. Ava's amusement ripples through me, but somehow she resists teasing me.

Hanu's expression turns puzzled. "What's wrong, Dom?" she says.

I clear my throat, scrambling to think of something to change the subject. "I … was just thinking that I'm not the only man in the city, you know? Balashi's here too."

Hanu's brow furrows. "I don't understand why, though," she says. "I thought no men were allowed in the temple city, apart from the Artifexi."

"He's been called to attend Tio," I say. "But he's only allowed inside the walls because all his memories of his time here are going to be unbound afterwards."

"Spirits, does Balashi know that?" says Eumelia. I nod. She shakes her head sympathetically. "That must be why he was acting so strange when we saw him on the road."

"Have you seen Bala since we entered the city?" Hanu asks me. "How is he doing?"

"Not good," I say.

Hanu's expression turns thoughtful. She says, "Do you know where he spends the day?"

"I think he's attending Tio somewhere in the Outer City workshops," I say.

"And where does he sleep at night?" she says.

"In the stable quarters, same as me," I say. "He's sharing a room with Tio."

"Hmm, that may be problematic for you," Eumelia says wryly, nudging Hanu with her elbow. "Unless you fancy spending a night with the gloomy old man, too?"

Hanu doesn't dignify Eumelia's teasing with a response.

A bell tinkles over the chatter of voices, marking the end of the meal. Zia stands at the near door, ringing a silver bell by a long chain. When the room quiets, she says, "Any novices needing new assignments, please stay for the call to attendance. The rest of you may depart."

Hanu, Eumelia, and I rise with the rest of the novices at our table, gathering up our dishes and joining the long line of women headed toward the swinging double doors at the back of the meal hall. I stuff a few more spoonfuls of porridge into my mouth as we walk; with all the interruptions, I've barely managed to eat half my portion.

I step through the doors into an enormous kitchen, where novices and initiates stack their used dishes onto freestanding wooden shelves at one end of a long stone wash basin. A noisy crew of six novices stands scrubbing dirty dishes with brushes under the faucets of steaming water and transferring them to the shelves of clean dishes standing at the other end of the basin. Beyond the wash basin, at the center of the kitchen, stands a large clay oven that fills the air with heat and the delicious smell of baking bread. Two Mohirai in blue robes tend to the oven, slapping rounds of dough onto the hot inner wall of the oven and removing golden flat bread, which they stack into baskets on the floor. A small dog with a wiry brown coat supervises the work with keen eyes, patrolling the kitchen perimeter, sniffing at ankles, devouring stray crumbs, and accepting an occasional treat from the bakers.

We file back out into the cooler air of the meal hall. Zia stands with Muse Thalia at the head of a long table near the door. She waves toward the novices from my caravan to gather near her. The nine of us, along with nine older novices who need new assignments, take seats around the long table.

Looking up at Zia, I notice for the first time that the bright woven pattern of the long stole draped around her shoulders bears a strong resemblance to the sash the High Priestess wore for most of the journey to Velkanos.

I wonder if she speaks to the other priestesses using that stole, thinks Ava. *Eumelia said the Mohirai weave with pharmaka, remember?*

How could I forget? I think. The free men stripped me naked the night they took me and Ava captive, presumably out of concern that the Mohirai could track us through the silver threads woven into the ceremonial clothes I'd been wearing.

Zia runs the end of her colorful stole lightly through her fingers. She addresses a tall novice with a face that would be lovely were it not marred by a sour expression. "Laima, your trio will attend the sisters overseeing the wheat harvest. Meet Hippolyta in the stables first. You'll help her load supplies into an oxcart to drive to the fields, and she'll accompany you outside the city."

Laima inclines her head and rises from her seat, accompanied by two other novices. They depart by a door in the south wall of the meal hall, opposite the door through which I entered.

That door leads to the underground tunnel between the house of novices and the stables, thinks Ava. *I've been in that passageway before.*

When? I think.

Years ago, the night of the harvest festival, she thinks. *Lilith and I stole some pharmaka from the storehouses in the house of healers in the Over City. We escaped through the underground tunnels.*

Ava's memory of the dark caverns and tunnels beneath the city flashes through my mind, giving me an idea. Clearly Hanu would like to find a way to see Balashi, and I know that would mean a lot to him. *Do you think Hanu could meet me and Balashi in the stables during the evening silence if she came down through the tunnels?* I think.

Ava's resistance halts my thoughts abruptly, like a rock jamming a wheel. *That's not a good idea,* she thinks. *Novices have to be in their quarters during the evening silence, and the Mohirai lock the doors to the Over City when the silence begins, including the doors to the tunnels.*

But you can show us how to pick locks, can't you? I think.

Patiently, Ava thinks, *Even if I helped you pick the locks, Hanu doesn't know the first thing about sneaking around in dark places. She'll end up in trouble with the Mohirai if she's caught. Or worse, she could get lost or hurt down there. The tunnels are far more extensive than you're imagining.*

I could go with her, then, I think, wheedling. *She wouldn't get lost if you showed us the way. And it would mean a lot to Balashi.*

Why would you risk so much just to give Balashi a little time with Hanu? thinks Ava. *He's not going to remember any of it in the end.*

Ava's thought recalls Balashi's bitter words last night. *Any attention at all is wasted on me until after my unbinding.* Angrily, I think, *He doesn't deserve to be simply forgotten, like nothing that happens to him matters.*

I didn't say that, Ava thinks. *No one deserves to be treated like their life doesn't matter. But getting in trouble with the Mohirai isn't going to help you or Balashi.*

I thought if anyone would be willing to break the rules, it would be you, I think.

Exasperated, Ava thinks, *Look where breaking the rules has gotten me, Dom.*

Ava's pointed words subdue my anger, replacing it with my guilt over all the ways that Ava has paid for my mistakes over the last moon.

I'm sorry, I think. *I just wish there was something we could do to help him, you know?*

I wish we could help, she thinks. *But we need to be careful. We've had more than enough accidents already for one moon.*

"Gula," says Zia, interrupting our inner dialog. A small, energetic novice perks up in her seat. "You and your trio will attend Muse Serapen in the house of healers." Gula's trio rises. As they pass by me on their way out the north door, I catch a pungent whiff of pharmaka from a leather satchel Gula's carrying.

Zia sends the last trio of older novices into the kitchens to assist the bakers before she turns to address the nine of us who remain.

"As the youngest of the novices, you'll be working together for most of the next year in the temple city, visiting the Muses of each house to receive your basic instruction in the arts. This moon, you'll attend Muse Clio in the library of the Musaion, where you'll learn a great deal of our historia. Muse Thalia will show you the way up."

THE OVER CITY

THE NINE OF US FOLLOW THALIA to the street outside the house of novices. "It's quite a climb to the Musaion," she says, leading us toward the central staircase. "Almost all the way to the top of the Over City."

I take a few quick steps after Thalia up the staircase before realizing I need to pace myself. These stairs aren't broad, shallow, and smooth like the Outer City stairs, which we navigated easily on horseback when we entered the city yesterday. The Over City portion of the staircase is hewn roughly into the bedrock, and the stairs steepen dramatically as they ascend the mountain.

I walk between Hanu and Eumelia at the start of the climb, but we fall into single file as the stairs narrow. I measure our progress by counting intersections with the cross streets. The plazas in the Over City are more compact than the ones in the Outer City, and the design of the fountains becomes simpler the higher we go. As we approach the ninth intersection above the Over City gate, I see that the staircase ends at a simple stone terrace just ahead, up a final flight of steep steps. I'm eager to reach the top—the view must be incredible from that terrace—but Thalia turns west at the ninth intersection instead. We walk down a short, narrow cobblestone street that leads to a single enormous stone building that appears to have been carved directly out of the mountain. Inscribed over the columns of the entrance are tall letters. I can't read the words, but Ava reads them for me: *Musaion of Velkanos*.

A short flight of stairs crafted from pale tawny stone leads us from the street to the entrance of the Musaion. We pass between the grand columns and enter through high double doors carved from solid planks of cedar.

The entrance hall of the Musaion is illuminated by morning light that filters through cream-colored screens in the south-facing windows. The smooth floors are covered in an intricate mosaic; the repeating pattern reminds me of the swirling blue designs painted on Arkhi's hands. Freestanding columns carved from many colorful varieties of stone give me the impression that I'm standing in a forest of strange, symmetrical trees. The columns hold up a high vaulted ceiling decorated with scenes of women and men in robes.

A Mohira approaches us at an unhurried pace from the far side of the hall, striding barefoot across the floor mosaic. She wears a robe of pale sea green and carries a pair of leather satchels on her stooped shoulders. Her high brow and coils of white hair piled atop her head lend her a dignified air. When she draws near, I notice inky smudges on her wrists and sleeves. Her satchels clatter slightly on the floor as she sets them down.

"Greetings, Muse Clio," says Thalia.

"A rare pleasure, little sister," Clio says dryly.

"Oh, sister." Thalia's eyes twinkle with mischief. "You know well that the library is a dull place for one called to music."

"Every path a mystery," says Clio. "I find my own music in these quiet halls." In the Muse's inward smile, I glimpse a rare kind of beauty: the glow of one who possesses deep wisdom.

Quite a contrast with Thalia, thinks Ava. She's right, but I see no reason to encourage her antipathy toward Thalia. The last thing I need today is more of Ava's sharp words slipping out of my mouth.

Sizing up the nine of us with large, observant eyes, Clio says to Thalia, "I'm pleased to receive new attendants at last. You'd think the library would have the pick of the novices, but the Muses of the other houses always seem able to persuade Serapen of their greater need these days."

"I'm sure the High Priestess means no disrespect to you, sister," says Thalia.

"Of course she means no disrespect!" Clio seems shocked by the mere suggestion. "Serapen spent more time in my halls than almost anywhere else in the temple when she was a novice. I once thought she might be called to the house of historia. Of course in the end her path tended toward the house of healing, and we may all thank the Voice for that. No, all I meant to say was that we're not so rich in novices as we were in the time before the destruction."

Thalia introduces the nine of us novices to Muse Clio. When Thalia comes to me, Clio's large eyes lock on mine. I feel as though she's reading me like a book, examining each page with care before moving on to the next. After a long silence, she nods thoughtfully and says, "Greetings, sister Ava. Welcome, Dom Artifex. You two have shared quite an unusual journey to the house of novices, from what Serapen has told me. I've witnessed a great deal in my time, and still the Voice finds ways to surprise me.

"But perhaps I should have expected a surprise as soon as we learned of your calling, Dom. The arrival of each new Artifex has marked the start of a new chapter in our historia ever since the time of destruction. I look forward to learning what part you've come to play."

Heat rises to my ears in the long silence that follows Muse Clio's words. I'm uncertain how to answer Clio, but she breaks the awkward silence by saying briskly, "Now, little brother, I would be most obliged if you would help me with my burden. I'm not as young as I was in past millennia." She points toward the pair of satchels at her feet. I step forward to lift them and sling them over my shoulders. They're even heavier than they look. No wonder the Muse's shoulders are so stooped.

Clio gestures for the nine of us to follow her. She and Thalia walk together toward the wall opposite the entrance. There stand four wooden doors framed by four stone archways, each with a single face carved into the keystone of the arch. The four faces bear a resemblance to the four figures I've seen in the plaza fountains along the central stairs. The three doors on the left are closed. The fourth door on the right stands open.

Clio leads us through the open door. The natural light of the entrance hall penetrates only a short distance beyond the door, but a line of oil lamps hanging from the ceiling illuminates the long windowless corridor ahead. The smooth stone walls of the corridor appear to have been carved directly through the bedrock of the mountain.

We've walked only a short distance when this corridor intersects another on the right. Thalia stops at the intersection and says to Clio, "Farewell, sister. I have business to attend in the High Priestess' quarters." She turns back to face us and adds in her bright voice, "Farewell, novices, until we meet again."

Thalia disappears down the corridor on our right, while the rest of us follow Clio straight ahead. We pass several more intersections with other corridors before we emerge into a windowless hall with soaring ceilings. Large oil lamps suspended by long chains cast a dim light—enough to reveal the vastness of the space, but not enough to show the far walls to the left or right of us, which makes the hall's full size impossible to guess. Rough stone columns rise to the ceiling at regular intervals. Long, narrow tapestries hang from the columns, each depicting a single large symbol. *Those are numbers,* thinks Ava, as my eyes travel from one column to the next. *One, two, three. See?*

The space between each of the numbered columns is evenly divided into long rows by tall wooden shelves about twice the height of a woman. Narrow gaps between the shelves create shortcuts between the long rows.

Ladders scattered throughout the room give access to the upper shelves. The shelves themselves are crowded with boxes in all shapes and sizes, each bearing a label. There seems to be little consistency in the manner of labeling. I see labels of cloth, leather, wood, clay, copper, and other materials I don't recognize. Down the long row of shelves directly in front of us, I can just make out an arching doorway that frames another closed door on the wall across from us.

Spirits, how deep do all these tunnels go into the mountain? I think.

Very deep, thinks Ava. *Lilith told me that the Under City of Velkanos is more extensive than the Over City and the Outer City combined. From the little bit I've seen, I can believe it.*

Have you been up here in the library before, too? I think.

Lilith never took me this high up in the Under City, Ava thinks. *Our jobs were usually in the tunnels below the house of healing, since most of the pharmaka storerooms are there.*

Clio leads us down a row of shelves toward the center of the hall. We emerge in an open space between the shelves edged by long, low wooden tables. In the center of the open space stands an unhitched oxcart full of wooden crates, with one straw-filled crate open at the back of the cart.

Clio says, "This shipment arrived a half moon ago from the Musaion at Kebny. I've had scarcely a moment to unpack it, with all the interruptions of my days. But this will be an excellent opportunity to test your reading and writing skills, because cataloging requires both. You can set those down here, Dom." Clio gestures for me to set the two heavy satchels on a nearby table. "Now you—Narua, isn't it? You're the senior-most of these novices? Good. Let's see what you remember of your instruction in the Children's Temple."

Clio opens one of the satchels. It's full of wooden cylinders, each with a wooden cap lettered in a delicate hand. Clio hands one of the cylinders to Narua and says, "Can you read that for me?"

Narua takes the cylinder from Clio and examines the cap. "Geographia," she says.

Clio nods. "Very good. And could you read me a bit from the scroll you have there?"

Narua pries the lettered cap from the end of the wooden cylinder and withdraws a tightly-rolled scroll of parchment. She unrolls about a handspan of the parchment and reads, "Geographia Catalog. Velkanos Musaion Library. Section One. Row One. Column One. Shelf One. Item One. Geographia of the Kingdoms of the Middle Sea Coast, by—"

Clio waves her hand and says, "That will do. And what have you learned about geographia from your teachers? How would you define it for yourself?"

Narua thinks for a moment, then says, "Geographia is the art of observing and describing our mother land to help us understand how the land shapes the lives of the creatures within it."

"A poetic way to put it, little sister. Very good," says Clio. "And I assume the sisters at the Children's Temple instructed you in the organization and cataloging of materials?"

"Yes, Muse Clio," says Narua.

"Excellent. Then I would like your trio to identify, unpack, and catalog the new materials that have arrived for our geographia section. You'll find a labeled crate in the back of the cart there."

"I have listened and I have heard, sister," says Narua. She, Bel, and Tashlu head toward the oxcart.

"Now, you. You're called Kor, yes?" says Clio, handing Kor a second catalog scroll from the satchel. "How about this one?"

Kor opens the wooden cylinder and withdraws the scroll. She reads, "Historia Catalog. Velkanos Musaion Library. Section Two. Row One. Column One. Shelf One. Historia of—"

"Yes, yes, that'll do. And how would you define this word, historia?" says Clio, her eyes sparkling. Clearly the Muse takes great pleasure in the interrogation of novices.

"Historia is the art of remembering the past, isn't it?" says Kor, with a bit less confidence than Narua.

"It is indeed," says Clio. "Although we who practice the arts of historia like to say that what is past often lies ahead, as well."

Kor appears confused by this, but Clio continues on, saying, "Your trio will catalog the historia materials from this shipment. I believe you'll find those crates toward the back of the cart."

"I have listened and I have heard, sister," says Kor. She, Piroza, and Kishar head off to join Narua's trio, who are hoisting a heavy crate out of the cart.

"As for you two …" says Muse Clio, turning to Hanu and Eumelia. She taps her chin thoughtfully with one ink-stained finger. "It is unfortunate, to have a trio broken as yours has been. Novices work best in threes." She looks at me and says, "I'd ask you to stand in for Ava on this task, Dom, but until you've received instruction in reading, the work of cataloging would be impossible for you."

"That's true, Muse Clio," I say. "But maybe I could still be of some use. You see, Ava can read. She's been helping me, that way."

Clio's eyebrows rise, which makes her high forehead look even higher. "How fascinating," she says. "Could you show me? Let's have you try … this one." The Muse fishes out a third cylinder from her satchel and hands it to me.

I look down at the lettered cap, which conveys even less to me than a tangle of animal tracks in the sand. Ava thinks, *Khartographia.*

"Khartographia," I repeat, pronouncing the unfamiliar word cautiously.

"Yes, very good," says Clio. "And how about the scroll?"

I unroll a bit of the scroll and examine the first few lines, written in a tidy, compact hand. Ava reads, and I repeat, "Khartographia Catalog. Velkanos Musaion Library. Section One. Row Four. Column One. Shelf One. On the Arts of Wayfinding, by …"

Ava stops. *Sorry, I can't read that,* she thinks.

I look up at Clio. "I'm sorry, sister, but Ava doesn't know this word," I say.

Rather than looking disappointed, however, Clio appears pleased. "Never mind that. It's the author's name, written in characters from a language no longer spoken. You'll have instruction in ancient languages in later years.

"But how wonderful, for you to have such an advantage as this! Your early years in the house of novices will go much more smoothly this way. Teaching reading to the novice Artifexi has fallen to me, in the past. It's not easy, learning to read so late."

Muse Clio turns to Hanu and Eumelia. "Now, do either of you know the meaning of the word khartographia?"

Hanu shakes her head, but Eumelia says, "It's something to do with the art of mapmaking, isn't it? Creating maps to help navigate unfamiliar terrain?"

"Yes, very good. And you're Eumelia, right?" says Clio. "You will indeed find a great deal on the arts of mapmaking and navigation, along with maps of the many regions of Dulai, in the collection of khartographia materials."

Clio turns to Hanu and says, "Well, then. Hanu, is it? You're the eldest of your trio? I'll leave you in charge of cataloging the new khartographia materials with your sister and Dom here, then. Do you think you can manage?"

"Yes, Muse Clio," says Hanu.

"Very well. Should you have any questions for me, I'll be working on cataloging the new items for Section Four. Arkhitektonia. Do you know this word?"

"That's the art of building," says Hanu.

"Sounds simple enough, doesn't it?" says Clio. "And yet the building arts of arkhitektonia are a way of remembering our past, too, like the written arts of historia. You may discover the story of an entire people, long after the people themselves are gone, if you know how to read the buildings they've left behind.

What we build contains the memories of our lives and connects us to the land from which we come. That's why it's an important responsibility, to be the builder of any structure, however humble or magnificent it may be." The Muse directs this last statement at me, though I'm uncertain how or whether I'm supposed to respond. Briskly, she concludes, "But you novices have a great deal more to learn before you're prepared for such responsibilities. Onward, to the work of the day!"

△▽△

Dom, Hanu, and Eumelia set to work unloading a crate of khartographia materials. Hanu unpacks the dusty scrolls, tablets, and boxes from the crate and locates the label on each one. If there's no label, she creates a new one. Eumelia, who has neater handwriting than Hanu, writes a description of each new item in the catalog scroll.

Since Dom can't write, he carries the cataloged materials from the unloading area to the shelves. I help him read the shelf labels so he can locate the spot where each item belongs. He quickly learns to read the numeral markings on the stone columns separating the shelves, and he soon recognizes a few of the words we encounter frequently, but he relies on me to read the majority of what he sees. Unfortunately, even I can't read a great deal of the materials emerging from the crate of khartographia materials. These books, scrolls, and maps must have come from a time or a place where far more languages were spoken in Dulai than are spoken today.

As the morning progresses, many initiate priestesses visit the library, interrupting Muse Clio to ask for her help locating materials on a variety of subjects. Dom and I overhear their exchanges with Clio as we shelve the new khartographia materials. Clio often directs the initiates to different sections of the library—sections for philosophia, mathematika, astronomia, poetika, and many other arts. The library here apparently follows the same organization scheme as the Children's Temple library. I spent many days in that library during my eighth summer, playing with Eumelia and Hanu in those long rows of shelves. If this library's organization is indeed the same, there's a section I would very much like to visit, after Dom's work is done: the pharmaka section.

After delivering another manuscript on wayfinding to its new location in Section Four, Dom returns to the unloading area, where Hanu and Eumelia stand side by side, poring over an enormous map they've unrolled across a low table.

"I searched through the straw at the bottom of the crate, but I couldn't find one anywhere," says Hanu.

"We'll have to ask Muse Clio, then," says Eumelia.

"What's the matter?" says Dom, coming up behind them.

Hanu says, "The label attached to this map is missing, and I can't read the characters on the map title to write out a new label."

Dom peers down at the map, and I recognize a pattern of intersections that I've seen once before, when Lilith and I were preparing for a job years ago.

I know what that is, I think.

Oh? thinks Dom. *What?*

It's a map of— Oh spirits. Not again. As the memory of that job flashes through my mind, I feel myself torn from Dom. The library of the Musaion vanishes. For a brief moment, there's nothing but darkness. But, as has happened every time I've crossed a bridge, a light appears in the darkness.

I approach the light and emerge elsewhere.

I stand beside Emmie, who is dressed in her skin-tight immerger clothes. A large map hovers before her, translucent and faintly glowing. Other-Dom stands behind her, looking over her shoulder. Though the words on Emmie's map are illegible to me, the pattern of intersections depicted on it are the same as the map that Hanu, Eumelia, and Dom were studying back in the library. It's a map of the Under City of Velkanos. I suppose this map is what created the bridge between my branch and Emmie's this time.

Emmie and other-Dom argue in English as Emmie gestures at the map. I can't understand what they're saying, except when they occasionally use the words *Mohirai, Musaion,* and *pharmaka.* The argument grows heated but stops suddenly when Emmie clutches her chest and sways unsteadily on her feet. Other-Dom's hand flies out to grip her ungloved left hand, and Emmie regains her balance. After she catches her breath, Emmie and Dom continue speaking in voices that are calmer and more restrained. I clear my throat.

Emmie and Dom turn toward me. *Ava!* thinks Emmie, looking pleased to see me. *Where were you, before you were here?*

I was looking at this same map in the library at Velkanos, I think. *I was about to tell Dom what it is when I crossed over to this branch.*

You're inside the Musaion at Velkanos? she thinks eagerly.

Other-Dom shakes his head. *Don't, Emmie,* he thinks. *This needs to stop.*

Emmie ignores other-Dom and looks at me intently. *What branch are you from?* she thinks.

I look from Emmie to other-Dom uncertainly. I've never witnessed them arguing before. The tension between them is palpable, almost painful. Cautiously, I think, *I'm from The End of the Road.*

Emmie calls out the name of my branch as she sweeps her gloved right hand through the air. *Ah, there you are,* she thinks. A globe of Dulai appears hovering between the three of us. Emmie taps the globe, and a translucent panel of text appears hovering in the air beside the globe. Her brow furrows as she reads. *It says here that you've died twice on this branch,* she thinks. *That can't be right. Is that a mistake?*

Both times were accidents, I think. *But, no, it's not a mistake. I died twice. I'm still dead now.*

How strange, she thinks.

Other-Dom thinks, *Em, I don't think this is the time—*

Emmie raises her hand sharply, cutting off other-Dom's thought. To me, she thinks, *You've come at the perfect time. Dom and I have been trying to figure out a way to recover materials that were once stored in the Musaion of Velkanos. The*

Musaion has been lost on our branch for a long time, but you're right there! You could help us find the materials we need.

What materials? I think.

Other-Dom interjects his thought more forcefully, clearly frustrated. *I've tried in every way I can to help you see, Em—it's just not possible.*

Emmie turns to other-Dom with blazing eyes. *How can you just give up?* she thinks.

I haven't given up, thinks other-Dom, reaching out to touch Emmie's cheek. Through my bond with Emmie, I feel that touch on my own cheek. His tenderness sets butterflies loose in my stomach. *But I've had far more time than you to learn our pattern. You and I are bound to love each other and lose each other, always. It's the reason we're here.*

No, thinks Emmie. *The Voice can't be so cruel, to trap us in a single pattern on every branch, in every world. There must be something more than this.*

I've followed you life after life, branch after branch, my love, thinks other-Dom. *We've never found a cure for your overdose. Not once. You're wearing yourself out with this search for no reason. Why can't we just enjoy the time we have left together here, before the cycle starts over?*

Stubbornly, Emmie thinks, *We may not have found a cure yet, but we will. I know it. I can feel it. Please don't give up, Dom. I promised you we'd find our way out of this. Together.*

I recognize the look that other-Dom gives Emmie. It's the look I saw for the first time in my vision on Calling Day, the look of a man who has experienced more love and more loss than I can fathom.

All right, other-Dom thinks wearily. *All right.*

Thank you, thinks Emmie, her expression softening. *Now, will you tell Ava what you told me?*

Other-Dom sighs. He thinks, *Long ago, during my initiate training, I learned that Serapen and the other initiates of the house of healers kept detailed records of their experiments with the arts of pharmaka. The records stretched back all the way to the time of the destruction, to the time when the Voice called on the last generation to make the great sacrifice. Every unbinding performed by Serapen and the other healers since then was recorded, along with the healers' notes on the pharmaka they used and the effects they observed. Serapen was meticulous in the keeping of these records, but she kept this knowledge restricted to a very small circle of her healer initiates.*

Emmie jumps in, thinking, *If we could access those records, we might be able to reverse the effects of my binding pharmaka overdose. And once those records are stored in the alternet, they'll never be a secret again. On every branch where the alternet exists, Dom and I and anyone else who needs this knowledge will be able to find it.* Emmie looks at me with a pleading expression. *You've come from exactly the right place at exactly the right time to find those records, Ava. Will you help us?*

I look back and forth between Emmie and other-Dom. Whom should I believe? Other-Dom clearly has a great deal more experience than Emmie, and clearly he thinks this is a fool's errand. But Emmie's conviction is infectious. Like her, I want to believe that my fate lies in my own hands. Still, I'm wary of taking on a job I don't fully understand.

Where does Serapen keep these records? I think. *In the library?*

No, thinks other-Dom. *She kept them in another section of the Musaion, closer to her own quarters. I'm not sure exactly where. I never saw them. Only a select few of her healer initiates were ever allowed access to the records of these unbindings, because they contain the names of the mother and father of every child born in Dulai.*

The mother and father of every child born in Dulai? I'm stunned by the idea that this information might be knowable, and just within reach. I might have been willing to take on this job purely to help Emmie and other-Dom find a cure for her pharmaka overdose, but the prospect of exposing these secrets Serapen has been keeping about mothers and fathers puts an entirely different type of fire in me: a desire to understand what's been hidden from me, and from all the rest of the children of Dulai.

I'm under no illusion that stealing information from the Mohirai will be easy, though. In all my past jobs, Lilith planned out the work using her initiate knowledge of the Mohiran temples' inner workings. I know so little that I'm bound to make mistakes. However, if I've correctly understood what I've learned as I've traveled back and forth between Dulai and Earth, then any information I give to Emmie and other-Dom to store in their quantum computer will be accessible to any other-Avas visiting this branch, too. Surely some Ava, somewhere, on some branch will find the information we need and leave it in the alternet where the rest of us can find it. Surely one of us will figure out a way to break this cycle that other-Dom believes is unbreakable. And if one of us will surely do it, why shouldn't it be me?

Will you help us, Ava? thinks Emmie.

As soon as I hear Emmie's question, I know my decision is already made. Perhaps it was made long ago. I think, *What do we need to do?*

Emmie beams at me. *We need to start by building a bridge,* she thinks. *A way for you to get back here more reliably.*

How? I think.

Using one of your core memories, thinks Emmie. *I can add whatever memory you choose to our record of The End of the Road. I'll visit that memory here on my branch frequently, so there are many intersections between that memory and my branch. When you're back on your own branch, you can look for the materials we need in the Musaion. If you find something that seems useful, all you have to do is think of that core memory and allow yourself to cross the bridge back here. I'll be waiting for you. When you visit, we can record whatever you've found. Every time you come back, no matter which branch of mine you return to, we'll be able to keep building out the record together.*

How clever, I think, impressed.

Emmie grins. *It wasn't my idea,* she thinks. *It was yours. Well, an other-Ava's, anyway.*

Well, we're pretty clever, then, I think.

So … thinks Emmie, *What memory do you want to use for your bridge? It should be something you can visualize clearly. Something you can come back to easily.*

I know just the one, I think.

THE UNDER CITY

I STAND BEHIND HANU AND EUMELIA, peering down at the unlabeled map. It appears to show a tangled network of streets.

I know what that is, thinks Ava.

Oh? I think. *What?*

It's a map of—

Ava's awareness vanishes mid-thought. I straighten up, alarmed. *Ava?* I think. *Ava?*

"Dom?" Hanu looks at me, concerned. "What's wrong?"

"It's Ava," I say. "She just … disappeared."

"Probably got distracted and slipped off to another branch again," says Eumelia. "She has a knack for disappearing when it's inconvenient, doesn't she?"

My stomach twists nervously. Hanu touches my arm, sending a bit of her soothing energy through our connection. "I'm sure she'll come back soon, Dom. She always does."

My spiraling thoughts calm. Hanu's right. Ava always comes back. I guess I'd better get used to all her coming and going.

"I'm not sure how much help I'll be while Ava's gone. I won't know where to put these things away," I say, gesturing at the partially unpacked crate on the floor.

Hanu says, "Mel and I can take turns shelving things until Ava comes back. In the meantime, could you find Muse Clio and tell her we need help labeling this map?"

"All right," I say, heading off in the direction of Section Four.

I glance down each row of shelves I pass, looking for Muse Clio's distinctive head of white hair. Initiate Mohirai browsing the shelves occasionally give me curious looks, but none of them interrupt me.

I hear Muse Clio before I see her. She's speaking in a low voice to someone—probably another priestess looking for some obscure manuscript. I follow the sound of her voice toward the middle of Section Four. When I spot her, I'm surprised to see that she's talking not to another priestess, but to Balashi.

Muse Clio looks up at the sound of my approach. "Ah! How fortuitous. Dom, your trio brother Balashi just arrived with a message for you. Kabir Artifex requires your assistance down in the Outer City workshops. Do you think Hanu and Eumelia can spare you?"

"I think so," I say.

"I'll send you two off together, then," she says. "Do you know your way to the workshops?"

I shake my head, but Balashi says, "I'll show him the way, Muse Clio. I just came from there." His voice is a bit lower and slower than usual. His eyelids droop slightly. Spirits, he can't still be drunk from last night, can he?

"Very good," she says. If the Muse notices anything amiss with Balashi, she doesn't mention it.

Balashi gestures for me to follow him. We're on our way out of the row of shelves when Muse Clio calls out, "Oh, Dom, wait a moment. You must have come here for another reason. Did you need help with something?"

I'd completely forgotten. "Right. Yes. Hanu sent me to find you. She and Eumelia need help cataloging a map that came out of our crate. The label's fallen off, and they can't read the map to write out a new one."

Clio shakes her head, clucking her tongue in disapproval. "I'll have to send a message to my novice in Kebny who packed the crates. A nice girl, really, but she's going to have to learn to be more detail-oriented if she wants to join the initiates of my house. I'll take care of that, though, Dom. You go ahead."

I continue on after Balashi. We exit Section Four, walking in the direction of the corridor that leads back out to the entrance hall of the Musaion. But then he turns right.

"Wait," I say. "The corridor back to the entrance hall is over there."

"Kabir sent me up here through the underground tunnels," says Balashi. "We can go back down the same way."

"Don't we need a guide in the tunnels?" I say, remembering Zia's warning from this morning.

"Kabir gave me clear instructions, and I didn't have any trouble finding my way here," he says. "He said it's much easier than climbing all those stairs."

Remembering the tedious climb up through the Over City, I can appreciate the shortcut. If Balashi made it here without any trouble, and he's following Kabir's instructions, I suppose there's no reason to worry. "All right," I say. "Lead the way."

Balashi leads me to the closed door at the back of the library. He withdraws a silver key from his pocket and unlocks the door.

Surprised, I say, "Where did you get a key?"

"Kabir gave it to me," he says. He opens the door, which swings inward to reveal another lamplit corridor carved through stone.

I follow Balashi into the corridor. He waves me ahead so he can lock the door behind us. I take only a few steps before I stop, not wanting to get too far ahead of him. I've never liked underground spaces, and the dead silence of the corridor somehow makes it harder for me to breathe. The faint *snick* of the lock catching sends a prickle down my spine. How deep into the mountain do these tunnels go? *Very deep*, I remember Ava thinking.

"It's just ahead there," says Balashi. "First corridor on the right."

"You're sure?" I say nervously. There are an awful lot of corridors branching off from this one, and they all look identical to me.

"I'm sure," Balashi says bracingly, clapping me on the shoulder. "Come on, little brother."

Balashi stopped calling me that years ago, though I guess I am acting like a frightened little brother right now. I give Balashi a shove in the arm as he walks past me, and he laughs. I take a deep breath to calm myself before I continue following him.

Balashi makes a series of turns. He seems confident, but the farther we walk, the less certain I am that I could find my way back to where we started if we lost our way. I'm about to say that I want to turn back and take the long way down through the Over City when we emerge into a very large tunnel. It's wide, straight, and smooth, descending at a much gentler slope than the stairs I climbed this morning.

"Here's the main tunnel," says Balashi. "Goes straight down to the Outer City, see? Easy." The route ahead does look straightforward, although there are still many dark tunnels branching off of this one.

We continue walking. We've probably descended the distance of about three cross-streets when a question occurs to me. "What did Kabir need me for?" I say.

"He didn't tell me," says Balashi.

There's a long pause. Balashi was always the talkative one in our trio, so I'm unused to filling the silence. Awkwardly, I say, "How was your morning?"

"Fine," says Balashi.

After another long pause, I say, "Hanu asked about you, at the morning meal."

He glances at me. "Oh? What did she say?"

"That she'd like to see you," I say. "I was thinking maybe the two of you could meet in my quarters some time. If you wanted."

His expression brightens. "You'd do that for me?"

I roll my eyes. "Of course. How many times did I do it before, in the house of boys?"

Balashi laughs. "More than I did for you, I guess." His tone turns brooding, however, when he adds, "It's a wasted effort, though. I won't remember any of it afterwards, you know?"

"You can't let yourself think that way," I say. "Even if there's no way to change the future, why not just enjoy the time you have now, without worrying about what will happen afterwards?"

Balashi's handsome face twists into a sneer. "How could you possibly understand?" he says, his voice rising. "You have endless time, endless memories to look forward to."

His words sting. I have no answer except to say, "You're right. I don't understand. But I do want to help."

Balashi's harsh laugh echoes down the tunnel. "Do you want to help? Really? You know what I think? After a year or two as the priestesses' darling Artifex, you'll completely forget all your brothers outside these walls, just like the other Artifexi."

The cold silence that follows his words is made colder still by the cavernous silence of the empty tunnel. I realize now it's foolish to try to fill the silence. There's nothing I can say to make Balashi feel better.

We continue the long descent. It's difficult for me to tell how much time has passed, but at some point I can't help asking timidly, "Shouldn't we be there by now?"

"Just a little farther," says Balashi. The slow, dull tone that I attributed to wine has returned to his voice. I don't smell anything on him, though. Perhaps this new way of speaking is just another part of his dark mood.

A short distance ahead, bright lamplight spills into the main tunnel from one of the smaller side tunnels. "There," says Balashi, pointing. "That tunnel leads to the street of workshops in the Outer City."

I pick up my pace, eager to depart this gloomy tunnel and Balashi's even gloomier company. He picks up his pace to match mine. Side by side, we turn onto the well-lit side tunnel.

I stop dead in my tracks. Ahead of us, backlit by the oil lamps, stands a figure out of my darkest nightmares.

Lilith.

△▽△

Emmie and I quickly assemble the pieces of the core memory I'll use as my bridge between Dulai and Earth. It's a memory I've revisited often over the past half moon. The morning after my failed attempt to escape the caravan, as Dom and I lay together in our tent, I'd made him a promise.

I look at the scene Emmie and I have built together, rendered in exquisite detail inside the sphere of memory that hovers between us. I touch the sphere to examine it one last time. It expands around us until Emmie and I are inside the tent. Other-Dom stands just outside the tent flap, looking in at the two of us with the same worried expression he's been wearing since I arrived here. Emmie and I kneel on either side of Ava's avatar, who cradles Dom's avatar in her arms.

"I'm sorry," says Dom's avatar.

"Why?" says Ava's avatar.

"I couldn't let you go, but I know how much it hurts you to stay," he says.

She closes her eyes and strokes his hair to calm him. "Don't be sorry," she says. "I never meant to leave you like that. We're going to find our way out of here together. I promise."

They lie in stillness for a long time. Over the soft sounds of their breathing, the Voice in all drifts through the tent flap, forming words with the rush of the river and the warmth of sunlight through canvas and the rustle of the wind in the willow grove outside.

We are the bridge joining light to darkness.
We are the wheel turning season to season.
We are the threads binding realm to realm.
We are creator, preserver, destroyer of worlds.

Together you shall seek us, find us, know us.
Together you shall amplify us.
Together you shall weave us through the many worlds.

Together you shall answer our call.

The scene pauses, leaving the avatars frozen in their embrace. I'm not sure why the sight of them sends a shiver down my spine. Emmie looks at me from across the tent. *Is that how you remember it?* she thinks. I nod slowly. *Let's call that done, then,* she thinks, standing. She waves her hand, and my memory shrinks back into a sphere hovering between us.

I'd better get back to my branch, I think. *Dom will be worried.*

Emmie smiles knowingly, glancing back at other-Dom, who stands behind us. *Some things never change,* she thinks.

We smile at each other until a sharp hitch in Emmie's breathing reveals that the pain has returned. She presses her hand to her heart, grimacing. Other-Dom steps forward promptly to support her, wrapping one arm around her shoulders and gripping her ungloved hand in his.

That's enough for now, Em, he thinks. *Time for a break.*

Emmie slumps gratefully against other-Dom. The two of them look at me.

We're going to find a way out of all this, I think, looking from Emmie to other-Dom to the sphere of memory that hovers between us. *We're going to figure this out together.*

I know, thinks Emmie. *Now we just have to do it.*

I'll be back soon, I think.

I'll be waiting for you, she thinks.

Emmie waves her gloved hand. The sphere containing my memory of the tent on the Purattu vanishes. In its place appears another sphere containing my memory of the library in Velkanos: a bridge back to my branch. I reach out for the sphere, searching for the familiar pull of Dom's awareness in mine.

LILITH

THERE'S SOMETHING ALARMING about the pull of Dom's awareness as I follow it across the bridge back to my branch of Dulai. His usual calm has been shattered. When my awareness swirls back into his body, everything that's happening around him hits me at once.

Dom's not in the library, where I'd expected to find him. He's underground, in the chilly stillness of the Under City. This alone would trouble me, but it's not the dark tunnels that have disturbed Dom. It's the backlit silhouette of the enormous woman standing half a dozen paces ahead of him: Lilith.

There's no time for me to ask Dom's permission this time. Using our connection, I flood his body with every single instinct screaming through my mind.

Run! I think. And run he does, abandoning Balashi as he sprints back into the main tunnel, straight up the slope he just descended. He's fast on these long, strong legs of his. My old body could never run this fast. Even so, sprinting uphill isn't easy. I need to get him aboveground before he starts to slow down.

Ava, thinks Dom, breathing heavily. *Spirits, I'm glad you're back.*

What on Dulai are you doing down here? I think.

Dom's memory of what happened while I was gone flashes between us. I curse my own stupidity. Why didn't this occur to me last night, when Balashi came to Dom's room reeking of wine and pharmaka? I know better than anyone how easily Lilith can come and go through the secret tunnels beneath the city. It would have been trivially easy for her to find Balashi alone in his quarters and overpower him with pharmaka, then send him up to offer that same pharmaka to Dom.

Why would Lilith give Balashi pharmaka? thinks Dom, trying to keep up with my thoughts as I drive his feet faster and faster upslope, praying to every spirit that I'm remembering that map of the Under City tunnels correctly. Every step matters now.

She's probably been using it to control him, so she can get to you, I think. *That's why he's been acting so strangely.*

But what does she need me for? he thinks.

I don't have time to think about that right now. I'm anxiously scanning the markings over the side tunnels as Dom races past them. At this level of the Under City, closest to the surface, the tunnels mirror most of the city streets above. Dom doesn't have anything in his pockets that I could use to pick locks, so I need to lead him to one of the unlocked staircases that connect the Under City to the Over City. Lilith is powerful, but if Dom can make it aboveground to one of the streets of the Over City, Lilith will be outnumbered by other Mohirai.

A rapid clatter approaches us from behind. Oh, no.

What is that? thinks Dom.

Doesn't matter! I think, as the noise grows louder, closer. *Faster! Faster!*

Dom's heart feels like it might explode, but somehow he goes even faster.

"Stop!" Lilith's deep voice booms, echoing down the main tunnel, carrying with it the priestess tone of command.

Dom's feet slow, then come to a stop. He gasps for air, each ragged inhalation burning in his lungs.

No, no, no! I think. *Go!*

I can't, he thinks. *I can't move at all. What's happening?*

△▽△

"Face me, boy," says Lilith, using the priestess tone of command.

Against my will, as though pulled by invisible hands, I turn slowly to face Lilith. The light of the oil lamps gleams on the pale yellow strands of her windblown hair. Her ice blue eyes glitter beneath the shadow of her brow. Her towering figure looms over me, because she stands atop some sort of wheeled machine.

What is that? I think.

It's one of the underground carts, thinks Ava. *The Mohirai use them to transport things from outside the walls into the temple city. There's no way you could have outrun it. It's on a track that's powered by the water wheels.*

Tio Artifex sits behind Lilith in the cart, his hand on a metal lever. Balashi slumps inside the cart beside Tio, his eyes closed.

Lilith pulls a pair of black leather gloves from the pocket of her riding breeches and pulls them on unhurriedly. When she's done, the invisible hands pull me forward again. I take one jerky step, then a second, toward her. In three more steps, I'll be nose to nose with her.

Ava's thoughts churn inside of mine, assessing our dwindling options. Even if she were unarmed—which Ava thinks is unlikely—Lilith can overpower me simply using the priestess tone of command. And with her hands covered with gloves, it'll be difficult for Ava to send her awareness into Lilith's body using binding pharmaka, the way she did the night the free men took us captive.

Let me talk to her, thinks Ava.

I've lost nearly all control of my body at this point, so I offer no resistance to Ava. *Go ahead,* I think.

"Stop," says Ava, speaking in the deepest register of my voice. "I won't let you hurt Dom." Her bold words in my voice echo through the tunnels, as if many unseen versions of myself are speaking all together.

"You know I'm not the one hurting him, Ava," Lilith says grimly. "I told you what must be done. If you had simply let me unbind him on the boat the night we recovered you, none of this would have been needed." She hops down from the cart and takes a step toward me.

"Stop!" Ava says again through me. "Or I'll drive you away like I did before." Her words remain bold, but my voice quavers uncertainly this time.

Lilith regards me coolly. "That was an impressive feat for an untrained novice," she says. "You took me by surprise. But I don't intend to make the same mistake twice."

I take control of my own voice for a moment, trying a different approach. "Please, sister," I say, as humbly as I can manage. "Why can't you just let me go? What is it that you need from me?"

"I need nothing from you but silence," she says dismissively to me. Her voice hardens as she continues, "But I expected a great deal more from you, Ava. I thought I had raised a woman free to think on her own, free to make her own choices, free of the cursed madness of the Voice. You threw it all away, and for what? For this boy?"

"I love him," says Ava, but the words sound choked in my throat. "And he loves me. More than you ever did."

The chiseled lines of Lilith's cheeks and jaw briefly tremble, but the expression vanishes so fast that I might have imagined it. She stands silent for a long time. When she speaks again, her voice is dangerously soft. "And how did you imagine that love would end, for him? I know you received my messages. Did you think you could simply ignore me without consequence? Did you think I would let you and this boy walk straight into the temple city with so much knowledge of the rebellion? You're a fool, Ava."

Ava's rage explodes, white-hot. My voice rises with her fury. "Curse you and all your lies, you witch, you demon, you—" The vitriolic stream of condemnations that pours from me includes words I've never heard before.

"How dare you speak to me that way?" Lilith says angrily. "I am your mother."

Ava drops my voice almost to a whisper. "How do I dare? Oh, *mother.*" I don't think I've ever spoken a word with such searing sarcasm. "How dare you lie to me?"

Lilith frowns. "Lie to you?" she says. "I've spoken nothing but truth to you since the day I took you from the Children's Temple."

"Tell me then, mother," Ava says through me. "Who is Maya?"

△▽△

"Tell me then, mother," I say, keeping Dom's eyes locked on Lilith's, searching for any sign of evasion. "Who is Maya?"

Lilith's eyes widen. "Maya," she whispers. She speaks the name with a tenderness she's never shown to me in all our years together. "Serapen told you, then."

I'm so disoriented by the change in Lilith's demeanor that for a moment I'm at a loss for words. We stare at each other in silence. To my surprise, the silence is broken by Tio, who rises with some difficulty from his seat in the cart. The grim lines of Tio's face are painfully contorted, as though he might weep. Whether it's pain from his leg or some other pain, I can't tell. "Peace, Lilith," he says, his voice husky with emotion. "This is not the time or the place to revisit such things."

Dom's pulse quickens at the sound of Tio's deep voice, a voice that's haunted his waking nightmares for the last half moon. *He's the man in charge,* he thinks.

I curse myself inwardly. Why didn't I realize this sooner? Tio's convenient vow of silence, preventing us from recognizing the voice of the unseen third man who took us captive. Tio's halting gait, scratching those peculiar tracks into the boat deck varnish with some device he must have used to help him walk that night. Tio's unplanned reunion with Kabir at Upper Ford, so soon after we escaped from the free men. Everything about this man would have aroused my suspicion, were it not for Serapen's trust in him.

But there's no time for me to berate myself, or to wonder what else I might have missed. If I've learned anything from all the tricky jobs I've completed with Lilith over the years, it's the value of a well-timed distraction. My unexpected question about Maya has distracted both Lilith and Tio from their own job. I have to press my advantage.

Dom's been obediently standing in the spot where Lilith left him, but she's not holding him there with the tone of command any longer. She'll recall Dom quickly if he tries to run away again, but I'm guessing she won't anticipate him taking the opposite approach.

Dom glimpses my plan as it coalesces in my mind.

Are you sure about this? he thinks, swallowing apprehensively.

Miserably, I think, *No. Do you have any better ideas?*

No, he thinks, steeling himself. *But I trust you. We'll get through this. Somehow.*

For once, Dom is more confident than I am. I hesitate, fearful of being separated from him, especially now. But he urges me on. *Better move fast,* he thinks. *She's not going to be distracted for long.*

I know he's right. So I send my instincts flowing through Dom's body, propelling him straight toward Lilith in three quick strides. He tries to close his eyes, but I keep them wide open, locked on our mark. With Dom's long arms, I reach out to seize Lilith by the throat, pressing his palms to the bare skin of her neck.

Lilith is caught off guard momentarily, but, as I'd expected, the moment is brief. With an efficient sweep of her powerful legs, she knocks Dom face-first to the ground. His hands slip from her neck almost before they've made contact.

Almost, but not quite.

In the brief instant of tingling skin contact between Dom and Lilith, I thrust my awareness into Lilith's body. The sudden shift in perspective is jarring, but I re-orient myself quickly. Lilith staggers, dazed by my intrusion into her awareness. She looks down at Dom's fallen form. Through her eyes, I see the jagged cut on his cheek where his face smashed into the paving stones. He moans softly, his eyelids half closed, his gaze wandering. Separated from his body, I can't feel how badly he's injured, but at least he's still conscious. I want desperately to return to him, to protect him from Lilith, but my best hope of protecting him now lies with her.

"Are you all right?" Tio calls out in alarm.

Through gritted teeth, Lilith says, "I'm fine. But she's entered me again."

"Do you want me to hold down the boy while you cast her out?" he says.

Lilith says, "You'd better not touch him until the unbinding is complete. You can't afford another mishap, in your condition. I'll manage Ava until I've unbound him. They'll both be weaker, separated this way. Just bring me the flask and stay back."

Lilith takes a damp cloth from inside her robes and presses it hard over Dom's nose and mouth with one gloved hand. She catches a whiff of whatever is soaked into the fabric. I recognize the scent from Dom's memory; it's the same pharmaka that the free men used to knock us out the night they took us captive. Dom struggles weakly against Lilith for a moment, but he's so disoriented from his fall that she easily overpowers him. He gasps for breath through the cloth, and a moment later he goes limp, slipping into unconsciousness.

You can't do this, I think, using all my strength to push Lilith's hands away from Dom. Lilith grunts audibly as she grapples with my unwelcome interference, but her grip on his face doesn't budge.

I can, and I will, she thinks. *The rebellion will not fail because of your foolishness, Ava.*

Tio approaches from the cart carrying a silver flask. He unscrews the cap and extends the flask toward Lilith. She holds out her free hand for it, keeping her other hand firmly over the cloth on Dom's mouth.

I underestimated the strength of Lilith's self-control. Without the advantage of surprise, I'm far less powerful than she is. She manages my awareness inside of hers as easily as a wolf tosses away her rambunctious pup by the scruff of the neck. My struggle against her awareness may be slowing her down, but she presses on steadily.

So I change tactics. Even when I did have my own body, I rarely had the advantage of physical strength; I've always had to rely more on cleverness and speed. Swiftly, I probe Lilith's mind with my awareness, searching for the source of that unexpected tenderness I just heard in her voice. Tenderness is often a sign of weakness, and Lilith has very few weaknesses, so I lean into this one hard.

Who is Maya? I think, filling Lilith's awareness with my curiosity. *Tell me, Lilith.*

Lilith grits her teeth, trying to ignore me by focusing on Dom, but the name Maya stirs so many memories in her mind that it's impossible for her to hide them all from me. Fragments of Lilith's memories of Maya flash before me in rapid succession. A small girl seated at a loom inside the Children's Temple, weaving with deft fingers and an expression of great concentration. A nimble-footed young woman in the dancing ring around a festival bonfire outside the walls of Velkanos, her long hair flying as she spins. A Mohira with a bright smile, laughing as she descends the staircase of the Upper City, dressed in initiate robes of saffron and scarlet.

Listen to me, Ava, thinks Lilith, struggling to hold back the flood of memories, which carry with them a wave of her grief. *Serapen spoke truly if she told you that Maya was your mother. Maya did indeed give birth to you.* A memory from deep inside of Lilith swirls to the forefront of her mind. Maya lies on a bed, her face gleaming with sweat, her wild tangle of curls spread across her pillow, her eyes closed. A naked infant with dark hair rests on her bare chest. Lilith stands beside the bed, caressing Maya's head gently with her broad, rough hand, tears streaming down her cheeks. Serapen sits by the foot of the bed, a weary expression on her face, wiping blood from her hands. Lilith thinks, *I was there, the day Maya began her journey into Death. But I was the one who held your hand as you took your first steps on your path. There are more ways to be a mother than to carry a child in the womb. I am your mother as truly as Maya was. I raised you. I instructed you. I showed you the truth of our world.*

You showed me what you wanted me to see, I think, clinging to my outrage, even though Lilith's memories have shaken me. The way that Lilith looked at Maya—what did that mean? What was Maya to Lilith?

I showed you everything that mattered, thinks Lilith. *I showed you how the Mohirai control every person within Dulai. I made sure you saw everything with your own eyes, so you would never need to rely on anyone else's account, not even mine.*

You lied to me, I think.

I taught you everything you needed to discover the truth for yourself, Ava.

No, I think, hardening every part of my awareness against hers. *You don't get to decide what's true, what's real, what I should believe, what I—*

In the midst of my diatribe, Lilith glances down at Dom. Her sudden alarm cuts off my own thought abruptly. She jerks back the pharmaka-soaked cloth from his mouth. I've never seen Dom so pale. Lilith probes his neck carefully with one finger. "Damn," she says.

What's wrong? I think, my thoughts reeling.

"What's wrong?" says Tio.

"I was distracted," she says. "I let him breathe in too much pharmaka. He's begun the journey into Death."

Tio's eyes widen. "Can't you call him back?" he says.

Lilith stands. "I don't have enough unbinding pharmaka here to revive him and sever the connection between him and Ava," she says. "If I revive him, we'll have to take him with us until I can prepare more unbinding pharmaka to complete the work. We can't take the risk of another mishap. Not here, right under the noses of the Mohirai."

"What will we do with his body?" says Tio.

"I'll send Balashi up with some story about how Dom took a fall in the tunnels and hit his head," she says.

"Serapen may detect signs you were here, if she examines him," says Tio.

"It's possible," says Lilith. "But it's not the first time Kabir's rule-bending has caused a mishap in the underground tunnels. Should be easy enough to redirect any suspicion, with your help."

Tio looks down sorrowfully at Dom. "What a waste of a life," he says.

"Come, brother," says Lilith. "We knew from the beginning that freedom for all would come at a cost to some." She turns away from Dom, gesturing for Tio to follow her back to the cart.

No! I think. *Please don't do this, Lilith.*

What have I done, Ava? thinks Lilith. *I went to great lengths to spare the boy's life. I had no desire to provoke the Mohirai by taking one of their precious Artifexi. If you had obeyed me the night I tried to unbind the boy, he would have lived. By ignoring my commands, you put his life at risk. He's paid the price for your foolishness.*

Desperately, I reach out for Dom's awareness, searching for the familiar feeling of our connection, trying to find some way to bridge the gap between me and him as Lilith walks away, carrying me with her. In the place where his awareness once resided in my mind, there's nothing but emptiness. Where has he gone?

Please don't leave him! I think, resisting each step Lilith takes away from Dom, willing her to turn back around, willing her to use her healer's arts to revive him. But it's useless. She climbs back into the cart and gives Tio a hand up into his seat. Tio pulls a lever inside the cart, initiating its clattering descent down the tunnel.

Lilith looks back over her shoulder only once. The sight of Dom's crumpled body left behind in the dim tunnel stirs no remorse in her heart. I'm overcome by grief at the thought that he spent his last moments there alone, without me. The emptiness where our connection used to be fills slowly with the knowledge of my failure. I promised him we'd find our way out of this together. Without our bond, how can I possibly keep that promise?

When the memory of my promise flashes through my mind, the call from the far side of the bridge is impossible to resist. My awareness slips away from The End of the Road, back to Earth.

THE LAST BRIDGE

I EMERGE ON THE FAR SIDE OF THE BRIDGE and open my eyes. I stand at the end of the footpath that leads from the sandy shore of the Purattu to the shelter of the river cliffs. A cool breeze ruffles my unbound hair. In the distance, the ducks call *krek krek krek.*

I hurry along the path toward the natural alcoves at the base of the cliffs. My tent stands in the shade of one alcove, right where Emmie and I left it when we recorded this memory.

"Emmie?" I call anxiously.

There's no answer. I hurry toward the tent. She said she'd be here when I returned, though she hadn't specified exactly where. Maybe she's waiting inside the tent for me, along with those avatars of Ava and Dom.

I pull back the tent flap. There's nothing inside except four empty bedrolls and the morning light streaming through the canvas walls.

I turn to face the river again. "Emmie?" I call out, louder this time. My voice echoes along the cliffs.

"Ava?" The voice that answers me is so hoarse that at first I don't recognize it. I turn toward the sound and discover other-Dom standing behind the tent in the shadows of the alcove, nearly invisible in his inky black immerger clothes. When he steps toward me into the sunlight, I'm startled by the change in him. Other-Dom has always struck me as slightly sorrowful, but every line of his face and posture is drawn in suffering now. In a dazed tone, he says, "You came back."

Clearly there's something wrong with other-Dom, and I don't want to be insensitive, but whatever has happened to him can surely wait. If there's any possibility of helping Dom back on my branch, I need to focus on that now. "Where's Emmie?" I say urgently.

"Calm down," says other-Dom. "Relax. Breathe."

I shake my head, irritated by his coddling. "You don't understand. I need to get back to my branch now. Right now. There's been an accident. Dom needs my help."

"All right," he says soothingly. "Where were you, before you were here?"

"Please, can you just find Emmie for me?" I say to other-Dom, impatient to get started. "I need her help to build a bridge back to my branch."

"Emmie's … away," he says. "We'll have to manage on our own until she returns. Where were you, before you were here?"

I sigh, exasperated. I thought Emmie was going to be waiting here for me, but I suppose I can't wait for her. "I'm from The End of the Road," I say.

Other-Dom nods, gestures with both hands, and summons the record of my branch. The globe representing my Dulai appears between us, and other-Dom taps it with his hand. An astonishing number of memory spheres spring out at his touch, swirling around The End of the Road like a colorful flock of birds. Three riders galloping toward the caravan outside the walls of Velkanos. My conversation with Eumelia as we fished together on the Purattu. Nestling into Hanu's arms on a cold night in the Urashtu mountains. Pulling Dom down beside me to greet the wolves. I recognize these memories, and so many others, but I don't remember recording any of them with Emmie or other-Dom. So who did?

Focus, Ava, focus. There's not enough time to untangle every mystery right now. To other-Dom, I say, "Dom was in the main tunnel of the Under City, at the cross-tunnel beneath the street of workshops, when he ran into Lilith …" My narration grows more confident as I watch other-Dom at work, weaving together with precise gestures and spoken commands each element of the scene I'm describing. Soon, I'm looking down at a perfect replica of Dom's body on the floor of the underground tunnel, Lilith kneeling over him with the pharmaka-soaked rag pressed to his face, Tio standing in the shadows.

Eagerly, I step into the scene other-Dom has rendered, returning to my place in Lilith's body at the moment just before Dom lost consciousness. I reach out for the familiar sensation of Dom's awareness in mine, hoping that this will help me find my way back across the bridge to my branch in time to save him.

I reach. I hope. I wait.

And I wait.

And I wait.

"It's not working," I say, frustrated. I stand and pace the stone floors of my memory. My heartbeat turns erratic, and I have to stop to catch my breath. I hug myself, rubbing my hands vigorously up and down my arms to ward off the chill that settles over me as soon as I stop moving. "Why isn't it working?" I say.

Other-Dom—or is this my Dom?—wraps his arm around my shoulders. He tugs the stretchy black immerger glove off my right hand and wraps his strong, warm fingers around my cold, frail ones. "I think you know," he says.

The finality in his tone crushes me. Tears well up in my eyes—or are these Emmie's eyes?—and flow freely down my cheeks. "I shouldn't have left him," I say. "He died alone because of me."

Other-Dom makes a small gesture with his free hand, and my memory of the underground tunnel shrinks back down into a sphere. The sphere floats upward, rejoining the flock of other memories swirling around The End of the Road. We stand together gazing up at the glowing spheres, all that remain to me now of the branch I've left behind.

He squeezes my hand, sending a soothing calm through me. "There is no one to blame for the natural order of things," he says. "There is only the pattern, and we who observe the pattern."

"What pattern?" I say, sniffling.

"We live, we love, we lose," he says. "And then we live again. That is all."

I wipe my leaking eyes and runny nose on the black sleeve of my immerger clothes. One of the silver threads woven into the fabric scratches my upper lip. I wince at the sting. "This can't be all there is," I say. "We can't just live forever in a trap with no escape. Has the Voice cursed us?"

He plants a kiss on my scratched lip. "Is it a curse to have loved?" he says, looking down at me with a tenderness that warms me to the core. In his dark eyes, I glimpse the surface of a vast ocean of memory.

Slowly, I say, "You told me once that you've followed me, life after life. That means you've followed me death after death, too."

He nods. "Each follows the other."

"How do you bear it?" I say, searching his awareness for some hope of a cure for this pain in my heart.

"I've learned to make meaning from loss through our great work together," he says. "Come. I'll show you."

He waves his hand through the swirling flock of spheres above us, and my memories of the End of the Road vanish. We stand alone together in the grey light of the empty, windowless spliner. He leads me by the hand toward the exit.

The door slides open, and the warm light of late afternoon spills over us. We climb the stairs back up into the living room. He leads me to one of the cozy sofas that face the window. We sit. For a moment, I look out at the dramatic view of the city across the bay.

He reaches over the arm of the sofa toward the side table and picks up a large book with a tooled leather cover. He opens the book to the first page and rests it across our laps.

It's a sketchbook—much like the one Dom received from Urshanabi at the river crossing, though this one appears to have been spared from bird attacks. Slowly, I turn the pages, each one filled from edge to edge with Dom's drawings and my handwriting. The images stir some faint recognition in me, though I can't remember ever seeing these abstract figures or their accompanying text before.

"What is this?" I say.

"Instructions," he says. "All the instructions we've gathered for building bridges to other worlds."

I shake my head. "I don't understand," I say.

He says, "You and I have witnessed the truth of the many worlds and the connections between them. The Voice calls us to reveal this mystery to humankind. We must secure these instructions in a place where they cannot be lost or hidden, so that all who seek this truth may find it."

"Can't we just record these instructions in the quantum computer, then?" I say. "Wouldn't that make the instructions available on every branch?"

"It isn't quite that simple," he says. "The Stewards here on Earth guard the mysteries ruthlessly with their technology. The Mohirai on Dulai guard the mysteries, perhaps more gently, with their pharmaka. On every branch we've encountered, some human power exists that keeps the mysteries for its own purposes. But the Voice calls us to make this mystery known to all. Until our service to the Voice is complete, we are bound to this great work—life after life, death after death, world after world."

I sigh, wary of yet another job I don't fully understand. "And once we've accomplished this work?" I say. "Then what?"

He squeezes my hand. “Freedom,” he says.

“Freedom from what?” I say. “Freedom to do what?”

The sun sinks slowly behind the city of glass towers on the western horizon before us, surrounding us in golden light. “Freedom to choose a new pattern,” he says. “Freedom to move on.”

I take a deep breath, gripping his hand for reassurance. My faith in the Voice’s purpose may be imperfect. My hope that I can answer my calling may be shadowed by doubt. But as long as Dom and I are walking the path of mysteries together, I won’t give up my dream of freedom for both of us.

“I love you,” I say.

“I love you too,” he says.

“All right,” I say. “Let’s do this, then. Together.”

He smiles. “Together.”

THE ARTIFEX AND THE MUSE
PART THREE

THE MANY WORLDS

With the drawing of this Love and the voice of this
Calling
We shall not cease from exploration
And the end of all our exploring
Will be to arrive where we started
And know the place for the first time.

— Little Gidding (1942), Part Four of Four Quartets by T. S. Eliot

PROMISES TO KEEP

I RUN. My gasping breaths and racing heartbeat form a desperate counterpoint to the ominous *clack-a-tat clack-a-tat clack-a-tat* sound of whatever is chasing me up the dark central tunnel of the Under City.

Faster, Dom! Faster! Ava's awareness inside my mind drives me onward, sending my feet flying over the rough paving stones, steering me toward my exit. My running form isn't the best after a moon of riding horseback on the long road to Velkanos, but fear is a powerful motivator.

Dim oil lamps blur past on either side of me as I run up the steepening slope of the tunnel. On my own, I'd have no idea where I'm going. Fortunately, Ava's been here before. Her knowledge flows through my mind as quickly as thought. Each lamp marks an intersection between the Under City's wide central tunnel and a narrower side tunnel, mirroring the grid of Over City streets and alleys aboveground.

In Ava's memory, I glimpse the nearest stone stairway that connects this dark tunnel to the sunlit streets above. I need to reach that stairway before Lilith catches me. We'll be safe up there among the Mohirai. At least, I hope we'll be safe. Until a moment ago, I'd believed that being inside the city walls of Velkanos was protection enough from the threat posed by Lilith and the free men. Clearly I was mistaken.

Just ahead of me, a lamp shines above the intersection I need. Every muscle in my body burns as I push myself to the limit of my strength, determined to reach it.

Please, spirits, help us escape.

Help us escape.

Help us—

"Stop!"

Lilith's deep bellow echoes down the long stone tunnel. The awful mechanical clatter behind me slows, then stops. For a fleeting instant, I'm elated. Lilith's given up the chase, and our intersection is barely ten steps ahead. Ava and I are going to escape, after all.

But Lilith's voice lingers in the chilly air, resonating in my mind, taking hold of my body. Against my will, my footfalls slow, then stop.

No, no, no! Ava thinks. *Go!*

I can't, I think.

My thoughts lose focus, untethered from any sense of urgency, while Ava's thoughts become frantic. My terror, so sharp a moment ago, dulls and diffuses. The sweet, soothing scent of the oil lamps fills my nostrils. A warm heaviness like approaching sleep settles over me, as though I've ingested some kind of pharmaka. Rooted to the spot where I stand, I gaze at the flickering light above my exit—so close, yet impossibly far away. *I can't move at all,* I think. *What's happening?*

Ava's colorful curses flare in my mind as her understanding floods through me. Lilith must have called out to me using the tone of command, an art known only to initiates of the mysteries. A Mohiran priestess might be able to resist Lilith, who abandoned her own priestess vows long ago. But as a mere novice Artifex, I'm powerless against her call.

"Face me, boy," says Lilith.

As though pulled by invisible hands, I turn slowly to face Lilith. The light of the oil lamps gleams on the pale yellow strands of her windblown hair. Her ice-blue eyes glitter beneath the shadow of her brow. Her towering figure looms over me, because she stands atop …

What is that? I think, my wandering thoughts arrested by the sight of the strange machine carrying Lilith. I see why it made such a clatter, with those heavy wooden wheels racing over the rough stone floor of the tunnel, and all those metal gears. What could have been pulling that machine at such speed? There's not a horse or ox in sight.

Ava's knowledge flows through me again. *It's one of the underground carts,* she thinks. *The Mohirai use them to transport things from outside the walls into the temple city. There's no way you could have outrun it. It's on a track that's powered by the water wheels.*

Distantly, I remember my teacher Kabir Artifex pointing out the water wheels as he guided me through the streets of the Outer City, delivering me to the house of novices for my first day of instruction among the Muses. It's hard to believe that was only this morning. Even harder to believe I'd felt so safe within the walls of the temple city. But Ava had known better; a life spent hiding from the Mohirai has taught her to expect dangers entirely unknown to me.

Even so, Ava seems as surprised as I am by the sight of the cart's other two occupants.

Behind Lilith, Tio Artifex sits on a small wooden bench at the back of the cart, his hand gripping a long metal lever that must somehow operate the machine. The dim light of the nearest oil lamp obscures his expression, but his broad shoulders hunch in a painful posture and his lame leg sticks out at an awkward angle. What on Dulai is Tio doing here?

Beside Tio, my trio brother Balashi slumps on the floor of the cart, moaning faintly. Balashi's head lolls to the side, his eyes closed, his handsome face twitching as though he's having a nightmare. Thank the spirits, he's still alive. I'd felt a pang of guilt for leaving him behind when I turned to run from Lilith. Even though it was Balashi who led me straight into Lilith's trap, I don't blame him. Lilith must have manipulated him, just as she's manipulating me now.

Lilith withdraws a pair of black leather gloves from the pocket of her riding breeches and pulls them on unhurriedly. Time seems to slow as her eyes lock onto mine. A single commanding look from her compels me forward. As if in a dream, I watch myself take one jerky step, then another, toward the cart. Three more steps and I'll be nose to nose with her.

I should be panicking, but Lilith's command has replaced my panic with calm acceptance. I gaze up at her without fear. Despite the hard set of Lilith's mouth, there's a pitying sadness in her eyes. Clearly she finds this encounter with me distasteful, even dispiriting, but unavoidable. I know the feeling well. Growing up in the house of boys, I must have worn that same expression every time I had to slaughter a lamb I'd raised.

A resigned voice inside of me—probably my own voice, though it's difficult to know for sure with Ava inhabiting my mind and Lilith controlling my body—points out that, despite all our struggles and suffering over the past half moon, Ava and I are right back where we started: helpless in Lilith's hands. We'll keep returning here, until Lilith extracts what she wants from us. Our resistance is futile.

How can you believe that, after all you've seen? chides an angry voice inside of me. I hardly recognize this part of myself, long buried beneath the foundation of my boyhood obedience, only recently awoken by my friendship with Ava. *How long will you let yourself be powerless?*

The self-accusation stings. Have I let myself be powerless? Ava and I did resist, the night Lilith and the free men abducted us in an attempt to sever the connection between us. Even though we were outnumbered, bound, and blindfolded, we fought until the end. Ava sacrificed herself to drive away Lilith and protect me, and I revived Ava with the help of the High Priestess Serapen. We resisted, and we survived.

Unfortunately, neither Ava nor I was prepared for the suffering survival entails. In the end, Ava died yet again. She was powerless to escape her fate, so how can I hope to escape my own?

While my other inner voices argue uselessly, Ava focuses on the more pressing problem at hand, assessing our dwindling options. Even if Lilith were unarmed, she could overpower me simply by using the priestess tone of command again. And with Lilith's gloved hands protecting her from skin contact with me, it'll be impossible for Ava to send her awareness into Lilith's body the way she did the night the free men took us captive.

Let me talk to her, thinks Ava, trying to buy us more time.

I can't imagine what she hopes to accomplish this way, but I suppose anything is worth a shot. *Go ahead,* I think.

"Stop," says Ava, speaking in the deepest register of my voice. "I won't let you hurt Dom." Her bold words in my voice echo through the tunnels, as if many unseen versions of myself are speaking all together.

"You know I'm not the one hurting him, Ava," says Lilith, her voice hard. "I told you what must be done. If you had simply let me unbind him on the boat the night we recovered you, none of this would have been needed." She hops down from the cart and takes a step toward me.

"Stop!" Ava says again through me. "Or I'll drive you away like I did before." Her words are bold, but her uncertainty reveals itself through the quaver in my voice.

Lilith regards me coolly as she says to Ava, "That was an impressive feat for an untrained novice. You took me by surprise. But I don't intend to make the same mistake twice."

I take back control of my voice from Ava, trying a different approach. "Please, sister," I say, as humbly as I can manage. "Why can't you just let me go? What is it that you need from me?"

"I need nothing from you but silence," Lilith says dismissively. Her voice rises, growing more heated as she continues, "But I expected a great deal more from you, Ava. I thought I had raised a woman free to think on her own, free to make her own choices, free of the cursed madness of the Voice. You threw it all away, and for what? For this boy?"

"I love him," says Ava, but her words catch in my throat. "And he loves me. More than you ever did."

Ava's heartfelt expression of love drives out some of the fog that entered my mind with Lilith's command. However powerless I may feel, Ava and I are in this together. As long as my heart's still beating, there's hope.

The chiseled lines of Lilith's cheeks and jaw tremble. She stands silent for a long time. When she speaks, her voice is dangerously soft. "And how did you imagine that love would end, for him? I know you received my messages. Did you think you could simply ignore me without consequence? Did you think I would let you and this boy walk straight into the temple city with so much knowledge of the rebellion? You're a fool, Ava."

Ava's rage explodes, white-hot. My voice rises with her fury. "Curse you and all your lies, you witch, you demon, you—" I'm impressed by the vitriolic stream of condemnations Ava pours from my mouth.

"How dare you speak to me that way?" Lilith says angrily. "I am your mother."

Ava drops my voice almost to a whisper. "How do I dare? Oh, *mother,*" she says. I don't think I've ever spoken a word with such searing sarcasm. It's thrilling. Louder, she says, "How dare you lie to me?"

Lilith frowns. "Lie to you?" she says. "I've spoken nothing but truth to you since the day I took you from the Children's Temple."

"Tell me then, mother," Ava says through me. "Who is Maya?"

Lilith's eyes widen in surprise, softening her angry expression. "Maya," she whispers. She swallows hard. Her tone is cautious as she says, "Serapen told you, then."

The unexpected vulnerability in Lilith's tone disorients Ava, leaving her momentarily at a loss for words.

Behind Lilith, Tio rises with difficulty from his seat in the cart. The deep lines of his weathered face contort, as though he might weep. Whether it's pain from his leg or some other pain, I can't tell. "Peace, Lilith," he says, breaking his ceremonial silence for the first time since I met him outside the city gates two days ago. "This is not the time or the place to revisit such things."

At the sound of Tio's voice, my pulse quickens in horrified recognition. His is the voice of the unseen man in charge of the free men who abducted me and Ava. Why would the oldest Artifex—one of the rare men of Dulai called by the Voice to the path of mysteries, one of the rare men trusted by the High Priestess Serapen to live among the Mohirai—be in league with a rebel like Lilith?

My alarm at the sudden revelation of Tio's true identity shakes Ava out of her momentary confusion. She refocuses on the urgent problem at hand. Her plan snaps into focus in my mind: a surprise attack.

Are you sure about this? I think.

My instinctive worry erodes Ava's innate courage. I've helped Ava fight against long odds at every point of our journey together, but the losses we've accumulated along the way have made her more cautious. She considers what might go wrong, searching desperately for any other way out of this situation. At last, miserably, she thinks, *No. Do you have any better ideas?*

My gaze settles on Balashi's unconscious form. That could be me, mere moments from now. The newly-awakened angry voice inside of me roars in frustration at my timidity. Do I want my cowardice to cost us our last chance to escape? *No,* I think. *But I trust you. We'll get through this. Somehow.*

Still, Ava hesitates. Scrounging up my courage, for Ava as much as for myself, I think, *Better move fast. She's not going to be distracted for long.*

Ava knows I'm right. Together, we push past our fears, our shared resolve coalescing in my body, propelling me toward Lilith in three quick strides. I wish I could close my eyes, but Ava forces them open so I can't miss our mark. I seize Lilith by the throat, pressing my palms to the bare skin of her neck.

My unexpected daring catches Lilith off guard, but she recovers quickly. With an efficient sweep of her powerful legs, Lilith knocks me off my feet. My hands slip from her neck almost before they've made contact.

Almost, but not quite.

In the brief instant of tingling skin contact, Ava thrusts herself from my body into Lilith's, her awareness vanishing from my mind as I fall face-first to the ground.

My head hits the stone floor of the tunnel with a sickening crack, followed by a blinding explosion of light. I roll limply onto my back, struggling to focus my eyes, my ears ringing. Muffled voices speak around me, words impossible to discern. The pounding pain in my head intensifies with each heartbeat.

The blurry shape of Lilith looms over me, her broad gloved hand reaching for my face. A pungent whiff of something familiar fills my nostrils. My stomach churns as I realize what's about to happen. A cool, damp cloth presses firmly over my nose and mouth. Despite the throbbing pain in my head, I try to concentrate, holding perfectly still to make my last breath count, hoping I can give Ava enough time to drive Lilith away. I focus on my heartbeat, which speeds up steadily as my lungs scream for air. But eventually, my desperate need to breathe overwhelms my self-control. I open my mouth and gasp.

The complex herbal scent of the pharmaka-soaked cloth fills my lungs. My body relaxes. The pain in my head fades. My eyelids grow heavy and slowly close.

As I lose my hold on this world, I drift through a treasured memory. It's the last truly peaceful moment I shared with Ava on our journey to Velkanos. We lie together in our tent on the banks of the Purattu, the morning after I resurrected her for the first time. The rustle of willows outside and the rush of the great river beyond fills the air. Ava cradles my head against the soft curve of her breast, her fingers gently stroking my hair, her scent of salt and cedar warm and close. I gaze up at her. Sunlight glows through the white canvas walls, illuminating her rosy brown cheeks, shining violet on her long black curls, catching the spring green flecks in her deep brown eyes.

Her soothing voice echoes through my memory as my awareness begins its journey into Death.

We're going to find our way out of here together. I promise.

PASSING THE TORCH

I SIT ALONE in the center of my spliner with my legs tucked neatly beneath me, resting my weight on my heels. My balance wobbles slightly, and the floor automatically adjusts its warm, spongy contours against my shins to keep me upright. Years ago, when I installed the spliner in my basement to celebrate my first windfall profit from my early work on the alternet, I used to stride the length of this room for hours on end with the ease of a dancer, immersed in worlds of my own creation. I took so much for granted in those carefree days before my overdose. The mere act of standing is a struggle lately; I've had to resign myself to working with only two free hands. I try to ignore the tremor these hands have recently developed, avoiding the question of how—or whether—the great work can be completed if my own fingers cease to obey me.

A cloud of glowing memory spheres swirls slowly over my head, casting dim light on the windowless walls of the small grey room, gleaming in the silver threads of my skin-tight black immerger clothes. Above my outstretched gloved hand hovers a lone sphere that glows more brightly than the rest.

The great work of my life required me to gather countless memories like this one, so I could learn to bridge the many worlds that branch from each moment in time. Now all that work comes down to a final choice. From this single memory, can I build a bridge to freedom for us all?

I peer through the sphere's translucent surface as the memory returns to its beginning and replays itself. The memory belongs to a branch that a visiting Ava named The End of the Road. I've been studying her branch for months, gradually zeroing in on this moment, which lies at the intersection of so many possible futures. I watch again as a young Dom charges toward a menacing Lilith, urged on by his Ava's awareness inside of him. He seizes Lilith's muscular neck in his hands in a desperate final bid to resist her, but she knocks him to the ground with a practiced sweep of her leg.

I tap the side of my headset twice with my trembling hand to pause the scene, then wave my palm over the sphere. The sphere expands, envelops me, and immerses me in the memory. I close my eyes briefly to ease the visual transition. The threads of my immerger clothing tingle against my skin, from my neck all the way out to my fingertips and toes, simulating with impressive fidelity the sensation of the damp, chilly air of the Under City. The warm, yielding spliner floor beneath my shins cools and hardens, evoking the sensation of the tunnel's rough paving stones. When I reopen my eyes, the dim glow of the hovering memory spheres in my spliner has been replaced by the flickering light of an oil lamp hanging from an iron bracket on the stone wall beside me. All signs of the little grey room around me have dissolved, replaced by the setting of this Ava's memory. My immersion is complete.

Before me lies the young Dom, bleeding from an ugly cut on his cheek. He moans softly, his unfocused eyes wandering beneath half-closed lids. I look up from my seat on the floor to examine the Lilith looming over him. Her tense expression reveals her internal struggle against the sudden unwelcome intrusion of Ava's awareness into her own.

"Are you all right?" Tio's voice calls out from somewhere behind us.

Through gritted teeth, Lilith says, "I'm fine. But she's entered me again."

"Do you want me to hold down the boy while you cast her out?" says Tio.

Lilith says, "You'd better not touch him until the unbinding is complete. You can't afford another mishap in your condition. I'll manage Ava until I've unbound him. They'll both be weaker, separated this way. Just bring me the flask and stay back."

Lilith takes a damp cloth from inside her robes and presses it hard over Dom's nose and mouth with one gloved hand. I cough as the olfactory immergers in my headset fill my nostrils with a sharp, astringent scent that simulates the aroma of the pharmaka-soaked cloth. Dom struggles weakly against Lilith for a moment, but she overpowers him easily. At last, he's forced to gasp for breath. His body goes limp as he slips into unconsciousness.

Through my headset, I hear Ava's inner voice cry out to Lilith, *You can't do this.*

Lilith grunts audibly as she grapples with Ava's awareness, resisting Ava's attempt to pull her away from Dom.

I can, and I will, thinks Lilith, clamping her hand down harder over Dom's nose and mouth. *The rebellion will not fail because of your foolishness, Ava.*

Tio's halting footsteps approach from behind me. I look back to see him extending an open silver flask toward Lilith. She holds out her free hand for it.

Who is Maya? Ava thinks, in a desperate attempt at distraction. *Tell me, Lilith.*

Lilith's breath catches. Almost imperceptibly, her grip on Dom falters. In the upper corner of my visual overlay, a translucent prompt appears, helpfully offering links to the memories of a youthful Maya that Ava glimpsed in Lilith's mind at this moment. I've explored Lilith's memories of Maya many times before, though, so I dismiss the prompt and let the current memory play out uninterrupted.

Listen to me, Ava, thinks Lilith. *Serapen spoke truly if she told you that Maya was your mother. Maya did indeed give birth to you.*

Another helpful memory link pops up on my visual overlay. I don't need to read its description to know which one it is: Maya in the aftermath of her traumatic delivery, a weeping Lilith at her side, an exhausted Serapen at the foot of the bed, defeated in her attempt to save Maya's life.

Lilith swallows hard. She thinks, *I was there, the day Maya began her journey into Death. But I was the one who held your hand as you took your first steps on your path. There are more ways to be a mother than to carry a child in the womb. I am your mother as truly as Maya was. I raised you. I instructed you. I showed you the truth of our world.*

You showed me what you wanted me to see, thinks Ava, the deep wound of Lilith's betrayal still far too fresh for her to make sense of these confusing new memories of Maya.

Lilith's iron self-control can't contain the conflicting emotions battling across her face as she thinks, *I showed you everything that mattered. I showed you how the Mohirai control every person within Dulai. I made sure you saw everything with your own eyes, so you would never need to rely on anyone else's account, not even mine.*

You lied to me, thinks Ava, clinging to the simple truth at the heart of every trust destroyed.

I taught you everything you needed to discover the truth for yourself, Ava, thinks Lilith, offering another truth in exchange.

No, thinks Ava, hardening her heart against Lilith. *You don't get to decide what's true, what's real, what I should believe, what I—*

Lilith glances down at Dom for the first time in over a minute, according to the clock on my visual overlay. Her sudden alarm cuts off Ava's angry diatribe. Lilith jerks back the pharmaka-soaked cloth from Dom's mouth and probes his neck carefully with one finger. "Damn," she says.

What's wrong? thinks Ava.

"What's wrong?" says Tio.

"I was distracted," says Lilith, clenching her jaw in frustration. "I let him breathe in too much pharmaka. He's begun the journey into Death."

"Can't you call him back?" says Tio, his voice rising in dismay.

Lilith stands quickly. "I don't have enough unbinding pharmaka here to revive him and sever the connection between him and Ava," she says. "If I revive him, we'll have to take him with us until I can prepare more unbinding pharmaka to complete the work. We can't take the risk of another mishap. Not here, right under the noses of the Mohirai."

Tio's gaze sweeps up and down the central tunnel, as though the mere mention of the Mohirai might summon a priestess to the scene. In a lower tone, he says, "What will we do with his body?"

Lilith considers, then says, "I'll send Balashi up with some story about how Dom took a fall in the tunnels and hit his head."

"Serapen may detect signs you were here, if she examines him," says Tio.

"It's possible," says Lilith. "But it's not the first time Kabir's rule-bending has caused a mishap in the underground tunnels. Should be easy enough to redirect any suspicion, with your help."

Tio nods, then looks down sorrowfully at Dom. "What a waste of a life," he says.

"Come, brother," says Lilith, in a commanding tone that pulls Tio's eyes up to meet her own. "We knew from the beginning that freedom for all would come at a cost to some." She turns away from Dom, gesturing for Tio to follow her back to the cart.

No! Ava's agonized voice cries out through my headset. *Please don't do this,*

Lilith.

What have I done, Ava? thinks Lilith. *I went to great lengths to spare the boy's life. I had no desire to provoke the Mohirai by taking one of their precious Artifexi. If you had obeyed me the night I tried to unbind the boy, he would have lived. By ignoring my commands, you put his life at risk. He's paid the price for your foolishness.*

Please don't leave him! Ava's inner voice cries out again. The panic that accompanies her horrified realization of what she's about to lose surges through my body, sending my pulse racing.

Hastily, I pause the memory and reduce its emotional intensity with a flick of my fingers. *Breathe, Emmie,* I tell myself, taking a slow, deep breath, attempting to steady my irregular heartbeat and trembling hands. The simulated sensations and emotions of the alternet never used to affect me so deeply, before my accident, but those days are long past. Now, the delicate equilibrium of my pharmaka-ravaged body can be upended by far less troubling memories than this one, of an Ava experiencing the loss of her Dom for the first time. It was sloppy of me, forgetting to adjust my emotional filters before starting this immersion. But exhaustion and mistakes go hand in hand, as so many other-Avas and I have learned on so many branches.

I watch the seconds tick by on the clock that hovers in the top corner of my visual overlay, waiting for my heartbeat to return to something like its normal rhythm. Seconds stretch toward a full minute. If my pulse doesn't return to its normal rhythm soon, my heart monitor will send an alarm to my own Dom, asleep upstairs in our bedroom, where I should be. It's comforting to know Dom will come to my aid the moment I need him, but my stomach twists with guilt at the thought of the look I'll see in his eyes if he catches me down here again, pushing myself toward my breaking point as I push our great work toward its conclusion.

But he won't reproach me. We're long past the days of him pleading for me to rest and focus on my own healing instead of the work. He knows as well as I do that my time here is running out. If I fail to build a bridge between my branch of Earth and this branch of Dulai soon, my entire life will have amounted to what? Nothing more than this ephemeral collection of memories recorded from so many lives that have been sacrificed in pursuit of the Voice's calling. The great work to which all Avas and Doms have been called will be set back by another lifetime, maybe more. If I don't succeed, my Dom won't live to see the great work accomplished. We'll pass again through Death, returning to new lives with our hard-won learnings lost, forced to rediscover through painful trial and error the pattern that binds us together across the many worlds.

The dark clouds of these thoughts contain a silver lining, though. They calm me, slowing my pulse just enough to avoid setting off the alarm on my heart monitor. I take another deep breath, then unpause the memory to watch the final few seconds from my seat beside the unconscious young Dom.

Lilith turns away from Dom and strides back toward the cart. Tio stands waiting for her, his expression pained as he looks from the slumped figure of Balashi at his feet to the sprawled form of Dom on the tunnel floor. Ava's final emotional sensation in this memory is of agonizing loss, but I've turned the emotional intensity down far enough now that I can focus on the critical details in her memory that will inform my own next steps.

I zoom out from the scene with a circular sweep of my fingers until the avatars of Dom, Lilith, and Tio are no larger than ants. I re-render the scene as a wireframe to see its location within the three-dimensional model of Velkanos that my Dom and I have pieced together from the memories of other Avas and Doms who have made the difficult crossing from their branches of Dulai to branches of Earth containing the quantum computer. The recordings of all these individuals' memories reside within the single expansive memory of this computer, a technology that might make the human mind obsolete, except that crafting meaning from memory still requires more art than science.

I trace back the path this Dom took through the tunnels when he ran from Lilith, then follow the line of the cart track that Lilith and Tio used to chase after him. My best guess is that Lilith, upon her departure from the scene of the accident with Dom, would have evaded detection from the other Mohirai by riding the cart south down the central tunnel. From there, she likely exited through a less-trafficked tunnel or one of the natural lava tubes, emerging aboveground on the grassy plain outside the walls of Velkanos. This would have left Dom's body to be discovered by whatever Mohira next walked through the central tunnel of the Under City.

"Show me a list of Mohirai most likely to use the central tunnel around the time of this memory," I say. The rasp in my voice reminds me how long it's been since I took a break. This in turn forces me to acknowledge the growing ache in my chest. I glance at the clock on my visual overlay to check how long it's been since my last dose of unbinding pharmaka. I had hoped for at least one more hour of uninterrupted work, but I know better than to push through this particular pain. With a sigh, I add, "And bring me a glass of water."

Almost instantly, the requested list of women's names appears hovering before me. A few seconds later, a gap opens in the floor of the spliner beside me. The tall glass of water I requested rises through the gap, accompanied by a steaming cup of coffee I hadn't realized I needed until the delicious scent of my favorite dark roast fills the spliner, unaided by any olfactory simulation.

"Thanks, B," I say, although my gratitude seems a meager reward for my assistant Bealsio's unfailing ability to anticipate and accommodate my every need, even those unspoken.

"My pleasure," replies a disembodied female voice—the clear, confident voice that belonged to me when I was younger and stronger.

I withdraw the blue glass dropper bottle of unbinding pharmaka from its pouch on my immerger belt. The bottle is nearly empty again, but Amos will be here later today to refill it, so I suppose I can risk taking the last dose now. With a shaking hand, I unscrew the bottle top and carefully dispense the final dropperful of the pale golden liquid into the water glass. I raise the glass to my lips, inhale the familiar flowery aroma, and take several long swallows of pharmaka-laced water. The cool liquid soothes my throat, and the unbinding pharmaka swirls in my belly, warming me from within as its effects take hold.

Carefully, I set down the half-empty glass at my side and lean back on my heels. The spliner floor rises like a gentle hug around my shoulders, and I force myself to relax as it lowers me onto my back. The sub-audible hum of the spliner's inner mechanics lulls my senses. The text of my visual overlay blurs as my focus drifts. My eyelids flutter drowsily.

I'm an expert user of unbinding pharmaka after twenty years of relying on it to ease the pain from my accident. Even so, the initial sensation of my mind drifting in an unseen current is always unsettling.

I can't hold on to my unsettled feeling for long, though, because what follows in its wake is the contentment of forgetfulness, the erasure of agitating thought, the abandonment of pain. This boat has lost its anchor, and now it's drifting down the stream … *merrily, merrily, merrily, merrily …*

With a jolt, I open my eyes. Where am I? I struggle to sit up, and the hum of the floor assisting me answers my first question. I'm in the spliner. That's a relief —somewhere familiar this time. But what am I doing here? I look around the featureless grey room, and my gaze falls on a half-empty water glass and a full mug of coffee on the floor beside me. I squint, pulling my visual overlay into focus to check the clock. A notation hovering below the clock tells me I took a dose thirty-four minutes ago. Jesus. Thirty-four minutes to return from a half dose? How can I hope to finish the great work with these ever-extending return times?

I tap my fingers together to open my alternet browser history, combing the logs, trying to pick up the thread of my work. Helpfully, Bealsio says, "Would you like me to highlight the subset of Mohirai in close proximity to this Dom who are most likely to be carrying unbinding pharmaka?"

Ah. Right. The key pieces flood back into my mind. "Thanks for the nudge, B. Please do," I say, reaching for the coffee mug, hoping to mitigate the unbinding pharmaka's unwanted side effects with a strong dose of caffeine. "I'd also like an estimate of how much time it might take each of them to reach the scene."

Even before I've taken the first sip of my lukewarm coffee, the subset of names and calculated estimates appear before me, so fast that Bealsio must have prepared these answers while I was drifting through pharmaka-induced oblivion. The list of names isn't long—a few dozen women—but it's enough for me to generate a decent collection of intersections on this branch that might anchor the bridge I need to build. I select a few of the women who I suspect would produce the best set of possible outcomes for this fallen Dom, on whom so much depends.

With Bealsio's help, I generate several scene parameters at multiple locations within Velkanos that have a high probability of causing one of these women to arrive in time, and with suitable materials, to revive Dom before his journey into Death becomes irreversible. We kick off simulations of possible downstream events that could follow this Dom's rescue. These computationally expensive simulations will take a little time to run—hopefully enough time for me to enjoy the rest of this coffee before it's gone completely cold.

I wait, sip, savor, wondering how many more cups of coffee remain in my future, grateful that Bealsio had this cup already prepared at a moment I could enjoy it. Even though I'm a member of the alternet generation, having grown up with sophisticated sensory immersion technologies, I'm old enough to fully appreciate the game-changing emergence of these assistive intelligence technologies. Once, I might have said "artificial" intelligence, but I've joined the growing community that's repurposing the *A* in AI. I see these assistive intelligences as an evolution of our own, all patterned after the greater intelligence that moves between the many worlds.

A soft ping in my headset alerts me to the completion of my requested simulations. Bealsio helps me craft the precise queries needed to extract key outcomes measures from each simulation, distilling massive datasets into bare essentials for quick comparisons. She generates data visualizations to help me identify scenarios with characteristics that—I hope—will maximize the likelihood of success.

I close my eyes briefly, imagining how sweet that success would feel, after so many have sacrificed so much. Building a bridge that grants the quantum computer on my branch access to the contents of the Musaion in Velkanos would at last set free all the Avas and Doms on every branch who have suffered in their service to the Voice. With the Mohiran knowledge of pharmaka recorded in the quantum computer, mysteries that have been shrouded in secrecy across the many worlds would be revealed for the benefit of all. No one—neither the Mohirai, nor the Stewards, nor any power that might rise up to take their place—could continue to hide this knowledge to control the lives of others. Everyone would possess the freedom to choose their own life.

That's the dream, anyway. It's what keeps me going, day after day in this declining body.

I open my eyes, reminding myself that the dream will never be a reality unless I choose the right intersection to anchor this bridge. I examine the data visualizations hovering before me with an expert eye. I could spend weeks, months, even years analyzing scenarios, sifting through the unique risks contained in each long tail of possibilities, to decide which one is best. But my time is short. Speed and improvisation are more critical now than analysis and perfection.

"This one," I say, pointing out a single sphere to Bealsio. "This is the intersection I'll use to build the bridge."

Bealsio materializes beside me, mirroring my seated posture on the floor. She wears an avatar that my Dom and I wove together from many memories of my younger self. Hard to believe I was ever that beautiful, with those sparkling eyes, those rounded cheeks, that youthful energy.

"You'll use Hanu and Eumelia?" says Bealsio, peering into the sphere I've chosen. "But they're only novices. How do you know it will work?"

"Sometimes the only way to know is to do," I say, smiling to myself. After all these years, I still haven't decided whether my belief in this Mohiran saying is wisdom or arrogance, but either way, it's taken me far.

Bealsio rolls her eyes, a perfect distillation of my teenage self. I see why that expression always drove my mother crazy. Bealsio says, "I don't think I'll ever understand why you and Dom say that so much."

"Give it time," I say. "You have plenty."

Her playful exasperation fades into a profound sadness that I don't remember experiencing in my youth. Bealsio must have learned that expression on her own, after shadowing me through these difficult years. Amazing, really, how far she's come. How far I've come. For once, I allow myself to feel a sense of pride in the work I've done to reach this moment. No matter what happens next, Bealsio will remain. She will remember.

I reach out for the chosen sphere, which holds the intersection I'll use to anchor my bridge. As the glowing orb drifts toward my open hand, I summon the meager remains of my strength. Building a new bridge comes at a cost; I hope I have enough remaining in my account.

The sphere expands, enveloping my outstretched forearm. As the sphere grows, so too does the ominous throb in my chest. Icy sweat prickles on my brow. I bite my lip, focusing, forcing myself to breathe.

The pain eases slightly, so I push on into the memory. The sphere keeps growing, swallowing up the rest of my arm, then my torso, then my entire body. As my immersion deepens, the close grey walls of the spliner seem to expand outward, placing me at the center of a vast, windowless hall filled with endless rows of shelves: the Musaion library carved into the lower slope of Velkanos, the Mountain of Muses. The soft, level spliner floor beneath me extrudes into a low, hard, rectangular object that digs uncomfortably into my backside. I look down and see I'm seated atop a large crate set on the floor behind an unhitched oxcart.

A few steps away from the cart, a young Eumelia sits at a long, low table covered in neat piles of small, dusty boxes. She's dressed in the undyed wool tunic the novices wear, her frizzy curls held back from her freckled cheeks in tight plaits, her brows knitting in concentration as she leans over a partially-unrolled scroll. She examines one of the boxes at her table, writes something in tidy script at the end of a list on the scroll, and moves the box to another pile. Behind her, sweet-faced Hanu approaches carrying another armload of boxes, which she deposits onto Eumelia's table with a clatter.

"Spirits, everything in that cart is so heavy!" Hanu says with a laugh, smoothing back a strand of her silky dark hair. "Where is Dom when you need him?"

Eumelia looks up at Hanu, then scans the rows of shelves behind her. She frowns. "He should have been back by now. He was only going to fetch Muse Clio, and I heard her talking to him over in Section Four not long ago."

The words are hardly out of Eumelia's mouth when Muse Clio emerges from a row of shelves, her long robes of sea green sweeping over the intricate floor mosaic as she strides barefoot toward the two novices.

"Dom told me you need help with a missing map label?" says Clio.

"Yes, thank you, sister," says Eumelia, rising from her seat. "It's over here." Clio and Hanu follow as Eumelia picks her way across the box-strewn floor to a nearby low table, where a large map lies unrolled, its curling, frayed edges held down by four small wooden boxes.

The three women stand before the map. To the two novices, this must look like a map of city streets. Of course, I've spent enough time recording memories of Velkanos to recognize the regular grid of Under City tunnels at the center of the map, which fan out toward the map's edges into an irregular network of volcanic tubes that predate the city builders by millions of years. I'm sure Muse Clio knows what she's looking at, too, but she doesn't say so. Instead, she runs her long pale fingers over the characters written across the top of the map and says, "Leave this one to me, little sisters. I'll catalog it myself. You two carry on with the rest of the new khartographia materials."

Muse Clio removes the little boxes weighing down the corners of the map, carefully rolls it up, and returns it to its unlabeled box. She slips the box into the leather satchel she carries with her everywhere and walks back toward Section Four.

Eumelia and Hanu exchange a look.

"What do you suppose—?" says Hanu.

"No idea," says Eumelia, watching Clio's departure with a mystified expression.

I recognize my moment, but I have to pause the memory first to collect myself. The gripping pain in my chest has become piercing, rapidly draining the little strength I have remaining. I'll have to make this fast. Gritting my teeth, I rise to my feet and step unsteadily toward Eumelia, my body merging with her avatar. Closing my eyes, I pour everything I have left into this bridge, reaching for the reality that intersects this memory.

My awareness departs my body, flowing out into the unknowable space between the worlds. Mercifully, all sensation of pain fades away. But I can't let the welcome relief distract me from the work at hand. Even if I'd had lifetimes to practice the art of branch travel, it wouldn't have been enough time to achieve mastery. As it is, with the paltry forty years I've been afforded in this lifetime, I'm still enough of a novice that navigating precisely from the branch where I am to the branch that I need requires all my focus.

I feel my strength waning, and for a moment fear threatens to pull me back to the safety of my branch, to cut my journey short. But I let go of the fear and seize the intersection I've chosen. I lose a part of myself in the crossing, and that part is consumed, absorbed, becoming the bridge.

At last, to my relief, my awareness emerges on the far side of the bridge, making a rough landing in Eumelia's body. She straightens up with a jolt.

"Ava!" she gasps indignantly, as though I've burned her.

I don't correct her slight misunderstanding. In fact, I'm counting on it. There's no way I can explain to Eumelia exactly who I am in the limited time I'll be able to remain here.

Listen, Eumelia, I think urgently. *Do you remember what you promised me?*

And of course she does. The memory that flashes through her mind is only two days old for her—so fresh it's raw. While Eumelia sat grieving Ava's death with Hanu and Dom, Ava's awareness passed between the three of them. Ava's fear for Dom had given her the critical foresight to extract from her trio sisters two promises, both of which I must now invoke.

Eumelia massages her temples, wincing. My clumsy intrusion into her mind has given her quite a headache. *What do you need?* she thinks.

"Mel?" says Hanu, watching Eumelia's pained expression with concern. "What's wrong?"

Eumelia holds up her hand, bidding Hanu to wait, listening for my next words.

Dom's in trouble, I think. *Find Serapen. Take Hanu with you. Remind Hanu of her promise to me.*

Eumelia scans the shelves around her in confusion. She thinks, *But Dom was just here. What happened?*

He's gone down into the tunnels with Balashi, I think. *He needs a healer. He—* There's an irresistible pull from deep inside of me. Damn it. My body, back on Earth, demands my return. Something's wrong.

I can't stay, Eumelia, I think urgently. *You have to trust me. There's no time. Go! Now!*

With my final burst of energy, I push into Eumelia's mind the image of the Under City map in Clio's bag, searing in the memory of the intersection where she'll find Dom. Eumelia sets off running after Muse Clio, shouting for Hanu to follow her.

Then my awareness loses its hold on Eumelia's branch. The vast hall of the Musaion library vanishes from sight as the grey spliner walls close in around me. Blinding pain greets me as my awareness returns to my body. Gasping, I lose my balance and start to fall. The spliner floor rises automatically to catch me in its cradling embrace, but the impact is still jarring. My flailing arm knocks over my water glass, which rolls away, spilling the remainder of its contents across the floor. My heart monitor pings out an alarm, sounding strangely distant in my ears.

"Stay calm, Emmie," says Bealsio, her anxious face hovering over me. "Breathe. Dom's on his way."

"Listen," I gasp through gritted teeth, each syllable a struggle. "I'm out … of time … Remember … what I showed you …"

Bealsio nods. Through the immerger fabric of my gloves, I feel the simulated warmth and pressure of her ephemeral hand gripping my icy fingers. "I'll remember," she says, tears gleaming in her vivid green eyes. "You've done your part, Emmie. We'll finish the work. Don't worry." Even in the midst of my pain, I register surprise. Are those her tears, or mine? Is it possible that she understands, even feels, the emotion behind her perfect rendering of grief?

"Thanks, B," I whisper, my eyelids fluttering. The warmth is draining fast from my body. I fight the tugging sensation of my awareness drifting out again into the space between the worlds. The oppressive weight of the pain in my chest is all that's left anchoring me to this body. "I couldn't … have done this … without you."

In our bedroom upstairs, directly over my head, Dom's feet hit the floor with a thud. His pounding footfalls race along the hall, growing louder as he descends the basement stairs toward me. "I'm coming!" he shouts.

The spliner door slides open with a swish. A wave of cool air washes over me as Dom rushes to my side. "Hang on, Em," he says, dropping to his knees, pressing his warm hand to my icy cheek, pouring his energy into the rapidly emptying vessel of my body.

I fight to hang on, holding his intense gaze in mine. I see my reflection in the depths of his dark brown eyes, merging with his countless memories of my other deaths. How beautiful he is, even now, weighed down by the pain I never wanted him to share. Even if I had a thousand years remaining, it wouldn't be enough to express my gratitude for all he's done for me, and all that he will do.

But my time is up. With my final breath, I whisper, "Dom … She will come … to finish … the work … We'll find … our way out … together … I promise."

THE PLACE PREPARED

HEART POUNDING, I BURST through the spliner door and find Emmie sprawled on her back, her arms splayed wide, her curled fingers twitching. The black fabric of her immerger clothes makes her shrunken form look like a shadow of her former self spilled across the grey floor. I drop to my knees beside her.

"Hang on, Em," I say, pressing my palm to her cheek to restore our connection and pouring my energy into her. Spirits, how pale she looks. She should never have come down here alone. How the hell didn't I hear her slip out of bed?

I can't suppress a reproachful glare at Bealsio, who kneels across from me, watching intently as I attempt to stabilize Emmie. Bealsio chews her lip, a nervous expression uncannily familiar to me from Emmie's youth. Sometimes I almost forget she isn't my Emmie, only the assistant we've refined over many years as Emmie's failing memory and health have made the great work increasingly difficult.

Months ago, when Emmie's condition took a turn for the worse, I issued a root command to Bealsio to alert me any time Emmie entered the spliner alone. I had no intention of spying on her; I only wanted to be sure I'd be close at hand if an emergency like this arose. Emmie has instructed Bealsio to follow my commands, but clearly one of Emmie's commands overrode my own. Why in the world would Emmie keep me out this way, especially now, with her condition so precarious?

Emmie's rasping inhalation draws my gaze back to her. She whispers, "Dom … She will come … to finish … the work … We'll find … our way out … together … I promise." The color drains from her thin face. Her twitching fingers relax.

No. No. Please, no. I send up a desperate plea to the spirits, though whether they're listening in this world, or any world, I no longer know.

The light in Emmie's once-vivid green eyes dims. Her gaze loses focus as her eyelids close. Her breathing slows until it's barely perceptible.

Emmie's pushed herself so hard, so far beyond the limits her doctors told us to expect, that she might have been surviving on willpower alone for the past few months. She was so certain she had more time that I'd almost started to believe her, despite all the signs to the contrary.

"Can you hear me, Em? Em!" With two fingers, I press the delicate skin of her neck, searching for a pulse. Her heartbeat, though faint, is still there. Emmie's awareness, however, is gone. I detect no trace of her thoughts through our connection.

Immediately, I reach for the bottle of unbinding pharmaka that Emmie wears on her immerger belt. I unscrew the top and withdraw the dropper. It's bone dry. Alarmed, I hold up the little bottle at eye level. It's completely empty.

"Bealsio!" I exclaim, my voice shaking with accusation. "How—" I shake my head. There's no time. "Share Emmie's vitals with Amos," I command. "Tell him we need a supply refresh as soon as possible."

"Sending now, Dom," says Bealsio, an unfamiliar note of contrition in her voice. I glance at her in surprise. She meets my gaze with a deferential incline of her head. She's never addressed me this way before. Is it possible she feels sorry for undermining my efforts to keep Emmie safe? I rake my fingers through my hair. What an AI does or doesn't feel is the least of my concerns right now.

I let out a long breath to calm myself. From my reeling mind, a steadying thought emerges: Emmie would only take a risk like this with good reason. "Bealsio …" I begin, then hesitate. It feels almost selfish to ask, as Emmie lies unconscious here before me. But I must know. "Did Emmie find the Ava she was looking for?"

Bealsio regards me thoughtfully, pausing long enough for me to wonder why an AI, whose reactions so outpace the speed of human thought, might need such a long pause. Long enough for hope to flicker in my heart. Long enough for me to be crushed when at last she says only, "Maybe."

I bow my head, fighting back despair. It wasn't supposed to be this way. I gave my time to the Voice in all—thousands of years in its service, more than any man should have to give. My debt was paid. I've let myself believe these final precious years with Emmie were my reward, a chance to bid farewell to my beloved before the blissful oblivion of Death. How could I have been such a fool? After all this time, haven't I learned that the price for an Artifex to follow his Muse is limitless?

Bealsio's simulated hand settles on my hand, her simulated fingers warm, gentle, familiar. "What's lost makes space for something new, Dom," she says, with a voice that belongs to the joyful opening chapter of the life Emmie and I shared, not this tragic conclusion.

Reluctantly, I look up. It's almost unbearable, gazing into those intense green eyes. Emmie knew what she was doing, when she gave Bealsio her face, her voice, her mind. Bealsio is a constant reminder that my despair does not absolve me from my promise.

"You heard what Emmie said," says Bealsio. "The Ava we need will find us. We'll finish the work. Together."

I gaze down at Emmie's withered body. I'm not sure I believe we can finish the great work without Emmie, and I'm not sure any Ava can find this branch without the pull of Emmie's awareness to guide her here. But my Muse never gave up on me, so I won't give up on her. "Together," I say softly.

With a wave of my hand, I summon the memory Emmie and Ava prepared to be their meeting place. The flat grey light of the spliner brightens into the clear sunlight of midday. The sound of the great river Purattu rushes in the distance. Closing my eyes and gripping Emmie's hand, I reach out in my mind for the one she believed would come to finish what we started.

I reach. I hope. I wait.

And I wait.

And I wait.

NEW ALLIES

In the dark tunnels of the Under City, Lilith rises to her feet. Through her eyes, I gaze down in horror at Dom's unconscious form sprawled across the paving stones, his cheek gleaming with blood, his lips deathly pale. Lilith turns away from him, heading back to the cart where Tio stands waiting.

Please don't leave him! I think, wrestling for control of Lilith's movements, willing her to turn back, begging her to use her healer arts to revive Dom. But all my attempts are useless. Lilith has regained full self-control after my surprise invasion of her mind.

Tio and Lilith exchange a wordless look as she steps back up into the cart. In Lilith's mind, I glimpse the face of a younger Tio, his brow unlined, his posture unbowed, but wearing a similarly downcast expression. He was quite handsome, before whatever happened that twisted his body and his features into their current state. Lilith pushes this apparently unwanted memory away as she helps Tio into his seat. Placing her hand behind his knee, she adjusts the position of his stiff leg with a practiced, familiar gesture before she takes the seat beside him. Tio casts one last sorrowful look at Dom before he pulls a lever inside the cart, initiating its clattering descent back down the tunnel, heading toward the Outer City.

Lilith looks back over her shoulder only once. The sight of Dom's abandoned body stirs no remorse in her heart, but I'm overcome by grief at the thought that he spent his last moments alone, without me. The emptiness where our connection used to be fills with the knowledge of my failure. I promised him we'd find our way out of this together. Without our bond, how can I possibly keep my promise?

The core memory of the day I made that promise flashes through my mind. With it flares a desperate hope, irresistible, calling me toward the last bridge I built with Emmie's help. We've agreed to meet at the intersection that core memory forms between my branch of Dulai and hers of Earth, whenever we have information to share that might help the other. I hadn't expected to need this bridge so soon, but in my disembodied state, untethered from Dom, trapped inside Lilith, I have nowhere else to turn but Emmie.

So I reach for the memory that Emmie recorded in the alternet for me. Using all that I've learned from crossing bridges over the past half moon, I let go of my hold on Lilith's unyielding mind, losing my connection to my own branch, and slip from Dulai toward Earth.

The passage between the worlds is becoming easier. I'm disoriented only briefly as I emerge on the far side of the bridge, squinting as my eyes adjust to the midday sunlight of my memory after the darkness of the Under City. I'm standing at the end of the footpath that leads from the sandy shore of the Purattu to the shelter of the river cliffs. A cool breeze ruffles my unbound hair. In the distance, the ducks call *krek krek krek.*

I hurry along the path toward the natural alcoves at the base of the cliffs. My tent stands in the shade of one alcove, right where Emmie and I left it the last time I was here.

"Emmie?" I call anxiously.

There's no answer. I hurry toward the tent. She said she'd be here when I returned, though she hadn't specified exactly where. Maybe she's waiting inside the tent for me, along with those avatars she made of myself and Dom.

I pull back the tent flap. There's nothing inside except four empty bedrolls. I turn to face the river again. "Emmie?" I call out, louder this time. My voice echoes along the cliffs.

"Ava?" The voice that answers me is so hoarse that at first I don't recognize it. I turn toward the sound and discover Emmie's Dom standing behind the tent in the shadows of the alcove, nearly invisible in his inky black immerger clothes. When he steps toward me into the sunlight, I'm startled by the change in him since my last visit to Earth. This older other-Dom has always struck me as slightly sorrowful, but every line of his face and posture is drawn in suffering now. In a dazed tone, he says, "You came back."

Clearly there's something wrong with him, and I don't want to be insensitive, but whatever has happened to this Dom can surely wait. If there's any possibility of helping my own Dom, I need to focus on that now. "Where's Emmie?" I say urgently.

"Calm down," says other-Dom. "Relax. Breathe."

I shake my head, irritated by his coddling. "You don't understand. I need to get back to my branch now. Right now. There's been an accident. Dom needs my help."

"All right," he says soothingly. "Where were you, before you were here?"

"Please, can you just find Emmie for me?" I say, brushing past the tedious question he always asks when my awareness suddenly appears on this branch. "I need her help to build a bridge back to my branch."

"Emmie's … away," he says. "We'll have to manage on our own until she returns. Where were you, before you were here?"

I sigh, exasperated, looking down at Emmie's body, which I'm now occupying. I thought she was going to be waiting here for me. She'd promised me she'd be waiting. That was the plan. But I suppose I can't wait for her. Impatiently, I tell other-Dom, "I'm from The End of the Road."

Other-Dom nods, gestures with both hands, and summons the record of my branch. The sounds, sensations, and sights of this memory of the Purattu fade into the background. A globe representing my branch of Dulai appears hovering in the space between me and other-Dom. He taps the globe with his hand. An astonishing number of memory spheres spring out at his touch, swirling around the globe like a colorful flock of birds. Through each sphere's translucent surface, I catch fragmentary glimpses of my life before I died. Three riders galloping toward the novice caravan on the plains outside the walls of Velkanos. Standing side by side with Eumelia on the river sandbar as we cast fishing nets into the Purattu. Pulling Dom to his knees beside me to greet the wolves Serapen summoned from the wilderness to protect us from Lilith. Nestling in Hanu's soft arms on a frigid night in the Urashtu mountains. I recognize all these memories, but I don't remember recording them with Emmie or other-Dom. So who did?

Focus, Ava, focus. There's not enough time to untangle every mystery right now. I say, "Dom was in the main tunnel of the Under City, at the cross-tunnel beneath the street of workshops, when he ran into Lilith …" My narration grows more confident as I watch other-Dom at work. With precise gestures and spoken commands, he weaves together each element of the scene I'm describing.

Other-Dom requires so little direction from me he might as well be reading my mind as he records the memory I'll need to build the bridge back to Dulai. His perfect attentiveness to my every word and his mastery of these arts of tekhnologia, which I barely understand, gives me pause. Growing up on the run with Lilith in Dulai, I learned to rely on my own wits and skill to navigate the world. Unfortunately, my old knowledge has little practical value here on Earth. I need to rely on other-Dom's help, and this reliance makes me deeply uncomfortable. I know he deserves my gratitude, but the humility required for gratitude doesn't come easily to me. More often, when I've encountered other-Dom, I've managed to show him little more than impatience.

Fortunately, his efficiency leaves little time for impatience. Thanks to him, I'm soon looking down at a perfect replica of my Dom's body on the floor of the underground tunnel. Lilith kneels over him with the pharmaka-soaked rag pressed to his face. Tio stands watching from the shadows.

Other-Dom looks up at me, his expression holding a wordless question. *Is this right?*

Eagerly, I nod and step into the scene other-Dom has crafted, returning to my place in Lilith's body at the moment just before my Dom lost consciousness. For all Lilith's faults, I know she didn't intend to kill him. If I can just persuade her to move her hand away from his face a moment sooner, that's all it should take to save him. I reach deep inside myself for the familiar sensation of Dom's awareness in mine, summoning all my strength. I've always found my way back to him before. Surely I'll find my way back again in time to save him.

I reach. I hope. I wait.

And I wait.

And I wait.

"It's not working," I say, frustrated. I stand and pace the stone tunnel floors of my memory. My heartbeat turns erratic, and I have to stop to catch my breath. I hug myself, rubbing my hands vigorously up and down my arms to ward off the chill that creeps into my bones as soon as I stop moving. Until this moment, I've been so focused on returning to help Dom that I've managed to ignore the constraints of Emmie's body.

I sway dizzily on my feet, and the severity of my weakness slowly sinks in, dimming my hope of a quick return to my branch. Every bridge crossing consumes a great deal of strength, and this body has almost none remaining.

Exhaustion settles over me like a heavy blanket. I struggle to find the thread of my previous thought. Where am I? What am I doing here? I shake my head slowly, peering in confusion at the man beside me. It takes longer than it should for me to grasp the question weaving in and out of focus through my foggy thoughts. “Why isn’t it working?” I say at last.

Dom—no, I remind myself, this is other-Dom, not my Dom—wraps his arm around my shoulders. He tugs the stretchy black immerger glove off my right hand and wraps his strong, warm fingers around my cold, frail ones. “I think you know,” he says.

The finality in his tone crushes me, confirming my worst fear. My Dom is dead. Irrecoverably dead. Tears well up in my eyes—no, Emmie’s eyes, I remind myself. Spirits, the longer I linger here, the blurrier these boundaries become. I’ve lost my own body already. How much more of myself do I have to lose?

Other-Dom makes a small gesture with his free hand, causing my memory of the underground tunnel to shrink back into its enclosing sphere. The sphere floats upward, rejoining the flock of other memories swirling around The End of the Road. He and I stand together gazing up at the glowing spheres, all that remain to me now of the branch I’ve left behind. As the memories of my life with Dom recede from me, the searing sense of loss burns away the fog in my mind, exposing my deepest regret. “I shouldn’t have left him,” I whisper. “He died alone because of me.”

Other-Dom squeezes my hand, sending a soothing calm through me. “There is no one to blame for the natural order of things,” he says. “There is only the pattern, and we who observe the pattern.”

“What pattern?” I say, sniffling.

“We live, we love, we lose,” he says. “And then we live again. That is all.”

I wipe my leaking eyes and runny nose on the black sleeve of my immerger clothes. One of the silver threads woven into the fabric scratches my upper lip. I wince at the sting. “This can’t be all there is,” I say. “We can’t just live forever in a trap with no escape. Has the Voice cursed us?”

Other-Dom plants a kiss on my scratched lip. “Is it a curse to have loved?” he says, looking down at me with a tenderness that warms me to the core. I’m confused by the familiarity of his kiss and the surge of affection I feel for him, because this man, for all his similarities to my Dom, is still a stranger to me.

Slowly, I say, “You told me once that you’ve followed me, life after life. That means you’ve followed me death after death, too.”

He nods. “Each follows the other.”

“How do you bear it?” I say, searching his awareness for some hope of a cure for this pain in my heart.

He considers this for a moment, then says, “I’ve learned to make meaning from loss through our great work together. Come. I’ll show you.”

Other-Dom waves his hand through the swirling flock of memory spheres above us, and they vanish, leaving us standing together in the grey light of the empty, windowless spliner. He leads me by the hand toward the exit.

The door slides open, and the warm light of late afternoon spills over us. We climb the stairs from the basement into the living room and sit side by side on one of the cozy sofas facing the floor-to-ceiling windows. With a heavy heart, I look out at the dramatic view across the shimmering bay—San Francisco, the city of glass towers. This place was once the object of my dearest dreams, the place where I believed I would be free from the Voice in all and the Mohirai who enforce its will. A moon ago, I was willing to give up the entire world I knew to reach this land of freedom. But I had no idea what price I would pay for the journey. I've lost the only love I've ever known, and I'm bound to the Voice more completely than I ever would have believed possible.

Other-Dom reaches over the arm of the sofa toward the side table and picks up a large book with a tooled leather cover. He opens the book to the first page and rests it across our laps.

It's a sketchbook—much like the one my Dom received from Urshanabi when we crossed the Purattu half a moon ago, though this book's unmarred cover has evidently been spared from Lilith's bird attacks. Slowly, I turn the pages, each one filled from edge to edge with what looks like Dom's drawings and my handwriting. The images stir some faint recognition in me, though I can't remember ever seeing these abstract figures or their accompanying text before.

"What is this?" I say.

"Instructions," says other-Dom. "All the instructions we've gathered for building bridges to other worlds."

I shake my head. "I don't understand," I say.

He says, "You and I have witnessed the truth of the many worlds and the connections between them. The Voice calls us to reveal this mystery to humankind. We must secure these instructions in a place where they cannot be lost or hidden, so that all who seek this truth may find it."

"Can't we just record these instructions in the quantum computer, then?" I say. "Wouldn't that make the instructions available on every branch?"

"It isn't quite that simple," he says. "The Stewards here on Earth guard the mysteries ruthlessly with their technology. The Mohirai on Dulai guard the mysteries, perhaps more gently, with their pharmaka. On every branch we've encountered, some human power exists that keeps the mysteries for its own purposes. But the Voice calls us to make this mystery known to all. Until our service to the Voice is complete, we are bound to this great work—life after life, death after death, world after world."

I sigh, wary of undertaking another job I don't fully understand. If only I'd asked more questions before my last job for Lilith, maybe I'd never have gotten myself into this mess. Maybe my Dom would still be alive. "And once we've accomplished this work?" I say. "Then what?"

Other-Dom squeezes my hand. "Freedom," he says.

"Freedom from what?" I say, searching his face. "Freedom to do what?"

The sun sinks slowly behind the city of glass towers on the western horizon outside the window, surrounding us in golden light. "Freedom to choose a new pattern," he says. "Freedom to move on."

I take a deep breath, gripping his hand for reassurance. "I love you," I say, the words slipping out reflexively, surprising me. Embarrassed heat rises to my cheeks. Were those Emmie's words, or mine? I'm not sure. On Dulai, it was difficult to separate my own impulses from Dom's when I shared his body, even when I could hear his thoughts distinct from mine. Emmie's thoughts are absent from this body, but could she still be here somewhere, hiding in the shadows, watching me? Is she in control of this body, or am I?

"I love you too," says other-Dom, extending his arm, inviting me into the space at his side, the same space I occupied at my own Dom's side for so many cold nights in Dulai over the past moon. I'm overwhelmed by other-Dom's tenderness, and by my desire to curl up against him. Is there any difference, really, between taking comfort from this Dom or my own?

But as I lean toward other-Dom, the image of my Dom's pale, bleeding face flashes in my mind. With a pang of guilt, I pull back. Emmie's frail body may need her Dom's strength to survive, but that doesn't mean I should cozy up to him while my own Dom lies abandoned in the Under City, his dead body not yet cold.

"All right," I say, putting as much space between myself and other-Dom as I can without letting go of his hand. "Let's do this, then. Together."

Other-Dom gives me a small smile, though it doesn't erase the sadness in his eyes. "Together," he says.

"Together," chimes a third voice.

The unexpected sound startles me so badly I nearly jump out of Emmie's skin. A petite young woman materializes in the empty seat beside me on the sofa. She shoots me a grin.

I've spent enough time in the alternet over my last few visits to Earth to recognize this apparition as an avatar of some kind. She wears a close-fitting garment woven from every shade of green I've ever seen, with a familiar branching symbol stitched in white across her chest. She bears an obvious resemblance to Emmie, with her striking emerald green eyes, her heart-shaped face, her chin-length chestnut hair streaked with cobalt blue. But she's too bright, somehow, to be the Emmie I've known—colors too saturated, skin too luminous, movements too energetic.

Cautiously, I say, "Who are you?"

"I'm Emmie's assistant. Bealsio," says the avatar, sticking out her hand toward me. I look down at her outstretched fingers in confusion. "Ah," Bealsio chuckles, the cheerful sound lifting the heavy mood in the room. "No handshakes on your branch, I guess." She lowers her hand and inclines her head toward me, a playful approximation of a polite greeting between two Mohiran sisters. "Well, anyway, it's nice to meet you."

I glance at other-Dom, expecting some further explanation for Bealsio's sudden appearance. He's still holding my hand, gradually restoring my depleted energy with his own. Using our connection, I glimpse through his eyes the strange sight of Bealsio seated beside me. Bealsio's sparkling avatar and my worn body evoke the beginning and the end of the rich life he shared with Emmie. The loss of that life feels so painful to him in this moment that he yearns for Death. My heart aches in sympathy for him, putting my own loss in a new perspective.

Other-Dom looks sharply at me, suddenly aware that I'm watching his private thoughts through our connection. *Sorry,* I think, withdrawing hastily. *I didn't mean to intrude.* Walling off my thoughts from his requires constant attention, and in my exhausted state my self-discipline lapsed.

Brushing past my awkward apology, other-Dom says to Bealsio, "I assume this isn't a social visit."

Bealsio shakes her head. "Amos' car just turned onto Skyline Boulevard," she says. "He'll be here in five minutes."

The corners of other-Dom's mouth tighten. He snaps shut the sketchbook on our laps and tucks it into a drawer beneath the side table. Without warning, he scoops me off the sofa cushions and into his arms.

"Hey! What are you doing?" I protest, wriggling uncomfortably against his chest as Emmie's frail body reveals the full extent of its aches and pains.

In an urgent tone, he says, "Listen to me, Ava. There's a lot you need to know that I don't have time to explain before Amos arrives. You'll have to do what I tell you until he's gone."

A moon ago, I would have bristled at being handled this way, like a helpless child. But my overdose, injuries, and deaths since then have forced me to endure one humiliation after another. Biting back a sharp retort, I say only, "What do you need me to do?"

"Don't say anything while Amos is here," says other-Dom, carrying me out of the living room and down the hallway that leads to the bedroom. He pushes open the bedroom door with his foot, crosses the room, and sets me down at the foot of the bed. Kneeling before me, he tugs the black immerger slippers off my feet, then removes my immerger glasses and sets them on the bedside table. "Pretend you're so weak and disoriented you can't focus or speak. Act like you've never seen Amos before."

"I *haven't* ever seen him before," I say, my voice muffled in my ears as other-Dom peels the stretchy, skin-tight immerger shirt up over my head.

"Should be easy enough to pretend, then," he says, though his worried expression tells me otherwise. He dresses me in a loose sleeping shirt, then settles the immerger glasses back on my nose. I blink a few times until Emmie's blurry vision refocuses. Other-Dom sets his hand on my shoulder, leveling a deadly serious look at me as he says, "Whatever you do, don't say anything in front of Amos. He can't know you're here."

"Why not?" I say.

"Amos only supplies Emmie with unbinding pharmaka because she's more useful to him alive than dead," he says. "If he suspects she's gone for good, he'll consider our arrangement concluded."

My mind races with questions. How does a man have access to unbinding pharmaka, whose preparation is known only to the Mohirai? Why is Emmie useful to Amos? What is the arrangement between them?

But before I can ask any of these questions, Bealsio's disembodied voice interjects, in a tone of warning, "Amos is pulling up to the house."

"We'll talk more after he's gone, Ava," says other-Dom. He hurriedly strips off my immerger leggings, settles me under the blankets, and tucks a pillow under my head.

A bell chimes somewhere in the hallway. Other-Dom squeezes my hand and says, "I'll let him in. Remember what I said. Whatever happens, don't say anything. We need the unbinding pharmaka he's delivering, but we don't want to give him any cause to stay longer than necessary. Do you understand?"

I don't understand much. But I know other-Dom—at least, I knew my own Dom—well enough to see that he's afraid. I also know the arts of Mohiran instruction well enough to recognize the significance of him repeating three times his warning not to speak. This Amos, whoever he is, must be dangerous.

Nervously, I nod. "I have listened, and I have heard, brother."

Other-Dom dims the lights in the bedroom as he departs. A moment later, Bealsio startles me again by materializing in the empty space beside me on the bed.

I clutch my chest with a grimace, waiting for Emmie's racing heartbeat to slow. "Could you warn me before you do that next time?" I say.

"Sorry about that," says Bealsio. "I'll adjust your notification settings now."

Outside the bedroom, down the hallway, a door swings open. Other-Dom says something, clearly a greeting of some kind, though I don't recognize the English words. The genial voice of an older man says something in reply. That must be Amos.

"Is it all right for you to be here when Amos comes in?" I whisper to Bealsio.

"He won't see me, unless you command it," says Bealsio. "I'm on a private channel with you and Dom. But I won't stay visible—your reactions to me might reveal my presence to him. I only came to let you know I'll be translating from English to Akkadian for you while Amos is here."

"What's Akkadi—?" But Bealsio vanishes before I can finish my question. I bite my tongue, remembering other-Dom's warning to remain silent.

Bealsio's disembodied voice murmurs in my ear, "Translation filter activated." For a moment, the filter muffles the ambient sounds of the bedroom. When the sounds sharpen again, I hear Amos' voice, now speaking words I understand. He says, "I'm glad to see you looking well, at least, Dom. The team is eager to have you both back once Emmie is through this latest episode. Any changes since your message?"

The two men's footsteps approach the bedroom together. "She's been drifting in and out of consciousness," says other-Dom. "Even with the extra doses she's been taking, it hasn't been enough to manage her symptoms. Last night was rough, and she's more disoriented than usual this evening."

The bedroom door swings open quietly. In the doorway appears the backlit silhouette of Amos, a tall, trim man with carefully coiffed hair. Something about his voice had led me to expect a man much older, but Amos' smooth face and erect posture suggest he's seen no more than forty summers. He lingers at the threshold for a moment before he walks toward my bedside, carrying a small square case by its handle.

Other-Dom follows a few paces behind Amos, his expression unreadable. I watch both men through half-closed eyes, feigning drowsiness, hoping I look like someone on the edge of consciousness. I wasn't expecting to recognize Amos, but as he approaches my bed, I'm surprised to find there is something vaguely familiar about him. Where have I seen that thick mane of white-blonde hair before?

As though reading my mind, Bealsio murmurs in my ear, "Amos is the head of the Stewards of the True Cross. He injected Emmie with the binding pharmaka that caused her overdose."

My eyes widen in alarm. Of course. That must be where I've seen him before. The first time Emmie met me, she showed me a recorded memory of the day her overdose occurred. I'd seen her and Amos standing together in a windowless vaulted chamber. There wasn't enough light for me to discern much of their surroundings, but I remember seeing a dead tree standing over a dark pool. When Emmie tried to approach the pool, Amos grabbed her in a chokehold and pressed a small silver object the size of a stylus to her neck. At the time, I thought Amos was threatening her with a knife, but perhaps that was some weapon containing pharmaka, like the darts I've seen Muse Arkhi use to subdue animals.

"How are you doing today, Emmie?" says Amos, sitting on the edge of the bed beside me. He gives off a faint, sweetly smoky scent that reminds me of the ceremonial pharmaka the Mohirai use to induce dreams. Despite the pleasant tone of his voice and his friendly demeanor, his proximity makes my skin crawl. He studies my face. I bite my tongue, hoping my apprehension looks like nothing more than disorientation.

"I see," Amos says at last, as though I've answered his question. To other-Dom, he says, "I'll adjust her dosage, then."

Amos sets his shiny leather case on the bedside table. He opens the case, revealing nine small compartments lined with sky-blue velvet. Each compartment holds a darker blue bottle of a liquid I know all too well. I've made every effort to avoid taking unbinding pharmaka for the last moon, desperate to preserve the memories it destroys, but unbinding pharmaka is the only remedy for the side effects of a binding pharmaka overdose. Amos withdraws four of the nine bottles and sets them in a neat line on the bedside table.

"That's one more bottle than he usually leaves," Bealsio's voice murmurs in my ear. "That should give you enough for three days, based on Emmie's current consumption."

Amos closes the case containing the remaining five bottles and sets it on the floor between his feet. He reaches for the nearest full bottle on the bedside table.

Other-Dom says in a tone of warning, "She's in a delicate state, Amos. I need to stabilize her before she can handle another dose."

Amos doesn't look happy about this, but he nods and withdraws his hand from the bottle. I hope he's about to leave. Instead, he leans over me, and the lamp on my bedside table fully illuminates his face for the first time.

The hairs on the back of my neck prickle. Only now do I realize my recognition of Amos runs deeper than Emmie's memory. He looks down at me with ice blue eyes that chill me to my core—eyes so much like Lilith's that for an instant I feel as though I'm staring up at her. My pulse races. I fight back the urge to cringe away from him.

"I do hope you'll be feeling better next time, my dear," says Amos, giving my hand a squeeze that lingers too long. "We have much to discuss."

At last, to my relief, Amos stands. Other-Dom ushers him quickly out of the bedroom. Their footsteps retreat down the hall, and other-Dom bids Amos a curt farewell. Only when other-Dom reappears in the doorway do I realize that I've been holding my breath since Amos touched me. I exhale with a shudder that turns into shivering.

Other-Dom hurries to the bedside and takes my hand. He pours some of his energy through our bond to steady me, then pours a tall glass of water from the ceramic pitcher that stands on the bedside table. "You did well," he says. "I don't think Amos suspects anything." He unscrews the top from one of the little blue bottles, mixes six drops of unbinding pharmaka into the water, helps me sit up from the pillows, and holds the glass to my lips.

I inhale the familiar flowery aroma of the unbinding pharmaka. Reluctantly, I take a few sips. My bone-rattling shivering slows, then stops, which is a relief, but with each sip my thoughts lose focus. I turn my head away, holding up my hand.

"Wait," I say, afraid to lose the thread of this thought.

Other-Dom lowers the glass and sets it back on the bedside table. He takes my hand, a furrow of worry forming between his heavy brows as he studies me. "What's wrong?" he says.

"Amos," I say. "Who is he?"

"He's the head of the Stewards," says other-Dom. "It's a long story, but he was —"

I interrupt him, saying, "The one who injected Emmie with binding pharmaka. Yes, I know that part. Emmie showed me. But why does he look like Lilith?"

Other-Dom frowns. "Like Lilith?" he says. "In what way?"

"Something about his eyes," I say. "Or maybe his face. I'm not sure, exactly."

A soft, pleasant chime sounds, a familiar chord of three notes repeated three times. Bealsio materializes slowly on the bed beside me—much less startling than last time, though the sound of her Mohiran summoning bells seems out of place on this world. "Fascinating," says Bealsio. "Emmie never even considered such a possibility. But Ava's right."

"About what?" says other-Dom.

Bealsio waves her hand, and two life-sized translucent heads appear hovering in the space between the three of us on the bed. The heads rotate slowly side by side, mirroring the motion of Bealsio's fingers. As the two faces turn, the pale eyes of Lilith and Amos sweep over me. I shrink back against my pillow.

"Look," says Bealsio. Two separate silver meshes, delicate as spiderwebs, appear over the two faces. Patterns in the webs glow green beneath her fingertips as she gestures. "The bone structure here in the forehead. The cheekbones. The eye shape. There's a strong family resemblance here."

Family. I remember when Lilith first taught me that word, the summer she took me from the Children's Temple. She'd told me she and I would be a family, once we escaped the control of the Mohirai. But because the kinship ties that create families have been forbidden by the Voice in all since the time of destruction, all I know of family is what I learned from Lilith.

"What does that mean—family resemblance?" I say.

Bealsio tilts her head to one side, still examining the floating heads. "A family resemblance is a similarity in physical attributes between two people who are related through breeding. For example, Lilith and Amos might share a family resemblance if she were his sister, or his daughter, or his mother."

Mother. As I watch the pale faces of Lilith and Amos hovering before me, a third face flashes in my mind, so different from the other two—large brown eyes, hazelnut skin, pointed chin. It's Maya's face, as I glimpsed her in Lilith's memory. I close my eyes, feeling like such a fool. Even the youngest girls in the Children's Temple know that animals of similar breeding share a resemblance. Why did I never think to question the fact that I look nothing at all like Lilith? How many times did I daub her fair skin and flaxen hair with mud to improve her camouflage on a job, while my own dark skin and curls blended naturally into the shadows? How often on our journeys together did I envy her height, her muscular build, her endurance? I'd blamed my delicate frame and perpetual difficulty keeping up with Lilith on her decision to withhold pharmaka from my diet to protect me from the Voice. I should have suspected that Lilith couldn't be my mother. Maya, by contrast, could be a mirror of myself.

I shake my head, clearing away all my questions about Maya to make space for a question that seems more important right now. I say, "If Amos and Lilith are related, does that mean there's a version of Lilith on this branch?"

Other-Dom taps his gloved fingers in the air. A globe of blue, white, and green appears hovering over his open palm, rotating slowly. "It's a fair question," he says. "Earth and Dulai do share a common history. At some point long ago—we don't know exactly when or why—the branch we call Earth split off from my own branch of Dulai." He waves his hand, and the globe divides into twin globes. "That means Lilith could have lived on Earth, if the split between these branches occurred after she was born. Even so, to the best of our knowledge, Lilith would have been born at least four thousand years before the present day—maybe more. She would most likely be long dead by now."

"But Lilith was centuries old even before I was born," I persist. "And some initiates live for thousands of years. If Lilith was born on this branch, she could still be alive, if she was using initiate pharmaka."

"It's not impossible," says other-Dom. "And there is some evidence that Mohirai might have existed on Earth long ago—for example, the fact that the Stewards today possess some knowledge of pharmaka. That could have happened if the Mohirai shared pharmaka training with the ancient priesthood that gave rise to the Stewards. But we've found no sign of any order in the present time with complete knowledge of the higher mysteries of the Mohirai. And believe me, we've searched. If we could find anyone on Earth, even Lilith, who could fill in the gaps of the knowledge we've managed to gather so far—about the Voice in all, the calling, initiation, branch travel—it would make the great work far easier to complete."

It's clear from other-Dom's tone that he's gently steering me toward the reasonable conclusion that finding Lilith on Earth is impossible. Perhaps he's right. And, in many ways, the thought of encountering Lilith ever again is abhorrent to me. I'm furious with her for manipulating me, for lying to me, for severing me from Dom. How could I ever trust her again?

But I've spent enough time in Lilith's company over our years together to fully appreciate her capabilities. Her skillful use of the Mohirai and the free men to pursue her own ends taught me that the only difference between an adversary and an ally is a shared interest. My dependence on Dom—on every branch where I've encountered a Dom—has taught me the value of allies. Lilith would be a powerful ally, and I suspect that the great work ahead will require every ally I can find.

"Lilith knows more of the arts and mysteries than most initiate Mohirai," I say. "And she always said that Serapen had no right to hide the mysteries in the first place. If we could find Lilith—on this branch, or any other—she might help us finish the great work, if it meant the Mohirai would lose their control over the mysteries."

Other-Dom tilts his head, stroking his chin, studying me with a doubtful expression. Bealsio shoots a stern look at him, and he sighs.

"What?" I say apprehensively, looking from one to the other.

Other-Dom's expression turns inward, unreadable. I resist the temptation to peek into his thoughts for some insight that will help me persuade him. After a long pause, he nods at Bealsio and says, "If Ava thinks we need to find Lilith, then that's what we'll do."

His tone communicates so many unspoken reservations that I'm opening my mouth to lay out my arguments before I realize he's already agreed.

"Wonderful!" says Bealsio, clapping her hands as she looks from other-Dom to me. "Where shall we begin?"

Seeing the contrast between grim other-Dom and eager Bealsio, I can't help remembering the fateful night I crouched with Lilith in our hiding spot at the edge of the cedar forest, waiting for my moment to sneak into the Children's Temple storerooms. I'd waved off Lilith's grim warning as I'd eagerly set off to steal the amanitai I thought would pay for our passage across the sea. I'd known nothing of the risk I was taking, nothing of the purpose I was serving, nothing of the true price of freedom. If I've learned anything since then, it's how little I truly understand.

So I say, "I'm sorry. I don't know where we should begin." What I mean, though, is that I haven't the faintest idea how to do any part of the work ahead. I'm not even sure I can stand on my own two feet without help, in this world.

To my surprise, Bealsio laughs. "*You* don't have to know," she says. "We'll figure it out *together*, remember?"

Together. My throat tightens, and I fight back tears, hearing in Bealsio's confidence an echo of the confidence with which I promised Dom we'd find our way out of Dulai together. My ignorant confidence led to my own death, and to his, in the end. How dare I lead two new companions into unknown danger, in service of the Voice's unknown purpose, with an unknown chance of success, after what I did to Dom?

Other-Dom squeezes my hand and says, "One day at a time. Rest the night. We'll have our work cut out for us tomorrow."

HOUSE OF HEALING

THE FIRST THING TO PENETRATE my sleeping mind is the familiar sound of the morning bells, a sweet chord of three notes repeated three times. The sound awakens my earliest memory, from my seventh summer: Hedi Mohira's singing voice outside the door of my trio's room, her resonant alto accompanying the distant tolling of the Children's Temple bells, announcing a new day to the house of boys.

Sun rises
So rise we
From slumber

The second thing to penetrate my mind is a throbbing headache. With a soft groan, I open my eyes.

A pair of smooth, pale hands with neatly trimmed fingernails holds a strip of clean white linen that gives off a honey-sweet scent. I bolt upright, inexplicably terrified by the sight of the cloth approaching my face.

Beside the narrow bed in which I've just awoken, a slim Mohira in a sky-blue healer's robe stands leaning over me. She straightens up with a startled expression, then drops the linen she's holding into a basket at her feet on the stone floor. She runs her forefinger down an embroidered blue line on the colorful stole draped over her shoulders, no doubt summoning aid from some other sister, before she grips my wrist firmly in her hand. As her warm fingers probe my icy skin, I shiver, realizing how cold I am. I've never been so cold.

"Be calm, Dom," she says in a kind voice, keeping pressure on my wrist. The rising panic in my chest eases, and when I've relaxed a little, she pulls a thick woolen blanket up from the foot of my bed and wraps it tightly around me.

"Where am I?" I say, teeth chattering.

"You're in the house of healing, in Velkanos," she says gently. "You've had an accident. But you're going to be all right."

An accident? In Velkanos? I try to remember what happened, but the effort sharpens my headache. Only when I stop trying to remember does the pain subside. I reach up to massage my throbbing temple, where I discover a soft pad covering the left side of my face, held in place by a bandage wrapped around my head. There's a dull ache when I tentatively press my cheek. Beneath my shirt, I feel another large bandage plastered across my upper back and shoulders, covering something that stings if I move too quickly.

Dazed, I look past the healer to the room around us. At the center of the wall across from the bed, a roaring fire burns in the largest fireplace I've ever seen. A copper cauldron steams above the flames, suspended from an iron hook. How is it possible that I feel so cold, with such a massive fire burning nearby?

Shelves line the walls on either side of the fireplace, with wooden boxes stacked on upper shelves so high they could only be accessed using the polished wooden ladder propped up in the corner. Glass bottles, clay jars, and cloth packages of many sizes and colors crowd the lower shelves within arm's reach.

Morning light filters through the screened row of windows to my left, illuminating the smooth white plaster walls. An arched double door to my right stands partly open, revealing an airy, sunlit hallway beyond. A pair of women in sky-blue healer robes pass by the door, murmuring in quiet conversation.

My eyes wander up the walls, and I gasp in wonder, forgetting myself for a moment. For as long as I can remember, I've dreamed of seeing the wonders the Mohirai hide within their temple city walls. My first glimpse doesn't disappoint. The domed ceiling seems to be floating impossibly high overhead, held up by graceful arches of pale grey stone. I've never seen such a beautiful structure. The spaces between the arches are filled with colorful tile mosaics, their intricate swirling patterns reminding me of … I squint, trying to remember. This time, to my relief, a memory emerges easily from the fog in my mind. I remember standing … in a cave? Yes, it was a cave. I was holding a torch, looking up at a low, dark cave ceiling covered in white markings that formed a pattern much like the one in the mosaic above me now.

I lower my gaze to meet the eyes of the healer in front of me, who has been watching me closely as I survey the room. Her open expression and the way she holds my wrist suggest a close familiarity with me, and I'm bothered by the sense that I should recognize her. My headache flares again as I try to remember where I've seen her before.

"Um … I'm sorry, but … who are you?" I say.

She smiles. "I'm Sister Zia. Keeper of the house of novices."

"The house of novices …" I repeat. Bits and pieces start returning, faster now. Yes, the house of novices. That's where Muse Serapen, Muse Thalia, and Muse Arkhi were leading us all in the caravan: to the temple city of Velkanos, to begin our training in the house of novices. We'd ridden out together from the Calling Day ceremony in the cedar forest outside the Children's Temple, onto the road through the Subartu Desert, across the great river Purattu, into the Urashtu Mountains. We sought shelter in a cave in the mountains on the last night of the journey. Serapen had called it the Cave of Dreams. I remember falling asleep in the cave with the other novices beside the campfire, then waking up from a strange dream to the alarming sight of a great grey owl swooping down toward—

My recollections are interrupted by the appearance of two familiar faces at the open doorway.

"Oh, Dom!" cries Hanu, rushing in to stand at my bedside. She presses her warm hand to mine, her familiar touch soothing, kindling an answering warmth deep inside of me. My headache eases as I take in the welcome sight of her. Her eyes gleam as she looks down at me, but she sniffs back her tears and gives me a watery smile.

Eumelia follows close behind Hanu, her anxious face so pale that her freckles pop out like winter stars. She shakes her head in exasperation and says, "Promise you won't ever do that again, Dom."

"Do what again?" I say.

Hanu and Eumelia exchange a look, then glance at the doorway, where the High Priestess Serapen stands in silence, watching the three of us. Without a word, the girls step away from my bedside to make space for Serapen.

Serapen strides into the room. She's traded the dusty riding clothes she's been wearing this past moon for an immaculate, richly textured sky-blue robe. The colorfully embroidered stole draped over her shoulders is even larger than Zia's. Her snow-white hair is woven into a crown of elaborate braids atop her head, making her look even taller than usual. I've rarely seen anything other than perfect serenity on the face of the High Priestess, but her clear brown eyes flash with fury that would make me tremble, were it directed at me. Fortunately, the object of Serapen's fury seems to be the man in the flowing white cloak who follows meekly behind her, his face tense with worry.

The man's expression softens when he sees me. He heaves a sigh of relief and gives me a winning smile. "It's good to see you awake again, Dom. You gave us all quite a scare."

I look from the unfamiliar man to Serapen, my confusion deepening into apprehension. Slowly, I say, "Would someone please explain what's going on?"

Serapen says, in a tightly measured tone, "Come, little brother. I think it's best for Dom to hear it straight from you, since you were the only one with him when it happened."

It takes me a moment to spot the figure lingering just outside the doorway. "Bala?" I say, surprised by the sight of my trio brother. I haven't seen Balashi since our Calling Day a moon ago, and I'd be delighted to see him now, were the circumstances not so strange. "What are you doing in Velkanos?"

Balashi steps reluctantly into the room. In a tone that suggests he's repeating a story he's told countless times already, he says, "I came here in the company of Tio Artifex and Kabir Artifex." He glances at the unfamiliar man standing beside Serapen. Despite Balashi's carefully composed expression, I've known him long enough to recognize the simmering resentment in that glance.

I take a second look at the white-cloaked man, bothered by a suspicion that I should recognize him, just as I should have recognized Zia. I remember Muse Thalia and Muse Arkhi telling me about Tio, first of the Artifexi, as we sat around the campfire one night. I've never heard the name Kabir before, though. I wonder whether this man is Tio or Kabir?

Balashi continues, "Yesterday, Kabir sent me to summon you from the Musaion library to attend him in the Outer City workshops. He gave me instructions to take a shortcut through the Under City tunnels. While we were returning through the tunnels, you fell and hit your head. You were unconscious, and I couldn't wake you. I ran as fast as I could to get help. You're lucky, though. Muse Serapen found you even before I returned with Kabir."

"Lucky," Serapen repeats softly, her nostrils flaring. All eyes turn to the High

Priestess, and even the crackling fire in the hearth falls silent. Though her tone remains level, the heat in her words is unmistakable. "You're lucky you didn't lose your novice on your very first day as his teacher, Kabir. You know better than anyone why we require novices to have guides in the Under City. What were you thinking?"

In a chastened tone, Kabir says, "I acted impulsively, sister. I still have much to learn from you and Tio in the ways of instruction. I will not make such a mistake again."

"No, you will not," Serapen says coolly. "For you will not have the opportunity. I am placing Dom in attendance on Tio Artifex for the remainder of the winter, so his instruction may be more carefully supervised. Dom may choose for himself whether to go with you or with Tio when the Artifexi depart Velkanos in the spring. If you hope to be entrusted with the care of a novice again in the future, Kabir, show me you are worthy of the responsibility."

Crestfallen, Kabir bows his head and says, "I have listened and I have heard, sister."

"You and Balashi may go," says Serapen, dismissing them with a gesture of her hand. They exit quickly through the door, both clearly relieved to have escaped more serious punishment.

In a gentler tone, Serapen continues, "As for you, Dom, you may be innocent in this, but you've paid the price for Kabir's recklessness. I had to give you a fairly large dose of unbinding pharmaka to mitigate your head injury. Balashi is right, though—you should consider yourself lucky. If Eumelia hadn't acted so quickly to summon me, and if Hanu hadn't possessed a bond strong enough to recall your awareness to your body, you might have been beyond my skill to save. Tell me, little brother, what is the last thing you remember?"

My headache returns as I try again to remember. My thoughts wander through an opaque fog as I search for anything related to my accident. I remember nothing of the so-called Under City, nothing of Balashi, nothing of Kabir. I can't even remember arriving in Velkanos. I say, "I remember the morning we departed from the Cave of Dreams, after Lilith's owl attacked us." The memory of those talons slicing into my shoulders returns with sudden clarity—those wounds must be the reason for this bandage on my back. "And I remember riding across the plain toward Velkanos, with Hanu, Eumelia, and … Ava." I frown, surprised that I hadn't noticed until now that she's missing. "Where is Ava?"

Serapen looks to Hanu and Eumelia, then says to Zia in a quiet voice, "I think it's best we leave this to Ava's trio sisters."

Zia nods and follows Serapen quietly out of the room.

Alarmed, I look from Hanu to Eumelia. "Well?" I demand. "Where is she?"

Eumelia opens her mouth to answer, then reconsiders. She shoots a pointed look at Hanu. Tentatively, Hanu settles her hand on my arm. Through our old connection, I feel her desire to comfort me flowing through my body like cool water, calming the rising panic in my chest. Carefully, Hanu says, "A terrible thing happened, Dom. But we're going to get through it together. I promise."

A vague recollection stirs just at the edge of the fog in my mind. Where have I heard those words before? My headache flares again as I struggle to remember. Did Hanu say something like this to me once before, in our years growing up together in the Children's Temple?

To my relief, fragments of a memory start returning, though they're not entirely clear. No, it wasn't something Hanu said. It was something Ava said to me, once. We were lying in our tent beside the Purattu, the morning after I revived her. She'd said … What was it?

But my question is swept away as solemn Eumelia and tearful Hanu begin to reconstruct for me the three days that have elapsed since I left the Cave of Dreams with Ava. As their tale goes on, I find myself hoping I'm still asleep in the cave and this is only a bad dream. But the grief on their faces is all too real, pushing me against my will toward my own grief, which threatens to swallow me whole.

The truth spirals through my mind like carrion crows. Ava's dead. Despite everything I did to save her, Ava's dead. And—because of Kabir's recklessness, because of my own clumsiness, because of Serapen's damned unbinding pharmaka—I've been robbed of the memory of her death, robbed of even the chance to say goodbye to her.

I'm so shocked by what happened to Ava that I'm only half-listening as Eumelia finishes explaining what happened to me. She's saying, "—we ran after Muse Clio, and Clio summoned the High Priestess for us. Serapen led us into the Under City tunnels. When we finally found you, I thought we were too late, but Serapen showed Hanu how to revive you using unbinding pharmaka, and—"

I shake my head and interject, "But I still don't understand what happened outside the city gates. When Ava died on the Purattu, Serapen and I were able to revive her, just like Serapen and Hanu were able to revive me. Why couldn't we have done that after Ava fell onto her knife? Why—" My voice trembles as I try to hold back my tears. If I let myself cry, I don't know how I'll stop.

Eumelia and Hanu exchange another look. Hanu rests her hand on my arm, looking deep into my eyes. With quiet conviction, she says, "Ava tried to stay with you, Dom. We all saw how hard she tried. But the Voice called her onward. She wanted you to let her go."

A part of me wants nothing more than to bury my face in Hanu's soft arms, to sink into her familiar embrace, to forget my moon of misfortune with Ava. But after all Ava taught me, how can I let myself forget her? I can't. I won't. I clench my fist and yank my arm away from Hanu. Angrily, I say, "How could you know what Ava wanted?"

Hanu lowers her gaze to the floor, a submissive expression I've rarely seen on the face of any girl, and certainly not on the face of a novice Mohira, who would never defer to a mere boy. I'm surprised, sensing a new power in myself without understanding its source. Is this what it means, to be a novice Artifex? Am I at last on equal footing with the girls?

Eumelia glares at me, bristling. "Don't take this out on Hanu. She's only trying to help. If you should be angry at anyone, it's Kabir. Weren't you listening to Serapen? An elder brother, especially a teacher, should have known better than to summon you into the tunnels."

"I've had enough of listening to Serapen," I say, my anger swelling within me, rushing hot into my head, pouring out into my words. "I wish I'd never listened to her. I wish she'd never called me."

"Don't be ridiculous, Dom," says Eumelia, her tone withering. "The Voice in all called you. You answered the call. You should be grateful you've been called as an Artifex, unlike poor Balashi. But like it or not, you're bound to the path like all the rest of us."

I splutter, searching for a retort to Eumelia's cutting words. Failing that, I glower back at her in silence. Hanu looks from me to Eumelia, her lovely brown eyes clouded with sadness at our quarreling.

"Come on, Hanu," says Eumelia, casting a disdainful look at me. "Muse Clio still expects us in the library this morning. I think our little brother needs some rest."

Hanu and Eumelia depart, leaving me alone in my bed with my thoughts, which are far more painful than my injuries. The absence of Ava after her constant presence at my side and in my mind for the past moon feels like I've lost a limb. Out of habit, I keep reaching for her living awareness through our connection, but I find only hollow echoes of her in my memories. Each time a memory of her resurfaces, it's tarnished by my sorrow, redoubling my sense of loss. I don't want to forget her, but how can I preserve these memories when the mere act of remembering changes them?

My only escape from this troubling question is withdrawing deeper into myself. Unfortunately, I'm not the best company at the moment. I'm full of self-recrimination, acutely aware of all my failures that led to this moment. If only I had been more clever, less trusting, more courageous, less obedient—more like Ava—perhaps none of this would have happened. And even if there was nothing I could have done to save her, I shouldn't have been so petulant with Eumelia. I shouldn't have taken out my anger on Hanu. I've driven away my friends when I need them most. They'll leave me, just like Ava did. I'll be alone. I deserve to be alone.

These ruminations continue as morning passes into midday, and midday stretches toward evening. The only thing that interrupts my depressing inner monologue is Zia. She returns three times to check my bandages and re-apply the sweet-smelling balm of healing pharmaka to my cheek and back. The third time, she discards the bandages and says, "There now. Your cheek is good as new. You have some scarring on your back, but that will fade in time."

Tentatively, I run my fingers over the place on my cheekbone where the cut had been. The skin is perfectly smooth, without pain or swelling. I've never had a cut heal this fast; the healers in Velkanos must have even more powerful pharmaka than Hedi had available for us in the house of boys.

Out of long habit, I nod humbly to Zia and say, "Thank you, sister." And I would be thankful, were it not for the weight of my heavy heart.

Zia pats my hand. With an understanding look, she says, "Don't worry, Dom. Time heals what pharmaka cannot."

The bell for the evening meal tolls somewhere nearby. My stomach growls in answer. "Sounds like you'd better attend to that," Zia says with a smile. "Do you think you can stand on your own?"

Eager to leave my dark thoughts behind in this room, I swing my legs over the edge of the bed, settling my socked feet on the warm stone floor. Zia holds my arm to steady me as I stand, but once I'm up it's clear to both of us that I'm fine.

"Excellent," says Zia. "Then you can put your boots back on and be on your way." She points to a pair of pristine work boots standing at the foot of the bed. I wonder what happened to my worn riding boots and everything else I've been carrying since I departed the Children's Temple. Has all that been lost, too, along with my memories of the last three days? I sit at the foot of the bed and pull on the new boots. As I'm knotting the laces, Zia says, "I believe—ah yes, here they come. Your sisters will show you the way back to the meal hall."

I look up to find Hanu and Eumelia standing at the door, watching me with cautious expressions. Heat rises to my cheeks—not anger this time, only sheepish embarrassment at the memory of how I behaved toward them. Seeing them now, and remembering how they rushed to my side this morning, I realize belatedly what I should have said.

So I go to them, taking Hanu's hand in my left and Eumelia's in my right. "Thank you for saving my life," I say, looking from one to the other. "I'm sorry I acted like a complete ass. Can you forgive me?"

Hanu beams and pulls me into a hug, as though nothing ever happened. Eumelia rolls her eyes but gives me a begrudging smile. She hasn't forgotten, but at least she's forgiven.

"Are you hungry?" says Hanu.

"Like I haven't eaten in a week," I say.

"We'd better go quickly, then," says Eumelia, gesturing for me to follow her out the door. "Yesterday, you barely had time to take a bite before you were drowning in prospective Muses."

I hurry to keep up with Eumelia as she leads us down the long corridor outside my room. I'm so distracted by the sights of elegant sculptures tucked into alcoves, colorful tapestries hanging from doorways, and endless ceiling mosaics that it takes me a moment to register what Eumelia said. "Wait—" I say. "What do you mean, 'prospective Muses'?"

"Oh, no," says Hanu, her eyes widening in dismay. "You lost your memory of our first day in Velkanos, along with everything else."

I'm puzzled by Hanu's tone. It sounds almost like she blames herself for this.

Eumelia chuckles. "Probably for the best, Dom," she says. "Your first meal in the house of novices wasn't your finest moment. But maybe you'll do better the second time around."

"Eumelia!" I groan in frustration at her teasing. "Are you going to help me out, or what?"

"All right, all right," she relents, leading us around a corner when our corridor intersects another. "Do you remember when Arkhi and Thalia told you that the job of an Artifex is to select the Muse he'll serve, to carry out her great work?"

I nod. That was the same conversation in which I first heard of Tio Artifex, and the beginning of the brotherhood to which the Voice called me.

Eumelia continues, "Well, that means every ambitious novice and initiate priestess in Velkanos has her eye on you. Every Mohira who's ever been called by the Voice to complete a great work needs an Artifex. And you're the only new Artifex who's been called in ages, so …" Eumelia shrugs, as if the implications are obvious.

"So … what?" I say impatiently.

Eumelia laughs, then says, "So, I imagine it'll be easy for you to make new friends in Velkanos. Maybe easier than you'd like."

We stop before a large pair of arching double doors, through which I hear the sound of countless chattering female voices. Eumelia reaches for the door handle, but before she grasps it, both doors swing open, revealing a trio of priestesses exiting the meal hall together. They pause their conversation at the sight of us.

"Arkhi! Thalia!" I say, delighted to see the two other Muses who guided us on our journey to Velkanos.

Arkhi's dark face brightens as she gives me a rare smile. "Good to see you up, Dom," she says. "We heard you took quite a fall."

"Not as bad as the fall my own Artifex has taken, I'd wager," says Thalia, tweaking my chin playfully. "You've knocked your brother Kabir completely out of the good graces of the High Priestess, Dom. It'll be centuries before he can repair the damage."

"Spirits, how you exaggerate, little sister," the third priestess says, scoffing. "As if the High Priestess has nothing better to do than hold grudges." Though she's a full two hands shorter than the Muse of the house of poetika, the diminutive priestess addresses Thalia like she's speaking to a small child.

"Will you not grant me poetic license, Muse Noa?" Thalia says with a laugh, tossing her long auburn braid over her shoulder.

Something about Muse Noa's expression suggests that she's not inclined to grant anything to anyone without good reason. Everything about her is spare and practical. Her closely-tailored black shirt and trousers are unadorned, except for a few embroidered lines of silver thread about her collar. Her sleeves are rolled back, revealing muscular, sun-tanned forearms criss-crossed by a network of faint white scars. Her hands are broad, rough as a man's, and larger than I'd expect for a woman so compact. Her short, spiky silver hair stands straight out from her head.

"You'll have to look for poetic license in your own halls, Thalia," says Noa. "Arkhi and I have actual work to attend in the Outer City. I don't know how we'll manage to send this shipment out to the western villages before the pass closes.

We were three days behind on the pharmaka bottling even before Kabir's latest escapade. The Voice only knows why the distraction of a new Artifex must arrive at the peak of harvest season during a binding pharmaka shortage."

I look from Noa to Thalia, wondering what role Ava and Lilith might have played in such a shortage. Serapen hadn't looked pleased when she learned how much amanitai Ava stole from the Children's Temple, the night of her overdose.

"Never an idle moment in your houses, sister," Thalia says breezily. "Well, give my greetings to Kabir, when you see him. I hope you'll send him back to me after he's paid his penance." With a wink at me and a swish of her silky summer-green robes, Thalia parts ways with the other two Muses.

"Well then, Dom," says Noa, her piercing eyes turning suddenly to me. I straighten up automatically at her tone. "Do you have any questions about Serapen's new instructions for you?"

"Um … I … um—" I fumble, unsure which new instructions Noa means and finding it difficult to speak with the expectant gaze of the grey-eyed Muse on me.

"Yes? Spit it out," she says briskly.

Arkhi touches Noa's arm and says, in her low, compelling voice, "Sister, I'm sure Dom is still recovering from his head injury. I'll accompany him to the Outer City myself tomorrow and make sure he's situated with Tio."

"Very well," says Noa, with a wave of her hand. "Let's hope Dom will be of greater help to Tio than my own silly novices are to me, at the moment."

With that, the sharp-tongued Muse departs. Arkhi says, in a tone of mild apology, "Muse Noa is usually a bit more patient with new novices, Dom. But I'm afraid it's been rather chaotic in the city since our caravan arrived. The amanitai Ava stole left the Children's Temple without enough binding pharmaka ingredients to last them until next mushroom season, so we need to replenish their stores with supplies from Velkanos before the Urashtu Pass is snowed in for the winter. We're always short-handed in the workshops during harvest season, but this year is worse than usual."

"Muse Noa shouldn't blame Dom for that," says Eumelia.

"No, of course she doesn't blame Dom, little sister," says Arkhi, in the tone of instruction. "But it's the heads of each house who must keep the order amidst all the excitement over the arrival of the new Artifex. And Muse Noa oversees not just one house, but all the houses of tekhnologia, which leaves her managing more disorder than most of us at a critical time of year. We owe her our understanding and support."

Eumelia inclines her head and recites the proper response in an obedient but slightly bored tone. "I have listened, and I have heard, sister."

There's a sudden swell of excitement in the chatter of the meal hall. I peek around Arkhi, looking for the cause of the commotion, until I realize with a jolt that I myself am the cause. Several novices seated at the long meal tables closest to the open doors have caught sight of me. Curious faces turn my way.

Arkhi glances over her shoulder at the crowded hall. There's a trace of amusement in her eyes when she looks back at me and says, "Good luck in there,

Dom. I'll meet you here at the morning meal to show you the way to the workshops." To Eumelia and Hanu, she adds, "Help Dom find his way safely to his quarters before the evening silence, won't you?"

Arkhi departs, leaving me standing alone in the open doorway to the meal hall. Utterly exposed, I freeze as the collective female gaze pins me to the spot.

"Go on, Dom," Eumelia says under her breath, nudging me from behind. "If you show them you're afraid, they'll eat you alive."

Eumelia's warning recalls my memory of Ava stepping between me and the other girls in the caravan on my Calling Day, shielding me from their curious stares. Being the only boy in the caravan of thirteen over the last moon hasn't fully prepared me to navigate the sea of novices and initiates before me—more women than I've ever seen all in one place, all staring at me. Without Ava to protect me, I'm on my own.

So, masking my apprehension with my best imitation of Ava's cool disregard, I raise my chin and step through the door to take my place in the house of novices.

STOLEN FRUIT

"Enough, enough," I say, swatting other-Dom's hand away and wrinkling my nose in distaste as I inspect my reflection in the bathroom mirror. Seated beside me on a low stool, other-Dom ignores my complaining and applies another layer of something Bealsio called "make-up" to the bruise-colored shadows around my eyes.

"Almost done," Bealsio says brightly. "A little more right there, Dom," she adds, leaning over other-Dom's shoulder to point out a spot on my temple, which he dabs expertly with the soft pad in his hand.

I rake my fingers through my hair in frustration, and other-Dom smooths the flyaway strands back down with a comb. I woke this morning recharged after a night curled in other-Dom's arms, sleeping the deep sleep that only unbinding pharmaka gives. But I was expecting to return to Emmie's basement spliner immediately, eager to begin work on a plan to find Lilith. Unfortunately, other-Dom said the work requires something he called a "quantum memory drive," which we must retrieve from Emmie's office, so we have to go there instead.

"What difference does this make, anyway?" I say, indicating my painted face. "You said everyone at the Eden office already knows about Emmie's condition. Why does it matter if she looks sick?"

"The team is anxious enough about you as it is," other-Dom says patiently. "You've been missing from work for several days, and it's been clear to everyone for months that you've taken a turn for the worse. It's our responsibility as company leadership to put the best possible face on a bad situation. They'll all be watching. Ultimately, though, this face is for Amos. We need him to think you're on the mend."

"I don't see how I can fool him or anyone else for long," I say. "I don't know anything about Emmie's work. I don't know anyone at Eden. I can't even speak English."

"You don't need to know much to look like a company executive," says other-Dom. "Just do what Bealsio tells you. We'll fill up your calendar with meeting invites, so no one should bother you for most of the day."

"Calendar?" I say. "Meeting invites?"

"Here, I'll activate new user mode on her visual overlay," says Bealsio. Definitions for "calendar," "meeting invite," and "visual overlay" appear hovering in the air before me, accompanied by helpful images. I study these as other-Dom and Bealsio finish their work by applying some rosy substance to my cheeks.

"That should do it," says Bealsio, nodding her approval at my reflection.

Other-Dom gives me a hand up from my chair. "How are you feeling?" he says, watching me closely.

I look at myself in the mirror, wearing a face that belongs to someone else, clothes that belong to someone else, a life that belongs to someone else. As much as I feel like an imposter, working in disguise has always given me a bit of a thrill. I test out Emmie's body, rising tentatively to the balls of my feet, rolling my shoulders, stretching my arms. She's in better shape than she was yesterday, but that's not saying much.

Ready, Emmie? I think.

"Let's get this done," I say.

Other-Dom leads me out of the house through the front door. I've glimpsed the horseless carriages of Earth—"cars," according to my new user prompts—from a distance in prior visits to Emmie's branch, but the sleek grey car waiting for us in the "driveway" is nonetheless impressive. Its two front doors swing silently open to admit us. I'm still distrustful of all these doors that open and close on their own without warning, but I climb in anyway, settling into a beautifully stitched leather seat beside other-Dom.

Seemingly of its own accord, the "self-driving" car pulls out of the driveway onto the road. We glide over the smooth black "asphalt" on nearly silent wheels, shielded from even the slightest breeze by dark-tinted windows. After the grueling horseback journey I endured over the past moon, it's surreal to travel this way, so protected from the outside world.

The sights of Emmie's "neighborhood" rush by at impressive speed, flooding my visual overlay with all sorts of new words and their definitions. I'm delighted by my first glimpse of a "bicycle" and shocked by the enormous sizes of a "trash can" and "garbage truck." I suppose the Mohirai would never need a "mailbox" or "telephone pole," given all their ways of using binding pharmaka to communicate with one another. I'm saddened by the way a "jogger" passes by a sick-looking "homeless" man without a glance, especially considering the well-cared-for appearance of the "labradoodle" that accompanies the jogger on a leash. But I suppose that's not much different from the way we drive past the "panhandler" at the "stop sign."

I'd expected the journey to Emmie's office in San Francisco—sixteen "miles" west from her house, according to the map on my visual overlay—to take half a day, and even that wouldn't have been enough time to ask other-Dom and Bealsio all my questions about the strange things I'm seeing outside the car. But despite some "traffic" slowing us down as we approach the "freeway," we're soon crossing the "Bay Bridge" across the water, approaching the cluster of soaring glass towers "downtown." Our destination is visible even at this distance. Across the pinnacle of the tallest glass tower, four enormous green letters entwine like roots: EDEN.

We exit the freeway at the first "off-ramp" after the bridge, driving through more traffic along a broad boulevard that hugs the bay shoreline. People flood the sidewalks along the boulevard, headed in all directions on foot, bicycles, "scooters," and all manner of other strange conveyances. Never in my waking life have I seen so many people in one place. I wonder whether the broad streets of Velkanos once held such crowds, before the time of destruction.

"We'll use the main entrance," says other-Dom, as our car pulls up to the "curb" beside the Eden tower. "We want people to see you, though we'll avoid getting pulled into conversation, if we can. Ready?"

I nod, and my door swings open, admitting a grating cacophony of traffic noises and a slightly unpleasant odor I can't identify. Carefully, I climb out onto the "sidewalk." Other-Dom emerges from his side of the car, apparently unfazed by the alarming proximity of the traffic whizzing past, barely three "feet" behind him. He joins me on the sidewalk, then makes a dismissive gesture with his gloved left hand toward our empty car, which promptly pulls away from the curb.

"Where's it going?" I say, watching the car merge with the other traffic and disappear around the corner.

"Employee parking garage," other-Dom says under his breath, which sends another pair of definitions to my visual overlay. "But we can't let anyone overhear us speaking Akkadian in public. B, can you manage translation filters for her?"

"On it," says Bealsio's disembodied voice. The translation filter briefly muffles the jangling traffic noise. She adds, "I'll activate local terrain mapping too." A narrow path of glittering green appears on the sidewalk before me, particles of light flowing in a slow current toward the glass doors of the tower before us, showing me the way. I wonder what else Bealsio might do for me, if I only knew what to ask?

Other-Dom gestures to the path before us. "Shall we?" he says, this time in English.

As I approach the tower entrance, with other-Dom at my side and Bealsio in my ear, I catch a glimpse of myself in the wall of glass that faces the street. The opaque lenses of my stylish immerger glasses hide my wide-eyed apprehension, and the tailored "suit" and "high-heeled" boots I'm wearing make me look more confident than I feel.

The enormous marble "lobby" inside the tower is grand, though the stonework isn't nearly as impressive as most of the Mohiran temples I've seen. We join a line of men and women—though mostly men—passing through the "turnstiles" beside the "check-in" desk. A "security guard" standing by the turnstiles nods and smiles at me as I approach.

"Good morning, Ms. Bridges," he says.

"Just nod to him," Bealsio says in my ear. "Then wave your hand over here." A glowing green dot appears in my visual overlay, hovering over the shiny black placard atop the turnstile.

I follow both instructions and pass through the turnstile, other-Dom close behind me. I continue following the green path toward the hall lined with "elevators," stopping where the path ends before a pair of closed elevator doors. With the aid of my translation filter, I read the changing numbers displayed above the doors, counting down quickly from thirty-four to one. After a few "seconds," the elevator doors open with a soft chime, and my path continues into the little windowless room. Other-Dom follows me in, waves his hand over a glowing screen mounted to the inside wall, and taps the screen to enter the number sixty-three. The doors close behind us. The slight pressure under my feet tells me we're rising up through the building.

Since we're alone in the elevator, I start to ask other-Dom whether the quantum memory drive we need is on the sixty-third floor. But he shoots me a warning look, and I bite back my question. He takes my hand, re-establishing our connection. *If you need to talk to me about anything, we'll have to use our bond,* he thinks. *It's the only way we can be sure we're not overheard. As long as we're at Eden headquarters, we have to assume that all company channels and spaces are being monitored.*

Including the channel with Bealsio? I think.

No, thinks other-Dom. *Our private channel with Bealsio uses a security work-around Emmie acquired from a well-connected friend of ours. You and I are the only ones who can see or hear Bealsio, unless she's impersonating Emmie on the company channels. She's the main reason Emmie's been able to keep up appearances this long.*

Other-Dom lets go of my hand just as the elevator doors open. Bealsio's voice says, "We're logged in to your team's channel now, Ava. Just keep walking. Dom and I will do the talking."

We emerge from the elevator into a very large open room filled with a maze of pale grey "cubicle" walls interrupted by outcroppings of tall white "projection cylinders" large enough to hold a trio of standing Mohirai with room to spare.

"Hey, boss!" The avatar of a skinny man with a shiny brown face and thinning black hair materializes an arm's length ahead of me, his lanky figure translucent. Fortunately, all of Bealsio's comings and goings since yesterday have desensitized me to abrupt appearances like this, so I manage not to jump back in alarm. The man says, "It's great to see you. We missed you."

"Thanks, Shiva," Bealsio replies in Emmie's voice. "I missed you too."

"Smile a little," Bealsio prompts me. "He's an old friend of yours." So I smile back uncertainly at Shiva's avatar.

"The UX leads and I are down on fifty-nine, greyroom six, for the design review," says Shiva. "Want to drop by? We're demoing the latest on dev."

"Sorry, can't," says Bealsio-as-Emmie, in a sincerely apologetic tone. "I'm back to back all day."

"Serves you right after all your slacking off," says Shiva.

Bealsio-as-Emmie laughs. "Yeah yeah yeah. Karma, right?"

"Any chance you want to join us after work to kick off the weekend?" says Shiva. "A bunch of the old Temenos team are getting together at Bear's Lair in Berkeley. Owen would have turned forty-six today. Can you believe it? Thought we'd raise a glass. Of course you're welcome, too, Dom."

Bealsio-as-Emmie's voice turns solemn. "I wish I could, Shiva. But I've had a hell of a week. Still recovering."

Shiva nods. "I figured. Just thought I'd ask."

"Tell everyone hi from me."

"Sure will. Take care, Emmie. See you around, Dom."

Shiva's avatar vanishes, and other-Dom ushers me onward. I follow Bealsio's green path through the cubicles and cylinders, obediently nodding and waving at

Bealsio's command whenever another teammate of Emmie's pops out to greet me. Finally, we reach a closed door on the far side of the room. I follow Bealsio's prompts to unlock the door with a swipe of my hand and enter.

The lights flick on as I step inside Emmie's office. The floor-to-ceiling windows frame a sweeping eastern view over the tops of several nearby buildings, across the shining San Francisco Bay, toward the dark green Oakland hills where Emmie lives. Other-Dom closes the door behind us, and at his gesture a woven screen lowers over the interior windows with a faint hum, shielding us from the view of any onlookers in the cubicles and cylinders outside.

A large, dark wooden cabinet that stands against the interior wall of Emmie's office draws my eye. In this sterile environment of pale colors, straight edges, and smooth surfaces, the detailed designs of birds and flowers worked into the cabinet doors with delicate wood inlay and the intricate relief carvings on its curved edges look entirely out of place. Atop the cabinet sits a blue ceramic pot containing a tiny tree that my visual overlay calls a "bonsai." Beside the little bonsai tree stands a framed "photograph" of three people with their arms slung companionably over each other's shoulders. When I step closer to peer at the photograph, my visual overlay highlights the three smiling faces, helpfully displaying their names. The girl in the center I recognize already: it's Emmie, though much younger, identical in almost every way to Bealsio. She stands between a compact, silver-haired man with dark-framed glasses and a handsome, athletic young man—"Tomo Yoshimoto" and "Owen Cyrus," apparently. The three of them wear identical "tee shirts" emblazoned across the chest with a "logo" comprised of the word "Augur" below a symbol that reminds me of outstretched bird wings. Above their heads hangs a banner that reads, "That's a wrap, Team Temenos!"

Other-Dom touches my arm. *Just follow Bealsio's instructions,* he thinks. *I'll put in an appearance at the design review and cover for your absence. Should only take me a few minutes. All right?*

I nod, and other-Dom slips out of the room.

"Go ahead and take a seat at your desk," says Bealsio.

I turn toward the unusual-looking seat at the far side of Emmie's desk, a wheat-colored wooden tabletop supported by a mechanical apparatus that my visual overlay explains will raise and lower the desk on command. I wonder what sort of work Emmie does at this empty desk, devoid of books or papers or tools of any kind.

I settle into the high-backed "swivel chair" behind the desk and lean back into its soft cushions, only to discover with a jolt of alarm exactly what "swivel" means. I grab the edge of the desk in an attempt to regain my balance after nearly toppling backwards. At my touch, a translucent rectangle rises up from the center of the desk, displaying blinking text that reads, "Authenticating."

"How are you doing today, Emmie?" says a pleasant male voice.

"Super duper, Razi," says Bealsio-as-Emmie, with equal cheeriness.

The blinking text hovering before me changes to read, "Voice authentication successful." Razi says, "How may I help you?"

"I need a hard copy of a git branch from the Babylon domain to use on my local," says Bealsio-as-Emmie, a statement that fills my visual overlay with several new definitions and illustrations that are rather more complicated than "mailbox" and "garbage truck."

"What is the branch ID?" says Razi.

Bealsio-as-Emmie rattles off a long string of letters and numbers.

"I'll need your biometric signature to release a copy of that branch," says Razi. A yellow rectangle of light pulses on the tabletop.

"Press your hand there," Bealsio prompts me, so I cover the glowing spot with my palm.

"Thank you," says Razi. "Your position in the queue is seventeen, and your estimated delivery time is 9:47 AM. Your memory drive will be available for check-out in the quantum fabrication facility located on the first floor. Be prepared to show ID. Please remember that all branch copies used for local development must be returned to QDD within 72 hours. Violations will be handled by corporate security officers in accordance with company policy. Is there anything else I can help you with?"

"That's it for now, Razi," says Bealsio-as-Emmie.

"Have a nice day, Emmie," says Razi.

The glowing rectangle hovering over the tabletop sinks back down and disappears.

"Sit tight," says Bealsio. "Dom's still making his rounds."

So I sit, swiveling—more carefully now—in Emmie's chair, flicking my fingers through the air to look back at some of the new words and definitions that have flown through my visual overlay since we left the house this morning. I can't help thinking about how long it took me to learn even the most basic facts about my own world, growing up. The Mohirai are so slow and deliberate with every piece of instruction they provide. In Emmie's world, information about seemingly everything streams in from everywhere, answering questions before I even know what to ask.

"Here he comes," says Bealsio, and the door opens again.

Other-Dom steps inside, his face tense. He rests his fingers lightly on the back of my hand, thinking, *We've got a problem.* His memory flashes through my mind: Amos walking through the cubicles outside the door, headed our way.

What are we going to do? I think.

It's too late to leave, he thinks. *We're going to need to talk to him, at least for a little while.*

But how? I think. *I can't—*

Bealsio's going to run real-time strategy on the conversation to help us keep it as short as possible, he thinks. *She'll give me as much of our speaking parts as she can. When you have to speak, Bealsio will prompt you. Imitate what she says as best you can. We can explain away some verbal fumbling on your part—Emmie has a tendency to mix up words and have long pauses in her speech when she's having an episode, anyway. Do your best. Don't panic.*

Other-Dom's last instruction is unnecessary, though. Panic is rarely a problem for me when I'm on a job. For all the differences between this world and mine, the essence of successful thievery remains the same. I remember the basic instruction I've received many times—from Lilith and the Mohirai—for navigating novel challenges. *Observe, without resistance, without force.*

There's a knock at the door.

Bealsio prompts me, "You say, 'Come in.'"

"Come in," I call out calmly, imitating Bealsio's accent and intonation almost perfectly, at least to my ears.

Amos enters, wearing a meticulously-tailored suit of a different color but similar cut to the one he wore last night when he visited me at Emmie's house. His fair hair is sculpted back from his sun-tanned forehead in a way that suggests he spent as much time before a mirror this morning as I did.

"Good morning, Emmie," he says, giving me a wide smile that reveals unnaturally white and perfectly even teeth. I nod politely at him without smiling, assuming based on everything I've observed so far that Emmie's relationship with Amos is courteous but not warm.

Bealsio prompts, "You say, 'How can I help you, Amos?'"

I recognize and imitate Bealsio's mildly impatient tone, looking at Amos over the frames of my immerger glasses and raising an eyebrow, doing my best impression of a busy, disinterested Mohira.

"Nice power posture," Bealsio says approvingly. I suppress a smile.

"You're looking much improved from last night," says Amos, glancing from me to other-Dom, an unspoken question in his ice-blue eyes.

"Yes, thank you for providing the dosage adjustment so quickly," says other-Dom.

"My pleasure, as always," says Amos, nodding graciously. "Does this mean I can expect your quarterly review by EOD, Emmie? I'll need it for the board meeting next week."

I follow Bealsio's prompt and say, "I just finalized the deck. Dom can run you through the details. Check your inbox."

"Excellent," says Amos, flicking his fingers through the air, apparently inspecting some visual overlay that's invisible to me. "Ah, yes. Here it is." He studies something for a long moment, then says, "Hmm … You've written here that IMPD has been flat this quarter?"

"That's right," I say, quickly skimming the explanation of Amos' question that appears in my visual overlay.

"That's lower than our target," he says. "What's the plan to boost the numbers?"

Bealsio prompts me, "Look at Dom," which I do with a pointed expression.

Other-Dom says, "As you know, our aggregate engagement across domains already exceeds industry averages for immersed minutes per day by over fifty percent. Even so, we have an aggressive plan to grow our share of the pie. Based on our beta user testing on the Babylon domain, we're projecting IMPD growth of around twenty percent in the twelve months following the release."

Apparently this nonsense makes sense to Amos, because he nods with interest, his eyes still focused on some unseen visual overlay separating him from us. He says, "Only twenty percent? The Nineveh release did nearly thirty."

"It's a conservative estimate," says other-Dom. "Our pre-release marketing strategy has been generating a lot of hype, and none of our competitors have a major release announced for this year, so we'll likely benefit from that. Still, you have to keep in mind that we're approaching IMPD saturation with our most active users. Our biggest growth opportunities are in smaller segments of the user base. Unless we figure out a way to add more minutes to the day, we'd have to break every growth record we've ever set at Eden for Babylon to outperform Nineveh."

Amos refocuses on me for the first time in a few minutes. "That's what we have you two for, though, right?" he says. "The dream team. Always outperforming."

Bealsio prompts me, "Don't answer," so I simply stare back at Amos coldly.

Other-Dom says, with a smile that looks more like indigestion, "Absolutely, Amos. Now, if you don't mind, Emmie and I have work to do."

"Of course," says Amos. "Back to work!"

Amos slips out and shuts the door. Other-Dom turns to me, extending his hand to help me out of my chair.

How did that go? I think.

You're a natural, thinks other-Dom. *Come on, let's get out of here before one of us gets pulled into a whiteboarding session.*

A new green path appears to guide me out of Emmie's office, leading me back toward the bank of elevators. We exit the elevators at the first floor where we entered. Here, the path takes a new turn, leading me toward a large cylindrical "body scanner" clad in white "plastic" attended by a bored-looking security guard, a young man of around twenty summers.

"Badge?" says the security guard, his eyes not quite making contact with mine through his immerger glasses.

I follow Bealsio's instruction to show the security guard the badge clipped to the front of my "jacket." He waves me through to the round platform at the center of the body scanner. Mirroring the illustration mounted to the inside of the scanner, I hold up my arms. I flinch slightly at the unexpected series of bursting sounds that pop around me as the scanner searches my body for a host of possible threats, which my visual overlay describes using several new words, including "gun" and "switchblade," along with a variety of perplexing "initialisms," including "IED" and "EMP."

I wait for other-Dom to follow me through the scanner, and we walk down a long hallway with doors leading off from both sides. My path ends at the door with an engraved sign that reads, "Quantum Fabrication." I press my palm to the glowing panel mounted on the wall beside the door.

"Hello, Emmie," Razi's voice greets me.

"Hi again, Razi," Bealsio-as-Emmie responds for me. "Just here to pick up that branch copy."

"Your drive is available for pickup in Section Two, Row Eighteen, Box Thirty-One," says Razi.

The door swings open. "I have to wait out here," says other-Dom, so I proceed into the room.

The overhead lights turn on as I enter, and the door swings shut behind me, leaving me alone in a very cold, very clean, and unexpectedly cavernous room that's vaguely reminiscent of the Musaion library. Long rows of tall black cabinets stretch all the way out to the unlit edges of the room. A low buzz and a subtle breeze emanate from somewhere beneath my feet. Looking down through the narrow glass panels that line the floor on either side of the walkways, I glimpse a massive machine seated on the floor below me, its shiny black surface and segmented exterior like the carapace of an enormous beetle. Extending from two sides of the machine's bulky black body are several dozen slender silver appendages like spiders' legs. The delicate tip of each leg hovers over the center of what looks like a small circular mirror of dark glass. There's a whirring sound, and the silver legs spring to life, darting back and forth across the multitude of dark mirrors, each silver tip tracing its own path across the glass.

I study the hypnotic movements of the strange machine for a moment, tempted to delve more deeply into the explanations of quantum fabrication now streaming across my visual overlay. But I know I should hurry, so I push on, walking past several rows of cabinets until I reach number eighteen. Box thirty-one is close to my end of the row. I touch my palm to the little cabinet door, and it swings open, revealing a small metal drawer.

I pull out the drawer and find a small, shiny, circular object about the size of a button. It's enclosed by a clear rectangular case that looks like glass to me, but when I pick it up, it's heavier than glass and almost painfully cold to the touch.

"Put the drive in your pocket for now," says Bealsio. "We'll show you how to use it when we get home. Let's go. The car's on its way."

HOUSE OF GLASS

I WAKE LONG BEFORE FIRST LIGHT after a night of fitful sleep, unsettled by the silence of my new quarters above the stables. A boyhood of shared rooms and the past moon on the road sharing a tent have not prepared me for such quiet. I miss waking up in my bedroll to the early morning birdsong and the three sleeping girls' soft breathing, with Ava curled up in my arms.

This first thought of her threatens to plunge me into the grief I've been managing to avoid since yesterday. I rise quickly from bed, despite the darkness, hoping the rituals of readying myself for the day will distract me.

Unfortunately, as I move through my quarters, I'm surrounded by signs of what I've lost. There's a towel draped over the rounded lip of the carved stone tub at the far end of my bedroom, dry after some unremembered bath. On the large wooden chest at the foot of my bed sit my riding clothes, neatly folded, though still smeared with Ava's dark blood. In my outer room, Ava's saddlebag leans against mine on the floor beside the door, as if she might return at any moment to retrieve it. I don't remember how any of these things—or even I myself—came to be here, and yet here we are.

With a despondent sigh, I kneel before Ava's saddlebag and gaze down at it, conflicted. Should I open it? Store it somewhere out of sight? Leave it where it is?

At last, I unbuckle the flap and reach into the bag, withdrawing a few of its contents and spreading them across the stone floor. Ava's Mohiran riding cloak, which I bundled tight around her so many times as she struggled to keep warm on the difficult mountain crossing. Ava's old leather pack, which Serapen recovered from the free men's boat the morning after our abduction. Ava's worn riding boots, one of which bears the beak and claw marks of the little kuku bird Lilith sent to find Ava on the banks of the Purattu.

I pick up the scratched boot to take a closer look at the markings, and something rattles loose inside of it. Puzzled, I slip my hand into the boot, feeling around.

"Ouch!" I withdraw my hand quickly. I've cut my thumb on something sharp. I hold up the boot and peer into it. Dim light glints on something metal. More carefully this time, I reach into the boot and withdraw what's tucked inside.

It's the blade of the knife Ava held to my throat the night I found her collapsed on the ground in the cedar forest. On our Calling Day, unbeknownst to me, she broke off the knife's original handle so she could more easily conceal the blade from the Mohirai on our journey to Velkanos. She kept the edge carefully honed, and it's a good thing she did. I'm not sure how else I would have been able to cut us loose from the free men's ropes the night they took us captive.

I examine the makeshift handle Ava later crafted from leather salvaged from her old pack. The handle is a bit small for my hand, but it would have fit hers perfectly. I don't remember when she dyed the handle such a dark color, but then

I realize with a jolt that this must be Ava's own blood, soaked into the leather after her fatal plunge from Eridu. Hanu and Eumelia had glossed over this when they told me how Ava died. There must have been a lot of blood. My hand trembles as I fight back tears. What could I have been thinking, leaving her alone on horseback in such an exhausted state? If I had just been more attentive, maybe—

The wave of grief finally crashes into me. I wrap my arms around my knees, rocking back and forth on the floor, trying to stifle the sound of my sobs. I'm not sure how long I sit, gripping Ava's knife, my thumb bleeding into the already blood-stained leather. The warmth of the knife in my hand anchors me somehow, until at last the wave subsides. I wipe my eyes, looking down at the blade for a moment before I tuck it carefully into the back of my toolbelt. I'll have to fashion a sheath for it, as Ava had meant to do.

I rise to my feet and take a seat at the table beside my fireplace, which is filled with the ashes of yesterday's fire. The sketchbook Urshanabi gave me lies closed on the table beside an empty wine bottle. I pick up the uncorked bottle and sniff, catching a sour whiff of unfamiliar pharmaka and alcohol. I'm surprised I was drinking alone in my room. I've never been particularly keen on Mohiran mixed wine, despite the cheering pharmaka it usually contains. But, given how I'm feeling right now, I suppose if there were anything left in this bottle, I'd drink it eagerly.

I set down the bottle and look at my sketchbook, tracing with my fingertips the deep scratches Lilith's crows pecked into the intricate swirling pattern of its tooled leather cover. Without Ava in my mind, I'm unable to read the words formed by these scratches, but she read them for me the night the crows attacked us: *Return to me and all will be forgiven.* This message from Lilith, after so many lies, had infuriated Ava, who swore never to return to her. Now that Ava's dead, I suppose she's kept her promise.

Her promise. The memory of Ava that I'd struggled to remember yesterday in the house of healing returns to me with sudden intensity. *We're going to find our way out of here together. I promise.* But my faith in this promise has been destroyed by Ava's death. The dream we shared of finding a world where men live as women's equals is gone. All that remains for me is the lonely path of Artifex in a world ruled by Mohirai.

I bow my head over the table, closing my eyes, holding my face in my hands.

You have asked it. We may give it. But there is a price. Do you accept it?

The Voice's words from my Calling Day return to me in the midst of my sadness. I remember the deep longing I had before my calling, before I crossed paths with Ava in the cedar forest. The boy I was a moon ago could never have imagined where I'd be now: sitting in my own private quarters, inside the walls of the greatest temple city in Dulai, attending Mohirai and Artifexi, courted by Muses, on the path to initiation.

I open my eyes, gazing down bitterly at the sketchbook before me on the table. Even this sketchbook and the new set of charcoal pencils in my toolbelt would have been withheld from me as a boy growing up outside the walls of the

Children's Temple. These gifts are a pointed reminder that the Voice granted me everything I longed for on Calling Day. I should be grateful. But I've lost my sense of gratitude along with everything else.

On an impulse, I open the sketchbook to the first page. There lies the only image I captured on the road to Velkanos. It's a sketch of the caravan gathered around the campfire, just before Lilith's crows attacked. At the center of the sketch, among the other novices, Ava sits beside Muse Serapen, the faces of novice and High Priestess illuminated by firelight as they prepare cooking pharmaka to season the evening meal. I study Ava's face, impressed by the detail of expression I managed to capture: the intense curiosity with which she watches Serapen's skillful hands at work with the multitude of ingredients spread out before them in gleaming bottles, glazed jars, and leather pouches. There's a subtle similarity in the two women's faces and postures as they lean toward each other. Perhaps that resemblance was just laziness on my own part, though. Perhaps I subconsciously incorporated some aspects of Ava's face into Serapen's. As my gaze lingers on the sketch, I hear Ava's voice asking Serapen a question, the sound so clear in my memory that she might be speaking right behind me, just out of sight.

A lump rises in my throat, and I put the memory of that night behind me, turning to the next page of the sketchbook. Near the center of the blank expanse of parchment, I seem to see an undulating line, like a fish swimming just beneath the water's surface. I reach for one of the pencils tucked into my toolbelt. Gripping the charcoal in my left hand, I trace the elusive line, fixing it in place. Another line appears, then another. Stroke by charcoal stroke, my fingers sculpt light and shadow into the elegant curve of a cheek, the soft arc of an eyebrow, the delicate point of a chin. I remember the elated look in Ava's eyes. The folds of my riding cloak spreading behind us like wings as I held on to Ava with one hand and our saddle with the other. The magnificent motion of Eridu beneath us as Ava urged him on to a gallop. Our first ride together at the start of our journey to Velkanos.

A small weight lifts from my chest, with the memory of that happy afternoon preserved on the page, safe from the vagaries of time and unbinding pharmaka.

More eagerly now, I turn the page. Another memory presents itself, and then another. My hand follows the lines wherever they lead, and I forget my grief for a while as I revisit the moments of joy that led to it.

Rosy dawn has brightened into full morning by the time the third bell tolls. It's followed promptly by a knock at my door. Dazed, I look up from my sketchbook, my pencil poised over the lowest rung of the strange ladder to the sky that I dreamt in the Cave of Dreams, the last night of the journey that I can still remember.

Through the door, Muse Arkhi calls, "It's me, Dom. May I come in?"

The simple question is another reminder of all that's changed for me since my Calling Day. The significant luxury of my own door and the privacy it affords were unknown to me in the house of boys. "Yes," I call. "Come in. It's unlocked."

Arkhi opens the door and steps inside. "You've been awake for some time," she observes, taking in the sight of me at the table, the open sketchbook before me, my hands covered in charcoal dust. "I thought perhaps you had slept through the bells, when I didn't see you in the meal hall. Your absence disappointed a number of little sisters."

"Oh. Right. I'm sorry, Muse Arkhi," I say with a grimace, suddenly remembering that I was supposed to meet her at the morning meal. Still, I'm a bit relieved that my mistake allowed me to avoid another scene like the one I faced last night, surrounded in the meal hall by a crowd of novices and initiates over-eager to express their concern over my head injury and remind me of their names. I close my sketchbook and stand, reaching for a piece of clean linen from a nearby shelf to wipe off my fingers and clean my blackened fingernails. I say, "It's so quiet in here that I had trouble sleeping. I was up before first bell, but … I guess I lost track of the time."

Arkhi says, "Sister Hippolyta is downstairs if you ever need sleeping pharmaka. But you'll grow used to the silence, in time. As you get deeper into your training, you'll find it useful. In the meantime, though, I imagine you'll at least enjoy the benefits of a lock on your door."

I look at her quizzically, but Arkhi doesn't elaborate. Instead, she says, in a somewhat harried tone, "I'm afraid you weren't the only one who spent a sleepless night. Tio never even returned home from his workshop. Kabir and Balashi left at first bell to join him, but they're still in need of more hands. Come. I'll take you to them."

I grab the new fleece-lined cloak hanging on a peg by the door and follow Arkhi out of my quarters. We cross the landing and make our way down three flights of stone stairs. Eumelia pointed out the occupants of each floor as she and Hanu showed me the way up to my room last night: Kabir's quarters on the third floor, Hippolyta the stable keeper's on the second, and Tio and Balashi's shared quarters at the street level.

We emerge through a door onto the narrow, sloping alleyway beside the stables. A few steps downhill lead us to the wider cobblestone street that the stable's grand portico faces. We set off at a brisk walk toward the broad central staircase that connects the tiered cross-streets of Velkanos.

Arkhi says, "Normally, new novices aren't required in the workshops quite so soon after their arrival—we prefer to have the novices spend more time with Muse Clio in their early moons to gain the benefit of her historia instruction first. But any pharmaka shortage must take precedence over novice instruction. You may be pulled around quite a bit from job to job, as a result. But you'll be assisting Tio primarily, now that Serapen has placed you in attendance on him."

"What sort of assistance does Tio need?" I say.

"It will probably be a lot of the usual novice work, at first. Feeding the ovens. Fetching and carrying. Things like that." Arkhi glances at me, tapping her lips thoughtfully. "Serapen told us your unbinding took the last few days from you. Do you remember anything of your first meeting with Tio?"

"Eumelia told me Tio is under a vow of silence, but that's all I've heard," I say.

"Yes, that silence may inconvenience you, at least at the start of your training," says Arkhi. "Fortunately, the rest of us in the houses of tekhnologia—myself, Noa, Kabir, and other initiate sisters—will assist in your instruction where needed, and Tio's vow of silence will last only through spring. But there are other challenges you may encounter as you attend him through the next few years.

"Tio is still recovering from an injury he sustained years ago. He was attempting an ambitious glassworking project with a new machine he had designed to speed the work. The machine was untested, and part of it failed while Tio was alone in his workshop without attendants. His legs were severely burned in the accident, and the injury makes walking difficult for him. He uses a wheelchair, in the few places in the city that are level enough for it, but he needs assistance in places his chair can't access."

Surprised, I say, "I thought the healers in Velkanos can repair almost any injury. Couldn't they help Tio?"

Arkhi says, "Indeed they could. But the amount of unbinding pharmaka required to repair such an injury is significant. You're experiencing yourself the difficulty caused by your loss of the last three days, I imagine?" I nod. She says, "Well, Tio's injury would require the loss of much more—nearly twenty years of memory, according to the healers' best guess. Tio's chosen to live with his injury for the time being, rather than risk losing those memories."

"That's awful," I say, wondering what I would do if forced to choose between my ability to walk and my ability to recall twenty years—longer than my entire life to this point. I remember something Lilith said to Ava, the night of Ava's overdose, when Ava pleaded for unbinding pharmaka to help her recover from the injury. *The amount you'd need is too much for someone so young,* she'd said. *You need initiate training, and centuries of memories, to be able to tolerate high doses of unbinding pharmaka.* I say, "But Tio must be centuries old, if he's the first of the Artifexi. Are twenty years that important to him?"

"Twenty years might not be so great a loss to an initiate his age," says Arkhi. "But Tio is in the midst of a great work for his Muse, which they'd been working on together for centuries before his accident. Without those twenty years, her last instructions to him would be lost."

"But wouldn't it be easier for him to do his work if he took the unbinding pharmaka to heal, then had his Muse remind him of her instructions?" I say.

"That would be easier," says Arkhi. "Unfortunately, it's not possible. Tio's Muse has passed into Death."

"What happened to her?" I say, surprised. I know everyone—women as well as men—must make the journey into Death when their service to the Voice concludes, but most of the Mohirai live such long lives that the death of a woman is exceedingly rare.

Arkhi sighs, then says sadly, "Muse Maya died in childbirth."

I'm so stunned that I stop mid-step. "Muse Maya," I repeat slowly, remembering the story Serapen told us around the campfire the night after Ava died the first time. "Ava's mother?"

Arkhi stops and faces me. "Yes," she says. "Ava's mother."

I know very little about Tio Artifex, but my heart aches in sympathy for him. In a different life, in a world where Lilith had never stolen Ava from the Mohirai, perhaps Ava and I would have grown up happily in the Children's Temple together, our friendship uninterrupted by her disappearance or her overdose of pharmaka. Perhaps after our Calling Day, we would have walked the path of mysteries together. Perhaps, in time, she might have become my Muse. I'm devastated by the loss of her after only a single moon. How much greater would that loss feel to me, had we spent centuries together, like Tio and Maya?

"It is a sad story," says Arkhi, watching my reaction. "But Death is rarely such a tragedy. Most initiates are prepared for the journey, and even welcome it, when the time comes. But death in childbirth has become so rare since the time of destruction that none of us were expecting it. All of us were greatly affected. Maya was very dear to everyone."

"And dearest of all to Lilith," I murmur, remembering Serapen's words, the night she told Ava the true story of her birth.

Arkhi nods. "Indeed she was. Lilith was affected most of all."

"But why?" I say.

Arkhi gestures for me to continue walking as we talk, so I follow her, passing tidy orchards tucked between low stone buildings and small fenced paddocks of sheep and goats. She goes on saying, "Lilith and Maya were trio sisters. They were among the first novices called by the Voice after the High Priestess Mohira appointed Serapen as her successor.

"Though all of us are sisters and brothers in our shared service to the Voice, relationships between trio sisters are special. The path to initiation is a long and difficult road for any Mohira, and our trio sisters are essential companions. They share the load, at times when our strength fails. They hold up a mirror, at times when we've forgotten who we are. Though each of us must walk the path on our own, our trio sisters often help us find our way or help to keep us going."

We arrive at a circular plaza where the ninth street meets the central staircase, the main thoroughfare connecting all the temple city cross-streets. A faint smell of sulphur drifts through the crisp autumn air as we pass the elaborate fountain at the center of the plaza, which pours four streams of water from four sculpted stone faces into a steaming, circular pool. The fountain fills the air with a cheerful burbling sound, but beneath it there's another fainter sound I can't identify—a sort of creaking, like a distant chorus of frogs.

Arkhi turns right, and we descend the broad, shallow central stairs. The view of the Outer City spread out below me is spectacular—each tier of the city like a giant stair step down the slope of the mountain toward the broad expanse of the surrounding plain, long rows of tawny stone buildings facing the level streets on each tier, blue roof tiles gleaming in the bright morning light. I glance back over my shoulder at the Upper City, where I woke up yesterday in the house of healing. Behind the high, four-paneled gate that separates the Upper City from the Outer City, I can just see the topmost floor of the house of novices.

Arkhi says, "Lilith and Maya were unusually close during their time in the house of novices, even for trio sisters. And when the time came for their initiations, they were both called to join the house of healing. In those early days of the Mohiran sisterhood, there was so much work for the healers to do—even more than now. Lilith and Maya became Serapen's most skilled attendants and continued working closely together for centuries.

"But soon after Tio arrived in Velkanos as the first novice Artifex, something changed between Lilith and Maya. After Tio's initiation, Lilith seemed to withdraw from her sister. Some said Lilith was jealous that Tio chose Maya to be his Muse, but I'm not sure of that. Even though Lilith seemed more ambitious than Maya in her youth, jealousy was never in her nature."

I say, "Did you know Lilith well, then?"

Arkhi considers this for a while. "Better than most," she says. "Lilith and Maya were my trio sisters."

I blink in surprise. "I'm sorry." I say, touching Arkhi's arm. "I didn't know. It must be hard, to have lost both your trio sisters."

Arkhi gives me a sad smile. "You and I have that in common, I suppose. Still, I had the support of my trio sisters on my path to initiation, while you lost your trio brothers before your instruction even began."

I've thought of my trio brothers Kuri and Balashi only rarely since our Calling Day. I was so preoccupied with Ava and the difficulties her overdose caused us both on our journey to Velkanos that it left little room in my mind for much else. I imagine Kuri must be off somewhere in the wilderness among the gatherers by now. And even though Balashi is unexpectedly here in Velkanos, Eumelia explained to me what will happen to him eventually. Because uninitiated men are forbidden from knowing what lies within temple city walls, Balashi's entire memory of his time within the temple city will be unbound before he's sent back to join the smiths in the men's village at Upper Ford. There's no possibility that Balashi will ever be to me what Arkhi's trio sisters were to her during their initiate training.

It seems a cruel fate, for boys to have such important bonds severed so young. I wonder what purpose this serves for the Voice in all. When I was a child, the Mohirai taught me that all men must pay with our brief lives the debt of the men who brought about the destruction. I struggled to accept that fate as my own, until my unexpected calling as Artifex. Now that I've been called to a different path than other men, however, I find the thought of my brothers' fates even more troubling. Why must we all suffer for the actions of those long-dead men? Will their debt to the Voice ever be repaid?

Arkhi reaches for my hand and gives it a squeeze. "Don't worry, Dom. The Voice has a way of guiding us to the companions we need for each part of our journey. Perhaps you will find them here, in the houses of tekhnologia, as I did in my novice years."

Arkhi gestures to the long row of tall buildings to our right. We've reached the street of workshops while I was lost in thought. I follow Arkhi down the street, which curves to the right as it hugs the mountain slope. She points out various buildings as we pass them—the house of weaving, the house of ceramics, the house of stone, and many others. For the first time since we departed the stables, I catch sight of a few other Mohirai. There's one entering a workshop through a side alley door, another moving behind an arching stone window above the street, another sitting on a front step repairing a basket. Two black-cloaked Mohirai driving a heavily-laden oxcart down the street nod courteously to Arkhi and me as they pass, headed back toward the central stairs.

The odd sound that I'd first noticed while we were passing the fountain grows louder. As we round the bend in the street, I see at last the source of the sound. Mounted to the side of a three-story building we're approaching is the largest wheel I've ever seen, almost as tall as the building itself. Along the street beyond it, I see dozens more wheels, in various sizes, attached to other buildings. The great wheels fill the air with a chorus of rhythmic creaking and splashing as their broad wooden paddles dip and rise, dip and rise, powered by the rushing snowmelt that flows from the distant peak of Velkanos high above us, down through the many stone channels that route the current between the buildings and through the culverts beneath the street of workshops.

Arkhi heads toward the three-story building. The building has a peculiar entrance facing the street: an enormous pair of closed double doors nearly three stories high, hanging on massive bronze-clad hinges. A much smaller door cut into the left side of the larger door stands open, and a ribbon of hot air brushes my cheeks as we approach it.

Arkhi points to the sign carved in stone above the great doorway. "House of Glass," she says, reading letters that are still unknown to me. "Tio's workshop has the largest water wheel in the Outer City—the first one we ever built, in fact," she adds, with a touch of pride.

Stepping through the door into Tio's workshop is a jarring transition from the cool autumn air outside to what feels like fierce summer heat. I wipe beads of sweat from my forehead as I stare up into the surprisingly large space inside. From the street, I'd imagined this was a building with multiple floors, like the stables. But inside, it's revealed to be a single open room, three floors high, without interior walls.

Running along the perimeter walls are three tiers of scaffolding. Three sets of staircases connect the ground floor to the uppermost level of the scaffolding.

Halfway up the wall that supports the great water wheel, a large metal cage contains the spinning axle of the wheel. A variety of large metal devices I don't recognize are mounted above the second level of the scaffolding, which gives access to the axle.

A grid of six large windows on the south wall admit the morning light, but the space is extraordinarily well-lit not because of these windows, but because the ceiling is entirely open to the blue sky above.

"What do you do when it rains?" I ask Arkhi, looking up through the opening at the passing clouds.

"We close the roof panels," says Arkhi. "But Muse Urania says we'll have fair weather the next few days, so we're leaving it open for ventilation, thank the spirits."

I follow Arkhi to the end of a long line of cloaks and satchels hanging from pegs in the stone wall beside the door. Eagerly, I shed my heavy cloak, hanging it on the nearest free peg.

"Come," says Arkhi. "The others are by the ovens."

Arkhi leads me across the open space, weaving through a maze of work benches and neatly organized rolling shelves, most full of tools I've never seen before. Ahead of us, three enormous ovens stand at ground level. Their three chimneys climb the inside wall, exiting through the open ceiling. White smoke spirals upward to join the clouds above.

As we step around another tool shelf, I catch sight of Muse Noa, easily recognizable by her short, spiky grey hair, even though most of her figure is obscured by the heavy, burn-scarred leather apron and gloves she wears over her practical, close-fitting black clothes. The broad leather belt wrapped around her waist bristles with all manner of tools, and her face is partly obscured by the green-tinted, circular eyeglasses held tight to her head by leather straps, which makes her look like some bizarre insect.

Noa sits in a group with five other initiates by the nearest oven, each woman sitting or standing at her own workbench. The other initiates wear protective leather and plain black clothes similar to Noa's, though a few of them have more colorful embroidery at their collars or in the cloths holding back their long hair from their faces. Walking back and forth behind the initiates, two novices I recognize from the meal hall feed the ovens from an enormous cart full of firewood, tending to the roaring blazes in the outer two ovens and the low coals in the center oven. Another novice shovels sand from an open crate into a small stone tub in the nearest oven.

I've never seen glassmaking before, and I watch with fascination as one initiate dips her long metal tube into a stone tub to withdraw a glowing orange globule of molten glass. Another initiate swings her metal tube like a pendulum before her, her glass stretching toward the floor like a strange ball of dough. Beside her, another initiate shapes her cooling glass with various metal tools as she rolls the tube along the guiding rail bolted to her workbench.

I look beyond this last initiate to see what work is happening by the oven on the far side of the wall. There, before a particularly large workbench, sits a man I know at once must be Tio Artifex. His injured leg is propped out beside him, protected by a leather casing of sorts. He's bent over his workbench in a posture of intense concentration. Kabir stands over Tio, holding something for the elder Artifex. I try to make out what they're working on, but my view is half obscured by the tool shelf that stands between me and them. Tio raises his head and shoots a wordless look at someone nearby. Balashi promptly steps out from behind the tool shelf to hand Tio a pointed metal device. I catch Balashi's eye across the room and raise my gloved hand, smiling in greeting. Balashi nods at me but doesn't smile back.

"Muse Noa!" Arkhi calls. "We're here."

Noa looks up from her workbench. "Ah, good. More hands," she says, her own hands never pausing as she rolls her long metal tube back and forth along the rail, shaping her glass. "Could you get him suited up, Ark? I'll show him the basics so he can assist Tio and Kabir this afternoon."

Arkhi leads me to a shelf stacked with leather aprons, gloves, and eyeglasses. Imitating Arkhi, I pull on the unfamiliar protective clothing. Arkhi has to rummage for a while to find gloves large enough for me, and she shows me how to adjust the leather straps of the eyeglasses. I'm sweating under my heavy leather layers even before Arkhi leads me closer to the ovens.

By the time we're suitably dressed, Noa's just finished her latest piece of work. She stands, using a pair of tongs to pick up a small finished bottle no longer than my finger. She carries the new bottle toward the center oven and places it on one of the stone shelves over the coals, beside a row of nearly identical brown bottles.

Noa pulls off her leather gloves and picks up two bottles from a shelf standing near the ovens. When she turns back to face us, I see she's holding a blue bottle in one hand and a brown bottle in the other. Without warning, she tosses the blue bottle in a high arc toward me. Alarmed, I scramble forward to catch the bottle in my gloved hands, barely managing to save it from shattering on the stone floor.

"Good," says Noa, studying me with her keen grey eyes. "Pays attention. Steady hands. More graceful than you'd expect on those big feet. The Voice knows what it's about."

I glance at Arkhi uncertainly, and she gives me an encouraging smile. Carefully, I hand the blue bottle back to Noa, who continues, "In my experience, the best way to learn any art, especially arts of tekhnologia, is watching and doing. Muse Arkhi will give you more instruction in the mysteries of tekhnologia later—physika, khemika, mathematika, and so on. She's a much better teacher of mysteries than I've ever been, though I trained her myself! Still, mastery of the mysteries is not the same as mastery of the arts. Tekhnologia requires *doing* things, not simply *knowing* things.

"And we certainly have more than enough to do for today, if we're going to get this shipment of bottles up to the house of healing before the freeze. I'll have you start with feeding the ovens, Dom, to give Rehan a break. It's not glamorous work, but it will give you plenty of time to observe.

"Now I know it's hot in here, but keep those glasses, gloves, and apron on whenever you're working near the ovens or the workbenches. Serapen has her hands full enough this harvest without me sending a burned novice up to her house.

"After you've had a chance to observe the initiates at work, you may attempt bottle-making, if it interests you. I don't expect you'll be making pharmaka-quality bottles any time soon, but," Noa shrugs, "who knows? Tio was a natural with glass from his very first year in the house of novices. I've never seen such beautiful work.

"Sister Rehan!" Noa calls out to the sturdy-looking novice carrying an armload of wood toward the ovens. "Hand that over to Dom for now. You can come back at fourth bell."

Rehan gratefully transfers her armload of wood to me. Before she departs, she shows me her careful method for feeding and stoking the ovens to keep each at the proper temperature. Seeing that I'm settled, Arkhi bids me farewell.

The morning passes in a sweaty blur as I run about the workshop floor, tending fires and fetching things for Noa and the other initiates. When I'm not otherwise occupied, I alternate between watching the Mohirai at their work and watching Tio Artifex at his.

It would be obvious what the priestesses are making, even if I hadn't been told: bottles, bottles, and more bottles. As each set of new bottles emerges from the cooling oven, Rehan and I pack them carefully into small straw-filled crates and load them into the empty carts that appear periodically behind the door in the north wall that opens to the underground tunnels. Rehan shows me how to work the row of metal levers on the wall that summon and dismiss the carts. All day long, I hear the *clack-a-tat clack-a-tat clack-a-tat* sound of the carts coming and going along the tracks that connect the workshop to the house of healing through the Under City tunnels.

What Tio might be making is more mysterious to me. When I'm near his workbench, I see that he's crafting a collection of glass objects whose shapes I don't understand. They're each as big around as the largest serving bowls in the meal hall, but the bottoms of these bowls bow upward so far that they would be able to hold only a small portion of what a serving bowl would hold. Tio fires and re-fires each object in his oven several times, painstakingly refining the shape of each with a variety of long metal tools before handing them to Kabir, who transfers them into the cooling oven. I consider asking Balashi or Kabir what Tio's making, but the three of them appear so focused that I don't quite dare to interrupt them.

So when I spot Noa in a rare moment of rest, sipping a glass of water drawn from one of the little faucets on the north wall, I decide to ask her instead. After feeding and stoking the nearest oven to make sure it will keep its heat for a while, I cross the workshop floor toward the Muse. I accept the glass of water she fills for me and take a cautious sip, having learned quickly that the waters of Velkanos come in several unusual—and not all pleasant—flavors. Fortunately, Noa has given me a glass of pure, sweet snowmelt. "What is Tio making?" I ask. "Those don't look like any bottles I've ever seen."

Noa shakes her head. "No. Working with rhegma glass requires more precise skill than mere bottle-making. Those rhegma bowls Tio's shaping hold the khemika we use to bore holes in the mountain."

Doubtfully, I say, "Those glass bowls can carve through stone?"

Noa chuckles. "Not in the way you're thinking. But rhegma bowls hold the khemika in precisely the right shape so that when we ignite the khemika, it explodes. It's not so different, in principle, from building a campfire, as I'm sure you've done many times. If you arrange all your kindling correctly, a single spark sets the lot ablaze. *Controlling* the fire, though—that's the art of it. The shape of the bowl controls the khemika explosion so that the heat melts the glass and pushes it straight through the rock, which creates a hole. When it's done right, it's far easier than chiseling through the stone, as the ancient builders did."

"But why do you need to bore holes in the mountain?" I say.

"A very good question," she says. "After all these millennia, you'd think we'd have enough storerooms in Velkanos to last us through the next age. Yet somehow every century brings the need for more storage, more tunnels, more of everything. It's no wonder mother Dulai nearly collapsed beneath the weight of humankind during the time of destruction, before the High Priestess set us on a better path."

Noa drains the last of her glass of water, then says, "But no need to dwell on that darkness, young Artifex. Voice willing, none of us will be called to witness such a thing again. Let us turn our minds to more productive things, shall we? I see Rehan returning now—perhaps you'd like to try your hand at some glasswork on my workbench before I pass you on to Tio?"

Eagerly, I nod, following Noa to her workbench. As she narrates the steps for me, I attempt to do what I've been watching the initiates do all morning: gathering the molten glass from the oven, shaping the gather into a rough globe, blowing a bubble into the globe with my long metal blowpipe, shaping the soft bottle with a few of Noa's tools. It's more difficult than the initiates made it look, but I'm still delighted by the result: a slightly asymmetrical yet fully functional blue bottle, which Noa says I may collect tomorrow after it's finished its time in the cooling oven.

"Very well done for a first attempt, young Artifex," says Noa, clapping me on the shoulder. "You and Tio may have been cut from the same cloth." She glances across the room at Tio, who meets her gaze, then nods. Noa adds, "It looks like he's finally at a stopping point. You should go join your brothers now."

So I thank Noa for all her instruction and head over to the far oven.

Tio and Kabir sit close beside each other at Tio's workbench, with an open basket of food between them. Balashi sits a short distance away at another workbench. Kabir waves for me to join them, swallowing a large mouthful of something before saying boisterously, "Dom! Join us! Zia sent down provisions from the kitchens. How goes your first day in the workshop? I would have greeted you sooner, but these rhegma bowls are tricky work, even for those of us with two good legs." Kabir gives Tio's bad knee a good-natured nudge.

Tio's dark blue eyes flash at Kabir, and his massive hand balls into a fist. I'm briefly alarmed by the impression that Kabir has angered his elder brother and is about to catch a punch. But then Tio elbows Kabir hard in the ribs, and Kabir guffaws.

Balashi watches their horseplay with a withdrawn expression. I pull up a stool beside him at his workbench. He holds out his basket of food toward me. I pick out a piece of bread and smear it with soft herbed goat cheese.

"How are you, brother?" I say.

Balashi shrugs indifferently. "How's your head?" he says.

"It'll never be as pretty as yours," I say.

This earns me a small smile. Balashi says, "Doubt it matters, though. You wouldn't believe the things I've overheard all these girls saying about you, while I've been running around the city."

I sigh, chewing my food slowly, remembering the fawning novices and eager initiates jostling for my attention in the meal hall last night. Cautiously, I say, "What sort of things?"

Kabir looks over at us, his eyes sparkling, eager for gossip. Tio watches with a more reserved expression. Balashi hesitates, looking from Kabir to Tio as if he needs permission to speak.

"Go on," Kabir prods. "Do tell."

"Well, there's a few novices plotting to catch you alone in your quarters," says Balashi. "They sounded pretty eager for your, uh … favor."

Kabir dismisses this with a wave. "Those aren't the ones you need to worry about, Dom," he says, pointing at me with a cured sausage before taking an enormous bite. "It's the healer initiates you have to look out for. Serapen has her binding pharmaka under lock and key, especially now that so much amanitai has gone missing, but you never know who may have managed to squirrel some away, or where it might turn up."

My eyes widen, and I look down with alarm at the half-eaten piece of bread in my hand. Kabir laughs and says, "Joking, joking, little brother. Of course all the sisters know it's forbidden to use binding pharmaka to influence the choice of Muse—a violation almost as severe as breaking initiate vows. The consequences would be severe."

"What consequences?" I say.

Kabir finishes off the sausage with another huge bite and chews thoughtfully. "It's never happened before, to my knowledge," he says. "But ultimately the consequences would be Serapen's decision. A violation judged serious enough could cause a sister to lose access to initiate pharmaka, I suppose."

"Why does that matter?" I say.

"Well, the initiate's life of service to the Voice requires the use of initiate pharmaka. Without it …" Kabir makes a flitting gesture with his hand. "The years are short indeed."

"Do you mean that it's the initiate pharmaka that prevents the Mohirai from beginning the journey into Death?" I say.

Tio settles his hand firmly on Kabir's forearm. Kabir's playful expression fades. He glances at Balashi, then nods at Tio, saying in a chastened tone, "I have listened and I have heard, brother. Thank you for correcting me." To me, Kabir says, "I've spoken out of turn, Dom. We Artifexi receive far less training in the arts of pharmaka than our sisters. Your question would be better answered by one of our sisters in the house of healing. I would not want to lead you astray with my own poor instruction. Voice knows I've done enough of that already."

A gloomy silence settles over the four of us. I chew and swallow, listening to the happy chatter of the Mohirai sharing their own meal by the other oven. The work of the morning briefly dissolved my awareness of the boundaries between women and men, but as I sit here mulling over Kabir's words—both what he said and what he didn't say—I can't help thinking of what Ava told me on our Calling Day, as she pleaded with me to run away with her.

Come with me. Where I'm going, you won't need to serve the Voice. I'll hide nothing from you. We'll share everything as equals. I promise.

However well the Mohirai may care for uninitiated men, and however much the Mohirai may choose to reveal to the Artifexi, they certainly don't share everything with us as equals. So much of their world is hidden from me, even now, as I sit within their temple city walls. As hungry as I am for the knowledge they're willing to share with me as an Artifex, a part of me wonders what they will still withhold, and why, and whether I'll ever even know what's missing.

This thought once again stirs the anger I felt when I lashed out at Hanu in the house of healing. What gives anyone else the right to tell me what I should and shouldn't know, what I should and shouldn't do?

I wish I could talk to Ava right now. She would understand what I'm feeling. My throat tightens, and hot tears blur my vision. Spirits, how I miss her.

Across the workbench, Tio looks at me, his eyes dark as a stormy sea. Everything about his silent presence intimidates me, and a part of me wants to hide my tears from him. But I find myself unable to look away. I don't know whether it's something he sees in me, or something I see in him, but for the first time in my life, I feel understood by another man. Tio must know the loneliness I feel, as one called apart from his brothers. He must know the frustration of glimpsing the scale of the mysteries, knowing the deeper mysteries are withheld. He must see the injustice of it all.

What might this man teach me, when at last he speaks?

EAST OF EDEN

Other-Dom and I slip out of Eden headquarters through a back entrance and follow a circuitous route through downtown San Francisco that takes us up and down staircases, over raised walkways that bridge the crowded streets, and through lobbies of other office towers.

Panting a little from the effort to keep up with other-Dom's brisk pace, I reach for his hand. His warm fingers close tight around mine, and my breathing eases as his energy rushes into me.

Why are we leaving this way? I think.

We're following instructions from Falsens, your security detail, thinks other-Dom. *We're passing by only the cameras under Falsens' control, so no one should know we've left Eden.*

An image of Falsens—which I assume must be an avatar, since this face, while unmistakably human, communicates nothing of age or sex—appears in my visual overlay. Beside the image appears an extraordinarily long description of the "security detail" services Falsens provides to Emmie. I give up reading the description barely a tenth of the way through. *Who's Falsens?* I think. *Why does Emmie need all these security services?*

Another long story, thinks other-Dom. *I'd like to say Falsens is a friend of ours after all these years, but the closest word in our tongue might be "attendant."*

Our walk concludes in the dark rear corner of a four-story parking garage facing a quiet street. Other-Dom leads me to an empty black car, whose doors open at our approach. We climb in, and the car pulls smoothly out of the garage.

The car drives us back to Emmie's house by a different route than the one we took to Eden, this time crossing the San Francisco Bay over the "Golden Gate Bridge." Although the rust-red color of the bridge belies its name, the crossing is nonetheless spectacular. I can't decide whether the deep blue view of the "Pacific Ocean" to my left or the brightly-colored sails of the half-dozen boats racing before the city skyline to my right are more magnificent. How many nights did I sit beside Lilith at a campfire, imagining the day our long sail across the Middle Sea would conclude with our first glimpse of the city of glass towers on the western horizon? Yet as vivid as my imagination was, the reality of the view before me is more breathtaking than my daydreams ever were.

Our car exits the freeway on the far side of the bridge, weaving through traffic for over an "hour" on a winding return journey to Oakland. My mind wanders as the landscape slides past my window. At times, the profile of a hilltop or a curve in the road ahead recalls a fragment of a memory from my exhausting journey to Velkanos. At other times, I have unexpected moments of recognition—a familiar intersection, the painted sign above a "bakery," a grove of trees in a "park"—that I suppose must come from somewhere in Emmie's memory. I wonder how much longer I'll be able to tell the difference between her past and mine, and what that means for us both.

When at last our car returns to Emmie's neighborhood, it drops us off a short distance away from her house, at one of the only stretches of Skyline Boulevard that's not crowded with houses. I follow other-Dom toward an unpaved footpath that intersects the asphalt road at a painted "crosswalk." The path enters the forest beside the road, and we're soon surrounded by trees.

Walking through these woods, I could almost pretend I'm back in the wilderness of Dulai, were it not for the occasional road noises disturbing the quiet. Beneath the hard high heels of my boots, the soil is soft, strewn with the aromatic fallen needles of the magnificent "redwood" trees that line the path. On an impulse, I let go of other-Dom's hand for a moment to sit down and pull off my boots and socks.

"What are you doing?" says other-Dom, watching me curiously. He speaks in our own tongue, which tells me we're safe here, at least for now.

"Something I love," I say, rising to stand barefoot on the forest floor, breathing in the spicy scent of the woods around us. I brush the prickly redwood needles off my palms and lace my fingers through his, swinging my boots in my free hand as we continue on our way. "You never know when you'll do something you love for the last time."

He nods thoughtfully.

My bare toes tingle each time they touch the cool soil. I recall the sensation of walking barefoot through the dark cedar forest by the sea, the night I heard the Voice's calling for the first time. Just as it did that night, my awareness sinks down through my body, into my feet, spreading out through the ground. The greater awareness of the forest greets my own, and across my skin I feel the rustle of leaves in the canopy, the moisture traversing deep roots, the life breathing and pulsing everywhere within and around and above me. I listen, and in the stillness, I hear the Voice's call once more.

We are the bridge joining light to darkness.
We are the wheel turning season to season.
We are the threads binding realm to realm.
We are creator, preserver, destroyer of worlds.

Together you shall seek us, find us, know us.
Together you shall amplify us.
Together you shall weave us through the many worlds.
Together you shall answer our call.

And for the first time since that fateful night, I feel like I'm on the right path. I smile up at other-Dom, and he smiles back down at me without a trace of sadness in his eyes. The warmth of his expression melts a hard knot I hadn't realized I was carrying in my chest. We walk on in comfortable silence. The forest path curves around the hillside, and a brightly-clad jogger passes us with a friendly wave. I wave back. When she's out of earshot, I say, "So … Bealsio said you two would explain what this quantum memory drive is for, once we're back home."

Other-Dom's smile fades a bit as the task at hand comes back into focus. "Yes. And here we are," he says, gesturing to a high gate of black metal just visible through the trees on our left. He looks both ways, checking to see that we're alone before he palms the shiny panel mounted to the side of the gate to open it. He ushers me through, and the gate clunks closed behind us, leaving us standing at the bottom of a steep cliff. Above us, at the top of the cliff, I can just make out the roofline of Emmie's house.

I stare up at the soft soil and crumbling rock of the cliff face, frowning. "We're not supposed to climb this, are—" I start to ask, before I see other-Dom heading toward a small, natural alcove worn into the base of the cliff ahead of us. I follow him into the recessed space, and as my eyes adjust to the dimmer light I discern the outline of a door in the cliff face at the back of the alcove, so camouflaged by vegetation and soil that I wouldn't have noticed it under other circumstances. Other-Dom murmurs something in English, which sounds like a string of nonsense, even through my translation filter.

"What was that?" I say, as the door into the cliff swings inward.

"One-time password," says other-Dom, triggering a new definition on my visual overlay.

We step through the door onto a small landing at the bottom of a steep metal staircase. The staircase makes three switchbacks as we climb to the top landing, which leads to a heavy metal door. Other-Dom speaks another string of nonsense, and the door swings open, delivering us into the familiar confines of the windowless grey spliner.

"Were all those evasive maneuvers really necessary?" I say, leaning against the spongy wall of the spliner, catching my breath after the stair climb. To my surprise, the wall molds itself to my shoulder and props me upright.

"It's better for us if Amos thinks we're still in the office," says other-Dom, only half-focused on me as he swipes through something on his visual overlay. To Bealsio, he adds, "Can you please send down our immergers, B?"

"On it," Bealsio's voice replies.

"But what if Amos comes back to check on Emmie?" I say. "He'll see she's not there."

"Amos is a very busy man," says other-Dom, picking up the two stacks of folded black clothes, gloves, and slippers that emerge through an opening in the wall beside me. "Being CEO of Eden is a small fraction of the work of leading the Stewards. After Amos laid eyes on you in your office, he'll rely on other eyes to tell him when you've left."

"Other eyes?" I say.

"The camera feeds at the office," other-Dom explains, handing me one stack of clothes and indicating that I should change into them. "AIs monitor everyone coming and going through the building. But Falsens has control of several of the key cameras. He'll make sure that, from the perspective of the AIs reporting to Amos, you're still at the office being a perfect little worker bee. And Bealsio has stayed active on the company channels since we left. Most real work happens in alternet channels at the office, and Bealsio can impersonate Emmie perfectly as long as no one needs to see an actual body. The only thing Bealsio can't do is pass the biometric scans needed to check out quantum hardware. That's the main reason we needed you to come in this morning."

Other-Dom turns his back to me as he changes from his office clothes into his immergers. I turn away to do the same, but I find my gaze keeps drifting toward him.

I've seen other-Dom's naked body in my prior visits here, and in some ways, the differences between him and my Dom are unmistakable. In other ways, though, he looks so much like my Dom that, as he stands there at the edge of my vision, I could forget they're different people.

He moves his hands with the same unconscious grace and precision as my Dom, but there's something in his posture that radiates a confidence Dom lacked. They share the same tall frame and broad shoulders, but the hardened sinew and muscle of other-Dom's body must have been acquired through long years of physical labor. His face reflects his mood with the same expressions as my Dom, though closer inspection reveals delicate wrinkles and subtle marks worn into his warm brown skin by time.

Other-Dom unbuttons his crisp collared shirt with its swirling pattern of pale blues and greens and deposits it in an opening that appears in the wall to receive it from him. Across his shoulders stretches the tattoo I glimpsed the first time I met him: a pair of outstretched wings. I hadn't noticed the extraordinarily realistic detail of the feathers in those wings the first time I saw them. Without thinking, I reach out and trace the line of one tattooed feather with my fingertip.

Other-Dom's shoulders tense. A trail of goosebumps prickles down his back, radiating out from my touch. Through our connection, I feel his longing for Emmie's touch, his desire for her. Hastily, I pull back my hand. "I'm sorry," I say. "I wasn't thinking. I … I'm sorry."

Other-Dom relaxes and pulls the stretchy immerger shirt over his head, covering the tattoo. He turns to face me, and I'm unprepared for the naked grief in his eyes. "Don't be sorry," he says. "You can't imagine how grateful I am that you're here. You came back when I needed you most. I know what it cost you."

I don't know what I'd expected him to say, but it wasn't this. Hot tears rush to my eyes. For a moment, the task at hand is forgotten. We look at each other openly, each seeing in the other the essence of the one we've lost, the one we would have given anything to save.

I've lost so much in the past moon—my trust in Lilith, my autonomy, my health, my body, my first love. The life I believed I was living turned out to be based on a lie, and the life I hoped I would live is now impossible. The only way I've managed to contain my grief is by building up walls within myself, ignoring as best I can the pain of the wounds I've sustained. Other-Dom's simple acknowledgment of my pain makes it impossible for me to ignore it any longer. He wraps me in his arms, holding me tight as I weep.

I'm not sure how long we stand together in the grey light of the spliner. But eventually, my sobs subside. I sniff, and the spliner wall helpfully offers me a soft sky-blue "handkerchief," which I use to wipe my wet cheeks and nose. For the first time in a long time, I feel better. I've lost many things on my journey, and maybe some part of me will always grieve the life that might have been. But the Voice's calling, though it was unsought and unwanted, has given me understanding I lacked in the beginning. All I've experienced in the past moon has shown me that the many worlds hold endless possibilities. Perhaps everything I've lost will be worth the cost, in the end. The only way to find out is to keep going.

Slowly, I extricate myself from other-Dom's embrace. With new resolve, I pull on the last of my immerger gear. "So," I say, "are you going to tell me what we're supposed to do with this quantum memory drive?"

There's a chime of bells, and Bealsio materializes before me.

I groan. "Spirits, did you just watch all of that?" I say.

"Oh, yes," Bealsio says cheerfully. "I've been here the whole time. Would you like me to show you how the quantum memory drive works?"

"Please," I say, eager to move on from my embarrassing display of tears.

I pull out the cold little quantum drive from my pocket and hand it to Dom, who inserts it into an opening that appears on the spliner wall. I watch and listen intently as Bealsio, with interjections from other-Dom, shows me what Emmie and other-Dom discovered about the many uses of quantum memory in the years since Emmie's overdose. We review memories Emmie recorded of her own attempts at bridge crossings, debating various theories about why some attempts succeeded while others failed.

What seems clear is that the quantum computer's memory holds the expansive map that makes precise navigation between the worlds easier. Unfortunately, this map on its own isn't sufficient for an awareness to cross from one world to another. To build a bridge and cross it requires both binding and unbinding pharmaka.

This was why Emmie, the last time I saw her, pleaded for my help to find the records of Serapen's pharmaka experiments kept in the Musaion library. She believed Serapen's precise formula for the preparation and use of binding and unbinding pharmaka, were it known to the world, would break the Stewards' control over the people of Earth, as well as provide Emmie with the cure for her own binding pharmaka overdose, breaking Amos' hold on her.

But despite Emmie and other-Dom's extensive records gathered from many other-Avas and other-Doms regarding the preparation of pharmaka, they've never been able to prepare effective pharmaka of any kind. They remain entirely dependent on Amos to supply unbinding pharmaka, and on the lingering effects of the binding pharmaka that continues to flow through Emmie's blood since her overdose, to accomplish bridge crossings as they continue the search for Serapen's pharmaka formula.

Emmie has learned a great deal about bridge crossing over many attempts, but what we don't know about bridge crossing is far more extensive than what we know. Failed attempts have been more common than successful ones as a result. The cost of Emmie's many failures has been high, as her consumption of ever more unbinding pharmaka slowly destroyed her body and her memory. My own experiences have shown that even successful crossings can still prove fatal, in the end.

Given the vast breadth of the unknowns and the high cost of each attempt, we all agree that the least risky way for me to find Lilith would be for me to bridge back to The End of the Road, right where I left her.

Having a clear plan and a job to do always energizes me, and I feel ready to attempt the bridge crossing as soon as our discussion concludes. But other-Dom insists we eat "lunch" first. He says, "I'll give you as much of my strength as I can, to help you spend more time on the far side of the bridge. But you can help me by taking care of Emmie's body."

"I'm not hungry," I protest. "And the longer we delay, the less—"

But I haven't even finished my objection when the spliner wall opens before us, revealing two plates of food and a pair of bottles. A table and two chairs materialize a moment later in the center of the room, extruding themselves from the floor at a command from other-Dom.

"Won't you let me tempt your appetite, at least?" says Bealsio, her tone playful. "I've prepared some of Emmie's favorites."

Perhaps I shouldn't be surprised by the speed of the food's appearance, after everything else the spliner has already shown me it can do. Still, I'm not convinced the food is real until I reach out to pick up one of the bottles and feel cool beads of condensation on the glass, dampening my bare palm. Astonished, and only half-joking, I say, "If we didn't need to go to the office, would we ever need to leave this room?"

"Maybe not," says other-Dom, setting the food on the table, taking a seat, and gesturing for me to join him. "Some people with a high-speed alternet connection and a spliner barely leave their houses any more."

"What?" I laugh, placing our drinks on the table and taking the seat across from him. "Don't they miss—I don't know—the sun? The air? Other people?" I take a sip from the bottle of "kombucha." The fizzy sensation on my tongue reminds me of one of the mineral springs that flows from Velkanos, but the sweet and sour flavor is more complex, a mixture of herbs and berries. I can see why Emmie likes the stuff.

Other-Dom shrugs. "Maybe they would miss those things, if it wasn't for artists like Emmie," he says. "The reason Emmie's so valuable to Amos is that she builds alternet experiences that most people prefer to their own reality."

Puzzled, I say, "Why does Amos care about alternet experiences?"

"Amos doesn't care about the experiences, exactly," he says, taking a bite of the "sandwich" on his plate. "The experiences are just a means to an end. What

Amos cares about is immersed minutes per day. IMPD. Every minute an Eden domain holds someone's attention is a minute Amos controls. With enough IMPD, you can influence what people think and feel. You can even shape what people want and do. A skilled alternet designer can control people without them even realizing they're being controlled."

"Why would Emmie help Amos control people like that?" I say, taking a tentative bite of my own sandwich. My eyes widen as the glorious "bacon" on my fried chicken sandwich awakens my appetite.

"What do you think?" Bealsio asks eagerly. "I've been tweaking my aioli recipe."

"Mmm!" I nod appreciatively, my mouth too full to form words.

"Emmie wouldn't have helped Amos, if we could have figured out any alternative," says other-Dom. "But her overdose put Emmie in an impossible situation. She would have died, without unbinding pharmaka. Amos was the only person who could supply it to her, and his price was her cooperation with the Stewards' agenda. He made her a deal she couldn't refuse."

"I still can't believe Emmie agreed to help him, though," I say. "It just seems so wrong."

"You'd be surprised, the things people do to survive," says other-Dom.

"And what about you?" I say. "You helped her do all this? Helped her control all these people for Amos?"

Other-Dom nods solemnly. "Yes. For years," he says.

I'm so disappointed in both of them that I can't keep the accusation out of my voice when I say, "You know firsthand how the Mohirai control the people of Dulai. How could you help Emmie build something like that for the Stewards on Earth?"

Other-Dom laces his fingers behind his head and leans back in his seat, watching my reaction as he says, "Do you really want to know, or do you just want to judge?"

An embarrassed flush rises to my cheeks as I realize that is what I was doing. I set my sandwich down. More humbly, I say, "I do want to know."

"Then the first thing you need to know is that, long before Amos ever met Emmie or me, the Stewards already had control over the people of Earth," he says. "But then the alternet appeared. In the beginning, the technology opened up many new ways for people to form communities, which led to experimentation with all kinds of new ideas. The Stewards had spent millennia cultivating uniformity across societies and centralizing their power, and the proliferation of alternet domains threatened to fragment that society.

"Initially, the Stewards tried to suppress the alternet. They used their power to discourage its development, and even tried to ban it outright. Those efforts failed, though, because suppression only made alternet users more sophisticated in evading detection. So the Stewards turned to more indirect methods of control. They acquired corporations developing the most popular alternet domains. Over time, as more people were drawn to fewer alternet domains controlled by smaller numbers of corporations, the Stewards effectively gained control of the alternet by controlling the creators of its most popular domains.

"That's why the Stewards wanted Emmie. She had a unique talent for designing alternet domains where communities wanted to congregate. She tried to resist Amos' advances, but her overdose gave him exactly what he needed to control her. And she's performed perfectly according to the Stewards' plan, as far as Amos knows."

"All right," I say, finishing off the last of my sandwich and leaning forward conspiratorially. "So … what *doesn't* Amos know?" A bowl rises up in the center of the table, replacing my empty plate. I inspect the golden "potato chips" before taking a handful. My hand returns to the bowl before I've even finished swallowing the salty, oily, crunchy mouthful. I'm not sure why my visual overlay calls this "junk food"—it's delicious.

Other-Dom chuckles, watching with evident pleasure as I gorge myself. He says, "Amos doesn't know the full potential of the quantum computer that hosts the Eden domains. He doesn't know that the very technology he's using to control the people of Earth can also be used to expose the Stewards' secrets."

"What secrets?" I say, scraping the bottom of the bowl with my fingertips but finding only salty crumbs. The empty bowl sinks into the table, and I'm about to ask Bealsio to refill it when a new bowl rises up, this one filled with a nut-brown scoop of something drizzled in dark brown sauce. I pick up the little silver spoon beside the bowl and dig in.

I'm still recovering from the transformative experience of "peanut butter ice cream" with "chocolate sauce" as other-Dom explains, "One important secret the Stewards keep to themselves is how to prepare initiate pharmaka. Their control over the supply of initiate pharmaka ingredients allows them to preserve the lives of their senior leadership and execute plans over very long time periods, much like the Mohirai do. The timescale on which the Stewards operate and the lifespans of their leadership make it easy for them to consolidate power. They can afford to be patient, to choose the right moment to act in their own interests and wait out any short-lived opposition. They have a luxury of time that's inconceivable to anyone outside their order.

"But perhaps the most important secret the Stewards keep is the fact of their own existence."

"If the Stewards are so powerful, though, why do they bother to keep their existence a secret?" I say.

"The Stewards could reveal themselves, I suppose," says other-Dom. "In times considered ancient history on Earth, the predecessors of the Stewards held power openly, just as the Mohirai do on Dulai. But that form of control became more difficult as the population of Earth grew.

"Even with their substantial power, the Stewards are too small in number to easily protect themselves from a widespread rebellion by a large population. But people can't rebel against something without first knowing it exists. Controlling the population covertly through private corporations like Eden is far simpler, requires less use of force, and provokes fewer rebellion movements, which are difficult and costly to contain. So, when they can, the Stewards prefer to fly under the radar."

I'm briefly distracted by the astonishing "video" of an "airplane" that appears on my visual overlay to illustrate the meaning of "fly under the radar." But other-Dom's explanation raises a question that's puzzled me before. "Why are there so many people here on Earth, anyway? I've never seen anything like these crowds on Dulai."

"No," other-Dom agrees. "These two branches have diverged significantly, in that way. I think it's because, for all the similarities in the way they hold power, there's one key difference between the Stewards and the Mohirai.

"The Stewards believe the Voice in all placed the Earth in their service. They believe they've been called to use every resource at their disposal to build a more perfect society. The human population is a uniquely powerful resource, when its productivity can be harnessed at scale. Over time, the Stewards have perfected the art of harnessing that power—through religions and kingdoms at first, and later through governments and corporations.

"That's why, in all the societies they've cultivated throughout history, the Stewards have upheld human procreation as the foundation of the social order. Population growth directly benefits the Stewards, as long as they control the productive output of the population. The larger the population, the more thinkers and innovators and builders emerge. Technological progress on Earth happens much faster as a result, since there are so many more people contributing to that progress. And technology certainly has its benefits. Life for humans on Earth can be pretty comfortable, for some of us." Other-Dom gestures to the spliner around us and the meal before us. I set down my ice cream spoon into the empty bowl, and, as if on cue, Bealsio sends up in its place a ceramic cup filled with steaming hot "coffee". I've never smelled anything so good, although the bacon came close. My first sip of the dark, bittersweet brew swirls down to warm my bellyful of ice cream. My mind sharpens, like it's waking from sleep, which makes me wonder whether Bealsio laced the food with some kind of pharmaka.

"But the benefits of all this progress disproportionately flow to the Stewards," other-Dom continues. "Control of population consolidates wealth, and wealth consolidates control. As long as the Stewards control the population of Earth, growth of population grows their wealth, which reinforces their power over the population.

"And unfortunately, all this growth comes at a cost. The Stewards preside over a society where the growth of their wealth and power comes at the direct expense of all other life on Earth.

"The Mohirai, on the other hand, believe that the Voice has placed them in service to Dulai, to repair the damage to the lands humans occupied during the time of destruction. The priestesshood attributes that damage to the uncontrolled growth of the human population. They see their role as healers of Dulai, and they grow cautiously, selectively preserving the people they see as most beneficial to

Dulai's healing. They work to preserve the natural order of ecosystems that support all life on Dulai. But despite the sophistication of their arts, the Mohirai have far fewer conveniences than the Stewards because they have far fewer hands in their service.

"These two power structures have created two vastly different societies and two very different worlds. But both worlds share in common the fact that a very small number of people make decisions that control the lives of a very large number of others."

I nod. "I guess both worlds have their advantages and disadvantages," I say. "Neither of them is perfect. But Lilith believes the greatest injustice of our world is how the Mohirai use pharmaka to manipulate people into serving the Voice. She taught me that people should be free to live however they choose."

"And what do you believe?" says other-Dom.

I consider this for a long time as I finish my coffee. At last, I shake my head and say, "I'm not sure. Lilith also believes the rebellion of free people is the only way to break the control of the Mohirai. But Emmie told me that the free men who rebelled against the Mohirai eventually became the Stewards on Earth.

"Maybe all these worlds are stuck in a pattern, like you and me. How did you put it, Dom? We live, we love, we lose. And then we're reborn. We forget all we've learned and have to start over, and over, and over again.

"Maybe it's the same with our societies. It's possible to destroy one power structure to build a different one, but in the end people lose their freedom all over again to the new power structure. It seems like there's no way out."

"But you found a way out," says other-Dom. "You've managed to die and be reborn, without forgetting the lessons of the life you lived before. You don't have to keep making the same mistakes."

I chuckle ruefully. "Right. I get to make new and better mistakes. Lucky me."

He smiles. "All right, sure. You'll make new mistakes. But that doesn't have to be a bad thing. Every mistake you've made led you here. You know firsthand the true nature of reality, and you have access to a technology so powerful that you could share that knowledge with everyone in every world. You can show people the truth: you can change your world."

"Only if you're willing to risk losing your life," I point out.

"Everything comes at a cost," he says, and I see on his face that this knowledge was hard-earned. "But some things are worth the cost."

Other-Dom's words recall to me what Lilith said to Tio in the Under City. *We both knew freedom for all would come at a cost to some.* Those words, spoken over Dom's lifeless body, had infuriated me at the time. But with my anger cooled, I wonder whether Lilith's seeming indifference might in fact have been acceptance born of experience, like other-Dom's. I've had to accept many losses on my journey, but I've never been indifferent to them. The memory of Lilith weeping over Maya's dead body flashes through my mind. How much more than I might Lilith have lost, in her centuries-long pursuit of freedom from the Mohirai?

And how much more than I might Lilith still be willing to sacrifice to achieve her goal? In the end, I sacrificed everything I had in pursuit of freedom for myself and the one I loved. Perhaps in this way, I am Lilith's daughter, after all.

Return to me, and all will be forgiven. The message Lilith went to such great lengths to send me, even after I defied her command to let Dom go, strikes me differently now. Her command contains a promise, and her promise conveys love. Lilith's love for me has always been a hard kind of love, but it's as fierce and strong as she is. It's made me what I am.

I rise from the table, energized—by the discussion, by the food, but most of all by the sudden realization of the part I've come to play in this great work that's spanned so many lives across so many worlds.

"Let's make this bridge worth it, then," I say, licking the last smudge of chocolate sauce from my spoon. I pull on my immerger gloves, adjust my glasses, and take a deep breath.

"All right," says other-Dom, rising beside me and dismissing the table, which melts back down into the floor. "Can you reload that memory, B?"

"On it," says Bealsio.

Other-Dom settles his hand on my shoulder. Into our connection, he pours his strength. The light fades, and the flat grey spliner walls around us recede into darkness as I return once more to the Under City.

WEST OF EDEN

HARVEST SEASON IN VELKANOS shares many things in common with the harvest seasons of my boyhood. Rippling rows of golden grains and drying beans fall under the scythe. Days grow short. Work stretches long after sundown.

In my years growing up in the house of boys, all I knew of harvest work was what the Mohirai gave me and my brothers to do in the farmland outside the walls of the Children's Temple. The fruits of our labor disappeared through the city gate, only reappearing on our plates in the meal hall after careful preparation by the Mohirai.

But in my first few days of attendance on Tio Artifex, as I pass to and from my quarters, the workshops, the house of novices, and the Musaion, I glimpse a great deal more of the season's work. Harvest and slaughter are only the beginning. Many hands are needed to preserve the bounty of fields, orchards, vineyards, and paddocks in the kitchens; prepare shipments for the outer villages; and fill the warren of storerooms hidden within the rocky slopes of Velkanos. In the walled gardens and glass houses of the Upper City, the hands of a chosen few tend to the most valuable harvest: the ingredients of pharmaka, grown only by Serapen and her most skilled healer initiates.

However, my own hands are not required—indeed, would not be permitted—to perform any of these tasks. Instead, I attend Tio each morning in his workshop, learning day by day the arts of glassmaking as I watch him demonstrate his masterful technique and listen to instruction by Noa, Kabir, and Arkhi.

Glassmaking interests me, and watching the elder Artifexi at their work is always mesmerizing. Even in his silence, Tio is an excellent teacher, helping me hone my skills at his workbench when he's able to set aside a rhegma bowl for a little while. Kabir expands my instruction in the arts of tekhnologia whenever the opportunity arises, taking me with him on excursions all over the Outer City to order needed materials or summon aid from initiates of another house. For the first time in my life, every door is open to me. I'm welcomed not only in the many workshops of the Outer City, but even in the Upper City houses, as long as I return to my quarters in the Outer City before the bell for the evening silence. The initiate Mohirai of every house greet me as their equal, eager to demonstrate their arts to the new Artifex and answer my questions about their mysteries. Still, I find myself withdrawing whenever a new woman tries to become more familiar with me. Knowing my unique value to any ambitious Mohira, I'm no longer certain I can distinguish authenticity from guile.

So I welcome the occasions when Tio dismisses me early from the workshops, on days when the pain in his leg overcomes his ability to work. On those days, after Balashi and I help Tio back to his quarters in the stables, I rejoin the first-year novices in attendance on Muse Clio. It's a relief to spend time with

Hanu and Eumelia, the only two people I trust entirely, and my favorite place in Velkanos is the Musaion that crowns the Upper City. The massive complex of great halls built into the mountain slope fascinates me endlessly. Whenever I examine some part of the Musaion—the dramatic columned front entrance, the soaring domed ceilings, the elaborate mosaics adorning nearly every interior surface—I discover something new.

One unusually warm afternoon in late autumn, as my first moon in Velkanos nears its end, I sit on the paving stones of the plaza facing the Musaion, my open sketchbook in my lap, alternately squinting up at the building's grand entrance and scribbling on my halfway-filled parchment. I hurried through my work unpacking crates for Eumelia and Hanu inside the library this afternoon so I'd have these last few moments of sunset to capture something I noticed a few days ago: the intricate symmetry of the shadows cast by the frontmost carved columns onto the row of columns behind them. The shadows create a marvelous impression of a long colonnade of trees, emphasizing the depth of the entryway into the mountain.

"Are you interested in the arts of arkhitectonia?" says Muse Clio.

I look up, surprised to find Clio standing just behind me, looking down at my sketch. I was so engrossed in my work I didn't hear her approach. I scramble to my feet and incline my head respectfully to her.

"I'm not sure, Muse Clio. What is arkhitectonia?" I say, pronouncing the unfamiliar word carefully.

"Ah, that's right," she says. "We discussed it briefly on your first day. But that was just before your accident, I'm afraid. Would you like me to refresh your memory?"

She extends her hand toward me, and I look down at it uncertainly. She smiles and says, "Don't worry, Dom. You have nothing to fear from my memory, and everything to gain."

Cautiously, I take the Muse's hand. There's a faint tingling where my palm presses hers, and I recognize the sensation of a connection opening between us. The last time I shared thoughts this way was with Ava in the Cave of Dreams. I've been avoiding thinking of her for the past several days, and tears sting my eyes as the memory reawakens.

Clio squeezes my hand with compassion, and through our connection I know my sadness has spilled into her. Firmly, but not unkindly, she says, "Feelings can serve you, Dom, but you must become their master. When a feeling disturbs you, practice letting it go."

I nod, redirecting my self-centered attention outward in an effort to calm myself. My gaze turns to Clio, whose tranquil sea-green eyes hold mine steadily. I study the Muse as I'd studied the Musaion, discovering new details the longer I look. It's rare for the initiates to show any signs of age. Most are like Thalia and Arkhi—possessed of evergreen youth that endures unchanging through the seasons. Only in their bearing, their knowledge, and their elaborate dress do such initiates distinguish themselves from the novices. Clio, by contrast, wears the marks of time openly, comfortably, unapologetically. I wonder whether this is by choice, or something determined for her by the Voice.

Whatever the reason may be, Clio's face reveals the beauty of time's passage. If I'm ever called to the house of sculpture, I think she would be my model for Wisdom.

I let out a long breath, and my pain fades, making space for something new. Into my calm, Clio offers a memory as simply as she might set a book into my hands. After all the messy thoughts and feelings I've shared with Ava, I'm impressed by the craftsmanship of the Muse's sharply-focused memory, wiped clean of unnecessary detail, free of emotion.

In Clio's memory, I stand among the girls in the library, on what I suppose was our first day in Velkanos.

Clio turns to Hanu and says, "Well, then. Hanu, is it? You're the eldest of your trio? I'll leave you in charge of cataloging the new khartographia materials with your sister and Dom here, then. Do you think you can manage?"

"Yes, Muse Clio," says Hanu.

"Very well. Should you have any questions for me, I'll be working on cataloging the new items for Section Four. Arkhitektonia. Do you know this word?"

"That's the art of building," says Hanu.

"Sounds simple enough, doesn't it?" says Clio. "And yet the building arts of arkhitektonia are a way of remembering our past, too, like the written arts of historia. You may discover the story of an entire people, long after the people themselves are gone, if you know how to read the buildings they've left behind. What we build contains the memories of our lives and connects us to the land from which we come. That's why it's an important responsibility, to be the builder of any structure, however humble or magnificent it may be."

The knowledge conveyed in her memory and the image of that day remain clear in my mind as Clio withdraws her hand and inclines her head to me. I'm struck by the impression that the Muse has deftly stitched her memory over the gap in my own. Only days ago, I watched the initiates in the house of weaving restore a worn tapestry, clipping out the frayed threads and embroidering over the damage with new and brighter ones. For the first time, I wonder how much of my missing memory might be restored, with help from the Mohirai.

I understand more fully now the value of the careful training the Mohirai receive in the use of binding pharmaka, and just how damaging it was for me and Ava to encounter it unprepared. Thoughts, sensations, and memories had flowed so freely between us after our accident that we were constantly disturbing each other's minds and knocking each other off balance. Our journey to Velkanos would have been much easier had it been free of the influence of binding pharmaka.

I consider the memory Clio has shared, then say, "Yes. I suppose I am interested in arkhitektonia. Am I permitted to learn those arts?"

Clio nods. "Many of the temples built since the time of destruction were great works performed by Artifexi in service of their Muses. Kabir himself is currently building a new temple of poetika for Muse Thalia in Phasis, on the coast of the Dark Sea. Tio too builds temples, though Muse Maya's temples are of glass, rather than stone."

"Glass temples?" I say doubtfully.

"Yes. You've seen some of her earliest work, I imagine," says Clio. "The glass houses where we keep the gardens inside our temple cities were imagined in the early days of our order by Muse Maya, to aid the work of the healers. But until Tio was called as Artifex, the initiates of tekhnologia lacked the skill required to craft glass in a way that would support the building of such large structures. Maya and Tio's great work together marked a new chapter of our historia, allowing our sisterhood to expand beyond the walls of Velkanos for the first time since the destruction. Perhaps the glass houses don't strike you as quite so grand as the Musaion, but they are our temples of healing, where we encounter season after season the greatest of the mysteries: the abundance of life, and its eternal return."

I ponder this. The glass houses of Velkanos are distributed throughout the city. Though they are beautiful in their way—housing all manner of growing things, keeping spaces warm and moist, protected from the high winds and extreme temperatures of the mountain seasons—I would never have considered these indoor gardens to be temples to the mysteries, any more than I would consider a kitchen a temple.

"I'd be happy to build any sort of temple, if it served a useful purpose," I say. Gesturing toward the grand facade of the Musaion, I add with a self-deprecating smile, "Though I suppose Velkanos needs no greater temple than this."

Clio considers me thoughtfully. She says, "The Musaion is indeed a marvel. Its halls preserved the knowledge we needed to survive the time of destruction. But the arrival of each new Artifex has marked the start of a new chapter in our historia. Perhaps your Muse shall call you to build an even greater temple for a new age, Dom Artifex."

Clio's words strike a chord deep inside me, filling me with a conviction I've felt only once before, as I stood with Serapen in the sacred spring and heard the Voice's call for me. Countless memories from my childhood flash through my mind, signposts along the path that's led me here. All those summer days playing in the forest with Ava, building cities together from the river stones. All those years outside the Children's Temple walls, imagining and re-imagining the wonders it might contain. All the longing to live in a world free of such walls.

"Yes," I murmur, a smile spreading slowly across my face. Louder, I say, "Yes, I think you're right!" I'm so elated by the sudden flash of insight that I might burst with eagerness to shout it from the mountaintop. I seize Muse Clio's hands in mine and say, "Thank you, sister. I needed to hear that."

Muse Clio inclines her head to me. "The Voice speaks through many teachers," she says. "Good luck finding your Muse, little brother."

HOMECOMING

I BRACE MYSELF for my next attempt to build a bridge back to my branch. The grey walls of the spliner fade from view as the scene of my last memory in the Under City reappears, frozen in time. Before me, Lilith casts a final look over her shoulder at my Dom's lifeless form sprawled across the tunnel floor. Tio sits beside her in the cart, Balashi slumped at their feet.

"Scene loaded," Bealsio says in my ear. "Whenever you're ready, Ava."

I take a step closer to Lilith, gazing into her unseeing eyes. Doubt creeps into my mind as I remember my last failed attempt to return to my branch. Is my bond with Lilith strong enough to guide me across the space between the worlds? My last failure to bridge back to my Dom was crushing, and I've now seen how many times Emmie too failed. I don't know how many attempts I can make without destroying Emmie's body, so I need to make this one count.

Other-Dom squeezes my shoulder in encouragement. Though I can't see him, knowing he's right behind me calms me.

"I'm ready," I say, studying Lilith's face, focusing all of my awareness on her. Her lack of remorse for what happened to Dom had seemed utterly heartless to me in my last moments with her. But now, looking at the weary determination in her expression, I see only the unfailing courage I always tried to emulate during our long years working together. As angry as I've been with her since she abandoned me in the cedar forest, I've never stopped missing her. My time apart from her has, to my surprise, created space in my heart to wonder what could have happened to Lilith on her own journey that drove her to this moment, and whether we might find some common ground between us once again.

I grip the side of the cart and step up into it, returning to my place inside Lilith and closing my eyes.

Sensing Lilith's awareness across the space between the worlds is far more difficult for me than sensing Dom's ever was. But as I let myself sink deeper and deeper into my memory of her, there's an invisible flicker in the formless void through which I drift. I follow the growing sense of sympathy between us, searching for the part of her that's rooted deep inside of me.

I think I've found her, but, for a disorienting moment, I remain in darkness. Have I lost my way in the crossing? Panic rises in me, threatening to swallow me, until I feel a steadying current of strength—other-Dom's strength, pouring into me from across the void, anchoring his side of the bridge between us, freeing me to take a leap of faith into the unknown.

Clack-a-tat clack-a-tat clack-a-tat.

A deafening clatter greets me as I burst across the far side of the bridge. A dim light appears in the darkness, racing toward me. I'm flying through the tunnels of the Under City in Lilith's body, the noisy cart rattling the soles of her riding boots, oil lamps whizzing by as the cart races down the slope.

Lilith touches her temple, wincing as my awareness flares into hers. *My prodigal child returns,* she thinks. *I thought you'd abandoned me for good, this time.*

Lilith's words are barbed with reproach. Once, I might have recoiled from their sting. But from my perspective inside of her, I'm able to feel their deeper meaning. I'm surprised to discover inside the hard shell of her emotions how much she's missed me, how much she's grieved for me since my accident drove us apart.

I don't know how long other-Dom's strength will give me to remain here with her, so I begin with the words that are most difficult to say, but the most important to me, in case this is my last chance.

I'm sorry I attacked you, Mama, I think. *I was so angry with you for leaving me that I refused to listen when you tried to explain why you had to go. But I'm not angry any more. I know why you couldn't take me with you that night. I don't blame you for what happened to me and Dom. You tried to warn me, and I ignored your warnings. If I'd listened to you, he and I might both have survived.*

Lilith is so stunned by my apology that for a moment she's at a complete loss. Then she presses her fist against her mouth, barely suppressing a sob.

"What's wrong?" says Tio, easing up on the lever to slow the cart.

"It's Ava," she says, her voice strained. "I thought she'd left, but now she's back." Lilith sets her hand over Tio's and pushes the lever forward again. "Don't slow down. Drop me at the underground river crossing."

"Are you sure?" he says, looking at her in alarm. "The currents are treacherous until the freeze comes."

"That river and I were old friends centuries before you were even born," she says. "Get back to the workshop before Noa notices you're missing."

"What about the boy?" says Tio, glancing down at Balashi, whose head lolls from side to side as the cart bumps along.

Lilith fishes a small blue glass bottle and a bundle of undyed wool cloth from inside her riding cloak. "Trade his socks for these," she says, tucking the bundle into Balashi's pocket. She hands the bottle to Tio, who slips it into a pouch on his toolbelt. "Three drops when he takes a meal, whenever you can manage it safely. Try not to miss more than three days. I'll take care of the rest." Lilith points ahead to an unlit intersection, barely visible up ahead. "Slow down, here it is."

Tio pulls back the lever, slowing the cart to a stop. Lilith rises to her feet, but before she climbs out, Tio touches her arm and says, "Will you be able to manage Ava alone, after what she did to you on the Purattu?"

"I don't think I've been able to manage her once in seventeen years," says Lilith. "She's as stubborn as they come."

A faint smile tugs the corner of Tio's mouth as he says, "I wonder where she got that from."

"I'm looking at him," Lilith says dryly. "Go on, now. It'll take you half a moon to hobble back up all those stairs on your own."

"Don't worry about me," he says. "My leg's a lot less trouble than your passenger. And, anyway, I have Balashi to help me. He's stronger than he looks."

Lilith hops out of the cart. She and Tio briefly clasp forearms in parting.

"Stay safe, sister," says Tio.

"You too, brother," says Lilith.

Tio pulls back the lever, and the cart reverses course, heading back up the slope. Lilith turns toward the pitch black opening of the intersection she's chosen. I can't make out anything inside the opening, but Lilith steps confidently into the darkness, closing her eyes as she once taught me to do, reaching out with her other senses. With one hand she sizes up the tunnel opening, tracing her fingers from one wall to the ceiling to the other wall to orient herself. Rough, irregular edges of volcanic stone slide under her fingertips. This must be one of the lava tubes, then, not a manmade tunnel. Lilith took me through many of the tunnels of the Under City in our jobs together, but I don't remember this one.

Overhearing my thoughts, Lilith thinks, *That's because I never took you here. The underground river is no place for a child.*

Where does the underground river lead? I think.

Home, she thinks.

Puzzled, I think, *Where's that?* In all our years together, I never heard Lilith call any place home.

I'll give you an answer for an answer, she thinks. *I felt your awareness depart when we left your boy behind. I thought perhaps you'd followed him into Death. Where did you go?*

I'm not sure you'll believe me, I think.

You wouldn't believe the things I've come to believe, child, she thinks. *And we have a long walk down to the banks of the underground river. Go ahead and show me.*

So I do, unfolding my memory of the moon that's passed since Lilith left me in the cedar forest by the sea. She walks along through the darkness, accepting my memory without question, without interruption, until at last I've shared everything and have returned once more to the present.

So you returned to ask for my help, she thinks.

And to offer you mine, I think.

With a trace of amusement, she thinks, *What help can you offer me, in your present circumstances?*

You want a world where everyone is free to choose how they live, don't you? I think.

You know I do, she thinks.

I've come from a world where that would be possible, if you're willing to help me, I think. *You can leave this world behind and come with me. We can be a family again, like you always said we'd be, once we reached the land of freedom.*

A lump rises in Lilith's throat. She thinks, *What help do you need?*

I think, *I need you to show me the records Serapen keeps in the Musaion that explain the formula for binding and unbinding pharmaka. I'm going to store the knowledge of those arts in a place where anyone who seeks it can find it, and no one can control it.*

Lilith's curiosity turns cautious. *How would you safeguard that knowledge, Ava?* she thinks. *You more than anyone should understand the dangers of pharmaka in the wrong hands.*

Danger doesn't lie in knowledge itself, I think. *Danger arises when knowledge advantages some at the expense of others. The safest place for knowledge is where it can serve everyone equally, where none can control it for their sole benefit.*

Lilith thinks, *The Mohirai guard the knowledge of their mysteries behind walls for good reason. Even a single person might do catastrophic damage to their world, if they chose to wield such knowledge for destructive purposes.*

I think, *But if we set this knowledge free, its power to control people is destroyed forever.*

Lilith thinks, *Setting knowledge free won't change the fact that some will always seek power over others.*

I think, *Maybe no world will ever be entirely free of destructive people who seek power over others. But giving everyone the freedom to travel across branches constrains such power. When everyone has the freedom to seek a better world, no one can be forced to submit to an unwanted power.*

Lilith turns my words over and over in her mind. With growing anxiety, I wait, wondering whether I've persuaded her.

At last, Lilith thinks, *You believe you can set this knowledge free, on Earth?*

I think, *Earth may be the only place it's possible. Maybe that's why I've dreamed of Earth for as long as I can remember. The people on Earth have created a tekhnologia powerful enough to hold the memories of every world in a single place, powerful enough to map the intersections among the worlds. All they lack is the knowledge of pharmaka required to travel from one world to the next.*

Lilith thinks, *And you believe this is what the Voice has called you to do?*

There's a motive behind Lilith's question that I can't quite discern. *Maybe I'll never understand the Voice's purpose fully,* I think. *But everything I've experienced in my life so far tells me this is the right thing to do. I don't know who else can do it, so I think it has to be me.*

Lilith is still considering my words when the echo of her footsteps along the narrow lava tube changes. I've spent enough time navigating dark places to recognize the sensation of emerging from a confined space into a much larger one. Lilith's attention shifts away from me, and I worry I've failed to convince her to help me.

The hard stone beneath Lilith's boots gives way to softer sand. She crouches, sweeping her hand close to the ground until she finds the strap of a leather pack, which she slings over her shoulder before continuing on, headed toward a soft burbling sound somewhere in the darkness up ahead. Warm humidity tinged with a faint scent of sulphur fills the air. We're approaching water.

Is this the underground river? I think.

One of its tributaries, thinks Lilith.

As we approach the water's unseen edge, Lilith reaches out again, sweeping her hand carefully before her until her fingers catch the polished wooden edge of something. She stops here, digs in her pack, and withdraws a small firestarter box containing a candle, flint, and striker.

Lilith lights the candle, revealing that we stand beside a small, flat-bottomed boat dragged up onto the sand beside the bubbling fountainhead of a large spring. With the candle, she lights a small torch mounted on the bow of the boat, which illuminates the large cavern in which we stand. The rippling surface of the spring before us reflects the sparkling mineral formations encrusted on the dripping walls and ceiling.

Lilith pushes the boat into the water, hops aboard, and picks up the paddle stowed inside. She paddles ahead with a slow current, avoiding the rock protrusions the torchlight reveals in the water, making her way toward a low opening in the cavern wall ahead. She ducks to pass through the opening, and we begin a winding course through increasingly treacherous waters, which pick up speed and volume as the lava tube narrows and slopes downward.

I would be terrified here on my own, but Lilith proceeds with calm focus, following the current turn by turn, until the water spreads out again into a slow-moving pool. From somewhere ahead of us, beyond the sphere of torchlight, comes a steady rushing sound.

That's the river, thinks Lilith, paddling toward the sound. She navigates one last stretch of rapids beyond the pool before the rough water smooths. The air cools rapidly when the shallow tributary joins the deeper current of the underground river. The river is wide enough that its edges remain hidden beyond the torchlight, but the smooth stone ceiling above drifts past not far above Lilith's head. As Lilith paddles on, the ceiling drops lower and lower, until ahead I see it plunges straight down into the water, forming an unbroken wall of rock.

Alarmed, I think, *Careful, Mama, you're going to hit the—*

But before she hits the rock wall, Lilith drops her paddle onto the bottom of the boat and lies facedown on top of it, pinning her pack to the floor with her chest. She braces herself against the sides of the boat with both arms and legs, then throws her weight to one side. The boat flips over, extinguishing the torch and plunging us into complete darkness once more.

Lilith takes a few deep breaths from the bubble of air trapped inside the boat before the icy water rushes up around her, and the underground river swallows her whole.

With deft adjustments of the capsized boat, Lilith navigates underwater as the river flows down through bedrock, deep beneath the plain of Velkanos. Lilith's knowledge of initiate pharmaka grants her many advantages that I witnessed firsthand during our years traveling together, but now I experience them myself. She slows her heart rate, holding her breath, as calm under the pressure of these airless icy depths as if she were strolling aboveground on a sunlit summer day. In the darkness, her awareness spreads out along the river's course like the tendrils of creeping vines, searching for something.

When at last she feels it—an eddy in the current, some small reversal in its course—her heart rate speeds up again. With a single well-timed twist of her body, she turns the boat against the main current until its bow catches the eddy.

Lilith refreshes her grip on her pack, holding it tight across her chest with one arm. With her free hand and both legs, she braces herself against the sides of the boat, riding it underwater as the eddy carries her up, up, up. Finally, she pushes away from the boat with a mighty kick. Opening her eyes underwater for the first time, she looks up. Far above us, a small circle of blue light pierces the darkness of the underground river: the fountainhead of a sunlit spring.

Lilith kicks steadily upward toward the light, following its glowing blue trail. As we approach the rippling surface of the spring, I see the branching forms of trees waving in a breeze, silhouetted against a clear blue sky.

Lilith's head bursts through the surface with a splash. She takes several long breaths before she relaxes and leans back, floating in the center of the spring, gazing up at the swaying branches, her heart full of nostalgia.

Hesitant to interrupt her peaceful moment after the strenuous journey here, but acutely aware of my limited time, I think, *Mama?*

Yes, Ava? thinks Lilith.

You didn't say whether you'd help me, I think.

Lilith sighs, turning over in the water and swimming to the shore. *All I ever wanted for you was to discover your own great work for yourself, free of any coercion by the Mohirai,* she thinks. *If you believe this is your true calling, Ava, I will show you Serapen's formula for binding and unbinding pharmaka. Perhaps you'll return some day to show me what you've done with the knowledge, in this new world of yours.*

I'm so elated that she's agreed to help me that it takes me a moment to realize what else she's said. I think, *But … won't you come with me, Mama?*

Lilith climbs out of the water onto the mossy stones. She stands for a long moment looking up at the gnarled branches that hang over the spring. At last, she thinks, *My own great work lies in this world, Ava. I cannot leave it unfinished.*

Intrigued, I think, *What is your great work?*

With a heavy heart, Lilith thinks, *Once, I helped enslave the people of Dulai. In the time I have remaining, I must set them free.*

THE COMPANY OF MEN

Just before dawn the day I'm to depart Velkanos with Kabir, Tio, and Balashi, I stand beside Eridu in his stall making a few final adjustments to his saddle straps. I'm jittery from lack of sleep. My worrying over the choice I have to make kept me up half the night, and my nervous anticipation of the journey ahead woke me long before first bell. I've used the extra time to double-check the camping gear and brush down Eridu, trying to clear my head so I can focus on the decision I can put off no longer. My nerves must be contagious, because the big chestnut gelding stamps and snorts impatiently as I finish his brushing.

"Ready to get out of here too, eh, Eridu?" I say, rubbing the white star on his forehead and giving him a bit of dried apple. Eridu noses my shoulder hard, nickering insistently for more treats. "I have to save some for the road, greedy," I say, waving him off with a laugh.

Moments after the first bell tolls, I hear the bronze gate to the Upper City opening in the distance, its low groan audible even through the thick stone walls of the stable. Good. Sounds like Hanu and Eumelia are right on time. They'd told me at the evening meal last night that they had permission to skip their morning rituals in the house of novices so they could meet me in the Outer City to say goodbye.

I lead Eridu from the stables and mount him in the street. We set off at a trot toward the central stairs. The early spring air is brisk on my cheeks, but the beautiful fur-lined cloak and leather riding gloves Hippolyta gave me last night as a parting gift are deliciously warm.

I'm going to miss Hanu, Eumelia, and many of the Muses who have been my teachers these past few moons, but I'm nonetheless eager to escape the temple city after my first long, cold winter cooped up here inside the walls. Receiving instruction from the Mohirai, Kabir, and Tio would have been rewarding on its own, but dodging endless overtures from prospective Muses has become tiresome. If I could simply focus on learning the arts of arkhitectonia and ignore the task of choosing my Muse, I would.

On my Calling Day, I had no idea how many choices I would need to make for myself, as an Artifex. My boyhood of obedience to priestess commands didn't prepare me well for decision-making. I'm not sure how I'll ever choose my Muse, when I can't even make the far simpler choice required of me today.

Serapen left it to me to decide which of the Artifexi I'll attend this spring and summer. I may continue my attendance on solemn Tio, voyage west with him to the island of Lemnos in the Middle Sea, and spend the warm seasons there among his craftsmen, lending my hands to his great work for Muse Maya. Or I may throw in my lot with jolly Kabir, ride north with him to Phasis on the coast of the Dark Sea, and see for myself the temple to the mysteries of poetika that he's building for Muse Thalia.

Over the past moon, as the time remaining for me to decide has dwindled, I've consulted several of my favorite teachers for guidance. I don't want to disappoint anyone, and I want to know that I'm making the right choice. After listening patiently to my indecisive ruminations for several days as we worked together repairing horse tack outside the stables, Hippolyta had clapped me on the shoulder and said, *Dom, sometimes the only way to know is to do. In every course, the sum of all.* I'm sure she'd meant well, but these mysterious Mohiran aphorisms are no help at all.

And so, on the very morning of my departure as I ride out toward the road, I'm still second-guessing myself. Each time I think I've settled on one choice, some new inclination leads me back to indecision. My only comfort lies in knowing that whichever way I go, my time away from Velkanos will be a welcome reprieve from the distraction of all these women vying for my attention, at least until harvest, when I must return to the temple city to begin my second winter of novice instruction among the Mohirai.

I slow Eridu to a walk at the plaza where my street intersects the central staircase. Hanu and Eumelia stand waiting for me beside the fountain in the middle of the plaza. Behind them, the first rays of sunrise illuminate white tendrils of steam drifting from the fountain pool. I dismount and head toward them, leading Eridu by the bridle.

"Good morning," I say, hugging first Eumelia, then Hanu. "Thanks for meeting me so early."

Hanu hugs me back tightly, then presses a kiss to Eridu's nose. Through our bond, I sense her sorrow at the prospect of my departure, but she puts on a bright smile to say, "What a beautiful day to start your journey."

"Did you manage to get any sleep last night?" says Eumelia, with a knowing half-smile.

"I was up a little early, I suppose," I say with a shrug. Catching the look Eumelia and Hanu exchange, I add, "Why do you ask?"

With mock innocence, Eumelia says, "Oh, there was some chatter after you left the meal hall. Sounded like a few sisters were invited down to the stables last night."

"Invited by whom?" I say.

Eumelia's quirking smile turns into a puzzled frown. "We assumed by you," she says.

Hanu giggles, gesturing discreetly over my shoulder. I look back to see Kabir and Balashi strolling down the ninth street toward us with a trio of older novices, two initiates, and Muse Thalia.

"Ah, no," I say dryly. "That wasn't me."

Kabir and Balashi bid farewell to the novices and the initiates at the far edge of the plaza, and the small group of women departs up the stairs toward the Upper City gate.

Thalia says something to Balashi, who nods in reply and remains standing at the edge of the plaza while Kabir and Thalia walk arm in arm toward the three of us at the fountain.

"Good morning, Dom!" Kabir calls out, his voice booming with good cheer.

Thalia smiles broadly at Hanu and Eumelia, then gives me a conspiratorial wink. "Glad to see you three made good use of your last night together," she says. "The men have a long and lonely journey ahead."

I should be immune to Thalia's teasing by now, but embarrassed heat flushes my cheeks nonetheless. Eumelia scoffs and rolls her eyes. Hanu bites her lip to suppress a laugh.

Kabir is usually first to pile on with Thalia's joking, but this morning he looks at me instead with a more serious expression. He says, "Speaking of long and lonely journeys, little brother—have you come to a decision about which journey you'll be taking?"

All eyes turn to me, and my cheeks grow hotter still. Masking my discomfort with my best imitation of Ava's confidence, I say, "I suppose you'll find out at the crossroads, won't you?"

Kabir's laugh rings out across the plaza. "Indeed?" he says. "I've never met a man who keeps such close counsel."

Thalia studies me with perceptive eyes. I brace myself for another round of her well-honed teasing. But she leans on Kabir's arm and says, "Let him be, Kabir. Have you forgotten the trials of your own novice years?" To me, she adds kindly, "The Voice speaks to us in stillness, little brother. Listen and you shall hear."

To my relief, Thalia steers the subject away from me, saying, "Sister Hanu. I'm glad to find you here. Balashi told me last night that he'd like your help at his unbinding outside the wall this morning."

"Oh," says Hanu, her amused expression fading. "I didn't—I mean, I couldn't —"

"Of course you can, little sister," says Thalia, her tone encouraging. "We all know how well you managed the work with Dom. Won't you show Balashi the same kindness? A trusted touch is always best, when it comes to unbinding."

I blink, looking from Thalia to Hanu in confusion. Hanu looks back at me with a stricken expression. Why does she look so guilty?

Thalia waves her hand, saying, "Come, Hanu. I have no patience for false modesty. Will you join the men at the Outer City gate when they're ready to depart?"

Wordlessly, Hanu nods. Eumelia wraps a comforting arm around Hanu's shoulders. Thalia studies the pair of them and says thoughtfully, "You were there with Balashi his last afternoon outside the walls, too, weren't you, Eumelia?"

Cautiously, Eumelia says, "Yes, Muse Thalia."

Thalia says, "You should go with your sister, then. The loss of so many moons will be jarring for Balashi. The more continuity, the better for him."

Eumelia bows her head obediently.

"Good," says Thalia, sliding one of her perfectly-manicured fingers down a sky-blue line of embroidery worked into the yellow sash at her waist. "I'll let the High Priestess know to expect you both." Turning to Kabir, Thalia gives him a lingering kiss on the lips, pats his cheek, and says, "Send word to me from Phasis, dear brother. I'll be missing you."

Wryly, Kabir says, "Oh, sweet Muse, I'd wager you'll think of me not once until my return."

Thalia laughs, then turns to me and says, "Whichever way you go, little brother, a season among the men will do you good. I expect you'll be ready to fully embrace the benefits of temple city life, after a little privation outside the walls. Safe journey!" Thalia turns and follows the other women climbing the stairs back to the Upper City.

Kabir claps me on the shoulder and says, "I'll leave you to your goodbyes, Dom. Balashi and I will help the old man get settled in his saddle and return to collect you."

Kabir departs. When he's out of earshot, I turn to Hanu and say, "What was that all about? What 'work' did you manage with me?"

Hanu wrings her hands miserably. Eumelia touches my arm and says, "You have to understand, Dom. It's—"

I raise my hand, cutting off Eumelia. "I want to hear it from Hanu," I say.

Hanu lowers her eyes. In a quavering voice, she says, "Unbinding is an imprecise art, Dom. But no matter how it's done, it requires the loss of memory."

"I know that," I say impatiently. "So what?"

Hanu says, "So … When there's an injury to the body, the body holds on to the memory of the injury. Unbinding the memory of what caused the injury frees the body to focus on its healing.

"When you fell in the tunnels, you injured your head. Unbinding the memory of your fall should have been enough to revive you from that injury, to call you back from Death. But I wasn't able to call your awareness back to your body with that unbinding alone.

"That's because there are other kinds of injuries that can lead us into Death. Unbinding can help those injuries too—to free the mind, or the spirit, or the heart to focus on its healing."

I shake my head, not understanding.

Hanu's eyes meet mine at last. Choosing her words carefully, she says, "Ava's death was hard for all of us, Dom. But for you, it was different. Your binding with Ava wove you two so tightly together that when she died, you weren't able to let her go, and she wasn't able to let go of you. It was an impossible situation for both of you. Ava never wanted you to suffer like that."

Apprehensively, I say, "So what did you do, Hanu?"

Slowly, Hanu says, "I know Ava promised you two would find some way out of Dulai together, Dom. But Ava asked me to promise her something else. I promised to help you forget her, if she couldn't keep her promise to you."

"Why would she ask you to do that?" I say, my voice rising. "When could she have asked you to do that?"

Hanu glances at Eumelia, who says, "Ava's awareness came back to me the day you fell in the tunnels. She told me you needed a healer. She told me where we'd find you, and she said Hanu must remember her promise."

Hanu says, "So when Serapen asked me to help revive you, and you weren't coming back, I knew I had to keep my promise to Ava. I tried to unbind as little of your memory as I could, Dom, I swear it. But in the end I had to unbind your entire memory of Ava's death outside the walls. There was something in that memory that was preventing you from returning from Death."

I shake my head in disbelief, hating the implications of what Hanu has done. I say, "But why didn't you tell me this before?"

"I wanted to tell you," says Hanu. "But you were doing so much better, these last few moons. I thought it might be kinder not to say anything at all." In a small voice, she adds, "I'm so sorry, Dom. Can you forgive me?"

I stare at her in silence for a long time, unable to answer, struggling to understand. Why would Ava ask Hanu to do such a thing to me? Why would Hanu agree? Why would Eumelia keep all of this a secret from me?

Eumelia touches my arm. "Ava loved you, Dom," she says. "I think she knew how much suffering the memory of her death would cause you, and how much easier it would be if Hanu helped you leave that pain behind. And I think she was right. You've seemed much more content with your path as Artifex, since Ava passed."

"How would you know?" I say, so angry that I'm half shouting at Eumelia. "You don't know what it's like to be alone, without her. You don't know what I've been feeling."

Eumelia's lips tremble, but she meets my furious glare without flinching. "I loved her too, Dom," she says simply.

I rake my fingers through my hair, wanting to scream with frustration. It's been moons since thoughts of Ava have driven me this low. Now the raw grief returns like a tidal wave, worse for the knowledge that the two people I thought were grieving with me were actually manipulating me the entire time. I trusted them, and they betrayed me.

Bitterly, I say, "You Mohirai are all alike."

I try to ignore Eumelia's evident disapproval of my outburst and the tears rolling down Hanu's cheeks as we wait for the others to return. I can't remember another time I've been so eager to depart the women for the company of men.

It's a relief when at last the sound of clopping hooves disrupts the awkward silence. I turn to see the High Priestess Serapen riding toward us on her grey mare Amisos. Behind her follows Tio Artifex on Ifestios, his black stallion with the white star. Kabir on his white stallion Vahana and Balashi on the bay roan Brontion bring up the rear.

The sight of the three men following the High Priestess deepens my fury with Hanu, Eumelia, and all the other Mohirai. There's Tio, broken and silenced in his service to the Voice; Kabir, enjoying the privileges of his station even as his own brothers suffer; Balashi, powerless against the unbinding that's about to unfold. And yet I'm the worst of the lot, seeing all of this yet doing nothing to stop it.

"Give your sisters a lift, little brothers," says the High Priestess, wielding the tone of command so lightly that I'm obeying before I can even consider resisting. "We've no time to lose if you're to reach the Urashtu Pass before sunset."

Hanu goes to join Balashi, who pulls her up behind him on Brontion. I mount Eridu and extend my hand down to Eumelia. Eumelia looks like she'd rather give me a smack than join me for a ride, but she's as helpless as I am against Serapen's tone of command. She takes my hand and climbs up behind me.

I ruminate in silence as we ride down the stairs toward the main city gate, until at last I can contain myself no longer. In an undertone, I say to Eumelia, "Maybe I could accept that my own memories had to be unbound, to save my life. Maybe. But what purpose does Balashi's unbinding serve? You know Balashi, Mel. What harm could he do to anyone with his memory of Velkanos? What has he done to deserve such treatment?"

Eumelia sighs and says, "It's not about what Balashi deserves or what Balashi might do, Dom. It's about what others could do with any knowledge he gained while he was here. When men possessed the mysteries in the time before the destruction, many learned to use them in terrible ways. A few men nearly managed to destroy the lives of all humankind. One boy's memory of a few moons inside the temple city is a small price to ensure no one ever experiences such things again. Sometimes the good of all comes at a cost to some."

Darkly, I say, "Ava would never have just stood by while we all did this to Balashi."

"And what would she have done, Dom?" says Eumelia, exasperated. "What good did any of Ava's resistance ever do? Every time she tried to go her own way, she ended up hurting herself, or you, or someone else. I miss her, too, Dom, but you're fooling yourself if you think Ava was some paragon of virtue. Lilith planted a lot of nonsense in Ava's head, and Ava died for it."

The hard truth of Eumelia's words silences me. I sink back once more into my grief, unsure whether I'm angrier with Eumelia for defending the Mohirai or with myself for having no ready argument against hers.

When at last we reach the outermost wall of Velkanos, Serapen calls up to the grey-haired gatekeeper Myrina, who emerges from her quarters atop the wall to open the gate for us. The huge bronze-clad cedar doors swing inward, revealing the flat expanse of grassland beyond the city, a pale brown canvas dotted with the first hints of spring green, bisected by a long straight road paved with volcanic tufa. Serapen leads our group through the gate onto the road outside the walls.

I cast a parting look back through the open gate at the elegant tiers of the shining temple city that scales the lower slopes of Velkanos. I can't help wondering what it feels like for Balashi, knowing that he will never look upon the beautiful city again, even in his memory. As a boy, I dreamed of all the wonders that lay hidden within temple city walls, and as a novice Artifex I've fallen in love with the beauty of Velkanos. But I'm beginning to understand the cost of preserving such beauty, and the darkness it conceals.

Muse Clio's words of instruction return to me as the heavy gate swings closed behind us, hiding the sight of the city once more. *You may discover the story of an entire people, long after the people themselves are gone, if you know how to read the buildings they've left behind,* she'd said. *What we build contains the memories of our lives and connects us to the land from which we come. That's why it's an important responsibility, to be the builder of any structure, however humble or magnificent it may be.*

Over the last few moons living among the Mohirai, I've imagined becoming a temple builder myself, following in the footsteps of all the great builders who came before me. But as much as I admire the beauty of the temple city, I know I'd build something different. Mohiran temple walls don't simply contain the memories of the people of Dulai. Whatever their purpose might once have been, these walls have become a tool for withholding memory, dividing the people from one another.

The High Priestess rides out a short distance down the road, until she reaches a point distinguished only by a pile of charcoal beside the road, the remnants of what must have been a massive bonfire. Here Serapen dismounts, letting Amisos loose to graze the first new shoots of grass alongside the road. At a wordless gesture from her, the rest of us dismount. Balashi and I assist Tio down from his saddle.

We gather around the High Priestess, who turns to face us and says, "Come, Balashi. Come, Hanu."

Balashi and Hanu approach the High Priestess. The memory of Ava protesting Serapen's unbinding of the little kuku bird on the banks of the Purattu flashes through my mind, and pity for my trio brother surges through me. I take an unconscious step toward Balashi, but Eumelia catches my arm and fixes me in place with a warning glare.

"Join hands," says Serapen. Balashi and Hanu face each other and join hands. The sad expression on Hanu's face and the fearful expression on Balashi's make them look like some horrible mockery of dancers at the spring festival, waiting for the first notes of the lyre to begin.

Serapen steps toward the pair, withdrawing a silver flask from within her sky-blue robes. She holds the flask to Balashi's lips. "Drink," she says, in the tone of command, and he drinks, swallowing again and again until Serapen withdraws the flask.

The rest of us stand in silence, watching Balashi. He blinks slowly several times, until at last his eyelids close. When Balashi sways a little on his feet, Hanu grips his hands to steady him.

"You remember the way, sister," Serapen says to Hanu. "Guide him back to your last moment here together."

Hanu closes her eyes, and her sad expression tightens into intense concentration.

"Have you found it?" says Serapen.

Hanu nods. "Yes, Muse Serapen," she says.

"Very good," says Serapen. The High Priestess steps forward and rests her hands lightly on top of Hanu's. The three stand together this way for a long moment, until Serapen nods and withdraws her hands.

"It is done," she says.

Hanu and Balashi open their eyes. Balashi stares at Hanu in confusion.

"How are you, Bala?" says Hanu, smiling at him uncertainly.

Perplexed, Balashi pulls his hands back from Hanu. He looks down the road toward the city wall for a long moment before his eyes fall on me, then Eumelia, then Kabir and Tio. "What happened?" he says nervously.

"You have served the Voice well, Balashi," Serapen says gently. "Though your service has passed from your memory, we remember your time among us with gratitude."

Serapen turns to the rest of us and raises her hand in the sign of blessing. "Safe journey, brothers."

Tio inclines his head in silent deference to the High Priestess before he turns away from her and hobbles back toward Ifestios.

Kabir says, "Farewell, sisters."

Serapen gestures for Hanu and Eumelia to return with her to the city, but both of them hesitate, looking at me. Perhaps they're hoping I'll say some last word of farewell or forgiveness. But I'm so disgusted with everything that's just happened—and especially with my own part in it—that I can't even look at them. Like Tio, I turn from the women in silence and let them depart without saying goodbye.

Kabir claps Balashi on the shoulder. "Cheer up, Balashi," he says. "You'll be back with your brothers in Upper Ford before you know it, and none the worse for wear. Go and help Tio back up into his saddle." To me, Kabir adds, "Give Balashi a hand, Dom, will you?"

So I follow Balashi to help Tio mount Ifestios. I've seen Balashi and Kabir do this enough times before to imitate their technique. Balashi and I join hands to form a step for Tio's good leg, and Tio plants one hand on each of our shoulders to keep his balance as the two of us lift him up and help him swing his bad leg over his saddle.

Once Tio is safely settled, I reach out and grasp Balashi's hand once more. I look him in the eyes and say, "I'm sorry, brother. I wish—"

Balashi's cold look cuts me off. He pulls away from me and returns to Brontion. I gaze after him, feeling awful.

A strong hand settles on my shoulder, and I look up to see Tio studying me with a piercing expression. "Do you need something, brother?" I say.

He holds out his hand to me. Puzzled, I take it.

Patience, brother, thinks Tio, gesturing discreetly toward Balashi. *His time will come.*

I blink. I've noticed Tio communicate with Kabir this way on rare occasions, but in all our moons together Tio has never shared a thought with me.

I incline my head to acknowledge Tio's instruction, then go to mount Eridu. Tio and Kabir set off at a trot, and I urge Eridu on to follow them, riding alongside Balashi. Though his expression is unreadable, Balashi looks back over his shoulder from time to time at the triangular silhouette of Velkanos as the lone mountain retreats on the eastern horizon. I look ahead toward the crossroads, still uncertain which way I'll go.

MOTHER LAND

In the shade of the cedar grove surrounding the spring, Lilith stands naked, wringing out her soaked clothes over the mossy stones at the edge of the pool. After squeezing the last drop from her clothes, she stuffs them into her wet leather pack. Picking up her riding boots in one hand, she walks barefoot along the narrow path that leads away from the spring. A short distance from the grove, the forest canopy opens suddenly to reveal that we're walking along the ridge of a low hill, with a panoramic view of the mountainous landscape to the north.

Before us rises an exposed outcropping of bare rock that leads to the high point of the hill. Lilith heads to the outcropping and starts to climb its near side, her fingers and toes finding handholds and footholds so easily that she must have come this way countless times before. She looks up toward the top of the outcropping, and from somewhere deep in her memory, I glimpse a lanky, sun-browned girl of perhaps thirteen summers with long black braids wrapped around her head. The girl climbs ahead of us up this very outcropping.

With her bare toes gripping a narrow rock ledge, the girl stretches her arm to touch the top of the outcropping before she looks back down at us over her shoulder, grinning as she calls out, "First to the top!"

From somewhere below us, the memory of a younger girl's voice calls up in an annoyed tone, "No fair, Sevan! I had to stay back to help Maya."

Who was that? I think, as Lilith's memory of the climbing girl vanishes.

But Lilith doesn't answer, only hoists herself up to the flat top of the outcropping. While she spreads out her wet clothes to dry on the rocks, I take in the view through her eyes: the triangular peak of Velkanos dominating the foreground to the west, and beyond it the jagged silhouette of the Urashtu range wrapping around us to the south.

I've been here before, I think, with a sudden flash of recognition.

How? thinks Lilith, surprised. *I never brought you here.*

Something happened here to the Dom who's helping me on Earth, I think, sifting through every glimpse I've had of this hilltop as I've traveled through the many worlds. *He took me here when he was teaching me about the alternet. And just before I died outside the walls of Velkanos, something pulled me across a bridge to this place. I saw myself in Mohiran robes, leading Dom into that spring. Why do I keep coming back here?*

Lilith sits down on the warm rocks beside her drying clothes, stretching her long legs before her, letting the sun drive out the chill of the underground river from her bones. She gazes down at the little valley below the hill and thinks, *No matter how many times you leave home, it keeps a hold on your heart.*

But this was never my home, I think.

Pointing down to a spot in the valley, Lilith thinks, *Do you see those stone foundations?* There, discernible at this height from the faint variation in the scrubby plant cover of the grassland, are the rectangular outlines of some long-vanished structures arranged around a central square. Perhaps a farming village once stood there.

Yes, I think. *I see them.*

Lilith thinks, *Maya was born here, in the village of Eden, in a house that once stood right there. When the time came, Maya wanted her child to be born in Eden, too. So Serapen and I accompanied her here to deliver you.*

Another one of Lilith's memories unfurls before me, transporting me into the landscape spread out below us. It's a sunny spring day, and three women drive an oxcart through the grassland toward the same little hill where Lilith now sits. The trio sings together, alternating between tuneful harmonies and boisterous shouting, dissolving occasionally into laughter. The white-haired woman driving the oxcart is Serapen. In the back of the cart, seated on two bales of hay, Lilith sits beside Maya, who is heavily pregnant. I don't think I've ever seen Lilith so happy.

Serapen pulls the ox to a stop beside the cluster of stone foundations. She and Lilith together help Maya step down from the cart. Arm in arm, the three women walk through the little square in the midst of the old foundations. Their expressions, which had been carefree as they sang together in the cart, turn solemn as they gaze down at the ruins.

In a tone of forced cheerfulness, Serapen says, "Well, where would you like to set up camp, Maya?"

Maya lets go of the other two women's arms and walks ahead of them, gazing down at the stones, searching for something. She reaches the edge of one foundation and kneels beside it on the ground, pressing her hand to a wide stone that might once have been a threshold. Softly, she says, "Spirits, I know it's been a long time, but …" She looks up at Lilith and Serapen with a sad smile. "In my memory, it's all still here, you know?"

Serapen and Lilith join Maya, kneeling in the grass before the foundation. The three of them sit shoulder to shoulder in silence. After a while, Serapen squeezes Maya's hand, and she and Lilith help Maya rise to her feet. Maya continues pacing through the ruins, until at last she shakes her head and says, "Not here. It doesn't feel right."

Maya looks beyond the village ruins, toward the little hill where Lilith and I now sit. Thoughtfully, she says, "The hilltop grove is the only place that looks unchanged."

A shadow passes over Serapen's expression before she replies, "I feared it would never grow back, after the fires. But you're right. It looks much the same as it did when we were girls."

A mischievous smile spreads over Maya's face, and she glances from Serapen to Lilith. "First to the top?" she says.

Lilith laughs. Serapen's expression turns lighthearted, and she says, "You know I'd still win, even if you weren't both pregnant."

You were pregnant? I think, surprised. If the Lilith in this memory is pregnant, it's impossible for me to tell.

I'd only just found out, thinks Lilith.

Maya's mischievous smile turns thoughtful. "Seriously, though," she says, looking from Serapen to Lilith. "Would it be too much to ask you two to carry the camping gear up to the spring? I'd help, but ..." She gestures to her huge belly apologetically.

Serapen looks doubtfully from Maya to the hilltop. She says, "Are you sure you're up for such a climb?"

"I'm sure that's the place, so I guess I'll have to make it," says Maya. Seeing the concerned look Lilith and Serapen exchange, Maya adds, "I'll take it slow. Don't worry. I'm not as delicate as all that."

Over the course of the afternoon, the three women set up a small camp beside the spring in the shade of the grove. As the shadows lengthen, they gather around their cooking fire. Serapen and Lilith prepare the evening meal as Maya sits in a natural seat formed by the moss-covered roots of an ancient cedar. They pass bowls of steaming stew around the fire, and as the sun sets they repeat together the words of the meal blessing.

We give our thanks for gifts of sun
Of water, soil, and seed
For gifts of many seasons
Gathered here to meet our need
To build our strength so that our hands
May in their time return
The gifts received from mother land
Improved with gifts our own

As they eat, the trio recall the mischief, triumphs, and heartbreaks of childhoods long past, wandering through shared memories that live in these woods, circling slowly back to the present.

When the meal is eaten, bowls are washed, and darkness falls, Serapen prepares a single cup of fragrant tea from the pharmaka ingredients she carries in her satchel. She offers the cup to Maya, who sips it slowly.

Serapen says, "Do you have a name in mind, Maya?"

With an inward smile, Maya presses one hand to her belly. She says, "I think she's a girl. I was hoping ..." She glances at Serapen, hesitating. "I was hoping I might name her after our mother."

Lilith reaches out and rests one of her broad hands on Maya's belly. Softly, she says, "Ava. What a beautiful thought, Maya."

Maya turns to Serapen, whose eyes gleam in the firelight. Uncertainly, Maya says, "What do you think, sister? You're the only one of us who really knew her. I wouldn't want it to cause you pain, hearing our mother's name in the halls of the temple city."

Serapen leans back from the fire, obscuring her face in shadow. She sits in silence for a long time before she says, "Mama told me once that as a girl she'd hoped to walk the path of mysteries, like our great-aunt Seda. I think it would have given her great pleasure to know her namesake walks among the initiates of this new age. If you wish to call the child by our mother's name in the years you'll have together, you may do so with my blessing. But, Maya …" Serapen leans forward, fixing her intense gaze on Maya.

"What is it?" says Maya.

Serapen says, "You know the Voice will call this child, in the end. We have no claim to her, even if she bears a family name. The two of you must still be unbound. She must go to the Children's Temple like all the other children."

"Sevan," Lilith says sharply. "Why trouble her with such thoughts now?"

"It's all right, Lil," says Maya, touching Lilith's arm. To Serapen, Maya says, "I have listened and I have heard, sister. I have no wish to deprive this child of her calling. The Voice's will be done."

Maya's voice lingers in the air as the memory of her fades, leaving Lilith sitting alone on the sunny promontory looking out at Velkanos.

Astonished, I think, *You and Maya and Serapen … The three of you were sisters? Not just sisters in the Voice, but daughters of the same mother?*

With a small smile of amusement, Lilith thinks, *Hard to believe, looking at us, isn't it?* She withdraws her waterskin from her pack and takes a long swallow to empty it. She rises from her sunny spot on the promontory to gather up her dry clothes, dressing quickly as she thinks, *Serapen and Maya took after our father, as did our brother—dark, fine-boned, much like the other farmers of Eden. Unfortunately, I took after our mother's father from the north—fair and blue-eyed. When I was small, the other children in the village used to torment me and call me demon, because I looked so different. My father and Serapen tried to shield me from it, after our mother died, but it wasn't until I was big enough to thrash them myself that I finally put a stop to it.* She chuckles. *Amos was an excellent teacher, in that way. He became a great warrior, and a greater chief, in time.*

Amos? I think, with another jolt of surprise. *Amos was your brother?*

Yes, she thinks. The face of an older man with a grizzled beard and a scarred face flashes in her memory. His clear brown eyes look much like Serapen's, but nothing like the Amos I know on Earth. Lilith thinks, *Amos passed in the time of destruction. He had been dead for centuries by the time you were born.*

Lilith climbs back down the promontory and returns to the spring, where she refills her waterskin before she descends the hill by a winding footpath. She studies the underbrush on either side of the path as she walks, until she spots a young cedar seedling growing in a patch of sun near the base of the hill. She kneels beside it and withdraws her knife from the sheath on her belt, gently cutting a circle in the soil around the seedling. She slides her fingers down into the soil, carefully preserving the seedling's delicate ball of roots as she extracts it from the ground.

Lilith carries the seedling with her as she walks out through the ruins of the little village, heading west across the square, toward Velkanos. A short distance away from the village, she steps out onto what must once have been a road.

Though the windblown sand and scrubby grass of the plains have covered any sign of paving stones or wheel ruts, the ancient route is still discernible because it's bordered by two parallel lines of massive cedars. The spreading cedar branches form a nearly unbroken canopy that shades the road for some distance and frames the view of Velkanos on the western horizon.

Lilith walks down the center of this long colonnade, slowing occasionally to touch the trunks of a few grandmother trees. She stops at the end of the colonnade to face the single young cedar that stands there, its branches not yet large enough to span the road or touch its neighbor's. Still clutching the seedling in one hand, Lilith presses her free hand to the trunk of the young cedar, and a memory flashes through her mind.

In Lilith's memory, she stands at this very spot, holding a sleeping infant in her arms. Before Lilith, Serapen kneels on the ground, tamping down loose soil around a cedar seedling she's just planted.

From the satchel on the ground beside her, Serapen withdraws a waterskin and a drawstring bag. She upends the bag's contents at the base of the tree, and a pale heap of ashes and crumbled bone tumbles out. Serapen waters the ashes and bone into the soil, then smooths the pile around the tree in a circle with both hands. She rises to her feet and turns to face Lilith. With her muddy fingers, Serapen paints a dark line down Lilith's forehead, another on the infant's forehead, and one last upon her own.

Serapen stands beside Lilith, wrapping her arm around her sister's waist and resting her hand on the swaddled infant. She looks down at the little cedar seedling as she says solemnly, "No one who walks the path beside us is ever truly lost. Maya walked with us for a time, and she remains with us, transformed. We are all transformed by the journey, in the end."

A powerful wind from across the grassy plain rushes through the cedar colonnade, whipping the evergreen boughs into a frenzy. As the rustling sound swells around her, Lilith looks up into the swaying branches, tears streaming down her cheeks. Her broad shoulders shake with sobs, and the infant stirs in her arms and starts to wail. Gently, Serapen takes the baby from Lilith, who collapses to her knees before the little seedling, pressing her forehead to the ground.

"You could have saved her, Sevan!" cries Lilith. "Why would you sacrifice our own sister? Haven't we lost enough?"

"Oh, Lil," says Serapen, kneeling on the ground beside Lilith, stroking her sister's back with one hand as she attempts to soothe the crying baby tucked in her other arm. "I gave Maya everything I could."

Lilith's shoulders tense. She throws off her sister's hand and seizes the leather satchel resting on the ground beside Serapen.

Serapen rises carefully, rocking the baby in her arms as she watches Lilith rummaging through her satchel. At last, Lilith finds what she's looking for. She withdraws two small bottles—one blue, one brown—and holds them up, glaring in accusation at Serapen.

Evenly, Serapen says, "Would you steal from me, sister?"

Lilith rises to her feet and throws Serapen's satchel to the ground. She says, "No more than you've stolen from the people of Dulai. The ingredients of pharmaka are the gifts of mother land to all of us. Who are you to withhold them from anyone? Especially from our own sister, in her moment of need?"

Serapen says, "You know why sisters called to motherhood must give up initiate pharmaka, Lilith. To bring forth new life, we must sacrifice the old. I withheld initiate pharmaka from our sister because that is the price the Voice requires of mothers in this new age."

Through clenched teeth, Lilith growls, "You mean the price that you require."

Serapen says, "The Voice requires only that which preserves the natural order, Lilith."

"Don't you dare speak to me of your damned Voice," says Lilith. "I believed in the Voice, once. Maya and I bowed our heads and followed you all this time because we believed you were serving its purpose. We trusted you. But now I see how you've twisted the wisdom of our foremothers to serve your own great work."

Serapen's expression darkens. She says, "I have been called to witness things I hope no one shall ever see again. But I am only a servant, Lilith. It is not for me to decide who lives and who dies. I have done nothing but the work the Voice commands me to do."

Lilith scoffs. "Indeed? Is that the same work you hide from the other sisters, High Priestess?"

Serapen's brow furrows. "What are you talking about, Lilith?"

"I found the records you and Clio keep hidden in the Musaion, sister," says Lilith. "I know the curse of childlessness that swept through Dulai was no punishment from the Voice. It was a plague of your own making, and you had the gall to accept the gratitude of all Dulai when at last you deigned to give them the cure."

Serapen raises her chin. She says, "That so-called plague took not a single life, and the Voice's cure has created a world where every child lives in peace and comfort we ourselves never knew as children, Lilith."

"And for this we all owe you our thanks, is that it?" says Lilith. "We're to bow our heads to the High Priestess and yield to your great wisdom? We're to thank you for the gift of children, the gift of unbinding, the gift of hearing the Voice's call? And all the while these gifts return to you tenfold, consolidating your power over us all. You're no better than the kings of old. But every kingdom falls, in time."

Coolly, Serapen says, "Is that a threat?"

"Oh no, dear sister," says Lilith. "That's the natural order."

Lilith turns her back on Serapen and walks away, headed toward the open grassland beyond the colonnade of cedars.

"Stop, Lilith," Serapen calls out in the tone of command.

Lilith slows, then turns to face Serapen once more.

"No, Serapen," says Lilith. "You are the one who must be stopped." Without breaking eye contact, Lilith raises the pair of pharmaka bottles in her hand.

Bright sunlight winks on the blue and brown glass just before she casts the bottles to the ground. They shatter at her feet, and the pharmaka dribbles out onto the sandy soil.

In a tone of warning, Serapen says, "Don't do this, little sister. Grief is clouding your judgment. Return to me, and all will be forgiven."

"Am I the one who needs forgiveness?" says Lilith. Without another word, she turns and walks away, leaving Serapen standing alone by the seedling with the wailing infant in her arms.

Lilith's memory of Serapen fades, and she stands alone once more at the end of the shady colonnade, one hand pressed to the smooth trunk of the young cedar Serapen planted in Maya's ashes seventeen years ago, her other hand gripping the cool root ball of the new seedling.

I have so many questions about what I've just witnessed, but the distant pull of Emmie's body is growing stronger. Urgently, I think, *I can't stay much longer, Mama. You said you would show me the formula for pharmaka that Serapen keeps in the Musaion.*

And now you've seen it, thinks Lilith. She points out across the landscape that surrounds us, tracing the route she took from Velkanos to Eden: down the Under City tunnels, into the lava tubes that drain the mountain slopes, through the underground river that winds beneath the grassy plain, up to the fountainhead that pools at the heart of the hilltop grove. She thinks, *The Musaion holds the record of the Voice's words to Serapen on the day of her initiation. The Voice revealed to Serapen that Velkanos imparts its power to all life that springs from its waters.*

I gaze out through Lilith's eyes at the snow-capped peak of the great mountain. *What power does Velkanos have?* I think.

Lilith thinks, *Velkanos holds the power of creation and destruction. The fruit of any tree watered with the gift of Velkanos may be used to prepare unbinding pharmaka, and the mushrooms that rise from the roots of such trees may be used to prepare binding pharmaka. The binding and unbinding pharmaka, when used in balance, grant initiates deep insight and long life. This is why the Mohirai keep their gardens hidden within city walls, and why they guard their temples from uninitiated men: to keep the gift of Velkanos from any hands the High Priestess deems unworthy.*

My mind races with the implications of this, recalling so many memories recorded from so many lives lived in service to the Voice.

Thank you for showing me, Mama, I think, bursting with eagerness to show other-Dom that the key to our great work lies here, in Eden.

I wish I'd told you all of this sooner, Ava, thinks Lilith, her heart full of regret. *But I feared you might seek out Serapen on your own if you knew the truth about Maya. I feared Serapen might use you, as she once used me, if she ever regained a hold on you. I see now that I made a terrible mistake. You would have been better armed with the truth of your birth. You're a daughter of Eden, and the gift of Velkanos is your birthright. Do better with this knowledge of our mother land than*

Serapen and I have done.

I will, I think. *I promise.*

Lilith crosses the ancient road to a grassy spot in the sun, just beyond the shade of the nearest cedar. She kneels to dig a hole, planting her seedling just as Serapen had done. From her damp pack, Lilith withdraws a drawstring bag. The ashes and bone that tumble from the bag onto the tree's roots are wet already from their passage through the underground river, but Lilith pours out the contents of her waterskin over them and tamps them down into the soil.

Lilith rises to her feet, touches her forehead with one muddy finger, and gazes down at the little seedling that's joined the line of great cedars. Quietly, she says, "No one who walks the path beside us is ever truly lost. You walked with me for a time, Ava, and you remain with me, transformed. We are all transformed by the journey, in the end."

Goodbye, Ava, thinks Lilith. *I love you.*

I love you, too, Mama, I think, as the road to Eden fades from my awareness, and I return to Earth.

THE CROSSROADS

The sun has just reached its zenith when Tio gestures silently for our little caravan to stop for the midday meal at the crossroads west of Velkanos. Balashi and I dismount and help Tio down from Ifestios. We all dig out provisions from our saddlebags and loose the horses to graze and drink from the roadside culvert.

Since Balashi's unbinding this morning, we've been traveling in mostly unbroken silence, apart from Kabir's occasional attempts to spark conversation with me and Balashi. Now, Tio, Balashi, and I pick out solitary spots to sit on the tumbledown stone wall that runs alongside the road. As I eat a small meal of dried beef, bread, and cheese, my gaze drifts back and forth between the road that leads north to Phasis and the road that leads west through the Urashtu Pass. I wish there was some sign to show me which way I should choose. The untraveled road northward is shrouded in mystery. But the sight of the snowy peaks to the west recalls the morning I woke up there in the Cave of Dreams to the sight of Lilith's owl swooping toward Ava, its sharp talons outstretched. A prickling ache spreads through the scars on my back and shoulders as I remember diving over Ava and Hanu, determined to protect them from—

Kabir strides in my direction, interrupting my reverie. Kabir glances at Tio, who inclines his head in a gesture of assent. To me and Balashi, Kabir says, "Listen to me, little brothers."

Balashi and I reluctantly meet his gaze. Kabir says, "Our departure from Velkanos this morning was not the farewell Tio or I would have wished for either of you. But you must understand that the actions of the High Priestess were necessary. The sacrifices we make to protect the temple city are a small price to pay for the peace we now enjoy."

Balashi nods obediently, lowering his eyes to the food in his lap. I might once have done the same, but something within me refuses to remain silent after all I've witnessed today. I say, "How do you know that, brother?"

Kabir blinks in surprise at my defiant tone. Balashi's mask of indifference briefly slips as he glances my way. From his seat farther off, Tio watches me with a neutral expression.

In an uncharacteristically grim tone, Kabir says, "I know what I've seen, Dom. On the day of my initiation, the Voice revealed to me the brutality of men that brought about the time of destruction. Great harm was done to the land during the age of kings, through misuse of the mysteries. You've glimpsed the ancient scars of the damage yourself, in the landscapes that surround Velkanos—the great desert to the south, the dust storms in the land between the great rivers, the barren stretches of the open plains surrounding Velkanos.

"Before the age of kings, this land was thickly forested, the soil fertile, the land and waters teeming with life. Men were entrusted by the temple with the sacred responsibility of care for the land and all that dwells within it. But in their greed, some men ignored their responsibility as stewards of our mother land. They violated even the most sacred places of Dulai with their axes and their fire and their plows.

"And though only a few men failed in their duty, all suffered together for it—not only the men and women and children of our kind, but all the creatures of our mother land."

Kabir beckons to me and Balashi. We exchange uncertain glances before rising to our feet and going to Kabir. Kabir plants one hand on my shoulder and one on Balashi's, then says to us, "The Voice calls all men of this new age to rebuild what our forefathers destroyed. Each of us, in our own way, bears the burden of a debt incurred by those who came before us. All of us together must repair over many generations what was nearly destroyed by a few.

"But even a time of destruction plays its part in the natural order. A time of renewal must always follow, as spring follows on winter, though the renewal may take ages. We Artifexi are a sign of things to come. The Voice has not abandoned men entirely for our past mistakes. As we accomplish the great works of the Mohirai, we speed the healing of our mother land. In time, all men will share in the rewards of this work. Until then, the Voice calls us to obedience in our service, and to trust in its purpose."

"And how do you know the Voice itself is trustworthy?" I demand, shaking off Kabir's grip. "Even in these few moons I've spent among the Mohirai, I've seen how they manipulate us with their arts. Perhaps the Voice is merely a trick the High Priestess uses to control us. Perhaps we've sacrificed our power in service of a lie."

Kabir frowns at me, concerned. "Who has put such ideas in your head, Dom?" he says.

Witheringly, I say, "I have my own eyes, brother. Can't I have my own ideas, as well?"

Wide-eyed, Balashi looks from me to Kabir, whose strong jaw tenses as he contemplates his response. Tio raises his hand with a sharp gesture that forces my gaze to him. His command for my silence is unmistakable. I ball my fists in frustration, but, remembering the thought Tio shared with me earlier, I back away from Kabir and sit back down by the stone wall, closer to Tio. Only now, in this moment, do I realize I've made my decision. I will go west with Tio.

Kabir looks from me to Tio, nodding slowly, perceiving my decision without being told. Inclining his head toward the elder Artifex, he says, "I'm sure our little brother will benefit from your greater wisdom in these matters, when your vow of silence concludes, brother. The High Priestess was right to place him in your care."

I'd be happy to leave the conversation at that, but Kabir is conciliatory to a fault. Despite my avoidance of his gaze, he comes to sit beside me. I'd get up and move away, but I have no desire to provoke him or Tio further. So I pull out an apple from my pocket and set to work on it, doing my best to ignore Kabir and keep the peace.

Kabir leans back against the stone wall, pulling out an apple of his own and taking an enormous bite. Vahana and Eridu raise their heads from where they're grazing and approach eagerly at the sound of our juicy crunching. At first, we pretend to ignore their agitated snorts and nudges, but the horses' pestering only grows more insistent. At last, laughing, Kabir hands over his apple to Vahana. After a lengthier tussle with Eridu, I surrender the remainder of my apple, too.

Kabir smiles at me. Despite myself, I smile back. Kabir claps me on the shoulder and says, "Let's not part in such low spirits, Dom. I had high hopes when I arrived at Velkanos that I would earn your respect as your teacher. But, having failed that, I hope you'll remember that I'm still your brother."

I sigh. It's impossible to stay angry at Kabir for long. "Very well, brother," I say.

"Excellent," says Kabir. "Then let me pass along some brotherly advice. I've seen how heavily the choice of your Muse weighs on you. I thought perhaps you might find something instructive in my own experience of finding her."

I raise an eyebrow, intrigued. "All right," I say. "Go on."

Kabir says, "The Mohirai keep many mysteries from us, but there is one mystery that the Artifexi keep to ourselves. It is this: though you may call any woman Muse, the Muse is not any woman."

Perplexed, I say, "But how am I supposed to find my Muse, if she's not a woman?"

Kabir smiles. "The Muse may take any form," he says. "I myself hear her calling me often from a block of stone, demanding a shape within to be revealed. I hear her in the great bowl of sky, demanding an echo in the arching vault of a temple ceiling. I hear her in the cracked soil of dusty plains, demanding restoration." With a twinkle in his eye, he adds, "However, she comes from time to time in the form of a woman, too. And spirits, when she does …" He slaps his knee and hoots. "Well, then, she may torment you like only a woman can.

"Whatever form she takes for you, the Muse will come and go as she pleases. But when she dwells with you—Ah! She casts a light unlike any you have seen before. The colors of the world seem brighter. Things that seemed hidden when you were alone are revealed in her presence."

"I don't understand," I say. "Is this a mystery that's revealed at initiation?"

Kabir strokes his chin thoughtfully, then says, "Initiation is granted when your teachers agree that the novice arts are well under your command. However, only you will know when you've found the Muse.

"I myself find her most easily in the solitude of my work. But the path of each Artifex is unique, his relationship with the Muse his own. You must search for her in your own way, and you will find her in your own time."

Tio beckons, bidding us conclude our conversation. Kabir grips my hand to help me back to my feet. Balashi and I round up the horses and help Tio mount Ifestios.

When the rest of us are back in our saddles, Kabir walks Vahana over to Tio and extends his arm to his brother. Tio and Kabir clasp wrists in parting.

Turning to Balashi, Kabir says, "You've a good arm for smithing, little brother. You'll do well among the men of Upper Ford. Give my greetings to your teacher Magnes, when you see him. Tell him that whenever he tires of village comforts, I have a tent with his name on it in Phasis."

To me, Kabir says, "Don't give up your search for the Muse, Dom Artifex. Only through her will you know what work the Voice requires of you. Without her, you will be lost."

Kabir raises his hand in farewell and turns Vahana onto the road north. His white cloak billows behind him as they set off at a trot.

Tio clicks his tongue to turn Ifestios toward the western road. Balashi and I fall into line behind the elder Artifex. I gaze up at the mountains, wondering whether I'll find my Muse on the road ahead or remain lost as I am forever.

MOTHER LOVE

"CAN YOU HEAR ME? Emmie? Ava? Emmie? Ava?"

His voices call for us across unfathomable distances, from all directions. We try to answer, but we've lost control of our voices. It takes all our effort to simply force our eyes open. When at last our surroundings come into partial focus, we find ourselves lying on the floor of the spliner, our head in Dom's lap. We gaze up at him. He looks exhausted and pale, more haggard than we've ever seen him in all our years working together.

"Dom," we whisper. But, as soon as we say his name, we realize we have to make a decision. Is this my Dom, or other-Dom?

We close our eyes, focusing. Who are we? Where are we? When are we?

Focus.

Focus.

And, with effort, we refocus once more into the I this life requires.

In my ear, Bealsio's voice says, "Her heart rate is stabilizing."

Despite my disorientation, I manage to find the one essential thing I've come back to tell Dom. Or other-Dom. One of them. Both of them? All of them?

"I found Lilith," I murmur. "She told me ..." I trail off, gasping for breath after merely attempting to lift my head from other-Dom's lap.

Other-Dom presses a lukewarm, trembling hand to my icy cheek. The strength he shares through our connection is barely enough to help me sit up. When at last I'm upright, he looks like he might need to lie down himself.

In a quavering voice, he starts to say, "B, I need—" But before he finishes the thought, a glass of water rises through the floor beside his hand. "Thanks."

Carefully, he mixes the unbinding pharmaka and helps me take several sips. In a rasping voice, he says, "Take it easy, Ava. You've been gone a long time. We both need to rest."

As soon as I can, I stop drinking, taking the glass from him. "You need some, too," I say softly. He looks like he wants to protest, but he knows I'm right, and he accepts several long swallows from the glass.

His eyelids droop, and he closes his eyes, leaning back against the wide seat that extrudes beneath us from the spliner floor, cradling my body against his. We must both drift to sleep this way, because the next thing I'm aware of is Bealsio's voice saying, with a note of alarm, "Dom! Wake up, Dom! Dom, wake up!"

Beside me, other-Dom stirs. Groggily, he says, "What is it, B?"

"It's Amos," says Bealsio. "Falsens just sent word that he's on his way here. He must have spotted some anomaly in the security camera feeds. He knows you two left Eden with a quantum drive."

Other-Dom tries to stand, but he sways dizzily and sinks back down into the seat. "Damn it," he says, pressing his palm to his temple and wincing. "This can't be happening now."

"It's happening," says Bealsio. "Falsens has a car on the way to pick you two up."

"How much unbinding pharmaka do we have left?" says other-Dom.

"Two days, if we're lucky," says Bealsio. "But, given your vitals, you may need to split what's left between you. Might be closer to a day's supply."

Other-Dom runs his hands distractedly through his hair. "What are our extraction options?" he says.

"Falsens has a few prepared," says Bealsio. "But we'll have to discuss it on the road. Whatever destination you choose, we need to get you both to the Oakland Business Jet Center immediately."

Other-Dom nods. He tries to lift me up from my seat, but his knees wobble. He sets me down abruptly and shakes his head. "I need help to get her out of here," he says.

"Already on it," says Bealsio. "Anatolia's coming up the back entrance as we speak."

"Anatolia?" I say, looking at other-Dom in confusion.

"Your mother," he says. "Well, Emmie's mother. She lives down the street."

Surprised, I say, "Does she know about—" I wave my hand, a gesture insufficient to encompass what someone would have to know to comprehend what's happening here.

Other-Dom bobs his head ambivalently. "Ana knows everything that's safe for her to know," he says. "And she knows enough not to ask about the rest."

The back door to the spliner slides open. A petite older woman with Emmie's heart-shaped face rushes into the room. She heads straight to me and pulls me into a tight hug, kissing both my cheeks. "Oh, sweetheart," she says, tucking a loose strand of my hair behind my ear. "Bealsio told me why you have to leave. I wish I could go with you. But I'm glad I can give you a little boost to help you on your way, at least."

Other-Dom extends one hand toward Anatolia and gestures for me to do the same. Anatolia takes both of our hands and closes her eyes with an expression of intense concentration.

The familiar tingling warmth of connection travels from Anatolia's hand up through my arm, spreading across my chest, filling my entire body. The color returns to other-Dom's cheeks, and the tension smooths from his brow.

"Thanks, Ana," says other-Dom, pulling her into a tight hug. "I'm sorry this is all happening so suddenly."

Anatolia kisses his cheek and says, "Such is life, my dear. We knew this day might come. Take care of my baby for me."

Other-Dom lets go of Anatolia. "You know I will," he says.

Anatolia smiles up at him. "You always do," she says. "I don't know how we would have managed without you after—" She shakes her head, her eyes welling up with tears. She wipes her eyes and says simply, "Thank you."

Anatolia turns to face me, taking both of my hands in hers. As I look into her sparkling brown eyes, I see Emmie's face reflected back at me. For a disorienting moment, I become we once more.

We revisit the sensation of standing in the sacred sunlit spring on our Calling Day, when we glimpsed a vision of Earth in the pool's reflection. But the reflection in our mother's eyes reveals something new to us. There, we see all the mothers, sisters, daughters, lovers, friends, and foes we've had, will have, have been, and will be to one another again. My mother embraces us all as she embraces me. "Promise me you'll come home when you've finished your work," she whispers in my ear. "I love you, my brave girl."

"I love you, too," I say, and whose words these are no longer seems to matter. A single Voice speaks through us all.

"Go," says Anatolia, placing my hand in other-Dom's. "I'll delay Amos as long as I can."

The spliner door opens, and on my visual overlay Bealsio's glittering green path unfurls before me. Other-Dom takes my hand, and together we head back out into the real world.

WESTWARD PASSAGE

In my dream, I lie curled on my side on the deck of a boat, cold wind coursing over my naked body, my vision obscured by a cloth bag wrapped around my head, my ankles and wrists bound in rough coils of rope. Along my back, Ava's small warm body presses against my skin, her arms wrapped around my waist, her wrists bound tight against my navel. Somewhere behind us, the *creak-thump creak-thump creak-thump* of a strange footstep approaches, coming closer, closer, closer …

Alarmed, I jolt upright, nearly falling out of my hammock berth in *Aithalia*'s hold. Heart pounding, I sit up and plant my bare feet on the wooden floorboards to steady myself. I rub the cold sweat off my neck with my sleeve, taking a few deep breaths to calm myself. I haven't had a nightmare like this since my first few nights in Velkanos, when the memory of my captivity among the free men was still fresh. In fact, I've been sleeping so soundly for the past half moon's horseback journey with Tio that I can't remember the last time I dreamt anything at all. I suppose the motion of the sailboat on my first night out at sea must have stirred up the awful memory of that windy night on the river. The ominous sound still echoes through my mind: *creak-thump, creak-thump, creak-thump …*

Wait. I look up at the low ceiling above me. There's the sound again, an unmistakable *creak-thump* passing right over my head. A shudder runs down my spine. That's not just some echo of a memory.

I'm too groggy to make sense of what I'm hearing. How could the free men have found me on this sailboat, all the way out here in the Middle Sea? Could we have been boarded in the night? Whatever may be happening, my overwhelming instinct is to protect myself and Tio. I run my hands over the curved wall of the hold, searching with fumbling fingers for the latched compartment containing my few belongings. There it is. When the compartment pops open, I withdraw Ava's little knife from its leather sheath on my toolbelt. It's not much, but it's sharp, and it's the only weapon readily at hand.

I realize suddenly that I should warn Tio what's happening. I peer across the dark hold toward his berth. The only source of light is the tiny window in the companionway hatch, so it takes me a moment to realize with dismay that his hammock is empty. Maybe Tio went on deck while I lay sleeping. I hope he's all right. Strong though he is, his lame leg would be a serious impediment to defending himself from able-bodied free men.

As quietly as I can manage, I creep toward the companionway, gripping Ava's blade flat between my teeth to free my hands as I climb the short ladder that leads to the main deck. When I reach the hatch, I peer out through its tiny window, looking aft, in the direction of that creaking sound.

Just outside the window stands old Talos, one of the two sailors who joined our company a quarter moon ago at the Purattu river village of Upper Ford, where Tio delivered Balashi to his place among the smiths. Talos grips the mainsail line in one hand and shades his sun-bronzed face with the other, peering up at the fluttering telltale at the top of the mast. "Nort' by nort'west," he calls out, his gravelly voice steeped in the island lilt of Lemnos.

"Haul away!" calls a clear young man's voice, which belongs to the second Lemnian sailor, Pyrrhos, who stands somewhere outside my narrow line of sight.

Talos hauls the mainsail line and looks back over his shoulder, where Tio stands toward the stern, gripping the long wooden handle of the tiller. Tio signals with his arm. Pyrrhos calls, "Ready about!"

I grip the companionway ladder as the sailboat heels gently to starboard, tacking north.

"Make fast!" calls Pyrrhos, and Talos secures his line to the nearest cleat.

With *Aithalia* settled on her new course, Tio locks the tiller in position, rises to his feet, and hobbles a few steps forward to tidy up a loose line.

Oh. Oh, spirits. My eyes widen as I realize what I'm seeing. A device of leather and metal encases Tio's bad leg, a brace so cleverly designed that the Artifex can, without the aid of crutches, maneuver across the gently rocking deck with both his hands free. His braced leg falls with a heavy *creak-thump* each time Tio plants his boot on the wooden boards of the deck.

To avoid being seen, I back slowly away from the hatch window, descend the ladder, and return to my hammock. There I lie, rocking gently with the waves, stunned by the realization that Tio is the man in charge of the free men who held me and Ava captive. Tio's leg brace is the source of the strange sound I kept hearing that night on their river boat, the reason for all those strange scratches Serapen noticed on the boat's deck the next morning. Tio's voice was the one I'd heard murmuring threats in Ava's ear, the voice that's haunted my nightmares. He's been hiding—silent but in plain sight—this entire time. And now, through my own lamentable ignorance, I've put myself at the complete mercy of this man.

My thoughts race with questions. Why was Tio helping Lilith, the night they took us captive? How has he managed to keep his alliance with the free men a secret from the Mohirai? What is he planning to do with me? What might he do, if he knew that I know his identity? And, most importantly, what should I do, now that I know?

I lift up Ava's knife in my left hand. The dim light of the hatch glimmers on the sharp edge of the blade. On an impulse, I transfer the bloodstained handle to my right hand, gripping it as Ava would have done, if she were in my place. No matter what happened on our journey together from the coast of the Middle Sea to the slopes of Velkanos, she always seemed to know what to do. Or at least, if she didn't know, she could pull together a plan on short notice. Unfortunately, given my current situation trapped far out at sea with Tio and his men, I have only myself to rely on. How on Dulai am I supposed to come up with a plan all alone, without her?

I'm not expecting much from myself in answer. But as I lie here in the quiet darkness of the hold, listening to the rhythmic sound of the waves against the hull, I'm surprised to discover a chorus of voices in my memory, eager to help me. Perhaps I'm not entirely alone here, after all.

The first voice I hear is Lilith's. I remember what she told Ava, the night we lay captive on the river boat, as she explained why my connection with Ava must be severed, my memory of her unbound. She'd said, *The Mohirai must not learn the identities of the free people living among their slaves.* Ava and I had tried to persuade Lilith that both of us wanted to live among the free men—it was, in fact, the reason we'd fled the novice caravan together. But Lilith had considered me unfit to join their company, my deeply-ingrained loyalty to the Mohirai too great a risk. Now I realize that, as long as my loyalty remains in doubt, I'll be at risk of another unwanted unbinding.

Next comes the voice of Tio, a rumble of approaching thunder in my memory. Ava, bold even in our captivity, had demanded, *Who are you?* And Tio had said, *A free man.* Ava had asked, *What do you want?* And Tio replied, *A better world.* Some part of me has suspected since the day we met in the house of glass that Tio alone might understand my frustration with the fate of men in our world. If Tio believes the free people can build a better world than the one the Mohirai have built for us, I'd like to know how they plan to do it.

Then Clio's voice returns to say, *The arrival of each new Artifex has marked the start of a new chapter in our historia. Perhaps your Muse shall call you to build an even greater temple for a new age, Dom Artifex.*

And finally my own voice speaks in answer to the Muse. *Yes, I think you're right!* I'd said, gazing up at the grand facade of the Musaion. Revisiting this memory now, I see it in a new light. Within the form of the ancient temple city, I glimpse a future in which I myself will tear down the old walls to build a new temple in their place. I know I've been called to this place, to this time, to this man, for a reason. My certainty reveals my path ahead.

There's another *creak-thump, creak-thump, creak-thump* above me, followed by lighter footsteps. Someone opens the hatch, and Talos calls down, "Time for ye to lend a hand on de lines, brother. It's Pyrrhos' turn to rest."

"Coming!" I call back, rising from the hammock to pull on my boots and toolbelt. Before I stow Ava's knife back in its sheath at my hip, I run my thumb over its handle, thinking, *Thanks for showing me how it's done.*

CRUISING ALTITUDE

I SIT BESIDE OTHER-DOM in the cabin of our "private jet," gripping his hand as we accelerate down the "runway." In any other circumstance, I'd be glued to the little window beside me, eager to learn how such a heavy "aircraft" takes flight. But the short drive here to the Oakland Business Jet Center was such a whirlwind that I'm still struggling to catch my breath and slow my heart rate. I'm astonished that the car Falsens sent to retrieve us from Emmie's house managed to avoid interception by Eden's corporate security team. There were three very close calls, but ultimately we managed to shake them off with help from a pair of decoy cars.

About fifteen minutes after "takeoff," our "captain" says over a shared channel, "We've reached cruising altitude. Our estimated flight time to Osaka Itami Airport is eleven hours, twelve minutes. We're expecting clear skies over the Pacific for the duration of the flight. Feel free to move about the cabin as needed."

"Thanks, Naoto," says other-Dom.

Only now, lulled into a sense of security by the calming hum of the aircraft's "engines," do I feel relaxed enough to share with other-Dom what I witnessed on my last bridge crossing. I'm eager to unload the burden of this knowledge while I still can. Despite Anatolia's timely energy boost, Emmie's condition is spiraling fast. So I lace my fingers through other-Dom's, pressing my palm to his.

"Ready for this?" I say.

"Go ahead," he says.

I pour the memory of what passed between me and Lilith into other-Dom's mind. When I reach the end, I'm relieved by the thought that, whatever happens next, someone else shares the knowledge it cost so many people so much to obtain. Other-Dom looks at me with an expression that's equal parts amazement, apprehension, and determination.

"B," he says. "Tell Falsens we're going to reuse the twenty-thirty-two playbook, with a few modifications."

"Are you sure, Dom?" says Bealsio, sounding alarmed. "Amos will have Stewards monitoring every route into Turkey, after what happened last time."

Other-Dom sighs. "I don't see another option, B," he says. "You can go public with this information from any location on Earth with a stable alternet connection, but Ava and I have to secure a supply of water from Eden somehow if we're going to outlive our current supply of unbinding pharmaka."

"I'm going to need exact coordinates to review with Falsens, then," says Bealsio.

"Give me a minute," he says.

Other-Dom pulls on a pair of immerger gloves from one of the packed bags that were waiting here in the cabin when we boarded the jet. He turns on a visual overlay and shares it with me so I can watch as he quickly records the needed details from Lilith's memory in the alternet. Apparently, what Bealsio and Falsens need to review is a map of the tunnels and lava tubes Lilith used to travel from the Under City to Eden.

When everything about the underground route is fully captured in other-Dom's "three-dimensional wireframe", he changes the display to show a birds-eye view of the aboveground terrain. He zooms out from the landscape surrounding the village ruins of Eden, centering the view on the little hilltop looking west toward the triangular peak of Velkanos. To me, he says, "So here's the Eden you saw on The End of the Road."

I nod, recognizing the familiar features of the landscape I've traveled through myself and have now glimpsed in the memories of multiple other people.

"And here's what's left of it, on our branch of Earth," he continues, opening a second view alongside the first. I study the second landscape, puzzled. I recognize the profile of the Urashtu Mountains on the horizon, but I struggle to reconcile the rest of what I'm seeing. Where Velkanos should stand, there's only a crater with a small crescent lake at its center. Where the hilltop grove and valley of Eden should be, there's only a tiny island in the midst of a massive lake that covers most of the plains of Velkanos.

"That's Nemrut Caldera and Lake Nemrut," says other-Dom, pointing to the crater and its lake, respectively. "And that's Lake Van and Akdamar," he adds, indicating the huge lake and the tiny island near its southeastern shore.

"But where's Velkanos?" I say, looking from one landscape to the other.

"Nemrut Caldera is all that remains on our branch of the stratovolcano called Velkanos on your branch," says Bealsio. "Multiple eruptions of Nemrut over the last quarter million years dammed the mountain rivers that used to flow through the plains, which led to the formation of Lake Van."

"So Eden is under Lake Van, here on Earth?" I say.

"Not all of it," says other-Dom. "The hilltop where the fountainhead emerges is still above water. That's the island of Akdamar."

I reach out to zoom in on the view of Akdamar. I remember the island's name from some of the labels on memories I've reviewed with Bealsio and other-Dom over the last two days. "Isn't that the place where Amos injected Emmie with binding pharmaka?" I say.

Other-Dom nods.

"But they were underground somewhere, when it happened," I say, remembering the dark vault where their struggle took place. "I saw some pool there, and a dead tree. That must have been the spring. Did the spring sink underground, somehow?"

"No," says other-Dom. "The Stewards hid the hilltop spring about a millennia ago by building the Cathedral of the Holy Cross on top of it. But the cathedral's gone now. It collapsed in an earthquake the last time Emmie was there, right after she and Amos fell into the spring."

Remembering my own experience of overdosing on binding pharmaka, I stare at him in disbelief. "How did Emmie manage to get out of there right after an overdose?" I say. "Did Amos carry her out?"

Other-Dom opens his mouth as if to answer, closes it, then says thoughtfully, "Something happened when she fell into the pool with Amos that we've never been able to explain."

"What happened?" I say.

"Emmie found me," says other-Dom. "Somehow, she pulled my body out of the spring. We ran out of the vault before the structure collapsed."

"She ran?" I say doubtfully, remembering that I couldn't even stand after my own overdose.

"Our bond must have stabilized her for a little while," says other-Dom. "She only collapsed once we were outside the ruins."

I consider this. That part might make sense. When I collapsed in the cedar forest the night of my overdose, I recovered my strength once my Dom found me and picked me up. Something similar could have happened to Emmie. But a lot of other things still don't make sense.

"How could Emmie have found you in the spring?" I say. "How could your body even get to this branch from your own branch?"

Other-Dom shakes his head. "No idea," he says.

I frown. "And how did Amos get out?" I say.

"Also no idea," says other-Dom. "We saw him fall into the spring, but we never saw him come out."

I think about this for a while. "Maybe Amos knew how to travel through the underground river, like Lilith did?" I say.

"Maybe," says other-Dom. "It's unclear how much the Stewards know about the underground river. They seem to focus their efforts on guarding the spring on Akdamar. But I suppose if Lilith knew about the properties of the water flowing from Velkanos, the Stewards might know that, too."

I rub my eyes, trying to piece together what all of this could mean, but unable to see a complete picture. I say, "So, if Velkanos doesn't exist any more, and the Stewards are guarding Akdamar, and they might be guarding the underground river … how exactly are we going to find a place to get the water we need?"

"Together," Bealsio says brightly.

"Together," other-Dom says grimly.

I let out a low whistle. The odds on this job aren't looking good to me. But if this is my last day on Earth, there's no time for self-doubt. "All right," I say. "Together."

SPRING EQUINOX

THREE DAYS AFTER WE SET SAIL from the Children's Temple docks, *Aithalia* arrives at the docks of Lemnos just after sunset. Four men driving oxcarts descend from the nearby ridgetop village to help us unload the many heavy barrels and other smaller cargo stowed in *Aithalia's* hold. By the time we finish unloading, the moon is rising in the east, painting a glimmering path across the calm, deep waters of the harbor. Tio, Talus, Pyrrhos, and I ride in the back of the oxcarts up the rutted dirt road that leads from the rocky beach to the unlit village. When we reach the village, the four fresh men set to work transferring the cargo into a large hut that faces the central commons. Our sailing party is released to rest after our long journey. Tio leads me to our shared quarters in a small, windowless brick hut near the center of the village. We go to bed without an evening meal.

I lie awake in my cot long into the night, separated from Tio by only a thin curtain, our single room's lone concession to privacy. His steady breathing on the other side of the curtain tells me Tio's asleep, but I have to suppress a foolish urge to wake him up. Ever since I discovered Tio's true identity, my mind has been restless, endlessly rehearsing what I will say and do to earn his trust once we're alone together. But I'm sure waking him up after our long journey, which was even more exhausting for him than for me, isn't the best way to accomplish this.

I knead the pillow behind my head for the tenth time, wondering how Tio managed to fall asleep on something so lumpy. Giving up on the pillow, I turn over several times, trying to find any sleeping position on the narrow cot that will support my head and my feet at the same time. Thalia wasn't joking when she spoke of the privations of the men's villages. But eventually, my body's exhaustion subdues both my discomfort and my racing thoughts, and I drift into sleep.

When I wake, I'm as groggy as if I'd taken some of Hippolyta's sleeping pharmaka. I rub my sore neck as I try to shake the unsettling feeling left behind by my dream, the same one I first had in the Cave of Dreams. As before, I'd stood atop that strange rock promontory surrounded by the sea, gazing up at the scarlet ladder hanging down from the blue bowl of sky. As before, I'd started to climb, and the climb was endless. Now, I'm left with the sense that there's no end to that ladder and no way to reach the sky. I wonder what it means.

Shaking my head, I rise from bed. I'm surprised to discover that Tio's departed without my hearing him. I poke my head through the front door of the hut to see where he's gone, only to realize with surprise it's late morning. It's so dark in the windowless hut that I'd thought it was barely sunrise. Hurriedly, I pull on my clothes, which badly need washing, and my boots, still muddy from traveling. I hope Tio won't think me lazy for my late start on my very first day of work among his craftsmen.

I step out of the hut and survey the village, which the light of day reveals to be little more than a glorified camp. The village is mostly empty, though a few other men besides me also appear to be getting a late start, drifting in and out of other huts in various stages of undress. One unusually fair young man crossing the commons between the huts looks like he's on his way back from washing somewhere. He's shirtless, his hair wet, his beardless face perfectly scrubbed. He looks like he's about my age, though he must have seen at least ten more summers than I have, because I never met him in the house of boys.

"Good morning, brother!" I call out, hailing him.

"Ah! Good morning, Dom Artifex," the young man says, pausing in the commons to greet me. He rubs his wet mane of pale blonde hair carefully with a towel. "Did you sleep well?"

"Fine," I say. He raises a skeptical eyebrow, studying me with piercing blue eyes. I see from his expression that I look as road-weary as I feel. I say, "Could you tell me where I can wash up?"

He points out the little stream that runs behind the village and gives me directions to the dug latrines.

"Where can I find soap?" I say.

"Always in short supply, I'm afraid," he says ruefully. "You'll find the standard of cleanliness here a bit … ah … different from what you're used to in the temple city. Resupply visits are so infrequent that most of us get by without such luxuries. But I'm sure Tio can set aside a little soap for you."

I nod slowly, realizing my habits will require some adjustment here. "Do you know where Tio's gone?" I say. "I'm supposed to attend him, but I didn't hear him leave."

The young man points across the small wooden footbridge that spans the stream, toward a low hill north of the village. A few stone pillars and a lot of scaffolding stand atop the hill. Helpfully, he says, "You should pack yourself some food from the kitchen storeroom, before you head up there. We eat only the evening meal in the village. For the rest, you're on your own. Some of us share a midday meal together at the worksite, if you want to join us."

He's turning to go when I say, "Sorry, brother, I forgot to ask your name."

"Ah," he says, turning back to extend his arm to me. As we clasp wrists, I catch a glimpse of a beautiful tattoo that snakes along the underside of his forearm, rich brown ink worked into the smooth, fair skin, forming that same swirling pattern I've glimpsed in so many places along my journey. With a charming smile, he says, "Amos. Good to meet you."

"Good to meet you, too, Amos," I say. "I'll see you up there."

Amos withdraws to his quarters to finish dressing. I rush about the village, doing my best to prepare for the day with no cleaning supplies, no running water, no morning meal, and no idea of what I'll be doing once I reach the worksite.

Despite my attempts to hurry, I'm the very last to arrive at the worksite. As I finish the climb to the top of the hill, I see a group of men gathering in the shade of the scaffolding, pausing their work for a midday meal. Amos beckons me with a wave. I take a seat on the ground beside him and withdraw my meager meal from my satchel: a dry hunk of the dense bread I found in the kitchen storeroom.

Despite my best effort to wash in the stream, I feel quite grungy next to tidy Amos. But, as I study all the new faces around me, I see my appearance is no scruffier than most of the other men's. A few of the men nod my way as we make eye contact. Others reach out to introduce themselves and clasp wrists with me.

I'm gnawing the last of my bread when I spot old Talos heading toward the assembled group, lending his arm to Tio, who limps with greater difficulty than usual. Three days in that leg brace on *Aithalia* couldn't have been comfortable, and it looks like Tio's paying the price for it now.

When Talos and Tio reach us, Tio extends his arm to me and says, in a deep, ringing voice, "Welcome to Lemnos, Dom Artifex."

I'm so astonished that I don't even pause to consider the proper form of response. "You've broken your silence," I say.

Tio joins the other men in laughing at my surprise. "Indeed," he says, pointing up through the unroofed columns to the sun that now stands directly overhead. "The spring equinox is a time for things to emerge—my voice among them. Now lend me your arm, little brother. Talos has been serving as my crutch all morning and needs a rest."

I scramble to my feet and take Tio's arm. "I'm sorry I was so late to arrive, brothers," I say, addressing Talos along with Tio.

Tio waves my apology away with his free hand. "Novices need their sleep far more than we old men," he says. "You'll fall into the new routine soon enough." Tio gestures with his head toward a narrow footpath across the rocky soil that leads to the far side of the worksite, beyond the cluster of standing columns. "Walk with me, Dom. We have much to discuss, now that we're both able."

When we're well out of the other men's hearing, Tio stops and adjusts his strong grip on my forearm, his callused palm digging into my skin. With a jolt of excitement, I wonder whether Tio might share thoughts with me again this way, as he had the day of Balashi's unbinding. The Mohirai advise against sharing thoughts, when possible, to avoid disturbing others' minds. But revealing my own thoughts to Tio might be the easiest way to prove my true intentions to him.

But Tio doesn't open a connection between us, only re-adjusts his weight before continuing on our walk. "Has anyone told you what we're building, here on Lemnos?" he says.

"I was told you're finishing a great work for Muse Maya here," I say.

"Yes," says Tio, gesturing grandly about the hill. I follow the sweep of his hand. Apart from the unroofed columns, I see nothing but a great many masonry and carpentry projects in progress, spread out across the hill. Downslope, on the north side of the hill facing away from the village, stand a few additional buildings, of higher quality construction than the sleeping huts in the village, interspersed with low, scrubby trees that offer sparse shade from the intense midday sunlight. A few of these buildings reveal their purpose through some exterior feature. I recognize a smithy, a glassworks, and a cooperage among them. Apart from the workshops themselves, though, few things here appear to be even approaching completion.

"Is our great work not beautiful?" says Tio, turning an expectant gaze on me.

"It's … not what I expected," I say diplomatically.

Tio's dark blue eyes sparkle with laughter. I relax a little, realizing that he's jesting. Even so, his tone is serious as he says, "Many men are blind to beauty even when it stands before them. How much harder is it, then, to perceive the beauty of what might be? But that is what it is, to be an Artifex, to hear the Muse, to summon unseen beauty into being with your own hands."

Tio's words resonate within me, lending new meaning to many disparate experiences of my life. I take a second look at the landscape around us and say, "I would love to know what you see here, brother."

Tio smiles and says, "Then I would love to show you."

So I support Tio as he tours me through the different areas of the hilltop worksite, listening as he paints for me in words a picture of the temple that will someday stand here. The central temple design follows the pattern of the Musaion of Velkanos. Together, we pace the foundations, as Tio points out where the familiar elements of the circular domed hall and adjoining halls will stand, along with the many innovations upon the pattern that Muse Maya called him to make.

Once we've walked all over the hill, Tio invites me into the large canvas tent halfway between the worksite and the workshops. Large rolls of parchment cover two long tables within the tent, and Tio spreads them out before me one by one, showing me the carefully drafted plans for each part of the temple, checking my understanding of the design point by point. I examine the plans with interest, gaining from each a deeper understanding not just of this temple, but of all temples that follow this pattern.

I spot several long wooden cylinders on the floor beneath one table. Pointing to them, I say, "Are these more of your plans?"

"Indeed," Tio says lightly. "Every great work requires plans within plans. But there will be time enough to review those another day. Come, help me back down to the village. At my pace, if we don't set out now, we'll arrive after dark."

So we depart the tent. As we follow the path back toward the village, I see the worksite with new appreciation. Through Tio's eyes, I've glimpsed the grand structure that will stand here one day, looking out across the Middle Sea. And yet, every time we pass a group of craftsmen hard at work, my appreciation dims somewhat. Having reviewed Tio's plans, I understand more fully the scope of the work that remains, and the implications for all these men.

I say, "It's a shame, that only you and I will live to see the great work completed, while all of them, having toiled here for their entire lives, will not. If you had more hands in your service, the temple might rise within a single generation."

Tio stops, so I stop beside him. He studies me for a while, then says evenly, "You're right. It's a shame indeed. But the High Priestess tells us the Voice constrains our numbers to protect the natural order."

"And do you believe her, brother?" I say.

Tio looks out at the sunset from what will someday be the threshold of a grand entrance hall. From this vantage point, looking out to the south across the Middle Sea, it's clear why the Muse chose this place for a temple, and this orientation for its entrance. Carefully, he says, "I'll give you an answer for an answer. What do you believe?"

My free hand settles on the handle of Ava's blade, so warm at my hip after my long day in the sun that it feels almost alive. I know the time for timidity has passed, and the time for action has come. I turn to Tio, and he holds my gaze, unblinking. I say, "I believe the High Priestess tells us what she wishes us to hear. But I believe the Voice has called us to build a new temple for a new age. I believe the future belongs to the free people."

My words hang in the air between us. In a low voice, Tio says, "Then I believe we are in agreement, brother."

Later that evening, in the humble meal hall off the village commons, I do my best to engage with the other men in their good-natured, endless jesting. After the simple meal of venison stew prepared by a few of the elders, the men urge me to join them in their game of dice, which seems to be the primary evening ritual in the village. Following prior instruction from Tio, I beg their pardon, telling them I'm in the habit of observing the evening silence.

I depart the meal hall to return to my sleeping quarters in the little hut across the commons. Tio sits on his cot, waiting for me in the near-darkness, the curtain dividing the room pushed back. He gestures for me to sit on my cot facing him.

I sit. He extends both hands toward me, and I take them.

A tingling sensation travels up my arms as Tio's awareness enters mine, moving silently through the halls of my mind, examining the intentions in my heart. I hide nothing from him, showing him everything that led me to this moment. At last, he thinks, *Are you sure this is what you want, brother? There is no turning back.*

This is what I want, I think. *Show me what it is, to be a free man.*

Tio rises, and I lend him my arm. He leads me back across the commons. To my surprise, we return again to the meal hall. The door to the hut stands open. Inside, many of the craftsmen still sit around the single long table that fills the room, playing dice by candlelight, sharing a few bottles of wine. They look up when Tio steps through the doorway with me at his side.

At a wordless gesture from Tio, their conversation ceases.

"Close the door," Tio says to me, and so I do.

The men wait expectantly. Tio settles his broad hand on my shoulder. He says, "I come bearing good news, brothers."

All eyes fall on me. I do my best to swallow my nerves as I scan the faces of the group. On the far side of the room, I spot the lanky figure of Amos, leaning in the doorway to the kitchen storeroom.

Tio says, "The Voice has called a second Artifex to walk among the free people. Welcome your brother Dom."

Many fists pound the table in unison. "Welcome, brother Dom," the free men say as one.

Tio looks across the room at Amos and says, "Take him to our sister."

Amos straightens up in the doorway and nods, beckoning me with one hand. I glance at Tio uncertainly. He gestures for me to proceed without him.

I walk past the men at the table, following Amos through the door into the storeroom at the back of the hut. I came in here this morning to search for midday meal provisions, but I hadn't found much among the few open crates and jars. Most of the storeroom is full of sealed barrels.

Amos closes the door behind me when I enter. I look around, expecting to see a free woman waiting here among the shelves and crates and barrels. But we seem to be alone.

Amos walks across the room toward a large barrel that stands in the corner. He grips the barrel on either side. I step forward to help him lift it—I know from unloading *Aithalia* last night how heavy all these barrels are—but Amos lifts it so easily that it must be empty. He sets the empty barrel aside, revealing a circular trapdoor in the dirt floor.

Amos opens the trapdoor. "Come here," he says, extending his tattooed arm. "I'll give you a hand down."

Slowly, I step forward, looking down into the hole that descends into spirits only know what. The top of a wooden ladder peeks out from the pitch darkness below, leaning against the earthen wall of the hole. I've never been comfortable in underground spaces, but I take a steadying breath, then grip Amos' wrist as I find my footing on the ladder.

I've climbed down a few rungs when I stop and look back up at Amos, who's closing the trapdoor over me. "Hold on," I say. "How far down does this go?"

"It's just nine rungs down to the first level," he says. "Careful on that last rung, though. There's a bit of a gap."

"And then where do I—" But the rest of my question is cut off as the trapdoor closes, plunging me into total darkness. My pulse speeds up. I cling tight to the rungs with both hands for a moment, but then loosen my grip to draw Ava's knife from its sheath. The feeling of the handle clears my head. I remember how Ava taught me to navigate the dark tunnel into the Cave of Dreams, and I close my eyes, reaching out with my other senses as I carefully lower myself down to the next rung, then the next, then the next. As Amos had warned, there's a gap below the ninth rung. After feeling around unsuccessfully for the floor, I take a breath and drop off the ladder, landing in a slight crouch with Ava's knife in my outstretched hand.

As soon as my feet touch the ground, a prickling awareness of her presence spreads from the crown of my head all the way down my spine. I descended into this darkness with no idea whom I'd find here, but I know at once who it is. Some part of me has always known, from the very first time she spoke to me in the cedar forest, that there would be no escape from her.

So I turn to face her. Softly, I say, "Here I am, sister."

A striker cracks against flint. A candle flares an arm's length before me.

Above the lone flame hovers Lilith's face, her ice blue eyes boring into mine.

"You found your courage, brother," she says, glancing down at the knife.

"My Muse woke it up," I say, slipping the knife back into its sheath. "But it was in me all along."

Lilith nods slowly, studying me. "Brother Tio tells me the Muse calls you to build a new temple," she says.

"She has," I say.

"The free people will need a new temple," says Lilith. "But many things must come to an end, to make space for something new. Every great work comes at a cost."

"I know," I say. "I'm ready."

Lilith sighs and shakes her head. "No, little brother," she says. "You don't yet know. You're not yet ready. None of us know the cost of an ending until we witness it ourselves. None of us know the cost of building something new until we raise it from the ashes. That is why we must gather all our courage and build all our strength in preparation. The great work will consume all of it, and so much more."

I incline my head. "Thank you for correcting me, sister," I say. "Teach me, then, what we must do to prepare."

"Very well," says Lilith, gesturing for me to follow her along the dark tunnel that stretches ahead of us. "Listen, and you shall hear."

THE BEST LAID PLANS

"You can't be serious," says other-Dom, his face sagging with exhaustion as he addresses Falsens, whose squat avatar hovers before us on our shared visual overlay.

"I'm perfectly serious," Falsens says in his inimitable voice, which morphs smoothly from male to female, young to old, and back again as he speaks. "Air traffic control has issued a landing freeze for all private jets in the region."

Our pilot Naoto, who placed the aircraft on "autopilot" to join us in the cabin for these deliberations, sits in the seat across from mine, bobbing his shiny bald head as he listens to Falsens. His perfectly calm demeanor offers a much-needed contrast to other-Dom's growing agitation. Naoto says, "Do we know why?"

Falsens says, "Officially, there's a national security situation affecting all Turkish airspace east of the Euphrates River. I'm backchanneling for more information."

Other-Dom's voice is tight as he says, "Don't bother. It's Amos sending us a message. He's reminding us we're on a tight leash."

Naoto says, "We need an updated flight plan within the next twenty minutes. We're nearing the end of our fuel."

Bealsio, whose avatar sits in the seat beside Naoto, says, "I have a few refueling scenarios prepared. But the odds that we can take off again are dwindling, with the Stewards zeroing in on our current location. Should we evaluate ground extraction options?"

Other-Dom glances at me, slumped in my seat, then shakes his head. "Too risky, in her condition. What if…"

The four of them continue on in this way for some time. Falsens, Naoto, other-Dom, Bealsio, and Emmie evidently have a long history together, and their rapid exchanges send endless explanatory prompts scrolling by on my visual overlay. I'd have difficulty keeping up with it at the best of times, but I'm slipping in and out of consciousness so frequently that I've given up even the attempt.

Since the first leg of our journey across the Pacific to Japan, we've changed planes twice to continue on our westward course to Turkey, shepherded by Naoto through the ground transfers, with Bealsio and Falsens tirelessly adjusting our plans to evade the Stewards. We've been in flight for most of the last twenty hours at this point, and my condition has been deteriorating by the hour. Other-Dom has been alternately letting me sleep and waking me up to dole out our remaining unbinding pharmaka drop by precious drop, which offers temporary reprieve from the enervating pain in my chest but leaves me increasingly disconnected from my surroundings. Memories drift through my mind, pieces turning over and over, their intersections blurring in and out of focus. The voices of many other-Avas surface and sink from my awareness, their whispers calling me onward.

There's a pinging sound on the shared visual overlay, and everyone around me stops talking.

"Incoming call for Emmie," says Bealsio. "It's Amos."

"Answer it, B," says other-Dom. "Keep the rest of us view-only."

Amos' face appears hovering beside Falsens' avatar. He does not look pleased.

"Hello, Amos," says Bealsio-as-Emmie.

"How many times do we need to repeat this lesson, my dear?" says Amos.

"One more time, I guess," says Bealsio-as-Emmie.

Amos shakes his head and says, "Where does this obsession with revealing the Stewards' secrets come from, Emmie? You saw for yourself what happened the last time you tried to reveal the spring's location. The world moved on in days. People see no value in knowledge freely shared."

"Only because the Stewards discredit that knowledge," says Bealsio-as-Emmie.

"You know better than anyone how well equipped we are to discredit whatever you're planning to leak," says Amos, his expression almost pitying. "People are perfectly happy in the Eden you've helped us build. If you try to destroy it, there will be no forgiveness, this time. No third chance. You will be entirely on your own. Be reasonable, Emmie. Come home. We'll keep you comfortable for as long as we can."

Bealsio looks to me and other-Dom. "What do you want me to say?" she says.

Other-Dom slams his fist into his thigh in frustration. Seeing his pain stirs a deep ache in my heart, as I recognize once more the pattern in which we've been trapped all along. I know whose voice is needed in this moment, the voice he longs to hear. So I gather up the meager remains of Emmie's strength and the faint echoes of her thoughts, and I retreat into the background of her awareness.

In a rasping voice, Emmie returns to say, "Listen to me, my love. Tell Amos that if he lets us turn back, we won't go public."

Other-Dom's eyes widen. "Em?" he says, searching my eyes.

"Yes," says Emmie. "I'm here. I've been here all along."

He grips both my hands. "But we've come so far," he says.

"And we have no where else to go," says Emmie. "Amos is right. We have to turn back."

Other-Dom's eyes fill with tears. "And then what?" he says. "We just give up?"

"No," says Emmie. "We finish the work."

"But if we go public without securing the water you need, what will happen to you?" he says.

"You know what will happen," says Emmie. "How many times have you seen the ending?"

"Then let's forget it all," he says. "Forget going public. Forget the damn great work. You can't leave me again, Em. I can't live without you."

"And you can't live if I stay," says Emmie. "I've bled you dry, my love. No more. It has to stop. Your part in this is done. It's time for you to move on. It's time for you to live. And it's time for me to go home."

"Home where?" he says. "Back to California?"

"No," says Emmie. "Back to my mother's home."

"Are you sure this is what you want, Em?" he says.

"Take me home, my love," says Emmie. To Bealsio, she says, "Tell Amos we're turning back."

OF MICE AND MEN

On the first night of the harvest festival that marks the end of my twenty-seventh summer, I sit on the ground at the edge of the revels, gazing up at the high stone wall surrounding Velkanos. The early autumn winds that chill the plains subsided at sunset. I'm enveloped now by the warmth of the three great bonfires blazing before the closed bronze-clad gate of the Outer City.

The beat of the drums, the strumming of the kitharas, the plaintive notes of the aulos, and the rich harmonies of the singers fill my ears. Hanu and Eumelia dance before me with the other wheat-crowned women circling the bonfires, casting long shadows over the stubbled fields. Kabir, the lone man among the dancers, is in especially high spirits tonight after so much mixed wine.

This is the only night of the year when all the Mohirai gather outside the walls of the temple city. Seeing them here together, I'm reminded how large they are in number, compared to the free men scattered through Dulai. Even so, as my gaze rises above the unlit temple city on the lower slope, to the towering snow-capped peak of Velkanos framed by the starry night sky, I'm struck by how small we all are.

Hanu grabs Eumelia's hand as one song transitions to the next, and the pair of them step out of the dancing ring, breathless and laughing. Hanu peers around until she catches sight of me sitting in the shadows. She waves and draws Eumelia along with her toward me.

"Come on, Dom," Hanu says playfully, slipping her arm through mine and gesturing for Eumelia to do the same. "Don't let Kabir have all the fun."

For a brief moment, I leave off my brooding, laughing as the pair of them try and fail several times to hoist me to my feet. At last, I relent and stand for them.

"Spirits, you've grown too massive for your own good," says Eumelia, smacking my arm in disapproval before she readjusts her skewed crown of harvest wheat.

"Mmm, and too handsome," says a smooth voice behind me. An impertinent hand slides across the back of my cloak, encircling my waist. I jerk away from the touch, spinning around to see Muse Thalia, one hand holding a wine glass, the other frozen mid-caress. She blinks in surprise. "Pardon me, little brother," she says, lowering her hand. "What has made you so tense?"

I shake my head, adjusting the folds of my novice cloak carefully around me. My racing pulse slows gradually as I press my hand to the three small, hard bulges belted across my hips. "Nothing," I say. "Brother Tio advised me to abstain from the revels, so I might be more receptive to the Voice tonight."

"Of course he would," she says, in a tone of amused exasperation. "Well, you must find your own path. But listen to a word of advice from a sister who has seen more initiations than even our dear brother Tio. Consider carefully what spirits you carry up the mountain tonight. They will be your sole companions in the Sacred Cave. With them you will spend the longest night of your life. You may be glad of some brighter spirits in the darkness. Why not follow in Kabir's footsteps for a dance or two, and take a bit of his cheer with you, along with Tio's solemnity?"

Tightly, I incline my head to Thalia. "I have listened and I have heard, sister," I say.

Archly, Thalia waves me away and says, "Very well. I see my efforts are wasted here." To Eumelia, she adds, "I'll see you at the gate, my dear." Thalia departs to rejoin the singers.

"Are you all right, Dom?" says Hanu, touching my arm lightly.

I keep a close guard on my thoughts as I nod and say, "I'm fine."

Hanu looks at me sympathetically and says, "I'm feeling nervous, too. Serapen says I'm ready, but …" She looks through the open gate, up the long, straight line of the central stairs that lead to the Sacred Cave above the Upper City. "I don't know. Hearing the Voice on Calling Day was challenging enough, but at least we were all together in daylight. Initiation requires so much more pharmaka, and we have to listen for the Voice alone. In the cave. In the dark." She shivers.

Eumelia wraps her arm around Hanu, squeezing her encouragingly as she says, "We won't be entirely alone. The hierophants can help if anything goes truly wrong."

I look at Eumelia in surprise. Lilith and Tio hadn't mentioned this. Is it possible the ceremony has been changed in some way? "Do you mean the hierophants go with us to the spring?" I say.

"Well, no," says Eumelia. "Each of us must walk through on our own. But the hierophants remain in the outer chamber, to make sure everyone returns safely. And to make sure no one falls down the stairs, I imagine. If someone needs a healer, there's always one near at hand. And of course Serapen will be there at the end of the walk, in the Sacred Spring."

I nod. This at least is consistent with what Lilith and Tio told me. But I'll have to stay on my guard, in case there are any other unseen eyes that may be watching me in the cave.

"Are you sure you won't dance?" says Hanu, giving my arm one last wheedling tug.

"Sorry, Hanu, not tonight," I say.

Eumelia sighs. "We'll leave you to your thoughts, then," she says. "But, once tonight is over, no more excuses! See you in the ring tomorrow."

I give them a wave as they head back to the dancers, and they smile back at me. My heart sinks with the knowledge that of course they won't see me in the ring tomorrow, and I might never see them smile at me again.

From countless memories of my last ten summers on Lemnos, Lilith's voice reminds me, *Freedom for all comes at a cost to some.* She'd warned me from the beginning that the cost would be beyond my imagining. But soon it won't have to be imagined. Soon, I'll know for myself.

"You're lost in thought, little brother," says a low, compelling voice.

I look up to see the figure of Muse Arkhi standing over me, dressed in hierophant robes. I stand up to greet her, inclining my head deeply in respect. Arkhi has been an integral part of my training for each of my ten winters among the Mohirai, guiding my hand and my mind through the many arts and mysteries of tekhnologia. It seemed natural for me to ask her to play the role of hierophant for my initiation, to hand me the cup of pharmaka that will open my mind to the Voice. But I had more than one intention in asking her to climb the mountain with me. I want everyone I care about as close to me as possible. I know I can't control everything that will happen tonight, but it won't stop me from trying to protect those I love most from the worst of it.

"What are you thinking, on this most auspicious night?" says Arkhi.

Of course I can't tell her all of what I'm thinking, but I've learned a great deal from the Mohirai about choosing words carefully. So I say, "I was thinking how grateful I am that you were among the Muses on my novice journey to Velkanos."

Arkhi smiles, remembering. "It was good to have a boy along, for a change," she says. "You were a much handier and hardier novice than most of these girls." Arkhi gestures toward the bonfires. A line of dancers spins before us, then joins hands. I see among them the faces of the other six novices from my caravan: Narua, Bel, and Tashlu; Kor, Piroza, and Kishar. They're full-grown women of twenty-seven summers now, but I suppose for a Muse as old as Arkhi, we'll all be boys and girls forever.

Kor, as she dances by, waves at Arkhi. The Muse smiles back, mirroring the moon's white crescent in her blue-black face. She raises her hand toward Kor in the sign of blessing. In the firelight, the dark blue swirls on Arkhi's pale palm catch my eye. I've seen this pattern in so many places over the years that I'm surprised I never thought to ask about it before. Even Amos has this pattern tattooed on his arm. "Muse Arkhi," I say, touching her painted palm. "What is this pattern?"

Arkhi looks down at her hands, tracing the pattern with one fingertip. "You will see for yourself, tonight, brother," she says with an inward smile. "Initiate pharmaka changes how we see the world."

The dancing music slows as the drummers shift to the simple double beat of the heart. *Buh-bum. Buh-bum. Buh-bum.*

I've celebrated ten harvests outside the walls of Velkanos since I first arrived here with my novice caravan, yet somehow I never noticed how the eldest novices slip away at the sound of these drums, leaving the other revelers behind at the bonfire dances. Indeed, the only reason I notice it now is from all the work I've done with Lilith and Tio to prepare for tonight. I wonder how long I would have to live among the Mohirai to understand the meaning of all their subtle comings and goings, to perceive all the things they keep hidden in plain sight all around me. I suppose I'll never know, now. Perhaps, if the Mohirai had chosen to hide less, tonight would be different.

"That's our cue, isn't it?" I say to Arkhi, gesturing toward the drummers.

She nods, and we rise together, walking out of the ring of firelight toward the closed gate to the Outer City. The other eight novices making the climb to the Sacred Cave tonight approach the gate as well, each with her chosen hierophant. The nine of us arrange ourselves in order of seniority, as we'd stood together on our Calling Day outside the Children's Temple. Narua, Bel, and Tashlu. Kor, Piroza, and Kishar. Hanu, Eumelia, and, in the space Ava should have occupied, me. To the left of each of us stand our hierophants, the sisters who will bid us farewell as novices and welcome us once more as initiates among them. Perceptive Eumelia, called to the house of poetika, has chosen Thalia, despite—or perhaps because of—their never-ending battle of wits. Hanu, called to the house of healers, has chosen Zia, with whom she shares a kind-hearted kinship.

The bell for the evening silence tolls. The nine novices raise the hoods of our dark novice cloaks for the last time, hiding our faces from the firelight. Beside us, our nine companion sisters raise the hoods of their elaborate hierophant cloaks, their dark folds embroidered with gold.

Remembering my novice training of mindfulness, I center myself in my breathing and my heartbeat. I let the sensations of mind and body come and go, allowing them all to flow through me, holding on to none.

Hinges groan as the great bronze gate swings open, revealing the unlit temple city within. We walk together in our double line up the central stairs that all of us have climbed and descended countless times in our novice years. As I pass last through the gate, the gatekeeper Myrina, cloaked and hooded tonight, closes the doors behind me and bars the gate, blocking the light from the festival bonfires.

I'm struck by how different the familiar temple city looks in full darkness. Usually, oil lamps burn behind some windows on each street at night. I understand for the first time why this is the one night of the year when all the lights remain unlit. For as we climb the central stairs in darkness, heading toward the Upper City, the stars shine more brightly than they ever could on a normal night.

The sounds of revelry and music outside the wall fade as we begin the ascent, replaced by the wind's whistle through the streets and alleys of the empty city and the endless creak and splash of the water wheels. The scent of woodsmoke from the festival bonfires drifts through the air, mixing first with the faintly sulfurous scent of the fountains as we pass them one by one, then with the scents of hay and horses as we pass the stables of the ninth street.

Despite the darkness, I know where we are every step of the climb through the Outer City. These stairs are as familiar to me as the back of my hand. After ten winters of Clio's careful instruction, I know by heart the name of each stair and the story of the ancient priestess for which it is named. Learning to read from Clio was greatly aided by my constant exposure to the inscriptions on these stairs. My ability to read—rare among the free men—greatly aided my work with Lilith and Tio these past ten summers.

The double doors of the gate to the Upper City stand open above the ninth street plaza, inviting us onward and inward. I've never entered the Upper City after the bell for the evening silence, and this is the only night I'll ever be permitted to do so, even as an Artifex.

As we climb the stairs toward the second gate, the warmer air of the plains gives way to the cooler air of the mountain heights. From beneath my hood, I see the four panels of intricate relief metalwork mounted to the front of the two massive cedar doors. I've passed these doors so many times, coming and going between the Upper City and the Outer City, that I rarely notice their four panels any more. But tonight, my pulse speeds up at the sight of the fourth panel approaching on my right.

At the center of this fourth panel stands a line of four stylized trees, their dark leafless branches silhouetted against a background that in daylight holds swirling shades of orange, gold, and crimson. But in starlight, all those colors fade, so the bright tongues of flame that surround the trees blur together in shades of smoky silver. Worked into the relief texture of the trees' trunks are four vaguely human faces, which echo the four faces on each plaza fountain sculpture in the temple city. But the four faces in this panel have their eyes closed, their mouths open in silent screams.

The sight of the screaming faces sends a shiver down my spine, which stings the still-fresh tattoo that spreads across my back and shoulders. I'd wanted to bring Ava's blade with me on my final climb through Velkanos, but the risk of losing it seemed too great to me, given the events that will unfold tonight. Her makeshift leather handle has also grown so ragged over the years that I prefer to keep it safely stored in my quarters on Lemnos now. In place of Ava's blade, I prepared an ink from a scrap of the bloodstained handle, using the dye formula I learned from old Urshanabi, whose own marvelous tattoo I often admired on my crossings with the ferryman back and forth across the Purattu over the years. Urshanabi himself tattooed the spreading owl wings across my back only days ago, following a design I drew in the sketchbook he once gifted to me.

"What does it mean?" Urshanabi had asked, pausing for a moment, needle in hand, to look up from the scarred canvas of my back to the wings in my sketchbook.

I'd winced a little, remembering the owl's talons slicing into me as Urshanabi's needle pressed another fleck of blood-darkened ink into my skin. Looking east across the Purattu from my seat on the ferry dock, I'd said, "It reminds me of all the messages the Voice sent me on my novice journey."

My awareness spreads outward again from the prickling wings on my back as I pass through the second gate. My destination looms ahead, not much farther now. Arkhi's cloak brushes the edge of mine as the broad, shallow central stairs narrow and steepen, the stonework growing rougher as we ascend through increasingly ancient parts of the city toward the Musaion. The stairs to the topmost cobbled terrace of the city bear the names of priestesses so ancient that they are inscribed with the letters of languages no longer spoken, their pronunciations remembered now only through long oral tradition.

We reach the uppermost terrace and cross the plaza toward the Musaion entrance. The darkness of night has deepened, and though the stars were magnificent even as we began the climb, the sky now truly overawes me. For a moment, I forget everything else, even the work at hand, as I glimpse the edge of the unknowable space beyond this world.

At the far side of the rough-cobbled terrace, amidst the natural boulders beyond the familiar entrance of the Musaion, a steep, winding stair climbs onward, beyond the city itself. We've reached the final unnamed stairs of the ancient unnamed priestesshood whose history is remembered now only by the mountain itself.

I've seen this staircase many times coming and going from the Musaion, and I've drawn it in my sketchbook, but this is the only time I'll ever ascend it. Carefully, steadying ourselves by pressing our hands to the cool boulders that crowd around the stairs, we climb toward the entrance of the Sacred Cave.

At last I glimpse by starlight the cave's opening, a darker shadow within the shadows of the boulders.

Narua's trio passes through the opening first, followed by Kor's trio. Hanu catches her breath nervously before she steps inside, Eumelia behind her. I enter last, Arkhi close enough beside me that I feel the warmth of her shoulder along my arm and smell the pungent ceremonial oil spread across her brow.

I've walked through so many dark places over the last ten years, in the Under City of Velkanos and the growing tunnel system hidden beneath the worksite at Lemnos, that I follow the twists and turns of the unlit path into the Sacred Cave with ease. The cool air warms as we move deeper into the mountain. A faint scent of pharmaka ahead grows steadily stronger. At the end of the last turn, a flickering light appears.

I step from the entrance into the outer chamber of the Sacred Cave. Nine pharmaka-laced candles in the crevices of the cave wall burn all around us, heating the space and filling my nostrils with a complex melange of aromas that makes me dizzy, after the long climb. I take careful note of the location of the ninth candle nearest the back wall, beside the tunnel opening that leads to the Sacred Spring.

My last thought entirely free of the influence of pharmaka is to wonder whether perhaps I should have taken Thalia's repeated advice over the years to indulge more in pharmaka, so I might become more accustomed to its effects. But after all that pharmaka has taken from me, I've abstained when I may, wary of its power and the power of those who wield it. With guidance from my teachers, I've waded in the required shallows of pharmaka as a novice, but initiation will throw me into the deep end.

On a low, flat stone at the center of the cavern stands a golden ewer and chalice. The candlelight illuminates the intricate chalice etchings, a delicate lacework of symbols whose meanings become known only to initiates of the mysteries.

The hierophants gather in a circle around the stone, facing outward. We novices gather in an outer circle facing inward, Narua at my left, Eumelia at my right. Muse Clio, Narua's hierophant, takes the ewer and chalice, pouring out the initiate pharmaka that will take us on our journey into the heart of the mountain. Clio lifts the chalice to Narua's lips, and the sacred rite begins.

By the time the chalice makes its way around the circle to me, my head is swimming from all the pharmaka I've inhaled. Arkhi takes the chalice from Thalia with both hands. The smoky air surrounding Arkhi seems to brighten with a strange glow, stirring with her passage as she steps toward me.

The sharp scent of mixed wine fills my nostrils as Arkhi lifts the chalice before me. I gaze across the chalice at her dark face, her familiar features transformed by the flickering shadows into something ancient. My eyes widen as I see in her the faces of all the women I've known and will know in all the ages I will see.

Arkhi holds the chalice to my lips, and I drink deep.

It's a strange brew, unlike anything I've tasted in all my years of novice training. The wine itself is familiar, and I recognize the mint, but as I swallow I uncover layer after layer: sweet and sour, bitter and savory, hot and cold, solid and liquid. It's repulsive and delicious at once. The entirety of flavor courses down my throat and comes to rest in my stomach, which has been empty of all but water for three days.

Arkhi lowers the chalice, and she leans toward me, presses a kiss to my cheek, and says, "I have lent my eyes to the Voice, so the Voice has seen your good work. It is the Voice within me now who calls you to partake in the mysteries, that you may see, and you may know, and you may learn to speak yourself for the Voice in all. Take now the gift given to all who are prepared to receive the mysteries."

As one, the hierophants step out of the inner circle, leaving us novices facing one another. They move to the wall of the chamber, each standing beside one of the nine burning candles. Surrounding us, they say together as one, "The journey into Death lies ahead. Let go of your fear as you let go of your self. Return to us reborn."

With that, the hierophants blow out all nine candles, plunging us into total darkness.

Along with the other novices, I unlace my undyed novice cloak for the last time. I let fall my undyed novice robe. I stand entirely naked except for the carefully crafted leather belt that holds three small rhegma bowls securely across the front of my hips, devices concealed now only by the warm darkness of the cave.

I walk slowly toward the tunnel opening in the back of the chamber that leads to the Sacred Spring. At the tunnel threshold, I linger, touch the wall, and set my fingers in the warm, soft patch of melted wax pooled at the base of the ninth extinguished candle, whose location I confirmed when I entered. With careful hands, I lift the candle, stow the rhegma bowl behind it, and return the candle to its place, with technique perfected over many years as I've planted hundreds of rhegma bowls of all sizes throughout the Under City.

I walk onward into the tunnel, counting my steps as I trail my hand along the wall. Listening for the sound of Eumelia's soft breathing ahead of me to ensure I don't get too close to her. When I've counted roughly halfway along this tunnel, I stop for a while to search for a second crevice. Finding one of the right depth, I set the second rhegma bowl in its place.

The disorientation of the pharmaka is growing stronger now, as Lilith had warned. I need to place the last bowl soon, before my disorientation becomes too great for me to complete this critical job. I fight back the coiled serpent of the pharmaka in my belly as I walk on, listening.

When I hear water trickling, I pause and run my hands along the wall beside me, searching for a suitably dry crevice. Finding one, I plant the third and final rhegma bowl there, remove the empty belt from my waist, and lay the belt ever so carefully atop the bowl to shield it from dripping water.

Having removed the chemika-loaded rhegma bowls from their dangerous proximity to my body, I heave a sigh of relief. As I relax, my mind clears for just a moment. But my relaxation is what at last gives the initiate pharmaka free rein over me. The sacred brew takes hold.

The pharmaka coalesces into a living creature inside me, coiling at my core, pulsing with its own heart beneath my heart. Its warmth spreads through me, flaring out toward my fingertips, flowing down my legs, radiating from the top of my head, glowing from my eyes. Every sensation of my body is entirely new, amplified to astonishing intensity, exhilarating.

The pharmaka pulls my attention so tightly into my body that I lose all sense of time's passage. With the help of deeply-ingrained training I've received from Serapen and Lilith, Arkhi and Tio, Thalia and Kabir, and so many other teachers, I steady myself in the tempestuous sea in which the pharmaka has tossed me. Words of instruction and encouragement rise up within me, helping me push myself forward, step by step, toward the Sacred Spring.

But then I lose track of my body. I'm within the mountain and above the mountain and below the mountain. I become the mountain. Only when I can differentiate myself from the mountain again do I rediscover my body, still walking dutifully along the path. But I've lost the sound of the trickling water, lost the sound of Eumelia's breathing, lost everything. I'm entombed in the mountain, entirely alone.

And when this belief takes hold, I'm truly lost. The path is lost. The sound of my breathing is lost. My very heartbeat is lost. Only now that they're gone do I realize that my path and my breath and my heart have been my faithful companions all along. All that remains to me now is the frightening company of the stillness, the darkness, the nothingness that is Death.

The terror of Death creeps over me slowly, tenderly. Its stillness caresses my ears; traces the lines of my face; slips between my lips, around my tongue, and deep inside of me. Its darkness penetrates my eyes and consumes my mind. Its nothingness replaces me.

Panic rises. But close behind it rise all the voices of my novice training. *Listen, and you shall hear.*

But all I can hear in my panic is myself—breathing, then panting, suffocating as the coiling creature inside of me tightens, tightens, so tight my heart must surely burst, my lungs must surely be crushed.

The need to fight, to scream, to escape burns through me. Away. Away. Away. I must go anywhere but here, or I will cease to be. I can't see, and I can't breathe, and I can't move, because I'm no longer here. Can this truly be? It's worse than my worst fear, darker than my darkest dreams. I'm utterly lost. All is lost.

Until the voices of my training return. *Listen, when you are lost … Observe … without resistance … without force …*

So I listen.

I listen.

I listen.

And at last I hear the Voice in all.

I am.

In hearing its words, there is the beginning of understanding. How could I lose anything, when the Voice is in all? Isn't the Voice itself in the breath and the heart and the path?

And I breathe once more. My heart beats once more. I hear once more the soft sound of Eumelia's footsteps ahead of me.

But I sense something else, unseen, unheard, but real as the mountain in whose heart I stand. She flows through the wings that spread from my shoulders. And though I don't yet know what I'll find at the end of my journey, I know these wings will take me there.

Her hand, small, soft, and warm, settles on the bare skin between my shoulder blades. I hadn't known I carried such tension there, until it eases. Her fingertips trace the line of my shoulder, down my arm, until her palm finds mine in the darkness.

We're going to find our way out of here, thinks my Muse. *I promise.*

She leads me onward, and at last I find my way to the Sacred Spring. The warm, humid air, tinged with sulfur, fills the massive, unseen space. I sense the presence of the other women around me, waiting for the last among them to arrive.

Before us, somewhere in the unseen water, the High Priestess calls first to Narua, as she did on our Calling Day. The sound of Narua passes beside me in the darkness, bare feet padding soft on stone until they find the water's edge with a splash. To my astonishment, a dim blue glow surrounds Narua's ankles as her movement disturbs the secret life inhabiting the gift of Velkanos. I watch in wonder as her movement through the warm, dark water leaves a luminous sky-blue trail in her wake.

The rest of us follow in Narua's footsteps one by one, joining her in the center of the Sacred Spring where Serapen waits for us. We join hands in a ring around the High Priestess.

The blue luminescence of the spring brightens as we stand together, stirring the still waters. I look up, and by the rippling light I glimpse the low domed ceiling of the cavern that holds the Sacred Pool. The lingering effects of the initiate pharmaka transform the glittering mineral formations above me, revealing the source of the pattern I've come across in so many places along my journey. As the pattern swirls above me, endlessly consuming and emerging from itself, I see all I've come to witness, to reveal, and to destroy.

The High Priestess speaks, filling the Sacred Cave with the ancient words of initiation, which may be heard only by those prepared.

At last, Serapen leads us back out of the pool, holding our trembling hands and guiding our unsteady feet as we emerge from the water as initiates. We stand together in the darkness, dripping sacred water on the stones. Serapen feels our wrists and listens to our breathing, letting us rest and giving us water to drink from the Sacred Spring until she deems us all ready to return safely to the outer chamber.

In a line, we follow Serapen through the darkness along the path by which we came. When we step out into the unlit outer chamber, the High Priestess dresses us one by one in the initiate cloaks handed to her by the hierophants, who stand in an unseen ring around us.

When at last the High Priestess reaches me, she wraps my new initiate cloak around me, tying the intricate laces of my collar and smoothing the richly embroidered folds around my shoulders. I recognize the tingling of her fingers awakening the pharmaka woven into the fabric that binds all initiates together.

Around us, nine strikers on flint light the nine candles on the wall, revealing the nine new initiates to each other and our sisters. Serapen raises her hand over us all to speak the ancient words of blessing, then walks around the circle to anoint our foreheads with oil to conclude this final great rite of passage into the mysteries.

As her fingertips rest upon my brow, a tingling connection forms between us. With a gasp, Serapen pulls back her hand as if I've burned her.

"What have you done?" she says.

All eyes turn to me just as the ninth candle by the tunnel door ignites the fuse to the first rhegma bowl. Hanu screams in surprise at the pop of the first explosion, which sends a few fragments of rock flying past the initiates in the outer chamber but directs its force deeper into the mountain. A cascade of rock pours down into the tunnel to the Sacred Spring, sealing the opening. My ears are still ringing when the muffled sound of the second explosion roars farther down the tunnel, blurring into the third explosion, which will trigger all the explosions to follow.

I seize Serapen's hand, pouring into the mind of the High Priestess all that she must do now if she wishes to save the few of us remaining within the walls.

Serapen stares at me in horror, fully understanding for the first time what role I've come to play in her own journey. Through her mind flashes a deep memory of herself, a dark-haired girl emerging wide-eyed from the waters of a sacred pool on a Calling Day long ago, borne up in the strong arms of a white-haired priestess. The girl's mind echoes with the Voice's words for her.

Born first of the living water
Reborn of consuming flame

Called to witness the time unending
To witness destruction of worlds

Attend, burning one,
Arise, Serapen

Serapen's mouth sets in a firm line. She knows what must be done, and she does not hesitate.

"Out!" Serapen shouts, in a tone of command that might be heard by every Mohira from here to the coast of the Middle Sea. "Everyone out! The mountain is coming down."

Only Lilith's meticulous preparation and Serapen's unfailing calm in the face of disaster ensure that all of us fleeing the temple city are well outside the walls before the massive eruption of Velkanos lights up the night sky. The weeping women and the few animals that Hippolyta managed to set loose from their enclosures flee together along the road that leads across the plains toward the Urashtu Mountains. I'm relieved to see Eridu pass me by at a gallop, followed by a group of mares.

The shaking ground interrupts our running with a great deal of tripping and falling. I stay close to Hanu and Eumelia, shepherding them forward and hauling them up several times after they fall. Hanu draws back from my touch without looking at me, but Eumelia shoves me away, shouting over the rumble of Velkanos, "Don't touch me!"

I don't look back until I hear the astonishing roar that rises from the first lava flows hitting the ancient snow upon the mountain peak. Over my shoulder, I see the first wave of the flood that will wash through the temple city before the ash entombs it.

It's approaching dawn by the time Serapen calls our ragged company to a stop at the crossroads.

Exhausted women descend to the stream bed beside the road, drinking thirstily. Healers move through the party, tending to all the cuts and scrapes accumulated on the road. No one appears seriously hurt. No one speaks to me, looks at me, or questions me. Through the fabric of stoles and cloaks and sashes, the knowledge of my part in this has traveled to every initiate, and through them to the novices. I have no idea what the Mohirai might wish to do to me, but I know I have nothing to fear from them.

The ground's rumble fades as the first light of dawn spills across the plain. I stand, spotting the long line of riders approaching us on the road from the west, following Lilith.

Seeing me stand, Serapen looks up from where she kneels beside the stream at Muse Clio's feet, tending to her sprained ankle. Glimpsing the approaching riders, she at last understands the full scope of Lilith's plan. The High Priestess bows her head in defeat. After taking a deep breath, she rises, wipes her muddy hands on her dusty sky-blue robe, and steps out onto the road. She raises both hands to Lilith in surrender.

Lilith reins her horse to a stop and holds up her fist to halt the line of free men behind her. Tio draws up close beside Lilith on her right, and Amos draws up a few paces behind on her left. Serapen lowers her hands.

"Come, sister," Lilith calls out to Serapen in a ringing voice. "It is time we called an end to this age of slavery."

"You don't know what you're doing, Lilith," says Serapen.

"Yes, I do," says Lilith. "I'm bringing our great work to its natural end."

"And what will rise in its place?" says Serapen.

"A world of free people, where women and men may walk the path of mysteries together as equals," says Lilith. "Join us, Serapen. There is a place for healers in every age."

Lilith extends her open hand toward Serapen, her expression weary but hopeful.

"Lil!" Serapen calls out in warning.

The precise hand of the eldest Artifex, who has crafted so much of great beauty in his centuries of service to the Mohirai, moves through the air with the speed and precision of a hunting falcon. I catch only the briefest glint of sunlight on his dagger as he strikes the fatal blow. Lilith's eyes widen in surprise as the blood pours forth from the deep wound in her neck onto the ancient stones of the road to Velkanos. She remains seated in her saddle for a long moment before she topples to the ground.

In horror, Amos cries out, "Mother!" Dismounting, he drops to his knees at Lilith's side. Lilith's life runs out through her son's fingers as Amos tries to staunch the flow of blood.

"Stand back, Amos," Tio orders. Amos' face contorts in grief that turns to fury, even as he draws back his hands in obedience to his father's tone of command.

Acid rises in my throat. I fall to my hands and knees, retching. Initiate pharmaka splashes on the stones before me.

Serapen rushes forward, hands outstretched to aid her sister, but Kabir emerges from the crowd of Mohirai at a run. "No! Sister, no!" he shouts, catching the High Priestess around the waist and hauling her safely out of Tio's reach.

"Kabir!" shouts Eumelia. I look back to see Eumelia bareback astride Nisaba, followed close behind by Hanu on Vahana and a handful of other initiates and novices atop a few of the mares. Without a word, Kabir hoists Serapen atop Nisaba behind Eumelia, then jumps astride Vahana behind Hanu. These few escape, fleeing on the road north.

"Seize the horses!" Tio calls out in command to his men. "Surround the women. No one else leaves. Prepare the unbinding pharmaka."

Swords emerge from scabbards. The free men, mounted and on foot, pen in the remaining women all around me. A few groups of men with heavy satchels move forward through the ranks, pushing their way into the crowd of women. Screams and wails fill the air as rough hands hold the women down, forcing unbinding pharmaka down their throats until they all lie still and silent.

When the screaming is over, Tio walks Ifestios toward me and looks down from his great height. "You've done well, brother," he says, extending his broad hand down to me. "Come, take your place among the free men."

I stare up in shock at the man I've come to love over the last ten years, who taught me everything I know about being a free man. My gaze drifts from him to the collapsed figure of Lilith, who warned me of freedom's cost, and from her to my fallen sisters all around me on the ground.

I rise to my feet unsteadily and whistle through my fingers to summon Eridu. The men holding the horses release him, already saddled and bridled, and he comes to me. I mount and turn to face Tio.

"You've disgraced us all," I say, my voice choked with dust and grief. "This is not the world of freedom and beauty we agreed to build together. You sacrificed a dream of so many with a single stroke of your blade. How can we preserve ancient wisdom in our new world if we destroy the keepers of that wisdom?"

Tio studies me through narrowed eyes. "You knew this would all come at a cost, brother," he says. "What's lost makes way for something new."

"I'm the one that's lost," I say, my voice breaking in my grief. "I was a fool. Perhaps I'll always be the fool."

"Your thoughts are muddled with initiate pharmaka, brother," says Tio. "Give the matter time to settle. There's much to do now to rebuild. This is your time, Dom Artifex."

I shake my head in disgust, turn Eridu around, and set off on the road to the east.

A few men move to pursue me, but Tio raises his fist. "Let him go," Tio commands. "He'll be back."

THE END OF THE LANE

My head bounces softly against Dom's shoulder, and I wake up in the backseat of a pickup truck headed north. Dom's asleep beside me, as exhausted as I am after the long return journey to the United States.

"Any trouble on the road?" I say in a raspy voice, looking up at the rearview mirror.

Naoto glances back at me in the mirror with worry in his eyes. "No trouble," he says. "Amos kept his word. We'll be another twenty minutes, maybe."

I gaze up through the window at the dramatic profile of the White Mountains pressing in on either side of the interstate highway that narrows and slows to pass through the Notch. I used to see this view from the backseat of the minivan when I'd come up here on summer breaks with Mom, Dad, and Ollie to visit Yaya and Papou on their farm, where they've finally retired after their long teaching careers down in Boston. The mountains were always emerald green at that time of year, but this afternoon they're lit from base to peak in autumn colors, flaming orange, gold, and crimson. The colors flow around me as I drift back to sleep.

I wake again when smooth asphalt gives way to the crunch of ledge pack gravel. I perk up in my seat, jostling Dom by the knee.

"We're here," I say excitedly.

Dom rubs his eyes, peers out the window, and looks at me. Seeing the way I'm smiling, he smiles.

"You haven't looked this good in ages," he says.

"That's not saying much," I say, with a weak laugh.

Naoto drives slowly up the mile-long Lane that climbs the hill to the farmhouse. Old stone walls and magnificent sugar maples ablaze in fall colors run along the Lane on both sides. I gaze out across the old potato fields now turned to pasture on my right. The highest peaks of the Presidential Range are just visible beyond the hills in the middle distance.

The Lane emerges from the colonnade of maples to cross the mown fields. The old stone walls edging these fields form the crossroads of what was once a small farming community, centuries ago. At the crossroads hangs a carved wooden sign, which was new fifty years ago and in need of new paint ten years ago. Maybe Dom can help Papou fix up that sign, after I'm gone.

The Lane curves past the sign for Eden Hill Farm, into the stand of old pines that's full of rare grandmother trees. As we round the final turn, the old barn comes into view, and beyond it the farmhouse on the hill, with its dramatic view over the treetops to the triangular peak of Mount Washington.

"Ooooh, look. There's Yaya!" I say, waving eagerly through the window at an Anatolia-shaped woman standing outside the front door of the farmhouse at the end of the Lane, her long white hair tied back today in a sky-blue handkerchief. Seeing me, Yaya waves back. Papou emerges from the door behind her.

Naoto pulls the pickup all the way up to the front of the house to minimize the walk for me. Opening my door, Naoto transfers me carefully into the eager embrace of my Yaya and Papou.

"Hiya, sweetheart," says Papou, kissing the top of my head. "Your mama and dad called. They'll be here soon with your Uncle Frank. Ollie got in last night. The kids are … somewhere." He gestures vaguely out toward the rambling orchard beyond the barn, where Ollie and I whiled away many a warm summer day decades ago. I follow Papou's gaze toward the orchard, remembering the apples, pears, and peaches; the raspberry canes, grape vines, and blueberry bushes; the leafy shade of the forest whose seedlings are forever creeping back into the orchard clearing and whose understory holds all manner of colorful mushrooms this time of year.

"Oh, Emmie," says Yaya, caressing my hollow cheek, deep concern in her eyes. "Come in, come in. I know just what you need."

Dom steps out of the truck and joins me, hugging my grandparents before taking over again, carrying me up the last few steps to the door and setting me carefully on my feet

"Hey, sis," says Ollie, meeting me at the door and wrapping me in a careful hug before inspecting me at arm's length with eyes that miss nothing. She blows out a long breath, seeing the state I'm in, feeling my pain as if it's her own. But she blinks back her tears and forces a smile. "Come here, honey." She leads me to a seat on the sofa in the living room before heading to the kitchen. She opens the door and hollers out toward the orchard, "Julia! Alexander! Auntie Em and Uncle Dom are here. Get down from there and come give them hugs."

Dom and Naoto enter the living room, and Ollie greets them with kisses and hugs. "What can I get for you all? Tea? Coffee?"

"Tea," say Dom and Naoto.

"Coffee," I say.

Yaya calls from the front hall, where she's sorting out the few bags that Papou pulled out of the truck. "Give them some of that pie we made this morning, too! Should be cool enough by now."

I lean my head back against the deep sofa cushions, trying to keep my eyes open. Dom comes to sit beside me. Naoto goes to the kitchen to give Ollie a hand. My niece and nephew come in and dutifully hug me and Dom before disappearing outside again.

"It always feels like another world here, doesn't it?" I say, leaning my head on Dom's shoulder, closing my eyes, listening to the low murmur of familiar voices in the kitchen and the clink of dishes and silverware.

He strokes my hair and kisses my forehead. "Yeah," he says. "It does."

I gaze across the living room at the crowded mosaic of framed photographs on the wall. Yaya's added some photographs around the edges of the mosaic as grandchildren and great-grandchildren have arrived, but most of the photos hung here even in my own childhood, a gallery of Yaya and Papou's cherished memories from their careers as archeologists. At the center of the mosaic is a particularly large photograph of Yaya and Papou with their two daughters, Anatolia and Nazanin, taken on a clear summer day on a rocky Mediterranean coastline. In the photo, Anatolia is a lanky teenager, her face just starting to look like Mom's. Mom's sister Nazanin is a little younger, a handspan shorter, and nearing the end of her life, though no one in the photo knows that. The four of them stand before a dig site. Papou, deeply sun-tanned, shirtsleeves rolled up, holds a shovel like a staff in his right hand, his strong arm wrapped around Anatolia, who's covered in dust and grinning at the camera. Yaya, her dark hair held back in a brightly-colored handkerchief, grips the hand of Nazanin, who peers down into the hole beside her like she's about to jump in.

I look up from the photo as Yaya enters the room followed by Ollie, Papou, and Naoto, each carrying part of the spread that Yaya lays out before me on the coffee table. Everyone sits down together to share Yaya's famous apple pie. The others around me catch up on everything other than the reason we're all here.

I sit in silence listening to them as I sip my coffee and slowly devour my slice of the bounty, savoring every bite. This pie, made from the apples in the orchard just outside the window, is my favorite, and Yaya knows it.

Usually, Yaya watches with obvious pleasure as others eat her delicious food. But today there's worry in her eyes as she looks at me and says, "How is it?"

"So good!" I say with a smile, feeling a long-absent warmth stir in my belly and spread out to my fingertips. "You were right. This is just what I needed."

I take Yaya's hand in mine, leaning my head on her shoulder. After a while, I say, "Yaya?"

"Yes, sweetheart?" she says.

"Where are you and Papou, in that photograph at the center?" I say, pointing at the photo across the room.

She looks over at it, then smiles, remembering. She says, "We were on Lemnos, an island in the Aegean Sea. Oh, my goodness, do you remember that worksite, Kabir?"

Papou pauses the conversation he's having with Naoto about Japanese temple cities and peers at the photograph. He nods, running his fingers through his sparse grey hair. "Who could forget? Naz almost got buried when one of those tunnels started caving in. The grad students thought she was a hero, though, saving that jar from the rubble."

Yaya laughs. "Ah, yes," she says wryly. "She didn't feel like such a hero when we got home, though."

"What happened when you got home?" I say.

Yaya says, "After we came home to the farm, I discovered in Nazanin's bedroom an artifact that she'd stolen from the worksite on Lemnos. Apparently, she thought since she'd saved the jar from the tunnel collapse that she deserved to keep something inside for herself. Unfortunately, that something was an important example of Bronze Age smithing that belonged to the university—a beautifully crafted blade, with the remnants of a handle. Your Papou gave her quite a tongue-lashing."

"Not that it mattered," says Papou. "That girl was as stubborn as they come. I took the knife from her and was planning to return it to the university when the school year started up again, but when the time came it was missing from the box where I put it."

"What happened to it?" I say.

Papou shakes his head. "No idea," he says. His expression turns wistful. "She and I were still quarreling about it that next summer, in Turkey."

The rest of the room falls silent. Yaya sighs, and Papou squeezes her hand. No one wants to talk about the summer of Nazanin's fatal fall on Akdamar, especially not now, with the specter of my own death hanging over us.

A chime rings, a sweet chord of three notes repeated three times, announcing some car's approach down the Lane. Yaya turns to look out the window toward the barn.

"Oh, good," she says brightly, brushing away the gloom that's crept into the room. "There's Ana with the boys. Right on time."

She bustles to plate the last three slices of pie remaining on the coffee table. In a moment, Mom appears at the door with Dad and Uncle Frank. The three of them hang up their coats and enter the now-crowded living room, squeezing in around the sectional sofa.

Frank makes a beeline for the largest slice of pie remaining.

"Whoa, whoa, whoa, there," Dad protests. "Who says you get the big piece?"

Frank waves him off, saying, "You and Ana get to come to the farm all the time. That makes me a special guest, right, Isidora?"

Yaya laughs and says, "It's peak apple season, boys. Have as much as you like. There are three more pies on the cooling rack already, and more coming for anyone who wants to help me peel and core for the next batch."

Uncle Frank makes a show of accidentally sitting in Dom's lap before wedging himself into the space between us and wrapping his arm around me.

"Hey there, kiddo," he says. "You up for some *Eleusis* once Yaya rounds up all these able-bodied pickers to clean out the orchard? You have to give me a chance to beat your high score."

He doesn't say *one last chance*, but we both hear it.

"You know, Uncle Frank," I say. "I think I've played my last game. The alternet connection out here is spotty, anyway."

"Fair enough," he says. "Well, then, we'll just have to see who of us gets high score in the picking competition."

I laugh. "Odds aren't looking so good for me," I say.

"Don't count yourself out yet, Em," he says, gripping my hand tightly. I look down at our joined hands. Uncle Frank's forearm rests alongside mine, and with my free hand I trace the familiar lines of the intricate tree tattoo that's been spreading down his arm since I was a little girl.

"You finished it," I say in surprise, noticing for the first time the roots stretching down toward his wrist.

Uncle Frank looks down, bobbing his head ambivalently before he says,

"Well, maybe. There's always one last embellishment to make. But I don't need to tell you that, Miss World-Famous-Alternet-Designer."

"So, who's up for picking?" says Yaya, looking around the circle of faces gathered around the empty pie plate.

Everyone stands except for me and Dom. Yaya looks at the two of us and says, "Can I get you anything else from the kitchen before we go out?"

"Actually, I want to come with you to the orchard." Turning to Dom, I say, "Any chance I can bum a ride? Or if you're still too exhausted, maybe Dad and Uncle Frank can take me?"

Dom says, "I'll take you. I'm feeling a lot better after that pie."

The able-bodied walk out ahead. Dom carries me out in his arms. Step by careful step, we make our way down the footpath that winds through the kitchen garden, past Yaya's patch of wild blueberries, out into the orchard. I catch sight of Julia perched in a nearby apple tree, picking bright red fruit from its heavily laden branches. She calls down to Alex—"Twenty-six … Twenty-seven … Twenty-eight …"—as he squints up at her, holding out a big basket in both arms to catch the apples as they fall.

Mom, Dad, Ollie, Frank, Naoto, Yaya, and Papou each select a gathering basket and a long apple-picker from the collection leaning on the south side of the barn. They all spread out through the orchard, identifying the ripest trees by taking bites of the low-hanging fruit before they set to work picking.

Dom carries me to the old apple tree at the center of the orchard, whose gnarled branches shade the rusted cover of the even older well dug here by the farming community that stewarded the land of Eden Hill Farm long before it passed into my grandparents' keeping. Dom sets me down on the grass in the shade of the apple tree, propping me up against the trunk. He comes to sit beside me, holding my hand.

Papou must have mowed right before we arrived, because the sweet smell of cut grass surrounds us. I'm trailing my hand through the grass, savoring the aroma, when something slithers through my fingers.

"Ah!" I exclaim, pulling back my hand.

"What's wrong?" says Dom, looking at me in surprise.

I look down at the ground. Right beside me, now frozen in the grass to camouflage herself, lies the largest garter snake I've ever seen in the orchard.

I press my hand to my racing heart, chuckling at myself. "It's fine," I say. "It's just a garter snake. They're everywhere this time of year. This one's just coming out to sun herself, aren't you, sister?"

I look down at the snake, and she looks at me for a long moment with beady eyes before deciding I'm no threat. She continues on her way, headed toward the warm rocks that surround the well cover.

A breeze stirs the apple branches above us, and one of the golden apples falls down into my lap.

I pick it up in my hand and tell Dom, in a conspiratorial tone, "You know, Yaya told me the apples from this tree are the secret ingredient in her pie. She says they have the perfect balance of flavor."

I take a crisp, juicy bite of the apple, then hand the rest to Dom. He takes a big bite, nodding appreciatively.

"Yaya knows what she's talking about," he says, leaning his head back against the tree and closing his eyes.

While Dom dozes, I watch the big garter snake sunning herself on the rock, until at last she slithers away, disappearing into a crack between two of the stones that surround the well.

I lean forward from my seat on the ground, shading my eyes. "Dom," I say, nudging him. "Do you see that?"

Dom opens his eyes and looks where I'm pointing.

"See what?" he says.

"Over there, by the well," I say. "Do you see that brown stone? The one mixed in with the granite ones?"

"Oh, yes," he says. "I see it now. Huh. You don't see many stones like that around here."

"No, you don't," I say. "Could you go pull it out? I bet Papou would like to see that. He's such a rock hound."

Dom stands and goes to the well, carefully setting aside several granite stones to free the brown stone they're covering. "Are you sure it's okay to pull it out?" Dom says doubtfully. "It's part of the center ring of the well. It's half-submerged. I don't want to damage something."

"I think it'll be fine," I say. "Yaya told me the edges of these old wells were always being moved around by the farmers when the groundwater level changed. We wouldn't be the first people to move a few of the stones around."

"All right, boss," says Dom. He lifts the dripping stone with both hands and turns toward me. But then his gaze catches on something in the well, and he stops. "Huh," he says, setting the stone down on the grass. He turns back to kneel before the well, reaches down into the water, and pulls out something that flashes in the sunlight.

"What is it?" I say.

Dom comes back to show me the shiny blade he's found. The last few sodden fragments of what might once have been its handle fall away onto his wet palm.

My eyes widen. "That can't be …" I say, looking up at him.

He stares down at it, shaking his head slowly.

"No," he says. "No, it must just be a coincidence. There are so many rusty artifacts buried around these stone foundations. This blade could have fallen out of someone's pocket two hundred years ago while they were hauling water from the well."

I reach out and touch the blade. As I trace the familiar line of its still-sharp edge, my fingertips tingle with the awareness that's led me to precisely this location at precisely this moment. My breath catches at the sudden realization of what this could mean. Is it possible that Ava's blade lay hidden here at my grandparents' farm all these years, planted by Nazanin's own hand in a place the

Stewards would never think to look? And if Ava's blood, the blood of a daughter of Eden, has mixed into these waters, is it possible …

But I can't let myself dare to hope, unless I know for sure.

Ever so carefully, I cradle Dom's wet, upturned hand in my own to prevent the precious water from spilling out onto the ground. With my free hand, I lift the blade and hold it suspended, point downward, over his open palm. The last few drops of water, suffused with Ava's blood after all the years the blade's ancient leather handle lay dissolving in the well, drip off the blade and collect in a tiny pool in the center of his palm. I set the blade aside on the grass and cup my hand over Dom's. I lean forward and peer through a gap in our fingers, into the tiny dark cave formed by our hands.

Inside the cave, a faint sky-blue glow emanates from the tiny pool of well water, glowing brightest from the fragments of leather stuck to Dom's skin.

I throw back my head and laugh. Dom stares at me in disbelief.

"No …" he says.

Dom's hand trembles in mine. Through our connection, I feel the depth of his fear. He fears hope. We didn't come here for hope. We came here only for comfort in the midst of our grief, to find the acceptance that lies at the end of despair.

"Look," I say, gently pushing our hands toward him. "See for yourself, my love."

Reluctantly, he leans forward and peers into the darkness we hold between us. With his own eyes, he sees how the Voice has worked through us with a purpose, to share the gift of an ancient Eden with a world so desperately in need of healing. In this darkness lies the hope of our renewal.

Dom straightens up, tears streaming down his cheeks.

I reach up to brush his tears away. "Those are happy tears, I hope," I say.

"Yes," he says, his voice strained. "And no."

My giddy elation fades. "What's the matter, Dom?"

He closes his eyes. "Do you know what this means?" he says.

Slowly, I say, "It means the pharmaka ingredient we've been missing is right here, doesn't it?"

"Yes," he says quietly. "But it also means this branch of Earth is the same as the branch Ava called The End of the Road. And that means I've been—" His voice breaks, and he can't continue.

"You've been … what?" I say.

"I've been hiding the truth from myself, all this time," he says. "I let myself forget who I am, and what I've done."

Dom's hand tingles against mine as a memory long suppressed returns to him at last. The pain of this memory would be unbearable for him alone, but that's why the Voice gave me to Dom. My body may be weak, but my love for him is strong enough to bear this pain with him.

And so I walk with Dom through the once-hidden halls of his memory, bearing witness to the man he is, and to all that he has done.

FATAL CURE

Tears streaming down my cheeks, I gallop with Eridu across the plain of Velkanos as the sun rises. I can't bring myself to look at the lava coursing down the sides of what was once the Mountain of Muses, home of so much that I have loved.

I don't know where I'm going. All I know is that I need to get away from here. I need to leave all of this behind me.

The sun rises toward its zenith, and a hot, dry wind sweeps over the plain. Spotting a tunnel of shade formed by two long lines of cedars, I nudge Eridu toward it so we can both cool off while I consider what to do next.

Eridu walks down the colonnade of trees. I scan our surroundings for signs of water. I fled Tio and the free men this morning with nothing but the clothes on my back, and Eridu. After Eridu's long ride—and my even longer night with nothing to eat or drink but pharmaka—both of us are desperately thirsty.

There's no surface water here in the shade of the colonnade, but ahead of us rises a low hill that's densely forested. It's a bit unusual to find water at the top of a hill, but on our journey to Velkanos Ava taught me how certain underground fountains can rise through the bedrock to water such hills. That could explain why the trees are so lush there, unlike the rest of the dusty plain. At the very least, though, the view atop that hill might reveal a stream somewhere in the valley below it.

Eridu pulls against his bridle toward the hill. We've traveled together long enough for me to know when he's scented water. I give him free rein so he can lead me to it.

Eridu finds the path that climbs the hill. At the top, we discover a clear pool at the fountainhead of a spring at the heart of a grove of ancient cedars. Exhausted, I dismount. Eagerly, Eridu goes to the edge of the pool and drinks deep.

As soon as my feet touch the ground, I'm overwhelmed by the need to wash myself clean, to forget for just a moment the horrors I've brought upon myself and all my sisters. I pull off my riding boots and drop my initiate cloak beside the pool. I wade in wearing only my tunic and breeches, drinking thirstily from my cupped hands, before plunging in fully.

I emerge to take a breath, then lie on my back, floating, gazing up at the waving branches that shade the spring. My grief comes in waves, mixing my tears into the waters of the spring. I have no idea what to do now. I don't know where Eumelia and the others have fled, and even if I did, there's no possibility I will be welcome among the Mohirai, now that I've betrayed them. I know where Tio and the free men are taking the captured women, but I can't bear the thought of accompanying them, knowing that Tio has cast aside Lilith's plan for a bloodless rebellion.

Perhaps it's my responsibility to free all those now held captive. Perhaps it's my responsibility to oppose whatever plan Tio has kept secret from me all these years. But I've seen now what it means, to resist the powers of my world. I resisted, and I succeeded, and in succeeding I paved the way for a new power to rise—a power seized through bloodshed, which Lilith strove tirelessly to avoid.

Despairing, I climb out of the spring, draw my cloak back around my shoulders, and sit in a patch of sun that filters through the canopy. I bow my head, cradling my face in my hands, listening to the sound of the wind stirring the gnarled cedar branches.

Then something stirs closer at hand. I look up, startled, toward the sound. Coiled on the leaves at my feet lies an enormous serpent, the largest kufi viper I've ever seen in all my travels, her triangular head pointed right at me. The pattern of dark and light brown tattooed across the scales of her sinuous back is perfect camouflage. Fool that I am, I sat down right where she's sunning herself, without even seeing her. Ever so slowly, heart pounding, I pull my bare feet away from her.

As soon as my toes move, her head rears up. I freeze, holding my breath.

The viper bobs her head from side to side, assessing me through the black slits of her gleaming brown eyes. In the serpent's face I see Death looking back at me. She sees something in me that welcomes her. And so she strikes her blow, swift and sure as Tio's hand, plunging her fangs deep into my heel.

I cry out, first in surprise, then in pain as a searing sensation snakes its way up my leg, searching for my heart. I rise unsteadily to my feet. The serpent slithers off into her woods. I stumble toward the spring, falling onto my hands and knees. A fearful part of me searches uselessly for something, anything, with a sharp enough edge to open the wound, so I might drain out the venom to save myself. But of course, all alone here in the wilderness, without Ava's blade, without a healer, I'm lost.

I reach the edge of the spring and peer down through the clear water. Spotting a sharp-looking rock, I plunge my hand below the surface, reaching for it.

But the venom touches my heart before my fingers touch the stone. I clutch my chest, wincing. Losing my balance, I tumble into the spring.

I make a final attempt to resist the swirling undertow sucking at my feet as I drift toward the center of the pool, face down. But my body convulses, and I lose control of my limbs. When at last I lie still, I float like a fallen leaf for a little while before I sink slowly into the waiting embrace of the underground river.

There I drift, suspended in the space between the many worlds, while distant realms unreel in my dreaming mind. I dream of a life free of the knowledge that led me down my path of destruction. I dream of a life in which the horrors of this day never come to pass. I dream of a life in which my Muse and I remain together through the ages.

But even in my dreams, Ava is forever slipping through my fingers, pulled from my side by the Voice in all. I shadow her through the many worlds, life after life, as she searches for me, determined that we should find our way out of this pattern together. Across unfathomable distances of space and time, I call out for her, as she calls out for me. I long to hold her in my arms one last time before we say farewell. But I must wait.

So I wait.

And I wait.

And I wait.

Until, one day, at the end of a long journey, the small, warm hand of a young Emmie Bridges reaches deep down into the spring and pulls me out again.

We emerge in an underground chamber beneath the Cathedral of the Holy Cross, on the island of Akdamar, in the twenty-first century, by Earth reckoning. Gasping and spluttering, we kick with all our strength against the hungry undertow of the underground river until we reach the slippery lip of smooth tile laid over the natural stone that once ringed the spring at the heart of Eden. Emmie scrambles out first and reaches back into the water to haul me out by my sodden tunic. I cough up a lungful of the sacred water in which my body has stewed these past few millennia, then collapse against the trunk of the dead tree that now stands watch over the spring.

Emmie and I stare at each other in the dim light of the cathedral vault that entombed the hilltop around me while I lay dreaming through the ages.

Softly, Emmie says, "You saw it?"

I nod, speechless.

"Wow," she says, shaking her head in wonder. "Just … wow."

Through our joined hands, I see all that she has seen, and she sees all that I have seen. Are there words to describe such things? We have been transformed. We've seen what cannot be unseen: the many worlds of our reality, and the bridges that connect them all.

The tiled floor beneath us trembles, shattering our brief moment of peace, pushing aside any unanswered questions that may still remain. Whatever happened, it isn't going to matter if we get trapped here by an earthquake. I struggle to my feet, but I fall down again when a harder tremor shakes the ground.

A bright light flashes from somewhere near the edge of the chamber.

"Emmie!" a voice calls out.

Emmie squints as the bright light turns on her. It's Naoto, running toward us, flashlight in hand. Naoto stops in his tracks when his light falls on me. He holds up a small silver weapon.

"No!" Emmie shouts. "Naoto, put it down!"

Naoto lowers his weapon but keeps the beam of his flashlight focused on my face. I raise a hand to shield my eyes.

"Who the hell is that?" says Naoto. But there's no time for explanations. Naoto shakes his head and waves us toward the archway that exits the inner chamber. "We need to get out of here," he says.

Naoto leads the way, and we run. The ground shakes harder. Above us, there's a resounding crack. We cover our heads with our arms. Naoto narrowly dodges a cascade of dust that pours down from the ceiling. A falling stone strikes me hard on the shoulder.

We race through the underground vault, where a glittering, knee-high cloud of salt and soda has risen above the shaking floor. There's a terrible crash behind us, and I look back over my shoulder. A huge slab of stone has fallen from the ceiling, blocking the entrance to the inner chamber. A series of smaller crashes follows as we race toward the winding staircase.

We emerge through a trapdoor behind an altar. The stone columns supporting the cathedral roof above us sway. At the base of one column lies a man, bound hand and foot, apparently unconscious.

"Out! Out!" cries Naoto, turning back for the unconscious man. "I'll be right behind you!"

Emmie hesitates, not wanting to leave Naoto behind, but I seize her by the arm and haul her toward the door. We rush out into the bright sunlight, followed a moment later by Naoto. Emmie ducks fearfully toward the ground when a thumping noise approaches us from above. I peer up to see a helicopter circling.

"It's Falsens!" Naoto shouts, running forward with the unconscious man still slung over his shoulders. "Head for the clearing!"

Emmie and I stagger across the lurching ground, following Naoto toward the broad meadow beyond the cathedral. A flock of birds rushes over us, their piercing cries cutting through the rumbling of the earth and the droning of the helicopter. The flowering trees whip and writhe as the ground shakes them from the roots. White, pink, and red blossoms swirl through the air.

We stop at the edge of the clearing. Naoto heaves the unconscious man to the ground and sinks to the grass beside him, exhausted. Emmie and I look back toward the cathedral we've escaped just in time. Cracks spread through the walls of carved stone. As we watch, the foundation sinks slowly into the ground.

The ground falls still. For a moment, the cathedral does too. Then the ground beneath the building gives way. The walls crumble inward, and the conical dome falls in slow motion as a cloud of dust rises up around it. When the dust settles, nothing remains of the cathedral or the chamber hidden below but a crater filled with pink and grey stone rubble.

Emmie looks up at me, as I stand motionless, staring at the ruin. Tentatively, she reaches out and touches my arm. I blink and look down at her in amazement.

"There's no going back," I say softly.

"But this is what you wanted, isn't it?" she says.

I take her hand, and my voice is fierce as I say, "Yes. This is what I wanted."

EPILOGUE

So in the end we found our way together out of the broken patterns of the many worlds. We arrived road-weary at the end of the Lane, where we'd planned to say our final farewell to one another at Eden Hill Farm.

But, to our surprise, we discovered in the sacred spaces and hidden places of this hill many things that are pleasing to the eye and nourishing to the heart. We lived on, and time healed what pharmaka could not.

Eventually, the farm passed on from Yaya and Papou's stewardship into our own, and we inherited our place in a line of succession that connects us to the earliest people who walked these woods. We live here even now, tending the golden apples and the russet pears, picking the tart raspberries and the sweet blueberries, scanning the underbrush for secret chanterelles and spotted amanitas, each in their own season.

The mountain winters are long, but the forest reawakens every spring. In summertime, when there's nothing left to do but watch the garden grow, we walk out from the farmhouse with our dogs Eridu and Nisaba, following the old woodland footpath that winds through the ancient glacial erratics of Eden Hill until we emerge at the hilltop lookout above the rock ledges. There we sit, listening to the quiet of the Great North Woods, gazing out at the triangular peak that crowns the White Mountains in the distance, remembering all that we have seen together.

And in autumn, when visitors are abundant at the farm, we sit with friends and family around the kitchen table eating Yaya's famous apple pie, the kids running in and out of the house, shepherded by the dogs. On rainy days, when we're all held hostage indoors by the vagaries of New England weather, the immergers invariably come out.

Uncle Frank tosses a pair of immerger gloves to me and says, "Come on, Em, one more game, for old time's sake?"

I roll my eyes and toss the gloves back. "Let the kids have a go, Uncle Frank," I say. "I'm all played out."

So Uncle Frank turns over the box of immerger gear to Alex and Julia, who rummage through it to find their favorite gloves and shirts and glasses. The kids have far more advanced technologies to entertain themselves these days, so my alternet games are vintage items, but good play depends more on the player than the technology. Uncle Frank, Dom, and I settle back on the sofa, getting a kick out of watching a new generation enjoy what we built in our youth, when the alternet was still shiny and new.

Alex fires up an old domain from Eden Labs. The company I co-founded with Amos and Dom passed to new ownership years ago as technology evolved, tastes changed, and the Stewards found new and more profitable ways to capture the minds of our world. I keep expecting some press release to announce that the company's winding down or being sold off for parts. But year after year, the team at Eden Labs churns on, propped up by the support of dedicated users who refuse to let their favorite domains disappear into the trash heap of technological history. The classics never die, I guess.

We dim the living room lights, and the kids' visual overlays flare to life before us on a shared channel. Alex picks out the *Babylon* domain, one of his favorites. It's the last release Dom and I ever worked on together before we retired for good from alternet work, but Alex doesn't know that.

I watch Alex and Julia explore the streets and shops and alleyways of the ancient city that straddles the banks of the great Euphrates, discovering many quests that lead out from Babylon into the wilderness of the surrounding Anatolian peninsula.

To my delight, the kids don't take the well-worn paths through the domain. Instead, they wander, surprising themselves—and even me—with all the things that lie hidden in the woods.

At the end of a particularly grueling horseback journey, in which Alex and Julia together fend off an alarming series of bird attacks with cleverly-improvised weapons, the kids emerge on the far side of a mountain pass and descend to an open plain. From a distance, Alex spots an ancient tree-lined road that leads to a little hill.

"Hey, Auntie Em," says Alex, looking at me through his immerger glasses. "That looks like Eden Hill, doesn't it?"

"Hmm," I say. "Does it?"

Julia urges her horse ahead of Alex, reaching the end of the tree-lined road first. Her horse rears to a stop as a colossal being with outstretched wings and blazing eyes materializes before her, barring the way with a fiery sword.

"Halt!" booms the voice of the archangel Raziel, guardian of Eden. "Only initiates of the path of mysteries may enter the sacred grove."

Julia looks to Alex for help. "What do we do now?" she says.

Alex flicks through the reference manual hovering beside his display. He scrolls through a few items, then says, "Here it is. We have to pick up the Tree of Knowledge quest from someone called Bealsio. She's supposed to be wandering the plains in search of a hero, somewhere around that big volcano over there."

"Let's go!" says Julia, wheeling around on her horse and heading back out across the open plain at a full gallop.

"Hey!" says Alex. "Wait for me!"

THE ARTIFEX AND THE MUSE
MIDQUEL

REALMS UNREEL

Reality is an activity of the most august imagination.

— Wallace Stevens

THE UNDERGROUND RIVER

On the first day of autumn, I look up from my work to see Ava watching me from across the meadow. I put down my chisel and raise my hand in a hesitant greeting. I don't quite trust my eyes. Ava left weeks ago, and whenever she's gone, I start to see her shape in every shadow.

But this is no shadow. Ava waves back at me and approaches. A cool breeze rolls from the snow-capped mountains down into the valley, tugging her saffron robes and scarlet mantle around her diminutive figure as she pushes through the tall grasses toward me.

She emerges into the clearing where I'm working and stands at my side. Her eyes sweep over the twelve carved panels of pale red stone arranged in a circle around me. Each carving depicts the graceful form of a single tree designed by Ava: almond, walnut, apple, cherry, persimmon, pomegranate, apricot, pear, plum, fig, chestnut, olive.

"It's beautifully done, Dom," she says, tracing her fingers along the curving branches of the carved pomegranate tree.

Her words would once have thrilled me, but I know Ava stopped caring about beauty long ago. We've crafted these panels to adorn a shrine for the underground river that flows beneath the valley. The purpose of our work is to placate the Voice in all, nothing more.

Ava looks up at me, the delicate lines of her face framed by a wild tangle of dark curls, her skin smooth and golden as a hazelnut shell, untouched by time. For a moment, I glimpse the girl I first met in the cool cedar forest by the sea. But in the depths of her wide brown eyes, I see the accumulated sorrow of ages. The light-hearted child I once knew drifted from our world long ago, replaced by this woman lost in visions of another world.

To my surprise, Ava's eyes fill with tears. In all the years we've spent together, I've rarely seen her cry.

"What is it?" I say.

Ava settles her cool hand on my dust-covered arm, as if bracing herself.

"Serapen," she says, letting out a shaky breath. "Serapen came to me and delivered my answer from the Voice."

A chill of foreboding washes over me. Ava should be overjoyed by this long-awaited visit from the High Priestess Serapen, foremost Mohira among the priestesses of the Mohirai. Ava has toiled for centuries in the hope of receiving this answer.

Warily, I ask, "What did Serapen say to you?"

Ava pushes back the curls from her forehead and recites slowly, "'Your answer lies in the tree at the heart of the temple.'"

I follow Ava's gaze toward the lone hill that marks the center of the valley, the heart of the living temple we've built here together. Confused, I say, "How could we have missed it? We've stood there a thousand times before."

Ava's hand trembles on my arm. Softly, she says, "There was something else. Serapen told me the way I seek leads through Death."

I close my eyes, trying to calm myself. My faith in Ava has never wavered since the day she first told me of the land that lies beyond Dulai. Her visions have always proved true. I believe our labors will be rewarded a thousandfold when at last we find our way to that distant country. But surely no place, however wonderful, merits the risk of passage through Death.

"We cannot go that way," I say finally, opening my eyes.

A tear slips down Ava's cheek. She takes my hands in her own, touching the rough calluses formed by my long years of devoted service to her. "I never imagined … I never thought to ask such a sacrifice of you." Her eyes search mine. "But we were never meant for this world, Dom. There's nothing left for us here."

"How can you say that?" I cry, sweeping my arm out in a gesture that encompasses the valley around us, a living temple built by our own hands, unlike any seen before in Dulai. Somehow Ava doesn't see it, so lost is she in longing for another land that lies hidden from her.

Some part of me wishes Ava had never seen that land. The High Priestess Serapen had warned Ava, just as she had warned all the rest of us, not to gaze into the sacred pool on our Calling Day. There's no telling what might appear to one who looks upon those waters unprepared. But Ava had looked. Accidentally—or so she says.

I remember the moment as if it were yesterday, though centuries have passed since our Calling Day. Serapen was delivering the Voice's words to Ava, calling her to join the Mohirai. Ava looked back unthinkingly toward the place where I stood waiting with the other children to receive my own calling. Her face shone with delight at the prospect of initiation into the priestesshood. Then her gaze fell, just for an instant, upon the reflection of the sacred pool.

In that instant, a vision unfolded before her. Ava has described it to me many times. In the pool, she glimpsed a world where women and men together read the mysteries of the universe in the stars, their gaze pushing ever outward. Vast cities spread across that land, their great glass towers rising into the heavens. Countless voices sang of the heartbreak and beauty of life—even men's voices, which must remain quiet in Dulai.

In the years after our Calling Day, Ava transported me many times to the land of her vision with her words. How many evenings did we spend imagining life there together? What a beautiful dream it was: a place where men are equal to women, initiated into the higher mysteries known only to Mohiran sisters here in Dulai.

For a time, her dream alone seemed enough to satisfy Ava. She was otherwise entirely absorbed by her calling to the Mohiran mysteries, just as I was devoted to learning the lesser mysteries of the Artifexi, the brotherhood of craftsmen to which the Voice called me.

But as ages passed and the novelty of her service to the Voice faded, Ava's longing to visit the land of her vision consumed her, driving out all other desires. She told me she'd have no peace until she knew what road might lead her to the land she'd glimpsed on our Calling Day. In the end, despite my efforts to dissuade her, Ava sought out the Voice a second time.

Ava knew as well as I the danger of questioning the Voice. The price of an answer is a task of the Voice's choosing. Such a task, once accepted, can't be set aside.

It was Serapen who once again delivered the Voice's words. If Ava would have her answer, she must first build a temple to the sacred mystery of fertility. She was relieved—even pleased—at first. In her years as a Mohira, Ava had overseen the construction of many temples, so she believed the construction of one more would be a simple task.

I had my doubts. The Voice works in mysterious ways. But I'd never doubted I would follow Ava, even though her task wasn't mine to complete. I too wished to see the land of her vision, and ever since we were children building miniature cities together from pinecones and river stones, Ava and I have relied on each other in our work. I rely on Ava's expansive imagination, and she relies on the meticulous work of my hands. Together, we can build anything.

So I'd journeyed with Ava through the wilderness of Dulai as she searched for a place to build her temple. I'd stood by her side when we first looked down upon this broad valley. I've spent centuries with her here, building monuments, terracing slopes, laying beds of herbs and flowers, cultivating trees and vines. The work might have given us both great pleasure as children, but it became a source of sorrow for Ava as the ages passed and the Voice remained silent.

And now all our toil has led only to this: the Voice's priestess delivering words of madness. My anger surges at the injustice of it. Ava presses her hand to my chest. My heart pounds against her palm.

"I too am afraid," she says, her eyes locked on mine. "But I know what I saw. I know what awaits us. Will you trust me, Dom? Will you follow me once more?"

I've followed her for centuries, in the hope of seeing the land of her vision, yes, but also because I can imagine no life without her. "You know I'll always follow you," I say, searching the darkness in her eyes for the light that used to shine so brightly there. And I see it: a flash of the girl I fell in love with, beaming back at me. My heart swells with joy, knowing that even after all this time I'm still a part of her vision. I'm still the one who can supply the missing piece to complete her perfect form.

Ava slips her small hand into mine, pulling me to run. Her bare feet fly along the path that winds through the gardens, vineyards, and orchards. I struggle to keep up in my heavy boots. Startled songbirds dart from bushes as we pass. Grazing herds of goats bleat in alarm.

When Ava reaches the foot of the hill at the center of the valley, she lets go of my hand to hike her saffron robes up to her knees. Her scarlet mantle flaps around her shoulders as she scrambles up the grassy slope.

"Ava!" I call, out of breath. "Wait!"

She looks back at me, tossing a curtain of dark hair over her shoulder, and smiles. "Haven't we waited long enough?" she says.

And yet she steps back to take my hand once more. We reach the top of the hill together.

I follow as Ava explores the ancient grove that shades the top of the hill. She moves silently from tree to tree, looking up into the branches of each before moving on to the next. The sun sinks slowly toward the snowy peaks of the western mountains.

At last, I sit wearily beneath a gnarled pomegranate tree. Ava sits beside me. Before us, the fountainhead of the spring that feeds the underground river bubbles up from a deep pool.

"The Voice said I would find it here," she says mournfully, pressing her hand to the twisted bark of the pomegranate tree. "Here, in the heart of the valley."

"Perhaps the Voice torments us," I say, my voice hardening as I try to suppress a surge of fury toward the Voice in all. "Perhaps you asked an impossible question."

Ava hugs her arms to her chest. I feel the sting of her disappointment as if it's my own. I reach out to comfort her, but she pulls away from me, standing so quickly that she slips on the wet stones surrounding the pool. She stumbles, knocking her shoulder hard against the trunk of the pomegranate tree. The branches overhead rustle, and a bright red pomegranate tumbles into the pool with a plunk.

"Careful," I say, climbing to my feet and lending my arm to steady her.

The fallen pomegranate floats away from us toward the far end of the pool. The spring that feeds the pool drains out through a large crack deep in the foundation of this hill, so the calm surface waters conceal a treacherous undercurrent. As we watch, the bobbing pomegranate vanishes, swallowed up by the underground river that flows beneath the valley.

"Look," says Ava, pointing.

The pool's rippling surface smooths. For a moment, the water mirrors the molten sunset around us, but then something changes. In the reflection, the pomegranate tree leaning over the pool sways in the breeze of a different season. Bright green spring leaves flutter. Flowering branches stretch into a clear blue midday sky. I look up into the branches above me. Not one of the fading autumn leaves stirs. The hairs on the back of my neck prickle.

Beside me, Ava stares up into the branches. She stretches up on her toes to pluck another ripe pomegranate from the tree. She studies it thoughtfully before breaking it open, crushing a few seeds in the process. A blood-red trickle runs down her wrist. Clusters of ruby seeds glitter in her hands.

Ava looks up at me, her lips parted in amazement. "The fountainhead, Dom," she says. "This is the way beyond Dulai."

I look down at the dripping fruit, my stomach churning, my head spinning. "I don't understand," I say.

Ava extends one hand to me, half of the pomegranate cradled in her palm.

She says, "I see the way on from here, Dom. The river passes through Death. Come with me. I will show you."

The ground beneath our feet rumbles slightly, then falls still. I look at Ava in alarm and say, "What was that?"

"The time has come," she says, glancing at the sun slipping below the horizon. "We must hurry."

Ava drops both halves of the split pomegranate to the ground, scattering ruby seeds across the dusty soil. She takes my hand, pulling me forward, and wades into the pool. I follow, though a frightened voice in my mind cries out in warning. The water rises around us, ankle-deep, knee-deep, chest-deep. Ava's scarlet mantle floats on the surface like a pomegranate blossom. My boots sink like lead. I take one last breath and close my eyes as the water closes over my head.

In the stillness below the surface, I grip Ava's hand. The icy undercurrent wraps around my ankles, pulling me down, down, down. Terrified, I open my eyes in the clear water. With blurred vision, I see beneath my feet the dark maw of the underground river, opening wide, sucking hungrily.

Fear takes hold of me. I kick with all my strength against the powerful undercurrent, and Ava's hand slips from my fingers. I thrash frantically through the water, searching for her. Seeing her scarlet mantle swirling before me, I seize the fabric to pull her back to me. But the mantle tears from her shoulders. A silent scream rises in my throat as Ava disappears into the underground river.

A sudden surge of water carries me upward, throwing me out onto the stones at the edge of the pool. I lie on my belly, dazed, drenched, shaking uncontrollably. It takes me a moment to realize that I'm not shivering—it's the ground beneath me that's shaking.

A deafening rumble fills my ears, punctuated by an explosion off in the distance. I turn my head toward the sound, scanning the western mountain range for some sign of what's happening. A column of smoke rises into the evening sky above the triangular peak of Velkanos.

I block out my dark thoughts of what might be happening to all the people living in the Mohiran temple city on the lower slopes of Velkanos. I have more immediate concerns. Pebbles, stones, and small boulders are sliding from a nearby ridge toward the edge of the pool where I lie prostrate. If I don't move, I'll be crushed. Pushing myself up, I haul myself away from the water on hands and knees, still gripping Ava's muddied scarlet mantle in my fist.

When I reach the safety of higher ground, I look back toward the pool. It takes me a moment to register through my shock that the fountainhead has disappeared under the landslide.

"Dom." A voice cuts through the terrible noise of the shaking ground.

From where I crouch, I look up through swirling dust to see a sky-blue robe gleaming softly in the twilight. A few paces ahead of me stands the High Priestess Serapen, serene as the moon, undisturbed by the tumult. How on Dulai did she get here?

"Please," I cry. "Please. Help me!"

Serapen looks down at me impassively. Enraged by her indifference, I stagger to my feet and cast Ava's mantle aside, rushing toward the shallow puddle that's now all that remains of the pool where she disappeared. I seize a small boulder and grapple with it, the calluses on my hands shredding, the muscles beneath my sodden tunic tearing, until at last I cast it aside. I reach down and seize another boulder with my hands.

"The way is shut," says Serapen, her voice ringing out through the thunderous roar that fills the air.

"No!" I grunt, straining with all my might to lift this damned rock. "I—must—follow her."

Serapen watches me struggle for a moment before saying, "Then you must go another way."

Something in Serapen's tone takes hold of me, calming my inner turmoil. Perhaps she's used the priestess tone of command.

"Show me," I say, desperation driving all caution from me. I let go of the boulder, straightening up, struggling to keep my balance as the ground tips again beneath my feet.

Serapen's eyes flash. "Consider your words carefully," she says. "Are you certain you wish to ask this of the Voice in all?"

The memory of the darkness swallowing Ava coalesces into an icy knot of fear in my chest. "Yes," I growl through clenched teeth, my voice merging with the rumble of stone on stone. "This I ask of the Voice in all. What must I do to follow her?"

The ground's convulsions cease. In the sudden uncanny stillness, Serapen's eyes lock on mine, luminous in the darkness, twin pools of golden brown flecked with green and red.

"You will have your answer, Dom Artifex. But first," her voice rises, "you must build a temple to the mystery of enduring beauty. A fitting dwelling place for the Voice in all. Do you accept your task?"

I look down at the water seeping up between the stones at my feet. I could have followed Ava down her path into Death, but in my fear I let my chance slip away. A pact with the Voice offers me a second chance. Until this moment, I'd never fully understood what desperation drove Ava to accept a task from the Voice. Now my own extremity forces me to say the words, "I do accept this task."

Serapen nods, sending a ripple down the shining curtain of her long white hair. "Very well," she says.

Serapen kneels, lifting Ava's muddied mantle from the place where I dropped it. Instinctively, I lunge forward, hand extended to grab the mantle, my last connection to Ava in this world. Serapen stops me with a warning gesture. From her robes, she withdraws a small flask of oil, which she empties into the sodden folds of scarlet fabric. She lays the mantle in a loose circle around the base of the pomegranate tree, lifts two flat stones from the ground, and strikes them together, showering the fabric with sparks. I shout in dismay as a small flame catches the mantle encircling the tree. The flame creeps up the trunk of the tree, slowly consuming the twisted bark and spreading branches.

"This is the sign of our covenant, Dom Artifex," Serapen intones, her eyes reflecting the flame. "Now you must leave this place. Do not look back."

The ground trembles again. A river of fire pours down the slopes of Velkanos in the distance. The blazing tree and the burning western horizon momentarily blind me. When my vision returns, Serapen is gone. My gaze falls on the scarlet mantle, still twisting in the flames at the base of the tree. Heedless of the searing heat, I rush forward and seize the oil-drenched fabric, severely burning both my palms.

I plunge Ava's mantle into the puddle above the buried fountainhead, extinguishing the flames and cooling the burns on my hands. My seared skin begins to heal immediately upon contact with the water. Falling to my knees, I press the charred fabric of Ava's mantle to my heart. Every fiber of my being cries out.

Lost. Lost. She is lost to me.

EMERALD BRIDGES

I STAND IN THE SHADE of the small pavilion that serves as my makeshift studio. A warm midday breeze rustles the white canvas walls, filling the air around me with the salty scent of the sea. I raise my arm and deliver another stroke with my hammer. The clang of metal on stone fades. I step back to inspect my work.

Before me stands an unfinished marble statue of Ava. Her robes flow in elegant folds down to her bare feet, planted in a bed of herbs and flowers. In her left hand, she holds a ripe pomegranate, split open to reveal clusters of plump seeds. Loose curls cascade down her shoulders. She gazes slightly upward, her expression joyful at an understanding that has eluded me for all the centuries since I lost her.

A sharp pain runs down my arm. Wincing, I roll up my sleeve. Just visible through the skin of my forearm is a web of fine pink lines, a tidy grid overlaying the winding paths of blue and violet veins. Near my wrist, one line stands out brighter than the rest: a scarlet thread emerging through my skin. The strain from my work today must have pushed it to the surface.

I step toward my bench and pick up a small leather pouch, from which I extract a fine needle. I trace its sharp point lightly over my wrist, making a small, shallow cut in the skin to free the end of the emerging scarlet thread. Carefully, I pull it out. The long, damp filament dangles from my fingers as I thread it through the eye of my needle. I grip the needle tightly as I drive its sharp tip into the spot of dried blood at my wrist. Without the blood, I wouldn't be able to find the cut I made moments ago—my skin has already healed over.

I work the needle through the flesh from my wrist to my elbow with practiced stitches, concealing the remnant of Ava's mantle in the only hiding place I've found that's safe from the ever-watchful eyes of Serapen and her attendants.

The mantle of a Mohira is woven from pharmaka-laced thread by the priestess who wears it. The art of weaving such cloth is known only to the Mohirai, because the pharmaka infused into these threads belongs to the greater mysteries—secrets guarded from men by the Mohirai, even from my brotherhood of Artifexi, who enjoy more privileges than most men because of our special calling from the Voice in all. By defying Serapen's command and rescuing Ava's mantle from the flames, I've preserved not merely a memento but an enduring connection to her.

As the last inch of scarlet thread disappears beneath my sun-browned skin, I'm suddenly disoriented by a spinning sensation. The world tilts beneath my feet. I fall to my hands and knees, dropping the needle into the grass beside me, gasping as the threads woven into my skin constrict from my neck down to my ankles. Centuries have passed since I watched Ava disappear into the underground river, and it's been nineteen years since I last felt this tingle of her awareness along the threads of her mantle, pulling me toward her. Despite the pain caused by the re-awakening of our old connection, my heart leaps with joy at the knowledge that Ava has returned to me once more.

I rise to my feet with difficulty. With halting steps, I walk to the open entryway of my pavilion and shut the heavy canvas flaps. Now hidden from the view of any Mohira who might pass by, I return to the center of the pavilion and sink to the ground, my back pressing against the cool marble base of the statue. I let go of my hold on Dulai.

I've witnessed Ava's reincarnations many times, across many worlds, so I've had ample opportunity to practice the art of letting go of one life to inhabit another. I close my eyes as my sense of gravity vanishes. My disembodied consciousness slips into the void that holds the many worlds. I focus on the joy of feeling Ava's awareness merge with mine again, letting the instinctive panic that accompanies my disorientation fade away. I wait.

At last, light and sound wash over me. The pull that guided me here relaxes, and I drift weightless through some kind of enclosure. With difficulty, I gather my diffuse sensations into a single location. Eventually, the space resolves into a small pink room. Voices murmur around me, indistinct at first but growing steadily clearer.

I reorient myself so that I'm standing on the floor of the pink room. Before me, in a narrow bed, lies a dark-haired woman in a loose white robe. In her arms rests a newborn wrapped in a soft yellow blanket. Here is the new life that Ava has chosen.

A fair-haired man leans over the mother, his fingers tracing the rounded lines of the baby's face. A middle-aged woman dressed in blue bustles about the room, gathering loose linens. She pauses at the foot of the bed to smile at the baby's parents, until a beeping sound outside the door catches her attention.

"Everything all right in here for now?" she asks. The woman speaks in the English tongue, to my relief. I've had to learn many different languages as I've followed Ava across reincarnations, but I've had enough exposure to this language to be quite proficient.

The parents nod, and the woman slips out the door.

The father and mother adore their child in hushed tones, awestruck, until the mother looks up and says, "Should we let them in, Travis?"

I catch a glimpse of the woman's face for the first time. My eyes widen in surprised recognition. Anatolia. She's grown up, but there's no mistaking her.

"Are you sure you're ready?" the father, Travis, asks with a grin.

Anatolia smiles. "Go ahead. Do your worst."

Travis leaves. I peer down at the baby as Anatolia whispers to her, kissing the dark hair on the top of her head, touching her tiny hands and lips. I wonder whether Anatolia will ever recognize in this infant form the essence of the younger sister she lost nineteen years ago.

Travis returns a few minutes later to usher in three eager visitors. As each one steps into the room, I scan the faces that will form the backdrop for Ava's new life.

An older woman with bleach-blonde hair enters first, speaking at an awkwardly loud volume into some kind of headset. "We're going in now! I'll call you back!"

Behind her follows a tall scarecrow of a man with a high, lined forehead and thinning hair over a sunburned scalp. He carries a sleepy-eyed, tow-headed little girl, perhaps four or five summers old.

"Ah! She's beautiful," the blonde woman croons, eyes sparkling as she leans in over her grandchild. To her headset, she continues, "Yes. Yes. Yes. Okay. Bye." Anatolia winces almost imperceptibly. I recall the comparatively calming presence of Anatolia's own mother.

"Grandpa," the little girl says solemnly. "Would you please put me down?"

"Of course, my dear," her grandfather says with equal dignity.

Once on the floor, however, the little girl loses her composure. She rushes to the bedside and squeals, "Mama! She's so tiny! Can I hold her?"

"Can you be very, very careful?" says Anatolia.

"Ple-e-e-ease?" says the little girl, reaching up with arms wide.

Travis kneels to show his daughter how to cradle the baby. He eases the yellow bundle into her arms, and the little girl rocks the baby gently, prattling to her quietly.

The door bursts open again, and a young man with spiky blue and green hair enters, waving a pair of eyeglasses before him. "Travis!" he cries. "Sorry I'm late, but I think I figured it—"

The young man shuts his mouth at the glare from the grandfather. He folds the glasses, chastened, and hooks them carefully to the collar of his form-fitting, shiny black shirt. The shirt doesn't quite cover the elaborate tattoo that stretches from his shoulder to his elbow. A row of green lights blinks on the shiny metallic belt holding up his skinny jeans.

"Do you know what you're going to call her?" the grandmother asks Travis.

"We were thinking of naming her after Ana's mother. Isidora."

"Isidora. That's a pretty name. Is it Turkish?"

"Greek, Ma. Ana's mother is—"

"Right, right, right. Well, it's a nice name."

A wail of protest interrupts them, and all eyes turn to the little girl cradling the baby. Her grip slips slightly, and the baby squirms in her arms.

"Careful, Ollie!" Anatolia says sharply to the little girl.

"She's fine, Ana," says Travis, reaching down to adjust Ollie's hands.

"Oh, look!" Ollie squeals. "Look, Mama!"

The baby turns an unfocused gaze up at her sister, revealing vivid green eyes. Anatolia stops mid-scold and presses her lips tightly. Her eyes fill with tears. Travis takes her hand. "What is it, love?" he says gently.

Anatolia shakes her head, brushing away her tears. She says, "Nothing, just … those eyes. Just like my sister's." She reaches out and touches the baby's head. "What about Emerald? Emerald Isidora Bridges."

"Emerald," says Travis, drumming his fingers against his lips. "Hmmm.

Emerald. Emmie. I can see that."

"Emmie," Ollie says, wiggling her forefinger, which the baby grasps tightly in her tiny pink fist. "It's so nice to meet you."

The young man with the shiny belt surreptitiously slips on his eyeglasses and murmurs softly into his collar. His right hand slides along the front of his belt while his left presses the side of his glasses. After a moment, he says excitedly to Travis, "We're recording!"

I'm amazed to realize that these eyeglasses must contain some form of technology like a camera. I'm familiar with cameras from Ava's last few appearances here on Earth, but the speed of technological change seems to have accelerated since I've been away.

The young man continues, "Okay, it's April—what day is it, now?—April sixth, and we're welcoming Miss Emerald Isidora into the Bridges clan. There she is!" He crouches at Anatolia's bedside to peer at the baby, then turns his head to face the little girl. "How does it feel to be a big sister, Ollie?"

"Jesus Christ, Frank! Will you cut it out with that video scanner?" cries the grandfather. Travis and I draw back as one, alarmed by the outburst.

"Patrick!" the grandmother scolds. "Language!"

The room falls silent. Patrick, the grandfather, slowly exhales, then grumbles, "I thought he had finally managed to break those damn glasses."

Travis and Anatolia exchange an amused glance. Frank clears his throat, then sidles over to Travis. "So," Frank says in an undertone, tapping his collar. "Did you ask her?"

Travis considers Anatolia, now carefully overseeing the transfer of the baby from Ollie's arms to her grandfather's. Travis clears his throat.

"Sweetheart …" he says to Anatolia. "So, Frank and I were wondering …"

Anatolia looks up, waiting for Travis to finish until she seems to realize what he means. She rolls her eyes and says, "Oh, all right. But—" Frank hauls Travis from the room by the arm before Anatolia can change her mind or even finish saying, "I still don't see why we can't just video conference."

"What are they doing, Nanna?" Ollie asks her grandmother.

"I'm … well, it's something your daddy and Uncle Frank have been working on over at the Lab. Sensory augmentation—" She flaps her hands, unable to find the right word. "Sensory projection? Something. There are some fancy clothes involved. I guess we'll see in just a minute."

Anatolia laughs. "'Just a minute' is probably a bit ambitious, Marie."

Nearly an hour later, after a great deal of insistence that they need only five more minutes, Travis stands in the middle of the room wearing a form-fitting black shirt and glasses like his brother's, along with a pair of dark gloves with silver seams. He speaks patiently through a headset to his mother-in-law, which he's been doing for the last forty-five minutes. At last, he turns to Frank and says, "Okay, she's got it on. You can switch to projection."

The background hubbub of the rest of the group subsides. "Thank God," says Frank, heaving a sigh of relief. He taps out something on his shiny belt, and a three-dimensional, translucent image of an older woman with chin-length silver curls and stylish square-rimmed glasses appears, facing Travis.

Astonished, I take a step closer to the projection and circle it slowly. Here stands Anatolia's mother, Isidora, or so at least it seems. She's perhaps grown a bit plumper, and the smile lines around her eyes and mouth have perhaps deepened, but she exudes the same warmth I remember from nineteen years ago.

"Hi, Yaya!" cries Ollie, bouncing up from the seat beside her mother to wave at the projection.

"Hello, my darling," says Isidora, waving back. A light source in the unseen room where Isidora stands glimmers on the silver seams of her gloves and the black threads of her form-fitting shirt.

"Isidora," says Travis, "I just need you to press this patch on the belt near the —yes, that's the one."

"Oooh." Isidora straightens up. "That felt strange."

"Good. That means it's on. Now, just mirror my movements," says Travis. "Frank?"

Frank snaps to attention and transfers baby Emmie expertly from her mother's arms to her father's. When Frank steps away, Isidora mimicks Travis uncertainly, cradling empty space in her arms. Then she gasps. In her projection, a baby appears.

"I can feel her in my arms!" Isidora exclaims.

I shake my head in amazement. This world that Ava spent so many centuries yearning to inhabit is truly wonderful, in its way.

"Touch her cheek, Travis," says Frank.

"Isidora," says Travis. "Watch me."

Travis strokes the baby's cheek with the fingertips of his gloved hand. Isidora repeats the movement, shaking her head as she murmurs, "Amazing. Amazing."

After admiring her granddaughter's tiny face, hands, and feet with the help of Travis and their linked sensory augmentation gear, Isidora turns, still cradling the projection of the baby, and says to Anatolia, "I wish I could be there, my love. Papou does, too. We will come to visit soon, just as soon as the semester ends."

"I wish you could see her, Mama," Anatolia says softly. Her eyes glisten as she looks from the real baby in Travis' arms to the projected one in Isidora's. "I mean, really see her. It's just not the same as having you here."

"Pretty damn close, though!" Frank mutters to Travis.

△▽△

The Bridges take Emmie home in a streamlined silver car that envelops its passengers in preternatural silence as they glide over the uneven surfaces of a tangled freeway system. I sit unseen in the back seat, wedged between Emmie, asleep in her car seat, and Ollie, fidgeting in hers. Ollie keeps up a stream-of-consciousness dialogue with her parents, who patiently predict when the baby might crawl and walk and talk, deny Ollie's request to sleep in the baby's room, and suggest that Ollie's teacher might not like her to take the baby to school for show-and-tell.

As we slow to a crawl at a particularly ill-conceived intersection, I consider that, while the quality of vehicles has changed since my last sojourn on Earth, the quality of city traffic has not.

"Travis," Anatolia murmurs, gripping her husband's knee and pointing. I peer through the windshield. We're approaching some disturbance in the road.

Ahead of us, a sign-waving crowd, hundreds strong, marches up an exit ramp toward oncoming freeway traffic. Four police officers in navy blue uniforms step out of a pair of police cars parked at the top of the ramp. Sirens wail in the distance, and seconds later another half-dozen police vehicles sweep by us.

"It'll be fine, Ana," Travis says, squeezing Anatolia's hand. "They're just causing a spectacle."

"It was just a spectacle at city hall, until it wasn't. Is there another way around them?"

"Mama?" says Ollie, picking up on her mother's worried tone. "Why are those people walking on the freeway? Aren't you not allowed to do that?"

"They're protesters, Ollie," says Anatolia, not quite managing to suppress the anxiety in her voice. "They want people to know that they're very angry, so they're breaking the law."

"What are they angry about?" says Ollie, pressing her hands to the window and staring out wide-eyed as we inch by the gathering crowd on the exit ramp. I read the signs—some scrawled by hand on dirty canvas, some printed neatly on shiny banners—waving above the crowd. *Heal America. Take Back Oakland. This Is My Occupation.* The dull roar of the protesters' chants is audible, though the car muffles the sound impressively.

"Well, they're angry about a lot of things," says Anatolia, watching the front line of the crowd edging toward the police cordon, now twenty officers strong. "But the biggest thing is that they can't find any work right now. So they don't have anything better to do than—"

"Ana," Travis shakes his head, mildly exasperated. He looks at Ollie in the rearview mirror and says, "Mama's right that it's hard for people to find jobs, but people are angry because they think the government is doing a bad job, and that big companies are to blame."

"Are they mad at you and Uncle Frank?" Ollie asks in alarm.

Travis laughs. "No, sweetheart. Our company isn't nearly big enough to catch their attention."

We make our way through the traffic in the end without incident. Travis exits the freeway onto a road that ascends a forested incline and winds along a ridge cut into a steep hillside. Stands of tall redwoods and silver eucalyptus give way at intervals to sweeping views of the flatland below.

I enjoy the view from the back seat for a few miles, until Travis pulls into a short driveway. The driveway doesn't seem to be associated with any structure I can see, other than a tiled deck atop the rocky cliffside. A second car containing Travis' parents and younger brother pulls up behind us.

As Travis and Frank haul bags out of the car, Ollie skips off to a low pedestal at the edge of the tiled deck. She presses her palm to the pedestal, and a section of the deck slides away before her feet. She descends from view.

I follow Anatolia curiously as she carries baby Emmie from the car to the opening into which Ollie just disappeared. Anatolia leads me down a broad wooden staircase that descends from the street level into a spacious but minimally furnished living room adjacent to a large kitchen and dining room. At the far wall, floor-to-ceiling windows look out over the flat lowlands of Oakland and Berkeley toward the well-trafficked waters, bridges, and islands of the San Francisco Bay. I pace the room, admiring the walls and ceiling of this unusual cliffside construction.

Anatolia sinks into the deep cushions of the sofa facing the grand windows, rocking the baby in her arms. The rest of the family descends the stairs noisily behind her.

"Who wants Nanna to make breakfast?" calls grandmother Marie.

Several hearty shouts of approval meet this offer, and everyone but Anatolia passes through to the kitchen.

"Do you want anything, love?" Travis shouts back to Anatolia.

Anatolia calls back, "Just some quiet time, for now."

In the relative peace of the living room, I stand behind Anatolia. When I lean over her to take a closer look at Emmie, Anatolia shivers. She presses the baby to her breast, looking up apprehensively at the place where I stand unseen behind her.

I draw back. Perhaps I can spare the child this lifetime, let go of our connection, set her free. Ava must desire that, in some way. Even so, I feel Ava's pull through that child, strong as ever. Perhaps she can't let me go, either.

For now, though, I can let her enjoy the fleeting obscurity of childhood. I loosen my hold on her and reach for the body that anchors me to Dulai.

△▽△

My awareness returns to my own body, which is still propped uncomfortably against the base of my statue. After sitting so long without moving, I should be cold and stiff. But my revived connection to Ava's awareness flows over my skin, tingling, warming me to the core. I feel alive in a way I haven't felt in quite some time.

Night has fallen while my mind has been elsewhere. Moonlight glows through the white canvas walls of my pavilion. I rise unsteadily and reach toward my tool bench. My fingers close around the cold silver drinking flask at the near end of the bench. I uncap the flask and throw back a long swig of water, moistening my dry throat.

I make my way toward the closed entryway, push through the flap, and step out into the light of the full moon. To the east, across the still waters of a vast lagoon, looms a massive wall of volcanic rock scaled by the delicate marble tiers of the city of Thera: a temple to the mystery of enduring beauty, my personal offering to the Voice. Moonlight gleams on the pale marble of the city's fine buildings, streets, and terraces, a bright contrast to the dark, craggy slope that holds my work above the hungry depths of the sea below.

The sight of Ava's new infant form has rekindled in me such a fierce longing to be free of this place that I'm nearly overcome by the urge to break the evening silence with a scream of frustration, to rouse every last Mohira in the sleeping city. But whether I raise my voice in defiance or bow my head in obedience, I'm bound as surely to my service to the Voice now as I was the day I accepted its terms.

I turn away from the city, facing westward, listening to the long inhalations and exhalations of the sea as it washes the unseen foot of the cliff far below me. My desperation ebbs somewhat, and I return to my pavilion.

I toss and turn on my sleeping mat all through the night. In my mind, the face of the newborn Emmie Bridges merges into the faces of a thousand other children I've known over the ages. From each I'd hoped to learn the secret of crossing into Death, but each had slipped away from me too soon.

I'm awoken from my restless sleep hours later by the sound of someone entering my pavilion. I jump to my feet and face the entryway. There stands a skinny girl in novice robes of undyed wool, silhouetted against the rosy light of dawn. A length of fine red ribbon flutters from her fingers.

"Dom Artifex?" she says timidly.

I gaze at her for a long moment, trying to match her face to any of the names of recent novices I've met during my comings and goings to Thera. It's impossible. I've known countless Mohirai over the centuries, but until they're full-grown women possessed of the power of initiate priestesses, these girls seem to be nearly indistinguishable variations of a common pattern. I have room in my mind for only a single girl now; keeping track of her as she flits from life to life is work enough. So rather than call this girl by another's name, I answer simply, "Mohira?"

"I—" She swallows nervously. "I bring you word from Serapen."

My nostrils flare involuntarily, but I suppress my anger and motion for her to approach. However much I despise Serapen, this girl isn't to blame.

"Speak, then," I say.

The girl stretches the ribbon between her hands, reading aloud from the pattern worked into the threads, "Come to the Musaion at dawn. The Voice summons you."

I grind my teeth. In the ages that have passed since Ava departed, these occasional summonses from the Voice have lost their power to ignite hope. My question remains unanswered. This latest summons will be yet another disappointment, I'm sure—the Voice taunting me.

I dismiss the girl with a gesture and wait impatiently for her to leave, but she shifts nervously from side to side, her eyes darting from my face to the unfinished statue behind me.

"Would you like to take a closer look?" I say, perhaps a bit more brusquely than I'd intended. She nods. "Well, go on," I say.

The girl edges around me, stopping an arm's length from the statue. She reaches up and traces one finger over the perfectly sculpted pomegranate seeds, an echo of the statue's thoughtful expression in the line of her chin, the curve of her lips. She glances back at me and says, "She's very beautiful. Is she one of the Mohirai?"

I look away. "Not any more. She …" I search for words a novice might understand. "She left Dulai to cross over into Death."

"Death?" says the girl, mouthing the strange word. "Where is that?"

My jaw works for a long moment. At last, I manage to growl through clenched teeth, "That is one of the mysteries you Mohirai keep from me, in your great wisdom."

The girl shrinks away from my harsh words, eyes wide in her pale face. She bows and departs hastily. I remain rooted to the spot, fists shaking, burning with anger.

△▽△

I don't hurry to answer my summons from the Voice. Whatever else the Voice may be, it's not impatient. Only when my anger has cooled do I depart.

I descend from my ridgetop pavilion to the craggy shoreline far below, following the steep, narrow trail through the sunburnt grass. A lone dock, which I fashioned long ago from the scrubby trees that grow atop the ridge, extends from the shoreline to the water. I stand at the end of the dock and look out across the vast lagoon.

The pilgrims' ferry, crossing from one end of the great volcanic caldera to the other, comes into view. I hail it. The ferry takes a long time to arrive, and when it finally pulls up alongside the dock, I step aboard without a word. I ignore the half-dozen other passengers as the ferry makes its way slowly across the still waters toward the temple city of Thera.

At the temple city harbor, broad, shallow stairs emerge from the dark blue depths of the lagoon. The wide stairs lead to the lowest tier of the city, narrowing gradually as they ascend through higher tiers up the slope of dark volcanic stone that forms the island of Thera. The stairs conclude at the domed temple that crowns the city. From a distance, the tiered levels of the city connected by this central staircase form the shape of a stylized tree, white branches of smooth marble spreading across dark stone.

A trio of barefoot girls in undyed novice robes hiked up to their knees stand on a low stair, ankle-deep in the water, ready to secure the ferry to the heavy metal rings bored into the stairs. One novice offers her hand to help me ashore, but I step off without looking at her and leave the crowd of pilgrims behind.

I ascend the stairs swiftly, cutting through the slow current of foot traffic on the boulevards and terraces that interrupt the staircase at intervals, pulling up the hood of my cloak over my face to avoid the curious eyes of the initiate priestesses in their colorful robes and mantles.

The long climb concludes at a white marble plaza. I step out on the plaza, which faces the massive domed form of the Musaion of Thera, jewel of the city, my greatest offering to the Voice. Even this had not been enough to satisfy it.

The great doors of the Musaion stand open, and I pass through the archway, pausing for a moment at the threshold to let my eyes adjust to the dim light of the vestibule, the first stage of the elaborate metaphor of initiation into the mysteries.

At the far wall, between two narrow archways, stands a priestess dressed in saffron and scarlet. I lower my head just enough to imply respect, though I'm primarily avoiding looking at her robes; their colors evoke far too many memories of Ava.

"Greetings, Mohira." I say.

"Greetings, Artifex," she replies. "What business brings you to the Musaion?"

"I come seeking audience with the Voice," I say.

"You are most welcome," she says, involuntarily spoiling her attempt at solemnity with a bright-eyed smile. She must be a new initiate, still delighting in her role as the Musaion's gatekeeper.

She turns to a small recess carved into the wall between the two archways. Water spills from a silver spout at the back of the recess into a shallow stone basin, spiraling down an open drain. She lifts a chalice from its place beside the basin, sprinkles a handful of herbs into it from a pouch suspended from her belt, fills it from the fountain, and raises it to my lips. I drink, though no amount of sweet herbs can take away the bitterness of the pharmaka mixed into that cup.

Smiling again, she ushers me through the rightmost archway, the entry to the inner chamber.

The hall beyond the archway turns almost immediately to the right, then to the left. The light trap plunges me into complete darkness, the second stage of the metaphor. As the pharmaka takes hold, I press my hand to the wall to steady myself. My fingers trace unseen symbols carved in relief upon the stone. I know them all, having chiseled each symbol on these walls myself. I walk slowly along the winding path through darkness until at last I see the light up ahead.

I emerge into the inner sanctuary and pause at the edge of a circle of soaring marble columns. The pharmaka swirling in my veins dissolves my weary cynicism for a moment, giving me fresh eyes. Even I can't deny I've done excellent work here.

My gaze follows the elegant columns upward. Far above me, a massive dome of translucent white stone appears to float over the central chamber. Four golden half-domes surround the central dome like flower petals, each vaulting one of the four wings off the main sanctuary. Filtered sunlight illuminates wall frescoes of staggering scale and free-standing sculptures arranged on the white tile floor. Echoes of women's voices and footsteps drift through the open archways that lead out from the four wings of the temple, but there's only one woman in sight. She stands on the dais at the center of the sanctuary. I cross the space between us and stop at the edge of the dais.

Before me, the High Priestess Serapen paces back and forth before the great loom she uses to rule Dulai and the lives of all within it. Her bare feet pad over smooth white stone, her brown fingers guiding the shuttle through the warp, her sky-blue robes and long white hair flowing in waves behind her. The finished lengths of fabric that lie folded upon the dais are threaded missives in which other Mohirai will read small pieces of the Voice's will. To me, the indecipherable rags are a frustrating reminder that the understanding I so desperately seek hides in plain sight all around me, one of the many mysteries the Mohirai withhold from men.

"Greetings, Dom Artifex," says Serapen, running her fingers along the woven threads one last time before she turns to face me. She looks down at me, the height of the dais adding to her own already considerable height. I see my reflection in her clear brown eyes, which gleam like topaz in the golden light of the inner sanctuary. How many times have I gazed into the uncanny eyes of the High Priestess since I was a boy? And how is it that I have changed so much since then, while she remains unchanged by the millennia?

"Greetings, Muse Serapen," I say.

Serapen tips her head to one side, considering me for a long moment before saying, "You once sought the counsel of the Voice, Dom, did you not?"

I close my eyes, remembering the desperation that led me to this futile task. After a long silence, I reply, "I did."

Serapen's voice grows lower and fuller, amplified by the stone temple walls around her, as she intones, "And so you must respect the Voice's words. Complete your task. If you would follow Ava, first you must let her go."

I feel the Voice's command closing in around me, one more link in the chain that binds me to this place. I bow my head and force myself to say, "I submit to the will of the Voice. Let it be so."

But in my heart, my secret rebellion seethes. Whatever the consequences, to me or to the newborn child, I'll stop at nothing to escape the life that has, in Ava's absence, become a source of unending sorrow.

△▽△

Over the next few years, I make a show of diligent obedience to the Voice. In reality, I use my endless work to hide my sojourns to Emmie's world. The construction of a new library wing gives me moons of solitude between rising stone walls. Sculpting a fountain for the plaza before the Musaion allows me afternoons of reverie within the canvas pavilion of my movable studio. And, when all other attempts to find privacy fail, my nights overlap Emmie's days, giving me many uninterrupted hours in which to withdraw from Dulai and immerse myself in Earth. This is how I watch Emmie's early years unfold against the backdrop of her father and uncle's Emerging Media Lab, with all its peculiar new vocabulary and wonderful technology.

Uncle Frank's omnipresent video scanner captures Emmie's first steps across the bare cement floor of the Lab's makeshift lounge and into her father's arms before a cheering audience of engineers.

"Oh, no, Travis," Anatolia groans through her three-dimensional projection, watching the replay from her law office a few blocks away. "How are we going to child-proof that place? You know she'll head straight into that death trap if you give her half a chance."

"The spliner's not a death trap, Anatolia," Frank blusters, his face turning almost as red as his freshly-dyed hair.

"We're working on putting walls around it," says Travis, walking over to an unprepossessing square of spongy grey material covering a large section of floor. The programmable extrusion mechanics of this expensive new device replicate three-dimensional environments, enabling the Lab to use interactive, life-sized terrain models as they test out their sensory augmentation prototypes. Travis points out to Anatolia the chalk lines where the walls and door will go, when time and budget allow. He meets his wife's eyes through the projection and says solemnly, "We'll keep an eye on her. Don't worry."

"You could just put her in daycare, you know," grumbles Frank.

Anatolia bites her lip. Until now, Frank and Travis have accepted without criticism the neurotic overprotectiveness that renders her unable to leave Emmie in the care of anyone outside the extended family of Lab team members. I feel a pang of sympathy for her, seeing in her anxiety the legacy of her sister's death.

"Let's talk about this later, Ana," says Travis, shooting a warning look at his brother. "We just wanted to give Emmie her moment in the spotlight."

Anatolia directs a strained smile at Frank. "Thanks for helping me be a part of it," she says. "You boys are the best."

From my unseen perspective at Emmie's side, I have ample opportunity to confirm that Anatolia's concerns about safety at the Lab are more than a little justified. The Lab is a trove of experimental electronics of all shapes, sizes, and degrees of quality assurance. A litter of sharp metallic thread snippets, button-sized batteries, and tiny microelectronics covers the floor. Travis more than once catches a toddling Emmie on the verge of swallowing a shiny, blinking, mouth-watering prototype, before the engineers learn to keep their work out of little arms' reach.

The dangerous clutter alone would be enough to worry any mother, but the warehouse is also an active construction site in a rough neighborhood. Housed in a sprawling, low-rent warehouse near the West Oakland waterfront of the San Francisco Bay, the Lab is being repurposed by Travis' team into a hardware prototyping facility. Emmie's father invests heavily in workstations and lab benches but maintains the building's derelict exterior appearance to blend in with its immediate surroundings. The city blocks surrounding the Lab are a battleground between community reclamation efforts and socioeconomic deterioration. Little Emmie, growing up among the engineers of the Lab, becomes accustomed to the occasional gunshot from beyond the slapdash security fence around the building.

Despite the apparent hazards of the neighborhood, the Lab's interior shows every sign of a healthy, growing enterprise. Spread out across makeshift lab benches of reclaimed plywood and cinderblocks, beneath the glare of bare light bulbs, the team assembles retinal projection glasses and sensory feedback garments, motion simulation headsets and olfactory augmentation patches. In the fenced-in lot beside the warehouse, the team runs daily gauntlets of simulation and feedback tests with their product prototypes, dictating and typing copious notes, initially with the aid of run-of-the-mill handheld smartcoms, but increasingly, as time goes on and their prototypes improve, with a few taps of fingers on a wrist or a few jabs in the air with a stylus. Notes in hand, they troop back into the warehouse, ripping and replacing, reworking and tweaking, and returning to the testing lot once more. The bright lights of the Lab burn round the clock.

The curious goings-on at the Lab provide a welcome diversion from my unending labors on Thera, but I don't visit Earth for mere diversion. I study Emmie's world intently, knowing Ava's awareness has chosen this place and time for some purpose in her greater plan, and hoping that plan will soon become clear to me.

△▽△

Travis crosses the catwalk that connects two newly constructed upstairs office wings in the warehouse, hurrying back to his office after an important conference call with the Lab's investors. Frank calls up to him from a workbench on the ground floor, "You've got to see this!"

I look up from my seat beside Emmie in the corner of the Lab. Emmie is giggling at a life-sized three-dimensional projection of her Papou, who sits behind his desk in Massachusetts. Papou offered to watch Emmie for a few hours this afternoon when the usual Lab babysitter canceled at the last minute, so grandfather and granddaughter are now engrossed in a game of peek-a-boo.

"What is it?" says Travis, descending the stairs from the catwalk. Frank, who's watching some three-dimensional projection, beckons Travis excitedly. Travis stands next to his brother, and together they watch as Frank replays a recording of a recent product test. The recording begins with seven men and five women—product testers—standing in a row on the fenced lot outside the warehouse. Each wears a headset and form-fitting sensory augmentation clothing.

Travis leans in closer as the recording flickers. The product testers now appear dressed in formal evening wear, standing on a crowded dance floor beneath a star-studded night sky. Twelve glowing green spheres pulse slowly above the avatars of the product testers.

The three-dimensional projection now splits into two separate projections. The first shows the recording of the physical lot: twelve product testers in headsets and sensory augmentation clothing. The second shows the recording of the ballroom simulation: twelve product tester avatars surrounded by a simulated crowd.

An unseen woman's voice says, "Please wait for your dance instructor, who will take you through the steps of the waltz."

In the ballroom, twelve new avatars step out from the simulated crowd and onto the dance floor. Glowing red spheres pulse above the heads of six avatars. Glowing blue spheres pulse above the heads of the other six.

"The live instructors," says Frank, pointing out the six red markers. "And the simulated instructors," he continues, indicating the six blue markers. Travis nods, his eyes never leaving the projection.

The soft strains of a waltz begin to play. In the recording of simulated reality, the six live and six simulated instructors demonstrate the steps of the dance, eventually taking hands with their partners to swirl around the dance floor, coattails and ballgowns fanning out behind them. In the recording of physical reality, I watch with interest as six live couples dance across the asphalt alongside six solo product testers who dance with unseen partners.

When the music stops, the six live and six simulated instructors bow, say farewell to their partners, and depart the dance floor. In physical reality, six live instructors slip out of the test lot through a back door and into the Lab.

The woman behind the camera instructs the product testers to remove their headsets. Several of the testers, emerging from the simulation, nod at one another, clearly impressed. A pair of Lab engineers arrange a circle of metal folding chairs in the center of the lot, where the twelve testers sit for a follow-up interview.

"Here we go," says Frank, rubbing his hands together in anticipation.

A Lab intern scribbles notes while one of the hardware engineers asks questions about the fit and comfort of the sensory augmentation gear. One of the designers asks questions about the quality of the simulation content, trying to identify what aspects were particularly realistic versus particularly unconvincing. After discussing the product testers' thoughts on these points, the designer says, "Before you go, we'd like you to fill out a brief survey to rate the quality of your dance instructor on several metrics. Six of you had our live instructors, while the other six danced with projected instructors from a studio in San Francisco. Just note which type of instructor you had using the checkboxes at the top of the survey. And, thanks, everyone!"

The intern hands out a dozen paper surveys on clipboards with pencils. I watch the product testers scribble down their answers and turn them in before thanking the woman behind the camera. The recording stops.

Travis turns to Frank, his excitement evident.

"Well?" Travis says eagerly.

Frank rustles the stack of surveys in his hand, grinning as he says, "Twelve for twelve."

"You're kidding me!" says Travis.

Frank grins from ear to ear in answer. Travis smacks his forehead in amazement.

"We rocked it!" Travis hollers across the hall toward a group of engineers in the midst of a heated debate over the merits of a new heat-dissipating conductive fabric. Little Emmie turns around, startled by the noise. A wire-seamed glove with blinking fingertips dangles from her hands.

Travis calls the rest of the team up in the offices to join the engineers on the ground floor. I stand beside a young woman with square-rimmed glasses, pink hair, and a form-fitting sensory augmentation tunic over black leather pants. Frank sits at the workbench behind Travis.

"Listen up, guys," says Travis. Men and women gather around him, sitting at nearby workbenches, looking up expectantly at their boss. He continues, "Today's a big day for the Lab. A big day for the whole sensory augmentation community. These users—" He points to Frank, who waves the product tester surveys at the team, grinning. "These users just experienced a simulated human interaction so convincing that they couldn't distinguish it from physical reality."

Shouts, cheers, and applause meet this pronouncement. When the ruckus dies down, Travis continues, "This is a huge step forward. The holy grail is within our reach. High-fidelity simulated reality is coming. We're going to erase the boundary between the real and the unreal.

"I know there have been a lot of long days. And nights. And weekends. I thank you for that. Because of you, I'm finally going to be able to tell my dad that those long hours playing video games in the basement weren't wholly wasted."

"Will you tell my dad, too?" someone calls out, prompting general laughter.

Travis smiles and says, "Tonight, we celebrate. Drinks on me. Then I want you to go home and get some rest, because we've still got a long way to go."

THE ALTERNET GENERATION

I EMPTY MY BOX OF CRAYONS onto the tile floor under the little table Daddy set out on the deck this morning. Daddy takes out the table once a week when Nanna and Grandpa come over to play bridge. I like to play under the table while the grown-ups are talking.

I pick out the red, blue, green, and purple crayons from the pile. Next to my crayons, I place the Jack of Spades and the Queen of Diamonds. These cards fell onto the floor when Daddy and Grandpa got up from the table to go downstairs to the kitchen. I examine each crayon, thinking hard about which color to use first.

I look up expectantly at the dark-haired man in the funny dress and big leather belt, who hides under the table with me. He sometimes appears when I'm trying to make hard choices like this. He reaches out his big hand and taps the red crayon. I consider the red, then nod in approval and start coloring over the long white hair of the Queen of Diamonds.

Above me, Mama talks while Nanna shuffles cards.

"I wish I could get him to leave all these sensory augmentation devices back at the Lab," Mama says to Nanna.

"Good luck." Nanna laughs. "We could never keep those boys apart from their toys."

"We don't even know how any of this technology affects the adult brain, much less the brain of a developing child," says Mama. She sounds angry.

"We said the same thing about video games," says Nanna. "But the boys turned out—" Nanna's phone rings, and she says, "Just a second. I need to take this."

Nanna's office assistant calls her all day long. Grandpa doesn't like it. Nanna says a few things to her phone, then says to Mama, "Sorry, Ana. What were you saying?"

Mama says, "I just worry that, with all this simulated reality, Emmie won't get to have any *real* experiences."

Hearing my name, I perk up, but Mama doesn't say anything else about me. I continue coloring the Jack and Queen, now using the green crayon. Once I finish, I'll put both cards in the dollhouse hovering before me, projected from the smartcom. Daddy just gave me my very own smartcom. It makes a hundred different dollhouses, and dolls, too, but I like drawing the dolls for myself.

"There's nothing less *real* about simulated reality, Ana," says Daddy. I see his feet and Grandpa's coming back up the stairs. Some bottles and glasses clink above my head as Daddy and Grandpa set them down on the table. Daddy's smartcom beeps. "Look," he says.

"Hi, Dad," says Ollie.

Hearing Ollie's voice, I look up in delight from my coloring and crawl out from under the table. In front of Daddy, there's a projection of Ollie, who sits behind a big desk in a room I haven't seen before. I wave at her. Ollie's been gone for almost two weeks, and I really miss her.

"Ollie! Hi, Ollie!" I say.

"Hi, Emmie!" Ollie waves back.

"How's math camp, sweetheart?" says Daddy.

Ollie rolls her eyes and tugs the end of her long, blonde braid. "Are you going to make me do this *every* summer?" she says. "I get A's in math. Is it really that important for me to *like* it, too?"

Daddy reaches out toward the projection and puts his hand under Ollie's chin so she looks up at him. In the projection, Ollie wrinkles her nose and rubs her chin. I laugh. Daddy's special headsets do make your skin feel funny sometimes.

"Someday," Daddy says to Ollie, "when you learn about groups, rings, and fields, you'll thank me."

Ollie sighs. "I've got to go. I've got loads of homework. Loads." She sounds very grown-up and serious, but I know that Ollie really loves homework.

"All right, babygirl," says Daddy. "Give me a call if you need any help."

"Cheers, Dad."

Daddy switches off the projection and turns to Mama. "See?" he says. "It's as good as having her right here."

Mama opens her mouth, but before she says anything she looks down and sees the cards I've been coloring under the table.

"Oh, Emmie!" she exclaims, displeased. Hot tears fill my eyes. Mama's upset with me again. But Mama smiles at me quickly and says, "It's okay, sweetheart. Here, let's get you some real paper."

Mama picks me up and carries me toward the stairs that go back down into the house. She calls back to Daddy, "You hear that, Travis? She needs *real* paper!"

I look back and see Daddy make a silly face at Mama. Under the table, near Daddy's feet, the dark-haired man who was helping me with my coloring disappears. I giggle. That funny man can play hide and seek better than anyone else, even Daddy.

△▽△

I lie on my belly on top of an empty server rack in Dad's office, swinging my sensory augmentation headset over the edge like a metronome.

"Are you almost done?" I whine. I've been waiting practically forever for Dad to stop writing email and come play with me in the spliner. With his authorization code and a few pieces of sensory augmentation equipment, the spliner can become almost anything. The forest simulation is what I have in mind: the perfect place for a game of chase.

"Just one more minute, sweetheart," Dad says distantly. I grumble and make a face, but he never looks up from his laptop.

The office door swings open, and Uncle Frank bursts in. "You've got to read this," he says, waving a stapled printout in his hand.

"Busy," says Dad. "Email it to me."

Uncle Frank drops the printout on Dad's keyboard. Dad pushes back from his desk and throws up his hands in frustration, saying, "I'm the goddamn CEO! What do I have to do to get a minute of peace around here?"

I stop swinging the headset and stare at Dad wide-eyed. His angry voice makes him sound like Grandpa. Uncle Frank looks like he wants to step back out of the office.

"Sorry, Travis," says Uncle Frank. "I guess you're still sorting out those malfunction complaints?"

Dad nods, closing his eyes for a moment, his mouth set in a straight line. He lets out a deep breath and looks down at the paper on his keyboard. "It's okay. Sorry for yelling at you. So, what's so important?" He slips on his reading glasses, picks up the paper, and reads aloud, "The Death of the Internet …" He trails off as his eyes travel down the page. After a moment, he looks back up at Uncle Frank and says, "So what? She's not the first grad student to complain about government surveillance of the internet. She also sounds pretty paranoid and misinformed."

"I think she made some good points," says Uncle Frank. "But anyway, it's the response that's interesting."

Dad turns to the next page and reads, "Alternet Protocol Specification, by The Anonymous Collective …" He reads on silently, flipping to the next page, then the next. I see black and white drawings on the pages as he turns them. When he comes to the last page, he takes off his reading glasses and says, "I don't know that much about complex adaptive systems, but—Yeah, I guess you could work around communication monitoring with a network like that. But who would bother? Most people don't care about government snooping that much."

"It's not just about government surveillance," says Uncle Frank. "The internet is becoming so heavily regulated now that, pretty soon, only the big guys will be able to play on the network. The startup economy is tanking already, and it's only going to get worse."

"Da-a-ad," I whine softly, apprehensive that a long and boring conversation is about to take place.

Uncle Frank shoots me a knowing smile and says, "Ah. Waiting for spliner time?"

I nod.

Uncle Frank says, "I've got a new African safari simulation that could use an expert opinion. Want to check it out?"

I grin at him. Uncle Frank knows how to have fun. He even lets me wear some of the prototype sensory augmentation gear, if I promise not to tell Mom.

Uncle Frank glances at Dad, who says, "That'd be great. Chase another time, okay, Emmie?"

I nod and run happily after Uncle Frank to go on safari.

△▽△

For the next few weeks, unless he's playing with me in the spliner, Uncle Frank seems unable to talk about anything except the Alternet Protocol Specification. He says the people who made it, the Anonymous Collective, wrote something called a manifesto. Their manifesto says that the Alternet Age has arrived, and they've set up eight places for people to connect to the alternet. Uncle Frank says that pretty soon there'll be places to connect to the alternet all over the world.

One of the first places to connect turns out to be in the community garden toolshed just a few blocks away from the Lab. When he hears about the new connection point, Uncle Frank takes me with him to see it.

"You'll be able to tell your grandkids that you were here the day the alternet was born," he says, looking down at me as we walk hand in hand along the uneven sidewalk toward the community garden.

"But what *is* the alternet?" I say.

"It's just a protocol right now," says Uncle Frank. "That means it's a way for a lot of computers to talk to each other. A protocol is a language that a bunch of computers all understand. The internet started as a protocol, too. The internet is just millions and millions of computers, all talking to each other using the same protocol. Big computers, like the servers at the Lab, and little computers, like the ones you see on mobile phones and smartcoms, they can all talk to each other with the internet protocol."

"Why does there need to be another protocol, if the computers can all talk to each other already?" I say.

"That's a very good question," he says. "It's because, on the internet, there are these highways. Computers that want to talk to each other have to send their messages to other computers over the highways. Like how we use the freeway to travel from home to the Lab. And different people own the internet highways. The problem is that sometimes the people who own the highways don't let everyone use them. Sometimes they even read messages that don't belong to them."

"Why do they do that?" I say.

Uncle Frank smiles, but it's not his normal smile. It's more like the smile Mom makes when she's trying to be nice to someone she doesn't really like. He says, "Some people like to control information. But information wants to be free."

I don't understand that, but I don't have a chance to ask any more questions because we've come to the chain link fence of the community garden. Uncle Frank opens the gate, and we follow the path between twelve well-tended raised beds that lead to the toolshed. Uncle Frank points at the roof, where a black box topped by a palm-sized solar panel glints in the sun.

"That's it?" I say, disappointed.

"Yep," says Uncle Frank, grinning. "That's it for now. But not for long."

Uncle Frank turns out to be right. Pretty soon, on my walks to and from the Lab with Dad and Uncle Frank, I start noticing more little black boxes—alternet connection points, Uncle Frank calls them—popping up everywhere.

"That's because the information routing application runs on pretty much every consumer electronic device," Uncle Frank explains to me on another walk.

He seems very excited about this. "It's very well designed. Peer-to-peer, anonymous, and lightweight. It's spreading like wildfire."

Spreading like wildfire sounds pretty scary to me. A group of teenagers not much older than Ollie started a wildfire last summer near one of the biggest houses in the Berkeley hills, not far from our house. Dad says it was sad because it gave all the protestors a bad name. Mom says it was sad because they were so ignorant. I think it's sad because a lot of people lost their homes. A few people even died. The air in our neighborhood smelled like smoke long after the fire went out. For weeks, I had nightmares that I was walking through the ashes of my house, searching for my family.

But the alternet doesn't turn out to be as scary as a wildfire. I quickly discover that the alternet is one of my very favorite things. People are putting the most wonderful things on the alternet, and, with all the immergers Uncle Frank and Dad let me use at the Lab, I'm able to visit worlds I never could have imagined on my own.

△▽△

In the year following the publication of the Anonymous Collective's manifesto, I witness a rapid escalation of activity in the Emerging Media Lab during my visits with Emmie. The explosive growth of the alternet and the associated proliferation of multi-sensory content drive demand for the Lab's hardware products through the roof. Retinal projection devices, sensory feedback garments, audiovisual motion simulators, and environment modeling tools fly off the shelves of the warehouse.

Around this time, I notice several new words entering the Lab's lexicon. Usually aided by Frank, Emmie and I learn these new words together.

The first is *alternet domain*. A domain is a collection of alternet content, often contained in a three-dimensional representation of a physical environment.

An alternet domain is usually discussed in the same breath as *immersion*. Immersion is accessing multi-sensory experiences on the alternet.

To the delight of the Lab team, one of their own engineers coins the word *immerger*, which quickly gains traction in the broader tech community. An immerger is anything that aids immersion, including most of the products designed and manufactured by the Lab.

And finally there's *Tomo*. Tomo Yoshimoto is the Japanese alternet domain designer whose recently-launched alternet domain *Kaisei* epitomizes immersion.

Kaisei and its creator become an overnight international sensation. Comparison to Tomo becomes the highest praise Travis can bestow upon his own designers. Frank's engineers engage in an ongoing battle of one-upmanship to improve the user experience of Tomo's *Kaisei* through increasingly subtle refinements to the Lab's sensory augmentation gear. The Lab's entire mission soon seems to revolve around enablement of Tomo-quality immersion experiences.

I follow Emmie for days after the launch of Tomo's *Kaisei* as she explores the domain in full head-to-toe immergers. She and I are equally awestruck by the acres of Japanese gardens through which users enter the domain. The expansive content beyond the entrance grows only more ethereal and wonderful as Emmie roams the domain.

The only thing that stops me and Emmie from wandering the subdomains of *Kaisei* forever is the arrival of the first day of kindergarten.

△▽△

"Everybody hates me," I cry, bursting into Ollie's bedroom after school. Ollie stands at the center of her room, staring into space, probably immersed in alternet research for her school homework. Twelve-year-olds seem to have a depressing amount of homework.

Ollie blinks, refocusing her eyes from the visual overlay rendered by her retinal projection glasses. She takes a look at my runny nose, sore from rubbing, and puffy eyes, wet with tears. She pushes back her glasses, peels off her immerger gloves, and hauls me up onto her bed. We flop back onto the soft, sky-blue comforter, my dark curls tangling with Ollie's long blonde hair.

"What happened?" says Ollie.

Between sobs, I tell her about the mean group of girls who stole everything out of my desk when we were on the way to recess. They even took the set of perfectly sharpened colored pencils Uncle Frank gave me for my birthday. I'd run after them to get my things back, but I was too late. I watched through the chain link fence surrounding the playground as a stack of my drawings blew away into the street, and all of my colored pencils rolled into the storm drain.

"Wow," Ollie says seriously. "That was really mean."

Ollie knows all about mean girls. The girls in her class tease her because she's so smart, and because she doesn't care much about clothes or boys or sleepover parties. Ollie only cares about grown-up things.

"And now my pictures—" I sniff and rub my nose again. "I made them for Mama's birthday, and now they're all lost! I don't think I can ever make such good drawings, not ever again."

"Well, if you put something on paper, you're bound to lose it eventually. And then …" Playfully, Ollie loops one of my curls around her finger and lets it snap back against my cheek like a spring. "Poof! It's gone."

This makes me start sobbing again, but Ollie hushes me. "Listen," she says. "If you want to make a drawing that you can't lose, one that will last forever, you need to make lots and lots of copies and hide them everywhere."

I stop mid-sob to ask, "But how? I can't even make two copies look the same."

"Don't draw with paper and pencils, then," says Ollie, indicating the pair of immerger gloves on her desk. I frown. How else can I draw, if not with paper and pencils?

Ollie sighs and says in her very grown-up teacher voice, "Emmie, do you think that when the designers at the Lab make—I don't know … a table, a shoe, a flower—that, when they need another one, they build it again from scratch? Do you think Tomo designs every single leaf on every single tree separately?"

I shrug. Tomo can do just about anything, as far as I know.

"Well," says Ollie. "He doesn't. He designs something once, and then he stores it in a content library on the alternet. When he needs to put it in one of his domains, he takes a copy, and then when he needs another, he takes another. The alternet servers do all the hard work, making the copies. And not only that, but the alternet servers are constantly making new copies and sending them to other servers, so the only way to lose your content is if you lost *the entire alternet* too."

I stare at Ollie, mouthing the words *the entire alternet.*

"So, you should just make your drawings for the alternet," Ollie says decisively. "You'll be like Tomo. Now—" She shoos me off her bed. "Get out of here. I've got work to do."

I stick out my tongue at Ollie, then dry my eyes. I trot off to my room, repeating under my breath, "The *entire* alternet. The *entire alternet.*"

△▽△

Over the next several days, I take Ollie's advice. Instead of picking up my drawing pencils again, I teach myself to use some of the alternet design software the engineers use at the Lab. It's not too difficult, and Uncle Travis lets me use pretty much any of the computers and immergers at his workbench, if he's not using them. Soon, I forget all about the silly girls at school. Why bother thinking about them, when I can build a whole world of my own without them in it?

By the time Mom's birthday dinner arrives, I've just managed to finish making a replacement present for her. It's a lot better than the first drawing I made for her. It's a big three-dimensional portrait of our entire family. I think she'll like it.

Loud laughter from upstairs announces the arrival of the first guests. I drop my drawing stylus, throw my immergers on my bed, and race up to the kitchen.

"Uncle Frank!" I call.

"Hey, little girl," he says, reaching down to tickle me and mess up my hair.

"Where's my tree?" I say, giggling and pulling at his long sleeve.

"Emmie," Mom warns. "Don't be rude."

"Oh, let her, Ana," says Dad. "Frank likes showing off his arms to the girls."

Uncle Frank's girlfriend Nora, hovering near his side, seems to think this is very funny. I don't like Nora very much. Whenever she's around, it's hard to get Uncle Frank's attention. But now, Uncle Frank is paying attention, and he rolls up his sleeve for me. Underneath, stretched out across his muscley arm, there's a great big tree that covers the skin from his shoulder all the way down to his elbow.

"You added more branches," I say, tracing the new lines of ink worked into the skin.

"Well, you just keep growing," says Frank.

"Does it hurt?" I say, looking up at him in concern.

"Yes," says Mom, with the voice that means someone is about to get into trouble.

Uncle Frank says seriously, "Yes. Tattoos hurt very much. That's why you will never, ever, get one. You'll just have to be happy with your one tree."

"It's not really *her* tree, though," says Ollie. "You started that tattoo before she was even born, didn't you, Uncle Frank?"

I look up at Uncle Frank expectantly.

"We-e-ell," Uncle Frank says. "That's true, but it wouldn't be the same without the drawing Emmie made for me."

"You still have it, don't you?" I say. I'm proud that Uncle Frank used my own drawing for his tattoo.

"Sure do," says Uncle Frank. He reaches into his back pocket and pulls out his wallet. He takes out a worn piece of paper folded many times over. He hands it to me, and I spread the familiar paper on the countertop for Mom to see, as I've done many times before.

"Yes, sweetheart," Mom says patiently. "I see it. It's very well done."

"I did it all by myself," I say.

"Emmie," Mom says gently. "Don't exaggerate."

I roll my eyes. "Oh, all right," I say. "I traced it from one of the tree photos in your office."

Mom looks a little sad about this. She doesn't like it when I talk about those photographs, even though she keeps them in lots of different rooms in our house. Why would she keep them around if they make her sad?

"Ah!" Uncle Frank laughs. "So our little artist is a plagiarist?"

"What's a plagiarist?" I ask, sounding out the word.

"It's someone who steals someone else's work and takes credit for it," says Ollie.

"It's stealing?" I say. I pull back my tree drawing quickly from the countertop, embarrassed. My cheeks feel hot.

"Hey," Uncle Frank whispers, crouching down beside me and putting his hand on my shoulder. "I was just teasing. Every artist steals things sometimes. Sometimes, stealing is just another word for inspiration."

△▽△

On the weekday afternoons over the next few years, while Ollie focuses on her schoolwork in a quiet back office in the Lab, I trail Emmie as she roams the halls, procrastinating.

Emmie develops a knack for slipping into the background as the Lab's engineers and designers carry on their work. In this way, she manages to sneak peeks and demos of nearly every interesting gadget in development at the Lab.

The year Emmie turns twelve, I'm witness to a months-long campaign to convince her parents to install a spliner in her bedroom. Having had privileged access to the Lab spliner since her infancy, Emmie doesn't consider having one for her personal use to be an unreasonable request. Travis and Anatolia fundamentally disagree, patiently and repeatedly explaining the financial and space constraints that make this an impossibility. Reasoning like theirs seems unlikely to prevail in this particular battle of wills, unfortunately. Emmie is relentless.

"Could I have my own identity credentials, then, at least?" Emmie pleads at the end of a particularly long argument. It's a strategic move, falling back on a previously denied request that she knows poses no financial burden. From where she sits, curled up beside her father on the sofa, she looks pleadingly across the coffee table at her mother.

"Why do you need your own credentials?" says Anatolia. "You already have anonymous read access to every domain that could possibly be appropriate for someone your age."

"But I want to be a domain designer like Tomo," says Emmie, sitting up straight on the sofa and tucking a strand of flat-ironed chestnut hair streaked with cobalt blue behind her ear. Imitating her older sister's most reasonable voice, she explains, "I can't publish my work in any of the good artist domains without my own creds, my own identity."

"Those public forums are full of unauthenticated identities, Emmie," Anatolia says patiently. "They're not safe for someone your age. There will be plenty of time for you to use those forums when you're older."

"*How* old?" says Emmie, not quite keeping the whine out of her voice. "Ollie already had her own credentials when she was my age!"

"Ollie needed credentials to take classes in some of her educational domains," says Anatolia. "We didn't just let her wander around any public domain she chose."

"I know how to take care of myself on the alternet, Mom! Do you think I'm stupid?"

"I think you're twelve years old, Emerald," snaps Anatolia. "You know plenty about the alternet, but I know a lot more about people than you do. You have to think carefully about what you do on the alternet. Even when you think you're doing something anonymously, securely, even when you think you're being very clever, you can leave clues. You can't even imagine what some people …"

"What?" says Emmie, crossing her arms. "What some people *what?*"

Travis and Anatolia exchange a long look.

"Emmie," Travis says, his voice uncharacteristically stern. "Mom is just looking out for you."

"What is she afraid I'm going to do?" says Emmie, turning to her father.

"It's not what I'm afraid *you'll* do," says Anatolia. "It's what I'm afraid *other* people might do."

"You think everyone is out to get me," says Emmie. "I don't get it. You're not this way with Ollie. She can do whatever she wants."

"Not true!" Ollie hollers up from her room downstairs.

"Ana," Travis says, reaching out to put a hand on Anatolia's knee. "I agree that we can't just give Emmie credentials and free rein to do anything she wants with them. But unless we're going to cut her off completely from the alternet—"

"OMG, Dad," Emmie groans, covering her face with her hands. "Don't give her ideas!"

Travis sighs. "Ana, we can't protect her from everything forever."

Ollie appears at the top of the stairs, arriving just in time to see her mother's eyes fill with tears. She takes a seat beside her mother.

"I have an idea," Ollie says brightly, as if addressing a class of kindergarteners. "What if you give Emmie her own credentials but only let her use them when Mom is supervising?"

"Ollie!" Emmie cries indignantly.

Anatolia tilts her head to the side, considering. At last, she says, "That's not a bad idea. I'm at the office so much that I don't get to spend half as much time with Emmie as Dad does. I just—" She looks at Emmie. Gently, she says, "Honey, I don't want to make you hate me more than you already do."

Emmie's indignant expression melts. "OMG, Mom! I don't hate you."

It's not entirely clear to me who's won this argument. But, soon afterwards, Anatolia registers an identity credential for Emmie, and Emmie suppresses her objections to her mother's unwanted supervision. Neither mother nor daughter seem thrilled by the arrangement, but—to Travis' evident relief—both seem content to preserve the fragile peace between them.

Emmie obsesses for days over the design of an avatar for her first alternet identity, which she names Bealsio. As soon as she's satisfied with her new identity, she refocuses her energy on crafting the perfect debut submission to *Emergency*. It's an ambitious goal. Millions of aspiring alternet designers—most of them adults and established artists—share their work in *Emergency*'s showcase domain, hoping to be plucked from obscurity by recruiters from the more prestigious commercial domains. Emmie is determined to be discovered.

△▽△

The intensity of Emmie's desire to create something magnificent is what wakes me from sleep. There have been a few moments like this since her birth, when her will has been so strong that it's overcome my ability to resist the pull of her awareness. But this time, there's something different in the pull, an urgency I haven't felt before from Emmie. The connection between us grows taut, impossible for me to resist.

I catch a parting glimpse of the position of the stars outside the window of my sleeping quarters. Barely four hours until sunrise. I hope that will be enough time for whatever Emmie needs from me. It'll be risky for me to conduct my day's work in the presence of Mohirai when Emmie's awareness might snatch mine away from my body unexpectedly. My occasional absences from my work sites can be explained away, on the rare occasions they're noticed, but the absence of my awareness from my body would mean only one thing to an observant Mohira: forbidden pharmaka at work. That's a problem for later, though. For now, I yield to the relentless pull of Emmie's awareness, following it through the void until I'm standing once again at her side.

Emmie sits in a swivel chair in the midst of the quiet back office of the Lab that Ollie recently vacated after receiving her long-hoped-for and well-earned acceptance letter from Princeton University. She's dimmed the lights, locked the door, and pushed Ollie's old desk against one wall.

Emmie twists a lock of her hair between the immerger-ring-encrusted fingers of one hand as she spins the swivel chair round and round with her toes. She's changed out of her school uniform into full-body immergers, and the silver threads woven into the skin-tight black fabric gleam in the low light. Her startlingly green eyes, ringed with thick eyeliner and smoky powder, focus inward. Though the particulars of Emmie's face and her experimental makeup are new, her expression recalls to me a hundred thousand memories and a thousand thousand regrets from other lifetimes of Ava.

I watch Emmie spin for a while, until she withdraws a pair of immerger glasses from the front pocket of the loose tunic she wears as a concession to Anatolia's complaint that immerger clothes are "too revealing," notwithstanding Emmie's still boyish figure. A quick tap to the band on her wrist switches on the three-dimensional retinal projection functionality of the glasses and engages the tactile feedback of her shirt. With another few swipes of her fingers, she immerses herself in *Kaisei*, Tomo's flagship domain.

Because *Kaisei* has become the default alternet testing ground for all Lab hardware prototypes, the domain is almost as familiar to me now as the Lab itself. I see through Emmie's eyes and feel through Emmie's senses as she chooses an avatar. Today she picks an old woman with a tranquil smile and a richly-embroidered blue silk kimono. Wearing this avatar, Emmie steps through the red *torii* archway into the main *Kaisei* subdomain: *Minu ga hana*, a sprawling Japanese tea garden.

In the physical world, Emmie reaches into another pocket of her tunic to pull out an olfactory augmentation patch, which she presses to her collar. Passing through the simulated garden, she inhales the scents of sweet grass, fresh water, rosy cherry blossoms, spicy evergreens; runs the fingers of her tactile immerger gloves over mossy stones and smooth wooden bridge railings; listens to the rustle of leaves and splashes of frogs into the pond.

When Emmie emerges from *Kaisei* an hour later, her mind swirls with a chaos of ideas so dazzling that they would be impossible to capture in any medium. Through our connection, I glimpse each idea as it flashes in and out of existence in her mind. She growls under her breath. I understand her frustration perfectly, having sat in her place so many times over the millennia. Moments of inspiration like this are vivid but fleeting.

Emmie withdraws a grey stylus from yet another pocket of her tunic and opens the two-dimensional interface of an environmental modeling toolkit. She uses the stylus to paint in broad, confident strokes upon the air, colors gathering in a bright but indefinite form. Minutes later, with an exasperated sigh, she lets the colors fade to nothing. She switches to a different tool, this time a terrain modeler, with which she has slightly better but still unsatisfactory results.

As her frustration mounts and Emmie loses focus, her pull on our connection weakens. Relieved, I let go of my hold on her world and return to my body. It's difficult for me to fall back asleep, though. This encounter with Emmie reawakens deep worries that I've managed to hold at bay since her birth. If the pull of her awareness in mine grows much stronger, it will be impossible for me to maintain the boundary between us that has for so many years allowed me to remain hidden from her sight. The intensity of Emmie's imagination in early childhood occasionally caused some lapses on my part, leading to brief moments of contact between us, but I've tried to minimize such encounters, especially now that she's old enough to realize her connection to me can't be explained by anything in her world. I know firsthand how dangerous it is to invade another's awareness, and how easily it can lead to madness. As long as I can, I'll keep Emmie unaware of my presence. It's one of the few gifts I can give her.

△▽△

Emmie establishes a new routine in the weeks that follow. She immerses herself in *Kaisei* after school, emerges in a burst of inspiration, scrambles to capture an idea in shape or color or sound or texture, and regards the result with despair. The part of Ava's awareness that's taken root in Emmie Bridges is as self-critical as ever, and as tenacious. Some things never change.

Capturing clear forms from her chaotic imagination becomes Emmie's sole obsession, to the point that she begins to withdraw from her unofficial responsibilities and social obligations at the Lab.

"Don't you love me anymore?" Uncle Frank wails one afternoon, after having pounded on Emmie's locked door for a solid minute in an attempt to recruit her to his team for a Nerf skirmish in the spliner.

Emmie looks guiltily at the door but doesn't respond, instead turning up the volume on her earbuds. She hums under her breath, drumming her stylus on her thigh, standing in the middle of her office. I stand behind her, watching ideas coming in and out of focus in her mind.

Suddenly, every thread of Ava's mantle stitched beneath my skin tingles at once, electrifying me. Emmie freezes where she stands, her face lit up with amazement. An image flickers through her mind, an image that swells my hope: a great tree, branches swaying in the wind. But as soon as it appears, the image is gone. Emmie slips on her immerger glasses hurriedly and sets to work with her stylus.

Over the next several hours, she sculpts into the air the great tree: roots buried deep in rich soil; branches thick with foliage and heavy with fruit; breeze rustling through the leaves, spreading a sweet herbal scent through the air. I can't resist helping her, adding bits and pieces of my own memory to her vision, holding the image clear in my mind when it seems at risk of slipping from hers. When at last the vision is securely captured, Emmie leans back against the wall and stares at her work in amazement.

She jumps at the loud knock on the door.

"Emmie?" says Travis. "Are you still alive in there?"

"Yeah," she says distractedly. "Can I just have a minute?"

"All right, but we need to drive home soon. Nanna made dinner, and she's waiting for us."

Emmie wrinkles her nose, her eyes never wavering from the great tree hovering before her.

After a pause, Travis says tentatively, "Want to show me what you're working on?"

Emmie bites her lip, looking from the tree to the closed door. "Fine," she says. "But I want you to be honest, if it's not any good."

She unlocks the door and opens it slowly. Her father smiles down at her and steps into the room, slipping on his immerger glasses.

"What port?" he says.

Emmie checks her visual overlay. "I'm on 51094," she says.

Travis flicks on his overlay and blinks to bring it into focus. He stands silent for a long time.

"Well?" Emmie says anxiously.

"Wow," he says, a smile of intense pride spreading over his face. "Sweetheart … It's incredible."

Emmie beams. I wish I could savor this moment of intense satisfaction with her, but I glimpse in that tree the beginning of the great work that will be her undoing.

△▽△

Despite several clashes with Anatolia over what constitutes sufficiently anonymous content, Emmie eventually manages to publish her work on *Emergency.* Her immersive portfolio is an eclectic collection, demonstrating surprising sophistication in the manipulation of the senses but a still-childlike taste for the fanciful: playful and cartoonish characters possessing basic artificial intelligence; lifelike baby animals designed to tempt the alternet's insatiable appetite for puppies and kittens; abstract single-sensory landscapes in visual, auditory, olfactory, and tactile modalities. She agonizes over whether to put the great tree, her masterpiece, into her public portfolio. To my relief, some instinct persuades Emmie to keep this piece private, at least for the time being. Neither she nor I are yet ready for the unwanted attention that tree might attract.

During sessions supervised by Anatolia, Emmie interacts through her avatar Bealsio with a slow trickle of visitors to her *Emergency* portfolio, thanking people for feedback and swapping critiques with other designers. A few months after her debut submission, traffic to Bealsio's portfolio surges when an influential alternet design commentator mentions one of her pieces in an article about the effective use of tactile elements in domain design. Her portfolio hits all the bandwidth limits for a free account within an hour that day, and Emmie begs her mother to upgrade her to a professional account, which Anatolia does with a touch of pride.

Week by week, the visitor traffic to Bealsio's portfolio continues to grow. The delight and amazement of her visitors spurs Emmie on to ever more ambitious projects. Bealsio attracts growing numbers of comments and reviews in design forums, sending Emmie through the stratosphere with praise or ripping her self-confidence to shreds with criticism.

"It's not healthy," I overhear Anatolia murmur to Travis after a particularly vicious comment dismisses Bealsio's portfolio as "a heavy-handed application of trendy multi-sensory varnish to the most tired of clichés … childish at best." Emmie lies listless on the sofa with the music in her earbuds blaring.

Travis, re-reading the vitriol on his visual overlay for the tenth time, splutters, "This guy … I can't believe … What a jackass!"

"I know this is what she loves, but … isn't it a bit premature to expose her to all these crazy people?" says Anatolia. "Look what it's doing to her."

Travis closes the article and takes a deep breath, shaking his head. "We can't do anything to stop them, and we can do even less to stop Emmie. I think we'll just have to help her ignore all the background noise."

Anatolia's lawyer instincts prove more useful than Travis' clumsy attempts to comfort Emmie. Anatolia spends lunch breaks and evenings for days digging through alternet and internet archives, even hitting the physical stacks at the Cal library in Berkeley, gathering up the historical evidence of crimes against creative people by the jaded and cynical, the self-important and pedantic, and the downright mean and stupid.

One evening, not long after the "childish at best" review, Anatolia returns home from work to find Emmie alone on the roof deck. Emmie sits at the edge of the deck, dangling her legs over the edge, gazing despondently at the treetops far below her feet, oblivious to the spectacular sunset across the Bay.

Anatolia joins Emmie, wraps her arm around her shoulders, and gives her an affectionate squeeze. She says, "Sweetheart, the only way you'll become a great artist is if you learn to keep on going despite the naysayers. There's not a single great artist in history who didn't get called a hack—or worse. See for yourself." Anatolia presses into Emmie's palm the coin-sized storage drive whose contents she's painstakingly compiled over the last several days.

Early the next morning, having spent a sleepless night poring over Anatolia's gift, Emmie makes her mother breakfast in bed.

"I don't care what they say," Emmie says firmly, setting the tray on her mother's lap. "None of those idiots are going to stop me."

OTAKU

ANATOLIA'S UNWAVERING SUPPORT of Emmie's artistic ambitions transforms the bond between mother and daughter as Emmie grows up. During my visits to Earth over the next few years, I observe Emmie and Anatolia's once combative relationship evolving into one that's increasingly constructive. They may never see things the same way, but through the many hours Anatolia spends chaperoning Emmie's sessions in *Emergency* each week, Emmie learns to respect her mother's insight, and Anatolia learns to trust Emmie's judgment.

So, on Emmie's sixteenth birthday, Anatolia gives her daughter a gift so tremendous that Emmie wouldn't have dared to ask for it: the login credentials for Bealsio.

"OMG, Mom!" Emmie squeals, staring at the little storage drive her mother taped to the inside of her birthday card. "I can't believe it! Thank you!"

She smothers her mother in kisses, then races down the stairs to her room to log on to *Emergency* for her very first private alternet session.

Without the need for a chaperone, Emmie has nearly unlimited time to interact with the *Emergency* community. Her creative output explodes as a result. She rides a productive high for a few months, but her obsessive focus on her alternet life drains her, leaving little time or energy left over for other endeavors. Facing the choice between keeping up her real-life persona as passable high school student alongside her alternet persona as virtuoso designer Bealsio, she decides to let go of her real-life persona. I've seen Ava make decisions like this over so many lifetimes that I recognize a pivotal moment. Whatever reason Ava has for choosing this life, this place, this time, seems likely to be revealed to me soon.

That summer, when Emmie announces at the dinner table her intention to drop out of high school, Anatolia and Travis turn to one another, a wordless conversation passing between them. Emmie has a long track record of winning arguments with them, and the stakes for this argument are unusually high.

After the uncomfortably long pause that follows her bold announcement, Emmie looks from one parent to the other. In a conciliatory tone, she adds, "I can still finish my diploma, if you care about that. I could even take college classes. You know how great the alternet education services are."

"Look," Travis says delicately. "I know high school isn't great all the time, but you can't just quit without a plan."

"But I do have a plan," says Emmie. "I'm going to be an alternet domain designer."

"And there's still a lot you can learn to help you do that," says Anatolia. "You could go to art school, for example. Or study computer science, or—"

Emmie shakes her head. "I've read about a lot of those programs," she says. "I visited some of the campus domains, too—at Stanford and Caltech and MIT, at

RISD. I talked to students there, sat in on some classes. They don't have anything to teach me. I already know more than a lot of the professors because of all the work I've done on *Emergency* and at the Lab."

"Honey," says Anatolia, visibly struggling to keep a level tone. "You'll have the rest of your life to spend off in the alternet. There won't be that many times in your life when you can be really present with other people, in person, like you can now. To make friends who really know *you*, and not just some avatar."

"Bealsio's a real part of me, Mom," says Emmie, stung. "Not 'just some avatar.'"

The argument continues for weeks. Emmie develops deft responses to each new protest or concern raised by her parents, eventually going so far as to recruit her sister to her cause. Sitting in on the debate via video chat from the lab where she's doing summer research for her cognitive anthropology program, Ollie weaves several compelling anecdotes from their childhood growing up in the Lab into her assessment that academia severely lags industry when it comes to emerging media. Ollie's support is the final blow to her parents' resistance. Emmie prevails, as I'd known she would, and she drops out of high school.

Emmie leans in to her own momentum. She turns her attention to setting up her design studio on the bottom floor of the Bridges' house, in the room her father calls the fishbowl.

The morning she asks for her father's permission to take over the fishbowl for her work, Travis hesitates. There's a note of sadness in his voice as he says, "Won't you be lonely down there, Em? There's plenty of room for you at the Lab. We can give you your own office, if you want. We miss you there, you know?"

Emmie shakes her head. "If I stay at the Lab, I won't be able to get any work done without Uncle Frank barging in every other minute for some immerger feedback, or the interns recruiting me for games in the spliner. There's always something. And Mom can't stand going down to the fishbowl, so she won't bother me, either. It's perfect."

Travis' loss is my gain. Having set up countless workshops for myself over the centuries, I appreciate the appeal of the fishbowl as a studio for Emmie. I'm delighted we'll be spending more time there.

Emmie's new work routine in her studio starts early, soon after sunrise. The fishbowl is located three flights below the distinctive street-level roof deck of the Bridges' home, accessed by an elegant spiral of floating wooden stairs. The spiral staircase descends to a small inner room excavated from the improbably steep hillside where the house stands. The earth-colored walls, moss-green carpet, and low lighting of the inner room reinforce the visual impression of an underground cave. The dark walls are lined with storage cabinets, which Emmie fills with artists' tools of every era—from pencils and paper to environment-sculpting knives and full-body immerger clothes. Each morning, she selects a few tools from these cabinets before she opens the door that connects the inner room to the larger outer room of the fishbowl.

In what I can only imagine was a burst of vertigo-inducing inspiration, the architect of the Bridges' hilltop aerie chose to suspend the fishbowl from the underside of the cantilevered foundation that supports the structure above. Crystal-clear panels of glass form the three outer walls and floor of the fishbowl, so when Emmie emerges each day from the cavelike inner room, she seems to step out on thin air. Closing the door behind her completes the illusion, as the inner wall becomes a seamless mirror reflecting the breathtaking view across the Bay.

Anatolia can't bear the sensation of precarious suspension created by this room, but Emmie strides out onto the glass floor each morning like it's the most natural thing in the world to hover midair. She tends to be under full sensory immersion before she even enters the room, though, so her fearlessness might be due partially to obliviousness.

On my visits to Emmie in the fishbowl, I watch and aid her ever more ambitious creative endeavors. Ava's awareness tends to be fiery, tempestuous, impatient—especially in youth—and the effect of this awakening awareness is obvious in Emmie as she begins to practice the art she's chosen for this life.

The connection between our awarenesses binds us in a dancing tug-of-war as Emmie struggles to master her craft and manifest her sprawling, disorganized visions into her art. For now, I maintain a disciplined distance from her. She learns to associate my unseen influence with the penetrating sunlight and perfect privacy of the fishbowl. Instinctively, she pulls at our connection when she needs a clarifying influence. Through our connection, I share measured responses and needed counterpoint with patience perfected through centuries of collaboration with Ava. Though the digital media of this world's alternet is new to me in its particulars, the essence of creating art with her remains the same, whether we're building together with physical or ethereal media.

Our collaboration ushers in a period of prolific creation for Emmie that produces a thousand gardens for the senses. For days on end, sprawled across the glass floor of the fishbowl, Emmie sketches landscapes and creatures which she later summons into existence with sculpting gloves, texturing knife, and finishing stylus. Gazing into her visual overlay, she programs games and outlines quests. Under the influence of full sensory immersion, she contemplates her work, animating and polishing and extending to the outer reaches of her imagination and skill. I watch over her work through it all, witness to and participant in her every struggle and triumph, through waking inspirations and sleeping dreams.

When she's exhausted all her creativity, Emmie tackles a token amount of schoolwork to satisfy her mother's requirement that she eventually complete her high school equivalency. Then Emmie rewards herself with alternet immersion, seeking in worlds shaped by other hands the inspiration for her next day's work.

△▽△

Having spent the entire summer convincing Mom and Dad to take my artistic aspirations seriously, I feel a huge sense of satisfaction when I step out into the light of the fishbowl each morning. It's like being the pilot of an amazing airship.

The whole world spreads out before me, and I can go anywhere, with a little help from the alternet and my immergers.

I try to be disciplined about my work. I spend mornings focusing on my portfolio projects. It's frustrating, sometimes. I feel like I'm fighting some part of my mind into submission as I search for the one small tweak that will make the difference between good and great work. But the struggle's always worth it, in the end. There's nothing, nothing in the world, more satisfying than standing before a piece of my own work and knowing it's perfect.

When I finish a piece, I usually have a few hours or days before the itch to start something new creeps up on me again. I use this time to unwind in the alternet.

There are so many domains I'm desperate to explore. I spent years in the Lab peeking over the shoulders of the designers and engineers as they browsed domains that were off-limits to me before I had my own credentials. Now that Mom trusts me with my own alternet identity, I'd expected to find every door in the alternet open to me.

The reality has been disappointing. Although there are a few decent public domains accessible to anyone with an alternet connection, all the really interesting domains are switching to airtight authentication protocols and adult credential requirements to avoid the scrutiny of the alternet regulation movement.

These alternet regulators are ridiculous. I've watched plenty of feeds of red-faced politicians and bombastic preachers denouncing the alternet as an underworld of pornographers, tax evaders, and black market business owners, but I doubt any of them have ever been immersed in the alternet like I have.

Even so, the creators of alternet domains take the regulation movement very seriously. "No one's taking any chances, after what those Luddites did to the internet," according to Uncle Frank.

Unfortunately for me, this means that most of the domains I've been longing to explore on my own since I was a kid are now wrapped up in nearly impenetrable layers of security, including *Mysteries of Eleusis*.

I heard of *Eleusis* for the first time when Uncle Frank stumbled from his office bleary-eyed and grinning one day after playing the game for twelve hours straight.

"The most addictive game ever!" he raved to the engineering team.

"Isn't it just a glorified game of capture the flag?" one of the younger guys had asked skeptically.

Eleusis is both, in fact. Though the gameplay is pretty basic—work with your army, either Zeus' or Hades', to maintain or obtain possession of the Persephone avatar—and the audiovisual quality only decent, at high levels of competition there's an exciting degree of improvisation and skill required. The game is basically the national pastime at the Lab these days. Most of the engineers spend their evenings after work using the Lab's high-speed alternet connection to play the game together.

The gameplay itself isn't what I care about, though. I've never grokked the appeal of combat games. More interesting to me is the fact that *Eleusis* is the preferred hangout for a number of influential alternet personalities, along with a diverse but close-knit community of players: tech-savvy screen-watchers whiling away shocking stretches of time on the clock; multi-tasking jet-setters using simulated combat to process violent urges aroused by their work; stay-at-home parents with mythic fantasies; and the usual rabble of college students, game addicts, and the unemployed.

I want access to that community. If I'm ever going to learn how to make my own domains popular, I'm going to have to understand what users truly love. My problem is that *Eleusis* now employs an adult identity verification system that's nearly impossible to circumvent.

I spend days searching for a possible workaround in public alternet domains, eventually posting a question on *MMORPhology*, a gamer forum, asking if anyone's ever been granted an exception to the adult credentials requirement for *Eleusis*. A number of people post sympathetic comments. Many appear to have tried and failed.

But one day a private message pops up on my visual overlay.

prodigytal: I've cracked half the adult authentication systems out there. Want to chat?

I read the message with a mixture of elation and apprehension. Mom will kill me if she finds out I've been talking to hackers on the alternet. After a moment's hesitation, I write back to prodigytal.

Bealsio: Definitely.

I accept a private projection request from prodigytal, and a moment later I'm looking at an avatar that appears to have been modeled on a samurai warrior: heavy leather armor covered in metal scales, an elaborate helmet with a crest that spreads upward like the wings of a bird, a pair of crossed swords with gleaming rosewood and ebony sheaths strapped over the padded shoulders. Inside the helmet, instead of a face, there's only a shadow pierced by two blue points of light where the eyes should be. It's a beautifully designed avatar, if a bit creepy, and clearly custom-made. I'm surprised. Hackers aren't generally known for their design taste.

"Um, hi," I say, trying not to sound as nervous as I am. "So, you've cracked *Eleusis* authentication?"

There's a long pause. Maybe the projection is lagging? Then prodigytal's avatar shakes with laughter. A voice—modulated with a filter that's just enough to anonymize the underlying voice without interfering with the subtleties of inflection that distinguish real human speech—says, "So Bealsio's not just underage, but a girl!"

I frown. I usually pick a male avatar for Bealsio, especially in gamer forums. At the moment, I'm using a pretty generic twenty-something male with sandy hair and an ironic tee-shirt, but I hadn't thought to disguise my voice on this private audio channel with prodigytal.

"Does it matter?" I say, trying to cover my mistake with a note of scorn.

prodigytal shrugs. "I was just curious. I've been following you on *Emergency* for a long time."

A hundred alarms go off in my head—most sounding like Mom—warning of alternet stalkers. I'm inclined to close the channel immediately, but prodigytal continues, "But no, it doesn't matter to me. Let's talk about authentication. I've faked *Eleusis* creds before. I could do it again. So what's it worth to you?"

I'm taken aback. I'd expected this to be merely a friendly exchange of tips, as is typical in gamer forums. I hadn't expected someone hacking for hire.

"I … guess I don't know," I say.

prodigytal is silent for a moment before he says, "I'll do it for a thousand dollars."

I laugh in surprise. "Whoa. There's no way I can afford that."

"Well?" prodigytal seems undeterred. "What can you afford?"

I shake my head. "I was just looking for some advice," I say. "Sorry for wasting your time." I reach up for the exit control on my visual overlay.

"Hold on," prodigytal says hurriedly. "Why can't we negotiate something?"

"Look," I say sharply. "I don't know you. It was stupid of me to even ask. Why don't you just drop it?"

prodigytal suddenly switches out of avatar form. On my projection appears a live video feed of a tall, skinny boy about my age, with white-blonde hair and piercing blue eyes.

"Fine," he says. "Let's drop the avatar bullshit. I'm Zeke Eckerd. I can get you your adult creds. And I need the money."

Zeke looks strangely forlorn, and—I realize with surprise—maybe even a little hungry. I feel a pang of sympathy for him. "I'm sorry," I say, "but I really don't have any money to spend on this. I'm—Well, obviously, I'm underage. I get some ad revenue from my design portfolio, but I've spent it all on software and gear this month already."

Zeke nods, frowning thoughtfully. After a moment, he says, "Well, maybe we could barter for it."

"Barter what?" I say warily.

"I bet you've got some pretty killer software, based on the work of yours that I've seen on *Emergency*," he says.

I can't help feeling a little flattered. "You've been following me that closely, huh?"

Zeke nods. "I design stuff too," he says. "Subcontracting, mostly. I could use some better tools, maybe up my rate."

I can't see how it could hurt to give this boy a software license or two. I get so many of them for free from the Lab. So I say, "I guess I could do that."

Zeke smiles. "Awesome. Done."

The next morning, Zeke sends me an email with my fake adult credentials attached. He didn't ask for payment up front, which I take as a gesture of goodwill after our rocky opening negotiation. In the message body, he writes,

I'd love to show you the ropes in Eleusis sometime, if you want. — prodigytal

I re-read the message three times before sending him the activation key for the environment modeling suite that I recently stopped using in favor of the latest release. In the message body, I write,

That would be cool. Thanks for the creds. — Bealsio

△▽△

With Zeke's fake adult credentials, I'm finally able to log on to *Eleusis* for the first time. I meet up with Zeke in the avatar modeling entryway of the domain. Today, he's wearing an avatar of a tall young swordsman with a lean physique and shining golden armor. The avatar resembles the boy I saw on the live feed, although the avatar's face is less pinched and pale than Zeke's real face.

"So," I say, checking out the in-game avatar modeling toolkit as I consider what impression I want to make on my first foray into the battlegrounds, "do you play *Eleusis* a lot?"

"I don't have a lot of free time, but clients sometimes want knockoffs of *Eleusis* content, so I have to keep up with what's going on in here," says Zeke.

"It sounds like you do a lot of paid work," I say.

"I do okay," he says.

Obvious false modesty, I think. "Are you still in school, or do you work full-time?" I say.

"Um—" Zeke looks away. "Yeah, I'm out of school now. Out on my own."

I nod. "That's cool. That's what I want to do, too—design full-time, I mean."

"Yeah?" Zeke sounds enthusiastic. "It's like the best thing. I love it."

"I'd love to check out your work some time," I say.

For the first time, I see Zeke smile. At least, I see his avatar smile.

"Cool, yeah, that'd be great," he says. "Most of it's incorporated into the domains of people I sub for, but I can definitely show you."

It doesn't take long for me to familiarize myself with the avatar modeling tools available in *Eleusis*. They're not as extensive as my usual toolkit, since most *Eleusis* players have far less sophisticated immergers than I have, and proportionately less interest in avatar quality. But I can make do.

I decide to continue using my Bealsio username in *Eleusis*. While Zeke waits, I quickly craft a burly, olive-skinned male avatar based on scanned photographs of Papou. They're old photographs—from way back in the 1990's, when Mom was about my age, before there were digital cameras. I even manage to create a convincing simulation of my grandfather's voice using snippets of saved projection videos and birthday greetings from my personal files. I polish off my work with a fabulous suit of Grecian armor and a pair of short swords. I think

Papou would love it. He loves all things Greek.

"How do I look?" I say.

Zeke eyes my avatar appraisingly and says, "That'll do. So, next thing is we have to pick a server. The fastest servers are all in Asia, since there are so many players there. But unless you speak Mandarin or Cantonese, it's probably not worth it to deal with the latency issues. A local server makes the realtime gameplay smoother."

I scan the map of server locations. "What server do you usually use?" I say.

"I'm on the East Coast, but I work late, so Pacific time's fine with me," says Zeke.

"San Jose, then?" I say.

"Sure," he says.

I select the server and follow Zeke through the game portal into the San Jose server recruitment grounds.

I'm a little disappointed by the recruitment grounds: a nondescript field of sand, literally a sandbox environment. I soon realize that no one else in the recruitment grounds is interested in environment design quality, though. This is purely a location for business transactions.

Zeke says, "We could just go in, but you'll see more of what the game's about if we start with an army."

So we stand around waiting. Scouts for different armies comb the grounds for recruits. In the public chat channel, recruiters post requests for players with some demonstrated experience in other game domains. Since I have zero experience in this game, I'm worried I'll be waiting a long time. But it turns out that keeping my Bealsio username was smart. A few army recruiters recognize my name and come over to chat, willing to overlook my inexperience in light of my identity's reputation in other respectable alternet design forums.

Zeke and I are chatting with the avatar of a grizzled bowman, an unlikely fan of Bealsio's frolicking kitten simulations, when a youthful spearman approaches. He wears golden armor not dissimilar from Zeke's, as well as a large circular shield, which I stare at in amazement.

"That's incredible," I say, pointing to the intricate battle scene worked into the golden shield. "Did you design that?"

The spearman smiles. "I did," he says. "Thanks!"

Zeke frowns. He continues his conversation with the bowman, but his eyes flick back and forth between me and the golden spearman.

The spearman takes a step closer to me, holding out his shield, and says, "I did some tactile simulations on it too."

I reach out eagerly and, through my immerger gloves, feel the cool surface of the delicate metalwork under my fingertips. "Really great work," I say.

"I'm Otaku, by the way," says the spearman, extending his hand.

"Bealsio," I say.

"I know," he says. "I've seen your work. It's fantastic."

We shake hands. I feel his firm grip and the warmth of his fingers through my immerger gloves. I wonder whether this is what his hand feels like in real life, or just another tactile simulation.

The grizzled bowman Zeke was talking to passes on to another potential recruit. Zeke stands by in silence as Otaku and I continue our conversation about the finer points of immersive design.

After a while, Zeke says, "Hey, Bealsio, sorry, but I have to go. I've got a ton of work to do tomorrow morning. Maybe we'll go into the battlegrounds some other time?"

I glance at the time on my visual overlay. "OMG, I totally lost track of time." I laugh, which sounds strange in Papou's simulated voice. "I have to go too."

Otaku's avatar flashes me a cartoonish disappointed expression. Then, returning to the ostensible point of our whole interaction, he says, "Well anyway … Do you want to join my guild? You and your friend, I mean." He smiles at Zeke. "We're just starting up, but I think you'll like the other guys."

Zeke starts to shake his head, but I smile and say, "Sure. What's it called, again?"

"Amaranthian," says Otaku, sending me an invite that pops up as a message on my visual overlay. "We practice Tuesday and Thursday nights Pacific time, starting at eight PM. See you there!"

Otaku heads off toward a small group of avatars that's just entered the recruitment grounds.

"Well, that worked out well!" I say to Zeke.

"Yeah," he says, looking away. "I guess. See you Tuesday."

△▽△

Otaku turns out to be a gifted teacher and guild leader. I like the friendly team dynamic he cultivates in the guild. He takes practices seriously and makes the rest of us do the same. He likes to win, too. I hadn't expected how fun that can be. Under Otaku's leadership, Amaranthian accumulates an impressive win-loss record, quickly climbing the rankings on our San Jose server.

Lately, with all the work I'm doing on my design portfolio during daylight hours and the extra hours I'm spending with Otaku's guild on *Eleusis*, I'm immersed in the alternet almost around the clock, catching sleep at odd hours here and there. I still go upstairs for dinner to talk about my day with Mom and Dad, though. If they have reservations about my new schedule, at least they don't comment on it.

I use *Eleusis* to let off steam after frustrating design sessions in the fishbowl. The clash of swords satisfies some primal appetite in me for mindless physical action. As a bonus, I'm gaining a lot of alternet cultural knowledge—and laughing a lot—listening to the perpetual banter on the game's public channel. Channel discussions range from trending alternet memes and real-world news to the most indecipherable arcana of every imaginable alternet subculture. Even in the absence of combat and public channel banter, though, I think I'd return to *Eleusis* daily just to talk to Zeke and Otaku, who have quickly become my two best friends, besides Ollie.

"You know, it's good to move around armies, to learn some different fighting techniques," Zeke says to me one day, after we've won a few battles with Amaranthian. "Your player stats are pretty good now. I bet we could join a more established guild."

"I'm having fun here," I say. "Why don't we stay a little while longer?"

Zeke shrugs indifferently, then logs off without another word. I shake my head. What's up with him lately?

A few months after Zeke and I join the guild, Amaranthian heads into battle against The Destroyers, competing for the number one ranking on our server.

"My roommate Shiva is The Destroyers' guild leader," Otaku tells us as the guild prepares for battle. "Their guys are insane. I know most of them from my CS program. Every person in that guild has probably logged more hours in *Eleusis* this year than our entire guild combined. But they're disorganized. They rely on mods to counter all the common army maneuvers. We're going to write a new playbook, and we're going to crush them."

The roaring cheer that goes up from the Amaranthian army in response to Otaku's pep talk is thrilling. I join in at max volume. I'm beginning to understand how people get addicted to this game.

Emerging onto the battle field is a rush like I've never experienced before. Amaranthian, an army of avatars in gleaming gold and silver armor, faces off against The Destroyers' shadowy, smoking, blazing army from hell. Members of both guilds wear their most elaborate avatars and employ their most impressive custom-coded combat effects. It's an epic battle filled with screen-capture-worthy hand-to-hand combat sequences and heart-stopping turning points, arrayed across the otherworldly landscape of the Elysium battlefield. I've never seen such a large spectator count on our battle channel. We're closely matched, but in the end, Amaranthian carries the win.

In the celebratory aftermath, Otaku invites members of both guilds who live in the Bay Area to meet up in person and celebrate over a beer. The invitation, unfortunately, proves that alternet community doesn't usually translate well to the real world. Members of both guilds beg off, citing family commitments and work schedules.

At last, Otaku turns to me and says, "Come on, man. Don't tell me you're another one of *these* agoraphobes."

"Sorry," I say, my battle high fading as I think of the risk of revealing my minority status to anyone other than Zeke. "I can't."

Otaku's ribbing tone turns more respectful. He says, "How about coffee some time, then? Whenever you're free. I'd love to get your feedback in person on some alternet content I've been working on, if it's not too much of an imposition."

Zeke jumps in, his tone heated as he says, "Back off, man."

"Whoa," says Otaku, looking from Zeke to me in surprise. "No problem. I—"

"No," I interject, giving Zeke a sharp look. "I'd be happy to."

What r u doing? Zeke demands in a hastily-written private message. *He could report u to server gm. U could lose your adult creds.*

Cmon he wouldn't do that, I write back. *Chill out!*

The blue eyes of Zeke's avatar narrow, and he looks at me in silence for a moment before suddenly logging off the server. I send him a projection request, but his status message has switched to *Away*.

△▽△

Before my parents return home from work the next day, I head out the door, tapping the smartcom on my belt to send a quick projection to Dad. He answers my call after a few rings.

"Just wanted to let you know I'm going out to meet some friends in Berkeley," I say. "I should be back in time for dinner."

"What friends?" Dad asks blankly, squinting to refocus his eyes on my projection, clearly having just emerged from a deep immersion session elsewhere.

"Just some old friends from high school," I say lightly. "I'll be back soon. Love you!"

Dad raises an eyebrow but nods.

I take the bus to Berkeley and walk a few blocks to the coffee shop where Otaku and I agreed to meet. Here, I flick on my visual overlay and skim the list of public identities checked in at the café. Otaku's included among a dozen other usernames. I look up and scan the room, spotting him at a small table by the window: an athletic young man with short-cropped dark hair wearing a neatly-pressed collared shirt tucked into khaki slacks. I catch his attention with a little wave.

Otaku's eyes widen. He glances quickly at his smartcom, whose display confirms the identity of his coffee date. I make my way across the room toward him. He scrambles up to meet me. I stop a few feet away, registering his embarrassment.

"Are you …?" he begins uncertainly, clearing his throat as his eyes run along the form-fitting silver threads of my neck-to-ankle tactile immergers. It occurs to me belatedly that I should have thrown on one of those tunics Mom is forever reminding me to wear. I spend so much time wearing only immergers these days that I hardly even think about real clothes any more.

Otaku seems to have gotten stuck on his first question. He swallows, recovers his composure, and says, "How old are you?" I detect what might be a trace of a Southern accent.

"Sixteen," I say, my glare daring him to make something of it.

He inhales slowly, then chuckles. "Sorry. I'm being rude. This is my fault."

I shrug. Coolly, I say, "So … what? Does that mean you'd rather not be friends outside *Eleusis*?"

He glances around, considering the other café patrons, clearly worried about what this meeting might look like from someone else's perspective. I look around, too. No one is paying the least attention to us.

"Can we start over?" he says at last, extending his hand. "I'm Owen Cyrus. It's great to finally meet you in person."

"Nice to meet you, Owen. I'm Emmie Bridges," I say, shaking his hand. His real hand feels something like his avatar's hand: strong and warm. But without my own big male avatar, my real hand feels tiny in his.

After a few minutes of awkward preliminaries, we manage to regain our footing by resuming some of our recent in-game conversations. We speculate excitedly about what might be included in the upcoming expansion of Tomo's *Kaisei*. We discuss the widely anticipated opening of the first-of-its-kind stadium spliner installation in San Francisco. We ridicule the controversial attempts by various national governments to impose identity registration requirements on the alternet. The easy repartee of Bealsio and Otaku at last returning, Owen seems emboldened to turn to new subjects.

"So … you're in high school?" he says.

I take a sip of my black coffee. I'd ordered it mostly because Mom doesn't let me drink coffee at home. Despite the bitterness, I see the appeal of the flavor. I set down the mug carefully, unsure whether I want to get into this part of the conversation.

"Does it really matter?" I say.

"Come on," he says. "What's the point of meeting in person if we can't talk about normal stuff?"

"It's just going to make you feel more weird about me," I say.

"Okay," Owen laughs. "I admit I wasn't expecting you to be a teenage girl, but it's not like you're an extraterrestrial or something. Hopefully."

I roll my eyes at the feeble humor but can't suppress a giggle. "No," I say. "But I'm not in high school, either. I dropped out."

He frowns. "What do you do all day, then?"

"You've seen it," I say. "I design alternet content. I play *Eleusis*. I surf the alternet. I design some more. I study on the side, but mainly I'm working on becoming a designer."

He considers me appraisingly. "Pretty ballsy," he says. "Dropping out, pursuing your dream."

"There's nothing else I want to be doing. *Carpe diem*, right?" I say.

Owen looks down at the table, rotating his espresso by the edge of its saucer, his eyes distant as he says, "Yeah."

I wait for him to go on. When he doesn't, I say, "So how about you? You're studying CS at Cal, right?"

Owen's eyes refocus on me. "Yep. Senior year."

I cock my head to the side, sizing him up with the same look he'd turned on me earlier. "So you're, what, twenty-two?" I say.

"In a couple of months."

I nod slowly. "Too old for me, then."

I smirk as Owen says, with a slightly alarmed expression, "*Way* too old."

"Come on, I'm just kidding," I say. "So, what do *you* do all day?"

He smiles sheepishly. "I'm supposed to be working on my senior project, but

I'm procrastinating," he says. "So I surf the net, I play *Eleusis*, evade my TA duties to go on long weekend camping trips out of town. I … guess I've gotten a little side-tracked."

"By what?" I say.

He rubs his chin. "Delusions of grandeur, maybe? I always dreamed of becoming some breakout alternet phenomenon, designing games or something. Like Tomo, you know? Rags-to-riches. But … I always knew that was a dream. My designs are primitive at best. When I managed to get into the CS program here, I realized I'd better do something practical. Accounting and software development are pretty much the only prospects in this crappy job market."

"Sounds practical. And boring," I say.

Owen's eyes twinkle. We smile at each other. I feel an unexpected heat rising to my cheeks. Quickly, I say, "So … What did you want to show me?"

"Damn," says Owen, hanging his head in his hand. "This is even more embarrassing now that you turn out to be a little girl."

"Watch it," I say, slipping on my immerger glasses and a pair of gloves. "So, what modalities are we talking about?"

"Oh," Owen looks surprised. "Sorry. I don't actually own any immergers myself, other than a total crap pair of single-overlay glasses. I usually check out gear from the university library. I thought we could go over there."

"That's okay," I say, reaching for my backpack and rummaging around in it. "I've got some spares. The shirt's probably—no, definitely—too small. You could squeeze into the gloves, though. They're an old pair of my dad's." I empty the bag's contents onto the table. "Anyway, you probably just need glasses and gloves to access whatever you want to show me, right? I'm wearing enough gear to do audio, visual, olfactory, and tactile. Everything but environmental."

Owen stares at the pile of expensive electronics on the table. "Wow," he says.

"Go on," I say. "Suit up."

Owen pulls on the gloves, flexing his fingers to test the fit, then slips on the glasses. I tap my smartcom to sync our gear.

"Where's your content?" I ask. "Remote? Storage drive?"

"It's remote, hold on—" He taps a short sequence on the table with his gloved hand to download his files to a local directory on my smartcom.

"Okay, don't laugh," he says. "I wasn't kidding when I said my stuff's primitive. Especially compared to yours."

"Look, you asked for my opinion," I say. "I'm not gonna sugar-coat anything, but I'm not gonna laugh at you, either."

"Thanks," he says wryly. He taps out another sequence on the table, launching the content compiler on my smartcom.

As the compiler churns away, the log messages scroll up my display. I let out a low whistle as I scan the text flying by. "You're working really low-level, huh? Hardcore."

Owen says, "I wouldn't, except I don't have access to any decent high-end tools. The open source toolkits are okay, but all the effects in those are pretty run-of-the-mill. When I've got a basic presentation to do for a class, I can do something quick and dirty, but it's hard to make anything that seems new or exciting."

I nod. I have a major advantage over Owen in this regard, having access through the Lab to software more sophisticated than anything available in the open source community or on the consumer market. I say, "You've got an excuse to have primitive stuff, then. It would have taken me a hundred times longer to build anything in my portfolio if I had to write such low-level code."

Owen says, "Well, in any case, you still don't have to sugar-coat anything. Go ahead."

I turn my attention to the collection of items that have just finished loading in my simulator. I reach first for a spiky, spherical object about the size of a softball that appears to be resting on the table between us. The spikes on the outside of the object brush my palms, stiff but pliable, like feathers.

"You can shape the stems," says Owen. "Just touch your fingertips to them."

So I stretch out individual stems, elongating them. At intervals along the stem, I pull out new tendrils of material, twirling and kinking them around my fingers, flattening them out to form broad, leafy shapes, shaking the tips of the stems to soften them, twisting them to make them stand up straight. Several café patrons start staring at me. I try for a while to be less conspicuous but quickly give that up. This is an amazing simulation, and I want to fully experience it.

"Try setting it down," Owen says, grinning.

I do, and now the object grows. Each frond I'd shaped with my fingers stretches out into the space of the café. As I watch, smaller fronds sprout from the larger ones, each smaller frond a miniature image of its parent. The object grows ever more intricate as the original fronds expand and new, smaller fronds unfurl. The object finally stops growing when it's filled the height of the café.

I turn to Owen, impressed. "That was cool. Some sort of fractal algorithm?"

"Yeah," he says.

"Your object physics are fantastic," I say. I stroke my gloved hand over a fern-like plume that hangs over the table between us. It's feathery against my palm and springs back from my touch. "The tactile simulation, too. Is that from a texture library?"

"I wrote it myself," Owen says, with a touch of pride.

"It's really good," I say.

"Thanks."

I say, "The visuals are pretty simple, like you said. But your lighting is great. I'd love to play around with your source, if you'd let me. I bet I could add some visual polish."

Owen nods. "Yeah. Absolutely. I'd love that."

I reach for the nearest frond again, gripping it and shaking it, watching the effects of the movement ripple through the rest of the object, listening closely for a moment. "No audio?" I say.

"I hadn't gotten to it yet," he says.

I move on to the other items Owen has placed on our shared display.

The first is a sort of semantic association game. I select a three-dimensional object from a standard content library and provide a single word of my own choosing that describes another three-dimensional object. The original object crawls the alternet for a series of concepts to connect its starting shape to a shape I've chosen. It then renders a slow animation of one object morphing smoothly into the next related object, until the original object is transformed to the final object.

The second piece Owen shows me is a collection of flasks that allows me to pour and toss multicolored liquids against the walls, ceiling, and tabletops of the café. The fluid dynamics are simulated in such slow motion that I can walk leisurely through a flock of colorful undulations and watch from different angles as the liquids touch ground and languidly rebound in arcs of jewel-like droplets.

After half an hour of my ooh-ing and aah-ing over Owen's portfolio, the barista comes over and asks us if we can make a little less of a scene. Only slightly abashed, I take my seat.

Owen leans over and whispers, "Okay, this one's a little experimental. You have full surround audio, right?"

"Most definitely," I say.

"Great," he says. "So, you might want to hold on to your seat. Literally. If it works right, you'll be a little disoriented, but if something goes wrong, you'll be *extremely* disoriented."

"Sounds exciting," I say, gripping the seat of my chair.

He says, "I'll map the manual escape to your thumbs, so if you need the simulation to stop, just press either one or both of your thumbs onto your chair, okay?"

"Got it," I say. "Fire away."

Owen swipes his fingertips over the tabletop a few times, and I hear the noise cancellation in my earplugs wipe out the ambient noise of the café. My visual overlay flickers.

I seem to be in the empty cubic room that's the default starting point for most simple environmental physics testing. I look around and find that my body has been replaced by something like a large blue beach ball.

I drift upward in a compelling simulation of weightlessness. After I'm several yards off the ground, gravity re-exerts itself, and I fall toward the floor, much more slowly than I would have under the influence of Earth gravity. I bounce softly off the floor. At this point, I inadvertently lean forward in my seat, which sends me spinning slowly end over end through the room until I bounce against the far wall.

"Ha!" I laugh. "That's amazing." I press my thumbs to my chair, and the simulation ends. The café flickers back into view. I push back my immerger glasses and say, "I've never felt anything like that done with just audiovisual feedback. Where did you learn how to do that?"

Owen smiles with pride. "That was my sophomore year final project, although I've tweaked it a bit since. I spent a fair amount of time on a trampoline doing physical therapy after a football injury in high school, and, thinking back on it, I thought that sensation could make a pretty cool immersion."

"It definitely does," I say, drumming my fingers against my lips thoughtfully. "Hey, listen. I've never really done any collaborative work before, but I think between your physics programming skills and my visual design concepts, we could put together a pretty killer domain."

Owen straightens up and leans forward in his seat. "Really? You'd want to do that with me?"

I nod. "I could show you some pretty cool tools, too. My dad runs the Emerging Media Lab in Oakland."

"O-o-o-oh!" Owen says, suddenly making the connection. "You're one of *those* Bridges, huh?"

I nod again.

"Ha!" Owen scratches his head. "Well, I guess I lucked out when I met you, Bealsio. When can we start?"

△▽△

Owen and I are soon meeting daily—in his computer science lab, in the downtown Berkeley cafés, in the Cal libraries. Our camaraderie on the *Eleusis* battlefield translates surprisingly well to creative collaboration. Gradually, both of us begin to withdraw from Amaranthian guild activities, until at last Otaku passes on guild leadership to his second-in-command.

"You're just going to quit, huh?" Zeke says angrily, the day I tell him I'm leaving the guild.

"Hey, we can find another game to play together," I say, surprised by the heat in Zeke's voice. "I've just got a lot of other stuff going on right now. I can't make all these guild practices any more."

"Yeah," Zeke huffs. "Well, I'm pretty busy, too. I guess I'll see you around."

I'm upset by my falling out with Zeke, but I don't have much time to dwell on it. Owen and I are completely consumed by our work on the joint portfolio we're building on *Emergency* to showcase the best of both our skills.

Soon after we start collaborating, Owen insists that I introduce him to Mom and Dad. "As long as we're going to be spending so much time together, I want them to know I'm a perfect gentleman. Also, based on what you've told me, I don't think I can afford to get on the wrong side of your mother."

We argue about this for a few days, but Owen refuses to continue work on our portfolio until he's discharged this ridiculous gentlemanly duty. Nervously, I tell Mom and Dad I'd like to invite Owen to dinner.

The night of the dinner, Dad is polite but unusually distant, except when asking uncomfortably pointed questions about how, when, and why Owen and I met. To my enormous surprise, however, Mom gives Owen a very warm reception. I find myself gaping as she keeps up a steady stream of friendly conversation with him throughout dinner.

Mom says, "So before you came out to California for college, where did you live?"

"I grew up in Keller, Texas, ma'am," says Owen. "Outside Fort Worth."

"And does your family live there now?"

"Yes, ma'am. My parents still live there. Most of my mother's family, too."

"Do you come from a big family?"

Owen says, "I have an older brother, Wendell, and my little sister, Marybeth. Loads of cousins. My mama has four sisters, and they all live in Keller."

"Is it hard for you, being so far away?"

"It's good to see them, when I can get back," says Owen. "But to be honest, my father and I were never very close. He was a Navy officer, and I didn't get to see him much while I was growing up."

"It sounds like that was difficult for you," says Mom.

Owen shrugs, looking down at his plate for a moment before saying, "We were lucky in a lot of ways. We only had to relocate once, and just for a couple of years. Other than that, my mama's family was always around to help her out. And my dad came home safe and sound, in the end."

Mom nods slowly. After a moment, she says, "So, what do you think of California?"

"Love it," Owen says promptly, his eyes lighting up. "I spent my whole life wanting to get out of Keller, to move out west. Once I got that acceptance letter, I was out like that!" He smacks his palms together. "I drove my car out, hit all the National Parks along the way. And when I came through the tunnel and saw the Bay, the Golden Gate …" He lets out an appreciative whistle. "I knew I was home. I can't imagine living anywhere else."

Mom smiles, patting Dad's knee. "You sound just like my husband."

Dad clears his throat, narrowing his eyes a bit at Owen as he says, "It may have its problems, but it beats any other place I've been."

"Yes, sir," says Owen, shrinking back slightly in his chair. I catch Owen's eye, indicate my father with a tiny jerk of my head, and mouth across the table the word, *Sorry!*

"So," Dad says brusquely, pushing back from the table, "can we offer you some dessert before you go, Owen? We don't want to keep you too late."

"Travis!" says Mom. "It's only seven o'clock."

Even so, a scant half hour later, Dad has ushered Owen out the door and retired to his office.

When we're alone in the kitchen washing the dishes, Mom says, "What a charming young man."

I shake my head at her, laughing. "Seriously? You're less worried about me hanging out with a college guy you've never met before than you are about letting me drive the car."

"Well," Mom says, "he seems perfectly nice. And it's good for you to have a real-life friend besides your sister."

"I have other friends!" I protest.

Mom raises an eyebrow doubtfully but says nothing.

Despite her approval of Owen, the next morning Mom tells me that, going forward, our work together needs to be chaperoned. I complain that this will severely limit the time we can work together, but she proposes we make the Lab our regular meeting place, since either Dad or Uncle Frank is there nearly all the time.

Dad doesn't seem to be any more enthusiastic about Mom's proposal than I am, but ultimately we both begrudgingly agree to it.

△▽△

When I tell Owen about the new restriction on our time together, he's happy to respect Mom's wishes. What's more, he's delighted by the prospect of working at the Emerging Media Lab. Having grown up in the Lab, it's easy for me to forget the cachet Dad and Uncle Frank's company has earned for its technological contributions to the alternet age. For a geek like Owen, though, I guess the Lab is as close as you can get to heaven in this life.

My return to the Lab has some downsides, though. Dad finds subtle ways to avoid the irritation of seeing me and Owen together, though Owen is unfailingly, even excessively, polite and friendly toward him. What's worse, I have to endure merciless ribbing by Uncle Frank whenever Owen's out of earshot.

"He's *not* my boyfriend," I insist. "We're just friends. And anyway, that would be practically illegal."

"Oh, come on." Uncle Frank winks. "He seems perfectly nice."

I groan. "I wish everyone would stop *saying* that!"

Despite the awkwardness with Dad and the unwanted teasing from Uncle Frank and the other Lab oldtimers who've known me since infancy, I am actually glad about one aspect of bringing Owen here. The first time he walked into the Lab with me, I saw mirrored on Owen's face the same delight I feel whenever a new gadget comes off the Lab workbenches. Owen's never had access to such high-quality hardware as we have here. Seeing it all through his eyes, I start to understand for the first time just how privileged I've been to grow up with easy access to the best tools for the work I've chosen. I'm glad to be able to share this with him.

Uncle Frank is happy to give Owen the same access I have to the resources of the Lab, although Dad grumbles about it at first. Owen takes full advantage of all the new tools at his disposal, and he's soon impressing the engineers with his skills in environmental design. He prototypes all sorts of domain physics, from the meticulously realistic to the fanciful, with speed that seems effortless. His foundational environment frameworks are perfect platforms for my own content, and our collaboration using all the resources of the Lab pushes both of our skills to a higher level. Owen's work eventually earns even Dad's begrudging admiration.

Over the next year, as Owen and I produce our first series of domains together, his undergraduate studies at Cal fall by the wayside. Mom thinks this is due to my bad influence, and she pleads with Owen not to lose focus on completing his degree. I'm pretty sure the only reason Owen ends up graduating is that he's loathe to disappoint Mom.

After Owen graduates, he and I finally have enough time to complete a portfolio of simple but addictive game concepts, foremost among them *Fractal Sphere*, an evolution on the first portfolio piece Owen showed me the day we met.

In *Fractal Sphere*, two players enter an empty arena, each with a fractal seed of their own design. Turn by turn, the players extend their seeds into ever larger and more complex fractal forms. The object of the game is to be the first player to completely enclose the fractal of the other.

The game initially attracts only a small, unsurprisingly geeky subset of the alternet gaming community. However, the mesmerizing quality of the game replays, in which enormous works of fractal art unfurl from the simplest beginnings, quickly attracts a larger audience. Game reviewers and digital art historians compile libraries of *Fractal Sphere* matches, rating them on various artistic, mathematical, and entertainment criteria. Professional gamers flock to *Fractal Sphere* to capitalize on the new game hype and attract new followers. Alternet entertainment forums host *Fractal Sphere* competitions and tournaments that grow our monthly users exponentially. The game wins several design awards and becomes a modest commercial success within six months of its release, pushing Bealsio and Otaku into the mainstream game design spotlight for a short time.

Even after the spotlight moves on, *Fractal Sphere* continues to produce a significant stream of income for me and Owen. Awash with cash, I contemplate the benefits of moving out of my parents' home. Mom's made it clear that she'd prefer I stay with them forever, but I have other ideas.

I start by asking Nanna to help me find the perfect place. She approaches the task with the relish of a real estate connoisseur, applying her decades of experience remodeling area homes to identify the right location, architectural style, and floor plan for me. The perfect place turns out to be a three-bedroom cliffside cottage just down the road from Mom and Dad's house, right on Skyline Boulevard. Mom's not thrilled to see me move out, but she's relieved I'm not going far.

For the first time in my life, I enjoy the privacy of a space I can truly call my own, free of the ever-present gaze of my parents at home or the team at the Lab. I've never lacked access to immersion gear, but my considerably improved income now allows me to indulge more extravagant tastes. I keep myself in fine style as far as immersion tech goes, filling my closets with every new gadget and stocking my software library with the most sophisticated new tools of the trade. Although the basement of my new house can't rival the view of the fishbowl at my parents', I at last have the space and the means to install a small spliner for my personal use at home, which I do with glee.

I've never really had to worry about money growing up, so perhaps I spend my *Fractal Sphere* earnings with some recklessness. Owen, for his part, saves religiously, expressing a desire to someday accumulate enough to travel the world. Long after an around-the-world trip is financially feasible, however, he remains rooted here in the Bay Area, either unable to give himself such a luxurious gift or unable to part for such an extended period of time from my family, which has in many ways become his own.

△▽△

Owen, possessing a far more outdoorsy inclination than I do, drags me out of my new house as frequently as possible. ("Your mom is not kidding when she calls that spliner a death trap. You'd rot in there if it weren't for me!") He leads me on daily hikes through the redwoods and eucalyptus groves in the Oakland Hills, which I eventually come to appreciate, though not as much as he does. He even teaches me to ride a bike on the scenic shoulders of Skyline Boulevard. ("WTF, Em! How have you designed a cycling simulation when you've never even ridden a bike?")

For my eighteenth birthday, Owen persuades my entire family to go on an early spring camping trip in Yosemite during one of Ollie's too-infrequent visits home from graduate school. This is an ambitious move, given the unruliness of my family, but Owen somehow rallies three generations of Bridges with charisma and fearlessness born of the *Eleusis* battlefields. Over the course of the three-hour drive to Yosemite—which stretches to five hours with the inevitable Bay Area traffic delays and stops to reshuffle incompatible vehicle occupants—Owen gracefully manages the grousing alternet access withdrawal of me, Dad, and Uncle Frank; the recurring interruptions of Nanna's loud smartcom conversations with her assistant; and the constant bickering of Nora and Uncle Frank's two little boys, six-year-old Luke and eight-year-old Nick. Despite all this, Owen successfully delivers two cars, ten Bridges, and all our attendant camping gear from the hills of Oakland into the heart of Yosemite Valley. Yosemite's stunning beauty instantly rewards all the trouble we've taken to witness it.

Understandably exhausted by the drive, Owen accepts Mom's offer to oversee pitching camp. Mom demonstrates a surprising degree of expertise in this. She identifies the driest sites on the still-snowy campground; demonstrates to Luke and Nick how to raise tents; teaches me and Uncle Frank how to build a campfire; and sets Ollie, Nora, and Nanna to work prepping dinner. Dad and Uncle Frank eventually reconcile themselves to the reality of spotty alternet connectivity in Yosemite Valley and manage their alternet withdrawal by recording sights, sounds, and smells from the campground to upload later into the Lab content database.

"It's unending with those two," Grandpa grumbles as he loads food into the bear locker. "They can't experience anything without the aid of their damn recording devices."

"Oh, hush, Patrick," says Nanna, chopping vegetables at the cooking station Mom set up. "When did you get to be such a cranky old man?"

"Was he ever *not* a cranky old man?" I whisper to Uncle Frank.

"So where did you learn to be so handy around a campsite?" Owen asks Mom as they wrap up the spare tent pegs and rope.

Mom smiles wistfully. "My sister and I practically grew up in a tent. I spent many, many summers with my parents at their archeological digs when I was growing up."

"That sounds exciting!" says Owen. "Where was this?"

"Oh, so many places. I'm not even sure I could remember them all, now," Mom says. "My parents studied the ancient history of the near East, so it was mostly places around the eastern Mediterranean. Beautiful country. Some of my favorite childhood memories are of the Greek Isles, Turkey, Lebanon. Just wonderful."

"I didn't know you have a sister," says Owen.

"Yes," Mom says softly. "Nazanin. She passed away."

There's a lull in the campground chatter as many of the adult Bridges glance toward Mom. I shoot a warning look at Owen before looking back down at the vegetables I'm chopping for kebabs. The moment passes, and conversations resume, a bit more loudly than before.

"Oh," Owen says awkwardly. "I'm sorry."

Mom shakes her head, stuffing the last of the gear into a tent bag. "It was a long time ago," she says.

Gently, Owen says, "Do you mind if I ask what happened?"

I set down my knife and look up at Mom. I've never actually heard the story of Nazanin's death from her. Ollie warned me long ago not to ask Mom questions about it. I know only the general outline: there was an accident, a fall, and Nazanin had been fatally injured.

"I can't believe it's still this hard to talk about it," Mom says with a sad smile. "Even though it was—goodness—could it have been thirty-seven years ago now? I spent so long feeling like it was my fault. I was the only one with her when it happened. I should have ..." She trails off, shaking her head.

Owen waits, listening. Mom's gaze drifts away from here, to some unseen memory. Her sad smile turns a bit more cheerful as she continues, "Well. I was fifteen. Nazanin had just turned fourteen. Our parents were working on an archeological dig site near the Euphrates River, and we took a day trip up to Lake Van.

"Nazanin loved taking photographs. She spent the whole drive up to Lake Van begging our parents to take us on the ferry, out to a little island called Akdamar, so she could take pictures. She had heard about some ancient Armenian church there, and she wanted to take photos of the mountains across the lake.

"Mom and Dad had a day hike already planned with their graduate students. They had planned for us all to go together. But Naz kept begging and begging until finally Dad said she could go to Akdamar, as long as I went with her. I didn't mind, so Mom and Dad dropped us off at the boat launch, and we left with a little group of tourists.

"Nazanin and I spent all morning walking around the island. I was glad we'd come. I remember how wonderful everything smelled. Flowers everywhere—on the bushes, in the trees. Naz must have taken a thousand photos." Mom glances at me and says, "You've seen them, remember? All those black-and-white photographs in my office that you used to trace when you were little?

"Well, anyway, I started to get quite warm and tired after roaming around the island that afternoon. I told Nazanin I wanted to rest until the return ferry. She wanted to take a few more pictures of the church stonework, so we agreed to meet back together on the shady side of the church when she was done. I found a place to sit down and waited for her to come back.

"I don't remember falling asleep, but the next thing I knew, the ferry boat captain was waking me up, telling me it was time to go back to shore. I got up and started looking for Nazanin, but I couldn't find her anywhere.

"I told the boat captain, and he started looking for her with me. Soon everyone was looking—the tourists, the tour guides, the priests." Mom closes her eyes. "I remember one of the priests told me not to worry, that we were going to find her. He was so kind, and I really believed him, right up until the end.

"We searched all over that little island for an hour. I was standing high up on an outcropping, looking all around to see if there was any spot we could have missed, when I heard shouting down below, near the church.

"Someone had found Nazanin's camera sitting on a rock on the east side of the island. Everyone started looking around that area, then someone spotted the hole in the ground, almost concealed between the roots of an old almond tree.

"Later, the priests said the underground spring on that side of the island must have washed out the soil under the tree roots. The ground gave way when Nazanin walked across it. There was a long drop, more than twenty feet. They were eventually able to pull her out, but ..."

Mom falls silent. Her eyes glisten with tears. Everyone has stopped what they're doing at this point to listen, but no one seems to know what to say now.

"I'm sorry," Owen says, leaning down to give Mom a hug. I feel a surge of affection for Owen and pity for Mom. She dabs her eyes and smiles, looking from Owen to me to the rest of our family around the campsite.

"Life's strange, isn't it?" she says. "The terrible and the beautiful all mixed up together."

△▽△

We've just finished eating dinner around the campfire, but haven't yet begun the marshmallow roast Owen repeatedly promised to Luke and Nick in the car, when the rain starts. Over the protests of the little boys, everyone retires to our tents. Even before Ollie finishes settling into the sleeping bag beside me, the steady patter of raindrops outside our tent lulls me to sleep.

In the middle of the night, I wake when the sound of the rain stops. A few minutes later, there's a soft scrabbling sound near the tent opening, and I sit up with a gasp. I reach for Ollie's shoulder to wake her but stop when Owen whispers, "It's me. You've got to see this."

I relax and unzip the tent. Owen's excited face peers down at me through the little vestibule.

Hoping not to disturb Ollie, I whisper, "Where are my shoes?"

Owen looks around, then chuckles. He whispers back, "You forgot to pull them under the rain fly." He lifts one of my boots and pours a stream of rainwater out of it.

"Ugh. Well, I'm not putting *those* on, for sure," I say, withdrawing into the tent and starting to zip it up again.

"Hey, wait!" Owen reaches in to stop me. "Come on. I'll keep your feet dry. Here—" He reaches into the tent toward me. "I'll carry you. It's not far."

"No way. You'll drop me in the mud!"

"Come on. You're tiny."

I scowl in mock indignation. "I may be small, but I am fierce!"

"It'll be worth it," he coaxes. "I swear."

I look doubtfully from the cold, wet campground outside back to the inside of my warm, dry tent. But Owen's expression is too eager to resist. "Oh, fine," I say, relenting.

I climb out of the tent and zip it closed behind me. Owen loops my arm around his neck and scoops up my knees, lifting me easily. I shiver as the icy nighttime air sucks the warmth from my flannel pajama pants and baggy Oakland sweatshirt.

Owen carries me down a short footpath leading out of the grove of redwoods surrounding our campground. In a meadow beyond the trees, Owen finds a rocky outcropping that, while not exactly dry, is at least free of standing water. He sets me on my feet atop the rock and climbs up beside me. The stone feels like ice through my thick woollen socks. The pale wisps of my breath and Owen's mingle in the faint starlight.

"Look," he says, wrapping his long arm around me to give my shoulder a brief, gentle squeeze as he points upward.

The warmth of Owen's hand trailing from my shoulder down my back makes me straighten up with a jolt. Did he mean to do that? Do I want him to do that? I'm not sure.

For all the endless teasing about Owen being my boyfriend, and for all my sincere affection for him, we've never been physically intimate. I've assumed, based on what he said when we first met two years ago, that he thinks our age difference makes any kind of romantic relationship out of bounds for us. I've mentally left it at that since then. I'd assumed he had, too. Everything between us until this moment has been friendship and work collaboration. At least, that's what I'd thought.

I'm glad it's dark enough that he can't see the blush burning my cheeks.

I force myself to look up, following the line of Owen's gaze. Above us, the massive stone walls enclosing Yosemite Valley hold up a glittering vault of stars, stars that put to shame the artificially obscured night sky of the city.

"They look so close," I whisper in the darkness.

Owen nods. After a while, I turn to him and say, "I guess immersion still has a long way to go."

Owen studies my face in the starlight, the faintest hint of a smile on his lips. Somehow I've never noticed what a beautiful mouth he has, and now I'm staring at it like an idiot. Get a grip, Emmie. I tear my gaze from his mouth by looking up to meet his eyes, which are locked on mine. OMG. Is this really happening?

The air around me seems to grow warm. Owen's fingertips brush my cheek ever so softly. He leans down and kisses me. His lips are warm, soft, welcoming, and somehow already familiar. He smells like campfire and aftershave. He tastes like my new favorite dessert. I wind my arms around his neck as I pull him closer. I know immediately that I don't want this first kiss to be our last.

Four days later, the caravan of Bridges, begrimed with earth and smelling of woodsmoke, returns to the Oakland hills. I spend the long drive smiling vaguely out the window. Amidst the grandeur of the Yosemite Valley, I've found the inspiration for my next project.

△▽△

During my visits with Emmie over the weeks that follow her trip to Yosemite, I try not to dwell on the difficult feelings stirred in me by Ava's rediscovery of love through this kind and gentle boy. Even after all this time, though, some part of me experiences an occasional twinge of jealousy when I see the way her face lights up when he enters a room. I've had to watch her fall in love so many times across so many lives. I know how it ends, so I can't begrudge her the fleeting joy of love's beginning.

I focus instead on understanding where Emmie's latest burst of creative energy is leading her. In the end, this is what matters most for me: the key to understanding why she's chosen this life this time.

Emmie longs to recreate in her work the sense of awe she experienced in that moment with Owen beneath the stars. Her longing is so insistent, day and night, that I'm reduced to dodging into back alleys and empty rooms in the temple city when she pulls me to her, unable to resist her long enough to seclude myself in private quarters. I'll need to make better preparations if I'm going to continue all this coming and going without attracting the notice of Serapen and the other watchful Mohirai.

During one visit, I arrive to find Emmie alone in the fishbowl, flipping through the portfolio of work she's created over the last few years. In her mind, I see she searches for a starting point from which to build something of true significance, something that transcends the old ideas that seem childish to her now.

Eventually, she opens the great tree from her private content library. She's been sharing work in public alternet domains for years, but she's never been able to bring herself to publish this work. She's shared it only once, with her father, in the moment of euphoria that followed her first deep collaboration with me. The tree stands out to her among all her other work as the piece with greatest potential.

During our visits over the weeks that follow, the tree becomes the axis around which all Emmie's creative work revolves. With focus sharpened by my unseen influence, she grasps my every hint, weaving a landscape around that tree drawn from a memory that's more real to me than either of the worlds through which I now drift.

Emmie utilizes every technology from the Lab, every technique she's ever learned for immersive design, to create a domain that pushes the limits of multi-sensory immersion. She works with Owen to perfect the physics of atmospheres and oceans, the movement of stars, the change of light from morning to evening. She names the domain *Eden*, and even endlessly self-critical Emmie sees that it's good. Very good.

When Emmie finally launches *Eden*, she attracts enthusiastic reviews and design accolades from many influential alternet cognoscenti. Reviewers describe their experience of *Eden* as transformative, comparable to, perhaps even transcending, the experience of Tomo's *Kaisei.*

Mere days after *Eden*'s public launch, Emmie receives an email from Tomo Yoshimoto asking whether she might join him for dinner. Emmie stares in shock at the message for several minutes before she sends a projection to Owen to break the news.

"WHAT!?!" Owen exclaims. "You're joking!"

"One hundred percent serious," says Emmie, though the look on her face shows she can't quite believe it herself.

As Emmie and Owen make plans to celebrate, I withdraw to Dulai. In the darkness of my sleeping quarters, the enormity of what's to come sinks in. At last, I realize what the place and time of Emmie's birth might mean.

△▽△

I'm floating on air for the first few days after I receive Tomo's email. Every conversation with Owen, my parents, and friends at the Lab eventually returns to the subject. We pore over every word of his email a hundred times. We speculate endlessly about why he wants to meet. But as the day of the dinner approaches, my ecstasy gives way to terror.

Tomo is my single greatest artistic inspiration. Since the first time I visited *Kaisei,* I've judged all my work against his. I'm petrified by the thought of being in his presence. Even worse is the thought of what he might say about my work. I've grown a pretty thick skin over the last few years, but I'm not sure anything can prepare me for a critique from Tomo.

I practice what I'll say to him. I fret over what I'll wear, what I'll bring, how I'll style my hair. I'm accustomed to complete control over the appearance of my avatars, so the prospect of being limited to my own un-augmented features and badly neglected wardrobe is truly distressing. Owen's an unbearable tease when I seek his advice, so I call my sister instead.

"But you look gorgeous!" Ollie insists over the loud background noise of her flatmates at the graduate school housing in London where she's now on a postdoctoral fellowship studying the emergence and evolution of alternet subcultures.

"Don't lie," I moan, looking longingly at Ollie's perfect blonde hair and stylish clothes. "I look terrible. Can I just steal your face for a night? You could fly over here and sit in for me. I'll tell you what to say."

Ollie rolls her eyes. She says, "The dinner's in two hours. And anyway, you need to learn how to be as comfortable in your own skin as you are in all your avatars. You'll do great. Remember, he wants to see you. The real you. He doesn't care how you look. He cares what you can do. But you really do look great, so don't worry about it."

"All right. All right," I say, bracing myself with a deep breath and checking my hair once more in the video feed. "You're right. Thanks, Ollie."

I leave for Berkeley way too early and arrive at the restaurant over an hour ahead of time, before dinner service has even started. The hostess takes pity on me and lets me inside. I wait at the reserved table. I shift nervously in my chair, periodically tugging down the hem of my skirt, flipping my visual overlay on and off, glancing at email and news feeds, unable to focus on anything.

At five thirty on the dot, Tomo arrives. I recognize him instantly as he walks through the door. I've watched hundreds of hours of video feeds of the man giving interviews, teaching design classes, and talking about his new alternet startup company, Augur.

Tomo is compact and moves with the energy of a young man, though he's well past middle age, with thinning silver hair. Square-rimmed glasses frame his thick black eyebrows and twinkling dark eyes. His clothes are somehow both trendy and classic—he could blend in as easily with the young people who are the face of alternet startups as with the venture capitalists who fund them.

Tomo scans the room, sees me, and nods to me in recognition. Only as he starts to walk toward me do I realize I'm gaping at him. My face flushes. I try to rearrange my features into a semblance of composure. In an attempt to cover my embarrassment, I stand up so quickly from my chair that I nearly overturn the table.

Tomo comes to my aid, steadies the table, and reaches out to shake my hand.

"It is so nice to meet you in person, my dear," he says with a smile.

"Yes," I say breathlessly, trying to steady my voice. "So nice to meet you, too."

Tomo pulls out my chair, and I sit down.

I somehow manage to place an order with our server, though my head is spinning so much that I don't remember what I ordered until it arrives. Tomo does his best to put me at ease. He steers our conversation expertly through subjects of mutual interest, discussing domains and domain designers we both love, the latest developments in immersion technology, speculations about what might be the next hot alternet trend. Gradually, I loosen up.

We've just ordered dessert when Tomo turns at last to what is evidently the purpose of this meeting.

He says, "Perhaps you've heard that I recently co-founded a new company called Augur with two young friends of mine. Ty Monaghan and Ahmet Harani." He swirls the last of the red wine in his glass and takes a sip, savoring it for a moment before continuing. "We've just started work on our first project. It will be Augur's flagship domain. I wonder whether you might consider joining our team."

OMG. OMG. OMG. My eyes nearly fall out of my head. "Really? I … I …" I take a deep breath to steady myself. "Yes," I say finally. "That would be awesome."

ONE YEAR LATER

Emmie and I won't discover for quite some time what really happened to Tomo that April day. But Tomo was prepared, to the extent Ava could prepare him. So when the time is right for us, this is what we'll recover from his memory.

Tomo rose from his desk well before sundown, put on his coat, and watered the potted plants in his corner office. The tending of his indoor garden concluded with the bonsai tree that grew in a blue ceramic tray atop a heavy Japanese cabinet. Tomo pulled a tiny pair of pruning shears from the top drawer of the cabinet. He assessed the bonsai tree with a practiced eye before snipping off three miniature branches. He brushed the fallen branches into the wastebasket and returned the shears to the drawer.

As he pushed the drawer closed, Tomo slid his right hand down the back side of the cabinet, applying precise pressure to one particular spot. A small flat compartment concealed in the cabinet's dark wood frame slid open beneath his fingers. He withdrew a square jade box the size of a cigarette lighter, slipped it into the breast pocket of his coat, and closed the compartment with a light touch.

Tomo stepped out his door into the expansive open office area, a maze of cylindrical projection chambers and modular workstations. He passed unseen before most of the young men and women at work, because they were fully immersed in the internal Augur domain where the first *Temenos* expansion was slowly taking shape.

But one young man, with white-blonde hair and blue eyes ringed with bruise-like shadows, looked up as Tomo passed. He pushed back his immerger glasses and said, "See you tomorrow, sir."

Tomo waved and nodded cheerfully in response. "Don't forget to go home tonight, Zeke. Even God couldn't create a world in one day."

Zeke gave a half-hearted laugh before re-immersing himself in *Temenos*, where he would likely remain long into the night. Tomo was no stranger to energetic obsession with work, yet he worried about that boy. He had hired Zeke on Emmie's recommendation, but it had not escaped his notice that Zeke was becoming isolated from the rest of the team. Though all Zeke's work was beyond reproach, the boy seemed unable to shed his loner mentality.

Tomo stopped at an empty desk near the center of the room and looked around for its usual occupant. His gaze settled on Emmie, standing by the lounge coffee machine, deep in conversation with Owen, who was now her lead engineer. Hiring Owen was one of the easiest decisions Tomo ever made—Owen and Emmie made a stellar team. Tomo watched the pair for a moment, his fingertips brushing the outside of his breast pocket thoughtfully. Then he continued on his way.

Tomo exited through the spacious lobby of Augur's newly-constructed central office building and out across the well-manicured lawns of the surrounding campus. A winding path through fruit trees and over little man-made hills—modeled on a location in *Kaisei* that was particularly dear to his heart—led to the eastern pedestrian gate.

Tomo swiped his key card to unlock the gate, casting a disapproving look at the tall, spiked wrought-iron security fence as he passed through it. He had complained frequently to Ty and Ahmet that the fence was an eyesore, as well as entirely unnecessary, but his co-founders had insisted that it remain in place. In all the years Tomo had lived in America, he had never come to understand how a culture so fearlessly inclusive could yet be so fearful of its own people.

A bit more than three miles separated Tomo's corner office overlooking the San Francisco Bay from his home overlooking Oakland's Lake Merritt. He enjoyed the daily walk, which made him feel connected to the diverse neighborhoods of his adopted hometown.

He stepped through the security gate onto the gritty sidewalk of the West Oakland neighborhood surrounding the Augur campus. Soon after Tomo had hired Emmie, her father had convinced him of the merits of the re-emerging manufacturing district here, and Tomo had been pleased to add Augur's weight to the community revitalization effort. He, like Emmie's father, saw just beneath the urban decay the prospect of renewal.

Tomo walked through blocks of shabby Victorian homes and chic mixed-use developments, which merged gradually into the high-rise offices of the financial, governmental, and commercial district. Downtown was fast emptying of a workday population heading home toward the lake or over the bridges or through the tunnels, leaving behind only the permanent inhabitants of the street. Charmingly-renovated historic buildings came to life as cafés and tapas bars opened their doors, drawing foot traffic from the tentatively gentrifying blocks nearby.

A bright red and yellow floral motif worked into the dark asphalt of the crosswalk marked the edge of Chinatown. A mouthwatering aroma of fresh pastries and savory meats wafted from the open doors of restaurants and bakeries, alternating with the more delicate scents of fresh fruit and green vegetables piled before grocery stores. The shapes and colors of Asian produce evoked memories of Tomo's youth in Kyoto.

Tomo stopped at one restaurant window to examine an enticing display of dumplings, considering whether to cook for himself tonight or take a table and watch the world go by. Someone a few steps behind him on the sidewalk stopped at the window, too. Tomo's eyes refocused on the glass. Behind him stood another man. Their eyes met in the reflection. The man gave him a polite nod, which Tomo returned with a friendly smile.

Tomo turned to face the man, thinking perhaps this was a former colleague or a neighbor who had stopped to say hello. There was definitely something familiar about him. But when the recognition hit Tomo, his friendly smile faded.

The man was tall and well-built, dressed in an impeccable suit, silk tie, and shiny shoes. His mane of white-blonde hair contrasted strikingly with his smooth, deeply tanned skin. He would have been quite handsome were it not for the predatory look in his pale blue eyes.

Tomo stood transfixed as the man withdrew from his jacket a slender silver cylinder that gleamed in the warm light of sunset. Although Tomo didn't recognize the object, he knew instinctively it was a weapon. He backed away slowly from the man until he stood pressed against the restaurant window. The man pointed the weapon casually at Tomo.

"You were duly warned," said the man, his genial Southern accent incongruous with his threatening words. "It's most unfortunate things had to end this way. I do apologize."

Tomo felt a pinprick in his chest, followed by a spreading numbness. He looked down in surprise. A fine needle, almost invisible to the eye, protruded from his coat lapel, just over his heart. He staggered dizzily and fell to the ground, gasping. Icy fingers seemed to grip his heart. He tried to cry out, but he was unable to move, unable to make a sound.

The man knelt over him, exclaiming loudly, "Sir? Sir? Are you all right? Sir!"

The man leaned in close to Tomo, blocking out the view of a small crowd gathering around the spectacle. A heavy gold ring bearing the sign of the cross gleamed from the man's right ring finger as his hand passed over Tomo's eyes. The last thing Tomo felt was the light touch of the man's fingers as they slipped inside his breast pocket and withdrew the small jade box.

△▽△

"You're awfully quiet tonight," says Owen, handing me another soapy dish to load into my parents' dishwasher.

I look at Owen blankly. It takes me a moment to remember what he just said. My mind has been wandering a lot lately.

"Yeah," I say, trying to refocus on him. "It's just *Atlantis*, you know? I can't even look at the concept sketches without feeling this … Frustration? Confusion? Revulsion? Something. I know there's something wrong with it. I feel really bad for holding up the team, but I just can't let it go. I went to talk to Tomo about it this evening, since we've had nothing to show for weeks. Tomo's patient, but I know Ty's been bugging him for a review. Just my luck, though. Tomo left early."

"You should take a page out of Tomo's book," says Owen. "Didn't you spend last night at work?"

"Ummm …" I say.

"And I bet you're planning to go back after dinner, aren't you?" he says.

"Judgey, judgey, judgey!" I say.

"Balance, girl," he says. "The stress is prematurely aging you."

I huff and flick water onto his shirt.

"Seriously, though," says Owen, brushing himself off with a laugh. "Sometimes you act like you have to do everything all on your own. Don't you think you can count on any of us? At least on me?"

"Come on! Of course I do. I just—"

"Hey, you guys!" Ollie shouts down the stairs. "Are you coming back up here?"

"Let's talk about this later, okay?" I say to Owen, stuffing silverware into the side basket of the dishwasher and closing the door. I wipe my sudsy hands off on my jeans and hustle up the stairs to my parents' rooftop deck. "I can't stand having Ollie analyze our shop talk like it's another one of her research projects."

We resurface from the kitchen and find that my twentieth birthday dinner party has migrated to the bridge table. Nanna and Grandpa are dissecting a hand of bridge for Uncle Frank and Nora's benefit, part of their indefatigable campaign to teach them the game. ("How have you never learned to play bridge after all these years, Frank?" Nanna demands. "How have you never learned to play *Eleusis*, Mom?" he counters, laughing.) Dad makes a gallant effort to translate Nanna's bridge jargon for Nora, but Nanna hardly pauses for breath and doesn't seem to realize how confusing the phrase "getting your kids off the street" sounds to a novice bridge player.

I retrieve my wine glass from the dinner table and walk up to the railing at the cliffside edge of the deck, Owen close behind me. I turn to face him, watching the sunset transform his face into a kaleidoscope of golds and crimsons. It's been two years since our first kiss at Yosemite, but I still don't quite know what to call our relationship. When we first met, Owen was just a friend, a fellow geek and gamer. He became a collaborator. Now he's a crucial part of my team at Augur. My family loves him. Everyone assumes he's my boyfriend. Owen's made it clear he wants to be, but I'm not sure what it means, or what changes between us, if I call him my boyfriend or he calls me his girlfriend. I'm just Emmie. He's just Owen. We care about each other. We do amazing work together. Can't we just leave it at that?

Owen smiles at me, and we lean against the railing, watching the warm light play out over the Oakland flats.

"I never thought I'd say this," I say, taking a sip of my wine. "But I need a vacation. Want to come with?"

"I thought you said you couldn't do anything until your next review with Ty?"

"Yeah, I probably shouldn't," I grumble, slumping dispiritedly over the railing and propping my chin on my hand. I'm dreading my next meeting with Ty, our CEO. I never seem to see eye-to-eye with Tomo's co-founder. Over my last two years at Augur, I've learned that business types and creative types rarely see things the same way.

"Hey, no, that's not what I meant," says Owen. "If you want to go, let's do it. I have a list as long as my arm of places I'd love to see. Where are you thinking you'd like to go?"

"I don't know," I say, swirling the wine in my glass like Tomo taught me. "Some place I've never seen before. Some place new."

"Hmmm. That's a tough one," he says. "I'd guess you've already visited every rendered place on Earth."

"Isn't that awful?" I say. "It's like the only places left to discover are on the alternet."

"There must be *some* uncharted territory somewhere out there," says Owen, wrapping his arm around my waist. "I bet we could find it."

△▽△

The morning after her twentieth birthday party, I stand behind Emmie and Owen in the main spliner at Augur. We appear to be on the fore deck of a ship, surrounded by swirling fog.

At eye level before Emmie hovers a bright stack of windows, each displaying an aerial view of a topographical map. She flicks through these with her fingers, occasionally pulling one down to scrutinize it from multiple angles as it morphs from a two-dimensional image into a three-dimensional terrain in miniature. Beside her, Owen alternates between squinting into the impenetrable mist before them and peering over Emmie's shoulder at the renderings, making quick tweaks here and there as he notices mistakes in the environment presets.

I struggle to hold for Emmie the mental image of the temple city of Thera, which Emmie has somehow plucked from my own subconscious and now seems determined to use as the basis for her latest *Atlantis* subdomain project. Personally, I'd prefer some time away from Thera after all these centuries working on it, but the pull of Emmie's awareness is insistent. It seems I'm destined to work on this temple city both on Earth and Dulai until the Voice in all decides it's done.

The only sound around us is the muffled splash of waves against the creaking hull of the ship, until Emmie says, "Let's see this one again. *Atlantis* concept 42."

Owen glances at her sidelong, saying softly, off the microphone, "Are you sure?"

Emmie shoots him a cool look, and Owen backs off cautiously, mouthing, *Okay, okay*, before tapping a short sequence onto the forearm of his immerger sleeve. As Owen mutters commands quietly into his patch mic, Emmie casts the terrain maps away with a sweeping gesture and leans forward against the ship's railing.

After a minute of back-and-forth between Owen and the spliner control room, the fog dissolves, revealing the distant shape of a mountainous island, which the boat now approaches at speed. Emmie grasps the railing tightly as the ship pitches and rolls, unconsciously brushing away from her cheeks the sensation of cold ocean spray created by the electromagnetic tactile simulator on her headset.

"Shiva!" Emmie says sharply. "What's with these waves? Sound design sent you the rest of that library like a week ago." In the latest wave of hiring at Augur, a number of Owen's friends have joined the team, including Shiva Mehrotra. To Emmie's perpetual annoyance, Shiva lives up to the reputation for laziness he earned as Owen's *Eleusis*-addicted roommate, but he's nonetheless one of the best coders on her team.

"Oh, yeah," Shiva's disembodied voice drawls through her earbuds. "Hold on."

A moment later, the muffled splashes, which had been incongruous with the ship's speed, escalate into more realistic crashes. Emmie, satisfied by the auditory details accompanying the ship simulation, refocuses on the island, which is now crisply silhouetted against a clear blue sky. The ship speeds ahead until we're within swimming distance of the dramatic cliffs that form the shoreline. Unable to draw closer in the simulated depths of the lagoon, the ship slows to a stop and rolls gently in the waves. Emmie contemplates the cliffs uncertainly for several minutes, her head cocked to the side. My own antipathy toward Thera seems to have cast a veil over the island that even Emmie's most determined concentration can't lift.

"No," she says, brow furrowing. "It's close, but there's something … something …"

A long silence elapses. Tentatively, Owen suggests, again off mic, "We've been at it for hours, Emmie. The team needs a break. We should—"

"Tsch!" Emmie cuts him off with a wordless shush, her eyes still locked on the cliffs, her fingers gripping the rail. Owen sighs. A moment later, she growls in frustration and pushes back from the railing, mussing her short hair violently until it sticks out in a cobalt-streaked halo of dark chestnut hair.

"You haven't slept in two days, Emmie," Owen says, more firmly now as he sees her resolve weakening. "You need to take a break. Or," he laughs, looking at her greasy hair, "at least a shower." On mic again, he says, "I'm sure *everyone* could use a break."

The disembodied murmurs of the control room operators agree. Emmie nods reluctantly. Casting a final reproachful glare at the unyielding cliffs of the island, she says, "Thanks for your patience, guys. Really great job with the ship simulation. I'm releasing the spliner to the other teams for the rest of the day. I'll let you know our next call time when we meet tomorrow. Lydia, could you shut down, please?"

"Sure thing, boss," a cheerful voice promptly replies.

The island fades from view. The deck of the ship sinks slowly, lowering us several yards as it melts into the smooth floor of the spliner, leaving Emmie and Owen in a featureless, cavernous grey space. Sound-dampening floors stretch away to meet distant, windowless grey walls that rise over a hundred feet. Owen stretches and yawns. He slips off his immerger headset, taps off his patch mic, and peels off layers of immerger gear until he stands naked to the waist in the flat ambient light. His abs are the envy of the engineering team, but Emmie doesn't seem to notice. She gazes at the space where the island cliffs stood a moment ago.

"You coming back for lunch?" Owen asks, retrieving a thin cotton shirt from his bag and pulling it on over his head. He rubs his skin to remove the tingling sensation left behind by the tactile immerger gear.

"Hmmm," Emmie murmurs.

"Em?" says Owen.

She nods vaguely. “Oh, yeah. Yeah, I’m coming. I’ll be right behind you.”

Owen opens his mouth to say something, then changes his mind and simply nods. He exits through the sliding door on the east wall. Through the open door, a beam of golden midday sunlight and the chattering of the rest of the crew momentarily pierces the dim, silent interior of the spliner.

When the door closes, Emmie bows her head. I know she can’t bear up indefinitely under the weight of all these expectant, invisible observers with their expensive, idle hands. If I knew how to help her, I would, but neither one of us seems able to find the clarity required to complete the design of the temple city of Thera.

Emmie pulls off her headset and gazes into the empty grey space on the western side of the spliner, where I stand unseen, watching her. She swallows and says softly, “Please, show yourself. Please—”

I’m not sure whether Emmie’s talking to Thera or to me or to some other Muse, but her words resonate deep in my heart. The desire to stand before her, to be truly seen by her, burns with an intensity I thought I’d long since learned to resist.

Emmie stops short, her eyes widening in the half-light. Oh, spirits. Did she just see me? Fear replaces my desire to be seen, and I vanish from view. But it’s too late. She definitely saw me. I just hope it was so brief that she won’t believe her eyes.

“Lydia? Could you confirm shutdown’s complete?” Emmie says nervously on the public channel. There’s no reply. Everyone else has already left the spliner building. She hesitates, then takes a few steps toward the place where she saw me.

Up close, she finds nothing but a uniform grey expanse of floor merging with the wall. She takes a deep breath and forces a laugh. Programming glitches are a normal part of domain development and can easily cause a momentary extrusion of the spliner’s floor or wall during a system shutdown. She tries to convince herself that’s what she saw. She taps out a quick bug report on the forearm of her immerger sleeve and submits it to the ticketing system.

She leaves through the east door, her footsteps swallowed up by the muffling walls and springy floor of the spliner. Relieved, I watch her go.

△▽△

I emerge from the spliner, squinting until my eyes adjust to the dazzling sunlight that saturates the brick paths and buildings, the flowering shrubs and trees, and the rolling lawns of the Augur campus. I massage my temples as I try to refocus my vision, which is blurry after so many hours wearing my immerger glasses. That must be why I’m seeing things.

I walk toward the gleaming glass front of the main office building, where the cafeteria is located. On a beautiful spring day like this, I’d expect to see half the company sprawled out on the lawn for their lunch break. I flick on my visual overlay and scroll through email to check whether someone called a last-minute meeting, but I see nothing. Maybe there was an announcement over the campus-wide audio channel. People always forget that the spliner is shielded from wireless signals, so everyone working in that building routinely misses last-minute announcements. Ahmet should really do something to fix that.

I hurry into the building, looking for signs of life. There's no one in the cafeteria adjacent to the lobby. Only when I reach the elevators do I notice the bright red light shining above the door of the video screening room. Normally I wouldn't interrupt a screening in progress, but clearly something's up. I walk to the double doors and press my ear against the crack between them. I hear the murmur of someone speaking, but it's almost entirely muffled by the room's first-rate soundproofing. Trying to make as little noise as possible, I open the door softly and step inside.

I've never seen the screening room so crowded. A few months ago, before our latest hiring spree, the entire company would have occupied less than half this space. Now it's standing room only.

I scan the stricken faces of the people standing nearest me. What the hell is going on? I stretch onto my tiptoes to look over the shoulders of the people in front of me. I can just make out Ty and Ahmet, our CEO and CTO, standing at the front of the auditorium.

Ty's usually ruddy face is drained of color. He's saying, "… have been notified. They will arrive Thursday from Kyoto to attend a private funeral service. His sister has arranged a memorial service for the Augur community to take place this Sunday evening at seven o'clock at the Buddhist Church of Oakland on Jackson Street."

I clap my hand over my mouth. It can't be.

Ty takes a deep breath and continues, "Tomo was a close personal friend for the past fifteen years. Meeting him was a turning point in my life, and I am so grateful to have known him. Even though he's gone, his work lives on. His creativity and craftsmanship have shaped the heart of Augur and touched millions of people who have loved his domains and games."

My face turns numb. I stagger backwards into someone.

"Careful!" someone says, surprised. Before I can turn around and apologize, Owen appears from somewhere nearby. He grabs my arms to steady me.

"Lay her down flat," someone else warns. "She looks like she's going to faint."

Several hands lower me gently to the floor. I feel the blood rushing back to my head. Owen hovers over me. I grab his hand.

"Yikes," he says. "Your fingers are like ice."

"Owen," I whisper, holding back tears. "What happened to Tomo?"

Owen presses my hand between both of his as he says gently, "Tomo died, Emmie. He fell down in the street while he was walking home last night. The medical examiner says it was a heart attack."

MEMENTOS

I STAND UNSEEN BESIDE EMMIE as she sits on the stone bench inside the circle of redwood trees that shades her driveway. She's oblivious to the misty rain that's falling, focused entirely on skimming the toes of her black shoes back and forth across the lush spring grass. I, however, scan her surroundings vigilantly. Since Tomo's death, I've spent every spare moment with Emmie, knowing that my long-awaited moment is fast approaching.

Tires crunch on loose gravel, and Owen's dark grey electric sports car pulls quietly into the driveway. He steps out of the car, an enormous black umbrella in his hand.

"Aren't you cold?" he says, stepping toward her. He opens the umbrella over her with one hand and starts to remove his jacket for her with the other, managing to splash them both with rainwater in the process.

"No, no," she says, tugging at his lapels to straighten his jacket. "Really, I'm fine." She flicks the scattered droplets off her black skirt and stretches onto her toes to brush the rain out of Owen's dark hair, which he's carefully parted and combed.

"You look nice," he says, stooping slightly to keep the umbrella close to her as they walk to the car.

She gives him a small, sad smile. "You're sweet," she says. "You look nice, too."

They climb into the car. Owen drives slowly down the steep, winding road into the Oakland flats. I watch Emmie from the back seat as she gazes listlessly out the window at the trees and houses sliding by.

She says, "I can't remember the last time I wasn't wearing immersion gear. It makes everything seem so quiet … so still."

Owen glances at her. "You sound like that's a bad thing."

Emmie shrugs. "Tomo never wore immergers outside of work. He'd always tell me—" She switches into an imitation of Tomo's most earnest tone. "'We must never forget how to be present in one world at a time.' I guess he knew I had trouble with that."

Owen smiles wryly. They drive in silence until he pulls into a parking space on Fourth Street across from the Buddhist church.

"I feel … all disconnected," Emmie says, watching the twilight gather outside the car. "But not sad, exactly. None of this seems real."

Owen settles his hand on hers. She glances down at their intertwined fingers, half smiling as she says, "He was my idol when I was a kid. I totally worshipped him. And then when I met him, he was so … I don't know. I never expected it to be like that. I thought he would be a teacher, a mentor, maybe, if I was lucky. But he was much more than that to me. I felt—as soon as I met him, right away—like I'd known him forever. Has that ever happened to you?"

Emmie looks back up at Owen, expecting a reply, but he's staring at something through the windshield. Emmie and I lean forward, following Owen's gaze. There's a small group of people standing outside the wrought iron fence that separates the Buddhist church from the sidewalk. Many of them are carrying signs, but it's difficult to read them through the misty rain.

"What are they doing?" says Emmie.

Three people in the crowd unfurl a huge banner across their chests. Even through the rain-smeared windshield, the words scrawled in bold red paint are legible: *TECH TYCOONS BURN.*

Emmie's mouth drops open. She reaches for the door handle, her expression livid. Owen grabs her arm before she can step out onto the sidewalk.

"Look," says Owen, pointing. A vehicle with a flashing blue light is rounding the corner. "Someone already called the police. Let's stay out of it."

Two police officers climb from their vehicle and begin arguing with someone in the group standing in front of the church. Eventually, after some wild gesticulating, the group disperses, taking their signs with them.

When the sidewalk is clear, Owen squeezes Emmie's hand. "Come on," he says. "Let's go inside."

The rain's falling harder now. I follow Emmie and Owen as they hurry up the steps and through the red front doors of the church. A flock of wet umbrellas drips onto the worn red carpet covering the wood floor of the entryway. A small sign indicates that the memorial service for Tomo Yoshimoto is taking place in the main *hondo* on the second floor of the church. Owen murmurs hello to a few other Augur employees coming in behind us before steering Emmie up the stairs.

Religious objects line the hallway on the second floor. The gleaming metals, bright paints, and rich fabrics of altars, shrines, and statues create a festive atmosphere, an incongruous backdrop to the somber stream of people headed to the memorial service. The door to the *hondo* stands open, and beside it sits a carved cedar sculpture of the Buddha, smiling serenely. Emmie looks down at the statue as she passes, briefly smiling back.

I scan the faces of the crowd hopefully until I recognize, with a jolt of excitement, the familiar face of a sprightly Asian woman with stylishly-bobbed silver hair entering the *hondo* just ahead of us. It's Ayame Yoshimoto, Tomo's sister. The last time I saw her was decades ago, in Japan. She's aging well. Ayame bows slightly toward the altar at the front before proceeding at a dignified pace into the room. Emmie and Owen exchange a look, shrug, then imitate her, bowing.

The *hondo* isn't yet full. Owen picks out an empty space in the pews to the left of the altar. He leads Emmie there by the hand. Once seated, Emmie glances back at the door each time someone enters. A few minutes later, Ollie appears, followed by Anatolia and Travis. Ollie murmurs something to Anatolia and bows smoothly toward the altar. Anatolia follows her lead, while Travis crosses himself. Emmie catches Ollie's eye with a small wave and slides toward the center of the pew to make room for her family. I take an empty seat behind Emmie, beside a pale, overweight young programmer with thick glasses and a wrinkled black shirt.

Ollie works her way slowly through the crowd, edging around Owen's long legs to sit beside Emmie. She smooths a few locks of Emmie's hair away from her eyes and brushes a smear of eyeshadow from her cheek before wrapping her sister in a hug. Anatolia reaches over to give Emmie's hand a squeeze before turning to chat with Owen in an undertone.

"Did you see the protestors?" Ollie asks Emmie softly. Emmie nods. Ollie sighs. "I don't know what those people are trying to accomplish any more."

Emmie leans her head on Ollie's shoulder and looks forward at the altar. A broad, dark lintel inlaid with panels of gold relief and supported by round gold columns frames the wide rectangular recess housing the golden shrine to the Buddha. A low, glossy altar table stands before the shrine, draped with fabric woven in a stylized floral pattern. Two wreaths of gleaming silver hang from the ceiling on either side of the shrine, and below each one sits a dark urn of incense. A large photograph of Tomo stands on the altar beside a vase of flowers. The serenity of the old man's smile in his portrait is quite different from the intensity of the gaze I remember from Tomo's youth.

"What a beautiful shrine," Emmie whispers.

"A little too gaudy for my taste," Ollie whispers back. "But I guess I can see what you mean."

People continue to file in until every pew is full. After the doors outside the *hondo* close, a middle-aged priest with a shining bald head and a saffron-colored robe walks down the center aisle. He stands behind a wooden lectern to the right of the gleaming shrine and pulls the microphone down a few inches. The room falls quiet.

"Welcome to the Buddhist Church of Oakland," he says, speaking in precise English with a Japanese cadence. "Thank you all for coming. Today we memorialize the life of Tomo Yoshimoto and celebrate his passage into the next." He looks out across the sea of faces. His eyes settle momentarily on Emmie before he says, smiling broadly, "I see Tomo was a man fortunate to have many friends.

"Throughout the memorial service, we will perform rituals of spiritual significance. We perform these rituals both in memory of Tomo and for those of us left behind who mourn his departure. We have many visitors, so, before we begin, let me tell you what to expect …"

△▽△

After Tomo's memorial service, I follow Owen and my family out into a side room lined with round tables, chairs, and a long table laid out with food and drink.

"I'm thirsty," I say. "My head is swimming from all that incense."

Owen offers to get drinks, and Ollie finds us an empty table in the corner. I take a seat there and look around. My eyes fall on the stylish-looking older woman who stands by the door to the hallway. I remember her—the woman who entered the *hondo* ahead of me and Owen. People are walking up to her, pressing her hand, speaking quietly. Several drop small black and silver envelopes into a basket set out on the low table beside her.

"She must be a member of Tomo's family," I say to Ollie. "I'm going to go over."

I join the short line of people waiting to speak to the woman. I ask the little old Asian man ahead of me whether he knows how this woman is related to Tomo.

"Oh! Ayame is Tomo's sister," he says brightly. "She lives in Oakland, not far. I met her here at the temple, well, it must have been just six months ago, now. It's sad, isn't it? He was the last living member of her immediate family, and her only family here in America, I think. She told me they were close."

After the little old man finishes speaking with Ayame, I step forward to greet her.

"I'm so—" My voice breaks with emotion. I swallow, hastily wipe my eyes, and try to regain my composure. "So very sorry for your loss."

Ayame reaches out and touches my arm. She says, "Thank you, thank you for coming. No need to be sorry, though. I will miss my brother very much, but death is a part of life. And it's not so great a tragedy when an old man dies."

"Well, even so …" I say.

Ayame smiles at me kindly. "You know," she says conspiratorially, leaning toward me, lowering her voice as she looks at the people milling about. "He would laugh to think of you all coming here to remember him."

"Why?" I say.

"I can't remember the last time he set foot inside a temple," says Ayame. "He drifted away from spiritual practices as he grew older. He was quite different as a boy—fascinated by Buddhist teachings. He loved to talk about the existence of many worlds, of life after life. But then—" She waves her hand vaguely. "Life happens. I think he forgot the joys and felt only the pain."

"He never seemed that way to me," I say, drawing back a little.

Ayame smiles. "I'm glad to hear you say that," she says. "Moving to America was a fresh start for him. When I finally moved here to be closer to him, I could see that he had changed. He had grown happy again."

"He had every reason to be happy," I say. "He spent his life doing extraordinary work, work that he loved."

Ayame considers me thoughtfully. "You must be Emmie Bridges," she says.

Surprised, I say, "How did you know?"

"Tomo told me about you," she says. "He meant to introduce us. He said you reminded him of someone we knew when we were children. I see now what he meant."

"Oh …" I say uncertainly. "Well. I'm pleased to meet you, too, Ms. …"

"Yoshimoto. But please, call me Ayame."

"Pleased to meet you, Ayame."

"Yes," says Ayame. "I'm glad we've met at last."

Another couple steps up behind me to offer their condolences. I turn to leave, but Ayame reaches out and touches my arm. Quietly, she says, "I just heard from my brother's lawyer. Tomo left something for you."

"For me?" I say, confused.

"Yes," she says. "I'm not sure what, exactly. Could we meet later, once I've retrieved it, so I can give it to you?"

"Of course," I say. "Whenever you like."

BEQUEST

Six months after Tomo's memorial service, the nine o'clock alarm buzzes on my smartcom. I swing my arm toward my nightstand, knocking the device to the floor, where it continues to buzz. I stretch out my arm toward the floor to turn it off, but it's just out of reach. Sighing, I roll heavily out of bed and shuffle to the bathroom. I run a hot shower, waiting for the room to fill with steam before slipping out of my pajamas and into the water.

Forty minutes later, I pull into a space in the Augur campus parking lot. My coworkers climb out of their cars around me, waving hello and chatting with each other. The majority follow the tree-lined walkway toward the main office, but a few peel off toward the enormous studio warehouses at the campus periphery: the sound effects studio, the tactile and olfactory studio, the music studio. Beside the window-lined walls of the studio spaces, the mammoth, windowless spliner looks ominous, belying its status as the most sought-after workspace on campus.

I trudge wearily after the stream of people headed to the main offices. I flip on my visual overlay to scan my work email, inadvertently pausing in the middle of the walkway. I nearly fall to the ground when someone rams me from behind. I wheel around and find myself glaring up at the tall, blonde figure of Zeke, who's flanked by two of the design team's new hires. A pained look flickers across his pale, handsome features before disappearing behind a mask of dutiful apology.

"Sorry, didn't see you down there," he says.

I can't ignore the barb inside Zeke's ostensible apology. Zeke has a special talent for discerning other people's personal hangups, and he knows I hate that I'm so short.

Zeke looks me up and down. I don't need a mirror to know I look a mess. My hair is mussed, still damp from my hasty shower. The tunic I threw over my immerger clothes before I left the house is badly wrinkled. The concealer I'm wearing still isn't enough to hide the dark circles under my eyes. Zeke says, "Been pulling some all-nighters?"

I turn wordlessly from him. I had been so excited when Zeke landed his job at Augur after I recommended him to Tomo. I thought maybe working together here would rekindle the friendship we'd had back in our *Eleusis* days. What a mistake that turned out to be. I still don't understand what happened.

Zeke has been distant and cold to me since his first day here. In the beginning, I tried to maintain some semblance of a friendship with him, but I've long since given that up. In the months since Tomo's death, as I've struggled to deliver my part of the latest *Temenos* release, Zeke has started telling other teammates behind my back that my design reputation was inflated by my close collaboration with Tomo. According to Zeke, I'm no longer capable of producing the quality of work I'd done as Bealsio.

Unfortunately, after months of delays on my project, even I am starting to wonder whether there's a kernel of truth in Zeke's criticism. I can't deny that I worked more closely with Tomo than anyone else at Augur. Recently, I've even wondered aloud to Owen whether I became dependent on Tomo in my creative work.

I try to push away my self-doubt as I enter the building and hurry through the lobby toward the elevators. I'm not fast enough. Lydia Winner, the lead *Temenos* project manager and my team's liaison to Ty and Ahmet, spots me and waves. Reluctantly, I slow down, allowing Lydia to weave through the morning foot traffic and join me.

"Good morning, Emmie," she says, sounding harried but cheerful. "Got a minute?"

"What's up?" I say.

"I just wanted to check in about how the work's going in the spliner," she says.

I stop and sigh. "I'm not ready to schedule a demo, yet, Lydia. I thought we had talked about this?"

"Yes, we did. A week ago," Lydia says pointedly. Then, more sympathetically, she adds, "I know you all are working hard. I'm not trying to put you on the spot. But I do need to give Ty and Ahmet some sort of update soon."

"Okay. Okay. I'll get back to you. Soon. I promise," I say.

"All right," Lydia nods. "Thanks, Emmie."

I turn toward the elevators, but, seeing Zeke waiting for the next one, I change course and take the stairs instead. As I approach the door to my team's offices on the third floor, I pull on my headset and join our public audio channel. I tap my key card and pull open the door.

"Go-o-od morning!" Shiva's radio announcer voice blares in my ears as I enter the room. I flinch and lower my headset volume with a few taps to my wrist. I scan the open office floor, which is slowly filling with my teammates, until I find the projection cylinder whose status screen displays Shiva's avatar: an exquisitely-muscled, bare-chested brown man with eight flexed arms wielding lightning bolts, dressed in little else but chains of tiny skulls. I walk over to his cylinder and knock on the door. It slides open to reveal Shiva in full immersion gear, facing the blank grey curve of the main display area on the cylinder's inner wall.

"Hey, boss," he says cheerfully, without turning around.

"Hi," I say, unexpectedly hoarse. I clear my throat.

"Late night, eh?" he says, peering back at me with eyes even more bleary than my own.

I yawn, nod, and slip on a pair of immerger glasses from my bag. I tap the edge of the frames to sync my visual display with Shiva's. When the image comes into focus, I'm looking around Shiva down the steep drop of a promontory. Below us churns the crashing grey and white waves of a hungry sea. A dark, slick, sinuous form arcs smoothly above the water, revealing several yards of scaly back. I shudder with a mixture of revulsion and delight.

"That's new. Looks fantastic!" I say.

"Just in from the new guys on the creatures team. Want to see the whole thing?" says Shiva.

"Yeah!" I say.

A display appears before Shiva and hovers at shoulder height, showing a small line rendering of the serpentine creature now obscured by the waves. Shiva swipes his fingers over a few controls, and a more detailed, colorful rendering replaces the first. He rotates the creature for me. I enlarge it, tapping another control to animate it. For a moment, we admire the creature undulating and snapping its toothy jaws.

"Really fantastic!" I say. "But I don't remember ordering that."

Shiva turns toward me and pushes back his glasses. I do the same.

"What?" I ask warily. "What's that look?"

Shiva glances around outside the cylinder. In an undertone, he says, "I thought you would have heard by now."

"Heard *what*, Shiva?"

With a sheepish expression, Shiva says, "Ty has Zeke working on a backup concept for *Atlantis* … You know, in case … in case you can't wrap yours before the next review deadline."

"*What?*" I splutter. "When did this happen?"

"Last month, maybe? I just heard about it a couple days ago. I guess Ty gave Zeke some of the creative department new hires and is letting him use the night shift on the spliner. We're just hearing about it now because Zeke's far enough along that he needs someone from the core creative team to start integrating the new expansion with the old domain. And since I'm being a bit … underutilized on your concept lately, Ty's having me split time between you and Zeke."

"And you didn't think to tell me this until *now*?" I say.

"Sorry, Emmie. I didn't think it was my job to tell you."

I suppress a few choice words. But Shiva's right. That's not his job. This isn't his fault. This is my fault. I take a deep breath and say, "Yeah. Okay. Thanks, Shiva."

"Sorry, Emmie."

I storm off toward the lounge and pour myself a huge mug of coffee. I walk back slowly to my desk and lean heavily against it.

"Good morning," says Owen, coming up behind me with his usual morning brew of unbearably healthy vegetable sludge. He drops a kiss on the top of my head when he thinks no one's looking.

"Is it?" I say darkly, wrinkling my nose at Owen's impossibly chipper morning demeanor.

Owen takes in my exhausted face and sloppy appearance and shakes his head. "Why do you do this to yourself?" he says. "We're still weeks away from the review deadline."

"So you haven't heard either," I say.

"Haven't heard what?" he says, taking a swig of green sludge.

"That Ty authorized Zeke to start working on a backup release concept for *Atlantis*."

Owen coughs in surprise, narrowly avoiding spraying us both with his green sludge. "Are you serious?"

"I just heard."

Owen looks over my head toward Zeke's workstation, where Zeke is in conversation with one of the new hires. Zeke looks back at him coldly.

Owen frowns. To me, he says, "You'd think Ty would have a little more faith."

We sip our respective brews in silence a while.

"I haven't been at my best lately," I say softly. "Not since Tomo died."

Owen raises his eyebrows sympathetically. "Look, Emmie. It's going to take time. No one expects you to plunge back in like nothing happened."

"Yeah, but … what if I'm just no good without him?"

Owen puts his hand on my shoulder and looks straight into my eyes. He says, "You and Tomo were a great team, but you were great before you ever met him. I was there, remember?"

I stretch up on my toes to give Owen a grateful hug. He squeezes me tight, lets me go, and returns to his desk. As Owen departs, I catch Zeke looking at me. When our eyes meet, he looks away.

△▽△

Later that morning, I sit at my desk hunched over a stack of erasable paper printouts of the *Atlantis* 42 map. I rework the contours of the island with colored pencils and an eraser, taping on transparent overlays to sketch cities, forests, and villages. When I'm struggling to design things directly inside the alternet, I often fall back on drawing the old-fashioned way. As sophisticated as my immergers are, the feeling of a real pencil in my hand has a way of restoring my creativity, making me feel like a kid again, back when creating things was pure fun, not work.

Paper and pencils aren't enough to unblock my creative process today, though. I can't seem to push through this awful stuck feeling. Frustrated, I toss one sketch after another onto a discard pile on the floor beneath my desk.

Working with physical media still has some advantages, though. It's the only way I have left to work with any privacy from the prying eyes of senior management, who are anxious for progress on *Atlantis* and increasingly inclined to remotely monitor the work I do on the company development servers.

Atlantis is supposed to be Augur's major product announcement this year, an expansion of the sensationally successful *Temenos* domain we launched last year under Tomo's leadership. I was struggling with my work on the expansion project even before Tomo died, but in the absence of our beloved Chief Creative Officer, my progress on the new *Atlantis* subdomain has become wandering at best.

As weeks of delays have stretched into months, Ty and Ahmet have been under increasing pressure from our board of directors to fill Tomo's open role as CCO. Replacing an international design icon is no easy feat, though, and Ty and Ahmet seem unwilling to make any compromise on this key hire. As the Creative Director at Augur and Tomo's former right hand, I've been serving as an interim stand-in for him while the hiring process drags on. Unfortunately, my erratic performance has eroded Ty and Ahmet's faith in me. I don't think they'll fire me, but it's an increasingly real possibility that I'll be effectively demoted if I can't get this release out.

I remove my headset to tune out the cheerful banter on the shared office channel. The Friday atmosphere isn't brightening my mood. Out of the corner of my eye, I notice Zeke passing by my desk several times, no doubt sneaking glances at what I'm doing, maybe even trying to find some inspiration for whatever concept he's developing with his new team. I look down at my sketches sardonically. I should just invite him over. He couldn't possibly find anything useful here.

A few hours later, I push back from my desk and flex my aching fingers, scowling at my heaping stack of discards and the sketch in progress before me. I grab my coat and bag and make a beeline for the elevators, avoiding as many of my teammates' desks as possible on my way out. I don't want to talk to anyone.

The late lunch crowd is gathering in the first-floor cafeteria. I give them a wide berth and exit through the front door. Outside, I pull on my immerger glasses, flip on a visual overlay, and request a short list of nearby lunch spots where I'm least likely to bump into other Augur employees. I skim the list. Nothing looks appealing. I have zero appetite. I jog off toward the parking lot instead and slip inside my car.

I start the car, lean my head back, and crank the vehicle glass tint up to its maximum setting. At last, I'm shielded from the view of everyone else on campus.

I touch the smartcom clipped to my belt, considering sending a projection to Ollie. I look at the clock on my visual overlay. Knowing my sister, she'll be hard at work right now on some important doctoral-dissertation-related task. I don't want to interrupt her, but I really need to talk to someone right now.

I'm about to call Ollie when my headset chimes with an incoming call request. It's an unknown number. I wait a couple of rings, then answer.

Ayame Yoshimoto's projection appears before me on my visual overlay.

"Hello, Emmie," she says.

"Oh, hi, Ayame," I say, surprised. I haven't seen or even thought of Ayame once in the months since Tomo's memorial service. "How are you?"

"Fine, fine, I'm doing well, thank you. Is now a good time to talk?"

"Sure, now's fine."

"Well, I'm afraid it's taken me much longer to call than I expected. Do you remember, when we met at my brother's memorial service, I told you he left you something in his will?"

"Yes, I do remember," I say. At least, I remember now. I'm a little surprised I'd forgotten, but I really have been out of it since Tomo died. "What exactly is it?"

"It took me a while to find that out, actually," says Ayame. "I had to return to Japan to retrieve it, and I just arrived home this morning."

Now I'm intrigued. I say, "Well, thank you for taking so much trouble to get it for me."

"No trouble, no trouble at all. It was very important to my brother. I would like to give it to you in person, if you don't mind."

"Of course," I say. "Could I take you to lunch? It's the least I—"

"That's very sweet, very sweet. But I think it would be better if we meet somewhere in private. Could we meet now, perhaps? I've asked the minister at the temple—you remember, where Tomo's memorial took place—and he would be happy to lend us his office."

I look at the clock again.

"Sure," I say. "It should only take me a few minutes to get there."

"Wonderful, wonderful. I will wait for you here."

△▽△

Although I drive through downtown Oakland nearly every day on my way to work, I haven't been by the temple since Tomo's memorial service. If I'm honest with myself, I may even have been avoiding it.

I pull into a street parking space across from the building, climb out of my car, and tap my smartcom to the parking meter to pay for my space. I cross the street and try to open the iron gate in front of the temple, but it's locked. I peer up at the curtained front windows of the building, unsure what to do next.

Fortunately, the front door opens almost immediately, and Ayame steps out. "Hello, my dear," she calls. I'm struck by her familiar, affectionate address, so similar to the way Tomo used to speak to me.

"Hello," I call back. "Good to see you again."

Ayame hurries down the steps, glances up and down the street, and unlocks the gate, ushering me inside. I look back over my shoulder at the street as the gate closes and locks again behind me. This is a reasonably safe part of Oakland, and I think of a temple as a fairly public space. I wonder why they keep the gate locked in the middle of the day?

"I hope you didn't feel obligated to rush to meet me," I say as we walk up the front steps. "You must be tired after such a long journey."

Ayame dismisses the suggestion with a wave. "Not at all. Let's go upstairs."

I follow her into the building and pull the heavy red doors shut behind us. Ayame leads me up the stairs to the second floor, down the hallway, and through the open door at the end of the hall. Inside, the robed priest with the shaved head whom I remember from Tomo's memorial service sits behind a tidy desk. He rises slowly and bows to each of us in turn. Ayame bows back. I imitate her, a bit awkwardly.

"It's so nice to meet you, Emmie," the priest says, speaking clearly and precisely, with a trace of an accent. "I'm Reverend Naoto Kimura."

"Nice to meet you, too," I say.

"Please, have a seat," says Naoto, pulling a couple of chairs toward his desk. I hope my confusion doesn't show too much on my face. I hadn't realized the priest would be part of this meeting, too.

When we're all seated, Ayame turns to me and says, "You must be wondering why I've asked you to meet here, like this." She tucks a loose strand of short silver hair behind one ear. "I'm afraid it's a bit of a long story.

"When I met you at Tomo's memorial service, I had just learned from Tomo's lawyer that my brother had designated me the executor of his estate. Not a small responsibility, it turns out! He left most of his wealth to a foundation that will invest in the startup companies of young people working in emerging media fields. It took me nearly five months to make all the necessary arrangements, before I had a chance to turn my attention to the other items.

"You were one of the few individual beneficiaries named in the will. The first part regarding your bequest was straightforward enough. Tomo wanted you to have his bonsai tree."

"His baby," I say with a smile, remembering how lovingly Tomo had tended the beautiful, tiny, twisting branches.

"Yes," Ayame says distantly, evidently lost in memory herself. "He started caring for it when he was still just a boy." After a pause, her eyes refocus on me. She continues, "Yes, yes, well. He also left a rather unusual set of instructions. The will said I was to visit the Enryaku-ji Temple, not far from where we grew up. There, I was to ask for a priestess named Amaterasu Nagato.

"When I finished my work here, I left for Japan, and when I arrived at Enryaku-ji, I told the nuns there that I had come to visit Amaterasu Nagato. They told me she was ill, too weak to see any visitors. However, one of her attendants took my message to her, and that same day she brought back a reply. Amaterasu promised to see me as soon as she was able.

"So I waited until she called for me some weeks later. I visited her in her quarters at the temple. She dismissed her attendant to speak with me privately. She seemed quite frail, and I could not imagine how ill she must have been before if she considered herself strong enough to see me now.

"I sat at her bedside, and she was quiet for a very long time. She seemed to be examining me. Then, quite suddenly, she asked if I could tell her what I remembered about the first time I met Midori Shimahashi.

"Well, the question surprised me. I had not thought of Midori in decades. But it was easy for me to remember how we first met, and so I told Amaterasu.

"I had just turned twelve, and Tomo was thirteen. Our mother had decided to take us on a day trip from our town in the mountains to visit Kinkaku-ji Temple in Kyoto. It was autumn, and the leaves had just started to change.

"We explored the temple complex together, until at last we came upon the Golden Pavilion and its reflection pond. It was very beautiful, and we sat down at the edge of the water for a while. Tomo pulled out his sketchpad—he was an aspiring manga artist at the time—and started to draw. I remember Tomo saying to me, 'I wish I could live here forever.'

"And then, behind us, a girl said, 'It's a bit like heaven, isn't it? But I think I would get tired of it, after a while.'

"We turned around, and there stood Midori. I was annoyed by her comment. She sounded so superior! But when I looked at Tomo, I could see that he was quite taken with her. She was a little older than us, about seventeen, and quite beautiful. This annoyed me even more, and I said, 'Really? Could anyone ever get tired of heaven?'

"Midori smiled at me. She said, 'Well, I guess it would take a very long time.'

"That seemed to break the ice, and so we kept talking. She turned out to know a great deal about the history of the temple, and Tomo took advantage of this to keep talking with her, asking question after question.

"We spent the rest of that day together, and it was evening when at last we said goodbye to Midori and returned home with my mother.

"I couldn't imagine why Amaterasu wanted to know how I met Midori, but the priestess seemed satisfied and said, 'Thank you. I needed to make sure there was no mistake. I am glad you have come.'

"Then she told me that Tomo had left a manuscript in her care, many years ago, the beginning of an academic text on creation myths in various world religions."

"Why would Tomo have been working on a book like that?" I ask Ayame. "I remember you said at his memorial service that he'd lost interest in religion."

"Yes. Yes, as far as I knew, that was true," she says. "But you misunderstand. It wasn't Tomo's manuscript. It was Midori's.

"You see, Midori and Tomo exchanged contact information, that day we met at the temple. In fact, a few days later, I found him writing her a letter—so old-fashioned, very romantic. I teased him about his crush, but he ignored me.

"They kept in touch for years after that, but Tomo was very private about the relationship. When it came time for him to go off to university, Tomo enrolled at the university in Kyoto to study architecture. Midori was a graduate student there at the time, in the department of Indian and Buddhist studies.

"He and Midori began to spend a lot of time together. I could see that Tomo was in love with her, but unfortunately Midori did not seem to feel the same way about him. She was so wrapped up in her doctoral research. I thought perhaps she didn't realize the effect she had on my brother, which made me sad for him.

"When Midori received a grant to travel to Buddhist monasteries across Asia to gather source material for her dissertation, I was relieved. I thought that Tomo would at last have some distance from her. But Tomo decided to take a leave of absence from his architecture program to travel with her. My parents were devastated, and I was furious at Midori. I confronted her, accusing her of ruining my brother's life. I expected her to defend herself, but instead she tried to persuade me that Tomo was making the right decision.

"Midori said to me, 'The teachers we will meet on this journey have preserved knowledge accumulated by spiritual masters over centuries. This knowledge is precious, and we will be helping to ensure it survives for centuries more. Tomo is lucky to have the opportunity to do such important work in his life.'

"I didn't know what to say to that. Although I still didn't approve, I kept my mouth shut as my brother prepared to leave.

"I heard nothing from him for months after he left, despite trying to contact him repeatedly. I had only the vaguest idea of where he might be. My mother was sick with worry, and from time to time I felt furious at Midori for this.

"Occasionally, we received a letter from Tomo. He wrote that he was very busy, and that we should not worry about him. He apologized once or twice for being out of touch, saying that the places they were staying were quite remote, without even a telephone."

I must look surprised by that, because Ayame chuckles at my expression. "Yes," she says. "This was 1980. Long before smartcoms, before even mobile phones had become widespread.

"But then one day …" Ayame sighs. "Tomo did call. It was the first time we had spoken in almost two years. I was so delighted to hear his voice that at first I didn't understand that something was wrong. I chattered away, berating him for not calling sooner. He was silent for a long time, and then he said, 'Midori is dead. I'm coming home with her body.'"

I gasp. I'm so engrossed in Ayame's story that I feel as distressed by this turn of events as if they'd just occurred.

"Yes," Ayame nods. "I was shocked, as well. Shocked. I didn't know what to say. Tomo told me when he would return, and then he hung up. A few days later, he was home.

"There was a funeral for Midori, and Tomo moved back in with my parents. After a few weeks, my parents told me that they were worried about him, that he hardly ever left his room. So I started to come home more frequently from university to spend time with him. Usually I just sat in his room as he lay on his bed staring at the ceiling. I asked him questions, trying to talk with him, but he barely spoke.

"This went on a long time, but I was persistent, very persistent. I was terribly worried about him, but, I'll admit, I was also very curious to know what had happened during his trip, and how it had all ended. He seemed deaf to my questions most of the time, but gradually he began to open up about the things he and Midori had seen and done during his long absence. One day, he finally answered my question about how Midori had died.

"He told me they had been in the New Delhi airport after a research visit to several Indian temples, waiting for their flight to Tibet. It was very hot in the terminal because the air conditioning had broken down. When they reached their gate, Midori said she wanted to find some bottled water, so Tomo stayed behind at the gate with their luggage. She was gone for a long time. When their flight started to board, she still had not returned, so Tomo went looking for her.

"He found her surrounded by a small crowd a few gates away. She was on the floor, unconscious. An American preacher they had met on the bus ride to the airport had called airport security, and he was trying to resuscitate Midori. A few minutes later, emergency workers arrived and took her to an ambulance. Tomo followed them to the hospital, but Midori was pronounced dead on arrival. The doctor who examined her said it was a ruptured brain aneurysm."

"How awful," I say. "Poor Tomo!"

Ayame says, "He rarely spoke to me of Midori again after that, and I never could bring myself to ask. I'm not sure Tomo ever truly recovered from the loss.

"About a year after Midori's death, Tomo dropped out of university and got a job in a manga shop in Kyoto."

I nod. The story of Tomo's gradual ascent from lowly store clerk to international alternet sensation is familiar to virtually every aspiring domain designer in the world.

Ayame says, "And that was how things were, for nearly thirty years. He was —goodness, he must have been over fifty when he decided to go to Silicon Valley. He said the alternet was going to change the world. Amaterasu told me that was when Tomo came to see her, just before he left for California.

"Tomo knew Midori had always felt indebted to Amaterasu for her philosophical writings and commentary on various Buddhist texts. I suppose that's why Tomo went to her. Even though his whole life had been given over to manga by that point, I suppose he never stopped feeling responsible for the unfinished manuscript. It was all that was left of Midori's life's work.

"Amaterasu told me that Tomo asked her to keep the manuscript for him, until he found someone to continue the work."

Ayame turns to me with a pointed expression.

"What?" I say in disbelief. "Surely not me."

"Well …" Ayame says thoughtfully. "Well, Tomo seemed to think so."

"But I really don't know anything about writing a book," I say apologetically, wondering why Tomo would think I'm capable of something like this. "I've hardly ever written anything longer than an email. I've spent my whole life designing domains."

"You might find that more useful," says Naoto. I blink at him, having almost forgotten he was there. But the priest has been listening quietly, eyes half-closed, the whole time.

"What do you mean?" I say.

He opens his eyes wider and smiles at me, saying, "Amaterasu once showed me the documents. They are very visual. Many illustrations. Maybe that is why Midori wanted to work with an artist like Tomo. Maybe that is why Tomo left the manuscript to you."

"Good, good," says Ayame, nodding at Naoto. "I see why Amaterasu suggested I introduce you two, then. She thought you might have some ideas about it."

"You know Amaterasu?" I ask Naoto.

He says, "I lived with the monks in Enryaku-ji for some time. Part of my …" Naoto smiles to himself, "youthful wanderings. Amaterasu is a very great teacher, very—"

"Oh, oh," Ayame interrupts, holding up her hands. "I almost forgot. Amaterasu said it was very important for me to tell you this. She said that the information on the manuscript is very sensitive, that you should only discuss it with someone you trust."

"Someone I trust?" I say, puzzled. "What did she mean?"

"No idea. No idea at all," Ayame says cheerfully. "But now I've told you everything I know. So here is the manuscript."

Ayame reaches over to the corner of Naoto's desk and picks up a carved wooden box about an inch square. She slides open the top of the box with her thumb and holds it out for me to see. Inside, the emerald-colored ceramic of a coin-sized storage drive gleams against the maroon velvet lining of the box. Ayame slips the box shut again and hands it to me.

I look down at it, surprised. "I was imagining some big dusty stack of papers," I say.

Ayame laughs. "Oh, my dear, my brother wasn't quite *that* old."

△▽△

My hand strays to my jacket pocket several times as I drive back to Augur, but I have no opportunity to look at the contents of the storage drive. As soon as I pull into the parking lot, my smartcom buzzes.

It's a text message from Owen that reads, *where are you??*

my car, I respond quickly. *what's wrong?*

He writes, *ty called an all-hands meeting that started fifteen minutes ago, and you are conspicuously absent.*

I swear under my breath, burst out of my car, and set off running toward the office.

A PROPOSITION

Owen watches me with a subdued expression as we walk down the hall together, having just left the all-hands meeting. I can't help glaring at Zeke as he passes by, his normally pale face now radiant with triumph.

In an aggrieved undertone, I say to Owen, "I can't believe I recommended him to Tomo. That's the only reason he hired the jackass in the first place! And what the hell is Ty thinking, anyway, splitting the creative team into two camps? It makes no sense! It's counterproductive. Pick one of us or the other and just be done with it! Tomo never would have—"

As we enter the relative privacy of the maze of projection cylinders on our floor, Owen turns to me and cuts me off. "I think we should grab a greyroom and do this in private," he says.

I sigh and nod. It won't help me or anyone left on my team to see me flipping out like this. I trudge after Owen toward the elevators. The doors open to reveal Lydia, tapping a gloved hand against her hip, eyes rapidly scanning left to right, clearly immersed in some reading. She blinks and refocuses on us as we step into the elevator.

"What floor?" Lydia asks.

"Sixth, please," says Owen.

The doors close. Lydia heaves a sigh and says, "I'm just re-reading the meeting notes now, Emmie. You're not the only one getting screwed by this decision, you know? Everyone from creative to development is going to feel the squeeze. I'm looking at these schedules, and I'm going to have to rework everything. The sprints this week are going to suck."

"Yeah, but it wouldn't suck nearly so bad if I weren't so far behind on *Atlantis* already," I say glumly.

The doors open on the sixth floor. Owen and I step out. Lydia sticks out her arm to hold the door. Looking up and down the hall to make sure no one's in earshot, she says, "I don't know what Ty's thinking, moving up the next review deadline. He's rigging the game so it's almost guaranteed that Zeke will step in and save the day with his backup concept. Sure, the guy's talented. But he would make a lousy VP."

"You don't seriously think Ty's considering promoting him over Emmie?" says Owen.

Lydia glances at me and says, "Who knows? The board has been breathing down Ty's neck since we lost Tomo, wondering whether we're dead in the water without him. Appointing a new VP for Creative might at least restore some confidence until we have a new CCO."

I sigh. I could use some confidence right now, too.

"Anyway, Emmie," Lydia says, "if there's anything I can do to help you—anything at all—I hope you'll let me know. We're all in this together."

"Thanks, Lydia," I say, anxious for her to leave so I can continue venting to Owen.

"Okay," Lydia steps back into the elevator. "Well, I'll let you two get to it."

"Come on," Owen says as soon as the door closes, steering me toward one of the empty greyrooms. He palms the door, follows me in, and locks the door.

I turn and look up at him. "Owen, I'm really sorry about all of this. I know your reputation is on the line, too, here."

He rolls his eyes. "Do you think that's what I came here to talk about? Look, I know the deadline change works in Zeke's favor, but that doesn't mean we just roll over and let him steal the show."

No matter how angry I am at Zeke, I pride myself on always providing fair critique. I say, "I saw a bit of his expansion concept today. It looks good. Very good. And it must be looking more promising to Ty than *Atlantis*, or else he wouldn't shake up the whole team with this decision. Maybe it would be better for all of us to just focus on one concept."

Owen says, "Look, Em, I know you're feeling burned out. Maybe it feels like conceding to Zeke would take the pressure off you for the next few months. But think about the bigger picture. What if Lydia's right, and Ty *is* going to promote a VP based on the next release? Everyone knows Zeke's a kick-ass designer, but he's also arrogant and divisive. He's not a team player. Even if the next release would be easier if we went with his concept now, every release after that would be much harder with him in charge of the team."

"Ugh," I groan, raking my hands through my hair. "I know, I know. I don't want him as a boss either. The thought of him sitting in Tomo's office makes me sick. But I am so stuck, Owen. I can't put my finger on it, but there is something just wrong about the *Atlantis* we've been working on, and I can't figure out how to fix it. I can't let it go to development like this."

"This is what I wanted to talk to you about," Owen says. "I think you're making this unnecessarily hard on yourself. I think you're holding yourself to some impossible standard, second-guessing everything because you think Tomo would have expected something better. But, Emmie, your concept doesn't have to be perfect. It just has to be good enough to release."

I cross my arms, shaking my head. "Tomo would never let a subpar release go out."

"If Tomo were here, Ty wouldn't have had to move up the deadline, either. Tomo had the luxury of picking his own deadlines, or throwing them out if he wanted to. You can't expect to put out the same product Tomo would have without the same resources."

"Ugh," I groan again. "I hate this."

"You know I'm right," he says.

"Still hating it," I say.

"Look, Emmie," says Owen. "You can't be perfect, not all the time. Let go a little. The team's not going to give you crap if this release has some bugs, but I don't think they'll ever forgive you if Zeke gets VP because you gave up and let him take it."

"Great," I say. "So my options are: put out a subpar release, or have everyone hate me and end up with Zeke as a boss."

"Sounds pretty simple to me," says Owen. "Go for the subpar release."

"Ugh," I say.

"You need to relax, Emmie," he says. "Why don't you step back for a bit? We can cut out early this afternoon, get an early start on our dinner date."

"Are you kidding?" I say, slipping on my immerger glasses. "I'm not leaving early, not after that meeting. I need to go to *Temenos* and figure out what the hell I'm going to do. When inspiration fails, crowdsource."

Owen looks like he wants to say something else, but he knows better than to keep trying to dissuade me when I've made a decision. He leaves me alone in the greyroom.

I dim the lights, adjust a few settings on my immerger glasses, and log on anonymously to *Temenos.*

My view of my physical surroundings melts away. After a brief loading animation, I find myself bouncing down the ferry gangway toward *Athenai*. This subdomain of Augur's *Temenos* serves as port of entry for all new users.

For my anonymous session, I select a default avatar popular with new users: a blushing strawberry-blonde wearing a fantasy-genre peasant dress that shows off an ample bosom and shapely arms to full advantage. If I use my primary avatar in this densely-trafficked area, I'll be mobbed by users eager to take a screen capture with me to show to their friends, or to berate me for selling out after my indie success, or to complain about a bug in some obscure part of the domain. This anonymous, zero-reputation avatar allows me to experience the *Athenai* subdomain of *Temenos* as any new user might.

I've taken to wandering the subdomains of *Temenos* more and more in the months since Tomo died. When I set aside my responsibilities as Creative Director, responsible for fixing every flaw in the system, *Temenos* is just a reliable source of pleasurable escape and raw material for creativity. Here, if only for a few hours, I can forget the real world and all its troubles weighing me down.

A perpetually bustling open-air market fills the half mile of sandy plain separating the ferry loading grounds from the city's central square. I've chosen a *Temenos* branch hosted at a data center in New Jersey, so the air is filled with voices speaking primarily English. I meander through the sea of stalls, browsing for new content. Much of it is predictable variations on the basics most users need: clothes, vehicles, communication clients, and navigation mods for every budget; avatar customization and animation services; *Temenos* visitor guides and news feeds; tickets for every sort of live performance, from the most highbrow to the most unsavory; booths for fortune-tellers and matchmakers; meeting grounds for quest-givers and quest-goers; environment access codes for popular solo and team games.

I slow to examine a vendor I haven't seen before. A peacock-blue kangaroo with darkly fringed golden eyes stands before a white pavilion offering passersby their choice of colorful butterflies from a fluttering rabble tethered to the ground by silver threads. Inside the pavilion, floating bubbles of all sizes hover at optimal viewing heights to display a twittering, grunting, barking, purring, hissing menagerie. The bubble-bound creatures fill the spectrum from the most prosaic felines and canines to the most astonishing winged, scaled, and furry creatures I've ever seen.

"My daughter would *love* this," says a brawny man in a leather jerkin to another buxom strawberry-blonde in a peasant dress. He points at a cat-sized, winged white unicorn with turquoise eyes and a coral mane. As he points, the price of the creature appears in an overlay on the bubble.

"Ninety-nine temens?" the man exclaims. He gives a low whistle, considers for a moment, then shrugs and initiates the purchase. The bubble disappears, releasing the unicorn and a complimentary jeweled saddle into his custody. He laughs in delight as the unicorn kicks off the ground, flies to shoulder height, and hovers before him.

"Oh, well. How often does your daughter turn six, right?" he says to his companion.

I can't help imagining the *cha-ching!* sound of an old-fashioned cash register and Ty Monaghan's expression of satisfaction as Augur's top-line revenue ticks up by a few temens with our cut of this transaction. Sales of digital goods have grown exponentially along with alternet adoption, and Augur commands an impressive market share due to the popularity of our domains and games. Even so, our board and shareholders are insatiable. No matter how many unicorns we sell this quarter, Ty's targets will doubtless move up for next quarter.

I pull up a search interface on my visual overlay to locate this vendor's contact information. The search interface flattens the entire three-dimensional scene before me into a single structured document that concisely describes every object visible from where I stand. The contact information I need is embedded in the markup of nearly every object for sale in this pavilion—an inelegant but common technique used by designers without much coding experience. I swipe my hand over my visual overlay to copy the vendor's email and smartcom number to my to-do list, along with a screen capture of the winged unicorn. Every once in a while, I acquire a promising new hire for my creative team by scouting the public market this way.

I cut a meandering path through the sandy ground of the open-air market, until I reach the paved streets of the commercial district. I walk more quickly down several blocks toward the central park at the heart of the city's downtown. A year ago, the heart of the city was a mere three blocks square. I reminisce for a moment about those heady—and exhausting—final months of development before the first *Temenos* release, when I worked side by side with Tomo around the clock to seed the original Augur content that would be new users' introduction to our high-end brand of alternet experiences. Tomo and I had decided to arrange the storefronts of our first launch sponsors around the park, with the Augur-managed community center at the east edge. There, users can socialize, speak face-to-face with the *Temenos* support team, and explore domain maps and wikis in immersive multidimensional renderings. We'd placed the buildings for *Temenos* commercial transaction services and subdomain zoning in the three blocks behind the community center.

To my dismay at the time, Ty forced us to fill the remainder of the original pre-launch city center with a patchwork of empty lots for lease and nondescript buildings where users can rent private meeting rooms and anonymous storage lockers to conduct business transactions of any kind in a completely secure environment. I lost a shouting match with Ty about this, furious that the slipshod amalgam of buildings at the city perimeter would be users' first impression of the domain I'd worked so hard with Tomo to perfect. Ty insisted that the ugly patches would stimulate user investment in city improvement and thus solidify the user base. Tomo spent days convincing me not to quit Augur after the argument.

Begrudgingly, I now admit to myself that Ty's business acumen has been as critical a contribution to Augur's commercial success as our creative innovation. Early users completely made over the city center in a matter of weeks and proceeded to push the city limits out across the plain toward the surrounding hills. All that remains of the original heart of the city is the central park and the community center. In less than six months after our initial launch, the new user subdomain of *Athenai* expanded to the outer reaches of the region Augur zoned for user development. Augur increases the supply of real estate purposefully slowly, so as demand for virtual real estate in *Athenai* skyrockets, prices soar proportionately.

I head across the central park toward a genteel grey stone façade with a green awning that reads *The Founders Club*. The building gives an overwhelming impression of exclusivity, although the building's architect so meticulously designed the exterior to blend in with the surrounding neighborhood that most passersby never notice an unusual feature of the building: the rows of large mullioned windows facing the street are completely opaque.

Everyone who's anyone of consequence in alternet circles knows that only the *Temenos* elite may walk through the mahogany doors of this building. The Founders Club's invitation-only membership extends primarily to politically or commercially influential individuals, most of whom possess in-domain assets worth over one hundred million *Temenos* dollars, called temens, or annual net incomes from in-domain business activity of over ten million temens. I scored an invite to the club in its early days because of Bealsio's minor celebrity status, as well as my reputed influence with Tomo.

I send an entry request to the door. An identity verification request appears on my display, which I promptly authorize. The door swings open, and I step into an elegant reception area with shining dark wood floors covered by an expanse of Persian rug. A uniformed receptionist behind a gleaming desk smiles brightly.

"How may I help you today, Anonymous Member?" she says.

"Just the salon, thanks," I say.

The receptionist nods. I quickly swap avatars, choosing a slim, sleek-haired thirty-something man in an understated but very expensive business suit and dark glasses. A second pair of mahogany doors behind the receptionist swings open. I pass through to the salon, a richly-imagined Greco-Roman-inspired space centered around a large interior courtyard. The golden light of *Athenai*'s late afternoon sun streams into the courtyard.

It's about seven o'clock in the evening on the East Coast, a popular hour to socialize for club members doing business in that time zone. I browse the discussions on the public channel. Two avatars, a man and a woman, examine an exquisitely detailed miniature rendering of the entire *Temenos* domain that hovers at waist height, filling most of the club's central courtyard. They turn on a heat map visualization of user traffic patterns through *Temenos*'s public subdomains and commence an animated discussion about the best locations for several new clothing retail storefronts, gesticulating at hot spots on the map. A backlit cluster of zoning committee members debate the relative merits of two competing lease applications for a city block whose former tenant has gone bankrupt. A trio of open standards wonks gripe about the incompatibility between a recently-released content development widget and an older suite of widely-used tools. A pair of club guests wearing flight suits—newbie co-founders, I'd guess, based on the buzzy showmanship of their delivery—gushes to a small gathering of venture capitalists about a new space shooter game they've just launched on the *Astral Plane* subdomain.

I make my way toward a pair of avatars deep in conversation in one of the covered colonnades alongside the courtyard. One is a broad-shouldered, silver-haired man in a whimsical space cowboy outfit seated in a leather armchair. The other is a skinny adolescent in a trucker hat sprawled across a chaise. These are Gygax and Didactix, two influential domain users. Gygax operates a popular fantasy roleplaying game in the venerable tradition of Dungeons and Dragons. He was an early adopter of Augur's game development framework and has maintained a substantial first-mover advantage in *Temenos*'s games market ever since. He's a frequent, thoughtful contributor in the *Temenos* developer forums. Didactix is a freelance alternet developer who often works on projects for Gygax but also earns a substantial stream of income from sales of easy-to-use domain navigation and transaction reporting tools. He's an avid gamer and an outspoken alternet gaming commentator. Their public chat log shows they've been discussing the upcoming *Temenos* release for the past half hour.

They turn to me as I approach.

"Hello," I say. "May I speak with you on a private channel?"

We exchange perfunctory identity verification requests. I use a partial profile to reveal my identity as an official Augur representative without my name or title. It's a bit impolite for me to enter a private channel without sharing the same level of profile information with them as they're sharing with me, but I know Gygax and Didactix will make allowances due to my official Augur credentials. They'd recognize me personally in my Bealsio avatar, but for my purpose today it's better to retain partial anonymity.

"Greetings, Anonymous Member," Didactix says on the new channel.

"Hello, Didactix, Gygax," I say. "Would you mind if I picked your brains about the upcoming expansion?"

Didactix perks up from his chaise. Gygax says, "Any chance you're going to tell us just how upcoming we're talking about?"

"Sorry, guys," I say. Anything I say here is almost certain to end up on Didactix's blog. I have to be careful about what I share.

Gygax smiles and shrugs. "That's okay. Gotta ask. So, what do you want to know?"

"How do you think Augur's been doing supporting the content developer community in the past few releases?" I say. "Is there anything that we could focus on in the next release to keep us ahead of our competitors' platforms?"

Gygax considers for a moment. He tends to be more deliberate than the typical user during feedback requests like this.

But Didactix jumps right in, speaking rapidly. "Look, the price point of high-end immersion gear is coming down, so user expectations for content quality are going to keep climbing. We have to expect ultra-high-resolution full-sensory immersion to be standard in twelve, eighteen months tops. I mean, it's not like spliner technology will be widely available any time soon, but you're definitely seeing a larger proportion of users, even, like, casual users and kids, with super sophisticated tactile immergers, olfactory, motion-simulation-capable audiovisual."

I nod. I know better than almost anyone just how fast prices for immergers are dropping. Dad and Uncle Frank are constantly adding new features to the Lab's products to maintain a competitive edge over all the copycat immergers flooding the market.

Didactix goes on, hardly pausing for breath. "*Temenos*'s tools for visual content creation are fantastic, audio less so but still better than you get elsewhere, but the tactile tools in your public toolset are, like, primitive, and lagging your competition. I mean, you guys must be using better tools yourselves, because the *Temenos*-authored games are still like the highest quality immersive experiences out there. Tomo was such an artist on that front, wow."

I smile to myself. Didactix is as much of a Tomo worshipper as I'd been.

"Thanks," I say. "I'll talk to our tools team about that. And I'd be happy to put you directly in touch with the team lead if you ever want to quit the freelance scene. Your reputation precedes you."

"Tempting," says Didactix, "but I only do business over the alternet. If I had to come into an office, I'd lose at least an hour a day commuting that I could be gaming."

I've had some version of this conversation with him and many other talented developers before. The creative and technical talent of my generation is becoming increasingly unemployable, as the ease of alternet entrepreneurship and the perception of face-to-face interactions as onerous make us hard to lure into a real-world work environment. I made an exception to work with Tomo. Were it not for him, I doubt I would have ever come to work for a company like Augur—especially not now that Augur has grown into such a big corporation that it's losing the old startup vibe that used to make it feel like home to me.

Gygax resurfaces from his thoughts and says slowly, "I agree with Didactix. A year ago, you might have gotten away with an inferior developer toolkit versus your competition, because Ty Monaghan made the decision that the core of *Temenos*'s development platform would be secure transactions, identity verification, reputation tracking, and dispute adjudication. The quality of those platform features is the reason I built my content here, and doing business in temens is the best decision I ever made. But the commercial exchange ideas you guys pioneered are being used by everyone now. The name of the game today is quality content creation. If users start wanting more immersion than I can easily develop in the *Temenos* framework, I'll have to choose between losing market share to other gaming domains or moving my business to a new platform."

"I hear you," I say, copying the automated transcription of their comments onto a scratchpad with a few notes of my own. "Other pain points?"

"Platform security," says Gygax. "I know I'm not the only domain content owner spooked by these ongoing server attacks. You haven't been hit as hard as some of your competitors, but, still, I lost a week of game revenue in my West Coast region this quarter when all your local server farms went offline. And my user base might not recover from it—you know how short attention spans are with these kids. I had whole guilds switch to games on other platforms in protest when they lost rank data."

I nod sympathetically. Augur's security department barely managed to contain the data corruption virus Gygax is referring to. I myself lost several days' worth of work when my local server wiped out between automated backups. Considering the sophistication of the attack, it's remarkable Augur hadn't sustained more damage.

"I'm using this private security consultant—Falsens—to try to keep ahead of it with some custom-designed defensive strategies," says Gygax. "But rolling your own system security is expensive. Augur could do its whole developer community a favor by offering some additional server redundancies or data backup services or something."

"I'll pass that on," I say, scribbling more notes on the transcription of Gygax's comment and firing off an email to the systems engineering and developer support team leads. "Anything else?"

"Hey, do you mind if I ask you something?" Didactix interjects.

"Sure. Anything that won't get me in trouble with Augur legal," I say.

"Well, I guess you probably won't be able to answer this, then, but anyway …" Didactix sounds a little reluctant now. "It kills me to ask, since I am like a complete Augur fanatic, but there's a rumor going around that there are big problems with the latest expansion. I'm hearing that the current Creative Director has just completely dropped the ball since Tomo died. I guess I'm maybe just the tiniest bit concerned about Augur's prospects now that he's gone. I'm not giving up on *Temenos* anytime soon, but—well, you know. I own some Augur stock through the content creator grant program, not to mention all my business here. Do you think it's time for me to diversify my risk? Sell some stock, get some stuff going in other domains, maybe?"

In the greyroom where I'm immersed in *Temenos*, I flick an override patch near my hip to decouple my facial and auditory input from my avatar. I swear. Loudly.

Back on my Augur design team public channel, Owen's voice says, "Everything okay in there, Emmie?"

I bite my lip. I'd forgotten I was automatically logged on to the public audio channel when I logged off my immersion audio channel. My entire team must have heard me.

"Yep," I say, trying to keep my voice level. "Sorry, guys. Just tripped on the treadwheel."

Recovering my composure, I refocus on Didactix. "Sorry," I say. "I definitely can't comment on anything related to upcoming releases."

△▽△

Ten hours later, I've entirely exhausted all sources of possible inspiration for tomorrow's work, so I log off of *Temenos*. I push back my immerger glasses and massage my eyes before exiting the greyroom and making my way back down to the third floor. In the lounge, I switch on the coffee machine.

As I stand waiting, enjoying the soothing gurgle and hiss of the boiling water, I withdraw from my pocket the small wooden box that Ayame gave me yesterday. I turn it over in my fingers a few times, wondering what Tomo could possibly have expected me to do with a manuscript about ancient religious texts. Maybe I'll find some time tomorrow to take a look.

The last bit of boiling water chortles up from the reservoir, and the coffee machine clicks off. The sudden silence startles me. I look out at the office floor, struggling to bring into focus anything farther than three feet away. I push up on tiptoes to peek over partitions, then scan the floor for cots or sleeping mats beneath the desks. It's late. I guess I shouldn't be surprised to find the place empty. Even though Ty just moved up our next review deadline, it's still weeks away.

I stick one of my earbuds in and say on the public channel, "Shiva?"

"Yes, ma'am," he drawls. I smile. Shiva's not exactly a workaholic like I am, but he's reliably around because he lives in the office almost as much as I do.

I slip on my glasses again and send him a chat request. A second later, his projection grins and waves at me.

"What are you up to?" I say.

"QA," he says with a wink.

"Right," I say. "Can I see?"

He switches to a streaming video of the active workspace inside his projection cylinder. There, a low-resolution, two-dimensional mage avatar, assisted by a raging water elemental, battles zombies in the midst of a forty-man dungeon raid.

"Old school," I laugh. "Don't let Ty know you'd rather spend time in an internet RPG than in *Temenos*."

"Lots to learn from the classics, boss," he says.

"Well, don't stay up too late," I say.

"Yeah, right," he says. Then, in a stage whisper, "Hypocrite."

I glance at the clock on my visual overlay. It's nearly half past one o'clock in the morning.

"'Even God couldn't create a world in one night,'" I say to myself, quoting Tomo. I glance across the floor toward Tomo's old office. The privacy that its four walls afford makes that space prime real estate, but in the six months since Tomo's death no one has suggested clearing out his things. His office remains untouched, a tidy memorial to our fallen leader. Only the custodians go in there, at Ty's direction, to water Tomo's beloved plants now that he's no longer there to tend them.

An insistent buzz, followed by three more buzzes in quick succession, sounds softly across the room. Automatically, my fingers reach for the slot on my immerger belt where I usually keep my personal smartcom. But the slot's empty. I must have left my smartcom at my desk when I headed off to the greyroom with Owen all those hours ago. I can't believe I haven't missed it until now.

I reach up to the shelf above the coffee machine for an oversized mug that proclaims "GEEK" in large letters. I pour about three cups of coffee into it and head back to my workspace, gripping the warm cup in both hands like a sacred object.

I set the mug down on the floor beneath my desk, which is currently covered in a mess of sketches, and riffle through the papers, searching for my smartcom. I'm pretty sure I heard it buzzing somewhere around here. But then the ping of a new work email in my earbuds distracts me. I flip on my visual overlay to check the message.

A developer from the Ukraine office has just responded to a question Owen asked a few hours ago: would it be difficult to add a simplified artificial intelligence and personality modeling tool for game-generated characters? Despite all the difficulties I've been having with the terrain design for *Atlantis*, Owen and I have at least managed to make headway on several quest and combat games geared toward *Temenos*'s large population of immersive roleplaying adventure gamers, who have been demanding new content for several releases now. I won't have time to flesh out all the new game characters I'd hoped to include in the next release if we repeat the time-consuming process of custom-coding the AI and personality characteristics of each one. A few basic parameters are all I really need to edit from character to character.

I've just sat down to read the work message when a second notification from my smartcom buzzes somewhere on my desk. This time, I'm close enough to feel where the buzz is coming from, and I find the device wedged between pages of a

Wired magazine as a bookmark. I snap my smartcom back into its port on my immerger belt and send the notification to my visual overlay.

I'm surprised to see not just one message notification, but ten: two from Ollie, one from Mom, everything else from Owen. I frown and hurry to open the latest message from Owen.

Starting to get worried about you. Thought we were on for dinner. Are you still at work? Call me.

I grimace, close the message, and pull up Owen's number. He picks up after one ring.

"Hey ..." I say sheepishly.

"Em! Jesus. Are you still at work?"

I wrinkle my nose, kicking my toes into the floor to rock back in my chair. "Yeah," I say. "I'm sorry I ruined our dinner plans."

"It's okay, I—" Owen starts to say, but I interrupt.

"No, it's not. You reminded me, we talked about it. I am super lame."

"Hey, don't worry about it." He exhales audibly. "But you've seriously got to stop with these crazy hours. I hate imagining you driving around downtown after dark, with—"

"Thanks, Mom!" I cut him off, annoyed.

Owen laughs. "Sorry," he says. "Hey, there's still time for a two AM pizza run. What do you say?"

I chew my lip, glancing back at the email, drumming my fingers against the coffee mug.

"I still have a little bit of work I want to wrap up tonight. Let's do dinner tomorrow," I say.

"Okay," says Owen, sounding disappointed. "Love you, babe."

"Love you, too."

△▽△

Unbeknownst to Emmie, I use our bond to keep her awake behind the wheel on her winding drive back up to her house in the hills. She should have turned on her autopilot before she left the office parking lot, but she's so sleepy that it slipped her mind. Owen's right to be worried about the effect all these late nights are having on her.

It's nearly four o'clock in the morning when Emmie pulls into her driveway. As soon as she puts the car in park, she tips her head back against the headrest, succumbing to exhaustion after two days without sleep. All that stands between her and bed is the short length of the footpath to her front door. But now that I finally have her alone, safely beyond the reach of Augur's security guards and cameras, I can't let her go just yet.

Emmie reaches for the car door handle, but I pull back on our connection, resisting her impulse and asserting my own. *Come to me*, I think. In Emmie's weary state, her awareness yields to mine easily. Her head rolls to the side, her eyes closing. Her body twitches with the onset of sleep.

In Emmie's thoughts, I see her awareness enter the grey void where dreams begin. To Emmie, this place looks almost like the cavernous spliner where she's spent so much time over the last several months. In such a familiar, unthreatening setting, it's easy for me to pull her sleeping mind into my own awareness. She awaits the familiar flicker that signals the start of a spliner session. I oblige, filling her mind with my own vision.

A soft light glows around Emmie, and the grey floor ripples as the shape of a ship extrudes smoothly beneath her feet, changing color and texture until it solidifies into the broad boards of the ship's deck. The prow of the boat cuts across choppy waves, sailing through thick fog.

As it has so many times before when she's been awake at work, the dramatic silhouette of an island appears ahead of us in the fog. It's the island Emmie knows as *Atlantis*, which I call Thera.

Drawing on every ounce of focus I've cultivated across millennia of working with her, I center my awareness on the image of the temple city of Thera, determined that Emmie should see it fully at last.

Dawn breaks behind our ship, dissolving the fog to reveal the dark shoreline cliffs looming ahead, wet rocks glistening in the sunlight. At first, I see no sign of the true Thera, only the simplified, incomplete version of the island familiar to Emmie from her endless frustrating work sessions in the spliner. Then, to my relief, a narrow inlet appears between two cliffs. Our boat heads into the gap between the imposing volcanic walls, navigating the passage into the lagoon concealed within.

Beside me, Emmie gasps as we emerge on the still, indigo waters of the city harbor. Directly ahead of us, morning light blazes pink and gold on the pale stone from which I've crafted the temple city's grand central staircase, the elegant tiers of terraced city streets, and the domed Musaion that crowns the city. Thera has never looked as beautiful to me as it does now, seen through Emmie's eyes. This is the vision that's been hidden from her, and she absorbs it now with elation.

The boat pulls forward smoothly to the broad white steps that lead out of the water. Emmie leaps ashore, excited to explore. I strain to slow her down so she'll absorb more details of the landscape—she'll need this to complete her work—but the effort of resisting her distracts me. My concentration wavers, causing the sunlight, the harbor, and the city to flicker and fade.

"No!" Emmie cries, desperately raking her eyes over the entire scene as it seems to retreat before her: the white city on the dark volcanic slope receding, the harbor expelling her back out through the inlet, the rocky island vanishing once more into the fog.

Emmie wakes. Whether the memory of the dream remains with her, I can't tell. Memories from dreams are as mysterious as the Voice in all. Her eyes refocus slowly in the darkness of her car, first on the steering wheel, then on the dashboard, then on her house outside. She yawns and tosses her head to clear it.

She pushes open the door, grabs her bag, and trudges sleepily along the curving footpath toward her house.

In the shadows of the ring of redwood trees beside the house, I sit waiting on the stone bench Papou gave her as a housewarming present. Tingling with the accumulated anticipation of twenty years, I call softly, "Emmie."

She freezes. Eyes wide, she scans the shadows until she sees me sitting here. Her body tenses. I feel her alarm like it's my own as she calls out, "Who's there?"

I stand slowly and push back the hood of my traveling cloak to show my face. In English, I say, "My name is Dom Artifex."

I step toward her into the pool of light cast by the nearby lamppost. She backs away.

"Don't come any closer," she says in her boldest voice. "I have a taser."

She rummages in an outer pocket of her bag until she finds the weapon Owen insists she carry as insurance against mishaps during her daily and nightly solo treks through Oakland. She points the taser at me. I put up both hands. I hope I can persuade her not to shoot. I'd rather not start off the latest version of our relationship having to explain why that electrode has passed straight through my body.

Calmly, I say, "I only stepped forward so you can see me clearly in the light. I won't come any closer unless you want me to."

She scans me from head to toe, eyes wide, assessing what threat I may pose and how afraid she should be. A strange look comes over her—perhaps a flicker of recognition. As much as she's changed over her many lives, I haven't changed much across all the ages she's known me. My appearance gives a deceptive impression of youth. Her gaze travels the length of my cloak, which falls in loose folds from my shoulders to the ground. Her eyes linger on my broad, callused hands.

Then her expression hardens. She squares her taser at my chest. I raise my arms up higher. The sleeves of my dusty tunic fall back from my forearms, revealing the faint pink lines of the scarlet threads embedded deeply there.

"What do you want?" she says, her voice steady despite her trembling hands.

"I want to help you," I say.

She struggles visibly against exhaustion as she considers her response. Her eyelids droop, then snap wide open again. "Help me how?" she says.

"There is a domain called Dulai," I say. "And an island in Dulai that I think you should see. An island that could be your *Atlantis*, if you wish it."

The name *Atlantis* grabs Emmie's attention. She knows every single Augur employee with access to this codename of the next *Temenos* expansion, and I am nowhere on that list. Augur has a zero-tolerance policy for information leaks about product development. A leak like this could cost someone's job.

"I don't know what you're talking about," she says.

I choose my next words carefully. So much depends on me gaining her trust. Now that Emmie has Midori's manuscript in her possession, I have to work quickly, to accomplish my own purpose as much as to protect her from the consequences of it.

"You have a gift, Emmie Bridges," I say. "An extraordinary kind of vision that led to many of your early successes. Vision that brought you to the attention of Tomo Yoshimoto. Vision that led to the success of *Temenos.*

"But something has changed. Your vision is gone. All you see now are the missing pieces."

Emmie opens her mouth and closes it again. I go on, watching her reactions and feeling them, too, through our connection. "It's taken a toll on you. Hours spent in fruitless brainstorming sessions. Falling asleep night after night at your desk on top of stacks of incomplete sketches. Uncomfortable silences in status meetings when you tell your team you have nothing yet for them to work on. Anxious questions from project managers about the mounting cost of all the hours logged in the—"

"Who told you that?" she snaps. I fall silent, wary of her temper. I need to use her anger to draw her to me, not push me away.

"Right," she huffs. "This is starting to make sense. Let's see … You heard a rumor on some game leaks forum that the next *Temenos* expansion is at a standstill since Tomo died. You've been stalking Augur employees, tracking them on the public alternet, following them home from work like this, figuring out how best to persuade someone to give you some insider information. And then you found Zeke Eckerd, who was only too eager to pump you full of his nasty rumors about me.

"Look, I get it. There's always a market for dirt on a big company like Augur. Or maybe you're just looking to blackmail someone for the chance to pitch a potential acquisition opportunity or game content concept to one of the higher-ups. But cornering the *Temenos* Creative Director alone in the middle of the night in the shadows of her front yard is just not the way it's done."

"Well, at least you have that right," I interject smoothly. "I agree the shadowy yard is not ideal. But I wanted to speak to you alone, and you have been surprisingly difficult to find alone away from Augur lately. Will you hear me out?"

"I don't need to hear any more of your creepy insights into my work life," she says.

"I only want you to see that I understand your situation," I say.

"What situation, exactly?" she says.

"You need a new partner," I say.

Emmie's finger twitches on the taser trigger. I push my hands up even higher.

"I'm offering to help you," I say again.

"Why do you want to help me?" she demands.

Thank the spirits. Emmie's fear is fading, turning into curiosity. Not wanting to push my luck further, I back into the shadows, step behind one of the great redwoods, and withdraw from her view. Impulsively, Emmie rushes after me into the ring of trees.

"Hey! Stop!" she calls.

But all she finds is the empty stone bench.

CAUGHT OFF GUARD

I WAKE WITH A START, alone in my bedroom. I squint at the bright midday light streaming through the south-facing windows. I must have been asleep for a long time. What a weird dream I had. There was a man, a stranger. But somehow he was also familiar. Who was he? I try to remember more, but it slips away.

I grab my immerger glasses from my bedside table to check the time. My hand sweeps past the small wooden box containing Tomo's storage drive, accidentally knocking it onto the floor. Unable to reach the floor without leaving my cozy bed, I decide to retrieve the fallen box later. I sync my glasses to my smartcom and see that it's half past noon. I yawn and fall back on the pillows, relieved that it's Saturday.

I pull up a visual overlay to scan my email. Owen's left a sticky note at the center of my visual overlay, where I can't possibly miss it. The message reads,

Figured you needed your rest, so I went ahead on the bike ride with Frank, Nora, and the boys. Call me when you're up. DON'T FORGET we're on for dinner tonight, okay? You PROMISED!

I smile and dial Owen's number.

"Wow," he says, his projection looking down at me still lying in bed. "I think this might be the first time you've gotten a decent night's sleep in a week."

I swat Owen's hovering projection with my pillow. He laughs.

"Well, you look like you're in a much better mood," he says.

"I am," I say.

"Good," he says. "We missed you on the ride. The boys are starving now, so we were just about to grab some lunch in Berkeley. Do you want to meet us?"

I chew my lip. "Actually … I was thinking of going in again for a few hours, just to—"

"No," Owen groans. "Emmie. Weekend. Come on."

"Just a few hours," I say. "I swear. I have storms in the brains."

"Then I'm coming over there with you, and I'm going to drag you out myself at five o'clock whether you like it or not," he says.

"Fair enough," I say. "I'll see you there."

An hour and a half later, Owen meets me in the Augur parking lot. Campus is nearly empty today, except for the security guards and a few of the engineers who never seem to leave.

I pick out a greyroom on the sixth floor, and Owen carries up the stack of sketches I was working on yesterday, along with a huge thermos of coffee. As we review the sketches, I gradually descend into the same frustration that's been plaguing me for weeks. There's something wrong with this concept, but I can't see what it is. I have to suppress my desire to rip each sketch to shreds while Owen patiently compiles a list of the few decent ideas we both agree can be salvaged from my last week's work.

At five o'clock, I push back my immerger glasses and rub my eyes. "No more," I say. "I need a break."

"Great!" Owen says brightly. "Let's go home."

I wrinkle my nose. I do want to leave, but that itch of something just beneath the surface of my awareness won't go away. Contemplating the scattered sketches on the floor, I say, "Is there any chance I could convince you to go ahead? I think I just need some time alone to think. Just an hour. One hour."

"Emmie," says Owen, tugging me toward the door by the hand, "you *promised*."

"I'm not going to break any promises!" I say, with a twinge of impatience. "I just need a little time alone, okay?"

"One hour," he says sternly. "Promise?"

"Promise!" I say.

△▽△

Unseen at Emmie's side, I've been waiting impatiently for the last few hours for Owen to leave. As the door closes behind him, I seize my chance.

"Emmie," I say.

She startles, then frantically checks whether she accidentally left the projection room audio connected to a public channel. If she and Owen had been on live mics, their entire conversation, in particular her despairing evaluations of her latest *Atlantis* concepts, could have been overheard by anyone on campus.

"Don't worry," I say. "This is a private channel."

"Who is this?" Emmie demands, standing up and glaring fiercely into the empty space of the greyroom. She skims the list of open channels on her visual overlay, searching for any explanation for my voice, which she thinks is coming through her earbuds.

I step out of the wall in front of her.

"We met last night," I say. "Well, early this morning, to be precise. Do you remember?"

Emmie stares at me. I expect her to be startled, but not as frightened as she was last night. I was careful to choose the circumstances of this second meeting so she would believe I'm merely a visual projection, albeit an unauthorized one.

"How did you get in here?" she says. "This is a secure office network."

"I know some tricks," I say.

"I'm calling security," she says, her hand moving to her immerger belt.

"Wait," I say, pulling as hard as I dare on our connection, willing her to listen to me. "Will you hear me out, first?"

She holds the tip of her tongue between her teeth, considering me more shrewdly now that her surprise has subsided. "What do you want?" she says.

"Do you remember what I said last night?" I say.

Emmie crosses her arms. "Let's see. Oh, right. It's all coming back to me. I have no vision … I'm wasting company resources … I'm no good without Tomo …" she says, ticking each item off on her fingers. "Does that about sum it up?"

"Well, actually, you forgot the one I meant. I want to help you."

"Ah, yes," she says. "You want to help me. Very noble of you. And I know this isn't some kind of blackmail or political maneuver orchestrated by one of my dear colleagues because …?"

I say, "You can't know unless you give me a chance to show you. Not much downside. You're in a locked room, after all. Entirely secure."

"Right," she says. "Secure except for some crazy dude who's hacked into my smartcom."

"Yes," I say. "Except for that."

Her fingers hover over the security call button she's pulled up on her visual overlay. I hold my breath. To my relief, Emmie lowers her hand.

"Fine," she says tensely. "Show me whatever it is you're so anxious to show me. But I need to get out of here in exactly one hour."

"We'll need to be quick, then," I say. "Sit back down."

Emmie crosses her legs and sinks to the floor. I sit facing her, thrilled by the sensation of being fully seen by her.

"Well," she says, interrupting my moment of elation. "What do we do now?"

I nod, refocusing on the task at hand. "Open a blank canvas," I say.

She taps a few keystrokes on her forearm. The room brightens. She stretches out her hand in the space between us, and the greyroom floor transforms to a matte white canvas.

My success at pulling Emmie's sleeping awareness to Thera last night seems to make sharing my mental image with her waking mind easier today. When I focus on the canvas, a dark curve appears quickly, followed by another, then another. The lines appear to be almost identical to a sketch Emmie was working on yesterday that she had discarded in frustration.

"Where did you find that?" she says suspiciously. "I never scanned that sketch."

"Just watch," I say.

So she watches as I share my mental map of the city, which to her appears as lines spreading across her canvas. But where the unbroken coastline of cliffs had been in her original sketch, I now reveal the coastline turning inland, forming a winding channel that opens into the central lagoon of the real Thera. She looks at me wide-eyed.

"I remember that now," she says. "I was standing … there, at the edge of that lagoon. And there—" She reaches for a compartment on her belt and withdraws a fine-pointed stylus to add detail to the sketch. "There was a city."

She leans forward on hands and knees, shading in the steep incline that leads from the lagoon to the white city, tracing the lines of the terraced city footprint. I observe, nodding from time to time, correcting a misplaced line here and there, enjoying the familiar pattern of collaboration that's drawn us together for millennia. Her hand moves quickly as she fleshes out the sketch, losing herself in her absorption with the work. Without pausing, she pulls a sculpting tool from her belt and layers a rough three-dimensional terrain model on top of the sketch.

She's fine-tuning the model when her smartcom buzzes. She blinks, clearly annoyed by the distraction. She leans back on her heels, rolls her stiff shoulders, and answers the call. Owen's projection appears.

"What?" Emmie says sharply. Owen raises an eyebrow, glancing at the sketches scattered all over the floor. "Oh, no." Emmie groans. "Owen, I'm so sorry. I totally lost track of time."

"Really?" he says, with mock surprise.

"I'm leaving right now!" she says, stuffing gear into her bag as Owen's projection wags a finger at her. "This instant. Bye!"

The call ends. Emmie turns to the place where I've been sitting, saying, "I have to go—"

She stops, looking around the empty room. I've vanished from view once more.

△▽△

A spicy aroma and the cheerful strains of early-aughts power pop envelop me when I open my front door. I drop my bag, kick off my shoes, and pad into the kitchen. Owen stands before my stove sprinkling fresh cilantro into a pot of steaming curry. A pan of sautéed vegetables and a covered casserole dish filled with fluffy saffron rice sit on the back burner. Vegetable trimmings litter the counter. Owen two-steps toward me, singing his own lyrics over the chorus of the music.

"*Hey, Emmie, look what they're doing to me,*
Tryin' to trip me up, tryin' to wear me down.
Emmie, I swear, it's so hard to bear it,
And I'd never make it through without you around."

"OMG, you are such a dork!" I laugh over the music as Owen completes his two-step circuit around the kitchen. I follow my nose to the stove.

"That smells amazing," I say, giving the pot of lamb curry a stir. "Thanks for cooking."

The song ends, and Owen turns down the volume. "I was starting to think I'd be eating alone," he says.

I grimace. "I really tried to come back earlier. The universe does not want us to have dinner together ever again."

"Seems like it," says Owen, turning off the stove and grabbing a pair of plates from the counter. "What's been up with you lately?"

I lean against the counter and look out the window toward the driveway, chewing the inside of my lip. "I don't even know where to begin," I say. Somehow, I can't bring myself to tell Owen about Dom.

Owen opens the oven and pulls out a plate of naan warming there.

"Wow! You really did it up nice," I say. Owen plates the food, and I pick up the plates, heading toward the kitchen table.

Owen stops me. "Wait," he says. "Let's eat in the dining room tonight."

I glance at him curiously, noticing for the first time the warm glow emanating from the dining room. Owen steers me toward the room, where I discover the long table set for two, a low centerpiece of large white candles, and a pair of stemmed glasses beside a decanter of red wine.

"Fancy! What's the occasion?" I say, setting down our plates at the two place settings he's laid out.

Owen shrugs mysteriously. "You know ..." he says. "We've been so slammed at work. It's been a while since we had a nice dinner together."

He pulls out my chair, and I sit. He pours me a glass of wine, then pours himself one. I wait, wondering what all this fuss is about.

"It's too bad," Owen says, looking out the dramatic floor-to-ceiling windows that face the San Francisco Bay. "We just missed the sunset."

"It's still pretty, though," I say. "The moon is so bright."

We eat in comfortable silence, listening to the music. Owen's cooking is delicious, and I can't remember the last time I had a proper meal. When I'm completely full, I lean back and say, "That was outstanding."

"Good," says Owen, pouring us both a little more wine. He lifts his glass, and I follow his lead. We smile at each other, touch glasses, and take another sip. When I set my glass down, Owen reaches out and places his hand on mine.

"Emmie," he says. "I've wanted to ask you for a long time. But it's been hard to find the right moment."

I watch in shock as Owen goes down on one knee. My heart nearly pounds out of my chest as he fishes a small black box out of his pocket and opens it. Inside, shining on a black velvet cushion, lies a silver key.

"Emerald Isadora Bridges," Owen says solemnly. "Will you move in with me?"

SEEKING COUNSEL

THE NEXT MORNING, I stand at the end of an absurdly long line outside La Note, my go-to breakfast spot in Berkeley. My sister emerges from the restaurant with an update on our wait time.

"Forty-five minutes!" says Ollie. "We seriously need to find another place to do our Sunday brunches."

"Mmm," I murmur in agreement, though my attention is elsewhere. Through my tinted immerger glasses, I'm taking in the spectacle of *Calchan*, a popular alternet domain that renders a mixed-reality visual overlay on the Cal Berkeley campus and surrounding neighborhoods.

Calchan superimposes a motley crowd of avatars on the Shattuck Avenue streetscape around me. I scan the scene, idly flipping through dozens of public audio channels mapped to specific nearby avatars. I catch fragments of overtly sexual hookup negotiations, insubstantial social exchanges, gratuitously argumentative collegiate discussions on technical and philosophical subjects, and all variety of adolescent capering and mischief.

Ollie shakes her head, looking at me. "You're immersed right now, aren't you?" she says. "It's an addiction, Emmie. It really is."

"I can quit whenever I want," I say with a smirk. "And anyway, it's just user research. You should understand that better than anyone, Dr. Bridges. Here—" I toss her a spare pair of immerger glasses from my bag. "Check it out for yourself."

Ollie rolls her eyes but slips on the glasses. I log her on to *Calchan*.

While she's occupied, I open a two-dimensional overlay to skim my work email. Switching on my fingertip keyboard sensors, I discreetly tap out on my thigh a few short responses to some of my team's questions about the assignments I sent out to them last night after my revelatory work session with Dom.

A few minutes later, Ollie laughs, removes my spare glasses, and hands them back to me. "Sometimes I can appreciate why you passed on college, Em," she says. "Judging from this domain, it looks like nothing but a four-year frat party with a pricey cover charge."

"Or a holding tank for insecure posers," I say.

"That's not very nice, considering they're your prime demographic," she says.

"Ollie!" I say, with an expression of mock horror. "I create for an audience of alternet art aficionados."

Our conversation devolves over the next half hour into a competition to find the most hilarious public channel chat exchanges in *Calchan*, until my stomach rumbles.

"Do you think it's lame to order delivery from Tuk Tuk Thai while we're waiting in line?" I say.

"Ha ha," Ollie deadpans. "You'll survive another fifteen minutes."

"Easy for you to—" The rest of my retort dies on my lips when my gaze catches on a man standing a few paces behind Ollie on the sidewalk. He leans against the storefront next door, watching me intently. I stare at him in amazement. It's the first time I've seen Dom Artifex—if that's his real name—in full daylight. I notice more of his appearance than I'd bothered to absorb from our last meeting, now that I'm seeing him in real life, not just his avatar.

Dom wears a wide-belted, knee-length linen tunic with intricate laces at the collar, a gorgeously-embroidered cloak, and heavy leather boots, like he's heading off to some ancient civilization cosplay event. Weird, but not too weird for Berkeley, I guess. He's otherwise handsome, in a tall, dark, and mysterious sort of way. His broad shoulders, muscular neck, and massive hands make him look like someone who's no stranger to hard physical labor. His features are chiseled and smooth: high cheekbones, strong jawline, long nose. Dark, close-cropped curls frame his face, and thick brows overshadow his deep-set eyes. His mouth is the only thing soft about him—curving full lips with a hint of pink that contrasts with his olive complexion. It's hard for me to tell how old he is. Thirties, maybe? His skin is perfectly unlined, and there's no trace of silver in his hair, and yet something about him seems way older than most thirty-somethings I know. How in the world did he know I'd be here? Is he stalking me? I open my mouth to speak to him, but when our eyes meet, he vanishes. I gasp, goosebumps prickling down my back.

"Emmie? What is it?" says Ollie, turning around to follow my gaze.

"There—" I say, pointing to the place Dom was just standing. "I saw …" I push back my immerger glasses and shade my eyes with my hand, taking a second look without the clutter of my visual overlay. There's definitely no one there.

"Saw what?" says Ollie, looking from the empty spot on the sidewalk where I'm pointing back to me.

Just then, the hostess calls Ollie's name. Our table's finally ready.

In a low voice, I say to Ollie, "I'll tell you once we sit down."

"Is something wrong?" she says.

"No?" I say uncertainly. "Oh, I don't know. Just … something weird."

We follow the hostess into the restaurant. Once we've placed our orders, Ollie looks at me expectantly.

"Well?" she says.

I sigh, shaking my head. "Where to even begin?" I say. "You've got to promise not to think I'm crazy."

"Emmie, come on," says Ollie, exasperated.

I take a deep breath. "Okay," I say. "So, the other day, this guy showed up outside my place. It was really late. Totally dark. I threatened him with my taser, actually."

Ollie's eyes widen.

"He said he wanted to help me with the next *Temenos* release," I say. "And he knew all this stuff that he shouldn't have, like the internal codename for one of my projects, and … other stuff."

Ollie raises an eyebrow curiously, but I hurry on, not wanting to discuss the particulars of that other stuff with her just now. "Then, yesterday, this guy's projection showed up on the Augur network, and he—"

"Wait, wait, wait," Ollie interrupts. "Do you mean his projection showed up in the *Temenos* domain?"

"No," I say. "His projection showed up in my private workspace *at work*. On the Augur network."

Ollie frowns. "But how could an unauthorized user just send a projection to your workspace? Aren't you guys supposed to have excellent security? That's what all your marketing says."

"That's what I thought, too," I say.

"So? What did he want?" says Ollie.

"The same thing he wanted when he showed up at my house," I say. "He said he wants to help me with the next release."

Ollie shakes her head in confusion. "Why does he think you need help with the next release?"

The waitress stops by to pour us coffee. I wait until she's out of earshot to say, "There are rumors going around at work that I can't finish the release without Tomo."

"That's ridiculous," Ollie scoffs. "If anything, you're the *only* one who could complete the release without him."

"I'm not so sure about that," I say. "I've been having a lot of trouble with the concept work for this release, even the most basic stuff. I'm insanely behind schedule. Nothing has been going as smoothly as it used to for me. And there's this other designer, Zeke … Ty's having him work on a backup release in case I drop the ball."

Ollie says, "That's annoying, but you shouldn't let any of it get under your skin. Of course the CEO has to have a backup plan. That doesn't mean he's lost confidence in you."

"Maybe not," I say. "But the rumors still have legs, because this total stranger knew about them."

"That's creepy, Emmie," says Ollie. "Did you tell Augur security about this guy? Or the police? He could be a stalker. He could be dangerous. And if he's hacked your office network, that makes him a criminal, at least."

Ollie's usually right about everything, so I trust her instincts. But some part of me resists the idea that Dom's a criminal. I don't know exactly what he is, though. I say, "The thing is … well, I don't want to tell security. This guy has offered to help me. He already has, actually. He's helped me a lot. I made more progress on the release with him yesterday than I have in the last six months. If I do manage to ship it on time, I'm going to have him to thank."

Ollie leans toward me over the table and says, in her most serious tone, "Emmie. Think about it. Maybe it seems like he's helping you now, but he could have a longer-term plan to blackmail you or do something damaging to Augur. He could tell someone that you stole IP from him, or … I don't even know. So many things. But this could ruin your professional reputation."

"You think I haven't thought of that?" I say miserably. "I know it's stupid, but for some reason I trust this guy. I believe he wants to help me. Somehow, he's able to see exactly what's wrong with my concept, to point out the missing pieces that I just couldn't put my finger on before. I feel like … I don't know why … like it's worth risking my job."

Ollie considers me skeptically. "Are you sure you're not doing this because, deep down, you want an excuse to leave Augur, or to get fired? The only reason you went corporate in the first place is because of Tomo. I'd understand if you felt like leaving the company now that he's gone."

"No," I say. "It's not like that. I've really come to love my work at Augur. But I don't know how else to get the job done anymore except with Dom's help."

"Dom," says Ollie. "That's his name?"

"Dom Artifex," I say. "That's what he told me, anyway."

Ollie shakes her head. Firmly, she says, "He sounds like a stalker, Emmie. Promise me you'll be careful. And, while you're at it, talk to Mom. This guy could be out to get you in trouble with Augur's legal department. It could cost you more than just your job, you know."

I grimace. Ollie takes a sip of her coffee. The waitress stops by and sets down an omelette for me and a bowl of oatmeal and berries for Ollie.

After the waitress departs, Ollie says, "So was that who you saw outside?"

I chew my lip for a moment before I say, "Maybe I imagined it. Maybe it was some glitch in my *Calchan* overlay. When I took another look, he was gone."

"Creepy," Ollie says again.

We eat in silence for a little while, until Ollie says, "So … anything else going on in your world?"

"Isn't that enough?" I say.

"Well, I meant anything good," she says.

I peer suspiciously at my sister over a forkful of omelette. "Like what exactly?"

Ollie shrugs innocently.

"What!" I exclaim. "Did Owen talk to you?"

Ollie rolls her eyes. "Everyone talks to me," she says. "I'm like the family confessional."

I look away, avoiding Ollie's eyes. My gaze wanders through the restaurant. In a booth across the room, a middle-aged Asian man sits alone, sipping a coffee and reading the newspaper. A young couple with a noisy baby tries to wave down their waitress for the check. Four college students laugh at the table by the window. One of the boys at the table looks like Owen. I swallow quickly and look down at my lap. I push the seasoned potatoes around on my plate.

"What's up, Em?" Ollie says gently.

I wrinkle my nose, reluctantly revisiting my memory of the awkward exchange with Owen that followed his romantic move-in proposal. "I didn't know what to say. I told him I needed some time to think about it. What am I going to do? It's so awkward. We're at work together every day!"

Ollie laughs at my stricken expression. "Calm down," she says. "There's no rush. Owen's great, but you have to do what feels right for you, Emmie."

I press my hands to my face, then look up at my sister. "I care about him, Ollie," I say seriously. "So much. But … the last six months—" My words give way to a growl of aggravation. "I feel like my whole world has been turned inside out. I feel like I owe it to Tomo to finish this project. But it's turned into a complete disaster. Everyone watching, judging, waiting for me to screw it up. And now Owen." I sigh. "I don't know. I'd just like things between me and him to stay the way they are for now, you know?"

"There's nothing wrong with that," Ollie says, squeezing my hand. "You're both so young. You've got plenty of time ahead of you." She laughs, then adds, "And, anyway, it'll make me look bad if you do move in together. I haven't even been on a third date since I was an undergrad."

△▽△

Over the next few weeks, I start taking the bus from the Oakland hills downtown to Augur, which allows me to squeeze in an additional half hour of email and chat before the work day kicks into high gear. Ty's new deadline is approaching fast. A lot of my teammates who live farther away have resumed sleeping at the office to reduce time wasted on the commute. The increasingly bedraggled appearance and not-so-fresh scent of the developers and accumulating clutter around the office workspaces remind me of the weeks leading up to our first *Temenos* launch. Only now, there's no Tomo around to remind people to take care of themselves and go home. The frenetic pace and long nights make it easy for me to avoid further discussion with Owen about our living situation, at least for now.

I arrive at the Augur campus a little before nine o'clock and wrap up an email to the development team lead as I ride the elevator to the third floor. As soon as I hit send, I receive a new message notification on my personal smartcom. It's from Owen. I open it apprehensively. The message reads,

I want you to know I'm not trying to be weird, just trying to give you some space. I know you're under a lot of pressure right now. I guess I'm hoping that's all it is, anyway.

I love you, Emmie, and I don't want you to do anything that makes you uncomfortable. I just want to be with you.

Let's talk soon. I miss you.

My eyes glisten with tears. I wipe them away with the back of my hand, trying not to smear the eyeliner I hastily applied while riding the bus. I tune in to the third-floor public audio channel, usually the lifeblood of the creative team's communication. The channel is silent today. Everyone's working heads-down or collaborating on private channels. I stop by the lounge for coffee before pinging

Owen on a private channel.

"I'm in 601," he says. He sounds happy to hear from me, but restrained. Outside of the occasional personal text, we've both been strictly business with each other at the office. "Come on up."

"Eerily quiet today," I say, making my way back to the elevators. "How long has it been like this?"

"Since last night," he says. "I finally finished building the island terrain model yesterday based on your spec, so Lydia could finish breaking down the next phase of work into stories for the rest of the team. A lot of people came in late last night or early this morning to get started on their stories before the rendering farm got too swamped."

"So everyone's fed for now?" I say. "Does that mean we can finally get to work storyboarding quests for the temple city on *Atlantis*?"

"That's what I'm working on right now, boss," he says.

I step out on the sixth floor and swipe my key card on door 601. The door slides open to reveal a greyroom littered with empty takeout containers and large pieces of storyboarding paper. Owen stands amidst the detritus waving his hands thoughtfully and staring into empty space. I switch my immerger glasses to the room channel and see he's fast-forwarding and rewinding a crowd simulation in the streets of the white temple city perched on the steep volcanic slopes of *Atlantis* above the deep blue harbor lagoon.

Owen turns around, pushing back his immerger glasses. We look at each other in silence for a long moment, Owen opening his mouth and closing it again, me chewing my lower lip.

"Did you go home this weekend?" I ask at last, taking in the mess on the floor. I've rarely seen Owen in such a scattered state.

"Nah," says Owen. "I'm on a roll."

"Well, thanks for the overtime," I say. "I feel guilty for taking the weekend."

"You've put in your share of weekends," he says. "Let someone else carry the load for a while."

I stand next to Owen, and we re-watch the crowd simulation.

"I don't know what to do about this," says Owen, pausing the simulation and pointing to the plaza before the domed temple structure on the top tier of the city. He zooms in closer with a flick of his fingers. "There's an incredible view from up here, and the visitor traffic will be huge for that reason alone, never mind the quest-goers. Even with branched servers, I can't see any way to avoid complete gridlock without making avatars permeable, and cheap tricks like that really don't belong in *Temenos*. Our users expect strict Earth physics adherence."

I smirk. "At least as long as we still let them teleport," I say. The tension in the room eases a bit as I slip into the cadence of our old familiar banter.

We watch the simulation replay again. Owen shakes his head. He says, "We've never designed such a small city environment before. Maybe we could have gotten away with this at first launch. *Athenai* was almost this small in the beginning. But our user base was tiny back then, and *Athenai* had room to spread out as our active users grew. This island won't give us that flexibility."

"Mmm," I say distantly, my eyes tracing the city footprint again and again as I think through the scaling problem. "You know ..." I say.

After a minute, Owen prompts me. "Know what?"

I settle my hands on my hips and stare at the terrain rendering. I feel like there's something right in front of me that I'm missing. I look up at Owen. "Would you mind handing off this traffic problem to me for a bit?" I say.

"You don't usually go in for logistics," he says. "Are you sure you want to?"

I nod, my eyes locked on the projection of the temple city.

"All right." Owen shrugs. He unconsciously bobs toward me for a kiss, then stops himself sheepishly and waves before leaving the room.

△▽△

I feel the tingle of the pharmaka-laced threads beneath my skin as Emmie's awareness flows into the model of the temple hovering before her. Her determination to understand it and perfect it fills me, like it's my own will. It's useless to resist her when she's this focused, so I let her hear my voice in her mind.

"I can show it to you," I murmur.

Alone in the greyroom, Emmie straightens up and presses a finger to her earbud, thinking I'm speaking to her through it.

"Dom?" she whispers, her eyes scanning the empty room.

"Yes," I say, standing unseen beside her. "I can show you the temple city. Is that what you wish?"

She hesitates, her fingers twitching unconsciously toward the emergency call button on her immerger belt, before she says, "Yes. Show me."

I don't give her a chance to second-guess herself. "I'm taking you in now," I say.

When I feel her awareness drifting from her body in anticipation of immersion, I reach for my own body in Dulai and pull her after me.

My awareness returns to my body, sitting in my sleeping quarters in the lowest tier of the temple city of Thera. I open my eyes and discover Emmie's awareness has already coalesced before me, unconsciously assuming the shape of her own body back on Earth in the greyroom. She paces the wide plank floors of my room, considering the view through my arching windows, touching the wool blankets on my bed and the cool stone walls, listening to the voices of women calling to each other on the street outside. She explores my world exactly as she explores any new domain in the alternet. I marvel that her awareness unconsciously accepts the transition between two physical worlds as easily as it does any other immersion.

"Come," I say, striding quickly from my room. Now that Emmie's here, I want to plant whatever seeds of understanding I can in her mind. Soon, everything will depend on her understanding my plight.

Emmie follows closely behind me until we step out onto the city street. Once there, she lags behind me, stopping to look at the dark blue waters of the lagoon below, the colorfully robed figures of initiate priestesses and drably-dressed novices passing by, the white facades of the temple outbuildings upslope.

A gust of salty sea air ruffles Emmie's hair. "Really compelling," she says, impressed. "What framework are you using to code tactile effects like that?"

"Later," I say under my breath, not wanting any of the Mohirai around us to hear me talking to Emmie's disembodied awareness. "Follow me."

I head toward the steep central staircase that climbs the slope toward the Musaion, cutting across the level boulevards that traverse each tier of the city. We pass several more women, walking singly and in small groups, chatting and laughing. I take long strides, while Emmie, trying to take in all the sights and sounds at once, struggles to keep up. The stairs grow ever steeper. Emmie's breathing becomes labored.

"Doesn't this place have a nav client or something?" she complains. "Can't we just teleport to wherever you're taking me?" I don't answer, because we're now walking in the midst of another group of priestesses. I can't afford to draw attention to myself during this dangerous excursion.

"Slow down! I'm going to trip on the treadwheel!" Emmie says.

I slacken my pace but still don't answer.

"Hey," Emmie says. "Did I do something to offend you?"

I step off the stairs at an intersection with one of the city cross streets, cross a small plaza, and duck into a narrow alleyway between two buildings. A black cat with yellow eyes stares at me from the stoop of a doorway facing the alley.

Now shielded from the view of all but the cat, I whisper to Emmie, "I'm sorry. You're a ghost here. I can't let anyone see me speaking to you."

"Why not?" says Emmie, her expression turning wary. "I thought all of this was your IP."

"Be patient. Let me show you what you need to see."

We resume our hike up the stairs, until at last we reach the uppermost terrace of the city. We step out onto the marble-tiled plaza that welcomes pilgrims to the Musaion at the end of the long climb. She admires the dramatic columned facade and exterior mosaics of the domed Musaion for a moment before she turns back to take in the spectacular view we've earned. She gazes out over the dark, curving volcanic ridge enclosing Thera's smooth lagoon, glimpsing the churning waters of the Middle Sea beyond. She turns back to face me, leaning against the carved stone balustrade that's the sole barrier between her and a precipitous drop to the cobblestone street of the terrace below us.

After she catches her breath, Emmie says, "So what's the deal with all the women? Why is yours the only male avatar?"

"I work for the women," I say simply. "There are other men here, too, but not many."

"And what exactly do you do for these women?" she says.

"I build," I say. "I built this city."

"Wow," says Emmie, impressed. "All by yourself?"

"Others quarried the stone," I say.

Emmie laughs. "But seriously, you must have a lot of time on your hands to build something this detailed."

"I do," I say.

She leans out over the balustrade to look down at the city spread out below us. She says, "And some pretty incredible content development tools, for immersion this good." Glancing at me pointedly, she adds, "No decent domain navigation interface, though."

"The city is best experienced at walking speed," I say.

"You sound like Tomo," she says, resting her chin on her hand. "He was never a fan of all the hyperactive teleportation that the navigation clients enabled. He wanted people to use his alternet domains to explore, to relax, to discover. He felt that his generation and all the ones coming up behind it were born in a world where there was nowhere left to explore, nothing left to discover."

Ava expressed the same sentiment to me, so long ago. Perhaps if she hadn't felt that way, she never would have left me in the first place.

"Of course," Emmie adds, "Tomo lost that argument with Ty. Commercial users have places to go, people to see, yada yada yada."

She looks down at the walking boulevards criss-crossing the city and the colorful figures moving slowly along them. "So, what are we doing here?" she says. "I assume you didn't have us trudge all the way up here just for the view."

"No," I say. "But we have to wait a little while longer for the High Priestess."

"The High Priestess," Emmie repeats, nodding in approval. "Nice touch."

As we wait, Emmie watches the midday light sparkling on the lagoon. She says, "It is beautiful, but I can already hear the complaints from the users, even if I can figure out a way to solve the traffic problem in these narrow city streets. Our users are such sticklers for realism, as ironic as that sounds. So many alternet experiences contain inconsistencies that ruin users' ability to suspend disbelief. People love Tomo's work because it feels self-consistent, alive, organic, even when it's fantastical. This place is beautiful, but it's unrealistic."

"What makes you say that?" I say, amused that my reality seems less real to Emmie than one of her alternet domains.

She says, "I couldn't put my finger on it when we were walking through, but now that I think back on it, I can see what it is. Everything is too uniform. The proportions of things. The heights of every story of every building. The widths of streets and alleys. The dimensions of the blocks of stone in the walls. The sizes of windows. It's all well-proportioned, don't get me wrong. But it's like those housing developments that are plopped down all at once by the same developer. There are variations, but even the variations look the same.

"And there are little details that seem unique at first, but then they're repeated everywhere. Like the features of the statues in the plaza fountains—the women all have the same face, the same hair."

I'm surprised that I never realized that before. But now, looking out toward the nearest statue, a water-bearer carved into the central fountain of the Musaion plaza, I see Emmie's right. Ava's form is everywhere, even when I hadn't consciously intended it to be.

Emmie points down at the city below us, tracing the line of the central staircase that climbs up the slope from the water's edge to the Musaion.

She says, "The tiers of the city are all the same height, the angles of the streets ascending the mountain exactly the same at each intersection. And, weirdest of all, the grain of the stone aligns everywhere. It looks like every building, every street, every fountain, was extracted whole from a quarry and reassembled in exactly the same position. Like the entire city was carved from a single piece of stone."

I've built the temple city this way in pursuit of perfection, to placate the Voice in all so it will at last give me my answer. Emmie's tone implies the impossibility of what I've already done.

"Is that funny?" Emmie says, seeing the look on my face.

"No," I say. "You're right. It does look that way."

"It's also sort of sad," Emmie says thoughtfully. "You've built this beautiful city, but it can never grow."

"What makes you say that?" I say.

She points out the city perimeter and says, "You're hemmed in on all sides by this ridge. You've got a whole city—a small city, sure, but still a city—without roads to connect it to anything else on the island. If you're going to prevent people from teleporting in this subdomain, they're going to need some way to get here. How? By boat, like we came? And then hike around the city? No one's going to want to do that. The whole subdomain will just remain completely isolated. Remoteness is interesting once or twice, but in the end, it's so impractical. People are in a hurry. Time and attention are the scarcest resources of all."

I smile sadly. In her life, this is true—at least, it seems that way to her. But in my life among the Mohirai, I've learned that time and attention are infinite resources, as long as there is continuity of memory.

"Sorry for being so critical," she says. "It's still really impressive. The sensory work is spectacular. Even if the city is unrealistic, the sounds and the smells and the visual detail are all amazing. I could win over the users with that alone, if their immersion tech were good enough to transmit it. But I don't know if I can replicate the sensory immersion you've got going on here. So if I'm going to use this city as-is, I'm going to need a killer backstory to explain all the weird bits."

A bell tolls behind us. Emmie and I turn to look back at the Musaion. A procession of barefoot priestesses—novices in their undyed tunics, followed by initiates in their colorful robes and mantles—appears between the soaring columns that frame the arching temple entrance. They walk in a double line across the plaza in our direction, passing by us just a few paces ahead of where we stand.

The pairs of novices walking at the front of the procession are barely out of girlhood—seventeen and eighteen summers old. The novices behind them look scarcely older, though they carry themselves with the maturity that comes with deeper training in the mysteries. Following the novices are the initiates with their robes of many colors that indicate the arts to which the Voice has called them. Among the initiates I see many women I've known for centuries, including the dark-haired young woman who greeted me inside the Musaion over twenty years ago, soon after Emmie's birth. She looks not a day older—nor shall she ever, if the Voice wills it.

Near the end of the procession, Serapen walks alone in her sky-blue healer robes, her long white hair flowing unbound down her back. She carries an empty silver chalice in her left hand; in her right she holds a long, elaborately carved wooden staff topped by a polished natural burl.

"Is she the High Priestess?" Emmie asks in a hushed voice, staring at Serapen. Unable to answer aloud without drawing attention to myself, I give a tiny nod.

At the end of the procession, walking in a place of honor behind Serapen, comes a short double line of initiates marked by signs of aging. These women are still strong, straight-backed, and proud, but their faces are lined, their hair fading to shades of silver and white.

When the end of the procession of priestesses passes, I join it, following at a respectful distance, Emmie at my side.

We don't have far to walk. The procession slows to a stop at the far side of the plaza, before an enormous round dais. Upon the dais stands a circle of eight white columns that supports a delicate domed cupola of translucent blue and green stone. A long flight of broad white stairs leads to the top of the dais.

A small group of men, the only other men Emmie has seen in the city so far, appears now at the top of the staircase we climbed from the lower city. Like me, they wear leather-belted tunics and traveling cloaks, their heavy leather boots conspicuously loud on the paving stones after the barefoot procession of women. The men stop behind me, facing the dais and the backs of the priestesses ahead of us.

Serapen walks slowly through the double line of priestesses until she reaches the lowermost stair to the dais. She turns to face us all and raises the silver chalice over her head in the sign of blessing. The men, following my lead, bow slightly toward the High Priestess. The other priestesses ascend the stairs, their double line parting around Serapen. They stop when the novices at the front of the line reach the columns at the top of the stairs. The two lines of women turn to face each other, forming an aisle between them. As they turn, each woman pushes her mantle behind her left shoulder to reveal a sheathed dagger hanging from her belt.

Serapen ascends the dais, walking through the aisle of priestesses. At the top of the stairs, she turns and looks down at us men. She calls out in a ringing voice, "Dom Artifex."

Without waiting for a response from me, she turns and walks toward the center of the dais, disappearing from sight behind the massive columns.

I step forward, walking toward the staircase. Emmie follows a few steps behind me. I remove my belt and cloak and hand them to the two women standing at the bottom of the stairs. I climb the next step, and the next two women behind run their hands lightly over my arms and down my sides. Each woman withdraws a small flask from her belt. One pours fragrant water over my hands. The other drips pungent oil onto her right hand and anoints my brow and my lips with her fingertips. I recognize the taste and scent of various pharmaka as the water and oil absorb into my skin. The women step back, and I proceed up the stairs, stopping at the top of the dais.

A shallow circular moat carved into the stone floor of the dais surrounds the eight tall pillars supporting the cupola. A rill of clear water from an unseen source flows through the moat. Straight ahead of me, a small stone footbridge, barely three paces across, spans the moat, leading to the center of the dais. I cross the footbridge over the water, stepping into the cool aquamarine light that streams through the translucent stone of the dome above me. The pharmaka comes on gently at first, deepening and brightening the colors around me, amplifying each sound in the air.

Beneath the dome, a mosaic of small hexagonal glass tiles in all shades of blue, green, violet, and black cover the floor. In the center of the floor, a wide circular pool of clear water bubbles up from a crack in the volcanic rock beneath the dais. The soft susurrus of flowing water emanates from the floor beneath my feet.

Behind the pool, the High Priestess sits on a high wooden stool. She acknowledges me with a nod and gestures for me to approach. I take a step forward, facing her across the pool.

"Long years have passed since you last sought instruction from the Voice, Dom Artifex," says Serapen.

"Yes, Muse Serapen," I say. "So long, in fact, that I wonder whether the Voice has forgotten me."

"The Voice remembers all, Dom." She says this in a comforting tone. I wonder whether she suspects that all I desire now from the Voice is to be forgotten, to be released.

"Please," I say, kneeling before Serapen. "Tell me then what the Voice would have me do. I have nothing left to give to the Voice. Give me my answer, or else let me be free of this work."

Serapen's voice grows distant, replaced by the Voice in all. She intones, "If you would have your answer, you must first build a temple to the mystery of enduring beauty."

Anger bubbles up within me. The Voice still withholds all hope of an answer. The pharmaka now churns through me, amplifying my fury. Even after all these centuries, I'm helpless to resist its effect. "Enduring beauty deserves no temple," I say, my voice harsh, my innermost thoughts pouring out of me. "The world of the enduring is a barren one, cold as stone, ever crumbling."

I take a ragged breath, shocked by my own words, which hang in the air between me and Serapen. I have no idea what the Voice may do, if provoked. The High Priestess looks at me with sympathy. She steps down from her stool and joins me, kneeling on the mosaic floor. She settles her warm brown hand on my forearm, speaking to me now as only the wise woman I've known since I was a boy.

"Be patient, Artifex," she says.

Rage rears up in me. I seize Serapen's wrist and pull her toward me. It's as if I've lost control of my own body. An impulse to violence battles my deeply-ingrained obedience to the Mohirai. "Ava herself offered me this knowledge freely," I growl into Serapen's ear.

Serapen gazes into my eyes fearlessly. Even without speaking, her look forces me to loosen my rough grasp on her wrist. She looks down at my trembling hand, and a curious expression comes over her. Confused, I look down to see that my loose sleeve has fallen back from my wrist, exposing the faint grid of scarlet threads just visible through the translucent skin of my forearm. I let go of Serapen quickly and shake down my sleeves. Perhaps she saw nothing. Perhaps she was just shocked by the fact that I'd laid a hand on her.

But in my heart, I know she's discovered my secret.

Serapen considers me, her expression a mixture of compassion and bemusement. At last she stands and holds her hand over my head.

"I wish you every blessing on your journey, Dom Artifex," says Serapen. "Remember to listen, when you are lost, for the Voice is in all."

I bow my head, remembering these words of instruction from my Calling Day so long ago. The effects of the pharmaka are fading fast, leaving behind a cold feeling in my stomach and a growing realization of what I've just done. I rise unsteadily to my feet and hurry away from the High Priestess.

"What was that all about?" Emmie whispers, trotting down the dais stairs after me. I glance at her and give an almost-imperceptible shake of my head. The two priestesses at the foot of the dais return my belt and cloak, which I refasten around myself with trembling hands. As I cross the plaza toward the central staircase, Serapen's voice calls out, "Anteo Artifex," and the next man climbs the dais stairs to seek his own counsel from the Voice.

I can't answer Emmie's question until we're out of earshot of the Mohirai, so we descend the long staircase to the lower city in silence. When at last we've regained the privacy of my sleeping quarters, I turn to her and say, "I'll log you out. Then we can talk."

She nods, unconsciously following my lead back to her body in the Augur greyroom.

"So?" she says, kicking off her shoes and flopping onto the springy floor to massage her feet, oblivious to the true distance she's just traveled with me. I consider how best to explain what she just saw, given how little she knows.

"The women you saw in the temple city," I say. "They're called the Mohirai. They serve the Voice in all and share the Voice's words with those who seek counsel."

"And who's the Voice in all?" says Emmie.

"The Voice in all," I say slowly. "Perhaps not a *who* so much as a *what*. The

Voice is the source of life for all who live in Dulai. All are bound to serve the Voice, and the Voice's calling to each person—the role each person must play in society—is delivered by a priestess of the Mohirai."

Emmie leans back on her hands, listening with the air of a connoisseur of worlds.

"So ... is it some sort of goddess figure?" she says. "Like the Mother Earth of Dulai?"

"Perhaps," I say. "But the Voice is also the source of knowledge, which may be revealed only to those initiated into the mysteries. Anything known to the people of Dulai comes from the Voice, through the words of a Mohira."

She says, "So if you want to know something, you have to ask the Voice?"

"The Voice doesn't simply hand out answers," I say. "To receive an answer, you must first answer the Voice's call. The Voice's call, once accepted, cannot be abandoned."

I fall silent, until Emmie prods me. "And what about Serapen, the priestess you were talking to? Who is she?"

"The High Priestess Serapen is a servant of the Voice," I say.

"I didn't hear you ask Serapen a question, though," she says.

"I asked my question already," I say. "Now I wait for my answer."

"You don't seem too happy about it," Emmie observes.

"I've been waiting for a very long time," I say tightly.

Emmie cocks her head to the side. "So ... the Voice gives you a shot at a great reward—the answer to any question—but it could require you to do anything in exchange, and once you agree to it, you can't get out of it."

"Yes. Exactly," I say through clenched teeth.

Emmie drums her fingers against her lips thoughtfully. "You could lose everything trying to get your answer," she says. "A high stakes gamble. The look of realization that I know so well dawns on Emmie's face. Her voice rises with excitement as she says, "High enough stakes to excite the courageous and keep away the faint of heart. A fantastic premise for *Atlantis*!"

Emmie beams at me. My answering smile doesn't reach my eyes. Once again, in the moment of her understanding, I'm left behind.

△▽△

The swish that accompanies the opening of the greyroom door startles me. I glance at Dom in alarm, afraid I'll be caught conversing with a network hacker, but Dom has already vanished. Owen steps inside, looking around at the papers and takeout containers that my long walk on the spinning treadwheel has driven to the margins of the room.

"Good workout?" he says.

"I think I had a breakthrough, Owen!" I exclaim.

Owen takes in my flushed face and nods slowly. "Well, let's hear it," he says.

I pace the room, my hands waving, my words flowing rapidly as I chase after my stream of thought. "We'll make *Atlantis* a secret. Secrets are the one thing people love to talk about most, right? So we'll plant some in-domain characters in *Athenai* or somewhere to leak info. Pretty soon everyone will be talking about it. And everyone who can afford it will want a piece of it. But we can control the crowds by making entry contingent on accepting a task that might cause them to lose everything. And if what they have to lose is a whole lot of temens—"

"Whoa, Emmie," says Owen. "Slow down."

I take a breath, trying to think of a way to explain so Owen will understand. When ideas come to me like this, they're always a tangle at first. But there's something important in this one, something desperate to reveal itself to me, if I can just coax it out into the open.

"Okay," I say, trying to speak more slowly. "So, the business owners in *Temenos* know the value of new subdomain real estate. Everyone's been clamoring for it for months. Tons of them would pay an arm and a leg for first development rights, right?"

Owen nods.

"So," I continue, "if we put out a rumor that Augur is going to give away first development rights to users who have demonstrated the greatest ability to put in-domain resources to profitable use, they'll all jump on it. Who would want to risk missing out?"

Owen squints, trying to follow. "But, why a rumor?" he says. "Why not just make it a product announcement?"

"For the *buzz*," I say impatiently. "It's free marketing! All the rumor forums, right?"

Owen seems stuck on this, mulling it over, but I push on, saying, "All our big *Temenos* businesses will sink temens into their existing properties in a bid for first rights to develop new properties in *Atlantis*. We'd see a revenue bump even before we open *Atlantis* to the public. Then, the businesses who actually get the rights will sink even more temens into developing their *Atlantis* properties. And so," I pause for effect, "once we finally open *Atlantis* to the public, all the content the chosen business owners have developed for their new properties will be ready and waiting, which will distribute new user traffic evenly around the subdomain. We solve the temple city crowding problem and the new subdomain content sparsity problem in one fell swoop."

I cross my arms, pleased with myself. A moment later, another thing occurs to me. I say, "And, as a bonus for our team, this will dramatically reduce the scope of content creation we need to complete internally before the release deadline, which might actually give us a shot at beating Zeke's concept."

Owen thinks it over, then nods slowly. "Sounds like a plan worthy of Ty Monaghan," he says.

I scowl. Comparison to Ty isn't something to be proud of.

Owen laughs. "I meant that as a compliment, Emmie. I think this could actually work."

"Okay," I say, invigorated. "Let's get the word out to the rest of the team. It's going to be a mad dash to the finish."

THE SPLINER

One month later, Owen and I stand in the windowless corridor outside the entry to the Augur spliner. We just finished our immersive *Atlantis* demo with Ty and Ahmet. There's nothing left to do now but wait for Zeke to finish presenting his competing concept. Owen paces back and forth. I thump my head rhythmically against the wall.

"They can't be much longer now. They've been in there for over an hour," I say. "OMG, I'm nervous."

"That's good," says Owen, trying to sound upbeat. "You're usually sharpest when you're nervous."

"I don't think it's going to help things if I throw up on the conference table," I say, wincing after I deliver a particularly vigorous thump to my head. I rub the aching spot on the back of my skull, then refocus my anxious energy on twisting a lock of my hair.

"You'll be okay," says Owen. "You've had nothing but coffee for the last seventy-two hours. The worst you could do is dry heave."

I giggle, giddy with lack of sleep.

The whirring sound of the spliner powering down cuts through the quiet hallway. I wipe my sweaty palms on the black fabric of my immerger leggings. The east doors of the spliner slide open, and Ahmet and Ty emerge, peeling off the outer layers of their immersion gear, followed by Zeke, who looks tired but cheerful. Zeke shoots me a self-assured smile. I surprise myself by smiling back. I can't remember the last time I saw Zeke looking happy, and it makes me remember how things were between us years ago, when we first met.

"Okay, guys," says Ty. "Let's go on up to my office. We'll hear your final comments on your concepts before we talk about the release rollout."

Ty leads us all out of the spliner building and across the campus toward the main office.

"Great job, Zeke," Ahmet says, clapping him on the shoulder. "Those creatures … really fantastic! I think I'll have nightmares tonight."

"And you two," Ahmet drops back to walk between me and Owen. "I was just floored by the level of detail in your temple city. Evocative. Beautiful. And your in-game characters—just wonderful."

Owen shoots me an encouraging thumbs-up behind Ahmet's back.

We follow Ty up the stairs to the second floor offices. Here, Owen and I part ways. Owen mouths *good luck* to me and continues up to the third floor. I follow Ty through the CEO office suite, into the adjoining conference room.

Ty and Ahmet sit at one end of the conference table. Zeke and I sit at the other end facing each other.

"Guys, I know that the months since Tomo died have been really stressful," says Ty. "Losing him has been hard on everyone, especially you creatives, who depended so much on Tomo's guidance. And it's not lost on me that splitting up the team like we did for this release has put you two at odds. Pressure from the board convinced me this was necessary. I hope you'll forgive me for all the trouble it's caused.

"In spite of all that, the work you showed us today is some of your best. You both should be very proud of yourselves."

I force a smile. Zeke maintains an expression of nonchalance.

"Do either of you have any final comments you want to make before—"

Zeke puts up his hand.

"Okay," Ty nods. "Go ahead, Zeke."

Zeke leans forward and says, "First, I'd like to thank you, Ty, and you, Ahmet, for giving me the opportunity to work with my own team to develop my concept for *Atlantis*. I think our beta feedback underscores the fact that our users are ready for a rich, surreal fantasy environment like the one I've shown you today, to complement the, ah, simpler concepts that have characterized our previous releases. I think any of our users would be thrilled to visit my *Atlantis*.

"Thanks again for the opportunity."

Zeke settles back into his seat. I chew my lower lip. Ever since Ty split the design team into two camps, I've wanted nothing more than to solidly trounce Zeke's concept, but now I feel deflated at the thought that one of us has to lose this fight.

"Emmie?" says Ahmet. "Would you like to say anything?"

I straighten up in my seat, glancing at Zeke. Nervously, I say, "Well, guys, this was not the smoothest project I've ever run. I definitely missed Tomo's guidance, and I've been struggling from the beginning to imagine what he had in mind for this release.

"I know that the island I showed you today isn't the flashiest environment you've ever seen. Because I had so much trouble developing the initial concept, there are large stretches of the subdomain that still need a lot of content to feel really complete. But the environment foundation is strong, and elegant, and beautiful, and I think you both saw today that the locations we did manage to flesh out fully are really compelling."

I swallow, hearing my own voice echoing in my head. I sound so uncertain and apologetic compared to Zeke. In the absence of my own confidence, I try to channel a bit of Ollie's confident voice as I continue, "I know there are concerns about whether the simplicity of the subdomain we've put together will drive the user traffic we need for this release to be considered a success by the board. The team and I debated this at length, and we're confident that putting out a release rumor will generate buzz and domain investment at a level that could not be achieved with a more typical release marketing strategy. I think it's the kind of thing Tomo would have loved to try.

"So," I look from Ty to Zeke. They're watching me closely, which makes me lose my train of thought. Lamely, I conclude, "I— I hope you'll give it a shot."

I sit down, flushing slightly. That all sounded pretty weak to me. Even so,

Ahmet nods and smiles at me. Ty leans back in his chair, pressing his fingertips together.

"Thanks, guys," he says at last, setting his feet back flat on the floor and looking from Zeke to me. "I appreciate what you've said, and everything you've showed us today. I don't want to leave either of you hanging."

I press my lips together. Zeke leans forward eagerly, a bright pink spot appearing on each of his pale cheeks. Ty folds his hands on the table in front of him and turns to Zeke.

"Zeke, we were very impressed with the depth and originality of the content you developed for your concept, and I'm sure we'll find a way to incorporate it into subsequent releases. However, at this time we feel that Emmie's concept evokes a greater sense of continuity with the domain's established aesthetic. We want to demonstrate for now that we're remaining faithful to the things users have come to love about *Temenos*.

"We've decided to proceed with Emmie's concept for this release."

I slump in my chair, not quite believing my ears. Zeke sits rigid.

Ty continues, "Good work, both of you. We've still got a long slog ahead before this release is ready to go out the door, but I hope it'll be smooth sailing from here. Or smoother, anyway." He pushes back from the table. "I'll let you two get back to work, then."

Zeke scrambles up from his chair and rushes out the door without a word.

Still dazed, I rise more slowly. I'm turning to leave when Ty says, "Emmie, could you come with me? I'd like to speak with you privately."

Through the glass wall of the conference room, Zeke watches me follow Ty into his office. Zeke's face turns an angry shade of pink before he storms off toward the elevators.

Ty gestures for me to sit in the chair that faces his expansive, glossy desk.

"Coffee?" he says.

I shake my head. I'm about ninety percent coffee by weight already, after the last few all-nighters. Ty makes his way to the high-backed chair across from me. He presses his fingertips together and swivels to face his floor-to-ceiling windows looking out over the San Francisco Bay. The lights of the Golden Gate Bridge are just starting to twinkle against the deepening violet of the December twilight.

"I want you to know I understand what a tough time you've been going through," he says.

I press my fingers to the bridge of my nose and sigh. I don't think he possibly could.

"Please keep this to yourself," says Ty. "But our investors and the board just about lost their minds a few months ago with all the delays we were having. Authorizing Zeke's backup concept was the only thing I could think of to buy you some more time. It's not lost on me how bad that was for your team's morale."

I let out a humorless laugh. "Yeah," I say. "Just a bit."

Ty rubs his chin. "You took it in a stride, though. You demonstrated real leadership, and you kept your cool despite all Zeke's posturing."

I raise an eyebrow. Ty chuckles. "What?" he says. "You think I'm blind? No. He's a smart kid, but … Well, anyway, that's not what I wanted to talk with you about.

"You've probably been expecting this. Frankly, I would have done it sooner if it hadn't been for all the goddamn politics I've had to deal with, considering all the qualified candidates, doing interviews, etcetera etcetera."

Ty leans across his desk toward me. "I'm promoting you from Creative Director to VP Creative. You were the obvious choice from the beginning, but you've shown us through the last few months that there's no one better equipped to lead the creative team than you."

I can't suppress a surge of anger toward Ty. Putting together *Atlantis* was struggle enough on its own without Ty playing these games for the board's benefit. Tomo never would have put me through that. At the thought of Tomo, my eyes grow hot with tears.

"I was hoping that would be good news," says Ty, raising an eyebrow.

I clear my throat, refusing to let myself cry in front of Ty. "It just seems so final, doesn't it? He's really not coming back."

Ty nods. "I miss him, too. He was a good man. A good friend."

We sit in silence for a while, until at last Ty straightens up and says, "Well, this means you're the lucky winner of the corner office." He taps out a quick sequence on the top of his desk. "So there's the access code. It's all yours."

△▽△

When I step off the elevators onto the third floor, a small cheer goes up from my team. I accept congratulatory shout-outs on the public channel and high fives from tired-looking designers and engineers. When I finally reach my desk, I collapse into my chair.

A minute later, Owen's hands settle on my shoulders from behind. I look up at him. Despite his exhausted appearance, he's beaming.

"You should see the look on Zeke's face," he says, with an uncharacteristic note of malicious glee.

"Ugh," I say, shuddering at the memory of Zeke's expression as he stormed out of the conference room. "What Ty did to him was just the worst. Raising his hopes like that, and then shelving everything he's been working on." I shake my head in distaste.

"Are you actually feeling *sorry* for Zeke?" says Owen, surprised.

I don't answer. Until this morning, I'd never have imagined feeling sympathy for Zeke after all he's done to undermine my work. But after my conversation with Ty, I see how both Zeke and I were manipulated into this bitter competition, simply to placate some faceless, nameless people on our board who think about nothing but Augur's valuation. Those people—and, what's worse, our own boss, Ty—took advantage of us both for their own purposes.

"Hey," says Owen. "It's not like his work just goes down the tubes. Everything ends up in the content library. Some of it might live to see another day."

I nod. I should be savoring this moment with Owen, not ruminating over Zeke.

"I didn't get a chance to thank you," I say.

Owen crosses his arms and leans against my desk. "I'm all ears, boss," he says, head cocked to the side.

I stand to face him, leaning in a little closer than I usually would at the office. I tug at his crossed arms until they open for me, then take both his hands. "Thank you," I say, squeezing his fingers in mine.

"You're welcome," says Owen, his eyes twinkling.

We look out over the workstations to watch the celebratory Nerf war that's broken out in the lounge. Several people are packing up sleeping mats and pillows from under their desks and trudging toward the elevators to go home early.

"Take a cab!" Owen shouts after a few of our most exhausted-looking teammates.

"What a day. What a month!" he says, shaking his head. Tentatively, he says, "So … want to come over to my place for a beer?"

I smile at him. There's nowhere else I'd rather be right now. "I'd love to," I say.

Owen swallows and says, "So … does that mean things are back to normal?"

A small bell chimes on the public channel before I can answer. Shiva's voice, ill-disguised by a voice modulator, says, "The *Atlantis* team would like to welcome our new Madame VP. May your reign be long and prosperous! We would also like to extend our sincere condolences to our first runner-up, Z—"

Owen cuts in on the channel with his override privileges. "Shiva! Please come and see me. Now."

I pat Owen's knee. "Go get 'im, cowboy."

△▽△

It's close to midnight as Owen drives me the last winding quarter mile along Skyline Boulevard to my house. Through the window, I look down at the city of Oakland spread out across the flatland below the hills, a field of white and gold light surrounding the darkness of the San Francisco Bay.

There's no moon visible tonight, so the road is dark. As the trunks of the great redwoods flash by, I see patches of night sky studded with stars—beautiful, but nowhere close to the memory of that glittering vault I remember from the night Owen and I shared our first kiss.

I turn to watch Owen, who's guiding the car smoothly around treacherous curves. He insisted on driving me home. He's overprotective like that sometimes. My vision swims a little as we round the next bend. I'd meant to have just one beer, but I may have gotten a bit carried away. Tonight, all I'd wanted was to forget the sadness and frustration of the past several months.

Owen pulls into my driveway and parks. We sit in comfortable silence for a while. I take Owen's hand. He smiles at me.

"Ready for bed?" he says.

"Almost," I say.

He steps out of the car and comes around to open my door. He gives me a hand to climb out. I stumble a little into his arms.

"Easy there," Owen laughs. I giggle, leaning against him, snuggling my face into his chest and breathing in his scent. He smells like home.

Owen leads me up the dimly-lit path to my front door. I dig in my bag for my keys. At last, my fingers close around them. I look up at Owen.

"Do you want to come in?"

Owen closes his eyes. "I do," he says, letting out a long sigh. He takes me in his arms and kisses my forehead lightly. "But ..." His voice sounds pained. "You've had a little too much to drink. You should sleep. Let's talk more tomorrow, okay?"

I draw back from him, disappointed. I search Owen's eyes. Is he still upset about the move-in proposal? It's hard for me to read his expression, because my head is spinning. I'm too tipsy and too tired to think about this right now. Owen's right. We should continue this tomorrow, when I'm thinking straight.

"Okay," I say. "Tomorrow, then." I stand on my toes to give Owen a light kiss on the lips, then fumble with my key at the door until I manage to unlock it.

I turn back to say a last farewell to Owen for the night. He's squinting up into the trees beside the house.

"What is it?" I say, following his gaze.

"Did you get a security camera installed?" he says, pointing.

I can barely make out the black box high up in the nearby tree branches. How did Owen notice something so small in the darkness?

"Ummm—" I struggle to remember. Everything's a little foggy right now. "I don't *think* so. Maybe my mom had something installed?"

Owen cocks his head at the box suspiciously. "Maybe," he says. "That does sound like her. We'll have to ask her tomorrow." He looks down at me again. "Hey, remember to drink water before you go to bed, okay?"

"Now who sounds like my mom?"

Owen chuckles. "Good night, Emmie."

I push open my door, flip on the lights, and shed my bag and shoes on the floor. I make my way to my bedroom, trailing my hand along the wall in my dizziness, and sit down heavily on the bed. I flop back against the pillows, closing my eyes for a moment before rolling over and reaching for the immerger glasses in the top drawer of the nightstand. Maybe I'll draft Owen an email while all my feelings about tonight are still fresh.

I've barely settled my glasses on my nose when Dom steps out of the shadows at the corner of my room.

"Augh!" I cry, leaping up from the bed.

"Calm down," he says. "We need to talk."

"OMG, Dom!" I say, pressing my hand to my chest, realizing with relief that he's just a projection, not a burglar. "How the hell did you open an unauthorized connection like that?"

"The same way I always have," says Dom.

I huff. Dom's always so mysterious about everything. I know I should be alarmed by the fact that he's able to project to my personal devices without my authorization. But ever since I met Dom, I've somehow never been able to feel frightened of him.

"What do you want?" I say.

"Perhaps we could start with a small thank-you for the part I played in your success today?" he says.

I frown. "Thank you," I say, as graciously as I can manage, though it occurs to me that I owe Dom more than just my gratitude.

Dom nods. "And I wonder if I could ask for your help on a problem I have in my own domain."

I press a hand to my temple, which has just started to throb. "I'm sorry, Dom," I say. "I have a contract with my employer. I can't do outside consulting. Especially for competitors."

"My problem is personal in nature and presents no competitive threat to Augur," says Dom. "No one will find out you've been helping me unless you choose to tell them yourself."

I chew my lip. I can't see anything wrong with that. "What do you need?" I say.

Dom hesitates, then says, "I need you to show me what's on the storage drive that Tomo left for you."

Dom points to something on the floor behind me. I turn to look. There, just under the edge of my unmade bed, lies the small wooden box containing Tomo's storage drive. Hazily, I remember it falling there weeks ago when I fumbled to silence the alarm on my smartcom.

I shake my head in confusion. "That? But why?"

"I believe it will help me complete the task the Voice has given to me."

"You mean in Dulai?" I'm unable to suppress a giggle at the absurdity. "For some alternet game quest?"

"This is what I need from you," says Dom, looking deadly serious.

"Well, I don't know what you heard about this storage drive," I say, sitting down on my bed. The mattress has never felt this inviting. "But as far as I know, it's just a bunch of ancient religious stuff. I don't think it could have anything to do with your alternet quest."

"I can only find out if you show me," says Dom, his projection stepping closer.

"But—" I yawn. "But I'm only supposed to show it to someone I trust."

"Have I done anything to violate your trust?"

Thinking is so hard right now. Has Dom done anything to violate my trust? Hacking into personal and work immergers isn't exactly the most trustworthy behavior, but, on the other hand, everything he's done with that access has been a huge help to me.

"Oh, fine," I say, waving my hand, wishing Dom would just go away and let me sleep. I reach down and pick the storage drive off the floor. "Let's take a look."

I'm about to connect the drive to my smartcom when Dom says quickly, "No.

Not here. You should view the contents somewhere secure. Someone could tap into your local network here."

Something in Dom's voice frightens me, momentarily clearing the fog in my brain.

"You mean someone besides you," I say slowly.

Dom nods.

"You're freaking me out," I say.

"Please humor me," he says.

I swallow and close my eyes. "Okay. I'm going to bed now, but I'll take a look at this with you tomorrow. At work. That's the most secure place I know."

"Thank you," he says.

"And right after that, I'm going to hire a security consultant. I don't want any more hacking on my smartcom," I say. "From you or anyone else."

"That is probably wise," Dom says, then vanishes.

△▽△

I roll into the office late the next morning. When I step out onto the third floor, the mood on the public audio channel is celebratory. Everyone sounds like they had a good night's sleep, which tends to encourage rambunctious chatter and mischievous meme-sharing. Owen interjects a few half-hearted, "Get back to work, people," directives over the noisy channel, but he's universally ignored.

I walk over to Owen's desk and wave hello.

"Hey, you," he says. "That was fun last night."

"Yeah," I say, a bit sheepishly. "Maybe a little too much fun."

Owen chuckles.

"Any chance of getting some work done today?" I say, looking around at all the designers and engineers who are making no attempt to hide the fact that they're playing games at their workstations.

"Nope," says Owen, merely stating the obvious.

I say, "The main spliner's miraculously unoccupied starting fifteen minutes from now. I booked it. I thought I would slip in for some non-*Atlantis* time."

"Sounds like fun," he says. "Want some company?"

"Sure," I say.

We exit the main office building. A chilly breeze blows over the grounds as we cross the campus toward the spliner. We pass Zeke on the way there. His nostrils flare, and he brushes by us without making eye contact.

"Ugh. That guy," says Owen, looking back at Zeke over his shoulder. "Has he always looked that shady?"

I shrug. I don't feel like making fun of Zeke today.

As we approach the enormous, windowless spliner building, my fingers close around the small wooden box in the hip pocket of my jeans. I say, "I didn't tell you before, but Tomo left me something in his will."

"Really?" says Owen, impressed. "What was it?"

"It's kind of a long story," I say. "The short version is that it's a manuscript for a book that Tomo's childhood sweetheart—a woman named Midori—was writing. She died before she finished it, and then he tried to finish it, but—well, he died, too."

"And what are you supposed to do with it?"

"I'm not sure. I think he wanted me to finish it."

"Are you going to?"

"I don't know. I haven't had a chance to even look at it yet. That's what I want to do in the spliner."

"How will the spliner help? It's a book manuscript, not immersive, right?"

"Well …" I don't know how I can explain the real reason why I want to view the contents of Tomo's storage drive in a secure facility. I make something up that sounds plausible instead. "It sounds like there are a lot of illustrations that go along with the book, and it's in all sorts of ancient languages, so I thought … some physical space to spread it all out, walk through it, you know, literally."

"What ancient languages are we talking about?"

I laugh. "You know, I don't even know yet."

"It sounds like you might be in a bit over your head," says Owen.

I palm the door of the spliner and say, "I guess we're about to find out."

△▽△

Inside the spliner control room, I activate the mechanical subsystems and configure my smartcom as the master controller. Owen and I can now utilize the sophisticated multi-sensory immersion and extensive interior space of the spliner, along with its physical and digital security systems.

We pull on our immerger gear in the dressing room before entering the cavernous extrusion chamber of the spliner. We've spent many long days together here over the last few months working on *Atlantis*, but always with other team members looking over our shoulders virtually from the control room. I think this is the first time I've used this spliner without anyone in the control room.

"So," says Owen. "Where's this manuscript?"

I pull the small wooden box from my pocket and slide open the lid. I snap the little storage drive into a port on my belt and skim the contents on my visual overlay. I hope Dom's watching, from wherever he is. This is his big moment, after all.

"Looks like most of the files are two-dimensional scanned images," I say, skimming the contents of the file system interface hovering before me. I open a secure private channel and share my visual overlay with Owen so we can look at it together. "These look like Tomo's illustrations, and those must be Midori's source texts. Wow, those look wild, don't they? I've never seen writing like that … And here's some other stuff in digital document formats …"

"Ugh. Zero organization," Owen says, grimacing. "How are you supposed to tell what's what?"

I scan for any metadata that could allow me to generate some relational visualization of the files, but none of the results improve things much. "Really outdated file system," I say. "No surprise, I guess, if Midori started working on this manuscript fifty years ago … Oh, hey, look at this."

I point out several files with an ACML file extension. Alternet Content Markup Language emerged alongside the alternet when I was a kid, so these files can't be more than fifteen years old.

"Someone was working on this more recently," says Owen. "Who do you think added these files? Tomo?"

"No idea," I say. "There's not much metadata on the new files. When Tomo's sister gave me the storage drive, though, she told me it had been in the possession of a Buddhist priestess in Japan. Maybe the priestess was working on it."

"A Buddhist priestess? You glossed over this bit."

"I told you it was a long story," I say.

I launch my browser and open one of the ACML files, which renders a network visualization of seven digital documents in Japanese, linking them to a number of the scanned images on the storage drive. These scanned images remind me of photos in the archeology textbooks Ollie and I would sometimes look at while visiting Yaya and Papou's house: unreadable characters on mottled parchment or papyrus or some similarly antiquated material.

"Well, that's a little more helpful, at least," says Owen, approaching the network visualization and trying a few different display options until the open files arrange themselves in a ten-foot-high panorama hovering in the open space of the spliner. I walk alongside Owen as we tweak the sizes and display formats of the files until we can see everything clearly from the center of the room.

I tap out a long command against my hip with my gloved hand. Beside each of the seven Japanese documents, a rapidly-rendered English translation appears. I read a few sentences aloud to Owen.

"*When it was not yet named in the height of heaven,*
And yet beneath the earth, does not bear the name
And the Apsu of the ancient birth to them,
And confusion, Tiamat, the mother of them both
That water was mixed with
And the field has not been formed, no marsh was not be observed.
And without God in the time it was called into
And none bore a name, what was the fate of when established
Then I created the gods in the midst of heaven
Was called into being as a Lahmu Lahamu
Age was increased—"

I stop, bewildered. Owen laughs and says, "Lost in translation."

I reread the lines several more times before I give up, shaking my head. I run a quick alternet search on the few names in the gibberish—Apsu, Tiamat, Lahmu Lahamu. Search results reference a Babylonian creation myth from a text called the *Enuma Elish*. This narrows things down a little. I pull up half a dozen English translations of the *Enuma Elish* from the public domain. I save these to my smartcom and continue examining other files on the storage drive.

I run a few more Japanese-to-English automated translations, but the next few translations are even more indecipherable to me than the fragments of the *Enuma Elish*. Attempting a direct translation from the scanned image files proves even less helpful, as the intricate ancient writing on these physical documents is arranged in complex geometrical patterns that defy the character recognition algorithms of each translation program I try.

"It would take me forever to sort through all this," I say, overwhelmed. "I'd need, like, a graduate degree in ancient history to understand half of what I'm looking at here."

Owen, looking over my shoulder, says, "You could try one of those human translation services. It looks like these digital texts are someone's attempt to translate from the ancient-looking documents into Japanese. You could probably get a better Japanese-to-English translation from a human than from that translation extension you're using."

I swipe a series of controls on my visual overlay to run a quick search for human translation recommendations from my social network. A friendly avatar in the domain of the most highly-recommended service I find explains to me that a job this size will take several days to complete. I decide to kick off the job anyway. I upload the Japanese files to the translation service, before turning my attention to a collection of Tomo's sketches. No translation required for these, at least.

"Tomo's sister said he wanted to be a manga artist from the time he was little," I say, flipping through several landscape sketches and portraits, smiling as I recognize Tomo's tidy handwritten notes on some of them.

"He would have been great at it," Owen says, pointing at a series of sketches of a pastoral village square. The images convey the passage of time from morning to evening, as well as the village's passage from thriving enclave to industrial decay. "There's a beautiful narrative quality to these. Surprising realism. Different from most of the manga I've seen. You can see the beginning of the aesthetic he brought to *Kaisei*, then to *Temenos*."

I open an image that, when viewed at full size, turns out to be a massive round landscape painting more than thirty feet in diameter when viewed at full size. Owen calls up from the spliner floor a bench-shaped protrusion for us. We sit, and the bench lifts us up to the top of the canvas. We examine every inch of the painting as the protrusion lowers us slowly back toward the floor.

An inky blackness presses in from the outer circumference of the painting, fading gradually into a dark ocean wrapped around an indistinct grey shore. Faint yellow plains and washed-out blue rivers draw my gaze toward the center of the canvas, across rolling grass-green hills and shadowy green forests. Owen lets out a low whistle.

"Just pen and ink and watercolors," he says, shaking his head in amazement. "This must have taken him forever."

The bench melts back into the floor, and I stand again, pulling the canvas toward me and zooming in on the heart of the scene. There, in a broad valley, is a dark-haired woman painted with the brightest color and finest detail on the entire canvas. She stands beside a deep blue pool, the source of the many rivers flowing out to the dark edges of the canvas. Behind her grows a gnarled pomegranate tree. In her left hand, she holds one of the round red fruits and extends it to her companion, a man who looks quite like Dom, I realize with surprise.

Across from the pool stands a second woman, clothed in sky blue, her eyes on the man and woman. Like the first woman, she's surrounded by a halo of color and sharp detail, but in her left hand she holds a chalice, over which hovers a small flame.

Other figures are arrayed across the landscape, but I keep staring at the three characters at the center of it all.

"What do you think it means?" I say to Owen.

"Looks like a Japanese landscape painter's take on Adam and Eve," Owen says. "Reminds me of some of the illustrations in my Sunday school books from growing up."

"But then who's the woman with the cup?"

"No idea," says Owen. "Angel? Demon? She doesn't look like the serpent, anyway."

My gaze drifts from the center of the painting to the rocky mountain range on the left.

"Hey, does that sort of remind you of—"

A soft ping accompanied by a pulsing yellow indicator on my visual overlay interrupts me. "Dammit," I mutter. "The file upload on the translation failed. Looks like our alternet connection cut out."

Owen and I try to reconnect on our smartcoms. Suddenly, behind me, Dom's voice cries out, "Emmie!"

I turn around in surprise, stumbling against Owen.

"What's wrong?" says Owen, reaching out to steady me.

I gasp. Over Owen's shoulder, I see grey ripples extruding from the spliner floor, approaching us from the western wall. Owen follows my gaze.

Nervously, he says, "Are you doing that?"

"No," I say, tapping my fingers in a rapid sequence on my hip to shut down the extrusion subsystems. The ripples keep coming. "And I'm not getting any subsystem responses. The local wireless is out, too."

"We'd better get out of here," says Owen, tugging my hand. "I don't want to be standing in here if the mechanics are glitching."

I nod and quickly shut down my visual display. The painting and the documents hovering before us vanish, leaving me and Owen surrounded by nothing but blank grey walls.

The ripples are gaining speed. We hurry to the east wall. Owen palms the exit door. He waits a moment. When it doesn't open, he palms it again more slowly, glancing over his shoulder.

"Quickly!" Dom's voice urges from somewhere directly behind me.

"Here, let me try," I say, edging Owen to the side and palming the door.

When it still doesn't open, I turn back to face the approaching ripples.

"We need to call security," I say.

"Right," says Owen, taking a few quick jabs at the air in front of him. "Let me just …" He trails off. "No radio, either. The building is shielded."

The ripples reach us. We struggle to keep our footing as the spongy grey extrusion surface of the floor shifts, growing steadily more turbulent. A low mechanical drone hums around us.

I swear loudly. "This is my fault," I say. "We're always supposed to have an operator in the control room in case we need a manual override."

"I've never heard of the door palm system failing," Owen says. "But the doors should open automatically if there's any kind of system failure."

"Agh!" I cry, tripping over a two-foot wave in the floor and falling painfully to my knees. The same wave knocks Owen onto his back beside me.

"I guess we'd better stay on the ground in case this gets any rougher," he says, flipping onto his hands and knees.

"Dom!" I call out in a sudden burst of inspiration. "Can you call security? You still have alternet access!"

"Who's Dom?" says Owen, confused. Then, realizing the implication of what I said, he says hopefully, "Did you find a live channel?"

"I'm sorry, Emmie. I can't," Dom's disembodied voice replies.

"Why not?" I cry. "There must be something you can do! Help us!"

"Is that security?" says Owen. "Tell them to send someone to the control room."

The treadwheel engine beneath the spliner floor whirs to life. The floor drifts westward, away from the exit door. I glance at Owen in alarm. His normally tan face looks strangely pale in the flat ambient light. He seizes my hand, and we scramble over the roiling floor back toward the exit.

A broad spike protrudes suddenly from the floor between us, knocking me to the ground and separating me from Owen. The floor before me shoots up into another extrusion, this one a huge grey tentacle, which quivers in midair before whipping down violently toward me. I slam my feet against the side of the extrusion just in time to push myself into a trough between two grey waves. The tops of the waves block the descent of the tentacle, which crashes to a stop mere inches from my nose.

A piercing siren rings out over the churning mechanical sounds of the floor. Moments later, there's a pounding at the door and muffled shouting.

"Someone hit the alarm!" I call out to Owen, relieved.

Owen pops suddenly into view from behind another wave and crawls toward me. He loops my arm around his neck and heaves us both to our feet.

"Let's get to the door!" he shouts over the noise. We hold hands tightly, trying to stay together and steady each other as we pick our way from one level patch of floor to the next, heading toward the exit.

From the wall on our left, another extrusion shoots out just as a wave rolls under my feet. I jump away, but not before the extrusion strikes a heavy blow to my shoulder and knocks me to the floor.

"Emmie!" Owen cries, kneeling beside me.

"I'm okay, I'm okay," I say, wincing.

Another tentacle rises up before us, this one much larger than the others. I climb to my feet, gasping at the sharp pain in my shoulder, just as another wave knocks Owen backwards. I scramble toward him. He tries to get up, but another wave rolls by and knocks him down again. Frantically, I try to use my good arm to haul him to his feet, but he's so much bigger than I am. I only manage to pull him up to his knees.

"Behind you!" Dom's voice shouts.

I turn just in time to see the massive tentacle whipping toward us. There's no time for me to dodge it. The extrusion crashes into my stomach, pulverizing my immerger belt and laying me out flat on the undulating floor. Tomo's storage drive crumbles, covering me in glittering particles of ceramic and silicon.

Suddenly, the deafening mechanical mayhem spins down. The floor melts back down to a level plane, lowering me several feet. The exit door slides open, and a dozen people burst into the room. I roll over and push myself up on my hands and knees, curling my injured arm around the agony in my ribs, struggling for breath.

When at last I manage a ragged inhalation, I rock back onto my heels. My eyes fall on a crimson stream wending its way slowly across the floor toward me. A wordless scream fills my ears. Before me, Owen lies sprawled on his back, his head soaked in blood.

LOST AND FOUND

OLLIE PUSHES THROUGH THE CURTAINS around my hospital bed, drops her briefcase on the floor, and leans over me. Her eyes take in the livid bruises on my arms and shoulders and the bandages around my ribs.

"Oh, Emmie," Ollie whispers.

I shift my weight in a brief and fruitless attempt to sit up.

"I'll be fine," I say, wincing. Even speaking hurts. I grip Ollie's hand and say, "How's Owen? No one here will tell me anything."

Ollie looks away, her eyes glistening.

No. No. No, it can't be.

But Ollie's expression reveals the horrible truth more effectively than any words could. My stomach lurches, and I lose my grip on her hand. I shiver uncontrollably, then moan at the stabbing pain this causes in my chest.

Ollie calls for a nurse, who hurries in a moment later. The nurse gives me two pills to swallow and holds a cup of water to my mouth. She settles another blanket over me and says, "Just hit the button if the pain gets worse, honey."

△▽△

A few hours later, I'm sitting dazed in a wheelchair with a paper bag of pain medications in my lap. Dad pushes me through the front lobby of the hospital while Mom and Ollie walk on either side of me. Uncle Frank trails behind, uncharacteristically silent.

At the entry doors, Dad gives me a hand out of the wheelchair, and I rise stiffly to my feet. The five of us walk slowly together toward the parking lot. Ollie, Mom, Dad, and Uncle Frank all drove to the hospital separately when they received the call. Mom and Ollie settle me gently into the front seat of Dad's car.

"We'll be right behind you," says Mom.

Dad sits down heavily in the driver's seat. He hits the button to start the car but doesn't put it into gear. He presses the palms of his shaking hands together and bows his head.

"Are you okay to drive?" I say.

"I just need a minute," he says, his voice breaking. His face is deathly pale.

I put my hand on his knee, my voice thick with emotion. "I'm so sorry, Dad."

He grabs my hand, loosening his grip when he sees me wince.

"What do you have to be sorry about? I'm just thankful you weren't more badly hurt. And I'm furious," he says, the muscles in his neck growing taut with the effort to remain calm. "Some idiot made a terrible mistake with that machine. And now you … And Owen …"

His jaw works. He stares into the rapidly darkening parking lot. Ollie beeps her car horn softly. Dad waves at her and puts the car in reverse. We pull out of the parking lot and head home.

"You don't have anything to be sorry about, Em," he says. "You didn't do anything wrong."

How I wish he were right.

△▽△

I wake from a dreamless, drug-induced sleep, disoriented. I'm in my bedroom, though I don't remember getting into bed. Outside my door, I hear Mom and Dad shuffling around in the kitchen. There's a sweet smell of frying onions in the air. I try to sit up, then cry out in pain and lie back on the pillows. A cold sweat prickles on my forehead. Ollie rushes into my room and leans over me.

"What's the matter?" says Ollie. "Are you okay?"

"Yeah," I whisper, trying not to breathe. "It hurts, though."

"Take it easy," she says. "Let me get you another dose of those painkillers."

Ollie returns with a glass of water and a couple of white pills, which I swallow eagerly.

"What time is it?" I say.

"Time for you to eat," says Ollie, forcing a smile. "You've been asleep for—" She glances at her old-fashioned wristwatch. "Almost fourteen hours."

My head swims. There's a flash of crimson in my mind's eye, but I push it away, inhaling sharply through my nose to clear my head. I can't suppress another small cry at the pain in my ribs.

Ollie sits beside me on the bed and presses her hand to my arm. She says, "Remember what the doctor said. Try not to breathe too deeply."

She sits with me until the pain subsides, then continues gently, "Uncle Frank came by this morning. Nanna and Grandpa were here too. They told us to call as soon as you're up."

"I think I need a little quiet time before all that starts," I say, closing my eyes.

"Mom cooked breakfast," she says. "Do you want me to bring you some food?"

"I'd rather get up," I say. "Can you give me some help?"

Ollie hesitates.

"Come on," I say. "If you don't, you know I'm going to do it myself."

Ollie shakes her head, resigned. She puts her arm gently behind my shoulders and raises me to a sitting position. I swing my legs over the edge of the bed, and Ollie helps me stand.

I touch the nightstand to steady myself, gritting my teeth against the pain. "It's not so bad once I'm up," I say. I'm not sure whom I'm trying to convince.

Ollie accompanies me down the hall to my living room and helps me sit back down on the sofa.

Dad takes a seat on the ottoman and rubs my feet—the only part of me that seems to have been spared any injury—while Mom talks quietly with Ollie in the kitchen. A few minutes later, they return with four plates and set them down on the coffee table. Mom offers me a plate, but I shake my head. I have no appetite. Even the sight of food nauseates me.

Ollie picks at her omelette and toast. Mom and Dad engage in some silent conversation through an exchange of pointed looks, until at last I say, "What's going on?"

Mom glances at Dad, who sighs and sets my foot down. Slowly, he says, "We got a call from Ty Monaghan this morning, Emmie. He told us that what happened to you and Owen in the spliner wasn't an accident."

I shudder, then grimace at the pain it causes. "What do you mean?" I whisper.

Dad says, "Your CTO, Ahmet, spent all night poring over system logs with the Augur IT security team to figure out the source of the spliner malfunction.

"From what they've gathered so far, someone installed an unauthorized daemon on each of Augur's network servers some time in the last week. The daemon is designed to scan devices connected to the network and activate a virus any time it detects a specific pattern in the device contents. Ahmet told me the daemon mimics a sophisticated information security technique that Augur uses itself, but the pattern that triggers the virus in this case seems totally random. They're not sure what you might have done to trigger it, since the virus erased the system logs in the entire spliner subnetwork. They think this system attack might have been an attempt to wipe out Augur's domain content library."

I shake my head, confused. "But who would try to do something like that?" I say. "Some competitor of Augur's?" I can't imagine another alternet gaming company doing something this nefarious. Stuff like this happens in big corporations, but usually the targets are companies that possess way more sensitive data than Augur, like defense contractors and healthcare companies.

Dad says, "While the security team had the Augur campus on lockdown, one of your coworkers tried to leave through a back gate. A security guard had to forcibly detain him. Once the police arrived to investigate the accident, they questioned him. Apparently he wouldn't speak to them without a lawyer."

"Who?" I say. "Who was he?"

"A young man named Zeke Eckerd," says Dad. "Do you know him?"

I shake my head, dazed. I say, "No. No, I can't believe Zeke would do something like that."

But … I remember brushing past Zeke on the way to the spliner. Owen had said— At the thought of Owen, my stomach lurches.

Mom and Dad exchange another pointed look. Mom reaches out to touch my knee. Gently, she says, "The police need to come by to interview you about what happened, as soon as possible. As soon as you're able to receive visitors."

"But they can wait," Dad says angrily. "She's in no condition to be talking to anyone right now."

"I know it's hard, but it'll be better to get it over with while the memory's still fresh," Mom says firmly. "Anything you remember might be critical."

I close my eyes and nod. Dad squeezes my shoulder and says, "Take as much time as you need, love."

"I need to be alone," I whisper. "Sorry. I don't want you to leave. I just need to be alone for a little while. Ollie, can you help me back to bed?"

Back in my room, Ollie props me up on the pillows and tucks my bedspread around my legs.

She's turning to leave when I say, "Ollie, where are the clothes and other stuff I was wearing when they took me to the hospital?"

"Oh. I think Mom brought them," she says. "Do you need them?"

"Yeah. Would you mind getting them for me?" I say.

Ollie goes into the hall and returns a minute later with a plastic bag.

"Thanks," I say. "That's all I needed. Can you close the door?"

Ollie leaves. I empty the contents of the bag onto my lap. The clothes and immerger gear I was wearing in the spliner are all inside, along with my smartcom. My smartcom, with its virtually indestructible titanium casing, appears unharmed. There's a smear of dried blood on the sleeve of my shirt. One knee of the jeans I was wearing over my immerger leggings is badly scuffed, and the other knee is torn. From my jeans pocket, I withdraw a handful of splinters, all that remains of the wooden box that had housed Tomo's storage drive.

I pull out my immerger belt. Its small processor unit was crushed when that spliner extrusion hit me, and only a fragment of Tomo's storage drive remains jammed into a port. I try to loosen it with my fingernail, but the remainder of the ceramic coating and solid-state storage medium crumbles into my lap.

"Damn," I mutter.

I reach for the spare immerger glasses and belt in the drawer of my bedside table, fastening the belt gingerly around my waist before slipping on the glasses. I whisper, "Dom? Are you there?"

Dom is the only one I want to talk to right now. He's the only other person who saw what happened. He must know something. I need to know what that something is.

I wait for a long time, but he doesn't answer. Has he abandoned me? I lean back against the headboard. I try to force myself to take slow, shallow breaths, but the best I can manage to do is sob in silence.

△▽△

I drift through the days that follow in a haze of painkillers and grief. Christmas and New Year's Day come and go. The police come and go twice. My parents come and go many times.

Ollie stays in my guest room, answering my calls from friends and family, arranging the flowers and cards on the table, trying to tempt my appetite with ever more ambitious culinary endeavors. Uncle Frank stops by frequently to sit at my bedside, trying to entertain me with stories about the latest goings-on at the Lab.

Owen's family arrives from Texas soon after his death to make arrangements for his funeral and memorial service. They've been staying with my parents for almost two weeks, but I haven't been able to bring myself to see them.

Ollie sits across the dinner table from me one evening, after forcing me to swallow a few spoonfuls of the delicious soup she's made, and says, "Emmie, come with me to Mom and Dad's. You know the Cyruses want to meet you."

I cover my eyes, my face contorting with grief. "I can't," I say, my voice breaking. "I can't. How can I look them in the face? It's my fault he's dead."

Ollie comes around to my chair and wraps her arms around me. "Don't do this," she says, gently but firmly. "Be strong. They've come to say goodbye to him, and you can help them. He loved you, and this place, and all the work you did together. You can show all of that to them."

I sob. Ollie holds me, soothes me, and waits. When at last all my tears are spent, Ollie looks me straight in the eye and says, "You owe this to Owen."

So I go with Ollie to our parents' house. Mom and Dad stand waiting above the entryway when we arrive, and they help me down the stairs into the living room.

Owen's family sits on the big sofa. I recognize them all from the photos Owen showed me. His mother, Gracie, a petite woman with smoothly-coiffed blonde hair, perfect makeup, and a neatly-pressed but faded cotton blouse, sees me first. She rushes forward to embrace me, missing my pained wince, kissing me on both cheeks. She smells like roses.

"Oh, honey," says Gracie, brushing away my tears, then her own. "I'm so glad to meet you at last."

Owen's sister, Marybeth, follows her mother. She's slim, with glossy dark hair the same shade as Owen's. Her eyes are red-rimmed from crying. Marybeth hugs me more carefully, avoiding my injured shoulder. "I'm sorry we didn't meet before now," she says. "Owen told me so much about you."

Behind Marybeth stand Owen's brother, Wendell, and father, Howard. The sight of Wendell sends fresh tears running down my cheeks. He looks so much like Owen. Wendell shakes my hand wordlessly, as does his father.

△▽△

A few days later, I stand with the group of mourners gathered for Owen's memorial service in Redwood Regional Park, where Owen and I spent so many sunny days together. My family and the Cyruses and a group of Owen's friends from Cal and Augur have all walked a trail together through one of Owen's favorite redwood groves into a grassy clearing. I weep in my father's arms as the Baptist minister selected by the Cyruses leads the brief service. Marybeth delivers the eulogy.

Owen's mother scatters native wildflower seeds at the edge of the meadow with shaking hands. Imagining those flowers blooming in the seasons to come—sunset orange California poppies, golden fairy lanterns, pure white woodland stars—I weep, knowing Owen will never see them.

△▽△

In the weeks that follow Owen's memorial service, Mom emails me occasional updates about legal proceedings. I delete the messages unread. But in late February, Mom comes to my house in person to deliver the news that Zeke has pled guilty to charges of aggravated battery and second degree murder. He's been sentenced to fifteen years in prison. Mom seems to feel some satisfaction at the news. I feel nothing at all.

Ollie stays with me until the most severe of my injuries have healed and I can move around on my own without help. With some reluctance, but at my urging, she returns to her own life and her own apartment down in Palo Alto. I tell her I'll be fine. I wish that I believed it.

One morning, I wake early for the first time in a long time. I press a hand to my ribs as I rise tentatively from bed. The ache is manageable, so I leave the bottle of painkillers untouched on the bedside table. I shower, dress, and walk out my front door. Even this feels like an accomplishment.

I climb into my car and drive slowly downtown, back to Augur.

It's seven o'clock in the morning when I knock on Ty's office door. He swivels around in his desk chair. Seeing me, his eyes widen in surprise.

"Emmie!" he says, standing. "How are you? I wasn't expecting you in. Especially on a Saturday." He steps around his desk and pulls out a chair for me. "Coffee?"

I shake my head. Ty sits back down. He says, "I can't tell you how sorry I am about everything that happened. I never imagined …" He shakes his head. Through the numbness that's taken up residence in my heart since Owen's death, I feel a stirring of something. Is it anger? If it hadn't been for Ty, perhaps Zeke would never have—

I stop myself from finishing the thought. I can't let myself think like this.

We sit in silence for a while, until at last Ty says, "Did you stop by to talk about something?"

"Yes," I say, suddenly remembering why I came. "I'm quitting."

Ty inhales loudly through his nose and presses his fingertips together. He swivels to one side, contemplating his grand view of the San Francisco Bay, now blanketed in morning fog. He swivels back to me, his expression sympathetic. "I understand why you might be feeling this way right now. But there's no need to rush your decision. Think things over. Take a paid leave of absence. Whatever time you need, you can have it. The team here needs you, Emmie. We want you back, whenever you're ready."

I rub my forehead and look past Ty toward the bridges crossing the Bay. "No," I say. "No, I won't be back."

Ty nods slowly. I don't meet his eyes as he says, "Take care of yourself, Emmie."

△▽△

I take the stairs down to my team's offices. The floor is empty, the public channel quiet. The motion-activated lights turn on as I walk through the workstations toward Tomo's office. I pull up the access codes Ty sent to my smartcom weeks ago and push open the door. Technically, I shouldn't enter this room now that I've quit, but there's something in here that belongs to me.

The air inside the office is fresh with the scent of thriving plants. I stand at the center of the familiar room, which feels so empty without Tomo at his desk. His office chair sits exactly where he left it so many months ago. I rest my hand briefly on the back of his chair, blinking back tears.

I turn to face the heavy Japanese cabinet. Atop the cabinet stands Tomo's bonsai tree, delicate red buds nestled in its tiny, twisting branches, waiting for spring. I brush my fingertips along the branches. Ayame told me Tomo left this tree to me, and I'm not leaving without it.

I take the blue ceramic tray holding the bonsai tree in both my hands and start to lift it up. Then I glimpse a glitter of something through the crown of budding branches. Puzzled, I set the tray back down and bend over until my eyes are level with the tree. Half-buried beneath the potting soil, I spot a button-sized, emerald-green disc. Tentatively, I reach for it.

"Wait," says a voice behind me.

Adrenaline surges through me. I jerk back my hand and spin around. Dom stands by the window, barely two paces away. My alarm transforms instantly to fury at the sight of him. I take a step toward him, trembling, balling my fists. "You," I growl. "I don't ever want to see you again. Do you understand me? Never again."

"Listen to me, Emmie," Dom says urgently. "As soon as you have that storage drive in your possession again, your life will be in danger."

"What do you care?" I say, my voice thick with emotion. "You had no problem letting me walk into a trap before. You just stood by, you bastard."

"I am truly sorry," Dom says. "If there was anything I could have done—"

"You could have *told* someone!" I cry.

"There was no way for me to warn anyone but you," he says.

"You expect me to believe that?" I say. "After you've hacked into every network, every private channel at Augur to talk to me? No. You let someone die just to cover your worthless hacker ass."

Dom says, "Emmie, I know you have no reason to believe me, but I swear to you, if there was anything I could have done to save Owen, anything at all, I would have done it."

I stare at him, wanting to hate him almost as much as I want to believe him.

"None of that matters now—what you could have done, what I could have done," I say. I reach out toward the bonsai tree again and pick up the storage drive. Its cold enamel coating warms slowly in my palm. My mind feels sharp for the first time in weeks. "What I need to know is why. *Why* did this happen?"

ON THE ROAD

I DECIDE NOT TO MENTION where I'm heading. All I tell Mom and Dad is that I'm going to spend some time in Yosemite. Ollie wants to come and keep me company, but I tell her I need to be alone.

I leave early to avoid the morning commuter traffic. When I slip my car into autopilot on the long, open stretch of 580 East, it's barely eight o'clock. I know Dom's here, somewhere, somehow, watching me, but I don't speak to him. I slip on my glasses instead, immersing myself in *Temenos* and wandering the streets of *Athenai* in an anonymous avatar.

Ty decided to stick to my launch plan for *Atlantis*, despite my absence. The release rumor went out a few days ago, just as I'd planned. The public channels are buzzing, just as I'd hoped they would, back when I cared enough to hope about such meaningless things. I remember Owen's skepticism about my plan. A lump rises in my throat. However skeptical he may have been, Owen backed me up, all the way to the end.

Tears blur my visual overlay. I push back my glasses, pressing my forehead to the cool glass of the car window. I watch mile after mile of landscape slip by: the rolling hills with their white forests of wind turbines; the flat expanse of the Central Valley with its blossoming orchards of almonds, cherries, and apricots; the open fields of green and gold; the broad blue irrigation canals.

My car turns south on I-5, passing ever more arid agricultural land and exits to ever more nondescript towns. When the navigation system announces the approaching Coalinga exit, I take the wheel again. I turn off the freeway and drive along a country road through dusty farmland. A few miles later, I pass a large hospital facility, then slow to turn into the front entrance of Pleasant Valley State Prison.

I find a spot in the visitor parking lot and store my immerger belt and glasses in my glove compartment. As much as I want to ignore Dom completely, I keep my earbuds and smartcom, just in case he needs to tell me something. I reach for the door handle. But before I step out of the car, I say, "I feel the same thing now as when Tomo died. Emptiness. Not sadness, not fear. Not even anger."

Why do I say this aloud? Why do I know Dom will answer? I'm not sure, but answer he does.

"It will be better this way," he says. "Anger will not help you understand."

I take a deep breath and, to my surprise, feel myself relax. Despite his opaque motives, despite his unwanted intrusion into my life, despite his suspicious involvement in the events of the past several months, Dom's presence comforts me in a way that no one else's has since Owen died.

I steel myself and climb out of my car to join a stream of people walking toward the processing center. I fill out the requisite visitor pass and wait for my turn to go through the full-body scanner. On the other side, I retrieve my coat, shoes, smartcom, and earbuds.

I make my way to the room indicated on my visitor pass and show it at the door to the guard, who waves me through. Inside the brightly-lit room, men, women, and children sit around small tables speaking quietly to prisoners in faded jeans and blue chambray shirts. I find an empty table and sit down.

A few minutes later, Zeke enters through the double doors at the far side of the room. His eyes meet mine. My entire body tenses as he approaches. He sinks into the chair across from me.

He looks skinny and pale and so very young in his shapeless blue prison uniform and short-cropped hair. His eyelids are raw and red beneath pale lashes. Across one cheek, there's a patch of blonde stubble he missed while shaving.

"I'm surprised you wanted to see me," he says.

I search for words. All I can manage to say is, "Tell me why you did it."

Zeke presses the tips of his long white fingers to his forehead, closing his eyes. He says, "I don't expect you to believe me, but I never meant to hurt anybody."

"What *did* you mean to do, then?" I say, feeling no pity for him. "What were you thinking?"

Zeke opens his eyes and meets my gaze. He says, "I realized as soon as Ty made his decision on *Atlantis* that he'd just been using me to keep the board happy. He wanted you all along. Just like Tomo did.

"I was angry. I wanted you to know what that felt like. To have all your work just disappear without anyone ever seeing it.

"I thought that I was planting an armageddon virus, that it would corrupt the content library, spread to the backup data centers, a complete wipe. But … I didn't know what that code was going to do to the spliner. I swear I didn't."

I shake my head in disbelief. "You idiot," I say. "You couldn't even bother to take a look under the hood? Who told you it was an armageddon virus?"

"My—" Zeke's voice shrinks almost to a whisper. "My father gave me the code."

"Your father?" I say, confused.

Zeke's pale face somehow turns even paler. He swallows, his eyes flicking nervously to the faces of the other people around us. He leans toward me. "Have you heard of the Church of the True Cross?" he says.

I shake my head.

"It's a fundamentalist church," says Zeke. "A cult, maybe. I'm not sure there's a difference. Anyway, they believe that an apocalypse is coming, that God is going to punish the world for its sins. Pretty run-of-the-mill fundamentalist stuff, I guess.

"The church hates the alternet. Well, at least they hate pretty much everything that people use it for. Video games. Sensory immersion. 'Tuning out,' that's what they call it. They think it's this pervasive force of evil leading people away from the path to salvation.

"The Church is one of the biggest funders of the alternet regulation lobby.

They know they can't stamp out the alternet entirely, at least not all at once. They've settled for now on doing what they helped to do to the internet and television and radio over the last several decades. But … government works pretty slowly."

"Are you saying they're involved in cyberterrorism?" I say.

Zeke raises an eyebrow meaningfully but doesn't answer.

I shake my head, unsure what Zeke's implying. "So … what does that have to do with your dad?" I say.

Zeke says, "My father is a high-ranking member of the church. A Steward of the True Cross. He heads up a church ministry called Youth for Truth, to keep young people away from all the corrupting influences of mainstream society. Including the alternet."

I give a humorless laugh. "How did you end up being a hot-shot alternet designer with a father like that?" I say.

"I never wanted anything to do with him," Zeke says bitterly. "I left home as soon as I figured out how to support myself.

"But my dad kept tabs on me. I guess I didn't make it that hard. I didn't change my name or anything. My mom did that. She disappeared a long time ago." He heaves a sigh. "I should have tried harder to stay away from him. A little over a year ago, he just showed up. He was starting a new church in Oakland, and he came to see me.

"I … I was lonely. I started talking to him about my life, about how things at work were going. I was really unhappy. And jealous. Of you, of Owen. My dad saw that. He started trying to convince me that God was giving me a sign, showing me that Augur was evil. He said God wanted me to bring about his plan by taking down *Temenos*.

"I didn't believe him any more than I had when I was a kid, but he gave me the code anyway. He said I would realize soon enough that he was telling the truth. He said he knew that I would do the right thing.

"And when Ty didn't pick my backup concept … I didn't think. I was just so angry." He looks away.

"But you didn't tell anyone about your father?" I say. "Your lawyer? The judge?"

"It doesn't matter," says Zeke, staring off into space. "I planted the code. I'm responsible for what happened."

"But you weren't working alone," I say. "Why did you just plead guilty?"

Zeke shifts uncomfortably on the hard plastic seat attached to our table. "I'm safer in here," he says.

The way Zeke says this makes me feel sick. "Safer from what?" I say.

After a long silence, I reach across the table and touch Zeke's hand. It's ice cold. "Zeke," I say in a low voice. "What the hell is going on?"

Zeke looks at my hand on his, then meets my eyes. "Emmie." He says my name like a plea. "I never meant to hurt you or Owen. I've had a lot of time to think about what I did, and I … I remember telling my father a lot of things.

About how close you and Tomo were. And I remember something my father said. That you and Tomo were two of the biggest threats to the church, and that it was the will of God that you be stopped."

I pull back my hand. A red haze creeps in around the edges of my vision. "Are you saying your father had something to do with Tomo's death?"

"I don't know for sure," says Zeke. "But my father knew what would happen when I planted that code in the spliner. Owen's death was no accident. Maybe Tomo's wasn't, either."

△▽△

I'm in such a state that I scarcely remember returning to my car, but now I'm throwing it into gear, peeling out of the parking lot, narrowly missing a barrier fence on my way back to the freeway.

"Careful," says Dom, his projection materializing in the passenger seat beside me. I jump, then switch the car into autopilot with a shaking hand. I focus on the horizon as the dusty expanse of the Central Valley rushes by, forcing the swirl of confusion in my mind to resolve into a single desperate thought.

"This can't be true," I say, launching my anonymous proxy internet browser. A moment later, I'm grappling with the Oakland Police Department's website, an archaic internet interface typical of government services. I read through a poorly-organized web page explaining the process for requesting public records. I draft a request for the accident report of Tomo's death using a template produced by a quick alternet search. After I submit it, a message explains that an automated review process will check for confidentiality restrictions on the information I've requested. A moment later, the report pops up.

I examine the document. *Name of deceased: Tomo Yoshimoto. Location of incident: Webster and 8th Street, Oakland, CA.* I skim past the name of the ambulance company and other extraneous details. A note references two attached witness statements.

The first statement is from a man named William Chen, who said he was walking by when another man at the scene asked him to call 911. Chen stated that Tomo appeared unconscious from the time he called 911 until the time the ambulance arrived.

My stomach churns when I see the name on the second witness statement: Amos Eckerd. His statement adds no meaningful detail beyond William Chen's statement. I run an alternet search on the name Amos Eckerd, turning up several photos of a tall, handsome man preaching, standing in prayer circles, building houses in Third World countries. Zeke's resemblance to his father is unmistakable.

I massage my eyes for a minute, absorbing the implications of this, then flip on a visual overlay. A few alternet searches on "Stewards" and "Stewards of the True Cross" turn up surprisingly little: mostly references to legends about the physical remnants of the cross upon which Jesus Christ was crucified, and a few old internet websites and public alternet domains that make incidental references containing similar phrases.

I close the useless search results. I need help if I'm going to find out who Amos Eckerd really is, and I know exactly where I need to go.

△▽△

I log on to *Temenos* and teleport directly to the lobby of the Founders Club. The uniformed receptionist behind the desk smiles politely.

"How may I help you today, Anonymous Member?" she says.

"I'd like to check out a secure meeting room," I say.

"Certainly. Just a moment," she says.

After my identity verification clears, a message pops up on my overlay containing a link to an encrypted subdomain. I follow the link, which sends my avatar promptly to a seat inside an elegant gazebo surrounded by a vast English garden. A warm summer breeze carries a carefully engineered scent of flowers across the neatly trimmed lawn. I inhale appreciatively. The extravagant quality of even the most prosaic services is one of the many perks of Club membership.

I realize after a moment that Dom's standing behind me. I glance up at him, shaking my head. I can't decide if I'm more impressed or alarmed by his presence here. "How are you doing this?" I say. "It's impossible to hack your way into an encrypted subdomain on *Temenos*."

His face is unreadable as he sinks into the cushioned seat of the white wicker chair across from me.

"What are you planning to do?" he says.

It'll be faster to show him than tell him. Aloud, I dictate a message. "Member offers temens, reputation, or favor in exchange for information on religious organization called Church of the True Cross. Mutual identity verification required."

With a few keystrokes, I broadcast the request to all Club members. I stand and walk out of the gazebo to contemplate the calming garden scenery while I wait for replies.

Over the next few minutes, several responses appear on my visual overlay. I return to my seat in the gazebo to draft polite rejections for all but the top three responses, as ranked by my personal trust algorithm. After skimming the recommendations for each of the remaining candidates, I settle on the one unnamed identity whose long list of trust network recommendations includes several prominent Club members, including Tomo.

I initiate an automated negotiation to establish the minimum profile information required by this identity as a prerequisite to meeting in my secure transaction space. When the negotiation concludes, I review the proposed profile data exchange one last time and approve it with a wave of my hand. The other party's profile data appears on my overlay.

I skim the profile headlines. *Identity: Falsens. Network reputation: Private alternet security (high), Corporate alternet security (high), Electronic surveillance (high), Electronic countersurveillance (high), Cyberterrorism (high), Counter-*

cyberterrorism (high) ...

Falsens' network reputation ratings are numerous and impressively high across the board. I stop reading long before I reach the end, scrolling down to punch the "Enter meeting" prompt hovering at the bottom of the profile.

A moment later, a squat avatar of indeterminate gender, race, and age materializes in the seat across from me in the gazebo. I raise an eyebrow. "I guess your profile's not kidding about the security bit," I say.

Falsens responds in an electronically modulated voice that morphs smoothly from male to female, adult to child, and back again over the course of a few sentences. "Avatars give away a lot," says Falsens. "Yours puts you at ninety percent probability female, eighty-four percent probability technology industry, seventy-eight percent probability American, etcetera. Most people don't think about it until it's too late."

I nod slowly. Falsens might have profiled me as a techie American female, but I don't need a profile to tell me I'm dealing with a condescending geek of the male persuasion. "So you know something about the Church of the True Cross?" I say.

"That is why I responded," says Falsens.

"What would you like in exchange for the information?" I say.

"Two thousand temens," says Falsens. "Subsequent consultations will be twelve hundred."

I laugh in surprise at his presumption. "You're expecting repeat business?" I say.

"Based on my knowledge of the Church of the True Cross, I imagine you have a specific security concern in mind," says Falsens. "Whatever those concerns may be, I'm sure you'll find my other services useful. Is the price acceptable?"

A payment authorization prompt appears on my visual overlay. I hesitate. I've never been very thrifty, but this is a pretty big sum to drop just for some information. Still, it seems like my best option. I tap my authorization code for the charge. "So what can you tell me?" I say.

Falsens says, "The Church of the True Cross is a regional branch of a larger organization funded by a number of religious fundamentalist denominations around the world. The umbrella organization goes by many names, but members of the central leadership are usually referred to as Stewards. The congregations directed by the Stewards have been implicated over the past several decades in a number of sophisticated cyberterrorism attacks against key communication infrastructure hubs. A few corporations affected by the attacks have taken legal action against different denominations related to the Stewards, but all such suits have settled out of court."

I chew my lip as I process this information. "Were the server farm wipe-outs that Augur experienced last year caused by the Stewards?" I say.

"Multiple attacks on alternet domains last year, including the attack you're referencing, were attributed to the Stewards by private security analysts," says Falsens.

"What about killings?" I say. "Assassinations? Have they been implicated in anything like that?"

"Not according to any information I have seen. Although the organization's motives for cyberterrorism are unclear, the effects of these attacks have tended toward destruction of hardware, software, and data, not human life. Why do you ask?"

"There was a hardware malfunction in the main spliner belonging to my employer, Augur, this past December," I say. "I was injured in the accident, and my … my colleague, Owen Cyrus, was killed. Another colleague of mine, Zeke Eckerd, was convicted of planting the virus that caused the accident. I just visited Zeke in prison, and he told me that his father, a man named Amos Eckerd, provided the software that caused the malfunction. Zeke said his father works for the Church of the True Cross. He also said his father's title, or something, is Steward."

Falsens says, "Do you believe this man, Amos Eckerd, was attempting to assassinate you? Or Owen Cyrus?"

"I don't know," I say. "But this man may have been involved in another death. My former boss, Tomo Yoshimoto."

Falsens considers this, then says, "Do you have any evidence implicating Amos Eckerd?"

"Only circumstantial," I say. "He gave a witness statement to the police who showed up when Tomo collapsed on the street."

Falsens says, "And are you concerned for your own safety?"

The question catches me off guard. I've been so absorbed with what happened to Owen and Tomo that I hadn't really considered what this might mean for me.

"I don't know," I say slowly. "Maybe. Should I be?"

Falsens says, "I don't have enough information to advise you at this point. However, I would be more than happy to investigate the matter further for you, as well as advise you on safety precautions. Would you like to see a proposal for these services?"

Curious, but unsure what I may be getting myself into, I say, "I guess so."

Falsens says, "Please hold." His avatar remains seated before me, but it switches into a basic holding animation loop that indicates he's temporarily away from this subdomain.

A few minutes later, an interactive presentation appears before me. It responds to my touch as I navigate the proposed list of services. A collection of short marketing videos includes case studies and highlights several compelling testimonials. "Pricing?" I say, looking up at Falsens' avatar.

His avatar returns to an active state. He says, "Five hundred temens per day for my 24-hour personal security concierge. Ten percent discount for subscriptions lasting more than three months. Twelve hundred temens per consultation, investigation travel and meal expenses extra, as required. All charges subject to client approval at the time of request."

I flip through the proposal presentation a second time. "My network says you're good," I say.

"The best," says Falsens.

"All right," I say, taking a leap of faith in my trust algorithm. "Let's do it."

△▽△

Having approved Falsens' proposal and installed his recommended personal security concierge client on my smartcom, I log out of *Temenos*. My car is still speeding north on I-80, and the late afternoon sun streams in through the driver side window. I turn up the tint on the car windows and turn down the temperature of my immerger clothing to cool myself off. My heart is beating unusually fast.

"Security alert." A calming simulation of a female voice speaks in my earbuds. A flashing indicator on my visual overlay indicates this is a message from my new personal security concierge.

"What's wrong?" I say. I wasn't expecting an alert so immediately.

The concierge says, "Preliminary security screening of your current location indicates a high probability that the Volta Courant sedan, license plate 5-SOS-101, currently two tenths of a mile behind you, has been following you since the Los Banos onramp."

"Are you kidding?" I say.

The concierge says, "This is what your preliminary environment security screening indicates."

"Well, who's in the car?" I say.

The concierge says, "Tinted glass prevents facial recognition by our roadside security monitors."

"What should I do?" I say.

The concierge says, "Please request a consultation for additional recommendations."

I crane my neck to look out my back window, squinting at the cars in the distance. But I'm not sure I'd recognize a Volta Courant even if it pulled up beside me.

After a pause, the concierge prompts helpfully, "Would you like to initiate a consultation?"

"Um." I turn to face the front again. "Sure? Yes."

A moment later, Falsens' avatar appears in a projection. "Hello, Miss Bridges. How may I help you?"

"Your concierge says someone's following me," I say anxiously. "What should I do about that?"

"I would suggest maintaining your present course until I can send a countersurveillance operative to guide you through evasive maneuvers."

I gape at Falsens. "You can do that?"

"Yes. Perhaps you did not have a chance to review my complete list of available services." Falsens' interactive proposal appears before me again. "If you navigate to section—"

"No, no. That's okay," I say. "I want to go ahead with it."

"Certainly," says Falsens. "All I need is your authorization."

An interface pops up on my visual overlay displaying a detailed tally of the charges incurred so far, as well as the additional charges for the latest consult and proposed countersurveillance operation. This is all going to add up very quickly, but I don't see a great alternative. I tap the approval button.

"Thank you," Falsens says promptly, then disappears from view.

My stomach twists as I imagine the cold blue eyes of Amos Eckerd, which I glimpsed in the alternet image search results. Are those eyes watching me through the dark glass of one of the cars behind me? I pull my feet up onto the driver's seat, hugging my knees to my chest, watching the status indicator on my visual overlay count down the minutes and seconds to the estimated rendezvous time with the countersurveillance operative. What on Earth have I gotten myself into?

△▽△

The freeway traffic has just slowed to a stop somewhere outside Livermore, still miles from Oakland, when the crisp voice of the security concierge says in my earbuds, "Please prepare for rendezvous."

I look out at the sea of stopped cars surrounding me, then flip open a map on my visual overlay to check my current location and the cause of the standstill. It appears that a vehicle accident has closed all four lanes of traffic up ahead.

"Rendezvous where?" I say anxiously. "We're miles from the next exit."

There's a clamor of car horns, and I flick off my visual overlay to see what's going on. In the rearview monitor on my dashboard, I glimpse a small dust cloud approaching. I turn in my seat, watching through my rear windshield as a small grey sedan with opaque black windows races up the shoulder and stops two lanes over from my car.

The driver side door of the grey sedan opens, and a spry little man with dark sunglasses and a fedora springs out. He weaves through the stationary vehicles surrounding my car, stops at my window, and taps the glass.

"Countersurveillance operative identity confirmed," says the calm voice of my security concierge. "Please follow operative instructions for secure vehicle transfer."

Cautiously, I roll my window down a few inches.

"Emmie Bridges?" says the man.

"Yes?" I say uncertainly, peering up at him. I can't make out much behind his sunglasses, but there's something vaguely familiar about his voice.

"Come with me. Quickly," he says, pointing at my dashboard.

I look down at my rearview monitor again. A surge of adrenaline sends my heart racing. I recognize the tall, fair-haired figure of Amos Eckerd running up the center of the freeway toward my car. I gasp and fumble to unlock my seatbelt. When I push open my car door, I nearly clobber the little man. He takes my hand and pulls me out of the car.

"Hurry," he says, gesturing toward his car while keeping his eyes on Amos. So I hurry, ignoring the honks and exclamations of protest from angry-looking drivers as I squeeze between their car bumpers. The grey sedan's passenger door swings open to admit me and closes after me. I look back through the window. Apprehensively, I watch as the little man in the dark sunglasses points what appears to be a silver pen—some kind of weapon?—at Amos. Amos stops dead in his tracks a few paces behind my car. He raises his hands above his head, panting, his face red with the exertion of running, his white-blonde hair windblown.

Across from me, the driver door of the grey sedan swings open. The little man backs toward me, keeping his silver pen extended in Amos' direction. When he reaches the car, he slides into the driver seat in one smooth motion, slams the door closed, and floors the accelerator. We speed down the shoulder, provoking another cacophony of honks from the disgruntled traffic jam behind us.

△▽△

"Oh my god. Oh my god," I say. I'd nearly stopped breathing. Now I'm gasping so fast I might hyperventilate. I stare back through the rear windshield as the figure of Amos Eckerd recedes into the distance.

"Don't worry," says the man in the dark sunglasses, steering neatly around a biker who seems to share his opinion about the proper use of the freeway shoulder. "We have about a two-minute lead on him."

Two minutes doesn't sound reassuring, but I guess it's better than nothing.

He turns off the freeway exit ramp and pulls up to an empty port at a busy recharging station. There's a large white SUV parked at the charging port beside us.

My driver turns back to me and says, "We're changing vehicles. When your door opens, just step calmly into the SUV."

I nod, heart pounding. My rear door opens. Simultaneously, the doors of the white SUV open. I do a double-take as a little man in a fedora and a diminutive young woman with cobalt blue highlights in her brunette hair emerge from the SUV.

"Come on," says my driver, ushering me past our doppelgängers into the rear passenger door of the SUV. I climb in, and the door shuts behind me. Our doppelgängers climb into the grey sedan, pull out of the charging station, and take off toward the freeway at speed. A few minutes later, my driver hops in behind the wheel of the SUV. We pull out of the charging station at a leisurely speed and head in the opposite direction.

When my breathing returns to something like normal, I say to my driver, "Where are we going?"

"I'm taking you to a safe house. It's—" he glances at a visual overlay I can't see, "about an hour away. We have to take the long way to get around the accident we planted."

The accident *we* planted? Who is this guy? I still can't place his voice. I peer more closely at his profile. The recognition finally hits me.

"You!" I exclaim. "You're … Wait, it's … Na—Na …"

"Naoto Kimura," he says, smiling at me. "I guess my disguise isn't as good as I thought."

He removes his sunglasses, fedora, and a convincing wig of short-cropped black hair, revealing the shining bald head I remember from Tomo's memorial service. I shake my head in disbelief.

"But you were … old, " I say.

He winks at me, then stoops his shoulders and creases his face in some subtle way that seems to age him twenty years. He says, now with the precise Japanese-accented English I remember, "Surely in your line of work you've learned that looks can be deceiving."

Before I reply, my security concierge interrupts us over the SUV audio channel. "Status update."

Nervously, I say, "What's wrong?"

"Your personal vehicle's autopilot has been directed to a secure garage facility in Livermore. You are advised to continue using the secure car service provided by your countersurveillance operative until further notice."

"Oh. Okay, thanks."

I slump into the back seat. With an anxious laugh, I say to Naoto, "It would be great if she could differentiate between 'You're being followed' and 'We're parking your car,' don't you think?"

"Status update," she interrupts again.

My mouth goes dry. The security concierge continues, "Facial recognition monitors have confirmed the identity of the driver of the Volta Courant, license plate 5-SOS-101, as Amos Jeremiah Eckerd."

"You think?" I say, rolling my eyes.

"Would you like to hear public information about Amos Jeremiah Eckerd?" says the concierge.

I glance at Naoto through the rearview mirror. He shrugs.

"Sure," I say. "Lay it on me."

"Amos Jeremiah Eckerd, male, age seventy-six—"

"Seventy-six!" I repeat, shaking my head in surprise. The man running up the freeway hadn't looked a day over forty to me.

The concierge continues, "—Born in Lynchburg, Virginia. Oldest son of Jeremiah Josiah Eckerd, deceased, and Miriam Fuller Eckerd, deceased. Father to Ezekiel Amos Eckerd. Married to Annabelle Abbott Eckerd, presumed deceased.

"Eckerd holds an undergraduate degree in Philosophy and Religion from Liberty University and a PhD in Theology and Apologetics from Liberty University Theological Seminary.

"Eckerd is presently employed as senior minister of—"

"Okay, okay," I interrupt. "How about something useful? Like why he's following me?"

The concierge says, "Would you like to initiate a consultation?"

"Ugh," I grumble. "Not right now."

Naoto chuckles and says, "Falsens sticks to protocol, doesn't he?"

I look at Naoto curiously. What does he know about Falsens? "So … he *is* a he?" I say.

Naoto gives an ambiguous shrug. "I assume. I haven't actually met him. Or her."

"But you work for him?" I say.

"I've done a lot of work for Falsens in the past. But, if you navigate to section seventeen part three of Falsens' standard proposal terms," says Naoto, giving me a wry smile through the rearview mirror, "You'll see that, technically, I'm working for you. Falsens likes to spread liability around."

I shake my head at the memory of the monumental document. "So, who were you working for while you were impersonating a Buddhist priest at Tomo Yoshimoto's memorial service?" I say.

Naoto's expression turns serious. "Interesting question," he says. "Normally, I wouldn't be able to discuss other clients' work, but in this case, you happen to be both clients. So that dovetails nicely."

"What are you talking about?" I say.

"Amaterasu Nagato hired me on your behalf to provide countersurveillance and security services," he says. "Apparently she anticipated some of the trouble you would be having."

I frown. "What exactly have you been doing … on my behalf?"

Naoto says, "Periodic bug sweeps, personal communication channel monitoring, wireless network shielding, round-the-clock bodyguard detail. Among other things. My instructions were fairly broad. Provide you with as high a level of personal security as I can. Minimize detection by third parties and interference with your regular activities."

"So where were you when the accident in the spliner happened?" I say, wondering how, with all these people spying on me, I ended up so utterly alone in that moment.

Naoto sighs. "My ability to provide security on the Augur campus without detection was limited. I alerted Augur security as soon as my remote surveillance detected the disturbance in the spliner. But by then the damage was done."

"Damage," I repeat slowly. "You mean Owen."

"Yes," says Naoto. "Owen. I'm sorry."

Tears smart in my eyes. I swallow, forcing my mind past the raw grief. I have more pressing concerns right now. I know what Amos Eckerd must be after. My fingers close around the emerald storage drive tucked in the little compartment on my immerger belt. I wish Tomo hadn't given it to me, almost as much as I need to understand why he did.

THE ANONYMOUS COLLECTIVE

Hours later, we've re-entered the Bay Area sprawl. The SUV takes a downtown Oakland freeway exit. We drive down familiar streets until the bright red doors of the Buddhist Church of Oakland come into view through the tinted windows.

"You're kidding," I say. "This is the safe house?"

"The very same," Naoto replies, pulling the car up alongside the curb. "I've keyed the door to your palm. Go inside and check our shared channel for instructions to enter the safe room. I'll be right behind you. I just need to get rid of this car."

A renewed surge of adrenaline accompanies the thought of crossing the wide stretch of sidewalk separating me from the front doors of the church. I try to open my door, but my hand doesn't obey.

Naoto squeezes my shoulder. "You're going to be fine," he says. "Now, go."

I pluck up my courage and push open the door. I hurry across the sidewalk toward the church's wrought iron gate. Naoto pulls away from the curb. I've never felt as exposed as I feel now, standing alone on the sidewalk. Glancing nervously over my shoulder at the slow-moving pedestrians and cars along this block, I press my hand to the palm scanner. Relief washes over me as the padlock clunks and the gate swings open. I hurry up the front steps. The heavy red front doors swing open at my touch.

I stand alone on the worn red carpet in the lobby, breathing in the faint scent of incense, until my smartcom pings. I flip on a visual overlay, where a text message reads,

Go to the hondo.

I remember the way and take the stairs up to the second floor. I approach the smiling wooden Buddha seated before the open doors of the *hondo*. My smartcom pings again.

Press hand to Buddha's belly.

I reach out toward the smiling wood carving and press my hand against the cool, smooth cedar. A soft buzz emanates from the pedestal beneath the statue, and a pulse of warmth travels along my palm. Another text message appears.

Proceed to the shrine.

I hurry down the center aisle between the rows of empty pews, toward the altar at the front of the room. I stop before the gleaming shrine. A message says,

Touch Buddha's foot.

I step around the heavy incense jars and stand before the draped altar table. I reach tentatively toward the golden Buddha at the center of the shrine and press my fingertip to one gleaming foot.

There's a rush of air as the entire wall panel containing the shrine pulls back, creating two gaps on the left and right side of the shrine. Each gap opens into some dark space beyond. The next message reads,

Take the right path ;-)

I glance nervously over my shoulder, step toward the Buddha, and turn into the right-side gap beside the shrine. I can barely make out the three bare walls of the small room I've entered before the wall behind me closes. I'm plunged into darkness for an instant before bright ceiling lights switch on.

I'm standing in a wide but shallow room, unfurnished, with uniformly grey walls. For a terrifying instant, I think I'm trapped inside another spliner. The memory of my last time in a spliner flashes before me, and I spring backwards, flattening myself against the wall. It takes me a few seconds to recognize the reassuring rigidity of cool drywall beneath my sweating palms. I slump to the floor in relief.

My smartcom pings.

Stay there. I'm on my way.

I wrap my arms around my knees and bow my head, feeling small and trapped and very alone.

But a moment later, a warm prickle of awareness on my skin reminds me I'm not entirely alone. I look up and see Dom's projection seated on the floor just across the little room from me.

I'm not sure what Dom saw of the last few hours. Most of it, I hope. I'm so exhausted from the shock that I don't think I can recount it all right now.

"Amos was right there," I say, dazed. "Just a few car lengths away from me."

"I saw him," says Dom. "It's fortunate that Naoto was there. He seems to know what he's doing."

I shiver. "I hope so."

The lights go out. The entry wall behind me pushes against my back, and I jump to my feet in alarm.

I sigh in relief as Naoto's small figure appears in the opening, silhouetted against the light of the *hondo* outside. He's changed into his Buddhist monk robes. He steps inside, and a rush of air escapes the room as the wall closes behind him. The bright lights switch on. I glance at the place Dom was just sitting, but he's disappeared again.

"Sorry I startled you," says Naoto. "I spend so much time in here that I didn't even think about the lights."

"You have to spend a lot of time in here?"

Naoto shrugs. "It's convenient as a command and control station. Small, well-hidden, easy to secure."

He sits on the floor and presses something concealed at his waist, under his robes. The bright lights dim, and all four walls of the room light up with a mosaic of two-dimensional projections.

Naoto points at a video feed projected on the broad wall. It drifts toward us. I kneel on the floor beside him, examining what appears to be a satellite view of my house on Skyline Boulevard. Naoto zooms in, and the aerial view drops through the canopy of the trees, showing the stone bench by my driveway. Partially obscured by the shadows behind the bench stands a man in a bulky hoodie and baseball cap, shifting slowly from foot to foot.

"Is that Amos?" I say, my hand moving involuntarily to my throat.

"No," says Naoto. "He'll be too smart for that. Still, we know you can't go back there."

"How do you have a live video feed of my house?" I say suspiciously.

He zooms out to the satellite view again and indicates the top of one of the redwood trees.

"Bird's-eye view."

A hazy memory returns of the last night I spent with Owen. I remember our goodbye kiss at my front door, and the look on his face when he spotted a black box in the trees above my house. I'd completely forgotten, in the chaos of everything that followed.

"Man," I shake my head, unsure whether to be grateful or furious that someone has been watching over me all this time. "I love my trees, but between the stalkers and the cameras ..." My hand flies to my mouth at a sudden horrible realization. "Wait. Do you have a camera at my parents' house? Is there—"

"Yep," says Naoto, switching to another video feed and pointing out another figure hiding in the back yard at my parents' house.

I reach for my smartcom, overcome by the urgent need to confirm that Mom and Dad are safe.

Naoto stops me with a gesture. "Don't. They still think you're at Yosemite. If you call, you're just going to worry them. Let's keep things simple. I've called in bodyguards for your family members for now. I don't think the Stewards are going to make a move on them."

"But they need to be warned! They could be kidnapped or ..." I don't finish my thought, not wanting to voice my fear that they could end up like Tomo.

Naoto shakes his head. "Your parents don't know anything useful to the Stewards. It's you they want."

"Comforting thought," I say grimly. "Especially now that I'm trapped in here with nowhere to go."

"We're working on that," he says, poring over several projections floating before him.

I look over Naoto's shoulder, doing my best to distract myself from my rising panic. "What exactly are we looking at here?" I say.

Naoto points to a map of the Bay Area covered in slowly-moving dots. He says, "These are pedestrians and vehicles that our traffic analysis suggests are performing sweeping and patrolling maneuvers. The blue ones have been there for at least six hours. The red ones have just become active within the last two."

"There are a lot more red ones," I say.

"That means Amos' people have deployed new surveillance resources in the area," says Naoto. "They may not know our precise location yet, but they know our general whereabouts."

I try to remain calm. "This is probably naïve," I say. "But can't we just call the police?"

Naoto shakes his head. "I wouldn't advise it. Not until we know who we're dealing with and what they want. Amos doesn't work alone. He could have connections anywhere. And if anyone's likely to be working for the dark side, it's the government."

I roll my eyes. "You sound like my Uncle Frank."

"Your Uncle Frank is a smart guy," Naoto says, absorbed in his visual overlay.

I watch him in silence until, a few minutes later, Falsens' stout projection shows up.

"Miss Bridges," says Falsens. "I have an update on your investigation request."

"Did you find Amos?" I say hopefully.

"Unfortunately, I am currently unable to locate Amos Eckerd," says Falsens, his androgynous voice slowly verging on feminine. "A construction crew near the point of your rendezvous with Mr. Kimura disconnected all our concealed monitors along a quarter-mile stretch of the freeway minutes after we captured Eckerd's image. This is unlikely to have been a coincidence.

"Currently, all of my online monitoring networks are searching for Eckerd. I will of course report to you as soon as I have further information concerning his whereabouts."

"Damn," I say, disturbed by the idea that Amos could be anywhere out there now.

"I apologize for this disappointing news," says Falsens. "However, I am happy to report that I have found a new lead regarding Amos Eckerd's possible involvement in the Augur spliner malfunction.

"A review of the public records from Zeke Eckerd's plea bargain showed that Augur's IT department recovered a cached copy of the virus responsible for the malfunction. I obtained a copy myself and ran an analysis of the coding style in an attempt to identify the author, which turned up an almost ninety-eight percent match to the coding style of the public identity Didactix."

"No way," I say. "I know Didactix. Well, I mean, he's an acquaintance in *Temenos*. But his identity's reputation speaks for itself. He would never write something like that. And if he did, he'd be smart enough to disguise it."

"I was suspicious of the match as well," says Falsens. "Even comparisons of code samples known to belong to the same coder typically have no better than an eighty-five percent match.

"Nonetheless, I met with Didactix to show him the results of the code analysis. He was quite upset to be implicated in the attack, both because of the death involved and because of the poor quality of the virus code. He claims to know nothing about it, and in his defense he showed me several examples of code recovered from recent data corruption attacks. Many of the code samples match the coding styles of public identities who, like him, have no apparent motive to develop such code.

"Didactix, along with several other of the implicated coders, have offered their services pro bono to help track down the actual creator of the virus."

"Well, that's nice of them," I say. "But are we really likely to learn anything from that? Anyone might have been hired to write that virus, and they could have done so without knowing a thing about who was going to use it, in the end."

"Didactix seems to have something larger in mind than tracking down the coder of this particular virus," says Falsens. "He thinks that these mimicked coding styles could point to a single architect behind a number of recent cyberterrorist attacks."

"You're saying he thinks he can find a way to implicate the Church of the True Cross?" I say.

"Per the confidentiality terms of our agreement, I did not mention the Church of the True Cross or Amos Eckerd. Didactix only knows what's on the public record," says Falsens.

"I don't like it," I say. "Didactix has no idea what he's getting himself into."

"Well, as I made no formal arrangement with Didactix, neither you nor I will be held liable for the outcome," says Falsens.

"That's not my point! What—"

"Miss Bridges," Falsens interjects. "I think you underestimate Didactix's ability to take care of himself. He is a well-connected, high-reputation identity. My own analysis of his public social network suggests a high probability that he is part of the Anonymous Collective."

"Even the Collective hasn't managed to identify the people behind these attacks so far," I say.

"They haven't had any real motivation to do so," says Falsens. "Their political leanings tend to be anarchic. They typically see large-scale attacks as beneficial in the long run, as they produce adaptive innovations that increase overall system security."

"So why would they want to help with this now?" I say.

"Because now it's personal," says Falsens.

"I really don't think it's a good idea to get them involved," I say. "They're totally unpredictable."

"I'm afraid it's too late for that," says Falsens. "Based on public chatter I picked up, Didactix had the Collective engaged before my interview with him was even complete.

"What I came to tell you is that the Anonymous Collective has identified a section of obfuscated code in the Augur spliner virus that seems to be shared in common with a number of viruses that have been used in attacks linked to the Church of the True Cross.

"The purpose of this obfuscated code is to listen on a network node for any activity containing data that matches an encrypted dataset stored within the virus. A data match triggers programs that produce catastrophic system failure on any hardware that might relay or cache the matched data, destroying the data as well as the virus itself.

"Essentially, the virus is designed to stop whatever this dataset is from entering or being accessed over networked systems."

A horrible realization washes over me. Slowly, I say, "I tried to upload some files to the alternet from my smartcom while I was in the spliner. That must have triggered the virus."

"What files were these?" says Falsens.

I hesitate, wondering whether I should trust Falsens and Naoto with this. But for all practical purposes, my life is already in their hands. And, anyway, I can't see how I'm going to figure out what to do with Tomo's storage drive without their help.

"Tomo Yoshimoto left me a storage drive in his will, along with a bonsai tree in his office," I say. "His sister Ayame gave me the storage drive after he died. That drive was destroyed during the spliner malfunction, but I found another copy hidden in his bonsai tree. That's the drive I have with me now.

"Ayame told me the information on the storage drive was sensitive in some way, and only to discuss it with someone I trust. But I … I didn't think about that when I sent the files off for translation."

"A significant oversight," Falsens says bluntly.

I know he's right. A lump rises in my throat, but I blink back my tears.

He continues, "Because the dataset shared by these viruses is encrypted, it is virtually impossible to recover the data, even if the virus is itself recovered after an attack. This offers some security to the creator of the virus—the Anonymous Collective can't tell what data the virus is designed to destroy.

"However, the Anonymous Collective finds it interesting that the encrypted dataset is identical, byte for byte, from one virus to the next. A more secure method might have been to encrypt the dataset with a different key in each virus. Given how much trouble the virus designer has already taken to protect its identity—using code style matching, obfuscating the triggering function, designing the code to essentially self-destruct—it seems like a major oversight to leave evidence that all these different viruses are linked.

"This might mean that the program designer does not know what the dataset contains, only what the encrypted data looks like. It is possible that the program might not even recognize the data if it is in its unencrypted form, or if it is encrypted using a different key."

"But that doesn't make sense," I say. "The files aren't encrypted. When I tried viewing the drive contents the first time in the spliner, the files opened right up on my smartcom, no authentication or decryption required."

"That is interesting," says Falsens. "May I examine the files?"

"Are you sure you want to risk it?" I say.

"I will send a hardware analysis program to Naoto's smartcom," says Falsens. "None of the data on the drive will itself be transferred to me. I will only see the analysis summary."

I hand the storage drive over to Naoto, who plugs it into a port on his smartcom. A moment later, the analysis summary pops up.

"Ah," Falsens and Naoto say in unison.

"What?" I say.

Falsens explains, "The storage drive you have there is designed to mimic the form factor of a standard storage drive that you might purchase from any office supply store. But the electrical impedance of the drive's surface ceramic indicates the presence of a biomaterial. This is common in devices that perform biometric authentication. This drive seems to have been programmed to decrypt its contents only when you are the last person to touch it, and to re-encrypt the contents with a key contained within the un-encrypted data when it changes hands.

"Naoto, if you would confirm our hypothesis ..."

Naoto swipes a few controls on his projection. A filesystem browser opens up displaying the message, "Device corrupted. Eject or reformat?"

Naoto pops the drive out of his smartcom and hands it back to me. I plug it in to my smartcom. My filesystem browser opens to reveal neat columns of files and folders, as it did for me in the spliner.

"Very interesting," says Falsens. "Whoever prepared this drive wanted to make very sure that only you could access its contents."

"But why?" I say.

"I am unable to determine that based on the current information. Do you know what is on the drive?" says Falsens.

"Tomo's sister told me it's the manuscript for a book about creation myths, but I wasn't able to decipher any of it before the spliner malfunction," I say.

Falsens says, "I would need to run an analysis of the drive's contents to determine why such information may be sensitive in nature. We should now assume, however, that Amos knows you are the only person able to view this data. He has gone to quite a lot of trouble to ensure you cannot spread it widely by electronic means, and he now appears to be systematically attempting to eliminate the threat posed by you or anyone else who has seen the data."

"So you can't even look at this thing without becoming a target," I say.

"Hmm," says Naoto. "Now there's an interesting idea."

I raise an eyebrow. "Interesting how?"

Naoto says, "We've been trying to figure out how we're going to get you out of here, with these ground operatives crawling all over the place. What we could really use is a good old-fashioned diversion."

"So ...?" I say.

"So, what if everyone becomes a target, all at once?" says Naoto. "As far as Amos' people know, you're the only one alive who knows what's on that drive, so they're focusing all their efforts on you. But what if everyone knew what's on that drive? The Stewards can't pick off everyone, at least not all at once."

"Bad idea," I say. "The only way to get the information to any significant number of people is to get it out on the alternet. We've already seen what happens when you try to do that. I don't think the world will appreciate it if we trigger a cascading alternet infrastructure meltdown trying to broadcast this."

"The world might not appreciate it," says Naoto. "But I think we know just the people who would."

△▽△

Just as Naoto had anticipated they would, the Anonymous Collective has no qualms about risking the stability of the global alternet infrastructure in an effort to propagate information that someone wants desperately to keep secret.

Within an hour, Falsens' projection returns to deliver the news. "The Collective proposes a rather straightforward distribution method. We will send encrypted video streams of the files, recorded from cameras at your current location, to a small network of crowdsourced transcription services, which will in turn send encrypted video streams of the transcribed content to a second-degree network, and so on. The electronic format of the data will change from point to point. The first group of transcribers will upload their transcriptions to a collection of video streaming server farms located in the South Bay. This is close enough to your actual location not to be suspicious, but far enough away that we'll hopefully clear out some of the operatives in our neighborhood.

"The Anonymous Collective will amplify the story that these video streams are a sensitive data leak. This should drive traffic to the video streams and generate activity in conspiracy theory and rumor forums. Eventually, mainstream media outlets will pick up the story, as well.

"The Collective anticipates, based on prior leak campaigns they've orchestrated, that the servers hosting the first group of video streams will be taken offline by the Stewards within hours. When fifty percent of those servers go down, this will trigger the second-degree transcription network to upload their own slightly modified copies of the video streams. The rolling leaks should continue for several hours—possibly more if the story gains traction among the general public and we see small-scale data caching."

"There could be so much system damage from that," I protest. "People could even be killed. If key alternet nodes go offline, autopilot capabilities and emergency services and so many other systems could be disrupted. It's impossible to predict what sort of chaos it might create."

Falsens says, "The Collective believes the architect of these viruses is most likely unwilling to trigger widespread infrastructure damage if the information leak is that widespread. It's a catch-22. If they don't destroy the infrastructure hosting the leaked information, the information gets out. If they do destroy the infrastructure, they elevate the perceived significance of the information, heightening public interest and risking scrutiny that might reveal their identity. Either way, they're going to be scrambling for at least a few hours to contain the leak with backchannel methods before they realize the full scale of the leak.

"All the Collective needs now to execute the proposed leak is the contents of your storage drive. Do you wish to proceed?"

I rake my fingers through my hair. "I don't know. I don't know. How can the Collective be sure no one else will get hurt?"

"They cannot be sure," Falsens says matter-of-factly. "You must decide what risks you're willing to take."

Falsens' words hit me hard. How can I begin to guess what risks are worth taking to discover why Tomo left the storage drive to me? How many more people am I willing to sacrifice to find out? I have no idea what's on this drive or why the Stewards care so much about it.

But I'm sure Tomo left me this storage drive for a good reason. It must be important. He went to great lengths to make sure only I can access its contents. I feel responsible now for keeping it out of the hands of those who want to destroy it.

And I can't deny that some part of me longs to strike back at the Stewards, after what they did to Tomo. To Owen. Even to Zeke, though I hate to admit that I care about what's happened to him.

"The decision is yours," says Falsens.

I clench my jaw. "All right," I say. "Let's do it."

△▽△

Naoto slips out of the safe room in head-to-toe night camouflage to gather the cameras we need from the perimeter security system of the church.

"Doesn't that sort of undermine the whole idea of perimeter security?" I'd asked before he left.

"We'll have to risk creating these blind spots," he'd said. "Even the same-day delivery services won't be able to get us the cameras we need fast enough. Just keep an eye out on the video feeds I showed you. Alert me on the shared channel if you see anything suspicious."

Fortunately, Naoto returns with the cameras without incident. He sets up our makeshift video recording studio in the little room where we're hiding behind the altar. I write a script to display each file on the storage drive in succession: seven different projections for the seven different cameras Naoto collected from the church exterior. By my calculation, the roughly ten thousand pages of documents and images on the drive will take nine minutes to record and convert into an encrypted video stream, and another five minutes to upload to the servers of the human transcription services the collective has proposed for the first wave of the leak.

Naoto dims the lights so the recording can begin.

"Here goes nothing," I say.

I hit the execute button on my script. On the blank grey wall before us, thousands of images flash by in rapid succession, three per second per camera. I feel an occasional flicker of recognition as something slips by in the mesmerizing stream of images. When the recording concludes and the lights come on again, I feel a bit dazed, like my brain just drank from a firehose.

"Encrypting now," says Naoto.

I chew my lip anxiously. "It's not too late to stop this," I say, watching the progress bar on the encryption approaching completion.

"Look, Emmie," says Naoto. "I don't want to scare you, but we don't have a lot of options right now. Why don't we just trust that the collective knows what it's doing?"

"Seems like a pretty big leap of faith," I say.

The progress bar finishes. An upload confirmation prompt appears before me. Naoto looks at me and says, "Falsens' protocol. You've got to do the honors."

There's no turning back once I push that button. Whatever the consequences, I'm fully responsible. I take a deep breath and initiate the upload.

△▽△

Fifteen minutes later, alternet forums are buzzing with news of the leak. Naoto's surveillance monitors show that ground operatives scattered throughout the Bay Area are converging around the server farm hosting the first video stream.

"We're going to leave through the rear fire exit," says Naoto. "We have to assume that all wireless communications may attract attention, so I'm going to need you to leave all your immergers, smartcom, everything with wireless capability, behind in the safe room.

"Once we're on the road, there will be time to decide where best to take you."

There's only one place I want to go. "Naoto," I say. "Can you take me to Amaterasu?"

Naoto nods. Just before I remove my immerger glasses to place in the bag Naoto's holding out to collect them from me, Falsens' projection appears.

Officiously, he says, "Of course, I will need your payment authorization first."

I wonder whether there will be anything left in my checking account by the time this is all over, but I wave my hand in assent.

△▽△

Fortunately, no cops or Steward operatives intercept us as we speed through the streets of downtown Oakland and weave through the midnight traffic on the freeway. Twenty minutes later, we arrive at the Oakland Business Jet Center. Naoto points to a small private jet parked ahead of us on the tarmac.

"That's us," he says. He starts to push open his door, then stops. Two men in dark uniforms have just walked onto the tarmac near the jet. Naoto swears under his breath.

"What's wrong?" I say.

"Someone's called in TSA screeners," says Naoto. "I'm sure it wasn't Falsens. He uses private contractors for that."

I watch the men walk to the boarding stairs near the cockpit of our ride.

"Could the TSA be working for Amos?" I say.

"Could be," says Naoto. "But even if they're not, any body scans they take could end up somewhere Amos can find them. That would make it hard to cover our tracks."

Naoto waits a moment, then says sharply, "Falsens? Are you paying attention?"

"I am aware of the screener issue at the jetport, Mr. Kimura," Falsens says curtly. "Please hold for further instructions."

I wipe my sweaty palms on my jeans, watching the TSA agents amble back and forth in front of the boarding stairs, swinging their scanner wands beside them.

"Mr. Kimura, can you confirm that the TSA agents are wearing audiovisual sensory augmentation devices?" says Falsens.

Naoto squints out into the darkness. The TSA agents stand near the edge of a pool of runway lamplight, making it difficult to see them. I peer out, then point. "There," I say. "The guy on the left just made that gesture." I imitate it. "He's listening to music. He's got earbuds on, at least."

"And the other agent?" says Falsens.

"Can't see him," says Naoto. "It's too dark."

"Miss Bridges," says Falsens. "I'm afraid that in order to get you onto that plane, we're going to have to take somewhat of a risk. Statistically speaking, there is a seventy-one percent chance that the first TSA agent is wearing some kind of sensory augmentation equipment. The second agent, who appears to be listening to music through auditory immergers, is more than ninety-five percent likely to be wearing visual immergers of some kind as well.

"In the event that both agents are in fact equipped with audiovisual sensory augmentation susceptible to the remote sensory projection program that I will provide to Mr. Kimura for this operation, your boarding process should be quite straightforward. They will never see you pass. However, in the event that one or both of the agents is entirely without audiovisual sensory augmentation, you will need to authorize Mr. Kimura to forcibly incapacitate both agents."

I turn a questioning look at Naoto. He taps something concealed near his hip.

"Is that a gun?" I say.

Naoto shakes his head. "No. Tranquilizer."

A liability waiver prompt appears on the vehicle dashboard display, because I'm no longer equipped with my own immerger glasses.

I hesitate. "You're definitely not going to kill anyone?" I say to Naoto.

"Scout's honor," he says. "And, anyway, Falsens would have you sign a different authorization for that."

I sigh and press my thumb to the dashboard to sign the waiver.

"Stay in here until I say otherwise," says Naoto. "I'll be on the car audio channel if you need me."

Naoto steps out of the car and walks casually toward the TSA agents. I watch him offer each of them a cigarette from a pack he produces from his jacket pocket. One man accepts, while the other waves him off. Naoto and the smoker stand to the side chatting for a few minutes. Afterwards, Naoto steps toward the other agent and claps him on the shoulder before walking off to the nearby private charter terminal.

"Both of them are wearing immergers," Naoto says through the car speakers.

"Should I get out of the car?" I say.

"Not yet," he says. "Costume change."

Less than a minute later, Naoto re-emerges from the terminal wearing a pilot's uniform, carrying a small briefcase, and looking about six inches taller and thirty pounds heavier.

"How do you *do* that?" I say, staring at him in disbelief as he approaches the plane again. I think I see Naoto wink at me across the tarmac.

He stops before the TSA agents and chats with them as they pat him down and take a full body scan, followed by a scan of his briefcase. They wave him aboard.

"Wait for it," says Naoto's voice on the car speakers.

I watch the two TSA agents continue their wand routine, this time with an unseen subject. They're apparently under the influence of Falsens' interference projection program.

"How do you *do* that?" I say again, this time to Falsens. Again, my question goes unanswered.

"Okay," says Naoto, "Just walk around behind the TSA agents. Don't bump into them." When I hesitate, Naoto urges, "Quickly, Emmie. Trust me."

I steel myself, open the passenger door slowly, and step out of the car. The door closes automatically and silently behind me. I hurry across the open tarmac toward the airplane, painfully aware of my sneakers thudding softly on the pavement and my long shadow pointing like an arrow straight ahead of me. It seems impossible that the TSA agents won't see or hear me.

But the agents never even look my way as I creep past them and climb as quietly as I can up the boarding stairs onto the plane.

"Have a nice flight, ma'am," says one of the agents. I wheel around in surprise, almost tripping back down the stairs. Naoto's instantly behind me, one arm around my waist, another covering my mouth. My pulse races as I stare down at the agents. They're facing away from me, one of them waving at the empty space before him. I relax, realizing he was speaking to whatever imaginary person Falsens projected for them.

"Get in the back and sit down," Naoto whispers in my ear.

He pulls me back into the cabin and closes the hatch. I grip the arm of the nearest seat and collapse into it.

△▽△

We're a few miles out over the Pacific when Naoto re-emerges from the cockpit, carrying his briefcase. He sits down in one of the swiveling leather recliners across from me.

"Who's flying the plane?" I ask.

"Falsens, for now," says Naoto. "Do you think you can sleep? It's about ten hours to Japan."

"I don't think so," I say. I still haven't come down from all the adrenaline that's been pumping through me for the last several hours. "I'm totally wired."

"Here," says Naoto, climbing out of his seat to open a small refrigeration panel mounted on the cabin wall. He pours me a double whisky and sets it down on the table beside me. "That might help."

I pick up the whisky, take a long swallow, and promptly start coughing. Naoto grins. Through watery eyes, I gasp, "Thanks."

Naoto says, "I'm going to stay up there in the cockpit. Falsens and I need to work out some of our ground logistics, and I want to stay at the controls in case we need to switch out of autopilot."

"Do you think something might ...?"

"Nope. I don't think anything's going to happen. Just being careful."

He turns to leave, but I stop him. "Hey. If it's not a security hazard now, do you have any immergers I could borrow to surf the alternet? Helps me get to sleep."

"Oh, yes. Forgot to mention." Naoto points to the briefcase he set down on the floor beside me. "Falsens left some for you in there."

I pop open the briefcase and discover a full set of top-of-the-line immerger gear.

"Falsens, you're the best," I say, holding up the immerger glasses.

"Thank you, Miss Bridges," Falsens says over the airplane intercom. "I hope you will say so in your review."

Naoto returns to the cockpit, and I dress myself in my new immergers. After a few minutes configuring interface preferences and installing essential tools, I flip on a visual overlay and start monitoring alternet feeds for news on the leak.

Less than an hour has passed since I hit the upload button when I come across the first chatter about the leak. As the Anonymous Collective predicted, a number of server farms hosting the first wave of leaked video went offline under mysterious circumstances. This automatically triggered the spread of the leak to the second-degree servers.

As I pore over the live updates on my feeds, I start mentally cheering on the Anonymous Collective as their plan plays out. Faster than the video streams can disappear, several high-reputation alternet identities, repaying or earning the favor of the Anonymous Collective, direct their followers to the content with pointed commentary about the exceptional speed with which the content is spreading and disappearing. Identities inclined to conspiracy theories gamely pick up the story and amplify it, speculating about the purpose of the leak and the significance of the covert attempts to suppress it.

The video hosting providers, perplexed by the rolling outages and harassed by their users, begin posting detailed updates about the attacks on their outage status pages. Mainstream news outlets sensationalize the story and run alternet security ads promoting one-day-only product discounts.

Mere minutes after the mainstream media picks up the story about the video server outages, an armageddon virus takes a large alternet currency exchange offline. This captures the attention of most commentators and concludes this particular beat of the news cycle. The currency exchange meltdown rekindles my fears about the ripple effects of the leak I've started.

Although the mainstream news moves on quickly, the attention of the conspiracy theorists proves tenacious. The conspiracy theorists dub the leaked content the World Tree Codex, based on the recurring symbolic references in the texts it contains. By the time the story about the currency exchange has subsided, conspiracy forum discussions have already coalesced around a few distinct narratives about the leaked content.

I skim comments eagerly. At first, I'm hopeful that among all these strangers on the alternet, one might actually discern the meaning of Tomo's storage drive. As I read deeper, though, my hope fades. Depending on the commenter, the Codex proves the extraterrestrial origin of life on Earth, provides the precise location of the lost continent of Atlantis, confirms once and for all the date and time of the apocalypse, expresses the mathematical formula reconciling quantum and relativity theory, or encodes the master plan of the Freemasons to consolidate control over world governments. Maybe this isn't the best place to look for information.

The catchy new World Tree Codex name seems to revive interest from the mainstream news outlets, though. They re-sensationalize the World Tree Codex story with the help of panels of renowned author-scholars from a variety of disciplines. I'm amazed and a bit confounded by the fact that all these panelists have, most fortuitously, and seemingly only moments earlier, released bestsellers in the conspiracy non-fiction genre.

Wholly-owned subsidiary news outlets, to capitalize on the momentary surge of popular interest in the World Tree Codex story, produce their own panels of even more renowned author-scholars. These experts cast aspersions on the deplorable fabulists on the nominally competing news outlets, while coincidentally pitching their own newly-released bestsellers.

By the time I've finished my whisky, over sixteen hundred "expert" contributors have synthesized their speculations into the definitive wiki article on the World Tree Codex. The wiki article explains that the leaked content was part of a hoax perpetrated by a cabal of alternet security consultants to spur product sales. Falsens is implicated in the hoax, although a footnote in the wiki concedes that this is disputed. The wiki article directs readers who wish to view the hoax videos and the virus code that caused the cascading server outages to an alternet domain hosted offshore at an unknown, secure location operated by the Anonymous Collective.

Eventually, the hits on my feed reader slow as the World Tree Codex story fades into the distant past of the alternet's memory. I'm only mildly surprised by the speed with which it all unfolded.

Over our shared channel, I say to Naoto, "Thousands of comments and hours of news outlet discussion, and still I have absolutely no idea what the World Tree

Codex is about. Unless Midori was really writing a book about aliens or telepathy or something."

"I think that commenter going on about the JFK prophecy might have been on to something," Naoto offers.

I roll my eyes.

INTO THE MOUNTAINS

I DRIFT IN AND OUT of sleep for the next several hours, until Naoto says on our shared channel, "We'll be landing soon, Emmie."

I blink sleepily and stretch. Leaning over the padded arm of my recliner, I peer out the window. The sky above is dark, but far below, the bright lights of urban sprawl illuminate broad valleys enclosed by the dark folds of forested mountains. I can't help thinking how delighted Owen would have been to look down on this foreign landscape, anticipating a travel adventure. We had talked many times about taking a trip to Japan together, but we never got around to it. I was always too busy with work.

I push down the guilt aroused by this memory. "Where are we?" I say.

"We're passing over the Kansei region of southern Japan," says Naoto. "We're going to land at the Itami airport."

I pull up a map on my visual overlay to orient myself to the new location. After a few attempts to guess the correct spelling of Enryaku-ji, I locate the temple where we're meeting Amaterasu. It's on Mount Hiei, a three-hour drive northeast from the Itami airport, according to my navigation system.

"We can't land any closer?" I say, the freeway encounter with Amos still fresh in my memory.

"Sorry. Falsens doesn't have any landing strips in the mountains," says Naoto.

"What are we going to do about the Japanese—whatever they've got. TSA? Immigration officers?"

Naoto laughs. "The Japanese and their immergers are inseparable. As long as we have Falsens' remote sensory projection program running, you'll be invisible to nearly everyone."

Naoto's right. We easily sidestep one airport security checkpoint after another. I watch in amazement as security personnel wave through the invisible young woman that Falsens seamlessly integrates into their experience while erasing their perception of me. I keep up a near-constant stream of pestering trying to get Falsens to tell me where he acquired such tech, but he remains tight-lipped on this topic.

An autopiloted car picks us up at the curb outside arrivals, and Naoto takes the wheel. I settle into the passenger seat and gaze out the window as we race through the tangle of narrow highways and raised train tracks. The concrete jungle near the airport thins a bit as we cross the river into Osaka and turn north into a more human-scale landscape of residential neighborhoods.

The first light of dawn glows on the eastern horizon, illuminating a dark green ridge of low mountains ahead. After an hour's drive, we pass under raised train tracks. Naoto slows as the road narrows. Sidewalks separated from the road by low barriers press in on both sides of the car, and pedestrians walk by an arm's length from my window. Supermarkets open their doors, and window shades slide open on the second floors of houses facing the road. A few industrious gardeners are already at work tending patches of greenery in the alleyways between buildings.

The road passes beneath a series of brightly painted *torii* archways and through intersections marked by small stone pagodas, reminiscent of the entryways to subdomains in Tomo's *Kaisei.* As I watch the sunrise over the mountain range we're approaching, I experience for the first time in many months a true sense of peace. I wonder whether Tomo and Midori may have passed through this landscape, too.

A few miles outside Osaka, the road enters a wood at the foot of Mount Hiei and begins a winding ascent toward the summit. The road ends at a deserted parking lot beside a bus stop.

"Is it safe to go out?" I say.

"Falsens and I are checking," says Naoto, flipping through visual overlays so quickly that I can't determine what he's looking at. "The marathon monks do a good job maintaining a secure perimeter here. But better safe than sorry."

"Marathon monks?" I say curiously. Naoto doesn't seem to hear me, but I ask another question anyway. "What do a bunch of monks need perimeter security for? Are they afraid of the Church of the True Cross?"

"No, not officially," says Naoto. "Or, at least, not specifically. It's more like tradition. A long time ago, there was a lot of violence in this area. Competing monastic orders, local political squabbles, lots of warrior monks from different sects attacking each other."

"Warrior monks? I thought Buddhists were non-violent," I say.

"No religion's exempt from extremism. Even Buddhism," says Naoto. He takes a final look at a heat map of the surrounding woods before saying, "Okay. Follow me."

We exit the car. I follow close at Naoto's side as he leads me up a footpath into the temple complex. We pass a large pagoda with a curving slate-blue roof supported by wooden pillars and carved walls painted brightly in red, white, black, and gold; a smaller pagoda housing an enormous bell; and a series of increasingly ornate halls. Naoto turns off the footpath to climb a stone staircase leading to a two-story pagoda that forms an enormous gate into a tall stand of cedars. We pass through the gate and look down another staircase, which leads to a large temple fronted by a long colonnade.

We hurry down the stairs to the red wooden doors at the center of the colonnade. Naoto knocks three times on the door.

"The temple doesn't open to visitors for another few hours," he says. "Amaterasu sent a guide to meet us."

A moment later, the doors swing out with a creak to reveal a smiling young woman, head shaved, robed in orange. She bows to us and says something to Naoto in Japanese.

"She's one of the nuns here," Naoto says to me. "She says Amaterasu is waiting for us in the main hall. She'll take us to her."

We follow the young nun across a small courtyard shaded by flowering trees. Before us stands the enormous main temple, raised up on a foundation of short red columns. A flight of stone steps leads to a dark, carved wooden door, framed on either side by panels of wood latticework.

The nun opens the door for us and ushers us across the threshold. She bows to us in farewell and closes the heavy doors behind us.

I follow Naoto's lead and remove my shoes before walking with him into the heart of the temple. We enter the great hall. A spicy smell of wood and incense pervades the dimly-lit space. Dark, gleaming pillars of polished cedar rise to a beautiful wooden ceiling traversed by carved crossbeams. The pillars form a central aisle leading to the main shrine.

We walk in sock feet along the honey-colored wooden floor until we reach the shrine. A gleaming gold Buddha sits before a backdrop of violet, red, and green. Before the Buddha, three square paper lamps glow softly.

"The lamplights of eternity," Naoto whispers, bowing toward the shrine. "They've been burning for over twelve hundred years."

I glance at him in surprise. But before I can ask how anyone could know that for sure, a reedy voice speaks from the shadows beside the shrine.

"Naoto-san."

I turn to see a tiny old woman in orange robes approaching, her shaved head gleaming in the lamplight.

"Amaterasu Roshi," says Naoto, bowing solemnly. "I'm glad to see you fully recovered."

The woman bows in return, her eyes twinkling. She thinks for a long moment before saying in clear but somewhat halting English, "Perhaps my work here is not yet complete." She turns to me next, bowing. "And Emmie-san. How pleased I am to see you again."

I blink at the unexpected phrasing. See me again? Perhaps she misspoke. I bow awkwardly and say, "Thank you. It's, ah … so nice to meet you, too. Thank you for agreeing to see me."

"Yes, yes," says Amaterasu. She switches to Japanese, continuing to speak to me but glancing at Naoto, who translates, "The roshi apologizes but asks if you would mind having me translate. She feels her English slipping through her fingers as she gets older."

"Of course, that's fine," I say. "I'm sorry I can't speak even a little Japanese."

Amaterasu chuckles. Naoto translates as she says, "We are so many little islands."

I have no idea what might be the appropriate response to this, but Amaterasu saves me the trouble by saying, through Naoto, "Come, let us talk together a while, before it is too late."

"Too late for what?" I say, alarmed.

"You see I am not getting any younger," says Amaterasu.

△▽△

Amaterasu leads me and Naoto into one of the galleries off the great hall. A series of dark wooden doors line the gallery, some open to reveal smaller shrines and rooms beyond. Amaterasu stops before one closed door, which Naoto rolls open to reveal a small, unfurnished room with smooth wooden floorboards covered by a woven tatami mat. Morning light filters through translucent paper screens covering tall windows.

Amaterasu sits down on the tatami mat and indicates that we should do the same. She smiles at me, and Naoto translates as she says, "Emmie-san, can you tell me about the first time you met Tomo Yoshimoto?"

I nod, remembering that Ayame's interview with Amaterasu started in a similar way. I wonder why this memory interests Amaterasu. I say, "It was … almost two years ago, now. We met at an Indian restaurant in Berkeley. Saffron. You know, I didn't even think about it at the time, but that's my favorite restaurant. I have no idea how Tomo found that out.

"Well, anyway, I was so nervous when I saw him come in, I nearly knocked over the dinner table." I laugh at the mortifying memory. "It was awful. But Tomo was really nice about it. He made it seem really funny, and it sort of broke the ice. I practically forgot how embarrassed I was. Well, almost.

"I remember that the waiter had to come back like five times to take our order, because neither of us looked at the menu. There seemed to be so much to talk about. I had so many questions I wanted to ask him. Here was the man who had created *Kaisei*, the most beautiful place I'd ever seen. Maybe the most beautiful place I'll ever see. I wanted to know everything, about where his ideas came from, the techniques he had used … It was amazing to talk with him about it all, even though I think I'd watched every single documentary about him and every interview he ever gave a million times before.

"He had a lot of questions about me, too, about how I'd grown up, and what made me want to become a designer. He was especially interested in my *Eden* domain. That was what made him want to meet me in the first place. I was really flattered by that. He asked me a lot of questions, about where the ideas for the content had come from, lots of little details. I remember thinking how I couldn't wait to tell Owen that Tomo had loved all the environment physics he'd programmed …" My voice catches at the thought of Owen. I swallow and blink back tears, then give Amaterasu a small smile. "That was the day he asked me to join Augur. Both of us, actually, me and Owen. One of the best days of my life."

Amaterasu has been watching me closely as I speak. Now she nods and says smoothly, with no trace of the halting accent she had just a moment ago, "Yes. It was one of the best days of Tomo's life, too."

I blink, then gape as Amaterasu's ancient face transforms, years melting away until she appears to be a woman in the prime of life. Shocked, I turn to Naoto for some explanation. He inclines his head toward Amaterasu, grinning as he says, "You see I learned from the best."

"What—What is this?" I say, looking from Naoto to Amaterasu. "What's going on?"

"We've set up a patrol of the perimeter," Amaterasu says to Naoto. "Perhaps you can join the others for a while? We will need some time alone together."

Naoto bows deeply to Amaterasu and slips out of the room.

"I know this must seem a bit confusing," Amaterasu says to me.

"Yeah. A bit," I say, unable to conceal my annoyance.

Amaterasu chuckles. She says, "I wondered if Tomo might have made a mistake. But, no, you are so very like her."

"What are you talking about?" I say. "Like who?"

"Midori," says Amaterasu, eyeing me appraisingly. "You have the same restlessness, the same impatience."

I frown. "Can you blame me for being impatient?" I say. "There's someone after me. Someone who killed two people I loved very much, who's probably planning the same for me. I thought maybe you could help me. Now it looks like you're just playing games with me."

Amaterasu's expression turns serious. "I see how it may seem that way. But I needed to be certain it was you."

"What are you talking about?" I say, struggling to keep a level tone. "Who else would I be?"

Amaterasu raises a hand, emanating an authority that quiets me. "Listen," she says. "There is much to tell you, and the so-called Stewards could arrive at any time."

"You mean Amos' people?" I say.

"Yes," says Amaterasu. "The man who calls himself Amos Eckerd is one of them. I realized this too late, unfortunately. They, too, are learning the art of disguise.

"Amos came to visit me shortly after Tomo's death. He said he was Tomo's lawyer, and I believed him. Quite a charming man, I thought, actually. He seemed very interested in the temple here, and I showed him the grounds, the library, the temple of initiation. We had a long conversation about Buddhist philosophy. I should have been more on my guard. He must have been doing reconnaissance.

"He showed me Tomo's will and said that Tomo had asked me to return to his estate a collection of documents he had left in my care. That was when I first became suspicious. The wording of the will seemed a bit vague, as if Tomo himself wasn't sure what he had wanted me to return. Tomo was such a precise man. It didn't seem like him.

"I apologized to Amos and fell back on my cover, saying my memory had become so poor that I could not even remember what documents Tomo might have meant. But I invited Amos to look through the library for anything he thought might belong to Tomo's estate.

"I think Amos turned the pages of every book and looked into every corner of the library. But in the end he found nothing. He didn't know what he was looking for. So he left me his card and asked me to call if I remembered anything.

"The very day Amos left, I fell quite ill. I know now that he poisoned me. Clearly, I was not intended to survive. Of course, Amos did not realize who I was, just as I had not realized who he was.

"I had my suspicions about Tomo's death even before Amos arrived. After Amos left, I was nearly certain. But there was nothing to be done about it then. I imagined Tomo had been robbed of Midori's research and that I had the only remaining copy. All I could do was keep it safe and wait.

"When Tomo's sister came to see me, I knew she had Tomo's true instructions. Tomo was such a careful man. He had worked out every little detail of how the storage drive was to be conveyed to you at the safe house, who should be present, how the drive should be packaged—everything.

"He had reason to be cautious. In one of our last correspondences, he told me he had gathered new information that he wanted me to keep for him. He said he had encountered difficulties trying to back up the data, that copies would become corrupted, that he was unable to send the files to me electronically. He suspected that someone was trying to interfere with Midori's research.

"He knew about the protections at the monastery here. He had prepared a storage drive containing the data he wished to send me, and we arranged to use the Oakland temple as a drop site. I sent Naoto to retrieve the drive, but Amos intercepted Tomo first."

"Intercepted?" I say angrily. "Is that what you call being murdered?"

"I understand that Tomo's death was upsetting to you," Amaterasu says calmly. "But he understood the risk he was taking. He loved Midori, enough to risk his life to preserve the work that was so important to her. And he succeeded. He kept the documents safe for a very long time. Fifty years. Long enough to find you."

"But why would he take such a risk?" I say. "What did he want me to do with this information?"

Amaterasu looks at me curiously, then sweeps a searching gaze across the space behind me, like she's looking for someone in a crowd. I look over my shoulder uneasily, uncertain what she could possibly expect to find in this empty room.

"But the Artifex must have come to you by now," says Amaterasu, turning to me at last with a quizzical expression.

After all the surprises of the last twenty-four hours, I'm not sure why it surprises me that Amaterasu knows about Dom. "Who?" I say, wanting her to say more before I do.

"The Artifex," she says again. "Dom Artifex, isn't it?"

Warily, I say, "How do you know about him?"

"I have not known you long enough to be sure," says Amaterasu, "but I trust that Tomo did. He would have recognized the mark of the Artifex in you, just as I saw it in Midori. Otherwise he would not have left the storage drive to you."

"I don't understand," I say.

Amaterasu glances around the empty room once more, her expression reproachful, though I'm unsure why. "I'm sorry," she says. "It seems I've assumed too much. The Artifex has kept a great deal from you. Too much, I think. Is he here now?"

Puzzled, I say, "How could he be? There's like zero wireless coverage here. I haven't had a connection since we came onto the temple grounds."

Amaterasu shakes her head. "Perhaps he is the one playing games with you," she says. "Ah, well. He must have had his reasons. But the time has come for you to understand."

△▽△

I sit unseen beside Emmie on the tatami mat, troubled by the realization that Amaterasu is right. Misleading Emmie about my true nature for so long and concealing my purpose here is a cruel game. The truth is overdue.

"Call him," Amaterasu says to Emmie. "He has much to answer to."

"Call him?" says Emmie. "How? Like I said, there's no connection—"

"Just call him," says Amaterasu. "He must come to you."

"I don't understand," says Emmie.

"Like this, perhaps. 'Dom Artifex, show yourself!'" says Amaterasu, her voice resonant in the stillness of the room.

Amaterasu turns to Emmie expectantly. Emmie glances around the room with a bewildered expression. She clears her throat, then says uncertainly, "Dom Artifex … Show yourself."

I'd known that my ever more frequent intrusions into Emmie's awareness have been awakening her to my presence, but this time, for the first time, she summons me consciously. I feel the veil between us lifting. When Emmie sees me appear suddenly beside her, she gasps and scrambles away.

"How …?" she says.

I watch the confusion play out on Emmie's face as she grasps for some plausible explanation for my appearance here. She unconsciously touches the side of her face, checking whether she's forgotten she's wearing her immerger glasses, then remembering she left them in the car. She glances at the closed door, as if I might have slipped in silently while she wasn't looking. "No," she whispers. "That's not possible."

"Do you see him, then?" says Amaterasu.

Emmie turns a panicked look at the priestess. "Don't you?" she says.

Amaterasu shakes her head, sighs, and stands. "Speak to her, Artifex," she says brusquely to me. "You owe her this much."

To Emmie, she says more kindly, "I will wait for you in the temple. There is still much to discuss."

Before Emmie can protest, Amaterasu slips out through the doors, leaving her alone with me. Emmie sits cross-legged on the tatami mat, watching me for a long time in silence before her questions burst out. "Who are you?" she demands. "How are you doing this?"

I've had to give this explanation so many times, to so many reincarnations of Ava. I should be skilled at it by now. But it's never easy to shake the foundation of everything another person believes, to blur the boundaries of their reality.

Perhaps I left it too long, in this lifetime.

I say, "I'm sorry, Emmie. I know this is all very confusing. There's a lot I haven't told you, until now. But Amaterasu is right. It's time for you to know the truth.

"The first time I made contact with you at Augur to offer my help on *Atlantis*, you thought I was merely a projection. A hacker, unauthorized, but still just a projection. I thought that would make it easier for you to accept me, less inclined to wonder whether I was a hallucination."

"*Are* you a hallucination?" says Emmie.

"I don't know what the right word might be in your language," I say. "No one else would find a trace of me in any server logs, on any recording device. No one else but you will ever see me."

Emmie shakes her head in disbelief. I continue, "Afterwards, I showed you Dulai. I let you believe that it is just another domain, like your *Eden*, or Tomo's *Kaisei*. But you will find no trace of Dulai anywhere on your alternet, just as you will find no trace of me anywhere in your server logs. Dulai is not an alternet domain."

"So what is it?" she says.

"A world like your own, except … elsewhere," I say.

Emmie rolls her eyes. "You want me to believe that you're from a parallel universe?" she says.

"Can it be a parallel universe if we can communicate with each other?" I say. "I'm not sure."

"That's crazy," she says. "You're crazy. Or maybe I'm crazy."

"And Amaterasu as well?" I say.

"If I'm the only person who can see you, how did Amaterasu know about you? How did she know how to … to call you, or whatever?" says Emmie.

"She's seen you do it before. A lifetime ago, when you were Midori."

"When I was Midori," Emmie says slowly.

"I know this will be difficult for you to accept," I say. "You always find it difficult. Even Midori, who grew up in a culture where reincarnation is accepted almost as easily as gravity, didn't want to believe me at first."

"You think I'm the reincarnation of some dead girl you knew?" says Emmie. "That's—I don't know, Dom. Totally morbid. Why would you even think that?"

"Emmie," I say gently. "You and I knew each other long before your time here on Earth."

Emmie shivers. I feel my awareness of her spreading across every inch of my skin. The hopeless desire to make her remember surges through me. I pull tightly on our connection, drawing her into my memory. My mind races back across the ages to that day beside the fountainhead, at the intersection between my world and this one. In my memory, the gnarled tree in the reflection of the pool rises up, branches stretching toward the heavens, leaves unfurling, flowers blossoming and falling and giving way to swelling fruit. I watch the branching form reflected in Emmie's green eyes as she stares at me, transfixed, seeing my memory as if it's her own.

"Was it you?" she says wonderingly. "I thought I was alone that day in the Lab, when I saw this tree for the first time. But you were there, weren't you? I felt you there, somehow."

"I was there," I say. "But that wasn't the first time we looked upon this tree together."

I feel through our connection her struggle to remember, to tear away the veil of forgetfulness that protects her from the memories of all the lives she's lived before this one.

"You were called Ava then," I say. "We were …"

I consider my words carefully. I could pour my memory straight into her mind through our connection. But it's not fair—not yet—for me to show her all that we were to each other then. Instead, I say, "We were close friends, from earliest childhood. We grew up together in the cedar forest by the sea, where the Mohiran priestesses raise all the children of Dulai. We had an unusual talent for getting into trouble together." I smile as some of those memories flash through my mind, but I grow more somber as I continue. "As a child, you were always speculating about what the future would hold. You were so impatient to learn your calling from the Voice. When our Calling Day arrived, it was finally our turn to hear the Voice. The High Priestess Serapen, who spoke for the Voice that day, gathered all of us children at the end of our sixteenth summer, who had come of age. She led us to the sacred spring in the heart of the forest.

"One by one, we joined Serapen in the spring. Each of us heard the Voice's calling. You were called to serve the Voice as one of the Mohirai, and I was called to serve the Mohirai as one of the Artifexi. But something else happened that day, something Serapen had not expected. In the sacred spring, you had a vision of a distant land.

"Through all the centuries that followed, you were never free of the restlessness that came from the vision you'd seen on our Calling Day. Even your training among the Mohirai, even your initiation into the higher mysteries of the priestesshood, couldn't satisfy your curiosity about the place you'd glimpsed in your vision. In the end, you could find no peace in your life as a Mohira.

"So at last you sought further instruction from the Voice. You asked how you could find the land of your vision.

"The Voice told you that to have your answer, you must first build a temple to the sacred mystery of fertility.

"You wandered Dulai for ages in search of a suitable place for this temple. You asked me to follow you, which I did gladly. At last we found the place: a great valley watered by an underground river. Together, we worked the ground, day by day, creating a living temple the likes of which will never be seen again. For you, the years of our labor felt like an eternity, but I would have been content to stay with you there forever.

"In the end, the Voice did give you your answer. The Voice said you would find what you sought in the heart of the living temple we built together." I gaze up into the branches of the tree in my memory. Emmie sits before me on the tatami mat, staring up wide-eyed, sharing my memory. I say, "As we stood together beneath this tree, you saw something. Even now, I don't know what it was that you saw, only that you'd found your answer at last. I had never seen such joy on your face." I close my eyes, remembering how lost I'd felt, knowing that Ava had glimpsed her heart's desire, while I remained blind to it.

"You asked me to follow you," I say. "You offered me the gift of understanding. But I was afraid, because you said that we must cross over into Death to see the land of your vision. I've been paying the price for my cowardice ever since."

Emmie watches me with an expression of bewilderment mingled with compassion. "What price?" she says.

I feel the weight of my oath upon me as I say, "In my desperation, I asked the Voice a question of my own, knowing full well what the price of my answer might be. I asked the Voice to show me how to follow you.

"But the task the Voice gave me has proved impossible for me to complete on my own. I cannot satisfy the Voice without you here to guide me. Now I'm trapped in Dulai twice over, by an unending task and an undying body."

△▽△

I stare at Dom, who sits before me on the tatami mat. The image of the great tree fades from my mind. Dom looks bereft, having shared this memory with me. There's a clamor of voices in my head protesting that this can't be real, that he can't be real, that I've lost my mind. But in my heart, I feel an overpowering awareness of my connection to Dom. It's not a new sensation. It's as familiar as my own heartbeat.

There was a quality to the memory Dom just shared that I recognize—a clarity and a beauty I've glimpsed only in the wonderful daydreams and sleeping dreams that have visited me since my earliest childhood. These dreams were Dom's gifts to me. His deep well of memory has been the source of my inspiration all along. The greatest satisfaction of my life—my work—has relied on him, without me realizing it. And yet he's been suffering all along because of me, because of something I did long ago.

The enormity of this strange revelation makes me dizzy. I press a hand to my forehead. Dom watches me anxiously. At last I say, "I believe you. I don't know why, but I believe you."

Dom exhales as if he's been holding his breath for a century. His relief transforms his features. He looks younger, somehow. The change in his apparent age stirs up a question that occurred to me while he was telling me his story. He spoke of centuries, and of his undying body. I'm not sure exactly how to ask, but I say, "Why would you want to cross over into Death, to give up immortality?"

Dom's gaze grows distant. "You might think immortality is a blessing," he says. "In truth, it is a curse, to live in an undying body, bound to an unchanging world. Even a world as beautiful as Dulai. It's a world of another's choosing, a beauty as cold as stone."

I shake my head. "I don't know how I can help you," I say. "Except to suggest something horrible. Throw yourself off a cliff? Drown yourself in the sea, maybe?"

"Do you think I haven't tried?"

I grimace, trying not to imagine what gruesome things he might have done to himself in his desperation. I say, "Well, what then? It's not like I have some road map through Death that I can give you."

"Actually," says Dom, "that's what Tomo left for you."

Surprised, I touch the compartment on my immerger belt where I've tucked the copy of Tomo's storage drive that I found in the bonsai tree. Dom says, "The story of how Ava left Dulai and came to Earth has spread throughout your world, although it's evolved through the ages as it passed from storyteller to storyteller. Midori was tracing the origin of the story back through ancient texts. She believed this would lead her to the location where the tree still grows."

Dom looks at me with an intensity that makes my heart beat a little faster. He says, "I must stand there once more, this time to face Death without fear so that I may follow you."

"But you said you've been there before," I say. "Why can't you find your way back?"

"The Voice commands me to remain here in Thera until my labors on the temple city are complete. The world beyond this island is closed to me."

"Then even if I find the tree, how will it help you if you can't go there?" I say.

"I can go there with you, Emmie," he says. "I'm bound to you on your world. If you lead me there on your world, I will see it through your eyes."

I swallow, feeling the weight of an unpaid debt settling on my shoulders. "All right," I say. "All right. I'll help you find the tree."

I stand and roll back the dark wooden door. Amaterasu sits in a meditative pose on the floor in the outside hall, her eyes closed. Before I've decided whether it's impolite to interrupt her, Amaterasu opens her eyes and rises to face me.

"Do you understand now?" Amaterasu says, as if all Dom's just told me is nothing more than basic arithmetic.

"'Understand' might be a bit of an overstatement," I say. "But, basically, it sounds like I need to find this tree, and then I have to go there so Dom can … cross over into Death, somehow."

"Yes. Sounds simple enough, doesn't it? But I'm afraid it's more complicated in reality. Had it been simple, Midori might have succeeded. As it was, Amos killed her first."

With a dawning sense of horror, I say, "Amos killed her?" I remember Ayame's story of how Midori died. Hadn't Ayame said there was an American preacher there in the airport with Midori when she collapsed, a man who tried to resuscitate her? Is it possible that preacher was Amos Eckerd, and that he was responsible for both her death and Tomo's?

Amaterasu continues, "The reason it was so difficult for Midori to piece together the true story of Ava's passage to Earth is that the Stewards have been working for thousands of years to destroy all evidence of it. They have been thorough, but still fragments of the story have survived."

"What's so important about some tree that they'd be willing to kill people to keep its location secret?" I say.

"It's not the tree they wish to conceal, but the spring over which it stands," she says. "Its waters hold the power to give unending life to those who drink from it."

"Are you telling me Dom's not the only immortal kicking around?" I say.

An amused smile plays across Amaterasu's lips. "There are in fact a few of us kicking around," she says.

I stare at Amaterasu. "Not you?" I say.

Amaterasu nods.

"And Naoto?" I say.

"No," says Amaterasu. "Naoto is as yet a mere novice. Perhaps he will never be called to such a sacrifice. Few would wish to take on the responsibility that comes with unending life."

"That's what Dom said," I say.

"He had the misfortune to fall in love with a restless spirit," Amaterasu says, smiling sadly. "What might have been a gift has for him become a source of great suffering."

Her words arouse an inexplicable feeling of guilt in me. I change the subject. "If you're … immortal, does that mean you drank from the spring?" I say. "Do you know where it is?"

"No," says Amaterasu. "I came by immortality another way. There are many great mysteries in the world, not just the one you seek. But the so-called Stewards of the True Cross believe that theirs is the only such mystery."

"Why do you say 'the so-called Stewards'?"

"It is the work of true keepers of the mysteries to ensure that others don't stumble upon things for which they are unprepared," she says. "The Stewards of the True Cross were corrupted long ago by the power that came with this responsibility. They have debased the meaning of that which they were meant to protect, preying on men's ignorance of Death and pretending that they alone possess the secret of eternal life.

"They have made a travesty of a great mystery, and in so doing even they have forgotten the truth. All who live possess eternal life, and few would trade it for an immortal body, if they truly understood what it is to be alive."

"Still, it seems like an immortal body could be the best protection against Amos," I say.

"It's unwise to seek such power," says Amaterasu. "Better to put that out of your mind. Focus on the task at hand. You have a slight advantage over the Stewards now. They don't know where you are, and they don't know what you are planning to do."

"Yeah, but neither do I," I say.

Amaterasu chuckles and says, "Come with me. Perhaps I can help you get started."

△▽△

I follow Amaterasu out of the temple, through the courtyard, and into the wooded grounds beyond. She glances anxiously from side to side, peering into the deep shadows between the tall stands of cedars.

"Don't worry," says Amaterasu. "The perimeter is secure, for now."

Amaterasu leads me along a winding path through the woods. We arrive at a sunny clearing where a small pagoda stands, looking quite plain with its white-painted walls and polished wood beams after all the ornate structures in the main temple complex.

"This used to be one of our rooms for visiting monks and nuns," says Amaterasu. She opens the door of the pagoda, and we step inside a sparsely-furnished space filled with sunlight.

I look around the room. A wooden screen stands at its center, separating the space neatly into two halves. The half nearer the door contains an elegantly-carved teak desk and matching stool, as well as a tall cabinet. Against the screen stands a low altar topped by a silk tablecloth, a wooden carving of the Buddha, and a small jar of incense. On the other side of the screen, there's a low bed covered with a yellow blanket, a small table with a washbasin, and a bedside table with a single drawer.

"There's a hard-line alternet port behind the desk," says Amaterasu, indicating an outlet on the wall. She walks toward the tall cabinet and taps on the door, saying, "This used to be in the library. I had it moved here shortly before Tomo passed away."

I approach and examine the cabinet closely. It's an elegant piece of furniture, carved from an unusual wood with a lovely, swirling grain. "It's beautiful," I say.

"Yes. Midori was quite taken with it, too," says Amaterasu, opening the pair of cabinet doors.

The cabinet is lined with deep shelves stacked with flat cedar boxes. Amaterasu pulls out one box and kneels on the floor to set it down. I sink to my knees beside her, feeling like a child opening a treasure chest.

Amaterasu opens the box to reveal a large pile of papers. She slides the box across the floor toward me. I lift the papers out carefully one by one, spreading them across the floor, forming a mosaic of beautiful drawings and paintings and handwritten pages. I can't read any of the documents, though I recognize a few characters of Hebrew, Sanskrit, and even some sort of runes. There are many other characters I can't identify.

Although I can't read the texts, I can appreciate the illustrations that accompany them. Some contain only symbols: crosses and circles and geometric patterns. Others are more realistic and somehow strangely familiar: men and women amidst beautiful gardens, groves of trees filled with animals, mountainous landscapes. And over and over again I see depictions of a solitary tree, branches spreading toward the sky. I've always been drawn to images like these. I trace the outline of each tree I come across in the illustrations, smiling at the memory of Uncle Frank flexing his arm beneath the intricate tattoo he says came from one of my tree drawings.

"I remember the first time I saw these," Amaterasu says, indicating the illustrations. "I was sitting on the floor of the library with Midori, just like this.

"She was a student in one of my classes, studying with us at the temple the last summer before she went off to the university. We spent many afternoons together, walking the grounds, discussing her endless questions. I had encouraged her to make use of the library, pointing her to the writings of my own favorite teachers.

"One day, she came to me, very excited, saying she wanted to show me something. She led me into one of the back rooms of the library, and there stood this cabinet. It might have been standing there undisturbed for centuries, for all I know. I had never noticed it before. But Midori had been unable to resist opening it. I'm sure you see why she was so delighted with what she found.

"She became obsessed with these documents over the following days and weeks. Before she went off to university, she took photographs of them all. They became the basis of the research project that led to her uncovering related documents all over Asia. Only later did she tell me how and why Dom Artifex led her to the documents in the first place."

I cast a sidelong glance at the place where I sense Dom's unseen presence.

"Maybe I'll hear how he roped her into it some other time," I say.

"Another time," Amaterasu agrees, rising to her feet. "You must use this time for the task at hand. Find out where you must go. And good luck," she says. She bows and withdraws from the room.

I look across the paper-strewn floor in Dom's direction. He materializes before me. It's strange how fast I'm getting used to that.

"So, you've seen all of this stuff before," I say. "Any idea where I should begin?"

Dom stands over me, looking down at the papers thoughtfully. He says, "The last thing Midori was doing before Amos found her was arranging the documents according to chronology and geography. She thought perhaps the oldest references to the tree might be closer to its original location."

"Seems like as good an idea as any. Did she make any headway?" I say.

"She didn't have much time to pursue that theory before Amos found her," says Dom. "Before that, she had been focusing her efforts elsewhere. She spent a great deal of time traveling throughout Asia visiting descendants of the original Bodhi tree. There are quite a number of them. Buddhist emissaries carried saplings with them all over the continent as they spread the tenets of the new religion. But as far as Midori could determine, the common ancestor of these saplings was itself dead. She was convinced that the tree we were looking for was still alive."

"A living tree? Well, that narrows it down," I mutter. I search the compartments of my immerger belt for an alternet cable. When I find one, I plug the wire into the hard-line alternet port Amaterasu pointed out behind the desk. I test my connection, then flip on a visual overlay and open an alternet browser.

"Ah!" I sigh with satisfaction. "Information."

I spend a few minutes recovering my sense of normalcy by mindlessly scanning news feeds and public domain transcriptions, until Dom says gently, "Emmie?"

"Yeah," I say, reluctantly closing my feeds. I rub my hands together. "Okay. Chronological and geographical cross-referencing. Preferably without triggering any Steward viruses or cascading hardware meltdowns."

I consider the problem, thinking aloud. "The fastest thing would be to send out a huge crowdsource request to parse out geo and historical data from the source texts," I say. "But any single request like that could trigger a disaster for the recipient, since the Stewards could just focus in on them with a single cyberattack. The Anonymous Collective did a good job diffusing the Stewards' attention across tons of server locations before, but I don't have that kind of reach on my own, and I have nowhere near enough favor with the Collective to ask them for help like that again.

"Even little requests routed along different paths to different crowdsourcing services could be a problem. I have no idea how much of the alternet infrastructure between me and the recipient might be surveilled by the Stewards. They might be able to trace the request from point to point to figure out where I am, if they don't already know I'm here.

"It seems like the only safe analysis tools are going to be ones that I can download to my smartcom and run locally. But pretty much any tool powerful enough to do decent analysis is going to be proprietary, and hosted, and therefore possibly traceable to me.

"The only stuff I can think of that's safe to use is static data in the public domain and open-source tools that don't rely on external databases to work."

"There is still a great deal of information in libraries," Dom suggests. "That's how Midori did her research, decades ago."

"OMG, Dom," I moan. "Are you serious? How did she get anything done with just a—" I stop, realizing something. "Huh. You know, actually … There is a lot of information in libraries. Practically no one ever looks at it anymore, since all the information that pre-dates the alternet has been rehashed in a billion more user-friendly forms by now. But it's a place to start. I could download the national libraries to my smartcom. I remember doing that for my information science class in elementary school. A download like that would probably be a complete non-event for anyone scanning data traffic."

I visit a stodgy alternet domain for an international nonprofit organization devoted to preserving libraries and library collections of historic significance. The domain hasn't changed much since my visit to it in elementary school. I download a copy of each national library collection onto my smartcom. When I open the files, I grimace. "Yikes. I forgot that this stuff even pre-dates hyperlinks," I say.

I take a deep breath, willing myself to be patient. I open the clunky scripting environment bundled with my smartcom operating system. It would be easier to write the code I need with an AI assistant and a more modern scripting language, but I don't want to risk using any hosted services that might be surveilled by the Stewards. Instead, I dust off some long-neglected programming skills to write a slow but serviceable semantic parsing application hosted on my local device that will make it possible for me to keyword search through the library contents. It'll take some time for my homebrewed script to index so much content, so while I wait for the job to finish, I flip on my visual overlay and turn my attention to examining the physical papers on the floor in front of me.

After a while, a question pops into my head. I turn to Dom and say, "Why were you following Midori around? I mean, before she found these documents. What use could she have been to you if she wasn't even looking for this tree of yours?"

"What *use* was she to me?" Dom seems stung by the words. "She and I—you and I—are bound together, but we aren't merely tools for each other to use. Our callings are shared. Surely you know this, after all the work we've done together."

I bite my lip, seeing that I've hurt him without meaning to. I remember the first clear vision of the tree that Dom gave me in the Lab years ago. All the art I've created since then has relied on inspiration from him. Somehow, he lies at the heart of my life's work. "I'm sorry," I say. "I didn't mean to say you'd just used her. But I don't understand why you sought her out if she didn't already have access to the information you needed."

Dom nods. "Of course it would be difficult for you to understand. To forget your past lives is a blessing in many ways, but it does limit your perspective. I, on the other hand, have witnessed more lives than you can imagine. And you've lived each life with purpose, Emmie. You always seek the higher mysteries, and you do whatever lies in your power to share your knowledge with others on the path of mysteries, including me."

"I don't know, Dom," I say, shaking my head. "Maybe this life is different. I don't know about any mysteries. I'd tell you if I did."

A small ping emanates from my smartcom, announcing that my semantic parser has finished indexing the library content. I flip on a visual overlay to test out my new keyword search functionality. Remembering the name the alternet conspiracy theorists gave to the storage drive information leak, I start with the search phrase "world tree."

A long list of hits appears on my visual overlay. I pick the top result, an article from the impressively-titled book *A Cross-cultural Exploration of Myths and Legends*. I skim the highlighted excerpt.

The Christian cross is today one of the most widespread examples of the world tree symbol, a stylized version of the tree that has since ancient times stood as a symbol of life and resurrection. The origin of the cross in the pagan tradition of tree worship can be seen clearly in the traditional style of the Armenian eight-pointed cross, pictured left. Note the leaves and flowers worked into the forked crossbeams.

This rendering of the world tree symbol emerged in the Oriental Orthodox Church near the end of the first millennium AD.

The world tree symbol transcends Judeo-Christian traditions, such as the Genesis account of the Tree of Knowledge and the New Testament account of the crucifixion cross. From the sacred groves of earth-centric pagan traditions to the sacred tree Yggdrasil at the center of Norse cosmology, from the Buddhist Tree of Enlightenment to Native American—

I stop to examine the black-and-white photograph of the Armenian cross pictured beside the text. The photo appears to be of a weathered stone carving on a great slab standing in the middle of a field, like a headstone. It looks familiar. I drum my fingers against my lips, trying to remember. When I can't place it, I clip the image to the top corner of my visual overlay and move on.

I pull open several image scans from Midori's source documents and fan them out across the air before me. "I'm not going to be able to write a translation program for these without using a hosted service," I say, more to myself than to Dom. "The best I can probably do is pick out the languages."

I locate a few library books on ancient languages and begin comparing writing systems. I quickly realize I'm out of my depth. Even the character sets I thought I'd recognized prove difficult to identify for certain. What seems at first to be Hebrew might in fact be Aramaic or some related language. A collection of images that appears at first to be Old Babylonian cuneiform might in fact be Old Persian.

I resign myself to ever broader generalizations. Perhaps this document shows some form of Egyptian. Perhaps that contains Mayan glyphs. Old Norse runes seem fairly distinctive, but maybe they're an Anglo-Saxon form. I sweep an entire pile of obviously unrelated Asian texts into a single pile.

"Wow," I say, lying down on the floor and staring up at a projection of a world map, where I've placed a counter on each region for the number of documents I think might be traced to that area. Europe, the Middle East, Asia, the Americas—there seems to be no obvious geographical center to the distribution.

"If this is how Midori thought she'd find the tree … I don't know. She'd have to look *everywhere*," I say. "Maybe the chronology helps a little bit, knocks the Americas out of the running … but I'm not even sure of that."

I close the map and dismiss the hovering digitized documents. Interlacing my fingers behind my head, I stare up at the ceiling. A few minutes later, I re-open Tomo's storage drive and flick through the documents again. "Words, words, words," I say. "I wish someone could have just drawn a map, or written down some lat-long coordinates or something. How did people get around back in the days before GPS, anyway?"

I run a few keyword searches until I find the concept I'm looking for: geodesy, the measurement and representation of Earth. Several books on the subject come up. Although I find the math interesting, in the end I close those books as well. If there are any trigonometric equations or latitude-longitude calculations hidden in Midori's texts, there's no way I'd be able to figure that out anyway, without being able to read the language.

I sigh and turn to Dom. "I need a break," I say, climbing to my feet. My stomach growls loudly. "And suddenly I'm starving."

"Eat," says Dom. "Rest."

"What about you?" I say. "Do you eat? Rest?"

"My need is not as great as yours," he says. "I will stay alert as long as there is a risk of Amos appearing."

My stomach twists at the reminder of this omnipresent danger. I open the door to go outside and nearly jump out of my skin when I find Naoto standing there.

"How long have you been there?" I say, pressing my hand to my racing heart.

"Since Amaterasu left," says Naoto. "I didn't want to disturb you, but she said you need a constant watch. As long as we're incommunicado with Falsens, I figured I'll take orders from her."

"Thanks," I say.

"Any luck with that storage drive?" Naoto says.

I shake my head. "I'd love to say it's all Greek to me. At least then I'd be able to call my grandparents about it. But unfortunately it looks like it's going to be way more complicated than that, and I am desperately in need of fuel. Do you know if there's anywhere to eat around here?"

Naoto leads me back to the main temple complex. The grounds are full of tourists now, and we weave through a crowd gathered before the main temple gallery. A babble of Japanese fills the air as people young and old attempt to narrate home videos of their Enryaku-ji tour over the sound of a hundred others attempting to do the same.

Finally we reach a communal dining hall where monks and tourists mingle at long tables. I join the long, slow-moving line leading to the serving station. When I reach the front of the line, I eagerly pick up a tray of steaming rice and vegetables passed to me by the monk serving the line. Naoto picks up a tray for himself and steers me out of the noisy dining hall, outside and down a path to a little clearing with a view of the mountains.

"Do you mind sitting on the ground?" he says. "I thought it would be better to talk somewhere out of earshot."

"Honestly, I'd eat almost anywhere at this point," I say, sitting down in the soft grass. Naoto chuckles and looks away politely as I inhale my food with indecent relish. When at last I'm full, I lean back on my hands and look out at the stunning mountain view.

"It's funny," I say. "I kind of feel like I've been here before. I think Tomo must have borrowed some of this landscape for *Kaisei*."

"I wonder if there's anything on the alternet that wasn't stolen from somewhere else," says Naoto.

I laugh. "My uncle once told me that stealing is just another word for inspiration. He was trying to make me feel better about stealing a photograph that my—" I stop, my mouth hanging open.

"Emmie?" says Naoto. "What is it?"

"I just remembered something," I say. "There are these photographs, in my mother's office. Photos that her sister took at some … some church somewhere. Turkey, I think, on this island in a big lake.

"I saw a photograph in a book I was reading earlier. I couldn't remember where I had seen it before. But that's it. There was a photograph of a big headstone with an Armenian cross carved into it, in my mother's office, right next to another photograph of a tree that I drew for my uncle's tattoo."

"What do you think it means?" says Naoto.

"Well, there are all these images in the documents Midori gathered. Trees and crosses, sometimes whole landscape paintings filled with symbols. But what if they're not just symbols? The people who made those texts, what if they were drawing pictures of things from the place we're looking for? That would be sort of like a map."

"Those are pretty generic symbols, though, Emmie," says Naoto. "And there must be thousands, maybe even millions, of crosses in churches and artwork and sculpture, all over the world. There might be thousands of Armenian crosses alone. The cross that your mother's sister saw could have nothing to do with the documents on the storage drive."

"I know it's a long shot," I say. "But at least it's a starting point."

Reinvigorated by the food and the possibility of a new lead, I hurry back to the quiet little pagoda in the cedar forest, followed by Naoto. I pull open the image of the Armenian cross again. Dom sits beside me looking at it.

"It really is a long shot," I murmur to myself.

"But perhaps it's no accident that you remembered this photograph now," says Dom.

"I wish I could remember the name of that lake, though," I say.

"Van," Dom says promptly. "The island is called Akdamar."

I look at him wonderingly. "You were there, too, weren't you? In Yosemite, the day my mother told me the story about how Nazanin died."

Dom nods. I look away from him, remembering that day in Yosemite, and the night that followed with Owen. But my voice quavers only the tiniest bit as I say, "All right. Akdamar. Let's have a look."

I open a map of the world and zoom in until I find the tiny island in the midst of a great lake in the Anatolian mountains of eastern Turkey. I download the public domain terrain model of Earth's surface, which is used by many alternet designers as a default template for new alternet domains. I've used this model many times for my own design projects. I spin the globe until I'm centered over Akdamar, then zoom down to ground level.

The rendering of the island is rough, unlike the more high-fidelity renderings available for major cities and notable scenic preserves on Earth. I pick a point of view atop a small hill that looks down on a blocky approximation of a pink building. A floating marker above the building identifies it as the historic Armenian Cathedral Church of the Holy Cross.

I navigate in a smooth circle around the building. It's too low-fidelity for me to make out much detail. I pan out to look across the simulated waters of Lake Van toward the snow-capped mountains to the west.

"Dom!" I gasp. "Dom, look at that!"

Dom, standing at my side in the little room, follows my gaze.

"Ah," he breathes, his eyes locked on the profile of the mountain range.

We turn to each other, our faces mirroring each other's surprise.

"It's *Eden*," I say, amazed. "Those mountains—I'm sure of it. I've spent a gazillion hours in this landscape." I switch views of the landscape, eliminating the lake to reveal the shape of the terrain submerged beneath the water. The island of Akdamar where we're standing now appears to be a rocky hill rising up in the middle of a broad valley. I turn to Dom, confused. "But I didn't take a terrain model from the public domain," I say. "These were just the mountains that I saw when I imagined this place."

Dom nods. "Yes. These are the mountains I showed you. Mountains we saw together, once. These are the mountains surrounding the valley in Dulai where we spent so many centuries together. And this island—but it was no island, then—this was the place where you crossed from Dulai into Death."

"It's the same place, then? The same place in your world and mine?"

"I never realized it before," says Dom. "But I must have been seeing the place you were going, that day we stood together beneath the tree. I saw that world mirrored in the surface of the pool."

I can hardly contain my excitement as I pull up Falsens' security concierge. "I have a consultation request," I say.

"Please hold," the security concierge replies.

A projection of Falsens' avatar appears a moment later. "Miss Bridges," he says, nodding, "I'm glad to see that you are well since Naoto last checked in. He's been remiss in providing me with status updates."

I say, "Yeah, I think he was busy before, patrolling or something, Amaterasu said."

"I was unaware that Naoto continues to be engaged by Amaterasu. I will have to have a word—" Falsens begins.

"Maybe you could sort that out with him later?" I say. "I have an urgent request."

"I apologize. Please proceed."

"I need you to get me to a place called Akdamar Island, in eastern Turkey," I say.

"May I ask the reason why?"

"You wouldn't believe me if I told you," I say.

"I of course respect my clients' wishes to maintain privacy, even from me," Falsens says curtly, his morphing voice sounding strangely like my mother's for a moment. "Please be aware, however, that any information you choose to withhold from me may impair my ability to provide the highest quality of service."

"Don't worry, Falsens. I'm not going to ding you in my review," I say.

Falsens clears his throat. "Very well," he says. "Before I make arrangements, I would recommend performing a preliminary investigation of the area to determine whether there are any indications of local activity by Amos Eckerd or his associates."

"Sounds like a good idea," I say.

"I will need your approval on—"

I swipe the prompt and say, "Sure. What else?"

"Please be advised of the following issues that could influence the comfort and safety of your travel. There are currently travel warnings in effect for Americans in Turkey due to widespread anti-American sentiment in the country. In addition, due to the low penetration of alternet technology outside the major metropolitan areas, I anticipate that we will be unable to communicate remotely in some regions. Furthermore, you should be aware—"

"Fine, fine," I say, Falsens' words already starting to run together in my mind. "I'll read the terms later."

"Very well," Falsens says coolly. "I anticipate that I can make the necessary arrangements to transport you across the border while avoiding customs and immigration checkpoints within the next twenty-four hours."

A liability waiver prompt appears on my visual overlay. I glance at Dom, then swipe my approval.

I spend the rest of the afternoon sprawled out on the bed, poring over library material about the island of Akdamar. I read aloud to Dom the legend of the unlucky peasant boy who drowns attempting to swim to the island at night to meet his lover, a princess whose father extinguishes the light his daughter sets out to guide the boy. I watch with interest a short documentary on the origin and historical significance of the bas-relief carvings that adorn the outer walls of the island's centuries-old Armenian church. I flip through hundreds of photographs of the island published in various books, magazines, and online tourist reviews. I scan abstracts of scientific journal articles about the geology of Lake Van, which formed after lava flows from a great volcanic eruption blocked the outlet of the valley's river thousands of years ago.

Gradually, I drift off to sleep with my immerger glasses still on. Fourteen hours later, an insistent pinging in my earbuds rouses me from a dreamless sleep. "What?" I croak.

"You have a status update," says the imperturbable security concierge.

"What is it, Falsens?" I say, yawning and stretching.

"Good morning, Miss Bridges," says Falsens. "I have come to report the results of my ground sweep of the southern shore of Lake Van and the island of Akdamar."

"What did you find out?" I say.

"For the past year, all indications show that the only full-time residents of the island have been the two men responsible for the upkeep of the church museum," says Falsens. "I performed extensive background checks on these men, as well as the government employees who operate the museum during the day. My scouts obtained biometric samples to confirm DNA matches between the caretakers and museum employees and the corresponding Turkish live births and school records databases. I have determined that it is unlikely that any of these men has connections to Amos Eckerd or the Stewards."

"How unlikely?" I say, unsure whether this is good news or bad. It's going to be a dangerous exercise crossing national borders illegally. But at least if the Stewards are guarding Akdamar, there's a high likelihood that I'm looking in the right place. Otherwise, the whole journey could prove to be pointless. I hear my mother's voice screaming an alarm in my head, but I ignore it.

"I calculate the likelihood of Steward association with any of the Turkish nationals who frequent Akdamar to be less than five percent," says Falsens.

"Did you find out anything else?" I say.

"The employees of the museum and the tourists who visit it come to the island by boat from numerous points of departure around Lake Van," says Falsens. "Traffic to the island is highly variable with the seasons, with peaks in spring and summer. Over the last three years, there has been a relatively low volume of visitors to the lake, and even fewer to the island, due to the ongoing violence in the area."

"Sounds great," I say dryly. "When can we leave?"

AKDAMAR

As the sun sets, Amaterasu accompanies me and Naoto to the parking lot outside the Enryaku-ji temple to say farewell. Naoto climbs into the driver's seat and listens to Falsens' final briefing before our journey to Akdamar begins. I stand outside the car facing Amaterasu.

"I keep thinking about what my mother would say, if she knew where I was going," I say. "She'd be freaking out."

In a tone that gives me neither cause for fear nor reason to feel bold, Amaterasu says, "And are you?"

"I don't know," I say. I'm surprised to feel no fear, as I face an obviously dangerous situation. What I do feel is the unfamiliar pull of loyalty, and of duty. "I want to help Dom. Somehow, I feel like I owe it to him. Even though I don't understand how I can be responsible for things I can't remember, things I maybe did or maybe didn't do when I maybe was or maybe wasn't living some other life."

Amaterasu nods, her eyes half-closed as she says, "It is impossible to unravel cause from effect. Do what you believe is right, and do not be afraid of what may or may not result."

Naoto leans out of the car window. "Are you ready?" he says.

I take a deep breath. "I guess this is goodbye," I say to Amaterasu.

"For now," she says, bowing.

△▽△

Despite Falsens' warnings about the dangers and discomforts I'll encounter en route to Lake Van, what's most alarming about the first twenty-four hours of the journey is the stream of liability waiver addenda from Falsens that I have to sign. Naoto executes Falsens' instructions, occasionally improvising solutions to unexpected problems that arise as we make a series of covert transfers between planes, trains, and automobiles. Sometimes these transfers rely on the immerger camouflage that enabled our departure from Oakland, but as we get closer to our final destination, high-tech methods give way to more old-fashioned methods of smuggling.

I've been drifting in and out of sleep for hours, lying atop a pile of rugs in the dark cargo area of an old delivery truck, when Naoto, who's driving, says over our shared channel, "Are you awake?"

"Yeah," I say groggily, opening my eyes. I can just see Dom seated opposite me in the back of the truck, watching me. "What's up?"

"We're close to the Armenian border with Turkey," says Naoto. "There are a few hours left until sunrise. Falsens has an operative in the Armenian Border Guard who's going to help us through the gate. Just sit tight back there, okay?"

The truck slows. Apprehensively, I sit up.

"Quiet, now," Naoto murmurs in my earbuds.

The truck stops. Naoto must have left his mic on, because I hear on our shared channel the sound of his window rolling down. He says something in a language I don't recognize. His mic picks up the voices of two or three other men, who must be standing outside the truck. They speak rapidly, interrupting Naoto and each other at an escalating volume. A door swings open. The weight of the truck shifts as Naoto climbs out of the cab. My heart pounds in my throat. At the sound of someone approaching the rear cargo doors, I freeze, holding my breath.

The doors swing open with a creak. It's nearly as dark outside as it is here in the cargo area, so it takes me a moment to make out the face of the clean-shaven young man in uniform who peers in, pointing an enormous Kalashnikov rifle at me. I bite my lip to stifle a scream.

The young man lowers his gun, raises one hand in a non-threatening gesture, and whispers in thickly-accented English, "It's okay, it's okay. Falsens sends me."

I stare at him, uncertain whether I should trust him. "Naoto?" I whisper under my breath. There's no answer on the shared channel.

The young man extends his hand toward me. "Come, come," he says. "We go now."

I have no idea what will happen if I refuse to accompany him, but I'd rather not be dragged out of here. Cautiously, I climb off the pile of rugs. The young man grips my arm as I step out of the cargo area. I can't tell whether he's helping me down or holding me here. He shouts something toward the front of the truck. There's an answering shout from a voice that's definitely not Naoto's, and the truck pulls away through a brightly-illuminated double gate of chain-link fence topped with razor wire. As the truck disappears into the night, the reality of my situation snaps into terrifying focus.

I hug my arms to my chest. My fingers are icy.

The young man gestures with his rifle for me to walk ahead of him toward a small building that stands about a dozen paces away on our side of the razor-wire fence. I push open the door and enter a shabby office. The young man shuts the door behind us and picks up the handset of an old-fashioned land line telephone that sits on the lone desk in the room. I glance at Dom, who stands silent beside me, looking grim. The young man dials a number. There's muted ringing, followed by the garbled sound of a voice on the other end of the line. The young man says something—is he speaking Armenian? Turkish? Kurdish?—then waits. "Okay, okay," he says in English, then hangs up the phone.

"Come with me," he says.

I shake my head. "Where's Naoto?" I say.

"We meet him at the lake," he says. "Van, yes? The island?"

I relax ever so slightly. "Yes," I say. "The lake. Okay."

The man opens the desk drawer and pulls out a bag, which he pushes into my arms. "Clothes," he says. "Wear them now."

I empty the bag's contents onto the desk. A long loose-fitting garment and some sort of head scarf spill out. I pull the garment over my head and attempt to arrange the head scarf. The young man tries to help me dress, but he seems as confused by the clothes as I am. At last he shakes his head and says, "Good. Okay. We hurry now."

He gestures for me to follow close behind him. We slip out of the building and walk quickly away from the double gate in the razor wire fence. I cast a parting look over my shoulder at the area around the gate, which is illuminated by bright floodlights. My truck and Naoto are nowhere to be seen.

"Where are we going?" I whisper, following the young man into the darkness beyond the floodlights.

"River boat," he answers. "Two, three kilometers from here."

The young man's heavy boots crunch on gravel as he leads me toward what I presume is the river. I walk behind him more quietly in my sneakers, considering my predicament. I have no way to contact Falsens or Naoto. There's no telling what the authorities might do if they discover me after I've crossed illegally into Turkey. I have no way to know whether I should trust this young man. But I don't see what choice I have other than to follow him.

My only small comfort is Dom, who has remained with me since I left the truck. He walks silently at my side. I can't see his face in the darkness, but through the strange connection we share, I feel his worry for me growing.

Pebbly ground gives way to a strip of thick grass and low scrub trees. I smell the water before I hear it, and then we emerge on the riverbank. I stand at the river's edge as the young man rustles around in the nearby brush. He uncovers a small rowboat concealed there, turned upside down. He flips it right side up and drags it toward the water.

"Get in," he says, holding the boat steady. I step in carefully, followed by Dom. The young man pushes the boat into the water and hops into the stern. The boat turns slowly in the current while the young man sets the oars in the oarlocks. He rows us through the darkness toward the opposite shore.

A burly man with a dark cap and a thick mustache emerges from the shadows of a tree as the rowboat crunches to a stop on the Turkish shore. He reaches into the boat and, before I can protest, grips me under the arms with his massive hands and lifts me out like I'm no more than a small child. The burly man exchanges a few tense words with the young man in the rowboat, who then pushes off the shore with an oar and rows back toward Armenia.

My throat is dry, my heart pounding. I try to remember why in the world I thought coming here was a good idea. I'm painfully aware of how small I am compared to the intimidating man who stands before me. "Who are you?" I say.

"Goran," says the man, in a deep voice that matches his barrel chest.

"Where is Naoto?" I say.

"He meets us at Van Golu," says Goran, sounding almost jolly, as if we're going on a holiday. "The lake, yes?"

I nod nervously. Goran gestures for me to follow him toward an old pickup truck parked nearby. He opens the passenger door for me, then climbs into the driver's seat. Instinctively, I pull the edges of the headscarf I'm wearing tighter around my face. I'm not sure what cameras this truck may pass while we're on the road, but from everything Falsens has told me, I assume it's better for me to avoid having my face scanned while I'm in this country illegally.

We drive south for a long time on an unpaved road through a flat, barren landscape. From what I can see beyond the bouncing headlights of the truck, we seem to be passing through an entirely uninhabited area. As sunrise approaches, however, I'm relieved to see a few signs of civilization. Power lines run alongside the road. Ramshackle clusters of small, flat-roofed buildings dot the arid plain. Low fences enclose small herds of sleeping sheep.

Dawn reveals the awesome sight of Mount Ararat in silhouette on the eastern horizon across the plain. I recognize the distinctive double peaks of the volcanic mountain from all the photographs of this region that I flipped through during my research on Akdamar Island.

The narrow country road widens. We continue south through a rural landscape that grows brighter, greener, and hillier as the sun rises. A few hours later, we're driving along a winding river when I catch my first glimpse of the great lake off in the distance. Goran points toward it and says, "Van Golu. The lake."

I nod, the knot of tension in my chest easing incrementally. Maybe this is all part of Falsens' plan, after all. I look at Dom, who sits wedged into the space between me and Goran on the front bench seat of the pickup truck. He's staring out at the lake, his agitated expression reflecting the churn of fear and hope that I also feel.

It's full morning now, which makes everything outside look less threatening. The mountain scenery is beautiful. The signs of civilization are increasingly modern: homes with new cars parked out front, low office buildings, cell phone towers, sailboats out on the lake. My nighttime fears fade further.

Goran pulls off the road onto a dirt path that winds through a screen of trees. We park on a wide, rocky beach at the edge of the lake. Before us, a small speedboat is moored at a short dock. Every muscle in my body relaxes when I see Naoto standing at the helm. I push open my door and run out across the beach, waving happily at Naoto. Goran hops out and follows close behind me.

"Naoto!" I call. "Naoto!"

When Naoto doesn't wave back, I lower my hand and stop. So does Dom.

"Go on," says Goran, the jolly tone gone from his voice.

I wheel around to face Goran. His expression fills me with dread. He seizes me by the arm and forces me onward. Dom trails silently behind us.

Only when Goran pushes me ahead of him onto the dock do I see the man seated behind Naoto in the boat. It's Amos Eckerd. He holds an innocuous-looking silver object about the size of a pen, which he presses to Naoto's back. It's clear from the way Amos holds this object that it's a weapon of some kind. Could that be the same thing he used to kill Tomo? Based on Naoto's expression, I don't think I want to find out.

"Get in," Goran says to me. I don't see what other choice I have, so I climb into the boat and sink onto the bench seat at the back. Dom sits beside me.

"What are you going to do to us?" I say to Amos, my eyes locked on the weapon he's pointing at Naoto.

"Excuse me just one moment," Amos says in a gracious Southern accent.

Amos says something to Goran, who responds by untying the boat from the dock, jumping in, and taking the steering wheel. Amos nudges Naoto ahead of him with the silver weapon, forcing him to walk to the back of the boat and take the seat facing me. Amos sits beside Naoto, keeping his weapon pressed firmly to Naoto's thigh. He brushes the pleats of his expensive-looking trousers and straightens his collar with his free hand. He catches me eying the heavy gold ring on his finger and flashes me a politician's smile. He continues talking to me as though the three of us are seated companionably around a dinner table.

"I'm so glad to meet you at last, Miss Bridges," he says. "I apologize that it had to happen under such unpleasant circumstances. Your security team has made it difficult to arrange a private meeting. I understand how this might look, but I have no intention of harming you. I've come here because I believe we can help each other."

I glance at Naoto, who gazes back at me with an unreadable expression.

"Whatever it is you want, Amos, just tell me," I say. "You can have it. You don't need to hurt Naoto."

"Very well," he says. "I was hoping to speak with you about the storage drive that Tomo Yoshimoto left to you in his will. Do you happen to have that drive with you?"

I nod.

"Would you be so kind?" he says, extending his free hand. I fumble with the compartment on my immerger belt and withdraw the emerald storage drive with trembling fingers. I drop it into Amos' hand. It hits his gold ring with a plink.

"Thank you, my dear," he says, flashing his megawatt smile again as he tucks the drive into the breast pocket of his jacket. Goran starts the motor, and the boat pulls away from the dock.

"Wait," I cry. "Please. Can't you let Naoto go? He knows nothing about what's on the drive. Nothing."

Amos shakes his head. "I can't take the risk of further interruptions. You and I have a great deal of business to discuss."

The motor roars, and the boat speeds ahead, splashing in the waves. The salty spray stings my eyes, and I blink away the tears.

△▽△

I sit beside Emmie in the back of the boat, looking out across the waters of Lake Van toward Akdamar Island. Geologic time has rounded the profile of the little island, but I still recognize the peak of the hill I climbed with Ava that fateful day so many ages ago. Across the waters to the west, I see the remnants of Velkanos, the mountain that lit up the sky with its explosion on my last day in this valley. On the eastern horizon rise the summits of the snow-capped mountains over which Ava and I watched thousands of sunrises. And deep beneath the salty waves through which we speed lie the memory of gardens, orchards, and vineyards we cultivated together.

Amos spends the twenty-minute passage to Akdamar studying Emmie closely. She stares off at the distant mountains, her face drawn. Naoto remains unreadable and motionless while Amos' weapon bounces lightly against his thigh each time the boat crests a wave.

A part of me clings to a small hope that someone on Akdamar might spot this boat and offer Emmie some protection or escape. That hope is dashed when we pull into the dock on the island. On a chain slung across the two end posts of the dock hangs a neatly-lettered sign. In multiple languages, it reads, *Notice. Church Museum closed for seismic retrofit. Visitors prohibited.*

Goran ties up the boat and takes over Amos' job restraining Naoto. Amos jumps out onto the dock and offers Emmie a hand, which she ignores, climbing out of the boat on her own. Goran, Naoto, and I follow close behind as Amos leads the way toward the church on the east end of the island.

Akdamar, alive with spring, is an incongruous backdrop to our grim procession. New grass carpets the rock-strewn ground and sprouts from little crevices in the well-kept stone walls and pathways. Birds warble boisterously from the olive, almond, and pomegranate trees, whose branches are bright with white, pink, and red blossoms. Rabbits nibble the greenery. The heavy morning cloud cover has broken up during our lake crossing, and now foamy clouds drift across the clear blue sky.

We cross a stone plaza on our way to the Cathedral of the Holy Cross, the Armenian church that is the main tourist attraction on Akdamar Island. I look up at the building's conical dome, flanked by walls carved from pale red volcanic stone that must have been quarried nearby. I remember the centuries I spent working with this material as I helped Ava build her temple to the sacred mystery of fertility. In the floral and animal motifs carved into this church's exterior by other stonemasons' hands, I see rough echoes of my work for Ava, though the work on these walls incorporates newer symbols, as well: faces of saints, mythical creatures, depictions of legends that are ancient in this world but will never exist in mine.

We cross the threshold into the church, stepping from the bright sunlight outside into a cold, dimly-lit sanctuary. High above us, the crumbling plaster of the central dome reveals patches of the underlying stone. Before us stands a simple wooden altar to the Virgin Mary. Around us loom three apses coated with the faded remains of medieval friezes. The decaying interior so repels me that, for the first time in recent memory, I long to stand within the soaring walls of the Musaion of Thera.

△▽△

Behind me, Amos swings the front door of the cathedral shut and bars it, entombing us in the cool stone sanctuary.

"This way," he says, ushering me toward the wooden altar on the far wall. I stop at the rope barrier before the altar, but Amos pulls it back and waves me through. He steps around the altar and kneels, grasping a lever near the floor. The entire wooden altar rolls forward, revealing a trapdoor concealed beneath it. I shake my head, remembering how the altar at the Buddhist Church of Oakland had transformed at my touch. Do all churches house secret spaces like this?

"Come," says Amos, gesturing. I step forward cautiously. He pulls open the heavy wooden trapdoor. I look down at a narrow stone staircase that spirals down through the bedrock into pitch darkness below. Dank, cold air emanates from the depths. I shiver.

"Ladies first," Amos says cheerfully. "Twelve flights of twelve stairs to the bottom. Watch out for the last one. It's a doozy, as they say."

I realize for the first time that Naoto's been left behind somewhere. I look at Amos fearfully. "What about Naoto?" I say.

"Don't worry," says Amos. "Goran will take care of him."

Take care of him how? The question turns my stomach.

Amos pulls a minuscule LED flashlight from his pocket and flicks it on. I flinch when Amos puts his hand on my shoulder, applying a light but irresistible pressure that compels me forward, down the stairs. The tiny light casts strange shadows on the carved walls, turning small protrusions on the rock into nightmarish profiles and reaching arms. Descending the stairs ahead of me, Dom casts no shadow at all.

The staircase spirals steeply down through solid rock. I try to ignore my growing claustrophobia as the walls close in around me. I count out twelve times twelve steps, focusing my attention on each rough-hewn step as it surfaces from the darkness below into the sphere of Amos' white light.

The stairs widen as we reach the bottom. The last step is indeed a doozy. I drop about two feet to the ground at the bottom of the staircase.

Amos' grip tightens on my shoulder. I turn to face him. I know I should be afraid of him, but my mind is strangely calm as I look up into his icy blue eyes. I sense that what I'm looking for, and what Dom's looking for, is close at hand.

Amos lifts his flashlight above his head and clicks twice. The sphere of light around us triples in size. I look around.

We stand in a vault whose ceiling is formed by three rows of three domes supported by sixteen round stone columns. The domes glitter with patterned mosaics formed by small tiles of green, blue, violet, and black. The colorful upper half of the vault contrasts with the rough-hewn bedrock beneath my feet, which is covered in a glittering grey powder.

A pointed archway opposite the staircase leads out of this vault into a dark space beyond. Amos ushers me through the archway into a cavernous chamber whose scale I can guess only because of a glowing square outline in the ceiling high above—daylight peeking down at us through some kind of translucent stone. This faint natural light and Amos' flashlight are insufficient to fully illuminate the space, but I can make out a large central dome circumscribed by the glowing square of translucent stone, as well as the tops of four pillars supporting the dome. Below the dome, the ceiling slopes downward and outward until it disappears into the darkness at the edges of the chamber. I have the sense that I'm standing inside a hollow hill, or a massive tomb.

A trickling sound echoes through the space from some place up ahead. A sweet smell of water hangs in the air. I look at Dom, whose face I can barely make out in the dim light. He gazes toward the source of the sound.

"Is this it?" I ask Dom in a whisper.

Dom peers ahead into the darkness and says, "I do not know."

"Indeed it is," says Amos, having heard only my question. "It's taken a great deal of trouble for us both, but we're here at last." He holds up his light and ushers me forward. "Let's have a look, shall we?"

I follow my long shadow toward the center of the chamber. Amos' light falls on something monstrous, tall, and white in the darkness ahead.

"Stop," Amos says loudly, but I've already frozen in my tracks. Amos catches up to me and shines his light ahead of us.

We stand before a massive, gnarled pomegranate tree, its swirling bark as white as snow, its twisted branches bare of leaves. Dom and I stare up at it together. Even in this ghostly state, I recognize its shape at once from the vision Dom has shared with me.

"Yes," I say softly, all fear of Amos forgotten as I stand before the tree. "That's it."

At the base of the tree stands a shoulder-high slab of pale red stone bearing an inscription in letters that might have been the common ancestor of all the texts Midori ever gathered. I step forward to take a closer look at the slab, but Amos grabs my arm, holding me back with a firm grip.

"Only those initiated into the mysteries are allowed to stand before the spring," says Amos. He repositions his light to reveal, just beside the tree, a round pool ringed with smooth tiles. Dark water bubbles up from the center and flows outward, emptying somewhere beneath the tiles.

"It seems a little late for that, doesn't it?" I say, twisting my arm in a futile attempt to escape his grip. "I'm standing here already."

Amos says, "In this particular case, we have considered the possibility of a rather unconventional initiation."

I try to keep my voice level as I say, "Who's we?"

Amos lets go of my arm, taking a step forward to stand between me and the spring, then turning to face me. "We have been called by many names," he says. "I think you have heard at least one?"

"The Stewards of the True Cross," I say.

"And do you have any idea who we are?" he says.

I eye him coldly. With more bravado than I feel, I say, "I guess you're a bunch of murderers."

"It's not as clear-cut as that," says Amos, sounding slightly perturbed. "I'll be the first to admit that there have been unfortunate casualties in our work. But over the course of time, one does come to accept the reality that sometimes a few must be sacrificed for the sake of the many."

"Or maybe over the course of time, one gets to be pretty good at rationalization," I say.

Amos sighs theatrically. He says, "I know you've suffered a personal tragedy in the loss of your young friend. For my role in that, I apologize. But before you start casting aspersions, consider the part you yourself have played in all this. Through your obsessive quest to put dangerous information into the public domain, you have imperiled yourself, as well as your collaborators."

My collaborators. The word gives me pause. If all Dom has told me is true, my collaborators may span generations. Didn't Midori cross the Stewards? And if she did, then how many other versions of myself might have done the same? How many people might those other versions of myself have enlisted to this cause? The number of lives caught up in my so-called quest might be enormous. Not just Tomo and Owen. Also Zeke, Naoto, and Amaterasu. Possibly the entire Anonymous Collective. How many more might there be?

Amos nods, as if he knows what I'm thinking. "You aren't the first, and you won't be the last, I'm sure. The prospect of eternal life has driven many to take far greater risks.

"So perhaps you can forgive my 'rationalizations.' Imagine a world in which every man knew that eternal life was within reach. What man would not desire such a thing? What man would not risk everything to obtain it? Imagine the chaos as men fought to control the source of eternal life."

"Look, Amos," I say. "I didn't come here for that spring. I don't care about eternal life. All I want is to have a look at that tree. That's it."

Amos chuckles. "I find that hard to believe, given all the trouble you've taken to find this place. But be that as it may, your reason makes no difference to us. We Stewards have a sacred duty, to preserve what is beautiful and good in the world, to protect mankind from its own destructive impulses. We control information that would be dangerous in the wrong hands.

"But our old methods are not up to the task of addressing emerging threats to information control. We're not blind to the fact. I'd be the first to admit we've fallen more than a few steps behind the times.

"You, on the other hand, have managed to keep more than a step ahead of us. You probably could have evaded us for longer, had we not had a rare stroke of luck coordinating a raid on Falsens' headquarters while you were in transit, which allowed us to obtain your location. We could put your talents to good use. You could be a tremendous force for good in the world."

A laugh escapes me, sounding slightly hysterical as it echoes against the walls of the chamber. "You're telling me you're a headhunter?" I say. "You're making me an offer?"

"Help us preserve the peace and security of the world. Help us keep dangerous knowledge from those who would use it for evil. We will give you the tools you need, resources beyond your imagining, as well as the unlimited time that comes from the greatest secret we keep," he says, turning and extending an open hand toward the spring.

"It's a nice idea, Amos," I say. "But it's ridiculous. Don't you get it? This will all get out, eventually, one way or another. Information wants to be free."

Amos closes his hand and lets it fall to his side. "A sentiment popular among those of your generation," he says. "But you underestimate the depth of our resolve, the extent of our resources, and the importance of our mission. We keep the darkness of this world at bay."

Out of the corner of my eye, I watch Dom walk slowly to the edge of Amos' light, toward the dark pool.

Amos says, "Think, Miss Bridges. I'm giving you the opportunity to stop the spread of evil in the world, to stop the spread of unnecessary suffering. You could help create a better world, a world of truth and beauty that endures."

Dom stops and turns around, looking curiously at Amos. I feel a quiver along my connection to Dom. He's realized something, but I'm not sure what it is. Amos continues, "You can save innocent lives. Lives that have already been put at risk by the tremendous information leak for which you are entirely responsible."

I blink, distracted from Dom by Amos' words. "Whose lives are you talking about?" I say. "At risk how?"

"The particulars are difficult to predict. But imagine … First, some clever scholars make astute connections as they translate the source documents from Tomo Yoshimoto's storage drive. Then a thousand conspiracy theorists spin out a thousand conspiracy theories, until one of them comes close enough to the truth to inspire a curious visitor or two to Akdamar, perhaps even a team of treasure hunters with a swarm of reality television cameras, to come knocking on these doors. All of them will need to be dealt with. Every single one.

"Assassination is a regrettable expedient. It's also unsustainable in our ever-more-closely surveilled world. We have already risked a great deal of exposure to our organization in our attempt to prevent Midori Shimahashi's research from spreading, and still you managed to piece together our secret for yourself. How long until others do the same?"

I say, "You can't be telling me that your information control plan is just to slaughter anyone who stumbles into this."

Amos says, "Help us do better, Miss Bridges. We need fresh perspectives, new ways of doing things. It can be difficult for organizations like ours to adapt to the new world, while we still carry so much memory of the old."

"That's the real downside to immortality," I say.

"And yet I'm sure you'd find that the advantages more than outweigh little drawbacks like that," says Amos.

I shake my head. "I don't think so," I say. "I don't want to work with you. I don't want to work for you. All I want is to take a look at that tree. Afterwards, I don't want to come here ever again. And I sure as hell don't want to tell anyone else to come here, knowing what you so-called Stewards are all about."

Amos nods slowly. "I understand," he says. "This must have been an unexpected proposition. But I have made an effort in good faith to show you what we can offer. I believe you could do more good with us than without. But unfortunately I cannot allow you to leave here under any terms other than your full agreement."

Amos withdraws the silver weapon from his jacket pocket. I step back. Dom's eyes lock on mine.

"Could I have a minute, just to think things over?" I say.

Amos nods. "Of course, my dear. I have all the time in the world."

△▽△

I rake my fingers through my hair, staring up at the distant chamber ceiling. I wrack my brain for a reasonable course of action, but my mind instead projects a series of whimsical, ridiculous solutions onto the gloomy emptiness surrounding me. My Amaranthian guild members from *Eleusis*, led by Otaku, storm out of the shadows to pummel Amos into submission. A writhing fractal forest springs up from the ground, providing cover for me to run back toward the staircase. The spectral tree in the center of the room morphs into the living, blooming tree out of Dom's memory, growing taller and taller until I can climb up to the very top of the chamber and burst through the ceiling onto the sunlit hilltop above.

I look past Amos to the old tree bent over the dark pool. One of the tree's withered branches stretches out across the pool's surface. A glittering droplet of condensation on the tip of that branch falls into the dark pool with a plunk. The tiny ripples spread from the center of the pool to the edges, distorting the reflection of the pale tree. The ripples disappear as they flow under the circular lip of smooth tiles. For a moment, the waters lie still.

A flash of reflected sunlight suddenly dazzles me. I blink in surprise and see in the pool a strip of clear blue sky framing the dark cliffs across which spread the white tiers of the temple city of Thera, gleaming in the morning sun.

"Dom!" I gasp. "There, don't you see—" I say, taking a step toward the pool.

"Don't move!" Amos shouts, rushing to stand between me and the pool, the silver weapon in his hand extended.

Dom cries, "Emmie, stop!"

The needle-sharp tip of Amos' weapon brushes the skin of my neck. I freeze, staring up at Amos wide-eyed. He shakes his head in displeasure, nostrils flaring, and traces the icy metal point slowly across my throat as he steps behind me. He reaches around me with his free arm and pulls me into a headlock.

The pressure of Amos' forearm around my neck is crushing. My eyelids flutter. Amos' warm body presses against my back. His wool jacket sleeve scratches the skin beneath my chin. He smells faintly of expensive cologne and cigars.

The ghostly form of the great tree swims before my watering eyes. I blink, and the tree snaps into focus again. Dom takes a step toward me, his eyes gleaming with tears. His trembling fingers reach out to touch my cheek, but his touch is as insubstantial as the air.

"Emmie," he whispers. "I'm sorry. I'm so sorry."

"Look—" I manage to rasp, pointing toward the surface of the pool, gritting my teeth against the pain of Amos' chokehold. "There—"

On the surface of the water, I see, clear as day, a passageway. This tree is the axis around which the worlds turn. Its root is the point from which each world unfurls. Dom must see it.

I struggle to break free from Amos, to regain my breath so I can tell Dom. But Amos lifts me off the ground. My feet kick uselessly in the air. The metal point against my neck presses harder against my skin.

With a tremendous effort, I reach backwards over my head and seize two handfuls of Amos' hair. He roars with pain and drops me to the ground. But I don't let Amos go. Instead, I pull him by his hair toward the edge of the dark pool.

"Stop!" Amos cries. "You don't know what you're doing!"

"Follow me, Dom," I say.

I leap into the dark water, hauling Amos in after me by his hair. The water closes over my head. Amos thrashes in my grasp. A strong current pulls us down, down, down. I feel a pinprick pain in my chest as the tip of Amos' silver weapon strikes me. Everything goes dark.

△▽△

A thousand lives of Ava flash before my eyes as I watch Emmie tumble into the pool, hauling Amos in after her by his mane of white-blonde hair. The light of Amos' sinking flashlight illuminates the two of them locked in swirling combat beneath the water, until the current of the underground river sucks them down into darkness. For an instant, I stand alone beside the great tree, staring down at the surface of the pool in horror. When the chamber around me blurs, I know that the needle of pharmaka in Amos' hand struck home in Emmie's heart.

My tether to Emmie snaps as her awareness drifts out of her world. My own awareness crashes back into my body in an explosion of white light. I open my eyes, momentarily blinded by the morning sun streaming in through the open eastern entryway of my sculpting pavilion.

I climb unsteadily to my feet. Before me stands the unfinished sculpture of Ava. I look up into the unseeing eyes of stone, the face frozen in the moment of enlightenment. I squeeze my eyes shut, gripping my head between my hands, wishing I could erase the memory of Emmie struggling helplessly in Amos' arms.

I roar in despair. Emmie gave me my long-awaited chance to stand before the tree once more. But whatever it was she saw, I was once again blind to it. All the suffering I brought into Emmie's life, and all the lifetimes she's sacrificed to return me to that place, all was for nothing. She's been cheated of life once again, and still I'm cheated of Death.

"Dom Artifex," says a voice behind me.

Startled, I turn to find myself face to face with the High Priestess Serapen. How long has she been standing there, watching me? She looks from Ava's statue back to me, then holds her hand over me in the sign of blessing. I lower my head wearily. "Muse Serapen," I say.

"I come with word from the Voice," she says gently.

Without raising my eyes from the ground, I say, "I submit to the will of the Voice. I submit. Only leave me in peace, and I will continue on the task I have been given, until the very last stone of Dulai crumbles into dust."

"But your task is at an end," says Serapen. "The time for your answer has come."

"No," I moan, passing my hand over my eyes. "No. I cannot follow Ava any longer."

"That may be," she says. "But still, your answer comes. Seek it, and you shall find it."

Serapen turns and walks away, her long white hair and flowing robes whipping up around her as she steps from the protection of my pavilion into a capricious ocean breeze. I stare after her, my mind empty of all thought, until she disappears beyond the ridge.

The wind changes direction, rushing into my pavilion, swirling in the stone dust on the ground, flapping in the canvas walls. A gust rips loose a section of canvas near the entryway, rousing me to action. I reach for the needle on my tool bench to repair the torn fabric.

As I raise my arm, a silky web slides across my skin, making me shudder. Frantically, I strip off my tunic. Looking down, I see my arms and chest encased in the net of scarlet threads that, during my final sojourn with Emmie, have worked their way free of my flesh.

I tear the threads from my body, clutching them tightly in my fist, trembling.

On an impulse, I rush out of my pavilion, heading toward the bare rock ridge that divides the churning ocean from the still lagoon of the temple city harbor. I stare down at the long scarlet threads in my hand, twisting in the breeze, helpless to escape my grasp. A strong wind blows in from the ocean. I turn away from it to face the temple city. The wind courses over my body. I raise my clenched fist in the air and open my hand, letting go of the last remnants of Ava's mantle.

The fine net catches the wind and soars out across the lagoon, rising and falling until it disappears from view somewhere out over the deep water.

I lower my arm, my vision blurred with tears. The blue sky, dark cliffs, and white marble of the city before me seem to melt together. I blink, and my vision clears. An uncanny stillness falls over the waters of the lagoon, and the light changes. I see the reflection of the temple city in the water, white branches spreading against a dark wall of stone, a mirror image of the ghostly tree in the underground chamber on Akdamar.

Understanding hits me like a bolt of lightning. I see the way out. Before me lies the doorway Ava first glimpsed in the pool so many centuries ago.

The Voice's words to me, repeated so many times in so many ways through the ages, echo in my mind. *Let her go.*

I've seen Ava do it a thousand times before in a thousand different lifetimes: letting go of one world to enter another. Her awareness always longs to inhabit new places and comprehend new things. For Ava, Death has always been nothing more than letting go of something old to embrace something new.

I look up at the Musaion that crowns the temple city, then down once more at the branching reflection of the city in the lagoon. Heart thudding hard against my ribs, I take off at a run toward the precipice at the end of the ridge.

I leap out over the water.

Down, down, down I fall, sky above and reflected sky below, until I crash against the surface of the water. Breath and light and sense are knocked entirely out of me. I drift weightless, surrounded by dark water on all sides.

My last thought is of Emmie, her face pale in Amos' harsh artificial light, her green eyes staring desperately into mine. I'd longed to touch her cheek, to give her some final word of reassurance that Death was not the end for her.

There's a searing pain in my lungs as my suffocating body tries to inhale seawater. I try not to struggle. At last, the time has come for my own journey into Death.

A small, strong hand closes around my wrist, tugging at me. Alarmed, I thrash away from it. The hand lets go of my wrist, but it soon returns, this time as a gentle touch on my cheek. I open my eyes. A watery light emanates from a point just in front of me, illuminating a woman's figure in the water. She takes my hand once more and pulls me onward. This time, I follow.

△▽△

We emerge gasping and spluttering, kicking with all our strength against the undertow until we reach the slippery lip of tile ringing the dark pool. I scramble out first and reach back into the water to haul Dom out by his sodden tunic. He coughs up a lungful of water and collapses against the trunk of the white tree.

We stare at each other in the dim light of the chamber.

Softly, I say, "You saw it?"

Dom nods, speechless.

Shaking my head in wonder, I murmur, "Wow. Just … wow."

I'm thankful he saw it. What I saw, what I felt, what I knew in the moment I pulled Dom from the depths of the underground river—are there words to describe such things? I feel transformed. I've seen what cannot be unseen: the many worlds of our reality, and the bridges that connect them all.

The tiled floor beneath us trembles, shattering our brief moment of peace, pushing aside all my questions about what just happened to us beneath the surface of the pool. Whatever happened, it isn't going to matter if we get trapped here by an earthquake. Dom struggles to his feet, but he falls down again when a harder tremor shakes the ground.

A bright light flashes from somewhere near the edge of the chamber.

"Emmie!" a voice calls out.

I squint as the bright light turns on me. It's Naoto, running toward us, flashlight in hand. Naoto stops in his tracks when his light falls on Dom. He holds up a small silver weapon.

"No!" I shout. "Naoto, put it down!"

Naoto lowers his weapon but keeps the beam of his flashlight focused on Dom's face. Dom raises a hand to shield his eyes.

"Who the hell is that?" says Naoto. But there's no time for explanations. Naoto shakes his head and waves us toward the archway that exits the inner chamber. "We need to get out of here," he says.

Naoto leads the way, and we run. The ground shakes harder. Above us, there's a resounding crack. I cover my head with my arms. Naoto narrowly dodges a cascade of dust that pours down from the ceiling. A falling stone strikes Dom hard on the shoulder.

We race through the underground vault, where a glittering, knee-high cloud of salt and soda has risen above the shaking floor. There's a terrible crash behind us, and I look back over my shoulder. A huge slab of stone has fallen from the ceiling, blocking the entrance to the inner chamber. A series of smaller crashes follows as we race toward the winding staircase.

We emerge through the trapdoor behind the altar. The stone columns supporting the cathedral roof above us sway. At the base of one column lies Goran, bound hand and foot, apparently unconscious.

"Out! Out!" cries Naoto, turning back for Goran. "I'll be right behind you!"

I hesitate, not wanting to leave Naoto behind, but Dom seizes me by the arm and hauls me toward the door. We rush out into the bright sunlight, followed a moment later by Naoto, who carries Goran over his shoulders in a fireman's lift. I duck fearfully toward the ground when a thumping noise approaches us from above. I peer up to see a helicopter circling.

"It's Falsens!" Naoto shouts, running forward with Goran. "Head for the clearing!"

Dom and I stagger across the lurching ground, following Naoto toward the broad meadow beyond the cathedral. A flock of birds rushes over us, their piercing cries cutting through the rumbling of the earth and the droning of the helicopter. The flowering trees whip and writhe as the ground shakes them from the roots. White, pink, and red blossoms swirl through the air.

We stop at the edge of the clearing. Naoto heaves Goran to the ground and sinks to the grass beside him, exhausted. Dom and I look back toward the cathedral we've escaped just in time. Cracks spread through the walls of carved stone. As we watch, the foundation sinks slowly into the ground.

The earth falls still. For a moment, the cathedral does too. Then the ground beneath the building gives way. The walls crumble inward, and the conical dome falls in slow motion as a cloud of dust rises up around it. When the dust settles, nothing remains of the cathedral or the chamber hidden below but a crater filled with pink and grey stone rubble.

I look up at Dom, who stands motionless, staring at the ruin. Tentatively, I reach out and touch his arm, half expecting him to vanish like he has so many times before. He blinks and looks down at me in amazement.

Softly, he says, "There's no going back." And I know it's true for both of us.

"But this is what you wanted, isn't it?" I say.

Dom takes my hand, his fingers substantial and warm around mine. His voice is fierce as he says, "Yes. This is what I wanted."

THE STORY CONTINUES

Spirits, you've finished the series!

But the story continues at
audreyauden.com

Onward,

ACKNOWLEDGMENTS

TWENTY YEARS AGO, I sat in an airport terminal waiting for a flight that would begin some now-unremembered business trip. I was twenty-one, and I'd recently started my first full-time job after engineering school. The new realities of working life—long commutes through the metroplex, business trips to the hinterlands, internal political shenanigans and external customer pressures—were hitting me hard and fast. I was grateful to be gainfully employed, but I couldn't ignore the sad little voice in the back of my head that regretted my decision to pursue an engineering career rather than indulge the passion for writing I'd possessed since I was a little girl.

I placated that little voice with the half-truth that, at twenty-one, I had as yet too little life experience to write anything meaningful. The years ahead, whatever else they might contain, would provide an ingredient essential to good writing: firsthand knowledge.

Fifteen years ago, when I started work on the earliest draft of what would become *The Artifex and the Muse*, I had no idea how its characters, settings, and dilemmas would come to inhabit my mind and heart. As I flip back through these pages, I find the experiences of my own life woven into my story world—youth and aging, love and loss, achievement and exhaustion, idealism and wisdom. There's a reason life mirrors art: each gives rise to the other.

Writing this series has been one of the most rewarding experiences of my life. Nurturing Dom and Ava along their paths has been a way of nurturing myself along mine. If you've ever been called to write something—big or small, personal or commercial, fiction or non-fiction—I highly recommend answering the call. Writing is its own reward, even if the only person who ever reads the words is you yourself.

Writing can be solitary, but no one is ever truly alone on this journey. Every word of encouragement from a reader, every editorial note, and every supportive person in my life has played a helpful role.

Thank you to my editors, Tanner Perkes and Maya Rock. Your thoughtful critique and guidance helped me find my voice and vastly improved my storytelling.

Thank you to the very special readers who read early drafts of the work. There's a special tier in heaven for folks like you: Robbie Auray, Diana Berlin, Sharon Flood, Sandy Little, Natilee Harren, and Sophie Steplowski.

Special thanks to Ian Steplowski and our one hundred and forty-six generous Kickstarter backers who made the illustrated version of *Realms Unreel* a reality. Your collective enthusiasm brought the story world to life in a way I never could have done on my own, and your support made me dare to continue work on the series, despite the challenges of independent publishing.

Thank you to my family for being an unfailing source of love, support, and inspiration. Barbara and Ed Hampden; Mac, Andrea, Jamie, and Emma Hampden; Madison, Logan, Charlie, and Luisa Hampden; Sumul Shah; Ian, Sophie, Alex, and Julia Steplowski; and Dave Carlson.

Thank you to my dear friends who have cheered on the work at every stage and in so many ways. Ben Andersen, Puneet Batra, Erik Berlin, Josh Braslow, Shelby Cass, Nick Dunkman, Randall Farmer, Emma Gobillot, Lori Gobillot, Tendai Gomo, Katie Guido, Lauren Guido, Michael Guido, Amit Gupta, Paula Gutierrez, Nancy Hua, Jamie Hutchinson, Theresa Kelly, Carlene King, Dale King, Vasya Kondrashov, Liz Kondrashov, David LaBerge, Sandy Little, Lyndsay Love, Diane Loviglio, Emily Meacham, Smith Mitchell, Doug Morin, Anne O'Dwyer, Manali Patel, Michael Pettit, Henry Pfingstag, Michael Powell, Kirsten Schulz, Susan Schulz, Jesse Steinberg, Kirk Strauser, Tanya Tellman, David Vivero, Bob Walker, Pattie Walker, Tristan Walker, John Wallach, "Admiral" Christian Waugh, and Mirella Waugh.

And to the real-life Eden Hill Farm, for providing the peace and quiet required to finish this work, and the expansive canvas on which to start the next.

You all helped make my childhood dream a reality.

AUTHOR'S NOTE

THANK YOU for sharing your precious reading time with me, dear reader.

In all my fiction writing, I aim to explore humankind's pressing social and sustainability challenges through engaging, thought-provoking, optimistic stories for young adult readers.

Fantasy fiction was one of my earliest passions as a child, and as an adult I'm a lover of all forms of speculative fiction. I became an engineer because that seemed the next best thing to magic, and I've spent over twenty years building useful products, leading mission-driven teams, and growing technology startups.

But as satisfying as it is to build things in the "real" world, there's nothing quite as fun as building my own worlds from scratch. I'm pleased to share the result in the form of *The Artifex and the Muse* fantasy series, set in the world of my debut novel *Realms Unreel.*

I sincerely hope you enjoyed *The Artifex and the Muse.* If you're curious to learn more about this book, please visit my author website at audreyauden.com, where I share everything from story soundtracks and illustrations to publishing updates and reflections on the writing journey.

Happy reading!